S0-ABA-747

SERVANT OF THE SHARD

The fact that this drow was not a simple instrument of chaos and destruction, as were so many of the demon lords, or an easily duped human—perhaps the most redundant thought the artifact had ever considered—only made him more interesting.

They had a long way to go together, Crenshinibon believed.

The artifact would find its greatest level of power.

The world would suffer greatly.

PROMISE OF THE WITCH-KING

Entreri went for his sword, but when the lich reached out with bony fingers, the assassin instead thrust his gloved hand out before him. Again Entreri screamed—in defiance, in denial, in rage—as another lightning bolt blasted forth.

Spots danced before his eyes, and waves of dizziness assailed him.

The floor and walls began to tremble with a low, rolling growl.

And he heard the taunting cackle of the lich.

ROAD OF THE PATRIARCH

"What a cunning system you have there," Entreri said. "You and all the other self-proclaimed royalty of Faerûn. By your conditions, you alone are kings and queens and lords and ladies of court. You alone matter, while the peasant grovels and kneels in the mud, and since you are 'rightful' in the eyes of this god or that, then the peasant cannot complain. He must accept his muddy lot in life and revel in his misery, all in the knowledge that he serves the rightful king."

Gareth's jaw tightened, and he ground his teeth as he continued to stare unblinking at Entreri.

"You should have had Kane kill me," Entreri continued, "back at the castle."

"I am not your judge," the king said.

"Just my executioner," replied the assassin.

R.A. SALVATORE

THE LEGEND OF DRIZZT®

See the appendix at the back of this book for a full list of FORGOTTEN REALMS® novels by R.A. Salvatore, and how to start, where to go next, and how they all fit together into one of the greatest fantasy epics in the history of the genre!

FORGOTTEN REALMS®

R.A. SALVATORE

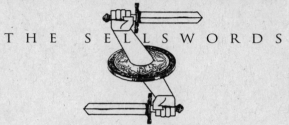
THE SELLSWORDS

SERVANT OF THE SHARD

PROMISE OF THE WITCH-KING

ROAD OF THE PATRIARCH

COVER ART BY
TODD LOCKWOOD

Wizards
OF THE COAST®

The Sellswords

©2010 Wizards of the Coast LLC

All characters in this book are fictitious. Any resemblance to actual persons, living or dead, is purely coincidental.

This book is protected under the copyright laws of the United States of America. Any reproduction or unauthorized use of the material or artwork contained herein is prohibited without the express written permission of Wizards of the Coast LLC.

Published by Wizards of the Coast LLC

FORGOTTEN REALMS, DUNGEONS & DRAGONS, D&D, WIZARDS OF THE COAST, their respective logos, and THE LEGEND OF DRIZZT are trademarks of Wizards of the Coast LLC in the U.S.A. and other countries.

Printed in the U.S.A.

Cover art by Todd Lockwood
Maps by Todd Gamble

Contains the complete text of the June 2005 edition of *Servant of the Shard,* the September 2006 edition of *Promise of the Witch-King,* and the July 2007 edition of *Road of the Patriarch.*

This Edition First Printing: December 2010

9 8 7 6 5 4 3 2 1

ISBN: 978-0-7869-5716-3
620-26413000-001-EN

U.S., CANADA,	EUROPEAN HEADQUARTERS
ASIA, PACIFIC, & LATIN AMERICA	Hasbro UK Ltd
Wizards of the Coast LLC	Caswell Way
P.O. Box 707	Newport, Gwent NP9 0YH
Renton, WA 98057-0707	GREAT BRITAIN
+1-800-324-6496	Save this address for your records.

Visit our web site at www.wizards.com

Welcome to Faerûn, a land of magic and intrigue, brutal violence and divine compassion, where gods have ascended and died, and mighty heroes have risen to fight terrifying monsters. Here, millennia of warfare and conquest have shaped dozens of unique cultures, raised and leveled shining kingdoms and tyrannical empires alike, and left long forgotten, horror-infested ruins in their wake.

A LAND OF MAGIC

When the goddess of magic was murdered, a magical plague of blue fire—the Spellplague—swept across the face of Faerûn, killing some, mutilating many, and imbuing a rare few with amazing supernatural abilities. The Spellplague forever changed the nature of magic itself, and seeded the land with hidden wonders and bloodcurdling monstrosities.

A LAND OF DARKNESS

The threats Faerûn faces are legion. Armies of undead mass in Thay under the brilliant but mad lich king Szass Tam. Treacherous dark elves plot in the Underdark in the service of their cruel and fickle goddess, Lolth. The Abolethic Sovereignty, a terrifying hive of inhuman slave masters, floats above the Sea of Fallen Stars, spreading chaos and destruction. And the Empire of Netheril, armed with magic of unimaginable power, prowls Faerûn in flying fortresses, sowing discord to their own incalculable ends.

A LAND OF HEROES

But Faerûn is not without hope. Heroes have emerged to fight the growing tide of darkness. Battle-scarred rangers bring their notched blades to bear against marauding hordes of orcs. Lowly street rats match wits with demons for the fate of cities. Inscrutable tiefling warlocks unite with fierce elf warriors to rain fire and steel upon monstrous enemies. And valiant servants of merciful gods forever struggle against the darkness.

A LAND OF
UNTOLD ADVENTURE

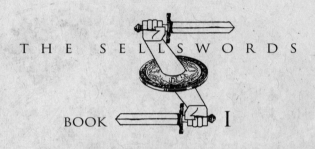

THE SELLSWORDS

BOOK I

SERVANT OF THE SHARD

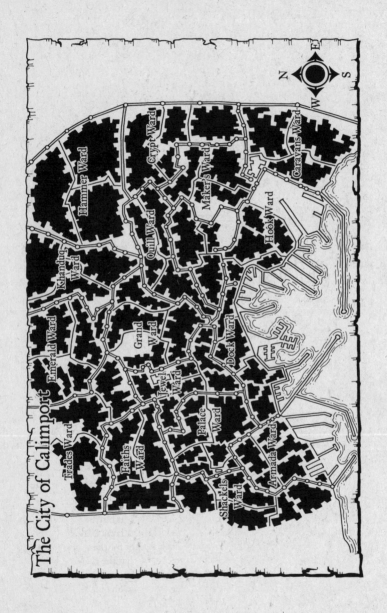

The City of Calimport

PROLOGUE

He glided through the noonday sunshine's oppressive heat, moving as if always cloaked in shadows, though the place had few, and as if even the ever-present dust could not touch him. The open market was crowded—it was always crowded—with yelling merchants and customers bargaining for every copper piece. Thieves were positioning themselves in all the best and busiest places, where they might cut a purse string without ever being noticed, or if they were discovered, where they could melt away into a swirling crowd of bright colors and flowing robes.

Artemis Entreri noted the thieves clearly. He could tell with a glance who was there to shop and who was there to steal, and he didn't avoid the latter group. He purposely set his course to bring him right by every thief he could find, and he'd pushed back one side of his dark cloak, revealing his ample purse—

—revealing, too, the jewel-decorated dagger that kept his purse and his person perfectly safe. The dagger was his trademark weapon, one of the most feared blades on all of Calimport's dangerous streets.

Entreri enjoyed the respect the young thieves offered him, and more than that, he demanded it. He had spent years earning his reputation as the finest assassin in Calimport, but he was getting older. He was losing, perhaps, that fine edge of brilliance. Thus, he came out brazenly—more so than he ever would have in his younger days—daring them, any of them, to make a try for him.

He crossed the busy avenue, heading for a small outdoor tavern that had many round tables set under a great awning. The place was bustling, but Entreri immediately spotted his contact, the flamboyant Sha'lazzi Ozoule with his trademark bright yellow turban. Entreri moved straight for the table. Sha'lazzi wasn't sitting alone, though it was obvious to Entreri that the three men seated with him were not friends of his, were not known to him at all. The others held a private conversation, chattering and chuckling, while Sha'lazzi leaned back, glancing all around.

Entreri walked up to the table. Sha'lazzi gave a nervous and embarrassed shrug as the assassin looked questioningly at the three uninvited guests.

1

"You did not tell them that this table was reserved for our luncheon?" Entreri calmly asked.

The three men stopped their conversation and looked up at him curiously.

"I tried to explain . . ." Sha'lazzi started, wiping the sweat from his dark-skinned brow.

Entreri held up his hand to silence the man and fixed his imposing gaze on the three trespassers. "We have business," he said.

"And we have food and drink," one of them replied.

Entreri didn't reply, other than to stare hard at the man, to let his gaze lock with the other's.

The other two made a couple of remarks, but Entreri ignored them completely and just kept staring hard at the first challenger. On and on it went, and Entreri kept his focus, even tightened it, his gaze boring into the man, showing him the strength of will he now faced, the perfect determination and control.

"What is this about?" one of the others demanded, standing up right beside Entreri.

Sha'lazzi muttered the quick beginning of a common prayer.

"I asked you," the man pushed, and he reached out to shove Entreri's shoulder.

Up snapped the assassin's hand, catching the approaching hand by the thumb and spinning it over, then driving it down, locking the man in a painful hold.

All the while Entreri didn't blink, didn't glance away at all, just kept visually holding the first one, who was sitting directly across from him, in that awful glare.

The man standing at Entreri's side gave a little grunt as the assassin applied pressure, then brought his free hand to his belt, to the curved dagger he had secured there.

Sha'lazzi muttered another line of the prayer.

The man across the table, held fast by Entreri's deadly stare, motioned for his friend to hold calm and to keep his hand away from the blade.

Entreri nodded to him, then motioned for him to take his friends and be gone. He released the man at his side, who clutched at his sore thumb, eyeing Entreri threateningly. He didn't come at Entreri again, nor did either of his friends make any move, except to pick up their plates and sidle away. They hadn't recognized Entreri, yet he had shown them the truth of who he was without ever drawing his blade.

"I meant to do the same thing," Sha'lazzi remarked with a chuckle as the three departed and Entreri settled into the seat opposite him.

Entreri just stared at him, noting how out-of-sorts this one always appeared. Sha'lazzi had a huge head and a big round face, and that put on a body so skinny as to appear emaciated. Furthermore, that big round face was always, always smiling, with huge, square white teeth glimmering in contrast to his dark skin and black eyes.

Sha'lazzi cleared his throat again. "Surprised I am that you came out for this meeting," he said. "You have made many enemies in your rise with the Basadoni Guild. Do you not fear treachery, O powerful one?" he finished sarcastically and again with a chuckle.

Entreri only continued to stare. Indeed he had feared treachery, but he needed to speak with Sha'lazzi. Kimmuriel Oblodra, the drow psionicist working for Jarlaxle, had scoured Sha'lazzi's thoughts completely and had come to the conclusion that there was no conspiracy afoot.

Of course, considering the source of the information—a dark elf who held no love for Entreri—the assassin hadn't been completely comforted by the report.

"It can be a prison to the powerful, you understand," Sha'lazzi rambled on. "A prison to *be* powerful, you see? So many pashas dare not leave their homes without an entourage of a hundred guards."

"I am not a pasha."

"No, indeed, but Basadoni belongs to you and to Sharlotta," Sha'lazzi returned, referring to Sharlotta Vespers. The woman had used her wiles to become Pasha Basadoni's second and had survived the drow takeover to serve as figurehead of the guild. And the guild had suddenly become more powerful than anyone could imagine. "Everyone knows this." Sha'lazzi gave another of his annoying chuckles. "I always understood that you were good, my friend, but never this good!"

Entreri smiled back, but in truth his amusement came from a fantasy of sticking his dagger into Sha'lazzi's skinny throat, for no better reason than the fact that he simply couldn't stand this parasite.

Entreri had to admit that he needed Sha'lazzi, though—and that was exactly how the notorious informant managed to stay alive. Sha'lazzi had made a living, indeed an art, out of telling anybody anything he wanted to know—for a price—and so good was he at his craft, so connected to every pulse beat of Calimport's ruling families and street thugs alike, that he had made himself too valuable to the often-warring guilds to be murdered.

"So tell me of the power behind the throne of Basadoni," Sha'lazzi remarked, grinning widely. "For surely there is more, yes?"

Entreri worked hard to keep himself stone-faced, knowing that a responding grin would give too much away—and how he wanted to grin at Sha'lazzi's honest ignorance of the truth of the new Basadonis. Sha'lazzi would never know that a dark elf army had set up shop in Calimport, using the Basadoni Guild as its front.

"I thought we had agreed to discuss Dallabad Oasis?" Entreri asked in reply.

Sha'lazzi sighed and shrugged. "Many interesting things to speak of," he said. "Dallabad is not one of them, I fear."

"In your opinion."

"Nothing has changed there in twenty years," Sha'lazzi replied. "There is nothing there that I know that you do not, and have not, for nearly as many years."

"Kohrin Soulez still retains Charon's Claw?" Entreri asked.

Sha'lazzi nodded. "Of course," he said with a chuckle. "Still and forever. It has served him for four decades, and when Soulez is dead, one of his thirty sons will take it, no doubt, unless the indelicate Ahdania Soulez gets to it first. An ambitious one is the daughter of Kohrin Soulez! If you came to ask me if he will part with it, then you already know the answer. We should indeed speak of more interesting things, such as the Basadoni Guild."

Entreri's hard stare returned in a heartbeat.

"Why would old Soulez sell it now?" Sha'lazzi asked with a dramatic wave of his skinny arms—arms that looked so incongruous when lifted beside that huge head. "What is this, my friend, the third time you have tried to purchase that fine sword? Yes, yes! First, when you were a pup with a few hundred gold pieces—a gift of Basadoni, eh?—in your ragged pouch."

Entreri winced at that despite himself, despite his knowledge that Sha'lazzi, for all of his other faults, was the best in Calimport at reading gestures and expressions and deriving the truth behind them. Still, the memory, combined with more recent events, evoked the response from his heart. Pasha Basadoni had indeed given him the extra coin that long-ago day, an offering to his most promising lieutenant for no good reason but simply as a gift. When he thought about it, Entreri realized that Basadoni was perhaps the only man who had ever given him a gift without expecting something in return.

And Entreri had killed Basadoni, only a few months ago.

"Yes, yes," Sha'lazzi said, more to himself than to Entreri, "then you asked about the sword again soon after Pasha Pook's demise. Ah, but he fell hard, that one!"

Entreri just stared at the man. Sha'lazzi, apparently just then beginning to catch on that he might be pushing the dangerous assassin too far, cleared his throat, embarrassed.

"Then I told you that it was impossible," Sha'lazzi remarked. "Of course it is impossible."

"I have more coin now," Entreri said quietly.

"There is not enough coin in all of the world!" Sha'lazzi wailed.

Entreri didn't blink. "Do you know how much coin is in all the world, Sha'lazzi?" he asked calmly—too calmly. "Do you know how much coin is in the coffers of House Basadoni?"

"House Entreri, you mean," the man corrected.

Entreri didn't deny it, and Sha'lazzi's eyes widened. There it was, as clearly spelled out as the informant could ever have expected to hear it. Rumors had said that old Basadoni was dead, and that Sharlotta Vespers and the other acting guildmasters were no more than puppets for the one who clearly pulled the strings: Artemis Entreri.

"Charon's Claw," Sha'lazzi mused, a smile widening upon his face. "So, the power behind the throne is Entreri, and the power behind Entreri is . . . well, a mage, I would guess, since you so badly want that particular sword. A mage, yes, and one who is getting a bit dangerous, eh?"

"Keep guessing," said Entreri.

"And perhaps I will get it correct?"

"If you do, I will have to kill you," the assassin said, still in that awful, calm tone. "Speak with Sheik Soulez. Find his price."

"He has no price," Sha'lazzi insisted.

Entreri came forward quicker than any cat after a mouse. One hand slapped down on Sha'lazzi's shoulder, the other caught hold of that deadly jeweled dagger, and Entreri's face came within an inch of Sha'lazzi's.

"That would be most unfortunate," Entreri said. "For you."

The assassin pushed the informant back in his seat, then stood up straight and glanced around as if some inner hunger had just awakened within him and he was now seeking some prey with which to sate it. He looked back at Sha'lazzi only briefly, then walked out from under the awning, back into the tumult of the market area.

As he calmed down and considered the meeting, Entreri silently berated himself. His frustration was beginning to wear at the edges of perfection. He could not have been more obvious about the roots of his problem than to so eagerly ask about purchasing Charon's Claw. Above all else, that weapon and gauntlet combination had been designed to battle wizards.

And psionicists, perhaps?

For those were Entreri's tormentors, Rai-guy and Kimmuriel—Jarlaxle's Bregan D'aerthe lieutenants—one a wizard and one a psionicist. Entreri hated them both, and profoundly, but more importantly he knew that they hated him. To make things worse Entreri understood that his only armor against the dangerous pair was Jarlaxle himself. While to his surprise he had cautiously come to trust the mercenary dark elf, he doubted Jarlaxle's protection would hold forever.

Accidents did happen, after all.

Entreri needed protection, but he had to go about things with his customary patience and intelligence, twisting the trail beyond anyone's ability to follow, fighting the way he had perfected so many years before on Calimport's tough streets, using many subtle layers of information and misinformation and blending the two together so completely that neither his friends nor his foes could ever truly unravel them. When only he knew the truth, then he, and only he, would be in control.

In that sobering light, he took the less than perfect meeting with perceptive Sha'lazzi as a distinct warning, a reminder that he could survive his time with the dark elves only if he kept an absolute level of personal control. Indeed, Sha'lazzi had come close to figuring out his current plight, had gotten half of it, at least, correct. The pie-faced man would obviously offer that information to any who'd pay well enough for it. On Calimport's streets these days many were scrambling to figure out the enigma of the sudden and vicious rise of the Basadoni Guild.

Sha'lazzi had figured out half of it, and so all the usual suspects would be considered: a powerful arch-mage or various wizards' guilds.

Despite his dour mood, Entreri chuckled when he pictured Sha'lazzi's expression should the man ever learn the other half of that secret behind Basadoni's throne, that the dark elves had come to Calimport in force!

Of course, his threat to the man had not been an idle one. Should Sha'lazzi ever make such a connection, Entreri, or any one of a thousand of Jarlaxle's agents, would surely kill him.

Sha'lazzi Ozoule sat at the little round table for a long, long time, replaying Entreri's every word and every gesture. He knew that his assumption concerning a wizard holding the true power behind the Basadoni rise was correct, but that was not really news. Given the expediency of the rise, and the level of devastation that had been enacted upon rival houses, common sense dictated that a wizard, or more likely many wizards, were involved.

What caught Sha'lazzi as a revelation, though, was Entreri's visceral reaction.

Artemis Entreri, the master of control, the shadow of death itself, had never before shown him such an inner turmoil—even fear, perhaps?—as that.

When before had Artemis Entreri ever touched someone in threat? No, he had always looked at him with that awful gaze, let him know in no uncertain terms that he was walking the path to ultimate doom. If the offender persisted, there was no further threat, no grabbing or beating.

There was only quick death.

The uncharacteristic reaction surely intrigued Sha'lazzi. How he wanted to know what had so rattled Artemis Entreri as to facilitate such behavior—but at the same time, the assassin's demeanor also served as a clear and frightening warning. Sha'lazzi knew well that anything that could so unnerve Artemis Entreri could easily, so easily, destroy Sha'lazzi Ozoule.

It was an interesting situation, and one that scared Sha'lazzi profoundly.

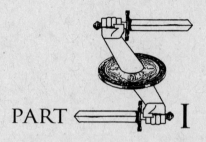

PART I

STICKING TO THE WEB

I live in a world where there truly exists the embodiment of evil. I speak not of wicked men, nor of goblins—often of evil weal—nor even of my own people, the dark elves, wickeder still than the goblins. These are creatures—all of them—capable of great cruelty, but they are not, even in the very worst of cases, the true embodiment of evil. No, that title belongs to others, to the demons and devils often summoned by priests and mages. These creatures of the lower planes are the purest of evil, untainted vileness running unchecked. They are without possibility of redemption, without hope of accomplishing anything in their unfortunately nearly eternal existence that even borders on goodness.

I have wondered if these creatures could exist without the darkness that lies within the hearts of the reasoning races. Are they a source of evil, as are many wicked men or drow, or are they the result, a physical manifestation of the rot that permeates the hearts of far too many?

The latter, I believe. It is not coincidental that demons and devils cannot walk the material plane of existence without being brought here by the actions of one of the reasoning beings. They are no more than a tool, I know, an instrument to carry out the wicked deeds in service to the truer source of that evil.

What then of Crenshinibon? It is an item, an artifact—albeit a sentient one—but it does not exist in the same state of intelligence as does a reasoning being. For the Crystal Shard cannot grow, cannot change, cannot mend its ways. The only errors it can learn to correct are those of errant attempts at manipulation, as it seeks to better grab at the hearts of those around it. It cannot even consider, or reconsider, the end it desperately tries to achieve—no, its purpose is forever singular.

Is it truly evil, then?

No.

I would have thought differently not too long ago, even when I carried the dangerous artifact and came better to understand it. Only recently, upon reading a long and detailed message sent to me from High Priest Cadderly Bonaduce of the Spirit Soaring, have I come to see the truth of the Crystal Shard, have I come to understand that the item itself is an anomaly, a mistake, and that its never-ending hunger for power and glory, at whatever cost, is merely a perversion of the intent of its second maker, the eighth spirit that found its way into the very essence of the artifact.

9

The Crystal Shard was created originally by seven liches, so Cadderly has learned, who designed to fashion an item of the very greatest power. As a further insult to the races these undead kings intended to conquer, they made the artifact a draw against the sun itself, the giver of life. The liches were consumed at the completion of their joining magic. Despite what some sages believe, Cadderly insists that the conscious aspects of those vile creatures were not drawn into the power of the item, but were, rather, obliterated by its sunlike properties. Thus, their intended insult turned against them and left them as no more than ashes and absorbed pieces of their shattered spirits.

That much of the earliest history of the Crystal Shard is known by many, including the demons that so desperately crave the item. The second story, though, the one Cadderly uncovered, tells a more complicated tale, and shows the truth of Crenshinibon, the ultimate failure of the artifact as a perversion of goodly intentions.

Crenshinibon first came to the material world centuries ago in the far-off land of Zakhara. At the time, it was merely a wizard's tool, though a great and powerful one, an artifact that could throw fireballs and create great blazing walls of light so intense they could burn flesh from bone. Little was known of Crenshinibon's dark past until it fell to the hands of a sultan. This great leader, whose name has been lost to the ages, learned the truth of the Crystal Shard, and with the help of his many court wizards, decided that the work of the liches was incomplete. Thus came the "second creation" of Crenshinibon, the heightening of its power and its limited consciousness.

This sultan had no dreams of domination, only of peaceful existence with his many warlike neighbors. Thus, using the newest power of the artifact, he envisioned, then created, a line of crystalline towers. The towers stretched from his capital across the empty desert to his kingdom's second city, an oft-raided frontier city, in intervals equating to a single day's travel. He strung as many as a hundred of the crystalline towers, and nearly completed the mighty defensive line.

But alas, the sultan overreached the powers of Crenshinibon, and though he believed that the creation of each tower strengthened the artifact, he was, in fact, pulling the Crystal Shard and its manifestations too thin. Soon after, a great sandstorm came up, sweeping across the desert. It was a natural disaster that served as a prelude to an invasion by a neighboring sheikdom. So thin were the walls of those crystalline towers that they shattered under the force of the glass, taking with them the sultan's dream of security.

The hordes overran the kingdom and murdered the sultan's family while he helplessly looked on. Their merciless sheik would not kill the sultan, though—he wanted the painful memories to burn at the man—but Crenshinibon took the sultan, took a piece of his spirit, at least.

Little more of those early days is known, even to Cadderly, who counts demigods among his sources, but the young high priest of Deneir is convinced that this "second creation" of Crenshinibon is the one that remains key to the present hunger of the artifact. If only Crenshinibon could have held its highest level of power. If only the crystalline towers had remained strong. The hordes would have been turned away, and the sultan's family, his dear wife and beautiful children, would not have been murdered.

Now the artifact, imbued with the twisted aspects of seven dead liches and with the wounded and tormented spirit of the sultan, continues its desperate quest to attain and maintain its greatest level of power, whatever the cost.

There are many implications to the story. Cadderly hinted in his note to me, though he drew no definitive conclusions, that the creation of the crystalline towers actually served as the catalyst for the invasion, with the leaders of the neighboring sheikdom fearful that their borderlands would soon be overrun. Is the Crystal Shard, then, a great lesson to us? Does it show clearly the folly of overblown ambition, even though that particular ambition was rooted in good intentions? The sultan wanted strength for the defense of his peaceable kingdom, and yet he reached for too much power.

That was what consumed him, his family, and his kingdom.

What of Jarlaxle, then, who now holds the Crystal Shard? Should I go after him and try to take back the artifact, then deliver it to Cadderly for destruction? Surely the world would be a better place without this mighty and dangerous artifact.

Then again, there will always be another tool for those of evil weal, another embodiment of their evil, be it a demon, a devil, or a monstrous creation similar to Crenshinibon.

No, the embodiments are not the problem, for they cannot exist and prosper without the evil that is within the hearts of reasoning beings.

Beware, Jarlaxle. Beware.

—Drizzt Do'Urden

CHAPTER

1

Dwahvel Tiggerwillies tiptoed into the small, dimly lit room in the back of the lower end of her establishment, the Copper Ante. Dwahvel, that most competent of halfling females—good with her wiles, good with her daggers, and better with her wits—wasn't used to walking so gingerly in this place, though it was as secure a house as could be found in all of Calimport. This was Artemis Entreri, after all, and no place in all the world could truly be considered safe when the deadly assassin was about.

He was pacing when she entered, taking no obvious note of her arrival at all. Dwahvel looked at him curiously. She knew that Entreri had been on edge lately and was one of the very few outside of House Basadoni who knew the truth behind that edge. The dark elves had come and infiltrated Calimport's streets, and Entreri was serving as a front man for their operations. If Dwahvel held any preconceived notions of how terrible the drow truly could be, one look at Entreri surely confirmed those suspicions. He had never been a nervous one—Dwahvel wasn't sure that he was now—and had never been a man Dwahvel would have expected to find at odds with himself.

Even more curious, Entreri had invited her into his confidence. It just wasn't his way. Still, Dwahvel suspected no trap. This was, she knew, exactly as it seemed, as surprising as that might be. Entreri was speaking to himself as much as to her, as a way of clarifying his thoughts, and for some reason that Dwahvel didn't yet understand, he was letting her listen in.

She considered herself complimented in the highest way and also realized the potential danger that came along with that compliment. That unsettling thought in mind, the halfling guildmistress quietly settled into a chair and listened carefully, looking for clues and insights. Her first, and most surprising, came when she happened to glance at a chair set against the back wall of the room. Resting on it was a half-empty bottle of Moonshae whiskey.

"I see them at every corner on every street in the belly of this cursed city," Entreri was saying. "Braggarts wearing their scars and weapons like badges of honor, men and women so concerned about reputation that they have lost sight of what it is they truly wish to accomplish. They play for the status and the accolades, and with no better purpose."

His speech was not overly slurred, yet it was obvious to Dwahvel that Entreri had indeed tasted some of the whiskey.

"Since when does Artemis Entreri bother himself with the likes of street thieves?" Dwahvel asked.

Entreri stopped pacing and glanced at her, his face passive. "I see them and mark them carefully, because I am well aware that my own reputation precedes me. Because of that reputation, many on the street would love to sink a dagger into my heart," the assassin replied and began to pace again. "How great a reputation that killer might then find. They know that I am older now, and they think me slower—and in truth, their reasoning is sound. I cannot move as quickly as I did a decade ago."

Dwahvel's eyes narrowed at the surprising admission.

"But as the body ages and movements dull, the mind grows sharper," Entreri went on. "I, too, am concerned with reputation, but not as I used to be. It was my goal in life to be the absolute best at that which I do, at out-fighting and out-thinking my enemies. I desired to become the perfect warrior, and it took a dark elf whom I despise to show me the error of my ways. My unintended journey to Menzoberranzan as a 'guest' of Jarlaxle humbled me in my fanatical striving to be the best and showed me the futility of a world full of that who I most wanted to become. In Menzoberranzan, I saw reflections of myself at every turn, warriors who had become so callous to all around them, so enwrapped in the goal, that they could not begin to appreciate the process of attaining it."

"They are drow," Dwahvel said. "We cannot understand their true motivations."

"Their city is a beautiful place, my little friend," Entreri replied, "with power beyond anything you can imagine. Yet, for all for that, Menzoberranzan is a hollow and empty place, bereft of passion unless that passion is hate. I came back from that city of twenty thousand assassins changed indeed, questioning the very foundations of my existence. What is the point of it, after all?"

Dwahvel interlocked the fingers of her plump little hands and brought them up to her lips, studying the man intently. Was Entreri announcing his retirement? she wondered. Was he denying the life he had known, the glories to which he had climbed? She blew a quiet sigh, shook her head, and said, "We all answer that question for ourselves, don't we? The point is gold or respect or property or power . . ."

"Indeed," he said coldly. "I walk now with a better understanding of who I am and what challenges before me are truly important. I know not yet where I hope to go, what challenges are left before me, but I do understand now that the important thing is to enjoy the process of getting there.

"Do I care that my reputation remains strong?" Entreri asked suddenly, even as Dwahvel started to ask him if he had any idea at all of where his road might lead—important information, given the power of the Basadoni Guild. "Do I wish to continue to be upheld as the pinnacle of success among assassins within Calimport?

"Yes, to both, but not for the same reasons that those fools swagger about the street corners, not for the same reasons that many of them will make a try for me, only to wind up dead in the gutter. No, I care about reputation because it allows me to be so much more effective in that which I choose to do. I care for celebrity, but only because in that mantle my foes fear me more, fear me beyond rational thinking and beyond the bounds of proper caution. They are afraid, even as they come after me, but instead of a healthy respect, their fear is almost paralyzing, making them continuously second-guess their own every move. I can use that fear against them. With a simple bluff or feint, I can make the doubt lead them into a completely erroneous position. Because I can feign vulnerability and use perceived advantages against the careless, on those occasions when I am truly vulnerable the cautious will not aggressively strike."

He paused and nodded, and Dwahvel saw that his thoughts were indeed sorting out. "An enviable position, to be sure," she offered.

"Let the fools come after me, one after another, an endless line of eager assassins," Entreri said, and he nodded again. "With each kill, I grow wiser, and with added wisdom, I grow stronger."

He slapped his hat, that curious small-brimmed black bolero, against his thigh, spun it up his arm with a flick of his wrist so that it rolled right over his shoulder to settle on his head, complementing the fine haircut he had just received. Only then did Dwahvel notice that the man had trimmed his thick goatee as well, leaving only a fine mustache and a small patch of hair below his lower lip, running down to his chin and going to both sides like an inverted T.

Entreri looked at the halfling, gave a sly wink, and strode from the room.

What did it all mean? Dwahvel wondered. Surely she was glad to see that the man had cleaned up his look, for she had recognized his uncharacteristic slovenliness as a sure signal that he was losing control, and worse, losing his heart.

She sat there for a long time, bouncing her clasped hands absently against her puckered lower lip, wondering why she had been invited to such a spectacle, wondering why Artemis Entreri had felt the need to open up to her, to anyone—even to himself. The man had found some epiphany, Dwahvel realized, and she suddenly realized that she had, too.

Artemis Entreri was her friend.

CHAPTER

2

Faster! Faster, I say!" Jarlaxle howled. His arm flashed repeatedly, and a seemingly endless stream of daggers spewed forth at the dodging and rolling assassin.

Entreri worked his jeweled dagger and his sword—a drow-fashioned blade that he was not particularly enamored of—furiously, with in and out vertical rolls to catch the missiles and flip them aside. All the while he kept his feet moving, skittering about, looking for an opening in Jarlaxle's superb defensive posture—a stance made all the more powerful by the constant stream of spinning daggers.

"An opening!" the drow mercenary cried, letting fly one, two, three more daggers.

Entreri sent his sword back the other way but knew that his opponent's assessment was correct. He dived into a roll instead, tucking his head and his arms in tight to cover any vital areas.

"Oh, well done!" Jarlaxle congratulated as Entreri came to his feet after taking only a single hit, and that a dagger sticking into the trailing fold of his cloak instead of his skin.

Entreri felt the dagger swing in against the back of his leg as he stood up. Fearing that it might trip him, he tossed his own dagger into the air, then quickly pulled the cloak from his shoulders, and in the same fluid movement, started to toss it aside.

An idea came to him, though, and he didn't discard the cloak but rather caught his deadly dagger and set it between his teeth. He stalked a semicircle about the drow, waving his cloak, a drow *piwafwi,* slowly about as a shield against the missiles.

Jarlaxle smiled at him. "Improvisation," he said with obvious admiration. "The mark of a true warrior." Even as he finished, though, the drow's arm starting moving yet again. A quartet of daggers soared at the assassin.

Entreri bobbed and spun a complete circuit, but tossed his cloak as he did and caught it as he came back around. One dagger skidded across the floor, another passed over Entreri's head, narrowly missing, and the other two got caught in the fabric, along with the previous one.

15

Entreri continued to wave the cloak, but it wasn't flowing wide anymore, weighted as it was by the three daggers.

"Not so good a shield, perhaps," Jarlaxle commented.

"You talk better than you fight," Entreri countered. "A bad combination."

"I talk because I so enjoy the fight, my quick friend," Jarlaxle replied.

His arm went back again, but Entreri was already moving. The human held his arm out wide to keep the cloak from tripping him, and dived into a roll right toward the mercenary, closing the gap between them in the blink of an eye.

Jarlaxle did let fly one dagger. It skipped off Entreri's back, but the drow mercenary caught the next one sliding out of his magical bracer into his hand and snapped his wrist, speaking a command word. The dagger responded at once, elongating into a sword. As Entreri came over, his sword predictably angled up to gut Jarlaxle, the drow had the parry in place.

Entreri stayed low and skittered forward instead, swinging his cloak in a roundabout manner to wrap it behind Jarlaxle's legs. The mercenary quick-stepped and almost got out of the way, but one of the daggers hooked his boot and he fell over backward. Jarlaxle was as agile as any drow, but so too was Entreri. The human came up over the drow, sword thrusting.

Jarlaxle parried fast, his blade slapping against Entreri's. To the drow's surprise, the assassin's sword went flying away. Jarlaxle understood soon enough, though, for Entreri's now free hand came forward, clasping Jarlaxle's forearm and holding the drow's weapon out wide.

And there loomed the assassin's other hand, holding again that deadly jeweled dagger.

Entreri had the opening and had the strike, and Jarlaxle couldn't block it or begin to move away from it. A wave of such despair, an overwhelming barrage of complete and utter hopelessness, washed over Entreri. He felt as if someone had just entered his brain and began scattering all of his thoughts, starting and stopping all of his reflexes. In the inevitable pause, Jarlaxle brought his other arm forward, launching a dagger that smacked Entreri in the gut and bounced away.

The barrage of discordant, paralyzing emotions continued to blast away in Entreri's mind, and he stumbled back. He hardly felt the motion and was somewhat confused a moment later, as the fuzziness began to clear, to find that he was on the other side of the small room sitting against the wall and facing a smiling Jarlaxle.

Entreri closed his eyes and at last forced the confusing jumble of thoughts completely away. He assumed that Rai-guy, the drow wizard who had imbued both Entreri and Jarlaxle with stoneskin spells that they could spar with all of their hearts without fear of injuring each other, had intervened. When he glanced that way, he saw that the wizard was nowhere to be seen. He turned back to Jarlaxle, guessing then that the mercenary had used yet another in his seemingly endless bag of tricks. Perhaps he had used his newest magical acquisition, the powerful Crenshinibon, to overwhelm Entreri's concentration.

"Perhaps you *are* slowing down, my friend," Jarlaxle remarked. "What a pity that would be. It is good that you defeated your avowed enemy when you did, for Drizzt Do'Urden has many centuries of youthful speed left in him."

Entreri scoffed at the words, though in truth, the thought gnawed at him. He had lived his entire life on the very edge of perfection and preparedness. Even now, in the middle years of his life, he was confident that he could defeat almost any foe—with pure skill or by out-thinking any enemy, by properly preparing any battlefield—but Entreri didn't want to slow down. He didn't want to lose that edge of fighting brilliance that had so marked his life.

He wanted to deny Jarlaxle's words, but he could not, for he knew in his heart that he had truly lost that fight with Drizzt, that if Kimmuriel Oblodra had not intervened with his psionic powers, then Drizzt would have been declared the victor.

"You did not outmatch me with speed," the assassin started to argue, shaking his head.

Jarlaxle came forward, his glowing eyes narrowing dangerously—a threatening expression, a look of rage, that the assassin rarely saw upon the handsome face of the always-in-control dark elf mercenary leader.

"I have *this!*" Jarlaxle announced, pulling wide his cloak and showing Entreri the tip of the artifact, Crenshinibon, the Crystal Shard, tucked neatly into one pocket. "Never forget that. Without it, I could likely still defeat you, though you are good, my friend—better than any human I have ever known. But with this in my possession . . . you are but a mere mortal. Joined in Crenshinibon, I can destroy you with but a thought. Never forget that."

Entreri lowered his gaze, digesting the words and the tone, sharpening that image of the uncharacteristic expression on Jarlaxle's always smiling face. *Joined in Crenshinibon? . . . but a mere mortal?* What in the Nine Hells did that mean? *Never forget that,* Jarlaxle had said, and indeed, this was a lesson that Artemis Entreri would not soon dismiss.

When he looked back up again, Entreri saw Jarlaxle wearing his typical expression, that sly, slightly amused look that conferred to all who saw it that this cunning drow knew more than he did, knew more than he possibly could.

Seeing Jarlaxle relaxed again also reminded Entreri of the novelty of these sparring events. The mercenary leader would not spar with any other. Rai-guy was stunned when Jarlaxle had told him that he meant to battle Entreri on a regular basis.

Entreri understood the logic behind that thinking. Jarlaxle survived, in part, by remaining mysterious, even to those around him. No one could ever really get a good look at the mercenary leader. He kept allies and opponents alike off-balance and wondering, always wondering, and yet, here he was, revealing so much to Artemis Entreri.

"Those daggers," Entreri said, coming back at ease and putting on his own sly expression. "They were merely illusions."

"In your mind, perhaps," the dark elf replied in his typically cryptic manner.

"They were," the assassin pressed. "You could not possibly carry so many, nor could any magic create them that quickly."

"As you say," Jarlaxle replied. "Though you heard the clang as your own weapons connected with them and felt the weight as they punctured your cloak."

"I *thought* I heard the clang," Entreri corrected, wondering if he had at last found a chink in the mercenary's never-ending guessing game.

"Is that not the same thing?" Jarlaxle replied with a laugh, but it seemed to Entreri as if there was a darker side to that chuckle.

Entreri lifted that cloak, to see several of the daggers—solid metal daggers—still sticking in its fabric folds, and to find several more holes in the cloth. "Some were illusions, then," he argued unconvincingly.

Jarlaxle merely shrugged, never willing to give anything away.

With an exasperated sigh, Entreri started out of the room.

"Do keep ever present in your thoughts, my friend, that an illusion can kill you if you believe in it," Jarlaxle called after him.

Entreri paused and glanced back, his expression grim. He wasn't used to being so openly warned or threatened, but he knew that with this one particular companion, the threats were never, ever idle.

"And the real thing can kill you whether you believe in it or not," Entreri replied, and he turned back for the door.

The assassin departed with a shake of his head, frustrated and yet intrigued. That was always the way with Jarlaxle, Entreri mused, and what surprised him even more was that he found that aspect of the clever drow mercenary particularly compelling.

That is the one, Kimmuriel Oblodra signaled to his two companions, Rai-guy and Berg'inyon Baenre, the most recent addition to the surface army of Bregan D'aerthe.

The favored son of the most powerful house in Menzoberranzan, Berg'inyon had grown up with all the drow world open before him—to the level that a drow male in Menzoberranzan could achieve, at least—but his mother, the powerful Matron Baenre, had led a disastrous assault on a dwarven kingdom, ending in her death and throwing all the great drow city into utter chaos. In that time of ultimate confusion and apprehension, Berg'inyon had thrown his hand in with Jarlaxle and the ever elusive mercenary band of Bregan D'aerthe. Among the finest of fighters in all the city, and with familial connections to still-mighty House Baenre, Berg'inyon was welcomed openly and quickly promoted, elevated to the status of high lieutenant. Thus, he was not here now serving Rai-guy and Kimmuriel, but as their peer, taken out on a sort of training mission.

He considered the human Kimmuriel had targeted, a shapely woman posing in the dress of a common street whore.

You have read her thoughts? Rai-guy signaled back, his fingers weaving an intricate pattern, perfectly complementing the various expressions and contortions of his handsome and angular drow features.

Raker spy, Kimmuriel silently assured his companion. *The coordinator of their group. All pass her by, reporting their finds.*

Berg'inyon shifted nervously from foot to foot, uncomfortable around the revelations of the strange and strangely powerful Kimmuriel. He hoped that Kimmuriel wasn't reading his thoughts at that moment, for he was wondering how Jarlaxle could ever feel safe with this one about. Kimmuriel could walk into someone's mind, it seemed, as easily as Berg'inyon could walk through an open doorway. He chuckled then but disguised it as a cough, when he considered that clever Jarlaxle likely had that doorway somehow trapped.

Berg'inyon decided that he'd have to learn the technique, if there was one, to keep Kimmuriel at bay.

Do we know where the others might be? Berg'inyon's hands silently asked.

Would the show be complete if we did not? came Rai-guy's responding gestures. The wizard smiled widely, and soon all three of the dark elves wore sly, hungry expressions.

Kimmuriel closed his eyes and steadied himself with long, slow breaths.

Rai-guy took the cue, pulling an eyelash encased in a bit of gum arabic out of one of his several belt pouches. He turned to Berg'inyon and began waggling his fingers. The drow warrior flinched reflexively—as most sane people would do when a drow wizard began casting in their direction.

The first spell went off, and Berg'inyon, rendered invisible, faded from view. Rai-guy went right back to work, now aiming a spell designed mentally to grab at the target, to hold the spy fast.

The woman flinched and seemed to hold for a second, but shook out of it and glanced around nervously, now obviously on her guard.

Rai-guy growled and went at the spell again. Invisible Berg'inyon stared at him with an almost mocking smile—yes, there were advantages to being invisible! Rai-guy continually demeaned humans, called them every drow name for offal and carrion. On the one hand, he was obviously surprised that this one had resisted the hold spell—no easy mental task—but on the other, Berg'inyon noted, the blustery wizard had prepared more than one of the spells. One, without any resistance, should have been enough.

This time, the woman took one step, and held fast in her walking pose.

Go! Kimmuriel's fingers waved. Even as he gestured, the powers of his mind opened the doorway between the three drow and the woman. Suddenly she was there, though she was still on the street, but only a couple of strides away. Berg'inyon leaped out and grabbed the woman, tugging her hard into the extra-dimensional space, and Kimmuriel shut the door.

It had happened so fast that to any watching on the street, it would have seemed as if the woman had simply disappeared.

The psionicist raised his delicate black hand up to the victim's forehead, melding with her mentally. He could feel the horror in there, for though her physical body had been locked in Rai-guy's stasis, her mind was working and she knew indeed that she now stood before dark elves.

Kimmuriel took just a moment to bask in that terror, thoroughly enjoying the spectacle. Then he imparted psionic energies to her. He built around her an armor of absorbing kinetic energy, using a technique he had perfected in Entreri's battle with Drizzt Do'Urden.

When it was done, he nodded.

Berg'inyon became visible again almost immediately, as his fine drow sword slashed across the woman's throat, the offensive strike dispelling the defensive magic of Rai-guy's invisibility spell. The drow warrior went into a fast dance, slashing and thrusting with both of his fine swords, stabbing hard, even chopping once with both blades, a heavy drop down onto the woman's head.

But no blood spewed forth, no groans of pain came from the woman, for Kimmuriel's armor accepted each blow, catching and holding the tremendous energy offered by the drow warrior's brutal dance.

It went on and on for several minutes, until Rai-guy warned that the spell of holding was nearing its end. Berg'inyon backed away, and Kimmuriel closed his eyes again as Rai-guy began yet another casting.

Both onlookers, Kimmuriel and Berg'inyon, smiled wickedly as Rai-guy produced a tiny ball of bat guano that held a sulfuric aroma and shoved it, along with his finger into the woman's mouth, releasing his spell. A flash of fiery light appeared in the back of the woman's mouth, disappearing as it slid down her throat.

The sidewalk was there again, very close, as Kimmuriel opened a second dimension portal to the same spot on the street, and Rai-guy roughly shoved the woman back out.

Kimmuriel shut the door, and they watched, amused.

The hold spell released first, and the woman staggered. She tried to call out, but coughed roughly from the burn in her throat. A strange expression came over her, one of absolute horror.

She feels the energy contained in the kinetic barrier, Kimmuriel explained. *I hold it no longer—only her own will prevents its release.*

How long? a concerned Rai-guy asked, but Kimmuriel only smiled and motioned for them to watch and enjoy.

The woman broke into a run. The three drow noted other people moving about her, some closing cautiously—other spies, likely—and others seeming merely curious. Still others grew alarmed and tried to stay away from her.

All the while, she tried to scream out, but just kept hacking from the continuing burn in her throat. Her eyes were wide, so horrifyingly and satisfyingly wide! She could feel the tremendous energies within her, begging release, and she had no idea how she might accomplish that.

She couldn't hold the kinetic barrier, and her initial realization of the problem transformed from horror into confusion. All of Berg'inyon's terrible beating came out then, so suddenly. All of the slashes and the stabs, the great chop and the twisting heart thrust, burst over the helpless woman. To those watching, it seemed almost as if she simply fell apart, gallons of blood erupting about her face, head, and chest.

She went down almost immediately, but before anyone could even begin to react, could run away or charge to her aid, Rai-guy's last spell, a delayed fireball, went off, immolating the already dead woman and many of those around her.

Outside the blast, wide-eyed stares came at the charred corpse from comrade and ignorant onlooker alike, expressions of the sheerest terror that surely pleased the three merciless dark elves.

A fine display. Worthy indeed.

For Berg'inyon, the spectacle served a second purpose, a clear reminder to him to take care around these fellow lieutenants himself. Even taking into consideration the high drow standards for torture and murder, these two were particularly adept, true masters of the craft.

CHAPTER

3

He had his old room back. He even had his name back. The memories of the authorities in Luskan were not as long as they claimed.

The previous year, Morik the Rogue had been accused of attempting to murder the honorable Captain Deudermont of the good ship *Sea Sprite,* a famous pirate hunter. Since in Luskan accusation and conviction were pretty much the same thing, Morik had faced the prospect of a horrible death in the public spectacle of Prisoner's Carnival. He had actually been in the process of realizing that ultimate torture when Captain Deudermont, horrified by the gruesome scene, had offered a pardon.

Pardoned or not, Morik had been forever banned from Luskan on pain of death. He had returned anyway, of course, the following year. At first he'd taken on an assumed identity, but gradually he had regained his old trappings, his true mannerisms, his connections on the streets, his apartment, and, finally, his name and the reputation it carried. The authorities knew it too, but having plenty of other thugs to torture to death, they didn't seem to care.

Morik could look back on that awful day at Prisoner's Carnival with a sense of humor now. He thought it perfectly ironic that he had been tortured for a crime that he hadn't even committed when there were so many crimes of which he could be rightly convicted.

It was all a memory now, the memory of a whirlwind of intrigue and danger by the name of Wulfgar. He was Morik the Rogue once more, and all was as it had once been . . . almost.

For now there was another element, an intriguing and also terrifying element, that had come into Morik's life. He walked up to the door of his room cautiously, glancing all about the narrow hallway, studying the shadows. When he was confident that he was alone, he walked up tight to the door, shielding it from any magically prying eyes, and began the process of undoing nearly a dozen deadly traps, top to bottom along both sides of the jamb. That done, he took out a ring of keys and undid the locks—one, two, three—then he clicked open the door. He disarmed yet another trap—this one explosive—then entered, closing and securing the door and resetting all the traps. The complete process took him more than ten minutes, yet he performed this ritual every time he came home. The dark elves had come into Morik's life, unannounced and uninvited. While they had promised him the treasure of a king if he performed their tasks, they had also promised him and had shown him the flip side of that golden coin as well.

Morik checked the small pedestal at the side of the door next. He nodded, satisfied to see that the orb was still in place in the wide vase. The vessel was coated with contact poison and maintained a sensitive pressure release trap. He had paid dearly for that particular orb—an enormous amount of gold that would take him a year of hard thievery to retrieve—but in Morik's fearful eyes, the item was well worth the price. It was enchanted with a powerful anti-magic dweomer that would prevent dimensional doors from opening in his room, that would prevent wizards from strolling in on the other side of a teleportation spell.

Never again did Morik the Rogue wish to be awakened by a dark elf standing at the side of his bed, looming over him.

All of his locks were in place, his orb rested in its protected vessel, and yet some subtle signal, an intangible breeze, a tickling on the hairs at the back of his neck, told Morik that something was out of place. He glanced all around, from shadow to shadow, to the drapes that still hung over the window he had long ago bricked up. He looked to his bed, to the tightly tucked sheets, with no blankets hanging below the edge. Bending just a bit, Morik saw right through the bottom of the bed. There was no one hiding under there.

The drapes, then, he thought, and he moved in that general direction but took a circuitous route so that he wouldn't force any action from the intruder. A sudden shift and quick-step brought him there, dagger revealed, and he pulled the drapes aside and struck hard, catching only air.

Morik laughed in relief and at his own paranoia. How different his world had become since the arrival of the dark elves. Always now he was on the edge of his nerves. He had seen the drow a total of only five times, including their initial encounter way back when Wulfgar was new to the city and they, for some reason that Morik still did not completely understand, wanted him to keep an eye on the huge barbarian.

He was always on his edge, always wary, but he reminded himself of the potential gains his alliance with the drow would bring. Part of the reason that he was Morik the Rogue again, from what he had been able to deduce, had to do with a visit to a particular authority by one of Jarlaxle's henchmen.

He gave a sigh of relief and let the drapes swing back, then froze in surprise and fear as a hand clamped over his mouth and the fine edge of a dagger came tight against his throat.

"You have the jewels?" a voice whispered in his ear, a voice showing incredible strength and calm despite its quiet tone. The hand slipped off of his mouth and up to his forehead, forcing his head back just enough to remind him of how vulnerable and open his throat was.

Morik didn't answer, his mind racing through many possibilities—the least likely of which seeming to be his potential escape, for that hand holding him revealed frightening strength and the hand holding the dagger at his throat was too, too steady. Whoever his attacker might be, Morik understood immediately that he was overmatched.

"I ask one more time; then I end my frustration," came the whisper.

"You are not drow," Morik replied, as much to buy some time as to ensure that this man—and he knew that it was a man and certainly no dark elf—would not act rashly.

"Perhaps I am, though under the guise of a wizard's spell," the assailant replied. "But that could not be—or could it?—since no magic will work in this room." As he finished, he roughly pushed Morik away, then grabbed his shoulder to spin the frightened rogue around as he fell back.

Morik didn't recognize the man, though he still understood that he was in imminent danger. He glanced down at his own dagger, and it seemed a pitiful thing indeed against the magnificent, jewel-handled blade his opponent carried—almost a reflection of the relative strengths of their wielders, Morik recognized with a wince.

Morik the Rogue was as good a thief as roamed the streets of Luskan, a city full of thieves. His reputation, though bloated by bluff, had been well-earned across the bowels of the city. This man before him, older than Morik by a decade, perhaps, and standing so calm and so balanced . . .

This man had gotten into his apartment and had remained there unobserved despite Morik's attempted scrutiny. Morik noted then that the bed sheets were rumpled—but hadn't he just looked at them, to see them perfectly smooth?

"You are not drow," Morik dared to say again.

"Not all of Jarlaxle's agents are dark elves, are they, Morik the Rogue?" the man replied.

Morik nodded and slipped his dagger into its sheath at his belt, a move designed to alleviate the tension, something that Morik desperately wanted to do.

"The jewels?" the man asked.

Morik could not hide the panic from his face.

"You should have purchased them from Telsburgher," the man remarked. "The way was clear and the assignment was not difficult."

"The way would have been clear," Morik corrected, "but for a minor magistrate who holds old grudges."

The intruder continued to stare, showing neither intrigue nor anger, telling Morik nothing at all about whether or not he was even interested in any excuses.

"Telsburgher is ready to sell them to me," Morik quickly added, "at the agreed price. His hesitation is only a matter of his fear that there will be retribution from Magistrate Jharkheld. The evil man holds an old grudge. He knows that I am back in town and wishes to drag me back to his Prisoner's Carnival, but he cannot, by word of his superiors, I am told. Thank Jarlaxle for me."

"You thank Jarlaxle by performing as instructed," the man replied, and Morik nervously shifted from foot to foot. "He helps you to fill his purse, not to fill his heart with good feelings."

Morik nodded. "I fear to go after Jharkheld," he explained. "How high might I strike without incurring the wrath of the greater powers of Luskan, thus ultimately wounding Jarlaxle's purse?"

"Jharkheld is not a concern," the man answered with a tone so assured that Morik found that he believed every word. "Complete the transaction."

"But . . ." Morik started to reply.

"This night," came the answer, and the man turned away and started for the door.

His hands worked in amazing circles right before Morik's eyes as trap after trap after lock fell open. It had taken Morik several minutes to get through that door, and that with an intricate knowledge of every trap—which he had set—and with the keys for the three supposedly difficult locks, and yet, within the span of two minutes, the door now swung open wide.

The man glanced back and tossed something to the floor at Morik's feet.

A wire.

"The one on your bottom trap had stretched beyond usefulness," the man explained. "I repaired it for you."

He went out then and closed the door, and Morik heard the clicks and sliding panels as all the locks and traps were efficiently reset.

Morik went to his bed cautiously and pulled the bed sheets aside. A hole had been cut into his mattress, perfectly sized to hold the intruder. Morik gave a helpless laugh, his respect for Jarlaxle's band multiplying. He didn't even have to go over to his trapped vase to know that the orb now within it was a fake and that the real one had just walked out his door.

Entreri blinked as he walked out into the late afternoon Luskan sun. He dropped a hand into his pocket, to feel the enchanted device he had just taken from Morik. This small orb had frustrated Rai-guy. It defeated his magic when he'd tried to visit Morik himself, as it was likely doing now. That thought alone pleased Entreri greatly. It had taken Bregan D'aerthe nearly a tenday to discern the source of Morik's sudden distance, how the man had made his room inaccessible to the prying eyes of the wizards. Thus, Entreri had been sent. He held no illusions that his trip had to do with his thieving prowess, but rather, it was simply because the dark elves weren't certain of how resistant Morik might be and simply hadn't wished to risk any of their brethren in the exploration. Certainly Jarlaxle wouldn't have been pleased to learn that Rai-guy and Kimmuriel had forced Entreri to go, but the pair knew that Entreri wouldn't go to Jarlaxle with the information.

So Entreri had played message boy for the two formidable, hated dark elves.

His instructions upon taking the orb and finishing his business with Morik had been explicit and precise. He was to place the orb aside and use the magical signal whistle Rai-guy had given him to call to the dark elves in faraway Calimport, but he wasn't in any hurry.

He knew that he should have killed Morik, both for the man's impertinence in trying to shield himself and for failing to produce the required jewels. Rai-guy and Kimmuriel would demand such punishment, of course. Now he'd have to justify his actions, to protect Morik somewhat.

He knew Luskan fairly well, having been through the city several times, including an extended visit only a few days before, when he, along with several other drow agents, had learned the truth of Morik's magic-blocking device. Wandering the streets, he soon heard the shouts and cheers of the vicious Prisoner's Carnival. He entered the back of the open square just as some poor fool was having his intestines pulled out like a great length of rope. Entreri hardly noticed the spectacle, concentrating instead on the sharp-featured, diminutive, robed figure presiding over the torture.

The man screamed at the writhing victim, telling him to surrender his associates, there and then, before it was too late. "Secure a chance for a more pleasant afterlife!" the magistrate screeched, his voice as sharp as his angry, angular features. "Now! Before you die!"

The man only wailed. It seemed to Entreri as if he was far beyond any point of even comprehending the magistrate's words.

He died soon enough and the show was over. The people began filtering out of the square, most nodding their heads and smiling, speaking excitedly of Jharkheld's fine show this day.

That was all Entreri needed to hear.

He moved shadow to shadow, following the magistrate down the short walk from the back of the square to the tower that housed the quarters of the officials of Prisoner's Carnival as well as the dungeons holding those who would soon face the public tortures.

He mused at his own good fortune in carrying Morik's orb, for it gave him some measure of protection from any wizard hired to further secure the tower. That left only sentries and mechanical traps in his way.

Artemis Entreri feared neither.

He went into the tower as the sun disappeared in the west.

"They have too many allies," Rai-guy insisted.

"They would be gone without a trace," Jarlaxle replied with a wide smile. "Simply gone."

Rai-guy groaned and shook his head, and Kimmuriel, across the room and sitting comfortably in a plush chair, one leg thrown over the cushioning arm, looked up at the ceiling and rolled his eyes.

"You continue to doubt me?" Jarlaxle asked, his tone light and innocent, not threatening. "Consider all that we have already accomplished here in Calimport and across the surface. We have agents in several major cities, including Waterdeep."

"We are *exploring* agents in other cities," Rai-guy corrected. "We have but one currently working, the little rogue in Luskan." He paused and glanced over at his psionicist counterpart and smiled. "Perhaps."

Kimmuriel chuckled as he considered their second agent now working in Luskan, the one Jarlaxle did not know had left Calimport.

"The others are preliminary," Rai-guy went on. "Some are promising, others not so, but none are worthy of the title of agent at this time."

"Soon, then," said Jarlaxle, coming forward in his own comfortable chair. "Soon! They will become profitable partners or we will find others—not so difficult a thing to do among the greedy humans. The situation here in Calimport . . . look around you. Can you doubt our wisdom in coming here? The gems and jewels are flowing fast, a direct line to a drow population eager to expand their possessions beyond the limited wealth of Menzoberranzan."

"Fortunate are we if the houses of Ched Nasad determine that we are undercutting their economy," Rai-guy, who hailed from that other drow city, remarked sarcastically.

Jarlaxle scoffed at the notion.

"I cannot deny the profitability of Calimport," the wizard lieutenant went on, "yet when we first planned our journey to the surface, we all agreed that it would show immediate and strong returns. As we all agreed it would likely be a short tenure, and that, after the initial profits, we would do well to reconsider our position and perhaps retreat to our own land, leaving only the best of the trading connections and agents in place."

"So we should reconsider, and so I have," said Jarlaxle. "It seems obvious to me that we underestimated the potential of our surface operations. Expand! Expand, I say."

Again came the disheartened expressions. Kimmuriel was still staring at the ceiling, as if in abject denial of what Jarlaxle was proposing.

"The Rakers desire that we limit our trade to this one section," Jarlaxle reminded, "yet many of the craftsmen of the more exotic goods—merchandise that would likely prove most attractive in Menzoberranzan—are outside of that region."

"Then we cut a deal with the Rakers, let them in on the take for this new and profitable market to which they have no access," said Rai-guy, a perfectly reasonable suggestion in light of the history of Bregan D'aerthe, a mercenary and opportunistic band that always tried to use the words "mutually beneficial" as their business credo.

"They are pimples," Jarlaxle replied, extending his thumb and index finger in the air before him and pressing them together as if he was squeezing away an unwanted blemish. "They will simply disappear."

"Not as easy a task as you seem to believe," came a feminine voice from the doorway, and the three glanced over to see Sharlotta Vespers gliding into the room, dressed in a long gown slit high enough to reveal one very shapely leg. "The Rakers pride themselves on spreading their organizational lines far and wide. You could destroy all of their houses and all of their known agents, even all of the people dealing with all of their agents, and still leave many witnesses."

"Who would do what?" Jarlaxle asked, but he was still smiling, even patting his chair for Sharlotta to go over and sit with him, which she did, curling about him familiarly.

The sight of it made Rai-guy glance again at Kimmuriel. Both knew that Jarlaxle was bedding the human woman, the most powerful remnant—along with Entreri—of the old Basadoni Guild, and neither of them liked the idea. Sharlotta was a sly one, as humans go, almost sly enough to be accepted among the society of drow. She had even mastered the language of the drow and was now working on the intricate hand signals of the dark elven silent code. Rai-guy found her perfectly repulsive, and Kimmuriel, though seeing her as exotic, did not like the idea of having her whispering dangerous suggestions into Jarlaxle's ear.

In this particular matter, though, it seemed to both of them that Sharlotta was on their side, so they didn't try to interrupt her as they usually did.

"Witnesses who would tell every remaining guild," Sharlotta explained, "and who would inform the greater powers of Calimshan. The destruction of the Rakers Guild would imply that a truly great power had secretly come to Calimport."

"One has," Jarlaxle said with a grin.

"One whose greatest strength lies in remaining secret," Sharlotta replied.

Jarlaxle pushed her from his lap, right off the chair, so that she had to move quickly to get her shapely legs under her in time to prevent falling unceremoniously on her rump.

The mercenary leader then rose as well, pushing right past Sharlotta as if her opinion mattered not at all, and moving closer to his more important lieutenants. "I once envisioned Bregan D'aerthe's role on the surface as that of importer and exporter," he explained. "This we have easily achieved. Now I see the truth of the human dominated societies, and that is a truth of weakness. We can go further—we *must* go further."

"Conquest?" Rai-guy asked sourly, sarcastically.

"Not as Baenre attempted with Mithral Hall," Jarlaxle eagerly explained. "More a matter of absorption." Again came that wicked smile. "For those who will play."

"And those who will not simply disappear?" Rai-guy asked, but his sarcasm seemed lost on Jarlaxle, who only smiled all the wider.

"Did you not execute a Raker spy only the other day?" Jarlaxle asked.

"There is a profound difference in defending our privacy and trying to expand our borders," the wizard replied.

"Semantics," Jarlaxle said with a laugh. "Simply semantics."

Behind him, Sharlotta Vespers bit her lip and shook her head, fearing that her newfound benefactors might be about to make a tremendous and very dangerous blunder.

From an alley not so far away, Entreri listened to the shouts and confusion coming from the tower. When he had entered, he'd gone downstairs first, to find a particularly unpleasant prisoner to free. Once he had ushered the man to relative safety, to the open tunnels at the back of the dungeons, he had gone upstairs to the first floor, then up again, moving quietly and deliberately along the shadowy, torch-lit corridors.

Finding Jharkheld's room proved easy enough.

The door hadn't even been locked.

Had he not just witnessed the magistrate's work at Prisoner's Carnival, Artemis Entreri might have reasoned with him concerning Morik. Now the way was clear for Morik to complete his task and proffer the jewels.

Entreri wondered if the escaped prisoner, the obvious murderer of poor Jharkheld, had been found in the maze of tunnels yet. What misery the man would face. A wry grin found its way onto Entreri's face, for he hardly felt any guilt about using the wretch for his own gain. The idiot should have known better, after all. Why would someone come in unannounced and at obvious great personal risk to save him? Why hadn't he even questioned Entreri while the assassin was releasing him from the shackles? Why, if he was smart enough to deserve his life, hadn't he tried to capture Entreri in his place, to put this unasked-for and unknown savior up in the shackles in his stead, to face the executioner? So many prisoners came through these dungeons that the gaolers likely wouldn't even have been aware of the change.

So, his fate was the thug's own to accept, and in Entreri's thinking, of his own doing. Of course, the thug would claim that someone else had helped him to escape, had set it all up to make it look like it was his doing.

Prisoner's Carnival hardly cared for such excuses.

Nor did Artemis Entreri.

He dismissed all thoughts of those problems, glanced around to ensure that he was alone, and placed the magic dispelling orb along the side of the alley. He walked across the way and blew his whistle. He wondered then how this might work. Magic would be needed, after all, to get him back to Calimport, but how might that work if he had to take the orb along? Wouldn't the orb's dweomer simply dispel the attempted teleportation?

A blue screen of light appeared beside him. It was a magical doorway, he knew, and not one of Rai-guy's, but rather the doing of Kimmuriel Oblodra. So that was it, he mused. Perhaps the orb wouldn't work against psionics.

Or perhaps it would, and that thought unsettled the normally unshakable Entreri profoundly as he moved to collect the item. What would happen if the orb somehow did affect Kimmuriel's dimension warp? Might he wind up in the wrong place—even in another plane of existence, perhaps?

Entreri shook that thought away as well. Life was risky when dealing with drow, magical orbs or not. He took care to pocket the orb slyly, so that any prying eyes would have a difficult time making out the movement in the dark alley, then strode quickly up to the portal, and with a single deep breath, stepped through.

He came out dizzy, fighting hard to hold his balance, in the guild hall's private sorcery chambers back in Calimport, hundreds and hundreds of miles away.

There stood Kimmuriel and Rai-guy, staring at him hard.

"The jewels?" Rai-guy asked in the drow language, which Entreri understood, though not well.

"Soon," the assassin replied in his shaky command of Deep Drow. "There was a problem."

Both dark elves lifted their white eyebrows in surprise.

"*Was,*" Entreri emphasized. "Morik will have the jewels presently."

"Then Morik lives," Kimmuriel remarked pointedly. "What of his attempts to hide from us?"

"More the attempts of local magistrates to seal him off from any outside influences," Entreri lied. "One local magistrate," he quickly corrected, seeing their faces sour. "The issue has been remedied."

Neither drow seemed pleased, but neither openly complained.

"And this local magistrate had magically sealed off Morik's room from outside, prying eyes?" Rai-guy asked.

"And all other magic," Entreri answered. "It has been corrected."

"With the orb?" Kimmuriel added.

"Morik proffered the orb," Rai-guy remarked, narrowing his eyes.

"He apparently did not know what he was buying," Entreri said calmly, not getting alarmed, for he recognized that his ploys had worked.

Rai-guy and Kimmuriel would hold their suspicions that it had been Morik's work, and not that of any minor official, of course. They would suspect that Entreri had bent the truth to suit his own needs, but the assassin knew that he hadn't given them anything overt enough for them to act upon—at least, not without raising the ire of Jarlaxle.

Again, the realization that his security was almost wholly based on the mercenary leader did not sit well with Entreri. He didn't like being dependent, equating the word with weakness.

He had to turn the situation around.

"You have the orb," Rai-guy remarked, holding out his slender, deceivingly delicate hand.

"Better for me than for you," the assassin dared to reply, and that declaration set the two dark elves back on their heels.

Even as he finished speaking, though, Entreri felt the tingling in his pocket. He dropped a hand to the orb, and his sensitive fingers felt a subtle vibration coming from deep within the enchanted item. Entreri's gaze focused on Kimmuriel. The drow was standing with his eyes closed, deep in concentration.

Then he understood. The orb's enchantment would do nothing against any of Kimmuriel's formidable mind powers, and Entreri had seen this psionic trick before. Kimmuriel was reaching into the latent energy within the orb and was exciting that energy to explosive levels.

Entreri toyed with the idea of waiting until the last moment then throwing the orb into Kimmuriel's face. How he would enjoy the sight of that wretched drow caught in one of his own tricks!

With a wave of his hand, Kimmuriel opened a dimensional portal, from the room to the nearly deserted dusty street outside. It was a portal large enough for the orb, but that would not allow Entreri to step through.

Entreri felt the energy building, building . . . the vibrations were not so subtle any longer. Still he held back, staring at Kimmuriel—just staring and waiting, letting the drow know that he was not afraid.

In truth this was no contest of wills. Entreri had a mounting explosion in his pocket, and Kimmuriel was far enough away so that he would feel little effect from it other than the splattering of Entreri's blood. Again the assassin considered throwing the orb into Kimmuriel's face, but again he realized the futility of such a course.

Kimmuriel would simply stop exciting the latent energy within the orb, would shut off the explosion as completely as dipping a torch into water snuffed out its flame. Entreri would have given Rai-guy and Kimmuriel all the justification they needed to utterly destroy him. Jarlaxle might be angry, but he couldn't and wouldn't deny them their right to defend themselves.

Artemis Entreri wasn't ready for such a fight.

Not yet.

He tossed the orb out through the open door and watched, a split second later, as it exploded into dust.

The magical door went away.

"You play dangerous games," Rai-guy remarked.

"Your drow friend is the one who brought on the explosion," Entreri casually replied.

"I speak not of that," the wizard retorted. "There is a common saying among your people that it is foolhardy to send a child to do a man's work. We have a similar saying, that it is foolhardy to send a human to do a drow's work."

Entreri stared at him hard, having no response. This whole situation was starting to feel like those days when he had been trapped down in Menzoberranzan, when he had known that, in a city of twenty thousand dark elves, no matter how good he got, no matter how perfect his craft, he would never be considered any higher in society's rankings than twenty thousand and one.

Rai-guy and Kimmuriel tossed out a few phrases between themselves, insults mostly, some crude, some subtle, all aimed at Entreri.

He took them, every one, and said nothing, because he could say nothing. He kept thinking of Dallabad Oasis and a particular sword and gauntlet combination.

He accepted their demeaning words, because he had to.

For now.

CHAPTER

MANY ROADS TO MANY PLACES

4

Entreri stood in the shadows of the doorway, listening with great curiosity to the soliloquy taking place in the room. He could only make out small pieces of the oration. The speaker, Jarlaxle, was talking quickly and excitedly in the drow tongue. Entreri, in addition to his limited Deep Drow vocabulary, couldn't hear every word from this distance.

"They will not stay ahead of us, because we move too quickly," the mercenary leader remarked. Entreri heard and was able to translate every word of that line, for it seemed as if Jarlaxle was cheering someone on. "Yes, street by street they will fall. Who can stand against us joined?"

"Us *joined?*" the assassin silently echoed, repeating the drow word over and over to make sure that he was translating it properly. *Us?* Jarlaxle could not be speaking of his alliance with Entreri, or even with the remnants of the Basadoni Guild. Compared to the strength of Bregan D'aerthe, these were minor additions. Had Jarlaxle made some new deal, then, without Entreri's knowledge? A deal with some pasha, perhaps, or an even greater power?

The assassin bent in closer, listening particularly for any names of demons or devils—or of illithids, perhaps. He shuddered at the thought of any of the three. Demons were too unpredictable and too savage to serve any alliance. They would do whatever served their specific needs at any particular moment, without regard for the greater benefit to the alliance. Devils were more predictable—were *too* predictable. In their hierarchical view of the world, they inevitably sat on top of the pile.

Still, compared to the third notion that had come to him, that of the illithids, Entreri was almost hoping to hear Jarlaxle utter the name of a mighty demon. Entreri had been forced to deal with illithids during his stay in Menzoberranzan—the mind flayers were an unavoidable side of life in the drow city—and he had no desire to ever, ever, see one of the squishy-headed, wretched creatures again.

He listened a bit longer, and Jarlaxle seemed to calm down and to settle more comfortably into his seat. The mercenary leader was still talking, just muttering to himself about the impending downfall of the Rakers, when Entreri strode into the room.

"Alone?" the assassin asked innocently. "I thought I heard voices."

He noted with some relief that Jarlaxle wasn't wearing his magical, protective eye patch this day, which made it unlikely that the drow had just encountered, or soon planned to encounter, any illithids. The eye patch protected against mind magic, and none in all the world were more proficient at such things as the dreaded mind flayers.

"Sorting things out," Jarlaxle explained, and his ease with the common tongue of the surface world seemed no less fluent than that of his native language. "There is so much afoot."

"Danger, mostly," Entreri replied.

"For some," said Jarlaxle with a chuckle.

Entreri looked at him doubtfully.

"Surely you do not believe that the Rakers can match our power?" the mercenary leader asked incredulously.

"Not in open battle," Entreri answered, "but that is how it has been with them for many years. They cannot match many, blade to blade, and yet they have ever found a way to survive."

"Because they are fortunate."

"Because they are intricately tied to greater powers," Entreri corrected. "A man need not be physically powerful if he is guarded by a giant."

"Unless the giant has more tightly befriended a rival," Jarlaxle interjected. "And giants are known to be unreliable."

"You have arranged this with the greater lords of Calimport?" Entreri asked, unconvinced. "With whom, and why was I not involved in such a negotiation?"

Jarlaxle shrugged, offering not a clue.

"Impossible," Entreri decided. "Even if you threatened one or more of them, the Rakers are too long-standing, too entrenched in the power web of all Calimshan, for such treachery against them to prosper. They have allies to protect them against other allies. There is no way that even Jarlaxle and Bregan D'aerthe could have cleared the opposition to such a sudden and destabilizing shift in the power structure of the region as the decimation of the Rakers."

"Perhaps I have allied with the most powerful being ever to come to Calimport," Jarlaxle said dramatically, and typically, cryptically.

Entreri narrowed his dark eyes and stared at the outrageous drow, looking for clues, any clues, as to what this uncharacteristic behavior might herald. Jarlaxle was often cryptic, always mysterious, and ever ready to grab at an opportunity that would bring him greater power or profits, and yet, something seemed out of place here. To Entreri's thinking, the impending assault on the Rakers was a blunder, which was something the legendary Jarlaxle never did. It seemed obvious, then, that the cunning drow had indeed made some powerful connection or ally, or was possessed of some deeper understanding of the situation. This Entreri doubted since he, not Jarlaxle, was the best connected person on Calimport's streets.

Even given one of those possibilities, though, something just didn't seem quite right to Entreri. Jarlaxle was cocky and arrogant—of course he was!—but never before had he seemed this self-assured, especially in a situation as potentially explosive as this.

The situation seemed only more explosive if Entreri looked beyond the inevitability of the downfall of the Rakers. He knew well the murderous power of the dark elves and held no doubt that Bregan D'aerthe would slaughter the competing guild, but there were so many implications to that victory—too many, certainly, for Jarlaxle to be so comfortable.

"Has your role in this been determined?" Jarlaxle asked.

"No role," Entreri answered, and his tone left no doubt that he was pleased by that fact: "Rai-guy and Kimmuriel have all but cast me aside."

Jarlaxle laughed aloud, for the truth behind that statement—that Entreri had been willingly cast aside—was all too obvious.

Entreri stared at him and didn't crack a smile. Jarlaxle had to know the dangers he had just walked into, a potentially catastrophic situation that could send him and Bregan D'aerthe fleeing back to the dark hole of Menzoberranzan. Perhaps that was it, the assassin mused. Perhaps Jarlaxle longed for home and was slyly facilitating the move. The mere thought of that made Entreri wince. Better that Jarlaxle kill him outright than drag him back there.

Perhaps Entreri would be set up as an agent, as was Morik in Luskan. No, the assassin decided, that would not suffice. Calimport was more dangerous than Luskan, and if the power of Bregan D'aerthe was forced away, he would not take such a risk. Too many powerful enemies would be left behind.

"It will begin soon, if it has not already," Jarlaxle remarked. "Thus, it will be over soon."

Sooner than you believe, Entreri thought, but he kept silent. He was a man who survived through careful calculation, by weighing scrupulously the consequences of every step and every word. He knew Jarlaxle to be a kindred spirit, but he could not reconcile that with the action that was being undertaken this very night, which, in searching it from any angle, seemed a tremendous and unnecessary gamble.

What did Jarlaxle know that he did not?

<hr/>

No one ever looked more out of place anywhere than did Sharlotta Vespers as she descended the rung ladder into one of Calimport's sewers. She was wearing her trademark long gown, her hair neatly coiffed as always, her exotic face painted delicately to emphasize her brown, almond-shaped eyes. Still, she was quite at home there, and anyone who knew her would not have been surprised to find her there.

Especially if they considered her warlord escorts.

"What word from above?" Rai-guy asked her, speaking quickly and in the drow tongue. The wizard, despite his misgivings about Sharlotta, was impressed by how quickly she had absorbed the language.

"There is tension," Sharlotta replied. "The doors of many guilds are locked fast this night. Even the Copper Ante is accepting no patrons—an unprecedented event. The streets know that something is afoot."

Rai-guy flashed a sour look at Kimmuriel. The two had just agreed that their plans depended mostly on stealth and surprise, that all of the elements of the Basadoni Guild and Bregan D'aerthe would have to reach their objectives nearly simultaneously to ensure that few witnesses remained.

How much this seemed like Menzoberranzan! In the drow city, one house going after another—a not-uncommon event—would measure success not only by the result of the actual fighting, but by the lack of credible witnesses left to produce evidence of the treachery. Even if every drow in the great city knew without doubt which house had precipitated the battle, no action would ever be taken unless the evidence demanding it was overwhelming.

But this was not Menzoberranzan, Rai-guy reminded himself. Up here, suspicion would invite investigation. In the drow city, suspicion without undeniable evidence only invited quiet praise.

"Our warriors are in place," Kimmuriel remarked. "The drow are beneath the guild houses, with force enough to batter through, and the Basadoni soldiers have surrounded the main three buildings. It will be swift, for they cannot anticipate the attack from below."

Rai-guy kept his gaze upon Sharlotta as his associate detailed the situation, and he did not miss a slight arch of one of her eyebrows. Had Bregan D'aerthe been betrayed? Were the Rakers setting up defenses against the assault from below?

"The agents have been isolated?" the drow wizard pressed to Sharlotta, referring to the first round of the invasion: the fight with—or rather, the assassinations of—Raker spies in the streets.

"The agents are not to be found," Sharlotta replied matter-of-factly, a surprising tone given the enormity of the implications.

Again Rai-guy glanced at Kimmuriel.

"All is in place," the psionicist reminded.

"Keego's swarm cramps the tunnels," Rai-guy replied, his words an archaic drow proverb referring to a long-ago battle in which an overwhelming swarm of goblins led by the crafty, rebellious slave, Keego, had been utterly destroyed by a small and sparsely populated city of dark elves. The drow had gone out from their homes to catch the larger force in the tight tunnels beyond the relatively open drow city. Simply translated, given the current situation, Rai-guy's words followed up Kimmuriel's remark. All was in place to fight the wrong battle.

Sharlotta looked at the wizard curiously, and he understood her confusion, for the soldiers of Bregan D'aerthe waiting in the tunnels beneath the Rakers' houses hardly constituted a "swarm."

Of course, Rai-guy hardly cared whether Sharlotta understood or not.

"Have we traced the course of the missing agents?" Rai-guy asked Sharlotta. "Do we know where they have fled?"

"Back to the houses, likely," the woman replied. "Few are on the streets this night."

Again, the less-than-subtle hint that too much had been revealed. Had Sharlotta herself betrayed them? Rai-guy fought the urge to interrogate her on the spot, using drow torture techniques that would quickly and efficiently break down any human. If he did so, he knew, he would have to answer to Jarlaxle, and Rai-guy was not ready for that fight . . . yet.

If he called it all off at that critical moment—if all the fighters, Basadoni and dark elf, returned to the guild house with their weapons unstained by Raker blood—Jarlaxle would not be pleased. The drow was determined to see this conquest through despite the protests of all of his lieutenants.

Rai-guy closed his eyes and logically sifted through the situation, trying to find some safer common ground. There was one Raker house far removed from the others, and likely only lightly manned. While destroying it would do little to weaken the structure and effectiveness of the opposition guild, perhaps such a conquest would quiet Jarlaxle's expected rampage.

"Recall the Basadoni soldiers," the wizard ordered. "Have their retreat be a visible one—instruct some to enter the Copper Ante or other establishments."

"The Copper Ante's doors are closed," Sharlotta reminded him.

"Then open them," Rai-guy instructed. "Tell Dwahvel Tiggerwillies that there is no need for her and her diminutive clan to cower this night. Let our soldiers be seen about the streets—not as a unified fighting force, but in smaller groups."

"What of Bregan D'aerthe?" Kimmuriel asked with some concern. Not as much concern, Rai-guy noted, as he would have expected, given that he had just countermanded Jarlaxle's explicit orders.

"Reposition Berg'inyon and all of our magic-users to the eighth position," Rai-guy replied, referring to the sewer hold beneath the exposed Raker house.

Kimmuriel arched his white eyebrows at that. They knew the maximum resistance they could expect from that lone outpost, and it hardly seemed as if Berg'inyon and more magic-users would be needed to win out easily in that locale.

"It must be executed as completely and carefully as if we were attacking House Baenre itself," Rai-guy demanded, and Kimmuriel's eyebrows went even higher. "Redefine the plans and reposition all necessary drow forces to execute the attack."

"We could summon our kobold slaves alone to finish this task," Kimmuriel replied derisively.

"No kobolds and no humans," Rai-guy explained, emphasizing every word. "This is work for drow alone."

Kimmuriel seemed to catch on to Rai-guy's thinking then, for a wry smile showed on his face. He glanced at Sharlotta, nodded back at Rai-guy, and closed his eyes. He used his psionic energies to reach out to Berg'inyon and the other Bregan D'aerthe field commanders.

Rai-guy let his gaze settle fully on Sharlotta. To her credit, her expression and posture did not reveal her thoughts. Still, Rai-guy felt certain she was wondering if he had come to suspect her or some other Raker informant.

"You said that our power would prove overwhelming," Sharlotta remarked.

"For today's battle, perhaps," Rai-guy replied. "The wise thief does not steal the egg if his action will awaken the dragon."

Sharlotta continued to stare at him, continued to wonder, he knew. He enjoyed the realization that this too-clever human woman, guilty or not, was suddenly worried. She turned for the ladder again and took a step up.

"Where are you going?" Rai-guy asked.

"To recall the Basadoni soldiers," she replied, as if the explanation should have been obvious.

Rai-guy shook his head and motioned for her to step down. "Kimmuriel will relay the commands," he said.

Sharlotta hesitated—Rai-guy enjoyed the moment of confusion and concern—but she did step back down to the tunnel floor.

Berg'inyon could not believe the change in plans—what was the point of this entire offensive if the bulk of the Rakers' Guild escaped the onslaught? He had grown up in Menzoberranzan, and in that matriarchal society, males learned how to take orders without question. So it was now for Berg'inyon.

He had been trained in the finest battle tactics of the greatest house of Menzoberranzan and had at his disposal a seemingly overwhelming force for the task at hand, the destruction of a small, exposed Raker house—an outpost sitting on unfriendly streets. Despite his trepidation at the change in plans, his private questioning of the purpose of this mission, Berg'inyon Baenre wore an eager smile.

The scouts, the stealthiest of the stealthy drow, returned. Only minutes before, they had been inserted into the house above through wizard-made tunnels.

Drow fingers flashed, the silent hand gesture code.

While Berg'inyon's confidence mounted, so did his confusion over why this target alone had been selected. There were only a score of humans in the small house above, and none of them seemed to be magic-users. According to the drow scouts' assessment they were street thugs—men who survived by keeping to favorable shadows.

Under the keen eyes of a dark elf, there were no favorable shadows.

While Berg'inyon and his army had a strong idea of what they would encounter in the house above them, the humans could not understand the monumental doom that lay below them.

You have outlined to the group commanders all routes of retreat? Berg'inyon's fingers and facial gestures asked. He made it clear from the fact that he signaled retreat with his left hand that he was referring to any possible avenues their enemies might take to run away.

The wizards are positioned accordingly, one scout silently replied.

The lead hunters have been given their courses, another added.

Berg'inyon nodded, flashed the signal for commencing the operation, then moved to join his assault group. His would be the last group to enter the building, but they were the ones who would cut the fastest path to the very top.

There were two wizards in Berg'inyon's group. One stood with his eyes closed, ready to convey the signal. The other positioned himself accordingly, his eyes and hands pointed up at the ceiling, a pinch of seeds from the Underdark selussi fungus in one hand.

It is time, came a magical whisper, one that seeped through the walls and to the ears of all the drow.

The magic-user eyeing the ceiling began his spellcasting, weaving his hands as if tracing joining semicircles with each, thumbs touching, little fingers touching, back and forth, back and forth, chanting quietly all the while.

He finished with a chant that sounded more like a hiss, and reached his outstretched fingers to the ceiling.

That part of the stone ceiling began to ripple, as if the wizard had stabbed his fingers into clear water. The wizard held the pose for many seconds. The rippling increased until the stone became an indistinct blur.

The stone above the wizard disappeared—was just gone. In its place was an upward reaching corridor that cut through several feet of stone to end at the ground floor of the Raker house.

One unfortunate Raker had been caught by surprise, his heels right over the edge of the suddenly appearing hole. His arms worked great circles as he tried to maintain his balance. The drow warriors shifted into position under the hole and leaped. Enacting their innate drow levitation abilities, they floated up, up.

The first dark elf floating up beside the falling Raker grabbed him by the collar and yanked him backward, tumbling him into the hole. The human managed to land in a controlled manner, feet first, then buckling his legs and tumbling to the side to absorb the shock. He came up with equal grace, drawing a dagger.

His face blanched when he saw the truth about him: dark elves—drow!—were floating up into his guild house. Another drow, handsome and strong, holding the finest-edged blade the Raker could ever have imagined, faced him.

Maybe he tried to reason with the dark elf, offering his surrender, but while his mouth worked in a logical, hide-saving manner, his body, paralyzed by stark terror, did not. He still held his knife out before him as he spoke, and since Berg'inyon did not understand well the language of the surface dwellers, he had no way of understanding the Raker's intent.

Nor was the drow about to pause to figure it out. His fine sword stabbed forward and slashed down, taking the dagger and the hand that held it. A quick retraction re-gathered his balance and power, and out went the sword again. Straight and sure, it tore through flesh and sliced rib, biting hard at the foolish man's heart.

The man fell, quite dead, and still wearing that curious, stunned expression.

Berg'inyon didn't pause long enough to wipe his blade. He crouched, sprang straight up, and levitated fast into the house. His encounter had delayed him no more than a span of a few heartbeats, and yet, the floor of the room and the corridor beyond the open door was already littered with human corpses.

Berg'inyon's team exited the room soon after, before the wizard's initial passwall spell had even expired. Not a drow had been more than slightly injured and not a human remained alive. The Raker house held no treasure when they were done—not even the few coins several of the guildsmen had secretly tucked under loose floorboards—and even the furniture was gone. Magical fires had consumed every foot of flooring and all of the partitioning walls. From the outside, the house seemed quiet and secure. Inside, it was no more than a charred and empty husk.

Bregan D'aerthe had spoken.

⊶═╫═⊷

"I accept no accolades," Berg'inyon Baenre remarked when he met up with Rai-guy, Kimmuriel, and Sharlotta. It was a common drow saying, with clear implications that the vanquished opponent was not worthy enough for the victor to take any pride in having defeated him.

Kimmuriel gave a wry smile. "The house was effectively purged," he said. "None escaped. You performed as was required. There is no glory in that, but there is acceptance."

As he had done all day, Rai-guy continued his scrutiny of Sharlotta Vespers. Was the human woman even comprehending the sincerity of Kimmuriel's words, and if so, did that allow her any insight into the true power that had come to Calimport? For any guild to so completely annihilate one of another's houses was no small feat—unless the attacking guild happened to be comprised of drow warriors who understood the complexities of inter-house warfare better than any race in all the world. Did Sharlotta recognize this? And if she did, would she be foolish enough to try to use it to her advantage?

Her expression now was mostly stone-faced, but with just a trace of intrigue, a hint to Rai-guy that the answer would be yes, to both questions. The drow wizard smiled at that, a confirmation that Sharlotta Vespers was walking onto very dangerous ground. *Quiensin ful biezz coppon quangolth cree, a drow*, went the old saying in Menzoberranzan, and elsewhere in the drow world. Doomed are those who believe they understand the designs of the drow.

"What did Jarlaxle learn to change his course so?" Berg'inyon asked.

"Jarlaxle has learned nothing of yet," Rai-guy replied. "He chose to remain behind. The operation was mine to wage."

Berg'inyon started to redirect his question to Rai-guy then, but he stopped in midsentence and merely offered a bow to the appointed leader.

"Perhaps later you will explain to me the source of your decision, that I will better understand our enemies," he said respectfully.

Rai-guy gave a slight nod.

"There is the matter of explaining to Jarlaxle," Sharlotta remarked, in her surprising command of the drow tongue. "He will not accept your course with a mere bow."

Rai-guy's gaze darted over at Berg'inyon as she finished, quickly enough to catch the moment of anger flash through his red-glowing eyes. Sharlotta's observations were correct, of course, but coming from a non-drow, an *iblith*—which was also the drow word for excrement—they intrinsically cast an insulting reflection upon Berg'inyon, who had so accepted the offered explanation. It was a minor mistake, but a few more quips like that against the young Baenre, Rai-guy knew, and there would remain too little of Sharlotta Vespers for anyone ever to make a proper identification of the pieces.

"We must tell Jarlaxle," the drow wizard put in, moving the conversation forward. "To us out here, the course change was obviously required, but he has secluded himself, too much so perhaps, to view things that way."

Kimmuriel and Berg'inyon both looked at him curiously—why would he speak so plainly in front of Sharlotta, after all?—but Rai-guy gave them a quick and quiet signal to follow along.

"We could implicate Domo and the wererats," Kimmuriel put in, obviously catching on. "Though I fear that we will then have to waste our time in slaughtering them." He looked to Sharlotta. "Much of this will fall to you."

"The Basadoni soldiers were the first to leave the fight," Rai-guy added. "And they will be the ones to return without blood on their blades." Now all three gazes fell upon Sharlotta.

The woman held her outward calm quite well. "Domo and the wererats, then," she agreed, thinking things through, obviously, as she went. "We will implicate them without faulting them. Yes, that is the way. Perhaps they did not know of our plans and coincidentally hired on with Pasha Da'Daclan to guard the sewers. As we did not wish to reveal ourselves fully to the coward Domo, we held to the unguarded regions, mostly around the eighth position."

The three drow exchanged looks, and nodded for her to continue.

"Yes," Sharlotta went on, gathering momentum and confidence. "I can turn this into an advantage with Pasha Da'Daclan as well. He felt the press of impending doom, no doubt, and that fear will only heighten when word of the utterly destroyed outer house reaches him. Perhaps he will come to believe that Domo is much more powerful than any of us believed, and that he was in league with the Basadonis, and that only House Basadoni's former dealings with the Rakers cut short the assault."

"But will that not implicate House Basadoni clearly in the one executed attack?" asked Kimmuriel, playing the role of Rai-guy's mouthpiece, drawing Sharlotta in even deeper.

"Not that we played a role, but only that we allowed it to happen," Sharlotta reasoned. "A turn of our heads in response to their increased spying efforts against our guild. Yes, and if this is conveyed properly, it will only serve to make Domo seem even more powerful. If we make the Rakers believe that they were on the edge of complete disaster, they will behave more reasonably, and Jarlaxle will find his victory." She smiled as she finished, and the three dark elves returned the look.

"Begin," Rai-guy offered, waving his hand toward the ladder leading out of their sewer quarters.

Sharlotta smiled again, the ignorant fool, and left them.

"Her deception against Pasha Da'Daclan will necessarily extend, to some level, to Jarlaxle," Kimmuriel remarked, clearly envisioning the web Sharlotta was foolishly weaving about herself.

"You have come to fear that something is not right with Jarlaxle," Berg'inyon bluntly remarked, for it was obvious that these two would not normally act so independently of their leader.

"His views have changed," Kimmuriel responded.

"You did not wish to come to the surface," Berg'inyon said with a wry smile that seemed to question the motives of his companions' reasoning.

"No, and glad will we be to see the heat of Narbondel again," Rai-guy agreed, speaking of the great glowing clock of Menzoberranzan, a pillar that revealed its measurements with heat to the dark elves, who viewed the Underdark world in the infrared spectrum of light. "You have not been up here long enough to appreciate the ridiculousness of this place. Your heart will call you home soon enough."

"Already," Berg'inyon replied. "I have no taste for this world, nor do I like the sight or smell of any I have seen up here, Sharlotta Vespers least of all."

"Her and the fool Entreri," said Rai-guy. "Yet Jarlaxle favors them both."

"His tenure in Bregan D'aerthe may be nearing its end," said Kimmuriel, and both Berg'inyon and Rai-guy opened their eyes wide at such a bold proclamation.

In truth, though, both were harboring the exact same sentiments. Jarlaxle had reached far in merely bringing them to the surface. Perhaps he'd reached too far for the rogue band to continue to hold much favor among their former associates, including most of the great houses back in Menzoberranzan. It was a gamble, and one that might indeed pay off, especially as the flow of exotic and desirable goods increased to the city.

The plan, however, had been for a short stay, only long enough to establish a few agents to properly facilitate the flow of trade. Jarlaxle had stepped in more deeply then, conquering House Basadoni and renewing his ties with the dangerous Entreri. Then, seemingly for his own amusement, Jarlaxle had gone after the most hated rogue, Drizzt Do'Urden. After completing his business with the outcast and stealing the mighty artifact Crenshinibon, he had let Drizzt walk away, had even forced Rai-guy to use a Lolth-bestowed spell of healing to save the miserable renegade's life.

And now this, a more overt grab for not profit but power, and in a place where none of Bregan D'aerthe other than Jarlaxle wished to remain.

Jarlaxle had taken small steps along this course, but he had put a long and winding road behind him. He brought all of Bregan D'aerthe further and further from their continuing mission, from the allure that had brought most of the members, Rai-guy, Kimmuriel, and Berg'inyon among them, into the organization in the first place.

"What of Sharlotta Vespers?" Kimmuriel asked.

"Jarlaxle will eliminate that problem for us," Rai-guy replied.

"Jarlaxle favors her," Berg'inyon reminded.

"She just entered into a deception against him," Rai-guy replied with all confidence. "We know this, and she knows that we know, though she has not yet considered the potentially devastating implications. She will follow our commands from this point forward."

The drow wizard smiled as he considered his own words. He always enjoyed seeing an *iblith* fall into the web of drow society, learning piece by piece that the sticky strands were layered many levels deep.

"I know of your hunger, for I share in it," Jarlaxle remarked. "This is not as I had envisioned, but perhaps it was not yet time."

Perhaps you place too much faith in your lieutenants, the voice in his head replied.

"No, they saw something that we, in our hunger, did not," Jarlaxle reasoned. "They are troublesome, often annoying, and not to be trusted when their personal gain is at odds with their given mission, but that was not the case here. I must examine this more carefully. Perhaps there are better avenues toward our desired goal."

The voice started to respond, but the drow mercenary cut short the dialogue, shutting it out.

The abruptness of that dismissal reminded Crenshinibon that its respect for the dark elf was well-placed. This Jarlaxle was as strong of will and as difficult to beguile as any wielder the ancient sentient artifact had ever known, even counting the great demon lords who had often joined with Crenshinibon through the centuries.

In truth, the only wielder the artifact had ever known who could so readily and completely shut out its call had been the immediate predecessor to Jarlaxle, another drow, Drizzt Do'Urden. That one's mental barrier had been constructed of morals. Crenshinibon would have been no better off in the hands of a goodly priest or a paladin, fools all and blind to the need to attain the greatest levels of power.

All that only made Jarlaxle's continued resistance even more impressive, for the artifact understood that this one held no such conscience-based mores. There was no intrinsic understanding within Jarlaxle that Crenshinibon was some evil creation and thus to be avoided out of hand. No, to Crenshinibon's reasoning, Jarlaxle viewed everyone and everything he encountered as tools, as vehicles to carry him along his desired road.

The artifact could build forks along that road, and perhaps even sharper turns as Jarlaxle wandered farther and farther from the path, but there would be no abrupt change in direction at this time.

Crenshinibon, the Crystal Shard, did not even consider seeking a new wielder, as it had often done when confronting obstacles in the past. While it sensed resistance in Jarlaxle, that resistance did not implicate danger or even inactivity. To the sentient artifact, Jarlaxle was powerful and intriguing, and full of the promise of the greatest levels of power Crenshinibon had ever known.

The fact that this drow was not a simple instrument of chaos and destruction, as were so many of the demon lords, or an easily duped human—perhaps the most redundant thought the artifact had ever considered—only made him more interesting.

They had a long way to go together, Crenshinibon believed.

The artifact would find its greatest level of power. The world would suffer greatly.

CHAPTER

THE FIRST THREADS
ON A GRAND TAPESTRY

5

O thers have tried, and some have even come close," said Dwahvel
Tiggerwillies, the halfling entrepreneur and leader of the only real halfling
guild in all the city, a collection of pickpockets and informants who regularly
congregated at Dwahvel's Copper Ante. "Some have even supposedly gotten
their hands on the cursed thing."

"Cursed?" Entreri asked, resting back comfortably in his chair—a pose
Artemis Entreri rarely assumed.

So unusual was the posture, that it jogged Entreri's own thoughts about
this place. It was no accident that this was the only room in all the city in
which Artemis Entreri had ever partaken of liquor—and even that only in
moderate amounts. He had been coming here often of late—ever since he had
killed his former associate, the pitiful Dondon Tiggerwillies, in the room next
door. Dwahvel was Dondon's cousin, and she knew of the murder but knew,
too, that Entreri had, in some respects, done the wretch a favor. Whatever ill
will Dwahvel harbored over that incident couldn't hold anyway, not when her
pragmatism surfaced.

Entreri knew that and knew that he was welcomed here by Dwahvel and
all of her associates. Also, he knew that the Copper Ante was likely the most
secure house in all of the city. No, its defenses were not formidable—Jarlaxle
could flatten the place with a small fraction of the power he had brought to
Calimport—but its safeguards against prying eyes were as fine as those of a
wizards' guild. That was the area, as opposed to physical defenses, where Dwahvel
utilized most of her resources. Also, the Copper Ante was known as a place to
purchase information, so others had a reason to keep it secure. In many ways,
Dwahvel and her comrades survived as Sha'lazzi Ozoule survived, by proving
of use to all potential enemies.

Entreri didn't like the comparison. Sha'lazzi was a street profiteer, loyal to
no one other than Sha'lazzi. He was no more than a middleman, collecting
information with his purse and not his wits, and auctioning it away to the
highest bidder. He did no work other than that of salesman, and in that regard,
the man was very good. He was not a contributor, just a leech, and Entreri

suspected that Sha'lazzi would one day be found murdered in an alley, and that no one would care.

Dwahvel Tiggerwillies might find a similar fate, Entreri realized, but if she did, her murderer would find many out to avenge her.

Perhaps Artemis Entreri would be among them.

"Cursed," Dwahvel decided after some consideration.

"To those who feel its bite."

"To those who feel it at all," Dwahvel insisted.

Entreri shifted to the side and tilted his head, studying his surprising little friend.

"Kohrin Soulez is trapped by his possession of it," Dwahvel explained. "He builds a fortress about himself because he knows the value of the sword."

"He has many treasures," Entreri reasoned, but he knew that Dwahvel was right on this matter, at least as far as Kohrin Soulez was concerned.

"That one treasure alone invites the ire of wizards," Dwahvel predictably responded, "and the ire of those who rely upon wizards for their security."

Entreri nodded, not disagreeing, but neither was he persuaded by Dwahvel's arguments. Charon's Claw might indeed be a curse for Kohrin Soulez, but if that was so it was because Soulez had entrenched himself in a place where such a weapon would be seen as a constant lure and a constant threat. Once he got his hands on the powerful sword, Artemis Entreri had no intention of staying anywhere near to Calimport. Soulez's chains would be his escape.

"The sword is an old artifact," Dwahvel remarked, drawing Entreri's attention more fully. "Everyone who has ever claimed it has died with it in his hands."

She thought her warning dramatic, no doubt, but the words had little effect on Entreri. "Everyone dies, Dwahvel," the assassin replied without hesitation, his response fueled by the living hell that had come to him in Calimport. "It is how one lives that matters."

Dwahvel looked at him curiously, and Entreri wondered if he had, perhaps, revealed too much, or tempted Dwahvel too much to go and learn even more about the reality of the power backing Entreri and the Basadoni Guild. If the cunning halfling ever learned too much of the truth, and Jarlaxle or his lieutenants learned of her knowledge, then none of her magical wards, none of her associates—even Artemis Entreri—and none of her perceived usefulness would save her from Jarlaxle's merciless soldiers. The Copper Ante would be gutted, and Entreri would find himself without a place in which to relax.

Dwahvel continued to stare at him, her expression a mixture of professional curiosity and personal—what was it?—compassion?

"What is it that so unhinges Artemis Entreri?" she started to ask, but even as the words came forth, so too came the assassin, his jeweled dagger flashing out of his belt as he leaped out of the chair and across the expanse, too quickly for Dwahvel's guards to even register the movement, too quickly for Dwahvel to even realize what was happening.

He was simply there, hovering over her, her hairy head pulled back, his dagger just nicking her throat.

But she felt it—how she felt the bite of that vicious, life-stealing dagger. Entreri had opened a tiny wound, yet through it Dwahvel could feel her very life-force being torn out of her body.

"If such a question as that ever echoes outside of these walls," the assassin promised, his breath hot on her face, "you will regret that I did not finish this strike."

He backed away then, and Dwahvel quickly threw up one hand, fingers flapping back and forth, the signal to her crossbowmen to hold their shots. With her other hand, she rubbed her neck, pinching at the tiny wound.

"You are certain that Kohrin Soulez still has it?" Entreri asked, more to change the subject and put things back on a professional level than to gather any real information.

"He had it, and he is still alive," the obviously shaken Dwahvel answered. "That seems proof enough."

Entreri nodded and assumed his previous posture, though the relaxed position did not fit the dangerous light that now shone in his eyes.

"You still wish to leave the city by secure routes?" Dwahvel asked.

Entreri gave a slight nod.

"We will need to utilize Domo and the were—" the halfling guildmaster started to say, but Entreri cut her short.

"No."

"He has the fastest—"

"No."

Dwahvel started to argue yet again. Fulfilling Entreri's request that she get him out of Calimport without anyone knowing it would prove no easy feat, even with Domo's help. Entreri was publicly and intricately tied to the Basadoni Guild, and that guild had drawn the watchful eyes of every power in Calimport. She stopped short, and this time Entreri hadn't interrupted her with a word but rather with a look, that all-too-dangerous look that Artemis Entreri had perfected decades before. It was the look that told his target that the time was fast approaching for final prayers.

"It will take some more time, then," Dwahvel remarked. "Not long, I assure you. An hour perhaps."

"No one is to know of this other than Dwahvel," Entreri instructed quietly, so that the crossbowmen in the shadows of the room's corners couldn't hear. "Not even your most trusted lieutenants."

The halfling blew a long, resigned sigh. "Two hours, then," she said.

Entreri watched her go. He knew that she couldn't possibly accede to his wishes to get him out of Calimport without anyone at all knowing of the journey—the streets were too well monitored—but it was a strong reminder to the halfling guildmaster that if anyone started talking about it too openly, Entreri would hold her personally responsible.

The assassin chuckled at the thought, for he couldn't imagine himself killing Dwahvel. He liked and respected the halfling, both for her courage and her skills.

He did need this departure to remain secret, though. If some of the others, particularly Rai-guy or Kimmuriel, found out that he had gone out, they would investigate and soon, no doubt, discern his destination. He didn't want the two dangerous drow studying Kohrin Soulez.

Dwahvel returned soon after, well within the two hours she had pessimistically predicted, and handed Entreri a rough map of this section of the city, with a route sketched on it.

"There will be someone waiting for you at the end of Crescent Avenue," she explained. "Right before the bakery."

"Detailing the second stretch your halflings have determined to be clear for travel," the assassin reasoned.

Dwahvel nodded. "My kin and other associates."

"And, of course, they will watch the movements as each map is collected," Entreri indicated.

Dwahvel shrugged. "You are a master of disguises, are you not?"

Entreri didn't answer. He set out immediately, exiting the Copper Ante and turning down a dark ally, emerging on the other side looking as though he had gained fifty pounds and walking with a pronounced limp.

He was out of Calimport within the hour, running along the northwestern road. By dawn, he was on a dune, looking down upon the Dallabad Oasis. He considered Kohrin Soulez long and hard, recalling everything he knew about the old man.

"Old," he said aloud with a sigh, for in truth, Soulez was in his early fifties, less than fifteen years older than Artemis Entreri.

The assassin turned his thoughts to the palace-fortress itself, trying to recall vivid details about the place. From this angle, all Entreri could make out were a few palm trees, a small pond, a single large boulder, a handful of tents including one larger pavilion, and behind them all, seeming to blend in with the desert sands, a brown, square-walled fortress. A handful of robed sentries walked around the fortress walls, seeming quite bored. The fortress of Dallabad did not appear very formidable—certainly nothing against the likes of Artemis Entreri—but the assassin knew better.

He had visited Soulez and Dallabad on several occasions when he had been working for Pasha Basadoni, and again more recently, when he had been in the service of Pasha Pook. He knew of the circular building within those square wall with its corridors winding in tighter and tighter circles toward the great treasury rooms of Kohrin Soulez, culminating in the private quarters of the oasis master himself.

Entreri considered Dwahvel's last description of the man and his place in the context of those memories and chuckled as he recognized the truth of her observations. Kohrin Soulez was indeed a prisoner.

Still, that prison worked well in both directions, and there was no way that Entreri could easily slip in and take that which he desired. The palace was a fortress, and a fortress full of soldiers specifically trained to thwart any attempts by the too-common thieves of the region.

The assassin thought that Dwahvel was wrong on one point, though. Kohrin himself, and not Charon's Claw, was the source of that prison. The man was so fearful of losing his prized weapon that he allowed it to dominate and consume him. His own fear of losing the sword had paralyzed him from taking any chances with it. When had Soulez last left Dallabad? the assassin wondered. When had he last visited the open market or chatted with his old associates on Calimport's streets?

No, people made their own prisons, Entreri knew, and knew well, for hadn't he, in fact, done the same thing in his obsession with Drizzt Do'Urden? Hadn't he been consumed by a foolish need to do battle with an insignificant dark elf who really had nothing to do with him?

Confident that he would never again make such an error, Artemis Entreri looked down upon Dallabad and smiled widely. Yes, Kohrin Soulez had done well to design his fortress against any would-be thieves skulking in from shadow to shadow or under cover of the darkness of night, but how would those many sentries fare when an army of dark elves descended upon them?

"You were with him when he learned of the retreat," Sharlotta Vespers asked Entreri the next night, soon after the assassin had quietly returned to Calimport. "How did Jarlaxle accept the news?"

"With typical nonchalance," Entreri answered honestly. "Jarlaxle has led Bregan D'aerthe for centuries. He is not one to betray that which is in his heart."

"Even to Artemis Entreri, who can read a man's eyes and tell him what he had for dinner the night before?" Sharlotta asked, grinning.

That smirk couldn't hold against the deadly calm expression that came over Entreri's face. "You do not begin to understand these new allies who have come to join with us," he said in all seriousness.

"To conquer us, you mean," Sharlotta replied, the first time since the take-over that Entreri had heard her even hint ill will against the dark elves. He wasn't surprised—who wouldn't quickly come to hate the wretched drow? On the other hand, Entreri had always known Sharlotta as someone who accepted whatever allies she could find, as long as they brought to her the power she so desperately craved.

"If they so choose," Entreri replied without missing a beat and in a most serious tone. "Underestimate any facet of the dark elves, from their fighting abilities to whether or not they betray themselves with expressions, and you will wind up dead, Sharlotta."

The woman started to respond but did not, fighting hard to keep an unchar-acteristic hopelessness off of her expression. He knew she was beginning to feel the same way he had during his journey to Menzoberranzan, the same way that he was beginning to feel once more, particularly whenever Rai-guy and Kim-muriel were around. There was something humbling about even being near these handsome, angular creatures. The drow always knew more than they should and always revealed less than they knew. Their mystery was only heightened by the undeniable power behind their often subtle threats. And always there was that damned condescension toward anyone who was not drow. In the current situation, where Bregan D'aerthe could obviously easily overwhelm the remnants of House Basadoni, Artemis Entreri included, that condescension took on even uglier tones. It was a poignant and incessant reminder of who was the master and who was the slave.

He recognized that same feeling in Sharlotta, growing with every passing moment, and he almost used that to enlist her aid in his secret scheme to take Dallabad and its greatest prize.

Almost—then Entreri considered the course and was shocked that his feel-ings toward Rai-guy and Kimmuriel had almost brought forth such a blunder as that. For all his life, with only very rare exceptions, Artemis Entreri had worked alone, had used his wits to ensnare unintentional and unwitting allies.

Cohorts inevitably knew too much for Entreri ever to be comfortable with them. The one exception he now made, out of simple necessity, was Dwahvel Tiggerwillies, and she, he was quite sure, would never double-cross him, not even under the questioning of the dark elves. That had always been the beauty of Dwahvel and her halfling comrades.

Sharlotta, however, was a completely different sort, Entreri now point-edly reminded himself. If he tried to enlist Sharlotta in his plan to go after Kohrin Soulez, he'd have to watch her closely forever after. She'd likely take the information from him and run to Jarlaxle, or even to Rai-guy and Kimmuriel, using Entreri's soon-to-be-lifeless body as a ladder with which to elevate herself.

Besides, Entreri did not need to bring up Dallabad to Sharlotta, for he had already made arrangements toward that end. Dwahvel would entice Sharlotta toward Dallabad with a few well-placed lies, and Sharlotta, who was predict-able indeed when one played upon her sense of personal gain, would take the information to Jarlaxle, only strengthening Entreri's personal suggestions that Dallabad would prove a meaningful and profitable conquest.

"I never thought I would miss Pasha Basadoni," Sharlotta remarked off-handedly, the most telling statement the woman had yet made.

"You hated Basadoni," Entreri reminded.

Sharlotta didn't deny that, but neither did she change her stance.

"You did not fear him as much as you fear the drow, and rightly so," Entreri remarked. "Basadoni was loyal, thus predictable. These dark elves are neither. They are too dangerous."

"Kimmuriel told me that you lived among them in Menzoberranzan," Sharlotta mentioned. "How did you survive?"

"I survived because they were too busy to bother with killing me," Entreri honestly replied. "I was *dobluth* to them, a non-drow outcast, and not worth the trouble. Also, it seems to me now that Jarlaxle might have been using me to further his understanding of the humans of Calimport."

That brought a chuckle to Sharlotta's thick lips. "I would hardly consider Artemis Entreri the typical human of Calimport," she said. "And if Jarlaxle had believed that all men were possessed of your abilities, I doubt he would have dared come to the city, even if all of Menzoberranzan marched behind him."

Entreri gave a slight bow, taking the compliment in polite stride, though he never had use for flattery. To Entreri's way of thinking, one was good enough or one wasn't, and no amount of self-serving chatter could change that.

"And that is our goal now, for both our sakes," Entreri went on. "We must keep the drow busy, which would seem not so difficult a task given Jarlaxle's sudden desire rapidly to expand his surface empire. We are safer if House Basadoni is at war."

"But not within the city," Sharlotta replied. "The authorities are starting to take note of our movements and will not stand idly by much longer. We are safer if the drow are engaged in battle, but not if that battle extends beyond house-to-house."

Entreri nodded, glad that Dwahvel's little suggestions to Sharlotta that other eyes might be pointing their way had brought the clever woman to these conclusions so quickly. Indeed, if House Basadoni reached too far and too fast, the true power of the house would likely be discovered. Once the realm of Calimshan came to that revelation, their response against Jarlaxle's band would be complete and overwhelming. Earlier on, Entreri had entertained just such a scenario, but he had come to dismiss it. He doubted that he, or any other *iblith* of House Basadoni, would survive a Bregan D'aerthe retreat.

That ultimate chaos, then, had been relegated to the status of a backup plan.

"But you are correct," Sharlotta went on. "We must keep them busy—their military arm, at least."

Entreri smiled and easily held back the temptation to enlist her then and there against Kohrin Soulez. Dwahvel would take care of that, and soon, and Sharlotta would never even figure out that she had been used for the gain of Artemis Entreri.

Or perhaps the clever woman would come to see the truth.

Perhaps, then, Entreri would have to kill her.

To Artemis Entreri, who had suffered the double-dealing of Sharlotta Vespers for many years, it was not an unpleasant thought.

CHAPTER

MUTUAL BENEFIT

6

Artemis Entreri surely recognized the voice but hardly the tone. In all the months he had spent with Jarlaxle, both here and in the Underdark, he had never known the mercenary leader to raise his voice in anger.

Jarlaxle was shouting now, and to Entreri's pleasure as much as his curiosity, he was shouting at Rai-guy and Kimmuriel.

"It will symbolize our *ascension,*" Jarlaxle roared.

"It will allow our enemies a focal point," Kimmuriel countered.

"They will not see it as anything more than a new guild house," Jarlaxle came back.

"Such structures are not uncommon," came Rai-guy's response, in calmer, more controlled tones.

Entreri entered the room then, to find the three standing and facing each other. A fourth drow, Berg'inyon Baenre, sat back comfortably against one wall.

"They will not know that drow were behind the construction of the tower," Rai-guy went on, after a quick and dismissive glance at the human, "but they will recognize that a new power has come to the Basadoni Guild."

"They know that already," Jarlaxle reasoned.

"They suspect it, as they suspect that old Basadoni is dead," Rai-guy retorted. "Let us not confirm their suspicions. Let us not do their reconnaissance for them."

Jarlaxle narrowed his one visible eye—the magical eye patch was over his left this day—and turned his gaze sharply at Entreri. "You know the city better than any of us," he said. "What say you? I plan to construct a tower, a crystalline image of Crenshinibon similar to the one in which you destroyed Drizzt Do'Urden. My associates here fear that such an act will prompt dangerous responses from other guilds and perhaps even the greater authorities of Calimshan."

"From the wizards' guild, at least," Entreri put in calmly. "A dangerous group."

Jarlaxle backed off a step in apparent surprise that Entreri had not readily gone along with him. "Guilds construct new houses all the time," the mercenary leader argued. "Some more lavish than anything I plan to create with Crenshinibon."

"But they do so by openly hiring out the proper craftsmen—and wizards, if magic is necessary," Entreri explained.

He was thinking fast on his feet here, totally surprised by Jarlaxle's dangerous designs. He didn't want to side with Rai-guy and Kimmuriel completely, though, because he knew that such an alliance would never serve him. Still, the notion of constructing an image of Crenshinibon right in the middle of Calimport seemed foolhardy at the very least.

"There you have it," Rai-guy cut in with a chortle. "Even your lackey does not believe it to be a wise or even feasible option."

"Speak your words from your own mouth, Rai-guy," Entreri promptly remarked. He almost expected the volatile wizard to make a move on him then and there, given the look of absolute hatred Rai-guy shot his way.

"A tower in Calimport would invite trouble," Entreri said to Jarlaxle, "though it is not impossible. We could, perhaps, hire a wizard of the prominent guild as a front for our real construction. Even that would be more easily accomplished if we set our sights on the outskirts of the city, out in the desert, perhaps, where the tower can better bask in the brilliant sunlight."

"The point is to erect a symbol of our strength," Jarlaxle put in. "I hardly wish to impress the little lizards and vipers that will view our tower in the empty desert."

"Bregan D'aerthe has always been better served by hiding its strength," Kimmuriel dared to interject. "Are we to change so successful a policy here in a world full of potential enemies? Time and again you seem to forget who we are, Jarlaxle, and *where* we are."

"We can mask the true nature of the tower's construction for a handsome price," Entreri reasoned. "And perhaps I can discern a location that will serve your purposes," he said to Jarlaxle, then turned to Kimmuriel and Rai-guy, "and alleviate your well-founded fears."

"You do that," Rai-guy remarked. "Show some worth and prove me wrong."

Entreri took the left-handed compliment with a quiet chuckle. He already had the perfect location in mind, yet another prompt to push Jarlaxle and Bregan D'aerthe against Kohrin Soulez and Dallabad Oasis.

"Have we heard any response from the Rakers?" Jarlaxle asked, walking to the side of the room and taking his seat.

"Sharlotta Vespers is meeting with Pasha Da'Daclan this very hour," Entreri replied.

"Will he not likely kill her in retribution?" Kimmuriel asked.

"No loss for us," Rai-guy quipped sarcastically.

"Pasha Da'Daclan is too intrigued to—" Entreri began.

"Impressed, you mean," corrected Rai-guy.

"He is too *intrigued,*" Entreri said firmly, "to act so rashly as that. He harbors no anger at the loss of a minor outpost, no doubt, and is more interested in weighing our true strength and intentions. Perhaps he will kill her, mostly to learn if such an act might illicit a response."

"If he does, perhaps we will utterly destroy him and all of his guild," Jarlaxle said, and that raised a few eyebrows.

Entreri was less surprised. The assassin was beginning to suspect that there was some method behind Jarlaxle's seeming madness. Typically, Jarlaxle would have been the type to find a way for his relationship to be mutually beneficial with a man as entrenched in the power structures as Pasha Da'Daclan of the Rakers. The mercenary dark elf didn't often waste time, energy, and valuable soldiers in destruction—no more than was necessary for him to gain the needed foothold. At this time, the foothold in Calimport was fairly secure, and yet Jarlaxle's hunger seemed only to be growing.

Entreri didn't understand it, but he wasn't too worried, figuring that he could find some way to use it to his own advantage.

"Before we take any action against Da'Daclan, we must weaken his outer support," the assassin remarked.

"Outer support?" The question came from both Jarlaxle and Rai-guy.

"Pasha Da'Daclan's arms have a long reach," Entreri explained. "I suspect that he has created some outer ring of security, perhaps even beyond Calimport's borders."

From the look on the faces of the dark elves, Entreri realized that he had just successfully laid the groundwork, and that nothing more needed to be said at that time. In truth, he knew Pasha Da'Daclan better than to believe that the old man would harm Sharlotta Vespers. Such overt revenge simply wasn't Da'Daclan's way. No, he would invite the continued dialogue with Sharlotta, because for the Basadonis to have moved so brazenly against him as to destroy one of his outer houses, they would, by his reasoning, have to have some new and powerful weapons or allies. Pasha Da'Daclan wanted to know if the attack had been precipitated by the mere cocksureness of the new leaders of the guild—if Basadoni was indeed dead, as the common rumors implied—or by well-placed confidence. The fact that Sharlotta herself, who in the event of Basadoni's death would certainly have been elevated to the very highest levels within the organization, had come out to him hinted, at least, at the second explanation for the attack. In that instance, Pasha Da'Daclan wasn't about to invite complete disaster.

So Sharlotta would leave Da'Daclan's house very much alive, and she would hearken to Dwahvel Tiggerwillies's previous call. When she returned to Jarlaxle late that night, the mercenary would hear confirmation that Da'Daclan had an ally outside the city, an ally, Entreri would later explain, whose location would be the perfect setting for a new and impressive tower.

Yes, this was all going along quite well, in the assassin's estimation.

"Silence Kohrin Soulez, and Pasha Da'Daclan has no voice outside of Calimport," Sharlotta Vespers explained to Jarlaxle that same evening.

"He needs no voice outside the city," Jarlaxle returned. "Given the information that you and my other lieutenants have provided, there is too much backing for the human right here within Calimport for us wisely to consider any course of true conquest."

"But Pasha Da'Daclan does not understand that," Sharlotta replied without hesitation.

It was obvious to Jarlaxle that the woman had thought this through quite extensively. She had returned from her meeting with Da'Daclan, and later meetings with her street informants, quite excited and animated. She hadn't really accomplished anything conclusive with Da'Daclan, but she had sensed that the man was on the defensive. He was truly worried about the state of complete destruction that had befallen his outer, minor house. Da'Daclan didn't understand Basadoni's new level of power, nor the state of control within the Basadoni Guild, and that too made him nervous.

Jarlaxle rested his angular chin in his delicate black hand. "He believes Pasha Basadoni to be dead?" he asked for the third time, and for the third time, Sharlotta answered, "Yes."

"Should that not imply a new weakness, then, within the guild?" the mercenary leader reasoned.

"Perhaps in your world," Sharlotta replied, "where the drow houses are ruled by Matron Mothers who serve Lolth directly. Here the loss of a leader implies nothing more than instability, and that, more than anything else, frightens rivals. The guilds do not normally wage war because to do so would be detrimental to all sides. This is something the old pashas have learned through years, even decades, of experience. It's something they have passed down to their children, or other selected followers, for generations."

Of course it all made sense to Jarlaxle, but he held his somewhat perplexed look, prompting her to continue. In truth, Jarlaxle was learning more about Sharlotta than about anything to do with the social workings of Calimport's underground guilds.

"As a result of our attack, Pasha Da'Daclan believes the rumors that speak of old Basadoni's death," the woman continued. "To Da'Daclan's thinking, if Basadoni is dead—or has at least lost control of the guild—then we are more dangerous by far." Sharlotta flashed her wicked and ironic smile.

"So with every outer strand we cut—first the minor house and now this Dallabad Oasis—we lessen Da'Daclan's sense of security," Jarlaxle reasoned.

"And make it easier for me to force a stronger treaty with the Rakers," Sharlotta explained. "Perhaps Da'Daclan will even give over to us the entire block about the destroyed minor house to appease us. His base of operations is gone from that area anyway."

"Not so big a prize," Jarlaxle remarked.

"Ah yes, but how much more respect will the other guilds offer to Basadoni when they learn that Pasha Da'Daclan turned over some of his ground to us after we so wronged him?" Sharlotta purred. Her continuing roll of intrigue, her building of level upon level of gain, heightened Jarlaxle's respect for her.

"Dallabad Oasis?" he asked.

"A prize in and of itself," Sharlotta was quick to answer, "even without the gains it will afford us in our game with Pasha Da'Daclan."

Jarlaxle thought it over for a bit, nodded, and, with a sly look at Sharlotta, nodded toward the bed. Thoughts of great gain had ever been an aphrodisiac for Jarlaxle.

Jarlaxle paced his room later that night, having dismissed Sharlotta that he could consider in private the information she had brought to him. According to the woman—who had been so ill-briefed by Dwahvel—Dallabad Oasis was working as a relay point for Pasha Da'Daclan, the exit for information to Da'Daclan's more powerful allies far from Calimport. Run by some insignificant functionary named Soulez, Dallabad was an independent fortress. It was not an official part of the Rakers or any other guild from the city. Soulez apparently accepted payment to serve as information-relay, and also, Sharlotta had explained, sometimes collected tolls along the northwestern trails.

Jarlaxle continued to pace, digesting the information, playing it in conjunction with the earlier suggestions of Artemis Entreri. He felt the telepathic intrusion of his newest ally then, but he merely adjusted his magical eye patch to ward off the call.

There had to be some connection here, some truth within the truth, some planned relationship between Dallabad's tenuous position and the mere convenience of this all. Hadn't Entreri earlier suggested that Jarlaxle conquer some place outside of Calimport where he could more safely set up a crystalline tower?

And now this: a perfect location practically handed over to him for conquest, a place so conveniently positioned for Bregan D'aerthe to make a double gain.

The mental intrusions continued. It was a strong call, the strongest Jarlaxle had ever felt through his eye patch.

He wants something, Crenshinibon said in the mercenary leader's head.

Jarlaxle started to dismiss the shard, thinking that his own reasoning could bring him to a clearer picture of this whole situation, but Crenshinibon's next statement leaped past the conclusions he was slowly forming.

Artemis Entreri has deeper designs here, the shard insisted. *An old grudge, perhaps, or some treasure within the obvious prize.*

"Not a grudge," Jarlaxle said aloud, removing the protective eye patch so that he and the shard could better communicate. "If Entreri harbored such feelings as that, then he would see to this Soulez creature personally. Ever has he prided himself on working alone."

You believe the sudden imposition of Dallabad Oasis, a place never before mentioned, into both the equation of the Rakers and our need to construct a tower to be a mere fortunate coincidence? the shard asked, and before Jarlaxle could even respond, Crenshinibon made its assessment clear. *Artemis Entreri harbors some ulterior motive for an assault against Dallabad Oasis. There can be no doubt. Likely, he knew that our informants would bring to us the suggestion that conquering Dallabad would frighten Pasha Da'Daclan and considerably strengthen our bargaining power with him.*

"More likely, Artemis Entreri arranged for our informants to come to that very conclusion," Jarlaxle reasoned, ending with a chuckle.

Perhaps he views this as a way toward our destruction, the shard imparted. *That he can break free of us and rule on his own.*

Jarlaxle was shaking his head before the full reasoning even entered his mind. "If Artemis Entreri wished to be free of us, he would find some excuse to depart the city."

And run as faraway as Morik the Rogue, perhaps? came the ironic thought.

It was true enough, Jarlaxle had to admit. Bregan D'aerthe had already proven that its arms on the surface world were long indeed, long enough, perhaps, to catch a runaway deserter. Still, Jarlaxle highly doubted the shard's last reasoning. First of all, Artemis Entreri was wise enough to understand that Bregan D'aerthe would not go blindly against Dallabad or any other foe. Also, to Jarlaxle's thinking, such a ploy to bring about Bregan D'aerthe's downfall on the surface would be far too risky—and would it not be more easily accomplished merely by telling the greater authorities of Calimshan that a band of dark elves had come to Calimport?

He offered all of the reasoning to Crenshinibon, building common ground with the artifact that the most likely scenario here involved the shard's second line of reasoning, that of a secret treasure within the oasis.

The drow mercenary closed his eyes and absorbed the Crystal Shard's feelings on these plausible and growing suspicions and laughed again when he learned that he and the artifact had both come to accept the conclusion and were of like mind concerning it. Both were more amused and impressed than angry. Whatever Entreri's personal motives, and whether or not the information connecting Dallabad to Pasha Da'Daclan held any truth or not, the oasis would be a worthy and seemingly safe acquisition.

More so to the artifact than to the dark elf, for Crenshinibon had made it quite clear to Jarlaxle that it needed to construct an image of itself, a tower to collect the brilliant sunlight.

A step closer to its ever-present, final goal.

CHAPTER
TURNING ADVANTAGE INTO DISASTER

7

Kohrin Soulez held his arm up before him, focusing his thoughts on the black, red-laced gauntlet that he wore on his right hand. Those laces seemed to pulse now, an all-too-familiar feeling for the secretive and secluded man.

Someone was trying to look in on him and his fortress at Dallabad Oasis.

Soulez forced his concentration deeper into the magical glove. He had recently been approached by a mediator from Calimport inquiring about a possible sale of his beloved sword, Charon's Claw. Soulez, of course, had balked at the absurd notion. He held this item more dear to his heart than he had any of his numerous wives, even above his many, many children. The offer had been serious, promising wealth beyond imagination for the single item.

Soulez had gained enough understanding of Calimport's guildsmen and had been in possession of Charon's Claw long enough to know what a serious offer, obviously refused and without room for bargaining, might bring, and so he was not surprised to find that prying eyes were seeking him out now. Since further investigation had whispered that the would-be purchaser might be Artemis Entreri and the Basadoni Guild, Soulez had been watching carefully for those eyes in particular.

They would look for weakness but would find none, and thus, he believed, they would merely go away.

As Soulez fell deeper into the energies of the gauntlet, he came to recognize a new element, dangerous only because it hinted that the would-be thief this time might not be so easily dissuaded. These were not the magical energies of a wizard he felt, nor the prayers of a divining priest. No, this energy was different than the expected, but certainly nothing beyond the understanding of Soulez and the gauntlet.

"Psionics," he said aloud, looking past the gauntlet to his lieutenants, who were standing at attention about his throne room.

Three of them were his own children. The fourth was a great military commander from Memnon, and the fifth was a renowned, and now retired, thief from Calimport. Conveniently, Soulez thought, a former member of the Basadoni Guild.

"Artemis Entreri and the Basadonis," Soulez told them, "if it is them, have apparently found access to a psionicist."

The five lieutenants muttered among themselves about the implications of that.

"Perhaps that has been Artemis Entreri's edge for all these years," the youngest of them, Kohrin Soulez's daughter, Ahdahnia, remarked.

"Entreri?" laughed Preelio, the old thief. "Strong of mind? Certainly. Psionics? Bah! He never needed them, so fine was he with the blade."

"But whoever seeks my treasure has access to the mind powers," said Soulez. "They believe that they have found an edge, a weakness of mine and of my treasure's, that they can exploit. That only makes them more dangerous, of course. We can expect an attack."

All five of the lieutenants stiffened at that proclamation, but none seemed overly concerned. There was no grand conspiracy against Dallabad among the guilds of Calimport. Kohrin Soulez had paid dearly to certify that information right away. The five knew that no one guild, or even two or three of the guilds banded together, could muster the power to overthrow Dallabad—not while Soulez carried the sword and the gauntlet and could render any wizards all but ineffective.

"No soldiers will break through our walls," Ahdahnia remarked with a confident smirk. "No thieves will slide through the shadows to the inner structures."

"Unless through some devilish mind power," Preelio put in, looking to the elder Soulez.

Kohrin Soulez only laughed. "They *believe* they have found a weakness," he reiterated. "I can stop them with this—" he held up the glove—"and of course, I have other means." He let the thought hang in the air, his smile bringing grins to the faces of all in attendance. There was a sixth lieutenant, after all, one little seen and little bothered, one used primarily as an instrument of interrogation and torture, one who preferred to spend as little time with the humans as possible.

"Secure the physical defenses," Soulez instructed them. "I will see to the powers of the mind."

He waved them away and sat back, focusing again on his mighty black gauntlet, on the red stitching that ran through it like veins of blood. Yes, he could feel the meager prying, and while he wished that the jealous folk would simply leave him to his business in peace, he believed that he would enjoy this little bit of excitement.

He knew that Yharaskrik certainly would.

Far below Kohrin Soulez's throne room, in deep tunnels that few of Soulez's soldiers even knew existed, Yharaskrik was already well aware that someone or something using psionic energies had breached the oasis. Yharaskrik was a mind flayer, an illithid, a humanoid creature with a bulbous head that resembled a huge brain, with several tentacles protruding from the part of his face where a nose, mouth, and chin should have been. Illithids were horrible to behold, and could be quite formidable physically, but their real powers lay in the realm of the mind, in psionic energies that dwarfed the powers of human practitioners, even of drow practitioners. Illithids could simply overwhelm an opponent with stunning blasts of mental energies, and either enslave the unfortunate victim, his mind held in a fugue state, or move in for a feast, attaching their horrid tentacles to the helpless victim and burrowing in to suck out brain matter.

Yharaskrik had been working with Kohrin Soulez for many years. Soulez considered the creature as much an indentured servant as a minion. He believed he had cut a fair deal with the creature after Soulez had apparently rendered Yharaskrik helpless in a short battle, capturing the illithid's mind blast within the magical netting of his gauntlet and thus leaving Yharaskrik open to a devastating counterstrike with the deadly sword. In truth, had Soulez gone for that strike, Yharaskrik would have melted away into the stone, using energies not directed against Soulez and thus beyond the reach of the gauntlet.

Soulez had not pressed the attack, though, as Yharaskrik's communal brain had calculated. The opportunistic man had struck a deal instead, offering the illithid its life and a comfortable place to do its meditation—or whatever else it was that illithids did—in exchange for certain services whenever they were needed, primarily to aid in the defense of Dallabad Oasis.

In all these years, Kohrin Soulez had never once harbored any suspicions that coming to Dallabad in such a capacity had been Yharaskrik's duty all along, that the illithid had been chosen among its strange kin to seek out and study the black and red gauntlet, as mind flayers were often sent to learn of anything that could so block their devastating energies. In truth, Yharaskrik had learned little of use concerning the gauntlet over the years, but the creature was never anxious about that. Brilliant illithids were among the most patient of all the creatures in the multiverse, savoring the process more than the goal. Yharaskrik was quite content in its tunnel home.

Some psionic force had tickled the illithid's sensibility, and Yharaskrik felt enough of the stream of energy to know that it was no other illithid psionically prying about Dallabad Oasis.

The mind flayer, as confident in his superiority as all of his kind, was more intrigued than concerned. He was actually a bit perturbed that the fool Soulez had captured that psychic call with his gauntlet, but now the call had returned, redirected. Yharaskrik had called back, bringing his roving mind eye down, down, to the deep caverns.

The illithid did not try to hide its surprise when it discerned the source of that energy, nor did the creature on the other end, a drow, even begin to mask his own stunned reaction.

Haszakkin! the drow's thoughts instinctively screamed, their word for illithid—a word that conveyed a measure of respect the drow rarely gave to any creature that was not drow.

Dyon G'ennivalz? Yharaskrik asked, the name of a drow city the illithid had known well in its younger days.

Menzoberranzan, came the psionic reply.

House Oblodra, the brilliant creature imparted, for that atypical drow house was well known among all the mind flayer communities of Faerûn's Underdark.

No more, came Kimmuriel's response.

Yharaskrik sensed anger there, and understood it well as Kimmuriel relayed the memories of the downfall of his arrogant family. There had been, during the Time of Troubles, a period when magic, but not psionics, had ceased to function. In that too-brief time, the leaders of House Oblodra had challenged the greater houses of Menzoberranzan, including mighty Matron Baenre herself. The energies shifted with the shifting of the gods, and psionics had become temporarily impotent, while the powers of conventional magic had returned. Matron Baenre's response to the threats of House Oblodra had wiped the structure and all of the family—except for Kimmuriel, who had wisely used his ties with Jarlaxle and Bregan D'aerthe to make a hasty retreat—from the city, dropping it into the chasm called the Clawrift.

You seek the conquest of Dallabad Oasis? Yharaskrik asked, fully expecting an answer, for creatures communicating through psionics often held their own loyalties to each other even above those of their kindred.

Dallabad will be ours before the night has passed, Kimmuriel honestly replied.

The connection abruptly ended, and Yharaskrik understood the hasty retreat as Kohrin Soulez sauntered into the dark chamber, his right hand clad in the cursed gauntlet that so interfered with psionic energy.

The illithid bowed before his supposed master.

"We have been scouted," Soulez said, getting right to the point, his tension obvious as he stood before the horrid mind flayer.

"Mind's eye," the illithid agreed in its physical, watery voice. "I sensed it."

"Powerful?" Soulez asked.

Yharaskrik gave a quiet gurgle, the illithid equivalent of a resigned shrug, showing his lack of respect for any psionicist that was not illithid. It was an honest appraisal, even though the psionicist in question was drow and not human, and tied to a drow house that was well known among Yharaskrik's people. Still, though the mind flayer was not overly concerned about any battle he might see against the drow psionicist, Yharaskrik knew the dark elves well enough to understand that the Oblodran psionicist would likely be the least of Kohrin Soulez's problems.

"Power is always a relative concept," the illithid answered cryptically.

Kohrin Soulez felt the tingling of magical energy as he ascended the long spiral staircase that took him back to the ground level of his palace in Dallabad. The guildmaster broke into a run, scrambling, muscles working to their limits and his old bones feeling no pain. He thought that the attack must already be underway.

He calmed somewhat, slowing and huffing and puffing to catch his breath. He came up into the guild house to find many of his soldiers milling about, talking excitedly, but seeming more curious than terrified.

"Is it yours, Father?" asked Ahdahnia, her dark eyes gleaming.

Kohrin Soulez stared at her curiously, and taking the cue, Ahdahnia led him to an outer room with an east-facing window.

There it stood, right in the middle of Dallabad Oasis, *within* the outer walls of Kohrin Soulez's fortress.

A crystalline tower, gleaming in the bright sunlight, an image of Crenshinibon, the calling card of doom.

Kohrin Soulez's right hand throbbed with tingling energy as he looked at the magical structure. His gauntlet could capture magical energy and even turn it back against the initiator. It had never failed him, but in just looking at this spectacular tower the guildmaster suddenly recognized that he and his toys were puny things indeed. He knew without even going out and trying that he could not hope to drag the magical energies from that tower, that if he tried, it would consume him and his gauntlet. He shuddered as he pictured a physical manifestation of that absorption, an image of Kohrin Soulez frozen as a gargoyle on the top rim of that magnificent tower.

"Is it yours, Father?" Ahdahnia asked again.

The eagerness left her voice and the sparkle left her eyes as Kohrin turned to her, his face bloodless.

Outside of Dallabad fortress's wall, under the shelter of a copse of palm trees and surrounded by globes of magical darkness, Jarlaxle called to the tower. Its outer wall elongated, and sent forth a tendril, a stairway tunnel that breached the darkness globes and reached to the mercenary's feet. Secure that his soldiers were all in place, Jarlaxle ascended the stairs into the tower proper. With a thought to the Crystal Shard, he retracted the tunnel, effectively sealing himself in.

From that high vantage point in the middle of the fortress courtyard, Jarlaxle watched the unfolding drama around him.

Could you dim the light? he telepathically asked the tower.

Light is strength, Crenshinibon answered.

For you, perhaps, the mercenary replied. *For me, it is uncomfortable.*

Jarlaxle felt a sensation akin to a chuckle from the Crystal Shard, but the artifact did comply and thicken its eastern wall, considerably dulling the light in the room. It also provided a floating chair for Jarlaxle, so that he could drift about the perimeter of the room, studying the battle that would soon unfold.

Notice that Artemis Entreri will partake of the attack, the Crystal Shard remarked, and it sent the chair floating to the northern side of the room. Jarlaxle took the cue and focused hard down below, outside the fortress wall, to the tents and trees and boulders. Finally, with helpful guidance from the artifact, the drow spotted the figure lurking about the shadows.

He did not do so when we planned the attack on Pasha Da'Daclan, Crenshinibon added. Of course, the Crystal Shard knew that Jarlaxle was considering the same thing. The implications continued to follow the line that Entreri had some secret agenda here, some private gain that was either outside of the domain of Bregan D'aerthe, or held some consequence within the second level of the band's hierarchy.

Either way, both Jarlaxle and Crenshinibon thought it more amusing than in any way threatening.

The floating chair drifted back across the small circular room, putting Jarlaxle in line with the first diversionary attack, a series of darkness globes at the top of the outer wall. The soldiers there went into a panic, running and crying out to reform a defensive line away from the magic, but even as they moved back—in fairly good order, Jarlaxle noted—the real attack began, bubbling up from the ground within the fortress courtyard.

Rai-guy had crossed the courtyard, ten difficult feet at a time, casting a series of passwall spells out of a wand. Now, from a natural tunnel that he had fortunately located below the fortress, the drow wizard enacted the last of those passwalls, vanishing a section of stone and dirt.

Immediately the soldiers of Bregan D'aerthe arose, floating with drow levitation into the courtyard, enacting darkness globes above them to confuse their enemies and to lessen the blinding impact of the hated sun.

"We should have attacked at night," Jarlaxle said aloud.

Daytime is when my power is at its peak, Crenshinibon responded immediately, and Jarlaxle felt the rest of the thought keenly. Crenshinibon was none-too-subtly reminding him that it was more powerful than all of Bregan D'aerthe combined.

That expression of confidence was more than a little disconcerting to the mercenary leader, for reasons that he hadn't yet begun to untangle.

Rai-guy stood in the hole, issuing orders to those dark elves running and leaping into levitation, floating up and eager for battle. The wizard was particularly animated this day. His blood was up, as always during a conquest, but he was not pleased at all that Jarlaxle had decided to launch the attack at dawn, a seemingly foolish trade-off of putting his soldiers, used to a world of blackness, at a disadvantage, for the simple gain of constructing a crystalline tower vantage point. The appearance of the tower was an amazing thing, without doubt, one that showed the power of the invaders clearly to those defending inside. Rai-guy did not diminish the value of striking such terror, but every time he saw one of his soldiers squint painfully as he rose up out of the hole into the daylight, the wizard considered his leader's continuing surprising behavior and gritted his teeth in frustration.

Also, the mere fact that they were using dark elves openly against the fortress seemed more than a bit of a gamble. Could they not have accomplished this conquest, as they had planned to do with Pasha Da'Daclan, by striking openly with human, perhaps even kobold soldiers, while the dark elves infiltrated more quietly? What would be left of Dallabad after the conquest now, after all? Almost all remaining alive within—and there would be many, since the dark elves led every assault with their trademark sleep-poisoned hand crossbow darts—would have to be executed anyway, lest they communicate the truth of their conquerors.

Rai-guy reminded himself of his place in the guild and knew it would take a monumental error on the part of Jarlaxle, one that cost the lives of many of Bregan D'aerthe, for him to rally enough support truly to overthrow Jarlaxle. Perhaps this would be that mistake.

The wizard heard a change in the timbre of the shouts from above. He glanced up, taking note that the sunlight seemed brighter, that the globes of magical darkness had gone away. The magically created shaft, too, suddenly disappeared, capturing a pair of levitating soldiers within it as the stone and dirt rematerialized. It lasted only a moment, as if something suddenly reached out and grabbed away the magic that was trying to dispel Rai-guy's vertical passwall dweomers. That moment was long enough to destroy utterly the two unfortunate drow soldiers.

The wizard cursed at Jarlaxle, but under his breath.

He reminded himself to keep safe and to see, in the end, if this attack, even if a complete failure, might not prove personally beneficial.

Kohrin Soulez fell back. His sensibilities were stung, both by the realization that these were dark elves that had come to secluded Dallabad, and by the magical counterattack that had overwhelmed his gauntlet. He had come out from the main house to rally his soldiers, the blood-red blade of Charon's Claw bared and waving, leaving streaks of ashy blackness in the air. Soulez had run to the area of obvious invasion, where globes of darkness and screams of pain and terror heralded the fighting.

Dispelling those globes was no major task for the gauntlet, nor was closing the hole in the ground through which the enemy continued to arrive, but Soulez had nearly been overwhelmed by a wave of energy that countered the countering energy he was exerting himself. It was a blast of magical power so raw and pure that he could not hope to contain it. He knew it had come from the tower.

The tower!

The dark elves!

His doom was at hand!

He fell back into the main house, ordering his soldiers to fight to the last. As he ran along the more deserted corridors leading to his private chambers, his dear Ahdahnia right behind him, he called out to Yharaskrik to come and whisk him away.

There was no answer.

"He has heard me," Soulez assured his daughter anyway. "We need only escape long enough for Yharaskrik to come to us. Then we will run out to inform the lords of Calimport that the dark elves have come."

"The traps and locks along the hallways will keep our enemies at bay," Ahdahnia replied.

Despite the surprising nature of their enemies, the woman actually believed the claim. These long corridors weaving along the somewhat circular main house of Dallabad were lined with heavy, metal-banded doors of stone and wood layers that could defeat most intrusions, wizardly or physical. Also, the sheer number of traps in place between the outer walls and Kohrin Soulez's inner sanctuary would deter and daunt the most seasoned of thieves.

But not the most clever.

Artemis Entreri had worked his way unnoticed to the base of the fortress's northern wall. It was no small feat—an impossible one under normal circumstances, for there was an open field surrounding the fortress, running nearly a hundred feet to the trees and tents and boulders, and several of the small ponds that marked the place—but this was not a normal circumstance. With a tower materializing *inside* the fortress, most of the guards were scurrying about, trying to find some answers as to whether it was an invading enemy or some secret project of Kohrin Soulez's. Even those guards on the walls couldn't help but stare in awe at that amazing sight.

Entreri dug himself in. His borrowed black cloak—a camouflaging drow *piwafwi* that wouldn't last long in the sun—offered him some protection should any of the guards lean over the twenty foot wall and look down at him.

The assassin waited until the sounds of fighting erupted from within.

To untrained eyes, the wall of Kohrin Soulez's fortress would have seemed a sheer thing indeed, all of polished white marble joints forming an attractive contrast to the brownish sandstone and gray granite. To Entreri, though, it seemed more of a stairway than a wall, with many seam-steps and finger-holds.

He was up near the top in a matter of seconds. The assassin lifted himself up just enough to glance over at the two guards anxiously reloading their crossbows. They were looking in the direction of the courtyard where the battle raged.

Over the wall without a sound went the *piwafwi*-cloaked assassin. He came down from the wall only a few moments later, dressed as one of Kohrin Soulez's guards.

Entreri joined in with some others running frantically around to the front courtyard, but he broke away from them as he came in sight of the fighting. He melted back against the wall and toward the open, main door, where he spotted Kohrin Soulez. The guildmaster was battling drow magic and waving that wondrous sword. Entreri kept several steps ahead of the man as he was forced to fall back. The assassin entered the main building before Soulez and his daughter.

Entreri ran, silent and unseen, along those corridors, through the open doors, past the unset traps, ahead of the two fleeing nobles and those soldiers trailing their leader to secure the corridor behind him. The assassin reached the main door of Soulez's private chambers with enough time to spare to recognize that the alarms and traps on this portal were indeed in place and to do something about them.

Thus, when Ahdahnia Soulez pushed open that magnificent, gold-leafed door, leading her father into his seemingly secure chamber, Artemis Entreri was already there, standing quietly ready behind a floor-to-ceiling tapestry.

The three Dallabad soldiers—well-trained, well-armed, and well-armored with shining chain and small bucklers—faced off against the three dark elves along the western wall of the fortress. The men, frightened as they were, kept the presence of mind to form a triangular defense, using the wall behind them to secure their backs.

The dark elves fanned out and came at them in unison. Their amazing drow swords—two for each warrior—worked circular attack routines so quickly that the paired weapons seemed to blur the line between where one sword stopped and the other began.

The humans, to their credit, held strong their position, offered parries and blocks wherever necessary, and suppressed any urge to scream out in terror and charge blindly—as some of their nearby comrades were doing to disastrous results. Gradually, talking quickly between them to analyze each of their enemy's movements, the trio began to decipher the deceptive and brilliant drow sword dance, enough so, at least, to offer one or two counters of their own.

Back and forth it went, the humans wisely holding their position, not following any of the individually retreating dark elves and thus weakening their own defenses. Blade rang against blade, and the magical swords Kohrin Soulez had provided his best-trained soldiers matched up well enough against the drow weapons.

The dark elves exchanged words the humans did not understand. Then the three drow attacked in unison, all six swords up high in a blurring dance. Human swords and shields came up to meet the challenge and the resulting clang of metal against metal rang out like a single note.

That note soon changed, diminished, and all three of the human soldiers came to recognize, but not completely to comprehend, that their attackers had each dropped one sword.

Shields and swords up high to meet the continuing challenge, they only understood their exposure below the level of the fight when they heard the clicks of three small crossbows and felt the sting as small darts burrowed into their bellies.

The dark elves backed off a step. Tonakin Ta'salz, the central soldier, called out to his companions that he was hit, but that he was all right. The soldier to Tonakin's left started to say the same, but his words were slurred and groggy. Tonakin glanced over just in time to see him tumble facedown in the dirt. To his right, there came no response at all.

Tonakin was alone. He took a deep breath and skittered back against the wall as the three dark elves retrieved their dropped swords. One of them said something to him that he did not understand, but while the words escaped him, the expression on the drow's face did not.

He should have fallen down asleep, the drow was telling him. Tonakin agreed wholeheartedly as the three came in suddenly, six swords slashing in brutal and perfectly coordinated attacks.

To his credit, Tonakin Ta'salz actually managed to block two of them.

And so it went throughout the courtyard and all along the wall of the fortress. Jarlaxle's mercenaries, using mostly physical weapons but with more than a little magic thrown in, overwhelmed the soldiers of Dallabad. The mercenary leader had instructed his killers to spare as many as possible, using sleep darts and accepting surrender. He noted, though, that more than a few were not waiting long enough to find out if any opponents who had resisted the sleep poison might offer a surrender.

The dark elf leader merely shrugged at that, hardly concerned. This was open battle, the kind that he and his mercenaries didn't see often enough. If too many of Kohrin Soulez's soldiers were killed for the oasis fortress to properly function, then Jarlaxle and Crenshinibon would simply find replacements. In any case, with Soulez chased back into his house by the sheer power of the Crystal Shard, the assault had already reached its second stage.

It was going along beautifully. The courtyard and wall were already secured, and the house had been breached at several points. Now Kimmuriel and Rai-guy at last came onto the scene.

Kimmuriel had several of the captives who were still awake dragged before him, forcing them to lead the way into the house. He would use his overpowering will to read their thoughts as they walked him and the drow through the trapped maze to the prize that was Soulez.

Jarlaxle rested back in the crystalline tower. A part of him wanted to go down and join in the fun, but he decided instead to remain and share the moment with his most powerful companion, the Crystal Shard. He even allowed the artifact to thin the eastern wall once more, allowing more sunlight into the room.

◦∗∗∗◦

"Where is he?" Kohrin Soulez fumed, stomping about the room. "Yharaskrik!"

"Perhaps he cannot get through," Ahdahnia reasoned. She moved nearer to the tapestry as she spoke.

Entreri knew he could step out and take her down, then go for his prize. He held the urge, intrigued and wary.

"Perhaps the same force from the tower—" Ahdahnia went on.

"No!" Kohrin Soulez interrupted. "Yharaskrik is beyond such things. His people see things—everything—differently."

Even as he finished, Ahdahnia gasped and skittered back across Entreri's field of view. Her eyes went wide as she looked back in the direction of her father, who had walked out of Entreri's very limited line of sight.

Confident that the woman was too entranced by whatever it was that she was watching, Entreri slipped down low to one knee and dared peek out around the tapestry.

He saw an illithid step out of the psionic dimensional doorway and into the room to stand before Kohrin.

A mind flayer!

The assassin fell back behind the tapestry, his thoughts whirling. Very few things in all the world could rattle Artemis Entreri, who had survived life on the streets from a tender young age and had risen to the very top of his profession, who had survived Menzoberranzan and many, many encounters with dark elves. One of those few things was a mind flayer. Entreri had seen a few in the dark elf city, and he abhorred them more than any other creature he had ever met. It wasn't their appearance that so upset the assassin, though they were brutally ugly by any but illithid standards. No, it was their very demeanor, their different view of the world, as Kohrin had just alluded to.

Throughout his life, Artemis Entreri had gained the upper hand because he understood his enemies better than they understood him. He had found the dark elves a bit more of a challenge, based on the fact that the drow were too experienced—were simply too good at conspiring and plotting for him to gain any real comprehension . . . any that he could hold confidence in, at least.

With illithids, though he had only dealt with them briefly, the disadvantage was even more fundamental and impossible to overcome. There was no way Artemis Entreri could understand that particular enemy because there was no way he could bring himself to any point where he could view the world as an illithid might.

No way.

So Entreri tried to make himself very small. He listened to every word, every inflection, every intake of breath, very carefully.

"Why did you not come earlier to my call?" Kohrin Soulez demanded.

"They are dark elves," Yharaskrik responded in that bubbling, watery voice that sounded to Entreri like a very old man with too much phlegm in his throat. "They are within the building."

"You should have come earlier!" Ahdahnia cried. "We could have beaten—" Her voice left her with a gasp. She stumbled backward and seemed about to fall. Entreri knew the mind flayer had just hit her with some scrambling burst of mental energy.

"What do I do?" Kohrin Soulez wailed.

"There is nothing you can do," answered Yharaskrik. "You cannot hope to survive."

"P-par-parlay with them, F-father!" cried the recovering Ahdahnia. "Give them what they want—else you cannot hope to survive."

"They will take what they want," Yharaskrik assured her, and turned back to Kohrin Soulez. "You have nothing to offer. There is no hope."

"Father?" Ahdahnia asked, her voice suddenly weak, almost pitiful.

"You attack them!" Kohrin Soulez demanded, holding his deadly sword out toward the illithid. "Overwhelm them!"

Yharaskrik made a sound that Entreri, who had mustered enough willpower to peek back around the tapestry, recognized to be an expression of mirth. It wasn't a laugh, actually, but more like a clear, gasping cough.

Kohrin Soulez, too, apparently understood the meaning of the reply, for his face grew very red.

"They are drow. Do you now understand that?" the illithid asked. "There is no hope."

Kohrin Soulez started to respond, to demand again that Yharaskrik take the offensive, but as if he had suddenly come to figure it all out, he paused and stared at his octopus-headed companion. "You knew," he accused. "When the psionicist entered Dallabad, he conveyed . . ."

"The psionicist was drow," the illithid confirmed.

"*Traitor!*" Kohrin Soulez cried.

"There is no betrayal. There was never friendship, or even alliance," the illithid remarked logically.

"But you *knew!*"

Yharaskrik didn't bother to reply.

"Father?" Ahdahnia asked again, and she was trembling visibly.

Kohrin Soulez's breath came in labored gasps. He brought his left hand up to his face and wiped away sweat and tears. "What am I to do?" he asked, speaking to himself. "What will . . ."

Yharaskrik began that coughing laughter again, and this time, it sounded clearly to Entreri that the creature was mocking pitiful Soulez.

Kohrin Soulez composed himself suddenly and glared at the creature. "This amuses you?" he asked.

"I take pleasure in the ironies of the lesser species," Yharaskrik responded. "How much your whines sound as those of the many you have killed. How many have begged for their lives futilely before Kohrin Soulez, as he will now futilely beg for his at the feet of a greater adversary than he can possibly comprehend?"

"But an adversary that you know well!" Kohrin cried.

"I prefer the drow to your pitiful kind," Yharaskrik freely admitted. "They never beg for mercy that they know will not come. Unlike humans, they accept the failings of individual-minded creatures. There is no greater joining among them, as there is none among you, but they understand and accept that fallibility." The illithid gave a slight bow. "That is all the respect I now offer to you, in the hour of your death," Yharaskrik explained. "I would throw energy your way, that you might capture it and redirect it against the dark elves—and they are close now, I assure you—but I choose not to."

Artemis Entreri recognized clearly the change that came over Kohrin Soulez then, the shift from despair to nothing-to-lose anger that he had seen so many times during his decades on the tough streets.

"But I wear the gauntlet!" Kohrin Soulez said powerfully, and he moved the magnificent sword out toward Yharaskrik. "I will at least get the pleasure of first witnessing your end!"

But even as he made the declaration, Yharaskrik seemed to melt into the stone at his feet and was gone.

"Damn him!" Kohrin Soulez screamed. "Damn you—" His tirade cut short as a pounding came on the door.

"Your wand!" the guildmaster cried to his daughter, turning to face her, in the direction of the floor-to-ceiling tapestry that decorated his private chamber.

Ahdahnia just stood there, wide-eyed, making no move to reach for the wand at her belt. Her expression changing not at all, she crumpled to the floor.

There stood Artemis Entreri.

Kohrin Soulez's eyes widened as he watched her descent, but as if he hardly cared for the fall of Ahdahnia other than its implications for his own safety, his gaze focused clearly on Entreri.

"It would have been so much easier if you had merely sold the blade to me," the assassin remarked.

"I knew this was your doing, Entreri," Soulez growled back at him, advancing a step, the blood-red blade gleaming at the ready.

"I offer you one more chance to sell it," Entreri said, and Soulez stopped short, his expression one of pure incredulity. "For the price of her life," the assassin added, pointing down at Ahdahnia with his jeweled dagger. "Your own life is yours to bargain for, but you'll have to make that bargain with others."

Another bang sounded out in the corridor, followed by the sounds of some fighting.

"They are close, Kohrin Soulez," Entreri remarked, "close and overwhelming."

"You brought dark elves to Calimport," Soulez growled back at him.

"They came of their own accord," Entreri replied. "I was merely wise enough not to try to oppose them. So I make my offer, but only this one last time. I can save Ahdahnia—she is not dead but merely asleep." To accentuate his point, he held up a small crossbow quarrel of unusual design, a drow bolt that had been tipped with sleeping poison. "Give me the sword and gauntlet—now—and she lives. Then you can bargain for your own life. The sword will do you little good against the dark elves, for they need no magic to destroy you."

"But if I am to bargain for my life, then why not do so with the sword in hand?" Kohrin Soulez asked.

In response, Entreri glanced down at the sleeping form of Ahdahnia.

"I am to trust that you will keep your word?" Soulez answered.

Entreri didn't answer, other than to fix the man with a cold stare.

There came a sharp rap on the heavy door. As if incited by that sound of imminent danger, Kohrin Soulez leaped forward, slashing hard.

Entreri could have killed Ahdahnia and still dodged, but he did not. He slipped back behind the tapestry and went down low, scrambling along its length. He heard the tearing behind him as Soulez slashed and stabbed. Charon's Claw easily sliced the heavy material, even took chunks out of the wall behind it.

Entreri came out the other side to find Soulez already moving in his direction, the man wearing an expression that seemed half crazed, even jubilant.

"How valuable will the drow elves view me when they enter to find Artemis Entreri dead?" he squealed, and he launched a thrust, feint and slash for the assassin's shoulder.

Entreri had his own sword out then, in his right hand, his dagger still in his left, and he snapped it up, driving the slash aside. Soulez was good, very good, and he had the formidable weapon back in close defensively before the assassin could begin to advance with his dagger.

Respect kept Artemis Entreri back from the man, and more importantly, from that devastating weapon. He knew enough about Charon's Claw to understand that a simple nick from it, even one on his hand that he might suffer in a successful parry, would fester and grow and would likely kill him.

Confident that he'd find the right opening, the deadly assassin stalked the man slowly, slowly.

Soulez attacked again with a low thrust that Entreri hopped back from, and a thrust high that the assassin ducked. Entreri slapped at the red blade with his sword and thrust at his opponent's center mass. It was a brilliantly quick routine that would have left almost any opponent at least shallowly stabbed.

He never got near to hitting Entreri. Then he had to scramble and throw out a cut to the side to keep the assassin, who had somehow quick-stepped to his right while slapping hard at the third thrust, at bay.

Kohrin Soulez growled in frustration as they came up square again, facing each other from a distance of about ten feet, with Entreri continuing that composed stalk. Now Soulez also moved, angling to intercept.

He was dragging his back foot behind him, Entreri noted, keeping ready to change direction, trying to cut off the room and any possible escape routes.

"You so desperately desire Charon's Claw," Soulez said with a chuckle, "but do you even begin to understand the true beauty of the weapon? Can you even guess at its power and its tricks, assassin?"

Entreri continued to back and pace—back to the left, then back to the right—allowing Soulez to shrink down the battlefield. The assassin was growing impatient, and also, the sounds on the door indicated that the resistance in the hallway had come to an end. The door was magnificent and strong, but it would not hold out long, and Entreri wanted this finished before Rai-guy and the dark elves arrived.

"You think I am an old man," Soulez remarked, and he came forward in a short rush, thrusting.

Entreri picked it off and this time came forward with a counter of his own, rolling his sword under Soulez's blade and sliding it out. The assassin turned and stepped ahead, dagger rushing forward, but he had to disengage from the powerful sword too soon. The angle of the parry was forcing the enchanted blade dangerously close to Entreri's exposed hand, and without the block, he had to skitter into a quick retreat as Soulez slashed across.

"I am an old man," Soulez continued, sounding undaunted, "but I draw strength from the sword. I am your fighting equal, Artemis Entreri, and with this sword you are surely doomed."

He came on again, but Entreri retreated easily, sliding back toward the wall opposite the door. He knew he was running out of room, but to him that only meant that Kohrin Soulez was running out of room, too, and out of time.

"Ah, yes, run back, little rabbit," Soulez taunted. "I know you, Artemis Entreri. I know you. Behold!" As he finished, he began waving the sword before him, and Entreri had to blink, for the blade began trailing blackness.

No, not trailing, the assassin realized to his surprise, but emitting blackness. It was thick ash that held in place in the air in great sweeping opaque fans, altering the battlefield to Kohrin Soulez's designs.

"I know you!" Soulez cried and came forward, sweeping, sweeping more ash screens into the air.

"Yes, you know me," Entreri answered calmly, and Soulez slowed. The timbre of Entreri's voice had reminded him of the power of this particular opponent. "You see me at night, Kohrin Soulez, in your dreams. When you look into the darkest shadows of those nightmares, do you see those eyes looking back at you?"

As he finished, he came forward a step, tossing his sword slightly into the air before him, and at just the right angle so that the approaching sword was the only thing Kohrin Soulez could see.

The room's door exploded into a thousand tiny little pieces.

Soulez hardly noticed, coming forward to meet the attack, slapping the apparently thrusting sword on top, then below and to the side. So beautifully angled was Entreri's toss that the man's own quick parry strikes, one countering the spin of the other, gave Soulez the illusion that Entreri was still holding the other end of the blade.

He leaped ahead, through the opaque fans of the sword's conjured ash, and struck hard for where he knew the assassin had to be.

Soulez stiffened, feeling the sting in his back. Entreri's dagger cut into his flesh.

"Do you see those eyes looking back at you from the shadows of your nightmares, Kohrin Soulez?" Entreri asked again. "Those are my eyes."

Soulez felt the dagger pulling at his life-force. Entreri hadn't driven it home yet, but he didn't have to. The man was beaten, and he knew it. Soulez dropped Charon's Claw to the floor and let his arm slip down to his side.

"You are a devil," he growled at the assassin.

"I?" Entreri answered innocently. "Was it not Kohrin Soulez who would have sacrificed his daughter for the sake of a mere weapon?"

As he finished, he was fast to reach down with his free hand and yank the black gauntlet from Soulez's right hand. To Soulez's surprise, the glove fell to the floor right beside the sword.

From the open doorway across the room came the sound of a voice, melodic yet sharp, and speaking in a language that rolled but was oft-broken with harsh and sharp consonant sounds.

Entreri backed away from the man. Soulez turned around to see the ash lines drifting down to the floor, showing him several dark elves standing in the room.

Kohrin Soulez took a deep, steadying breath. He had dealt with worse than drow, he silently reminded himself. He had parlayed with an illithid and had survived meetings with the most notorious guildmasters of Calimport. Soulez focused on Entreri then, seeing the man engaged in conversation with the apparent leader of the dark elves, seeing the man drifting farther and farther from him.

There, right beside him, lay his precious sword, his greatest possession—an artifact he would indeed protect even at the cost of his own daughter's life.

Entreri moved a bit farther from him. None of the drow were advancing or seemed to pay Soulez any heed at all.

Charon's Claw, so conveniently close, seemed to be calling to him.

Gathering all his energy, tensing his muscles and calculating the most fluid course open to him, Kohrin Soulez dived down low, scooped the black, red-stitched gauntlet onto his right hand, and before he could even register that it didn't seem to fit him the same way, scooped up the powerful, enchanted sword.

He turned toward Entreri with a growl. "Tell them that I will speak with their leader . . ." he started to say, but his words quickly became a jumble, his tone going low and his pace slowing, as if something was pulling at his vocal chords.

Kohrin Soulez's face contorted weirdly, his features seeming to elongate in the direction of the sword.

All conversation in the room stopped. All eyes turned to stare incredulously at Soulez.

"T-to the Nine . . . Nine Hells with y-you, Entreri!" the man stammered, each word punctuated by a croaking groan.

"What is he doing?" Rai-guy demanded of Entreri.

The assassin didn't answer, just watched in amusement as Kohrin Soulez continued to struggle against the power of Charon's Claw. His face elongated again and wisps of smoke began wafting up from his body. He tried to cry out, but only an indecipherable gurgle came forth. The smoke increased, and Soulez began to tremble violently, all the while trying to scream out.

Nothing more than smoke poured from his mouth.

It all seemed to stop then, and Soulez stood staring at Entreri and gasping.

The man lived just long enough to put on the most horrified and stunned expression Artemis Entreri had ever seen. It was an expression that pleased Entreri greatly. There was something too familiar in the way in which Soulez had abandoned his daughter.

Kohrin Soulez erupted in a sudden, sizzling burst. The skin burned off his head, leaving no more than a whitened skull and wide, horrified eyes.

Charon's Claw hit the hard floor again, making more of a dull thump than any metallic ring. The skull-headed corpse of Kohrin Soulez crumpled in place.

"Explain," Rai-guy demanded.

Entreri walked over and, wearing a gauntlet that appeared identical to the one Kohrin Soulez had but not a match for the other since it was shaped for the same hand, reached down and calmly gathered up his newest prize.

"Pray I do not go to the Nine Hells, as you surely will, Kohrin Soulez," the deadly assassin said to the corpse. "For if I see you there, I will continue to torment you throughout eternity."

"Explain!" Rai-guy demanded more forcefully.

"Explain?" Entreri echoed, turning to face the angry drow wizard. He gave a shrug, as if the answer seemed obvious. "I was prepared, and he was a fool."

Rai-guy glared at him ominously, and Entreri only smiled back, hoping his amused expression would tempt the wizard to action.

He held Charon's Claw now, and he wore the gauntlet that could catch and redirect magic.

The world had just changed in ways that the wretched Rai-guy couldn't begin to understand.

CHAPTER

8

T he tower will remain. Jarlaxle has declared it," said Kimmuriel. "The fortress weathered our attack well enough to keep Dallabad operating smoothly, and without anyone outside of the oasis even knowing that an assault had taken place."

"Operating," Rai-guy echoed, spitting the distasteful word out. He stared at Entreri, who walked beside him into the crystal tower. Rai-guy's look made it quite clear that he considered the events of this day the assassin's doing and planned on holding Entreri personally responsible if anything went wrong. "Is Bregan D'aerthe to become the overseers of a great toll booth, then?"

"Dallabad will prove more valuable to Bregan D'aerthe than you assume," Entreri replied in his stilted use of the drow language. "We can keep the place separate from House Basadoni as far as all others are concerned. The allies we place out here will watch the road and gather news long before those in Calimport are aware. We can run many of our ventures from out here, farther from the prying eyes of Pasha Da'Daclan and his henchmen."

"And who are these trusted allies who will operate Dallabad as a front for Bregan D'aerthe?" Rai-guy demanded. "I had thought of sending Domo."

"Domo and his filthy kind will not leave the offal of the sewers," Sharlotta Vespers put in.

"Too good a hole for them," Entreri muttered.

"Jarlaxle has hinted that perhaps the survivors of Dallabad will suffice," Kimmuriel explained. "Few were killed."

"Allied with a conquered guild," Rai-guy remarked with a sigh, shaking his head. "A guild whose fall we brought about."

"A very different situation from allying with a fallen house of Menzoberranzan," Entreri declared, seeing the error in the dark elf's apparent internal analogy. Rai-guy was viewing things through the dark glass of Menzoberranzan, was considering the generational feuds and grudges that members of the various houses, the various families, held for each other.

"We shall see," the drow wizard replied, and he motioned for Entreri to hang back with him as Kimmuriel, Berg'inyon, and Sharlotta started up the staircase to the second level of the magical crystalline tower.

"I know that you desired Dallabad for personal reasons," Rai-guy said when the two were alone. "Perhaps it was an act of vengeance, or that you might wear that very gauntlet upon your hand and carry that same sword you now have sheathed on your hip. Either way, do not believe you've done anything here I don't understand, human."

"Dallabad is a valuable asset," Entreri replied, not backing away an inch. "Jarlaxle has a place where he can safely construct and maintain the crystalline tower. There was gain here to be had by all."

"Even to Artemis Entreri," Rai-guy remarked.

In answer, the assassin drew forth Charon's Claw, presenting it horizontally to Rai-guy for inspection, letting the drow wizard see the beauty of the item. The sword had a slender, razor-edged, gleaming red blade, its length inscribed with designs of cloaked figures and tall scythes, accentuated by a black blood trough running along its center. Entreri opened his hand enough for the wizard to see the skull-bobbed pommel, with a hilt that appeared like whitened vertebrae. Running from it toward the crosspiece, the hilt was carved to resemble a backbone and rib-cage, and the crosspiece itself resembled a pelvic skeleton, with legs spread out wide and bent back toward the head, so that the wielder's hand fit neatly within the "bony" boundaries. All of the pommel, hilt and crosspiece was white, like bleached bones—perfectly white, except for the eye sockets of the skull pommel, which seemed like black pits at one moment and flared with red fires the next.

"I am pleased with the prize I earned," Entreri admitted.

Rai-guy stared hard at the sword, but his gaze inevitably kept drifting toward the other, less-obvious treasure: the black, red-stitched gauntlet on Entreri's hand.

"Such weapons can be more of a curse than a blessing, human," the wizard remarked. "They are possessed of arrogance, and too often does that foolish pride spill over into the mind of the wielder, to disastrous result."

The two locked stares, with Entreri's expression melting into a wry grin. "Which end would you most like to feel?" he asked, presenting the deadly sword closer to Rai-guy, matching the wizard's obvious threat with one of his own.

Rai-guy narrowed his dark eyes, and walked away.

Entreri held his grin as he watched the wizard move up the stairs, but in truth, Rai-guy's warning had struck a true chord to him. Indeed, Charon's Claw was strong of will—Entreri could feel that clearly—and if he was not careful with the blade always, it could surely lead him to disaster or destroy him as it had utterly slaughtered Kohrin Soulez.

Entreri glanced down at his own posture, reminding himself—a humble self-warning—not to touch any part of the sword with his unprotected hand.

Even Artemis Entreri could not deny a bit of caution against the horrific death he had witnessed when Charon's Claw had burned the skin from the head of Kohrin Soulez.

"Crenshinibon easily dominates the majority of the survivors," Jarlaxle announced to his principal advisors a short while later in an audience chamber he had crafted of the second level the magical tower. "To those outside of

Dallabad Oasis, the events of this day will seem like nothing more than a coup within the Soulez family, followed by a strong alliance to the Basadoni Guild."

"Ahdahnia Soulez agreed to remain?" Rai-guy asked.

"She was willing to assume the mantle of Dallabad even before Crenshinibon invaded her thoughts," Jarlaxle explained.

"Loyalty," Entreri remarked under his breath.

Even as the assassin was offering the sarcastic jibe, Rai-guy admitted, "I am beginning to like the young woman more already."

"But can we trust her?" Kimmuriel asked.

"Do you trust me?" Sharlotta Vespers interjected. "It would seem a similar situation."

"Except that her guildmaster was also her father," Kimmuriel reminded.

"There is nothing to fear from Ahdahnia Soulez or any of the others who will remain at Dallabad," Jarlaxle put in, forcefully, thus ending the philosophical debate. "Those who survived and will continue to do so belong to Crenshinibon now, and Crenshinibon belongs to me."

Entreri didn't miss the doubting look that flashed briefly across Rai-guy's face at the moment of Jarlaxle's final proclamation, and in truth, he, too, wondered if the mercenary leader wasn't a bit confused as to who owned whom.

"Kohrin Soulez's soldiers will not betray us," Jarlaxle went on with all confidence. "Nor will they even remember the events of this day, but rather, they will accept the story we tell them to put forth as truth, if that is what we choose. Dallabad Oasis belongs to Bregan D'aerthe now as surely as if we had installed an army of dark elves here to facilitate the operations."

"And you trust the woman Ahdahnia to lead, though we just murdered her father?" Kimmuriel said more than asked.

"Her father was killed by his obsession with that sword; so she told me herself," Jarlaxle replied, and as he spoke, all gazes turned to regard the weapon hanging easily at Entreri's belt. Rai-guy, in particular, kept his dangerous glare upon Entreri, as if silently reiterating the warnings of their last conversation.

The wizard meant those warnings to be a threat to Entreri, a reminder to the assassin that he, Rai-guy, would be watching Entreri's every move much more closely now, a reminder that he believed that the assassin had, in effect, used Bregan D'aerthe for the sake of his personal gain—a very dangerous practice.

"You do not like this," Kimmuriel remarked to Rai-guy when the two were back in Calimport.

Jarlaxle had remained behind at Dallabad Oasis, securing the remnants of Kohrin Soulez's forces and explaining the slight shift in direction that Ahdahnia Soulez should now undertake.

"How could I?" Rai-guy responded. "Every day, it seems that our purpose in coming to the surface has expanded. I had thought that we would be back in Menzoberranzan by this time, yet our footpads have tightened on the stone."

"On the sand," Kimmuriel corrected, in a tone that showed he, too, was not overly pleased by the continuing expansion of Bregan D'aerthe's surface ventures.

Originally, Jarlaxle had shared plans to come to the surface and establish a base of contacts, humans mostly, who would serve as profiteering front men for the trading transactions of the mercenary drow band. Though he had never specified the details, Jarlaxle's original explanation had made the two believe that their time on the surface would be quite limited.

But now they had expanded, had even constructed a physical structure, with more apparently planned, and had added a second base to the Basadoni conquest. Worse than that, both dark elves were thinking, though not openly saying, perhaps there was something even more behind Jarlaxle's continuing shift of attitude. Perhaps the mercenary leader had erred in taking a certain relic from the renegade Do'Urden.

"Jarlaxle seems to have taken a liking to the surface," Kimmuriel went on. "We all knew that he had tired somewhat of the continuing struggles within our homeland, but perhaps we underestimated the extent of that weariness."

"Perhaps," Rai-guy replied. "Or perhaps our friend merely needs to be reminded that this is not our place."

Kimmuriel stared at him hard, his expression clearly asking how one might "remind" the great Jarlaxle of anything.

"Start at the edges," Rai-guy answered, echoing one of Jarlaxle's favorite sayings, and favorite tactics for Bregan D'aerthe. Whenever the mercenary band went into infiltration or conquest mode, they started gnawing at the edges of their opponent—circling the perimeter and chewing, chewing—as they continued their ever-tightening ring. "Has Morik yet delivered the jewels?"

***

There it lay before him, in all its wicked splendor.

Artemis Entreri stared long and hard at Charon's Claw, the fingers on both of his unprotected hands rubbing in against his moist palms. Part of him wanted to reach out and grasp the sword, to effect now the battle that he knew would soon enough be fought between his own willpower and that of the sentient weapon. If he won that battle, the sword would truly be his, but if he lost. . . .

He recalled, and vividly, the last horrible moments of Kohrin Soulez's miserable life.

It was exactly that life, though, that so propelled Entreri in this seemingly suicidal direction. He would not be as Soulez had been. He would not allow himself to be a prisoner to the sword, a man trapped in a box of his own making. No, he would be the master, or he would be dead.

But still, that horrific death. . . .

Entreri started to reach for the sword, steeling his willpower against the expected onslaught.

He heard movement in the hallway outside his room.

He had the glove on in a moment and scooped up the sword in his right hand, moving it to its sheath on his hip in one fluid movement even as the door to his private chambers—if any chambers for a human among Bregan D'aerthe could be considered private—swung open.

"Come," instructed Kimmuriel Oblodra, and he turned and started away.

Entreri didn't move, and as soon as the drow realized it, he turned back.

Kimmuriel had a quizzical look upon his handsome, angular face. That look of curiosity soon turned to one of menace, though, as he considered the standing, but hardly moving assassin.

"You have a most excellent weapon now," Kimmuriel remarked. "One to greatly complement your nasty dagger. Fear not. Neither Rai-guy nor I have underestimated the value of that gauntlet you seem to keep forever upon your right hand. We know its powers, Artemis Entreri, and we know how to defeat it."

Entreri continued to stare, unblinking, at the drow psionicist. A bluff? Or had resourceful Kimmuriel and Rai-guy indeed found some way around the magic-negating gauntlet? A wry smile found its way onto Entreri's face, a look bolstered by the assassin's complete confidence that whatever secret Kimmuriel might now be hinting of would do the drow little good in their immediate situation. Entreri knew, and his look made Kimmuriel aware as well, that he could cross the room then and there, easily defeat any of Kimmuriel's psionically created defenses with the gauntlet, and run him through with the mighty sword.

If the drow, so cool and so powerful, was bothered or worried at all, he did a fine job of masking it.

But so did Entreri.

"There is work to be done in Luskan," Kimmuriel remarked at length. "Our friend Morik still has not delivered the required jewels."

"I am to go and serve as messenger again?" Entreri asked sarcastically.

"No message for Morik this time," Kimmuriel said coldly. "He has failed us."

The finality of that statement struck Entreri profoundly, but he managed to hide his surprise until Kimmuriel had turned around and started away once more. The assassin understood clearly, of course, that Kimmuriel had, in effect, just told him to got to Luskan and murder Morik. The request did not seem so odd, given that Morik apparently was not living up to Bregan D'aerthe's expectations. Still, it seemed out of place to Entreri that Jarlaxle would so willingly and easily cut his only thread to a market as promising as Luskan without even asking for some explanation from the tricky little rogue. Jarlaxle had been acting strange, to be sure, but was he as confused as that?

It occurred to Entreri even as he started after Kimmuriel that perhaps this assassination had nothing to do with Jarlaxle.

His feelings, and fears, were only strengthened when he entered the small room. He came in not far behind Kimmuriel but found Rai-guy, and Rai-guy alone, waiting for him.

"Morik has failed us yet again," the wizard stated immediately. "There can be no further chances for him. He knows too much of us, and with such an obvious lack of loyalty, well, what are we to do? Go to Luskan and eliminate him. A simple task. We care not for the jewels. If he has them, spend them as you will. Just bring me Morik's heart." As he finished, he stepped aside, clearing the way to a magical portal he had woven, the blurry image inside showing Entreri the alleyway beside Morik's building.

"You will need to remove the gauntlet before you stride through," Kimmuriel remarked, slyly enough for Entreri to wonder if perhaps this whole set-up was but a ruse to force him into an unguarded position. Of course, the resourceful assassin had considered that very thing on the walk over, so he only chuckled at Kimmuriel, walked up to the portal, and stepped right through.

He was in Luskan now, and he looked back to see the magical portal closing behind him. Kimmuriel and Rai-guy were looking at him with expressions that showed everything from confusion to anger to intrigue.

Entreri held up his gloved hand in a mocking wave as the pair faded out of sight. He knew they were wondering how he could exercise such control over the magic-dispelling gauntlet. They were trying to get a feel for its power and its limitations, something that even Entreri had not yet figured out. He certainly didn't mean to offer any clues to his quiet adversaries, thus he had changed from the real magical gauntlet to the decoy that had so fooled Soulez.

When the portal closed he started out of the alleyway, changing once again to the real gauntlet and dropping the fake one into a small sack concealed under the folds of his cloak at the back of his belt.

He went to Morik's room first and found that the little thief had not added any further security traps or tricks. That surprised Entreri, for if Morik was again disappointing his merciless leaders he should have been expecting company. Furthermore, the thief obviously had not fled the small apartment.

Not content to sit and wait, Entreri went back out onto Luskan's streets, making his way from tavern to tavern, from corner to corner. A few beggars approached him, but he sent them away with a glare. One pickpocket actually went for the purse he had secured to his belt on the right side. Entreri left him sitting in the gutter, his wrist shattered by a simple twist of the assassin's hand.

Sometime later, and thinking that it was about time for him to return to Morik's abode, the assassin came into an establishment on Half-Moon Street known as the Cutlass. The place was nearly empty, with a portly barkeep rubbing away at the dirty bar and a skinny little man sitting across from him, chattering away. Another figure among the few patrons remaining in the place caught Entreri's attention.

The man was sitting comfortably and quietly at the far left end of the bar with his back against the wall and the hood of his weathered cloak pulled over his head. He appeared to be sleeping, judging from his rhythmic breathing, the hunch of his shoulders, and the loll of his head, but Entreri caught a few tell-tale signs—like the fact that the rolling head kept angling to give the supposedly sleeping man a fine view of all around him—that told him otherwise.

The assassin didn't miss the slight tensing of the shoulders when that angle revealed his presence to the supposedly sleeping man.

Entreri strode up to the bar, right beside the nervous, skinny little man, who said, "Arumn's done serving for the night."

Entreri glanced over, his dark eyes taking a full measure of this one. "My gold is not good enough for you?" he asked the barkeep, turning back slowly to consider the portly man behind the bar.

Entreri noted that the barkeep took a long, good measure of him. He saw respect coming into Arumn's eyes. He wasn't surprised. This barkeep, like so many others, survived primarily by understanding his clientele. Entreri was doing little to hide the truth of his skills in his graceful, solid movements. The man pretending to sleep at the bar said nothing, and neither did the nervous one.

"Ho, Josi's just puffing out his chest, is all," the barkeep, Arumn, remarked, "though I had planned on closing her up early. Not many looking for drink this night."

Satisfied with that, Entreri glanced to the left, to the compact form of the man pretending to be asleep. "Two honey meads," he said, dropping a couple of shining gold coins on the bar, ten times the cost of the drinks.

The assassin continued to watch the "sleeper," hardly paying any heed at all to Arumn or nervous little Josi, who was constantly shifting at his other side. Josi even asked Entreri his name, but the assassin ignored him. He just continued to stare, taking a measure, studying every movement and playing them against what he already knew of Morik.

He turned back when he heard the clink of glass on the bar. He scooped up one drink in his gloved right hand, bringing the dark liquid to his lips, while he grasped the second glass in his left hand, and instead of lifting it, just sent it sliding fast down the bar, angled slightly for the outer lip, perfectly set to dump onto the supposedly-sleeping man's lap.

The barkeep cried out in surprise. Josi Puddles jumped to his feet, and even started toward Entreri, who simply ignored him.

The assassin's smile widened when Morik, and it was indeed Morik, reached up at the last moment and caught the mead-filled missile, bringing his hand back and wide to absorb the shock of the catch and to make sure that any liquid that did splash over did not spill on him.

Entreri slid off the barstool, took up his glass of mead and motioned for Morik to go with him outside. He had barely taken a step, though, when he sensed a movement toward his arm. He turned back to see Josi Puddles reaching for him.

"No, ye don't!" the skinny man remarked. "Ye ain't leavin' with Arumn's glasses."

Entreri watched the hand coming toward him and lifted his gaze to look Josi Puddles straight in the eye, to let the man know, with just a look and just that awful, calm and deadly demeanor, that if he so much as brushed Entreri's arm with his hand, he would surely pay for it with his life.

"No, ye . . ." Josi started to say again, but his voice failed him and his hand stopped moving. He knew. Defeated, the skinny man sank back against the bar.

"The gold should more than pay for the glasses," Entreri remarked to the barkeep, and Arumn, too, seemed quite unnerved.

The assassin headed for the door, taking some pleasure in hearing the barkeep quietly scolding Josi for being so stupid.

The street was quiet outside, and dark, and Entreri could sense the uneasiness in Morik. He could see it in the man's cautious stance and in the way his eyes darted about.

"I have the jewels," Morik was quick to announce. He started in the direction of his apartment, and Entreri followed.

The assassin thought it interesting that Morik presented him with the jewels—and the size of the pouch made Entreri believe that the thief had certainly met his master's expectations—as soon as they entered the darkened room. If Morik had them, why hadn't he simply given them over on time? Certainly Morik, no fool, understood the volatile and extremely dangerous nature of his partners.

"I wondered when I would be called upon," Morik said, obviously trying to appear completely calm. "I have had them since the day after you left but have gotten no word from Rai-guy or Kimmuriel."

Entreri nodded, but showed no surprise—and in truth, when he thought about it, the assassin wasn't really surprised at all. These were drow, after all. They killed when convenient, killed when they felt like it. Perhaps they had sent Entreri here to slay Morik in the hopes that Morik would prove the stronger. Perhaps it didn't matter to them either way. They would merely enjoy the spectacle of it.

Or perhaps Rai-guy and Kimmuriel were anxious to clip away at the entrenchment that Jarlaxle was obviously setting up for Bregan D'aerthe. Kill Morik and any others like him, sever all ties, and go home. He lifted his black gauntlet into the air, seeking any magical emanations. He detected some upon Morik and some other minor dweomers in and around the room, but nothing that seemed to him to be any kind of scrying spell. It wasn't that he could have done anything about any spells or psionics divining the area, anyway. Entreri had come to understand already that the gauntlet could only grab at spells directed at him specifically. In truth, the thing was really quite limited. He might catch one of Rai-guy's lightning bolts and hurl it back at the wizard, but if Rai-guy filled the room with a fireball. . . .

"What are you doing?" Morik asked the distracted assassin.

"Get out of here," Entreri instructed. "Out of this building and out of the city altogether, for a short while at least."

The obviously puzzled Morik just stared at him.

"Did you not hear me?"

"That order comes from Jarlaxle?" Morik asked, seeming quite confused. "Does he fear that I have been discovered, that he, by association, has been somehow implicated?"

"I tell you to begone, Morik," Entreri answered. "I, and not Jarlaxle, nor, certainly, Rai-guy or Kimmuriel."

"Do I threaten you?" asked Morik. "Am I somehow impeding your ascension within the guild?"

"Are you that much a fool?" Entreri replied.

"I have been promised a king's treasure!" Morik protested. "The only reason I agreed—"

"Was because you had no choice," Entreri interrupted. "I know that to be true, Morik. Perhaps that lack of choice is the only thing that saves you now."

Morik was shaking his head, obviously upset and unconvinced. "Luskan is my home," he started to say.

Charon's Claw came out in a red and black flash. Entreri swiped down beside Morik, left and right, then slashed across right above the man's head. The sword left a trail of black ash with all three swipes so that Entreri had Morik practically boxed in by the opaque walls. So quickly had he struck, the dazed and dazzled rogue hadn't even had a chance to draw his weapon.

"I was not sent to collect the jewels or even to scold and warn you, fool," Entreri said coldly—so very, very coldly. "I was sent to kill you."

"But . . ."

"You have no idea the level of evil with which you have allied yourself," the assassin went on. "Flee this place—this building *and* this city. Run for all your life, fool Morik. They will not look for you if they cannot find you easily—you are not worth their trouble. So run away, beyond their vision and take hope that you are free of them."

Morik stood there, encapsulated by the walls of black ash that still magically hung in the air, his jaw hanging open in complete astonishment. He looked left and right, just a bit, and swallowed hard, making it clear to Entreri that he had just then come to realize how overmatched he truly was. Despite the assassin's previous visit, easily getting through all of Morik's traps, it had taken this display of brutal swordsmanship to show Morik the deadly truth of Artemis Entreri.

"Why would they . . . ?" Morik dared to ask. "I am an ally, eyes for Bregan D'aerthe in the northland. Jarlaxle himself instructed me to . . ." He stopped at the sound of Entreri's laughter.

"You are *iblith*," Entreri explained. "Offal. Not of the drow. That alone makes you no more than a plaything to them. They *will* kill you—I am to kill you here and now by their very words."

"Yet you defy them," Morik said, and it wasn't clear from his tone if he had come around yet truly to believe Entreri or not.

"You are thinking that this is some test of your loyalty," Entreri correctly guessed, shaking his head with every word. "The drow do not test loyalty, Morik, because they expect none. With them, there is only the predictability of actions based in simple fear."

"Yet you are showing yourself disloyal by letting me go," Morik remarked. "We are not friends, with no debt and little contact between us. Why do you tell me this?"

Entreri leaned back and considered that question more deeply than Morik could have expected, allowing the thief's recognition of illogic to resonate in his thoughts. For surely Entreri's actions here made little logical sense. He could have been done with his business and back on his way to Calimport, without any real threat to him. By contrast, and by all logical reasoning, there would be little gain for Entreri in letting Morik walk away.

Why this time? the assassin asked himself. He had killed so many, and often in situations similar to this, often at the behest of a guildmaster seeking to punish an impudent or threatening underling. He had followed orders to kill people whose offense had never been made known to him, people, perhaps, similar to Morik, who had truly committed no offense at all.

No, Artemis Entreri couldn't quite bring himself to accept that last thought. His killings, every one, had been committed against people associated with the underworld, or against misinformed do-gooders who had somehow become entangled in the wrong mess, impeding the assassin's progress. Even Drizzt Do'Urden, that paladin in drow skin, had named himself as Entreri's enemy by preventing the assassin from retrieving Regis the halfling and the magical ruby pendant the little fool had stolen from Pasha Pook. It had taken years, but to Entreri, killing Drizzt Do'Urden had been the justified culmination of the drow's unwanted and immoral interference. In Entreri's mind and in his heart, those who had died at his hands had played the great game, had tossed aside their innocence in pursuit of power or material gain.

In Entreri's mind, everyone he had killed had indeed deserved it, because he was a killer among killers, a survivor in a brutal game that would not allow it to be any other way.

"Why?" Morik asked again, drawing Entreri from his contemplation.

The assassin stared at the rogue for a moment, and offered a quick and simple answer to a question too complex for him to sort out properly, an answer that rang of more truth than Artemis Entreri even realized.

"Because I hate drow more than I hate humans."

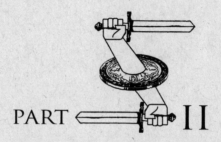

PART II

WHICH THE TOOL?
WHICH THE MASTER?

E ntreri again teamed with Jarlaxle?

What an odd pairing that seems, and to some (and initially to me, as well) a vision of the most unsettling nightmare imaginable. There is no one in all the world, I believe, more crafty and ingenious than Jarlaxle of Bregan D'aerthe, the consummate opportunist, a wily leader who can craft a kingdom out of the dung of rothé. Jarlaxle, who thrived in the matriarchal society of Menzoberranzan as completely as any Matron Mother.

Jarlaxle of mystery, who knew my father, who claims a past friendship with Zaknafein.

How could a drow who befriended Zaknafein ally with Artemis Entreri? At quick glance, the notion seems incongruous, even preposterous. And yet, I do believe Jarlaxle's claims of the former and know the latter to be true—for the second time.

Professionally, I see no mystery in the union. Entreri has ever preferred a position of the shadows, serving as the weapon of a high-paying master—no, not master. I doubt that Artemis Entreri has ever known a master. Rather, even in the service of the guilds, he worked as a sword for hire. Certainly such a skilled mercenary could find a place within Bregan D'aerthe, especially since they've come to the surface and likely need humans to front and cover their true identity. For Jarlaxle, therefore, the alliance with Entreri is certainly a convenient thing.

But there is something else, something more, between them. I know this from the way Jarlaxle spoke of the man, and from the simple fact that the mercenary leader went so far out of his way to arrange the last fight between me and Entreri. It was for the sake of Entreri's state of mind, no less, and certainly as no favor to me, and as no mere source of entertainment for Jarlaxle. He cares for Entreri as a friend might, even as he values the assassin's multitude of skills.

There lies the incongruity.

For though Entreri and Jarlaxle have complementary professional skills, they do not seem well matched in temperament or in moral standards—two essentials, it would seem, for any successful friendship.

Or perhaps not.

Jarlaxle's heart is far more generous than that of Artemis Entreri. The mercenary can

83

be brutal, of course, but not randomly so. Practicality guides his moves, for his eye is ever on the potential gain, but even in that light of efficient pragmatism, Jarlaxle's heart often overrules his lust for profit. Many times has he allowed my escape, for example, when bringing my head to Matron Malice or Matron Baenre would have brought him great gain. Is Artemis Entreri similarly possessed of such generosity?

Not at all.

In fact, I suspect that if Entreri knew that Jarlaxle had saved me from my apparent death in the tower, he would have first tried to kill me and turned his anger upon Jarlaxle. Such a battle might well yet occur, and if it does, I believe that Artemis Entreri will learn that he is badly overmatched. Not by Jarlaxle individually, though the mercenary leader is crafty and reputedly a fine warrior in his own right, but by the pragmatic Jarlaxle's many, many deadly allies.

Therein lies the essence of the mercenary leader's interest in, and control of, Artemis Entreri. Jarlaxle sees the man's value and does not fear him, because what Jarlaxle has perfected, and what Entreri is sorely lacking in, is the ability to build an interdependent organization. Entreri won't attempt to kill Jarlaxle because Entreri will need Jarlaxle.

Jarlaxle will make certain of that. He weaves his web all around him. It is a network that is always mutually beneficial, a network in which all security—against Bregan D'aerthe's many dangerous rivals—inevitably depends upon the controlling and calming influence that is Jarlaxle. He is the ultimate consensus builder, the purest of diplomats, while Entreri is a loner, a man who must dominate all around him.

Jarlaxle coerces. Entreri controls.

But with Jarlaxle, Entreri will never find any level of control. The mercenary leader is too entrenched and too intelligent for that.

And yet, I believe that their alliance will hold, and their friendship will grow. Certainly there will be conflicts and perhaps very dangerous ones for both parties. Perhaps Entreri has already learned the truth of my departure and has killed Jarlaxle or died trying. But the longer the alliance holds, the stronger it will become, the more entrenched in friendship.

I say this because I believe that, in the end, Jarlaxle's philosophy will win out. Artemis Entreri is the one of this duo who is limited by fault. His desire for absolute control is fueled by his inability to trust. While that desire has led him to become as fine a fighter as I have ever known, it has also led him to an existence that even he is beginning to recognize as empty.

Professionally, Jarlaxle offers Artemis Entreri security, a base for his efforts, while Entreri gives Jarlaxle and all of Bregan D'aerthe a clear connection to the surface world.

But personally, Jarlaxle offers even more to Entreri, offers him a chance to finally break out of the role that he has assumed as a solitary creature. I remember Entreri upon our departure from Menzoberranzan, where we were both imprisoned, each in his own way. He was with Bregan D'aerthe then as well, but down in that city, Artemis Entreri looked into a dark and empty mirror that he did not like. Why, then, is he now returned to Jarlaxle's side?

It is a testament to the charm that is Jarlaxle, the intuitive understanding that that most clever of dark elves holds for creating desire and alliance. The mere fact that Entreri is apparently with Jarlaxle once again tells me that the mercenary leader is already winning the inevitable clash between their basic philosophies, their temperament and moral standards. Though Entreri does not yet understand it, I am sure, Jarlaxle will strengthen him more by example than by alliance.

Perhaps with Jarlaxle's help, Artemis Entreri will find his way out of his current empty existence.

Or perhaps Jarlaxle will eventually kill him.

Either way, the world will be a better place, I think.

—Drizzt Do'Urden

CHAPTER

CONTROL AND COOPERATION

9

The Copper Ante was fairly busy this evening, with halflings mostly crowd-ing around tables, rolling bones or playing other games of chance and all whispering about the recent events in and around the city. Every one of them spoke quietly, though, for among the few humans in the tavern that night were two rather striking figures, operatives central to the recent tumultuous events.

Sharlotta Vespers was very aware of the many stares directed her way, and she knew that many of these halflings were secret allies of her companion this night. She had almost refused Entreri's invitation for her to come and meet with him privately here, in the house of Dwahvel Tiggerwillies, but she recognized the value of the place. The Copper Ante was beyond the prying eyes of Rai-guy and Kimmuriel, a condition necessary, so Entreri had said, for any meeting.

"I can't believe you openly walk Calimport's streets with that sword," Sharlotta remarked quietly.

"It is rather distinctive," Entreri admitted, but there wasn't the slightest hint of alarm in his voice.

"It's a well-known blade," Sharlotta answered. "Anyone who knew of Kohrin Soulez and Dallabad knows he would never willingly part with it, yet here you are, showing it to all who would glance your way. One might think that a clear connection between the downfall of Dallabad and House Basadoni."

"How so?" Entreri asked, and he took pleasure indeed at the look of sheer exasperation that washed over Sharlotta.

"Kohrin is dead and Artemis Entreri is wearing his sword," Sharlotta remarked dryly.

"He is dead, and thus the sword is no longer of any use to him," Entreri flip-pantly remarked. "On the streets, it is understood that he was killed in a coup by his very own daughter, who, by all rumors, had no desire to be captured by Charon's Claw as was Kohrin."

"Thus it falls to the hands of Artemis Entreri?" Sharlotta asked incredulously.

"It has been hinted that Kohrin's refusal to sell at the offered price—an absurd amount of gold—was the very catalyst for the coup," Entreri went on,

86

leaning back comfortably in his chair. "When Ahdahnia learned that he refused the transaction. . . ."

"Impossible," Sharlotta breathed, shaking her head. "Do you really expect that tale to be believed?"

Entreri smiled wryly. "The words of Sha'lazzi Ozoule are often believed," he remarked. "Inquiries to purchase the sword were made through Sha'lazzi only days before the coup at Dallabad."

That set Sharlotta back in her chair as she tried hard to digest and sort through all of the information. On the streets, it was indeed being said that Kohrin had been killed in a coup—Jarlaxle's domination of the remaining Dallabad forces through use of the Crystal Shard had provided consistency in all of the reports coming out of the oasis. As long as Crenshinibon's dominance held out, there was no evidence at all to reveal the truth of the assault on Dallabad. If Entreri had spoken truly—and Sharlotta had no reason to think that he had not—the refusal by Kohrin to sell Charon's Claw would be linked not to any theft or any attack by House Basadoni, but rather as one of the catalysts for the coup.

Sharlotta stared hard at Entreri, her expression a mixture of anger and admiration. He had covered every possible aspect of his procurement of the coveted sword beforehand. Sharlotta, given her understanding of Entreri's relationship with the dangerous Rai-guy and Kimmuriel, held no doubts that Entreri had helped guide the dark elves to Dallabad specifically with the intent of collecting that very sword.

"You weave a web with many layers," the woman remarked.

"I have been around dark elves for far too long," Entreri casually replied.

"But you walk the very edge of disaster," said Sharlotta. "Many of the guilds had already linked the downfall of Dallabad with House Basadoni, and now you openly parade about with Charon's Claw. The other rumors are plausible, of course, but your actions do little to distance us from the assassination of Kohrin Soulez."

"Where stands Pasha Da'Daclan or Pasha Wroning?" Entreri asked, feigning concern.

"Da'Daclan is cautious and making no overt moves," Sharlotta replied. Entreri held his grin private at her earnest tones, for she had obviously taken his bait. "He is far from pleased with the situation, though, and the strong inferences concerning Dallabad."

"As they all will be," Entreri reasoned. "Unless Jarlaxle grows too bold with his construction of crystalline towers."

Again he spoke with dramatically serious tones, more to measure Sharlotta's reaction than to convey any information the woman didn't already know. He did note a slight tremor in her lip. Frustration? Fear? Disgust? Entreri knew that Rai-guy and Kimmuriel were not happy with Jarlaxle, and that the two independent-minded lieutenants, perhaps, were thinking that the influences of the sentient and dominating Crystal Shard might be causing some serious problems. They had sent him after Morik to weaken the guild's presence on the surface, obviously, but why, then, was Sharlotta still alive? Had she thrown in with the two potential usurpers to Bregan D'aerthe's dark throne?

"The deed is completed now and cannot be undone," Entreri remarked. "Indeed I did desire Charon's Claw—what warrior would not?—but with

Sha'lazzi Ozoule spreading his tales of a generous offer to buy being refused by Kohrin, and with Ahdahnia Soulez speaking openly of her disdain for her father's choices, particularly concerning the sword, it all plays to the advantage of Bregan D'aerthe and our work here. Jarlaxle needed a haven to construct the tower, and we gave him one. Bregan D'aerthe now has eyes beyond the city, where we might watch all mounting threats that are outside of our immediate jurisdiction. Everyone wins."

"And Entreri gets the sword," Sharlotta remarked.

"Everyone wins," the assassin said again.

"Until we step too far, and too boldly, and all the world unites against us," said Sharlotta.

"Jarlaxle has lived on such a precipice for centuries," Entreri replied. "He has not stumbled over yet."

Sharlotta started to respond but held her words at the last moment. Entreri knew them anyway, words taken from her by the quick give and take of the conversation, the mounting excitement and momentum bringing a rare unguarded moment. She was about to remark that never in all those centuries had Jarlaxle possessed Crenshinibon, the clear inference being that never in those centuries had Crenshinibon possessed Jarlaxle.

"Say nothing of our concerns to Rai-guy and Kimmuriel," Entreri bade her. "They are fearful enough, and frightened creatures, even drow, can make serious errors. You and I will watch from afar—perhaps there is a way out of this if it comes to an internal war."

Sharlotta nodded, and rightly took Entreri's tone as a dismissal. She rose, nodded again, and moved out of the room.

Entreri didn't believe that nod for a moment. He knew the woman would likely go running right to Rai-guy and Kimmuriel, attempting to bend this conversation her way. But that was the point of it all, was it not? Entreri had just forced Sharlotta's hand, forced her to show her true alliances in this ever-widening web of intrigue. Certainly his last claim, that there might be a way out for the two of them, would ring hollow to Sharlotta, who knew him well, and knew well that he would never bother to take her along with him on any escape from Bregan D'aerthe. He'd put a dagger in her back as surely as he had killed any previous supposed partners, from Tallan Belmer to Rassiter the wererat. Sharlotta knew that, and Entreri knew she knew it.

It did occur to the assassin that perhaps Sharlotta, Rai-guy, and Kimmuriel were correct in their apparent assessment that Crenshinibon was having unfavorable influences on Jarlaxle, that the artifact was leading the cunning mercenary in a direction that could spell doom for Bregan D'aerthe's surface ambitions. That hardly mattered to Entreri, of course, who wasn't sure the retreat of the dark elves back to Menzoberranzan would be such a bad thing. What was more important, to Entreri's thinking, were the dynamics of his relationship with the principles of the mercenary band. Rai-guy and Kimmuriel were notorious racists and hated him as they hated anyone who was not drow—more, even, because Entreri's skill and survival instincts threatened them profoundly. Without Jarlaxle's protection, it wasn't hard for Artemis Entreri to envision his fate. While he felt somewhat bolstered by his acquisition of Charon's Claw, the bane of wizards, he hardly thought it evened the odds in any battle he might find with the duo of the drow wizard-cleric and psionicist. If those two wound up in command of Bregan D'aerthe, with over a hundred drow warriors at their immediate disposal . . .

Entreri didn't like the odds at all.

He knew, without doubt, that Jarlaxle's fall would almost immediately precede his own.

Kimmuriel walked along the tunnels beneath Dallabad with some measure of trepidation. This was a *haszakkin,* after all, an illithid—unpredictable and deadly. Still, the drow had come alone, had deceived Rai-guy that he might do so.

There were some things that psionicists alone could understand and appreciate.

Around a sudden bend in the tunnel, Kimmuriel came upon the bulbous-headed creature, sitting calmly on a rock against the back end of an alcove. Yharaskrik's eyes were closed, but he was awake, Kimmuriel knew, for he could feel the mental energy beaming out from the creature.

I chose well in siding with Bregan D'aerthe, it would seem, the illithid telepathically remarked. *There was never any doubt.*

The drow are stronger than the humans, Kimmuriel agreed, using the illithid's telepathic link to impart his exact thoughts.

Stronger than these *humans,* Yharaskrik corrected.

Kimmuriel bowed, figuring to let the matter drop there, but Yharaskrik had more to discuss.

Stronger than Kohrin Soulez, the illithid went on. *Crippled, he was, by his obsession with a particular magical item.*

That brought some understanding to Kimmuriel, some logical connection between the mind flayer and the pitiful gang of Dallabad Oasis. Why would a creature as great as Yharaskrik waste its time with such inferior beings, after all?

You were sent to observe the powerful sword and the gauntlet, he reasoned.

We wish to understand that which can sometimes defeat our attacks, Yharaskrik freely admitted. *Yet neither item is without limitations. Neither is as powerful as Kohrin Soulez believed, or your attack would never have succeeded.*

We have discerned as much, Kimmuriel agreed.

My time with Kohrin Soulez was nearing its end, said Yharaskrik, a clear inference that the illithid—creatures known as among the most meticulous of all in the multiverse—believed that it had learned every secret of the sword and gauntlet.

The human, Artemis Entreri, confiscated both the gauntlet and Charon's Claw, the drow psionicist explained.

That was his intent, of course, the illithid replied. *He fears you and wisely so. You are strong in will, Kimmuriel of House Oblodra.*

The drow bowed again.

Respect the sword named Charon's Claw, and even more so the gauntlet the human now wears on his hand. With these, he can turn your powers back against you if you are not careful.

Kimmuriel imparted his assurances that Artemis Entreri and his dangerous new weapon would be closely watched. *Are your days of watching the paired items now ended?* he asked as he finished.

Perhaps, Yharaskrik answered.

Or perhaps Bregan D'aerthe could find a place suited to your special talents, Kimmuriel offered. He didn't think it would be hard to persuade Jarlaxle of such an arrangement. Dark elves often allied with illithids in the Underdark.

Yharaskrik's pause was telling to the perceptive and intelligent drow. "You have a better offer?" Kimmuriel asked aloud, and with a chuckle.

Better it would be if I remained to the side of events, unknown to Bregan D'aerthe other than to Kimmuriel Oblodra, Yharaskrik answered in all seriousness.

The response at first confused Kimmuriel and made him think that the illithid feared that Bregan D'aerthe would side with Entreri and Charon's Claw if any such conflict arose between Yharaskrik and Entreri, but before he could begin to offer his assurances against that, the illithid imparted a clear image to him, one of a crystalline tower shining in the sun above the palm trees of Dallabad Oasis.

"The towers?" Kimmuriel asked aloud. "They are just manifestations of Crenshinibon."

Crenshinibon. The word came to Kimmuriel with a sense of urgency and great importance.

It is an artifact, the drow telepathically explained. *A new toy for Jarlaxle's collection.*

Not so, came Yharaskrik's response. *Much more than that, I fear, as should you.*

Kimmuriel narrowed his red-glowing eyes, focusing carefully on Yharaskrik's thoughts, which he expected might confirm the fears he and Rai-guy had long been discussing.

Weave into the thoughts of Jarlaxle, I cannot, the illithid went on. *He wears a protective item.*

The eye patch, Kimmuriel silently replied. *It denies entrance to his mind by wizard, priest, or psionicist.*

But such a simple tool cannot defeat the encroachment of Crenshinibon, Yharaskrik explained.

How do you know of the artifact?

Crenshinibon is no mystery to my people, for it is an ancient item indeed, and one that has crossed the trails of the illithids on many occasions, Yharaskrik admitted. *Indeed, Crenshinibon, the Crystal Shard, despises us, for we alone are quite beyond its tempting reach. We alone as a great race are possessed of the mental discipline necessary to prevent the Crystal Shard from its greatest desires of absolute control. You, too, Kimmuriel, can step beyond the orb of Crenshinibon's influence and easily.*

The drow took a long moment to contemplate the implications of that claim, but naturally, he quickly came to the conclusion that Yharaskrik was relating that psionics alone might fend the intrusions of the Crystal Shard, since Jarlaxle's potent eye patch was based in wizardly magic and not the potent powers of the mind.

Crenshinibon's primary attack is upon the ego, the illithid explained. *It collects slaves with promises of greatness and riches.*

Not unlike the drow, Kimmuriel related, thinking of the tactics Bregan D'aerthe had used on Morik.

Yharaskrik laughed a gurgling, bubbly sound. *The more ambitious the wielder, the easier he will be controlled.*

But what if the wielder is ambitious yet ultimately cautious? Kimmuriel asked, for never had he known Jarlaxle to allow his ambition to overrule good judgment—never before, at least, for only recently had he, Rai-guy, and others come to question the wisdom of the mercenary leader's decisions.

Some lessers can deny the call, the illithid admitted, and it was obvious to Kimmuriel that Yharaskrik considered anyone who was not illithid or who was not at least a psionicist a lesser. *Crenshinibon has little sway over paladins and goodly priests, over righteous kings and noble peasants, but one who desires more—and who of the lesser races, drow included, does not?—and who is not above deception and destruction to further his ends, will inevitably sink into Crenshinibon's grasp.*

It made perfect sense to Kimmuriel, of course, and explained why Drizzt Do'Urden and his "heroic" friends had seemingly put the artifact away. It also explained Jarlaxle's recent behavior, confirming Kimmuriel's suspicions that Bregan D'aerthe was indeed being led astray.

I would not normally refuse an offer of Bregan D'aerthe, Yharaskrik imparted a moment later, after Kimmuriel had digested the information. *You and your reputable kin would be amusing at the least—and likely enlightening and profitable as well—but I fear that all of Bregan D'aerthe will soon fall under the domination of Crenshinibon.*

And why would Yharaskrik fear such a thing, if Crenshinibon becomes leader in order to take us in the same ambitious direction that we have always pursued? Kimmuriel asked, and he feared that he already knew the answer.

I trust not the drow, Yharaskrik admitted, *but I understand enough of your desires and methods to recognize that we need not be enemies among the cattle humans. I trust you not, but I fear you not, because you would find no gain in facilitating my demise. Indeed, you understand that I am connected to the one community that is my people, and that if you killed me you would be making many powerful enemies.*

Kimmuriel bowed, acknowledging the truth of the illithid's observations.

Crenshinibon, however, Yharaskrik went on, *acts not with such rationality. It is all-devouring, a scourge upon the world, controlling all that it can and consuming that which it cannot. It is the bane of devils, yet the love of demons, a denier of laws for the sake of the destruction wrought by chaos. Your Lady Lolth would idolize such an artifact and truly enjoy the chaos of its workings—except of course that Crenshinibon, unlike her drow agents, works not for any ends, but merely to devour. Crenshinibon will bring great power to Bregan D'aerthe—witness the new willing slaves it has made for you, among them the very daughter of the man you overthrew. In the end, Crenshinibon will abandon you, will bring upon you foes too great to fend. This is the history of the Crystal Shard, repeated time and again through the centuries. It is unbridled hunger without discipline, doomed to bloat and die.*

Kimmuriel unintentionally winced at the thoughts, for he could see that very path being woven right before the still-secretive doorstep of Bregan D'aerthe.

91

All-devouring, Yharaskrik said again. *Controlling all that it can and consuming that which it cannot.*

And you are among that which it cannot, Kimmuriel reasoned.

"As are you," Yharaskrik said in its watery voice. "Tower of Iron Will and Mind Blank," the illithid recited, two typical and readily available mental defense modes that psionicists often used in their battles with each other.

Kimmuriel growled, understanding well the trap that the illithid had just laid for him, the alliance of necessity that Yharaskrik, obviously fearing that Kimmuriel might betray him to Jarlaxle and the Crystal Shard, had just forced upon him. He knew those defensive mental postures, of course, and if the Crystal Shard came after him, seeking control, now that he knew the two defenses would prevent the intrusions, he would inevitably and automatically summon them up. For, like any psionicist, like any reasoning being, Kimmuriel's ego and id would never allow such controlling possession.

He stared long and hard at the illithid, hating the creature, and yet sympathizing with Yharaskrik's fears of Crenshinibon. Or, perhaps, it occurred to him that Yharaskrik had just saved him. Crenshinibon would have come after him, to dominate if not to destroy, and if Kimmuriel had discovered the correct ways to block the intrusion in time, then he would have suddenly become an enemy in an unfavorable position, as opposed to now, when he, and not Crenshinibon, properly understood the situation at hand.

"You will shadow us?" he asked the illithid, hoping the answer would be yes.

He felt a wave of thoughts roll through him, ambiguous and lacking any specifics, but indicating clearly that Yharaskrik meant to keep a watchful eye on the dangerous Crystal Shard.

They were allies, then, out of necessity.

"I do not like her," came the high-pitched, excited voice of Dwahvel Tiggerwillies. The halfling shuffled over to take Sharlotta's vacated seat at Entreri's table.

"Is it her height and beauty that so offend you?" Entreri sarcastically replied.

Dwahvel shot him a perfectly incredulous look. "Her dishonesty," the halfling explained.

That answer raised Entreri's eyebrow. Wasn't everyone on the streets of Calimport, Entreri and Dwahvel included, basically a manipulator? If a claim of dishonesty was a reason not to like someone in Calimport, then the judgmental person would find herself quite alone.

"There is a difference," Dwahvel explained, intercepting a nearby waiter with a wave of her hand and taking a drink from his laden tray.

"So it comes back to that height and beauty problem, then," Entreri chided with a smile.

His own words did indeed amuse him, but what caught his fancy even more was the realization that he could, and often did, talk to Dwahvel in such a manner. In all of his life, Artemis Entreri had known very few people with whom he could have a casual conversation, but he found himself so at ease with Dwahvel that he had even considered hiring a wizard to determine if she was using some charming magic on him. In fact, then and there, Entreri clenched his gloved fist, concentrating briefly on the item to see if he could determine any magical emanations coming from Dwahvel, aimed at him.

There was nothing, only honest friendship, which to Artemis Entreri was a magic more foreign indeed.

"I have often been jealous of human women," Dwahvel answered sarcastically, doing well to keep a perfectly straight face. "They are often tall enough to attract even ogres, after all."

Entreri chuckled, an expression from him so rare that he actually surprised himself in hearing it.

"There is a difference between Sharlotta and many others, yourself included," Dwahvel went on. "We all play the game—that is how we survive, after all—and we all deceive and plot, twisting truths and lies alike to reach our own desired ends. The confusion for some, Sharlotta included, lies in those ends. I understand you. I know your desires, your goals, and know that I impede those goals at my peril. But I trust as well that, as long as I do not impede those goals, I'll not find the wrong end of either of your fine blades."

"So thought Dondon," Entreri put in, referring to Dondon Tiggerwillies, Dwahvel's cousin and once Entreri's closest friend in the city. Entreri had murdered the pitiful Dondon soon after his return from his final battle with Drizzt Do'Urden.

"Your actions against Dondon did not surprise him, I assure you," Dwahvel remarked. "He was a good enough friend to you to have killed you if he had ever found you in the same situation as you found him. You did him a favor."

Entreri shrugged, hardly sure of that, not even sure of his own motivations in killing Dondon. Had he done so to free Dondon from his own gluttonous ends, from the chains that kept him locked in a room and in a state of constant incapacity? Or had he killed Dondon simply because he was angry at the failed creature, simply because he could not stand to look at the miserable thing he had become any longer?

"Sharlotta is not trustworthy because you cannot understand her true goals and motivations," Dwahvel continued. "She desires power, yes, as do many, but with her, one can never understand where she might be thinking that she can find that power. There is no loyalty there, even to those who maintain consistency of character and action. No, that one will take the better deal at the expense of any and all."

Entreri nodded, not disagreeing in the least. He had never liked Sharlotta, and like Dwahvel, he had never even begun to trust her. There were no scruples or codes within Sharlotta Vespers, only blatant manipulation.

"She crosses the line every time," Dwahvel remarked. "I have never been fond of women who use their bodies to get that which they desire. I've got my own charms, you know, and yet I have never had to stoop to such a level."

The lighthearted ending brought another smile to Entreri's face, and he knew that Dwahvel was only half joking. She did indeed have her charms: a pleasant appearance and fine, flattering dress, as sharp a wit as was to be found, and a keen sense of her surroundings.

"How are you getting on with your new companion?" Dwahvel asked.

Entreri looked at her curiously—she did have a way of bouncing about a conversation.

"The sword," Dwahvel clarified, feigning exasperation. "You have it now, or it has you."

"*I have it,*" Entreri assured her, dropping his hand to the bony hilt.

Dwahvel eyed him suspiciously.

"I have not yet fought my battle with Charon's Claw," Entreri admitted to her, hardly believing that he was doing so, "but I do not think it so powerful a weapon that I need fear it."

"As Jarlaxle believes with Crenshinibon?" Dwahvel asked, and again, Entreri's eyebrow lifted high.

"He constructed a crystalline tower," the ever-observant halfling argued. "That is one of the most basic desires of the Crystal Shard, if the old sages are to be believed."

Entreri started to ask her how she could possibly know of any of that, of the shard and the tower at Dallabad and of any connection, but he didn't bother. Of course Dwahvel knew. She always knew—that was one of her charms. Entreri had dropped enough hints in their many discussions for her to figure it all out, and she did have an incredible number of other sources as well. If Dwahvel Tiggerwillies learned that Jarlaxle carried an artifact known as Crenshinibon, then there would be little doubt that she would go to the sages and pay good coin to learn every little-known detail about the powerful item.

"He thinks he controls it," Dwahvel said.

"Do not underestimate Jarlaxle," Entreri replied. "Many have. They all are dead."

"Do not underestimate the Crystal Shard," Dwahvel returned without hesitation. "Many have. They all are dead."

"A wonderful combination then," Entreri said matter-of-factly. He dropped his chin in his hand, stroking his smooth cheek and bringing his finger to a pinch at the small tuft of hair that remained on his chin, considering the conversation and the implications. "Jarlaxle can handle the artifact," he decided.

Dwahvel shrugged noncommitally.

"Even more than that," Entreri went on, "Jarlaxle will welcome the union if Crenshinibon proves his equal. That is the difference between him and me," he explained, and though he was speaking to Dwahvel, he was, in fact, really talking to himself, sorting out his many feelings on this complicated issue. "He will allow Crenshinibon to be his partner, if that is necessary, and will find ways to make their goals one and the same."

"But Artemis Entreri has no partners," Dwahvel reasoned.

Entreri considered the words carefully, and even glanced down at the powerful sword he now wore, a sword possessed of sentience and influence, a sword whose spirit he surely meant to break and dominate. "No," he agreed. "I have no partners, and I want none. The sword is mine and will serve me. Nothing less."

"Or?"

"Or it will find its way into the acid mouth of a black dragon," Entreri strongly assured the halfling, growling with every word, and Dwahvel wasn't about to argue with those words spoken in that tone.

"Who is the stronger then," Dwahvel dared to ask, "Jarlaxle the partner or Entreri the loner?"

"I am," Entreri assured her without the slightest hesitation. "Jarlaxle might seem so for now, but inevitably he will find a traitor among his partners who will bring him down."

"You never could stand the thought of taking orders," Dwahvel said with a laugh. "That is why the shape of the world so bothers you!"

"To take an order implies that you must trust the giver of such," Entreri retorted, and the tone of his banter showed that he was taking no offense. In fact, there was an eagerness in his voice rarely heard, a true testament to those many charms of Dwahvel Tiggerwillies. "That, my dear little Dwahvel, is why the shape of the world so bothers me. I learned at a very young age that I cannot trust in or count on anyone but myself. To do so invites deceit and despair and opens a vulnerability that can be exploited. To do so is a weakness."

Now it was Dwahvel's turn to sit back a bit and digest the words. "But you have come to trust in me, it would seem," she said, "merely by speaking with me such. Have I brought out a weakness in you, my friend?"

Entreri smiled again, a crooked smile that didn't really tell Dwahvel whether he was amused or merely warning her not to push this observation too far.

"Perhaps it is merely that I know you and your band well enough to hold no fear of you," the cocky assassin remarked, rising from his seat and stretching. "Or maybe it is merely that you have not yet been foolish enough to try to give me an order."

Still that grin remained, but Dwahvel, too, was smiling, and sincerely. She saw it in Entreri's eyes now, that little hint of appreciation. Perhaps their talks were a bit of weakness to Entreri's jaded way of thinking. The truth of it, whether he wanted to admit it or not, was that he did indeed trust her, perhaps more deeply than he had ever trusted anyone in all of his life. At least, more deeply than he had since that first person—and Dwahvel figured that it had to have been a parent or a close family friend—had so deeply betrayed and wounded him.

Entreri headed for the door, that casual, easy walk of his, perfect in balance and as graceful as any court dancer. Many heads turned to watch him go—so many were always concerned with the whereabouts of deadly Artemis Entreri.

Not so for Dwahvel, though. She had come to understand this relationship, this friendship of theirs, not long after Dondon's death. She knew that if she ever crossed Artemis Entreri, he would surely kill her, but she knew, too, where those lines of danger lay.

Dwahvel's smile was indeed genuine and comfortable and confident as she watched her dangerous friend leave the Copper Ante that night.

CHAPTER

10

M y master, he says that I am to pay you, yes?" the slobbering little brown-skinned man said to one of the fortress guards. "Kohrin Soulez is Dallabad, yes? My master, he says I pay Kohrin Soulez for water and shade, yes?"

The Dallabad soldier looked to his amused companion, and both of them regarded the little man, who continued bobbing his head stupidly.

"You see that tower?" the first asked, drawing the little man's gaze with his own toward the crystalline structure gleaming brilliantly over Dallabad. "That is Ahdahnia's tower. Ahdahnia Soulez, who now rules Dallabad."

The little man looked up at the tower with obvious awe. "Ah-dahn-ee-a," he said carefully, slowly, as if committing it to memory. "Soulez, yes? Like Kohrin."

"The daughter of Kohrin Soulez," the guard explained. "Go and tell your master that Ahdahnia Soulez now rules Dallabad. You pay her, through me."

The little man's head bobbed frantically. "Yes, yes," he agreed, handing over the modest purse, "and my master will meet with her, yes?"

The guard shrugged. "If I get around to asking her, perhaps," he said, and he held his hand out, and the little man looked at it curiously.

"If I find the time to bother to tell her," the guard said pointedly.

"I pay you to tell her?" the little man asked, and the other guard snorted loudly, shaking his head at the little man's continuing stupidity.

"You pay me, I tell her," the guard said plainly. "You do not pay me, and your master does not meet with her."

"But if I pay you, we . . . he, meets with her?"

"If she so chooses," the guard explained. "I will tell her. I can promise no more than that."

The little man's head continued to bob, but his stare drifted off to the side, as if he was considering the options laid out before him. "I pay," he agreed, and handed over another, smaller, purse.

The guard snatched it away and bounced it in his hand, checking the weight, and shook his head and scowled, indicating clearly that it was not enough.

"All I have!" the little man protested.

"Then get more," ordered the guard.

96

The little man hopped all about, seeming unsure and very concerned. He reached for the second purse, but the guard pulled it back and scowled at him. A bit more shuffling and hopping, and the little man gave a shriek and ran off.

"You think they will attack?" the other guard asked, and it was obvious from his tone that he wasn't feeling very concerned about the possibility.

The group of six wagons had pulled into Dallabad that morning, seeking reprieve from the blistering sun. The drivers were twenty strong, and not one of them seemed overly threatening, and not one of them even looked remotely like any wizard. Any attack that group made against Dallabad's fortress would likely bring only a few moments of enjoyment to the soldiers now serving Ahdahnia Soulez.

"I think that our little friend has already forgotten his purse," the first soldier replied. "Or at least, he has forgotten the truth of how he lost it."

The second merely laughed. Not much had changed at the oasis since the downfall of Kohrin Soulez. They were still the same pirating band of toll collectors. Of course the guard would tell Ahdahnia of the wagon leader's desire to meet with her—that was how Ahdahnia collected her information, after all. As for his extortion of some of the stupid little wretch's funds, that would fade away into meaninglessness very quickly.

Yes, little had really changed.

"So it is true that Kohrin is dead," remarked Lipke, the coordinator of the scouting party, the leader of the "trading caravan."

He glanced out the slit in his tent door to see the gleaming tower, the source of great unease throughout Calimshan. While it was no great event that Kohrin Soulez had at last been killed, nor that his daughter had apparently taken over Dallabad Oasis, rumors tying this event to another not-so-minor power shift among a prominent guild in Calimport had put the many warlords of the region on guard.

"It is also true that his daughter has apparently taken his place," Trulbul replied, pulling the padding from the back collar of his shirt, the "hump" that gave him the slobbering, stooped-over appearance. "Curse her name for turning on her father."

"Unless she had no choice in the matter," offered Rolmanet, the third of the inner circle. "Artemis Entreri has been seen in Calimport with Charon's Claw. Perhaps Ahdahnia sold it to him, as some rumors say. Perhaps she bartered it for the magic that would construct that tower, as say others. Or perhaps the foul assassin took it from the body of Kohrin Soulez."

"It has to be Basadoni," Lipke reasoned. "I know Ahdahnia, and she would not have so viciously turned against her father, not over the sale of a sword. There is no shortage of gold in Dallabad."

"But why would the Basadoni Guild leave her in command of Dallabad?" asked Trulbul. "Or more particularly, how would they leave her in command, if she holds any loyalty to her father? Those guards were not Basadoni soldiers," he added. "I am sure of it. Their skin shows the weathering of the open desert, as with all the Dallabad militia, and not the grime of Calimport's streets. Kohrin

Soulez treated his guild well—even the least of his soldiers and attendants always had gold for the gambling tents when we passed through here. Would so many so quickly abandon their loyalties to the man?"

The three looked at each other for a moment and burst into laughter. Loyalty had never been the strong suit of any of Calimshan's guilds and gangs.

"Your point is well taken," Trulbul admitted, "yet it still does not seem right to me. Somehow there is more to this than a simple coup."

"I do not believe that either of us disagrees with you," Lipke replied. "Artemis Entreri carries Kohrin's mighty sword, yet if it is a simple matter that Ahdahnia Soulez decided that the time had come to secure Dallabad Oasis for herself, would she so quickly part with such a powerful defensive item? Is this not the time when she will likely be most open to reprisals?"

"Unless she hired Entreri to kill her father, with payment to be Charon's Claw," Rolmanet reasoned. He was nodding as he improvised the words, thinking that he had stumbled onto something very plausible, something that would explain much.

"If that is so, then this is the most expensive assassination Calimshan has known in centuries," Lipke remarked.

"But if not that, then what?" a frustrated Rolmanet asked.

"Basadoni," Trulbul said definitively. "It has to be Basadoni. They extended their grasp within the city, and now they have struck out again, hoping it to be away from prying eyes. We must confirm this."

The others were nodding, reluctantly it seemed.

⊷══⊶

Jarlaxle, Kimmuriel, and Rai-guy sat in comfortable chairs in the second level of the crystalline tower. An enchanted mirror, a collaboration between the magic of Rai-guy and Crenshinibon, conveyed the entire conversation between the three scouts, as it had followed the supposedly stupid little hunched man from the moment he had handed his purses over to the guard outside the fortress.

"This is not acceptable," Rai-guy dared to remark, turning to face Jarlaxle. "We are grasping too far and too fast, inviting prying eyes."

Kimmuriel sent his thoughts to his wizardly friend. *Not here. Not within the tower replica of Crenshinibon.* Even as he sent the message, he felt the energies of the shard tugging at him, prying around the outside of his mental defenses. With Yharaskrik's warnings echoing in his mind, and surely not wanting to alert Crenshinibon to the truth of his nature at that time, Kimmuriel abruptly ceased all psionic activity.

"What do you plan to do with them?" Rai-guy asked more calmly. He glanced at Kimmuriel, relaying to his friend that he had gotten the message and would heed the wise thoughts well.

"Destroy them," Kimmuriel reasoned.

"Incorporate them," Jarlaxle corrected. "There are a score in their party, and they are obviously connected to other guilds. What fine spies they will become."

"Too dangerous," Rai-guy remarked.

"Those who submit to the will of Crenshinibon will serve us," Jarlaxle replied with utmost calm. "Those who do not will be executed."

Rai-guy didn't seem convinced. He started to reply, but Kimmuriel put his hand on his friend's forearm and motioned for him to let it go.

"You will deal with them?" Kimmuriel asked Jarlaxle. "Or would you prefer that we send in soldiers to capture them and drag them before the Crystal Shard for judgment?"

"The artifact can reach their minds from the tower," Jarlaxle replied. "Those who submit will willingly slay those who do not."

"And if those who do not are the greater?" Rai-guy had to ask, but again, Kimmuriel motioned for him to be quiet, and this time, the psionicist rose and bade the wizard to follow him away.

"With the changes in Dallabad's hierarchy and the tower so evident, we will have to remain fully on our guard for some time to come," Kimmuriel did say to Jarlaxle.

The mercenary leader nodded. "Crenshinibon is ever wary," he explained.

Kimmuriel smiled in reply, but in truth, Jarlaxle's assurances were only making him more nervous, were only confirming to him that Yharaskrik's information concerning the devastating Crystal Shard was, apparently, quite accurate.

The two left their leader alone then with his newest partner, the sentient artifact.

Rolmanet and Trulbul blinked repeatedly as they exited their tent into the stinging daylight. All about them, the other members of their band worked methodically, if less than enthusiastically, brushing the horses and camels and filling the waterskins for the remaining journey to Calimport.

Others should have been out scouting the perimeter of the oasis and doing guard counts on Dallabad fortress, but Rolmanet soon realized that all seventeen of the remaining force was about. He also noticed that many kept glancing his way, wearing curious expressions.

One man in particular caught Rolmanet's eye. "Did he not already fill those skins?" Rolmanet quietly asked his companion. "And should he not be at the east wall, counting sentries?" As he finished, he turned to Trulbul, and his last words faded away as he considered his companion, the man standing quietly, staring up at the crystalline tower with a wistful look in his dark eyes.

"Trulbul?" Rolmanet asked, starting toward the man but, sensing that something was amiss, changing his mind and stepping away instead.

An expression of complete serenity came over Trulbul's face. "Can you not hear it?" he asked, glancing over to regard Rolmanet. "The music . . ."

"Music?" Rolmanet glanced at the man curiously, and snapped his gaze back to regard the tower and listened carefully.

"Beautiful music," Trulbul said rather loudly, and several others nearby nodded their agreement.

Rolmanet fought hard to steady his breathing and at least appear calm. He did hear the music then, a subtle note conveying a message of peace and prosperity, promising gain and power and . . . demanding. Demanding fealty.

"I am staying at Dallabad," Lipke announced suddenly, coming out of the tent. "There is more opportunity here than with Pasha Broucalle."

Rolmanet's eyes widened in spite of himself, and he had to fight very hard to keep from glancing all around in alarm or from simply running away. He was gasping now as it all came clear to him: a wizard's spell, he believed, charming enemies into friends.

"Beautiful music," another man off to the side agreed.

"Do you hear it?" Trulbul asked Rolmanet.

Rolmanet fought very hard to steady himself, to paint a serene expression upon his face, before turning back to stare at his friend.

"No, he does not," Lipke said from afar before Rolmanet had even completed the turn. "He does not see the opportunity before us. He will betray us!"

"It is a spell!" Rolmanet cried loudly, drawing his curved sword. "A wizard's enchantment to ensnare us in his grip. Fight back! Deny it, my friends!"

Lipke was at him, slashing hard with his sword, a blow that skilled Rolmanet deftly parried. Before he could counter, Trulbul was there beside Lipke, following the first man's slash with a deadly thrust at Rolmanet's heart.

"Can you not understand?" Rolmanet cried frantically, and only luck allowed him to deflect that second attack.

He glanced about as he retreated steadily, seeking allies and taking care for more enemies. He noted another fight over by the water, where several men had fallen over another, knocking him to the ground and kicking and beating him mercilessly. All the while, they screamed at the man that he could not hear the music, that he would betray them in this, their hour of greatest glory.

Another man, obviously resisting the tempting call, rushed away to the side, and the group took up the chase, leaving the beaten man facedown in the water.

A third fight erupted on the other side.

Rolmanet turned to his two opponents, the two men who had been his best friends for several years now. "It is a lie, a trick!" he insisted. "Can you not understand?"

Lipke came at him hard with a cunning low thrust, followed by an upward slash, a twisting hand-over maneuver, and yet another upward slash that forced Rolmanet to lean backward, barely keeping his balance. On came Lipke, another straight-ahead charge and thrust, with Rolmanet quite vulnerable.

Trulbul's blade slashed across, intercepting Lipke's killing blow.

"Wait!" Trulbul cried to the astonished man. "Rolmanet speaks the truth! Look more deeply at the promise, I beg!"

Lipke was fully into the coercion of the Crystal Shard. He did pause, only long enough to allow Trulbul to believe that he was indeed reflecting on the seeming inconsistency here. As Trulbul nodded, grinned, and lowered his blade, Lipke hit him with a slashing cut that opened wide his throat.

He turned back to see Rolmanet in full flight, running to the horses tethered beside the water.

"Stop him! Stop him!" Lipke cried, giving chase. Several others came in as well, trying to cut off any escape routes as Rolmanet scrambled onto his horse and turned the beast around, hooves churning the sand. The man was a fine rider, and he picked his path carefully, and they could not hope to stop him.

He thundered out of Dallabad, not even pausing to try to help the other resister, who had been cut off, forced to turn, and would soon be caught and overwhelmed. No, Rolmanet's path was straight and fast, a dead gallop down the sandy road toward distant Calimport.

Jarlaxle's thoughts, and those of Crenshinibon, angled the magical mirror to follow the retreat of the lone escapee.

The mercenary leader could feel the power building within the crystalline tower. It was a quiet humming noise as the structure gathered in the sunlight, focusing it more directly through a series of prisms and mirrors to the very tip of the pointed tower. He understood what Crenshinibon meant to do, of course. Given the implications of allowing someone to escape, it seemed a logical course.

Do not kill him, Jarlaxle instructed anyway, and he wasn't sure why he issued the command. *There is little he can tell his superiors that they do not already know. The spies have no idea of the truth behind Dallabad's overthrow, and will only assume that a wizard . . .* He felt the energy continuing to build, with no conversation, argument or otherwise, coming back at him from the artifact.

Jarlaxle looked into the mirror at the fleeing, terrified man. The more he thought about it, the more he realized that he was right, that there was no real reason to kill this one. In fact, allowing him to return to his masters with news of such a complete failure might actually serve Bregan D'aerthe. Likely these were no minor spies sent on such an important mission as this, and the manner in which the band was purely overwhelmed would impress—perhaps enough so that the other pashas would come to Dallabad openly to seek truce and parlay.

Jarlaxle filtered all of that through his thoughts to the Crystal Shard, reiterating his command to halt, for the good of the band, and secretly, because he simply didn't want to kill a man if he did not have to,

He felt the energy building, building, now straining release.

"Enough!" he said aloud. "Do not!"

"What is it, my leader?" came Rai-guy's voice, the wizard and his sidekick psionicist rushing back into the room.

They entered to see Jarlaxle standing, obviously angry, staring at the mirror.

Then how that mirror brightened! There was a flash as striking, and as painful to sensitive drow eyes, as the sun itself. A searing beam of pure heat energy shot out of the tower's tip, shooting down across the sands to catch the rider and his horse, enveloping them in a white-yellow shroud.

It was over in an instant, leaving the charred bones of Rolmanet and his horse lying on the empty desert sands.

Jarlaxle closed his eyes and clenched his teeth, suppressing his urge to scream out.

"Impressive display," Kimmuriel said.

"Fifteen have come over to us, and it would seem the other five are dead," Rai-guy remarked. "The victory is complete."

Jarlaxle wasn't so sure of that, but he composed himself and turned a calm look upon his lieutenants. "Crenshinibon will discern those who are most easily and completely dominated," he informed the wary pair. "They will be sent back to their guild—or guilds, if this was a collaboration—with a proper explanation for the defeat. The others will be interrogated—and they will willingly submit to all of our questions—so that we might learn everything about this enemy that came prying into our affairs."

Rai-guy and Kimmuriel exchanged a glance that Jarlaxle did not miss, a clear indication that they had seen him distressed when they had entered. What they might discern from that, the mercenary leader did not know, but he wasn't overly pleased at that moment.

"Entreri is back in Calimport?" he asked.

"At House Basadoni," Kimmuriel answered.

"As we should all be," Jarlaxle decided. "We will ask our questions of our newest arrivals and give them over to Ahdahnia. Leave Berg'inyon and a small contingent behind to watch over the operation here."

The two glanced at each other again but offered no other response. They bowed and left the room.

Jarlaxle stared into the mirror at the blackened bones of the man and horse.

It had to be done, came the whisper of Crenshinibon into his mind. *His escape would have brought more curious eyes, better prepared. We are not yet ready for that.*

Jarlaxle recognized the lie for what it was. Crenshinibon feared no prying, curious eyes, feared no army at all. The Crystal Shard, in its purest of arrogance, believed that it would simply convert the majority of any attacking force, turning them back on any who did not submit to its will. How many could it control? Jarlaxle wondered. Hundreds? Thousands? Millions?

Images of domination, not merely of the streets of Calimport, not merely of the city itself, but of the entire realm, flittered through his thoughts as Crenshinibon "heard" the silent questions and tried to answer.

Jarlaxle shifted his eye patch and focused on it, lessening the connection with the artifact, and tightened his willpower to try to keep his thoughts as much to himself as possible. No, he knew, Crenshinibon had not killed the fleeing man for fear of any retribution. Nor had it struck out with such overwhelming fury against that lone rider because it did not agree with the merits of Jarlaxle's arguments against doing so.

No, the Crystal Shard had killed the man precisely because Jarlaxle had ordered it not to do so, because the mercenary leader had crossed over the line of the concept of partner and had tried to assume control.

That Crenshinibon would not allow.

If the artifact could so easily disallow such a thing, could it also step back over the line the other way?

The rather disturbing notion did not bring much solace to Jarlaxle, who had spent the majority of his life serving as no man's, nor Matron Mother's, slave.

"We have new allies under our domination, and thus we are stronger," Rai-guy remarked sarcastically when he was alone with Kimmuriel and Berg'inyon.

"Our numbers grow," Berg'inyon agreed, "but so too mounts the danger of discovery."

"And of treachery," Kimmuriel added. "Witness that one of the spies, under the influence of Jarlaxle's artifact, turned against us when the fighting started. The domination is not complete, nor is it unbreakable. With every unwitting soldier we add in such a manner, we run the risk of an uprising from within. While it is unlikely that any would so escape the domination and subsequently cause any real damage to us—they are merely humans, after all—we cannot dismiss the likelihood that one will break free and escape us, delivering the truth of the new Basadoni Guild and of Dallabad to some of the guilds."

"We already have agreed upon the consequences of Bregan D'aerthe being discovered for what it truly is," Rai-guy added ominously. "This group came to Dallabad looking specifically for the answers behind the facade, and the longer we stretch that facade, the more likely that we will be discovered. We are forfeiting our anonymity in this foolish quest for expansion."

The other two remained very silent for a long while. Then Kimmuriel quietly asked, "Are you going to explain this to Jarlaxle?"

"Should we be addressing this problem to Jarlaxle," Rai-guy countered, his voice dripping with sarcasm, "or to the true leader of Bregan D'aerthe?"

That bold proclamation gave the other two even more pause. There it was, set out very clearly, the notion that Jarlaxle had lost control of the band to a sentient artifact.

"Perhaps it is time for us to reconsider our course," Kimmuriel said somberly.

Both he and Rai-guy had served under Jarlaxle for a long, long time, and both understood the tremendous weight of the implications of Kimmuriel's remark. Wresting Bregan D'aerthe from Jarlaxle would be something akin to stealing House Baenre away from Matron Baenre during the centuries of her iron-fisted rule. In many ways, Jarlaxle, so cunning, so layered in defenses and so full of understanding of everything around him, might prove an even more formidable foe.

Now the course seemed obvious to the three, a coup that had been building since the first expansive steps of House Basadoni.

"I have a source who can offer us more information on the Crystal Shard," Kimmuriel remarked. "Perhaps there is a way to destroy it or at least temporarily to cripple its formidable powers so that we can get to Jarlaxle."

Rai-guy looked to Berg'inyon and both nodded grimly.

Artemis Entreri was beginning to understand just how much trouble was brewing for Jarlaxle and therefore for him. He heard about the incident at Dallabad soon after the majority of the dark elves returned to House Basadoni, and knew from the looks and the tone of their voices that several of Jarlaxle's prominent underlings weren't exactly thrilled by the recent events.

Neither was Entreri. He knew that Rai-guy's and Kimmuriel's complaints were quite valid, knew that Jarlaxle's expansionist policies were leading Bregan D'aerthe down a very dangerous road indeed. When the truth about House Basadoni's change and the takeover of Dallabad eventually leaked out—and Entreri was now harboring few doubts that it would—all the guilds and all the lords and every power in the region would unite against Bregan D'aerthe. Jarlaxle was cunning, and the band of mercenaries was indeed powerful—even more so with the Crystal Shard in their possession—but Entreri held no doubts that they would be summarily destroyed, every one.

No, the assassin realized, it wouldn't likely come to that. The groundwork had been clearly laid before them all, and Entreri held little doubt that Kimmuriel and Rai-guy would move against Jarlaxle and soon. Their scowls were growing deeper by the day, their words a bit bolder.

That understanding raised a perplexing question to Entreri. Was the Crystal Shard actually spurring the coup, as Lady Lolth often did among the houses in Menzoberranzan? Was the artifact reasoning that perhaps either of the more volatile magic-using lieutenants might be a more suitable wielder? Or was the coup being inspired by the actions of Jarlaxle under the prodding, if not the outright influence, of Crenshinibon?

Either way, Entreri knew that he was becoming quite vulnerable, even with his new magical acquisitions. However he played through the scenario, Jarlaxle alone remained the keystone to his survival.

The assassin turned down a familiar avenue, moving inconspicuously among the many street rabble out this evening, keeping to the shadows and keeping to himself. He had to find some way to get Jarlaxle back in command and on strong footing. He needed for Jarlaxle to be in control of Bregan D'aerthe—not only of their actions but of their hearts as well. Only then could he fend a coup—a coup that could only mean disaster for Entreri.

Yes, he had to secure Jarlaxle's position. Then he had to find a way to get himself far, far away from the dark elves and their dangerous intrigue.

The sentries at the Copper Ante were hardly surprised to see him and even informed him that Dwahvel was expecting him and waiting for him in the back room.

She had already heard of the most recent events at Dallabad, he realized, and he shook his head, reminding himself that he should not be surprised, and also reminding himself that it was just her amazing ability for the acquisition of knowledge that had brought him to Dwahvel this evening.

"It was House Broucalle of Memnon," Dwahvel informed him as soon as he entered and sat on the plush pillows set upon the floor opposite the halfling.

"They were quick to move," Entreri replied.

"The crystalline tower is akin to a huge beacon set out on the wasteland of the desert," Dwahvel replied. "Why do your compatriots, with their obvious need for secrecy, so call attention to themselves?"

Entreri didn't answer verbally, but the expression on his face told Dwahvel much of his fears.

"They err," Dwahvel concurred with those fears. "They have House Basadoni, a superb front for their exotic trading business. Why reach further and invite a war that they cannot hope to win?"

Still Entreri did not answer.

"Or was that the whole purpose for the band of drow to come to the surface?" Dwahvel asked with sincere concern. "Were you, too, perhaps, misinformed about the nature of this band, led to believe that they were here for profit— mutual profit, potentially—when in fact they are but an advanced war party, setting the stage for complete disaster for Calimport and all Calimshan?"

Entreri shook his head. "I know Jarlaxle well," he replied. "He came here for profit—mutual profit for those who work along with him. That is his way. I do not think he would ever serve in anything as potentially disastrous as a war party. Jarlaxle is not a warlord, in any capacity. He is an opportunist and nothing more. He cares little for glory and much for comfort."

"And yet he invites disaster by erecting such an obvious, and obviously inviting, monument as that remarkable tower," Dwahvel answered. She tilted her plump head, studying Entreri's concerned expression carefully. "What is it?" she asked.

"How great is your knowledge of Crenshinibon?" the assassin asked. "The Crystal Shard?"

Dwahvel scrunched up her face, deep in thought for just a moment, and shook her head. "Cursory," she admitted. "I know of its tower images but little more."

"It is an artifact of exceeding power," Entreri explained. "I am not so certain that the sentient item's goals and Jarlaxle's are one and the same."

"Many artifacts have a will of their own," Dwahvel stated dryly. "That is rarely a good thing."

"Learn all that you can about it," Entreri bade her, "and quickly, before that which you fear inadvertently befalls Calimport." He paused and considered the best course for Dwahvel to take in light of fairly recent events. "Try to find out how Drizzt came to possess it, and where—"

"What in the Nine Hells is a Drizzt?" Dwahvel asked.

Entreri started to explain but just stopped and laughed, remembering how very wide the world truly was. "Another dark elf," he answered, "a dead one."

"Ah, yes," said Dwahvel. "Your rival. The one you call 'Do'Urden.' "

"Forget him, as have I," Entreri instructed. "He is only relevant here because it was from him that Jarlaxle's minions acquired the Crystal Shard. They impersonated a priest of some renown and power, a cleric named Cadderly, I believe, who resides somewhere in or around the Snowflake Mountains."

"A long journey," the halfling remarked.

"A worthwhile one," Entreri replied. "And we both know that distance is irrelevant to a wizard possessing the proper spells."

"This will cost you greatly."

With just a twitch of his honed leg muscles, a movement that would have been difficult for a skilled fighter half his age, Entreri rose up tall and fearsome before Dwahvel, then leaned over and patted her on the shoulder—with his gloved right hand.

She got the message.

CHAPTER

GROUNDWORK

11

I t is what you desired all along, Kimmuriel said to Yharaskrik.

The illithid feigned surprise at the drow psionicist's blunt proposition. Yharaskrik had explaining to Kimmuriel how he might fend the intrusions of the Crystal Shard. The illithid desired that the situation be brought to this very point all along.

Who will possess it? Yharaskrik silently asked. *Kimmuriel or Rai-guy?*

Rai-guy, the drow answered. *He and Crenshinibon will perfectly complement one another—by Crenshinibon's own impartations to him from afar.*

So you both believe, the illithid responded. *Perhaps, though, Crenshinibon sees you as a threat—a likely and logical assumption—and is merely goading you into this so that you and your comrades might be thoroughly destroyed.*

I have not dismissed that possibility, Kimmuriel returned, seeming quite at ease. *That is why I have come to Yharaskrik.*

The illithid paused for a long while, digesting the information. *The Crystal Shard is no minor item,* the creature explained. *To ask of me—*

A temporary reprieve, Kimmuriel interrupted. *I do not wish to pit Yharaskrik against Crenshinibon, for I understand that the artifact would overwhelm you.* He imparted those thoughts without fear of insulting the mind flayer. Kimmuriel understood that the perfectly logical illithids were not possessed of ego beyond reason. Certainly they believed their race to be superior to most others, to humans, of course, and even to drow, but within that healthy confidence there lay an element of reason that prevented them from taking insult to statements made of perfect logic. Yharaskrik knew that the artifact could overwhelm any creature short of a god.

There is, perhaps, a way, the illithid replied, and Kimmuriel's smile widened. *A Tower of Iron Will's sphere of influence could encompass Crenshinibon and defeat its mental intrusions, and its commands to any towers it has constructed near the battlefield. Temporarily,* the creature added emphatically. *I hold no illusions that any psionic force short of that conducted by a legion of my fellow illithids could begin to permanently weaken the powers of the great Crystal Shard.*

"Long enough for the downfall of Jarlaxle," Kimmuriel agreed aloud. "That is all that I require." He bowed and took his leave then, and his last words echoed in his mind as he stepped through the dimensional doorway that would bring him back to Calimport and the private quarters he shared with Rai-guy.

The downfall of Jarlaxle! Kimmuriel could hardly believe that he was a party to this conspiracy. Hadn't it been Jarlaxle, after all, who had offered him refuge from his own Matron Mother and vicious female siblings of House Oblodra, and who had then taken him in and sheltered him from the rest of the city when Matron Baenre had declared that House Oblodra must be completely eradicated? Aside from any loyalty he held for the mercenary leader, there remained the practical matter of the problem of decapitating Bregan D'aerthe. Jarlaxle above all others had facilitated the rise of the mercenary band, had brought them to prominence more than a century before, and no one in all the band, not even self-confident Rai-guy, doubted for a moment how important Jarlaxle was politically for the survival of Bregan D'aerthe.

All those thoughts stayed with Kimmuriel as he made his way back to Rai-guy's side, to find the drow thick into the plotting of the attacks they would use to bring Jarlaxle down.

"Your new friend can give us that which we require?" the eager wizard-cleric asked as soon as Kimmuriel arrived.

"Likely," Kimmuriel replied.

"Neutralize the Crystal Shard, and the attack will be complete," Rai-guy said.

"Do not underestimate Jarlaxle," Kimmuriel warned. "He has the Crystal Shard now and so we must first eliminate that powerful item, but even without it, Jarlaxle has spent many years solidifying his hold on Bregan D'aerthe. I would not have gone against him before the acquisition of the artifact."

"But it is just that acquisition that has weakened him," Rai-guy explained. "Even the common soldiers fear this course we have taken."

"I have heard some remark that they cannot believe our rise in power," Kimmuriel argued. "Some have proclaimed that we will dominate the surface world, that Jarlaxle will take Bregan D'aerthe to prominence among the weakling humans, and return in glory to conquer Menzoberranzan."

Rai-guy laughed aloud at the proclamation. "The artifact is powerful, I do not doubt, but it is limited. Did not the mind flayer tell you that Crenshinibon sought to reach its limit of control?"

"Whether or not the fantasy conquest can occur is irrelevant to our present situation," Kimmuriel replied. "What matters is whether or not the soldiers of Bregan D'aerthe believe in it."

Rai-guy didn't have an argument for that line of reasoning, but still, he wasn't overly concerned. "Though Berg'inyon is with us, the drow will be limited in their role in the battle," he explained. "We have humans at our disposal now and thousands of kobolds."

"Many of the humans were brought into our fold by Crenshinibon," Kimmuriel reminded. "The Crystal Shard will have little difficulty in dominating the kobolds, if Yharaskrik cannot completely neutralize it."

"And we have the wererats," Rai-guy went on, unfazed. "Shapechangers are better suited to resisting mental intrusions. Their internal strife denies any outside influences."

"You have enlisted Domo?"

Rai-guy shook his head. "Domo is difficult," he admitted, "but I have enlisted several of his wererat lieutenants. They will fall to our cause if Domo is eliminated. To that end, I have had Sharlotta Vespers inform Jarlaxle that the wererat leader has been speaking out of turn, revealing too much about Bregan D'aerthe, to Pasha Da'Daclan, and we believe to the leader of the guild that came to investigate Dallabad."

Kimmuriel nodded, but his expression remained concerned. Jarlaxle was a tough opponent in games of the mind—he might see the ruse for what it was, and use Domo to turn the wererats back to his side.

"His actions now will be telling," Rai-guy admitted. "Crenshinibon, no doubt, will want to believe Sharlotta's tale, but Jarlaxle will desire to proceed more cautiously before acting against Domo."

"You believe that the wererat leader will be dead this very day," Kimmuriel reasoned after a moment.

Rai-guy smiled. "The Crystal Shard has become Jarlaxle's strength and thus his weakness," he said with a wicked grin.

⊷══⊶

"First the gauntlet and now this," Dwahvel Tiggerwillies said with a profound sigh. "Ah, Entreri, what shall I ever do for extra coin when you are no more?"

Entreri didn't appreciate the humor. "Be quick about it," he instructed.

"Sharlotta's actions have made you very nervous," Dwahvel remarked, for she had observed the woman busily working the streets during the last few hours, with many of her meetings with known operatives of the wererat guild.

Entreri just nodded, not wanting to share the latest news with Dwahvel—just in case. Things were moving fast now, he knew, too fast. Rai-guy and Kimmuriel were laying the groundwork for their assault, but at least Jarlaxle had apparently caught on to some of the budding problems. The mercenary leader had summoned Entreri just a few moments before, telling the man that he had to go and meet with a particularly wretched wererat by the name of Domo. If Domo was in on the conspiracy, Entreri suspected that Rai-guy and Kimmuriel would soon have a hole to fill in their ranks.

"I will return within two hours," Entreri explained. "Have it ready."

"We have no proper material to make such an item as you requested," Dwahvel complained.

"Color and consistency alone," Entreri replied. "The material does not need to be exact."

Dwahvel shrugged.

Entreri went out into Calimport's night, moving swiftly, his cloak pulled tight around his shoulders. Not far from the Copper Ante, he turned down an alley. Then after a quick check to ensure that he was not being followed, he slipped down an open sewer hole into the tunnels below the city.

A few moments later, he stood before Jarlaxle in the appointed chamber.

"Sharlotta has informed me that Domo has been whispering secrets about us," Jarlaxle remarked.

"The wererat is on the way?"

Jarlaxle nodded. "And likely with many allies. You are prepared for the fight?"

Entreri wore the first honest grin he had known in several days. Prepared for a fight with wererats? How could he not be? Still he could not dismiss the source of Jarlaxle's information. He realized that Sharlotta was working both ends of the table here, that she was in tight with Rai-guy and Kimmuriel but was in no overt way severing her ties to Jarlaxle. He doubted that Sharlotta and her drow allies had set this up as the ultimate battle for control of Bregan D'aerthe. Such intricate planning would take longer, and the sewers of Calimport would not be a good location for a fight that would grow so very obvious.

Still . . .

"Perhaps you should have stayed at Dallabad for a while," Entreri remarked, "within the crystalline tower, overseeing the new operation."

"Domo hardly frightens me," Jarlaxle replied.

Entreri stared at him hard. Could he really be so oblivious to the apparent underpinnings of a coup within Bregan D'aerthe? If so, did that enhance the possibility that the Crystal Shard was indeed prompting the disloyal actions of Rai-guy and Kimmuriel? Or did it mean, perhaps, that Entreri was being too cautious here, was seeing demons and uprisings where there were none?

The assassin took a deep breath and shook his head, clearing his thoughts.

"Sharlotta could be mistaken," the assassin did say. "She would have reasons of her own to wish to be rid of troublesome Domo."

"We will know soon enough," Jarlaxle replied, nodding in the direction of a tunnel, where the wererat leader, in the form of a huge humanoid rat, was approaching, along with three other ratmen.

"My dear Domo," Jarlaxle greeted, and the wererat leader bowed.

"It is good that you came to us," Domo replied. "I do not enjoy any journeys to the surface at this time, not even to the cellars of House Basadoni. There is too much excitement, I fear."

Entreri narrowed his eyes and considered the wretched lycanthrope, thinking that answer curious, at least, but trying hard not to interpret it one way or the other.

"Do the agents of the other guilds similarly come down to meet with you?" Jarlaxle asked, a question that surely set Domo back on his heels.

Entreri stared hard at the drow now, catching on that Crenshinibon was instructing Jarlaxle to put Domo on his guard, to get him thinking of any potentially treasonous actions that they might be more easily read. Still, it seemed to him that Jarlaxle was moving too quickly here, that a little small talk and diplomacy might have garnered the necessary indicators without resorting to any crude mental intrusions by the sentient artifact.

"On those rare occasions when I must meet with agents of other guilds, they often do come to me," Domo answered, trying to remain calm, though he betrayed his sudden edge to Entreri when he shifted his weight from one foot to the other. The assassin calmly dropped his hands to his belt, hooking his wrists over the pommels of his two formidable weapons, a posture that seemed more relaxed and comfortable, but also one that had him in touch with his weapons, ready to draw and strike.

"And have you met with any recently?" Jarlaxle asked.

Domo winced, and winced again, and Entreri caught on to the truth of it.

The artifact was trying to scour his thoughts then and there.

The three wererats behind the leader glanced at each other and shifted nervously.

Domo's face contorted, began to form into his human guise, and went back almost immediately to the trapping of the wererat. A low, feral growl escaped his throat.

"What is it?" one of the wererats behind him asked.

Entreri could see the frustration mounting on Jarlaxle's face. He glanced back to Domo curiously, wondering if he had perhaps underestimated the ugly creature.

Jarlaxle and Crenshinibon simply could not get a fix on the wererat's thoughts, for the Crystal Shard's intrusion had brought about the lycanthropic internal strife, and that wall of red pain and rage had now denied any access.

Jarlaxle, growing increasingly frustrated, stared at the wererat hard.

He betrayed us, Crenshinibon decided suddenly.

Jarlaxle's thoughts filled with doubt and confusion, for he had not seen any such revelation.

A moment of weakness, came Crenshinibon's call. *A flash of the truth within that wall of angry torment. He betrayed us . . . twice.*

Jarlaxle turned to Entreri, a subtle signal, but one that the eager assassin, who hated wererats profoundly, was quick to catch and amplify.

Domo and his associates caught it, too, and their swords came flashing out of their scabbards. By the time they'd drawn their weapons, Entreri was on the charge. Charon's Claw waved in the air before him, painting a wall of black ash that Entreri could use to segment the battleground and prevent his enemies from coordinating their movements.

He spun to the left, around the ash wall, ducking as he turned so that he came around under the swing of Domo's long and slender blade. Up went the assassin's sword, taking Domo's far and wide. Entreri, still in a crouch, scrambled forward, his dagger leading.

Domo's closest companion came on hard, though, forcing Entreri to skitter back and slash down with his sword to deflect the attack. He went into a roll, over backward, and planted his right hand, pushing hard to launch him back to his feet, working those feet quickly as he landed to put him in nearly the same position as when he had started. The foolish wererat followed, leaving Domo and its two companions on the other side of the ash wall.

Behind Entreri, Jarlaxle's hand pumped once, twice, thrice, and daggers sailed past Entreri, barely missing his head, plunging through the ash wall, blasting holes in the drifting curtain.

On the other side came a groan, and Entreri realized that Domo's companions were down to two.

A moment later, down to one, for the assassin met the wererat's charge full on, his sword coming up in a rotating fashion, taking the thrusting blade aside. Entreri continued forward, and so did the wererat, thinking to bite at the man.

How quickly it regretted that choice when Entreri's dagger blade filled its mouth.

A sudden second thrust yanked the creature's head back, and the assassin disengaged and quickly turned. He saw yet another of the beasts coming fast through the ash wall and heard the footsteps of a retreating Domo.

Down he went into a shoulder roll, under the ash wall, catching the ankles of the charging wererat and sending it flying over him to fall facedown right before Jarlaxle.

Entreri didn't even slow, rolling forward and back to his feet and running off full speed in pursuit of the fleeing wererat. Entreri was no stranger to the darkness, even the complete blackness of the tunnels. Indeed, he had done some of his best work down there, but recognizing the disadvantage he faced against infravision-using wererats, he held his powerful sword before him and commanded it to bring forth light—hoping that it, like many magical swords, could produce some sort of glow.

That magical glow surprised him, for it was a light of blackish hue and nothing like Entreri had ever seen before, giving all the corridor a surrealistic appearance. He glanced down at the sword, trying to see how blatant a light source it appeared, but he saw no definitive glow and hoped that meant that he might use a bit of stealth, at least, despite the fact that he was the source of the light.

He came to a fork and skidded to a stop, turning his head and focusing his senses.

The slight echo of a footfall came from the left, so on he ran.

Jarlaxle finished the prone wererat in short order, pumping his arm repeatedly and hitting the squirming creature with dagger after dagger. He put a hand in his pocket, on the Crystal Shard, as he ran through the gap in the ash wall, trying to catch up with his companion.

Guide me, he instructed the artifact.

Up, came the unexpected reply. *They have returned to the streets.*

Jarlaxle skidded to a stop, puzzled.

Up! came the more emphatic silent cry. *To the streets.*

The mercenary leader rushed back the other way, down the corridor to the ladder that would take him back up through the sewer grate and into the alley outside the neighborhood of the Copper Ante.

Guide me, he instructed the shard again.

We are too exposed, the artifact returned. *Keep to the shadows and move back to House Basadoni—Artemis Entreri and Domo lie in that direction.*

Entreri rounded a bend in the corridor, slowing cautiously. There, standing before him, was Domo and two more wererats, all holding swords. Entreri started forward, thinking himself seen, and figuring to attack before the three could organize their defenses. He stopped abruptly, though, when the ratman to Domo's left whispered.

"I smell him. He is near."

111

"Too near," agreed the other lesser creature, squinting, the tell-tale red glow of infravision evident in its eyes.

Why did they even need that infravision? Entreri wondered. He could see them clearly in the black light of Charon's Claw, as clearly as if they were all standing in a dimly lit room. He knew that he should go straight in and attack, but his curiosity was piqued now and so he stepped out from the wall, in clear view, in plain sight.

"His smell is thick," Domo agreed. All three were glancing about nervously, their swords waving. "Where are the others?"

"They have not come but should have been here," the one to his left answered. "I fear we are betrayed."

"Damn the drow to the Nine Hells, then," Domo said.

Entreri could hardly believe they could not see him—yet another wondrous effect of the marvelous sword. He wondered if perhaps they could see him had they been focusing their eyes in the normal spectrum of light, but that, he realized, had to be a question for another day. Concentrating now on moving perfectly silently, he slid one foot, and then the other, ahead of him, moving to Domo's right.

"Perhaps we should have listened more carefully to the dark elf wizard," the one to the left went on, his voice a whisper.

"To go against Jarlaxle?" Domo asked incredulously. "That is doom. Nothing more."

"But . . ." the other started to argue, but Domo began whispering harshly, sticking his finger in the other's face.

Entreri used their distraction to get right up behind the third of the group, his dagger tip coming against the wererat's spine. The creature stiffened as Entreri whispered into its ear. "Run," he said.

The ratman sped off down the corridor, and Domo stopped his arguing long enough to chase his fleeing soldier a few steps, calling threats out after him.

"Run," said Entreri, who had shifted across the way to the side of the remaining lesser wererat.

This one, though, didn't run, but let out a shriek and spun, its sword slashing across at chest level.

Entreri ducked below the blade easily and came up with a stab that brought his deadly jeweled dagger under the wererat's ribs and up into its diaphragm. The creature howled again, but then spasmed and convulsed violently.

"What is it?" Domo asked, spinning about. "What?"

The wererat fell to the floor, twitching still as it died. Entreri stood there, in the open, dagger in hand. He called up a glow from his smaller blade.

Domo jumped back, bringing his sword out in front of him. "Dancing blade?" he asked quietly. "Is this you, wizard drow?"

"Dancing blade?" Entreri repeated quietly, looking down at his glowing dagger. It made no sense to him. He looked back to Domo, to see the glow leave the wererat's eyes as he shifted from ratman, to nearly human form. Likewise his vision shifted from the infrared to the normal viewing spectrum.

He nearly jumped out of his boots again, as the specter of Artemis Entreri came clear to him. "What trick is that?" the wererat gasped.

Entreri wasn't even sure how to answer. He had no idea what Charon's Claw was doing with its black light. Did it block infravision completely but apparently hold a strange illuminating effect that was clearly visible in the normal spectrum? Did it act like a black campfire then, even though Entreri felt no heat coming from the blade? Infravision could be severely limited by strong heat sources.

It was indeed intriguing—one of so many riddles that seemed to be presenting themselves before Artemis Entreri—but again, it was a riddle to be solved another day.

"So you are without allies," he said to Domo. "It is you and I alone."

"Why does Jarlaxle fear me?" Domo asked as Entreri advanced a step.

The assassin stopped. "Fear you? Or loathe you? They are not the same thing, you know."

"I am his ally!" Domo protested. "I stood beside him, even against the advances of his lessers."

"So you said to him," Entreri remarked, glancing down at the still-twitching, still-groaning form. "What do you know? Speak it clearly and quickly, and perhaps you will walk out of here."

Domo's rodent eyes narrowed angrily. "As Rassiter walked away from your last meeting?" he asked, referring to one of his greatest predecessors in the wererat guild, a powerful leader who had served Pasha Pook along with Entreri, and whom Entreri had subsequently murdered—a deed never forgotten by the wererats of Calimport.

"I ask you one last time," Entreri said calmly.

He caught a slight movement to the side and knew that the first wererat had returned, waiting in the shadows to leap out at him. He was hardly surprised and hardly afraid.

Domo gave a wide, toothy smile. "Jarlaxle and his companions are not as unified a force as you believe," he teased.

Entreri advanced another step. "You must do better than that," he said, but before the words even left his mouth, Domo howled and leaped at him, stabbing with his slender sword.

Entreri barely moved Charon's Claw, just angled the blade to intercept Domo's and slide it off to the side.

The wererat retracted the strike at once, thrust again, and again. Each time Entreri, with barely any motion at all, positioned his parry perfectly and to a razor-thin angle, with Domo's sword stabbing past him, missing by barely an inch.

Again the wererat retracted and this time came across with a great slash.

But he had stepped too far back, and Entreri had to lean only slightly backward for the blade to swish harmlessly past before him.

The expected charge came from Domo's companion in the shadows to the side, and Domo played his part in the routine perfectly, rushing ahead with a powerful thrust.

Domo didn't understand the beauty, the efficiency, of Artemis Entreri. Again Charon's Claw caught and turned the attack, but this time, Entreri rolled his hand right over, and under the outside of Domo's blade. He pulled in his gut as he threw Domo's blade up high, and brought forth another wall of ash, blackening the air between him and the wererat. Following his own momentum, Entreri went into a complete spin, around to the right. As he came back square with

Domo he brought his right arm swishing down, the sword trailing ash, while his left crossed his body over the down-swing, launching his jeweled dagger right into the gut of the charging wererat.

Charon's Claw did a complete circuit in the air between the combatants, forming a wide, circular wall. Domo came ahead right through it with yet another stubborn thrust, but Entreri wasn't there. He dived to the side into a roll and came up and around with a powerful slash at the legs of the wererat still struggling with the dagger in its belly. To the assassin's surprise and delight, the mighty sword sheared through not only the wererat's closest knee, but through the other as well. The creature tumbled to the stone, howling in agony, its life-blood pouring out freely.

Entreri hardly slowed, spinning about and coming up powerfully, slapping Domo's sword out wide yet again, and snapping Charon's Claw down and across to pick off a dagger neatly thrown by the wererat leader.

Domo's expression changed quickly then, his last trick obviously played. Now it was Entreri's turn to take the offensive, and he did so with a powerful thrust high, thrust center, thrust low routine that had Domo inevitably skit-tering backward, fighting hard merely to keep his balance.

Entreri, leaping ahead, didn't make it any easier on the overmatched creature. His sword worked furiously, sometimes throwing ash, sometimes not, and all with a precision designed to limit Domo's vision and options. Soon he had the wererat nearly to the back wall, and a glance from Domo told Entreri that he wasn't thrilled about the prospect of getting cornered.

Entreri took the cue to slash and slash again, bringing up a wall of ash per-pendicular to the floor then perpendicular to the first, an L-shaped design that blocked Domo's vision of Entreri and his vision of the area to his immediate right.

With a growl, the wererat went right with a desperate thrust, thinking that Entreri would use the ash wall to try to work around him. He hit only air. Then he felt the assassin's presence at his back, for the man, anticipating the anticipation, had simply gone around the other way.

Domo threw his sword to the ground. "I will tell you everything," he cried. "I will—"

"You already did," Entreri assured him and the wererat stiffened as Charon's Claw sliced through his backbone and drove on to the hilt, coming out the front just below Domo's ribs.

"It . . . hurts," Domo gasped.

"It is supposed to," Entreri replied, and he gave the sword a sudden jerk, and Domo gasped, and he died.

Entreri tore his blade free and rushed to retrieve his dagger. His thoughts were whirling now, as Domo's confirmation of some kind of an uprising within Bregan D'aerthe incited a plethora of questions. Domo had not been Jarlaxle's deceiver, nor was he in on the plotting against the mercenary leader—of that much, at least, Entreri was pretty sure. Yet it was Jarlaxle who had prompted this attack on Domo.

Or was it?

Wondering just how much the Crystal Shard was playing Jarlaxle's best interests against Jarlaxle, Artemis Entreri scrambled out of Calimport's sewers.

"Beautiful," Rai-guy remarked to Kimmuriel, the two of them using a mirror of scrying to witness Artemis Entreri's return to House Basadoni. The wizard broke the connection almost immediately after, though, for the look upon the cunning assassin's face told him that Entreri might be sensing the scrying. "He unwittingly does our bidding. The wererats will stand against Jarlaxle now."

"Alas for Domo," Kimmuriel said, laughing. He stopped abruptly, though, and assumed a more serious demeanor. "But what of Entreri? He is formidable— even more so with that gauntlet and sword—and is too wise to believe that he would be better served in joining our cause. Perhaps we should eliminate him before turning our eyes toward Jarlaxle."

Rai-guy thought it over for just a moment, and nodded his agreement. "It must come from a lesser," he said. "From Sharlotta and her minions, perhaps, as they will be little involved in the greater coup."

"Jarlaxle would not be pleased if he came to understand that we were going against Entreri," Kimmuriel agreed. "Sharlotta, then, and not as a straight-forward command. I will plant the thought in her that Entreri is trying to eliminate her."

"If she came to believe that, she would likely simply run away," Rai-guy remarked.

"She is too full of pride for that," Kimmuriel came back. "I will also make it clear to her, subtly and through other sources, that Entreri is not in the favor of many of Bregan D'aerthe, that even Jarlaxle has grown tired of his independence. If she believes that Entreri stands alone in some vendetta or rivalry against her, and that she can utilize the veritable army at her disposal to destroy him, then she will not run but will strike and strike hard." He gave another laugh. "Though unlike you, Rai-guy, I am not so certain that Sharlotta and all of House Basadoni will be able to get the job done."

"They will keep him occupied and out of our way, at least," Rai-guy replied. "Once we have finished with Jarlaxle . . ."

"Entreri will likely be far gone," Kimmuriel observed, "running as Morik has run. Perhaps we should see to Morik, if for no other reason than to hold him up as an example to Artemis Entreri."

Rai-guy shook his head, apparently recognizing that he and Kimmuriel had far more pressing problems than the disposition of a minor deserter in a faraway and insignificant city. "Artemis Entreri cannot run far enough away," he said determinedly. "He is far too great a nuisance for me ever to forget him or forgive him."

Kimmuriel thought that statement might be a bit extravagant, but in essence, he agreed with the sentiment. Perhaps Entreri's greatest crime was his own ability, the drow psionicist mused. Perhaps his rise above the standards of humans alone was the insult that so sparked hatred in Rai-guy and in Kimmuriel. The psionicist, and the wizard as well, were wise enough to appreciate that truth.

But that didn't make things any easier for Artemis Entreri.

CHAPTER

12

"Layer after layer!" Entreri raged. He pounded his fist on the small table in the back room of the Copper Ante. It was still the one place in Calimport where he could feel reasonably secure from the ever-prying eyes of Rai-guy and Kimmuriel—and how often he had felt those eyes watching him of late! "So many layers that they roll back onto each other in a never-ending loop!"

Dwahvel Tiggerwillies leaned back in her chair and studied the man curiously. In all the years she had known Artemis Entreri, she had never seen him so animated or so angry—and when Artemis Entreri was angry, those anywhere in the vicinity of the assassin did well to take extreme care. Even more surprising to the halfling was the fact that Entreri was so angry so soon after killing the hated Domo. Usually killing a wererat put him in a better mood for a day at least. Dwahvel could understand his frustration, though. The man was dealing with dark elves, and though Dwahvel had little real knowledge of the intricacies of drow culture, she had witnessed enough to understand that the dark elves were the masters of intrigue and deception.

"Too many layers," Entreri said more calmly, his rage played out. He turned to Dwahvel and shook his head. "I am lost within the web within the web. I hardly know what is real anymore."

"You are still alive," Dwahvel offered. "I would guess, then, that you are doing something right."

"I fear that I erred greatly in killing Domo," Entreri admitted, shaking his head. "I have never been fond of wererats, but this time, perhaps, I should have let him live, if only to provide some opposition to the growing conspiracy against Jarlaxle."

"You do not even know if Domo and his wretched, lying companions were speaking truthfully when they uttered words about the drow conspiracy," Dwahvel reminded. "They may have been doing that as misinformation that you would take back to Jarlaxle, thus bringing about a rift in Bregan D'aerthe. Or Domo might have been sputtering for the sake of saving his own head. He knows your relationship with Jarlaxle and understands that you are better off as long as Jarlaxle is in command."

Entreri just stared at her. Domo knew all of that? Of course he did, the assassin told himself. As much as he hated the wererat, he could not dismiss the creature's cunning in controlling that most difficult of guilds.

"It is irrelevant anyway," Dwahvel went on. "We both know that the ratmen will be minor players at best in any internal struggles of Bregan D'aerthe. If Rai-guy and Kimmuriel start a coup, Domo and his kin would do little to dissuade them."

Entreri shook his head again, thoroughly frustrated by it all. Alone he believed that he could outfight or out-think any drow, but they were not alone, were never alone. Because of that harmony of movement within the band's cliques, Entreri could not be certain of the truth of anything. The addition of the Crystal Shard was merely compounding matters, blurring the truth about the source of the coup—if there was a coup—and making the assassin honestly wonder if Jarlaxle was in charge or was merely a slave to the sentient artifact. As much as Entreri knew that Jarlaxle would protect him, he understood that the Crystal Shard would want him dead.

"You dismiss all that you once learned," Dwahvel remarked, her voice soothing and calm. "The drow play no games beyond those that Pasha Pook once played—or Pasha Basadoni, or any of the others, or all of the others together. Their dance is the same as has been going on in Calimport for centuries."

"But the drow are better dancers."

Dwahvel smiled and nodded, conceding the point. "But is not the solution the same?" she asked. "When all is a facade. . . ." She let the words hang out in the air, one of the basic truths of the streets, and one that Artemis Entreri surely knew as well as anyone. "When all is a facade . . . ?" she said again, prompting him.

Entreri forced himself to calm down, forced himself to dismiss the overblown respect, even fear, he had been developing toward the dark elves, particularly toward Rai-guy and Kimmuriel. "In such situations, when layer is put upon layer," he recited, a basic lesson for all bright prospects within the guild structures, "when all is a facade, wound within webs of deception, the truth is what you make of it."

Dwahvel nodded. "You will know which path is real, because that is the path you will make real," she agreed. "Nothing pains a liar more than when an opponent turns one of his lies into truth."

Entreri nodded his agreement, and indeed he felt better. He knew that he would, which was why he had slipped out of House Basadoni after sensing that he was being watched and had gone straight to the Copper Ante.

"Do you believe Domo?" the halfling asked.

Entreri considered it for a moment, and nodded. "The hourglass has been turned, and the sand is flowing," he stated. "Have you the information I requested?"

Dwahvel reached under the low dust ruffle of the chair in which she was sitting and pulled out a portfolio full of parchments. "Cadderly," she said, handing them over.

"What of the other item?"

Again the halfling's hand went down low, this time producing a small sack identical to the one Jarlaxle now carried on his belt, and, Entreri knew without even looking, containing a block of crystal similar in appearance to Crenshinibon.

Entreri took it with some trepidation, for it was, to him, the final and irreversible acknowledgment that he was indeed about to embark upon a very dangerous course, perhaps the most dangerous road he had ever walked in all his life.

"There is no magic about it," Dwahvel assured him, noting his concerned expression. "Just a mystical aura I ordered included so that it would replicate the artifact to any cursory magical inspection."

Entreri nodded and hooked the pouch on his belt, behind his hip so that it would be completely concealed by his cloak.

"We could just get you out of the city," Dwahvel offered. "It would have been far cheaper to hire a wizard to teleport you far, far away."

Entreri chuckled at the thought. It was one that had crossed his mind a thousand times since Bregan D'aerthe had come to Calimport, but one that he had always dismissed. How far could he run? Not farther than Rai-guy and Kimmuriel could follow, he understood.

"Stay close to him," Dwahvel warned. "When it happens, you will have to be the quicker."

Entreri nodded and started to rise, but paused and stared hard at Dwahvel. She honestly cared how he managed in this conflict, he realized, and the truth of that—that Dwahvel's concern for him had little to do with her own personal gain—struck him profoundly. It showed him something he'd not known often in his miserable existence—a friend.

He didn't leave the Copper Ante right away but went into an adjoining room and began ruffling through the reams of information that Dwahvel had collected on the priest, Cadderly. Would this man be the answer to Jarlaxle's dilemma and thus Entreri's own?

Frustration more than anything else guided Jarlaxle's movements as he made his swift way back to Dallabad, using a variety of magical items to facilitate his silent and unseen passage, but not—pointedly not—calling upon the Crystal Shard for any assistance.

This was it, the drow leader realized, the true test of his newest partnership. It had struck Jarlaxle that perhaps the Crystal Shard had been gaining too much the upper hand in their relationship, and so he had decided to set the matter straight.

He meant to take down the crystalline tower.

Crenshinibon knew it, too. Jarlaxle could feel the artifact's unhappy pulsing in his pouch, and he wondered if the powerful item might force a desperate showdown of willpower, one in which there could emerge only one victor.

Jarlaxle was ready for that. He was always willing to share in responsibility and decision-making, as long as it eventually led to the achievement of his own goals. Lately, though, he'd come to sense, the Crystal Shard seemed to be altering those very goals. It seemed to be bending him more and more in directions not of his choosing.

Soon after the sun had set, a very dark Calimshan evening, Jarlaxle stood before the crystalline tower, staring hard at it. He strengthened his resolve and mentally bolstered himself for the struggle that he knew would inevitably ensue. With a final glance around to make certain that no one was nearby, he reached into his pouch and took out the sentient artifact.

No! Crenshinibon screamed in his thoughts, the shard obviously knowing exactly what it was the dark elf meant to do. *I forbid this. The towers are a manifestation of my—of our strength and indeed heighten that strength. To destroy one is forbidden!*

Forbidden? Jarlaxle echoed skeptically.

It is not in the best interests of—

I decide what is in my best interests, Jarlaxle strongly interrupted. *And now it is in my interest to tear down this tower.* He focused all his mental energies into a singular and powerful command to the Crystal Shard.

And so it began, a titanic, if silent, struggle of willpower. Jarlaxle, with his centuries of accumulated knowledge and perfected cunning, was pitted squarely against the ages-old dweomer that was the Crystal Shard. Within seconds of the battle, Jarlaxle felt his will bend backward, as if the artifact meant to break his mind completely. It seemed to him as if every fear he had ever harbored in every dark corner of his imagination had become real, stalking inexorably toward his thoughts, his memories, his very identity.

How naked he felt! How open to the darts and slings of the mighty Crystal Shard!

Jarlaxle composed himself and worked very hard to separate the images, to single out each horrid manifestation and isolate it from the others. Then, focusing as much as he possibly could on that one vividly imagined horror, he counterattacked, using feelings of empowerment and strength, calling upon all of those many, many experiences he had weathered to become this leader of Bregan D'aerthe, this male dark elf who had for so long thrived in the matriarchal hell that was Menzoberranzan.

One after another the nightmares fell before him. As his internal struggles began to subside, Jarlaxle sent his willpower out of his inner mind, out to the artifact, issuing that singular, powerful command:

Tear down the crystalline tower!

Now came the coercion, the images of glory, of armies falling before fields of crystalline towers, of kings coming to him on their knees, bearing the treasures of their kingdoms, of the Matron Mothers of Menzoberranzan anointing him as permanent ruler of their council, speaking of him in terms previously reserved for Lady Lolth herself.

This second manipulation was, in many ways, even more difficult for Jarlaxle to control and defeat. He could not deny the allure of the images. More importantly, he could not deny the possibilities for Bregan D'aerthe and for him, given the added might that was the Crystal Shard.

He felt his resolve slipping away, a compromise reached that would allow Crenshinibon and Jarlaxle both to find all they desired.

He was ready to release the artifact from his command, to admit the ridiculousness of tearing down the tower, to give in and reform their undeniably profitable alliance.

But he remembered.

This was no partnership, for the Crystal Shard was no partner, no real, controllable, replaceable and predictable partner. No, Jarlaxle reminded himself. It was an artifact, an enchanted item, and though sentient it was a created intelligence, a method of reasoning based upon a set and predetermined goal. In this case, apparently, its goal was the acquisition of as many followers and as much power as its magic would allow.

While Jarlaxle could sympathize, even agree with that goal, he reminded himself pointedly and determinedly that he would have to be the one in command. He fought back against the temptations, denied the Crystal Shard its manipulations as he had beaten back its brute force attack in the beginning of the struggle.

He felt it, as tangible as a snapping rope, a click in his mind that gave him his answer.

Jarlaxle was the master. His were the decisions that would guide Bregan D'aerthe and command the Crystal Shard.

He knew then, without the slightest bit of doubt, that the tower was his to destroy, and so he led the shard again to that command. This time, Jarlaxle felt no anger, no denial, no recriminations, only sadness.

The beaten artifact began to hum with the energies needed to deconstruct its large magical replica.

Jarlaxle opened his eyes and smiled with satisfaction. The fight had been everything he had feared it would be, but in the end, he knew without doubt he had triumphed. He felt the tingling as the essence of the crystalline tower began to weaken. Its binding energy would be stolen away. Then the material bound together by Crenshinibon's magic would dissipate to the winds. The way he commanded it—and he knew that Crenshinibon could comply—there would be no explosions, no crashing walls, just fading away.

Jarlaxle nodded, as satisfied as with any victory he had ever known in his long life of struggles.

He pictured Dallabad without the tower and wondered what new spies would then show up to determine where the tower had gone, why it had been there in the first place, and if Ahdahnia was, therefore, still in charge.

"Stop!" he commanded the artifact. "The tower remains, by *my* word."

The humming stopped immediately and the Crystal Shard, seeming very humbled, went quiet in Jarlaxle's thoughts.

Jarlaxle smiled even wider. Yes, he would keep the tower, and he decided in the morning he would construct a second one beside the first. The twin towers of Dallabad. Jarlaxle's twin towers.

At least two.

For now the mercenary leader did not fear those towers, nor the source that had inspired him to erect the first one. No, he had won the day and could use the mighty Crystal Shard to bring him to new heights of power.

And Jarlaxle knew it would never threaten him again.

⊷━━┼━⊷

Artemis Entreri paced the small room he had rented in a nondescript inn far from House Basadoni and any of the other street guilds. On a small table to the side of the bed was his black, red-stitched gauntlet, with Charon's Claw lying right beside it, the red blade gleaming in the candlelight.

Entreri was not certain of this at all. He wondered what the innkeeper might think if he came in later to find Entreri's skull-headed corpse smoldering on the floor.

It was a very real possibility, the assassin reminded himself. Every time he used Charon's Claw, it showed him a new twist, a new trick, and he understood sentient magic well enough to understand that the more powers such a sword possessed, the greater its willpower. Entreri had already seen the result of a defeat in a willpower battle with this particularly nasty sword. He could picture the horrible end of Kohrin Soulez as vividly as if it had happened that very morning, the man's facial skin rolling up from his bones as it melted away.

But he had to do this and now. He would soon be going against the Crystal Shard, and woe to him if, at that time, he was still waging any kind of mental battle against his own sword. With just that fear in mind, he had even contemplated selling the sword or hiding it away somewhere, but as he considered his other likely enemies, Rai-guy and Kimmuriel, he realized that he had to keep it.

He had to keep it, and he had to dominate it completely. There could be no other way.

Entreri walked toward the table, rubbing his hands together, then bringing them up to his lips, and blowing into them.

He turned around before he reached the sword, thinking, thinking, seeking some alternative. He wondered again if he could sell the vicious blade or hand it over to Dwahvel to lock in a deep hole until after the dark elves had left Calimport and he could, perhaps, return.

That last thought, of being chased from the city by Jarlaxle's wretched lieutenants, fired a sudden anger in the assassin, and he strode determinedly over to the table. Before he could again consider the potential implications, he growled and reached over, snapping up Charon's Claw in his bare hand.

He felt the immediate tug—not a physical tug, but something deeper, something going to the essence of Artemis Entreri, the spirit of the man. The sword was hungry—how he could feel that hunger! It wanted to consume him, to obliterate his very essence simply because he was bold enough, or foolish enough, to grasp it without that protective gauntlet.

Oh, how it wanted him!

He felt a twitching in his cheek, an excitement upon his skin, and wondered if he would combust. Entreri forced that notion away and concentrated again on winning the mental battle.

The sentient sword pulled and pulled, relentlessly, and Entreri could hear something akin to laughter in his head, a supreme confidence that reminded him that Charon's Claw would not tire, but he surely would. Another thought came, the realization that he could not even let go of the weapon if he chose to, that he had locked in this combat and there could be no turning back, no surrender.

That was the ploy of the devilish sword, to impart a sense of complete hopelessness on the part of anyone challenging it, to tell the challenger, in no uncertain terms, that the fight would be to the bitter and disastrous end. For so many before Entreri, such a message had resulted in a breaking of the spirit that the sword had used as a springboard to complete its victory.

But with Entreri, the ploy only brought forth greater feelings of rage, a red wall of determined and focused anger and denial.

"You are mine!" the assassin growled through gritted teeth. "You are a possession, a thing, a piece of beaten metal!" He lifted the gleaming red blade before him and commanded it to bring forth its black light.

It did not comply. The sword kept attacking Entreri as it had attacked Kohrin Soulez, trying to defeat him mentally that it might burn away his skin, trying to consume him as it had so many before him.

"You are mine," he said again, his voice calm now, for while the sword had not relented its attack, Entreri's confidence that he could fend that attack began to rise.

He felt a sudden sting within him, a burning sensation as Charon's Claw threw all of its energy into him. Rather than deny it he welcomed that energy and took it from the sword. It mounted to a vibrating crescendo and broke apart.

The black light appeared in the small room, and Entreri's smile gleamed widely within it. The light was confirmation that Entreri had overwhelmed Charon's Claw, that the sword was indeed his now. He lowered the blade, taking several deep breaths to steady himself, trying not to consider the fact that he had just come back from the very precipice of obliteration.

That did not matter anymore. He had beaten the sword, had broken the sword's spirit, and it belonged to him now as surely as did the jeweled dagger he wore on his other hip. Certainly he would ever after have to take some measure of care that Charon's Claw would try to break free of him, but that was, at most, a cursory inconvenience.

"You are mine," he said again, calmly, and he commanded the sword to dismiss the black light.

The room was again bathed in only candlelight. Charon's Claw, the sword of Artemis Entreri, offered no arguments.

Jarlaxle *thought* he knew. Jarlaxle *thought* that he had won the day.

Because Crenshinibon made him think that. Because Crenshinibon wanted the battle between the mercenary leader and his upstart lieutenants to be an honest one, so that it could then determine which would be the better wielder.

The Crystal Shard still favored Rai-guy, because it knew that drow to be more ambitious and more willing, even eager, to kill.

But the possibilities here with Jarlaxle did not escape the artifact. Turning him within the layers of deception had been no easy thing, but indeed, Crenshinibon had taken Jarlaxle exactly to that spot where it had desired he go.

At dawn the very next morning, a second crystalline tower was erected at Dallabad Oasis.

CHAPTER

13

You understand your role in every contingency?" Entreri asked Dwahvel at their next meeting, an impromptu affair conducted in the alley beside the Copper Ante, an area equally protected from divining wizards by Dwahvel's potent anti-spying resources.

"In every contingency that you have outlined," the halfling replied with a warning smirk.

"Then you understand every contingency," Entreri answered without hesitation. He returned her grin with one of complete confidence.

"You have thought *every* possibility through?" the halfling asked doubtfully. "These are dark elves, the masters of manipulation and intrigue, the makers of the layers of their own reality and of the rules within that layered reality."

"And they are not in their homeland and do not understand the nuances of Calimport," Entreri assured her. "They view the whole world as an extension of Menzoberranzan, an extension in temperament, and more importantly, in how they measure the reactions of those around them. I am *iblith*, thus inferior, and thus, they will not expect the turn their version of reality is about to take."

"The time has come?" Dwahvel asked, still doubtfully. "Or are you bringing the critical moment upon us?"

"I have never been a patient man," Entreri admitted, and his wicked grin did not dissipate with the admission but intensified.

"Every contingency," Dwahvel remarked, "thus every layer of the reality you intend to create. Beware, my competent friend, that you do not get lost somewhere in the mixture of your realities."

Entreri started to scowl but held back the negative thoughts, recognizing that Dwahvel was offering him sensible advice here, that he was playing a most dangerous game with the most dangerous foes he had ever known. Even in the best of circumstances, Artemis Entreri realized that his success, and therefore his very life, would hang on the movements of a split second and would be forfeited by the slightest turn of bad luck. This culminating scenario was not the precision strike of the trained assassin but the desperate move of a cornered man.

Still, when he looked at his halfling friend, Entreri's confidence and resolve were bolstered. He knew that Dwahvel would not disappoint him in this, that she would hold up her end of the reality-making process.

"If you succeed, I'll not see you again," the halfling remarked. "And if you fail, I'll likely not be able to find your blasted and torn corpse."

Entreri took the blunt words for the offering of affection that he knew they truly were. His smile was wide and genuine—so rare a thing for the assassin.

"You will see me again," he told Dwahvel. "The drow will grow weary of Calimport and will recede back to their sunless holes where they truly belong. Perhaps it will happen in months, perhaps in years, but they will eventually go. That is their nature. Rai-guy and Kimmuriel understand that there is no long-term benefit for them or for Bregan D'aerthe in expanding any trading business on the surface. Discovery would mean all-out war. That is the main focus of their ire with Jarlaxle, after all. So they will go, but you will remain, and I will return."

"Even if the drow do not kill you now, am I to believe that your road will be any less dangerous once you're gone?" the halfling asked with a snort that ended in a grin. "Is there any such road for Artemis Entreri? Not likely, I say. Indeed, with your new weapon and that defensive gauntlet, you will likely take on the assassinations of prominent wizards as your chosen profession. And, of course, eventually one of those wizards will understand the truth of your new toys and their limitations, and he will leave you a charred and smoking husk." She chuckled and shook her head. "Yes, go after Khelben, Vangerdahast, or Elminster himself. At least your death will be painlessly quick."

"I did say I was not a patient man," Entreri agreed.

To his surprise, and to the halfling's as well, Dwahvel then rushed up to him and leaped upon him, wrapping him in a hug. She broke free quickly and backed away, composing herself.

"For luck and nothing more," she said. "Of course I prefer your victory to that of the dark elves."

"If only the dark elves," Entreri said, needing to keep this conversation lighthearted.

He knew what awaited him. It would be a brutal test of his skills—of all of his skills—and of his nerve. He walked the very edge of disaster. Again, he reminded himself that he could indeed count on the reliability of one Dwahvel Tiggerwillies, that most competent of halflings. He looked at her hard then and understood that she was going to play along with his last remark, was not going to give him the satisfaction of disagreeing, of admitting that she considered him a friend.

Artemis Entreri would have been disappointed in her if she had.

"Beware that you do not catch yourself within the very layers of lies that you have perpetrated," Dwahvel said after the assassin as he started away, already beginning to blend seamlessly into the shadows.

Entreri took those words to heart. The potential combinations of the possible events was indeed staggering. Improvisation alone might keep him alive in this critical time, and Entreri had survived the entirety of his life on the very edge of disaster. He had been forced to rely on his wits, on complete improvisation, dozens of times, scores of times, and had somehow managed to survive. In his mind, he held contingency plans to counter every foreseeable event. While he kept confidence in himself and in those he had placed strategically around him, he did not for one moment dismiss the fact that if one eventuality materialized that he had not counted on, if one wrong turn appeared before him and he could not find a way around that bend, he would die.

And, given the demeanor of Rai-guy, he would die horribly.

⊶═══⊷

The street was busy, as were most of the avenues in Calimport, but the most remarkable person on it seemed the most unremarkable. Artemis Entreri, wearing the guise of a beggar, kept to the shadows, not moving suspiciously from one to another, but blending invisibly against the backdrop of the bustling street.

His movements were not without purpose. He kept his prey in sight at every moment.

Sharlotta Vespers attempted no such anonymity as she moved along the thoroughfare. She was the recognized figurehead of House Basadoni, walking bidden into the domain of dangerous Pasha Da'Daclan. Many suspicious, even hateful eyes cast more than the occasional glance her way, but none would move against her. She had requested the meeting with Da'Daclan, on orders from Rai-guy, and had been accepted under his protection. Thus, she walked now with the guise of complete confidence, bordering on bravado.

She didn't seem to realize that one of those watching her, shadowing her, was not under any orders from Pasha Da'Daclan.

Entreri knew this area well, for he had worked for the Rakers on several occasions in the past. Sharlotta's demeanor told him without doubt that she was coming for a formal parlay. Soon enough, as she passed one potential meeting area after another, he was able to deduce exactly where that meeting would take place. What he did not know, however, was how important this meeting might be to Rai-guy and Kimmuriel.

"Are you watching her every step with your strange mind powers, Kimmuriel?" he asked quietly

His mind worked through the contingency plans he had to keep available should that be the case. He didn't believe that the two drow, busy with planning of their own, no doubt, would be monitoring Sharlotta's every move, but it was certainly possible. If that came to pass, Entreri realized that he would know it, in no uncertain terms, very soon. He could only hope that he'd be ready and able to properly adjust his course.

He moved more quickly then, outpacing the woman by taking the side alleys, even climbing to one roof, and scrambling across to another and to another.

Soon after, he reached the house bordering the alley he believed Sharlotta would turn down, a suspicion only heightened by the fact that a sentry was in position on that very roof, overlooking the alley on the far side.

As silent as death, Entreri moved into position behind the sentry, with the man's attention obviously focused on the alleyway and completely oblivious to him. Working carefully, for he knew that others would be about, Entreri spent some amount of time casing the entire area, locating the two sentries on the rooftops across the way and one other on this side of the alley, on the adjoining roof of a building immediately behind the one Entreri now stood upon.

He watched those three more than the man directly in front of him, measured

125

their every movement, their every turn of the head. Most of all, he gauged their focus. Finally, when he was certain that they were not attentive, the assassin struck, yanking his victim back behind a dormer.

A moment later, all four of Pasha Da'Daclan's sentries seemed in place once more, all of them honestly intent on the alleyway below as Sharlotta Vespers, a pair of Da'Daclan's guards at her back, turned into the alleyway.

Entreri's thoughts whirled. Five enemy soldiers, and a supposed comrade who seemed more of an enemy than the others. He didn't delude himself into thinking that these five were alone. Da'Daclan's stooges probably included a significant portion of the scores of people milling about on the main avenue.

Entreri went anyway, rolling over the edge of the roof of the two-story building, catching hold with his hand, stretching to his limit, and dropping agilely to the surprised Sharlotta's side.

"A trap," he whispered harshly, and he turned to face the two soldiers following her and held up his hand for them to halt. "Kimmuriel has a dimensional portal in place for our escape on the roof."

Sharlotta's facial expression went from surprise to anger to calm so quickly, each one buried in her practiced manner, that only Entreri caught the range of expressions. He knew that he had her befuddled, that his mention of Kimmuriel had given credence to his outlandish claim that this was a trap.

"I will take her from here," Entreri said to the guards. He heard movement farther along and across the alley, as two of the other three sentries, including the one on the same side of the alley as Entreri, came down to see what was going on.

"Who are you?" one of the soldiers following Sharlotta asked skeptically, his hand going inside his common traveling cloak to the hilt of a finely crafted sword.

"Go," Entreri whispered to Sharlotta.

The woman hesitated, so Entreri prompted her retreat in no uncertain terms. Out came the jeweled dagger and Charon's Claw, the assassin throwing back his cloak, revealing himself in all his splendor. He leaped forward, slashing with his sword and thrusting with his dagger at the second soldier.

Out came the swords in response. One picked off the swipe of Charon's Claw, but with the man inevitably retreating as he parried. That had been Entreri's primary goal. The second soldier, though, had less fortune. As his sword came forth to parry, Entreri gave a subtle twist of his wrist and looped his dagger over the blade, then thrust it home into the man's belly.

With others closing fast, the assassin couldn't follow through with the kill, but he did hold the strike long enough to bring forth the dagger's life-stealing energies to let the man know the purest horror he could ever imagine. The soldier wasn't really badly wounded, but he fell away to the ground, clutching his belly and howling in terror.

The assassin broke back, turning away from the wall where Sharlotta Vespers was scrambling to gain the roof.

The one who had fallen back from the sword slash came at Entreri from the left. Another came from the right, and two rushed across the alleyway, coming straight in. Entreri started right, sword leading, then turned back fast to the left. Even as the four began to compensate for the change—a change that was not completely unexpected—the assassin turned back fast to the right, charging in hard just as that soldier had begun to accelerate in pursuit.

The soldier found himself in a flurry of slashing and stabbing. He worked his own blades, a sword and dirk, quite well. The soldier was no novice to battle, but this was Artemis Entreri. Whenever the man moved to parry, Entreri altered the angle. His fury kept the ring of metal in the air for a long few seconds, but the dagger slipped through, gashing the soldier's right arm. As that limb drooped, Entreri went into a spin, Charon's Claw coming around fast to pick off a thrust from the man coming in at his back, then continuing through, over the wounded man's lowered defense, slashing him hard across the chest.

Also on that maneuver, Entreri's devilish sword trailed out the black ash wall. The line was horizontal, not vertical, so that ash did not impede the vision of his adversaries, but still the mere sight of it hanging there in midair gave them enough pause for Entreri to dispatch the man who had come in on his right. Then the assassin went into a wild flurry, sword waving and bringing up an opaque wall.

The remaining three soldiers settled back behind it, confused and trying to put some coordination into their movements. When at last they mustered the nerve to charge through the ash wall, they discovered that the assassin was nowhere to be found.

Entreri watched them from the rooftop, shaking his head at their ineptness, and also at the little values offered by this wondrous sword—a weapon to which he was growing more fond with each battle.

"Where is it?" Sharlotta called to him from across the way.

Entreri looked at her quizzically.

"The doorway?" Sharlotta asked. "Where is it?"

"Perhaps Da'Daclan has interfered," Entreri replied, trying to hide his satisfaction that apparently Rai-guy and Kimmuriel were not closely monitoring Sharlotta's movements. "Or perhaps they decided to leave us," he added, figuring that if he could throw a bit of doubt into Sharlotta Vespers' view of the world and her dark elven compatriots, then so be it.

Sharlotta merely scowled at that disturbing thought.

Noise from behind told them that the soldiers in the alleyway weren't giving up and reminded them that they were on hostile territory here. Entreri ran past Sharlotta, motioning for her to follow, then made the leap across the next alleyway to another building, then to a third, then down and out the back end of an alley, and finally, down into the sewers—a place that Entreri wasn't thrilled about entering at that time, given his recent assassination of Domo. He didn't remain underground for long, coming up in the more familiar territory beyond Da'Daclan's territory and closer to the Basadoni guild house.

Still leading, Entreri made his way along at a swift pace until he reached the alleyway beside the Copper Ante, where he abruptly stopped.

Seeming more angry than grateful, obviously doubting the sincerity of the escape and the very need for it, Sharlotta continued past, hardly glancing his way.

Until the assassin's sword came out and settled in front of her neck. "I think not," he remarked.

Sharlotta glanced sidelong at him, and he motioned for her to head down the alley beside Dwahvel's establishment.

"What is this?" the woman asked.

"Your only chance at continuing to draw breath," Entreri replied. When she still didn't move, he grabbed her by the arm, and with frightening strength yanked her in front of him heading down the alley. He pointedly reminded her to keep going, prodding her with his sword.

They came to a tiny room, having entered through a secret alley entrance. The room held a single chair, into which Entreri none-too-gently shoved Sharlotta.

"Have you lost what little sense you once possessed?" the woman asked.

"Am I the one bargaining secret deals with dark elves?" Entreri replied, and the look Sharlotta gave him in the instant before she found her control told him volumes about the truth of his suspicions.

"We have both been dealing as need be," the woman indignantly answered.

"Dealing? Or double-dealing? There is a difference, even with dark elves."

"You speak the part of a fool," snapped Sharlotta.

"Yet you are the one closer to death," Entreri reminded, and he came in very close, now with his jeweled dagger in hand, and a look on his face that told Sharlotta that he was certainly not bluffing here. Sharlotta knew well the life-stealing powers of that horrible dagger. "Why were you going to meet with Pasha Da'Daclan?" Entreri asked bluntly.

"The change at Dallabad has raised suspicions," the woman answered, an honest and obvious—if obviously incomplete—response.

"No suspicions that trouble Jarlaxle, apparently," Entreri reasoned.

"But some that could turn to serious trouble," Sharlotta went on, and Entreri knew that she was improvising here. "I was to meet with Pasha Da'Daclan to assure him the situation on the streets, and elsewhere, will calm to normal."

"That any expansion by House Basadoni is at its end?" Entreri asked doubtfully. "Would you not be lying, though, and would that not invite even greater wrath when the next conquest falls before Jarlaxle?"

"The next?"

"Have you come to believe that our suddenly ambitious leader means to stop?" Entreri asked.

Sharlotta spent a long while mulling that one over. "I have been told that House Basadoni will begin pulling back, to all appearances, at least," she said. "As long as we encounter no further outside influences."

"Like the spies at Dallabad," Entreri agreed.

Sharlotta nodded—a bit too eagerly, Entreri thought.

"Then Jarlaxle's hunger is at last sated, and we can get back to a quieter and safer routine," the assassin remarked.

Sharlotta did not respond.

Entreri's lips curled up into a smile. He knew the truth of it, of course, that Sharlotta had just blatantly lied to him. He would never have put it past Jarlaxle to have played such opposing games with his underlings in days past, leading Entreri in one direction and Sharlotta in another, but he knew that the mercenary leader was in the throes of Crenshinibon's hunger now, and given the information supplied by Dwahvel, he understood the truth of that. It was a truth very different from the lie Sharlotta had just outlined.

Sharlotta, by going to Da'Daclan and claiming that Jarlaxle had been behind the meeting, which meant that Rai-guy and Kimmuriel certainly had been, confirmed to Entreri that time was indeed running short.

He stepped back and paused, digesting all of the information, trying to reason when and where the actual in-fighting might occur. He noted, too, that Sharlotta was watching him very carefully.

Sharlotta moved with the grace and speed of a hunting cat, rolling off the chair to one knee, drawing and throwing a dagger at Entreri's heart, and bolting for the room's other, less remarkable doorway.

Entreri caught the dagger in midflight, turned it over in his hand and hurled it into that door with a thump, to stick, quivering, before Sharlotta's widening eyes.

He grabbed her and turned her roughly around, hitting her with a heavy punch across the face.

She drew out another dagger—or tried to. Entreri caught her wrist even as it came out of its concealed sheath, turning a quick spin under the arm and tugging so violently that all of Sharlotta's strength left her hand and the dagger fell harmlessly to the floor. Entreri tugged again, and let go. He leaped around in front of the woman, slapping her twice across the face, and grabbed her hard by the shoulders. He ran her backward, to crash back into the chair.

"Do you not even understand those with whom you play these foolish games?" he growled in her face. "They will use you to their advantage, and discard you. In their eyes you are *iblith,* a word that means "not drow," a word that also means offal. Those two, Rai-guy and Kimmuriel, are the greatest racists among Jarlaxle's lieutenants. You will find no gain beside them, Sharlotta the Fool, only horrible death."

"And what of Jarlaxle?" she cried out in response.

It was just the sort of instinctive, emotional explosion the assassin had been counting on. There it was, as clear as it could be, an admission that Sharlotta had fallen into league with two would-be kings of Bregan D'aerthe. He moved back from her, just a bit, leaving her ruffled in the chair.

"I offer you one chance," he said to her. "Not out of any favorable feelings I might hold toward you, because there are none, but because you have something I need."

Sharlotta straightened her shirt and tunic and tried to regain some of her dignity.

"Tell me everything," Entreri said bluntly. "All of this coup—when, where, and how. I know more than you believe, so try none of your foolish games with me."

Sharlotta smirked at him doubtfully. "You know nothing," she replied. "If you did, you'd know you've come to play the role of the idiot."

Even as the last word left her mouth, Entreri was there, back against her, one hand roughly grabbing her hair and yanking her head back, the other, holding his awful dagger point in at her exposed throat. "Last chance," he said, so very calmly. "And do remember that I do not like you, dearest Sharlotta."

The woman swallowed hard, her eyes locked onto Entreri's deadly gaze.

Entreri's reputation heightened the threat reflected in his eyes to the point where Sharlotta, with nothing to lose and no reason for loyalty to the dark elves, spilled all she knew of the entire plan, even the method Rai-guy and Kimmuriel planned to use to incapacitate the Crystal Shard—some kind of mind magic transformed into a lantern.

None of it came as any surprise to Entreri, of course. Still, hearing the words spoken openly did bring a shock to him, a reminder of how precarious his position truly had become. He quietly muttered his litany of creating his own reality within the strands of the layered web and reminded himself repeatedly that he was every bit the player as were his two opponents.

He moved away from Sharlotta to the inner door. He pulled free the stuck dagger and banged hard three times on the door. It opened a few moments later and a very surprised looking Dwahvel Tiggerwillies bounded into the room.

"Why have you come?" she started to ask of Entreri, but she stopped, her gaze caught by the ruffled Sharlotta. Again she turned to Entreri, this time her expression one of surprise and anger. "What have you done?" the halfling demanded of the assassin. "I'll play no part in any of the rivalries within House Basadoni!"

"You will do as you are instructed," the assassin replied coldly. "You will keep Sharlotta here as your comfortable but solitary guest until I return to permit her release."

"Permit?" Dwahvel asked doubtfully, turning from Entreri to Sharlotta. "What insanity have you brought upon me, fool?"

"The next insult will cost you your tongue," Entreri said coldly, perfectly playing the role. "You will do as I've instructed. Nothing more, nothing less. When this is finished, even Sharlotta will thank you for keeping her safe in times when none of us truly are."

Dwahvel stared hard at Sharlotta as Entreri spoke, making silent contact. The human woman gave the slightest nod of her head.

Dwahvel turned back to the assassin. "Out," she ordered.

Entreri looked to the alleyway door, so perfectly fitted that it was barely an outline on the wall.

"Not that way . . . it opens only in," Dwahvel said sourly, and she pointed to the conventional door. "That way." She moved up to him and pushed him along, out of the room, turning to close and lock the door behind them.

"It has come this far already?" Dwahvel asked when the two were safely down the corridor.

Entreri nodded grimly.

"But you are still on course for your plan?" Dwahvel asked. "Despite this unexpected turn?"

Entreri's smile reminded the halfling that nothing would be, or could be, unexpected.

Dwahvel nodded. "Logical improvisation," she remarked.

"You know your role," Entreri replied.

"And I thought I played it quite well," Dwahvel said with a smile.

"Too well," Entreri said to her as they reached another doorway farther along the wall up the alleyway. "I was not joking when I said I would take your tongue."

With that, he went out into the alley, leaving a shaken Dwahvel behind. After a moment, though, the halfling merely chuckled, doubting that Entreri would ever take her tongue, whatever insults she might throw his way.

Doubting, but not sure—never sure. That was the way of Artemis Entreri.

Entreri was out of the city before dawn, riding hard for Dallabad Oasis on a horse he'd borrowed without the owner's permission. He knew the road well. It was often congested with beggars and highwaymen. That knowledge didn't stop the assassin, though, didn't slow his swift ride one bit. When the sun rose over his left shoulder he only increased his pace, knowing that he had to get to Dallabad on time.

He'd told Dwahvel that Jarlaxle was back at the crystalline tower, where the assassin now had to go with all haste. Entreri knew the halfling would be prompt about her end of the plan. Once she released Sharlotta. . . .

Entreri put his head down and drove on in the growing morning sunlight. He was still miles away, but he could see the sharp focus at the top of the tower . . . no, tower*s*, he realized, for he saw not one, but two pillars rising in the distance to meet the morning light.

He didn't know what that meant, of course, but he didn't worry about it. Jarlaxle was there, according to his many sources—informants independent of, and beyond the reach of Rai-guy and Kimmuriel and their many lackeys.

He sensed the scrying soon after and knew he was being watched. That only made the desperate assassin put his head down and drive the stolen horse on at greater speeds, determined to beat the brutal, self-imposed timetable.

"He goes to Jarlaxle with great haste, and we know not where Sharlotta Vespers has gone," Kimmuriel remarked to Rai-guy.

The two of them, along with Berg'inyon Baenre, watched the assassin's hard ride out from Calimport.

"Sharlotta may remain with Pasha Da'Daclan," Rai-guy replied. "We cannot know for certain."

"Then we should learn," said an obviously frustrated and nervous Kimmuriel.

Rai-guy looked at him. "Easy, my friend," he said. "Artemis Entreri is no threat to us but merely a nuisance. Better that all of the vermin gather together."

"A more complete and swift victory," Berg'inyon agreed.

Kimmuriel thought about it and held up a small square lantern, three sides shielded, the fourth open. Yharaskrik had given it to him with the assurance that, when Kimmuriel lit the candle and allowed its glow to fall over Crenshinibon, the powers of the Crystal Shard would be stunted. The effects would be temporary, the illithid had warned. Even confident Yharaskrik held no illusions that anything would hold the powerful artifact at bay for long.

But it wouldn't take long, Kimmuriel and the others knew, even if Artemis Entreri was at Jarlaxle's side. With the artifact shut down, Jarlaxle's fall would be swift and complete, as would the fall of all of those, Entreri included, who stood beside him.

This day would be sweet indeed—or rather, this night. Rai-guy and Kimmuriel had planned to strike at night, when the powers of the Crystal Shard were at their weakest.

"He is a fool, but one, I believe, acting on honest fears," Dwahvel Tiggerwillies said to Sharlotta when she joined the woman in the small room. "Find a bit of sympathy for him, I beg."

Sharlotta, the prisoner, looked at the halfling incredulously.

"Oh, he's gone now," said Dwahvel, "and so should you be."

"I thought I was your prisoner," the woman asked.

Dwahvel chuckled. "Forever and ever?" she asked with obvious sarcasm. "Artemis Entreri is afraid, and so you should be too. I know little about dark elves, I admit, but—"

"Dark elves?" Sharlotta echoed, feigning surprise and ignorance. "What has any of this to do with dark elves?"

Dwahvel laughed again. "The word is out," she said, "about Dallabad and House Basadoni. The power behind the throne is well-known around the streets."

Sharlotta started to mumble something about Entreri, but Dwahvel cut her short. "Entreri told me nothing," she explained. "Do you think I would need to deal with one as powerful as Entreri for such common information? I am many things, but I do not number fool among them."

The woman settled back in her chair, staring hard at the halfling. "You believe you know more than you really know," she said. "That is a dangerous mistake."

"I know only that I want no part of any of this," Dwahvel returned. "No part of House Basadoni or of Dallabad Oasis. No part of the feud between Sharlotta Vespers and Artemis Entreri."

"It would seem that you are already a part of that feud," the woman replied, her sparkling dark eyes narrowing.

Dwahvel shook her head. "I did and do as I had to do, nothing more," she said.

"Then I am free to leave?"

Dwahvel nodded and stood aside, leaving the path to the door open. "I came back here as soon as I was certain Entreri was long gone. Forgive me, Sharlotta, but I would not make of you an ally if doing so made Entreri an enemy."

Sharlotta continued to stare hard at the surprising halfling, but she couldn't argue with the logic of that statement. "Where has he gone?" she asked.

"Out of Calimport, my sources relay," Dwahvel answered. "To Dallabad, perhaps? Or long past the oasis—all the way along the road and out of Calimshan. I believe I might take that very route, were I Artemis Entreri."

Sharlotta didn't reply, but silently she agreed wholeheartedly. She was still confused by the recent events, but she recognized clearly that Entreri's supposed "rescue" of her was no more than a kidnapping of his own, so he could squeeze information out of her. And she had offered much, she understood to her apprehension. She had told him more than she should have, more than Rai-guy and Kimmuriel would likely find acceptable.

She left the Copper Ante trying to sort it all out. What she did know was that the dark elves would find her and likely soon. The woman nodded, recognizing the only real course left open before her, and started off with all speed for House Basadoni. She would tell Rai-guy and Kimmuriel of Entreri's treachery.

⊷━━⊶

Entreri looked at the sun hanging low in the eastern sky and took a deep, steadying breath. The time had passed. Dwahvel had released Sharlotta, as arranged. The woman, no doubt, had run right to Rai-guy and Kimmuriel, thus setting into motion momentous events.

If the two dark elves were even still in Calimport.

If Sharlotta had not figured out the ruse within the kidnapping, and had gone off the other way, running for cover.

If the dark elves hadn't long ago found Sharlotta in the Copper Ante and leveled the place, in which case, Dallabad and the Crystal Shard might already be in Rai-guy's dangerous hands.

If, in learning of the discovery, Rai-guy and Kimmuriel hadn't just turned around and run back to Menzoberranzan.

If Jarlaxle still remained at Dallabad.

That last notion worried Entreri profoundly. The unpredictable Jarlaxle was, perhaps, the most volatile on a long list of unknowns. If Jarlaxle had left Dallabad, what trouble might he bring to every aspect of this plan? Would Kimmuriel and Rai-guy catch up to him unawares and slay him easily?

The assassin shook all of the doubts away. He wasn't used to feelings of self-doubt, even inadequacy. Perhaps that was why he so hated the dark elves. In Menzoberranzan, the ultimately capable Artemis Entreri had felt tiny indeed.

Reality is what you make of it, he reminded himself. He was the one weaving the layers of intrigue and deception here, so he—not Rai-guy and Kimmuriel, not Sharlotta, not even Jarlaxle and the Crystal Shard—was the one in command.

He looked at the sun again, and glanced to the side, to the imposing structures of the twin crystalline towers set among the palms of Dallabad, reminding himself that this time he, and no one else, had turned over that hourglass.

Reminding himself pointedly that the sand was running, that time was growing short, he kicked his horse's flanks and leaped away, galloping hard to the oasis.

CHAPTER

14

Entreri kept the notion that he had come to steal the Crystal Shard foremost in his mind. All he thought of was that he'd come to take it as his own, whatever the cost to Jarlaxle, though he made certain that he kept a bit of compassion evident whenever he thought of the mercenary leader. Entreri replayed that singular thought and purpose over and over again, suspecting that the artifact, in this place of its greatest power, would scan those thoughts.

Jarlaxle was waiting for him on the second floor of the tower in a round room sparsely adorned with two chairs and a small desk. The mercenary leader stood across the way, directly opposite the doorway through which Entreri entered. Jarlaxle put himself as far, Entreri noted, as he could be from the approaching assassin.

"Greetings," Entreri said.

Jarlaxle, curiously wearing no eye patch this day, tipped his broad-brimmed hat and asked, "Why have you come?"

Entreri looked at him as if surprised by the question, but turned the not-so-secret notion in his head to one appearing as an ironic twist: Why have I come indeed!

Jarlaxle's uncharacteristic scowl told the assassin that the Crystal Shard had heard those thoughts and had communicated them instantly to its wielder. No doubt, the artifact was now telling Jarlaxle to dispose of Entreri, a suggestion the mercenary leader was obviously resisting.

"Your course is that of the fool," Jarlaxle remarked, struggling with the words as his internal battle heightened. "There is nothing here for you."

Entreri settled back on his heels, assuming a pensive posture. "Then perhaps I should leave," he said.

Jarlaxle didn't blink.

Hardly expecting one as cunning as Jarlaxle to be caught off guard, Entreri exploded into motion anyway, a forward dive and roll that brought him up in a run straight at his opponent.

Jarlaxle grabbed his belt pouch—he didn't even have to take the artifact out—and extended his other hand toward the assassin. Out shot a line of pure white energy.

134

Entreri caught it with his red-stitched gauntlet, took the energy in, and held it there. He held some of it, anyway, for it was too great a power to be completely held at bay. The assassin felt the pain, the intense agony, though he understood that only a small fraction of the shard's attack had gotten through.

How powerful was that item? he wondered, awestruck and thinking that he might be in serious trouble.

Afraid that the energy would melt the gauntlet or otherwise consume it, Entreri turned the magic right back out. He didn't throw it at Jarlaxle, for he hardly wanted to kill the drow. Entreri loosed it on the wall to the dark elf's side. It exploded in a blistering, blinding, thunderous blow that left both man and dark elf staggering to the side.

Entreri kept his course straight, dodging and parrying with his blade as Jarlaxle's arm pumped, sending forth a stream of daggers. The assassin blocked one, got nicked by a second, and squirmed about two more. He then came on fast, thinking to tackle the lighter dark elf.

He missed cleanly, slamming the wall behind Jarlaxle.

The drow was wearing a displacement cloak, or perhaps it was that ornamental hat, Entreri mused, but only briefly, for he understood that he was vulnerable and came right around, bringing Charon's Claw in a broad, ash-making sweep that cut the view between the opponents.

Hardly slowing, Entreri crashed straight through that visual barrier, his straightforwardness confusing Jarlaxle long enough for him to get by—and properly gauge his attack angle this time—close enough to work his own form of magic.

With skills beyond those of nearly any man alive, Entreri sheathed Charon's Claw, drew forth his dagger in his gloved hand, and pulled out his replica pouch with his other. He spun past Jarlaxle, deftly cutting the scrambling drow's belt pouch and catching it in the same gloved hand, while dropping the false pouch at the mercenary's feet.

Jarlaxle hit him with a series of sharp blows then, with what felt like an iron maul. Entreri went rolling away, glancing back just in time to pick off another dagger, then to catch the next in his side. Groaning and doubled over in pain, Entreri scrambled away from his adversary, who held, he now saw, a small warhammer.

"Do you think I need the Crystal Shard to destroy you?" Jarlaxle confidently asked, stooping over to retrieve the pouch. He held up the warhammer then and whispered something. It shrank into a tiny replica that Jarlaxle tucked up under the band of his great hat.

Entreri hardly heard him and hardly saw the move. The pain, though the dagger hadn't gone in dangerously far, was searing. Even worse, a new song was beginning to play in his head, a demand that he surrender himself to the power of the artifact he now possessed.

"I have a hundred ways to kill you, my former friend," Jarlaxle remarked. "Perhaps Crenshinibon will prove the most efficient in this, and in truth, I have little desire to torture you."

Jarlaxle clasped the pouch then, and a curious expression crossed his face.

Still, Entreri could hardly register any of Jarlaxle's words or movements. The artifact assailed him powerfully, reaching into his mind and showing such overwhelming images of complete despair that the mighty assassin nearly fell to his knees sobbing.

Jarlaxle shrugged and rubbed the moisture from his hand on his cloak, and produced yet another of his endless stream of daggers from his enchanted bracer. He brought it back, lining up the killing throw on the seemingly defenseless man.

"Please tell me why I must do this," the drow asked. "Was it the Crystal Shard calling out to you? Your own overblown ambitions, perhaps?"

The images of despair assailed him, a sense of hopelessness more profound than anything Entreri had ever known.

One thought managed to sort itself out in the battered mind of Artemis Entreri: Why didn't the Crystal Shard summon forth its energy and consume him then and there?

Because it cannot! Entreri's willpower answered. Because I am now the wielder, something that the Crystal Shard does not enjoy at all!

"Tell me!" Jarlaxle demanded.

Entreri summoned up all his mental strength, every ounce of discipline he had spent decades grooming, and told the artifact to cease, simply commanded it to shut down all connection to him. The sentient artifact resisted, but only for a moment. Entreri's wall was built of pure discipline and pure anger, and the Crystal Shard was closed off as completely as it had been during those days when Drizzt Do'Urden had carried it. The denial that Drizzt, a goodly ranger, had brought upon the artifact had been wrought of simple morality, while Entreri's was wrought of simple strength of will, but to the same effect. The shard was shut down.

And not an instant too soon, Entreri realized as he blinked open his eyes and saw a stream of daggers coming at him. He dodged and parried with his own dagger, hardly picking anything off cleanly, but deflecting the missiles so that they did not, at least, catch him squarely. One hit him in the face, high on his cheekbone and just under his eye, but he had altered the spin enough so that it slammed in pommel first and not point first. Another grazed his upper arm, cutting a long slash.

"I could have killed you with the return bolt!" Entreri managed to cry out.

Jarlaxle's arm pumped again, this dagger going low and clipping the dancing assassin's foot. The words did register, though, and the mercenary leader paused, his arm cocked, another dagger in hand, ready to throw. He stared at Entreri curiously.

"I could have struck you dead with your own attack," Entreri growled out through teeth gritted in pain.

"You feared you would destroy the shard," Jarlaxle reasoned.

"The shard's energy cannot destroy the shard!" Entreri snapped back.

"You came in here to kill me," Jarlaxle declared.

"No!"

"To take the Crystal Shard, whatever the cost!" Jarlaxle countered.

Entreri, leaning heavily back against the wall now, his legs growing weak from pain, mustered all his determination and looked the drow in the eye—though he did so with only one eye, for his other had already swollen tightly closed. "I came in here," he said slowly, accentuating every word, "making you believe, through the artifact, that such was my intent."

Jarlaxle's face screwed up in one of his very rare expressions of confusion, and his dagger arm began to slip lower. "What are you about?" he asked, his anger seemingly displaced now by honest curiosity.

"They are coming for you," Entreri vaguely explained. "You have to be prepared."

"They?"

"Rai-guy and Kimmuriel," the assassin explained. "They have decided that your reign over Bregan D'aerthe is at its end. You have exposed the band to too many mighty enemies."

Jarlaxle's expression shifted several times, through a spectrum of emotions, confusion to anger. He looked down at the pouch he held in his hand.

"The artifact has deceived you," Entreri said, managing to straighten a bit as the pain at last began to wane. He reached down and, with trembling fingers, pulled the dagger out of his side and dropped it to the floor. "It pushes you past the point of reason," he went on. "And at the same time, it resents your ability to . . ."

He paused as Jarlaxle opened the pouch and reached in to touch the shard—the imitation item. Before he could begin again, Entreri noted a shimmering in the air, a bluish glow across the room. Then, suddenly, he was looking out as if through a window, at the grounds of Dallabad Oasis.

Through that portal stepped Rai-guy and Kimmuriel, along with Berg'inyon Baenre and another pair of Bregan D'aerthe soldiers.

Entreri forced himself to straighten, growled away the pain, knowing that he had to be at his best here or he would be lost indeed. He noted, then, even as Rai-guy brought forth a curious-looking lantern, that Kimmuriel had not dismissed his dimensional portal.

They were expecting the tower to fall, perhaps, or Kimmuriel was keeping open his escape route.

"You come unbidden," Jarlaxle remarked to them, and he pulled forth the shard from his pouch. "I will summon you when you are needed." The mercenary leader stood tall and imposing, his gaze locked onto Rai-guy. His expression was one of absolute competence, Entreri thought, one of command.

Rai-guy held forth the lantern, its glow bathing Jarlaxle and the shard in quiet light.

That was it, Entreri realized. That was the item to neutralize the Crystal Shard, the tip in the balance of the fight. The intruders had made one tactical error, the assassin knew, one Entreri had counted on. Their focus was the Crystal Shard, as well as it should have been, along with the assumption that Jarlaxle's toy would be the dominant artifact.

You see how they would deny you, Entreri telepathically imparted to the artifact, tucked securely into his belt. *Yet these are the ones you call to lead you to deserved glory?*

He felt the artifact's moment of confusion, felt its reply that Rai-guy would disable it only thereby to possess it, and that . . .

In that instant of confusion, Artemis Entreri exploded into motion, sending a telepathic roar into Crenshinibon, demanding that the tower be brought crumbling down. At the same time he leaped at Jarlaxle and drew forth Charon's Claw.

Indeed, caught so off its guard, the shard nearly obeyed. A violent shudder ran through the tower. It caused no real damage, but was enough of a shake to put Berg'inyon and the other two warriors, who were moving to intercept Entreri, off their balance and to interrupt Rai-guy's attempt to cast a spell.

Entreri altered direction, rushing at the closest drow warrior, batting the sword of the off-balance dark elf aside and stabbing him hard. The dark elf fell away, and the assassin brought his sword through a series of vertical sweeps, filling the air with black ash, filling the room with confusion.

He dived toward Jarlaxle into a sidelong roll. Jarlaxle stood transfixed, staring at the shard he held in his hand as if he had been betrayed.

"Forget it," the assassin cried, yanking Jarlaxle aside just as a hand crossbow dart—poisoned, of course—whistled past. "To the door," he whispered to Jarlaxle, shoving him forward. "Fight for your life!"

With a growl, Jarlaxle put the shard in his pouch and went into action beside the slashing, fighting assassin. His arm flashed repeatedly, sending a stream of daggers at Rai-guy, where they were defeated, predictably, by a stoneskin enchantment. Another barrage was sent at Kimmuriel, who merely absorbed their power into his kinetic barrier.

"Just give it to them!" Entreri cried unexpectedly. He crashed against Jarlaxle's side, taking the pouch back and tossing it to Rai-guy and Kimmuriel, or rather past the two, to the far edge of the room beyond Kimmuriel's magic door. Rai-guy turned immediately, trying to keep the mighty artifact in the glow of his lantern, and Kimmuriel scrambled for it. Entreri saw his one desperate chance.

He grabbed the surprised Jarlaxle roughly and pulled him along, charging for Kimmuriel's magical portal.

Berg'inyon met the charge head on, his two swords working furiously to find a hole in Entreri's defenses. The assassin, a rival of Drizzt Do'Urden, was no stranger to the two-handed style. He neatly parried while working around the skilled drow warrior.

Jarlaxle ducked fast under a swing by the other soldier, pulled the great feather from his magnificent hat, put it to his lips, and blew hard. The air before him filled with feathers.

The soldier cried out, slapping the things away. He hit one that did not so easily move and realized to his horror that he was now facing a ten-foot-tall, monstrous birdlike creature—a diatryma.

Entreri, too, added to the confusion by waving his sword wildly, filling the air with ash. He always kept his focus, though, kept moving around the slashing blades and toward the dimensional portal. He could easily get through it alone, he knew, and he had the real Crystal Shard, but for some reason he didn't quite understand, and didn't bother even to think about, he turned back and grabbed Jarlaxle again, pulling him behind.

The delay brought him some more pain. Rai-guy managed to fire off a volley of magic missiles that stung the assassin profoundly. Those the wizard had launched Jarlaxle's way, Entreri noted sourly, were absorbed by the broach on the band in his hat. Did this one ever run out of tricks?

"Kill them!" Entreri heard Kimmuriel yell, and he felt Berg'inyon's deadly sword coming in fast at his back.

Entreri found himself rolling, disoriented, out onto the sand of Dallabad, out the other side of Kimmuriel's magical portal. He kept his wits about him enough to keep scrambling, grabbing the similarly disoriented Jarlaxle and pulling him along.

"They have the shard!" the mercenary protested.

"Let them keep it!" Entreri cried back.

Behind him, on the other side of the portal, he heard Rai-guy's howling laughter. Yes, the drow wizard thought he now possessed the Crystal Shard, the assassin realized. He'd soon try to put it to use, no doubt calling forth a beam of energy as Jarlaxle had done to the fleeing spy. Perhaps that was why no pursuit came out of the portal.

As he ran, Entreri dropped his hand once more to the real Crystal Shard. He sensed that the artifact was enraged, shaken, and understood that it had not been pleased when Entreri had gone near to Jarlaxle, thus bringing it within the glow of Rai-guy's nullifying light.

"Dispel the magical doorway," he commanded the item. "Trap them and crush them."

Glancing back he saw that Kimmuriel's doorway, half of it within the province of Crenshinibon's absolute domain, was gone.

"The tower," Entreri instructed. "Bring it tumbling down and together we will construct a line of them across Faerûn!"

The promise, spoken so full of energy and enthusiasm, offering the artifact the very same thing it always offered its wielders, was seized upon immediately.

Entreri and Jarlaxle heard the ground rumbling beneath their feet.

They ran on, across the way to a campground beside the small pond of Dallabad. They heard cries from behind them, from soldiers of the fortress, and the cries of astonishment before them from traders who had come to the oasis.

Those cries only multiplied when the traders saw the truth of the two approaching, saw a dark elf coming at them!

Entreri and Jarlaxle had no time to engage the frightened, confused group. They ran straight for the horses that were tethered to a nearby wagon and pulled them free. In a few seconds, with a chorus of angry shouts and curses behind them, the duo charged out of Dallabad, riding hard, though Jarlaxle looked more than a little uncomfortable atop a horse in bright daylight.

Entreri was a fine rider, and he easily paced the dark elf, despite his posture, which was bent over and to the side in an attempt to keep his blood from flowing freely.

"They have the Crystal Shard!" Jarlaxle cried angrily. "How far can we run?"

"Their own magic defeated the artifact," Entreri lied. "It cannot help them now in their pursuit."

Behind them the first tower crashed down, and the second toppled atop the first in a thunderous explosion, all the binding energies gone, and all the magic fast dissipating to the wind.

Entreri held no illusions that Rai-guy and Kimmuriel, or their henchmen, had been caught in that catastrophe. They were too quick and too cunning. He could only hope that the wreckage had diverted them long enough for he and Jarlaxle to get far enough away. He didn't know the extent of his wounds, but he knew that they hurt badly, and that he felt very weak. The last thing he needed then was another fight with the wizard and psionicist or with a swordsman as skilled as Berg'inyon Baenre.

Fortunately, no pursuit became evident as the minutes turned to an hour, and both horses and riders had to slow to a stop, fully exhausted. In his head, Entreri heard the chanting promises of Crenshinibon, whispering to him to construct another tower then and there for shelter and rest.

He almost did it and wondered for a moment why he was even thinking of disagreeing with the Crystal Shard, whose methods seemed to lead to the very same goals that he now held himself.

With a smile of comprehension that seemed more a grimace to the pained assassin, Entreri dismissed the notion. Crenshinibon was clever indeed, sneaking always around the edges of opposition.

Besides, Artemis Entreri had not run away from Dallabad Oasis into the open desert unprepared. He slipped down from his horse, to find that he could hardly stand. Still, he managed to slip his backpack off his shoulders and drop it to the ground before him, then drop to one knee and pull at the strings.

Jarlaxle was soon beside him, helping him to open the pack.

"A potion," Entreri explained, swallowing hard, his breath becoming labored.

Jarlaxle fiddled around in the pack, producing a small vial with a bluish-white liquid within. "Healing?" he asked.

Entreri nodded and motioned for it.

Jarlaxle pulled it back. "You have much to explain," he said. "You attacked me, and you gave them the Crystal Shard."

Entreri, his brow thick with sweat, motioned again for the potion. He put his hand to his side and brought it back up, wet with blood. "A fine throw," he said to the dark elf.

"I do not pretend to understand you, Artemis Entreri," said Jarlaxle, handing over the potion. "Perhaps that is why I do so enjoy your company."

Entreri swallowed the liquid in one gulp, and fell back to a sitting position, closing his eyes and letting the soothing concoction go to work mending some of his wounds. He wished he had about five more of the things, but this one would have to suffice—and would, he believed, keep him alive and start him on the mend.

Jarlaxle watched him for a few moments, and turned his attention to a more immediate problem, glancing up at the stinging, blistering sun. "This sunlight will make for our deaths," he remarked.

In answer, Entreri shifted over and stuck his hand into his backpack, soon producing a small scale model of a brown tent. He brought it in close, whispered a few words, and tossed it off to the side. A few seconds later, the model expanded, growing to full-size and beyond.

"Enough!" Entreri said when it was big enough to comfortably hold him, the dark elf, and both of their horses.

"Not so hard to find on the open desert," Jarlaxle remarked.

"Harder than you believe," Entreri, still gasping with every word, assured him. "Once we're inside, it will recede into a pocket dimension of its own making."

Jarlaxle smiled. "You never told me you possessed such a useful desert tool," he said.

"Because I did not, until last night."

"Thus, you knew that it would come to this, with us out running in the open desert," the mercenary leader reasoned, thinking himself sly.

Far from arguing the point, Entreri merely shrugged as Jarlaxle helped him to his feet. "I hoped it would come to this," the assassin said.

Jarlaxle looked at him curiously, but didn't press the issue. Not then. He looked back in the direction of distant Dallabad, obviously wondering what had become of his former lieutenants, wondering how all of this had so suddenly come about. It was not often that the cunning Jarlaxle was confused.

"We have that which we desired," Kimmuriel reminded his outraged companion. "Bregan D'aerthe is ours to lead—back to the Underdark and Menzoberranzan where we belong."

"It is not the Crystal Shard!" Rai-guy protested, throwing the imitation piece to the floor.

Kimmuriel looked at him curiously. "Was our purpose to procure the item?"

"Jarlaxle still has it," Rai-guy growled back at him. "How long do you believe he will allow us our position of leadership? He should be dead, and the artifact should be mine."

Kimmuriel's sly expression did not change at the wizard's curious choice of words—words, he understood, inspired by Crenshinibon itself and the desire to hold Rai-guy as its slave. Yes, Yharaskrik had done well in teaching the drow psionicist the nuances of the powerful and dangerous artifact. Kimmuriel did agree, though, that their position was tenuous, given that mighty Jarlaxle was still alive.

Kimmuriel had never really wanted Jarlaxle as an enemy—not out of friendship to the older drow but out of simple fear. Perhaps Jarlaxle was already on his way back to Menzoberranzan, where he would rally the remaining members of Bregan D'aerthe, far more than half the band, against Rai-guy and Kimmuriel and those who might follow them back to the drow city. Perhaps Jarlaxle would call upon Gromph Baenre, the archmage of Menzoberranzan himself, to test his wizardly skills against those of Rai-guy.

It was not a pleasant thought, but Kimmuriel understood clearly that Rai-guy's frustration was far more involved with the wizard's other complaint, that the Crystal Shard and not Jarlaxle had gotten away.

"We have to find them," Rai-guy said a moment later. "I want Jarlaxle dead. How else might I ever know a reprieve?"

"You are now the leader of a mercenary band of males housed in Menzoberranzan," Kimmuriel replied. "You will find no reprieve, no break from the constant dangers and matron games. This is the trapping of power, my companion."

Rai-guy's returning expression was not one of friendship. He was angry, perhaps more so than Kimmuriel had ever seen him. He wanted the artifact desperately. So did Yharaskrik, Kimmuriel knew. Should they find a way to catch up to Jarlaxle and Crenshinibon, he had every intention of making certain that the illithid got it. Let Yharaskrik and his mighty mind flayer kin take control of Crenshinibon, study it, and destroy it. Better that than having it in Rai-guy's hands back in Menzoberranzan—if it would even agree to go to Menzoberranzan, for Yharaskrik had told Kimmuriel that the artifact drew much of its power from the sunlight. How much more on his guard might Kimmuriel have to remain with Crenshinibon as an ally? The artifact would never accept him, would never accept the fact that he, with his mental disciplines, could deny it entrance and control of his mind.

He was tempted to work against Rai-guy now, to foil the search for Jarlaxle however he might, but he understood clearly that Jarlaxle, with or without the Crystal Shard, was far too powerful an adversary to be allowed to run free.

A knock on the door drew him from his contemplation. It opened, and Berg'inyon Baenre entered, followed by several drow soldiers dragging a chained and beaten Sharlotta Vespers behind them. More drow soldiers followed, escorting a bulky and imposing ratman.

Kimmuriel motioned for Sharlotta's group to move aside, that he could face the ratman directly.

"Gord Abrix at your service, good Kimmuriel Oblodra," the ratman said, bowing low.

Kimmuriel stared at him hard. "You lead the wererats of Calimport now?" he asked in his halting command of the common tongue.

Gord nodded. "The wererats in the service of House Basadoni," he said. "In the service of—"

"That is all you need to know, and all that you would ever be wise to speak," Rai-guy growled at him and the wererat, as imposing as he was, inevitably shrank back from the dark elves.

"Get him out of here," Kimmuriel commanded the drow escorts, in his own language. "Tell him we will call when we have decided the new course for the wererats."

Gord Abrix managed one last bow before being herded out of the room.

"And what of you?" Kimmuriel asked Sharlotta, and the mere fact that he could speak to her in his own language reminded him of this woman's resourcefulness and thus her potential usefulness.

"What have I done to deserve such treatment?" Sharlotta, stubborn to the end, replied.

"Why do you believe you had to do anything?" Kimmuriel calmly replied.

Sharlotta started to respond, but quickly realized that there was really nothing she could say against the simple logic of that question.

"We sent you to meet with Pasha Da'Daclan, a necessary engagement, yet you did not," Rai-guy reminded her.

"I was tricked by Entreri and captured," the woman protested.

"Failure is failure," Rai-guy said. "Failure brings punishment—or worse."

"But I escaped and warned you of Entreri's run to Jarlaxle's side," Sharlotta argued.

"Escaped?" Rai-guy asked incredulously. "By your own words, the halfling was too afraid to keep you and so she let you go."

Those words rang uncomfortably in Kimmuriel's thoughts. Had that, too, been a part of Entreri's plan? Because had not Kimmuriel and Rai-guy arrived at the crystalline tower in Dallabad at precisely the wrong moment for the coup? With the Crystal Shard hidden away somewhere and an imitation playing decoy to their greatest efforts? A curious thought, and one the drow psionicist figured he might just take up with that halfling, Dwahvel Tiggerwillies, at a later time.

"I came straight to you," Sharlotta said plainly and forcefully, speaking then like someone who had at last come to understand that she had absolutely nothing left to lose.

"Failure is failure," Rai-guy reiterated, just as forcefully.

"But we are not unmerciful," Kimmuriel added immediately. "I even believe in the possibility of redemption. Artemis Entreri put you in this unfortunate position, so you say, so find him and kill him. Bring me his head, or I shall take your own."

Sharlotta held up her hands helplessly. "Where to begin?" she asked. "What resources—"

"All the resources and every soldier of House Basadoni and of Dallabad, and the complete cooperation of that rat creature and its minions," Kimmuriel replied.

Sharlotta's expression remained skeptical, but there flashed a twinkle in her eyes that Kimmuriel did not miss. She was outraged at Artemis Entreri for all of this, at least as much as were Rai-guy and Kimmuriel. Yes, she was cunning and a worthy adversary. Her efforts to find and destroy Entreri would certainly aid Kimmuriel and Rai-guy's efforts to neutralize Jarlaxle and the dangerous Crystal Shard.

"When do I begin?" Sharlotta asked.

"Why are you still here?" Kimmuriel asked.

The woman took the cue and began scrambling to her feet. The drow guards took the cue, too, and rushed to help her up, quickly unlocking her chains.

CHAPTER

DEAR DWAHVEL

15

A h, my friend, how you have deceived me," Jarlaxle whispered to Entreri, whose wounds had far from healed, leaving him in a weakened, almost helpless state. As Entreri had floated into semiconsciousness, Jarlaxle, possessed of the magic to heal him fully, had instead taken the time to consider all that had happened.

He was in the process of trying to figure out if Entreri had saved him or damned him when he heard an all-too familiar call.

Jarlaxle's gaze fell over Entreri and a great smile widened on his black-skinned face. Crenshinibon! The man had Crenshinibon! Jarlaxle replayed the events in his mind and quickly figured that Entreri had done more than simply cut the pouch loose from Jarlaxle's belt in that first, unexpected attack. No, the clever—so clever!—human had switched Jarlaxle's pouch for an imitation pouch, complete with an imitation Crystal Shard.

"My sneaky companion," the mercenary remarked, though he wasn't sure if Entreri could hear him or not. "It is good to know that once again, I have not underestimated you!" As he finished, the mercenary leader went for Entreri's belt pouch, smiling all the while.

The assassin's hand snapped up and grabbed Jarlaxle by the arm.

Jarlaxle had a dagger in his free hand in the blink of an eye, prepared to stab it through the nearly helpless man's heart, but he noted that Entreri wasn't pressing the attack any further. The assassin wasn't reaching for his dagger or any other weapon, but rather, was staring at Jarlaxle plaintively. In his head, Jarlaxle could hear the Crystal Shard calling to him, beckoning him to finish this man off and take back the artifact that was rightfully his.

He almost did it, despite the fact that Crenshinibon's call wasn't nearly as powerful and melodious as it had been when he had been in possession of the artifact.

"Do not," Entreri whispered to him. "You cannot control it."

Jarlaxle pulled back, staring hard at the man. "But you can?"

"That is why it is calling to you," Entreri replied, his breath even more labored than it had been earlier, and blood flowing again from the wound in his side. "The Crystal Shard has no hold over me."

"And why is that?" Jarlaxle asked doubtfully. "Has Artemis Entreri taken up the moral code of Drizzt Do'Urden?"

Entreri started to chuckle, but grimaced instead, the pain nearly unbearable. "Drizzt and I are not so different in many ways," he explained. "In discipline, at least."

"And discipline alone will keep the Crystal Shard from controlling you?" Jarlaxle asked, his tone still one of abject disbelief. "So, you are saying that I am not as disciplined as either of—"

"No!" Entreri growled, and he nearly came up to a sitting position as he tightened his side against a wave of pain.

"No," he said more calmly a moment later, easing back and breathing hard. "Drizzt's code denied the artifact, as does my own—not a code of morality, but one of independence."

Jarlaxle fell back a bit, his expression going from doubtful to curious. "Why did you take it?"

Entreri looked at him and started to respond but wound up just grimacing. Jarlaxle reached under the folds of his cloak and produced a small orb, which he held out to Entreri as he began to chant.

The assassin felt better almost immediately, felt his wound closing and his breathing easier to control. Jarlaxle chanted for a few seconds, each one making Entreri feel that much better, but long before the healing had been completely facilitated, the mercenary stopped.

"Answer my question," he demanded.

"They were coming to kill you," Entreri replied.

"Obviously," said Jarlaxle. "Could you not have merely warned me?"

"It would not have been enough," Entreri insisted. "There were too many against you, and they knew that your primary weapon would be the artifact. Thus, they neutralized it, temporarily."

Jarlaxle's first instinct was to demand the Crystal Shard again, that he could go back and repay Rai-guy and Kimmuriel for their treachery. He held the thought, though, and let Entreri go on.

"They were right in wanting to take it from you," the assassin finished boldly.

Jarlaxle glared at him but just for a moment.

"Step back from it," Entreri advised. "Shut out its call and consider the actions of Jarlaxle over the last few tendays. You could not remain on the surface unless your true identity remained secret, yet you brought forth crystalline towers! Bregan D'aerthe, for all of its power, and with all of the power of Crenshinibon behind it, could not rule the world—not even the city of Calimport—yet look at what you tried to do."

Jarlaxle started to respond several times, but each of his arguments died in his throat before he could begin to offer them. The assassin was right, he knew. He had erred, and badly.

"We cannot go back and try to explain this to the usurpers," the mercenary remarked.

Entreri shook his head. "It was the Crystal Shard that inspired the coup against you," he explained, and Jarlaxle fell back as if slapped. "You were too cunning, but Crenshinibon figured that ambitious Rai-guy would easily fall to its chaotic plans."

"You say that to placate me," Jarlaxle accused.

"I say that because it is the truth, nothing more," Entreri replied. Then he had to pause and grimace as a spasm of pain came over him. "And, if you take the time to consider it, you know that it is. Crenshinibon kept you moving in its preferred direction but not without interference."

"The Crystal Shard did not control me, or it did. You cannot have it both ways."

"It did manipulate you. How can you doubt that?" Entreri replied. "But not to the level that it knew it could manipulate Rai-guy."

"I went to Dallabad to destroy the crystal tower, something the artifact surely did not desire," Jarlaxle argued, "and yet, I could have done it! All interference from the shard was denied."

He continued, or tried to, but Entreri easily cut him short. "You *could* have done it?" the assassin asked incredulously.

Jarlaxle stammered to reply. "Of course."

"But you did not?"

"I saw no reason to drop the tower as soon as I knew that I could . . ." Jarlaxle started to explain, but when he actually heard the words coming out of his mouth, it hit him, and hard. He had been duped. He, the master of intrigue, had been fooled into believing that he was in control.

"Leave it with me," Entreri said to him. "The Crystal Shard tries to manipulate me, constantly, but it has nothing to offer me that I truly desire, and thus, it has no power over me."

"It will wear at you," Jarlaxle told him. "It will find every weakness and exploit them."

Entreri nodded. "Its time is running short," he remarked.

Jarlaxle looked at him curiously.

"I would not have spent the energy and the time pulling you away from those wretches if I did not have a plan," the assassin remarked.

"Tell me."

"In time," the assassin promised. "Now I beg of you not to take the Crystal Shard, and I beg of you, too, to allow me to rest."

He settled back and closed his eyes, knowing full well that the only defense he would have if Jarlaxle came at him was the Crystal Shard. He knew that if he used the artifact, it would likely find many, many ways to weaken his defenses and the effect might be that he would abandon his mission and simply let the artifact become his guide.

His guide to destruction, he knew, and perhaps to a fate worse than death.

When Entreri looked at Jarlaxle, he was somewhat comforted, for he saw again that clever and opportunistic demeanor, that visage of one who thought things through carefully before taking any definitive and potentially rash actions. Given all that Entreri had just explained to the mercenary drow, the retrieval of Crenshinibon would have to fall into that very category. No, he trusted that Jarlaxle would not move against him. The mercenary drow would let things play out a bit longer before making any move to alter a situation he obviously didn't fully comprehend.

With that thought in mind, Entreri fell fast asleep.

Even as he was drifting off, he felt the healing magic of Jarlaxle's orb falling over him again.

The halfling was surprised to see her fingers trembling as she carefully unrolled the note.

"Why Artemis, I did not even know you could write," Dwahvel said with a snicker, for the lines on the parchment were beautifully constructed, if a bit spare and efficient for Dwahvel's flamboyant flair. "My dear Dwahvel," she read aloud, and she paused and considered the words, not certain how she should take that greeting. Was it a formal and proper heading, or a sign of true friendship?

It occurred to the halfling then how little she really understood what went on inside of the heart of Artemis Entreri. The assassin had always claimed that his only desire was to be the very best, but if that was true why didn't he put the Crystal Shard to devastating use soon after acquiring it? And Dwahvel knew that he had it. Her contacts at Dallabad had described in detail the tumbling of the crystalline towers, and the flight of a human, Entreri, and a dark elf, whom Dwahvel had to believe must be Jarlaxle.

All indications were that Entreri's plan had succeeded. Even without her eyewitness accounts and despite the well-earned reputations of his adversaries, Dwahvel had never doubted the man.

The halfling moved to her doorway and made certain it was locked. Then she took a seat at her small night table and placed the parchment flat upon it, holding down the ends with paperweights fashioned of huge jewels, and read on, deciding to hold her analysis for the second read through.

My dear Dwahvel,

> *And so the time has come for us to part ways, and I do so with more than a small measure of regret. I will miss our talks, my little friend. Rarely have I known one I could trust enough to so speak what was truly on my mind. I will do so now, one final time, not in any hopes that you will advise me of my way, but only so that I might more clearly come to understand my own feelings on these matters . . . but that was always the beauty of our talks, was it not?*
>
> *Now that I consider those discussions, I recognize that you rarely offered any advice. In fact, you rarely spoke at all but simply listened. As I listened to my own words, and in hearing them, in explaining my thoughts and feelings to another, I came to sort them through. Was it your expressions, a simple nod, an arched eyebrow, that led me purposefully down different roads of reasoning?*
>
> *I know not.*
>
> *I know not—that has apparently become the litany of my existence, Dwahvel. I feel as if the foundation upon which I have built my beliefs and actions is not a solid thing, but one as shifting as the sands of the desert. When I was younger, I knew all the answers to all the questions. I existed in a world of surety and certainty. Now that I am older, now that I have seen four decades of life, the only thing I know for certain is that I know nothing for certain.*

147

It was so much easier to be a young man of twenty, so much easier to walk the world with a purpose grounded in—

Grounded in hatred, I suppose, and in the need to be the very best at my dark craft. That was my purpose, to be the greatest warrior in all of the world, to etch my name into the histories of Faerûn. So many people believed that I wished to achieve that out of simple pride, that I wanted people to tremble at the mere mention of my name for the sake of my vanity.

They were partially right, I suppose. We are all vain, whatever arguments we might make against the definition. For me, though, the desire to further my reputation was not as important as the desire—no, not the desire, but the need—truly to be the very best at my craft. I welcomed the increase in reputation, not for the sake of my pride, but because I knew that having such fear weaving through the emotional armor of my opponents gave me even more of an advantage.

A trembling hand does not thrust the blade true.

I still aspire to the pinnacle, fear not, but only because it offers me some purpose in a life that increasingly brings me no joy.

It seems a strange twist to me that I learned of the barren nature of my world only when I defeated the one person who tried in so many ways to show that very thing to me. Drizzt Do'Urden—how I still hate him!—perceived my life as an empty thing, a hollow trapping with no true benefit and no true happiness. I never really disagreed with his assessment, I merely believed that it did not matter. His reason for living was ever based upon his friends and community, while mine was more a life of the self. Either way, it seems to me as if it is just a play, and a pointless one, an act for the pleasure of the viewing gods, a walk that takes us up hills we perceive as huge, but that are really just little mounds, and through valleys that appear so very deep, but are really nothing at all that truly matters. All the pettiness of life itself is my complaint, I fear.

Or perhaps it was not Drizzt who showed me the shifting sands beneath my feet. Perhaps it was Dwahvel, who gave to me something I've rarely known and never known well.

A friend? I am still not certain that I understand the concept, but if I ever bother to attempt to sort through it, I will use our time together as a model.

Thus, this is perhaps a letter of apology. I should not have forced Sharlotta Vespers upon you, though I trust that you tortured her to death as I instructed and buried her far, far away.

How many times you asked me my plans, and always I merely laughed, but you should know, dear Dwahvel, that my intent is to steal a great and powerful artifact before other interested parties get their hands upon it. It is a desperate attempt, I know, but I cannot help myself, for the artifact calls to me, demands of me that I take it from its current, less-than-able wielder.

So I will have it, because I am indeed the best at my craft, and I will be gone, far, far from this place, perhaps never to return.

Farewell, Dwahvel Tiggerwillies, in whatever venture you attempt. You owe me nothing, I assure you, and yet I feel as if I am in your debt.

The road before me is long and fraught with peril, but I have my goal in sight. If I attain it, nothing will truly bring me any harm.
Farewell!

—AE

Dwahvel Tiggerwillies pushed aside the parchment and wiped a tear from her eye, and laughed at the absurdity of it all. If anyone had told her months before that she would regret the day Artemis Entreri walked out of her life, she would have laughed at him and called him a fool.

But here it was, a letter as intimate as any of the discussions Dwahvel had shared with Entreri. She found that she missed those discussions already, or perhaps she lamented that there would be no such future talks with the man. None in the near future, at least.

Entreri would also miss those talks by his own words. That struck Dwahvel profoundly. To think that she had so engaged this man—this killer who had secretly ruled Calimport's streets off and on for more than twenty years. Had anyone ever become so close to Artemis Entreri?

None who were still alive, Dwahvel knew.

She reread the ending of the letter, the obvious lies concerning Entreri's intentions. He had taken care not to mention anything that would tell the remaining dark elves that Dwahvel knew anything about them or the stolen artifact, or anything about his proffering of the Crystal Shard. His lie about his instructions concerning Sharlotta certainly added even more security to Dwahvel, buying her, should the need arise, some compassion from the woman and her secret backers.

That thought sent a shudder along Dwahvel's spine. She really didn't want to depend on the compassion of dark elves!

It would not come to that, she realized. Even if the trail led to her and her establishment, she could willingly and eagerly show Sharlotta the letter and Sharlotta would then see her as a valuable asset.

Yes, Artemis Entreri had taken great pains to cover Dwahvel's efforts in the conspiracy, and that, more than any of the kind words he had written to her, revealed to her the depth of their friendship.

"Run far, my friend, and hide in deep holes," she whispered.

She gently rerolled the parchment and placed it in one of the drawers of her crafted bureau. The sound of that closing drawer resonated hard against Dwahvel's heart.

She would indeed miss Artemis Entreri.

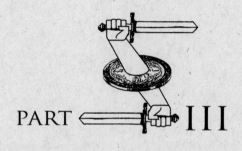

PART III

NOW WHAT?

There is a simple beauty in the absolute ugliness of demons. There is no ambiguity there, no hesitation, no misconception, about how one must deal with such creatures. You do not parlay with demons. You do not hear their lies. You cast them out, destroy them, rid the world of them—even if the temptation is present to utilize their powers to save what you perceive to be a little corner of goodness.

This is a difficult concept for many to grasp and has been the downfall of many wizards and priests who have errantly summoned demons and allowed the creatures to move beyond their initial purpose—the answering of a question, perhaps—because they were tempted by the power offered by the creature. Many of these doomed spellcasters thought they would be doing good by forcing the demons to their side, by bolstering their cause, their army, with demonic soldiers. What ill, they supposed, if the end result proved to the greater good? Would not a goodly king be well advised to add "controlled" demons to his cause if goblins threatened his lands?

I think not, because if the preservation of goodness relies upon the use of such obvious and irredeemable evil to defeat evil, then there is nothing, truly, worth saving.

The sole use of demons, then, is to bring them forth only in times when they must betray the cause of evil, and only in a setting so controlled that there is no hope of their escape. Cadderly has done this within the secure summoning chamber of the Spirit Soaring, as have, I am sure, countless priests and wizards. Such a summoning is not without peril, though, even if the circle of protection is perfectly formed, for there is always a temptation that goes with the manipulation of powers such as a balor or a nalfeshnie.

Within that temptation must always lie the realization of irredeemable evil. Irredeemable. Without hope. That concept, redemption, must be the crucial determinant in any such dealings. Temper your blade when redemption is possible, hold it when redemption is at hand, and strike hard and without remorse when your opponent is beyond any hope of redemption.

Where on that scale does Artemis Entreri lie, I wonder? Is the man truly beyond help and hope?

Yes, to the former, I believe, and no to the latter. There is no help for Artemis Entreri because the man would never accept any. His greatest flaw is his pride—not the boasting

153

pride of so many lesser warriors, but the pride of absolute independence and unbending self-reliance. I could tell him his errors, as could anyone who has come to know him in any way, but he would not hear my words.

Yet perhaps there may be hope of some redemption for the man. I know not the source of his anger, though it must have been great. And yet I will not allow that the source, however difficult and terrible it might have been, in any way excuses the man from his actions. The blood on Entreri's sword and trademark dagger is his own to wear.

He does not wear it well, I believe. It burns at his skin as might the breath of a black dragon and gnaws at all that is within him. I saw that during our last encounter, a quiet and dull ache at the side of his dark eyes. I had him beaten, could have killed him, and I believe that in many ways he hoped I would finish the task and be done with it, and end his mostly self-imposed suffering.

That ache is what held my blade, that hope within me that somewhere deep inside Artemis Entreri there is the understanding that his path needs to change, that the road he currently walks is one of emptiness and ultimate despair. Many thoughts coursed my mind as I stood there, weapons in hand, with him defenseless before me. How could I strike when I saw that pain in his eyes and knew that such pain might well be the precursor to redemption? And yet how could I not, when I was well aware that letting Artemis Entreri walk out of that crystalline tower might spell the doom of others?

Truly it was a dilemma, a crisis of conscience and of balance. I found my answer in that critical moment in the memory of my father, Zaknafein. To Entreri's thinking, I know, he and Zaknafein are not so different, and there are indeed similarities. Both existed in an environment hostile and to their respective perceptions evil. Neither, to their perceptions, did either go out of his way to kill anyone who did not deserve it. Are the warriors and assassins who fight for the wretched pashas of Calimport any better than the soldiers of the drow houses? Thus, in many ways, the actions of Zaknafein and those of Artemis Entreri are quite similar. Both existed in a world of intrigue, danger, and evil. Both survived their imprisonment through ruthless means. If Entreri views his world, his prison, as full of wretchedness as Zaknafein viewed Menzoberranzan, then is not Entreri as entitled to his manner as was Zaknafein, the weapons master who killed many, many dark elves in his tenure as patron of House Do'Urden?

It is a comparison I realized when first I went to Calimport, in pursuit of Entreri, who had taken Regis as prisoner (and even that act had justification, I must admit), and a comparison that truly troubled me. How close are they, given their abilities with the blade and their apparent willingness to kill? Was it, then, some inner feelings for Zaknafein that stayed my blade when I could have cut Entreri down?

No, I say, and I must believe, for Zaknafein was far more discerning in whom he would kill or would not kill. I know the truth of Zaknafein's heart. I know that Zaknafein was possessed of the ability to love, and the reality of Artemis Entreri simply cannot hold up against that.

Not in his present incarnation, at least, but is there hope that the man will find a light beneath the murderous form of the assassin?

Perhaps, and I would be glad indeed to hear that the man so embraced that light. In truth, though, I doubt that anyone or anything will ever be able to pull that lost flame of compassion through the thick and seemingly impenetrable armor of dispassion that Artemis Entreri now wears.

—Drizzt Do'Urden

CHAPTER

16

Danica sat on a ledge of an imposing mountain beside the field that housed the magnificent Spirit Soaring, a cathedral of towering spires and flying buttresses, of great and ornate windows of multicolored glass. Acres of grounds were striped by well-maintained hedgerows, many of them shaped into the likeness of animals, and one wrapping around and around itself in a huge maze.

The cathedral was the work of Danica's husband, Cadderly, a mighty priest of Deneir, the god of knowledge. This structure had been Cadderly's most obvious legacy, but his greatest one, to Danica's reasoning, were the twin children romping around the entrance to the maze and their younger sibling, sleeping within the cathedral. The twins had gone running into the hedgerow maze, much to the dismay of the dwarf Pikel Bouldershoulder. Pikel, a practitioner of the druidic ways—magic that his surly brother Ivan still denied—had created the maze and the other amazing gardens.

Pikel had gone running into the maze behind the children screaming, *"Eeek!"* and other such Pikelisms, and pulling at his green-dyed hair and beard. His maze wasn't quite ready for visitors yet, and the roots hadn't properly set.

Of course, as soon as Pikel had gone running in, the twins had sneaked right back out and were now playing quietly in front of the maze entrance. Danica didn't know how far along the confusing corridors the green-bearded dwarf had gone, but she had heard his voice fast receding and figured that he'd be lost in the maze, for the third time that day, soon enough.

A wind gust came whipping across the mountain wall, blowing Danica's thick mop of strawberry blond hair into her face. She blew some strands out of her mouth and tossed her head to the side, just in time to see Cadderly walking toward her.

What a fine figure he cut in his tan-white tunic and trousers, his light blue silken cape and his trademark blue, wide-brimmed, and plumed hat. Cadderly had aged greatly while constructing the Spirit Soaring, to the point where he and Danica honestly believed he would expire. Much to Danica's dismay Cadderly had expected to die and had accepted that as the sacrifice necessary for the construction of the monumental library. Soon after he had completed the construction of the main building—the details, like the ornate designs of the many doors and the golden leaf work around the beautiful archways, might never be completed—the aging process had reversed, and the man had grown younger almost as fast as he'd aged. Now he seemed a man in his late twenties with a spring in his step, and a twinkle in his eye every time he glanced Danica's way. Danica had even worried that this process would continue, and that soon she'd find herself raising four children instead of three.

He eventually grew no younger, though, stopping at the point where Cadderly seemed every bit the vivacious and healthy young man he had been before all the trouble had started within the Edificant Library, the structure that had stood on this ground before the advent of the chaos curse and the destruction of the old order of Deneir. The willingness to sacrifice everything for the new cathedral and the new order had sufficed in the eyes of Deneir, and thus, Cadderly Bonaduce had been given back his life, a life so enriched by the addition of his wife and their children.

"I had a visitor this morning," Cadderly said to her when he moved beside her. He cast a glance at the twins and smiled all the wider when he heard another frantic call from the lost Pikel.

Danica marveled at how her husband's gray eyes seemed to smile as well. "A man from Carradoon," she replied, nodding. "I saw him enter."

"Bearing word from Drizzt Do'Urden," Cadderly explained, and Danica turned to face him directly, suddenly very interested. She and Cadderly had met the unusual dark elf the previous year and had taken him back to the northland using one of Cadderly's wind-walking spells.

Danica spent a moment studying Cadderly, considering the intense expression upon his normally calm face. "He has retrieved the Crystal Shard," she reasoned, for when last she and Cadderly had been with Drizzt and his human companion, Catti-brie, they had spoken of just that. Drizzt promised that he would retrieve the ancient, evil artifact and bring it to Cadderly to be destroyed.

"He did," Cadderly said.

He handed a roll of parchment sheets to Danica. She took them and unrolled them. A smile crossed her face when she learned of the fate of Drizzt's lost friend, Wulfgar, freed from his prison at the clutches of the demon Errtu. By the time she got to the second page, though, Danica's mouth drooped open, for the note went on to describe the subsequent theft of the Crystal Shard by a rogue dark elf named Jarlaxle, who had sent one of his drow soldiers to Drizzt in the guise of Cadderly.

Danica paused and looked up, and Cadderly took back the parchments. "Drizzt believes the artifact has likely gone underground, back to the dark elf city of Menzoberranzan, where Jarlaxle makes his home," he explained.

"Well, good enough for Menzoberranzan, then," Danica said in all seriousness.

She and Cadderly had discussed the powers of the sentient shard at length, and she understood it to be a tool of destruction—destruction of the wielder's enemies, of the wielder's allies, and ultimately of the wielder himself. There had never been, and to Cadderly's reasoning, could never be, a different outcome where Crenshinibon was concerned. To possess the Crystal Shard was, ultimately, a terminal disease, and woe to all those nearby.

Cadderly was shaking his head before Danica ever finished the sentiment. "The Crystal Shard is an artifact of sunlight, which is perhaps, in the measure of symbolism, its greatest perversion."

"But the drow are creatures of their dark holes," Danica reasoned. "Let them take it and be gone. Perhaps in the Underdark, the Crystal Shard's power will be lessened, even destroyed."

Again Cadderly was shaking his head. "Who is the stronger?" he asked. "The artifact or the wielder?"

"It sounds as if this particular dark elf was quite cunning," Danica replied. "To have fooled Drizzt Do'Urden is no easy feat, I would guess."

Cadderly shrugged and grinned. "I doubt that Crenshinibon, once it finds its way into the new wielder's heart—which it surely will unless this Jarlaxle is akin in heart to Drizzt Do'Urden—will allow him to retreat to the depths," he explained. "It is not necessarily a question of who is the stronger. The subtlety of the artifact is its ability to manipulate its wielder into agreement, not dominate him."

"And the heart of a dark elf would be easily manipulated," Danica reasoned.

"A typical dark elf, yes," Cadderly agreed.

A few moments of quiet passed as each considered the words and the new information.

"What are we to do, then?" Danica asked at length. "If you believe that the Crystal Shard will not allow a retreat to the sunless Underdark, then are we to allow it to wreak havoc on the surface world? Do we even know where it might be?"

Still deep in thought, Cadderly did not answer right away. The question of what to do, of what their responsibilities might be in this situation, went to the very core of the philosophical trappings of power. Was it Cadderly's place, because of his clerical power, to hunt down the new wielder of the Crystal Shard, this dark elf thief, and take the item by force, bringing it to its destruction? If that was the case, then what of every other injustice in the world? What of the pirates on the Sea of Fallen Stars? Was Cadderly to charter a boat and go out hunting them? What of the Red Wizards of Thay, that notorious band? Was it Cadderly's duty to seek them out and do battle with each and every one? Then there were the Zhentarim, the Iron Throne, the Shadow Thieves. . . .

"Do you remember when we met here with Drizzt Do'Urden and Catti-brie?" Danica asked, and it seemed to Cadderly that the woman was reading his mind. "Drizzt was distressed when we realized that our summoning of the demon Errtu had released the great beast from its banishment—a banishment handed out to it by Drizzt years before. What did you tell Drizzt about that to calm him?"

"The releasing of Errtu was no major problem," Cadderly admitted again. "There would always be a demon available to a sorcerer with evil designs. If not Errtu, then another."

"Errtu was just one of a number of agents of chaos," Danica reasoned, "as the Crystal Shard is just another element of chaos. Any havoc it brings would merely replace the myriad other tools of chaos in wreaking exactly that, correct?"

Cadderly smiled at her, staring intently into the seemingly limitless depths of her almond-shaped brown eyes. How he loved this woman. She was so much his partner in every aspect of his life. Intelligent and possessed of the greatest discipline Cadderly had ever known, Danica always helped him through any difficult questions and choices, just by listening and offering suggestions.

"It is the heart that begets evil, not the instruments of destruction," he completed the thought for her.

"Is the Crystal Shard the tool or the heart?" Danica asked.

"That is the question, is it not?" Cadderly replied. "Is the artifact akin to a summoned monster, an instrument of destruction for one whose heart was already tainted? Or is it a manipulator, a creator of evil where there would otherwise be none?" He held out his arms, having no real answer for that. "In either case, I believe I will contact some extra-planar sources and see if I can locate the artifact and this dark elf, Jarlaxle. I wish to know the use to which he has put the Crystal Shard, or perhaps even more troubling, the use to which the Crystal Shard plans to put him."

Danica started to ask what he might be talking about, but she figured it out before she could utter the words, and her lips grew very thin. Might the Crystal Shard, rather than let this Jarlaxle creature take it to the lightless Underdark, use him to spearhead an invasion by an army of drow? Might the Crystal Shard use the position and race of its new wielder to create havoc beyond anything it had ever known before? Even worse for them personally, if Jarlaxle had stolen the artifact by using an imitation of Cadderly, then Jarlaxle certainly knew of Cadderly. If Jarlaxle knew, the Crystal Shard knew—and knew, too, that Cadderly might have information about how to destroy it. A flash of worry crossed Danica's face, one that Cadderly could not miss, and she instinctively turned to regard her children.

"I will try to discover where he might be with the artifact, and what trouble they together might already be causing," Cadderly explained, not reading Danica's expression very well and wondering, perhaps, if she was doubting him.

"You do that," the more-than-convinced woman said in all seriousness. "Right away."

A squeal from inside the maze turned them both in that direction.

"Pikel," the woman explained.

Cadderly smiled. "Lost again?"

"Again?" Danica asked. "Or still?"

They heard some rumbling off to the side and saw Pikel's more traditional brother, Ivan Bouldershoulder, rolling toward the maze grumbling with every step. "Doo-dad," the yellow-bearded dwarf said sarcastically, referring to Pikel's pronunciation of his calling. "Yeah, Doo-dad," Ivan grumbled. "Can't even find his way out of a hedgerow."

"And you will help him?" Cadderly called to the dwarf.

Ivan turned curiously, noting the pair, it seemed, for the first time. "Been helpin' him all me life," he snorted.

Both Cadderly and Danica nodded and allowed Ivan his fantasy. They knew well enough, if Ivan did not, that his helping Pikel more often caused problems for both of the dwarves. Sure enough, within the span of a few minutes, Ivan's calls about being lost echoed no less than Pikel's. Cadderly and Danica, and the twins sitting outside the devious maze, thoroughly enjoyed the entertainment.

A few hours later, after preparing the proper sequence of spells and after checking on the magical circle of protection the young-again priest always used when dealing with even the most minor of the creatures of the lower planes, Cadderly sat in a cross-legged position on the floor of his summoning chamber, chanting the incantation that would bring a minor demon, an imp, to him.

A short while later, the tiny, bat-winged, horned creature materialized in the protection circle. It hopped all about, confused and angry, finally focusing on Cadderly. It spent some time studying the man, no doubt trying to get some clues to his demeanor. Imps were often summoned to the material plane, sometimes for information, other times to serve as familiars for wizards of evil weal.

"Deneir?" the imp asked in a coughing, raspy voice that Cadderly thought seemed both typical and fitting to its smoky natural environment. "You wear the clothing of a priest of Deneir."

The creature was staring at the red band on his hat, Cadderly knew, on which was set a porcelain-and-gold pendant depicting a candle burning above an eye, the symbol of Deneir.

Cadderly nodded.

"Ahck!" the imp said and spat upon the ground.

"Hoping for a wizard in search of a familiar?" Cadderly asked slyly.

"Hoping for anything other than you, priest of Deneir," the imp replied.

"Accept that which has been given to you," Cadderly said. "A glimpse of the material plane is better than none, after all, and a reprieve from your hellish existence."

"What do you want, priest of Deneir?"

"Information," Cadderly replied, but even as he said it, he realized that his questions would be difficult indeed, perhaps too much so for so minor a demon. "All that I require of you is that you give to me the name of a greater demonic source, that I might bring it forth."

The imp looked at him curiously, tilting its head as a dog might, and licking its thin lips with a pointed tongue.

"Nothing greater than a nalfeshnie," Cadderly quickly clarified, seeing the impish smile growing and wanting to limit the power of whatever being he next summoned. A nalfeshnie was no minor demon, but was certainly within Cadderly's power to control, at least long enough for him to get what he needed.

"Oh, I has a name for you, priest of Deneir . . ." the imp started to say, but it jerked spasmodically as Cadderly began to chant a spell of torment. The imp fell to the floor, writhing and spitting curses.

"The name?" Cadderly asked. "And I warn you, if you deceive me and try to trick me into summoning a greater creature, I will dismiss it promptly and find you again. This torment is nothing compared to that which I will exact upon you!"

He said the words with conviction and with strength, though in truth, it pained the gentle man to be doing even this level of torture, even upon a wretched imp. He reminded himself of the importance of his quest and bolstered his resolve.

"Mizferac!" the imp screamed out. "A glabrezu, and a stupid one!"

Cadderly released the imp from his spell of torment, and the creature gave a beat of its wings and righted itself, staring at him coldly. "I did your bidding, evil priest of Deneir. Let me go!"

"Be gone, then," said Cadderly, and even as the little beast began fading from view, offering a few obscene gestures, Cadderly had to toss in, "I will tell Mizferac what you said concerning its intelligence."

He did indeed enjoy that last expression of panic on the face of the little imp.

Cadderly brought Mizferac in later that same day and found the towering pincer-armed glabrezu to be the embodiment of all that he hated about demons. It was a nasty, vicious, conniving, and wretchedly self-serving creature that tried to get as much gain as it could out of every word. Cadderly kept their meeting short and to the point. The demon was to inquire of other extra-planar creatures about the whereabouts of a dark elf named Jarlaxle, who was likely on the surface of Faerûn. Furthermore, Cadderly put a powerful geas on the demon, preventing it from actually walking the material world, but retreating only back to the Abyss and using sources to discern the information.

"That will take longer," Mizferac said.

"I will call on you daily," Cadderly replied, putting as much anger without adding any passion whatsoever as he could into his timbre. "Each passing day I will grow more impatient, and your torment will increase."

"You make a terrible enemy in Mizferac, Cadderly Bonaduce, Priest of Deneir," the glabrezu replied, obviously trying to shake him with its knowledge of his name.

Cadderly, who heard the mighty song of Deneir as clearly as if it was a chord within his own heart, merely smiled at the threat. "If ever you find yourself free of your bonds and able to walk the surface of Toril, do come and find me, Mizferac the fool. It will please me greatly to reduce your physical form to ash and banish your spirit from this world for a hundred years."

The demon growled, and Cadderly dismissed it, simply and with just a wave of his hand and an utterance of a single word. He had heard every threat a demon could give and many times. After the trials the young priest had known in his life, from facing a red dragon to doing battle with his own father, to warring against the chaos curse, to, most of all, offering his very life up as sacrifice to his god, there was little any creature, demonic or not, could say to him that would frighten him.

He recalled the glabrezu every day for the next tenday, until finally the fiend brought him some news of the Crystal Shard and the drow, Jarlaxle, along with the surprising information that Jarlaxle no longer possessed the artifact, but traveled in the company of a human, Artemis Entreri, who did.

Cadderly knew that name well from the stories that Drizzt and Catti-brie had told him in their short stay at the Spirit Soaring. The man was an assassin, a brutal killer. According to the demon, Entreri, along with the Crystal Shard and the dark elf Jarlaxle, was on his way to the Snowflake Mountains.

Cadderly rubbed his chin as the glabrezu passed along the information—information that he knew to be true, for he had enacted a spell to make certain the demon had not lied to him.

"I have done as you demanded," the glabrezu growled, clicking its pincer-ended appendages anxiously. "I am released from your bonds, Cadderly Bonaduce."

"Then begone, that I do not have to look upon your ugly face any longer," the young priest replied.

The demon narrowed its huge eyes threateningly and clicked its pincers. "I will not forget this," it promised.

"I would be disappointed if you did," Cadderly replied casually.

"I was told that you have young children, fool," Mizferac remarked, fading from view.

"Mizferac, *ehugu-winance!*" Cadderly cried, catching the departing demon before it had dissipated back to the swirling smoke of the Abyss. Holding it in place by the sheer strength of his enchantment, Cadderly twisted the demon's physical form painfully by the might of his spell.

"Do I smell fear, human?" Mizferac asked defiantly.

Cadderly smiled wryly. "I doubt that, since a hundred years will pass before you are able to walk the material plane again." The threat, spoken openly, freed Mizferac of the summoning binding—and yet, the beast was not freed, for Cadderly had enacted another spell, one of exaction.

Mizferac created magical darkness to fill the room. Cadderly fell into his own chanting, his voice trembling with feigned terror.

"I can smell you, foolish mortal," Mizferac remarked, and Cadderly heard the voice from the side, though he guessed correctly that Mizferac was using ventriloquism to throw him off guard. The young priest was fully into the flow of Deneir's song now, hearing every beautiful note and accessing the magic quickly and completely. First he detected evil, easily locating the great negative force of the glabrezu—then another mighty negative force as the demon gated in a companion.

Cadderly held his nerve and continued casting.

"I will kill the children first, fool," Mizferac promised, and it began speaking to its new companion in the guttural tongue of the Abyss—one that Cadderly, through the use of another spell that he had enacted before he had ever brought Mizferac to him this day, understood perfectly. The glabrezu told its fellow demon to keep the foolish priest occupied while it went to hunt the children.

"I will bring them before you for sacrifice," Mizferac started to promise, but the end of the sentence came out as garbled screams as Cadderly's spell went off, creating a series of spinning, slicing blades all around the two demons. The priest then brought forth a globe of light to counter Mizferac's darkness. The spectacle of Mizferac and its companion, a lesser demon that looked like a giant gnat, getting sliced and chopped was revealed.

Mizferac roared and uttered a guttural word—one designed to teleport him away, Cadderly assumed. It failed. The young priest, so strong in the flow of Deneir's song, was the quicker. He brought forth a prayer that dispelled the demon's magic before Mizferac could get away.

A spell of binding followed immediately, locking Mizferac firmly in place, while the magical blades continued their spinning devastation.

"I will never forget this!" Mizferac roared, words edged with outrage and agony.

"Good, then you will know better than ever to return," Cadderly growled back.

He brought forth a second blade barrier. The two demons were torn apart, their material forms ripped into dozens of bloody pieces, thus banishing them from the material plane for a hundred years. Satisfied with that, Cadderly left his summoning chamber covered in demon blood. He'd have to find a suitable spell from Deneir to clean up his clothes.

As for the Crystal Shard, he had his answers—and it seemed to him a good thing that he had bothered to check, since a dangerous assassin, an equally dangerous dark elf, and the even more dangerous Crystal Shard were apparently on their way to see him.

He had to talk to Danica, to prepare all the Spirit Soaring and the order of Deneir, for the potential battle.

CHAPTER

A CALL FOR HELP

17

"There is something enjoyable about these beasts, I must admit," Jarlaxle noted when he and Entreri pulled up beside a mountain pass.

The assassin quickly dismounted and ran to the ledge to view the trail below—and to view the band of orcs he suspected were still stubbornly in pursuit. The pair had left the desert behind, at long last, entering a region of broken hills and rocky trails.

"Though if I had one of my lizards from Menzoberranzan, I could simply run away to the top of the hill and over the other side," the drow went on. He took off his great plumed hat and rubbed a hand over his bald head. The sun was strong this day, but the dark elf seemed to be handling it quite well—certainly better than Entreri would have expected of any drow under this blistering sun. Again the assassin had to wonder if Jarlaxle might have a bit of magic about him to protect his sensitive eyes. "Useful beasts, the lizards of Menzoberranzan," Jarlaxle remarked. "I should have brought some to the surface with me."

Entreri gave him a smirk and a shake of his head. "It will be hard enough getting into half the towns with a drow beside me," he remarked. "How much more welcoming might they be if I rode in on a lizard?"

He looked back down the mountainside, and sure enough, the orc band was still pacing them, though the wretched creatures were obviously exhausted. Still, they followed as if compelled beyond their control.

It wasn't hard for Artemis Entreri to figure out exactly what might be so compelling them.

"Why can you not just take out your magical tent, that we can melt away from them?" Jarlaxle asked for the third time.

"The magic is limited," Entreri answered yet again.

He glanced back at Jarlaxle as he replied, surprised that the cunning drow would keep asking the same question. Was Jarlaxle, perhaps, trying to garner some information about the tent? Or even worse, was the Crystal Shard reaching out to the drow, subtly asking him to goad Entreri in that direction? If they did take out the tent and disappear, after all, they would have to reappear in the same place. That being true, had the Crystal Shard figured out how to send its telepathic call across the planes of existence? Perhaps the next time Entreri and Jarlaxle used the plane-shifting tent, they would return to the material plane to find an orc army, inspired by Crenshinibon, waiting for them.

"The horses grow weary," Jarlaxle noted.

"They can outrun orcs," Entreri replied.

"If we let them run free, perhaps."

"They're just orcs," Entreri muttered, though he could hardly believe how persistent this group remained.

He turned back to Jarlaxle, no longer doubting the drow's claim. The horses were indeed tired—they had been riding a long day before even realizing the orcs were following their trail. They had ridden the beasts practically into the desert sands in an effort to get out of that barren, wide-open region as quickly as possible.

Perhaps it was time to stop running.

"There are only about a score of them," Entreri remarked, watching their movements as they crawled over the lower slopes.

"Twenty against two," Jarlaxle reminded. "Let us go and hide in your tent, that the horses can rest, and come out and begin the chase anew."

"We can defeat them and drive them away," Entreri insisted, "if we choose and prepare the battlefield."

It surprised the assassin that Jarlaxle didn't look very eager about that possibility. "They're only orcs," Entreri said again.

"Are they?" Jarlaxle asked.

Entreri started to respond but paused long enough to consider the meaning behind the dark elf's words. Was this pursuit a chance encounter? Or was there something more to this seemingly nondescript band of monsters?

"You believe that Kimmuriel and Rai-guy are secretly guiding this band," Entreri stated more than asked.

Jarlaxle shrugged. "Those two have always favored using monsters as fodder," he explained. "They let the orcs—or kobolds, or whatever other creature is available—rush in to weary their opponents while they prepare the killing blow. It is nothing new in their tactics. They used such a ruse to take House Basadoni, forcing the kobolds to lead the charge and take the bulk of the casualties."

"It could be," Entreri agreed with a nod. "Or it could be a conspiracy of another sort, one with its roots in our midst."

It took Jarlaxle a few moments to sort that out. "Do you believe that I have urged the orcs on?" he asked.

In response, Entreri patted the pouch that held the Crystal Shard. "Perhaps Crenshinibon has come to believe that it needs to be rescued from our clutches," he said.

"The shard would prefer an orcish wielder to either you or me?" Jarlaxle asked doubtfully.

"I am not its wielder, nor will I ever be," Entreri answered sharply. "Nor will you, else you would have taken it from me our first night on the road from Dallabad, when I was too weak with my wounds to resist. I know this truth, so do you, and so does Crenshinibon. It understands that we are beyond its reach now, and it fears us, or fears me, at least, because it recognizes what is in my heart."

He spoke the words with perfect calm and perfect coldness, and it wasn't hard for Jarlaxle to figure out what he might be talking about. "You mean to destroy it," the drow remarked, and his tone made the sentence seem like an accusation.

"And I know how to do it," Entreri bluntly admitted. "Or at least, I know someone who knows how to do it."

The expressions that crossed Jarlaxle's handsome face ranged from incredulity to sheer anger to something less obvious, something buried deep. The assassin knew that he had taken a chance in proclaiming his intent so openly with the drow who had been fully duped by the Crystal Shard and who was still not completely convinced, despite Entreri's many reminders, that giving up the artifact had been a good thing to do. Was Jarlaxle's unreadable expression a signal to him that the Crystal Shard had indeed gotten to the drow leader once again and was even then working through, and with, Jarlaxle to find a way to get rid of Entreri's bothersome interference?

"You will never find the strength of heart to destroy it," Jarlaxle remarked.

Now it was Entreri's turn to wear a confused expression.

"Even if you discover a method, and I doubt that there is one, when the moment comes, Artemis Entreri will never find the heart to be rid of so powerful and potentially gainful an item as Crenshinibon," Jarlaxle proclaimed slyly. A grin widened across the dark elf's face. "I know you, Artemis Entreri," he said, grinning still, "and I know that you'll not throw away such power and promise, such beauty as Crenshinibon!"

Entreri looked at him hard. "Without the slightest hesitation," he said coldly. "And so would you, had you not fallen under its spell. I see that enchantment for what it is, a trap of temporary gain through reckless action that can only lead to complete and utter ruin. You disappoint me, Jarlaxle. I had thought you smarter than this."

Jarlaxle's expression, too, turned cold. A flash of anger lit his dark eyes. For just a moment, Entreri thought his first fight of the day was upon him, thought the dark elf would attack him. Jarlaxle closed his eyes, his body swaying as he focused his thoughts and his concentration.

"Fight the urge," the assassin found himself whispering under his breath. Entreri the consummate loner, the man who, for all his life, had counted on no one but himself, was surely surprised to hear himself now.

"Do we continue to run, or do we fight them?" Jarlaxle asked a moment later. "If these creatures are being guided by Rai-guy and Kimmuriel, we will learn of it soon enough—likely when we are fully engaged in battle. The odds of ten-to-one, of even twenty-to-one, against orcs on a mountain battlefield of our choosing does not frighten me in the least, but in truth, I do not wish to face my former lieutenants, even two-against-two. With his combination of wizardly and clerical powers, Rai-guy has variables enough to strike fear into the heart of Gromph Baenre, and there is nothing predictable, or even understandable, about many of Kimmuriel Oblodra's tactics. In all the years he has served me, I have not begun to sort the riddle that is Kimmuriel. I know only that he is extremely effective."

"Keep talking," Entreri muttered, looking back down at the orcs, who were much closer now, and at all the potential battlefield areas. "You are making me wish that I had left you and the Crystal Shard behind."

He caught a slight shift in Jarlaxle's expression as he said that, a subtle hint that perhaps the mercenary leader had been wondering all along why Entreri had bothered with both the theft and the rescue. If Entreri meant to destroy the Crystal Shard anyway, after all, why not just run away and leave it and the feud between Jarlaxle and his dangerous lieutenants behind?

"We will discuss that," Jarlaxle replied.

"Another time," Entreri said, trotting along the ledge to the right. "We have much to do, and our orc friends are in a hurry."

"Headlong into doom," Jarlaxle remarked quietly. He slid off of his horse and moved to follow Entreri.

Soon after, the pair had set up in a location on the northeastern side of the range, the steepest ascent. Jarlaxle worried that perhaps some of the orcs would come up from the other paths, the same ones they had taken, stealing from them the advantage of the higher ground, but Entreri was convinced that the artifact was calling out to the creatures insistently, and that they would alter their course to follow the most direct line to Crenshinibon. That line would take them up several high bluffs on this side of the hills, and along narrow and easily defensible trails.

Sure enough, within a few minutes of attaining their new perch, Entreri and Jarlaxle spotted the obedient and eager orc band, scrambling over stony outcroppings below them.

Jarlaxle began his customary chatting, but Entreri wasn't listening. He turned his thoughts inward, listening for the Crystal Shard, knowing that it was calling out to the orcs. He paid close heed to its subtle emanations, knowing them all too well from his time in possession of the item, for though he had denied the Crystal Shard, had made it as clear as possible that the artifact could offer him nothing, it had not relented its tempting call.

He heard that call now, drifting out over the mountain passes, reaching out to the orcs and begging them to come and find the treasure.

Halt the call, Entreri silently commanded the artifact. *These creatures are not worthy to serve either you or me as slaves.*

He sensed it then, a moment of confusion from the artifact, a moment of fleeting hope—there, Entreri knew without the slightest of doubts, Crenshinibon did desire him as a wielder!—followed by . . . questions. Entreri seized the moment to interject his own thoughts into the stream of the telepathic call. He offered no words, for he didn't even speak Orcish, and doubted that the creatures would understand any of the human tongues he did speak, but merely imparted images of orc slaves, serving the master dark elf. He figured Jarlaxle would be a more imposing figure to orcs than he. Entreri showed them one orc being eaten by drow, another being beaten and torn apart with savage glee.

"What are you doing, my friend?" he heard Jarlaxle's insistent call, in a loud voice that told him his drow companion had likely asked that same question several times already.

"Putting a little doubt into the minds of our ugly little camp-followers," Entreri replied. "Joining Crenshinibon's call to them in the hopes that they will hardly sort out one lie from the other."

Jarlaxle wore a perplexed expression indeed, and Entreri understood all the questions that were likely behind it, for he was harboring many of the same doubts. One lie from another indeed. Or were the promises of Crenshinibon truly lies?

the assassin had to ask himself. Even beyond that fundamental confusion, the assassin understood that Jarlaxle would, and had to, fear Entreri's motivations. Was Entreri, perhaps, shading his words to Jarlaxle in a way that would make the mercenary drow come to agree with Entreri's assessment that he, and not the dark elf, should carry the Crystal Shard?

"Ignore whatever doubts Crenshinibon is now giving to you," Entreri said matter-of-factly, reading the dark elf's expression perfectly.

"Even if you speak the truth, I fear that you play a dangerous game with an artifact that is far beyond your understanding," Jarlaxle retorted after another introspective pause.

"I know what it is," Entreri assured him, "and I know that it understands the truth of our relationship. That is why the Crystal Shard so desperately wants to be free of me—and is thus calling to you once more."

Jarlaxle looked at him hard, and for just a moment, Entreri thought the drow might move against him.

"Do not disappoint me," the assassin said simply.

Jarlaxle blinked, took off his hat, and rubbed the sweat from his bald head again.

"There!" Entreri said, pointing down to the lower slopes, to where a fight had broken out between different factions among the orcs. Few of the ugly brutes seemed to be trying to make peace, as was the way with chaotic orcs. The slightest spark could ignite warfare within a tribe of the beasts that would continue at the cost of many lives until one side was simply wiped out. Entreri, with his imparted images of torture and slavery and images of a drow master, had done more than flick a little spark. "It would seem that some of them heeded my call over that of the artifact."

"And I had thought this day would bring some excitement," Jarlaxle remarked. "Shall we join them before they kill each other? To aid whichever side is losing, of course."

"And with our aid, that side will soon be winning," Entreri reasoned, and Jarlaxle's quick response came as no surprise.

"Of course," said the drow, "we are then honor-bound to join in with the side that is losing. It could be a complicated afternoon."

Entreri smiled as he worked his way around the ledge of the current perch, looking for a quick way down to the orcs.

By the time the pair got close to the fighting, they realized that their estimates of a score of orcs had been badly mistaken. There were at least fifty of the beasts, all running around in a frenzy now, whacking at each other with abandon, using clubs, branches, sharpened sticks, and a few crafted weapons.

Jarlaxle tipped his hat to the assassin, motioned for Entreri to go left, and went right, blending into the shadows so perfectly that Entreri had to blink to make sure they were not deceiving him. He knew that Jarlaxle, like all dark elves, was stealthy. Likewise he knew that while Jarlaxle's cloak was not the standard drow *piwafwi*, it did have many magical qualities. It surprised him that anyone, short of using a wizard's invisibility spell, could find a way so to completely hide that great plumed hat.

Entreri shook it off and ran to the left, finding an easy path of shadows through the sparse trees, boulders, and rocky ridges. He approached the first group of orcs—four of the beasts squared up in battle, three against one. Moving silently, the assassin worked his way around the back of the trio, thinking to even up the odds with a sudden strike. He knew he was making no noise, knew he was hiding perfectly from tree to tree to rock to ridge. He had performed attacks like this for nearly three decades, had perfected the stealthy strike to an unprecedented level—and these were only orcs, simple, stupid brutes.

How surprised Entreri was, then, when two of the fighting trio howled and leaped around, charging right for him. The orc they had been fighting, with complete disregard to the battle at hand, similarly charged at the assassin. The remaining orc opponent promptly cut it down as it ran past.

Hard-pressed, Entreri worked his sword left and right, parrying the thrusts of the two makeshift spears and shearing the tip off one in the process. He was back on his heels, in a position of terrible balance. Had he been fighting an opponent of true skill he surely would have been killed, but these were only orcs. Their weapons were poorly crafted and their tactics were utterly predictable. He had defeated their first thrusts, their only chance, and yet, still they came on, headlong, with abandon.

Charon's Claw waved before them, filling the air with an opaque wall of ash. They plunged right through—of course they did!—but Entreri had already skittered to the left, and he spun back behind the charge of the closest orc, plunging his dagger deep into the creature's side. He didn't retract the blade immediately, though he had broken free. He could have made an easy kill of the second stumbling orc. No, he used the dagger to draw out the life-force from the already dying creature, taking that life-force into his own body to speed the healing of his own previous wounds.

By the time he let the limp creature drop to the ground, the second orc was at him, stabbing wildly. Entreri caught the spear with the crosspiece of his dagger and easily turned it up high, over his shoulder, and ducked and stepped ahead, shearing across with a great sweep of Charon's Claw. The orc instinctively tried to block with its arm, but the sword cut right through the limb, and drove hard into the orc's side, splintering ribs and tearing a great hole in its lung, all the way to its heart.

Entreri could hardly believe that the third of the group was still charging at him after seeing how easily and completely he had destroyed its two companions. He casually planted his left foot against the chest of the drooping, dead creature impaled on his sword, and waited for the exact moment. When that moment came, he turned the dead orc and kicked it free, dropping it in the path of its charging, howling companion.

The orc tripped, diving headlong past Entreri. The assassin stabbed up hard with the dagger, catching the orc under the chin and driving the blade up into its head. He bent as the heavy orc continued its facedown dive, ending with him holding the creature's head from the ground and the orc twitching spasmodically as it died.

A twist and yank tore the dagger free, and Entreri paused only long enough to wipe both his blades on the dead beast's back before running off in pursuit of other prey.

His stride was more tempered this time, though, for his failure in approaching the trio from behind bothered him greatly. He believed he understood what had happened—the Crystal Shard had called out a warning to the group—but the thought that carrying the cursed item left him without his favored mode of attack and his greatest ability to defend himself was more than a little unsettling.

He charged across the side of the rock facing, picking shadows where he could find them but worrying little about cover. He understood that with the Crystal Shard on his belt, he was likely as obvious as he would be sitting beside a blazing campfire on a dark night. He came past one small area of brush onto the lower edge of sloping, bare stone. Cursing the open ground but hardly slowing, Entreri started across.

He saw the charge of another orc out of the corner of his eye, the creature rushing headlong at him, one arm back and ready to launch a spear his way.

The orc was barely five strides away when it threw, but Entreri didn't even have to parry the errant missile, just letting it fly harmlessly past. He did react to it, though, with dramatic movement, and that only spurred on the eager orc attacker.

It leaped at the seemingly vulnerable man, a flying tackle aimed for Entreri's waist. Two quick steps took the assassin out of harm's way, and he swished his sword down onto the orc's back as it flew past, cracking the powerful weapon right through the creature's backbone. The orc skidded down hard on its face, its upper torso and arms squirming wildly, but its legs making no movement of their own.

Entreri didn't even bother finishing the wretched creature. He just ran on. He had a direction sorted for his run, for he heard the unmistakable laughter of a drow who seemed to be having too much fun.

He found Jarlaxle standing atop a boulder amidst the largest tumult of battling orcs, spurring one side on with excited words that Entreri could not understand, while systematically cutting down their opponents with dagger after thrown dagger.

Entreri stopped in the shadow of a tree and watched the spectacle.

Sure enough, Jarlaxle soon changed sides, calling out to the other orcs, and launching that endless stream of daggers at members of the side he had just been urging on.

The numbers dwindled, obviously so, and eventually, even the stupid orcs caught on to the deadly ruse. As one, they turned on Jarlaxle.

The drow only laughed at them all the harder as a dozen spears came his way—every one of them missing the mark badly due to the displacement magic in the drow's cloak and the bad aim of the orcs. The drow countered, throwing one dagger after another. Jarlaxle spun around on his high perch, always seeking the closest orc, and always hitting home with a nearly perfect throw.

Out of the shadows came Entreri, a whirlwind of fury, dagger working efficiently, but sword waving wildly, building walls of floating ash as the assassin sliced up the battlefield to suit his designs. Inevitably, Entreri worked his way into a situation that put him one-on-one against an orc. Just as inevitably, that creature was down and dying within the span of a few thrusts and stabs.

Entreri and Jarlaxle walked slowly back up the mountain slope soon after, with the drow complaining at the meager take of silver pieces they had found on the orcs. Entreri was hardly listening, was more concerned with the call that had brought the creatures to them in the first place—the plea, the scream, for help from Crenshinibon. These were just a rag-tag band of orcs, but what more powerful creatures might the Crystal Shard find to come to its call next?

"The call of the shard is strong," he admitted to Jarlaxle.

"It has existed for centuries," the drow answered. "It knows well how to preserve itself."

"That existence is soon to end," Entreri said grimly.

"Why?" Jarlaxle asked with perfect innocence.

The tone more than the word stopped Entreri cold in his tracks and made him turn around to regard his surprising companion.

"Do we have to go through this all over again?" the assassin asked.

"My friend, I know why you believe the Crystal Shard to be unacceptable for either of us to wield, but why does that translate into the need to destroy it?" Jarlaxle asked. He paused and glanced around, and motioned for Entreri to follow and led the assassin to the edge of a fairly deep ravine, a remote valley. "Why not just throw it away then?" he asked. "Toss it from this cliff and let it land where it may?"

Entreri stared out at the remote vale and almost considered taking Jarlaxle's advice. Almost, but a very real truth rang clear in his mind. "Because it would find its way back to the hands of our adversaries soon enough," he replied. "The Crystal Shard saw great potential in Rai-guy,"

Jarlaxle nodded. "Sensible," he said. "Ever was that one too ambitious for his own good. Why do you care, though? Let Rai-guy have it and have all of Calimport, if the artifact can deliver the city to him. What does it matter to Artemis Entreri, who is gone from that place, and who will not return anytime soon in any event? Likely, my former lieutenant will be too preoccupied with the potential gains he might find with the artifact in his hands even to worry about our whereabouts. Perhaps freeing ourselves of the burden of the artifact will indeed save us from the pursuit we now fear at our backs."

Entreri spent a long moment musing over that reasoning, but one fact kept nagging at him. "The Crystal Shard knows I wish to see it destroyed," he replied. "It knows that in my heart I hate it and will find some way to be rid of the thing. Rai-guy knows the threat that is Jarlaxle. As long as you live, he can never be certain of his position within Bregan D'aerthe. What would happen if Jarlaxle reappeared in Menzoberranzan, reaching out to old comrades against the fools who tried to steal the throne of Bregan D'aerthe?"

Jarlaxle offered no response, but the twinkle in his dark eyes told Entreri that his drow companion would like nothing more than to play out that very scenario.

"He wants you dead," Entreri said bluntly. "He needs you dead, and with the Crystal Shard at his disposal, that might not prove to be an overly difficult task."

The twinkle in Jarlaxle's dark eyes remained, but after a moment's thought, he just shrugged and said, "Lead on."

Entreri did just that, back to their horses and back to the trails that would take them to the northeast, to the Snowflake Mountains and the Spirit Soaring. Entreri was quite pleased with the way he had handled Jarlaxle, quite pleased in the strength of his argument for destroying the Crystal Shard.

But it was all just so much dung, he knew, all a justification for that which was in his heart. Yes, he was determined to destroy the Crystal Shard, and would see the artifact obliterated, but it was not for any fear of retribution or of pursuit. Entreri wanted Crenshinibon destroyed simply because the mere existence of the dominating artifact revolted him. The Crystal Shard, in trying to coerce him, had insulted him profoundly. He didn't hold any notion that the wretched world would be a better place without the artifact, and hardly cared whether it would be or not, but he did believe that he would more greatly enjoy his existence in the world knowing that one less wretched and perverted item such as the Crystal Shard remained in existence.

Of course, as Entreri harbored these thoughts, Crenshinibon realized them as well. The Crystal Shard could only seethe, could only hope that it might find someone weaker of heart and stronger of arm to slay Artemis Entreri and free it from his grasp.

CHAPTER

18

It was Entreri," Sharlotta Vespers said with a sly grin as she examined the orc corpse on the side of the mountain a couple days later. "The precision of the cuts . . . and see, a dagger thrust here, a sword slash there."

"Many fight with sword and dirk," the wererat, Gord Abrix, replied. The wretch, wearing his human form at that time, moved his hands out wide as he spoke, revealing his own sword and dagger hanging on his belt.

"But few strike so well," Sharlotta argued.

"And these others," Berg'inyon Baenre agreed in his stilted command of the common tongue. He swung his arm about to encompass the many orcs lying dead around the base of a large boulder. "Wounds consistent with a dagger throw—and so many of them. Only one warrior that I know of carries such a supply as that."

"You are counting wounds, not daggers!" Gord Abrix argued.

"They are one and the same in a fight this frantic," Berg'inyon reasoned. "These are throws, not stabs, for there is no tearing about the sides of the cuts, just a single fast puncture. And I think it unlikely that anyone would throw a few daggers at one opponent, somehow run down and pull them free, then throw them at another."

"Where are these daggers, then, drow?" the wererat leader asked doubtfully.

"Jarlaxle's missiles are magical in nature and disappear," Berg'inyon answered coldly. "His supply is nearly endless. This is the work of Jarlaxle, I know—and not his best work, I warn both of you."

Sharlotta and Gord Abrix exchanged nervous glances, though the wererat leader still held that doubting expression.

"Have you not yet learned the proper respect for the drow?" Berg'inyon asked him pointedly and threateningly.

Gord Abrix went back on his heels and held his empty hands up before him.

Sharlotta eyed him closely. Gord Abrix wanted a fight, she knew, even with this dark elf standing before him. Sharlotta hadn't really seen Berg'inyon Baenre in action, but she had seen his lessers, dark elves who had spoken of this young Baenre with the utmost respect. Even those lessers would have had little trouble in slaughtering the prideful Gord Abrix. Yes, Sharlotta realized then and there, her own self-preservation would depend upon her getting as far away from Gord Abrix and his sewer dwellers as possible, for there was no respect here, only abject hatred for Artemis Entreri and a genuine dislike for the dark elves. No doubt, Gord Abrix would lead his companions, wererat and otherwise, into absolute devastation.

Sharlotta Vespers, the survivor, wanted no part of that.

"The bodies are cold, the blood dried, but they have not been cleanly picked," Berg'inyon observed.

"A couple of days, no more," Sharlotta added, and she looked to Gord Abrix, as did Berg'inyon.

The wererat nodded and smiled wickedly. "I will have them," he declared. He walked off to confer with his wererat companions, who had been standing off to the side of the battleground.

"He will have a straight passageway to the realm of death," Berg'inyon quietly remarked to Sharlotta when the two were alone.

Sharlotta looked at the drow curiously. She agreed, of course, but she had to wonder why, if the dark elves knew this, they were allowing Gord Abrix to hold so critical a role in this all-important pursuit.

"Gord Abrix thinks he will get them," she replied, "both of them, yet you do not seem so confident."

Berg'inyon chuckled at the remark—one he obviously believed absurd. "No doubt, Entreri is a deadly opponent," he said.

"More so than you understand," Sharlotta, who knew the assassin's exploits well, was quick to add.

"And yet he is still, by any measure, the easier of the prey," Berg'inyon assured her. "Jarlaxle has survived for centuries with his intelligence and skill. He thrives in a land more violent than Calimport could ever know. He ascends to the highest levels of power in a warring city that prevents the ascent of males. Our wretched companion Gord Abrix cannot understand the truth of Jarlaxle, nor can you, so I tell you this now—out of the respect I have gained for you in these short tendays—beware that one."

Sharlotta paused and stared long and hard at the surprising drow warrior. Offering her respect? The notion pleased her and made her fearful all at once, for Sharlotta had already learned to try to look beneath every word uttered by her dark elf comrades. Perhaps Berg'inyon had just paid her a high and generous compliment. Perhaps he was setting her up for disaster.

Sharlotta glanced down at the ground, biting her lower lip as she fell into her thoughts, sorting it all out. Perhaps Berg'inyon was setting her up, she reasoned again, as Rai-guy and Kimmuriel had set up Gord Abrix. As she thought of the mighty Jarlaxle and the item he possessed, she came to realize, of course, that there was no way Rai-guy could believe Gord Abrix and his ragged wererat band could possibly bring down the great Entreri and the great Jarlaxle. If that came to pass, then Gord Abrix would have the Crystal Shard in his possession, and what trouble might he bring about before Rai-guy and Kimmuriel could take it away from him? No, Rai-guy and Kimmuriel did not believe that the wererat leader would get anywhere near the Crystal Shard, and furthermore, they didn't want him anywhere near it.

Sharlotta looked back up at Berg'inyon to see him smiling slyly, as if he had just followed her reasoning as clearly as if she had spoken it aloud. "The drow always use a lesser race to lead the way into battle," the dark elf warrior said. "We never truly know, of course, what surprises our enemies might have in store."

"Fodder," Sharlotta remarked.

Berg'inyon's expression was perfectly blank, was absent of any sense of compassion at all, giving Sharlotta all the confirmation she needed.

A shudder coursed up Sharlotta's spine as she considered the sheer coldness of that look, dispassionate and inhuman, a less-than-subtle reminder to her that these dark elves were indeed very different, and much, much more dangerous. Artemis Entreri was, perhaps, the closest creature she had ever met in temperament to the drow, but it seemed to her that, in terms of sheer evil, even he paled in comparison. These long-lived dark elves had perfected the craft of efficient heartlessness to a level beyond human comprehension, let alone human mimicry. She turned to regard Gord Abrix and his eager wererats, and made a silent vow then to stay as far away from the doomed creatures as possible.

The demon writhed on the floor in agony, its skin smoking, its blood boiling.

Cadderly did not pity the creature, though it pained him to have to lower himself to this level. He did not enjoy torture—even the torture of a demon, as deserving a creature as ever existed. He did not enjoy dealing with the denizens of the lower planes at all, but he had to for the sake of the Spirit Soaring, for the sake of his wife and children.

The Crystal Shard was coming to him, was coming for him, he knew, and his impending battle with the vile artifact might prove to be as important as his war had been against *Tuanta Quiro Miancay,* the dreaded Chaos Curse. It was as important as his construction of the Spirit Soaring, for what lasting effect might the remarkable cathedral hold if Crenshinibon reduced it to rubble?

"You know the answer," Cadderly said as calmly as he could. "Tell me, and I will release you."

"You are a fool, priest of Deneir!" the demon growled, its guttural words broken apart as spasm after spasm wracked its physical form. "Do you know the enemy you make in Mizferac?"

Cadderly sighed. "And so it continues," he said, as if he were speaking to himself, though well aware that Mizferac would hear his words and understand the painful implications of them with crystalline clarity.

"Release me!" the glabrezu demanded.

"Yokk tu Mizferac be-enck do-tu," Cadderly recited, and the demon howled and jerked wildly about the floor within the perfectly designed protective circle.

"This will take as long as you wish," Cadderly said coldly to the demon. "I have no mercy for your kind, I assure you."

"We . . . want . . . no . . . mercy," Mizferac growled. Then a great spasm wracked the beast, and it jerked wildly, rolling about and shrieking curses in its profane, demonic language.

Cadderly just quietly recited more of the exaction spell, bolstering his resolve with the continual reminder that his children might soon be in mortal danger.

"Ye wasn't lost! Ye was playing!" Ivan Bouldershoulder roared at his green-bearded brother.

"Doo-dad maze!" Pikel argued vehemently.

The normally docile dwarf's tone took his brother somewhat by surprise. "Ye getting talkative since ye becomed a doo-dad, ain't ye?" he asked.

"Oo oi!" Pikel shrieked, punching his fist in the air.

"Well, ye shouldn't be playin' in yer maze when Cadderly's at such dark business," Ivan scolded.

"Doo-dad maze," Pikel whispered under his breath, and he lowered his gaze.

"Yeah, whatever ye might be callin' it," grumbled Ivan, who had never been overly fond of his brother's woodland calling and considered it quite an unnatural thing for a dwarf. "He might be needin' us, ye fool." Ivan held up his great axe as he spoke, flexing the bulging muscles on his short but powerful arm.

Pikel responded with one of his patented grins and held up a wooden cudgel.

"Great weapon for fighting demons," Ivan muttered.

"Sha-la—" Pikel started.

"Yeah, I'm knowin' the name," Ivan cut in. "Sha-la-la. I'm thinking that a demon might be callin' it kind-lind-ling."

Pikel's grin drooped into a severe frown.

The door to the summoning chamber pulled open and a very weary Cadderly emerged—or tried to. He tripped over something and sprawled facedown to the floor.

"Oops," said Pikel.

"Me brother put one o' his magic trips on the doorway," Ivan explained, helping the priest back to his feet. "We was worryin' that a demon might be walkin' out."

"So of course, Pikel would trip the thing to the floor and bash it with his club," Cadderly said dryly, pulling himself back to his feet.

"Sha-la-la!" Pikel squealed gleefully, completely missing the sarcasm in the young cleric's tone.

"Ain't one coming, is there?" Ivan asked, looking past Cadderly.

"The glabrezu, Mizferac, has been dismissed to its own foul plane," Cadderly assured the dwarves. "I brought it forth again, thus rescinding the hundred year banishment I had just exacted upon it, to answer a specific question, and with that done, I had—and have, I hope—no further need of it."

"Ye should've kept him about just so me and me brother could bash him a few times," said Ivan.

"Sha-la-la!"' Pikel agreed.

"Save your strength, for I fear we will need it," Cadderly explained. "I have learned the secret to destroying the Crystal Shard, or at least, I have learned of the creature that might complete the task."

"Demon?" Ivan asked.

"Doo-dad?" Pikel added hopefully.

Cadderly, shaking his head, started to reply to Ivan, but paused to put a perfectly puzzled expression over the green-bearded dwarf. Embarrassed, Pikel merely shrugged and said, "Ooo."

"No demon," he said to the other dwarf at length. "A creature of this world."

"Giant?"

"Think bigger."

Ivan started to speak again, but paused, taking in Cadderly's sour expression and studying it in light of all that they had been through together.

"Let me guess one more time," the dwarf said.

Cadderly didn't answer.

"Dragon," Ivan said.

"Ooo," said Pikel.

Cadderly didn't answer.

"Red dragon," Ivan clarified.

"Ooo," said Pikel.

Cadderly didn't answer.

"Big red dragon," said the dwarf. *"Huge* red dragon! Old as the mountains."

"Ooo," said Pikel, three more times.

Cadderly merely sighed.

"Old Fyren's dead," Ivan said, and there was indeed a slight tremor in the tough dwarf's voice, for that fight with the great red dragon had nearly been the end of them all.

"Fyrentennimar was not the last of its kind, nor the greatest, I assure you," Cadderly replied evenly.

"Ye're thinking that we got to take the thing to another of the beasts?" Ivan asked incredulously. "To one bigger than old Fyren?"

"So I am told," explained Cadderly. "A red dragon, ancient and huge."

Ivan shook his head, and snapped a glare over Pikel, who said, "Ooo," once again.

Ivan couldn't help but chuckle. They had met up with mighty Fyrentennimar on their way to find the mountain fortress that housed the minions of Cadderly's own wicked father. Through Cadderly's powerful magic, the dragon had been "tamed" into flying Cadderly and the others across the Snowflake Mountains. A battle deeper in those mountains had broken the spell though, and old Fyren had turned on its temporary masters with a vengeance. Somehow, Cadderly had managed to hold onto enough magical strength to weaken the beast enough for Vander, a giant friend, to lop off its head, but Ivan knew, and so did the others, that the win had been as much a feat of luck as of skill.

"Drizzt Do'Urden told ye about another of the reds, didn't he?" Ivan remarked.

"I know where we can find one," Cadderly replied grimly.

Danica walked in, then, her smile wide—until she noted the expressions on the faces of the other three.

"Poof!" said Pikel and he walked out of the room, muttering squeaky little sounds.

A puzzled Danica watched him go. Then she turned to his brother.

"He's a doo-dad," Ivan explained, "and fearin' no natural creature. There ain't nothin' less natural than a red dragon, I'm guessing, so he's not too happy right now." Ivan snorted and walked out behind his brother.

"Red dragon?" Danica asked Cadderly.

"Poof," the priest replied.

CHAPTER

19

Entreri frowned when he glanced from the not-too-distant village to his ridiculously plumed drow companion. The hat alone, with its wide brim and huge diatryma feather that always grew back after Jarlaxle used it to summon a real giant bird, would invite suspicion and likely open disdain, from the farmers of the village. Then there was the fact that the wearer was a dark elf. . . .

"You really should consider a disguise," Entreri said dryly, and shook his head, wishing he still had a particular magic item, a mask that could transform the wearer's appearance. Drizzt Do'Urden had once used the thing to get from the northlands around Waterdeep all the way to Calimport disguised as a surface elf.

"I have considered a disguise," the drow replied, and to Entreri's—temporary—relief, he pulled the hat from his head. A good start, it seemed.

Jarlaxle merely brushed the thing off and plopped it right back in place. "You wear one, as well," the drow protested to Entreri's scowl, pointing to the small-brimmed black hat Entreri now wore. The hat was called a bolero, named after the drow wizard who had given it its tidy shape and had imbued it, and several others of the same make, with certain magical properties.

"Not the hat!" the frustrated Entreri replied, and he rubbed a hand across his face. "These are simple farmers, likely with very definite feelings about dark elves—and likely, those feelings are not favorable."

"For most dark elves, I would agree with them," said Jarlaxle, and he ended there, and merely kept riding on his way toward the village, as if Entreri had said nothing to him at all.

"Hence, the disguise," the assassin called after him.

"Indeed," said Jarlaxle, and he kept on riding.

Entreri kicked his heels into his horse's flanks, spurring the mount into a quick canter to bring him up beside the elusive drow. "I mean that you should consider wearing one," Entreri said plainly.

"But I am," the drow replied. "And you, Artemis Entreri, above all others, should recognize me! I am Drizzt Do'Urden, your most hated rival."

"What?" the assassin asked incredulously.

"Drizzt Do'Urden, the perfect disguise for me," Jarlaxle casually replied. "Does not Drizzt walk openly from town to town, neither hiding nor denying his heritage, even in those places where he is not well-known?"

"Does he?" Entreri asked slyly.

"Did he not?" Jarlaxle quickly replied, correcting the tense, for of course, as far as Artemis Entreri knew, Drizzt Do'Urden was dead.

Entreri stared hard at the drow.

"Well, did he not?" Jarlaxle asked plainly. "And it was Drizzt's nerve, I say, in parading about so openly, that prevented townsfolk from organizing against him and slaying him. Because he remained so obvious, it became obvious that he had nothing to hide. Thus, I use the same technique and even the same name. I am Drizzt Do'Urden, hero of Icewind Dale, friend of King Bruenor Battlehammer of Mithral Hall, and no enemy of these simple farmers. Rather, I might be of use to them, should danger threaten."

"Of course," Entreri replied. "Unless one of them crosses you, in which case you will destroy the entire town."

"There is always that," Jarlaxle admitted, but he didn't slow his mount, and he and Entreri were getting close to the village now, close enough to be seen for what they were—or at least, for what they were pretending to be.

There were no guards about, and the pair rode in undisturbed, their horses' hooves clattering on cobblestone roads. They pulled up before one two-story building, on which hung a shingle painted with a foamy mug of mead and naming the place as

Gent eman Briar's Good y
P ace of Si ing

in lettering old and weathered.

"Si ing," Jarlaxle read, scratching his head, and he gave a great and dramatic sigh. "This is a gathering hall for those of melancholy?"

"Not sighing," Entreri replied. He looked at Jarlaxle, snorted, and rolled off the side of his horse. "Sitting, or perhaps sipping. Not sighing."

"Sitting, then, or sipping," Jarlaxle announced, looping his right leg over his horse, and rolling over backward off the mount into a somersault to land gracefully on his feet. "Or perhaps a bit of both! Ha!" He ended with a great gleaming smile.

Entreri stared at him hard yet again, and just shook his head, thinking that perhaps he would have been better off leaving this one with Rai-guy and Kimmuriel.

A dozen patrons were inside the place, ten men and a pair of women, along with a grizzled old barkeep whose snarl seemed to be eternally etched upon his stubbly face, a locked expression amidst the leathery wrinkles and acne scars. One by one, the thirteen took note of the pair entering, and inevitably, each nodded or merely glanced away, and shot a stunned expression back at the duo, particularly at the dark elf, and sent a hand to the hilt of the nearest weapon. One man even leaped up from his chair, sending it skidding out behind him.

Entreri and Jarlaxle merely tipped their hats and moved to the bar, making no threatening movements and keeping their expressions perfectly friendly.

"What're ye about?" the barkeep barked at them. "Who're ye, and what's yer business?"

"Travelers," Entreri answered, "weary of the road and seeking a bit of respite."

"Well, ye'll not be finding it here, ye won't!" the barkeep growled. "Get yer hats back on yer ugly heads and get yer arses out me door!"

Entreri looked to Jarlaxle, who seemed perfectly unperturbed. "I do believe we will stay a bit," the drow stated. "I do understand your hesitance, good sir . . . good Eman Briar," he added, remembering the sign.

"Eman?" the barkeep echoed in obvious confusion.

"Eman Briar, so says your placard," Jarlaxle answered innocently.

"Eh?" the puzzled man asked, then his old yellow eyes lit up as he caught on. "*Gentle*man Briar," he insisted. "The L's all rotted away. *Gentleman* Briar."

"Your pardon, good sir," the charming and disarming Jarlaxle said with a bow. He gave a great sigh and threw a wink at Entreri's predictable scowl. "We have come in to sigh, sit, and sip, a bit of all three. We want no trouble and bring none, I assure you. Have you not heard of me? Drizzt Do'Urden of Icewind Dale, who reclaimed Mithral Hall for dwarven King Bruenor Battlehammer?"

"Never heard o' no Drizzit Dudden," Briar replied. "Now get ye outta me place afore me friends and me haul ye out!" His voice rose as he spoke, and several of the gathered men did, as well, moving together and readying their weapons.

Jarlaxle glanced around at the lot of them, smiling, seeming perfectly amused. Entreri, too, was quite entertained by it all, but he didn't bother looking around, just leaned back on his barstool, watching his friend and trying to see how Jarlaxle might wriggle out of this one. Of course, the ragged band of farmers hardly bothered the skilled assassin, especially since he was sitting next to the dangerous Jarlaxle. If they had to leave the town in ruin, so be it.

Thus, Entreri did not even search the ever-present silent call of the imprisoned Crystal Shard. If the artifact wanted these simple fools to take it from Entreri, then let them try!

"Did I not just tell you that I reclaimed a dwarven kingdom?" Jarlaxle asked. "And mostly without help. Hear me well, Gent Eman Briar. If you and your friends here try to expel me, your kin will be planting more than crops this season."

It wasn't so much what he said as it was the manner in which he said it, so casual, so confident, so perfectly assured that this group could not begin to frighten him. The men approaching slowed to a halt, all of them glancing to the others for some sign of leadership.

"Truly, I desire no trouble," Jarlaxle said calmly. "I have dedicated my life to erasing the prejudices—rightful conceptions, in many instances—that so many hold for my people. I am not merely a weary traveler, but a warrior for the causes of common men. If goblins attacked your fair town, I would fight beside you until they were driven away, or until my heart beat its last!" His voice continued a dramatic climb. "If a great dragon swooped down upon your village, I would brave its fiery breath, draw forth my weapons and leap to the parapets. . . ."

"I think they understand your point," Entreri said to him, grabbing him by the arm and easing him back to his seat.

Gentleman Briar snorted. "Ye're not even carryin' no weapon, drow," he observed.

"A thousand dead men have said the same thing," Entreri replied in all seriousness. Jarlaxle tipped his hat to the assassin. "But enough banter," Entreri added, hopping from his seat and pulling back his cloak to reveal his two fabulous weapons, the jeweled dagger and the magnificent Charon's Claw with its distinctive bony hilt. "If you mean to fight us, then do so now, that I can finish this business and still find a good meal, a better drink, and a warm bed before the fall of night. If not, then go back to your tables, I beg, and leave us in peace, else I'll forget my delusional paladin friend's desire to become the hero of the land."

Again, the patrons glanced nervously at each other, and some grumbled under their breaths.

"Gentleman Briar, they await your signal," Entreri remarked. "Choose well which signal that will be, or else find a way to mix blood with your drink, for you shall have gallons of it pooling about your tavern."

Briar waved his hand, sending his patrons retreating to their respective tables, and gave a great snort and snarl.

"Good!" Jarlaxle remarked, slapping his leg. "My reputation is saved from the rash actions of my impetuous friend. Now, if you would be so kind as to fetch me a fine and delicate drink, Gentleman Briar," he instructed, pulling forth his purse, which was bulging with coins.

"I'm servin' no damned drow in me tavern," Briar insisted, crossing his thin but muscled arms over his chest.

"Then I will gladly serve myself," Jarlaxle answered without hesitation, and he politely tipped his great plumed hat. "Of course, that will mean fewer coins for you."

Briar stared at him hard.

Jarlaxle ignored him and stared instead at the fairly wide selection of bottles on the shelves behind the bar. He tapped a delicate finger against his lip, scrutinizing the colors, and the words of the few that were actually marked.

"Suggestions?" he asked Entreri.

"Something to drink," the assassin replied.

Jarlaxle pointed to one bottle, uttered a simple magical command, and snapped his finger back, and the bottle flew from the shelf to his waiting grasp. Two more points and commands had a pair of glasses sitting upon the bar before the companions.

Jarlaxle reached for the bottle. The stunned and angry Briar snapped his hand out to grab the dark elf's arm.

He never got close.

Faster than Briar could possibly react, faster than he could think to react, Entreri snapped his hand on the barkeep's reaching arm, slamming it down to the bar and holding it fast. In the same fluid motion, the assassin's other hand came, holding the jeweled dagger, and Entreri plunged it hard into the wooden shelf right between Gentleman Briar's fingers. The blood drained from the man's ruddy face.

"If you persist, there will be little left of your tavern," Entreri promised in the coldest, most threatening voice Gentleman Briar had ever heard. "Enough to build a proper box to bury you in, perhaps."

"Doubtful," said Jarlaxle.

The drow was perfectly at ease, hardly paying attention, seeming as though he had expected Entreri's intervention all along. He poured the two drinks and eased himself back, sniffing, and sipping his liquor.

Entreri let the man go, glanced around to make sure that none of the others were moving, and slid his dagger back into its sheath on his belt.

"Good sir," Jarlaxle said. "I tell you one more time that we have no argument with you, nor do we wish one. Our road behind us has been long and dry, and the road before us will no doubt prove equally harsh. Thus we have entered your fair tavern in this fair village. Why would you think to deny us?"

"The better question is, why would you wish to be killed?" Entreri put in.

Gentleman Briar looked from one to the other and threw up his hands in defeat. "To the Nine Hells with both of ye," he growled, spinning away.

Entreri looked to Jarlaxle, who merely shrugged and said, "I have already been there. Hardly worth a return visit." He took up his glass and the bottle and walked away. Entreri, with his own glass, followed him across the room to the one free table in the small place.

Of course, the two tables near that one soon became empty as well, when the patrons took up their glasses and other items and scurried away from the dark elf.

"It will always be like this," Entreri said to his companion a short while later.

"It had not been so for Drizzt Do'Urden of late, so my spies indicated," the drow answered. "His reputation, in those lands where he was known, outshone the color of his skin in the eyes of even the small-minded men. So, soon, will my own."

"A reputation for heroic deeds?" Entreri asked with a doubting laugh. "Are you to become a hero for the land, then?"

"That, or a reputation for leaving burned-out villages behind me," Jarlaxle replied. "Either way, I care little."

That brought a smile to Entreri's face, and he dared to hope then that he and his companion would get along famously.

Kimmuriel and Rai-guy stared at the mirror enchanted for divining, watching the procession of nearly a score of ratmen, all in their human guise, trotting into the village.

"It is already tense," Kimmuriel observed. "If Gord Abrix plays correctly, the townsfolk will join with him against Entreri and Jarlaxle. Thirty-to-two. Fine odds."

Rai-guy gave a derisive snort. "Strong enough odds, perhaps, so that Jarlaxle and Entreri will be a bit weary before we go in to finish the task," he said.

Kimmuriel looked to his friend but, thinking about it, merely shrugged and grinned. He wasn't about to mourn the loss of Gord Abrix and a bunch of flea-infested wererats.

"If they do get in and get lucky," Kimmuriel remarked, "we must be quick. The Crystal Shard is in there."

"Crenshinibon is not calling to Gord Abrix and his fools," Rai-guy replied, his dark eyes gleaming with anticipation. "It is calling to me, even now. It knows we are close and knows how much greater it will be when I am the wielder."

Kimmuriel said nothing, but studied his friend intently, suspecting that if Rai-guy achieved his goal, he and Crenshinibon would likely soon be at odds with Kimmuriel.

◄═══►

"How many does the tiny village hold?" Jarlaxle asked when the tavern doors opened and a group of men walked in.

Entreri started to answer flippantly, but held the thought and scrutinized the new group a bit more closely. "Not that many," he answered, shaking his head.

Jarlaxle followed the assassin's lead, studying the movements of the new arrivals, studying their weapons—swords mostly, and more ornate than anything the villagers were carrying.

Entreri's head snapped to the side as he noted other forms moving about the two small windows. He knew then, beyond any doubt.

These are not villagers, Jarlaxle silently agreed, using the intricate sign language of the dark elves, but moving his fingers much more slowly than normal in deference to Entreri's rudimentary understanding of the form.

"Ratmen," the assassin whispered in reply.

"You hear the shard calling to them?"

"I smell them," Entreri corrected. He paused a moment to consider whether the Crystal Shard might indeed be calling out to the group, a beacon for his enemies, but he just dismissed the thought, for it hardly mattered.

"Sewage on their shoes," Jarlaxle noted.

"Vermin in their blood," the assassin spat. He got up from his seat and took a step out from the table. "Let us begone," he said to Jarlaxle, loudly enough for the closest of the dozen ratmen who had entered the tavern to hear.

Entreri took a step toward the door, and a second, aware that all eyes were upon him and his flamboyant companion, who was just then rising from his seat. Entreri took a third step, then . . . he leaped to the side, driving his dagger into the heart of the closest ratman before it could begin to draw its sword.

"Murderers!" someone yelled, but Entreri hardly heard, leaping forward and drawing forth Charon's Claw.

Metal rang out loudly as he brutally parried the swinging sword of the next closest wererat, hitting the blade so hard that he sent it flying out wide. A quick reversal sent Entreri's sword slashing out to catch the ratman across the face, and it fell back, clutching its torn eyes.

Entreri had no time to pursue, for all the place was in motion then. A trio of ratmen, swords slashing the air before them, were closing fast. He waved Charon's Claw, creating a wall of ash, and leaped to the side, rolling under a table. The ratmen reacted, turning to pursue, but by the time they had their bearings, Entreri came up hard, bringing the table with him, launching it into their faces. Now he cut down low, taking a pair out at the knees, the fine blade cleanly severing one leg and nearly a second.

Ratmen bore down on him, but a rain of daggers came whipping past the assassin, driving them back.

Entreri waved his sword wildly, making a long and wavy vision-blocking wall. He managed a glance back at his companion to see Jarlaxle's arm furiously

182

pumping, sending dagger after dagger soaring at an enemy. One group of ratmen, though, hoisted a table, as had Entreri, and used it as a shield. Several daggers thumped into it, catching fast. Bolstered by the impromptu shield, the group charged hard at the drow.

Too occupied suddenly with more enemies of his own, including a couple of townsfolk, Entreri turned his attention back to his own situation. He brought his sword up parallel to the floor, intercepting the blade of one villager and lifting it high. Entreri started to tilt the blade point up, the expected parry, which would bring the man's sword out wide. As the farmer pushed back against the block, Entreri fooled him by bringing up the hilt instead, turning the blade down and forcing the man's sword across his body. Faster than the man could react with any backhand move, Entreri snapped his hand, his weapon's skull-capped pommel, into the man's face, laying him low.

Back across came Charon's Claw, a mighty cut to intercept the sword of another, a ratman, and to slide through the parry and take the tip from another farmer's pitchfork. The assassin followed powerfully, stepping into his two foes, his sword working hard and furiously against the ratman's blade, driving it back, back, and to the side, forcing openings.

The jeweled dagger worked fast as well, with Entreri making circular motions over the broken pitchfork shaft, turning it one way and another and keeping the inexperienced farmer stumbling forward and off his balance. He would have been an easy kill, but Entreri had other ideas.

"Do you not understand the nature of your new allies?" he cried at the man, and as he spoke, he worked his sword even harder, slapping the blade against the wererat's sword to bat it slightly out of angle, and slapping the flat of the blade against the wererat's head. He didn't want to kill the creature, just to tempt the anger out of it. Again and again, the assassin's sword slapped at the wererat, bruising, taunting, stinging.

Entreri noted the creature's twitch and knew what was coming.

He drove the wererat back with a sudden but shortened stab, and went fully at the farmer, looping his dagger over and around the pitchfork, forcing it down at an angle. He went in one step toward the farmer, drove the wooden shaft down farther, forcing the man at an awkward angle that had him leaning on the assassin. Entreri broke away suddenly.

The farmer stumbled forward helplessly and Entreri had him in a lock, looping his sword arm around the man and turning him as he came on so that he was then facing the twitching, changing wererat.

The man gave a slight gasp, thinking his life was at its end, but caught fully in Entreri's grasp, a dagger at his back but not plunging in, he calmed enough to take in the spectacle.

His scream at the horrid transformation, as the wererat's face broke apart, twisted and wrenched, reforming into the head of a giant rodent, rent the air and brought all attention to the sight.

Entreri shoved the farmer toward the wrenching, changing ratman. To his satisfaction, he saw the farmer drive the broken pitchfork shaft through the beast's gut.

Entreri spun away with many more enemies still to fight. The farmers were standing perplexed, not knowing which side to take. The assassin knew enough about the shape-changers to understand that he had started a chain reaction here, that the enraged and excited wererats would look upon their transformed kin and likewise revert to their more primal form.

He took a moment to glance Jarlaxle's way then and saw the drow up in the air, levitating and turning circles, daggers flying from his pumping arm. Following their paths, Entreri saw one wererat, and another, stumble backward under the assault. A farmer grabbed at his calf, a blade deeply embedded there.

Jarlaxle purposely hadn't killed the human, Entreri noted, though he surely could have.

Entreri winced suddenly as a barrage of missiles soared back up at Jarlaxle, but the drow anticipated it and let go his levitation, dropping lightly and gracefully to the floor. He drew out two daggers as a host of opponents rushed in at him, grabbing them from hidden scabbards on his belt and not his enchanted bracer in a cross-armed maneuver. As he brought his arms back to their respective sides, Jarlaxle snapped his wrists and muttered something under his breath. The daggers elongated into fine, gleaming swords.

The drow planted his feet wide and exploded into motion, his arms pumping, his swords cutting fast circles, over and under, at his sides, chopping the air with popping, whipping sounds. He brought one across his chest, then the next, spinning them wildly, then went up high with one, turning his hand to put the blade over his head and parallel with the floor.

Entreri's expression soured. He had expected better of his drow companion. He had seen this fighting style many times, particularly among the pirates who frequented the seas off Calimport. It was called "swashbuckling," a deceptive, and deceptively easy, fighting technique that was more show than substance. The swashbuckler relied on the hesitance and fear of his opponents to afford him opportunities for better strikes. While often effective against weaker opponents, Entreri found the style ridiculous against any of true talent. He had killed several swashbucklers in his day—two in one fight when they had inadvertently tied each other up with their whirling blades—and had never found them to be particularly challenging.

The group of wererats coming in at Jarlaxle at that moment apparently didn't have much respect for the technique either. They quickly rushed around the drow, forming a box, and came in at him alternately, forcing him to turn, turn, and turn some more.

Jarlaxle was more than up to the task, keeping his spinning swords in perfect harmony as he countered every testing thrust or charge.

"They will tire him," Entreri whispered under his breath as he worked away from his newest opponents. He was trying to pick a path that would bring him to his drow friend that he might get Jarlaxle out of his predicament. He glanced back at the drow then, hoping he might get there in time, but honestly wondering if the disappointing Jarlaxle was still worth the trouble.

He gasped, first in confusion, and then in admiration.

Jarlaxle did a sudden back flip, twisting as he somersaulted so that he landed facing the opponent who had been at his back. The wererat stumbled away, hit twice by shortened stabs—shortened because Jarlaxle had other targets in mind.

The drow rolled around, falling into a crouch, and exploded out of it with a devastating double thrust at the wererat opposite. The creature leaped back, throwing its hips behind it and slapping its blade down in a desperate parry.

Before he could even think about it, Entreri cried out, thinking his friend doomed, for one sword-wielding wererat charged from Jarlaxle's direct left, another from behind and to the right, leaving the drow no room to skitter away.

"They reveal themselves," Kimmuriel said with a laugh. He, Rai-guy, and Berg'inyon watched the action through a dimensional portal that in effect put them in the thick of the fighting.

Berg'inyon thought the spectacle of the changing wererats equally amusing. He leaped forward, then, catching one farmer who was inadvertently stumbling through the portal, stabbing the man once in the side, and shoving him back through and to the tavern floor.

More forms rushed by, more cries came in at them, with Kimmuriel and Berg'inyon watching attentively and Rai-guy behind them, his eyes closed as he prepared his spells—a process that was taking the drow wizard longer because of the continuing, eager call of the imprisoned Crystal Shard.

Gord Abrix flashed by the door.

"Catch him!" Kimmuriel cried, and the agile Berg'inyon leaped through the doorway, grabbed Gord Abrix in a debilitating lock, and dived back through with the wererat in tow. He kept Gord Abrix held firmly out of the way, the wererat crying protests at Kimmuriel.

But the drow psionicist wasn't listening, for he was focused fully on his wizard companion. His timing in closing the door had to be perfect.

Jarlaxle didn't even try to get out of there, and Entreri realized, he had expected the attacks all along, had baited them.

Down low, his left leg far in front of his right, both arms and blades fully extended before him, Jarlaxle somehow managed to reverse his grip, and in a sudden and perfectly balanced momentum shift, the drow came back up straight. His left arm and blade stabbed out to the left. The sword in his right hand was flipped over in his hand so that when Jarlaxle turned his fist down, the tip was facing behind him, cocking straight back.

Both charging wererats halted suddenly, their chests ripped open by the perfect stabs.

Jarlaxle retracted the blades, put them back into their respective spins, and turned left, the whirling blades drawing lines of bright blood all over the wounded wererat there, and completing the turn, slashing the wererat behind him repeatedly and finishing with a powerful crossing backhand maneuver that took the creature's head from its shoulders.

Thus disintegrating Entreri's ideas about the weakness of the swashbuckling technique.

The drow rushed past into the path of the first wererat he had struck, his spinning swords intercepting his opponent's, and bringing it into the spin with them. In a moment, all three blades were in the air, turning circles, and only two of them, Jarlaxle's, were still being held. The third was kept aloft by the slapping and sliding of the other two.

Jarlaxle hooked the hilt of that sword with the blade of one of his own, angled it out to the side and launched it into the chest of another attacker, knocking him back and to the floor.

He went ahead suddenly and brutally, blades whirling with perfect precision, to take the wererat's arm, then drop the other arm limply to its side with a well-placed blow to the collarbone, then slash its face, then its throat.

Up came Jarlaxle's foot, planting against the staggered wererat's chest, and he kicked out, knocking the creature to its back and running over it.

Entreri had meant to get to Jarlaxle's side, but instead, the drow came rushing up to Entreri's side, uttering a command under his breath that retracted one of his swords to dagger size. He quickly slid the weapon back to its sheath, and with his free hand grabbed Entreri by the shoulder and pulled him along.

The puzzled assassin glanced at his companion. More wererats were piling into the tavern, through the windows, through the door, but those remaining farmers were falling back now, moving into purely defensive positions. Though more than a dozen wererats remained, Entreri did not believe that he and this amazingly skilled drow warrior would have any trouble at all tearing them apart.

Furthermore and even more puzzling, Jarlaxle had their run angled for the closest wall. While putting a solid barrier at their backs might be effective in some cases against so many opponents, Entreri thought this ridiculous, given Jarlaxle's flamboyant, room-requiring style.

Jarlaxle let go of Entreri then and reached up to the top of his huge hat.

From somewhere unseen in the strange hat, he brought forth a black disk made of some fabric Entreri did not know and sent it spinning at the wall. It elongated as it went, turning flat side to the wooden wall, then it hit . . . and stuck.

And it was no longer a disk of fabric, but rather a hole—a real hole—in the wall.

Jarlaxle pushed Entreri through, dived through right behind him, and paused only long enough to pull the magical hole out behind him, leaving the wall solid once more.

"Run!" the dark elf cried, sprinting away, with Entreri right on his heels.

Before Entreri could even ask what the drow knew that he did not, the building exploded into a huge and consuming fireball that took the tavern, took all of those wererats still scrambling about the entrances and exits, and took the horses, including Entreri's and Jarlaxle's, tethered anywhere near to the place.

The pair went flying to the ground but got right back up, running full speed out of the village and back into the shadows of the surrounding hills and woodlands.

They didn't even speak for many, many minutes, just ran on, until Jarlaxle finally pulled up behind one bluff and fell against the grassy hill, huffing and puffing.

"I had grown fond of my mount," he said. "A pity."

"I did not see the spellcaster," Entreri remarked.

"He was not in the room," Jarlaxle explained, "not physically, at least."

"Then how did you sense him?" Entreri started to ask, but he paused and considered the logic that had led Jarlaxle to his saving conclusion. "Because Kimmuriel and Rai-guy would never take the chance that Gord Abrix and his cronies would get the Crystal Shard," he reasoned. "Nor would they ever expect the wretched wererats ever to be able to take the thing from us in the first place."

"I have already explained to you that it is a common tactic for the two," Jarlaxle reminded. "They send their fodder in to engage their enemies, and Kimmuriel opens a window through which Rai-guy throws his potent magic."

Entreri looked back in the direction of the village, at the plume of black smoke drifting into the air. "Well thought," he congratulated. "You saved us both."

"Well, you at least," Jarlaxle replied, and Entreri looked back at him curiously, to see the drow waggling the fingers of one hand against his cheek, showing off a reddish-gold ring that Entreri had not noticed before.

"It was just a fireball," Jarlaxle said with a grin.

Entreri nodded and returned that grin, wondering if there was anything, anything at all, that Jarlaxle was not prepared for.

CHAPTER

BALANCING PRUDENCE
AND DESIRE

20

Gord Abrix gasped and fell over as the small globe of fire soared past him, through the doorway, and into the tavern. As soon as it went through, Kimmuriel dropped the dimensional door. Gord Abrix had seen fireballs cast before and could well imagine the devastation back in the tavern. He knew he had just lost nearly a score of his loyal wererat soldiers.

He came up unsteadily, glancing around at his three dark elf companions, unsure, as he always seemed to be with this group, of what they might do next.

"You and your soldiers performed admirably," Rai-guy remarked.

"You killed them," Gord Abrix dared to say, though certainly not in any accusatory tone.

"A necessary sacrifice," Rai-guy replied. "You did not believe that they would have any chance of defeating Artemis Entreri and Jarlaxle, did you?"

"Then why send them?" the frustrated wererat leader started to ask, but his voice died away as the question left his mouth, the reasoning dissipated by his own internal reminders of who these creatures truly were. Gord Abrix and his henchmen had been sent in for just the diversion they provided, to occupy Entreri and Jarlaxle while Rai-guy and Kimmuriel prepared their little finish.

Kimmuriel opened the dimensional door then, showing the devastated tavern, charred bodies laying all about and not a creature stirring. The drow's lip curled up in a wicked smile as he surveyed the grisly scene, and a shudder coursed Gord Abrix's spine as he realized the fate he had only barely escaped.

Berg'inyon Baenre went through the door, into what remained of the tavern room, which was more outdoors than indoors now, and returned a moment later.

"A couple of wererats still stir but barely," the drow warrior informed his companions.

"What of our friends?" Rai-guy asked.

Berg'inyon shrugged. "I saw neither Jarlaxle nor Entreri," he explained. "They could be among the wreckage or could be burned beyond immediate recognition."

Rai-guy considered it for a moment, and motioned for Berg'inyon and Gord Abrix to go back to the tavern and snoop around.

"What of my soldiers?" the wererat asked.

"If they can be saved, pull them back through," Rai-guy replied. "Lady Lolth will grant me the power to healing them . . . should I choose to do so."

Gord Abrix started for the dimensional doorway, and paused and glanced back curiously at the obscure and dangerous drow, not sure how to sort through the wizard-cleric's words.

"Do you believe our prey are still in there?" Kimmuriel asked Rai-guy, using the drow tongue to exclude the wererat leader.

Berg'inyon answered from the doorway. "They are not," he said with confidence, though it was obvious he hadn't found the time yet to scour the ruins. "It would take more than a diversion and a simple wizard's spell to bring down that pair."

Rai-guy's eyes narrowed at the affront to his spellcasting, but in truth, he couldn't really disagree with the assessment. He had been hoping he could catch his prey easily and tidily, but he knew better in his heart, knew that Jarlaxle would prove a difficult and cagey quarry.

"Search quickly," Kimmuriel ordered.

Berg'inyon and Gord Abrix ran off, poking through the smoldering ruins.

"They are not in there," Rai-guy said to his psionicist friend a moment later.

"You agree with Berg'inyon's reasoning?" Kimmuriel asked.

"I hear the call of the Crystal Shard," Rai-guy explained with a snarl, for he did indeed hear the renewed call of the artifact, the prisoner of stubborn Artemis Entreri. "That call comes not from the tavern."

"Then where?" Kimmuriel asked.

Rai-guy could only shake his head in frustration. Where indeed. He heard the pleas, but there was no location attached to them, just an insistent call.

"Bring our henchmen back to us," the wizard instructed, and Kimmuriel went through the doorway, returning a moment later with Berg'inyon, Gord Abrix, and a pair of horribly burned, but still very much alive, wererats.

"Help them," Gord Abrix pleaded, dragging his torched friends to Rai-guy. "This is Poweeno, a close advisor and friend."

Rai-guy closed his eyes and began to chant, and opened his eyes and held his hand out toward the prone and squirming Poweeno. He finished his spell by waggling his fingers and uttering another line of arcane words, and a sharp spark crackled from his fingertips, jolting the unfortunate wererat. The creature cried out and jerked spasmodically, howling in agony as smoking blood and gore began to ooze from its layers of horrible wounds.

A few moments later, Poweeno lay very still, quite dead.

"What . . . what have you done?" Gord Abrix demanded of Rai-guy, the wizard already into spellcasting once more.

When Rai-guy didn't answer, Gord Abrix made a move toward him, or at least tried to. He found his feet stuck to the floor, as if he was standing in some powerful glue. He glanced about, his gaze settling on Kimmuriel. He recognized from the drow's satisfied expression that it was indeed the psionicist holding him fast in place.

"You failed me," Rai-guy explained opening his eyes and holding one hand out toward the other wounded wererat.

"You just said we performed admirably," Gord Abrix protested.

"That was before I knew that Jarlaxle and Artemis Entreri had escaped," Rai-guy explained.

He finished his spell, releasing a tremendous bolt of lightning into the other wounded wererat. The creature flipped over weirdly, then rolling into a fetal position, fast following its companion to the grave.

Gord Abrix howled and drew forth his sword, but Berg'inyon was there, smashing the blade away with his own, fine drow weapon. The warrior looked to his two drow companions. On a nod from Rai-guy, he slashed Gord Abrix across the throat.

The wererat, his feet still stuck fast, sank to the floor, staring helplessly and pleadingly at Rai-guy.

"I do not accept failure," the drow wizard said coldly.

"King Elbereth has sent the word out wide to our scouts," the elf Shayleigh assured Ivan and Pikel when the two dwarven emissaries arrived in Shilmista Forest to the west of the Snowflake Mountains. Cadderly had sent the dwarves straight out to their elf friends, confident that anyone approaching would surely be noticed by King Elbereth's wide network of scouts.

Pikel gave a sound then, which seemed to Ivan to be more one of trepidation than one of hope, though Shayleigh had just given them the assurances they had come here to get.

Or had she?

Ivan Bouldershoulder studied the elf maiden carefully. With her violet eyes and thick golden hair hanging far below her shoulders, she was undeniably beautiful, even to the thinking of a dwarf whose tastes usually ran to shorter, thicker, and more heavily bearded females. There was something else about Shayleigh's posture and attitude, though, about the subtle undertone of her melodious voice.

"Ye're not to kill 'em, ye know," Ivan remarked bluntly.

Shayleigh's posture did not change very much. "You yourself have named them as ultimately dangerous," she replied, "an assassin and a drow."

Ivan noted that the ominous flavor of her voice increased when she named the dark elf, as if the creature's mere race offended her more than the profession of his traveling companion.

"Cadderly's needin' to talk to 'em," Ivan grumbled.

"Can he not speak to the dead?"

"Ooo," said Pikel and he hopped away suddenly, disappearing briefly into the underbrush, and reemerging with one hand behind his back. He hopped up to stand before Shayleigh, a disarming grin on his face. "Drizzit," he reminded, and he pulled his hand around, revealing a delicate flower he had just picked for her.

Shayleigh could hardly hold her stern demeanor against that emotional assault. She smiled and took the wildflower, bringing it to her nose that she could smell its beautiful fragrance. "There is often a flower among the weeds," she said, catching on to Pikel's meaning. "As there may be a druid among a clan of dwarves. That does not mean there are others."

"Hope," said Pikel.

Shayleigh gave a helpless chuckle.

"Ye get yer heart in the right place," Ivan warned, "so says Cadderly, else the Crystal Shard'll find yer heart and twist it to its own needs. It's a big bit o' hope he's puttin' on ye, elf."

Shayleigh's sincere smile was all the assurance he needed.

⊶══⊷

"Brother Chaunticleer has outlined a grand scheme for keeping the children busy," Danica said to Cadderly. "I will be ready to leave as soon as the artifact arrives."

Cadderly's expression hardly seemed to support that notion.

"You did not think I would let you go visit an ancient dragon without me beside you, did you?" Danica asked, sincerely wounded.

Cadderly blew a sigh.

"We've met one before and would have had no trouble at all with it if we had not brought it along with us across the mountains," the woman reminded.

"This time may be more difficult," Cadderly explained. "I will be expending energy merely in controlling the Crystal Shard at the same time I am dealing with the beast. Worse, the artifact will also be speaking to the dragon, I am sure. What better wielder for an instrument of chaos and destruction than a mighty red dragon?"

"How strong is your magic?" Danica asked.

"Not that strong, I fear," Cadderly replied.

"All the more reason that I, and Ivan and Pikel, must be with you," Danica remarked.

"Without the aid of Deneir, do you give any of us a chance of battling such a wyrm?" the priest asked sincerely.

"If Deneir is not with you, you will need us to drag you out of there and quickly," the woman said with a wide smile. "Is that not what your friends are supposed to do?"

Cadderly started to respond, but he really couldn't say much against the look of determination, and of something even more than that—of serenity—stamped across Danica's fair face. Of course she meant to go with him, and he knew he couldn't possibly prevent that unless he left magically and with great deception. Of course, Ivan and Pikel would travel with him as well, though he had to wince when he considered the would-be druid, Pikel, facing a red dragon. They did not want to disturb the great beast any more than to borrow its fiery breath for a single burst of fire. Pikel, so dedicated to the natural, might not be so willing to walk away from a dragon, which was perhaps the greatest perversion of nature in all the world.

Danica cupped her hand under Cadderly's chin then and tilted his head back up so that he was eyeing her directly as she moved very close to him.

"We will finish this and to our satisfaction," she said, and she kissed him gently on the lips. "We have battled worse, my love."

Cadderly didn't begin to deny her words, or her presence, or her determination to go along on this important and dangerous journey. He brought her closer and kissed her again and again.

"We are too busy elsewhere," Sharlotta Vespers tried to explain to Kimmuriel and Rai-guy. The pair were not pleased to learn that Dallabad had somehow been infiltrated by spies of great warlords from Memnon.

The dark elves exchanged concerned looks. Sharlotta had insisted repeatedly that every spy had been caught and killed, but what if she were wrong? What if even one spy had escaped to tell the warlords in Memnon the truth about the change at Dallabad? Or what if other spies had now discerned the real power behind the overthrow of House Basadoni?

"Every danger that Jarlaxle has sown may soon come to harvest," Kimmuriel said to his companion in the drow tongue.

While Sharlotta understood the words well enough, she surely didn't catch the subtleties of the common drow saying, one that referred to revenge taken on a drow house for crimes against another house. Kimmuriel's words were a stern warning, a reminder that Jarlaxle's involvement with Crenshinibon may have left them all vulnerable, no matter what remedial steps they now took.

Rai-guy nodded and stroked his chin, whispering something under his breath that the others could not catch. He stepped forward suddenly to stand right before Sharlotta, bringing his hands up in front of him, thumb-to-thumb. He uttered another word, and a gout of flame burst forth, engulfing the surprised woman's head. She slapped at the fire and screamed, running around the room, and dived to the floor, rolling.

"Make sure that all others who know too much are similarly uninformed," Rai-guy said coldly, as Sharlotta finally died on the floor at his feet.

Kimmuriel nodded, his expression grim, though a hint of an eager grin did turn up the edges of his thin lips.

"I will open the portal back to Menzoberranzan," the wizard explained. "I hold no love for this place and know now, as do you, that our potential gains here do not outweigh the risk to Bregan D'aerthe. I do not even consider it a pity that Jarlaxle foolishly overstepped the bounds of rational caution."

"Better that he did," Kimmuriel agreed. "That we can be on our way to the caverns where we truly belong." He glanced down at Sharlotta, her head blackened and smoking, and smiled once more. He bowed to his companion, his friend of like mind, and left the room, eager to begin the debriefing of others.

Rai-guy also left the room, though through another door, one that led him to the staircase to the basement of House Basadoni, where he could relax more privately in secure chambers. His words of retreat to Kimmuriel followed his every step.

Logical words. Words of survival in a place grown too dangerous.

But still . . . there remained a call in his head, an insistent intrusion, a plea for help.

A promise of greatness beyond his comprehension.

Rai-guy settled into a comfortable chair in his private room, reminding himself continually that a return to Menzoberranzan was the correct move for Bregan D'aerthe, that the risk of remaining on the surface, even in pursuit of the powerful artifact, was too great for the potential gains.

Soon after, the exhausted drow fell into a sort of reverie, as close to true sleep as a dark elf might know.

And in that "sleep," the call of Crenshinibon came again to Rai-guy, a plea for help, for rescue, and a promise of great gain in return.

That predictable call was soon magnified a hundred times over, with even greater promises of glory and power, with images not of magnificent crystalline towers on the deserts of Calimshan, but of a tower of the purest opal set in the center of Menzoberranzan, a black structure gleaming with inner heat and energy.

Rai-guy's reminders of prudence could not hold against that image, against the parade of Matron Mothers, the hated Triel Baenre among them, coming to the tower to pay homage to him.

The dark elf's eyes popped open wide. He collected his thoughts and sprang from the chair, moving quickly to locate Kimmuriel, to alter the psionisict's instructions. Yes, he would open the gate back to Menzoberranzan, and yes, much of Bregan D'aerthe would return to their home.

But Rai-guy and Kimmuriel were not finished here just yet. They would remain with a strike force until the Crystal Shard had found a proper wielder, a dark elf wizard-cleric who would bring to the artifact its greatest level of power, and who would take from it the same.

⊲━━━━⊳

In a dark chamber far under Dallabad Oasis, Yharaskrik silently congratulated himself on altering the promises of the Crystal Shard more greatly to entice Rai-guy. Kimmuriel had informed Yharaskrik of the change in Bregan D'aerthe's plans, but though Yharaskrik had outwardly accepted that change, the illithid was not willing to let the artifact go running off unchecked just yet. Through great concentration and mind control, Yharaskrik had been able to catch the subtle notes of the artifact's quiet call, but the illithid had not been able to begin to backtrack that call to the source.

Yharaskrik needed Bregan D'aerthe a bit longer, though the illithid recognized that once the drow band had fulfilled its purpose in locating the Crystal Shard, he and Rai-guy would likely be on opposite sides of the inevitable battle.

Let that be as it may, Yharaskrik realized. Kimmuriel Oblodra, a fellow psionicist who understood the deeper truths about Crenshinibon's shortcomings, would surely stand on his side of the battlefield.

CHAPTER

THE MASK OF A GOD

21

Why would you live in a desert, when such beauty is so near?" Jarlaxle asked Entreri.

The pair had moved quickly in the days after the disaster at Gentleman Briar's tavern, with Entreri even enlisting one wizard they found in an out-of-the-way tower magically to transport them many miles closer to their goal of the Spirit Soaring and the priest, Cadderly.

It didn't hurt, of course, that Jarlaxle seemed to have an inexhaustible supply of gold coins.

Now the Snowflake Mountains were in clear sight, towering before them. Summer was on the wane, and the wind blew chill, but Entreri could hardly argue Jarlaxle's assessment of the landscape. It surprised the assassin that a drow would find beauty in such a surface environment. They looked down on a canopy of great and ancient trees that filled a long, wide vale nestled right up against the Snowflake's westernmost slopes. Even Entreri, who seemed to spend most of his time denying beauty, could not deny the majesty of the mountains themselves, tall and jagged, capped with bright snow gleaming brilliantly in the daylight.

"Calimport is where I make my living," Entreri answered after a while.

Jarlaxle snorted at the thought. "With your skills, you could make your home anywhere in the world," he said. "In Waterdeep or in Luskan, in Icewind Dale or even here. Few would deny the value of a powerful warrior in cities large and villages small. None would evict Artemis Entreri—unless, of course, they knew the man as I know him."

That brought a narrow-eyed gaze from the assassin, but it was all in jest, both knew—or perhaps it wasn't. Even in that case, there was too much truth to Jarlaxle's statement for Entreri rationally to take offense.

"We must swing around the mountains to the south to get to Carradoon, and the trails leading us to the Spirit Soaring," Entreri explained. "A few days should have us standing before Cadderly, if we make all haste."

"All haste, then," said Jarlaxle. "Let us be rid of the artifact, and . . ." He paused and looked curiously at Entreri.

Then what?

That question hung palpably in the air between them, though it had not been spoken. Ever since they had fled the crystalline tower in Dallabad, the pair had run with purpose and direction—to the Spirit Soaring to be rid of the dangerous artifact—but what, indeed, awaited them after that? Was Jarlaxle to return to Calimport to resume his command of Bregan D'aerthe? both wondered. Entreri knew at once as he pondered the possibility that he would not follow his dark elf companion in that case. Even if Jarlaxle could somehow overcome the seeds of change sown by Rai-guy and Kimmuriel, Entreri had no desire to be with the drow band again. He had no desire to measure his every step in light of the knowledge that the vast majority of his supposed allies would prefer it if he were dead.

Where would they go? Together or apart? Both were contemplating that question when a voice, strong yet melodic, resonant with power, drifted across the field to them.

"Halt and yield!" it said.

Entreri and Jarlaxle glanced over as one to see a solitary figure, a female elf, beautiful and graceful. She was approaching them openly, a finely crafted sword at her side.

"Yield?" Jarlaxle muttered. "Must everyone expect us to yield? And halt? Why, we were not even moving!"

Entreri was hardly listening, was focusing his senses on the trees around them. The elf maiden's gait told him much, and he confirmed his suspicions almost immediately, spotting one, and another, elf archer among the boughs, bows trained upon him and his companion.

"She is not alone," the assassin whispered to Jarlaxle, though he tried to keep the smile on his face as he spoke, an inviting expression for the approaching warrior.

"Elves rarely are," Jarlaxle replied quietly. "Particularly when they are confronting drow."

Entreri couldn't hold his smile, facing that simple truth. He expected the arrows to begin raining down upon them at any moment.

"Greetings!" Jarlaxle called loudly. He swept off his hat, making a point to show his heritage openly.

Entreri noted that the elf maiden did wince and slow briefly at the revelation, for even from her distance—and she was still thirty strides away—Jarlaxle, without the visually overwhelming hat, was obviously drow.

She came a bit closer, her expression holding perfectly calm and steady, revealing nothing. It occurred to Entreri then that this was no chance meeting. He took a moment to listen for the silent call of Crenshinibon, to try to determine if the Crystal Shard had brought in more opponents to free it from Entreri's grasp.

He sensed nothing unusual, no contact at all between the artifact and this elf.

"There are a hundred warriors about you," the elf maiden said, stopping some twenty paces from the pair. "They would like nothing better than to pierce your tiny drow heart with their arrows, but we have not come here for that—unless you so desire it."

"Preposterous!" Jarlaxle said, quite animatedly. "Why would I desire such a thing, fair elf? I am Drizzt Do'Urden of Icewind Dale, a ranger, and of heart not unlike your own, I am sure!"

The elf's lips grew very thin.

"She does not know of you, my friend," Entreri offered.

"Shayleigh of Shilmista Forest knows of Drizzt Do'Urden," Shayleigh assured them both. "And she knows of Jarlaxle of Bregan D'aerthe, and of Artemis Entreri, most vile of assassins."

That made the pair blink more than a few times. "Must be the Crystal Shard telling her," Jarlaxle whispered to his companion.

Entreri didn't deny that, but neither did he believe it. He closed his eyes, trying to sense some connection between the artifact and the elf maiden again, and again he found nothing. Nothing at all.

But how else could she know?

"And you are Shayleigh of Shilmista?" Jarlaxle asked politely. "Or were you, perchance, speaking of another?"

"I am Shayleigh," the elf announced. "I, and my friends gathered in the trees all around you, were sent out here to find you, Jarlaxle of Bregan D'aerthe. You carry an item of great importance to us."

"Not I," the drow said, feigning confusion and glad that he could further mask that confusion by speaking truthful words.

"The Crystal Shard is in the possession of Jarlaxle and Artemis Entreri," Shayleigh stated definitively. "I care not which of you carries it, only that you have it."

"They will strike fast," Jarlaxle whispered to Entreri. "The shard coaxes them in. No parlay here, I fear."

Entreri didn't get that feeling, not at all. The Crystal Shard was not calling to Shayleigh, nor to any of the other elves. If it had been, that call had undoubtedly been completely denied.

The assassin saw Jarlaxle making some subtle motions then—the movements of a spell, he figured—and he put a hand on the dark elf's arm, holding him still.

"We do indeed possess the item you claim," Entreri said to Shayleigh, stepping up ahead of Jarlaxle. He was playing a hunch here, and nothing more. "We are bringing it to Cadderly of the Spirit Soaring."

"For what purpose?" Shayleigh asked.

"That he may rid the world of it," Entreri answered boldly. "You say that you know of Drizzt Do'Urden. If that is true, and if you know Cadderly of the Spirit Soaring as well—which I believe you do—then you likely know that Drizzt was bringing this very artifact to Cadderly."

"Until it was stolen from him by a dark elf posing as Cadderly," Shayleigh said determinedly and in a leading tone. In truth, that was about as much as Cadderly had told her about how this particular pair had come to acquire the artifact.

"There are reasons for things that a casual observer might not understand," Jarlaxle interjected. "Be satisfied with the knowledge that we have the Crystal Shard and are delivering it, rightfully so, to Cadderly of the Spirit Soaring, that he might rid the world of the menace that is Crenshinibon."

Shayleigh motioned to the trees, and her companions walked out from the shadows. There were dozens of grim-faced elves, warriors all, armed with crafted bows and wearing fine weapons and gleaming, supple armor.

"I was instructed to deliver you to the Spirit Soaring," Shayleigh explained. "It was not clear whether or not you had to be alive. Walk swiftly and silently, make no movements that indicate any hostility, and perhaps you will live to see the great doors of the cathedral, though I assure you that I hope you do not."

She turned then and started away. The elves began to close in on the dark elf and his assassin companion, with their bows still in hand and arrows aimed for the kill.

"This is going better than I expected," Jarlaxle said dryly.

"You are an eternal optimist, then," Entreri replied in the same tone. He searched all around for some weakness in the ring of elves, but he saw only swift, inescapable death stamped on every fair face.

Jarlaxle saw it, too, even more clearly. "We are caught," he remarked.

"And if they know all the details of our encounter with Drizzt Do'Urden. . . ." Entreri said ominously, letting the words hang in the air.

Jarlaxle held his wry smile until Entreri had turned away, hoping that he wouldn't be forced to reveal the truth of that encounter to his companion. He didn't want to tell Entreri that Drizzt was still alive. While Jarlaxle believed Entreri had gone beyond that destructive obsession with Drizzt, if he was wrong and Entreri learned the truth, he would likely be fighting for his life against the skilled warrior.

Jarlaxle glanced around at the many grim-faced elves and decided he already had enough problems.

As the meeting at the Spirit Soaring wore on, Cadderly fired back a testy remark concerning the feelings between the drow and the surface elves when Jarlaxle implied that he and his companion really couldn't trust anyone who brought them in under a guard of a score of angry elves.

"But you have already said that this is not about us," Jarlaxle reasoned. He glanced over at Entreri, but the assassin wasn't offering any support, wasn't offering anything at all.

Entreri hadn't spoken a word since they'd arrived, and neither had Cadderly's second at the meeting, a confident woman named Danica. Indeed, she and Entreri seemed cut of similar stuff—and neither of them seemed to like that fact. They had been staring, glowering at each other for nearly the entire time, as if there was some hidden agenda between them, some personal feud.

"True enough," Cadderly finally admitted. "In another situation, I would have many questions to ask of you, Jarlaxle of Menzoberranzan, and most of them far from complimentary toward your apparent actions."

"A trial?" the dark elf asked with a snort. "Is that your place, then, Magistrate Cadderly?"

The yellow-bearded dwarf behind the priest, obviously the more serious of the two dwarves, grumbled and shifted uncomfortably. His green-bearded brother just held his stupid, naive smile. To Jarlaxle's way of thinking, where he was always searching for layers under lies, that smile marked the green-bearded dwarf as the more dangerous of the two.

Cadderly eyed Jarlaxle without blinking. "We must all answer for our actions," he said.

"But to whom?" the drow countered. "Do you even begin to believe that you can understand the life I have lived, judgmental priest? How might you fare in the darkness of Menzoberranzan, I wonder?"

He meant to continue, but both Entreri and Danica broke their silence then, saying in unison, "Enough of this!"

"Ooo," mumbled the green-bearded dwarf, for the room went perfectly silent. Entreri and Danica were as surprised as the others at the coordination of their remarks. They stared hard at each other, seeming on the verge of battle.

"Let us conclude this," Cadderly said. "Give over the Crystal Shard and go on your way. Let your past haunt your own consciences then, and I will be concerned only with that which you do in the future. If you remain near to the Spirit Soaring, then know that your actions are indeed my province, and know that I will be watching."

"I tremble at the thought," Entreri said, before Jarlaxle could utter a similar, though less blunt, reply. "Unfortunately, for all of us, our time together has only just begun. I need you to destroy the wretched artifact, and you need me because I carry it."

"Give it over," Danica said, eyeing the man coldly.

Entreri smirked at her. "No."

"I am sworn to destroy it," Cadderly argued.

"I have heard such words before," Entreri replied. "Thus far, I am the only one who has been able to ignore the temptation of the artifact, and therefore, it remains with me until it is destroyed." He felt an inner twinge at that, a combination of a plea, a threat, and the purest rage he had ever known, all emanating from the imprisoned Crystal Shard.

Danica scoffed as if his claim was purely preposterous, but Cadderly held her in check.

"There is no need for such heroics from you," the priest assured Entreri. "You do not need to do this."

"I do," Entreri replied, though when he looked to Jarlaxle, it seemed to him as if his drow companion was siding with Cadderly.

Entreri could certainly see that point of view. Powerful enemies pursued them, and the Crystal Shard itself was not likely to be destroyed without a terrific battle. Still, Entreri knew in his heart that he had to see this through. He hated the artifact profoundly. He needed to see this controlling, awful item be utterly obliterated. He didn't know why he felt so strongly, but he did, plain and simple, and he wasn't giving over the artifact not to Cadderly or to Danica, not to Rai-guy and Kimmuriel, not to anyone while he still had breath in his body.

"I will finish this," Cadderly remarked.

"So you say," the assassin answered sarcastically and without hesitation.

"I am a priest of Deneir," Cadderly started to protest.

"I name supposedly goodly priests among the least trustworthy of all creatures," Entreri interrupted coldly. "They are on my scale just below troglodytes and green slime, the greatest hypocrites and liars in all the world."

"Please, my friend, do not temper your feelings," Jarlaxle said dryly.

"I would have thought that such a distinction would belong to assassins, murderers, and thieves," Danica remarked, her tone and expression making her hatred for Artemis Entreri quite evident.

"Dear girl, Artemis Entreri is no thief," Jarlaxle said with a grin, hoping to diffuse some of the mounting tension before it exploded—and he and his companion found themselves squared off against the formidable array within this room and without, where scores of priests and a group of elves were no doubt discussing the arrival of the two less-than-exemplary characters with more than a passing concern.

Cadderly put a hand on Danica's arm, calming her, and took a deep breath and started to reason it all out again.

Again Entreri cut him short. "However you wish to parse your words, the simple truth is that I possess the Crystal Shard, and that I, above all others who have tried, have shown the control necessary to hold its call in check.

"If you wish to take the artifact from me," Entreri continued, "then try, but know that I'll not give it over easily—and that I will even utilize the powers of the artifact against you. I wish it destroyed—you wish it destroyed, so you say. Thus, we do it together."

Cadderly paused for a long while, glanced over at Danica a couple of times, and to Jarlaxle, and neither offered him any answers. With a shrug, the priest looked back at Entreri.

"As you wish," he agreed. "The artifact must be engulfed in magical darkness and breathed upon by an ancient and huge red dragon."

Jarlaxle nodded, but then stopped, his dark eyes going wide. "Give it to him," he said to his companion.

Artemis Entreri, though he had no desire to face a red dragon of any size or age, feared more the consequence of Crenshinibon's becoming free to wield its power once more. He knew how to destroy it now—they all did—and the Crystal Shard would never suffer them to live, unless that life was as its servant.

That possibility Artemis Entreri loathed most of all.

Jarlaxle thought to mention that Drizzt Do'Urden had shown equal control, but he held the thought silent, not wanting to bring up the drow ranger in any context. Given Cadderly's understanding of the situation, it seemed obvious to Jarlaxle that the priest knew the truth of his encounter with Drizzt, and Jarlaxle did not want Entreri to discover that his nemesis was still alive—not now, at least, with so many other pressing issues before him.

Jarlaxle considered blurting it all out, on a sudden thought that speaking the truth plainly would heighten Entreri's willingness to be done with all of this, to give over the shard that he and Jarlaxle could pursue a more important matter—that of finding the drow ranger.

Jarlaxle held it back, and smiled, recognizing the source of the inspiration as a subtle telepathic ruse by the imprisoned artifact.

"Clever," he whispered, and merely smiled as all eyes turned to regard him.

Soon after, while Cadderly and his friends made preparations for the journey to the lair of some dragon Cadderly knew of, Entreri and Jarlaxle walked the grounds outside of the magnificent Spirit Soaring, well aware, of course, that many watchful eyes were upon their every move.

"It is undeniably beautiful, do you not agree?" Jarlaxle asked, looking back at the soaring cathedral, with its tall spires, flying buttresses, and great, colored windows.

"The mask of a god," Entreri replied sourly.

"The mask or the face?" asked the always-surprising Jarlaxle.

Entreri stared hard at his companion, and back at the towering cathedral. "The mask," he said, "or perhaps the illusion, concocted by those who seek to elevate themselves above all others and have not the skills to do so."

Jarlaxle looked at him curiously.

"A man inferior with the blade or with his thoughts can still so elevate himself," Entreri explained curtly, "if he can impart the belief that some god or other speaks through him. It is the greatest deception in all the world, and one embraced by kings and lords, while minor lying thieves on the streets of Calimport and other cities lose their tongues for so attempting to coax the purses of others."

That struck Jarlaxle as the most poignant and revealing insight he had yet pried from the mouth of the elusive Artemis Entreri, a great clue as to who this man truly was.

Up to that point, Jarlaxle had been trying to figure out a way that he could wait behind while Entreri, Cadderly, and whomever Cadderly chose to bring along went to face the dragon and destroy the artifact.

Now, because of this seemingly unrelated glimpse into the heart of Artemis Entreri, Jarlaxle realized he had to go along.

CHAPTER

IN THE EYE OF THE BEHOLDER

22

The great beast lay at rest, but even in slumber did the dragon seem a terrible and wrathful thing. It curled catlike, its long tail running up past its head, its huge, scaly back rising like a giant wave and sinking in a great exhalation that sent plumes of gray smoke from its nostrils and injected a vibrating rumble throughout the stone of the cavern floor. There was no light in the rocky chamber, save the glow of the dragon itself, a reddish-gold hue—a hot light, as if the beast were too full of energy and savage fires to hold it all in with mere scales.

On the other end of the scrying mirror, the six unlikely companions—Cadderly, Danica, Ivan, Pikel, Entreri, and Jarlaxle—watched the dragon with a mixture of awe and dread.

"We could use Shayleigh and her archers," Danica remarked, but of course, that was not possible, since the elves had absolutely refused to work alongside the dark elf for any purpose whatsoever and had returned to their forest home in Shilmista.

"We could use King Elbereth's entire army," Cadderly added.

"Ooo," said Pikel, who seemed truly mesmerized by the beast, a great wyrm at least as large and horrific as old Fyrentennimar.

"There is the dragon," Cadderly said, turning to Entreri. "Are you certain you still wish to accompany me?" His question ended weakly, though, given the eager glow in Artemis Entreri's eyes.

The assassin reached into his pouch and brought forth the Crystal Shard.

"Witness your doom," he whispered to the artifact. He felt the shard reaching out desperately and powerfully—Cadderly felt those sensations as well. It called to Jarlaxle first, and indeed, the opportunistic drow did begin physically to reach for it, but he resisted.

"Put it away," Danica whispered harshly, looking from the green-glowing shard to the shifting beast. "It will awaken the dragon!"

"My dear, do you expect to coax the fiery breath from a dragon that remains asleep?" Jarlaxle reminded her, but Danica turned an angry glare at him.

Entreri, hearing the Crystal Shard's call clearly and recognizing its attempt, understood that the woman spoke wisely, though, for while they would indeed have to wake the beast, they would be far better served if it did not know why. The assassin looked at the artifact and gave a confident, cocky grin, and dropped it back into his pouch and nodded for Cadderly to disenchant the scrying mirror.

"When do we go?" the assassin asked Cadderly, and his tone made it perfectly clear that he wasn't shaken in the least by the sight of the monstrous dragon, made it clear that he was eager to be done with the destruction of the vile artifact.

"I have to prepare the proper spells," Cadderly replied. "It will not be long."

The priest motioned for Danica and his other friends to escort their two undesirable companions away then, though he only dropped the image from the scrying mirror temporarily. As soon as he was alone, he called up the dragon cave again, after placing another spell upon himself that allowed him to see in the dark. He sent the roving eye of the scrying mirror all around the large, intricate lair.

There were many great cracks in the floor, he noted, and when he followed one down, he came to recognize that a maze of tunnels and chambers lay beneath the sleeping wyrm. Furthermore, Cadderly wasn't convinced that the dragon's cave was very secure structurally. Not at all.

He'd have to keep that well in mind while choosing the spells he would bring with him to the home of this great beast known as Hephaestus.

<hr />

Rai-guy, deep in concentration, his eyes closed, allowed the calls of Crenshinibon to invade his thoughts fully. He caught only flashes of anger and despair, the pleas for help, the promises of ultimate glory.

He saw some other images, as well, particularly one of a great curled red dragon, and he heard a word, a name echoing in his head: Hephaestus.

Rai-guy knew he had to act quickly. He settled back in his private chamber beneath House Basadoni and prayed with all his heart to his Lady Lolth, telling her of the Crystal Shard, and of the glorious chaos the artifact might allow him to bring to the world.

For hours, Rai-guy stayed alone, praying, sending away any who knocked at his door—Berg'inyon and Kimmuriel among them—with a gruff and definitive retort.

Then, when he believed he'd caught the attention of his dark Spider Queen, or at least the ear of one of her minions, the wizard fell into powerful spellcasting, opening an extra-planar gate.

As always with such a spell, Rai-guy had to take care that no unwanted or overly powerful planar denizens walked through that gate. His suspicions were correct, though, and indeed, the creature that came through the portal was one of the yochlol. These were the handmaidens of Lolth, beasts that more resembled half-melted candles with longer appendages than the Spider Queen herself.

Rai-guy held his breath, wondering suddenly and fearfully if he had erred in letting on about the artifact. Might Lolth desire the artifact herself and instruct Rai-guy to deliver it to her?

"You have called for help from the Lady," the yochlol said, its voice watery and guttural all at once, a dual-toned and horrible sound.

"I wish to return to Menzoberranzan," Rai-guy admitted, "and yet I cannot at this time. An instrument of chaos is about to be destroyed . . ."

"Lady Lolth knows of the artifact, Crenshinibon, Rai-guy of House Teya-chumet," the yochlol replied, and the title the creature bestowed upon him surprised the drow wizard-cleric.

He had indeed been a son of House Teyachumet—but that house of Ched Nasad had been obliterated more than a century before. A subtle reminder, the drow realized, that the memory of Lolth and her minions was long indeed.

And a warning, perhaps, that he should take great care about how he planned to put the mighty artifact to use in the city of Lolth's greatest priestesses.

Rai-guy saw his dreams of domination over Menzoberranzan melt then and there.

"Where will you retrieve this item?" the handmaiden asked.

Rai-guy stammered a reply, his thoughts elsewhere for the moment. "Hephaestus's lair . . . a red dragon," he said. "I know not where . . ."

"Your answer will be given," the handmaiden promised.

It turned around and walked through Rai-guy's gate, and the portal closed immediately, though the drow wizard had done nothing to dispel it.

Had Lolth herself been watching the exchange? Rai-guy had to wonder and to fear. Again he understood the futility of his dreams of conquest over Menzoberranzan. The Crystal Shard was powerful indeed, perhaps powerful enough for Rai-guy to manipulate or otherwise unseat enough of the Matron Mothers for him to achieve a position of tremendous power, but something about the way the yochlol had spoken his full name told him he should be careful indeed. Lady Lolth would not permit such a change in the balance of Menzoberranzan's power structure.

For just a brief moment, Rai-guy considered abandoning his quest to retrieve the Crystal Shard, considered taking his remaining allies and his gains and retreating to Menzoberranzan as the coleader, along with his friend, Kimmuriel, of Bregan D'aerthe.

A brief moment it was, for the call of the Crystal Shard came rushing back to him then, whispering its promises of power and glory, showing Rai-guy that the surface was not so forbidding a place as he believed. With Crenshinibon, the dark elf could carry on Jarlaxle's designs, but in more appropriate regions—a mountainous area teeming with goblins, perhaps—and build a magnificent and undyingly loyal legion of minions, of slaves.

The drow wizard rubbed his slender black fingers together, waiting anxiously for the answer the yochlol had promised him.

⊰═══⊱

"You cannot deny the beauty," Jarlaxle remarked, he and Entreri again sitting outside of the cathedral, relaxing before their journey. Both were well aware that many wary gazes were focused upon them from many vantage points.

"Its very purpose denies that beauty," Entreri replied, his tone showing that he had little desire to replay this conversation yet again.

Jarlaxle studied the man closely, as if hoping that physical scrutiny alone would unlock this apparently dark episode in Artemis Entreri's past. The drow wasn't surprised by Entreri's dislike of "hypocritical" priests. In many ways, Jarlaxle agreed with him. The dark elf had been alive for a long, long time, and had often ventured out of Menzoberranzan—and had known the movements of practically every visitor to that dark city—and he had seen enough of the many varied religious sects of Toril to understand the hypocritical nature of many so-called priests. There was something far deeper than that looming here within Artemis Entreri, though, something visceral. It had to be an event in Entreri's past, a deeply disturbing episode involving a priest. Perhaps he had been wrongly accused of some crime and tortured by a priest, who often served as jailers for the smaller communities of the surface. Perhaps he had known love once, and that woman had been stolen from him or had been murdered by a priest.

Whatever it was, Jarlaxle could clearly see the hatred in Entreri's dark eyes as the man looked upon the magnificent—and it was magnificent, by any standards—Spirit Soaring. Even for Jarlaxle, a creature of the Underdark, the place lived up to its name, for when he gazed upon those soaring towers, his very soul was lifted, his spirit enlightened and elevated.

Not so for his companion, obviously, and yet another mystery of Artemis Entreri for Jarlaxle to unravel. He did indeed find this man interesting.

"Where will you go after the artifact is destroyed?" Entreri asked unexpectedly.

Jarlaxle had to pause, both fully to digest the question and to consider his answer—for in truth, he really had no answer. "*If* we destroy it, you mean," he corrected. "Have you ever dealt with the likes of a red dragon, my friend?"

"Cadderly has, as I'm sure have you," Entreri replied.

"Only once, and I truly have little desire ever to speak with such a beast again," Jarlaxle said. "One cannot reason with a red dragon beyond a certain level, because they are not creatures with any definitive goals for personal gain. They see, they destroy, and take what is left over. A simple existence, really, and one that makes them all the more dangerous."

"Then let it see the Crystal Shard and destroy it," Entreri remarked, and he felt a twinge then as Crenshinibon cried out.

"Why?" Jarlaxle asked suddenly, and Entreri recognized that his ever-opportunistic friend had heard that silent call.

"Why?" the assassin echoed, turning to regard Jarlaxle fully.

"Perhaps we are being premature in our planning," Jarlaxle explained. "We know how to destroy the Crystal Shard now—likely that will be enough for us to use against the artifact to bend it continually to our will."

Entreri started to laugh.

"There is truth in what I say, and a gain to be had in following my reasoning," Jarlaxle insisted. "Crenshinibon began to manipulate me, no doubt, but now that we have determined that you, and not the artifact, are truly the master of your relationship, why must we rush ahead to destroy it? Why not determine first if you might control the item enough for our own gain?"

"Because if you know, beyond doubt, that you can destroy it, and the Crystal Shard knows that, as well, there may well be no need to destroy it," Entreri played along.

"Exactly!" said the now-excited dark elf.

"Because if you know you can destroy the crystalline tower, then there is no possible way that you will wind up with two crystalline towers," Entreri replied sarcastically, and the eager grin disappeared from Jarlaxle's black-skinned face in the blink of an astonished eye.

"It did it again," the drow remarked dryly.

"Same bait on the hook, and the Jarlaxle fish chomps even harder," Entreri replied.

"The cathedral is beautiful, I say," Jarlaxle remarked, looking away and pointedly changing the subject.

Entreri laughed again.

Delay him, then, Yharaskrik imparted to Kimmuriel when the drow told the illithid the plan to intercept Jarlaxle, Entreri, and the priest Cadderly and his friends at the lair of Hephaestus the red dragon.

Rai-guy will not be deterred in any way short of open battle, Kimmuriel explained. *He will have the Crystal Shard at all costs.*

Because the Crystal Shard so instructs him, Yharaskrik replied.

Yet it seems as if he has freed himself, partially at least, from its grasp, Kimmuriel argued. *He dismissed many of the drow soldiers back to our warren in Menzoberranzan and has systematically relinquished our holdings here on the surface.*

True enough, the illithid admitted, *but you are fooling yourself if you believe that the Crystal Shard will allow Rai-guy to take it to the lightless depths of the Underdark. It is a relic that derives its power from the light of the sun.*

Rai-guy believes that a few crystalline towers on the surface will allow the artifact to channel that sunlight power back to Menzoberranzan, Kimmuriel explained, for indeed, the drow wizard had told him of that very possibility—a possibility that Crenshinibon itself had imparted to Rai-guy.

Rai-guy has come to see many possibilities, Yharaskrik's thoughts imparted, and there was a measure of doubt, translated into sarcasm, in the illithid's response. *The source of those varied and marvelous possibilities is always the same.*

It was a point on which Kimmuriel Oblodra, who now found himself caught in the middle of five dangerous adversaries—Rai-guy, Yharaskrik, Jarlaxle, Artemis Entreri, and the Crystal Shard itself—did not wish to dwell. There was little he could do to alter the approaching events. He would not go against Rai-guy, out of respect for the wizard-cleric's prowess and intelligence, and also because of his deep relationship with the drow. Of his potential enemies, Kimmuriel feared Yharaskrik least of all. With Rai-guy at his side, he knew the illithid could not win. Kimmuriel could neutralize Yharaskrik's mental weaponry long enough for Rai-guy to obliterate the creature.

While he held respect for the manipulative powers of the Crystal Shard and knew that the mighty artifact would not be pleased with any psionicist, Kimmuriel was honestly beginning to believe that the artifact was indeed a fine match for Rai-guy, a joining that would be of mutual benefit. Jarlaxle hadn't been able to control the artifact, but Jarlaxle had not been properly forewarned about its manipulative powers. Kimmuriel doubted that Rai-guy would make that same mistake.

Still, the psionicist believed that all would be simpler and cleaner if the Crystal Shard were indeed destroyed, but he wasn't about to go against Rai-guy to ensure that event.

He looked at the illithid and realized that he already had gone against his friend, to some extent, merely by informing this bulbous-headed creature, who was certainly an enemy of Rai-guy, that Rai-guy meant to enter an alliance with the Crystal Shard.

Kimmuriel bowed to Yharaskrik out of respect, and floated away on psionic winds, back to House Basadoni and his private chambers. Not far down the hall, he knew, Rai-guy was awaiting his answer from the yochlol and plotting his strike against Jarlaxle and the fallen leader's newfound companions.

Kimmuriel had no idea where he was going to fit into all of this.

CHAPTER

THE FACE OF DISASTER

23

Artemis Entreri eyed the priest of Deneir with obvious mistrust as Cadderly walked up before him and began a slow chant. Cadderly had already cast prepared defensive spells upon himself, Danica, Ivan, and Pikel, but it occurred to Entreri that the priest might use this opportunity to get rid of him. What better way to destroy Entreri than to have him face the breath of a dragon errantly thinking he had proper magical defenses against such a firestorm?

The assassin glanced over at Jarlaxle, who had refused Cadderly's aid, claiming he had his own methods. The dark elf nodded to him and waggled his fingers, silently assuring Entreri that Cadderly had indeed placed the antifire enchantment upon him.

When he was done, Cadderly stepped back and inspected the group. "I still believe that I can do this better alone," he remarked, drawing a scowl from both Danica and Entreri.

"If it was as simple as erecting a fire barrier and tossing out the artifact for the dragon to breathe upon, I would agree," Jarlaxle replied. "You may need to goad the beast to breathe, I fear. Wyrms are not quick to use their most powerful weapon."

"When it sees us all, it will more likely loose its breath," Danica reasoned.

"Poof!" agreed Pikel.

"Contingencies, my dear Cadderly," said Jarlaxle. "We must allow for every contingency, must prepare for every eventuality and turn in the game. With an ancient and intelligent wyrm, no variable is unlikely."

Their conversation ended as they both noted Pikel hopping about his brother, sprinkling some powder over the protesting and slapping Ivan, while singing a whimsical song. He finished with a wide smile, and hopped up and whispered into Ivan's ear.

"Says he got a spell of his own to add," the yellow-bearded dwarf remarked. "Put one on meself and on himself, and's wondering which o' ye others'll be wantin' one."

"What type of spell?"

"Another fire protection," Ivan explained. "Says doo-dads can do that."

That brought a laugh to Jarlaxle—not because he didn't believe the dwarf's every word, but because he found the entire spectacle of a dwarven druid quite charming. He bowed to Pikel and accepted the dwarf's next spellcasting. The others followed suit.

"We will be as quick as possible," Cadderly explained, moving them all to the large window at the back of the room on a high floor in one of the Spirit Soaring's towering spires. "Our goal is to destroy the item and nothing more. We are not to battle the beast, not to raise its ire, and," he looked at Entreri and Jarlaxle as he finished, "surely not to attempt to steal anything from mighty Hephaestus.

"Remember," the priest added, "the enchantments upon you may diminish one blast of Hephaestus's fire, perhaps two, but not much more than that."

"One will be enough," Entreri replied.

"Too much," muttered Jarlaxle.

"Does everyone know his or her role and position when we enter the dragon's main chamber?" Danica asked, ignoring the grumbling drow.

No questions came back at her. Taking that as an affirmative answer, Cadderly began casting yet again, a wind-walking spell that soon carried them out of the cathedral and across the miles to the south and east to the caverns of mighty Hephaestus. The priest didn't magically walk them in the front door, but rather soared along deeper chambers, the understructure of the cavern complex, coming into a large antechamber to the dragon's main lair.

When he broke the spell, depositing their material forms in the cavern, they could hear the great sighing sound of the sleeping wyrm, the huge intake and smoky exhalation.

Jarlaxle put a finger to pursed lips and inched ahead, as silent as could be. He disappeared around an outcropping of stone, and came right back in, actually clutching the wall to steady himself. He looked at the others and nodded grimly, though there could be no doubt he had seen the beast simply from the expression on his normally confident face.

Cadderly and Entreri led the way, Danica and Jarlaxle followed, with the Bouldershoulder brothers behind. The tunnel behind the outcropping wound only for a short distance, and opened up widely into a huge cavern, its floor crisscrossed by many cracks and crevices.

The companions hardly noticed the physical features of that room, though, for there before them, looming like a mountain of doom, lay Hephaestus, its red-gold scales gleaming from its own inner heat. The beast was huge, even curled as it was, its size alone mocking them and making every one of them want to fall to his knees and pay homage.

That was one of the traps in dealing with dragons, that awe-inspiring aura of sheer power, that emanation of helplessness to all who would look upon their horrible splendor.

These were not novice warriors, though, trying to make a quick stab at great fame. These were seasoned veterans, every one. Each, with the exception of Artemis Entreri, had faced a beast such as Hephaestus before. Despite his inexperience in this particular arena, nothing in all the world—not a dragon, not an arch-devil, not a demon lord—could take the heart from Artemis Entreri.

The wyrm's eye, seeming more like that of a cat than a lizard, with a green iris and a slitted pupil that quickly widened to adjust to the dim light, popped open as soon as the group entered. Hephaestus watched their every movement.

"Did you think to catch me sleeping?" the dragon said quietly, which still made its voice sound like an avalanche to the companions.

Cadderly called out a cueing word to his companions, and snapped his fingers, bringing forth a magical light that filled all the chamber.

Up snapped Hephaestus's great horned head, the pupils of its eyes fast thinning. It turned as it rose, to face the impertinent priest directly.

To the side, Entreri eased the Crystal Shard out of his pouch, ready to throw it before the beast as soon as Hephaestus seemed about to loose its fiery breath. Jarlaxle, too, was ready, for his job in this was to use his innate dark elf powers to bring forth a globe of darkness over the artifact as the flames consumed it.

"Thieves!" the dragon roared. Its voice shook the chamber and sent shudders through the floor—a poignant reminder to Cadderly of the instability of this place. "You have come to steal the treasure of Hephaestus. You have prepared your proper spells and wear items of magic that you consider powerful, but are you truly prepared? Can any mere mortal truly be prepared to face the awful splendor that is Hephaestus?"

Cadderly tuned out the words and fell into the song of Deneir, seeking some powerful spell, some type of mighty magical chaos, perhaps, as he had once used against Fyrentennimar, that he could trick the beast and be done with this. His best spells against the previous dragon had been of reverse aging, lessening the beast with mighty spellcasting, but he could not use those this time, for so doing would diminish the dragon's breath as well, and defeat their very purpose in being there. He had other magic at his disposal, though, and the Song of Deneir rang triumphantly in his head. Along with that song, though, the priest heard the calls of Crenshinibon, discordant notes in the melody and surely a distraction.

"Something is amiss," Jarlaxle whispered to Entreri. "The beast expected us and anticipates our movements. It should have risen with attacks, not words."

Entreri glanced at him, and back at Hephaestus, the great head swaying back and forth, back and forth. He glanced down at the Crystal Shard, wondering if it had betrayed them to the beast.

Indeed, Crenshinibon was sending forth its plea at that time, to the beast and against Cadderly's spellcasting, but it had not been the Crystal Shard that had warned Hephaestus of intruders. No, that distinction fell to a certain dark elf wizard-cleric, hiding in a tunnel across the way along with a handful of drow companions. Right before Cadderly and the others had wind-walked into the lair, Rai-guy had sent a magical whisper to Hephaestus, a warning of intruders and a suggestion that these thieves had come with magic designed to use the creature's own breath against it.

Now Rai-guy waited for the appearance of the Crystal Shard, for the moment when he and his companions, including Kimmuriel, could strike hard and begone, their prize in hand.

◄┼──┼►

"Thieves we are, and we'll have your treasure!" shouted Jarlaxle. He used a language that none of the others, save Hephaestus, understood, a tongue of the red dragons, and one that the great wyrms believed that few others could begin to master. Jarlaxle, using a whistle that he kept on a chain around his neck, spoke it with perfect inflection. Hephaestus's head snapped down in line with him, the wyrm's eyes going wide.

Entreri dived aside in a roll, coming right back to his feet.

"What did you say?" the assassin asked.

Jarlaxle's fingers worked furiously. *He thinks that I am another red dragon.*

There seemed a long, long moment of absolute quiet, of a gigantic hush before a more gigantic storm. Then everything exploded into motion, beginning with Cadderly's leap forward, his arm extended, finger pointing accusingly at the beast.

"Hephaestus!" the priest roared at the appropriate moment of spellcasting. "Burn me if you can!"

It was more than a dare, more than a challenge, and more than a threat. It was a magical compulsion, launched through a powerful spell. Though fore-warned by some vague suggestions against the action, Hephaestus sucked in its tremendous breath, the force of the intake drawing Cadderly's curly brown locks forward onto his face.

Entreri dived ahead and pulled forth Crenshinibon, tossing it to the floor before the priest. Jarlaxle, even as Hephaestus tilted back its head, came forward with the great exhalation and produced his globe of darkness.

No! Crenshinibon screamed in Entreri's head, so powerful and angry a call that the assassin grabbed at his ears and stumbled aside, dazed.

The artifact's call was abruptly cut off.

Hephaestus's head came forward, a great line of fire roaring down, mocking Jarlaxle's globe, mocking Cadderly and all his spells.

◄┼──┼►

Even as the globe of darkness came up over the Crystal Shard, Rai-guy grabbed at it with a spell of telekinesis, a sudden and powerful burst of snatching power that sent the item flying fast across the way, past Hephaestus, who was seemingly oblivious to it, and down the corridor to the hiding wizard-cleric's waiting hand.

Rai-guy's red-glowing eyes narrowed as he turned to regard Kimmuriel, for it had been Kimmuriel's task to so snatch the item—a task the psionicist had apparently neglected.

I was not fast enough, the psionicist's fingers waggled at his companion.

But Rai-guy knew better, and so did Crenshinibon, for the powers of the mind were among the quickest of magic to enact. Still staring hard at his companion, Rai-guy began spellcasting once more, aiming for the great chamber.

◄┼──┼►

On and on went the fiery maelstrom, and in the middle of it stood Cadderly, his arms out wide, praying to Deneir to see him through.

Danica, Ivan, and Pikel stared at him intently, praying as well, but Jarlaxle was more concerned with his darkness, and Entreri was looking more to Jarlaxle.

"I hear not the continuing call of Crenshinibon!" Entreri cried hopefully above the fiery roar.

Jarlaxle was shaking his head. "The darkness should have been consumed by the artifact's destruction," he cried back, sensing that something was terribly, terribly wrong.

The fires ended, leaving a seething Hephaestus still staring at the unharmed priest of Deneir. The dragon's eyes narrowed to threatening slits.

Jarlaxle dispelled his darkness globe, and there remained no sign of Crenshinibon among the bubbling, molten stone.

"We done it!" Ivan cried.

"Home!" Pikel pleaded.

"No," insisted Jarlaxle.

Before he could explain, a low humming sound filled the chamber, a noise the dark elf had heard before and one that didn't strike him as overly pleasant at that dangerous moment.

"A magical dispel!" the dark elf warned. "Our enchantments are threatened!"

This left them, they all realized, in a room with an outraged, ancient, huge red dragon without many of their protections in place.

"What d' we do?" Ivan growled, slapping the handle of his battle axe across his open palm.

"Wee!" Pikel answered.

"Wee?" the perplexed yellow-bearded dwarf echoed, his face screwed up as he stared at his green-haired brother.

"Wee!" Pikel said again, and to accentuate his point, he grabbed Ivan by the collar and ran him a short distance to the side, to the edge of a crevice, and leaped off, taking Ivan on the dive with him.

Hephaestus's great wings beat the air, lifting the huge wyrm's front half high above the floor. Its hind legs clawed at the floor, digging deep gullies in the stone.

"Run away!" Cadderly cried, agreeing wholeheartedly with Pikel's choice. "All of you!"

Danica rushed forward, as did Jarlaxle, the woman rolling into a ready crouch before the wyrm. Hephaestus wasted not a second in snapping its great maw down at her. She scrambled aside, coming up from her roll in a crouch again, taunting the beast.

Cadderly couldn't watch it, reminding himself that he simply had to trust in her. She was buying him precious moments, he knew, that he might launch another magical attack or defensive spell, perhaps, at Hephaestus. He fell into the song of Deneir again and heard its notes more clearly this time, as he sorted through an array of spells to launch.

He heard a scream, Danica's scream, and he looked up to see Hephaestus's fiery breath drive down upon her, striking the stone floor and spraying up in an inverted fan of fires.

Cadderly, too, cried out, and reached desperately into the song of Deneir for the first spell he could find that would alter that horrible scene, the first enchantment he could think of to stop it.

He brought forth an earthquake.

Even as it started—a violent shudder and rumbling, like waves on a pond, lifting and rolling the floor—Jarlaxle drew the dragon's attention his way by hitting the beast with a stream of stinging daggers.

Entreri, too, moved—and surprised himself by going ahead instead of back, toward the spot where Hephaestus had just breathed.

There, too, there was only bubbling stone.

Cadderly called out for Danica, desperately, but his voice fell away as the floor collapsed beneath him.

"Let us begone, and quickly," Kimmuriel remarked, "before the great wyrm recognizes that there were more than those six intruders in its lair this day."

He and the other drow had already moved some distance down the tunnel, away from the main chamber. Leaving altogether seemed a prudent suggestion, one that had Berg'inyon Baenre and the other five drow soldiers nodding eagerly, but one that, for some reason, did not seem acceptable to the stern Rai-guy.

"No," he said firmly. "They must all die, here and now."

"As the dragon will likely kill them," Berg'inyon agreed, but Rai-guy was shaking his head, indicating that such a probability simply wasn't good enough for him.

Rai-guy and Crenshinibon were already fully into their bonding by then. The Crystal Shard demanded that Cadderly and the others, these infidels who understood the secret to its destruction, be killed immediately. It demanded that nothing concerning the group be left to chance. Besides, it telepathically coaxed Rai-guy, would not a red dragon be an enormous asset to add to Bregan D'aerthe?

"Find them and kill them, every one!" Rai-guy demanded emphatically.

Berg'inyon considered the command, and broke his soldiers into two groups and ran off with one group, the other heading a different direction. Kimmuriel spent a longer time staring hard at Rai-guy, seeming less than pleased. He, too, disappeared eventually, seemed simply to fall through the floor.

Leaving Rai-guy alone with his newest and most beloved ally.

In an alcove off to the side of the tunnel where Rai-guy stood, Yharaskrik's less-than-corporeal form slid through the stone and materialized, the illithid's Crenshinibon-defeating lantern in its hand.

CHAPTER

CHAOS

24

With skills honed to absolute perfection, Danica had avoided the flames by a short distance, close enough so that her skin was bright red on the left side of her face. No magic would aid Danica now, she knew, only her thousands and thousands of hours of difficult training, those many years she had spent perfecting her style of fighting and, more importantly, dodging. Danica had no intention of battling the great wyrm, of striking out in any offensive manner against a beast she doubted she could even hurt, let alone slay. All her abilities, all her energy and concentration, was solely on the defensive now, her posture a balanced crouch that would allow her to skitter out to either side, ahead, or back.

Hephaestus's fang-filled jaws snapped down at her with a tremendous clapping noise, but the dragon hit only air as the monk dived out to the right. A claw followed, a swipe that surely would have cut Danica into pieces, except that she altered the momentum of her roll to go straight back in a sudden retreat.

Then came the breath, another burst of fire that seemed to go on and on forever. Danica had to dive and roll a couple of times to put out the flames on the back side of her clothing. Sensing that Hephaestus had noted her escape and would adjust the line of fiery breath, she cut a fast corner around a jag in the wall, throwing herself flat against the stone behind the protective rock.

She noted two figures then. Artemis Entreri was running her way, but leaping short of her position into a wide crevice that had opened with Cadderly's earthquake. The strange dark elf, Jarlaxle, skittered behind the dragon, and to Danica's astonishment, launched a spell Hephaestus's way. A sudden arc of lightning caught the dragon's attention and gave Danica a moment of freedom. She didn't waste it.

Danica ran flat out, leaping even as the spinning Hephaestus swept its great tail around to squash her. She disappeared into the same crevice as had Artemis Entreri.

She knew as soon as she crossed the lip of the crack that she was in trouble—but still far less trouble, she supposed, than she would have found back in the dragon's lair. The descent twisted and turned, lined with broken and often sharp-edged, stone. Again Danica's training came into play, her hands and legs working furiously to buffer the blows and slow her descent. Some distance down, the crack opened into a chamber, and Danica had nothing to hold onto for the last twenty feet of her drop. Still, she coordinated her movements so that she landed feet first, but with her legs turned slightly, propelling her into a sidelong somersault. She tumbled over and over again, her roll absorbing the momentum of the fall.

She came up to her feet a few moments later, and there before her, leaning on a wall looking bruised but hardly battered, stood Artemis Entreri. He was staring at her intently and held a lit torch in his hand but tossed it aside as soon as Danica took note of him.

"I had thought you consumed by the first of Hephaestus's fires," the assassin remarked, coming away from the wall and drawing both sword and dagger, the smaller blade glowing with a white, fiery light.

"One cannot always get what one most wants," the woman answered coldly.

"You have hated me since the moment you saw me," the assassin remarked, ending with a chuckle to show that he hardly cared.

"Long before that, Artemis Entreri," Danica replied coldly, and she advanced a step, eyeing the assassin's weapons intently.

"We know not what enemies we will find down here," Entreri explained, but he knew even as he said the words, as he looked upon Danica's mask of hatred, that no explanation would suffice, that anything short of his surrender to her would invite her wrath. Artemis Entreri had little desire to battle the woman, to do any unnecessary fighting down here, but neither would he shy from any fight.

"Indeed," was all that Danica answered. She continued coming forward.

This had been coming for some time, both knew, and despite the fact that they were both separated from their respective companions, despite the fact that an angry dragon was barely fifty feet above their heads, and all of it in a cavern that seemed on the verge of complete collapse, Danica saw this encounter as more than an opportunity but a necessity.

For all his logic and common sense, Artemis Entreri really wasn't disappointed by her feelings.

As soon as Hephaestus began its stunningly fast spin, Jarlaxle had to question the wisdom of his distracting lightning bolt. Still, the drow had reacted as any ally would, taking the beast's attention so that both Entreri and the woman might escape.

In truth, after the initial shock of seeing an outraged red dragon turning at him, Jarlaxle wasn't overly worried. Despite the powerful dispel that had saturated the room—too powerful a spell for any dragon to cast, the mercenary leader recognized—Jarlaxle remained confident that he possessed enough tricks to get away from this one.

Hephaestus's great jaws snapped down at the drow, who was standing perfectly still and seemed an easy target. The magic of Jarlaxle's cloak forced the wyrm to miss, and Hephaestus roared all the louder when its head slammed into a solid wall.

Next, predictably, came the fiery breath, but even as Hephaestus began its great exhale, Jarlaxle waggled a ringed finger, opening a dimension door that brought him behind the dragon. He could have simply skittered away then, but he wanted to hold the beast at bay a little bit longer. Out came a wand, one of several the drow carried, and it spewed a gob of greenish semiliquid at the very tip of Hephaestus's twitching tail.

"Now you are caught!" Jarlaxle proclaimed loudly as the fiery breath at last ceased.

Hephaestus spun around again, and indeed, the wyrm's tail looped about, its end stuck fast by the temporary but incredibly effective goo.

Jarlaxle let fly another wad from the wand, this one smacking the dragon in the face.

Of course, then Jarlaxle remembered why he had never wanted to face such a beast as this again, for Hephaestus went into a terrific frenzy, issuing growls through its clamped mouth that resonated through the very stones of the cavern. It thrashed about so wildly its tail tore the stone from the floor.

With a tip of his wide-brimmed hat, the mercenary drow called upon his magical ring again, one of the last portal-enacting enchantments it could offer, and disappeared back behind the wyrm, a bit further along the wall than he had been before his first dimension door. There was another exit from the room back there, one that Jarlaxle suspected would bring him to some old friends.

Some old friends who likely had the Crystal Shard, he knew, for certainly it had not been destroyed by Hephaestus's first breath, certainly it had been magically stolen away right before the powerful magic-defeating spell had filled the room.

The last thing Jarlaxle wanted was for Rai-guy and Kimmuriel to get their hands on the Crystal Shard and, undoubtedly, come looking for him once more.

He was out of the cavern a moment later, the thunderous sounds of Hephaestus's thrashing thankfully left behind. He reached up into his marvelous hat and brought forth a piece of black cloth in the shape of a small bat. He whispered a few magical words and tossed it into the air. The cloth swatch transformed into a living, breathing creature, a servant of its creator that fluttered back to Jarlaxle's shoulder. The drow whispered some instructions into its ear and tossed it up before him again, and his little scout flew off into the gloom.

"We will take Hephaestus as our own," Rai-guy whispered to the Crystal Shard, the drow considering all the great gains that might be made this day. Logically, the dark elf knew he should be well on his way out of the place, for could Kimmuriel and the others really defeat Jarlaxle and the powerful companions he had brought to the dragon's lair?

Rai-guy smiled, hardly afraid, for how could he be fearful with Crenshinibon in his possession? Soon, very soon, he knew, he would be allied with a great wyrm. He turned and started down the wide tunnel toward the main chamber of Hephaestus's lair.

He noticed some movement off to the side, in an alcove, and Crenshinibon screamed a warning in his head.

Yharaskrik stepped out, not ten paces away. The tentacles around the illithid's mouth were waving menacingly.

"Kimmuriel's friend, no doubt," the dark elf remarked, "who betrayed Kohrin Soulez."

Betrayal implies alliance, Yharaskrik telepathically answered. *There was no betrayal.*

"If you were to venture here with us, then why not do so openly?" the drow asked.

I came for you, not with you, the ever-confident illithid answered.

Rai-guy understood well what was going on, for the Crystal Shard was making its abject hatred of the creature quite apparent in his thoughts.

"The drow and your race have been allied many times in the past," Rai-guy remarked, "and rarely have we found reason to do battle. So it should be now."

The wizard wasn't trying to talk the illithid out of any rash actions out of fear—far from it. He was thinking he might have, perhaps, made another powerful connection here, one that could be exploited.

The screaming in his mind, Crenshinibon's absolute hatred of the mind flayer, made that alliance seem less likely.

And even less likely a moment later, when Yharaskrik lit the magical lantern and aimed its glow Crenshinibon's way. The protests in the drow wizard's mind faded far, far away.

The artifact will be brought back before the dragon, came Yharaskrik's telepathic call. It was a psionically enhanced command, and one that had Rai-guy involuntarily taking a step toward the main chamber once more.

The cunning dark elf had survived more than a century in the hostile territory of his own homeland, and he was no novice to any type of battle. He fought back against the compelling suggestion and rooted his feet to the floor, turning back to regard the octopus-headed creature, his red-glowing eyes narrowing threateningly.

"Release the Crystal Shard and perhaps we will let you live," Rai-guy said.

It must be destroyed! Yharaskrik screamed into his mind. *It is an item of no gain, of loss to all, even to itself.* As the creature finished, it held the lantern up even higher and advanced a step, its tentacles wriggling out, reaching for Rai-guy hungrily though the drow was still too far away for any physical attack, but not out of range for psionic attacks, the drow found out a split second later, even as he began casting his own spell.

A blast of stunning and confusing energy washed over him, reached into him, and scrambled his mind. He felt himself falling over backward, watched almost helplessly as his line of vision rolled up the wall, and to the high ceiling.

He called for Crenshinibon, but it was too far away, lost in the swirl of the magical lantern's glow. He thought of the illithid, of those horrid tentacles burrowing under his skin, reaching for his brain.

Rai-guy steadied himself and fought desperately, finally regaining his balance and glancing back to see Yharaskrik very close—too close, those tentacles almost touching him.

He nearly exploded into the motion of yet another spellcasting, but he recognized that he had to be more subtle here, that he had to make the creature believe he was defeated. That was the secret of battling illithids, as many drow had been trained. Play upon their arrogance. Yharaskrik, like all of its kind, would hardly be able to comprehend that an inferior creature like a drow had somehow resisted its psionic attacks.

Rai-guy worked a simple spell, with subtle movements, and all the while feigning helplessness.

It must be done! the illithid screamed in his thoughts. The tentacles moved toward Rai-guy's face, and Yharaskrik's hand reached for the Crystal Shard.

Rai-guy released his spell. It was not a devastating blast, not a rumble of some great explosion, not a bolt of lightning nor a gout of fire. A simple gust of wind came from the drow's hand, a sharp and surprising burst that snapped Yharaskrik's tentacles back across its ugly face, that blew the creature's robes back behind it and forced it to retreat a step.

That blew out the lantern.

Yharaskrik glanced down, thought to summon some psionic energy to relight the lantern, and looked up and thought to strike Rai-guy with another psionic blast of scrambling energy, fearing some second spellcasting.

As quickly as the illithid could begin to do either of those things, a wave of crushing emotions washed over it, a Crenshinibon-imparted flood of despair and hopelessness, and, paradoxically of hope, with subtle promises that all could be put right, with greater glory gained for all.

Yharaskrik's psionic defenses came up almost immediately, dulling the Crystal Shard's demanding call.

A jolt of energy, the shocking grasp of Rai-guy, caught the illithid on the chest, lifted it from the ground, and sent it sprawling backward to the floor.

"Fool!" Rai-guy growled. "Do you think I need Crenshinibon to destroy the likes of you?"

Indeed, when Yharaskrik looked back at the drow wizard, thinking to attack mentally, he stared at the end of a small black wand. The illithid let go the blast anyway, and indeed it staggered Rai-guy backward, but the drow had already enacted the power of the wand. It was a wand similar to the one Jarlaxle had used to pin down Hephaestus's tail and momentarily clamp the dragon's mouth shut.

It took Rai-guy a long moment to fight through this burst of scrambling energy, but when he did stand straight again, he laughed aloud at the spectacle of the illithid splayed out on the floor, held in place by a viscid green glob.

The mental domination from Crenshinibon began on the creature anew, wearing at its resolve. Rai-guy walked to tower over Yharaskrik, to look the helpless mind flayer in the bulbous eye, letting it know in no uncertain terms that this fight was at its end.

⊶═══⊷

She had no apparent weapon, but Entreri knew better than to ask for her surrender, knew well enough what this skilled warrior was capable of. He had battled fighting monks before, though not often, and had always found them full of surprises. He could see the honed muscles of Danica's legs twitching eagerly, the woman wanting badly to come at him.

"Why do you hate me so?" the assassin asked with a wry grin, halting his advance a mere three strides from Danica. "Or is it, perhaps, that you simply fear me and are afraid to show it? For you should fear me, you understand."

Danica stared at him hard. She did indeed hate this man, and had heard much about him from Drizzt Do'Urden, and even more—and even more damning—testimony from Catti-brie. Everything about him assaulted her sensibilities. To Danica, finding Artemis Entreri in the company of dark elves seemed more an indictment of the dark elves.

"But perhaps we would do better to settle our differences when we are far, far from this place," Entreri offered. "Though our fight is inevitable in your eyes, is it not?"

"Logic would so dictate to both," Danica replied. As she finished the sentence, she came forward in a rush, slid down to the floor beneath Entreri's extending blade, and swept him from his feet. "But neither of us is a slave to wise thinking, are we, foul assassin?"

Entreri accepted the trip without resistance, indeed, even helped the flow of Danica's leg along by tumbling backward, throwing himself into a roll, and lifting his feet up high to get them over her swinging leg. He didn't quite get all the way back to his feet before reversing momentum, planting his toes, and throwing himself forward in a sudden, devastating rush.

Danica, still prone, angled herself to put her feet in line with the charging Entreri, then rolled back suddenly and with perfect timing to get one foot against the assassin's inner thigh as he fell over her, his sword reaching for her gut. With precision born of desperation, Danica rolled back up onto her shoulders, every muscle in her torso and legs working in perfect coordination to drive Entreri away, to keep that awful sword back.

He went up and over, flying past Danica and dipping his head at the last moment to go into a forward roll. He came back to his feet with a spin, facing the monk, who was up and charging, and stopping cold in her tracks as she faced again the deadly sword and its dagger companion.

Entreri felt the adrenaline coursing through his body, the rush of a true challenge. As much as he realized the foolishness of it all, he was enjoying this.

So was the woman.

The sound of a voice came from the side, the melodious call of a dark elf. "Do slay each other and save us the trouble," Berg'inyon Baenre explained, entering the small area along with a pair of dark elf companions. All three of them carried twin swords that gleamed with powerful enchantments.

Coughing and bleeding from a dozen scrapes, Cadderly pulled himself out of the rockslide and stumbled across a small corridor. He fished in a pouch to bring forth his light tube, a cylindrical object with a continual light spell cast into it, the enchantment focused into an adjustable beam out one end. He had to find Danica. He had to see her again. That last image of her, the dragon's fiery breath falling over her, had him dizzy with fear.

What would his life be without Danica? What would he say to the children? Everything about the life of Cadderly Bonaduce was wrapped inextricably around that wonderful and capable woman.

Yes, capable, he pointedly told himself again and again, as he staggered along in the dusty corridor, pausing only once to cast a minor spell of healing upon a particularly deep cut on one shoulder. He bent over and coughed again, and spat out some dirt that had gotten into his throat.

He shook his head, muttered again that he had to find her, and stood straight, pointing his light ahead—pointing his light so that it reflected off of the black skin of a drow.

That beam stung Kimmuriel Oblodra's sensitive eyes, but he was not caught unawares by it.

It all fell into place quickly for the intelligent priest. He had learned much of Jarlaxle in speaking with the drow and his assassin companion and had deduced much more with information gleaned from denizens of the lower planes. He was indeed surprised to see another dark elf—who could not be?—but he was far from overwhelmed.

The drow and Cadderly stood ten paces apart, staring at each other, sizing each other up. Kimmuriel reached for the priest's mind with psionic energy—enough energy to crush the willpower of a normal man.

But Cadderly Bonaduce was no normal human. The manner in which he accessed his god, the flowing song of Deneir, was somewhat akin to the powers of psionics. It was a method of the purest mental discipline.

Cadderly could not lash out with his mind, as Kimmuriel had just done, but he could surely defend against such an attack, and furthermore, he surely recognized the attack for what it was.

He thought of the Crystal Shard then, of all he knew about it, of its mannerisms and its powers.

The drow psionicist waved a hand, breaking the mental connection, and drew out a gleaming sword. He enacted another psionic power, one that would physically enhance him for the coming fight.

Cadderly did no similar preparations. He just stood staring at Kimmuriel and grinning knowingly. He cast one simple spell of translation.

The drow regarded him curiously, inviting an explanation.

"You wish Crenshinibon destroyed as much as I," the priest remarked, his magic translating the words as they came out of his mouth. "You are a psionicist, the bane of the Crystal Shard, its most hated enemy."

Kimmuriel paused and stared hard, with his physical and his mental eye. "What do you know, foolish human?" he asked.

"The Crystal Shard will not suffer you to live for long," Cadderly said, "and you know it."

"You believe I would help a human against Rai-guy?" Kimmuriel asked incredulously.

Cadderly didn't know who this Rai-guy might be, but Kimmuriel's question made it obvious that he was a dark elf of some power and importance.

"Save yourself, then, and leave," Cadderly offered, and he said it with such calm and confidence that Kimmuriel narrowed his eyes and regarded him even more closely.

Again came the psionic intrusions. This time Cadderly let the drow in somewhat, guided his probing mind's eye to the song of Deneir, let him see the truth of the power of the harmonious flow, let him see the truth of his doom should he persist in this battle.

The psionic connection again went away, and Kimmuriel stood up straight, staring hard at Cadderly.

"I am not normally this generous, dark elf," Cadderly said, "but I have greater problems before me. You hold no love for Crenshinibon and wish it destroyed perhaps more passionately than do I. If it is not, if your companion, this Rai-guy you spoke of, is allowed to possess it, it will be the end of you. So help me if you will in destroying the Crystal Shard. If you and your kin intend to return to your lightless home, I will in no way interfere."

Kimmuriel held his impassive pose for a short while, and smiled and shook his head. "You will find Rai-guy a formidable foe," he promised, "especially with Crenshinibon in his possession."

Before Cadderly could begin to respond, Kimmuriel waved his hand and became something less than corporeal. That transparent form turned and simply walked through the stone wall.

Cadderly waited a long moment and breathed a huge sigh of relief. How he had improvised there and bluffed. The spells he had prepared this day were for dealing with dragons, not dark elves, and the power of that one was substantial indeed. He had felt that keenly with the psionic intrusions.

Now he had a name, Rai-guy, and now his fears about the truth of Hephaestus's breathing had been confirmed. Cadderly, like Jarlaxle, understood enough about the mighty relic to know that if the breath had destroyed Crenshinibon, everyone in the area would have known it in no uncertain terms. Now Cadderly could guess easily enough where and how the Crystal Shard had gone. Knowing that there were other dark elves about, compounding the problem of one very angry red dragon, didn't make him feel any better about the prospects for his three missing friends.

He started away as fast as he dared, and fell again into the song of Deneir, praying for guidance to Danica's side.

⊛══╪═⊛

"Always I seem doomed to protect those I most despise," Entreri whispered to Danica, motioning with his hand for the woman to shift over to the side.

The dark elves broke ranks. One moved to square off against Danica, and Berg'inyon and one other headed for the assassin. Berg'inyon waved his companion aside.

"Kill the woman, and quickly," he said in the drow tongue. "I wish to try this one alone."

Entreri glanced over at Danica and held up two fingers, pointing to the two that would go for her, and pointing to her. The woman gave a quick nod, and a great deal passed between them in that instant. She would try to keep the two dark elves busy, but both understood that Entreri would have to be done with the third quickly.

"I have often wondered how I would fare against Drizzt Do'Urden," Berg'inyon said to the assassin. "Now that I will apparently never get the chance, I will settle for you, Drizzt's equal by all accounts."

Entreri bowed. "It is good to know that I serve some value for you, cowardly son of House Baenre," he said.

He knew as he came back up that Berg'inyon wouldn't hesitate in the face of those words. Still, the sheer ferocity of the drow's attack nearly had Entreri beaten before the fight ever really began. He leaped back, staying up on his heels, skittering away as the two swords came in hard, side by side down low, then low again, then high, then at his belly. He jumped back once, twice, thrice, then managed to bat his sword across those of Berg'inyon on the fourth double-thrust, hoping to drive the blades down low. This was no farmer he faced, and no orc or wererat, but a skilled, veteran drow warrior. Berg'inyon kept his left-handed sword pressing up against the assassin's blade, but dropped his right into a quick circle, then came up and over hard.

The jeweled dagger hooked it and turned it aside at the last second. Entreri rolled his other hand over, the tip of his own sword going toward Berg'inyon. He didn't follow through with the thrust, though, but continued the roll, bringing his blade down and around under the drow's, and stabbing straight ahead.

Berg'inyon quickly turned his left-hand blade across his body and down, disengaged his right from the dagger and brought it across over the left, further driving Entreri's sword down. In the same fluid motion, the skilled drow rolled his right-hand blade up and over his crossing left, the blade going forward at the assassin's head, a brilliant move that Berg'inyon knew would be the end of Artemis Entreri.

Across the way, Danica fared no better. Her fight was a mixture of pure chaos and lightning fast, almost violent movement. The woman crouched and dropped, sprang up hard, and rushed side to side, avoiding slash after slash of drow blades. These two were nowhere near as good as the one across the way battling her companion, but they were dark elves after all, and even the weakest of drow warriors was skilled by surface standards. Furthermore, they knew each other well and complemented each other's movements with deadly precision, preventing Danica from getting any real counterattacks. Every time one came ahead in a rush that seemed to offer the woman some hope of rolling past his double-thrusting blades, or even skittering in under them and kicking at a knee, the companion drow beat her to the potential attack zone, two gleaming swords holding her at bay.

With those long blades and precise movements, they were working her to exhaustion. She had to react, to overreact even, to every thrust and slash. She had to leap away from a blade sent across by a mere flick of a drow wrist.

She looked over at Entreri and the other drow, their blades ringing in a wild song and with the dark elf seeming, if anything, to be gaining an advantage. She knew she had to try something dangerous, even desperate.

Danica came ahead in a rush, and cut left suddenly, bursting out to the side though she had only three strides to the wall. Seeing her apparently caught, the closest dark elf cut fast in pursuit, stabbing at . . . nothing.

Danica ran right up the wall, turning over as she went and kicking out into a backward somersault that brought her down and to the side of the pursuing dark elf. She fell low as she landed and spun around viciously, one leg extended to kick out the dark elf's legs.

She would have had him, but there was his companion, swords extended, blade driving deeply into Danica's thigh. She howled and scrambled back, kicking futilely at the pursuing dark elves.

A globe of darkness fell over her. She slammed her back against the stone and had nowhere left to go.

He ran along, with the less-than-corporeal Kimmuriel Oblodra following close behind.

"You seek an exit?" the drow psionicist asked with a voice that seemed impossibly thin.

"I seek my friends," Cadderly replied.

"They are out of the mountain, likely," Kimmuriel remarked, and that slowed the priest considerably.

For indeed, would not Danica and the dwarves search for a way out of the mountain—and there were many easy exits from the lower tunnels, Cadderly knew from his searching of the place before this journey. Dozens of corridors crisscrossed down there, but a quiet pause and a lifted and wetted finger would show the drafts of air. Certainly Ivan and Pikel would have little trouble in finding their way out of the underground maze, but what of Danica?

"Something comes this way," Kimmuriel warned, and Cadderly turned to see the drow shrink back against the wall, and stand perfectly still, seeming simply to disappear.

Cadderly knew the drow wouldn't aid him in any fight and would likely even join in if the approaching footsteps were those of Kimmuriel's dark elf companions.

They were not, Cadderly knew almost as soon as that worry cropped up, for these were not the steps of any stealthy creature.

"Ye stupid doo-dad!" came the roar of a familiar voice. "Droppin' me in a hole, and one full o' rocks!"

"Ooo oi!" Pikel replied as they came bounding around the bend in the tunnel, right into the path of Cadderly's light beam.

Ivan shrieked and started to charge, but Pikel grabbed him and pulled him down, whispering into his ear.

"Hey, ye're right," the yellow-bearded dwarf admitted. "Damned drows don't use light."

Cadderly came up beside them. "Where is Danica?"

Any relief the two dwarves had felt at the sight of their friend disappeared immediately.

"Help me find her!" Cadderly said to the dwarves and to Kimmuriel, as he spun around.

Kimmuriel Oblodra, apparently fearing that Cadderly and his companions would not be safe traveling company, was already long gone.

His smile, a wicked grin indeed, widened as one of his blades came up over the other, for he knew that Entreri had nothing left with which to parry. Out went Berg'inyon's killing stab.

But the assassin was not there!

Berg'inyon's thoughts whirled frantically. Where had he gone? How were his weapons still in place with the previous parries? He knew Entreri could not have moved far, and yet, he was not there.

The angle of the sudden disengage clued Berg'inyon in to the truth, told the drow that in the same moment Berg'inyon had executed the roll, Entreri had also come forward, but down low, using Berg'inyon's own blade as the visual block.

The dark elf silently congratulated the cunning human, this man rumored to be the equal of Drizzt Do'Urden, even as he felt the jeweled dagger sliding into his back, reaching for his heart.

"You should have kept one of your lackeys with you," Entreri whispered in the drow's ear, easing the dying Berg'inyon Baenre to the floor. "He could have died beside you."

The assassin pulled free his dagger and turned around to consider the woman. He saw her get slashed, saw her skitter away, saw the globe fall over her.

Entreri winced as the two dark elves—too far away for him to offer any timely assistance—rolled out in opposite directions, flanking the woman and rushing into that darkness, swords before them.

Just a split second before the darkness fell, the dark elf standing before Danica to the right began to execute a roll farther that way, spinning a circle to bring him around quickly and with momentum, the only clue for Danica.

The other one, she guessed, was moving to her left, but both were surely coming in at a tight enough angle to prevent her from rushing straight ahead between them. Those three options: left, right, and ahead, were unavailable, as was moving back, for the stone of the wall was solid indeed.

She sensed their movements, not specifically, but enough to realize that they were coming in fast for the kill.

One option presented itself. One alone.

Danica leaped straight up, tucking her legs under her, so full of desperation that she hardly felt the burn of the wound in her thigh.

She couldn't see the double-thrust low attack of the drow to her right, nor the double-thrust high attack from the one on the left, but she felt the disturbance below her as she cleared both sets of blades. She came up high in a tuck, and kicked out to both sides with a sudden and devastating spreading snap of her legs.

She connected on both sides, driving a foot into the forehead of the drow on her right, and another into the throat of the drow on her left. She pressed through to complete extension, sending both dark elves flying away. She landed in perfect balance and burst ahead three running steps. A forward dive brought her rolling out of the darkness. She came up and around—to see the dark elf now on her left, and the one she had kicked on the forehead, still staggering backward out of the darkness globe and into the waiting grasp of Artemis Entreri.

The drow jerked suddenly, violently, and Entreri's fine sword exploded through his chest. The assassin held it there for a moment, let Charon's Claw work its demonic power, and the dark elf's face began to smolder, burn, and roll back from his skull.

Danica looked away, focusing on the darkness, waiting for the other dark elf to come rushing out. Blood was pouring from her wounded leg, and her strength was fast receding.

She was too lightheaded a moment later to hear the final gurgling of the drow dying in the darkness globe, its throat too crushed to bring in anymore air, but even if she had heard that reassuring sound, it would have done little to bolster her hopes.

She could not hold her footing, she knew, or her consciousness.

Artemis Entreri, surely no ally, was still very much alive, and very, very close.

Yharaskrik was overwhelmed. The combination of Rai-guy's magic and the continuing mental attack of the Crystal Shard had the illithid completely overmatched. Yharaskrik couldn't even focus its mental energies enough at that moment to melt away through the stone, away from the imprisoning goo.

"Surrender!" the drow wizard-cleric demanded. "You cannot escape us. We will take your word that you will promise fealty to us," the drow explained, oblivious to the shadowy form that darted out behind him to retrieve an item. "Crenshinibon will know if you lie, but if you speak of honest fealty, you will be rewarded!"

Indeed, as the dark elf proclaimed those words, Crenshinibon echoed them deep in Yharaskrik's mind. The thought of servitude to Crenshinibon, one of the most hated artifacts for all of the mind flayers, surely repulsed the bulbous-headed creature, but so, too, did the thought of obliteration. That was precisely what Yharaskrik faced. The illithid could not win, could not escape. Crenshinibon would melt its mind even as Rai-guy blasted its body.

I yield, the illithid telepathically communicated to both of its attackers.

Rai-guy relented his magic and considered Crenshinibon. The artifact informed him that Yharaskrik had truthfully surrendered.

"Wisely done," the drow said to the illithid. "What a waste your death would be when you might bolster my army, when you might serve me as liaison to your powerful people."

"My people hate Crenshinibon and will not hear those calls," Yharaskrik said in its watery voice.

"But you understand differently," said the drow. He spoke a quick spell, dissolving the goo around the illithid. "You see the value of it now."

"A value above that of death, yes," Yharaskrik admitted, climbing back to its feet.

"Well, well, my traitorous lieutenant," came a voice from the side. Both Rai-guy and Yharaskrik turned to see Jarlaxle perched a bit higher on the wall, tucked into an alcove.

Rai-guy growled and called upon Crenshinibon mentally to crush his former master. Even as he started that silent call, up came the magical lantern. Its glow fell over the artifact, defeating its powers.

Rai-guy growled again. "You need do more than defeat the artifact!" he roared and swept his arm out toward Yharaskrik. "Have you met my new friend?"

"Indeed, and formidable," Jarlaxle admitted, tipping his wide-brimmed hat in deference to the powerful illithid. "Have you met mine?" As he finished, his gaze aimed to the side, further along the wide tunnel.

Rai-guy swallowed hard, knowing the truth before he even turned that way. He began waving his arms wildly, trying to bring up some defensive magic.

Using his innate drow abilities, Jarlaxle dropped a globe of darkness over the wizard and the mind flayer, a split second before Hephaestus's fiery breath fell over them, immolating them in a terrible blast of devastation.

Jarlaxle leaned back and shielded his eyes from the glow of the fire, the reddish-orange line that so disappeared into the blackness.

Then there came a sudden sizzling noise, and the darkness was no more. The tunnel reverted to its normal blackness, lightened somewhat by the glow of the dragon. That light intensified a hundred times over, a thousand times over, into a brilliant glow, as if the sun itself had fallen upon them.

Crenshinibon, Jarlaxle realized. The dragon's breath had done its work, and the binding energy of the artifact had been breached. In the moment before the glare became too great, Jarlaxle saw the surprised look on the reptilian face of the great wyrm, saw the charred corpse of his former lieutenant, and saw a weird image of Yharaskrik, for the illithid had begun to melt into the stone when Hephaestus had breathed. The retreat had done little good, since Hephaestus's breath had bubbled the stone.

It was soon too bright for the eyes of the drow. "Well fired . . . er, breathed," he said to Hephaestus.

Jarlaxle spun around, slipped through a crack at the back of the alcove, and sprinted away not a moment too soon. Hephaestus's terrible breath came forth yet again, melting the stone in the alcove, chasing Jarlaxle down the tunnel, and singeing the seat of his trousers.

He ran and ran in the still-brightening light. Crenshinibon's releasing power filled every crack in every stone. Soon Jarlaxle knew he was near the outside wall, and so he utilized his magical hole again, throwing it against the wall and crawling through into the twilight of the outside beyond.

That area, too, brightened immediately and considerably, seeming as if the sun had risen. The light poured through Jarlaxle's magical hole. With a snap of his wrist, the drow took the magic item away, closing the portal and dimming the area to natural light again—except for the myriad beams shooting out of the glowing mountain in other places.

"Danica!" came Cadderly's frantic call behind him. "Where is Danica?"

Jarlaxle turned to see the priest and the two bumbling dwarves—an odd pair of brothers if ever the drow had seen one—running toward him.

"She went down the hole after Artemis Entreri," Jarlaxle said in a comforting tone. "A fine and resourceful ally."

"Boom!" said Pikel Bouldershoulder.

"What's the light about?" Ivan added.

Jarlaxle looked back to the mountain and shrugged. "It would seem that your formula for defeating the Crystal Shard was correct after all," the drow said to Cadderly.

He turned with a smile, but that look was not reflected on the face of the priest. He was staring back at the mountain with horror, wondering and worrying about his dear wife.

CHAPTER

THE LIGHT AT THE END OF THE TUNNEL

25

Hephaestus was an intelligent dragon, smart enough to master many powerful spells, to speak the tongues of a dozen races, to defeat all of the many, many foes who had come against it. The dragon had lived for centuries, gaining wisdom as dragons do, and in that depth of wisdom, Hephaestus recognized that it should not be staring at the brilliance of the Crystal Shard's released energy.

But the dragon could not turn away from the brilliance, from the sheerest and brightest, the purest power it had ever seen.

The wyrm marveled as a skeletal shadow rolled out of the brilliantly glowing object, then another, and a third, and so on, until the specters of seven long-consumed liches danced about the destroyed Crystal Shard, as they had danced around the object during its dark creation.

Then, one by one, they dissipated into nothingness.

The dragon stared incredulously, feeling the honest emotions as clearly as if it were empathically bound to the next form that flowed out of the artifact, the shadow of a man, hunched and broken with sadness. The stolen soul of the long-dead sheik sat on the floor, staring at the stone forlornly, an aura so devastated flowing out from the shadow that Hephaestus the Merciless felt a twinge in its cold heart.

That last specter, too, thinned to nothingness, and, finally, the light of the Crystal Shard dimmed.

Only then did Hephaestus recognize the depth of its mistake. Only then did the ancient red dragon realize that it was now totally blind, its eyes utterly destroyed by the pureness of the power released.

The dragon roared—how it roared! The greatest scream of anger, of rage, that ever-angry Hephaestus had ever issued. In that roar, too, was a measure of fear, of regret, of the realization that the wyrm could not dare go forth from its lair to pursue the intruders who had brought this cursed item before it, could not go out from the confines to the open world where it would need its eyes as well as those other keen senses to truly thrive, indeed to survive.

Hephaestus's olfactory senses told the wyrm that it had at least destroyed the drow and the illithid that had been standing in the corridor a few moments before. Taking that satisfaction in the realization that it was likely the only satisfaction Hephaestus could hope to find this day, the wyrm retreated to the large chamber secretly and magically concealed behind its main sleeping hall, the chamber where there was only one possible entrance, and the one where the dragon kept its piled hoard of gold, gems, jewels, and trinkets.

There the outraged but defeated wyrm curled up again, desiring sleep, peaceful slumber among its hoarded riches, hoping that the passing years would cure its burned eyes. It would dream, yes it would, of consuming those intruders, and it would set its great intelligent mind to work at solving the problem of blindness if the slumber did not bring the desired cure.

Cadderly nearly leaped for joy when the form came rushing out of the tunnels, but when he recognized the running man for who he was, Artemis Entreri, and noted that the woman slung across his shoulders was hardly moving and was covered in blood, his heart sank fast.

"What'd ye do to her?" Ivan roared, starting forward, but he found that he was moving slowly, as if in a dream. He looked to Pikel and found that his brother, too, was moving with unnatural sluggishness.

"Be at ease," Jarlaxle said to them. "Danica's wounds are not of Entreri's doing."

"How can ye know?" Ivan demanded.

"He would have left her dead in the darkness," the drow reasoned, and the simple logic of it did indeed calm the volatile brothers a bit.

Cadderly, though, ran on. As he was beyond the parameters of Jarlaxle's spell when it was cast, he was not slowed in the least. He rushed up to Entreri, who, upon seeing his approach, had stopped and turned one shoulder down, moving Danica to a standing, or at least leaning, position.

"Drow blade," the assassin said as soon as Cadderly got close enough to see the wound—and the feeble attempt at tying it off the assassin had made.

The priest went to work at once, falling into the song of Deneir, bringing forth all the healing energies he could find. Indeed, he discovered to his absolute relief that his love's wounds were not so critical, that she would certainly mend and quickly enough.

By the time he finished, the Bouldershoulders and Jarlaxle had arrived. Cadderly looked up at the dwarves and smiled and nodded, and turned a puzzled expression on the assassin.

"Her actions saved me in the tunnels," Entreri said sourly. "I do not enjoy being in anyone's debt." That said, he walked away, not once looking back.

Cadderly and his companions, including Danica, caught up to Entreri and Jarlaxle later on that day, after it became apparent, to everyone's relief, that Hephaestus would not be coming out of its lair in pursuit.

"We are returning to the Spirit Soaring with the same spell that brought us here," the priest announced. "It would be impolite, at least, if I did not offer you magical transport for the journey back."

Jarlaxle looked at him curiously.

"No tricks," Cadderly assured the cagey drow. "I hold no trials over either of you, for your actions have been no less than honorable since you came to my domain. I do warn you both, however, that I will tolerate no—"

"Why would we wish to return with you?" Artemis Entreri cut him short. "What in your hole of falsehood is for our gain?"

Cadderly started to respond—in many directions all at once. He wanted to yell at the man, to coerce the man, to convert the man, to destroy the man—anything he could do against that sudden wall of negativism. In the end, he said not a word, for indeed, what at the Spirit Soaring would be for the benefit of these two?

Much, he supposed, if they desired to mend their souls and their ways. Entreri's actions with Danica did hint that there might indeed be a possibility of that in the future. On a whim, the priest entered Deneir's song and brought forth a minor spell, one that revealed the general weal of those he surveyed.

A quick look at Entreri and Jarlaxle was all he needed to confirm that the Spirit Soaring, Carradoon, Shilmista Forest, and all the region about that section of the Snowflake Mountains would be better off if these two went in the opposite direction.

"Farewell, then," he said with a tip of his hat. "At least you found the opportunity to do one noble act in your wretched existence, Artemis Entreri." He walked by the pair, Ivan and Pikel in tow.

Danica took her time, though, eyeing Entreri with every step. "I am not ungrateful for what you did when my wound overcame me," she admitted, "but neither would I shy from finishing that which we started in the tunnels below Hephaestus's lair."

Entreri started to say, "To what end?" but changed his mind before the first word had escaped his lips. He merely shrugged, smiled, and let the woman pass.

"A new rival for Entreri?" Jarlaxle remarked when the four had gone. "A replacement for Drizzt, perhaps?"

"Hardly," Entreri replied.

"She is not worthy, then?"

The assassin only shrugged, not caring enough to try to determine whether she was or not.

Jarlaxle's laugh brought him from his contemplation.

"Growth," the drow remarked.

"I warn you that I'll tolerate little of your judgments," Entreri replied.

Jarlaxle laughed all the harder. "Then you plan to remain with me."

Entreri looked at him hard, stealing the mirth, considering a question that he could not immediately answer.

"Very well, then," Jarlaxle said lightheartedly, as if he took the silence as confirmation. "But I warn you, if you cross me, I will have to kill you."

"That will be difficult to do from beyond the grave," Entreri promised.

Jarlaxle laughed once more. "When I was young," he began, "a friend of mine, a weapon master whose ultimate frustration was that he believed I was the better fighter—though in truth, the one time I bested him was more good fortune than superior skill—remarked to me that at last he had found one who would grow to be at least my equal, and perhaps my superior, a child, really, who showed more promise as a warrior than any before.

"That weapon master's name was Zaknafein—you may have heard of him," Jarlaxle went on.

Entreri shook his head.

"The young warrior he spoke of was none other than Drizzt Do'Urden," Jarlaxle explained with a grin.

Entreri tried hard to show no emotion, but his inner feelings at the surprise betrayed him a tiny bit, and certainly enough for Jarlaxle to note it. "And did the prophecy of Zaknafein come true?" Entreri asked.

"If it did, does that hold any revelation for Artemis Entreri?" Jarlaxle asked slyly. "For would discovering the relative strength of Drizzt and Jarlaxle tell Entreri anything pertinent? How does Artemis Entreri believe he measures up against Drizzt Do'Urden?" Then the critical question: "Does Entreri believe he truly defeated Drizzt?"

Entreri looked at Jarlaxle long and hard, but as he stared, his expression inevitably softened. "Does it matter?" he answered, and that indeed was the answer that Jarlaxle most wanted to hear from his new, and, to his way of thinking, long-term companion.

"We are not yet done here," Jarlaxle announced then, changing the subject abruptly. "There is one group lingering about, fearful and angry. Their leader has decided that he cannot leave yet, not with things as they stand."

Entreri didn't ask, but just followed Jarlaxle as the dark elf made his way around the outcroppings of mountain stone. The assassin fell back a few steps when he saw the group Jarlaxle had spoken of: four dark elves led by a dangerous psionicist. Entreri put his hands immediately to the hilt of his deadly dagger and sword. A short distance away, Jarlaxle and Kimmuriel spoke in the drow tongue, but Entreri could make out most of their words.

"Do we battle now?" Kimmuriel Oblodra asked when Jarlaxle neared.

"Rai-guy is dead, the Crystal Shard destroyed," Jarlaxle replied. "What would be the purpose?"

Entreri noted that Kimmuriel did not wince at either proclamation.

"Ah, but I guess that you have tasted the sweetness of power, yes?" Jarlaxle asked with a chuckle. "You are seated at the head of Bregan D'aerthe now, it would seem, and you suppose all by yourself. You have little desire to relinquish your garnered position?"

Kimmuriel started to shake his head—it was obvious to Entreri that he was about to try to make peace here with Jarlaxle—but the surprising Jarlaxle cut short Kimmuriel's response. "Very well then!" Jarlaxle said dramatically. "I have little desire for yet another fight, Kimmuriel, and I accept and understand that my actions of late have likely earned me too many enemies within the ranks of Bregan D'aerthe for my return as leader."

"You are surrendering?" Kimmuriel asked doubtfully, and he seemed even more on his guard then, as did the foot-soldiers standing behind him.

"Hardly," Jarlaxle replied with another chuckle. "And I warn you, if you continue to do battle with me, or even to pursue me and track my whereabouts, I will indeed challenge you for the position you have rightly earned."

Entreri listened intently, shaking his head, certain that he must be getting some of the words, at least, very wrong.

Kimmuriel started to respond, but stuttered over a few words, and just gave up with a great sigh.

"Do well with Bregan D'aerthe," Jarlaxle warned. "I will rejoin you one day and will demand of you that we share the leadership. I expect to find a band of mercenaries as strong as the one I now willingly leave behind." He looked to the other three. "Serve him with honor."

"Any reunion between us will not be in Calimport," Kimmuriel assured him, "nor anywhere else on the cursed surface. I am bound for home, Jarlaxle, back to the caverns that are our true domain."

Jarlaxle nodded, as did the three foot-soldiers.

"And you?" Kimmuriel asked.

The former mercenary leader only shrugged and smiled again. "I cannot know where I most wish to be because I have not seen all that there is."

Again, Kimmuriel could only stare at his former leader curiously. In the end, he merely nodded and, with a snap of his fingers and a thought, opened a dimensional portal through which he and his three minions passed.

"Why?" Entreri asked, moving up beside his unexpected companion.

"Why?" Jarlaxle echoed.

"You could have returned with them," the assassin clarified, "though I'd have never gone with you. You chose not to go, not to resume control of your band. Why would you give that up to remain out here, to remain beside me?"

Jarlaxle thought it over for a few moments. Then, using words that Entreri himself had used before, he said with a laugh, "Perhaps I hate drow more than I hate humans."

In that instant, Artemis Entreri could have been blown over by a gentle breeze. He didn't even want to know how Jarlaxle had known to say that.

EPILOGUE

For days, Entreri and Jarlaxle wandered the region, at last happening upon a town where the folk had heard of Drizzt Do'Urden and seemed, at least, to accept the imposter Jarlaxle's presence.

In the nondescript and ramshackle little common house that served as a tavern, Artemis Entreri discovered a posting that he found, in light of his present situation, somewhat promising.

"Bounty hunters?" Jarlaxle asked with surprise when Entreri presented the posting to him. The drow was sitting in a corner, sipping wine and with his back to the corner. "A call by the forces of justice for bounty hunters?"

"A call by someone," Entreri corrected, sliding into a chair across the table. "Whether it begets justice or not seems of little consequence."

Jarlaxle looked at him with a wry grin. "Does it?" he said, seeming less than convinced. "And what gain did you derive, then, from carrying Danica from the tunnels?"

"The gain of keeping a powerful priest from becoming an enemy," the pragmatic Entreri answered coldly.

"Or perhaps there was more," said Jarlaxle. "Perhaps Artemis Entreri had not the heart to let the woman die alone in the darkness."

Entreri shrugged as if it did not matter.

"How many of Artemis Entreri's victims would be surprised?" Jarlaxle asked, pressing the point.

"How many of Artemis Entreri's victims deserved better than they found?" the assassin retorted.

There it was, Jarlaxle knew, the justification for a life lived in the shadows. To a degree, the drow, who had survived among shadows darker than anything Entreri had ever known, couldn't rightfully disagree. Perhaps, in that context, there was more to the measure of Artemis Entreri. Still, the transformation of this killer to the side of justice seemed a curious and odd occurrence.

"Artemis the Compassionate?" he had to ask.

Entreri sat perfectly still for a moment, digesting the words. "Perhaps," he said with a nod. "And perhaps if you keep saying foolish things, I will show you some compassion and kill you quickly. Then again, perhaps not."

Jarlaxle enjoyed a great laugh at that, at the absurdity of it all, of the new-found life that loomed before him. He understood Entreri well enough to take the man's threats seriously, but in truth, the dark elf trusted Entreri the way he would trust one of his own brothers.

However, Jarlaxle Baenre, the third son of Matron Baenre, once sacrificed to Lady Lolth by his mother and his siblings, knew better than to trust his own brother.

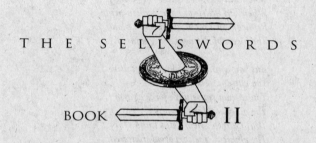

THE SELLSWORDS

BOOK II

PROMISE OF THE WITCH-KING

TO KILL THE WITCH-KING

When Gareth's holy sword did flash on high
When Zhengyi's form was shattered.
A blackened flame of detritus
His corporeal form a'tattered.
When did victory's claim ring loudly
When did hearts of hope swollen pride
Rejoice brave men, at Gareth's blow
The pieces of Zhengyi flung wide.

But you cannot kill what is not alive
You cannot strike a notion
You cannot smite with force of arm
The magic of dark devotion.
Thus Gareth's sword did undo
The physical, the corporeal shattered.
The Witch-King focus was denied
The magical essence scattered.

So hearken you children to Mother's words
Walk straight to Father, follow.
For a piece of Zhengyi watches you
In dark Wilderness's hollow.

PRELUDE

The smallish man skated along the magically greased, downward sloping corridor, his feet moving in short stabs to continue scrabbling ahead and keep him upright—no easy task. Wisps of smoke rose from his battered traveling cloak and a long tear showed down the side of his left pant leg, with bright blood oozing beneath.

Artemis Entreri slid into the right hand wall and rolled along it, not using it to break his dizzying dash, for to do so would be to allow the lich to catch sight of him.

And that, above all else, the assassin did not want.

He came around from one roll and planted his arms hard against the wall before him, then shoved out, propelling him diagonally down the narrow hallway. He heard the sound of flames roaring behind him, followed by the strained laughter of Jarlaxle, his drow companion. Entreri recognized that the confident dark elf was trying to unnerve the pursuer with that cackle, but even Entreri heard it for what it was: a discordant sound unevenly roiling above a bed of complete uneasiness.

Few times in their months together had Entreri heard any hint of worry from the collected dark elf, but there was no mistaking it, and that only reinforced his own very real fears.

He was well beyond the illumination of the last torch set along the long corridor by then, but a sudden and violent flash from behind him brightened the way, showing him that the corridor ended abruptly a dozen feet beyond and made a sharp right turn. The assassin took full note of that perpendicular course, his only chance, for in that flash, he saw clearly the endgame of the lich's nasty trap: a cluster of sharpened spikes sticking out from the wall.

Entreri hit the left hand wall and again went into a roll. On one turn, he sheathed his trademark jeweled dagger, and on the next he managed to slip his sword, Charon's Claw, into its scabbard on his left hip. With his hands free, he better controlled his skid along the wall. The floor was more slippery than an icy decline in a windless cavern in the Great Glacier itself, but the walls were smooth and solid stone. His hands worked hard each time he came around,

and his feet skidded and spun in place as he rolled his shoulders to keep himself upright. He approached the sharp turn and the abrupt, deadly ending.

He yelled as another thunderous explosion rocked the corridor behind him. The assassin shoved off with all his strength as he came around, timing it perfectly for maximum effect. Turning, he threw his upper body forward to strengthen the movement, cutting him across the hallway to the side passage. As soon as his feet slid off that main corridor, he stumbled, for the magical grease abruptly ended. He caught the corner and pulled himself back to it, going in hard, face up against the wall. He glanced back only once, and in the dim light could see the sharp, barbed tips of the deadly spikes.

He started to peek around, back the way he had come, but he nearly cried out in surprise to see a flailing form charging past him. He tried to grab at Jarlaxle, but the drow eluded him, and Entreri thought his companion doomed on the end of the spikes.

But Jarlaxle didn't hit the spikes. Somehow, some way, the drow pulled up short, whipped to the left, and slammed hard into the wall opposite Entreri. The assassin tried to reach out but yelped and fell back behind the corner as a bolt of blue-white lightning streaked past, exploding in a shower of stinging sparks as it crashed against the back wall, shearing off several of the spikes in the process.

Entreri heard the cackle of the lich creature, an emaciated skeletal form, partially covered in withered and stretched skin. He resisted the urge to sprint away down this side corridor and growled in defiance instead.

"I knew you'd get me killed!" he snapped at Jarlaxle.

Trembling with fury, Entreri leaped back into the middle of the main, slippery corridor.

"Come on then, spawn of Zhengyi!" the assassin roared.

The lich came into sight, black tattered robes fluttering out behind it, lipless face, rotted brown and skeletal white, grinning wide.

Entreri went for his sword, but when the lich reached out with bony fingers, the assassin instead thrust his gloved hand out before him. Again Entreri screamed—in defiance, in denial, in rage—as another lightning bolt blasted forth.

Entreri felt as if he was in a hot, stinging wind. He felt the burn and tingle of tremendous energies bristling around him. He was down on his knees but didn't know it. He had been thrown back to the wall, just below the spikes, but he didn't even register the firm footing of the base of the back wall against his feet. He was still reaching forward with the enchanted glove, arm shaking badly, sparks of blue and white spinning in the air and disappearing into the glove.

None of it registered to the assassin, whose teeth were clenched so forcefully that he couldn't even yell any louder than a throaty growl.

Spots danced before his eyes, and waves of dizziness assailed him.

He heard the taunting cackle of the lich.

Instinctively, he shoved off the wall, angling back to his left and the side corridor. He got one foot planted on that non-greased surface and sprang back up. He drew his sword, blinded still, and scrambled along the side passage's edge, then leaped out as fast and as far as he could, swiping Charon's Claw wildly and having no idea if he was anywhere near the lich.

He was.

The dark blade came down, sparks dancing around it, for the glove had caught the bulk of the energy from the lightning bolt and released it back through the metal of its companion sword.

The lich, surprised at how far and how fast the opponent had come, threw an arm up to block, and Charon's Claw sheared it off at the elbow. Entreri's strike would have destroyed the creature then, except the impact with the arm provided the conduit for the release of the lightning's energy.

Again the explosion sent Entreri sliding back to the wall to slam in hard and low.

The shrieking of the lich forced the assassin to reach out and retrieve his scattered senses. He turned himself around, his hand slapping the floor until he once again grasped the hilt of Charon's Claw. He looked up the corridor just in time to see the lich retreating, cloak aflame.

"Jarlaxle?" the assassin asked, glancing back to his right, to where the drow had been pressed up against the wall.

Confused to see only the wall, Entreri looked back into the corner, expecting to see a charred lump of drow.

But no, Jarlaxle was just . . . gone.

Entreri stared at the wall and inched himself into the corridor opposite. Off the greased section, he regained his footing and nearly jumped out of his boots when he saw two red eyes staring at him from within the stone of the opposite corridor.

"Well done," said the drow, pressing forward so that the outline of his face appeared in the stone.

Entreri stood there stunned. Somehow Jarlaxle had melded with the stone, as if he had turned the wall into a thick paste and pressed himself inside. Entreri didn't really know why he was so surprised—had his companion ever done anything within the realm of the ordinary?

A loud *click* turned his attention back the other way, up the hall. He knew it immediately as the latch on the door at the top of the ramp, where he and Jarlaxle had met up with, and been chased away by, the lich.

The floor and walls began to tremble with a low, rolling growl.

"Get me out of here," Jarlaxle called to him, the drow's voice gravelly and bubbly, as if he was speaking from under liquid stone, which, in fact, he was. He pushed forth one hand, reaching out to Entreri.

The thunder grew around them. Entreri poked his head around the corner. Something bad was coming.

The assassin snapped up Jarlaxle's offered hand and tugged hard but found to his surprise that the drow was tugging back.

"No," Jarlaxle said.

Entreri glanced back up the sloping, curving hallway and his eyes went so wide they nearly fell out of his head. The thunder came in the form of a waist-high iron ball rolling fast his way.

He paused and considered how he might dodge, when before his eyes, the ball doubled in size, nearly filling the corridor.

With a shriek, the assassin fell back into the side passage, stumbled, and spun around. He glanced at Jarlaxle's form receding into the stone once more, but he had no time to stop and ponder whether his companion could escape the trap.

Entreri turned and scrambled, finally setting his feet under him and running for his life.

The explosion behind him as the massive iron ball collided with the end wall had him stumbling again, the jolt bringing him to his knees. He glanced back to see that the impact had taken most of the ball's momentum but had not ended its roll. It was coming on again, slowly, but gathering momentum.

Entreri scrambled on all fours, cursing at Jarlaxle yet again for bringing him to this place. He got his feet under him and sprinted away, putting distance between himself and the ball. That wouldn't hold, he knew, for the ball was gaining speed, and the corridor wound along and down the circular tower for a long, long way.

He sprinted and looked for some way out. He shouldered each door as he passed but was not surprised to discover that the trap had sealed the portals. He looked for a place where the ceiling was higher, where he might climb and let the ball pass under him.

But there was nothing.

He glanced back to see if the ball hugged one wall or the other, that he might slide down beside it, but to his amazement, if not his surprise, the ball grew yet again, until its sides practically scraped the walls.

He ran.

The shaking made his teeth hurt in his mouth. Inside the stone, every reverberation as the sphere smashed the wall echoed within Jarlaxle's very being. He felt it to his bones.

For a moment, there was only blackness, then the ball began to recede, rolling along the adjacent corridor.

Jarlaxle took a couple of deep breaths. He had survived that one but feared he might need to find a new companion.

He started to push out of the stone again but stopped when he heard a familiar wheezing laughter.

He fell back, his eyes gazing out through a thin shield of stone, and the lich stood before him. The drow didn't dare breathe or move.

The lich wasn't looking at him but stared down the corridor, cackling victoriously. To Jarlaxle's great relief, the powerful undead creature began moving away, gliding as if it was floating on water.

Jarlaxle wondered if he could just press backward out of the tower then simply levitate to float to the ground and be gone from the place. He noticed the obvious wounds on the lich, though, inflicted by Entreri's reversal of the lightning bolt and the heavy strike of Charon's Claw, and another possibility occurred to him.

He had come with the idea of treasure after all, and it would be such a shame to leave empty handed.

He let the lich glide down around the bend. Then the drow began to push out from the wall.

"It has to be an illusion," Artemis Entreri told himself repeatedly. Iron balls didn't *grow*, after all, but how could it be? It was so real, in sound, shape, and feeling . . . how could any illusion so perfectly mimic such a thing?

The trick to beating an illusion was to set your thoughts fully against it, Entreri knew, to deny it, heart and soul. He glanced back again, and he knew that such was not a possibility.

He tried to block out the mounting thunder behind him. He put his head down and sprinted, forcing himself to recall all the details of the corridor before him. No longer did he try to shoulder the doors, for they were closed to him and he was only losing time in the futile effort.

He pulled the small pack from his back as he ran. He produced a silken cord and grapnel and tossed the bag to the floor behind him, hoping against hope that it would interrupt the gathering momentum of the stone ball.

It didn't. The ball flattened it.

Entreri didn't allow his thoughts to drift back to the rolling menace, but rather, worked the cord frantically, finding its length, picturing the spot in the corridor still some distance ahead, gauging the length he'd need.

The floor shook beneath him. He thought every step would be his last, with the sphere barreling over him.

Jarlaxle had once told him that even an illusion could kill a man if he believed in it.

And Entreri believed in it.

His instincts told him to throw himself flat to the floor off to the side, in the prayer that there would be enough room for him between the sharp corner and the rounded edge of his pursuer. He never found the heart to follow that, though, and he quickly put it out of his mind, focusing instead on the one best chance that lay before him.

Entreri readied the cord as he sprinted for all his life. He bounded around the next bend, the ball right behind. He ran past where the wall at his right-hand side dropped into a waist-high railing, opening into the center of the large tower, with the hallway continuing to circle along its perimeter.

Out went the grapnel, expertly thrown to loop around the large chandelier that was set in the top of the tower's cavernous foyer.

Entreri continued to run flat out. He had no choice, for to stop was to be crushed. The cord was set firmly in his hands, and when the slack wore out he let it force him to veer to the right. It yanked him right over the railing as the rolling iron sphere rushed past, ever so slightly clipping him on the shoulder as he swooped out into the air. He spun in tight circles within the larger circles of the rope's momentum.

He managed to watch the continued descent of the ball, thumping down along the edges, but was quickly distracted by a more ominous creaking from above.

Entreri scrambled, hands working to free up and drop the rope below him. He started his slide with all speed, hand-running down the rope. He felt a sudden jerk, then another as the decorated crystal chandelier pulled free of the ceiling.

Then he was falling.

The door stood slightly ajar. Given the trap he'd set off, there was no reason for the "innkeeper" to believe any of the intruders would be able to get up to it. Still, the drow drew out a wand and expended a bit of its magic. The door and the jamb glowed a solid and unbroken light blue, revealing no traps, magical or mechanical.

Jarlaxle moved up and gingerly pushed through.

The room, the top floor of the tower, was mostly bare. The gray stone walls were unadorned, sweeping in a semi-circle behind a singular large, wide-backed chair of polished wood. Before that seat lay a book, opened atop a pedestal.

No, not a pedestal, Jarlaxle realized as he crept in closer. The book was suspended on a pair of thick tendrils that reached down to the floor of the room and right into the stone.

The drow grinned, knowing that he had found the heart of the construction, the magical architect of the tower itself. He moved in and around the book, giving it a wide berth, then came up on it beside the chair. He glanced at the writing from afar and recognized a few magical runes there. A quick recital of a simple spell brought those runes into better focus and clarity.

He moved closer, drawn in by the power of the tome. He noted then that there were images of runes in the air above it, spinning and dipping to the pages below. He scanned a few lines then dared to flip back to the beginning.

"A book of creation," he mumbled, recognizing some of the early passages as common phrases for such dweomers.

He clasped the book and tried to pull it free, but it would not budge.

So he went back to reading, skimming really, looking for some hint, for some clue as to the secrets of the tower and its undead proprietor.

"You will find not my name in there," came a high-pitched voice that seemed on the verge of keening, a voice held tenuously, like a high note, ready to crack apart into a shivering screech.

Jarlaxle silently cursed himself for getting so drawn in to the book. He regarded the lich, who stood at the open door.

"Your name?" he asked, suppressing his honest desire to scream out in terror. "Why would I desire to know your name, O rotting one?"

"Rot implies death," said the lich. "Nothing could be farther from the truth."

Jarlaxle slowly moved back behind the chair, wanting to put as much distance and as many obstacles between himself and that awful creature as possible.

"You are not Zhengyi," the drow remarked, "yet the book was his."

"One of his, of course."

Jarlaxle offered a tip of his hat.

"You think of Zhengyi as a creature," the lich explained through its ever-grinning, lipless teeth, "as a singular entity. That is your error."

"I know nothing of Zhengyi."

"That much is obvious, or never would you have been foolish enough to come in here!" The lich ended with a sudden upswing in volume and intensity, and it pointed its bony fingers.

Greenish bolts of energy erupted from those digits, one from each, flying through the air, weaving and spinning around the book, the tentacle pedestal, and the chair to explode into the drow.

That was the intent, at least, but each magical bolt, as it approached, swirled to a specific spot on the drow's cloak, just below his throat and to the side, over his collarbone, where a large brooch clasped his cloak. That brooch swallowed the missiles, all ten, without a sound, without a trace.

"Well played," the lich congratulated. "How many can you contain?"

As the undead creature finished speaking, it sent forth another volley.

Jarlaxle was moving then, spinning away from the chair, straight back. The magic missiles swarmed at his back like so many bees, but again, as they neared him, they veered and swooped around him to be swallowed by the brooch.

The drow cut to the side, and as he turned halfway toward his enemy, his arm pumped feverishly. With each retraction, his magical bracer fed another dagger into his hand, which he promptly sent spinning through the air at the lich. So furious was his stream that the fourth dagger was in the air before the first ever struck home.

Or tried to strike home, for the lich was not unprotected. Its defensive wards stopped the daggers just short of the mark and let them fall to the ground with a *clang*.

The lich cackled, and the drow enveloped it in a globe of complete and utter darkness.

A ray of green energy burst from the globe and Jarlaxle was glad indeed that he had moved fast. He watched the ray burrow through the tower wall, disintegrating the stone as it went.

Entreri tucked his feet in tight and angled them to the side so that when he hit, he spun over sidelong. He drew his head in tight and tucked his shoulder, allowing himself to roll over again and again, absorbing the energy of the fifteen foot drop.

He continued to roll, putting as much distance as possible between himself and the point of the chandelier's impact, where glass and crystal shattered and flew everywhere.

When he finally came up to his feet, Entreri stumbled and winced. One ankle threw sharp pains up his leg. He had avoided serious injury but had not escaped unscathed.

Nor had he actually "escaped," he realized a moment later.

He was in the foyer of the tower, a wide, circular room. To the side, high above, the stone ball continued its rumbling roll. Before him, beyond the shattered chandelier and just past the bottom of those perimeter stairs, sat the sealed doorway through which he and Jarlaxle had entered the magical construction. To one side stood the great iron statue the pair had noted when first they had entered, a construct Jarlaxle had quickly identified as a golem.

They had to take care, Jarlaxle had told Entreri, not to set off any triggers that would animate the dangerous iron sentry.

Entreri learned now that they had apparently done just that.

Metal creaked and groaned as the golem came to life, red fires appearing in its hollow eyes. It took a great stride forward, crunching crystal and flattening the twisted metal of the fallen chandelier. It carried no weapon, but Entreri realized that it needed none, for it stood more than twice his height and weighed in at several thousand pounds.

"How do I hurt that?" the assassin whispered and drew forth his blades.

The golem strode closer and breathed forth a cloud of noxious, poisonous fumes.

Far too nimble to be caught by that, Entreri whirled aside. He saw an opening on the lumbering creature and knew that he could get in fast and strike hard.

But he ran instead, making all speed for the sealed doorway.

The golem's iron legs groaned in protest as it turned to pursue.

Entreri hit the door with his shoulder, though he knew it wouldn't open. He exaggerated the impact, though, and moved as if in terrified fury to break through.

On came the golem, focusing solely on him. He waited until the last second and darted along the wall to the left as the golem smashed in hard against the unyielding door. The sentry turned and pursued, iron arms reaching out for the assassin.

Entreri held his ground—for a few moments, at least—and he launched a barrage of swings and stabs that had the golem confused and standing in place for just . . .

. . . long enough.

The assassin bolted out to his left, out toward the center of the room.

The rolling metal sphere thundered down the last expanse of stairs and crashed hard against the back of the unwitting iron golem, driving the construct forward and to the floor, then bouncing across it, denting and twisting the iron. The ball continued rolling on its way, but most of its momentum had been played out on the unfortunate construct.

In the middle of the room, Entreri watched the twitching golem. It tried to rise, but its legs were crushed to uselessness, and it could do no more than lift its upper torso on one arm.

Entreri started to put his weapons away but paused at a sound from above.

He looked up to see many of the ceiling decorations, gargoylelike statues, flexing their wings.

He sighed.

━━━◆━━━

His darkness globe blinked out and Jarlaxle found himself once again facing the awful undead creature. He looked from the lich to the book and back again.

"You were alive just a few short tendays ago," the dark elf reasoned.

"I am still alive."

"Your existence might stretch the meaning of the word."

"You will soon enough know what it does and does not mean," the lich promised and it raised its bony hands to begin casting another spell.

"Do you miss the feel of the wind upon your living skin?" the drow asked, trying hard to sound truly curious and not condescending. "Will you miss the touch of a woman or the smell of springtime flowers?"

The lich paused.

"Is undeath worth it?" Jarlaxle went on. "And if it is, can you show me the path?"

Few expressions could show on the mostly skeletal face of the lich, of course, but Jarlaxle knew incredulity when he saw it. He kept his eyes locked with the creature's but angled his feet quietly to get him in line for a charge at the book.

"You speak of minor inconveniences against the power I have found," the lich roared at him.

Even as the creature howled, the drow sprang forward, a dagger appearing in one of his hands. He half-turned a page, laughed at the lich, and tore it out, confident that he had found the secret.

A new tear appeared in the lich's ragged cloak.

Jarlaxle's eyes widened and he began to work furiously, tearing page after page, driving his knife into the other half of the tome.

The lich howled and trembled. Pieces of its robe fell away and chips appeared in its bones.

But it wasn't enough, the drow realized, and he knew his error when the torn pages revealed something hidden within the book: a tiny, glowing violet gem in the shape of a skull. That was the secret, he realized, the tie between the undead lich and the tower. That skull was the key to the whole construction, to the unnatural remnant of Zhengyi, the Witch-King.

The drow reached for it, but his hand blistered and was thrown aside. The drow stabbed at it, but the dagger splintered and flew away.

The lich laughed at him. "We are one! You cannot defeat the tower of Zhengyi nor the caretaker he has appointed."

Jarlaxle shrugged and said, "You could be right."

Then he dropped another globe of darkness over the again-casting lich. The drow slipped on a ring that stored spells as he went. Considering the unearthliness of his foe, he thought to himself, hot or cold? then quickly chose.

He chose correctly. The spell he loosed from the ring covered his body in a shield of warm flames just as the lich blasted forth a conical spray of magical cold so intense that it would have frozen him solid in mid-stride.

Jarlaxle had won the moment, but only the moment, he knew, and in the three choices that loomed before him—counter with offensive magic, leap forth and physically strike, or flee—only one made any practical sense.

He pulled the great feather from his cap and dropped it with a command word that summoned from it a gigantic, flightless bird, an eight-foot avian creature with a thick neck and a deadly and powerful hooked beak. With a thought, the drow sent his summoned diatryma into battle, and he followed its course but broke off its wake as it barreled into the darkness globe.

Jarlaxle prayed that he had angled himself correctly and prayed again that the lich hadn't shut the door. He breathed a lot easier when he came out of the darkness to find himself in the corridor once more, running free.

And running fast.

⊫═══⊪

Oily liquid, the blood of gargoyles, dripped out from the channel along the red blade of Charon's Claw. One winged creature flopped about on the floor, mortally wounded but refusing to stop its futile thrashing. Another dived for

Entreri's head as he sprinted across the floor. He ducked low, then lower, then threw himself forward in a roll, fast approaching another of the creatures as it set down on the floor before him.

He came up at full speed, launching himself forward, sword leading.

The gargoyle's stonelike hand swept across, parrying the thrust, and Entreri lowered his shoulder and barreled in hard. The powerful creature hardly moved, and Entreri grunted when he took the brunt of the damage from the collision himself. The assassin's dagger flashed hard into the gargoyle's gut. Entreri growled and leaped back, tearing his hand up as he did and opening a long gash. He started to strike with Charon's Claw again but at the last moment leaped off to the side.

A swooping gargoyle went right past him, slamming headlong into its wounded companion.

Entreri slashed back behind the flying creature, drawing Charon's Claw hard across the passing gargoyle's back. The creature shrieked, and its gutted companion grunted and stumbled backward. Entreri couldn't pursue the tangled creatures, however, for another gargoyle came down fast at him, forcing him back.

He threw himself into a sidelong roll, going right under a table and hard into the base of a long rectangular box standing upright against the wall. He came up with the table above him, lifting it and hoisting it away.

The box creaked open behind him.

The assassin shook his head and glanced back to see a fleshy humanoid creature peering out at him from inside the box. It was larger than he, larger than any man ought to be.

Another golem, he knew, but one of stitched flesh rather than sculpted iron.

The creature reached out and the assassin scrambled away, turning back just long enough to slash Charon's Claw against one of the golem's forearms.

The golem stepped out in pursuit, and behind it, Entreri saw the back of the box, the false bottom, swing wide to reveal a second flesh golem.

"Lovely," the assassin said, diving yet again to avoid another swooping gargoyle.

He glanced up and saw more gargoyles forming, growing across the high ceiling. The tower was coming to life and hatching an army to defend itself.

Entreri sprinted across the foyer but pulled up short as he saw another form coming down at him. He skipped back a few steps and readied his sword, then he recognized the newest opponent.

Jarlaxle tipped his hat, all but stopping his rapid descent, and he gently touched down to the floor.

Entreri spun around and drove his sword again across the outstretched arms of the pursuing flesh golem.

"Glad you found your way here at last," the assassin grumbled.

"But I fear I did not come alone," Jarlaxle warned, his words turning the assassin back around.

The dark elf's gaze led Entreri's up to the high balcony where the lich ran toward the descending stairs.

The lich stopped at the top of the steps and began waggling its bony fingers in the air.

"Stop the beast!" Entreri cried.

He launched a more forceful routine against the golem, slashing Charon's Claw across and using its magic to bring forth a cloud of black ash. With that optical barrier hanging in the air, Entreri rushed by the first golem and stabbed the second one hard.

"We must be leaving," Jarlaxle called to him, as Entreri dived again to avoid a swooping gargoyle.

"The door is sealed!" Entreri shouted back.

"Come, and be quick!" replied the dark elf.

Entreri turned as he went and watched a series of green bolts soar out from the lich's fingers, weaving and darting down. Five struck Jarlaxle—or would have except that they were gathered up by the magic of his brooch—while the other five soared unerringly for Entreri.

The assassin tossed Charon's Claw into the air and held forth his gauntleted hand, absorbing the missiles one after another. He caught his sword and looked back to see Jarlaxle's slender fingers beckoning to him. Up above, the lich charged down the stairs.

Entreri ducked at the last moment, barely avoiding a heavy swipe by one of the golems that would have likely torn his head from his shoulders. He growled and ran at the drow, sheathing his sword as he went.

Jarlaxle grinned, tipped his hat, bent his knees, and leaped straight up.

Entreri leaped, too, catching Jarlaxle by the belt as the drow's levitation sped him upward, dragging Entreri along.

Below, the golems reached and swung futilely at the empty air. From the side came the attack of a gargoyle, the creature clawing hard at Entreri's legs. The assassin deftly retracted, just ahead of the claws, and kicked the gargoyle hard in the face.

He did little damage, however, and the gargoyle came back fast and hard—or started to, but then turned upright, wings beating furiously as Entreri reached out with his gauntlet and sent forth the missiles the lich had just thrown his way. The magic darts crackled into the gargoyle's black skin, making the creature jerk this way and that.

It started right back at the levitating pair, however, and from above came the shrieks of more gargoyles, already "grown" and ready to swoop down from on high.

But the companions had reached the railing by then, and Jarlaxle grabbed on and pulled himself over, Entreri coming fast behind.

"Run back up!" the drow cried. "There is a way!"

Entreri stared at him for a moment, but with gargoyles coming from above and beyond the railing and the lich reversing and running back up the stairs at them, Jarlaxle's order seemed fairly self-evident.

They sprinted back up the sloping corridor, gargoyles flapping at their heels, forcing Entreri to stop with practically every step and fend the creatures off.

"Quickly!" Jarlaxle called.

Entreri glanced at the drow, saw him with wand in his hand, and could only imagine what catastrophe might be contained within that slender item. The assassin bolted ahead.

Jarlaxle pointed the wand behind Entreri and spoke the triggering command word.

A wall of stone appeared in the corridor, blocking it from wall to wall, floor to ceiling. Behind it, they heard the thud as a gargoyle collided with it then the scratching noises as the frustrated creatures clawed at the unyielding stone.

"Run on," Jarlaxle told his companion. "The golems can batter through it in time, and it won't slow the lich at all."

"Cheery," said Entreri.

He sprinted past Jarlaxle and didn't wait for the drow to catch up. He did glance back as the corridor bent out of sight of the wall of stone, and he saw Jarlaxle's warning shining true, for the lich drifted into sight, moving right through the stone barrier.

The door to the tower's apex room was closed but not secured and Entreri shouldered through. He pulled up abruptly, staring at the partially torn book and the glow emanating from its central area. He felt a shove on his back.

"Go to it, quickly!" Jarlaxle bade him.

Entreri ran up to and around the book and its tentacle pedestal. There he saw the glowing skull clearly, pulsing with light and with power.

A thunderous retort slammed the stone door, which Jarlaxle had shoved closed, and it swung in, wisps of smoke rising from a charred point in its center. Beyond it and down the corridor came the lich, magically gliding, eyes glowing, teeth locked in that perpetual undead grin.

"There is no escape," came the creature's words, carried on a cold breath that swept through the room.

"Grab the skull," Jarlaxle instructed.

Entreri reached with his left hand and felt a sudden and painful sting.

"With the gauntlet!" Jarlaxle implored him.

"What?"

"The gauntlet!" shouted the drow, and he staggered and jolted to and fro as a series of green-glowing missiles struck at him. His brooch swallowed the first couple, then it glowed and smoked as the remaining missiles stabbed at him. Two quick steps moved the drow out of the lich's view, and Jarlaxle dived down and rolled to the side of the room.

That left Entreri staring through the open doorway at the lich, cognizant that he had become the primary target of the horrid creature.

But Entreri didn't dive aside. He knew he had nowhere to run and so dismissed the thought out of hand. Staring at his approaching enemy, his face full of determination with not a shred of fear, the assassin raised his gloved hand and dropped it over the glowing skull.

The lich halted as abruptly and completely as if it had smacked into a solid wall.

Entreri didn't see it, however, for the moment his magic-eating glove fell over the throbbing skull, jolts of power arced into the assassin. The muscles in his right arm knotted and twisted. His teeth slammed together, taking the tip off his tongue, and began to chomp uncontrollably, blood spitting out with each opening. His body stiffened and jerked in powerful spasms as red and blue energy bolts crackled and sparked through the gauntlet.

"Hold it fast!" Jarlaxle implored him.

The drow rolled back in sight of the lich, who stood thrashing and clawing at the air. Patches of shadow seemed to grab at the undead creature and eat at it, compacting him, diminishing him.

"You cannot defeat the power of Zhengyi!" the lich growled, words staggered and uneven.

Jarlaxle's laugh was cut short as he glanced back at the snapping and jerking form of Entreri, who shuddered on the edge of disaster, as if he would soon be thrown across the room and through the tower wall. His eyes bulged weirdly, seeming as if they might pop right out. Blood still spilled from his mouth and trickled from his ear as well, and his arm twisted, shoulder popping out of its socket, muscles straining so tightly that they seemed as if they might simply tear apart.

Growls escaped the assassin's mouth. He grimaced, strained, and fought with all his strength and all his willpower. Within the resonance of the growls came the word "No," oft repeated.

It was a challenge. It was a contest.

Entreri met it.

He held on.

Out in the hall, the lich wailed and scratched at the empty air, and with each passing moment, it seemed to diminish just a bit more.

The tower began to sway. Cracks appeared in the walls and floors.

Jarlaxle ran up beside his companion but took care not to touch him.

"Hold on," the drow implored.

Entreri roared in rage and clamped all the tighter. Smoke began to rise from the gauntlet.

The tower swayed more. A great chunk fell out of one wall, and sunlight beamed in.

Out in the hallway, the lich screamed.

"Ah yes, my friend, hold on," Jarlaxle whispered.

The skull pulled out of the book, held fast in the smoldering glove. Entreri managed to turn his hand over and stare at it for just a moment.

Then the tower fell apart beneath him.

Entreri felt a hand on his shoulder. He glanced aside.

Jarlaxle grinned and tipped his hat.

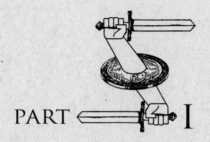

PART I

LEGACY OF INTRIGUE

By the time he'd left the crumbling tower, Jarlaxle had already secured the magical skull gem in an undetectable place: an extra-dimensional pocket in one of the buttons of his waistcoat designed to shield magical emanations. Even so, the drow wasn't confident that the item would remain undetected, for it verily throbbed with arcane energy.

Still, he took it with him—leaving his familiar waistcoat would have been more conspicuous—when he went to the palace-tower of Ilnezhara soon after the collapse of the Zhengyi construction. He found his employer lounging in one of her many easy chairs, her feet up on a decorated ottoman and her shapely legs showing through a high slit in her white silk gown that made the material flow down to the floor like a ghostly extension of the creamy-skinned woman. She flipped her long, thick blond hair as Jarlaxle made his entrance, so that it framed her pretty face. It settled covering one of her blue eyes, only adding to her aura of mystery.

Jarlaxle understood that it was all a ruse, of course, an illusion of magnificent beauty. For Ilnezhara's true form was covered in copper-colored scales and sported great horns and a mouth filled with rows of fangs each as long as the drow's arm. Illusion or not, however, Jarlaxle certainly appreciated the beauty reclining before him.

"It was a construct of Zhengyi," the dragon-turned-woman stated, not asked.

"Indeed it would seem," the drow answered, flipping off his wide-brimmed hat to reveal his bald head as he dipped a fancy bow.

"It was," Ilnezhara stated with all certainty. "We have traced its creation while you were away."

"Away? You mean inside the tower. I was away at your insistence, please remember."

"It was not an accusation, nor were we premature in sending you and your friend to investigate. My sister happened upon some more information quite by accident and quite unexpectedly. Still, we do not know how this construct was facilitated, but we know now, of course, that it was indeed facilitated, and we know by whom."

"It was a book, a great and ancient tome," Jarlaxle replied.

Ilnezhara started forward in her chair but caught herself. There was no denying the sparkle of interest in her blue eyes, so the drow let the tease hang in the air. He stood calm and unmoving, allowing a moment of silence slip past, forcing Ilnezhara's interest.

"Produce it then."

251

"I cannot," he admitted. "The tower was constructed by the magic of the book and controlled by the power of a lich. To defeat the latter, Artemis and I had to destroy the former. There was no other way."

Ilnezhara winced. "That is unfortunate," she said. "A book penned by Zhengyi would be most interesting, beneficial . . . and profitable."

"The tower had to be destroyed. There was no other way."

"Had you killed the lich, the effect would have been the same. The tower would have died, if not fallen, but no more of its defenses would have risen against you. Perhaps my sister and I might even have given the tower to you and Entreri as an expression of our gratitude."

Despite the empty promise, there was more than a little hint of frustration in the dragon's voice, Jarlaxle noted.

"An easy task?" he replied, letting his voice drip with sarcasm.

Ilnezhara harrumphed, waved her hand dismissively, and said, "It was a minor mage from Heliogabalus, a fool named Herminicle Duperdas. Could a man with such a name frighten the great Jarlaxle? Perhaps my sister and I overestimated you and your human friend."

Jarlaxle dipped another bow. "A minor mage in life, perhaps, but a lich is a lich, after all."

Again, the dragon harrumphed, and rolled her blue eyes. "He was a middling magic-user at most—many of his fellow students considered him a novice. Even in the undead state, he could not have proven too formidable for the likes of you two."

"The tower itself was aiding in his defense."

"We did not send you two in there to destroy the place, but to scout it and pilfer it," Ilnezhara scolded. "We could have easily enough destroyed it on our own."

"Pray do, next time."

The dragon narrowed her eyes, reminding Jarlaxle that he would be wise to take more care.

"If we do not benefit from your services, Jarlaxle, then we do not need you," Ilnezhara warned. "Is that truly the course you desire?"

A third bow came her way. "No, milady. No, of course not."

"Herminicle found the book and underestimated it," Ilnezhara explained, seeming as if she had put the disagreement out of her mind. "He read it, as foolish and curious wizards usually will, and it consumed him, taking his magic and his life-force as its own. The book bound him to the tower as the tower bound itself to him. When you destroyed the bonds—the book—you stole the shared force from both, sending both tower and lich to ruin."

"What else might we have done?"

"Had you killed the lich, perhaps the tower would have crumbled," came another female voice, one a bit deeper, less feminine, and less melodious than that of Ilnezhara. Jarlaxle wasn't really surprised to see Tazmikella walk out from behind a screen at the back of the large, cluttered room. "But likely not, though you would have destroyed the force that had initially given it life and material. In either event, the danger would have passed, but the book would have remained. Hasn't Ilnezhara already told you as much?"

"Please learn this lesson and remember it well," Ilnezhara instructed, and she teasingly added, " for next time."

"Next time?" Jarlaxle didn't have to feign interest.

"The appearance of this book confirms to us what we already suspected," Tazmikella explained. "Somewhere in the wastelands of Vaasa, a trove of the Witch-King has been uncovered. Artifacts of Zhengyi are revealing themselves all about the land."

"It has happened before in the years since his fall," Ilnezhara went on. "Every so often, one of the Witch-King's personal dungeons is found, one of his cellars opened wide, or a tribe of monsters is defeated, only for the victors to find among the beasts weapons, wands, or other magical items of which the stupid creatures had no comprehension."

"We suspected that one of Zhengyi's libraries, perhaps his only library, has recently been pilfered," added Tazmikella. "A pair of books on the art of necromancy—true tomes and not the typical ramblings of self-important and utterly foolish wizards—were purchased in Halfling Downs not a month ago."

"By you, I presume," said Jarlaxle.

"By our agents, of course," Ilnezhara confirmed. "Agents who have been more profitable than Jarlaxle and Entreri to date."

Jarlaxle laughed at the slight and bowed yet again. "Had we known that destroying the lich might have preserved the book, then we would have fought the beastly creature all the more ferociously, I assure you. Forgive us our inexperience. We have not long been in this land, and the tales of the Witch-King are still fresh to us."

"Inexperience, I suspect, is not one of Jarlaxle's failings," said Tazmikella, and her tone revealed to the drow her suspicions that perhaps he was holding back something from his recent adventure in the tower.

"But fear not, I am a fast study," he replied. "And I fear that I—we—cannot replicate our errors with this tower should another one appear." He held up a gauntlet, black with red stitching, and turned it over to show the hole in the palm. "The price of an artifact in defeating the magic of the book."

"The gauntlet accompanying Entreri's mighty sword?" asked Tazmikella.

"Aye, though the sword has no hold over him with or without it. In fact, since his encounter with the shade, I do believe the sword fancies him. Still, our excursion proved quite costly, for the gauntlet had many other valuable uses."

"And what would you have us do about that?" asked Ilnezhara.

"Recompense?" the drow dared ask. "We are weakened without the gauntlet, do not doubt. Our defenses against magic-users have just been greatly depleted. Certainly that cannot be beneficial, given our duties to you."

The sisters looked to each other and exchanged knowing smiles.

"If this tome has surfaced, we can expect other Zhengyian artifacts," Tazmikella said.

"That the tome made its way this far south tells us that someone in Vaasa has uncovered a trove of Zhengyi's artifacts," Ilnezhara added. "Such powerful magical items do not like to remain dormant. They find a way to resurface, again and again, to the bane of the world."

"Interesting . . ." the drow started, but Tazmikella cut him short.

"More so than you understand," she insisted. "Gather your friend, Jarlaxle, for the road awaits you—one that we might all find quite lucrative."

It was not a request but a demand, and since the sisters were, after all, dragons, it was not a demand the drow meant to ignore. He noted something else in the timbre of the sisters' voices, however, that intrigued him at least as much as the skull-shaped remnant of the Zhengyian construct. They were feigning excitement, as if a great adventure and potential gain awaited them all, but behind that, Jarlaxle clearly heard something else.

The two mighty dragons were afraid.

In the remote, cold northland of Vaasa, a second skull, a greater skull, glowed hungrily. It felt the fall of its little sister in Damara keenly, but not with the dread of one who had lost a family member. No, distant events were simply the order of things. The other skull, the human skull, was minor and weak.

What the distant remnant of the Witch-King's godliness had come to know above all else was that the powers could awaken—that the powers would awaken. Too much time had passed in the short memories of the foolish humans and those others who had defeated Zhengyi. Already they were willing to ply their wisdom and strength against the artifacts of a being so much greater than they, a being far beyond their comprehension. Their hubris led them to believe that they could attain that power.

They did not understand that the Witch-King's power had come from within, not from without, and that his remnants, "the essence of magic scattered," "the pieces of Zhengyi flung wide," in the songs of the silly and naïve bards, would, through the act of creation, overwhelm them and take from them even as they tried to gain from the scattering of Zhengyi.

That was the true promise of the Witch-King, the one that had sent dragons flocking to his side.

The tiny skull found only comfort. The tome that held it was found, the minds about it inquisitive, the memories short. The piece of essence flung wide would know creation, power, and life in death.

Some foolish mortal would see to that.

The dragon growled without sound.

CHAPTER

THE COMPANY

1

Parissus, the Impilturian woman, winced as the red-bearded dwarf drew a bandage tight around her wounded forearm.

"You better be here to tell me that you've decided to deliver the rest of our bounty," she said to the soldier sitting across the other side of the small room where the cleric had set up his chapel. Her appearance, with broad shoulders and short-cropped, disheveled blonde hair, added menace to her words, and anyone who had ever seen Parissus wield her broadsword would say that sense of menace was well-placed.

The man, handsome in a rugged manner, with thick black hair and a full beard, and skin browned by many hours out in the sun, seemed quite amused by it all.

"Don't you smile, Davis Eng," said the woman's female companion, a half-elf, much smaller in build than Parissus.

She narrowed her gaze then widened her eyes fiercely—and indeed, those eyes had struck fear into many an enemy. Light blue, almost gray, Calihye's eyes had been the last image so many opponents had seen. Those eyes! So intense that they made many ignore the hot scar on the woman's right cheek, where a pirate's gaff hook had caught her and nearly torn her face off, tearing a jagged line from her cheek through the edge of her thin lips and to the middle of her chin. Her eyes seemed even more startling because of the contrast between them and her long black hair, and the angular elf's features of a face that, had it not been for the scar, could not have been considered anything but beautiful.

Davis Eng chuckled. "What do you think, Pratcus?" he asked the dwarf cleric. "That little wound of hers seem ugly enough to have been made by a giant?"

"It's a giant's ear!" Parissus growled at him.

"Small for a giant," Davis Eng replied, and he fished into his belt pouch and produced the torn ear, holding it up before his eyes. "Small for an ogre, I'd say, but you might talk me out of the coin for an ogre's bounty."

"Or I might cut it out of your hide," said Calihye.

"With your fingernails, I hope," the soldier replied, and the dwarf laughed.

Parissus slapped him on the head, which of course only made him laugh all the louder.

255

"Every tenday it's that same game," Pratcus remarked, and even surly Calihye couldn't help but chuckle a bit at that.

For indeed, every tenday when it came time for the payout of the bounties, Davis Eng, she, and Parissus played their little game, arguing over the number of ears—goblin, orc, bugbear, hobgoblin, and giant—the successful hunting pair had delivered to the Vaasan Gate.

"Only a game because that one's meaning to pocket a bit of Ellery's coin," Calihye said.

"*Commander* Ellery," Davis Eng corrected, and his voice took on a serious tone.

"That, or he can't count," said Parissus, and she groaned again as Pratcus tugged the bandage into place. "Or can't tell the difference between an ogre and a giant. Yes, that would be it, I suppose, since he's not set foot outside of Damara in years."

"I did my fighting," the man argued.

"In the Witch-King War?" Parissus snapped back. "You were a child."

"Vaasa is not nearly as untamed as she was after the fall of the Witch-King," said Davis Eng. "When I first joined the Army of Bloodstone, monsters of every sort swarmed over these hills. If King Gareth had seen fit to pay a bounty in those first months, his treasury would have been cleared of coin, do not doubt."

"Kill any giants?" asked Calihye, and the man glared at her. "You're sure they weren't ogres? Or goblins, even?"

That brought another laugh from Pratcus.

"Bah, that one's always had a problem in measuring things," Parissus added. "So they're saying in Ironhead's Tavern and in Muddy Boots and Bloody Blades. But he's not one for consistency, I'm thinking, because if he's measuring now like he's measuring then, sure that he'd be certain we'd given him a titan's ear!"

Pratcus snorted and jerked, and Parissus ended with a squeal as he inadvertently twisted the bandage.

Calihye was laughing too, and after a moment, even Davis Eng joined in. He had never been able to resist those two, when all was said and done.

"I'll call it a giant, then," he surrendered. "A *baby* giant."

"I noted nothing on the bounty charts about age," Calihye said as Davis Eng began to count out the coins.

"A kill is a kill," Davis Eng agreed.

"You've been taking a particular interest in our earnings these last tendays," Calihye said. "Is there a reason?"

Pratcus started to chuckle, tipping the women off. Parissus pulled her hand back from him and glowered at him. "What do you know?"

Pratcus looked at Davis Eng, who similarly chuckled and nodded.

"Yer friend's passed Athrogate," the dwarf priest explained, and he glanced over at Calihye. "He'll be back in a couple o' tendays, and he's not to be pleased that all his time away has put him in back o' Calihye in bounties earned."

The look that crossed between Parissus and Calihye was one more of concern than of pride. Was that honor really a desired one, considering the disposition of Athrogate and his known connections to the Citadel of Assassins?

"And you, Parissus, are fast closing in on the dwarf," Davis Eng added.

Davis Eng tossed a small bag of silver to Calihye and said, "He'll fume and harrumph and run about in a fury when he gets back. He'll make stupid little rhymes about you both. Then he'll go out and slaughter half of the monsters in Vaasa, just to put you two in your place. He'll probably hire wagons out, just to carry back the ears."

Neither woman broke a smile.

"Ah, but these two can pace Athrogate," Pratcus said.

Davis Eng laughed and so did Calihye, and Parissus a moment later. Could anyone truly pace Athrogate?

"He's got a fire inside of him that I've never seen the likes of before," Calihye admitted. "And never does he run faster than when there's a hundred enemies standing in his way."

"But we're there, right beside him, and I mean to pass him, too," Parissus said, allowing her pride to finally spill forth. "When our fellow hunters look at the board outside of Ironhead's, they're going to see the names Parissus and Calihye penned right there on top!"

"Calihye and Parissus," the half-elf corrected.

Davis Eng and Pratcus burst into laughter.

"Only because we're being generous on this last kill," said Davis Eng.

"It was a giant!" both women said together.

"After that," the soldier replied. "You two were dead before you got to the wall, had not Commander Ellery rushed out. That alone should negate the bounty."

"So says yourself, bluster-blunder!" Calihye roared in defiance. "We had the goblins beat clean. Was your own fellow who wanted a piece of the fight for himself. He's the one Ellery needed saving."

"*Commander* Ellery," came a call from the doorway, and all four heads turned to regard the important woman herself, striding into the room.

Pratcus tried to appear sober and respectful, but giggles kept escaping his mouth as he tugged hard to tighten down Parissus's bandage.

"Commander Ellery," Calihye said in deference, and she offered a slight bow in apology. "A title well-earned, though all titles seem to fall hard from my lips. I beg your pardon, Commander Ellery, Lady Dragonsbane."

"Given the occasion, your indiscretion is of no concern," said Ellery, trying not to appear flushed by the complimentary use of her surname, Dragonsbane, a name of the greatest renown all across the Bloodstone Lands. Technically, Ellery's last name was Peidopare, though Dragonsbane immediately preceded that name, and the half-elf's use of the more prominent family name was certainly as great a compliment as anyone could possibly pay to Ellery. She was tall and slim, but there was nothing frail about her frame, for she had seen many battles and had wielded her heavy axe since childhood. Her eyes were wide-set and bright blue, her skin tanned, but still delicate, and dotted with many freckles about her nose. Those did not detract from her beauty, though, but rather enhanced it, adding a touch of girlishness to a face full of intensity and power. "I wanted to add this to the bounty." She pulled a small pouch from her belt and tossed it to Calihye. "An additional reward from the Army of Bloodstone for your heroic work."

"We were discussing whether Athrogate would be pleased when he returns," Davis Eng explained, and that thought brought a grin to Ellery's face.

"I expect he'll not take the demotion to runner-up as well as Mariabronne accepted Athrogate's ascent."

"With all respect to Athrogate," Parissus remarked, "Mariabronne the Rover has more Vaasan kills to his credit than all three of us together."

"A point hard to argue, though the ranger accepts no bounty and takes no public acclaim," said Davis Eng, and the way he spoke made it apparent that he was drawing a distinction between Mariabronne the Rover, a name legendary throughout Damara, and the two women.

"Mariabronne made both his reputation and his fortune in the first few years following Zhengyi's demise," Ellery added. "Once King Gareth took note of him and knighted him, there was little point for Mariabronne to continue to compete in the Vaasan bounties. Perhaps our two friends here, and Athrogate, will find similar honor soon."

"Athrogate knighted by King Gareth?" Davis Eng said, and Pratcus was bobbing so hard trying to contain his laughter at the absurd image those words conjured that he nearly fell right over.

"Well, perhaps not that one," Ellery conceded, to the amusement of them all.

Something just didn't feel right, didn't smell right.

His face showed the hard work, the battles, of more than twenty years. He was still handsome, though, with his unkempt brown locks and his scruffy beard. His bright brown eyes shone with the luster of youth more fitting of a man half his age, and that grin of his was both commanding and mischievous, a smile that could melt a woman on the spot, and one that the nomadic warrior had often put to good use. He had risen through the ranks of the Bloodstone Army in those years during the war with the Witch-King, and had moved beyond even those accolades upon his release from the official service of King Gareth after Zhengyi's fall.

Mariabronne the Rover, he was called, a name that almost every man, woman, and child in Damara knew well, and one that struck a chord of fear and hatred in the monsters of Vaasa. For the ending of his service in the Bloodstone Army had only been the beginning of Mariabronne's service to King Gareth and the people of the two states collectively known as the Bloodstone Lands. Working out of the northern stretches of the Bloodstone Pass, which connected Vaasa and Damara through the towering Galena Mountains, Mariabronne had served as tireless bodyguard to the workers who had constructed the massive Vaasan Gate. More than anyone else, even more so than the men and women surrounding King Gareth himself, Mariabronne the Rover had worked to tame wild Vaasa.

The progress was slow, so very slow, and Mariabronne doubted he'd see Vaasa truly civilized in his lifetime. But ending the journey wasn't the point. He could not solve all the ills of the world, but he could help his fellow men walk the path that would eventually lead to that.

But something smelled wrong. Some sensation in the air, some sixth sense, told the ranger that great trials might soon be ahead.

It must have been Wingham's summons, he realized, for had the old half-orc ever bade someone to his side before? Everything with Wingham—Weird

Wingham, he was called, and proudly called himself—prompted suspicion, of course, of the curious kind if not the malicious. But what could it be, Mariabronne wondered? What sensation was upon the wind, darkening the Vaasan sky? What omen of ill portent had he noted unconsciously out of the corner of his eye?

"You're getting old and timid," he scolded himself.

Mariabronne often talked to himself, for Mariabronne was often alone. He wanted no partner for his hunting or for his life, unless it was a temporary arrangement, a warm, soft body beside him in a warm, soft bed. His responsibilities were beyond the call of his personal desires. His visions and aspirations were rooted in the hope of an entire nation, not the cravings of a single man.

The ranger sighed and shielded his eyes against the rising sun as he looked east across the muddy Vaasan plain that morning. Summer had come to the wasteland, though the breeze still carried a chilly bite. Many of the more brutish monsters, the giants and the ogres, had migrated north hunting the elk herds, and without the more formidable enemies out and about, the smaller humanoid races—orcs and goblins, mostly—were keeping out of sight, deep in caves or high up among the rocks.

As he considered that, Mariabronne let his gaze linger to the left, to the south, and the vast wall-fortress known as the Vaasan Gate. Her great portcullis was up, and the ranger could see the dark dots of adventurers issuing forth to begin the morning hunt.

Already there was talk of constructing more fortified keeps north of the great gate, for the numbers of monsters there were declining and the bounty hunters could no longer be assured of their silver and gold coins.

Everything was going as King Gareth had planned and desired. Vaasa would be tamed, mile by mile, and the two nations would merge as the single entity of Bloodstone.

But something had Mariabronne on edge. Some feeling warned him far in the recesses of his mind, that the dark had not been fully lifted from the wild land of Vaasa.

"Wingham's summons is all," he decided, and he moved back to the sheltered dell and began to collect his gear.

Commander Ellery paced the top of the great wall that was the Vaasan gate a short while later. She hardly knew these two women, Calihye and Parissus, who had ascended so far and so fast among the ranking of bounty hunters, and in truth, Ellery was not fond of the little one, Calihye. The half-elf's character was as scarred as her formerly pretty face, Ellery knew. Still, Calihye could fight with the best of the warriors at the gate and drink with them as well, and Ellery had to admit, to herself at least, that she took a bit of private glee at seeing a woman attain the highest rank on the bounty board.

They had all been laughing about Athrogate's reaction, but Ellery understood that it truly was no joke. She knew the dwarf well, though few realized that the two had forged such a partnership of mutual benefit, and she understood that the dwarf, whatever his continual bellowing laughter might indicate, did not take well to being surpassed.

But all accolades to Calihye, and soon to Parissus, the niece of Gareth Dragonsbane thought. However she might feel about the little one—and in truth, the big one was a bit crude for Ellery's tastes, as well—she, Athrogate, and everyone else at the Vaasan Gate had to admit their prowess. Calihye and Parissus were fine fighters and better hunters. Monstrous prey had thinned severely about the Vaasan Gate, but those two always seemed to find more goblins or orcs to slaughter. Rare was the day that Calihye and Parissus left the fortification to return without a bag of ears.

And yes, it did sit well with Ellery that a pair of women, among the few at the Vaasan Gate, had achieved so much. Ellery knew well from personal experience how difficult it was for a woman, even a dwarf female, to climb the patriarchal ranks of the warrior class, either informally as a bounty hunter or formally in the Army of Bloodstone. She had earned her rank of commander one fight and one argument at a time. She had battled for every promotion and every difficult assignment. She had earned her mighty axe from the hand of the ogre who wielded it and had earned the plume in her great helmet through deed and deed alone.

But there were always those voices, whispers at the edges of her consciousness, people insisting under their breath that the woman's heritage, boasting of both the names of Tranth and particularly of Dragonsbane, served as explanation for her ascent.

Ellery moved to the northern lip of the great wall, planted her hands on the stone railing and looked out over the wasteland of Vaasa. She served under many men in the Army of Bloodstone who had not seen half the battles she had waged and won. She served under many men in the Army of Bloodstone who did not know how to lead a patrol, or set a proper watch and perimeter around an evening encampment. She served under many men in the Army of Bloodstone whose troops ran out of supplies regularly, all on account of poor planning.

Yet those doubting voices remained, whispering in her head and beating in heart.

CHAPTER

LOOKING IN THE MIRROR

2

"You are a weapon of disproportion," Artemis Entreri whispered. He sat on the edge of his bed in the small apartment, staring across the room at his signature weapon, the jeweled dagger. It hung in the wall an inch from the tall mirror, stuck fast from a throw made in frustration just a moment before. Its hilt had stopped quivering, but the way the candlelight played on the red garnet near the base of the pommel made it seem as if the weapon was still moving, or as if it was alive.

It does not satisfy you to wound, Entreri thought, *or even to kill. No, that is not enough.*

The dagger had served Entreri well for more than two decades. He had made his name on the tough streets of Calimport, clawing and scratching from his days as a mere boy against seemingly insurmountable obstacles. He had been surrounded by murderers all of his life, and had bettered them at their own game. The jeweled dagger hanging in the wall had played no small part in that. Entreri could use it to do more than wound or kill; he could use its vampiric properties to steal the very life-force from a victim.

But beyond proportion, he thought. *You must take everything from your victims—their lives, their very souls. What must it be like, this nothingness you bring?*

Entreri snorted softly and helplessly at that last self-evident question. He shifted on the bed just a bit, moving himself so that he could see his reflection in the tall, ornate mirror. When first he had awakened, hoisting the dagger in his hand to let fly, he had taken aim at the mirror, thinking to shatter the glassy reminder out of existence. Only at the last second had he shifted his aim, putting the dagger into the wall instead.

Entreri hated the mirror. It was Jarlaxle's prize, not his. The drow spent far too much time standing in front of the glass, admiring himself, adjusting his hat so that its wide brim was angled just right across his brow. Everything was a pose for that one, and no one appreciated Jarlaxle's beauty more than did Jarlaxle himself. He'd bring his cloak back over one shoulder and turn just so, then reverse the cloak and strike a pose exactly opposite. Similarly, he'd move his eye patch from left eye to right, then back again, coordinating it with the cloak. No detail of his appearance was too minor to escape Jarlaxle's clever eye.

But when Artemis Entreri looked into the mirror, he found himself faced with an image he did not like. He didn't appear anywhere near his more than four decades of life. Fit and trim, with finely-honed muscles and the lean athleticism of a man half his age, few who looked upon Entreri would think him beyond thirty. At Jarlaxle's insistence and constant badgering, he kept his black hair neatly trimmed and parted, left to right, and his face was almost always clean-shaven except for the small mustache he had come to favor. He wore silk clothes, finely cut and fit—Jarlaxle would have it no other way.

There was one thing about Entreri's appearance, however, that the meticulous and finicky drow could not remedy, and as he considered the tone of his skin, the grayish quality that made him feel as if he should be on display in a coffin, Entreri's gaze inevitably slipped back to that jeweled dagger. The weapon had done that to him, had taken the life essence from an extra-dimensional humanoid known as a shade and had drawn it into Entreri's human form.

"It's never enough for you to simply kill, is it?" Entreri asked aloud, and his gaze alternated through the sentence from the dagger to his image in the mirror and back again.

"On the contrary," came a smooth, lyrical voice from the side. "I pride myself on killing only when necessary, and usually I find that to be more than enough to sate whatever feelings spurred me to the deed in the first place."

Entreri turned his head to watch Jarlaxle enter the room, his tall black leather boots clacking loudly on the wooden floor. A moment ago, those boots were making not a whisper of sound, Entreri knew, for Jarlaxle could silence them or amplify them with no more than a thought.

"You look disheveled," the drow remarked. He reached over to the dark wood bureau and pulled Entreri's white shirt from it, then tossed it to the seated assassin.

"I just awakened."

"Ah, the tigress I brought you last night drove you to slumber."

"Or she bored me to sleep."

"You worry me."

If you knew how often the thought of killing you entered my mind, Entreri thought, but stopped as a knowing smirk widened on Jarlaxle's face. Jarlaxle was guessing his thoughts, he knew, if not reading them in detail with some strange magical device.

"Where is the red-haired lass?"

Entreri looked around the small room and shrugged. "I suspect that she left."

"Even with sleep caking your eyes, you remain the perceptive one."

Entreri sighed and glanced back at his dagger, and at his reflection, the side-by-side images eliciting similar feelings. He dropped his face into his hands and rubbed his bleary eyes.

He lifted his head at the sound of banging to see Jarlaxle using the pommel of a dagger to nail some ornament in place on the jamb above the door.

"A gift from Ilnezhara," the drow explained, stepping back and moving his hands away to reveal the palm-sized charm: a silvery dragon statuette, rearing, wings and jaws wide.

Entreri wasn't surprised. Ilnezhara and her sister Tazmikella had become their benefactors, or their employers, or their companions, or whatever else Ilnezhara and Tazmikella wanted, so it seemed. The sisters held every trump in the relationship because they were, after all, dragons.

Always dragons lately.

Entreri had never laid eyes upon a dragon until he'd met Jarlaxle. Since that time, he had seen far too many of the beasts.

"Lightning of the blue," Jarlaxle whispered to the statuette, and the figurine's eyes flared with a bright, icy blue light for just a moment then dimmed.

"What did you just do?"

Jarlaxle turned to face Entreri, his smile beaming. "Let us just say that it would not do to walk through that doorway without first identifying the dragon type."

"Blue?"

"For now," the drow teased.

"How do you know I won't change it on you when you're out?" Entreri asked, determined to turn the tables on the cocky dark elf.

Jarlaxle tapped his eye patch. "Because I can see through doors," he explained. "And the eyes will always give it away." His smile disappeared, and he glanced around the room again.

"You are certain that the tigress has gone?" he asked.

"Or she's become very, very small."

Jarlaxle cast a sour expression Entreri's way. "Is she under your bed?"

"You wear the eye patch. Just look through it."

"Ah, you wound me yet again," said the drow. "Tell me, my friend, if I peer into your chest, will I see but a cavity where your heart should be?"

Entreri stood up and pulled on his shirt. "Inform me if that is the case," he said, walking over to tug his jeweled dagger out of the wall, "that I might cut out Jarlaxle's heart to serve as replacement."

"Far too large for the likes of Entreri, I fear."

Entreri started to respond, but found that he hadn't the heart for it.

"There is a caravan leaving in two days," Jarlaxle informed him. "We might not only find passage to the north but gather some gainful employ in the process. They are in need of guards, you see."

Entreri regarded him carefully and curiously, not quite knowing what to make of Jarlaxle's sudden, ceaseless promotion of journeying to the Gates of Damara, the two massive walls blocking either end of the Bloodstone Pass through the Galena Mountains into the wilderlands of neighboring Vaasa. This campaign for a northern adventure had begun soon after the pair had nearly been killed in their last escapade, and that battle in the strange tower still had Entreri quite shaken.

"Our bona fides, my friend," said the drow, and Entreri's face screwed up even more curiously. "Many a hero is making a name for himself in Vaasa," Jarlaxle explained. "The opportunities for wealth, fame, and reputation are rarely so fine."

"I thought our goal was to make our reputation on the streets of Heliogabalus," Entreri replied, "among potential employers."

"And current employers," Jarlaxle agreed. "And so we shall. But think how much service and profit we might gather from a heroic reputation. It will elevate us from suspicion, and perhaps insulate us from punishment if we are caught in an indiscreet action. A few months at the Vaasan Gate will elevate our reputations more than a few years here in Heliogabalus ever could."

Entreri's eyes narrowed. There had to be something more to this, he knew. They had been in Damara for several months now, and had known about the "opportunities" for heroes in the wilderlands of Vaasa from the beginning—how could they not when every tavern and half the street corners of the city of Heliogabalus were plastered with notices claiming as much? Yet only recently, only since the near disaster in the tower, had Jarlaxle taken to the notion of traveling to the north, something Entreri found quite out of character. Work in Vaasa was difficult, and luxuries nonexistent, and Entreri knew all too well that Jarlaxle prized luxury above all else.

"So what has Ilnezhara told you about Vaasa that has so intrigued you?" Entreri asked.

Jarlaxle's smile came in the form of a wry grin, one that did not deny Entreri's suspicions.

"You know of the war?" the drow asked.

"Little," Entreri admitted. "I have heard the glory of King Gareth Dragonsbane. Who could not, in this city that serves as a shrine to the man and his hero companions?"

"They did battle with Zhengyi, the Witch-King," the drow explained, "a lich of tremendous power."

"And with flights of dragons," Entreri cut in, sounding quite bored. "Yes, yes, I have heard it all."

"Many of Zhengyi's treasures have been uncovered, claimed, and brought to Damara," said Jarlaxle. "But what they have found is a pittance. Zhengyi possessed artifacts, and a hoard of treasure enough to entice flights of dragons to his call. And he was a lich. He knew the secret."

"You hold such aspirations?" Entreri didn't hide the disgust in his voice.

Jarlaxle scoffed at the notion. "I am a drow. I will live for centuries more, though centuries have been born and have died in my lifetime. In Menzoberranzan there is a lich of great power."

"The Lichdrow Dyrr, I know," Entreri reminded him.

"The most wretched creature in the city, by most accounts. I have dealt with him on occasion, enough to know that practically the entirety of his efforts are devoted to the perpetuation of his existence. He has bought eternity for himself, so he is terrified of losing it. It is a wretched existence, as cold as his skin, and a solitary state of being that knows no like company. How many wards must he weave to feel secure, when he has brought himself to the point where he might lose too much to comprehend? No, lichdom is not something I aspire to, I assure you."

"Neither do I."

"But do you realize the power that would come from possessing Zhengyi's knowledge?" the drow asked. "Do you realize how great a price aging kings, fearing their impending death, would pay?"

Entreri just stared at the drow.

"And who can tell what other marvels Zhengyi possessed?" Jarlaxle went on. "Are there treasuries full of powerful magical charms or dragon-sized mounds of gemstones? Had the Witch-King weapons that dwarf the power of your own Charon's Claw?"

"Is there no purpose to your life beyond the act of acquisition?"

That rocked Jarlaxle back on his heels—one of the very few times Entreri had ever seen him temporarily rattled. But of course it passed quickly.

"If it is, it's the purpose of both my life and yours, it would seem," the drow finally retorted. "Did you not cross the face of Faerûn to hunt down Regis and the ruby pendant of Pasha Pook?"

"It was a job."

"One you could have refused."

"I enjoy the adventure."

"Then let us go," said the drow, and he waved his arm in an exaggerated motion at the door. "Adventure awaits! Experiences beyond any we have known, perhaps. How can you resist?"

"Vaasa is an empty frozen tundra for most of the year and a puddle of muddy swamp the rest."

"And below that tundra?" the drow teased. "There are treasures up there beyond our dreams."

"And there are hundreds of adventurers searching for those treasures."

"Of course," the drow conceded, "but none of them know how to look as well as I."

"I could take that two ways."

Jarlaxle put one hand on his hip, turned slightly, and struck a pose. "And you would be correct on both counts," he assured his friend. The drow reached into his belt pouch and brought forth a corn bread cake artistically topped with a sweet white and pink frosting. He held it up before his eyes, a grin widening on his face. "I do so know how to find, and retain, treasure," he said, and he tossed the delicacy to Entreri with the explanation, "A present from Piter."

Entreri looked at the cake, though he was in no mood for delicacies, or any food at all.

"Piter," he whispered.

He knew the man himself was the treasure to which Jarlaxle was referring and not the cake. Entreri and Jarlaxle had liberated the fat chef, Piter McRuggle, from a band of inept highwaymen, and Jarlaxle had subsequently set the man and his family up at a handsome shop in Heliogabalus. The drow knew talent when he saw it, and in Piter, there could be no doubt. The bakery was doing wonderful business, lining Jarlaxle's pockets with extra coin and lining his notebooks with information.

It occurred to Artemis Entreri that he, too, might fall into Jarlaxle's category of found and retained treasures. It was pretty obvious which of the duo was taking the lead and who was following.

"Now, have I mentioned that there is a caravan leaving in two days?" Jarlaxle remarked with that irresistible grin of his.

Entreri started to respond, but the words died away in his throat. What was the point?

Two days later, he and Jarlaxle were rode sturdy ponies, guarding the left flank of a six-wagon caravan that wound its way out of Heliogabalus's north gate.

CHAPTER

LIFE IN FUGUE

3

Entreri crawled out of his tent, rose to his feet and stretched slowly and to his limits. He twisted as he reached up high, the sudden stab in his lower back reminding him of his age. The hard ground didn't serve him well as a bed.

He came out of his stretch rubbing his eyes then glanced around at the tent-filled plain set between towering walls of mountains east and west. Just north of Entreri's camp loomed the gray-black stones and iron of the Vaasan Gate, the northern of the two great fortress walls that sealed Bloodstone Valley north and south. The Vaasan Gate had finally been completed, if such a living work could ever truly be considered finished, with fortresses on the eastern and western ends of the main structure set in the walls of the Galena Mountains. the gate served as the last barrier between Entreri and the wilderness of Vaasa. He and Jarlaxle had accompanied the caravan through the much larger of the two gates, the Damaran Gate, which was still under construction in the south. They had ridden with the wagons for another day, moving northwest under the shadow of the mountain wall, to Bloodstone Village, home of King Gareth—though the monarch was under pressure to move his seat of power to the largest city in the kingdom, Heliogabalus.

Not wanting to remain in that most lawful of places, the pair had quickly taken their leave, moving again to the north, a dozen mile trek that had brought them to the wider, relatively flat area the gathered adventurers had collectively named the Fugue Plane. A fitting title, Entreri thought, for the namesake of the Fugue Plane was rumored to be the extra-dimensional state of limbo for recently departed souls, the region where the newly dead congregated before their final journey to Paradise or Torment. The place between the heavens and the hells.

The tent city was no less a crossroads, for south lay Damara—at peace, united, and prosperous under the leadership of the Paladin King—while north beyond the wall was a land of wild adventure and desperate battle.

And of course, he and Jarlaxle were heading north.

All manner of ruffians inhabited the tent city, the types of people Entreri knew well from his days on Calimport's streets. Would-be heroes, every one—men and a few women who would do anything to make a name for themselves.

How many times had the younger Entreri ventured forth with such people? And more often than not, the journey had ended with a conflict between the members of the band. As he considered that, Entreri's hand instinctively went to the dagger sheathed on his hip.

He knew better than to trust ambitious people.

The smell of meat cooking permeated the dew-filled morning air. Scores of breakfast fires dotted the field, and the lizardlike hiss of knives being sharpened broke the calls of the many birds that flitted about.

Entreri spotted Jarlaxle at one such breakfast fire a few dozen yards to the side. The drow stood amidst several tough-looking characters: a pair of men who looked as if they could be brothers—or father and son possibly, since one had hair more gray than black—a dwarf with half his beard torn away, and an elf female who wore her golden hair braided all the way down her back. Entreri could tell by their posture that the four weren't overly confident in the unexpected presence of a dark elf. The positioning of their arms, the slight turn of their shoulders, showed that to a one they were ready for a quick defensive reaction should the drow make any unexpected movements.

Even so, it appeared as if the charming Jarlaxle was wearing away those defenses. Entreri watched as the dark elf dipped a polite bow, pulling off his grand hat and sweeping the ground. His every movement showed an unthreatening posture, keeping his hands in clear sight at all times.

A few moments later, Entreri could only chuckle as those around Jarlaxle began to laugh—presumably at a joke the drow had told. Entreri watched, his expression caught somewhere between envy and admiration, as the elf female began to lean toward Jarlaxle, her posture clearly revealing her increasing interest in him.

Jarlaxle reached out to the dwarf and manipulated his hand to make it seem as if he had just taken a coin out of the diminutive fellow's ear. That brought a moment of confusion, where all four of the onlookers reflexively brought a hand to their respective belt pouches, but it was quickly replaced by howls of laughter, with the younger of the men slapping the dwarf on the back of his head.

The mirth and Entreri's attention were stolen when the thunder of hooves turned the attention of all of them to the north.

A small but powerful black horse charged past the tents, silver armor strapped all about its flanks and chest. Its rider was similarly armored in shining silver plates, decorated with flowing carvings and delicate designs. The knight wore a great helm, flat-topped and plumed with a red feather on the left-hand side. As the horse passed Entreri's position, he noted a well-adorned battle-axe strapped at the side of the thick, sturdy saddle.

The horse skidded to a stop right in front of Jarlaxle and his four companions, and in that same fluid motion the rider slid down to stand facing the drow.

Entreri eased his way over, expecting trouble.

He wondered if the newcomer, tall but slender, might have some elf blood, but when the helm came off and a thick shock of long, fiery red hair fell free, tumbling down her back, Entreri realized the truth of it.

He picked up his pace and moved within earshot and also to get a better look at her face, and what he saw surely intrigued him. Freckled and dimpled, the knight's complexion clashed with her attire, for it did not seem to fit the garb of a warrior. By the way she stood, and the way she had ridden and dismounted so gracefully despite her heavy armor, Entreri could see that she was seasoned and tough—when she had to be, he realized. But those features also told him that there was another side to her, one he might like to explore.

The assassin pulled up short and considered his own thoughts, surprised by his interest.

"So the rumors are true," the woman said, and he was close enough to hear. "A drow elf."

"My reputation precedes me," Jarlaxle said. He flashed a disarming grin and dipped another of his patented bows. "Jarlaxle, at your service, milady."

"Your reputation?" the woman scoffed. "Nay, dark-skinned one. A hundred whispers speak of you, rumors of the dastardly deeds we can expect from you, certainly, but nothing of your reputation."

"I see. And so you have come to verify that reputation?"

"To witness a dark elf in our midst," the woman replied. "I have never seen such a creature as you."

"And do I meet with your approval?"

The woman narrowed her eyes and began to slowly circle the drow.

"Your race evokes images of ferocity, and yet you seem a frail thing. I am told that I should be wary—terrified, even—and yet I find myself less than impressed by your stature and your hardly-imposing posture."

"Aye, but watch his hands," the dwarf chimed in. "He's a clever one with them slender fingers, don't ye doubt."

"A cutpurse?" she asked.

"Madame, you insult me."

"I ask of you, and I expect an honest answer," she retorted, a tremor of anger sliding into the background of her solid but melodious voice. "Many in the Fugue are known cutpurses who have come here by court edict, to work the wilderness of Vaasa and redeem themselves of their light-fingered sins."

"But I am a drow," Jarlaxle replied. "Do you think there are enough monsters in all of Vaasa that I might redeem the reputation of my heritage?"

"I care nothing for your heritage."

"Then I am but a curiosity. Ah, but you so wound me again."

"A feeling you would do well to acquaint yourself with. You still have not answered my question."

Jarlaxle tilted his head and put on a sly grin.

"Do you know who I am?" the woman asked.

"The way you ask makes me believe that I should."

The woman looked past the drow to the female elf.

"Commander Ellery, of the Army of Bloodstone, Vaasan Gate," the elf recited without pause.

"My full name."

The elf stuttered and seemed at a loss.

"I am Commander Ellery Tranth Dopray Kierney Dragonsbane Peidopare," the woman said, her tone even more imperious than before.

"Labeling your possessions must prove a chore," the drow said dryly, but the woman ignored him.

"I claim Baron Tranth as my uncle; Lady Christine Dragonsbane, Queen of Damara, as my cousin; and King Gareth Dragonsbane himself as my second cousin, once removed."

"Lady Christine and King Gareth?"

The woman squared her shoulders and her jaw.

"Cousins in opposite directions, I would hope," said Jarlaxle.

That brought a less imperious and more curious stare.

"I would hate to think that the future princes and princesses of Damara might carry on their shoulders a second head or six fingers on each hand, after all," the drow explained, and the curious look turned darker. "Ah, but the ways of royalty."

"You mock the man who chased demon lord Orcus across the planes of existence?"

"Mock him?" Jarlaxle asked, bringing one hand to his chest and looking as if he had just been unexpectedly slapped. "Nothing could be farther from the truth, good Commander Ellery. I express relief that while you claim blood relations to both, their own ties are not so close. You see?"

She steeled her gaze. "I will learn of your reputation," she promised.

"You will wish then that you included D'aerthe in your collection of names, I assure you," the drow replied.

"Jarlaxle D'aerthe?"

"At your service," he said, sweeping into yet another bow.

"And you will be watched closely, drow," Commander Ellery went on. "If your fingers get too clever, or your mannerisms too disruptive, you will learn the weight of Bloodstone judgment."

"As you will," Jarlaxle conceded.

As Ellery turned to leave, he dipped yet another bow. He managed to glance over at Entreri as he did, offering a quick wink and the flash of a smile.

"I leave you to your meal," Ellery said to the other four, pulling herself back into her saddle. "Choose wisely the company you keep when you venture forth into Vaasa. Far too many already lay dead on that wasteland tundra, and far too many lay dead because they did not surround themselves with reliable companions."

"I will heed well your words," Jarlaxle was quick to reply, though they had not been aimed at him. "I was growing a bit leery of the short one anyway."

"Hey!" said the dwarf, and Jarlaxle flashed him that disarming grin.

Entreri turned his attention from the group of five to watch the woman ride away, noting most of all the respectful reactions to her from all she passed.

"She is a formidable one," he said when Jarlaxle appeared at his side a moment later.

"Dangerous and full of fire," Jarlaxle agreed.

"I might have to kill her."

"I might have to bed her."

Entreri turned to regard the drow. Did anything ever unsettle him? "She is a relative of King Gareth," Entreri reminded him.

Jarlaxle rubbed his slender fingers over his chin, his eyes glued to the departing figure with obvious intrigue.

He uttered only a single word in reply: "Dowry."

"Lady Ellery," said Athrogate, a dwarf renowned in the underworld of Damara as a supreme killer. He wore his black beard parted in the middle, two long braids of straight hair running down to mid-chest, each tied off at the end with a band set with a trio of sparkling blue gemstones. His eyebrows were so bushy that they somewhat covered his almost-black eyes, and his ears so large that many speculated he would be able to fly if only he learned how to flap them. " 'E's made hisself some fine company already. Be watchin' that one, I'm tellin' ye. Watchin' or killin' him, for if ye're not, then he's to be killin' us, don't ye doubt."

"It is an interesting turn, if it is anything at all beyond mere coincidence," admitted Canthan Dolittle, a studious looking fellow with beady eyes and a long straight nose. His hair, as much gray as brown, was thin, with a large bald spot atop his head that had turned bright red from a recent sunburn. The nervous, slim fellow rubbed his fingertips together as he spoke, all the while subtly twitching.

"To assume is to invite disaster," the third and most impressive of the group advised. Most impressive to those who knew the truth of him, that is, for the archmage Knellict wore nondescript clothing, with his more prized possessions stored safely away back at the Citadel of Assassins.

Athrogate licked his lips nervously as he regarded the mighty wizard, second only to Timoshenko, the Grandfather of Assassins, in that most notorious guild of killers. As an agent of Tightpurse, the leading thieves guild of Heliogabalus, Athrogate had been assigned to ride along with Jarlaxle and Entreri to Bloodstone Village, and to report to Canthan in the Fugue. He had been quite surprised to find Knellict at the camp. Few names in all the northern Realms inspired fear like that of the archmage of the Citadel of Assassins.

"Have you learned any more of the drow?" Canthan asked. "We know of his dealings with Innkeeper Feepun and the murder of the shade, Rorli."

"And the murder of Feepun," Knellict said.

"You have proof it was brought about by these two?" a surprised Canthan asked.

"You have proof it was not?"

Canthan backed off, not wanting to anger the most dangerous man in the Bloodstone Lands.

"Information of their whereabouts since the incident with Rorli has been incomplete," Knellict admitted.

"They been quiet since then from all that we're seein'," Athrogate replied, his tone revealing that he was eager to please. Though he was answering Canthan, his brown eyes kept darting over to regard Knellict. The archmage, however, quiet and calm, was simply impossible to read. "They done some dealin's with a pair o' intrestin' lady pawnbrokers, but we ain't seen 'em buy nothin' worth nothin'. Might be that they be lookin' more for lady charms than magic charms, if ye're gettin' me meanin'. Been known to fancy the ladies, them two be, especially the dark one."

Canthan glanced back at Knellict, who gave the slightest of nods.

"Keep close and keep wary," Canthan told Athrogate. "If you need us, place your wash-clothes as we agreed and we will seek you out."

"And if yerself's needing me?"

"We will find you, do not doubt," Knellict intervened.

The archmage's tone was too even, too controlled, and despite a desire to hold a tough facade, Athrogate shuddered. He nearly fell over as he bobbed in a bow then scurried away, ducking from shadow to shadow.

"I sense something more about the human," Knellict remarked when he and Canthan were alone.

"I expect they are both formidable."

"Deserving of our respect, indeed," Knellict agreed. "And requiring more eyes than those of the dolt Athrogate."

"I am already at work on the task," Canthan assured his superior.

Knellict gave a slight nod but kept staring across the tent city at Jarlaxle and Entreri as they walked back to their campsite.

Tightpurse had been ready to move on the pair back in Heliogabalus and would have—likely to disastrous results for Tightpurse, Knellict figured—had not the Citadel of Assassins intervened. At the prodding of Knellict, Timoshenko had decided to pay heed to the pair, particularly to that most unusual dark elf who had so suddenly appeared in their midst. Drow were not a common sight on the surface of Toril, and less common in the Bloodstone Lands than in most other regions. Less common in Damara, at least, a land that was quickly moving toward stable law and order under the reign of Gareth Dragonsbane and his band of mighty heroes. Zhengyi had been thrown down, flights of dragons destroyed, and the demon lord Orcus's own wand had been blasted into nothingness. Gareth was only growing stronger, the tentacles of his organizations stretching more ominously in the consolidation of Damara's various feudal lords. He had made no secret of his desire to bring Vaasa under his control as well, uniting the two lands as the single kingdom of Bloodstone. To that end, King Gareth's Spysong network of scouts was growing more elaborate with each passing day.

Timoshenko and Knellict suspected that Vaasa would indeed soon be tamed, and were that to occur, would there remain in all of the region a place for the Citadel of Assassins?

Knellict did well to hide his frown as he considered yet again the continuing trends in the Bloodstone Lands. His eyes did flash briefly as he watched the pair, drow and human, disappear into their tent.

There was a different feeling to the air the moment Jarlaxle and Entreri walked out of the Vaasan side of the wall fortress. The musty scent of peat and thawing decay filled the nostrils of the two, carried on a stiff breeze that held a chilly bite, though summer was still in force.

"She's blowing strong off the Great Glacier today," Entreri had heard one of the guards remark.

He could feel the bone-catching chill as the wind gathered the moisture from the sun-softened ice and lifted it across the muddy Vaasan plain.

"A remarkable place," Jarlaxle noted, scanning the sea of empty brown from under the wide brim of his outrageous hat. "I would send armies forth to do battle to claim this paradise."

The drow's sarcasm didn't sit well with Entreri. He couldn't agree more with the dreary assessment. "Then why are we here?"

"I have already explained that in full."

"You hold to a strange understanding of the term. 'in full.' "

Jarlaxle didn't look at him, but Entreri took some satisfaction in the drow's grin.

"By that, I presume that you mean you have explained it as well as you believe I need to know," Entreri went on.

"Sometimes the sweetest juices can be found buried within the most mundane of fruits."

Entreri glanced back at the wall and let it go at that. They had come out on a "day jaunt," as such excursions were known at the Vaasan Gate, a quick scout and strike mission. All newcomers to the Vaasan Gate were given such assignments, allowing them to get a feel for the tundra. When first the call had gone out for adventurers, there had been no guidance offered for their excursions into the wild. Many had struck right out from the gate and deep into Vaasa, never to be heard from again. But the Army of Bloodstone was offering more instruction and control, and offering it in a way more mandatory than suggestive.

Entreri wasn't fond of such rules, but neither did he hold much desire to strike out any distance from the gate. He did not wish to find his end seeking the bottom of a bottomless bog.

Jarlaxle turned slowly in a circle, seeming to sniff the air as he did. When he came full around, pointing again to the northeast, the general direction of the far-distant Great Glacier, he nodded and tipped his hat.

"This way, I think," the drow said.

Jarlaxle started off, and with a shrug, having no better option, Entreri started after him.

They stayed among the rocky foothills of the Galena Mountains, not wanting to try the muddy, flat ground. That course left them more vulnerable to goblin ambushes, but the pair were not particularly afraid of doing battle against such creatures.

"I thought there were monsters aplenty to be found and vanquished here," Entreri remarked after an hour of trudging around gray stones and across patches of cold standing water. "That is what the posted notices in Heliogabalus claimed, is it not?"

"Twenty gold pieces a day," Jarlaxle added. "And all for the pleasure of killing ten goblins. Yes, that was the sum of it, and perhaps the lucrative bounty proved quite effective. Could it be that all the lands about the gate have been cleared?"

"If we have to trek for miles across this wilderness, then my road is back to the south," said Entreri.

"Ever the optimist."

"Ever the obvious."

Jarlaxle laughed and adjusted his great hat. "Not for many more miles," he said. "Did you not notice the clear sign of adversaries?"

Entreri offered a skeptical stare.

"A print beside the last puddle," Jarlaxle explained.

"That could be days old."

"It is my understanding that such things are not so lasting here on the surface," the drow replied. "In the Underdark, a boot print in soft ground might be a millennium old, but up here. . . ."

Entreri shrugged.

"I thought you were famous for your ability to hunt down enemies."

"That comes from knowing the ways of folk, not the signs on the ground. I find my enemies through the information I glean from those who have seen them."

"Information gathered at the tip of your dagger, no doubt."

"Whatever works. But I do not normally hunt the wilderness in pursuit of monsters."

"Yet you are no stranger to the signs of such wild places," said the drow. "You know a print."

"I know that something made an impression near the puddle," Entreri clarified. "It might have been today, or it might have been several days ago—anytime since the last rain. And I know not what made it."

"We are in goblin lands," Jarlaxle interrupted. "The posted notices told me as much."

"We are in lands full of people pursuing goblins," Entreri reminded.

"Ever the obvious," the drow said.

Entreri scowled at him.

They walked for a few hours, then as storm clouds gathered in the north, they turned back to the Vaasan Gate. They made it soon after sunset, and after a bit of arguing with the new sentries, managed to convince them that they, including the dark elf, had left that same gate earlier in the day and should be re-admitted without such lengthy questioning.

Moving through the tight, well-constructed, dark brick corridors, past the eyes of many suspicious guards, Entreri turned for the main hall that would take them back to the Fugue and their tent.

"Not just yet," Jarlaxle bade him. "There are pleasures a'many to be found here, so I have been told."

"And goblins a'many to kill out there, so you've been told."

"It never ends, I see."

Entreri just stood at the end of the corridor, the reflection of distant campfires twinkling in Jarlaxle's eyes as he looked past his scowling friend.

"Have you no sense of adventure?" the drow asked.

"We've been over this too many times."

"And yet still you scowl, and you doubt, and you grump about."

"I have never been fond of spending my days walking across muddy trails."

"Those trails will lead us to great things," Jarlaxle said. "I promise."

"Perhaps when you tell me of them, my mood will improve," Entreri replied, and the dark elf smiled wide.

"These corridors might lead us to great things, as well," the drow answered. "And I think I need not tell you of those."

Entreri glanced back over his shoulder out at the campfires through the distant, opened doors. He chuckled quietly as he turned back to Jarlaxle, for he knew that resistance was hopeless against that one's unending stream of persuasion. He waved a hand, indicating that Jarlaxle should lead on, then moved along behind him.

There were many establishments—craftsmen, suppliers, but mostly taverns—in the Vaasan Gate. Merchants and entrepreneurs had been quick to the call of Gareth Dragonsbane, knowing that the hearty adventurers who went out from the wall would often be well-rewarded upon their return, given the substantial bounty on the ears of goblins, orcs, ogres and other monsters. So too had the ladies of the evening come, displaying their wares in every tavern, often congregating around the many gamblers who sought to take the recent earnings from foolish and prideful adventurers.

All the taverns were much the same, so the pair moved into the first in line. The sign on the wall beside the doorway read: "Muddy Boots and Bloody Blades," but someone had gouged a line across it and whittled in: "Muddy Blades and Bloody Boots" underneath, to reflect the frustrations of late in even finding monsters to kill.

Jarlaxle and Entreri moved through the crowded room, the drow drawing more than a few uncomfortable stares as he went. They split up as they came upon a table set with four chairs where only two men were sitting, with Jarlaxle approaching and Entreri melting back in to the crowd.

"May I join you?" the drow asked.

Looks both horrified and threatening came back at him. "We're waiting on two more," one man answered.

Jarlaxle pulled up a chair. "Very well, then," he said. "A place to rest my weary feet for just a moment then. When your friends arrive, I will take my leave."

The two men glanced at each other.

"Be gone now!" one snarled, coming forward in his chair, teeth bared as if he meant to bite the dark elf.

Next to him, his friend put on an equally threatening glower, and crossed his large arms over his strong chest, expression locked in a narrow-eyed gaze. His eyes widened quickly, though, and his arms slid out to either side—slow, unthreatening—when he felt the tip of a dagger against the small of his back.

The hard expression on the man who'd leaned toward Jarlaxle similarly melted, for under the table, the drow had drawn a tiny dagger, and though he couldn't reach across with that particular weapon, with no more than a thought, he had urged the enchanted dirk to elongate. Thus, while Jarlaxle hadn't even leaned forward in his chair, and while his arms had not come ahead in the least, the threatening rogue felt the blade tip quite clearly, prodding against his belly.

"I have changed my mind," Jarlaxle said, his voice cold. "When your friends arrive, they will need to find another place to repose."

"You smelly . . ."

"Hardly."

". . . stinking drow," the man went on. "Drawing a weapon in here is a crime against King Gareth."

"Does the penalty equate to that for gutting a fool?"

"Stinking drow," the man repeated. He glanced over at his friend then put on a quizzical expression.

"One at me back," said the other. "I'm not for helping ye."

The first man looked even more confused, and Jarlaxle nearly laughed aloud at the spectacle, for behind the other man stood the crowd of people that filled every aisle in Muddy Boots and Bloody Blades, but none appeared to be taking any note of him. Jarlaxle recognized the gray cloak of the nearest man and knew it to be Entreri.

"Are we done with this foolery?" Jarlaxle asked the first man.

The man glared at him and started to nod then shoved off the table, sliding his chair back.

"A weapon!" he cried, leaping to his feet and pointing at the drow. "He drew a weapon!"

A tumult began all around the table, with men spinning and leaping into defensive stances, many with hands going to their weapons, and some, like Entreri, using the moment to melt away into the crowd. Like all the taverns at the Vaasan Gate, however, Muddy Boots and Bloody Blades anticipated such trouble. Within the span of a couple of heartbeats—the time it took Jarlaxle to slide his own chair back and hold up his empty hands, for the sword had shrunken to nothingness at his bidding—a group of Bloodstone soldiers moved in to restore order.

"He poked me with a sword!" the man cried, jabbing his finger Jarlaxle's way.

The drow pasted on a puzzled look and held up his empty hands. Then he adjusted his cloak to show that he had no sword, no weapon at all, sheathed at his belt.

That didn't stop the nearest soldier from glowering at him, though. The man bent low and did a quick search under the table.

"So clever of you to use my heritage against me," Jarlaxle said to the protesting man. "A pity you didn't know I carry no weapon at all."

All eyes went to the accuser.

"He sticked me, I tell ye!"

"With?" Jarlaxle replied, holding his arms and cape wide. "You give me far too much credit, I fear, though I do hope the ladies are paying you close heed."

A titter of laughter came from one side then rumbled into a general outburst of mocking howls against the sputtering man. Worse for him, the guards seemed less than amused.

"Get on your way," one of the guards said to him, and the laughter only increased.

"And his friend put a dagger to me back!" the man's still-seated companion shouted, drawing all eyes to him. He leaped up and spun around.

"Who did?" the soldier asked.

The man looked around, though of course Entreri was already all the way to the other side of the room.

"Him!" the man said anyway, pointing to one nearby knave. "Had to be him."

A soldier moved immediately to inspect the accused, and indeed the man was wearing a long, slender dirk on his belt.

"What foolishness is this?" the accused protested. "You would believe that babbling idiot?"

"My word against yours!" the other man shouted, growing more confident that his guess had been accurate.

"Against *ours,* you mean," said another man.

More than a dozen, all companions of the newly accused man, came forward.

"I'm thinking that ye should take more care in who ye're pointing yer crooked fingers at," said another.

The accuser was stammering. He looked to his friend, who seemed even more ill at ease and helpless against the sudden turn of events.

"And I'm thinking that the two of you should be going," said the accused knave.

"And quick," added another of his rough-looking friends.

"Sir?" Jarlaxle asked the guard. "I was merely trying to take some repose from my travels in Vaasa."

The soldier eyed the drow suspiciously for a long, long while, then turned away and started off.

"You cause any more disturbances and I'll put you in chains," he warned the man.

"But . . ."

The protesting victim ended with a gasp as the soldier behind him kicked him in the behind, drawing another chorus of howls from the many onlookers.

"We're not for leaving!" the man's companion stubbornly decreed.

"Ye probably should be thinking that one over a bit more," warned one of the friends of the man he had accused, stealing his bluster.

It all quieted quickly, and Jarlaxle took a seat at the vacant table, waving a serving wench over to him.

"A glass of your finest wine and one of your finest ale," he said.

The woman hesitated, her dark eyes scanning him.

"No, he was not falsely accusing me," Jarlaxle confided with a wink.

The woman blushed and nearly fell over herself as she moved off to get the drinks.

"By this time, another table would have opened to us," said Entreri, taking a seat across from the drow, "without the dramatics."

"Without the *enjoyment*," Jarlaxle corrected.

"The soldiers are watching us now."

"Precisely the point," explained the drow. "We want all at the Vaasan Gate to know of us. Reputation is exactly the point."

"Reputation earned in battle with common enemies, so I thought."

"In time, my friend," said Jarlaxle. His smile beamed at the young woman, who had already returned with the drinks. "In time," he repeated, and he gave the woman a piece of platinum—many times the price of the wine and ale.

"For tales of adventure and those we've yet to make," he said to her slyly, and she blushed again, her dark eyes sparkling as she considered the coin. Her smile was shy but not hard to see as she scampered off.

Jarlaxle turned and held his glass up to Entreri then repeated his last sentence as a toast.

Defeated yet again by the drow's undying optimism, Entreri tapped his glass with his own and took a long and welcomed drink.

CHAPTER

4

Arrayan Faylin pulled herself out of her straw bed, dragging her single blanket along with her and wrapping it around her surprisingly delicate shoulders. That distinctly feminine softness was reflective of the many surprises people found when looking upon Arrayan and learning of her heritage.

She was a half-orc, like the vast majority of residents in the cold and wind-swept city of Palishchuk in the northeastern corner of Vaasa, a settlement in clear view of the towering ice river known as the Great Glacier.

Arrayan had human blood in her as well—and some elf, so her mother had told her—and certainly her features had combined the most attractive qualities of all her racial aspects. Her reddish-brown hair was long and so soft and flowing that it often seemed as if her face was framed by a soft red halo. She was short, like many orcs, but perhaps as a result of that reputed elf blood, she was anything but stocky. While her face was wide, like that of an orc, her other features—large emerald green eyes, thick lips, narrow angled eyebrows, and a button nose—were distinctly un-orcish, and that curious blend, in Arrayan's case, had a way of accenting the positives of the attributes from every viewing angle.

She stretched, yawned, shook her long, reddish-brown hair back from her face, and rubbed her eyes.

As the mental cobwebs of sleep melted away, Arrayan's excitement began to mount. She moved quickly across the room to her desk, her bare feet slapping the hard earth floor. Eagerly she grabbed her spellbook from a nearby shelf, used her other hand to brush clear the center area of the desk then slid into her chair, hooking her finger into the correct tab of the organized tome and flipping it open to the section entitled "Divination Magic."

As she considered the task ahead of her, her fingers began trembling so badly that she could hardly turn the page.

Arrayan fell back in her seat and forced herself to take a long, deep breath. She went over the mental disciplines she had learned several years before in a wizard's tower in distant Damara. If she could master control as a teenager, certainly in her mid-twenties she could calm her eagerness.

A moment later, she went back to her book. With a steady hand, the wizard examined her list of potential spells, discerned those she believed would be the most useful, including a battery of magical defenses and spells to dispel offensive wards before they were activated, and began the arduous task of committing them to memory.

A knock on her door interrupted her a few minutes later. The gentle nature of it, but with a sturdiness behind it to show that the light tap was deliberate, told her who it might be. She turned in her chair as the door pushed open, and a huge, grinning, tusky face poked in. The half-orc's wide eyes clued Arrayan in to the fact that she had let her blanket wrap slip a bit too far, and she quickly tightened it around her shoulders.

"Olgerkhan, well met," she said.

It didn't surprise her how bright her voice became whenever that particular half-orc appeared. Physically, the two seemed polar opposites, with Olgerkhan's features most definitely favoring his orc side. His lip was perpetually twisted due to his huge, uneven canines, and his thick forehead and singular bushy brow brought a dark shadow over his bloodshot, jaundiced eyes. His nose was flat and crooked, his face marked by small and uneven patches of hair, and his forehead sloped out to peak at that imposing brow. He wasn't overly tall, caught somewhere between five-and-a-half and six feet, but he appeared much larger, for his limbs were thick and strong and his chest would have fit appropriately on a man a foot taller than he.

The large half-orc licked his lips and started to move his mouth as if he meant to say something.

Arrayan pulled her blanket just a bit tighter around her. She really wasn't overly embarrassed; she just didn't give much thought to such things, though Olgerkhan obviously did.

"Are they here?" Arrayan asked.

Olgerkhan glanced around the room, seeming puzzled.

"The wagons," Arrayan clarified, and that brought a grin to the burly half-orc's face.

"Wingham," he said. "Outside the south gate. Twenty colored wagons."

Arrayan returned his smile and nodded, but the news did cause her a bit of trepidation. Wingham was her uncle, though she had never really seen him for long enough stretches to consider herself to be close to him and his traveling merchant band. In Palishchuk, they were known simply as "Wingham's Rascals," but to the wider region of the Bloodstone Lands, the band was called "Weird Wingham's Wacky Weapon Wielders."

"The show is everything," Wingham had once said to Arrayan, explaining the ridiculous name. "All the world loves the show." Arrayan smiled even wider as she considered his further advice that day when she was but a child, even before she had gone to Damara to train in arcane magic. Wingham had explained to her that the name, admittedly stupid, was a purposeful calling card, a way to confirm the prejudices of the humans, elves, dwarves, and other races. "Let them think us stupid," Wingham had told her with a great flourish, though Wingham always spoke with a great flourish. "Then let them come and bargain with us for our wares!"

Arrayan realized with a start that she had paused for a long while. She glanced back at Olgerkhan, who seemed not to have noticed.

"Any word?" she asked, barely able to get the question out.

Olgerkhan shook his thick head. "They dance and sing but little so far," he explained. "Those who have gone out to enjoy the circus have not yet returned."

Arrayan nodded and jumped up from her seat, moving swiftly across the room to her wardrobe. Hardly considering the action, she let her blanket fall—then caught it at the last moment and glanced back sheepishly to Olgerkhan.

He averted his eyes to the floor and crept back out of the room, pulling the door closed.

He was a good one, Arrayan realized, as she always tried to remind herself.

She dressed quickly, pulling on leather breeches and a vest, and a thin belt that held several pouches for spell components, as well as a set of writing materials. She started for the door but paused and pulled a blue robe of light material from the wardrobe, quickly removing the belt then donning the robe over her outfit. She rarely wore her wizard robes among her half-orc brethren, for they considered the flowing garment with its voluminous sleeves of little use, and the only fashion the males of Palishchuk seemed to appreciate came from her wearing less clothing, not more.

The robe was for Wingham, Arrayan told herself as she refitted the belt and rushed to the door.

Olgerkhan was waiting patiently for her, and she offered him her arm and hurried him along to the southern gate. A crowd had gathered there, flowing out of the city of nearly a thousand residents. Filtering her way through, pulling Olgerkhan along, Arrayan finally managed to get a glimpse of the source of the commotion, and like so many of her fellow Palishchukians, she grinned widely at the site of Weird Wingham's Wacky Weapon Wielders. Their wagon caravan had been circled, the bright colors of the canopies and awnings shining brilliantly in the glow of the late-summer sun. Music drifted along the breeze, carrying the rough-edged voice of one of Wingham's bards, singing a tale of the Galena Mountains and Hillsafar Hall.

Like all the rest swept up in the excitement, Arrayan and Olgerkhan found themselves walking more swiftly then even jogging across the ground, their steps buoyed by eagerness. Wingham's troupe came to Palishchuk only a few times each year, sometimes only once or twice, and they always brought with them exotic goods bartered in faraway lands, and wondrous tales of distant heroes and mighty villains. They entertained the children and adults alike with song and dance, and though they were known throughout the lands as difficult negotiators, any of the folk of Palishchuk who purchased an item from Weird Wingham knew that he was getting a fine bargain.

For Wingham had never forgotten his roots, had never looked back with anything but love on the community that had worked so hard to allow him and all the other half-orcs of his troupe to shake off the bonds of their heritage.

A pair of jugglers anchored the main opening into the wagon circle, tossing strange triple-bladed knives in an unbroken line back and forth to each other, the weapons spinning over the heads of nervous and delighted Palishchukians as they entered or departed. Just inside the ring, a pair of bards performed, one playing a curved, flutelike instrument while the other sang of the Galenas. Small kiosks and racks of weapons and clothing filled the area, and the aroma of a myriad of exotic perfumes and scented candles aptly blanketed the common smell of rot in the late summer tundra, where plants grew fast and died faster through the short mild period, and the frozen grip on the topsoil relinquished, releasing the fragrance of seasons past.

For a moment, a different and rarely felt aspect of Arrayan's character filtered through, and she had to pause in her step to bask in the vision of a grand ball in a distant city, full of dancing, finely dressed women and men. That small part of her composite didn't hold, though, when she noticed an old half-orc, bent by age, bald, limping, but with a sparkle in his bright eyes that could not help but catch the eye, however briefly, of any young woman locking stares with him.

"Mistress Maggotsweeper!" the old half-orc cried upon seeing her.

Arrayan winced at the correct recital of her surname, one she had long ago abandoned, preferring her Elvish middle name, Faylin. That didn't turn her look sour, though, for she knew that her Uncle Wingham had cried out with deep affection. He seemed to grow taller and straighter as she closed on him, and he wrapped her in a tight and powerful hug.

"Truly the most anticipated, enjoyable, lovely, wonderful, amazing, and most welcome sight in all of Palishchuk!" Wingham said, using the lyrical barker's voice he had so mastered in his decades with his traveling troupe. He pushed his niece back to arms' length. "Every time I near Palishchuk, I fear that I will arrive only to discover that you are off to Damara or somewhere other than here."

"But you know that I would return in a hurry if I learned that you were riding back into town," she assured him, and his eyes sparkled and his crooked smile widened.

"I have ridden back with some marvelous finds again, as always," Wingham promised her with an exaggerated wink.

"As always," she agreed, her tone leading.

"Playing coy?"

At Arrayan's side, Olgerkhan grunted disapprovingly, even threateningly, for "coy"—*koi* in the Orcish tongue—was the name of a very lewd game.

Wingham caught the hint in the overprotective warning and backed off a step, eyeing the brutish Olgerkhan without blinking. Wingham hadn't survived the harshness of Vaasa for so many years by being blind to any and every potential threat.

"Not *koi*," Arrayan quickly explained to her bristling companion. "He means sly, sneaky. My uncle is implying that I might know something more than I am telling him."

"Ah, the book," said Olgerkhan.

Arrayan sighed and Wingham laughed.

"Alas, I am discovered," said Arrayan.

"And I thought that your joy was merely at the sight of me," Wingham replied with feigned disappointment.

"It is!" Arrayan assured him. "Or would be. I mean . . . there is no . . . Uncle, you know . . ."

Though he was obviously enjoying the sputtering spectacle, Wingham mercifully held up a hand to calm the woman.

"You never come out to find me on the morning of the first day, dear niece. You know that I will be quite busy greeting the crowd. But I am not surprised to see you out here this day, this early. Word has preceded me concerning Zhengyi's writing."

"Is it truly?" Arrayan asked, hardly able to get the words out of her mouth.

She practically leaped forward as she spoke them, grabbing at her uncle's shoulders. Wingham cast a nervous glance around them.

"Not here, girl. Not now," he quietly warned. "Come tonight when the wagons' ring is closed and we shall speak."

"I cannot wait for—" Arrayan started to say, but Wingham put a finger over her lips to silence her.

"Not here. Not now.

"Now, dear lady and gentleman," Wingham said with his showman's flourish. "Do examine our exotic aromas, some created as far away as Calimshan, where the wind oft carries mountains of sand so thick that you cannot see your hand if you put it but an inch from your face!"

Several other Palishchukian half-orcs walked by as Wingham spoke, and Arrayan understood the diversion. She nodded at her uncle, though she was truly reluctant to leave, and pulled the confused Olgerkhan away. The couple browsed at the carnival for another hour or so then Arrayan took her leave and returned to her small house. She spent the entirety of the afternoon pacing and wringing her hands. Wingham had confirmed it: the book in question was Zhengyi's.

Zhengyi the Witch-King's own words!

Zhengyi, who had dominated dragons and spread his darkness across all the Bloodstone Lands. Zhengyi, who had mastered magic and death itself. Mighty beings such as the Witch-King did not pen tomes idly or carelessly. Arrayan knew that Wingham understood such things. The old barker was no stranger to items of magical power. The fact that Wingham wouldn't even discuss the book publicly told Arrayan much; he knew that it was a special item. She had to wait, and the sunset couldn't come fast enough for her.

When it arrived, when finally the bells began to signal the end of the day's market activity, Arrayan grabbed a wrap and rushed out her door. She wasn't surprised to find Olgerkhan waiting for her, and together they moved swiftly through the city, out the southern gate, and back to Wingham's circled wagons.

The guards were ushering out the last of the shoppers, but they greeted Arrayan with a nod and allowed her passage into the ring.

She found Wingham sitting at the small table set in his personal wagon, and at that moment he seemed very different from the carnival barker. Somber and quiet, he barely looked up from the table to acknowledge the arrival of his niece, and when she circled him and regarded what lay on the table before him, Arrayan understood why.

There sat a large, ancient tome, its rich black cover made of leather but of a type smoother and thicker than anything Arrayan had ever seen. It invited touching for its edges dipped softly over the pages they protected. Arrayan didn't dare, but she did lean in a bit closer, taking note of the various designs quietly and unobtrusively etched onto the spine and cover. She made out the forms of dragons, some curled in sleep, some rearing and others in graceful flight, and it occurred to her that the book's soft covering might be dragon hide.

She licked her dry lips and found that she was suddenly unsure of her course. Slowly and deliberately, the shaken woman took the seat opposite her uncle and motioned for Olgerkhan to stay back by the door.

A long while passed, and Wingham showed no signs of breaking the silence.

"Zhengyi's book?" Arrayan mustered the courage to ask, and she thought the question incredibly inane, given the weight of the tome.

Finally, Wingham looked up at her and gave a slight nod.

"A spellbook?"

"No."

Arrayan waited as patiently as she could for her uncle to elaborate, but again, he just sat there. The uncustomary behavior from the normally extroverted half-orc had her on the edge of her seat.

"Then what—?" she started to ask.

She was cut short by a sharp, "I don't know."

After yet another interminable pause, Arrayan dared to reach out for the tome. Wingham caught her hand and held it firmly, just an inch from the black cover.

"You have equipped yourself with spells of divination this day?" he asked.

"Of course," she answered.

"Then seek out the magical properties of the tome before you proceed."

Arrayan sat back as far as she could go, eyeing her uncle curiously. She had never seen him like this, and though the sight made her even more excited about the potential of the tome, it was more than a little unsettling.

"And," Wingham continued, holding fast her hand, "you have prepared spells of magical warding as well?"

"What is it, uncle?"

The old half-orc stared at her long and hard, his gray eyes flashing with intrigue and honest fear.

Finally he said, "A summoning."

Arrayan had to consciously remember to breathe.

"Or a sending," Wingham went on. "And no demon is involved, nor any other extra-planar creatures that I can discern."

"You have studied it closely?"

"As closely as I dared. I am not nearly proficient enough in the Art to be attempting such a tome as this. But I know how to recognize a demon's name, or a planar's, and there is nothing like that in this tome."

"A spell of divination told you as much?"

"Hundreds of such spells," Wingham replied. He reached down and produced a thin black metal wand from his belt, holding it up before him. "I have burned this empty—thrice—and still my clues are few. I am certain that Zhengyi used his magic to conceal something . . . something magnificent. And certain I am, too, that this tome is a key to unlocking that concealed item, whatever it might be."

Arrayan pulled her hand free of his grasp, started to reach for the book, but changed her mind and crossed both of her hands in her lap. She sat alternately staring at the tome and at her uncle.

"It will certainly be trapped," Wingham said. "Though I have been able to find none—and not for lack of trying!"

"I was told that you only recently found it," said Arrayan.

"Months ago," replied Wingham. "I spoke of it to no one until I had exhausted all of my personal resources on it. Also, I did not want the word of it to spread too wide. You know that many would be interested in such a tome as this, including more than a few powerful wizards of less than sterling reputation."

Arrayan let it all sink in for a moment, and she began to grin. Wingham had waited until he was nearing Palishchuk to let the word slip out of Zhen-gyi's tome because he had planned all along to give it to Arrayan, his powerful magic-using niece. His gift to her would be her own private time with the fascinating and valuable book.

"King Gareth will send investigators," Wingham explained, further confirming Arrayan's suspicions. "Or a group, perhaps, whose sole purpose will be to confiscate the tome and return it to Bloodstone Village or Heliogabalus, where more powerful wizards ply their craft. Few know of its existence—those who have heard the whispers here in Palishchuk and Mariabronne the Rover."

Arrayan perked up at the mention of Mariabronne, a tracker whose title was nearing legendary status in the wild land. Mariabronne had grown quite wealthy on the monster-ear bounty offered at the Vaasan Gate, so it was rumored. He knew almost everyone, and everyone knew him. Friendly and plain-spoken, cunning and clever, but disarmingly simple, the ranger had a way of putting people—even those well aware of his reputation—into a position of underestimating him. Arrayan had met him only twice, both times in Palishchuk, and had found herself laughing at his many tales, or sitting wide-eyed at his recounting of amazing adventures. He was a tracker by trade, a ranger in service to the ways of the wilderness, but by Arrayan's estimation, he was possessed of a bard's character. There was mischief behind his bright and curious eyes to be sure.

"Mariabronne will ferry word to Gareth's commanders at the Vaasan Gate," Wingham went on, and the sound of his voice broke Arrayan from her contemplations.

His smile as she looked up to regard him told the woman that she had betrayed quite a few of her feelings with her expressions, and she felt her cheeks grow warm.

"Why did you tell anyone?" she asked.

"This is too powerful a tome. Its powers are beyond me."

"And yet you will allow me to inspect it?"

"Your powers with such magic are beyond mine."

Arrayan considered the daunting task before her in light of the deadline Wingham's revelations to Mariabronne had no doubt put upon her.

"Fear not, dear niece, my words to Mariabronne were properly cryptic—more so even than the whispers I allowed to drift north to Palishchuk, where I knew they would find your ears. He likely remains in the region and nowhere near the Gate, and I fully expect to see him again before he goes to Gareth's commanders. You will have all the time you need with the tome."

He offered Arrayan a wink then motioned to the black-bound book.

The woman stared at it but did not move to turn over its cover.

"You have not prepared any magical wards," Wingham reasoned after a few long moments.

"I did not expect . . . it is too . . ."

Wingham held up his hand to stop her. Then he reached back behind his chair and pulled out a leather bag, handing it across to Arrayan.

"Shielded," he assured her as she took it. "No one watching you, even with a magical eye, will understand the power of the item contained within this protected satchel."

Arrayan could hardly believe the offer. Wingham meant to allow her to take the book with her! She could not hide her surprise as she continued to consider her uncle, as she replayed their long and intermittent history. Wingham didn't know her all that well, and yet he would willingly hand over what might prove to be the most precious item he had ever uncovered in his long history of unearthing precious artifacts? How could she ever prove herself worthy of that kind of trust?

"Go on, niece," Wingham bade her. "I am not so young and am in need of a good night's sleep. I trust you will keep your ever-curious uncle informed of your progress?"

Hardly even thinking of the movement, Arrayan lifted out of her chair and leaned forward, wrapping Wingham with her slender arms and planting a huge kiss on his cheek.

CHAPTER

BODY COUNT

5

Entreri came leaping down the mountainside, springing from stone to stone, never keeping his path straight. He was hardly aware of his movements, yet every step was perfect and in complete balance, for the assassin had fallen into a state of pure battle clarity. His movements came with fluid ease, his body reacting just below his level of consciousness perfectly in tune with what he instinctively determined he needed to do. Entreri moved at a full sprint as easily on the broken, jagged trail down the steep slope of the northern Galena foothills, a place where even careful hikers might turn an ankle or trip into a crevice, as if he was running across a grassy meadow.

He skipped down along a muddy trail as another spear flew over his head. He started around a boulder in his path, but went quickly up its side instead, then sprang off to the left of the boulder to the top of another large stone. A quick glance back showed him that the goblins were closing on his flank, moving down easier ground in an attempt to cut him off before he reached the main trail.

A thin smile showed on Entreri's face as he leaped from that second boulder back to the ground, rushing along and continuing to veer to the west, his left.

The crackle of a thunderbolt back the other way startled him for a moment, until he realized that Jarlaxle had engaged the monsters with a leading shot of magic.

Entreri brushed the thought away. Jarlaxle was far from him, leaving him on his own against his most immediate enemies.

On his own. Exactly the way Artemis Entreri liked it.

He came to a straight trail running north down the mountainside and picked up his pace into a full run, with goblins coming in from the side and hot on his heels. As he neared the bottom of the trail, he spun and swiped his magical sword in an arc behind him, releasing an opaque veil of dark ash from its enchanted, blood-red blade. As he came around to complete the spin, Entreri fell forward into a somersault, then turned his feet as he rolled back up, throwing his momentum to the side and cutting a sharp turn behind one boulder. He hooked his fingers as he skidded past and caught himself, then threw himself flat against the stone and held his breath.

A slight gasp told the assassin the exact position of his enemies. He drew his jeweled dagger, and as the first goblin flashed past, he struck, quick and hard, a jab that put the vicious blade through the monster's ribs.

The goblin yelped and staggered, lurching and stumbling, and Entreri let it go without further thought. He came out around the rock in a rush and dived to his knees right before the swirl of ash.

Goblin shins connected on his side, and the monster went tumbling. A third came close behind, tangling with the previous as they crashed down hard.

Entreri scrambled forward and rolled over, coming to his feet with his back to the remaining ash. Without even looking, he flipped his powerful sword in his hand and jabbed it out behind him, taking the fourth goblin in line right in the chest.

The assassin turned and retracted his long blade, snapping it across to pick off a thrusting spear as the remaining goblin pair composed themselves for a coordinated attack.

"Getsun innk's arr!" one goblin instructed the other, which Entreri understood as "Circle to his left!"

Entreri, dagger in his right hand, sword in his left, went down in a crouch, weapons out wide to defend against both.

"Beenurk!" the goblin cried. "Go more!"

The other goblin did as ordered and Entreri started to turn with it, trying to appear afraid. He wanted the bigger goblin to focus on his expression, and so it apparently did, for Entreri sneakily flipped the dagger over in his grip then snapped his hand up and out. He was still watching the circling goblin when he let fly at the other one, but he knew that he had hit the mark when the bigger goblin's next command came out as nothing more than a blood-filled gurgle.

The assassin slashed his sword across, creating another ash field, then leaped back as if meaning to retrieve his dagger. He stopped in mid-stride, though, and reversed momentum to charge back at the pursuing goblin. He rolled right over the goblin's thrusting sword, going out to the humanoid's right, a complete somersault that landed Entreri firmly back on his feet in a low crouch. As he went, he flipped Charon's Claw from his left hand to his right. He angled the blade perfectly so that when he stood, the blade came up right under the goblin's ribs.

His momentum driving him forward, Entreri lifted the goblin right from the ground at the tip of his fine sword, the creature thrashing as it slid down the blade.

Entreri snapped a retraction, then spun fast, bringing the blade across evenly at shoulder level, and when he came around, the fine sword crossed through the squealing goblin's neck so cleanly that its head remained attached only until the creature fell over sideways and hit the ground with a jolt.

The assassin leaped away, grabbing at the dagger hilt protruding from the throat of the kneeling, trembling goblin. He gave a sudden twist and turn as he yanked the weapon free, ensuring that he had taken the creature's throat out completely. By then, the two he had tripped were back up and coming in—though tentatively.

Entreri watched their eyes and noted that they were glancing more often to the side than at him. They wanted to run, he knew, or they were hoping for reinforcements.

And the latter was not a fleeting hope, for Entreri could hear goblins all across the mountainside. Jarlaxle's impetuousness had dropped them right into the middle of a tribe of the creatures. They had only seen three at the campfire, milling around a boiling kettle of wretched smelling stew. But behind that campfire was a concealed cave opening.

Jarlaxle hadn't heard Entreri's warning, or he hadn't cared, and their sudden assault had brought forth a stream of howling monsters.

He was outnumbered two to one, but Entreri had the higher ground, and he used it to facilitate a sudden, overpowering attack. He came forward stabbing with his sword then throwing it out across to the left, and back to the right. He heard the ring of metal on metal as the goblin off to his right parried the backhand with its own sword, but that hardly interrupted Entreri's flow.

He strode forward, sending Charon's Claw in a motion down behind him, then up over his shoulder. He came forward in a long-reaching downward swipe, one designed to cleave his enemy should the goblin leap back.

To its credit, it came forward again.

But that was exactly what Entreri had anticipated.

The goblin's sword stabbed out—and a jeweled dagger went against the weapon's side and turned it out, altering the angle just enough to cause a miss. His hand working in a sudden blur, Entreri sent his dagger up and over the blade, then down and around, twisting as he went to turn the sword out even more. He slashed Charon's Claw across to his right as he did, forcing the other goblin to stay back, and continued his forward rush, again rolling his dagger, turning the sword even farther. And yet again, he rolled his blade, walking it right up the goblin's sword. He finally disengaged with a flourish, pulling his dagger in close, then striking out three times in rapid succession, drawing a grunt with each successive hit.

Bright blood widening around the three punctures, the goblin staggered back.

Confident that it was defeated, Entreri had already turned by that point, his sword working furiously to fend the suddenly ferocious attacks by the other goblin. He parried a low thrust, a second heading for his chest, and picked off a third coming in at the same angle.

The goblin screamed and pressed a fourth thrust.

Entreri flung his dagger.

The goblin moaned once then went silent. Its sword tip drifted toward the ground as its gaze, too, went down to consider the dagger hilt protruding from its chest.

It looked back at Entreri. Its sword fell to the ground.

"My guess is that it hurts," said the assassin.

The goblin fell over dead.

Entreri kicked the dead creature over onto its back then tugged his dagger free. He glanced up the mountainside to the continuing tumult, though he saw no new enemies there. Back down the mountain, he noted that the first goblin that had passed him, the one he had stung in the side, had moved off.

A flash of fire to the side caught his attention. He could only imagine what carnage Jarlaxle was executing.

Jarlaxle ran to the center of a clearing, goblins closing in all around him, spears flying at him from every direction.

His magical wards handled the missiles easily enough, and he was quite confident that the crude monsters possessed none of sufficient magical enhancement to get through the barriers and actually strike him. A dozen spears came out at him and were harmlessly deflected aside, but closely following, coming out from behind every rock surrounding the clearing, it seemed, came a goblin, weapon in hand, howling and charging.

Apparently, the reputation of the dark elves was lost on that particular group of savages.

As he had counted on their magical deficiencies to render their spears harmless, so did Jarlaxle count on the goblins' intellectual limitations. They swarmed in at him, and with a shrug Jarlaxle revealed a wand, pointed it at his own feet, and spoke a command word.

The ensuing fireball engulfed the drow, the goblins, and the whole of the clearing and the rocks surrounding it. Screams of terror accompanied the orange flames.

Except there were no flames.

Completely ignoring his own illusion, Jarlaxle watched with more than a little amusement as the goblins flailed and threw themselves to the ground. The creatures thrashed and slapped at flames, and soon their screams of terror became wails of agony. The dark elf noted some of the dozen enemies lying very still, for so consumed had they been by the illusion of the fireball that the magic had created through their own minds the same result actual flames from such a blast might have wrought.

Jarlaxle had killed nearly half the goblins with a single simple illusion.

Well, the drow mused, not a simple illusion. He had spent hours and hours, burning out this wand through a hundred recharges, to perfect the swirl of flames.

He didn't pat himself on the back for too long, though, for he still had half a dozen creatures to deal with. They were all distracted, however, and so the drow began to pump his arm, calling forth the magic of the bracer he wore on his right wrist to summon perfectly weighted daggers into his hand. They went out in a deadly stream as the drow turned a slow circle.

He had just completed the turn, putting daggers into all six of the thrashing goblins—and into three of the others, just to make sure—when he heard the howling approach of more creatures.

Jarlaxle needed no magical items. He reached inside himself, into the essence of his heritage, and called forth a globe of absolute darkness. Then he used his keen hearing to direct him out of the clearing off to the side, where he slipped from stone to stone away from the goblin approach.

◆▬▬▬◆

"Will you just stop running?" Entreri asked under his breath as he continued his dogged pursuit of the last wounded goblin.

The blood trail was easy enough to follow and every so often he spotted the creature zigzagging along the broken trail below him. He had badly stung the creature, he believed, but the goblin showed no sign of slowing.

Entreri knew that he should just let the creature bleed out, but frustration drove him on.

He came upon one sharp bend in the trail but didn't turn. He sprang atop the rock wall lining the ravine trail and sprinted over it, leaping across another crevice and barreling on straight down the mountainside. He saw the winding trail below him, caught a flash of the running goblin, and veered appropriately, his legs moving on pure instinct to keep him charging forward and in balance along stones and over dark holes that threatened to swallow him up. He tripped more than once, skinning a knee and twisting an ankle, but never was it a catastrophic fall. Hardly slowing with each slight stumble, Entreri growled through the pain and focused on his prey.

He crossed the snaking path and resisted the good sense to turn and follow its course, again cutting across it to the open, rocky mountainside. He crossed the path again, and a few moments later came up on the fourth bend.

Certain he was ahead of his foe, he paused and caught his breath, adjusted his clothing, and wiped the blood from his kneecap.

The terrified, wounded goblin rounded a bend, coming into view. So intent on the trail behind it, the wretch never even saw Entreri as it ran along.

"You could have made this so much easier," Entreri said, drawing his weapons and calmly approaching.

The assassin's voice hit the goblin's sensibilities as solidly as a stone wall would have smacked its running form. The creature squealed and skidded to an abrupt stop, whined pitifully, and fell to its knees.

"Pleases, mister. Pleases," it begged, using the common tongue.

"Oh, shut up," the killer replied.

"Surely you'll not kill a creature that so eloquently begs for its life," came a third voice, one that only surprised Entreri momentarily—until he recognized the speaker.

He had no idea how Jarlaxle might have gotten down that quickly, but he knew better than to be surprised at anything Jarlaxle did. Entreri sheathed his sword and grabbed the goblin by a patch of its scraggly hair, yanking its head back violently. He let his jeweled dagger slide teasingly across the creature's throat, then moved it to the side of the goblin's head.

"Shall I just take its ears, then?" he asked Jarlaxle, his tone showing that he meant to do no such thing and to show no such mercy.

"Always you think in terms of the immediate," the drow replied, and he moved up to the pair. "In those terms, by the way, we should be fast about our business, for a hundred of this one's companions are even now swarming down the mountainside."

Entreri moved as if to strike the killing blow, but Jarlaxle called out and stopped him.

"Look to the long term," the drow bade him.

Entreri cast a cynical look Jarlaxle's way.

"We are competing with a hundred trackers for every ear," the drow explained. "How much better will our progress become with a scout to guide us?"

"A scout?" Entreri looked down at the sniveling, trembling goblin.

"Why of course," said Jarlaxle, and he walked over and calmly moved Entreri's dagger away from the goblin's head. Then he took hold of Entreri's other hand

and gently urged it from its grip on the goblin's hair. He pushed Entreri back a step then bent low before the creature.

"What do you say to that?" he asked.

The dumbfounded goblin stared at him.

"What is your name?"

"Gools."

"Gools? A fine name. What do you say, Gools? Would you care to enter into a partnership with my friend and me?"

The goblin's expression did not change.

"Your job will be quite simple, I assure you," said the drow. "Show us the way to monsters—you know, your friends and such—then get out of our way. We will meet you each day—" he paused and looked around—"right here. It seems a fine spot for our discussions."

The goblin seemed to be catching on, finally. Jarlaxle tossed him a shiny piece of gold.

"And many more for Gools where that came from. Interested?"

The goblin stared wide-eyed at the coin for a long while then looked up to Jarlaxle and slowly nodded.

"Very well then," said the drow.

He came forward, reaching into a belt pouch, and brought forth his hand, which was covered in a fine light blue chalky substance. The dark elf reached for the goblin's forehead.

Gools lurched back at that, but Jarlaxle issued a stern warning, bringing forth a sword in his other hand and putting on an expression that promised a painful death.

The drow reached for the goblin's forehead again and began drawing there with the chalk, all the while uttering some arcane incantation—a babbling that any third-year magic student would have known to be incoherent blather.

Entreri, who understood the drow language, was also quite certain that it was gibberish.

When he finished, Jarlaxle cupped poor Gools's chin and forced the creature to look him right in the eye. He spoke in the goblin tongue, so there could be no misunderstanding.

"*I have cast a curse upon you,*" he said. "*If you know anything of my people, the drow, then you understand well that this curse will be the most vicious of all. It is quite simple, Gools. If you stay loyal to me, to us, then nothing will happen to you. But if you betray us, either by running away or by leading us to an ambush, the magic of the curse will take effect. Your brains will turn to water and run out your ear, and it will happen slowly, so slowly! You will feel every burn, every sting, every twist. You will know agony that no sword blade could ever approach. You will whine and cry and plea for mercy, but nothing will help you. And even in death will this curse torment you, for its magic will send your spirit to the altar of the Spider Queen Lolth, the Demon Goddess of Chaos. Do you know of her?*"

Gools trembled so badly he could hardly shake his head.

"*You know spiders?*" Jarlaxle asked, and he walked his free hand over the goblin's sweaty cheek. "*Crawly spiders.*"

Gools shuddered.

"*They are the tools of Lolth. They will devour you for eternity. They will bite*"—he pinched the goblin sharply—*"you a million million times. There will be no release from the burning of their poison."*

He glanced back at Entreri, then looked the terrified goblin in the eye once more.

"Do you understand me, Gools?"

The goblin nodded so quickly that its teeth chattered with the movement.

"Work with us, and earn gold," said the drow, still in the guttural language of the savage goblins. He flipped another gold piece at the creature. Gools didn't even move for it, though, and the coin hit him in the chest and fell to the dirt. *"Betray us and know unending torture."*

Jarlaxle stepped back, and the goblin slumped. Gools did manage to retain enough of his wits to reach down and gather the second gold piece.

"Tomorrow, at this time," Jarlaxle instructed. Then, in Common, he began, "Do you think—?"

He stopped and glanced back up the mountainside at the sudden sound of renewed battle.

Entreri and Gools, too, looked up the hill, caught by surprise. Horns began to blow, and goblins squealed and howled, and the ring of metal on metal echoed on the wind.

"Tomorrow!" Jarlaxle said to the goblin, poking a finger his way. "Now be off, you idiot."

Gools scrambled away on all fours, finally put his feet under him, and ran off.

"You really think we'll see that one ever again?" Entreri asked.

"I care little," said the drow.

"Ears?" reminded Entreri.

"You may wish to earn your reputation one ear at a time, my friend, but I never choose to do things the hard way."

Entreri started to respond, but Jarlaxle held up a hand to silence him. The drow motioned up the mountainside to the left and started off to see what the commotion was all about.

"Now I know that I have walked into a bad dream," Entreri remarked.

He and Jarlaxle leaned flat against a rock wall, overlooking a field of rounded stone. Down below, goblins ran every which way, scrambling in complete disarray, for halflings charged among them—dozens of halflings riding armored war pigs.

The diminutive warriors swung flails, blew horns, and threw darts, veering their mounts in zigzagging lines that must have seemed perfectly chaotic to the poor, confused goblins.

From their higher vantage point, however, Entreri and Jarlaxle could see the precision of the halflings' movements, a flowing procession of destruction so calculated that it seemed as if the mounted little warriors had all blended to form just a few singular, snakelike creatures.

"In Menzoberranzan, House Baenre sometimes parades its forces about the streets to show off their discipline and power," Jarlaxle remarked. "These little ones are no less precise in their movements."

Entreri had not witnessed such a parade in his short time in the dark elf city, but in watching the weaving slaughter machine of the halfling riders, he easily understood his companion's point. It was easy, too, for the pair to determine the timeline of the one-sided battle, and so they began making their way down the slope, Jarlaxle leading Entreri onto the stony field as the last of the goblins was cut down.

"Kneebreakers!" the halflings cried in unison, as they lined their war pigs up in perfect ranks. A few had been injured, but only one seemed at all seriously hurt, and halfling priests were already hard at work attending to him.

The halflings' self-congratulatory cheering stopped short, though, when several of them loudly noted the approach of two figures, one a drow elf.

Weapons raised in the blink of an eye, and shouts of warning told the newcomers to hold their ground.

"*Inurree waflonk,*" Jarlaxle said in a language that Entreri did not understand. As he considered the curious expressions of the halflings, however, and remembered his old friend back in Calimport, Dwahvel Tiggerwillies, and some of her linguistic idiosyncrasies, he figured out that his friend was speaking the halfling tongue—and, apparently, quite fluently. Entreri was not surprised.

"Well fought," Jarlaxle translated, offering a wink to Entreri. "We watched you from on high and saw that the unorganized goblins hadn't a chance."

"You do realize that you're a dark elf, correct?" asked one of the halflings, a burly little fellow with a brown mustache that curled in circles over his cheeks.

Jarlaxle feigned a look of surprise as he held one of his hands up before his sparkling red eyes.

"Why, indeed, 'tis true!" he exclaimed.

"You do realize that we're the Kneebreakers, correct?"

"So I heard you proclaim."

"You do realize that we Kneebreakers have a reputation for killing vermin, correct?"

"If you did not, and after witnessing that display, I would spread the word myself, I assure you."

"And you do realize that dark elves fall into that category, of course."

"Truly? Why, I had come to believe that the civilized races, which some say include halflings—though others insist that halflings can only be thought of as civilized when there is not food to be found—claim superiority because of their willingness to judge others based on their actions and not their heritage. Is that not one of the primary determining factors of civility?"

"He's got a point," another halfling mumbled.

"I'll give him a point," said yet another, that one holding a long (relatively speaking), nasty-tipped spear.

"You might also have noticed that many of the goblins were already dead as you arrived on the scene," Jarlaxle added. "It wasn't infighting that slew them, I assure you."

"You two were battling the fiends?" asked the first, the apparent leader.

"Battling? Slaughtering would be a better term. I do believe that you and your little army here have stolen our kills." He did a quick scan and poked his finger repeatedly, as if counting the dead. "Forty or fifty lost gold pieces, at least."

The halflings began to murmur among themselves.

"But it is nothing that my friend and I cannot forgive and forget, for truly watching your fine force in such brilliant maneuvering was worthy of so reasonable an admission price," Jarlaxle added.

He swept one of his trademark low bows, removing his hat and brushing the gigantic diatryma feather across the stones.

That seemed to settle the halfling ranks a bit.

"Your friend, he does not speak much?" asked the halfling leader.

"He provides the blades," Jarlaxle replied.

"And you the brains, I presume."

"I, or the demon prince now standing behind you."

The halfling blanched and spun around, along with all the others, weapons turning to bear. Of course, there was no monster to be seen, so the whole troupe spun back on a very amused Jarlaxle.

"You really must get past your fear of my dark-skinned heritage," Jarlaxle explained with a laugh. "How else might we enjoy our meal together?"

"You want us to feed you?"

"Quite the contrary," said the drow. He pulled off his traveling pack and brought forth a wand and a small wineskin. He glanced around, noting a small tumble of boulders, including a few low enough to serve as tables. Motioning that way, he said, "Shall we?"

The halflings stared at him dubiously and did not move.

With a great sigh, Jarlaxle reached into his pack again and pulled forth a tablecloth and spread it on the ground before him, taking care to find a bare spot that was not stained by goblin blood. He stepped back, pointed his wand at the cloth, and spoke a command word. Immediately, the center area of the tablecloth bulged up from the ground. Grinning, Jarlaxle moved to the cloth, grabbed its edge, and pulled it back, revealing a veritable feast of sweet breads, fruits, berries, and even a rack of lamb, dripping with juices.

A row of halfling eyes went so wide they seemed as if they would fall out and bounce along the ground together.

"Being halflings, and civilized ones at that, I assume you have brought a fair share of eating utensils, plates, and drinking flagons, correct?" said the drow, aptly mimicking the halfling leader's manner of speaking.

Some of the halflings edged their war pigs forward, but the stubborn leader held up his hand and eyed the drow with suspicion.

"Oh, come now," said Jarlaxle. "Could you envision a better token of my friendship?"

"You came from the wall?"

"From the Vaasan Gate, of course," Jarlaxle answered. "Sent out to scout by Commander Ellery Tranth Dopray Kierney Dragonsbane Peidopare herself."

Entreri tried hard not to wince at the mention of the woman's name, for he thought his friend was playing a dangerous game.

"I know her well," said the halfling leader.

"Do you?" said the drow, and he brightened suddenly as if it all had just fallen in place for him. "Could it be that you are the renowned Hobart Bracegirdle himself?" he gasped.

The halfling straightened and puffed out his chest with pride, all the answer the companions needed.

"Then you must dine with us," said Jarlaxle. "You must! I . . ." He paused and gave Entreri a hard look. "We," he corrected, "insist."

Again the hard look, and from that prodding, he did manage to pry a simple "Indeed" out of the assassin.

Hobart looked around at his companions, most of them openly salivating.

"Always could use a good meal after a battle," he remarked.

"Or before," said another of the troupe.

"Or during," came a deadpan from Jarlaxle's side, and the drow's face erupted with a smile as he regarded Entreri.

"Charm is a learned skill," Jarlaxle whispered through his grin.

"So is murder," the human whispered back.

Entreri wasn't exactly comfortable sitting in a camp with dozens of drunken halflings. He couldn't deny that the ale was good, though, and few races in all the Realms could put out a better selection of tasty meats than the halflings, though the food from their packs hardly matched the feast Jarlaxle had magically summoned. Entreri remained silent throughout the meal, enjoying the fine food and wine, and taking the measure of his hosts. His companion, though, was not so quiet, prodding Hobart and the others for tales of adventure and battle.

The halflings were more than willing to comply. They spoke of their rise to fame, when King Gareth first claimed the throne and the Bloodstone Lands were even wilder than their present state.

"It is unusual, is it not, for members of your race to prefer the road and battle to comfortable homes?" Jarlaxle asked.

"That's the reputation," Hobart admitted.

"And we're knowing well the reputation of dark elves," said another of the troupe, and all of the diminutive warriors laughed, several raising flagons in toast.

"Aye," said Hobart, "and if we're to believe that reputation, we should have killed you out on the slopes, yes?"

"To warrior halfling adventurers," Jarlaxle offered, lifting his flagon of pale ale.

Hobart grinned. "Aye, and to all those who rise above the limitations of their ancestors."

"Huzzah!" all the other halflings cheered.

They drank and toasted some more, and some more, and just when Entreri thought the meal complete, the main chef, a chubby fellow named Rockney Hamsukker called out that the lamb was done.

That brought more cheers and more toasts, and more—much more—food.

The sun was long gone and still they ate, and Jarlaxle began to prod Hobart again about their exploits. Story after story of goblins and orcs falling to the Kneebreakers ensued, with Hobart even revealing the variations on the "swarm," the "weave," and the "front-on wallop," as he named the Kneebreaker battle tactics.

"Bah," Jarlaxle snorted. "With goblins and orcs, are tactics even necessary? Hardly worthy opponents."

The camp went silent, and a scowl spread over Hobart's face. Behind him, another Kneebreaker stood and dangled his missile weapon, a pair of iron balls fastened to a length of cord for the outsiders to clearly see.

Entreri stopped his eating and stared hard at that threatening halfling, quickly surmising his optimum route of attack to inflict the greatest possible damage on the largest number of enemies.

"In numbers, of course," Jarlaxle clarified. "For most groups, numbers of goblinkin could prove troublesome. But I have watched you in battle, you forget?"

Hobart's large brown eyes narrowed.

"After your display on the stony field, good sir Hobart, you will have a difficult time of convincing me that any but a great number of goblinkin could prove of consequence to the Kneebreakers. Did those last goblins even manage a single strike against your riders?"

"We had some wounded," Hobart reminded him.

"More by chance than purpose."

"The ground favored our tactics," Hobart explained.

"True enough," Jarlaxle conceded. "But am I to believe that a troupe so precise as your own could not easily adapt to nearly any terrain?"

"I work very hard to remind my soldiers that we live on the precipice of disaster," Hobart declared. "We are one mistake from utter ruin."

"The warrior's edge, indeed," said the drow. "I do not underestimate your victories, of course, but I know there is more."

Hobart hooked his thick thumbs into the sides of his shining plate mail breastplate.

"We've been out a long stretch," he explained. " 'Twas our goal to return to the Vaasan Gate with enough ears to empty Commander Ellery's coffers."

"Bah, but you're just looking to empty Ellery from her breeches!" another halfling said, and many chortled with amusement.

Hobart looked around, grinning, at his companions, who murmured and nodded.

"And so we shall—the coffers, I mean."

The halfling leader snapped his stubby fingers in the air and a nervous, skinny fellow at Jarlaxle and Entreri's right scrambled about, finally producing a large bag. He looked at Hobart, returned the leader's continuing smile, then overturned the bag, dumping a hundred ears, ranging in size from the human-sized goblins' ears, several that belonged to creatures as large as ogres, and a pair so enormous Jarlaxle could have worn either as a hat.

Hobart launched back into his tales, telling of a confrontation with a trio of ogres and another ogre pair in the company of some hobgoblins. He raised his voice, almost as a bard might sing the tale, when he reached the climactic events, and the Kneebreakers all around him began to cheer wildly. One halfling pair stood up and re-enacted the battle scene, the giant imposter leaping up on a rock to tower over his foes.

Despite himself, Artemis Entreri could not help but smile. The movements of the halflings, the passion, the food, the drink, all of it, reminded him so much of some of his closest friends back in Calimport, of Dwahvel Tiggerwillies and fat Dondon.

The giant died in Hobart's tale—and the halfling giant died on the rock with great dramatic flourish—and the entire troupe took up the chant of "Kneebreakers! Kneebreakers!"

They danced, they sang, they cheered, they ate, and they drank. On it went, long into the night.

Artemis Entreri had perfected the art of sleeping light many years before. The man could not be caught by surprise, even when he was apparently sound asleep. Thus, the stirring of his partner had him wide awake in moments, still some time before the dawn. All around them, the Kneebreakers snored and grumbled in their dreams, and the few who had been posted as sentries showed no more signs of awareness.

Jarlaxle looked at Entreri and winked, and the assassin nodded curiously. He followed the drow to the sleeping halfling with the bag of ears, which was set amid several other bags of equal or larger size next to the halfling that served as the pack mule for the Kneebreakers. With a flick of his long, dexterous fingers, Jarlaxle untied the bag of ears. He slid it out slowly then moved silently out of camp, the equally quiet Entreri close behind. Getting past the guards without being noticed was no more difficult than passing a pile of stones without having them shout out.

The pair came to a clearing under the light of the waning moon. Jarlaxle popped a button off of his fine waistcoat, grinning at Entreri all the while. He pinched it between his fingers, then snapped his wrist three times in rapid succession.

Entreri was hardly surprised when the button elongated and widened, and its bottom dropped nearly to the ground, so that it looked as if Jarlaxle was holding a stovepipe hat that would fit a mountain giant.

With a nod from Jarlaxle, Entreri overturned the bag of ears and began scooping them into Jarlaxle's magical button bag. The drow stopped him a couple of times, indicating that he should leave a few, including one of the giant ears.

A snap of Jarlaxle's wrist then returned his magical bag to its inauspicious button form, and he put it on the waistcoat in its proper place and tapped it hard, its magic re-securing it to the material. He motioned for Entreri to move away with him then produced, out of thin air of course, a dust broom. He brushed away their tracks.

Entreri started back toward the halfling encampment, but Jarlaxle grabbed him by the shoulder to stop him. The drow offered a knowing wink and drew a slender wand from an inside pocket of his great traveling cloak. He pointed the wand at the discarded bag and the few ears, then spoke a command word.

A soft popping sound ensued, accompanied by a puff of smoke, and when it cleared, standing in place of the smoke was a small wolf.

"Enjoy your meal," Jarlaxle instructed the canine, and he turned and headed back to camp, Entreri right behind. The assassin glanced back often, to see the summoned wolf tearing at the ears, then picking up the bag and shaking it all about, shredding it.

Jarlaxle kept going, but Entreri paused a bit longer. The wolf scrambled around, seeming very annoyed at being deprived of a further meal, Entreri reasoned, for it began to disintegrate, its temporary magic expended, reducing it to a cloud of drifting smoke.

The assassin could only stare in wonder.

They had barely settled back into their blankets when the first rays of dawn peeked over the eastern horizon. Still, many hours were to pass before the halflings truly stirred, and Entreri found some more much-needed sleep.

The sudden tumult in camp awakened him around highsun. He groggily lifted up on his elbows, glancing around in amusement at the frantic halflings scrambling to and fro. They lifted stones and kicked remnants of the night's fire aside. They peeked under the pant legs of comrades, and often got kicked for their foolishness.

"There is a problem, I presume," Entreri remarked to Jarlaxle, who sat up and stretched the weariness from his body.

"I do believe our little friends have misplaced something. And with all the unorganized commotion, I suspect they'll be long in finding it."

"Because a bag of ears would hear them coming," said Entreri, his voice as dry as ever.

Jarlaxle laughed heartily. "I do believe that you are beginning to figure it all out, my friend, this journey we call life."

"That is what frightens me most of all."

The two went silent when they noted Hobart and a trio of very serious looking fellows staring hard at them. In procession, with the three others falling respectfully two steps behind the Kneebreaker commander, the group approached.

"Suspicion falls upon us," Jarlaxle remarked. "Ah, the intrigue!"

"A fine and good morning to you, masters Jarlaxle and Entreri," Hobart greeted, and there was nothing jovial about his tone. "You slept well, I presume."

"You would be presuming much, then," said Entreri.

"My friend here, he does not much enjoy discomfort," explained Jarlaxle. "You would not know it from his looks or his reputation, but he is, I fear, a bit of a fop."

"Every insult duly noted," Entreri said under his breath.

Jarlaxle winked at him.

"An extra twist of the blade, you see," Entreri promised.

"Am I interrupting something?" Hobart asked.

"Nothing you would not be interrupting in any case if you ever deign to speak to us," said Entreri.

The halfling nodded then looked at Entreri curiously, then similarly at Jarlaxle, then turned to regard his friends. All four shrugged in unison.

"Did you sleep the night through?" Hobart asked.

"And most of the morning, it would seem," Jarlaxle answered.

"Bah, 'tis still early."

"Good sir halfling, I do believe the sun is at its zenith," said the drow.

"As I said," Hobart remarked. "Goblin hunting's best done at twilight. Ugly little things get confident when the sun wanes, of course. Not that they ever have any reason to be confident."

"Not with your great skill against them, to be sure."

Hobart eyed the drow with clear suspicion. "We're missing something," he explained. "Something you'd be interested in."

Jarlaxle glanced Entreri's way, his expression not quite innocent and wide-eyed, but more curious than anything else—the exact look one would expect from someone intrigued but fully ignorant of the theft. Entreri had to fight hard to keep his own disinterested look about him, for he was quite amused at how perfectly Jarlaxle could play the liars' game.

"Our bag of ears," said Hobart.

Jarlaxle blew a long sigh. "That is troubling."

"And you will understand why we have to search you?"

"And our bedrolls, of course," said the drow, and he stepped back and held his cloak out wide to either side.

"We'd see it if it was on you," said Hobart, "unless it was magically stored or disguised." He motioned to one of the halflings behind him, a studious looking fellow with wide eyes, which he blinked continually, and thin brown hair sharply parted and pushed to one side. Seeming more a scholar than a warrior, the little one drew out a long blue wand.

"To detect magic, I presume," Jarlaxle remarked.

Hobart nodded. "Step apart, please."

Entreri glanced at Jarlaxle then back to the halfling. With a shrug he took a wide step to the side.

The halfling pointed his wand, whispered a command, and a glow engulfed Entreri for just a moment then was gone.

The halfling stood there studying the assassin, and his wide eyes kept going to Entreri's belt, to the jeweled dagger on one hip then to the sword, power-fully enchanted, on the other. The halfling's face twisted and contorted, and he trembled.

"You would not want either blade to strike you, of course," said Jarlaxle, catching on to the silent exchange where the wand was clueing the little wizard in to just how potent the human's weapons truly were.

"You all right?" Hobart asked, and though the wand-wielder could hardly draw a breath, he nodded.

"Turn around, then," Hobart bid Entreri, and the assassin did as he was asked, even lifting his cloak so the prying little scholar could get a complete picture.

A few moments later, the wand-wielder looked at Hobart and shook his head.

Hobart held his hand out toward Jarlaxle, and the other halfling lifted his wand. He spoke the command once more and the soft glow settled over a grin-ning Jarlaxle.

The wand-wielder squealed and fell back, shading his eyes.

"What?" Hobart asked.

The other one stammered and sputtered, his lips flapping, and kept his free hand up before him.

Entreri chuckled. He could only imagine the blinding glow of magic that one saw upon the person of Jarlaxle!

"It's not . . . there's . . . I mean . . . never before . . . not in King Gareth's own . . ."

"What?" Hobart demanded.

The other shook his head so rapidly that he nearly knocked himself over.

"Concentrate!" demanded the Kneebreaker commander. "You know what you're looking for!"

"But . . . but . . . but . . ." the halfling managed to say through his flapping lips.

Jarlaxle lifted his cloak and slowly turned, and the poor halfling shielded his eyes even more.

"On his belt!" the little one squealed as he fell away with a gasp. His two companions caught him before he tumbled, and steadied him, straightening him and brushing him off. "He has an item of holding on his belt," the halfling told Hobart when he'd finally regained his composure. "And another in his hat."

Hobart turned a wary eye on Jarlaxle.

The drow, grinning with confidence, unfastened his belt—with a command word, not through any mundane buckle—and slid the large pouch free, holding it up before him.

"This is your point of reference, yes?" he asked the wand-wielder, who nodded.

"I am found out, then," Jarlaxle said dramatically, and he sighed.

Hobart scowled.

"A simple pouch of holding," the drow explained, and tossed it to Hobart. "But take care, for within lies my precious Cormyrean brandy. I know, I know, I should have shared it with you, but you are so many, and I feared its potent effect on ones so little."

Hobart pulled the bottle from the pouch and held it up to read the label. His expression one of great approval, he slid it back into the pouch. Then he rummaged through the rest of the magical container, nearly climbing in at one point.

"We share the brandy, you and I, a bit later?" Jarlaxle proposed when Hobart was done with the pouch.

"Or if that hat of yours is holding my ears, I take it for my own, drink just enough to quench my thirst and use the rest as an aid in lighting your funeral pyre."

Jarlaxle laughed aloud. "I do so love that you speak directly, good Sir Brace-girdle!" he said.

He bowed and removed his hat, brushing it across the ground, then spun it to Hobart.

The halfling started to fiddle with it, but Jarlaxle stopped him with a sharp warning.

"Return my pouch first," he said, and the four halflings looked at him hard. "You do not wish to be tinkering with two items of extra-dimensional nature."

"Rift. Astral. Bad," Entreri explained.

Hobart stared at him then at the amused drow and tossed the pouch back to Jarlaxle. The Kneebreaker commander began inspecting the great, wide-brimmed hat, and after a moment, discovered that he could peel back the underside of its peak.

"A false compartment?" he asked.

"In a sense," Jarlaxle admitted, and Hobart's expression grew curious as the flap of cloth came out fully in his hand, leaving the underside of the peak intact, with no compartment revealed. The halfling then held up the piece of black cloth, a circular swatch perhaps half a foot in diameter.

Hobart looked at it, looked around, casually shrugged, and shook his head. He tossed the seemingly benign thing over his shoulder.

"No!" Jarlaxle cried, but too late, for the spinning cloth disk elongate in the air and fell at the feet of Hobart's three companions, widening and opening into a ten foot hole.

All three squealed and tumbled in.

Jarlaxle put his hands to his face.

"What?" Hobart asked. "What in the six hundred and sixty-six layers of the Abyss?"

Jarlaxle slipped his belt off and whispered into its end, which swelled and took on the shape of a snake's head. The whole belt began to grow and come alive.

"They are all right?" the drow casually asked of Hobart, who was at the edge of the hole on his knees, shouting down to his companions. Other Kneebreakers had come over as well, staring into the pit or scrambling around in search of a rope or a branch to use as a ladder.

Jarlaxle's snake-belt slithered over the edge.

Hobart screamed and drew his weapon, a beautifully designed short sword with a wicked serrated edge.

"What are you doing?" he cried and seemed about to cleave the snake.

Jarlaxle held up his hand, bidding patience. Even that small delay was enough, for the fast-moving and still growing snake was completely in the pit by then, except for the tip of its tail, which fastened itself securely around a nearby root.

"A rope of climbing," the drow explained. Hobart surveyed the scene. "Have one take hold and the rope will aid him in getting out of the pit."

It took a few moments and another use of the wand to confirm the claim, but soon the three shaken but hardly injured halflings were back out of the hole. Jarlaxle walked over and calmly lifted one edge of the extra-dimensional pocket. With a flick of his wrist and a spoken command, it fast reverted to a cloth disk that would fit perfectly inside the drow's great hat. At the same time, the snake-rope slithered up Jarlaxle's leg and crawled around his waist, obediently winding itself inside the belt loops of his fine trousers. When it came fully around, the "head" bit the end of the tail and commenced swallowing it until the belt was snugly about the drow's waist.

"Well . . ." the obviously flustered Hobart started to say, staring at the wand-wielder. "You think . . " Hobart tried to go on. "I mean, is there . . . ?"

"I should have killed you in Calimport," Entreri said to Jarlaxle.

"For the sake of a flustered halfling, of course," the drow replied.

"For the sake of my own sanity."

"Truer than you might realize."

"A-anything else you need to look at on that one?" Hobart finally managed to sputter.

The wand-wielder shook his head so forcefully that his lips made popping and smacking noises.

"Consider my toys," Jarlaxle said to Hobart. "Do you really believe that your ears are of such value to me that I would risk alienating so many entertaining and impressive newfound friends in acquiring them?"

"He's got a point," said the halfling standing next to Hobart.

"All the best to you in your search, good Sir Bracegirdle," said Jarlaxle, taking his hat back and replacing the magical cloth. "My offer for brandy remains."

"I expect you would favor a drink right now," Entreri remarked. "Though not as much as that one," he added, indicating the flabbergasted, terrified, and stupefied wand-wielder.

"Medicinal purposes," Jarlaxle added, looking at the trembling little halfling.

"He's lucky you didn't strike him blind," added Entreri.

"Would not be the first time."

"Stunning."

CHAPTER

6

Black spots circled and danced before her eyes and a cold sweat was general about her body, glistening, it seemed, from every pore.

Arrayan tried to stand straight and hold fast to her concentration, but those spots! She put one foot in front of the other, barely inching her way to the door across the common room of her tiny home.

Three strides will take me to it, she thought, a sorry attempt at willing herself to shake her state of disorientation and vertigo and just take the quick steps.

The knocking continued even more insistently.

Arrayan smiled despite her condition. From the tempo and frantic urgency of the rapping, she knew it was Olgerkhan. It was always Olgerkhan, caring far too much about her.

The recognition of her dear old friend emboldened Arrayan enough for her to fight through the swirling black dots of dizziness for just a moment and get to the door. She cracked it open, leaning on it but painting an expression that tried hard to deny her weariness.

"Well met," she greeted the large half-orc.

A flash of concern crossed Olgerkhan's face as he regarded her, and it took him a long moment to reply, "And to you."

"It is far too early for a visit," Arrayan said, trying to cover, though she could tell by the position of the sun, a brighter spot in the typically gray Palishchuk sky, that it was well past mid-morning.

"Early?" Olgerkhan looked around. "We will go to Wingham's, yes? As we agreed?"

Arrayan had to pause a moment to suppress a wave of nausea and dizziness that nearly toppled her from the door.

"Yes, of course," she said, "but not now. I need more sleep. It's too early."

"It's later than we agreed."

"I didn't sleep well last night," she said. The effort of merely standing there was starting to take its toll. Arrayan's teeth began to chatter. "You understand, I'm sure."

The large half-orc nodded, glanced around again, and stepped back.

Arrayan moved her hand and the weight of her leaning on the door shut it hard. She turned, knowing she had to get back to her bed, and took a shaky step away, then another. The inching along wouldn't get her there in time, she knew, so she tried a quick charge across the room.

She got one step farther before the floor seemed to reach up and swallow her. She lay there for a long moment, trying to catch her breath, trying with sheer determination to stop the room from spinning. She would have to crawl, she knew, and she fought hard to get to her hands and knees to do just that.

"Arrayan!" came a shout from behind her, and it sounded like it was a hundred miles away.

"Oh my, Arrayan," the voice said in her ear a moment later, cracking with every word. Arrayan hardly registered the voice and barely felt powerful Olgerkhan sweep her into his arms to carry her gently to her bed.

He continued to whisper to her as he pulled a blanket up over her, but she was already far, far away.

"Knellict will not be pleased if we fail in this," Canthan Dolittle said to Athrogate upon the dwarf's return to their small corner table in Muddy Boots and Bloody Blades.

"How many times ye meaning to tell me that, ye dolt?" asked the black-bearded dwarf.

"As many as it takes for you to truly appreciate that—"

Canthan sucked in his breath and held his tongue as Athrogate rose up over the edge of the table, planting both of his calloused hands firmly on the polished wood. The dwarf kept coming forward, leaning over so near to the studious man that the long braids of his beard and the gem-studded ties settled in Canthan's lap. Canthan could feel the heat and smell the stench of the dwarf's breath in his face.

"Knellict is—" Canthan started again.

"A mean son of a pig's arse," Athrogate finished for him. "Yeah, I'm knowin' it all too well, ye skinny dolt. Been the times when I've felt the sting of his crackling fingers, don't ye doubt."

"Then we must not forget."

"Forget?" Athrogate roared in his face.

Canthan blanched as all conversation around their table stopped. The dwarf, too, caught on to the volume of his complaint, and he glanced back over his shoulder to see several sets of curious eyes focusing on him.

"Bah, what're ye lookin' at, lest it be yer doom?" he barked at them. Athrogate held no small reputation for ferocity at the Vaasan Gate, having dominated the hunt for bounty ears for so many months, and having engaged in more than a dozen tavern brawls, all of which had left his opponents far more battered than he. The dwarf narrowed his eyes, accentuating his bushy eyebrows all the more, and gradually sank back into his chair. When the onlookers finally turned their attention elsewhere, Athrogate wheeled back on his partner. "I ain't for forgetting nothing," he assured Canthan.

"Forgive my petulance," said Canthan. "But please, my short and stout friend, never again forget that you are here as my subordinate."

The dwarf glowered at him.

"And I am Knellict's underling," Canthan went on, and this mention of the powerful, merciless archmage did calm Athrogate somewhat.

Canthan was indeed Knellict's man, and if Athrogate moved on Canthan, he'd be facing a very angry and very potent wizard in a short amount of time. Knellict had left the Fugue and gone back to the Citadel of Assassins, but Knellict could move as quickly as he could unexpectedly.

"We ain't to fail in this," the dwarf grumbled, coming back to the original point. "Been watching them two closely."

"They go out into Vaasa almost every day. Do you follow?"

The dwarf snorted and shook his head. "I ain't for meeting no stinking drow elf out there in the wilds," he explained. "I been watching them on their return. That's enough."

"And if they don't return?"

"Then they're dead in the bogs and all the better for us," Athrogate replied.

"They are making quite a reputation in short order," said Canthan. "Every day they come in with ears for bounty. They are outperforming much larger groups, by all reports, and indeed have long since surpassed the amount of coin handed out at the Vaasan Gate for bounty in so short a time—a performance until very recently pinnacled by yourself, I believe."

Athrogate grumbled under his breath.

"Very well, then, though I would have hoped that you would trail them through all their daily routines," said Canthan.

"Ye thinking they got contacts in the wastelands?"

"It remains a possibility. Perhaps the drow elves have risen form their Underdark holes to find a spot in Vaasa—they have been known to seize similar opportunities."

"Well, if that Jarlaxle fellow's got drow friends in Vaasa, then I'm not for going there." He fixed Canthan's surprised expression with a fierce scowl. "I'm tougher'n any drow elf alone," he growled, "but I'm not for fighting a bevy o' the damned tricksters!"

"Indeed."

Athrogate paused for a long time, letting that "indeed" sink in, trying to gauge if there was any sarcasm in the word or if it was honest acceptance and agreement.

"Besides," he said at length, "Hobart's boys been seeing them often, as've others. Rumors're sayin' that Jarlaxle's got himself a goblin scout what's leadin' him to good hunting grounds."

"That cannot sit well with Hobart," Canthan reasoned. "The Kneebreakers view goblins as vermin to be killed and nothing more."

"A lot o' them pair's not sitting well with Hobart of late, so I'm hearin'," Athrogate agreed. "Seems some o' them halflings're grumbling about the ears Entreri and Jarlaxle're bringing in. Seems them halflings lost a bunch o' their own earned ears."

"A pair of thieves? Interesting."

"It'd be a lot more interestin' and a lot easier to figure it all out if yer friends would get us some history on them two. They're a powerful pair—it can't be that they just up and started slaughterin' things. Got to be a trail."

"Knellict is fast on the trail of that information, do not doubt," said Canthan. "He is scouring the planes of existence themselves in search of answers to the dilemma of Artemis Entreri and this strange drow, Jarlaxle. We will have our answers."

"Be good to know how nasty we should make their deaths," grumbled the dwarf.

Canthan just clucked and let it go. Indeed, he suspected that Knellict would send him a message to do just that and be rid of the dangerous pair.

So be it.

⊷════⊶

Olgerkhan grunted and sucked in his breath as poor Arrayan tried to eat the soup he'd brought. Her hand shook so badly she spilled most of the steaming liquid back into the bowl long before the large spoon had come up level with her mouth. Again and again she tried, but by the time the spoon reached her mouth and she sipped, she could barely wet her lips.

Finally Olgerkhan stepped forward and took Arrayan's shaking hand.

"Let me help you," he offered.

"No, no," Arrayan said. She tried to pull her hand away but didn't have much strength behind it. Olgerkhan easily held on. "It is quite . . ."

"I am your friend," the large half-orc reminded her.

Arrayan started to argue, as the prideful woman almost always did when someone fretted over her, but she looked into Olgerkhan's eyes and her words were lost in her throat. Olgerkhan was not a handsome creature by any standards. He favored his orc heritage more than his human, with a mouth that sported twisted tusks and splotchy hair sprouting all about his head and face. He stood crooked, his right shoulder lower than his left, and farther forward. While his muscled, knotted limbs exuded strength, there was nothing supple or typically attractive about them.

But his eyes were a different matter, to Arrayan at least. She saw tenderness in those huge brown orbs, and a level of understanding well beyond Olgerkhan's rather limited intelligence. Olgerkhan might not be able to decipher mystical runes or solve complex equations, but he was not unwise and never unsympathetic.

Arrayan saw all of that, staring at her friend—and he truly was the best friend she had ever known.

Olgerkhan's huge hand slid down her forearm to her wrist and hand, and she let him ease the spoon from her. As much for her friend's benefit as for her own, Arrayan swallowed her pride and allowed Olgerkhan to feed her.

She felt better when he at last tipped the bowl to her mouth, letting her drink the last of its contents, but she was still very weak and overwhelmed. She tried to stand and surely would have fallen had not her friend grabbed her and secured her. Then he scooped her into his powerful arms and walked her to her bed, where he gently lay her down.

As soon as her head hit her soft pillow, Arrayan felt her consciousness slipping away. She noted a flash of alarm on her half-orc friend's face, and as blackness closed over her, she felt him shake her, gently but insistently, several times.

A moment later, she heard a thump, and somewhere deep inside she understood it to be her door closing. But that hardly mattered to Arrayan as the darkness enveloped her, taking her far, far away from the land of waking.

Olgerkhan's arms flailed wildly as he scrambled down the roads of Palishchuk, heading to one door then another, changing direction with every other step. Palishchuk was not a close-knit community; folk kept to themselves except in times of celebration or times of common danger. Olgerkhan didn't have many friends, and all but Arrayan, he realized, were out hunting that late-summer day.

He gyrated along, gradually making his way south. He banged on a couple more doors but no one answered, and it wasn't until he was halfway across town that he realized the reason. The sound of the carnival came to his ears. Wingham had opened for business.

Finding direction, Olgerkhan sprinted for the southern gate and to the wagon ring. He heard Wingham barking out the various attractions to be found and charged in the direction of his voice. Pushing through the crowd he inadvertently bumped into and nearly ran over poor Wingham. The only thing that kept the barker up was Olgerkhan's grasping hands.

Large guards moved for the pair, but Wingham, as his senses returned, waved them away.

"Tell me," he implored Olgerkhan.

"Arrayan," Olgerkhan gasped.

As he paused to catch his breath, the half-orc noticed the approach of a human—he knew at first glance that it was a full human, not a half-orc favoring the race. The man looked to be about forty, with fairly long brown hair that covered his ears and tickled his neck. He was lean but finely muscled and dressed in weathered, dirty garb that showed him to be no stranger to the Vaasan wilderness. His bright brown eyes, so striking against his ruddy complexion and thick dark hair, gave him away. Though Olgerkhan had not seen him in more than two years, he recognized the human.

Mariabronne, he was called, a ranger of great reputation in the Bloodstone Lands. In addition to his work at the Vaasan Gate, Mariabronne had spent the years since Gareth's rise and the fall of Zhengyi patrolling the Vaasan wilds and serving Palishchuk as a courier to the great gates and as a guide for the half-orc city's hunting parties.

"Arrayan?" Wingham pressed. He grabbed Olgerkhan's face and forced the gasping half-orc to look back at him.

"She's in bed," Olgerkhan explained. "She's sick."

"Sick?"

"Weak . . . shaking," the large half-orc explained.

"Sick or exhausted?" Wingham asked and began to nod.

Olgerkhan stared at him, confused, not knowing how to answer.

"She tried the magic," Mariabronne whispered at Wingham's side.

"She is not without magical protections," said Wingham.

"But this is Zhengyi's magic we are speaking of," said the ranger, and Wingham conceded the point with a nod.

"Bring us to her, Olgerkhan," Wingham said. "You did well in coming to us."

He shouted some orders at his compatriots, telling them to take over his barker's spot, and he, Mariabronne, and Olgerkhan rushed out from the wagon ring and back into Palishchuk.

CHAPTER

DREAMERS

7

Entreri rocked his chair up on two legs and leaned back against the wall. He sipped his wine as he watched the interaction between Jarlaxle and Commander Ellery. The woman had sought the drow out specifically, Entreri knew from her movements, though it was obvious to him that she was trying to appear as if she had not. She wasn't dressed in her armor, nor in any uniform of the Army of Bloodstone, and seemed quite the lady in her pink dress, subtly striped with silvery thread that shimmered with every step. A padded light gray vest completed the outfit, cut and tightly fitted to enhance her womanly charms. She carried no weapon—openly, at least—and it had taken Entreri a few minutes to even recognize her when first he'd spotted her among the milling crowd. Even on the field when she had arrived in full armor, dirty from the road, Entreri had thought her attractive, but now he could hardly pull his eyes from her.

When he realized the truth of his feelings it bothered him more than a little. When had he ever before been distracted by such things?

He studied her movements as she spoke to Jarlaxle, the way she leaned forward, the way her eyes widened, sparkling with interest. A smile, resigned and helpless, spread across the assassin's face and he briefly held out his glass in a secret toast to his dark elf companion.

"This chair and that chair free o' bums?" a gruff voice asked, and Entreri looked to the side to see a pair of dirty dwarves staring back at him.

"Well?" the other one asked, indicating one of the three empty chairs.

"Have the whole table," Entreri bade them.

He finished his drink with a gulp then slipped from his seat and moved away along the back wall. He took a roundabout route so as to not interrupt Jarlaxle's conversation.

<hr/>

"Well met to you, Comman—*Lady* Ellery," Jarlaxle said, and he tipped his glass of wine to her.

"And now you will claim that you didn't even recognize me, I expect."

"You underestimate the unique aspect of your eyes, good lady," said the drow. "In a full-face helm, I expect I would not miss that singular beauty."

Ellery started to respond but rocked back on her heels for just an instant.

Jarlaxle did well to mask his grin.

"There are questions I would ask of you," Ellery began, and her voice gained urgency when the drow turned away.

He spun right back, though, holding a second glass of wine he had apparently found waiting on the bar. He held it out to the woman, and she narrowed her eyes and glanced around suspiciously. How was it that the second glass of wine had been waiting there?

Yes, I knew you would come to me, Jarlaxle's smile clearly revealed when Ellery accepted the drink.

"Questions?" the drow prompted the obviously flabbergasted woman a few moments later.

Ellery tried to play it calm and collected, but she managed to dribble a bit of wine from the corner of her mouth and thought herself quite the clod while wiping it.

"I have never met a dark elf before, though I have seen a pair from afar and have heard tales of a half-drow making a reputation for herself in Damara."

"We do have a way of doing that, for good or for ill."

"I have heard many tales, though," Ellery blurted.

"Ah, and you are intrigued by the reputation of my dark race?"

She studied him carefully, her eyes roaming from his head to his feet and back up again. "You do not appear so formidable."

"Perhaps that is the greatest advantage of all."

"Are you a warrior or a wizard?"

"Of course," the drow said as he took another sip.

The woman's face crinkled for a brief moment. "It is said that drow are masters of the arts martial," she said after she recovered. "It is said that only the finest elf warriors could do individual battle against the likes of a drow."

"I expect that no elves who sought to prove such a theory are alive to confirm or deny."

Ellery's quick smile in response clued Jarlaxle in to the fact that she was catching on to his wit—a manner that was always a bit too dry and unrelenting for most surface dwellers.

"Is that a confirmation or a boast?" she asked.

"It just is."

A wicked smile grew on the woman's face. "Then I say again, you do not look so formidable."

"Is that an honest observation or a challenge?"

"It just is."

Jarlaxle held out his glass and Ellery tapped hers against it. "Some day, perhaps, you will happen upon me in Vaasa and have your answer," Jarlaxle said. "My friend and I have found some success in our hunts out there."

"I have noted your trophies," she said, and again her eyes scanned the drow head to toe.

Jarlaxle laughed aloud. He quieted quickly, though, under the intensity of Ellery's stare, her bright eyes boring into his.

"Questions?" he asked.

"Many," she answered, "but not here. Do you think that your friend will be well enough without you?"

As she asked, both she and Jarlaxle turned to the table in the back corner, where the drow had left Entreri, only to find that he was gone.

When they looked back at each other, Jarlaxle shrugged and said, "Answers."

They left the bustle of Muddy Boots and Bloody Blades behind, Jarlaxle following the woman as she easily navigated the myriad corridors and hallways of the wall complex. They moved down one side passage and crossed through the room where monster ears were exchanged for bounty. Moving toward the door at the rear of the chamber gave the drow an angle to see behind the desks, and he spotted a small chest.

He made a note of that one.

The door led the pair into another corridor. A right turn at a four-way intersection led them to another door.

Ellery casually fished a key out of a small belt pouch, and Jarlaxle watched her curiously, his senses more acutely attuning to his surroundings. Had the warrior woman planned their encounter from the beginning?

"A long way to walk for the answers to a few questions," he remarked, but Ellery just glanced back at him, smiling.

She grabbed a nearby torch and took it with her into the next chamber, moving along the wall to light several others.

Jarlaxle's smile widened along with his curiosity as he came to recognize the purpose of the room. Dummies stood silently around the perimeter and archery targets lined the far wall. Several racks were set here and there, all sporting wooden replicas of various weapons.

Ellery moved to one such rack and drew forth a wooden long sword. She studied it for a moment then tossed it to Jarlaxle, who caught it in one hand and sent it into an easy swing.

Ellery drew out a second blade and lifted a wooden shield.

"No such shield for me?" the drow asked.

With a giggle, Ellery tossed the second sword his way. "I have heard that your race favors a two-bladed fighting style."

Jarlaxle caught the tossed blade with the edge of the first wooden sword, breaking its fall, balancing it, then sending it into a controlled spin.

"Some do," he replied. "Some are quite adept with long blades of equal length."

A flick of his wrist sent the second sword spinning skyward, and the drow immediately disregarded it, looking over at Ellery, placing his remaining sword tip down on the floor, tucking one foot behind his other ankle and assuming a casual pose on the planted blade.

"Myself, I prefer variety," he added with more than a little suggestion in his tone.

As he finished, he caught the dropping second blade in his free hand.

Ellery eyed him cautiously, then led his gaze to the weapons' rack. "Is there another you'd prefer?"

"Prefer? For?"

The woman's eyes narrowed. She strapped the shield onto her left arm, then reached over and drew a wooden battle-axe from the rack.

"My dear Lady Ellery," said Jarlaxle, "are you challenging me?"

"I have heard so many tales of the battle prowess of your race," she replied. "I will know."

Jarlaxle laughed aloud. "Ah yes, answers."

"Answers," Ellery echoed.

"You presume much," said the drow, and he stepped back and lifted the two blades before him, testing their weight and balance. He sent them into a quick routine, spinning one blade over the other, then quick-thrusting the second. He retracted the blades immediately, bringing them to rest at his side. "What interest would I have in doing battle with you?"

Ellery let the axe swing easily at the end of her arm. "Are you not curious?" she asked.

"About what? I have already seen far too many human warriors, male and female." He sent one of the wooden swords in a spin again, then paused and offered a coy glance at Ellery. "And I am not impressed."

"Perhaps I can change your mind."

"Doubtful."

"Do you fear to know the truth?"

"Fear has nothing to do with it. You brought me here to satisfy your curiosity, not mine. You ask of me that I reveal something of myself to you, for your sake. You will reveal your battle prowess at the reward of satisfying your curiosity. For me, there is . . . ?"

Ellery straightened and stared at him sourly.

"The chance to win," she said a moment later.

"Winning means little," said the drow. "Pride is a weakness, don't you know?"

"Jarlaxle does not like to win?"

"Jarlaxle likes to survive," the drow replied without hesitation. "That is not so subtle a difference."

"Then what?" Ellery asked, impatience settling into her tone.

"What?"

"What is your price?" she demanded.

"Are you so desperate to know?"

She stared at him hard.

"A lady of your obvious charms should not have to ask such a question," the drow said.

Ellery didn't flinch. "Only if you win."

Jarlaxle cocked his head to the side and let his eyes roam the woman's body. "When I win, you will take me to your bedchamber?"

"You will not win."

"But if I do?"

"If that is your price."

Jarlaxle chuckled. "Pride is a weakness, my lady, but curiosity . . ."

Ellery stopped him by banging the axe hard against her shield.

"You talk too much," she said as she strode forward.

She lifted her axe back over her shoulder, and when Jarlaxle settled into a defensive stance, she charged in.

She pumped her arm as if to strike but stepped ahead more forcefully with her opposite foot and shield-rushed instead, battering at the drow's weapons left to right. She started to step in behind that momentum, the usual move, but then pivoted instead, spinning around backward and dropping low. She let her weapon arm out wide, axe level and low as she came around.

Had he expected the move, Jarlaxle could have easily stepped in behind the shield and stabbed her.

But he hadn't expected it, and he knew as Ellery came around, forcing him to leap the sailing axe, that the woman had judged his posture perfectly. He had underestimated her, and she knew it.

Jarlaxle fell back as Ellery came up fast and pressed the attack, chopping her axe in a more straightforward manner. He tried to counter, thrusting his right sword out first, then his left, but the woman easily blocked the first with her shield and deftly parried the second out wide on one downswing with her axe.

Jarlaxle snapped his right hand across, however, batting the side of that axe hard, then rolled his left hand in and over, again smacking the same side of the axe. He did a quick drum roll on the weapon, nearly tearing it from Ellery's hand and forcing it out wider with every beat.

But Ellery reacted properly, rolling her shield shoulder in tight and bulling ahead to force too much of a clench for Jarlaxle to disarm her.

"If I win, I will have you," the drow said.

Ellery growled and shoved out hard with her shield, driving him away.

"And what will Ellery claim if she wins?" Jarlaxle asked.

That stopped the woman even as she began to charge in once more. She settled back on her heels and peered at the drow from over the top of her shield.

"If I win," she began and paused for effect then added, *"I* will have *you."*

Jarlaxle's jaw might have hit the floor, except that Ellery's shield would surely have caught it, for the woman used the moment of distraction to launch another aggressive charge, barreling in, shield butting and axe slashing. It took every bit of Jarlaxle's speed and agility for him to keep away from that axe, and he only managed it by rolling to the side and allowing Ellery to connect with the shield rush. The drow used the momentum to get away, throwing himself back and into a roll. He came lightly to his feet and side-stepped fast, twisting as he went to avoid a wild slash by the woman.

"Ah, but you cheat!" he cried and he kept backing, putting considerable ground between the two. "My good lady, you steal all of my incentive. Should I not just drop my weapons and surrender?"

"Then if I win, I deny you!" she cried, and she charged.

Jarlaxle shrugged, and whispered, "Then you will not win."

The drow dodged left, then fast back to the right as Ellery tried to compensate, and though she tried to maintain her initiative, she found herself suddenly barraged by a dizzying array of thrusts, slashes, and quick, short stabs. At one point, Jarlaxle even somehow moved his feet out in front and dropped to the floor, sweeping her legs out. She didn't fall directly but stumbled, twisting and turning.

It was futile, though, for she went down to the floor.

Her agility served her well then, as she rolled to the side and got up to one knee in time to intercept the drow's expected charge. She parried and blocked the first wave of attacks, and even managed to work her way back to a standing position.

Jarlaxle pressed the attack, his blades coming at her from a dizzying array of angles. She worked her arms furiously, positioning her shield, turning her axe, and she dodged and backed, twisting to avoid those cunning strikes that managed to slip through her defenses. On a couple of occasions, the woman saw an opening and could have pressed the attack back the other way.

But she didn't.

She played pure defense and showed the drow a series of apparent openings, only to close them fast as Jarlaxle tried to press in. At one point, her defense was so quick that the drow overbalanced and his great hat slipped down over his eyes. For just a moment, though, for he swept one hand up, pulled the hat from his head and tossed it aside. Beads of perspiration marked his bald head.

He laughed and came on hard again, pressing the attack until he had Ellery in full flight away from him.

"You are young, but you fight like a drow veteran," Jarlaxle congratulated after yet another unsuccessful attack routine.

"I am not so young."

"You have not seen thirty winters," the drow protested.

The grin that creased Ellery's wide face made her look even younger. "I spent my childhood under the shadow of the Witch-King," she explained. "Bloodstone Village knew war continually from the Vaasan hordes. No child there was a stranger to the blade."

"You were taught well," Jarlaxle said.

He straightened and brought one sword up in salute.

Not ready to let such an obvious opening pass, Ellery leaped ahead, axe swinging wildly.

Halfway into that swing, she realized that she had been baited, and so she laughed helplessly as she saw her target easily spinning to the side. Her laugh became a yelp when the flat of Jarlaxle's wooden sword slapped hard against her rump.

She started to whirl around to face him, but he was too quick, and she got slapped hard again, and a third time before the drow finally disengaged and leaped back.

"By all measures, that should be scored as a victory," Jarlaxle argued. "For if my blades were real, I could have hamstrung you thrice over."

"Your blows were a bit high for that."

"Only because I did not wish to sting your legs," he answered, and he arched his eyebrow suggestively.

"You have plans for them?"

"Of course."

"If you are so eager then you should let me win. I promise, you would find it more enjoyable."

"You said you would deny me."

"I have changed my mind."

Jarlaxle straightened at that, his swords coming down to his sides. He looked at her, smiled, shrugged, and dropped his blades.

Ellery howled and leaped forward.

But the drow had planned his disarmament carefully and precisely, dropping the swords from on low so that they fell perfectly across his feet. A quick hop and leg tuck sent both swords flying back to his hands, and he landed in a spin, blades swiping across to slap hard at Ellery's axe. Jarlaxle rolled in right behind the stumbling woman's outstretched arms, and right behind the stumbling woman, catching her from behind and with one arm wrapped around, his sword tight against her throat.

"I prefer to lead," he whispered into her ear.

The drow could feel her shivering under the heat of his breath, and he had a marvelous view of her breasts heaving from the exertion of the fight.

Ellery slumped, her axe falling to the floor. She reached across, unstrapped her shield, and tossed it aside.

Jarlaxle inhaled deeply, taking in her scent.

She turned and grabbed at him hard, pressing her lips against his. She would only let him lead so far, it seemed.

Jarlaxle wasn't about to complain.

———※———

Entreri didn't know if he was supposed to be walking so freely through the corridors of the Vaasan Gate, but no guards presented themselves to block his progress. He had no destination in mind; he simply needed to walk off his restlessness. He was tired, but no bed could lure him in, for he knew that no bed of late had offered him any real rest.

So he walked, and the minutes rolled on and on. When he found a side alcove set with a tall ladder, he let his curiosity guide him and climbed. More corridors, empty rooms, and stairwells greeted him above and he kept on his meandering way through the dark halls of this massive fortress. Another ladder took him to a small landing and a door, loose-fitting and facing east, with light glowing around its edges. Curious, Entreri pushed it open.

He felt the wind on his face as he stared into the first rays of dawn, reaching out from the Vaasan plain and crawling over the valleys and peaks of the Galenas, lighting brilliant reflections on the mountain snow.

The sun stung Entreri's tired eyes as he walked out and along the parapet of the Vaasan Gate. He paused often, stood and stared, and cared not for the passage of time. The wall top was more than twenty feet wide at its narrowest points and swelled to more than twice that width in some spots, and from there Entreri truly came to appreciate the scope of the enormous construction. Several towers dotted the length of the wall stretching out before the assassin to the east, and he noted the occasional sentry, leaning or sitting. Still with no indication that he should not be there, he walked out of the landing and along the top of the great wall, some forty or fifty feet above the wasteland stretching out to the north. His eyes remained in that direction primarily, rarely glancing south to the long valley running between the majestic Galenas. He could see the tents of the Fugue, even his own, and he wondered if Jarlaxle had gone back there but thought it more likely that Ellery had offered him a more comfortable setting.

The curious couple did not remain in his thoughts any more than did the southland. The north held his attention and his eyes, where Vaasa stretched out before him like a flattened, rotting corpse. He veered that way in his stroll, moving nearer to the waist-high wall along the edge so that he could better take in the view of Vaasa awakening to the dawn's light.

There was a beauty there, Entreri saw, primal and cold: hard-edged stones, sharp-tipped skeletons of long dead trees, and the soft, sucking bogs. Blasted by war, torn by the march of armies, scalded by the fires of wizard spells and dragon breath, the land itself, the soul of Vaasa, had survived. It had taken all the hits and blasts and stomping boots and had come out much as it had been before.

So many of those who had lived there had perished, but Vaasa had survived.

Entreri passed a sentry, sitting half asleep and with his back against the northern wall. The man looked at him with mild curiosity then nodded as the assassin strode past him.

Some distance away, Entreri stopped his walk and turned fully to survey the north, resting his hands on the waist-high wall that ran the length of the gate. He looked upon Vaasa with a mixture of affection and self-loathing—as if he was looking into a mirror.

"They think you dead," he whispered, "because they do not see the life that teems beneath your bogs and stones, and in every cave, crack, and hollow log. They think they know you, but they do not."

"Talking to the land?" came a familiar voice, and Entreri found his moment of contemplation stolen away by the approach of Jarlaxle. "Do you think it hears you?"

Entreri considered his friend for a moment, the bounce in his gait, the bit of moisture just below the brim of his great hat, the look of quiet serenity behind his typically animated expression. Something more was out of place, Entreri realized, before it even fully registered to him that Jarlaxle's eye patch had been over the other eye back in the tavern.

Entreri could guess easily enough the route that had at last taken Jarlaxle to the wall top, and only then did the assassin truly appreciate that several hours had passed since he had left his friend in Muddy Boots and Bloody Blades.

"I think there are some who would do well to hear me less," he answered, and turned his eyes back to Vaasa.

Jarlaxle laughed and moved right beside him on the wall, leaning on the rail with his back to the northern land.

"Please do not let my arrival here disturb your conversation," said the drow.

Entreri didn't reply, didn't even look at him.

"Embarrassed?"

That did elicit a dismissive glance.

"You have not slept," Jarlaxle remarked.

"My sleep is not your concern."

"Sleep?" came the sarcastic response. "Is that what you would call your hours of restlessness each night?"

"My sleep is not your concern," Entreri said again.

"Your lack of sleep is," the drow corrected. "If the reflexes slow. . . ."

"Would you like a demonstration?"

Jarlaxle yawned, drawing another less-than-friendly glare. The drow returned it with a smile—one that was lost on Entreri, who again stared out over the muddy Vaasan plane. Jarlaxle, too, turned and leaned to the north, taking in the preternatural scene. The morning fog swirled in gray eddies in some places, and lifted up like a waking giant in others.

Indeed, Vaasa did seem as if a remnant of the time before the reasoning races inhabited the world. It seemed a remnant of a time, perhaps, before any creatures walked the lands at all, as if the rest of the world had moved along without carrying Vaasa with her.

"A forgotten land," Jarlaxle remarked, glancing at Entreri.

The assassin returned that look, even nodded a bit, and the drow was surprised to realize that Entreri had understood his reference exactly.

"What do you see when you look out there?" Jarlaxle asked. "Wasted potential? Barrenness where there should be fertility? Death where there should be life?"

"Reality," Artemis Entreri answered with cold finality.

He turned and offered one stern look to the drow then walked past him.

Jarlaxle heard the uncertainty in Entreri's voice, sensed that the man was off-balance. And he knew the source of that imbalance, for he had played no small part in ensuring that Idalia's flute had found its way into Artemis Entreri's hand.

He stayed at the rail for some time, soaking in the scene before him, remembering the night just passed, and considering his always dour friend.

Most of all, the dark elf wondered what he might do to dominate the first, recreate the second, and alter the third.

Always wondering, always thinking.

CHAPTER
8

Arrayan had to pause and consider the question for a long while before answering. Where had she left the book? The woman felt the fool, to be sure. How could she have let something that powerful out of her sight? How could she not even remember where she'd placed it? Her mind traced back to the previous night, when she had dared start reading the tome. She remembered casting every defensive spell she knew, creating intricate wards and protections against the potentially devastating magic Zhengyi had placed on the book.

She looked back at the table in the center of the room, and she knew that she had cracked open the book right there.

A sense of vastness flooded her memories, a feeling of size, of magic, and a physical construct too large to be contained within.

"I took it out," she said, turning back to Wingham and Mariabronne. "Out of here."

"You left it somewhere beyond your control?" Wingham scolded, his voice incredulous. He leaped up from his seat, as if his body was simply too agitated to be contained in a chair. "An item of that power?"

Mariabronne put a hand on Wingham's arm to try to calm him. "The book is out of the house," he said to Arrayan. "Somewhere in Palishchuk?"

Arrayan considered the question, trying desperately to scour her memories. She glanced over at Olgerkhan, needing his always rock-solid support.

"No," she answered, but it was more a feeling than a certainty. "Out of the city. The city was . . . too small."

Wingham slipped back into his seat and for a moment seemed to be gasping for breath. "Too small? What did you create?"

Arrayan could only stare at him. She remembered leaving the house with the book tucked under her arm, but only vaguely, as if she were walking within a dream. Had it been a dream?

"Have you left the house since your return from your journey with the book?" Mariabronne asked.

The woman shook her head.

"Any sense of where you went?" the ranger pressed. "North? South near Wingham's caravan?"

"Not to Uncle Wingham," Arrayan replied without pause.

Wingham and Mariabronne looked at each other.

"Palishchuk only has two gates open most of the time," Mariabronne said. "South and north."

"If not south, then. . . ." said Wingham.

Mariabronne was first to stand, motioning for the others to follow. Olgerkhan moved immediately to Arrayan's side, offering her a shawl to protect her from the chilly wind in her weakened form.

"How could I have been so foolish?" the woman whispered to the large half-orc, but Olgerkhan could only smile at her, having no practical answers.

"The book's magic was beyond your control, perhaps," Mariabronne replied. "I have heard of such things before. Even the great Kane, for all his discipline and strength of will, was nearly destroyed by the Wand of Orcus."

"The wand was a god's artifact," Arrayan reminded him.

"Do not underestimate the power of Zhengyi," said Mariabronne. "No god was he, perhaps, but certainly no mortal either." He paused and looked into the troubled woman's eyes. "Fear not," he said. "We'll find the book and all will be put right."

The city was quiet that late afternoon, with most of the folk still off in the south at Wingham's circus. The quartet saw almost no one as they made their way to the north gate. Once there, Mariabronne bent low before Arrayan and bade her to lift one foot. He inspected her boot then studied the print she'd just made. He motioned for the others to hold and went to the gate then began poking around, studying the tracks on the muddy ground.

"You left and returned along the same path," he informed Arrayan. The ranger pointed to the northeast, toward the nearest shadows of the Great Glacier, the towering frozen river that loomed before them. "Few others have come through this gate in the last couple of days. It should not be difficult to follow your trail."

Indeed it wasn't, for just outside the area of the gate, Arrayan's footprints, both sets, stood out alone on the summer-melted tundra. What was surprising for Mariabronne and all the others, though, was how far from the city Arrayan's trail took them. The Great Glacier loomed larger and larger before them as they trudged to the northeast, and more directly north. The city receded behind them and night descended, bringing with it a colder bite to the wind. The air promised that the summer, like all the summers before it so far north, would be a short one, soon to end. An abrupt change in the weather would freeze the ground in a matter of days. After that, the earth would be held solid for three quarters of the year or more. It was not unknown for the summer thaw to last less than a single month.

"It's no wonder you were so weary," Wingham said to Arrayan some time later, the miles behind them.

The woman could only look back at him, helpless. She had no idea she'd been so far from the city and could only barely remember leaving her house.

The foursome came up on a ridge, looking down on a wide vale, a copse of trees at its low point down the hill before them and a grouping of several large stones off to the right.

Arrayan gasped, "There!"

She pointed, indicating the stones, the memory of the place flooding back to her.

Mariabronne, using a torch so he could see the tracks, was about to indicate the same direction.

"No one else has come out," the ranger confirmed. "Let us go and collect the book that I might bring it to King Gareth."

Arrayan and Olgerkhan caught the quick flash of shock on Wingham's face at that proclamation, but to his credit, the shrewd merchant didn't press the issue just then.

Mariabronne, torch in hand, was first to move around the closest, large boulder. The others nearly walked into his back when they, too, moved around the corner only to discover that the ranger had stopped. As they shuffled to his side to take in the view before him, they quickly came to understand.

For there was Zhengyi's book, suspended in the air at about waist height by a pair of stone-gray tentacles that rolled out from its sides and down to, and into, the ground. The book was open, with only a few pages turned. The foursome watched in blank amazement as red images of various magical runes floated up from the open page and dissipated in the shimmering air above the book.

"What have you done?" Wingham asked.

Mariabronne cautiously approached.

"The book is reading itself," Olgerkhan observed, and while the statement sounded ridiculous as it was uttered, another glance at the book seemed to back up the simple half-orc's plain-spoken observation.

"What is that?" Wingham asked as Mariabronne's torchlight extended farther back behind the book, revealing a line of squared gray stone poking through the tundra.

"Foundation stones," Arrayan answered.

The four exchanged nervous glances, then jumped as a spectral hand appeared in mid-air above the opened book and slowly turned a single page.

"The book is excising its own dweomers," Arrayan said. "It is enacting the magic Zhengyi placed within its pages."

"You were but a catalyst," Wingham added, nodding his head as if it was all starting to make sense to him. "It took from you a bit of your life-force and now it is using that to facilitate Zhengyi's plans."

"What plans?" asked Olgerkhan.

"The magic was in the school of creation," Arrayan replied.

"And it is creating a structure," said Mariabronne as he moved the length of the foundation stones. "Something large and formidable."

"Castle Perilous," muttered Wingham, and all three looked at him with great alarm, for that was a name not yet far enough removed from the consciousness of the region for any to comfortably hear.

"We do not yet know anything of the sort," Mariabronne reminded him. "Only that the book is creating a structure. Such artifacts are not unknown. You have heard of the work of Doern, of course?"

Arrayan nodded. The legendary wizard Doern had long ago perfected a method of creating minor extra-dimensional towers adventurers could summon to shield them from the dangers and hardships of the open road.

"It is possible that Zhengyi created this tome, perhaps with others like it, so that his commanders could construct defensible fortresses without the need of muscle, tools, supplies, and time," Mariabronne reasoned, edging ever closer to the fascinating book. "It could be, Wingham, that your niece Arrayan has done nothing more than build herself a new and impressive home."

Wingham, too, moved to the book, and from up close the rising, dissipating runes showed all the more clearly. Individual, recognizable characters became visible. Wingham started to wave his hand over the field of power above the opened book.

What little hair the old half-orc had stood on end and he gave a yelp then went flying back and to the ground. The other three were there in a moment, Arrayan helping him to sit up.

"It seems that Zhengyi's book will protect itself," Mariabronne remarked.

"Protect itself while it does what?" Wingham asked, his teeth chattering from the jolt.

All four exchanged concerned glances.

"I think it is time for me to ride to the Vaasan Gate," Mariabronne said.

"Past time," Arrayan agreed.

Mariabronne and Wingham dropped Arrayan and Olgerkhan at the woman's house then went to the south gate of Palishchuk and to Wingham's wagons beyond.

"My horse is stabled in the city," Mariabronne protested repeatedly, but Wingham kept waving the thought and the words away.

"Just follow," he instructed. "To all our benefit."

When they arrived at Wingham's wagon, the old half-orc rushed inside, returning almost immediately with a small pouch.

"An obsidian steed," he explained, reaching into the leather bag and pulling forth a small obsidian figurine depicting an almost skeletal horse with wide, flaring nostrils. "It summons a nightmare that will run tirelessly—well, at least until the magic runs out, but that should be long after the beast has taken you to the Vaasan Gate."

"A nightmare?" came the cautious response. "A creature of the lower planes?"

"Yes, yes, of course, but one controlled by the magic of the stone. You will be safe enough, mighty ranger."

Mariabronne gingerly took the stone and cradled it in his hands.

"Just say 'Blackfire,' " Wingham told him.

"Blackfi—" Mariabronne started to reply, but Wingham cut him short by placing a finger over his lips.

"Speak it not while you hold the stone, unless you are ready to be ridden yourself," the half-orc said with a chuckle. "And please, do not summon the hellish mount here in my camp. I do so hate when it chases the buyers away."

"And eats more than a few, I am sure."

"Temperamental beast," Wingham confirmed.

Mariabronne tapped his brow in salute and started away, but Wingham grabbed him by the arm.

"Discretion, I beg," the old half-orc pleaded.

Mariabronne stared at him for a long while. "To diminish Arrayan's involvement?"

"She began it," Wingham said, and he glanced back toward the city as if Arrayan was still in sight. "Perhaps she is feeding it with her very life-force. The good of all might weigh darkly on the poor girl, and she is without fault in this."

Again Mariabronne paused a bit to study his friend. "The easy win, at the cost of her life?" he asked, and before Wingham could answer, he added, "Zhengyi's trials have often proved a moral dilemma to us all. Mayhaps we could defeat this construct, and easily so, but at the cost of an innocent."

"And the cost of our own souls for making that sacrifice," said Wingham.

Mariabronne offered a comforting smile and nodded his agreement. "I will return quickly," he promised.

Wingham glanced back to the north again, as if expecting to see a gigantic castle looming over the northern wall of the city.

"That would be wise," he whispered.

Just south of Wingham's wagon circle, Mariabronne lifted the obsidian steed in both his cupped hands. "Blackfire," he whispered as he placed the figurine on the ground, and he nearly shouted as the stone erupted in dancing black and purple flames. Before he could react enough to fall back from the flames, though, he realized that they weren't burning his flesh.

The flames flared higher. Mariabronne watched, mesmerized.

They leaped to greater proportions, whipping about in the evening breeze, and gradually taking the form of a horse, a life-sized replica of the figurine. Then the fires blew away, lifting into the air in a great ball that puffed out to nothingness, leaving behind what seemed to be a smoking horse. The indistinct edges of wispy smoke dissipated, and a more solid creature stood before the ranger, its red eyes glaring at him with hate, puffs of acrid smoke erupting from its flared nostrils, and gouts of black flame exploding from its hooves as it pawed at the ground.

"Blackfire," Mariabronne said with a deep exhale, and he worked very hard to calm himself.

He reminded himself of the urgency of his mission, and he moved slowly and deliberately, fully on guard and with his hand on the pommel of Bayurel, his renowned bastard sword, a solid, thick blade enchanted with a special hatred for giantkin.

Mariabronne swallowed hard when he came astride the nightmare. He gingerly reached up for the creature's mane, which itself seemed as if it was nothing more than living black fire. He grabbed tightly when he felt its solidity, and with one fluid move, launched himself upon the nightmare's back. Blackfire wasted no time in rearing and snorting fire, but Mariabronne was no novice to riding, and he held firm his seat.

Soon he was galloping the fiery steed hard to the south, the shadows of the Galenas bordering him on his left, the city of Palishchuk and the Great Glacier fast receding behind him. It was normally a five-day journey, but the nightmare didn't need to rest, didn't let up galloping at all. Miles rolled out behind the ranger. He took no heed of threats off to the side of the trail—a goblin campfire or the rumble of a tundra yeti—but just put his head down and let the nightmare speed him past.

After several hours, Mariabronne's arms and legs ached from the strain, but all he had to do was conjure an image of that magical book and the structure it was growing, all he had to do was imagine the danger that creation of the Witch-King might present, to push past his pain and hold fast his seat.

He found that Wingham's estimation was a bit optimistic, however, for he felt the weakening of the magic in his mount as the eastern sky began to brighten with the onset of dawn. No stranger to the wilderness, Mariabronne pulled up in his ride and scanned the area about him, quickly discerning some promising spots for him to set a camp. Almost as soon as he dismounted, the nightmare became a wavering black flame then disappeared entirely.

Mariabronne took the obsidian figurine from the ground and felt its weight in his hand. It seemed lighter to him, drained of substance, but even as he stood there pondering it, he felt a slight shift as the weight increased and its magic began to gather. In that way the figurine would tell him when he could call upon its powers again.

The ranger reconnoitered the area, enjoyed a meal of dried bread and salted meat then settled in for some much needed sleep.

He awoke soon after mid-day and immediately went to the figurine. It was not yet fully recovered, he recognized, but he understood implicitly that he could indeed summon the nightmare if he so desired. He stepped back and surveyed the area more carefully under the full light of day. He glanced both north and south, measuring his progress. He had covered nearly half the ground to the Vaasan gate in a single night's ride—thrice the distance he could have expected with a living horse on the difficult broken ground, even if he had been riding during the daylight hours.

Mariabronne nodded, glanced at the figurine, and replaced it in his pouch. He resisted the stubborn resolve to begin hiking toward the Vaasan Gate and instead forced himself to rest some more, to take a second meal, and to go through a regimen of gently stretching and preparing his muscles for another night's long ride. Before the last rays of day disappeared behind the Vaasan plain in the west, the ranger was back upon the hellish steed, charging hard to the south.

He made the great fortress, again without incident, just before the next dawn.

Recognized and always applauded by the guards of the Army of Bloodstone, Mariabronne found himself sharing breakfast with the Honorable General Dannaway Bridgestone Tranth, brother of the great Baron Tranth who had stood beside Gareth in the war with the Witch-King. Rising more on his family's reputation than through any deed, Dannaway served as both military commander and mayor of the eclectic community of the Vaasan Gate and the Fugue.

Normally haughty and superior-minded, Dannaway carried no such pretensions in his conversations with Mariabronne the Rover. The ranger's fame had more than made him worthy to eat breakfast with the Honorable General, so Dannaway believed, and that was a place of honor that Dannaway reserved for very few people.

For his part, and though he never understood the need of more than a single eating utensil, Mariabronne knew how to play the game of royalty. The renowned warrior, often called the Tamer of Vaasa, had oft dined with King Gareth and Lady Christine at their grand Court in Bloodstone Village and at the second palace in Heliogabalus. He had never been fond of the pretension and the elevation of class, but he understood the practicality, even necessity, of such stratification in a region so long battered by conflict.

He also understood that his exploits had put him in position to continue to better the region, as with this very moment, as he recounted the happenings in Palishchuk to the plump and aging Honorable General. Soon after he had begun offering the details, Dannaway summoned his niece, Commander Ellery, to join them.

Dannaway gave a great, resigned sigh, a dramatic flourish, as Mariabronne finished his tale.

"The curse of Zhengyi will linger on throughout my lifetime and those of my children, and those of their children, I do fear," he said. "These annoyances are not uncommon, it seems."

"Let us pray that it is no more than an annoyance," said Mariabronne.

"We have trod this path many times before," Dannaway reminded him, and if the general was at all concerned, he did not show it. "Need I remind you of the grand dragon statue that grew to enormous proportions in the bog north of Darmshall, and . . .what? Sank into the bog, I believe.

"And let us not forget the gem-studded belt discovered by that poor young man on the northern slopes of the Galenas," Dannaway went on. "Yes, how was he to know that the plain gray stone he found the belt wrapped around, and carelessly threw aside after strapping on the belt, was actually the magical trigger for the twenty-five fireball-enchanted rubies set into the belt? Were it not for the witnesses—his fellow adventurers watching him from a nearby ridge—we might never have known the truth of that Zhengyian relic. There really wasn't enough left of the poor man to identify."

"There really wasn't anything left of the man at all," Ellery added.

A mixture of emotions engulfed Mariabronne as he listened to Dannaway's recounting. He didn't want to minimize the potential danger growing just north of Palishchuk, but on the other hand he was somewhat relieved to recall these other incidents of Zhengyian leftovers, tragic though several had been. For none of the many incidents had foretold doom on any great scale, a return of Zhengyi or the darkness that had covered the Bloodstone Lands until only eleven years ago.

"This is no minor enchantment, nor is it anything that will long remain unnoticed, I fear. King Gareth must react, and quickly," the ranger said.

Dannaway heaved another overly dramatic sigh, cast a plaintive look at Ellery, and said, "Assemble a company to ride with Mariabronne back to Palishchuk."

"Soldiers alone?" the woman replied, not a hint of fear or doubt in her strong, steady voice.

"As you wish," the general said.

Ellery nodded and looked across at the ranger with undisguised curiosity. "Perhaps I will accompany you personally," she said, drawing a look of surprise from her uncle. "It has been far too long since I have looked upon Palishchuk, in any case, nor have I visited Wingham's troupe in more than a year."

"I would welcome your company, Commander," Mariabronne replied, "but I would ask for more support."

Dannaway cut in, "You do not believe I would allow the Commander of the Vaasan Gate Militia to travel to the shadows of the Great Glacier alone, do you?"

Mariabronne fell back as if wounded, though of course it was all a game.

"The Rover," Dannaway said slyly. "It is not a title easily earned, and you have earned it ten times over by all accounts."

"Honorable General, Mariabronne's reputation . . ." Ellery started to intervene, apparently not catching on to the joke.

Dannaway stopped her with an upraised hand. "The Rover," he said again. "It is the title of a rake, though an honorable one. But that is not my concern, my dear Ellery. I do not fear for you in Mariabronne's bed, nor in the bed of any man. You are a Paladin of Bloodstone, after all.

"Nay, the Rover is also a remark on the nature of this adventurer," Dannaway went on, obviously missing Ellery's sour expression. "Mariabronne is the scout who walks into a dragon's lair to satisfy his curiosity. King Gareth would have used young Mariabronne to seek out Zhengyi, no doubt, except that the fool would have strolled right up to Zhengyi and asked him his name for confirmation. Fearless to the point of foolish, Mariabronne?"

"Lack of confidence is not a trait I favor."

Dannaway laughed raucously at that then turned to Ellery. "Bring a small but powerful contingent with you, I beg. There are many dragon lairs rumored in the Palishchuk region."

Ellery looked at him long and hard for a time, as if trying to make sense of it all.

"I have several in mind, soldiers and otherwise," she said, and Mariabronne nodded his satisfaction.

With another grin and bow to Dannaway, he took his leave so that he could rest up for the ride back to the north. He settled in to the complimentary room that was always waiting for him off the hallway that housed the garrison's commanders. He fell asleep hoping that Dannaway's casual attitude toward the construct was well-warranted.

He slept uneasily though, for in his heart, Mariabronne suspected that this time the remnant of Zhengyi might be something more.

You are a Paladin of Bloodstone, after all.

Ellery couldn't prevent a wince from tightening her features at that remark, for it was not yet true—and might never be, she knew, though many others, like Dannaway, apparently did not. Many in her family and among the nobles awaited the day when she would demonstrate her first miracle, laying on hands to heal the wounded, perhaps. None of them doubted it would happen soon, for the woman held a sterling reputation and was descended from a long line of such holy warriors.

Ellery's other friends, of course, knew better.

Well away from the general, she moved from foot to foot, betraying her nervousness.

"I can defeat him if need be," she told the thin man standing in the shadow of the wall's angular jag. "I have taken the measure of his skill and he is as formidable as you feared."

"Yet you believe you can kill him?"

"Have you not trained me in exactly that art?" the woman replied. "One strike, fatal? One move, unstoppable?"

"He is superior," came the thin voice of the thin man, a scratching and wheezing sound, but strangely solid in its confident and deathly even tone.

Ellery nodded and admitted, "Few would stand against him for long, true."

"But Ellery is among those few?"

"I do not make that claim," she replied, trying hard to not sound shaken. Then she added the reminder, as if to herself and not to the thin man, "My axe has served me well, served King Gareth well, and served you well."

That brought a laugh, again wheezy and thin, but again full of confidence—well-earned confidence, Ellery knew.

"An unlikely continuum of service," he observed. She could see the man's smirk, stretching half out of the shadows. "You do not agree?" asked the thin man, and Ellery, too, smirked and found humor in the irony.

Few would see the logic of her last statement, she realized, because few understood the nuance of politics and practicality in Damara and Vaasa.

"Speak it plainly," the thin man bade her. "If the need arises, you are confident that you can defeat the drow elf, Jarlaxle?"

The woman straightened at the recriminating tone. She didn't glance around nervously any longer, but stared hard at her counterpart.

"He has a weakness," she said. "I have seen it. I can exploit it. Yes. He will not be able to defeat that which you have trained me to execute."

The thin man replied, "Ever were you the fine student."

Emboldened, Ellery bowed at the compliment.

"Let us hope it will not come to that," the thin man went on. "But they are a hard pair to read, this drow and his human companion."

"They travel together and fight side by side, yet the human seems to hold the black-skinned one in contempt," Ellery agreed. "But I see no weakness there that we might exploit," she quickly added, as her counterpart's countenance seemed to brighten with possibility. "A blow against one is a blow against both."

The thin man paused and absorbed that reasoning for a short while, and she was far from certain he agreed.

"The ranger is an excitable one," he said, shifting the subject. "Even after twenty years of hunting the Vaasan wilderness, Mariabronne is easily agitated."

"This is a relic of Zhengyi he has discovered. Many would consider that reason to become agitated."

"You believe that?"

"Wingham believes that, so says Mariabronne, and not for the purposes of making a deal, obviously, or the half-orc opportunist would have quietly sold the artifact."

That had the thin man leaning back more deeply into the shadows, the darkness swallowing almost all of his fragile form. He brought his hands up before him, slender fingertips tap-tapping together.

"Wingham is no fool," the shadowy figure warned.

"He knows magic, if nothing else," Ellery replied. "I would trust his judgment on this."

"So Zhengyi left a book," muttered the thin man, "a book of power."

"A book of creation, so says Mariabronne."

"You will go to Palishchuk?"

"I will."

"With an appointed escort of your choosing?"

"Of course. Mariabronne will lead a small group in the morning."

"You know whom to choose?"

Ellery didn't even try to hide her surprise when she said, "You wish a place on the caravan?"

The thin man tapped his fingers together a few more times, and in the shadows, Ellery could see him nodding.

"Your exploits have not gone unnoticed," Ellery said to Jarlaxle that night, back in Muddy Boots and Bloody Blades.

"If they had, I would be deeply wounded," the drow replied, tipping his glass and offering a lewd wink.

Ellery blushed despite herself, and Jarlaxle thought her red hair only accentuated the sudden color in her cheeks.

"I travel to Palishchuk tomorrow," she said, composing herself.

"I have heard of this place, Palishchuk—half-orcs, correct?"

"Indeed, but quite civilized."

"We should celebrate your departure."

"Our departure."

That caught the drow off his guard, but of course, he didn't show it.

"I am assembling a troupe to make the journey," she explained. "Your exploits have not gone unnoticed."

"Nor have they been accomplished alone."

"Your friend is invited as well."

As she spoke of Entreri, the pair of them turned together to regard the man who stood beside the bar, a mug of ale growing warm on the counter before him, and his typical background sneer hidden just behind his distanced expression. He wore his gray cloak back over one shoulder, showing the fine white shirt that Ilnezhara had given him before the journey to the Vaasan Gate and also revealing the jeweled hilt of his fabulous dagger, sheathed on his hip. It did not escape the attention of Jarlaxle and Ellery that those around Entreri were keeping a respectful step back, were affording him more personal space than anyone else in the bar.

"He has that quality," Jarlaxle mused aloud.

He continued to admire Entreri even as Ellery looked at him for an explanation. But the drow didn't bother to voice his observation. Entreri was far from the largest man in the tavern and had made no aggressive moves toward anyone, yet it was obvious that those around him could sense his strength, his competence. It had to be his eyes, Jarlaxle presumed, for the set of his stare spoke of supreme concentration—perhaps the best attribute of a true warrior.

"Will he go?" the drow heard Ellery ask, and from her tone, it was apparent to him that it was not the first time she had posed the question.

"He is my friend," Jarlaxle replied, as if that description settled everything. "He would not let me walk into danger alone."

"Then you agree?"

Jarlaxle turned to her and grinned wickedly. "Only if you promise me that I will not be cold in the night wind."

Ellery returned his smile then placed her drink down on the table beside them.

"At dawn," she instructed, and she started away.

Jarlaxle grabbed her arm and said, "But I am cold."

"We are not yet on the road," she said.

Ellery danced from his grasp and moved across the floor and out of the tavern.

Jarlaxle continued to grin as he considered her curves from that most advantageous angle. The moment she was out of sight, he snapped his gaze back at Entreri and sighed, knowing the man would resist his persuasion, as always.

It was going to be a long night.

Looking splendid in her shining armor, shield strapped across her back and axe set at her side, Ellery sat upon a large roan mare at the head of the two wagon caravan. Mariabronne rode beside her on a bay. A pair of mounted soldiers complimented them at the back of the line, two large and angry looking men. One of them was the bounty clerk, Davis Eng, the other an older man with gray hair.

The two women driving the first wagon were not of the Army of Bloodstone, but fellow mercenaries from the local taverns. One Jarlaxle knew as Parissus of Impiltur, large-boned, round-faced, and with her light-colored hair cropped short. Often had he and Entreri heard the woman boasting of her exploits, and she did seem to take great pleasure in herself.

The other was one that Jarlaxle couldn't help but know, for her name sat atop the board listing bounty payouts. She called herself Calihye and was a half-elf with long black hair and a beautiful, angular face—except for that angry-looking scar running from one cheek through the edge of her thin lips and to the middle of her chin. When she called out to Commander Ellery that she was ready to go, Jarlaxle and his human companion—surprised to find themselves assigned to driving the second wagon—heard a distinct lisp, undoubtedly caused by the scar across her lips.

"Bah!" came a grumble from the side. "Hold them horses, ye dolts be durned. I'm huffin' and puffin' and me blood's but to burn!"

All watched as a dwarf rambled across the short expanse from the gate, his muscled arms bare and pumping in cadence with his determined strides, his black beard wound into two long braids. He had a pair of odd-looking morning stars strapped in an **X** across his back, their handles reaching up and wide beyond the back of his bushy head. Each ended in a spiked metal ball, the pair bouncing and rolling at the end of their respective chains in similar cadence to the pumping movements. While that was normal enough, the material of the weapons gleamed a dullish and almost translucent gray. Glassteel, they were, a magical construct of rare and powerful properties.

"Ye ask me to go, and so I'm for going, but then ye're not for waiting, so what're ye knowin'? Bah!"

"Your pardon, good Athrogate," said Commander Ellery. "I thought that perhaps you had changed your mind."

"Bah!" Athrogate snorted back.

He walked to the back of the open wagon, pulled a bag from his belt and tossed it inside—which made a second dwarf already in the wagon dodge aside—then grabbed on with both his hands and flipped himself up and over to take a seat beside a thin, fragile-looking man.

Jarlaxle noted that with some curiosity, thinking that a dwarf would normally have chosen the seat beside the other dwarf, which remained open. There were only three in the back of the wagon, which could have held six rather easily.

"They know each other," the drow remarked to Entreri, indicating the dwarf and the man.

"You find that interesting?" came the sarcastic remark.

Jarlaxle just gave a "Hmm," and turned his attention back to the reins and the horses.

Entreri glanced at him curiously, then considered the obnoxious dwarf and the frail-looking man again. Earlier, Jarlaxle had reasoned that the man must be a sage, a scholar brought on to help decipher the mystery of whatever it was that they were going to see in this northern city of Palishchuk.

But that dwarf was no scholarly type, nor did he seem overly curious about matters cerebral. If he and the man knew each other, as Jarlaxle had reasoned, then might there be more to the man than they had presumed?

"He is a wizard," Entreri said quietly.

Jarlaxle looked over at the assassin, who seemed unaware of the movement as he clenched and unclenched his right hand, upon which he had not long ago worn the enchanted gauntlet that accompanied his sword. The magic-defeating gauntlet was lost to him, and it likely occurred to Entreri, in considering the wizard, that he might wish he was wearing it before their journey was over. Though the man had done nothing to indicate any threat toward Entreri, the assassin had never been, and never would be, comfortable around wizards.

He didn't understand them.

He didn't want to understand them.

Usually, he just wanted to kill them.

Ellery motioned to them all and she and Mariabronne began walking their horses out to the north, the wagons rolling right behind, the other two soldiers falling in to flank Entreri and Jarlaxle's supply wagon.

Jarlaxle began to talk, of course, noting the landscape and telling tales of similar places he had visited now and again. And Entreri tuned him out, of course, preferring to keep his focus on the other nine journeying beside him and the drow.

For most of his life, Artemis Entreri had been a solitary adventurer, a paid killer who relied only upon himself and his own instincts. He felt a distinct discomfort with the company, and surely wondered how the drow had ever convinced him to go along.

Perhaps he wondered why Jarlaxle had wanted to go in the first place.

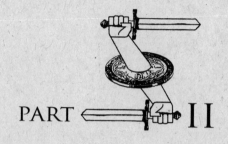

PART II

JARLAXLE'S ROAD

Jarlaxle left Ilnezhara and Tazmikella excitedly discussing the possibilities of Zhengyi's library a short while after the fall of the lich's tower. As soon as he had exited the dragon's abode, the drow veered from the main road that would take him back to Heliogabalus proper. He wandered far into the wilderness, to a grove of dark oaks, and did a quick scan of the area to ensure that no one was about. He leaned back against a tree and closed his eyes, and replayed in his thoughts the conversation, seeing again the sisters' expressions as they rambled on about Zhengyi.

They were excited, of course, and who could blame them? But there was something else in the look of Ilnezhara when first she had spoken to him about the crumbled tower. A bit of fear, he thought again.

Jarlaxle smiled. The sisters knew more about Zhengyi's potential treasures than they were letting on, and they feared the resurfacing artifacts.

Why would a dragon fear anything?

The wince on Ilnezhara's face when he told her that the book had been destroyed flashed in his thoughts, and he realized that he'd do well to keep his treasure—the tiny skull gem—safely hidden for a long, long time. Ilnezhara hadn't completely believed him, he suspected, and that was never a good thing when dealing with a dragon. He knew without doubt that the dragon sisters would try to confirm that he was speaking the truth. Of course, as was their hoarding nature, the dragons would desire such a tome as the one that had constructed the tower, but that expression on Ilnezhara's face spoke to something beyond so simple and obvious a desire.

Despite his better instincts the drow produced the tiny glowing skull, just for a moment. He clutched it tightly in his hand and let his thoughts flow into the magic, accepting whatever road the skull laid out before him. Kimmuriel, the psionicist dark elf Jarlaxle had left to command his mercenary band, Bregan D'aerthe, had long ago taught him a way of getting some sense of the purpose of a magical item. Of course Jarlaxle already knew a portion of the skull's properties, for it had no doubt been a large part of creating the tower. He understood logically that the skull had been the conduit between the life-force of that fool Herminicle and the creation power of the tome itself.

All hints of color faded from Jarlaxle's vision. Even in the dark of night he recognized that he was moving into a sort of alternate visual realm. He recoiled at first, fearing that the skull was taking his life-force, was draining him of living energy and moving him closer to death.

He fast realized that such was not the case, however. Rather, the power of the skull was allowing his sensibilities to enter the nether realm.

He sensed the bones of a dead squirrel right below his feet, and those of many other creatures who had died in that place. He felt no pull to them, however, just a recognition, an understanding that they were there.

But he did feel a pull, clearly so, and he turned and walked out of the grove, letting the skull guide him.

Soon he stood in the remains of an ancient, forgotten cemetery. A couple of stones might have been markers, or perhaps they were not, but Jarlaxle knew with certainty that it was a cemetery, where any other wanderer who happened upon the place might not guess.

Jarlaxle felt the long-buried corpses, buried in neat rows. They were calling to him, he thought . . .

No, he realized, and he opened his eyes wide and looked down at the skull. They weren't calling to him, they were waiting for him to call to them.

The drow took a deep and steadying breath. He noted the remains of a dwarf and a halfling, but when he concentrated on them, he understood that they were not connected in any way but by the ground in which they rested and were connected in no way to the dark elf.

This skull was focused in its power. It held strength over humans—alive and dead, so it would seem.

"Interesting," Jarlaxle whispered to the chilly night air, and he subconsciously glanced back in the direction of Ilnezhara's tower.

Jarlaxle held the glowing item up before his twinkling eyes.

"If I had initially found the tome and had enacted the creation power with my life-force, would the skull that grew within the pages have been that of a drow?" he asked. "Could a dragon have made a skull that would find its connection to long-dead dragons?"

He shook his head as he spoke the words aloud, for they just didn't sound correct to him. The disposition of the skull predated the construction of the tower and had been embedded within the book before the foolish human Herminicle had found it. The book was predetermined to that end result, he believed.

Yes, that sounded better to the aged and magically-literate dark elf. Zhengyi held great power over humans and had also commanded an army of the dead, so the tales said. The skull was surely one of his artifacts to affect that end.

Jarlaxle glanced back again in the direction of the distant tower.

It was no secret that Zhengyi had also commanded flights of dragons—disparate wyrms, somehow brought together under a singular purpose and under his control.

The drow's smile widened and he realized that a journey to Vaasa was indeed in his future.

Happily so.

CHAPTER

THE WIND ON THE ROAD

9

We'll keep close to the foothills," Ellery said to Jarlaxle, pulling her horse up beside the bouncing wagon. "There have been many reports of monsters in the region and Mariabronne has confirmed that they're about. We'll stay in the shadows away from the open plain."

"Might our enemies not be hiding in wait in those same shadows?" Jarlaxle asked.

"Mariabronne is with us," Ellery remarked. "We will not be caught by surprise." She smiled with easy confidence and turned her horse aside.

Jarlaxle set his doubting expression upon Entreri.

"Yes," the assassin assured him, "almost everyone I've killed uttered similar last words."

"Then I am glad once again that you are on my side."

"They've often said that, too."

Jarlaxle laughed aloud.

Entreri didn't.

The going was slower on the more uneven ground under the shadows of the Galenas, but Ellery insisted and she was, after all, in command. As the sun began its lazy slide down the western sky, the commander ordered the wagons up into a sheltered lea between mounds of tumbled stones and delegated the various duties of setting the camp and defenses. Predictably, Mariabronne went out to scout and the pair of soldiers set watch-points—though curiously, Entreri thought, under the guidance of the dwarf with the twin morning stars. Even more curious, the thin sage sat in contemplation off to the side of the main encampment, his legs crossed before him, his hands resting on his knees. It was more than simple meditation, Entreri knew. The man was preparing spells they might need for nighttime defense.

Similarly, the other dwarf, who had introduced himself as Pratcus Bristlebeard, built a small altar to Moradin and began calling upon his god for blessing. Ellery had covered both the arcane and the divine.

And probably a little of both with Jarlaxle, Entreri thought with a wry grin.

The assassin went out from the main camp soon after, climbing higher into the foothills and finally settling on a wide boulder that afforded him a superb view of the Vaasan lowlands stretching out to the west.

He sat quietly and stared at the setting sun, long rays slanting across the great muddy bog, bright lines of wetness shining brilliantly. Dazzling distortions turned the light into shimmering pools of brilliance, demanding his attention and drawing him into a deeper state of contemplation. Hardly aware of the movement, Entreri reached to his belt and drew forth a small, rather ordinary-looking flute, a gift of the dragon sisters Ilnezhara and Tazmikella.

He glanced around quickly, ensuring that he was alone, then lifted the flute to his lips and blew a simple note. He let that whistle hang in the air then blew again, holding it a little longer. His delicate but strong fingers worked over the instrument's holes and he played a simple song, one he had taught himself or one the flute had taught to him; he couldn't be certain of which. He continued for a short while, letting the sound gather in the air around him, bidding it to take his thoughts far, far away.

The flute had done that to him before. Perhaps it was magic or perhaps just the simple pleasure of perfect timbre, but under the spell of his playing, Artemis Entreri had several times managed to clear his thoughts of all the normal clutter.

A short while later, the sun much lower in the sky, the assassin lowered the flute and stared at it. Somehow, the instrument didn't sound as fine as on those other occasions he'd tested it, nor did he find himself being drawn into the flute as he had before.

"Perhaps the wind is countering the puff of your foul breath," Jarlaxle said from behind him.

The drow couldn't see the scowl that crossed Entreri's face—was there ever to be a time when he could be away from that pestering dark elf?

Entreri laid the flute across his lap and stared off to the west and the lowering sun, the bottom rim just touching the distant horizon and setting off a line of fires across the dark teeth of the distant hills. Above the sun, a row of clouds took on a fiery orange hue.

"It promises to be a beautiful sunset," Jarlaxle remarked, easily scaling the boulder and taking a seat close beside the assassin.

Entreri glanced at him as if he hardly cared.

"Perhaps it is because of my background," the drow continued. "I have gone centuries, my friend, without ever witnessing the cycles of the sun. Perhaps the absence of this daily event only heightens my appreciation for it now."

Entreri still showed no hint of any response.

"Perhaps after a few decades on the surface I will become as bored with it as you seem to be."

"Did I say that?"

"Do you ever say anything?" Jarlaxle replied. "Or does it amuse you to let all of those around you simply extrapolate your words from your continuing scowls and grimaces?"

Entreri chortled and looked back to the west. The sun was lower still, half of it gone. Above the remaining semicircle of fire, the clouds glowed even more fiercely, like a line of fire churning in the deepening blue of the sky.

"Do you ever dream, my friend?" Jarlaxle asked.

"Everyone dreams," Entreri replied. "Or so I am told. I expect that I do, though I hardly care to remember them."

"Not night dreams," the drow explained. "Everyone dreams, indeed, at night. Even the elves in our Reverie find dream states and visions. But there are two types of dreamers, my friend, those who dream at night and those who dream in the day."

He had Entreri's attention.

"Those night-dreamers," Jarlaxle went on, "they do not overly concern me. Nighttime dreams are for release, say some, a purging of the worries or a fanciful flight to no end. Those who dream in the night alone are doomed to mundanity, don't you see?"

"Mundanity?"

"The ordinary. The mediocre. Night-dreamers do not overly concern me because there is nowhere for them to rise. But those who dream by day . . . those, my friend, are the troublesome ones."

"Would Jarlaxle not consider himself among that lot?"

"Would I hold any credibility at all if I did not admit my troublesome nature?"

"Not with me."

"There you have it, then," said the drow.

He paused and looked to the west, and Entreri did too, watching the sun slip lower.

"I know another secret about daydreamers," Jarlaxle said at length.

"Pray tell," came the assassin's less-than-enthusiastic reply.

"Daydreamers alone are truly alive," Jarlaxle explained. He looked back at Entreri, who matched his stare. "For daydreamers alone find perspective in existence and seek ways to rise above the course of simple survival."

Entreri didn't blink.

"You do daydream," Jarlaxle decided. "But only on those rare occasions your dedication to . . . to what, I often wonder? . . . allows you outside your perfect discipline."

"Perhaps that dedication to perfect discipline is my dream."

"No," the drow replied without hesitation. "No. Control is not the facilitation of fancy, my friend, it is the fear of fancy."

"You equate dreaming and fancy then?"

"Of course! Dreams are made in the heart and filtered through the rational mind. Without the heart . . ."

"Control?"

"And only that. A pity, I say."

"I do not ask for your pity, Jarlaxle."

"The daydreamers aspire to mastery of all they survey, of course."

"As I do."

"No. You master yourself and nothing more, because you do not dare to dream. You do not dare allow your heart a voice in the process of living."

Entreri's stare became a scowl.

"It is an observation, not a criticism," said Jarlaxle. He rose and brushed off his pants. "And perhaps it is a suggestion. You, who have so achieved discipline, might yet find greatness beyond a feared reputation."

"You assume that I want more."

"I know that you need more, as any man needs more," said the drow. He turned and started down the back side of the boulder. "To live and not merely to survive—that secret is in your heart, Artemis Entreri, if only you are wise enough to look."

He paused and glanced back at Entreri, who sat staring at him hard, and tossed the assassin a flute, seemingly an exact replica of the one Entreri held across his lap.

"Use the real one," Jarlaxle bade him. "The one Ilnezhara gave to you. The one Idalia fashioned those centuries ago."

Idalia put a key inside this flute to unlock any heart, Jarlaxle thought but did not speak, as he turned and walked away.

Entreri looked at the flute in his hands and at the one on his belt. He wasn't really surprised that Jarlaxle had stolen the valuable item and had apparently created an exact copy—no, not exact, Entreri understood as he considered the emptiness of the notes he had blown that day. Physically, the two flutes looked exactly alike, and he marveled at the drow's work as he compared them side by side. But there was more to the real creation of Idalia.

A piece of the craftsman's heart?

Entreri rolled the flute over in his hands, his fingers sliding along the smooth wood, feeling the strength within the apparent delicateness. He lifted the copy in one hand, the original in the other, and closed his eyes. He couldn't tell the difference.

Only when he blew through the flutes could he tell, in the way the music of the real creation washed over him and through him, taking him away with it into what seemed like an alternate reality.

<hr/>

"Wise advice," a voice to the side of the trail greeted Jarlaxle as he moved away from his friend.

Not caught by surprise, Jarlaxle offered Mariabronne a tip of his great hat and said, "You listened in on our private conversation?"

Mariabronne shrugged. "Guilty as charged, I fear. I was moving along the trail when I heard your voice. I meant to keep going, but your words caught me. I have heard such words before, you see, when I was young and learning the ways of the wider world."

"Did your advisor also explain to you the dangers of eavesdropping?"

Mariabronne laughed—or started to, but then cleared his throat instead. "I find you a curiosity, dark elf. Certainly you are different from anyone I have known, in appearance at least. I would know if that is the depth of the variation, or if you are truly a unique being."

"Unique among the lesser races, such as humans, you mean."

This time, Mariabronne did allow himself to laugh.

"I know about the incident with the Kneebreakers," he said.

"I am certain that I do not know of what you speak."

"I am certain that you do," the ranger insisted. "Summoning the wolf was a cunning turn of magic, as returning enough of the ears to Hobart to ingratiate yourself, while keeping enough to build your legend was a cunning turn of diplomacy."

"You presume much."

"The signs were all too easily read, Jarlaxle. This is not presumption but deduction."

"You make it a point to study my every move, of course."

Mariabronne dipped a bow. "I and others."

The drow did well to keep the flicker of alarm from his delicate features.

"We know what you did, but be at ease, for we pass no judgment on that particular action. You have much to overcome concerning the reputation of your heritage, and your little trick did well in elevating you to a position of respectability. I cannot deny any man, or drow, such a climb."

"It is the end of that climb you fear?" Jarlaxle flashed a wide smile, one that enveloped the whole spectrum from sinister to disarming, a perfectly non-readable expression. "To what end?"

The ranger shrugged as if it didn't really matter—not then, at least. "I judge a person by his actions alone. I have known halflings who would cut the throat of an innocent human child and half-orcs who would give their lives in defense of the same. Your antics with the Kneebreakers brought no harm, for the Kneebreakers are an amusing lot whose reputation is well solidified, and they live for adventure and not reputation, in any case. Hobart has certainly forgiven you. He even lifted his mug in toast to your cleverness when it was all revealed to him."

The drow's eyes flared for just a moment—a lapse of control. Jarlaxle was unused to such wheels spinning outside his control, and he didn't like the feeling. For a moment, he almost felt as if he was dealing with the late Matron Baenre, that most devious of dark elves, who always seemed to be pacing ahead of him or even with him. He quickly replayed in his mind all the events of his encounters with the Kneebreakers, recalling Hobart's posture and attitude to see if he could get a fix upon the point when the halfling had discovered the ruse.

He brought a hand up to stroke his chin, staring at Mariabronne all the while and mentally noting that he would do well not to underestimate the man again. It was a difficult thing for a dark elf to take humans and other surface races seriously. All his life Jarlaxle had been told of their inferiority, after all.

But he knew better than that. He'd survived—and thrived—by rising above the limitations of his own prejudices. He affirmed that again, taking the poignant reminder in stride.

"The area is secure?" he asked the ranger.

"We are safe enough."

The drow nodded and started back for the camp.

"Your words to Artemis Entreri were well spoken," Mariabronne said after him, halting him in his tracks. "The man moves with the grace of a true warrior and with the confidence of an emperor. But only in a martial sense. He is one and alone in every other sense. A pity, I think."

"I am not sure that Artemis Entreri would appreciate your pity."

"It is not for him that I express it but for those around him."

Jarlaxle considered the subtle difference for just a moment then smiled and tipped his hat.

Yes, he thought, Entreri would take that as a great compliment.

More's the pity.

The ground was uneven, sometimes soft, sometimes hard, and full of rocks and mud, withered roots and deep puddles. The drivers and riders in the wagons bounced along, rocking in the uneven sway of the slow ride, heads lolling as they let the jolts play out. Because of the continual jarring, it took Entreri a few moments to detect the sudden vibration beneath his cart, sudden tremors building in momentum under the moving wheels. He looked to Jarlaxle, who seemed similarly awakening to the abrupt change.

Beside the wagon, Ellery's horse pawed the ground. Across and to the front, the horse of one guard reared and whinnied, hooves slashing at the air.

Mariabronne locked his horse under tight control and spurred the creature forward, past Ellery and Entreri's wagon then past the lead wagon.

"Ride through it and ride hard!" the ranger shouted. "Forward, I say! With all speed!"

He cracked his reigns over one side of his horse's neck then the other, spurring the animal on.

Entreri reached for the whip, as did the woman driving the front wagon. Jarlaxle braced himself and stood up, looking around them, as Ellery regained control of her steed and chased off after Mariabronne.

"What is it?" Entreri bade his companion.

"I'm feeling a bump and a bit of a shake," yelled Athrogate from the back of the wagon in front. "I'm thinkin' to find a few monsters to break!"

Entreri watched the dwarf bring forth both his morning stars with a blazing, fluid movement, the balls immediately set to spinning before him.

Athrogate lost all concentration and rhythm a split second later, however, as the ground between the wagons erupted and several snakelike creatures sprang up into the air. They unfurled little wings as they lifted, hovering in place, little fanged mouths smiling in hungry anticipation.

The horse reared again and the poor rider could hardly hold on. Up leaped a snake-creature, right before his terror-wide eyes. He instinctively threw his hands before his face as the serpent spat a stream of acid into his eyes.

Down he tumbled, his weapon still sheathed aside his terrified, leaping horse, and all around him more winged snakes sprang from holes and lifted into the air.

Streams of spittle assaulted the man, setting his cloak smoldering with a dozen wisps of gray smoke. He screamed and rolled as more and more acid struck him, blistering his skin.

His horse leaped and bucked and thundered away, a group of snakes flying in close and hungry pursuit.

Beside the gray-haired man, Davis Eng kept his horse under control and crowded in to try to shield his fallen comrade, but more and more winged snakes came forth from the ground, rising up to intercede. Out came Davis Eng's broadsword, and a quick slash folded one of the hovering snakes around the blade and sent it flying away as he finished through with his great swing.

But another snake was right there, spitting into the soldier's face, blinding him with its acid. He swept his blade back furiously, whipping it about in a futile effort to keep the nasty little creatures at bay.

More venom hit the man and his mount. Another pair of snakes dived in from behind and bit hard at the horse, causing it to rear and shriek in pain. The soldier held on but lost all thoughts of helping his prostrated companion. That prone man continued to squirm under a barrage of acidic streams. He clawed at the ground, trying to get some traction so that he could propel himself away.

But a snake dived onto his neck, wrapping its body around him and driving its acid-dripping fangs into his throat. He grabbed at it frantically with both hands, but other snakes dived in fast and hard, spitting and biting.

Entreri shouted out, and the horses snorted and bucked in terror and swerved to the right, moving up along the uneven and rising foothill.

"Hold them!" Jarlaxle cried, grabbing at the reigns.

The wagon jolted hard, its rear wheel clipping a stone and diving into a deep rut. The horse team broke free, pulling the harness from the frame and taking both Jarlaxle and Entreri with them—for the moment at least. Both kept their sensibilities enough to let go as they came forward from the jolt and tug, and neither was foolish enough to try to resist the sudden momentum. They hit the ground side by side, Entreri in a roll and the drow landing lightly on his feet and running along to absorb the shock.

Entreri came up to his feet in a flash, sword and dagger in hand and already working. He set opaque veils of ash in the air around him, visually shielding himself from the growing throng of winged snakes.

Streams of acidic spittle popped through the sheets of black ash, but the assassin was not caught unaware. Already turning and shifting to avoid the assault, he burst through hard, catching the snakes by surprise as they had tried to catch him. A slash of Charon's Claw took down a pair, and a stab of his jeweled dagger stuck hard into the torso of a third. That snake snapped its head forward to bite at the assassin's wrist, but Entreri was a flash ahead of it, twisting his hand down and flicking the blade to send the creature flying away.

Before the creature had even cleared from the blade, the assassin was on the defensive again, slashing his sword to fend a trio of diving serpents and to deflect three lines of acid.

More came at him from the other side, and he knew he could never defeat them all. He surrendered his ground, leaping back down the hill toward the two dwarves and the thin man, who had formed a triangular defensive posture in the back of the rolling wagon.

Athrogate's twin morning stars moved in a blur, spiked metal balls spinning fast at the end of their respective chains. He worked them out and around with tremendous precision, never interrupting their flow, but cunningly altering their angles to clip and send spinning any snakes that ventured too close. Athrogate let out a series of rhyming curses as he fought, for lines of acidic spittle assaulted him, sending wisps of smoke from his beard and tunic.

Pratcus stood behind him, deep in prayer, and every now and then he called out to Moradin then gently touched his wild bodyguard, using healing magic to help repair some of his many wounds.

To the side of the cleric, the thin man waggled his fingers, sending forth bolts of energy that drove back the nearest creatures.

Entreri knew he had to catch that wagon.

"Make way!" he cried, cutting fast to the side, coming up even with the back of the wagon as he leaped atop a rock.

Athrogate turned fast, giving him safe passage onto the bed. Before the dwarf could yell, "Hold the flank!" Entreri went right past him, between the other dwarf and the thin man. He scrambled over the bench rail to take a seat between the two drivers, both of whom were ducking and screaming in pain.

Entreri threw the hood of his cloak up over his head and grabbed the reins from Calihye. The half-elf woman was obviously blinded and almost senseless.

"Keep them away from me!" he shouted to the trio behind.

He bent low in the seat, urging the horses on faster.

Parissus, sitting to Entreri's right, mumbled something and slumped in hard against him, causing him to twist and inadvertently tug the reins and slow the team. With a growl, Entreri shoved back, not quite realizing that the woman had lost all consciousness. She tumbled back the other way and kept going, right over the side. Entreri grabbed at her but couldn't hold her and hold the team in its run.

He chose the wagon.

The woman rolled off, falling under the front wheel with a grunt, then a second grunt as the back wheel bounced over her.

Calihye cried out and grabbed at Entreri's arm, yelling at him to stop the wagon.

He turned to glower at her, to let her know in no uncertain terms that if she didn't immediately let go of him, he'd toss her off the other side.

She fell back in fear and pain then screamed again as another stream of acidic venom hit her in the face, blistering one cheek.

Hold on! Hold on!

That was all the poor, confused Davis Eng could think as the assault continued. Gone were his hopes for aiding his fallen friend, for he rode on the very edge of doom, disoriented, lost in a sea of hovering, biting, spitting serpents. Lines of blood ran down his arms and along the flanks of his horse, and angry blisters covered half his face.

"Abominations of Zhengyi!" he heard his beloved commander yell from somewhere far, far away—too distant to aid him, he knew.

He had to find a direction and bolt his horse away, but how could he begin to do anything but hold on for all his life?

His horse reared, whinnied, and spun on its hind legs. Then something hit it hard from the side, stopping the turn, and the soldier lurched over and could not hold on.

But a hand grabbed him hard and yanked him upright, then slid past him and grabbed at his reigns, straightening him and his horse out and leading them on.

So great was Mariabronne's control of his mount that the horse accepted the stinging hits from the abominations, accepted the collision with Davis Eng's horse, and carried on exactly as the ranger demanded, finding a line out of there and galloping away.

On the ground behind Mariabronne, the fallen soldier kept squirming and rolling, but he was obviously beyond help. It pained Mariabronne greatly to abandon him, but there was clearly no choice, for dozens of snake creatures slithered around him, biting him repeatedly, filling his veins with their venom.

The horses could outrun the creatures, Mariabronne knew, and that was this other soldier's—and his own—only hope.

The warrior woman cried out, bending low and slashing her axe through the air as her horse thundered on toward the soon-to-be-overwhelmed drow. He worked his arms frantically—and magnificently, Ellery had to admit—sending a stream of spinning daggers at the nearby snakes. He spun continually as well, his cloak flying wide and offering more than nominal protection against the barrage of acidic venom flying his way. Still, he got hit more than once and grimaced in pain, and Ellery was certain that he couldn't possibly keep up the seemingly endless supply of missiles.

She bent lower, winced, and nearly fell from her seat as a stream of caustic fluid struck the side of her jaw, just under the bottom edge of her great helm. She kept her wits about her enough to send her axe swiping forward to tear the wing from another of the snakes, but a second got in over the blade and dived hard onto her wrist and hand. Hooked fangs came forth and jabbed hard through Ellery's gauntlet.

The knight howled and dropped her axe then furiously shook her hand, sending both the gauntlet and the serpent tumbling away. She shouted to the drow and drove her steed on toward him, reaching out her free hand for his.

Jarlaxle caught her grip, his second hand working fast down low with a dagger, and Ellery's surprise was complete when she found herself sliding back from her seat rather than tugging the drow along. Some magic had gripped the dark elf, she realized, for his strength was magnified many times over and he did not yield a step as her horse galloped by.

She was on the ground in a flash, stunned and stumbling, but Jarlaxle held her up on her feet.

"What . . . ?" she started to ask.

The drow jerked her in place in front of him, and Ellery noted faint sparkles in the air around them both, a globe of some sort.

"Do not pull away!" he warned.

He lifted his other hand to show her a black, ruby-tipped wand in his delicate fingers.

The woman's eyes went wide with fear as she glanced over Jarlaxle's shoulder to see a swarm of snakes flying at them.

Jarlaxle didn't show the slightest fear. He just pointed his wand at the ground and uttered a command that dropped a tiny ball of fire from its end.

Ellery instinctively recoiled, but the drow held her fast in his magically-enhanced iron grip.

She recoiled even more when the fireball erupted all around her, angry flames searing the air. She felt her breath sucked out of her lungs, felt the sudden press of blazing heat, and all around her and the drow, the globe sparked and glowed in angry response.

But it held. The killing flames could not get through. Outside that space, though, for a score of feet all around, the fires ate hungrily.

Serpents fell flaming to the ground, charred to a crisp before they landed. Off to the side, the wagon Entreri and Jarlaxle had unceremoniously abandoned flared, the corn in the supply bags already popping in the grip of the great flames. Across the other way, the body of the fallen soldier crackled and charred, as did the dozen serpents that squirmed atop it.

A puff of black smoke billowed into the air above the warrior and the drow. The wagon continued to burn, sending a stream up as well, its timbers crackling in protest.

But other than that, the air around them grew still, preternaturally serene, as if Jarlaxle's fireball had cleansed the air itself.

⊷═╫═⊷

A wave of heat flashed past Entreri—the hot winds of Jarlaxle's fireball. He heard the thin man in the wagon behind him yell out in the surprise, followed by Athrogate's appreciative, "Good with the boom for clearin' the room!"

If the assassin had any intention of slowing and looking back, though, it was quickly dismissed by the plop of acidic spittle on the hood of his cloak and the flapping of serpent wings beside his ear.

Before he could even move to address that situation, he heard a thrumming sound followed by a loud *whack* and the sight of the blasted serpent spiraling out to the side. The thrumming continued and Entreri recognized it as Athrogate's morning stars, the dwarf working them with deadly precision.

"I got yer back, I got yer head," came the dwarf's cry. "Them snakes attack ye, they wind up dead!"

"Just shut up and kill them," Entreri muttered under his breath—or so he thought. A roar of laughter from Athrogate clued him in that he had said it a bit too loudly.

Another serpent went flying away, right past his head, and Entreri heard a quick series of impacts, each accompanied by a dwarf's roar. Entreri did manage to glance to the side to see the remaining woman, fast slipping from consciousness, beginning to roll off the side of the wagon. With a less-than-amused grimace, Entreri grabbed her and tugged her back into place beside him.

Entreri then glanced back and saw Athrogate running around in a fury. His morning stars hummed and flew, splattering snakes and tossing them far

342

aside, launching them up into the air or dropping them straight down to smack hard into the ground.

Behind the two dwarves the thin man stood at the back of the wagon, facing the way they had come and waggling his fingers. A cloud of green fog spewed forth from his hands, trailing the fast-moving wagon.

The serpents in close pursuit pulled up and began to writhe and spasm when they came in contact with the fog. A moment later, they began falling dead to the ground.

"Aye!" the other dwarf cried.

"Poison the air, ye clever wizard?" said Athrogate. "Choking them stinkin', spittin' liza—"

"Don't say it!" Entreri shouted at him.

"What?" the dwarf replied.

"Just shut up," said the assassin.

Athrogate shrugged, his morning stars finally losing momentum and dropping down at the end of their respective chains.

"Ain't nothing left to hit," he remarked.

Entreri glared at him, as if daring him to find a rhyming line.

"Ease up the team," the thin man said. "The pursuit is no more."

Entreri tugged the reigns just a bit and coaxed the horses to slow. He turned the wagon to the side and noted the approach of Mariabronne and the wounded soldier, the ranger still handling both their mounts. Entreri moved around a bit more onto the flat plain, allowing himself a view of the escape route. The wizard's killing cloud of green fog began to dissipate, and the distant burning wagon came more clearly into sight, a pillar of black smoke rising into the air.

Beside him, Calihye coughed and groaned.

Mariabronne handed the soldier's horse over to the care of Athrogate then turned his own horse around and galloped back to the body of the other fallen woman. Looking past him, Entreri noted that the other soldier was dead, for the man's charred corpse was clearly in sight.

From the sight of the fallen woman, all twisted, bloody, and unmoving, the assassin gathered that they had lost two in the encounter.

At least two, he realized, and to his own surprise, a quiver of alarm came over him and he glanced around, calming almost immediately when he noted Jarlaxle off to the other side, up in the foothills, calmly walking toward them. He noted Ellery, too, a bit behind the drow, moving after her scared and riderless mount.

The wounded woman on the ground groaned and Entreri turned to see Mariabronne cradling her head. The ranger gently lifted her battered form from the mud and set her over his horse's back then slowly led the mount back to the wagon.

"Parissus?" Calihye asked. She crawled back into a sitting position, widened her eyes, and called again for her friend, more loudly. "Parissus!"

The look on Mariabronne's face was not promising. Nor was the lifeless movement of Parissus, limply bouncing along.

"*Parissus?*" the woman beside Entreri cried again, even more urgently as her senses returned. She started past the assassin but stopped short. "You did this to her!" she cried, moving her twisted face right up to Entreri's.

Or trying to, for when the final word escaped her lips, it came forth with a gurgle. Entreri's strong hand clamped against her throat, fingers perfectly positioned to crush her windpipe. She grabbed at the hold with both hands then dropped one low—to retrieve a weapon, Entreri knew.

He wasn't overly concerned, however, for she stopped short when the tip of the assassin's jeweled dagger poked in hard under her chin.

"Would you care to utter another accusation?" Entreri asked.

"Be easy, boy," said Athrogate.

Beside him, the other dwarf began to quietly chant.

"If that is a spell aimed at me, then you would be wise to reconsider," said Entreri.

The dwarf cleric did stop—but only when a drow hand grabbed him by the shoulder.

"There is no need for animosity," Jarlaxle said to them all. "A difficult foe, but one vanquished."

"Because you decided to burn them, and your companion," accused the shaken, shivering half-elf soldier.

"Your friend was dead long before I initiated the fireball," said the drow. "And if I had not, then I and Commander Ellery would have suffered a similar fate."

"You do not know that!"

Jarlaxle shrugged as if it did not matter. "I saved myself and Commander Ellery. I could not have saved your friend, nor could you, in any case."

"Abominations of Zhengyi," said Mariabronne, drawing close to the others. "More may be about. We have no time for this foolishness."

Entreri looked at the ranger, then at Jarlaxle, who nodded for him to let the half-elf go. He did just that, offering her one last warning glare.

Calihye gagged a bit and fell back from him, but recovered quickly. She scrambled from the wagon bench and over to her fallen companion. Mariabronne let her pass by, but looked to the others and shook his head.

"I got some spells," the dwarf cleric said.

Mariabronne walked away from the horse, leaving the woman with her fallen friend. "Then use them," he told the dwarf. "But I doubt they will be of help. She is full of poison and the fall broke her spine."

The dwarf nodded grimly and ambled past him. He grabbed at the smaller Calihye, who was sobbing uncontrollably, and seemed as if she would melt into the ground beside the horse.

"Parissus . . ." she whispered over and over.

"A stream of drats for being her," Athrogate muttered.

"At least," said Jarlaxle.

The sound of an approaching horse turned them all to regard Ellery.

"Mariabronne, with me," the commander instructed. "We will go back and see what we can salvage. I need to retrieve my battle-axe and we have another horse running free. I'll not leave it behind." She glanced at the fallen woman, as Pratcus and Calihye were easing her down from the horse. "What of her?"

"No," Mariabronne said, his voice quiet and respectful.

"Put her in the wagon then, and get it moving along," Ellery instructed.

Her callous tone drew a grin from Entreri. He could tell that she was agitated under that calm facade.

"I am Canthan," he heard the thin man tell Jarlaxle. "I witnessed your blast. Most impressive. I did not realize that you dabbled in the Art."

"I am a drow of many talents."

Canthan bowed and seemed impressed.

"And many items," Entreri had to put in.

Jarlaxle tipped his great hat and smiled.

Entreri didn't return his smile, though, for the assassin had caught the gaze of Calihye. He saw a clear threat in her blue-gray eyes. Yes, she blamed him for her friend's fall.

"Come along, ye dolts, and load the wagon!" Athrogate roared as Mariabronne and Ellery started off. "Be quick afore Zhengyi attacks with a dragon! *Bwahaha!*"

"It will be an interesting ride," Jarlaxle said to Entreri as he climbed up onto the bench beside the assassin.

"'Interesting' is a good word," Entreri replied.

CHAPTER

WITH OPEN HEART

10

"At ease, my large friend," Wingham said, patting his hands in the air to calm the half-orc.

But Olgerkhan would not be calmed. "She's dying! I tried to help, but I cannot."

"We don't know that she's dying."

"She's sick again, and worse now than before," Olgerkhan continued. "The castle grows and its shadow makes Arrayan sick."

Wingham started to respond again but paused and considered what Olgerkhan just said. No doubt the somewhat dim warrior was making only a passing connection, using the castle to illustrate his fears for Arrayan, but in that simple statement Wingham heard a hint of truth. Arrayan had opened the book, after all. Was it possible that in doing so, she had created a magical bond between herself and the tome? Wingham had suspected that she'd served as a catalyst, but might it be more than that?

"Old Nyungy, is he still in town?" the merchant asked.

"Nyungy?" echoed Olgerkhan. "The talespinner?"

"Yes, the same."

Olgerkhan shrugged and said, "I haven't seen him in some time, but I know his house."

"Take me to it, at once."

"But Arrayan . . ."

"To help Arrayan," Wingham explained.

The moment the words left his mouth, Olgerkhan grabbed his hands and pulled him away from the wagon, tugging him to the north and the city. They moved at full speed, which meant the poor old merchant was half-running and half-flying behind the tugging warrior.

In short order, they stood before the dilapidated door of an old, three-story house, its exterior in terrible disrepair, dead vines climbing halfway up the structure, new growth sprouting all over it with roots cracking into the foundation stones.

Without the slightest pause, Olgerkhan rapped hard on the door, which shook and shifted as if the heavy knocks would dislodge it from its precarious perch.

"Easy, friend," Wingham said. "Nyungy is very old. Give him time to answer."

"Nyungy!" Olgerkhan yelled out.

He thumped the house beside the door so hard the whole of the building trembled. Then he moved his large fist back in line with the door and cocked his arm.

He stopped when the door pulled in, revealing a bald, wrinkled old man, more human than orc in appearance, save teeth too long to fit in his mouth. Brown spots covered his bald pate, and a tuft of gray hair sprouted from a large mole on the side of his thick nose. He trembled as he stood there, as if he might just fall over, but in his blue eyes, both Olgerkhan and Wingham saw clarity that defied his age.

"Oh, please do not strike me, large and impetuous child," he said in a wheezing, whistling voice. "I doubt you'd find much sport in laying me low. Wait a few moments and save yourself the trouble, for my old legs won't hold me upright for very long!" He ended with a laugh that fast transformed into a cough.

Olgerkhan lowered his arm and shrugged, quite embarrassed.

Wingham put a hand on Olgerkhan's shoulder and gently eased him aside then stepped forward to face old Nyungy.

"Wingham?" the man asked. "Wingham, are you back again?"

"Every year, old friend," answered the merchant, "but I have not seen you in a decade or more. You so used to love the flavors of my carnival . . ."

"I still would, young fool," Nyungy replied, "but it is far too great a walk for me."

Wingham bowed low. "Then my apologies for not seeking you out these past years."

"But you are here now. Come in. Come in. Bring your large friend, but please do not let him punch my walls anymore."

Wingham chuckled and glanced at the mortified Olgerkhan. Nyungy began to fade back into the shadows of the house, but Wingham bade him to stop.

"Another time, certainly," the merchant explained. "But we have not come for idle chatter. There is an event occurring near to Palishchuk that needs your knowledge and wisdom."

"I long ago gave up the road, the song, and the sword."

"It is not far to travel," Wingham pressed, "and I assure you that I would not bother you if there was any other way. But there is a great construct in process—a relic of Zhengyi's, I suspect."

"Speak not that foul name!"

"I agree," Wingham said with another bow. "And I would not, if there was another way to prompt you to action."

Nyungy rocked back a bit and considered the words. "A construct, you say?"

"I am certain that if you climbed to your highest room and looked out your north window, you could see it from here."

Nyungy glanced back into the room behind him, and the rickety staircase ascending the right-hand wall.

"I do not much leave the lowest floor. I doubt I could climb those stairs." He was grinning when he turned back to Wingham, then kept turning to eye Olgerkhan. "But perhaps your large friend here might assist me—might assist us both, if your legs are as old as my own."

Wingham didn't need the help of Olgerkhan to climb the stairs, though the wooden railing was fragile and wobbly, with many balusters missing or leaning out or in, no longer attached to the rail. The old merchant led the way, with Olgerkhan carrying Nyungy close behind and occasionally putting his hand out to steady Wingham.

The staircase rose about fifteen feet, opening onto a balcony that ran the breadth of the wide foyer and back again. Across the way, a second staircase climbed to the third story. That one seemed more solid, with the balusters all in place, but it hadn't been used in years, obviously, and Wingham had to brush away cobwebs to continue. As the stairs spilled out on the south side of the house, Wingham had to follow the balcony all the way back around the other side to the north room's door. He glanced back when he got there, for Nyungy was walking again and had lost ground with his pronounced limp. Nyungy waved for him to go on, and so he pressed through the door, crossing to the far window where he pulled aside the drape.

Staring out to the north, Wingham nearly fell over, for though he had expected to view the growing castle, he didn't expect how dominant the structure would be from so far away. Only a few days had passed since Wingham had ventured to the magical book and the structure growing behind it, and the castle was many times the size it had been. Wingham couldn't see the book from so great a distance, obviously, but the circular stone keep that grew behind it was clearly visible, rising high above the Vaasan plain. More startling was the fact that the keep was far to the back of the structure, centering a back wall anchored by two smaller round towers at its corners. From those, the walls moved south, toward Palishchuk, and Wingham could see the signs of a growing central gatehouse at what he knew would be the front wall of the upper bailey.

Several other structures were growing before the gatehouse as well, an outer bailey and a lower wall already climbed up from the ground.

"By the gods, what did he do?" old Nyungy asked, coming up beside Wingham.

"He left us some presents, so it would seem," Wingham answered.

"It seems almost a replica of Castle Perilous, curse the name," Nyungy remarked.

Wingham looked over at the old bard, knowing well that Nyungy was one of the few still alive who had glimpsed that terrible place during the height of Zhengyi's power.

"A wizard did this," Nyungy said.

"Zhengyi, as I explained."

"No, my old friend Wingham, I mean now. A wizard did this. A wizard served as catalyst to bring life to the old power of the Witch-King. Now."

"Some curses are without end," Wingham replied, but he held back the rest of his thoughts concerning Arrayan and his own foolishness in handing her the book. He had thought it an instruction manual for necromancy or golem creation or a history, perhaps. He could never have imagined the truth of it.

"Please come out with me, Nyungy," Wingham bade.

"To there?" the old man said with a horrified look. "My adventuring days are long behind me, I fear. I have no strength to do battle with—"

"Not there," Wingham explained. "To the house of a friend: my niece, who is in need of your wisdom at this darkening hour."

Nyungy looked at Wingham with unveiled curiosity and asked, "The wizard?" Wingham's grim expression was all the answer the older half-orc needed.

Wingham soon found that Olgerkhan had not been exaggerating in his insistence that the old merchant go quickly to Arrayan. The woman appeared many times worse than before. Her skin was pallid and seemed bereft of fluid, like gray, dry paper. She tried to rise up from the bed, where Olgerkhan had propped her almost to a sitting position with pillows, but Wingham could see that the strain was too great and he quickly waved her back to her more comfortable repose.

Arrayan looked past Wingham and Olgerkhan to the hunched, elderly half-orc. Her expression fast shifted from inviting to suspicious.

"Do you know my friend Nyungy?" Wingham asked her.

Arrayan continued to carefully scrutinize the old half-orc, some spark of distant recognition showing in her tired eyes.

"Nyungy is well-versed in the properties of magic," Wingham explained. "He will help us help you."

"Magic?" Arrayan asked, her voice weak.

Nyungy came forward and leaned over her. "Little Arrayan Maggotsweeper?" he said. The woman winced at the sound of her name. "Always a curious sort, you were, when you were young. I am not surprised to learn that you are a wizard—and a mighty one, if that castle is any indication."

Arrayan absorbed the compliment just long enough to recognize the implication behind it then her face screwed up with horror.

"I did not create the castle," she said.

Nyungy started to respond, but he stopped short, as if he had just caught on to her claim.

"Pardon my mistake," he said at last.

The old half-orc bent lower to look into her eyes. He bade Olgerkhan to go and fetch her some water or some soup, spent a few more moments scrutinizing her, then backed off as the larger half-orc returned. With a nod, Nyungy motioned for Wingham to escort him back into the house's front room.

"She is not ill," the old bard explained when they had moved out of Arrayan's chamber.

"Not sick, you mean?"

Nyungy nodded. "I knew it before we arrived, but in looking at her, I am certain beyond doubt. That is no poison or disease. She was healthy just a few days ago, correct?"

"Dancing lightly on her pretty feet when she first came to greet me upon my arrival."

"It is the magic," Nyungy reasoned. "Zhengyi has done this before."

"How?"

"The book is a trap. It is not a tome of creation, but one of *self*-creation. Once one of suitable magical power begins to read it, it entraps that person's life essence. As the castle grows, it does so at the price of Arrayan's life-force, intellect, and magical prowess. She is creating the castle, subconsciously."

"For how long?" Wingham asked, and he stepped over and glanced with concern into the bedroom.

"Until she is dead, I would guess," said Nyungy. "Consumed by the creation. I doubt that the merciless Zhengyi would stop short of such an eventuality out of compassion for his unwitting victim."

"How can we stop this?" Wingham asked.

Nyungy glanced past him with concern then painted a look of grim dread on his face when he again met Wingham's stare.

"No, you cannot," Wingham said with sudden understanding.

"That castle is a threat—growing, and growing stronger," reasoned Nyungy. "Your niece is lost, I fear. There is nothing I can do, certainly, nor can anyone else in Palishchuk, to slow the progression that will surely kill her."

"We have healers."

"Who will be powerless, at best," answered the older half-orc. "Or, if they are not, and offer Arrayan some relief, then that might only add to the energy being channeled into the growth of Zhengyi's monstrosity. I understand your hesitance here, my friend. She is your relation—beloved, I can see from your eyes when you look upon her. But do you not remember the misery of Zhengyi? Would you, in your false compassion, help foster a return to that?"

Wingham glanced back into the room once more and said, "You cannot know all this for sure. There is much presumption here."

"I know, Wingham. This is not mere coincidence. And you know, too." As he finished, Nyungy moved to the counter and found a long kitchen knife. "I will be quick about it. She will not see the strike coming. Let us pray it is not too late to save her soul and to diminish the evil she has unwittingly wrought."

Wingham could hardly breathe, could hardly stand. He tried to digest Nyungy's words and reasoning, looking for some flaw, for some sliver of hope. He instinctively put his arm out to block the old half-orc, but Nyungy moved with a purpose that he had not known in many, many years. He brushed by Wingham and into the bedroom and bade Olgerkhan to stand aside.

The large half-orc did just that, leaving the way open to Arrayan, who was resting back with her eyes closed and her breathing shallow.

Nyungy knew much of the world around Palishchuk. He had spent his decades adventuring, touring the countryside as a wandering minstrel, a collector of information and song alike. He had traveled extensively with Wingham for years as well, studying magic and magical items. He had served in Zhengyi's army in the early days of the Witch-King's rise, before the awful truth about the horrible creature was fully realized. Nyungy didn't doubt his guess about the insidious bond that had been created between the book and the reader, nor did he question the need for him to do his awful deed before the castle's completion.

His mind was still sharp; he knew much.

What he did not comprehend was the depth of the bond between Arrayan and Olgerkhan. He didn't think to hide his intent as he brandished that long knife and moved toward the helpless woman.

Something in his eyes betrayed him to Olgerkhan. Something in his forward, eager posture told the young half-orc warrior that the old half-orc was about no healing exercise—at least, not in any manner Olgerkhan's sensibilities would allow.

Nyungy lurched for Arrayan's throat and was stopped cold by a powerful hand latching onto his forearm. He struggled to pull away, but he might as well have been trying to stop a running horse.

"Let me go, you oaf!" he scolded, and Arrayan opened her eyes to regard the two of them standing before her.

Olgerkhan turned his wrist over, easily forcing Nyungy's knife-hand up into the air, and the old half-orc grimaced in pain.

"I must . . . You do not understand!" Nyungy argued.

Olgerkhan looked from Nyungy to Wingham, who stood in the doorway.

"It is for her own good," Nyungy protested. "Like bloodletting for poison, you see?"

Olgerkhan continued to look to Wingham for answers.

Nyungy went on struggling then froze in place when he heard Wingham say, "He means to kill her, Olgerkhan."

Nyungy's eyes went wide and wider still when the young, strong half-orc's fist came soaring in to smack him in the face, launching him backward and to the floor, where he knew no more.

CHAPTER

11

"Hurry!" Calihye shouted at Entreri. "Drive them harder!"

Entreri grunted in reply but did not put the whip to the team. He understood her desperation, but it was hardly his problem. Across a wide expanse of rocky ground with patches of mud, far up ahead, loomed the low skyline of Palishchuk. They were still some time away from the city, Entreri knew, and if he drove the team any harder, the horses would likely collapse before they reached the gates.

Jarlaxle sat beside him on the bench, with Athrogate next to him, far to Entreri's left. Pratcus sat in the back, along with Calihye and the two wounded, the soldier Davis Eng and Calihye's broken companion, Parissus.

"Harder, I say, on your life!" Calihye screamed from behind.

Entreri resisted the urge to pull the team up. Jarlaxle put a hand on his forearm, and when he glanced at the drow, Jarlaxle motioned for him to not respond.

In truth, Entreri wasn't thinking of shouting back at the desperate woman, though the thought of drawing his dagger, leaping back, and cutting out her wagging tongue occurred to him more than once.

A second hand landed on the assassin's other shoulder, and he snapped his cold and threatening glare back the other way, face-to-face with Pratcus.

"The lady Parissus is sure to be dying," the dwarf explained. "She's got moments and no more."

"I cannot drive them faster than—" Entreri started to reply, but the dwarf cut him short with an upraised hand and a look that showed no explanation was needed.

"I'm only telling ye so ye don't go back and shut the poor girl up," Pratcus explained. "Them half-elves are a bit on the lamenting side, if ye get me meaning."

"There is nothing you can do for the woman?" Jarlaxle asked.

"I got all I can handle in keeping Davis Eng alive," Pratcus explained. "And he weren't hurt much at all in comparison, except a bit o' acid burns. It's the damn bites she got. So many of 'em. Poisoned they were, and a nasty bit o' the stuff. And Parissus, she'd be dying without the poison, though I'm sure there's enough to kill us all running through her veins."

"Then have Athrogate smash her skull," Entreri said. "Be done with it, and done with her pain."

"She's far beyond any pain, I'm thinking."

"More's the pity," said Entreri.

"He gets like that when he's frustrated," Jarlaxle quipped.

He received a perfectly vicious look from Entreri and of course, the drow responded with a disarming grin.

"That soldier gonna live, then?" asked Athrogate, but Pratcus could only shrug.

Behind them all, Calihye cried out.

"Saved me a swat," Athrogate remarked, understanding, as did they all from the hollow and helpless timbre of the shriek that death had at last come for Parissus.

Calihye continued to wail, even after Pratcus joined her and tried to comfort her.

"Might be needing a swat, anyway," Athrogate muttered after a few moments of the keening.

Ellery pulled her horse us beside the rolling wagon, inquiring of the cleric for Parissus and her soldier.

"Nasty bit o' poison," Entreri and Jarlaxle heard the dwarf remark.

"We're not even to the city, and two are down," Entreri said to the drow.

"Two less to split the treasures that no doubt await us at the end of our road."

Entreri didn't bother to reply.

A short while later, the Palishchuk skyline much clearer before them, the troupe noted the circle of brightly colored wagons set before the city's southern wall. At that point, Mariabronne galloped past the wagon, moving far ahead.

"Wingham the merchant and his troupe," Ellery explained, coming up beside Entreri.

"I do not know of him," Jarlaxle said to her.

"Wingham," Athrogate answered slyly, and all eyes went to him, to see him holding one of his matched glassteel morning stars out before him, letting the spiked head sway and bounce at the end of its chain with the rhythm of the moving wagon.

"Wingham is known for trading in rare items, particularly weapons," Ellery explained. "He would have more than a passing interest in your sword," she added to Entreri.

Entreri grinned despite himself. He could imagine handing the weapon over to an inquiring "Wingham," whoever or whatever a "Wingham" might be. Without the protective gauntlet, an unwitting or weaker individual trying to hold Charon's Claw would find himself overmatched and devoured by the powerful, sentient item.

"A fine set of morning stars," Jarlaxle congratulated the dwarf.

"Finer than ye're knowing," Athrogate replied with a grotesque wink. "Putting foes to flying farther than ye're throwing!"

Entreri chortled.

"Fine weapons," Jarlaxle agreed.

"Enchanted mightily," said Ellery.

Jarlaxle looked from the rocking morning star back to the commander and said, "I will have to pay this Wingham a visit, I see."

"Bring a sack o' gold!" the dwarf hollered. "And a notion to part with it!"

"Wingham is known as a fierce trader," Ellery explained.

"Then I really will have to pay him a visit," said the drow.

Pratcus waddled back up to lean between Entreri and the drow. "She's gone," he confirmed. "Better for her that it went quick, I'm thinking, for she weren't to be using her arms or legs e'er again."

That did make Entreri wince a bit, recalling the bumps as the wagon had bounced over poor Parissus.

"What of Davis Eng?" Ellery asked.

"He's a sick one, but I'm thinking he'll get back to his feet. A few tendays in the bed'll get him up."

"A month?" Ellery replied. She did not seem pleased with that information.

"Three gone," Entreri mumbled to the drow, who didn't really seem to care.

Ellery obviously did, however. "Keep him alive, at all cost," she instructed then she turned her horse aside and drove her heels into its flanks, launching it away.

Accompanied by the continuing sobs of Calihye, Entreri took the wagon the rest of the way to Palishchuk. On Ellery's orders, he rolled the cart past Wingham's circus and to the city's southern gate, where they were given passage without interference—no doubt arranged by Mariabronne, who had long ago entered the city.

They pulled up beside a guardhouse, just inside the southern gate, and stable hands and attendants came to greet them.

"I promise you that I will not forget what you did," Calihye whispered to Entreri as she moved past him to climb down from the wagon.

Jarlaxle again put a hand on the assassin's forearm, but Entreri wasn't about to respond to that open threat—with words anyway.

Entreri rarely if ever responded to threats with words. In his thoughts, he understood that Calihye would soon again stand beside Parissus.

A trio of city guards hustled out to collect Davis Eng, bidding Pratcus to go with them. Another couple came out to retrieve the body of Parissus.

"We have rooms secured inside, though we'll not be here long," Ellery explained to the others. "Make yourself at ease; take your rest as you can."

"You are leaving us?" the drow asked.

"Mariabronne has left word that I am to meet him at Wingham's circus," she explained. "I will return presently with word of our course."

"Your course," Calihye corrected, drawing all eyes her way. "I'm through with you, then."

"You knew the dangers when you joined my quest," Ellery scolded, but not too angrily, "as did Parissus."

"I'm to be no part of a team with that one," Calihye retorted, tipping her chin in Entreri's direction. "He'll throw any of us to our doom to save himself. A wonder it is that even one other than him and that drow survived the road."

Ellery looked at the assassin, who merely shrugged.

"Bah! But yer friend fell and flees to the Hells," Athrogate cut in. "We're all for dyin', whate'er we're tryin', so quit yer cryin'! *Bwahaha!*"

Calihye glowered at him, which made him laugh all the more. He waddled away toward the guardhouse, seeming totally unconcerned.

"He is one to be wary of," Jarlaxle whispered to Entreri, and the assassin didn't disagree.

"You agreed to see this through," Ellery said to Calihye. She moved over as she spoke, and forcibly turned the woman to face her. "Parissus is gone and there's naught I, or you, can do about it. We've a duty here."

"Your own duty, and mine no more."

Ellery leveled a hard stare at her.

"Will I be finding myself an outlaw in King Gareth's lands, then, because I refuse to travel with a troupe of unreliables?"

Ellery's look softened. "No, of course not. I will ask of you only that you stay and look over Davis Eng. It seems that he'll be journeying with us no farther as well. When we are done with Palishchuk, we will return you to the Vaasan Gate—with Parissus's body, if that is your choice."

"And my share is still secure?" the woman dared ask. "And Parissus's, which she willed to me before your very eyes?"

To the surprise of both Entreri and Jarlaxle, Ellery didn't hesitate in agreeing.

"An angry little creature," Jarlaxle whispered to his friend.

"A source of trouble?" Entreri mused.

"Mariabronne has returned," Wingham informed Olgerkhan when he found the large half-orc back at Nyungy's house. "He has brought a commander from the Vaasan Gate, along with several other mercenaries, to inspect the castle. They will find a way, Olgerkhan. Arrayan will be saved."

The warrior looked at him with undisguised skepticism.

"You will join them in their journey," Wingham went on, "to help them in finding a way to defeat the curse of Zhengyi."

"And you will care for Arrayan?" Olgerkhan asked with that same evident doubt. He glanced to the side of the wide foyer, to a door that led to a small closet. "You will protect her from him?"

Wingham glanced that way, as well. "You put the great Nyungy in a closet?"

Olgerkhan shrugged, and Wingham started that way.

"Leave him in there!" Olgerkhan demanded.

Wingham spun back on him, stunned that the normally docile—or controllable, at least—warrior had so commanded him.

"Leave him in there," Olgerkhan reiterated. "I beg of you. He can breathe. He is not dangerously bound."

The two stared at each other for a long while, and it seemed to Olgerkhan as if Wingham was fighting an internal struggle over some decision. The old merchant started to speak a couple of times, but kept stopping short and finally just assumed a pensive pose.

"I will not care for Arrayan," Wingham said decided at last.

"Then I will not leave her."

Wingham stepped toward Olgerkhan, reaching into his coat pocket as he did. Olgerkhan leaned back, defensive, but calmed when he noted the objects Wingham had produced: a pair of rings, gold bands with a clear gemstone set in each.

"Where is she?" Wingham asked. "Back at her house?"

Olgerkhan stared at him a bit longer, then shook his head. He glanced up the stairs then led the way to the first balcony. In a small bedroom, they came upon Arrayan, lying very still but breathing with a smooth rhythm.

"She felt better, a bit," Olgerkhan explained.

"Does she know of Nyungy?"

"I told her that he was with you, looking for some answers."

Wingham nodded, then moved to his niece. He sat on the bed beside her, blocking much of Olgerkhan's view. He bent low for a moment then moved aside.

Olgerkhan's gaze was drawn to the woman and to the ring Wingham had placed on her finger. The clear gem sparkled for a brief moment then it went gray, as if smoke had somehow filtered into the gemstone. It continued to darken as Olgerkhan moved closer, and by the time he gently lifted Arrayan's hand for a closer inspection, the gem was as inky black as onyx.

The warrior looked at Wingham, who stood with his hand out toward Olgerkhan, holding the other ring.

"Are you strong enough to share her burden?" Wingham asked.

Olgerkhan looked at him, not quite understanding. Wingham held up the other ring.

"These are Rings of Arbitration," the old merchant explained. "Both a blessing and a curse, created long ago by magic long lost to the world. Only a few pairs existed, items crafted for lovers who were bound body and soul."

"Arrayan and I are not—"

"I know, but it does not matter. What matters is what's in your heart. Are you strong enough to share her burden, and are you willing to die for her, or beside her, should it come to that?"

"I am. Of course," Olgerkhan answered without the slightest hesitation.

He reached for Wingham and took the offered ring. With but a fleeting glance at Arrayan, he slid the ring on his finger. Before he even had it in place, a profound weariness came over him. His vision swam and his head throbbed with a sharp pain. His stomach churned from the waves of dizziness and his legs wobbled as if they would simply fold beneath him. He felt as if a taloned hand had materialized within him and had begun to tug at his very life-force, twanging that thin line of energy so sharply and insistently that Olgerkhan feared it would just shatter, explode into a scattering of energy.

He felt Wingham's hand on him, steadying him, and he used the tangible grip as a guide back to the external world. Through his bleary vision he spotted Arrayan, lying still but with her eyes open. She moved one arm up to brush back her thick hair, and even through the haze it was apparent to Olgerkhan that the color had returned to her face.

He understood it all then, so clearly. Wingham had asked him to "share her burden."

That thought in mind, the half-orc growled and forced the dizziness aside, then straightened his posture, grabbed Wingham's hand with his own, and pointedly moved it away. He looked to the old merchant and nodded. Then he glanced down at his ring and watched as a blood-red mist flowed into it and swirled in the facets of the cut stone. The mist turned gray, but a light gray, not the blackness he had seen upon poor Arrayan's finger.

He glanced back at the woman, at her ring, and saw that it, too, was no longer onyx black.

"Through the power of the rings, the burden is shared," Wingham whispered to him. "I can only hope that I have not just given a greater source of power to the growing construct."

"I will not fail in this," Olgerkhan assured him, though neither of them really knew what "this" might actually mean.

Wingham moved over and studied Arrayan, who was resting more comfortably, obviously, though she had again closed her eyes.

"It is a temporary reprieve," the merchant said. "The tower will continue to draw from her, and as she weakens, so too will you. This is our last chance—our only chance—to save her. Both of you will go with Mariabronne and Gareth's emissary. Defeat the power that has grown dark on our land, but if you cannot, Olgerkhan, then there is something else you must do for me."

The large half-orc stood attentively, staring hard at old Wingham.

"You must not let the castle have her," Wingham explained.

"Have her?"

"Consume her," came the reply. "I cannot truly comprehend what that even means, but Nyungy, who is wiser than I, was insistent on this point. The castle grows through the life-force of Arrayan, and the castle has made great gains because we did not know what we battle. Even now, we cannot understand how to defeat it, but defeat it you must, and quickly. And if you cannot, Olgerkhan, I will have your word that you will not let the castle consume my dear Arrayan!"

Olgerkhan's gaze went to Arrayan again as he tried to sort through the words, and as Wingham's meaning finally began to dawn on him, his soft appearance took on a much harder edge. "You ask me to kill her?"

"I ask for your mercy and demand of you your strength."

Olgerkhan seemed as if he would stride over and tear Wingham's head from his shoulders.

"If you cannot do this for me then . . ." Wingham began, and he lifted Arrayan's limp arm and grabbed at the ring.

"Do not!"

"Then I will have your word," said the merchant. "Olgerkhan, there is no choice before us. Go and do battle, if battle is to be found. Mariabronne is wise in the ways of the world, and he has brought an interesting troupe with him, including a dark elf and a wizened sage from Damara. But if the battle cannot be won, or won in time, then you must not allow the castle to take Arrayan. You must find the strength to be merciful."

Olgerkhan was breathing in rough pants by then, and he felt his heart tearing apart as he looked at his dear Arrayan lying on the bed.

"Put her hand down," Olgerkhan said at length. "I understand and will not fail in this. The castle will not have Arrayan, but if she dies at my hand, know that I will fast follow her to the next world."

Wingham slowly nodded.

"Better this than to enter the castle beside that troublesome dwarf," said Davis Eng, his voice weak with poison.

Herbalists had come to him, and Pratcus had worked more spells over him. He would survive, they all agreed, but it would be some time before he even had the strength to return to the Vaasan Gate, and it would likely be tendays before he could lift his sword again.

"Athrogate?" Calihye asked.

"A filthy little wretch."

"If he heard you say that, he'd crush your skull," the woman replied. "The finest fighter at the wall, so it was said, and there's more than a little magic in those morning stars he swings so cleverly."

"Strength of arm is one thing. Strength of heart another. Has one so fine ever thought to enlist in the Army of Bloodstone?"

"By serving at the wall, he serves the designs of King Gareth," Calihye reminded.

Flat on his back, Davis Eng lifted a trembling hand and waved that notion away.

Calihye persisted. "How many monster ears has he delivered to your Commander Ellery, then? And those of giants, too. Not many can lay claim to felling a giant in single combat, but it's one that Athrogate all too easily brandishes."

"And how do you know he was alone? He's got that skinny friend of his— more trouble than the dwarf!"

"And more dangerous," said Calihye. "Speak not ill of Canthan in my presence."

Davis Eng lifted his head enough to glower at her.

"And be particularly wise to do as I say as you lie there helplessly," the woman added, and that made the man lay his head back down.

"I didn't know you were friends."

"Me and Canthan?" The woman snorted. "The more ground's between us, the calmer beats my heart. But like your dwarf, that one is better on my side than my opponent's." She paused and moved across the small room to the fire pit, where a kettle of stew simmered. "You want more?"

The man waved and shook his head. It already seemed as though he was falling far, far away from the conscious world.

"Better to be out here, indeed," Calihye said—to herself, for Davis Eng had lapsed into unconsciousness. "They're for going into that castle, so I'm hearing, and that's no place I'm wanting to be, Athrogate and Canthan beside me or not."

"But did you not just say that the dwarf was a fine warrior?" came a different voice behind her, and the woman froze in place. "And the skinny one even more dangerous?"

Calihye didn't dare turn about; she knew from the proximity of the voice that the newcomer could take her down efficiently if she threatened him. How had he gotten so near? How had he even gotten into the room?

"Might I even know who's addressing me?" she dared ask.

A hand grabbed her shoulder and guided her around to look into the dark eyes of Artemis Entreri. Anger flared in Calihye's eyes, and she had to fight the urge to leap upon the man who had allowed her friend to fall beneath the wagon wheels.

Wisdom overcame the temptation, though, for in looking at the man, standing so at ease, his hands relaxed and ready to bring forth one of his ornamented weapons in the blink of an eye, she knew that she had no chance.

Not now. Not with her own weapons across the way next to Davis Eng's bed.

Entreri smiled at her, and she knew that her glance at the sleeping soldier had betrayed her.

"What do you want?" she asked.

"I wanted you to keep on speaking, that I could hear what I needed to hear and be on my way," Entreri replied. "Since that is not an option, apparently, I decided to bid you continue."

"Continue what?"

"Your appraisal of Athrogate and Canthan, to start," said the assassin. "And any information you might offer on the others."

"Why should I offer anyth—"

She bit off the last word, and nearly the tip of her tongue as faster than her eye could even follow, the assassin had his jeweled dagger in his hand and tip-in against the underside of her chin.

"Because I do not like you," Entreri explained. "And unless you make me like you in the next few minutes, I will make your death unbearable."

He pressed in just a bit harder, forcing Calihye up on her tip-toes.

"I can offer gold," she said through her gritted teeth.

"I will take whatever gold of yours I want," he assured her.

"Please," she begged. "By what right—"

"Did you not threaten me out on the road?" he said. "I do not let such chatter pass me by. I do not leave enemies alive in my wake."

"I am not your enemy," she rasped. "Please, if you let me show you."

She lifted one hand as if to gently stroke him, but he only grinned and pressed that awful dagger in more tightly, breaking the skin just a bit.

"I don't find you charming," Entreri said. "I don't find you alluring. It annoys me that you are still alive. You have very little time left."

He let the dagger draw a bit of the half-elf's life-force into its vampiric embrace. Calihye's eyes widened in an expression so full of horror that the assassin knew he had her undivided attention.

He reached up with his other hand, planted it on her chest, and retracted the dagger as he unceremoniously shoved her back and to the side of the cooking pit.

"What would you ask of me?" Calihye gasped, one hand clutching her chin as if she believed she had to contain her life's essence.

"What more is there to know of Athrogate and Canthan?"

The woman held up her hands as if she didn't understand.

"You battle monsters for your living, yet you fear Canthan," said Entreri. "Why?"

"He has dangerous friends."

"What friends?"

The woman swallowed hard.

"Two beats of your fast-beating heart," said Entreri.

"They say he is associated with the citadel."

"What citadel? And do understand that I grow weary of prying each word from your mouth one at a time."

"The Citadel of Assassins."

Entreri nodded his understanding, for he had indeed heard whispers of the shadowy band, living on after the fall of Zhengyi, digging out their kingdom in the shadows created by the brilliance of King Gareth's shining light. They were not so different than the pashas Entreri had served for so long on the streets of Calimport.

"And the dwarf?"

"I know not," said Calihye. "Dangerous, of course, and mighty in battle. That he even speaks to Canthan frightens me. That is all."

"And the others?"

Again the woman held up her hand as if she did not understand.

"The other dwarf?"

"I know nothing of him."

"Ellery?" he asked, but he shook his head even as the name left his lips, doubting there was anything the half-elf might tell him of the red-haired commander. "Mariabronne?"

"You have not heard of Mariabronne the Rover?"

A glare from Entreri reminded her that it really wasn't her place to ask the questions.

"He is the most renowned traveler in Vaasa, a man of legend," Calihye explained. "It is said that he could track a swift-flying bird over mountains of empty stone. He is fine with the blade and finer with his wits, and always he seems in the middle of momentous events. Every child in Damara can tell you tales of Mariabronne the Rover."

"Wonderful," the assassin muttered under his breath. He moved across the room to Calihye's sword belt, hooked it with his foot and sent it flying to her waiting grasp.

"Well enough," he said to her. "Is there anything more you wish to add?"

She looked from the sword to the assassin and said, "I cannot travel with you—I am charged with guarding Davis Eng."

"Travel? Milady, you'll not leave this room. But your words satisfied me. I believe you. And I assure you, that is no small thing."

"Then what?"

"You have earned the right to defend yourself."

"Against you?"

"While I suspect you would rather fight him,"—he gave a quick glance at the unconscious Davis Eng—"I do not believe he is up to the task."

"And if I refuse?"

"I will make it hurt more."

Calihye's look moved from one of uncertainty to that primal and determined expression Entreri had seen so many times before, the look that a fighter gets in her eye when she knows there is no escape from the battle at hand. Without blinking, without taking her gaze from him for one second, Calihye drew her sword from its scabbard and presented it defensively before her.

"There is no need for this," she remarked. "But if you must die now, then so be it."

"I do not leave enemies in my wake," Entreri said again, and out came Charon's Claw.

He felt a slight tug at his consciousness from the sentient weapon but put the intrusion down with a thought. Then he came on, a sudden and brutal flurry of movement that sent his dagger out ahead and his sword sweeping down.

Calihye snapped her blade up to block, but Entreri shifted the angle at the last minute, making the sword flash by untouched—until, that is, he reversed the flow and slapped it hard against the underside of her sword, bringing forth a yelp of surprise to accompany the loud ringing of metal.

Entreri hit her sword again as she tried to bring it to bear, then retreated a step.

The woman slipped back behind the fire pit and glanced at Entreri from above the glow. Her gaze went down to the cooking pot, just briefly.

Enough for Entreri.

Charon's Claw came across vertically as Calihye broke for the pot, launching it and the tripod on which it stood forward to send hot stew flying. She followed with a howl, one that turned to surprise as she saw the wall of black ash Entreri's sword had created.

Still, she could not halt her momentum as she leaped the small fire pit, and she followed the pot through the ash wall, bursting out with a wild slashing of her sword to drive the no-doubt retreating intruder back even farther.

Except that he was not there.

"How?" Calihye managed to say even as she felt the explosion of pain in her kidney.

Fire burned through her and before she regained her sensibilities she was on her knees. She tried to turn her shoulders and send her sword flashing back behind her, but a boot stopped her elbow short, painfully extending her arm, and the sword flew from her hand.

She felt the heavy blade settle onto her collarbone, its evil edge against the side of her neck.

Entreri knew he should just be done with her then and there. Her hatred on the road had sounded as a clear warning bell to him that she might one day repay him for the perceived wrong.

But something washed over him in that moment, strong and insistent. He saw Calihye in a different light, softer and vulnerable, one that made him reconsider his earlier words to her—almost. He looked past the scar on her face and saw the beauty that was there beneath. What had driven a woman such as her to so hard a road, he wondered?

He retracted the sword, but instead of bringing it in to take his enemy's head, he leaned in very close to her, his breath hot in her ear.

Disturbed by his emotions, Entreri roughly shook them away.

"Remember how easily you were beaten," he whispered. "Remember that I did not kill you, nor did I kill your friend. Her death was an unfortunate accident, and would that I could go back to that frantic moment and catch her before she fell, but I cannot. If you cannot accept that truth then remember this."

The assassin brought the tip of his awful dagger up against her cheek, and the woman shuddered with revulsion.

"I will make it hurt, Calihye. I will make you beg me to be done with it, but. . . ."

It took Calihye a few moments to realize that the cold metal of the demonic blade was no longer against her skin. She slowly dared to open her eyes then even more slowly dared to turn back.

The room was empty save for Davis Eng, who lay with his eyes wide and terror-filled, obviously having witnessed the last moments of the one-sided fight.

CHAPTER

12

By the time Entreri caught up to Jarlaxle and the others, they were camped on a hillock beyond Palishchuk's northern wall. From that vantage point, the growing black castle was all too clear to see.

"When I left here last it was no more than foundation stones, and seemingly for a structure much smaller than this," Mariabronne informed them in hushed tones. "Wingham named it a replica of Castle Perilous, and I fear now that he was correct."

"And you once glanced upon that awful place," Ellery said.

"Well, if none are in there, then we'll make it our halls!" roared Athrogate. "Got me some friends to be guardin' our walls!"

"Got you a habit to bring on your fall," Jarlaxle muttered under his breath, but loud enough for Athrogate to hear, which of course only brought a burst of howling laughter from the wild-eyed dwarf.

"Good grief," said the drow.

"Only kind I'm likin'!" Athrogate said without missing a beat.

"I doubt it is uninhabited or's to stay that way for long," Pratcus put in. "I can feel the evilness emanating from the thing—a beacon call, I'm guessing, for every monster in this corner o' Vaasa."

Entreri looked over at Jarlaxle and the pair exchanged knowing glances. The strange castle, as with the similar tower they'd previously encountered, likely needed no garrison from without. That tower had nearly killed them both, had destroyed perhaps his greatest artifact in the battle. Entreri wondered how much more formidable might the castle be, for it was many times the size of that single tower.

"Whatever your feeling, good dwarf, and whatever our fears, it is of course incumbent upon us to investigate more closely," Canthan put in. "That is our course, is it not, Commander Ellery?"

Entreri caught something in the undertones of Canthan's words. A familiarity?

"Indeed, our duty seems clear to that very course," Ellery replied.

It seemed to Entreri that she was being a bit too formal with the thin wizard, a bit too standoffish.

"In the morning then," Mariabronne said. "Wingham said he would meet us here this night and he is not one to break his word."

"And so he has not," came a voice from down the hill, and the troupe turned as one to regard the old half-orc trudging up the side of the hillock, arm-in-arm with a woman whose other arm was locked with that of another half-orc, a large and hulking specimen.

Normally, Entreri would have focused on the largest of the group, for he carried himself like a warrior and was large enough to suggest that he presented a potential threat. But the assassin was not looking at that one, not at all, his eyes riveted to the woman in the middle. She seemed to drift into the light of their campfire like some apparition from a dream. Though arm-in-arm with both men flanking her, she seemed apart from them, almost ethereal. There was something familiar about her wide, flat face, about the sparkle in her eyes and the tilt of her mouth as she smiled, just a bit nervously. There was something warm about her, Entreri sensed somewhere deep inside, as if the mere sight of her had elicited memories long forgotten and still not quite grasped of a better time and a better place.

She glanced his way and was locked by his gaze. For a long moment, there seemed a tangible aura growing in the air between them.

"As promised, Mariabronne, I have brought my niece Arrayan Faylin and her escort Olgerkhan," Wingham said, breaking the momentary enchantment.

Arrayan blinked, cleared her throat, and pulled her gaze away.

"The book was lost to us for a time," Mariabronne explained to the others. "It was Arrayan who discovered it and the growth about it north of the city. It was she who first recognized this dark power and alerted the rest of us."

Entreri looked from the woman to Jarlaxle, trying hard to keep the panic out of his expression. Memories of the tower outside of Heliogabalus buried those of that distant and unreachable warmth, and the fact that the woman was somehow connected to that evil construct of the Witch-King's stung Entreri's sensibilities.

He paused and considered that sensation.

Why should he care?

The look Entreri gave to Arrayan when Wingham introduced her was not lost upon Jarlaxle.

Nor had it been lost on the large escort at Arrayan's other side, the drow noted.

Jarlaxle, too, had been caught a bit off guard when first he glanced Wingham's niece, for the attractive woman was hardly what he had expected of a half-orc. She clearly favored her human heritage far more than her orc parent or grandparent, and more than that, Jarlaxle saw a similarity in Arrayan to another woman he had known—not a human, but a halfling.

If Dwahvel Tiggerwillies had a human cousin, Jarlaxle mused, she would look much like Arrayan Faylin.

Perhaps that had helped to spark Entreri's obvious interest.

Jarlaxle thought the whole twist perfectly entertaining. A bit dangerous, perhaps, given the size of Arrayan's escort, but then again, Artemis Entreri could certainly take care of himself.

The drow moved to join his companion as the others settled in around the northern edge of the hilltop. Entreri was on the far side, keeping watch over the southern reaches, the short expanse of ground between the encampment and the city wall.

"A castle," Entreri muttered as Jarlaxle moved to crouch beside him. "A damned castle. Ilnezhara told you of this."

"Of course not," the drow replied.

Entreri turned his head and glared at him. "We came north to Vaasa and just happened to stumble upon something so similar to that which we had just left in Damara? An amazing coincidence, wouldn't you agree?"

"I told you that our benefactors believed there might be treasures to find," the drow innocently replied. He moved closer and lowered his voice as he added, "The appearance of the tower in the south indicated that other treasures might soon be unearthed, yes, but I told you of this."

"Treasures?" came the skeptical echo. "That is what you would call this castle?"

"Potentially . . ."

"You've already forgotten what we faced in that tower?"

"We won."

"We barely escaped with our lives," Entreri argued. He followed Jarlaxle's concerned glance back to the north and realized that he had to keep his voice down. "And for what gain?"

"The skull."

"For my gauntlet? Hardly a fair trade. And how do you propose we do battle with this construct now that the gauntlet is no more? Has Ilnezhara given you some item that I do not know about, or some insight?"

Jarlaxle fought very hard to keep his expression blank. The last thing he wanted to do at that moment, given the nature of Entreri's glance at Arrayan, was explain to him the connection between Herminicle the wizard, Herminicle the lich, and the tower itself.

"A sense of adventure, my friend," was all Jarlaxle said. "A grand Zhengyian artifact, a tome, perhaps, or perhaps some other clue, awaits us inside. How can we not explore that possibility?"

"A dragon's lair often contains great treasures, artifacts even, and by all reasoning such a hunt would constitute the greatest of adventures," Entreri countered with understated sarcasm. "When we are done here, perhaps our 'benefactors' will hand us maps to their distant kin. One adventurous road after another."

"It is a thought."

Entreri just shook his head slowly and turned to gaze back at the southland and the distant wall of Palishchuk.

Jarlaxle laughed and patted him on the shoulder then rose and started away.

"There are connections among our companions that we do not yet fully understand," Entreri said, causing the dark elf to pause for just a moment.

Jarlaxle was glad that his companion remained as astute and alert as ever.

"What's it about, ye skinny old lout?" Athrogate roared as he approached Canthan on the far western side of the hillock, where the wizard had set up his tent—an ordinary inverted V-shaped affair suitable for one, or perhaps for two, if they were as thin as the wizard.

"Be silent, you oaf," Canthan whispered from inside the tent. "Come in here."

Athrogate glanced around. The others seemed perfectly content and busy with their own affairs. Pratcus and Ellery worked at the fire, cooking something that smelled good, but in truth, there was no food that didn't smell good to Athrogate. On the northern end of the flat-topped hill, Arrayan and Olgerkhan sat staring off into the darkness, while across the way to the south, that damned dark elf had gone to join his swarthy friend. Mariabronne was off somewhere in the night, Athrogate knew, along with the odd half-orc Wingham.

With a shrug, the black-bearded dwarf dropped to his knees and crawled into Canthan's tent. There was no light in there, other than the distant glow of the campfire, but Athrogate needed no more than that to realize he was alone in the tent. But where had Canthan's voice come from?

"What're ye about?" Athrogate asked.

"Be silent, fool, and come up here."

"Up?" As he moved toward the voice, Athrogate's face brushed into a rope hanging down from the apex of the tent. "Up?"

"Climb the rope," came a harsh whisper from above.

It seemed silly to the dwarf, for if he had stood up, his head would have lifted the tent from the ground. He had been around Canthan long enough to understand the wizard's weird ways, however, and so, with another shrug, he grasped the rope and started to climb. As soon as his bent legs lifted off the ground, Athrogate felt as if he had left the confines of the tent. Grinning mischievously, the dwarf pumped his powerful arms more urgently, hand-walking up the rope. Where he should have bumped into the solid barrier of the tent roof, he found instead a strange foggy area, a magical rift between the dimensions. He charged through and ran out of rope—it simply ended in mid-air!

Athrogate threw himself into a forward roll, landing on a soft rug. He tumbled to a sitting position and found himself in a fairly large room, perhaps a dozen feet square, and well-furnished with many plush rugs, a couple of hardwood chairs, and a small pedestal atop which sat a crystal ball. Canthan peered into the orb.

"Well," said Athrogate, "if ye was to bring such goodies as these, then why'd ye make a tent fit for a dwarf on his knees?"

Canthan waved at him with impatience, and the dwarf sighed at the dismissal of his hard-earned cleverness. He shrugged it away, stood, and walked across the soft carpet to take a seat opposite the skinny wizard.

"Naked halflings?" he asked with a lewd wink.

"Our answers, from Knellict, no less," Canthan said, once again invoking the name of the imposing wizard to steal the grin from Athrogate's smug expression.

The dwarf moved his face up to the crystal ball, staring in. His wildly distorted face filled the globe and brought a yelp from Canthan, who fell back and glowered at him.

"Ain't seein' nothing, except yerself," said Athrogate. "And ye're skinnier than e'er!"

"A wizard might look into the ball. A dwarf can only look through it."

"Then why'd ye call me up here?" Athrogate asked, settling back in the chair. He glanced around the room again, and noted a blazing hearth across the way with a pot set in it. "Got anything good for eating?"

"The citadel's spies have searched far and wide for answers," Canthan explained. "All the way to Calimport."

"Never heard of it. That a place?"

"On Faerûn's far southwestern shores." Canthan said, though Athrogate was not at all impressed. "That is where our friends—and they haven't even changed their names—originated from. Well, the drow came from Menzoberranzan."

"Never heard of it, either."

"It does not matter," the wizard replied. "The two of them were in Calimport not so long ago, accompanied by many other dark elves from the Underdark."

"Heard o' that, and yep, that'd be where them dark elves come from."

"Shut up."

The dwarf sighed and shrugged.

"They tried to conquer the back streets of the city," Canthan said.

"Streets wouldn't give up, would they?"

Again, the wizard narrowed his eyes and glared at the dwarf. "They went against the thieves' guilds, which are much like our own citadel. This Jarlaxle person sought to control the cutpurses and killers of Calimport."

Athrogate considered that for a few moments, then took on a more serious expression. "Ye think they come here wanting the same thing?"

"There is no indication that they brought any allies with them, from all we've seen," explained the wizard. "Perhaps they have been humbled and understand their place among us. Perhaps not, and if not. . . ."

"Yeah, I know, we kill 'em to death in battle," the dwarf said, seeming almost bored.

"Ellery is ready to deal with the drow."

"Bah, I can swat 'em both and be done with it."

Canthan came forward in a rush, his eyes wide, his expression wild. "Do not underestimate them!" he warned. "This is no ordinary duo. They have traveled the breadth of Toril, and for a drow to do so openly is no small matter."

"Yeah, yeah, yeah," Athrogate agreed, patting his gnarled hand in the air to calm the volatile wizard. "Take care and caution and all that. Always that."

"Unlike your typical methods."

"Ones that got me where I am." He paused and hopped up, then did a quick inspection of himself, even seeming to count his fingers. "With all me pieces intact, and what do ye know about that?"

"Shut up."

"Keep saying it."

"You forget why we came out here? Knellict sent us with a purpose."

"Yeah, yeah, yeah."

"You just be ready," said Canthan. "If it comes to blows, then we can hope that Ellery will finish the drow. The other one is your task."

Athrogate snapped his fingers in the air.

Even with Athrogate still sitting there, Canthan started to go on, to work through a secondary plan, just in case. But he stopped short, realizing from the dwarf's smug expression that powerful Athrogate really didn't think it necessary.

In truth, and in considering the many enemies he had watched Athrogate easily dispatch, neither did Canthan.

Commander Ellery ran to the eastern edge of the hillock. To her left loomed the growing replica of Castle Perilous, Palishchuk to her right seeming diminished by the sheer grandiosity of the new construction. Before her rose the northeastern peaks of the Galenas, running north to collide with the gigantic floe of the Great Glacier. Ellery squinted and ducked lower, trying to alter the angle of the black horizon, for she caught a movement down there in the near pitch blackness.

"What was it, then?" asked Pratcus the dwarf, hustling up beside her.

Ellery shook her head and slowly pulled the axe from her the harness on her back.

Across the way, Entreri and Jarlaxle took note, too, as did Olgerkhan and Arrayan.

A form blacker than the shadows soared up at the commander, flying fast on batlike wings.

Ellery fell back with a yelp, as did Pratcus, but then, acting purely on instinct, the woman retracted her axe arm, took up the handle in both hands, and flung the weapon end-over-end at her approaching assailant.

The axe hit with a dull thud and crackle, and the winged creature lurched higher into the air. Ellery ducked low as it came over her.

"Demons!" Pratcus howled when he saw the beast in the glow of their campfire, light glistening off its clawed hands and feet, and its horned, hideous head. It was humanoid with wide wings. Taller than Pratcus, but shorter than Ellery, the creature was both solid and sinewy.

"Gargoyles," Jarlaxle corrected from across the way.

The obsidian beast clawed at Ellery's axe, which she had embedded deep into its chest, dark blood flowing from either side of the sharp gash. It remained outstretched horizontally for a bit longer, but then tumbled head down and crashed and rolled across the hilltop.

Ellery was on it in a flash.

"More coming!" she yelled.

She skidded down to her knees beside the fallen gargoyle, grasped her axe in both hands, and tore it free.

Behind her, Pratcus was already spellcasting, calling on the magic of Dumathoin, the dwarf god, the Keeper of Secrets under the mountain. He finished with a great flourish, lifting his arms high and wide, and as he spoke the last syllable of the spell, a burst of brilliant light filled the air around him, as if the sun itself had risen.

And in that light, the dwarf and the others saw that Ellery's words were on the mark, for dark shapes fluttered this way and that at the edges of the glowing magic.

"So the fun begins," Entreri said to Jarlaxle.

He drew his sword and dagger and charged forward into the fray, veering as he went, though he was hardly aware of it, to move closer to the woman Arrayan.

"Form defenses!" Ellery yelled. A call from Mariabronne somewhere down the hill turned her and the others. "Tight formations!" she cried as she sprinted off to the lip of the rise, then disappeared into the night.

Entreri dipped forward into a roll as a gargoyle dived for him, the creature's hind claws slashing at the air above the assassin. He came up with a slash and clipped the gargoyle's foot before it rushed out of range.

Entreri couldn't follow, for a second was upon him, arms slapping wildly. The creature tried to come forward to bite or gore with its horn, but Entreri's sword came up and around, forcing it back and bringing both of its arms over to the assassin's left.

Entreri stepped forward and right, feinting with his dagger as he went by. The gargoyle turned to roll behind him, but the assassin switched weapons, sword to his left, dagger to his right and with a reverse grip. He stepped forward with his left foot, but dug it in and stopped short, reversing his momentum, turning back into the closing gargoyle.

A claw raked his shoulder, but it was not a serious wound. The assassin willingly traded that blow with his own, burying his dagger on a powerful backhand deep into the center of the gargoyle's chest.

For good measure, Entreri drew some of the gargoyle's life-force through his vampiric blade, and he felt the soothing warmth as his wound fast mended.

As he withdrew and turned again, Entreri let fly a backhand with his sword as well, creasing the creature's face and sending it crashing to the ground. He completed the spin, bringing his hands together, and when he righted himself, he had his weapons back in their more comfortable positions, Charon's Claw in his right, jeweled dagger in his left.

Entreri glanced right to see Arrayan, Olgerkhan, and the dwarf Pratcus formed into a solid defensive triangle, then back to the left where Jarlaxle crouched and pumped his arm, sending a stream of daggers at a gargoyle as it flew past. The creature pulled up, wings wide to catch the air. It hovered for a second, accepting another stinging hit, then pivoted in mid-air and dived hard at the drow.

Jarlaxle met Entreri's glance for just a second, offered an exaggerated wink, then created a globe of darkness, completely obscuring his form and the area around him.

Entreri couldn't help but wince as the gargoyle dived into it full speed.

Any thoughts he had of going to his friend were short-lived, though, and he instinctively dropped and rolled, slashing his sword to fend another of the horned creatures.

Still another was on the ground and charging at him, its limp telling him that it was the same one he had earlier slashed.

Entreri bent his knees and lifted his hips from the ground, arching his back. With a snap of his finely-toned muscles, he flipped himself up to his feet, and met the charge with a sidelong swipe that forced the gargoyle to pull up short.

The second dropped behind him, but the assassin was not caught off guard. He turned as the creature landed, dagger thrusting—not with any chance to hit, but merely to keep the gargoyle back a stride.

Over and around went his sword, right to left, then back left to right, and in that second roll, he had the gargoyle's eyes and arms following the blade. Back went the sword the other way again, and the gargoyle had to twist even more off balance.

Entreri let the blade go all the way over until its tip was straight down. He turned with it and under it, lifting it and the gargoyle's arms high. Again the creature tried to twist away, but Entreri's movement had leaned him in at the creature. He let himself fall at the gargoyle, thrusting his dagger into the creature's side as he went.

The assassin easily regained his balance, using the weight of the gargoyle to steady his fall. He tore his dagger free as he spun back to face the second, pursuing gargoyle.

Across came the sword, and the gargoyle leaped high, wings beating, to get above it. Entreri let the sword flow its opaque black ash and he went forward as the gargoyle passed over him. He ducked low under the ash wall and waved the sword back behind him to create a second one.

Then, even as the gargoyles turned together to consider the puzzle, Entreri burst forth through the veil, sword stabbing right, dagger thrusting left. He cut fast to the right, where he had scored a hit, and came in with a dagger stab to the creature's gut, followed by a half turn that allowed him to bash the howling gargoyle's face with the pommel of Charon's Claw. He reversed his grip on the dagger as he pulled it free then jabbed it back once, twice, thrice, into the wounded beast.

He leaped forward as if to meet the second gargoyle, his ruse forcing the creature to break its momentum, but Entreri stopped short and whirled, his sword coming across at shoulder level to take the head from the wounded beast.

Entreri let himself fall over backward, timing it perfectly with the renewed approach of the second, which leaped above him as it charged past.

Up he stabbed with his sword, gashing the gargoyle beside the knee, and he rolled back, coming up to his feet behind the creature as it struggled to turn around.

Too slow.

Entreri took the thing in its kidney with his dagger, and the gargoyle howled and leaped away, spinning as it went.

But the assassin was right there with it, Charon's Claw coming across low-to-high. The gargoyle tried to block and lost an arm for the effort.

It hardly noticed that, however, for the assassin pressed in, his dagger scoring a hit on the gargoyle's hip. Entreri hooked and tugged as he fast retracted, dropping his left foot far back and pulling the gargoyle forward just a bit.

Close enough for Charon's Claw. Across came the assassin's right hand, the mighty sword creasing the gargoyle from face to wounded hip.

It shrieked, an unearthly sound indeed, and stumbled back a step, then another. It tried to beat its wings to lift away, but it was too late for that, and with a confused look at the assassin, it fell over dead.

Bolts of luminescent green flared from Arrayan's fingers, burning into a charging gargoyle. One after another, her magically-created missiles reached out and seared the creature, and with each, its steps toward her became more unsteady.

Still, watching the woman, Pratcus feared that the gargoyle would rush over her. He shook the sight away—she would have to hold!—and continued his magical casting, leaping toward Olgerkhan as he did battle with two of the creatures, his heavy club smashing at their reaching, clawed hands. Bluish magic flowed from Pratcus and into the large half-orc. Healing energy stemmed the flow of blood from a wound the half-orc had suffered in the first exchange.

A shout from the side turned the dwarf on his heel, just in time to see the gargoyle collide with Arrayan, both going down in a heap. The dwarf leaped in and slugged the gargoyle in the back of its horned head with his mailed fist. He knew even as he connected that Arrayan's missiles had already finished the job, though. He grabbed the dead thing's shoulders and yanked it off the woman, then took Arrayan's hand and tugged her to her feet.

Blood ran freely from Arrayan's broken nose, but the dwarf had no time for that at the moment. He turned and began his spellcasting, and Arrayan did, too, though her arcane chant was slurred by the blood in her mouth.

Her missiles fired first, reaching out and swerving to either side of Olgerkhan to alternately slam the creatures he was frantically battling.

"Close your eyes!" Pratcus yelled an instant before his spell went off.

A burst of brilliant light filled the area around the battle, and Olgerkhan and both gargoyles recoiled in horrified surprise. Before the large half-orc or Arrayan could question the dwarf's tactic, however, the purpose became apparent, for the gargoyle to Olgerkhan's left began flailing helplessly at the air, obviously blinded.

Olgerkhan went for the one on the right instead. He swiped his heavy club across in front of him. As it went out far to the left, he let go with his trailing hand. He rolled the club under his left arm as he continued his swing, bringing it in behind his back, where he caught it again with his right. He rolled the weapon over so that its butt was sticking out before him, recaptured it closer to the leading edge with his left hand, and thrust if forward into the midsection of the leaping gargoyle as he, too, strode ahead.

The devastating impact doubled the gargoyle over, and Olgerkhan stepped away fast and slid his club back so that both his hands were on its handle again. With a roar, the brutish half-orc brought it in a great overhand swipe that cracked against the back of the gargoyle's head and drove it face down to the ground.

Olgerkhan went for the second gargoyle, and Pratcus was already casting another healing spell for the warrior, when Arrayan yelped and flew forward, hit hard by the head butt of yet another diving creature.

Pratcus turned his attention to the gargoyle standing at his side, of course, but not before noting that Olgerkhan, too, arched his back in sudden pain, though nothing had hit him there. With no time to sort through the puzzle, the dwarf launched a sidelong swipe with his small mace.

The gargoyle caught it by the handle, just under the spiked head, but that was exactly what the dwarf had expected. Pratcus's muscled legs uncoiled, launching him into the creature, and he let fly a left jab that crunched the gargoyle squarely in the face. That, not the mace, was Pratcus's preferred method of attack, for he wore heavy metal gauntlets powerfully enchanted for battle.

The dwarf continued to bore in, pressing his face into the gargoyle's chest. He let go of his mace and began driving his fists one after another into the gargoyle's midsection, each heavy blow bringing forth a gasping growl and lifting the gargoyle from the ground.

Beside him, Arrayan re-oriented herself to the battle.

A heavy thump brought her attention to Olgerkhan, his club sending the blind gargoyle into a sidelong spin, so brutal was the blow.

Arrayan caught movement out of the corner of her eye and grabbed at her pouch where she kept her spellcasting ingredients. She waved her hand and called forth her magic, and the air above and to the side of Olgerkhan filled with stringy, weblike strands. Arrayan had nothing upon which to set her web, so it didn't stop the descent of the gargoyle, but by the time the creature hit the ground between her and Olgerkhan, it was all tangled and fighting furiously to pull free of the sticky filaments.

Its predicament only worsened when a second gargoyle flew past Arrayan, tumbling down at the entangled one's feet and tripping it up. Right behind that battered form came Pratcus, howling his battle cry.

And Olgerkhan was there, too, driving his club down with heavy chops that shattered gargoyle bone.

Those chops quickly diminished, though, and Pratcus turned to question the large half-orc. The words stuck in the dwarf's mouth, however, when he realized that Olgerkhan was gasping for breath, exhausted and struggling.

The dwarf eyed him with curiosity, not quite understanding. The warrior had suffered no serious hits, and the fight had barely begun.

Shaking his head, Pratcus could only turn and look for something else to hit.

⊕━━━⊕

Entreri wondered why he even bothered to stand up again after yet another roll beneath the reaching claws of a diving gargoyle. He also wondered why in the Nine Hells the warrior dwarf and the thin wizard hadn't yet joined the fray. He figured that would soon enough be remedied, in any case, as a gargoyle swept down into the wizard's small tent, tearing through the fabric with abandon.

But the two were not in there.

Entreri's eyes narrowed as the tent fell away, leaving the gargoyle standing confused before a rope hanging in mid-air. The gargoyle tugged then climbed. Its head and shoulders disappeared into an extra-dimensional pocket.

There was a brilliant flash of flame, and the decapitated body of the gargoyle tumbled to the ground. Out of thin air leaped Athrogate, one of his morning stars smoking.

"Give me the boys and yerself fights the girls," he roared. "For everyone knows there's claws in them curls! *Bwahaha!*"

Entreri prayed that a dozen gargoyles would throttle the little beast.

A pair seemed as if they would do exactly that, soaring down fast, but the dwarf's spinning morning stars kept them at bay, and a searing bolt of lightning flashed out from the extra-dimensional pocket.

From across the way, Entreri marked that lightning blast clearly, for so intense was the power that the gargoyles were incinerated and thrown away. He saw Canthan's face peeking out above the rope, and he knew then that the frail-looking wizard was not one to be taken lightly.

A third gargoyle, on the ground, charged at the dwarf, who howled and charged right back. The creature came in and snapped its head forward to gore with its horn, but Athrogate leaped and similarly head-butted, forcing an impact with the creature's forehead before it could bring the horn in line.

Dwarf and gargoyle bounced back, both standing staring at each other, and seeming as if on shaky legs.

Athrogate yelled, *"Bwahaha!"* again, snorted and launched a wad of spit into the gargoyle's face.

"Mark ye with spit so I know where to hit!" he cried.

The dwarf went into a sudden spin, coming around with a leading morning star that crunched against the stunned gargoyle's face. The creature's head snapped back. Its arms out wide, the gargoyle arched its back and stared up at the dark sky.

Athrogate twisted his torso as he continued his spin so that his arms were on the diagonal, and his second morning star's spiked head came in on the gargoyle descending from on high.

The creature jolted down and seemed to bounce, and it appeared as if it would just fall over.

The dwarf was taking no chances, though, or was just enjoying it all too much. He put the weapons in tighter alternating spins above his head, slamming the gargoyle several times, driving it back, back, until he finally just let the dead thing fall to the ground.

"Bwahaha!" the dwarf yelled as he charged in the direction of Pratcus and the two half-orcs.

He cut back suddenly, though, his heavy boots digging ruts in the ground.

Entreri shook his head and started the same way, but he pulled up as the dwarf halted and turned around. He knew what had gotten Athrogate's attention, and a lump appeared in his throat as he watched a quartet of gargoyles diving at the drow's globe of darkness.

"Jarlaxle!" he cried.

The assassin winced as the gargoyles disappeared into the impenetrable shadow.

Howls and screams, shrieks of pain and bloodthirsty hunger, erupted from within.

Entreri found it hard to breathe.

"Get there, dwarf," he heard himself whispering.

CHAPTER

THE LIVING CASTLE

13

Pratcus could tell that the half-orcs beside him were faltering, and he frantically cheered them on with both words and prayers. He called upon his god to bless his allies and sent waves of healing magic into them, sealing their wounds.

But still they floundered. Arrayan threw out bursts of destructive magical energy, but her repertoire fast diminished, and many of her magical attacks were no more than cantrips, minor spells that inconvenienced an enemy more than they truly hurt it. No one could question the determination and bravery of Olgerkhan, standing strong as rock against the current of the gargoyle river—at least at first. Eventually the large half-orc seemed more a mound of sand, cracking and weakening, his very solidity seeming to lessen.

Something was wrong, Pratcus knew. Either the pair was not nearly as formidable as they had initially seemed, or their strength was draining far too quickly.

The gargoyles seemed to sense it, too. They came on more furiously and more directly, and Pratcus fell back as one crossed over Olgerkhan, the half-orc's sluggish swing not coming close to intercepting it, and dived at the cleric.

Pratcus threw his hands up defensively, expecting to be overwhelmed, but he noticed the gargoyle jerk awkwardly, then again. As the dwarf dodged aside, the creature didn't react but just kept its current course, slamming face-first into the ground.

Pratcus's eyes widened as he noted two feathered arrows protruding from the dead gargoyle's side. The dwarf scrambled to the northern lip of the hillock and saw his two missing companions battling furiously. Ellery guarded Mariabronne's flank, her mighty axe cutting great sweeps through the air, taking the reaching limbs from any gargoyles who ventured too near. With the warrior-woman protecting him, Mariabronne, the legendary Rover of Vaasa, put his great bow to deadly use, sending lines of arrows soaring into the night sky, almost every one finding its mark in the hide of a hovering gargoyle.

"I need ye!" Pratcus yelled down, and the two heroes heeded the call and immediately charged the dwarf's way. Even that movement was perfectly coordinated, with Ellery circling around Mariabronne, protecting his rear and both flanks, while the ranger's bow *twanged* in rapid order, clearing any enemies from before them.

They joined Pratcus not a moment too soon, for Olgerkhan was near to collapse. The half-orc, down on one knee, barely managed to defend himself against a gargoyle that would have soon killed him had not Mariabronne's arrow taken the thing in the throat.

Beside the large half-orc, Arrayan, her spells depleted, stood with dagger in hand. She slashed wildly, her every movement off-balance and exaggerated, her every cut leaving openings in her defenses that any novice warrior could easily exploit.

Ellery leaped to Arrayan's side as the gargoyle bore down on the half-orc woman, its arms out wide to wrap her in its deadly embrace.

That momentum halted when an overhand chop put the warrior-woman's axe head deep into the gargoyle's chest.

Arrayan fell back with a squeal, tripping to the ground. Ellery noted a second creature's approach and tried desperately to tear her axe free, but it got hooked on one of the dead creature's ribs. Ellery reached across with her shield to fend it off but knew she was vulnerable.

The gargoyle's shriek was not one of hungry victory, however, but of pain and surprise, as a pair of arrows knifed into its chest.

Ellery managed to glance back and offer an appreciative nod to Mariabronne.

The ranger didn't notice, for he was already sighting his next target, bow drawn and arrow ready to fly.

Beside him, Pratcus breathed a sigh of relief.

Athrogate could not get to the globe in time, and Entreri watched helplessly as the four gargoyles disappeared into the darkness. Howls and shrieks erupted immediately, a flurry of claws slapping at flesh and a cacophony of opposing screeches, blending and melding into a macabre song of death.

"Jarlaxle," Entreri whispered, and he knew again that he was alone.

"They do make a mess of it," remarked a familiar voice, and Entreri nearly jumped out of his boots when he noted the dark elf standing next to him.

Jarlaxle held a thin metallic wand tipped with a ruby. He reached out and spoke a command word, and a tiny pill of fire arched out at the globe of darkness.

Noting the angle of the fiery pea and the approach of Athrogate, it seemed to Entreri almost as if the drow was tossing it to the roaring dwarf. Entreri thought to yell out a warning to Athrogate, but he knew that his call could do nothing to deter the committed warrior.

The pea disappeared into the darkness.

So did the dwarf.

A burst of flame lit the night, erupting from the globe, and when it was done, the darkness was gone and six gargoyles lay smoldering on the ground.

Athrogate ran out the other side, trailing wisps of smoke and a stream of colorful curses.

"Tough little fellow," Jarlaxle remarked.

"More's the pity," said Entreri.

Across the way, Canthan poked his head out of his extra-dimensional pocket and watched the goings-on with great amusement. He saw Ellery and Mariabronne charge to the aid of the dwarf cleric and the two half-orcs and was distracted by the roar of Athrogate—that one was always roaring!—as the dwarf bounded toward a globe of darkness.

It was a drow's globe, Canthan knew, and if the dark elf was inside it, the wizard could only hope the gargoyles would make fast work of him.

A familiar sight, usually one leaving his own hands, crossed into his field of vision, right to left, and he backtracked it quickly to see the dark elf standing beside Entreri, wand in hand.

A glance back made Canthan wince for his gruff ally, but it was one of instinct and reaction, certainly not of sympathy for the dwarf.

Athrogate came through the fireball, of course, smoking and cursing.

Canthan hardly paid him any heed, for his gaze went back to Jarlaxle. Who was this drow elf? And who was that deadly sidekick of his, standing amidst the inedible carrion of dead gargoyles? The wizard didn't lie to himself and insist that he wasn't impressed. Canthan had served Knellict for many years, and in the hierarchy of the Citadel of Assassins, survival meant never underestimating either your friends or your foes.

"Why are you here, drow?" Canthan whispered into the night air.

At that moment, Jarlaxle happened to turn his way and obviously spotted him, for the drow gave a tip of his great plumed hat.

Canthan chewed his lip and silently cursed himself for the error. He should have cast an enchantment of invisibility before poking his head out.

But the drow would have seen him anyway, he suspected.

He gave a helpless sigh and grabbed the rope, rolling out so that he landed on his feet. A glance around told him that the fight was over, the gargoyles destroyed, and so with a snap of his fingers, he dismissed his extra-dimensional pocket.

"The castle is alive," Olgerkhan said.

He was bent over at the waist, huffing and puffing, and it seemed to the others that it was all he could do to hold his footing and not sink down to his knees. At his side, Arrayan put a hand on his shoulder, though she seemed equally drained.

"And already more gargoyles are . . . growing," said old Wingham, coming up the northern side of the hill. "On the battlements, I mean. Even as that force flew off into the night, more began to take shape in their vacated places."

"Well now, there is a lovely twist," Canthan remarked.

"We must tear down the castle," declared Pratcus. "By the will o' Moradin, no such an abomination as that will stand! Though I'm guessing that Dumathoin'd be wanting to find out how the magic o' the place is doing such a thing."

"A high wall of iron and stone," Mariabronne said. "Tear it down? Has Palishchuk the capability to begin such a venture as that?" From his tone, it was clear that the ranger's question was a rhetorical one.

"We are fortunate that this group flew our way," said Wingham. "What havoc might they have wrought upon the unsuspecting folk of Palishchuk?"

"Unsuspecting no more, then," the ranger agreed. "We will set the defenses."

"Or prepare the runnin'," put in a snickering Athrogate.

"King Gareth will send an army if need be," said Ellery. "Pratcus is correct. This abomination will not stand."

"Ah, but would we not all be the fools to attack an armored turtle through its shell?" said Jarlaxle, turning all eyes, particularly those of Entreri, his way.

"Ye got a better idea?" Athrogate asked.

"I have some experience with these Zhengyian constructs," the drow admitted. "My friend and I defeated a tower not unlike this one, though much smaller of course, back on the outskirts of Heliogabalus."

Athrogate raised an eyebrow at that. "Ye were part o' that? A few days afore ye—*we* left on the caravan to Bloodstone Pass? That big rumble in the east?"

"Aye, good dwarf," Jarlaxle replied. " 'Twas myself and good Entreri here who laid low the tower and its evil minions."

"Bwahaha!"

Entreri just shook his head as Jarlaxle dipped a low bow.

"The way to win," the drow said as he straightened, "is from the inside. Crawl in through the hard shell to the soft underbelly."

"Soft? Now there's a word," remarked an obviously flustered and suspicious Entreri, and when Jarlaxle glanced his way, he saw that his friend was none too happy. And none too trusting, his dark eyes throwing darts at the drow.

"We're listening, good drow," Mariabronne prompted.

"The castle has a king—a life-force holding it together," Jarlaxle explained, though of course he had no idea if he was on target or not.

Certainly the tower back in Heliogabalus had crumbled when the gem had been plucked from the book, and the sisters told him that killing the lich would have served the same purpose, but in truth, he had no more than a guess concerning the much grander structure—and if the structure was so much bigger, then what of its "king"?

"If we destroy this life-force, the tower—the castle—will unbind," the drow went on. "All that will be left will be a pile of stone and metal for the blacksmiths and stonemasons to forage through." He noted as he finished that both Arrayan and Olgerkhan shifted uneasily.

That told him a lot.

"Perhaps it would be better to alert King Gareth," a doubting Mariabronne replied.

"Master Wingham can send runners from Palishchuk to that end," Commander Ellery declared. "For now, our course is clear—through the shell then and to the soft insides."

"So says yerself," blustered Athrogate.

"So I do, good dwarf," said Ellery. "I will enter the castle at dawn." She paused and glanced at each of them in turn. "I brought you out here for just an eventuality such as this. Now the enemy is clear before us. Palishchuk cannot wait for word to get to Bloodstone Village and for an army to be assembled. And so I go in. I will not command any of you to follow, but—"

"Of course you will not have to," Jarlaxle interrupted, and when all eyes turned his way again, he dipped another bow. "We ventured forth for just an eventuality such as this, and so by your side, we stand." By *his* side, Jarlaxle could feel Entreri's gaze boring into him.

"Bwahaha!" Athrogate bellowed again.

"Yes, of course we must investigate this further," said Canthan.

"By Dumathoin!" said Pratcus.

"All of you, then," Wingham remarked, "with Arrayan and Olgerkhan, you will vanquish this menace. Of that I am sure."

"Them two?" Athrogate asked with a great *"Harrumph."*

"They represent the finest of Palishchuk," Wingham replied.

"Then get the whole damn town running now, and save yerself the trouble!"

"Easy, good dwarf," said Canthan.

"We'll be spending more time dragging them two about than hunting the enemy," Athrogate grumbled. "I ain't for—"

"Enough, good dwarf," said Canthan.

Arrayan moved from Olgerkhan's side to face the furious dwarf.

"We will not fail in this," she said.

"Bah!" Athrogate snorted, and he turned away.

"Two replacements for us," Entreri whispered to Jarlaxle as they moved back across the hilltop to their respective bedrolls.

"You would not wish to miss this grand adventure, of course."

"You knew about it all along," the assassin accused. "The sisters sent us up here for precisely this."

"We have already been through this," replied the drow. "A library has been opened, obviously, and so the adventure unwinds."

"The tower we defeated wouldn't serve as a guardhouse for this structure," Entreri warned. "And that lich was beyond us."

"The lich is destroyed."

"So is my glove."

Jarlaxle stopped walking and stared at his friend for a few moments.

"A fine point," he conceded finally, "but worry not, for we'll find a way."

"That is the best answer you can find?"

"We always do find a way."

"And we always shall, I suppose?"

"Of course."

"Until the last time. There will be only one last time."

Jarlaxle considered that for a few moments.

Then he shrugged.

"First time them two fall down will only be giving me a softer place to put me boot," Athrogate grumbled, sitting on the torn fabric that used to be Canthan's tent.

He rambled on with his unceasing complaints, but the wizard wasn't listening. Canthan's eyes were focused across the way, where Wingham was sitting with Arrayan and Olgerkhan.

Something wasn't right with those two.

"What? What?" the dwarf asked him, apparently taking heed of the fact that he wasn't being listened to and not much enjoying it.

Canthan began to cast a quick spell, and a translucent shape, somewhat like an ear, appeared floating in mid-air before him. He puffed on it and it drifted away, gliding toward the conversation on the northern side of the encampment. The female, Arrayan, moved off, leaving Wingham alone with the brutish Olgerkhan.

And with Canthan, though of course Wingham didn't know that.

"You know our deal," the old half-orc said, his tone grave.

"I know."

"It must not get too far gone," Wingham said. "There can be no delay, no staying of your hand if the killing blow is needed."

"I know!" the larger half-orc growled.

"Olgerkhan, I am as wounded by this possibility as are you," Wingham said. "This is neither my choice nor my desire. We follow the only road possible, or all is already lost."

His voice trailed off and Olgerkhan held his response as Arrayan moved back to them.

"Interesting," mumbled Canthan.

"What? *What?*" bellowed Athrogate.

"Nothing, perhaps," said the wizard, turning to face his friend. He glanced back across the way as he added, "Or perhaps everything."

Face down, his arms bound behind him, his head hooded, Nyungy had all but given up hope. Resigned to his doom, he wasn't even crying out anymore.

But then a hand grabbed his hood and gently pulled it back, and the old sage found himself staring into the face of his friend.

"How many days?" he gasped through his dry, cracked lips.

"Only two," Wingham replied. "I tried to get to you earlier, but Olgerkhan . . ." He finished with a sigh and held up his wrists, cut cord still hanging from them.

"Your young friend has gone mad!"

"He protects the girl."

"Your niece." There was no missing the accusation in that tone. Wingham looked at Nyungy hard, but only for a moment, then moved around and began to untie him. "To simply murder—"

"It is not murder, as she brought it on herself."

"Unwittingly."

"Irrelevant. You would see the city endangered for the sake of one girl?" asked the sage. Again Wingham held up his wrists, but Nyungy was too sly to fall for that ruse. "You play a dangerous game here, Wingham."

Wingham offered a sigh and said, "The game was begun before ever I knew the dangers, and once set in motion, there was no other course before us."

"You could have killed the girl and been done with it."

Wingham paused for just a moment. "Come," he bade his old friend. "We must prepare the city."

"Where is the girl?"

"Heroes have come from the Vaasan Gate."

"Where is the girl?"

"She went into the castle."

Nyungy's eyes widened and he seemed as if he might simply fall over.

"With Commander Ellery, niece of Gareth Dragonsbane," Wingham explained, "and with Mariabronne the Rover."

Nyungy continued to stare, then nodded and asked, "Olgerkhan is with her?"

"With instructions to not allow the structure to take her. At all costs."

The old sage considered it all for some time. "Too dangerous," he decided with a shake of his head, and he started walking past Wingham.

"Where are you going?"

"Didn't you just say that we had to go and prepare the city? But prepare it for what? To defend, or to run?"

"A little of both, I fear," Wingham conceded.

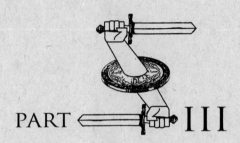

PART III

SECRETS WITHIN
SECRETS WITHOUT

Many times during his journey back to the apartment he shared with Entreri, Jarlaxle fished the violet-glowing gem out of his pocket. Many times he held it up before his eyes, pondering the possibilities hidden inside its skull-like facets as he vividly recalled the sensations at the graveyard. It was a power, necromancy, of which Jarlaxle knew little, and one that piqued his curiosity. What gains might he realize from that purple gem?

The book that had hidden it had been destroyed. Gone too was the tower it had created from feeding on the life-force of Herminicle. All that remained was rubble and scraps. But the gem survived, and it thrummed with power. It was the real prize. The book had been the icing, as sweet as anything Piter spread on his creations, but the gem, that violet skull, was the cake itself. If its powers could be harnessed and utilized. . . .

To build another tower, perhaps?

To find a better connection to the dead? For information, perhaps?

To find allies among the dead?

The dark elf could hardly contain his grin. He so loved new magical toys to examine, and his near-disastrous companionship with the infamous artifact Crenshinibon, the Crystal Shard, had done little to dampen his insatiable curiosity. He wished that Kimmuriel was available to him, for the drow psionicist could unravel the deepest of magical mysteries with ease. If only Jarlaxle had found the skull gem before his last meeting with his lieutenant.

But he would have to wait tendays for their next appointed rendezvous.

"What can you do for me?" he whispered to the skull gem, and perhaps it was his imagination, but the item seem to flare with eagerness.

And that Zhengyian artifact was of little consequence, comparatively speaking, if the fear in Ilnezhara's eyes was any indication. What other treasures lay up there in wait for him and Entreri? What other toys had Zhengyi left scattered about to bring mischief to his vanquishers?

Power to topple a king, perhaps?

Or power to create a king?

That last thought hung in the air, waiting for the drow to grab it and examine it.

He considered the road he and Entreri had traveled to get to Heliogabalus in the still untamed Bloodstone Lands. Wandering adventurers they were, profiteers in heroes' *clothing. Living free and running free, turning their backs to the wind, whichever way that wind was blowing. No purpose led them, save the drow's desire for a new experience, some excitement different from that which had surrounded him for so many centuries. For Entreri, the same?*

No, Jarlaxle thought. It wasn't the lure of new experiences that guided Entreri, but some other need that the assassin likely didn't even understand himself. Entreri didn't know why he stayed by Jarlaxle's side along their meandering road.

But Jarlaxle knew, and he knew, too, that Entreri would stay with him as that road led them farther to the north to the wilds of Vaasa and the promise of greater treasure than even the skull gem.

How might Entreri react if Jarlaxle decided they should stay for some time—forever, perhaps, as measured in the life of a human? If Zhengyian artifacts fell into their hands, the power to tear down a kingdom or to build one, would Entreri willingly participate?

"One journey at a time," Jarlaxle decided, even as he came upon the wooden staircase that led to the balcony of their second story apartment. The sun was up by then, burning through the heavy mist of the eastern sky.

Jarlaxle paused there to consider the parting words of the two dragon sisters:

"The secrets of Zhengyi were greater than Zhengyi. The folk of Damara, King Gareth most of all, pray that those secrets died with the Witch-King," Ilnezhara had said with certainty.

"But now we know that they did not," Tazmikella had added. "Some of them, at least, have survived."

Jarlaxle remembered the words and recalled even more vividly the timbre with which they were spoken, the reverence and even fear. He recalled the look in their respective eyes, sparkling with eagerness, intrigue, and terror.

"With all due respect, King Gareth," Jarlaxle said to the misty morning air, "let us hope that little was destroyed."

He glanced down the street to the little shop where he had set up Piter the baker. Its doors weren't open yet, but Jarlaxle knew that his portly friend would not refuse him admittance.

A short while later, he started up the staircase, knowing that the first battle along his new road, that of convincing the sour, still-hurting Entreri, lay behind his multi-trapped door.

CHAPTER

14

So complete was the castle construction that by the time the nine companions approached the front gates the next morning, they found a fanciful and well-designed flagstone walkway leading to them. On the walls to either side of the closed portcullis, half-formed gargoyles leered at the approaching troupe, and in the few minutes it took them to reach the portcullis, those statues grew into an even more defined form.

"They will be ready to launch into the sky again this night," Mariabronne noted. "Wingham would do well to force Palishchuk into a strong defensive posture."

"For all the good that'll do 'em," Athrogate grumbled.

"Then let us be quick about our task," Ellery replied.

"We heroes," Entreri muttered under his breath, so that only Jarlaxle, standing right beside him at the back of the line, could hear.

The drow was about to respond, but he felt a sudden tug at his sensibilities. Not sure what that might mean, Jarlaxle put a hand over the magical button on his waistcoat, wherein he had stored the skull gem. A look of concern flashed over his angular face. Could it be that the magical gems could call to each other? Had he erred in bringing his skull gem near to the new construct?

Mariabronne was first to the portcullis, its iron spikes as thick as his arms. He peered through the bars at the castle's lower bailey.

"It appears empty," he reported as the others came up beside him. "I can get a grapnel over the wall, perhaps, and locate the hoist."

"No need," Canthan said, and the thin wizard nodded at Athrogate.

"Bah!" the dwarf snorted and he moved up and gently nudged Mariabronne aside. "Gonna pop out me guts, ye stupid mage."

"We all have our uses," Canthan replied to him. "Some of us attend to them without so much blather, however."

"Some of ye sit back and wiggle yer fingers while some of us stop clubs with our faces."

"Good that there's not much beauty to steal then."

"Bah!"

The other seven listened with some amusement, but the banter struck Entreri and Jarlaxle more poignantly.

"Those two sound a bit familiar," Entreri lamented.

"Though not as witty, of course, and therein lies the rub," said the drow.

Athrogate spat in his hands and grabbed at the portcullis, knees bent. He grunted and tried to straighten, to no effect, so he gave another roar, spat in his hands again, and reset his grip.

"A little help, if ye might," he said.

Mariabronne grabbed the portcullis on one side of the dwarf, while both Pratcus and Olgerkhan positioned themselves on the other side.

"Not yerselves, ye bunch o' dolts," the dwarf grumbled.

Behind them, Canthan completed the words of a spell and a wave of energy rolled out from the wizard's hands to encompass the dwarf. Muscles bulged and bones crackled as they grew, and Athrogate swelled to the size of a large man, and continued to grow.

"And again!" the dwarf demanded, his voice even more resonant.

Canthan uttered a second enchantment, and soon Athrogate was the size of an ogre, his already muscular arms as thick as old trees.

"Bah!" he growled in his booming bass voice, and with a roar of defiance, he began to straighten his legs.

The portcullis groaned in protest, but the dwarf pressed on, bringing it up from the ground.

"Get ye going!" he howled, but even as he said it, even as Entreri and Ellery both made to dive under, Athrogate growled and began to bend, and the other three couldn't begin to slow the descent of the huge barrier.

Entreri, the quicker by far to the ground, was also the quicker to halt his movement and spin back, and he managed to grab the diving Ellery as he went and deflect her enough so that she did not get pinned under the heavy spiked gate as it crashed back to earth. The commander cried out, as did Arrayan and Pratcus, but Canthan merely chuckled and Jarlaxle, caught up in the curious sensations of the skull gem, hadn't even heard the call or noticed the lifting of the portcullis, let alone the near loss of one of their companions. When he looked at Athrogate, suddenly so much larger than before, his eyes widened and he fell back several steps.

"Oh, ye son of a bar whore!" Athrogate cursed, and it did not miss Jarlaxle's notice that Entreri shot the dwarf a quick glance that would have curdled milk. Because of the gate's swift descent, the drow wondered? Or was it those few words? Very rarely did Jarlaxle glimpse into the depths of the puzzle that was Artemis Entreri, for the disciplined assassin rarely wore his emotions in his expression.

Every now and then, though. . . .

Athrogate stormed about, rubbing his calloused hands together and repeatedly tightening his belt, a great and decorated girdle with a silver buckle set with crossed lightning bolts.

"By the gods, dwarf," Mariabronne said to Athrogate. "I do believe that you were lifting that practically by yourself, and that our helping hands were of little or no consequence. When you bent, I felt as if a mountain was descending upon me."

"Wizard's spell," Athrogate grumbled, though he hardly sounded convinced.

"Then I pray you cast the enchantment on us others," Mariabronne bade Canthan. "This gate will rise with ease in that case."

"My spells are exhausted," the wizard said, as unconvincingly as the dwarf.

Jarlaxle looked from Canthan to Athrogate, sizing them up. No doubt the spell of enlargement had played some role, but that was not the source of the dwarf's incredible strength. Again Athrogate went to his belt, tightening it yet another notch, and the drow smiled. There were girdles said to imbue their wearer with the strength of a giant, the greatest of which were the storm giants that threw lightning bolts across mountain peaks. Jarlaxle focused on Athrogate's belt buckle and the lightning bolts it displayed.

Athrogate went back to stand in front of the portcullis, hands on hips and staring at it as if it were a betraying wife. Once or twice he started to reach out and touch the thick bars, but always he retracted his hands and grumbled.

"I ain't about to lift it," he finally admitted.

The dwarf grumbled again and nodded as the first of Canthan's enlargement dweomers wore off, reducing him to the size of a large man. By the time Athrogate sighed and turned about, he was a dwarf again. Intimidating, to be sure, but still a dwarf.

"Over the wall, then," said Mariabronne.

"Nah," the dwarf corrected.

He pulled his twin morning stars off of his back and set them to twirling, glassteel gleaming dully in the soft morning light. He brought the handle of the one in his left hand up before his face and whispered something. A reddish-gray liquid began to ooze from the small nubs on the striking ball, coating the whole of the business end of the weapon. Then he brought up the right-hand weapon and similarly whispered, and the liquid oozed forth on that one too, only the gooey stuff was blue-gray instead of red.

"Get back, ye dolt," he said when Ellery moved near to investigate. "Ye're not for wanting to get any o' this on that splendid silver armor o' yers. *Haha!*"

His laugh became a growl and he put his morning stars up in whistling spins above his head. Then he turned a complete circuit, gathering momentum, and launched the red-covered weapon head in a mighty swing against one of the portcullis's vertical bars. He followed with a smash from the other weapon, one that created an explosion that shook the ground beneath the feet of all the stunned onlookers. Another spin became a second thunderous retort, the dwarf striking—one, two, and always with the red-colored morning star leading—a perpendicular bar.

Another hit took that crossing, horizontal bar again. To the amazement of all save Canthan, who stood watching with a sour expression, the thick cross bar broke in half, midway between two vertical spikes. Athrogate back went to work on his initial target, one of those spikes.

The red-colored weapon head clanged against it, about eye level with the furious, wildly-dancing dwarf, followed by a strike with the bluish one a bit lower down.

The spike bent outward. Athrogate hit it again in the same place, once, twice, and the spike fell away, leaving enough room for the companions to squeeze through and into the castle bailey.

Athrogate came to a sudden stop, his morning star heads bouncing around him. He planted his hands on his hips and inspected his handiwork then gave a nod of acceptance.

"For a bit of a kick is why ye got me hired. Anything else ye're wantin' blasting while I got 'em fired?"

Seven stunned expressions and the look of one bored wizard came back at him, eliciting a roaring, *"Bwahaha!"*

"Would that he slips with both and hits himself repeatedly in the face," Entreri muttered to Jarlaxle.

"So then when he's gone, my friend Entreri can take his place?" the drow quipped back.

"Shut up."

"He is a powerful ally."

"And a mighty enemy."

"Watch him closely, then."

"From behind," Entreri agreed.

Entreri did just that, staring hard at the dwarf, who stood with hands on hips, gazing through the gap he had hammered in the portcullis. The power of those swings, magic and muscle, were noteworthy, the assassin knew, as was the ease with which Athrogate handled his weapons. Entreri didn't particularly like the dwarf and wanted to throttle him with every stupid rhyme, but the assassin respected the dwarf's martial prowess. He suspected that he would soon come to blows with Athrogate, and he was not looking forward to the appointment.

Before the group, beyond the corridor cutting between the two small gate-houses, the castle's lower bailey opened wide. To either side of the gatehouse corridor they could see openings: stairwells leading to the wall top, with perhaps inner tunnels snaking through the wide walls.

"Left, right, or center?" Athrogate asked. "Best we quickly enter."

"Will you stop that?" Entreri demanded, and he got a typical, *"Bwahaha!"* in reply.

"The book is straight back, yes?" Mariabronne asked Arrayan, who was standing at his side.

The woman paused for a moment and tried to get her bearings. Her eyes fixed upon the central keep, the largest structure in the castle, which loomed beyond the inner bailey wall.

"Yes," she said, "straight back. I think."

"Do better than that," Canthan bade her, but Arrayan had only a weak and apologetic expression in response.

"Then straight ahead," Ellery told the dwarf.

Entreri noticed that Jarlaxle moved as if to say something in protest. The drow stayed silent, though, and noted the look the assassin was offering his way.

"Be ready," Jarlaxle quietly warned.

"What do you know?"

Jarlaxle only shrugged, but Entreri had been around the drow long enough to understand that he would not have said anything if he wasn't quite sure that trouble was looming. In looking at the castle, the dark stones and hard iron, Entreri had the same feeling.

◄━━━►

They moved through the gates and halted on the muddy courtyard, Athrogate at the lead, Pratcus and Ellery close behind. Jarlaxle paused as soon as he slipped through the portcullis, and swayed with a sudden weakness. An overwhelming feeling of power seemed to focus its sentient attention on him. He looked at Arrayan and knew immediately that it was not her. The castle had progressed far beyond her.

The drow's eyes went to the ground ahead, and in his mind he looked down, down, past the skeletons buried in the old graveyard, for that is what the place once had been. He visualized tunnels and a great chamber. He knew that something down there was waiting for him.

The others took no note of Jarlaxle's delay, for they were more concerned with what lay ahead. A few stone buildings dotted the open bailey: a stable against the left-hand wall immediately inside, a blacksmith's workshop situated in the same place on the right, and a pair of long, low-ceilinged barracks stretching back from both side walls to the base of the taller wall that blocked the inner bailey. The only free-standing structure was a round, two-story, squat tower, set two-thirds of the way across the courtyard before the gates of the inner wall.

Mariabronne moved up beside Ellery and motioned to the tower. The commander nodded her agreement and waved for Athrogate to lead the way.

"I would not . . ." Jarlaxle started to say, but his words were buried by Athrogate's sudden shout.

All eyes turned to the dwarf as he leaped back—or tried to, for a skeletal hand had thrust up through the soft summer tundra dirt to hold fast his ankle. Athrogate twisted, yelped, and went tumbling to the ground. He was back to his feet almost as soon as he landed, though, leaping up and shouting out again, but in rage, not surprise.

The skeletal hand clawed higher into the air, a bony arm coming out to the elbow.

Athrogate's morning star smashed it to dust.

But the skeleton's other hand prodded through the soil to the side, and as the dwarf moved to smash that one he cried, *"Hunnerds!"*

Perhaps it was an exaggeration borne of shock, or perhaps it was an accurate assessment, for all across soft ground of the outer bailey, the skeletal hands of long-dead humanoids clawed up through the hard soil.

Athrogate finished the skeleton's second hand and charged ahead, roaring, "Skinny bones to grind to dust!"

And Pratcus leaped up right beside him. Presenting his anvil-shaped holy symbol, the priest swore, "By the wisdom of Moradin, the grace of Dumathoin and the strength of Clangeddin, I damn thee foul beasts to dust!"

One skeleton, half out of its hole, vibrated under waves of unseen energy, its bony frame rattling loudly. But the others, all across the way, continued to claw their way free of the turf.

Black spots danced before Jarlaxle's eyes, and his head thrummed with a rhythmic chanting, an arcane and evil-sounding cant, calling to the skeletons. The skull-shaped gem in his button seemed to gain weight and substance then, and he felt it vibrating on his chest. Through its power the drow keenly sensed the awakening around him, and understood the depth of the undead parade. From the sheer strength of the call, he expected that the place had served as a burial ground for the Palishchuk half-orcs, or their orc ancestors, for centuries.

Hundreds of skeletal teeth rattled in the drow's thoughts. Hundreds of long-dead voices awakened once more in a communal chanted song. And there remained that one, deeper, larger force, overwhelming with its strength.

He felt a squeeze on his biceps and cried out, then spun and used the magic of his bracer to drop a dagger into his hand. He started to strike but felt his wrist grabbed suddenly, brutally. Jarlaxle opened his eyes as if awakening from a bad dream, and there stood a confused and none-too-happy Artemis Entreri, holding him arm and wrist, and staring at him dumbfounded.

"No, it is all right," the dark elf assured him as he shook his head and pulled away.

"What are you seeing?" Entreri asked. "What do you know?"

"That we are in trouble," the drow answered, and together, the pair turned to face the rising onslaught.

"Cleave with your sword, don't stab," the drow informed Entreri.

"Good to have you looking out for me," Entreri sarcastically replied before he leaped forward and slashed across at an approaching skeleton.

Charon's Claw cut through the reaching monster's ribs to slam hard against its backbone. Entreri expected the blow to cut the skinny undead monstrosity in half, but the skeleton staggered a couple of steps to the side and came on again.

And again Entreri hit it, even harder.

Then again as the stubborn creature relentlessly moved in.

The assassin fell back a step, then dived sidelong as a brilliant bolt of lightning flashed before him, blasting through the skeleton.

The bony monster staggered several steps with that hit, and a pair of ribs fell away, along with one arm. But still it came on, heading toward the disbelieving Jarlaxle and the slender wand the drow held.

Entreri waded in and cracked the skeleton's skull with a two-handed downward chop.

Finally, the undead creature fell to the ground, its bony frame folding up into a neat pile.

"Not your ordinary animations," Jarlaxle remarked.

"We are in trouble," Entreri agreed.

Pratcus stared at his anvil-shaped silver holy symbol as if it had deceived him. The dwarf's lip quivered and he whispered the name of his gods, one after another, the trembling in his voice begging them for an explanation.

"Blunt weapons!" he heard Mariabronne cry. "Shatter their bones!"

But the dwarf priest stood there, shaking his head in disbelief.

A bony hand came out of the ground and grabbed him by the ankle, but Pratcus, still muttering, easily managed to yank his foot away. A second hand clawed forth from the ground and in the torn turf between them, the top of a skull appeared.

Pratcus howled, and he held the screaming note, leaped into the air, and dropped straight down, his metal-shod fist leading in a pile-driving punch atop the skull. He felt the bone crackle beneath him, but the angry dwarf, far from satisfied, put his feet under him again. He leaped up and bashed the skull again, smashing his hand right through it.

The reaching fingers on the skeletal hands shivered and bent over, becoming very still.

"Good enough for ye, ye devils," the confused and angry dwarf remarked then he slugged the skull yet again.

Mariabronne didn't draw his long sword but instead brought forth a small mace. Relying more on speed and skill than on brute force, the ranger whirled, slapping repeatedly at a pair of skeletons coming in at him. None of the blows was heavy in nature, but chip after chip fell away as Mariabronne, seeming almost like a king's drummer, rattled off dozens of strikes.

Beside him, Ellery didn't bother changing weapons, as her heavy-bladed axe was equally devastating to bone as to flesh. Fragments of rib or arm or leg splintered under her devastating chops. But still the skeletons came on, undeterred and unafraid, and for every one that Ellery or Mariabronne broke apart, two more took its place.

Behind them Olgerkhan worked his club frantically and Arrayan fired off a series of minor magic spells, glowing missiles of pure energy, mostly. But neither were overly effective, and both half-orcs were obviously tiring quickly again.

Olgerkhan shielded Arrayan with his sizeable bulk and grunted more in pain than battle rage as bony fingers raked at his flesh. Then he howled in terror as one skeleton slipped past him. It had an open path to Arrayan.

The large half-orc tried to turn and catch up but was surprised to learn that he didn't have to, for the animated undead monster did not approach the woman.

Olgerkhan believed he knew why. He closed on the skeleton and smashed it with all his strength anyway, not wanting the others to take note of its aversion to Arrayan.

Of all the companions, none was better equipped to deal with such creatures than was Athrogate. His spinning morning stars, though he hadn't placed any of the enchantments upon them, devastated the skeletal ranks, each strike reducing bone to dust or launching a skull from its perch atop a bony spine.

The dwarf truly seemed to be enjoying himself as he leaped ahead of the others into the midst of the skeletal swarm. His weapons worked in a devastating blur, and white powder filled the air around him, every explosive hit accompanied by his howling laughter.

Canthan stayed close to his diminutive companion the whole time. The wizard enacted only one more spell, summoning a huge, disembodied, semi-translucent hand that floated in mid-air before him.

A skeleton rushed in at him and the five-fingered guardian grasped it, wrapping huge digits around its bony frame. With a grin and a thought, Canthan commanded the hand to squeeze, and the skeleton shattered beneath the power of its grip.

The hand, closed into a fist, darted across as a second skeleton approached the wizard. The spell effect slugged the creature hard and sent it flying away.

"Press on," Mariabronne ordered. "The keep is our goal—our only goal!"

But the ranger's words were lost to the wind a moment later, when Olgerkhan faltered and cried out. Mariabronne turned to see the large half-orc slump to one knee, his half-hearted swings barely fending the clawing skeletons.

"Dwarves, to him!" the ranger cried.

Pratcus took up the charge, throwing himself at the skeletons crushing in around Olgerkhan, but Athrogate was too far away and too wildly engaged to begin to extract himself.

Similarly, Jarlaxle had lagged behind back by the wall. The drow showed no eagerness to wade out into the mounting throng of undead, despite the fact that his companion, though his weapons were ill-suited for battling skeletons, had moved toward the half-orcs before the ranger had even cried out.

Canthan, too, did not go for Olgerkhan and Arrayan, but instead slipped to one side as the ranger and Ellery turned and went for the half-orcs. Canthan retreated to the position held clear by Jarlaxle. With a thought, the wizard sent his enchanted hand back out behind him, gigantic fingers flicking aside skeletons. It reached Athrogate, who looked at it with some curiosity. Then it grabbed the dwarf and lifted him from his feet. The hand sped him in fast pursuit of its wizard master.

Mariabronne, Ellery, and Pratcus formed a defensive triangle around Olgerkhan, beating back the skeletons' assault. Entreri, meanwhile, grabbed Arrayan by the arm and started to pull her away, slashing aside any undead interference.

"Come along," he ordered the woman, but he felt her lagging behind, and when he glanced at her, he understood why.

Arrayan collapsed to the ground.

Entreri sheathed his weapons, slipped his arm around her shoulders, then slid his other arm under her knees and hoisted her. Slipping in and out of consciousness, Arrayan still managed to put her arms around Entreri's neck to help secure the hold.

The assassin ran off, zigzagging past the skeletons.

Behind Entreri, when a break finally presented itself, Mariabronne grabbed

Olgerkhan and ushered him to his feet. Still, when the ranger let him go, the half-orc nearly fell over again.

"I do so enjoy baby-sitting," Canthan muttered as Entreri carried the nearly unconscious Arrayan beside him.

Entreri scowled, and for a moment both Jarlaxle and Canthan thought he might lash out at the insulting wizard.

"Is she wounded?" the drow asked.

Entreri shrugged as he considered the shaky woman, for he saw no obvious signs of injury.

"Yes, pray tell us why our friend Arrayan needs to be carried around when there is not a drop of her blood spilled on the field," Canthan put in.

Again Entreri scowled at him. "Tend to your friend, wizard," he said, a clear warning, as the disembodied hand floated in and deposited a very angry Athrogate on the ground before them.

"Join up and battle to the keep!" Mariabronne called to the group.

"Too many," Jarlaxle shouted back. "We cannot fight them on the open field. Our only hope is through the wall tunnels."

Mariabronne didn't immediately answer, but one look across the field showed him and the three with him that the drow's observations were on target. For dozens of skeletons were up and approaching and more clawing skeletal hands were tearing through practically every inch of turf across the outer bailey.

"Clear a path for them," Canthan ordered Athrogate.

The dwarf gave a great snort and set his morning stars to spinning again. Canthan's huge magical hand worked beside him, and soon the pair had cleared the way for Mariabronne and the other three to rejoin those at the wall.

Jarlaxle disappeared into the left-hand gatehouse, then came back out a few moments later and motioned for them all to follow. Shielded by Canthan's magical hand, holding back the undead horde, all nine slipped into the gatehouse and into the tunnel beyond. A heavy door was set at the end of that tunnel, which Mariabronne closed and secured not a moment too soon, for before the ranger had even turned around to regard the other eight, the clawing of skeletal fingers sounded on the portal.

"An auspicious beginning, I would say," said Canthan.

"The castle protects itself," Jarlaxle agreed.

"It protects many things, so it would seem," Canthan replied, and he managed a sly glance Arrayan's way.

"We cannot continue like this," Mariabronne scolded. "We are fighting in pockets, protective of our immediate companions and not of the group as a whole."

"Might be that we didn't think some'd be needin' so much damn protecting," Athrogate muttered, his steely-eyed gaze locked on the two half-orcs.

"It is what it is, good dwarf," said the ranger. "This group must find harmony and unity if we are to reach the keep and find our answers. We are here together, nine as one."

"Bah!"

"Therein lies our only hope," said Mariabronne.

To the apparent surprise of Athrogate, Canthan agreed. "True enough," the wizard said, cutting the dwarf's next grunt short. "Nine as one and working toward a single goal."

The timbre of his voice was less than convincing, and it didn't pass the notice of both Entreri and Jarlaxle that Canthan had cast a glance Arrayan's way as he spoke.

CHAPTER

SPITTING MONSTERS

15

The tunnel through the wall was narrow and short, forcing everyone other than Athrogate and Pratcus to stoop low. Poor Olgerkhan had to bend nearly in half to navigate the corridor, and many places were so narrow that the broad-shouldered half-orc had to turn sideways to slip through. They came to a wider area, a small circular chamber with the corridor continuing as before out the other side.

"Stealth," Jarlaxle whispered. "We do not want to get into a fight in these quarters."

"Bah!" Athrogate snorted, quite loudly.

"Thank you for volunteering to take the lead," Entreri said, but if that was supposed to be any kind of negative remark to the boisterous and fearsome dwarf, it clearly missed the mark.

"On we go, then!" Athrogate roared and he rambled out of the room and along the corridor, his morning stars in his hands and bouncing along. The weapons often clanged against the stone walls and every time one did, the others all held their breath. Athrogate, of course, only howled with laughter.

"If we kill him correctly, he will block the corridor enough for us to escape," said Entreri, who was third in line, just behind the dwarves and just ahead of Jarlaxle.

"There is nothing waiting for us behind," Pratcus reminded.

"Leaving without that one would constitute a victory," said Entreri, and Athrogate laughed all the louder.

"On we go then!" he roared again. "Hearty dwarves and feeble men. Now's the time for kind and kin, together banded for the win! *Bwahaha!*"

"Enough," Entreri growled, and just then they came upon a wider and higher spot in the uneven corridor, and the assassin set off. A stride, spring, and tuck sent him right over Pratcus's head, and Athrogate let out a yelp and spun as if he expected Entreri to set upon him with his weapons.

As Athrogate turned, however, Entreri went by, and by the time the confused dwarves stopped hopping about and focused ahead once more, the assassin was nowhere to be found.

"Now what was that all about?" Athrogate asked of Jarlaxle.

"He is not my charge, good dwarf."

"He's running out ahead, but for what?" the dwarf demanded. "To tell our enemies we're here?"

"I expect that you have done a fine enough job of that without Artemis Entreri's help, good dwarf," the drow replied.

"Enough of this," said Mariabronne from behind Ellery, who was right behind the drow. "We have not the time nor the luxury of fighting amongst ourselves. The castle teems with enemies as it is."

"Well, where'd he go, then?" asked the dwarf. "He scouting or killing? Or a bit of both?"

"Probably more than a bit," Jarlaxle replied. "Go on, I pray you, and with all speed and with all the stealth you might muster. We will find adversity this day at every corner—I pray you don't invite more than we will happen upon without your . . . enthusiasm."

"Bah!" snorted Athrogate.

He spun around and stomped off—or started to, for barely had he gone two strides, coming up fast on a sharp bend in the corridor, when a form stepped out to block his way.

It was humanoid and fleshy, as tall as a man, but stocky like a dwarf, with massive fleshy arms and twisted, thick fingers. Its head sat square and thick on a short stump of a neck, its pate completely hairless, and no light of life shone in its cold eyes. It came right at Athrogate without hesitation, the biggest clue of all that the creature wasn't truly alive.

"What're ye about?" the dwarf started to ask, indicating that he, unlike Pratcus and Jarlaxle behind him, didn't quite comprehend the nature of the animated barrier. "What?" the dwarf asked again as the creature fast approached.

"Golem!" Jarlaxle cried.

That broke all hesitation from Athrogate, and he gave a howl and leaped ahead, eager to meet the charge. A quick overhand flip of the morning stars, one after the other, got them past the slow-moving creature's defenses.

Both slapped hard against the thick bare flesh, and both jolted the golem.

But neither really seemed to hurt the creature nor slow it more than momentarily.

Pratcus fell back for fear of getting his head crushed on a backswing as Athrogate launched himself into a furious series of arm-pumping, shoulder-spinning attacks. His morning stars hummed and struck home, once then again.

And still the golem pressed in, slapping at him, grabbing at him.

The dwarf dodged a crossing punch, but the move put him too close to the left hand wall, and the ball head of his weapon rang loudly off the stone, halting its rhythmic spin. Immediately, the golem grabbed the morning star's chain.

Athrogate's other arm pumped fast, and he scored a hit with his second weapon across the golem's cheek and jaw. Bone cracked and flesh tore, and when the ball bounced away, it left the golem's face weirdly distorted, jaw hanging open and torn.

Again, though, the golem seemed to feel no pain and was not deterred. It tugged back, and stubborn Athrogate refused to let go of his weapon and was lifted from his feet and pulled in.

A small crossbow quarrel whipped past him as he flew, striking the golem in the eye.

That brought a groan, and a pool of mucus popped out of the exploded orb, but the golem did not relent, yanking the dwarf right in to its chest and enwrapping Athrogate in its mighty arms.

The dwarf let out a yelp of pain, not for the crushing force as yet, but because he felt a point ramming into his armor, as if the golem was wearing a spiked shield across its chest.

Then the stabbing pain was gone and the golem began to squeeze. For all of his strength, Athrogate thought in an instant that he would surely be crushed to death. Then he got stabbed again, and he cried out.

Pratcus was fast to him, calling to Moradin and throwing waves of magical healing energy into the tough warrior. Behind the cleric, Jarlaxle reloaded and let fly another bolt, scoring a hit in the golem's other eye to blind the creature entirely.

The drow pressed himself flat against the corridor wall as he shot, allowing Mariabronne an angle to shoot past him with his great bow. A heavier, more deadly arrow knifed into the golem's shoulder.

Athrogate yelped as he was prodded again and again. He didn't understand; what weapon was this strange creature employing?

And why did the golem suddenly let him go?

He hit the floor and hopped backward, bowling Pratcus over in the process.

Then the dwarf understood, as the stabbing blade popped forth from the golem's chest yet again.

Athrogate recognized that red steel sword tip. The dwarf gave a laugh and started back at the golem but stopped abruptly and put his hands on his hips, watching with great amusement as the sword prodded through yet again.

Then it retracted and the golem collapsed in a heap.

Artemis Entreri reached down and wiped his sword on the fleshy pile.

"Ye could've warned us," Athrogate said.

"I yelled out, but you were too loud to hear," the assassin replied.

"The way is clear to the keep at the wall's corner," Entreri explained. "But once we go through that door, onto the building's second story balcony, we'll be immediately pressed."

"By?" asked Mariabronne.

"Gargoyles. A pair of them." He kicked at the destroyed golem and added, "More, if any are in wait behind the tower's northern door that will take us along the castle's eastern wall."

"We should lead with magic and arrows," Mariabronne remarked, and he looked alternately at Canthan and Jarlaxle.

"Just move along, then," said the thin wizard. "The longer we tarry, the more fighting we will find, I expect. The castle is creating defenses as we stand and chatter—spitting monsters."

"And regenerating them, if the gargoyles are any indication," said Mariabronne.

"Looking like a good place for training young dwarf warriors, then," Athrogate chimed in. "Pour a bit o' the gutbuster down their throats and set 'em to fighting and fighting and fighting. Something to be said for never running out o' monster faces to crush."

"When we're done with it, you can have it, then," Jarlaxle assured the brutish little warrior. "For your children."

"Haha! All thirty of them are already out and fighting, don't ye doubt!"

"A sight I'll have to one day witness, I'm sure."

"Haha!"

"May we go on and be done with this?" asked Canthan, and he motioned to Entreri. "Lead us to the room and clear the door for me."

Entreri gave one last glance at the annoying dwarf then started off along the corridor. It widened a bit, and ramped up slightly, ending in a heavy wooden, iron-banded door. Entreri glanced back at the group, nodded to confirm that it was the correct room, then turned around and pushed through the door.

Immediately following him, almost brushing his back, came a fiery pea. It arced into the open tower room, over the balcony. Just as it dropped from sight below the railing, it exploded, filling the entire tower area with a great burst of searing flame.

Howls came from within and from without. Athrogate rubbed his boots on the stone for traction and went tearing through the door, morning stars already spinning. He was met by a gargoyle, its wings flaming, lines of smoke rising from the top of its head. The creature clawed at him, but half-heartedly, for it was still dazed from the fireball.

Athrogate easily ducked that grasp, spun, and walloped the gargoyle in the chest with his morning star.

Over the railing it went, and with a second gargoyle fast following as Athrogate rambled along.

Into the room went Pratcus, Jarlaxle—wearing a concerned expression—close behind, with Ellery and Mariabronne pressing him.

Canthan came next, chuckling under his breath and glancing this way and that. As he crossed to the threshold, though, a hand shot out from the side, grabbing him roughly by the collar.

There stood Artemis Entreri, somehow hidden completely from sight until his sudden movement.

"You thought I went into the room," he said.

Canthan eyed him, his expression going from surprise to a hint of fear to a sudden superior frown. "Remove your hand."

"Or your throat?" Entreri countered. "You thought I went into the room, yet you launched your fireball without warning."

"I expected that you would be wise enough not to get in the way of a battle mage," Canthan retorted, a double-edged timbre to his voice to match the double edge of his words.

The mounting sound of battle inside rolled out at the pair, along with Olgerkhan's insistence that they get out of the way.

Neither Entreri nor Canthan bothered to look the half-orc's way. They held their pose, staring hard at each other for a few moments.

"I know," Canthan teased. "Next time, you will not wait to ask questions."

Entreri stole his grin and his comfort, obviously, when he replied, "There will be no next time."

He let go of the mage, giving him a rough shove as he did. With a single movement, leaping into the room, he brought forth both his dagger and sword.

His first thought as he came up on his battling companions was to get out of Canthan's line of fire.

Over the railing he went, landing nimbly on the lip of the balcony beyond. Up on one foot, he pointed the toe of the other and slid it into the gap between the bottom of the railing and the floor.

He rolled forward off the ledge. As he swung down to the lowest point, he tightened his leg to somewhat break the momentum, then pulled his locked foot free and tucked as he spun over completely, dropping the last eight feet to the tower floor. Immediately a trio of gargoyles and a flesh golem descended upon him, but they were all grievously damaged from the fireball. None of the gargoyles had working wings, and one couldn't lift its charred arms up to strike.

That one led the way to Entreri, ducking its head and charging in with surprising ferocity.

Charon's Claw halted that charge, creasing the creature's skull and sending it hopping back and down to a sitting position on the floor. It managed to cast one last hateful glance at Entreri before it rolled over dead.

The look only brought a grin to the assassin's face, but he didn't, couldn't, dwell on it. He went into a furious leaping spin, dagger stabbing and sword slashing. The creatures were limping, slow, and Entreri just stayed ahead of them, darting left and right, continually turning them so that they bumped and tangled each other. And all the while his dagger struck at them, and his sword slashed at them.

The balcony above was quickly secured as well, with Athrogate and his mighty swipes launching yet another gargoyle into the air. That one almost hit Entreri as it crashed down, but he managed to get back behind the falling creature. It hit the floor right in front of him, and the flesh golem, closing in, tripped over it.

Charon's Claw cleaved the lunging golem's head in half.

Entreri darted out to the right, staying under the balcony. He saw Mariabronne and Ellery on the stone stairway that lined the tower's eastern, outer wall, driving a battered and dying gargoyle before them.

The gargoyles saw them too, and one rushed their way.

Entreri made short work of the other, taking off its one working arm with a brutal sword parry, then rushing in close and driving his dagger deep into the creature's chest. He twisted and turned the blade as he slid off to the side, then brought Charon's Claw across the gargoyle's throat for good measure.

The creature went into a frenzy, thrashing and flailing, blood flying. It had no direction for its attacks, though, and Entreri simply danced away as it wound itself to the floor, where it continued its death spasms.

Entreri came up behind the second gargoyle, which was already engaged with the ranger, and drove his sword through its spine.

"Well fought," said Mariabronne.

"By all," Ellery quickly added, and Entreri got the distinct impression that the woman did not appreciate the ranger apparently singling him out above her.

She didn't look so beautiful to Entreri in that moment, and not just because she had taken a garish hit on one shoulder, the blood flowing freely down her right arm.

Pratcus hustled down next, muttering with every step as he closed on the wounded woman. "Sure'n me gods're getting sick o' hearing me call," he cried. "How long can we keep this up, then?"

"Bah!" Athrogate answered. "Forever and ever!"

To accentuate his point, the wild dwarf leaped over to one broken gargoyle, the creature pitifully belly-crawling on the floor, its wings and most of its torso ravaged by the flames of Canthan's fireball. The gargoyle noted his approach and with hate-filled eyes tried to pull itself up on its elbows, lifting its head so that it could spit at Athrogate.

The dwarf howled all the louder and more gleefully, and brought his morning stars in rapid order crunching down on the gargoyle's head, flattening it to the floor.

"Forever and ever," Athrogate said again.

Entreri cast a sour look in Jarlaxle's direction as if to say, "He'll get us all killed."

The drow merely shrugged and seemed more amused with the dwarf than concerned, and that worried Entreri all the more.

And frustrated him. For some reason, the assassin felt vulnerable, as if he could be wounded or killed. As he realized the truth of his emotions, he understood too that never before had he harbored such feelings. In all the battles and deadly struggles of the past three decades of his life, Artemis Entreri had never felt as if his next fight might be his last.

Or at least, he had never cared.

But suddenly he did care, and he could not deny it. He glanced at Jarlaxle again, wondering if the drow had found some new enchantment to throw over him to so put him off-balance. Then he looked past Jarlaxle to the two Palishchuk half-orcs. They stood against the outer southern wall, obviously trying to stay small and out of the way. Entreri focused his gaze on Arrayan, and he had to resist the urge to go over to her and assure her that they would get through this.

He winced as the feeling passed, and he dropped his hand to Charon's Claw and lifted the blade a few inches from its scabbard. He sent his thoughts into the sword, demanding its fealty, and it predictably responded by assailing him with a wall of curses and demands of its own, telling him that he was inferior, assuring him that one day he would slip up and the sword would dominate him wholly and melt the flesh from his bones as it consumed his soul.

Entreri smiled and slid the sword away, his moment of empathy and shared fear thrown behind.

"If the castle's resources are unlimited, ours are not," Canthan was saying as Entreri tuned back into the conversation. From the way the mage muttered the words and glanced at Athrogate, Entreri knew that the dwarf was still proclaiming that they could fight on until the end of time.

"But neither can we wait and recuperate," Ellery said. "The castle's defenses will simply continue to regenerate and come against us."

"Ye have a better plan, do ye?" asked Pratcus. "Not many more spells to be coming from me lips. I bringed a pair o' scrolls, but them two're of minor healing powers, and I got a potion to get yer blood flowing straight but just the one. I used more magic in the wagon run from the flying snakes and more magic in the fight on the hill than I got left in me heart and gut. I'll be needing rest and prayers to get any more."

"How long?" asked Ellery.

"Half a night's sleep."

Ellery, Mariabronne, and Canthan were all shaking their heads.

"We don't have that," the commander replied.

"On we go," Athrogate declared.

"You sound as if you know our course," said Ellery.

Athrogate poked his hand Arrayan's way. "She said she found that book out here, over by where that main keep now stands," he reasoned. "We were going for that, if I'm remembering right."

"We were indeed," said Mariabronne. "But that is only a starting place. We don't truly know what the book is, nor do we know if it's still there."

"Bah!" Athrogate snorted.

"It is still there," replied a quiet voice from the side, and the group turned as one to regard Arrayan, who seemed very, very small at that moment.

"What d'ye know?" Athrogate barked at her.

"The book is still there," Arrayan said. She stood up a bit straighter and glanced over at Olgerkhan for support. "Uncle Wingham didn't tell you everything."

"Then perhaps you should," Canthan replied.

"The tower . . . all of this, was created by the book," Arrayan explained.

"That was our guess," Mariabronne cut in, an attempt to put her at ease, but one that she pushed aside, holding her hand up to quiet the ranger.

"The book is part of the castle, rooted to it through tendrils of magic," Arrayan went on. "It sits open." She held her palms up, as if she was cradling a great tome. "Its pages turn of their own accord, as if some reader stands above it, summoning a magical breeze to blow across the next sheaf."

As Canthan suspiciously asked Arrayan how she might know all of this, Entreri and Jarlaxle glanced at each other, neither surprised, of course.

Entreri swallowed hard, but that did not relieve the lump in his throat. He turned to Arrayan and tried to think of something to say to interrupt the conversation, for he knew what was coming and knew that she should not admit . . .

"It was I who first opened Zhengyi's book," she said, and Entreri sucked in his breath. "Uncle Wingham bade me to inspect it while Mariabronne rode to the Vaasan Gate. We hoped to give you a more complete report when you arrived in Palishchuk."

Olgerkhan shifted nervously at her side, a movement not lost on any of the others.

"And?" Canthan pressed when Arrayan did not continue.

Arrayan stuttered a couple of times then replied, "I do not know."

"You do not know what?" Canthan snapped back at her, and he took a stride her way, seeming so much more imposing and powerful than his skinny frame could possibly allow. "You opened the book and began to read. What happened next?"

"I . . ." Arrayan's voice trailed off.

"We've no time for your cryptic games, foolish girl," Canthan scolded.

Entreri realized that he had his hands on his weapons and realized too that he truly wanted to leap over and cut Canthan's throat out at that moment.

Or rush over and support Arrayan.

"I started to read it," Arrayan admitted. "I do not remember anything it said—I don't think it *said* anything—just syllables, guttural and rhyming."

"Good!" Athrogate interrupted, but no one paid him any heed.

"I remember none . . . just that the words, if they were words, found a flow in my throat that I did not wish to halt."

"The book used you as its instrument," Mariabronne reasoned.

"I do not know," Arrayan said again. "I woke up back at my house in Palishchuk."

"And she was sick," Olgerkhan piped in, stepping in front of the woman as if daring anyone to make so much as an accusation against her. "The book cursed her and makes her ill."

"And so Palishchuk curses us by making us take you along?" Canthan said, and his voice did not reveal whether he was speaking with complete sarcasm or logical reasoning.

"You can all run from it, but she cannot," Olgerkhan finished.

"You are certain that it is at the main keep?" Mariabronne asked, and though he was trying to be understanding and gentle, there was no missing the sharp edge at the back of his voice.

"And why did you not speak up earlier?" demanded Canthan. "You would have us fighting gargoyles and fiends forever? To what end?"

"No!" Arrayan pleaded. "I did not know—"

"For one who practices the magical arts, you seem to know very little," the older wizard scolded. "A most dangerous and foolhardy combination."

"Enough!" said Mariabronne. "We will get nowhere constructive with this bickering. What is past is past. We have new information now and new hope. Our enemy is identified beyond these animates it uses as shields. Let us find a path to the keep and to the book, for there we will find our answers, I am certain."

"Huzzah your optimism, ranger," Canthan spat at him. "Would you wave King Gareth's banner before us and hire trumpeters to herald our journey?"

That sudden flash of anger and sarcasm, naming the beloved king no less, set everyone on their heels. Mariabronne furrowed his brow and glared at the mage, but what proved more compelling to Jarlaxle and Entreri was the reaction of Ellery.

Far from the noble and heroic commander, she seemed small and afraid, as if she was caught between two forces far beyond her.

"Relation of Dragonsbane," Jarlaxle whispered to his companion, a further warning that something wasn't quite what it seemed.

"The keep will prove a long and difficult run," Pratcus intervened. "We gotta be gathering our strength and wits about us, and tighten our belts'n'bandages. We know where we're going, so where we're going's where we're goin'."

"Ye said that right!" Athrogate congratulated.

"A long run and our only run," Mariabronne agreed. "There we will find our answers. Pray you secure that door above, good Athrogate. I will scout the northern corridor. Recover your breath and your heart. Partake of food and drink if you so need it, and yes, tighten your bandages."

"I do believe that our sadly poetic friend just told us to take a break," Jarlaxle said to Entreri, but the assassin wasn't even listening.

He was thinking of Herminicle and the tower outside of Heliogabalus.

He was looking at Arrayan.

Jarlaxle looked that way too, and he stared at Entreri until he at last caught the assassin's attention. He offered a helpless shrug and glanced back at the woman.

"Don't even think it," Entreri warned in no ambiguous voice. He turned away from Jarlaxle and strode to the woman and her brutish bodyguard.

An amused Jarlaxle watched him every step of the way.

"A fine flute you crafted, Idalia the monk," he whispered under his breath.

He wondered if Entreri would agree with that assessment or if the assassin would kill him in his sleep for playing a role in the grand manipulation.

"I would have a moment with you," Entreri said to Arrayan as he approached.

Olgerkhan eyed him with suspicion and even took a step closer to the woman.

"Go and speak with Commander Ellery or one of the dwarves," Entreri said to him, but that only made the brutish half-orc widen his stance and cross his arms over his massive chest, scowling at Entreri from under his pronounced brow.

"Olgerkhan is my friend," Arrayan said. "What you must say to me, you can say to him."

"Perhaps I wish to listen more than speak," said Entreri. "And I would prefer if it were just we two. Go away," he said to Olgerkhan. "If I wanted to harm Arrayan, she would already be dead."

Olgerkhan bristled, his eyes flaring with anger.

"And so would you," Entreri went on, not missing a beat. "I have seen you in battle—both of you—and I know that your magical repertoire is all but exhausted, Lady Arrayan. Forgive me for saying, but I am not impressed."

Olgerkhan strained forward and seemed as if he would leap atop Entreri.

"The book is draining you, stealing your life," the assassin said, after glancing around to make sure no others were close enough to hear. "You began a process from which you cannot easily escape."

Both of the half-orcs rocked off-balance at the words, confirming Entreri's guess. "Now, will you speak with me alone, or will you not?"

Arrayan gazed at him plaintively, then turned to Olgerkhan and bade him to go off for a few minutes. The large half-orc glowered at Entreri for a moment, but he could not resist the demands of Arrayan. Staring at the assassin every step of the way, he moved off.

"You opened the book and you started reading, then found that you could not stop," Entreri said to Arrayan. "Correct?"

"I . . . I think so, but it is all blurry to me," she replied. "Dreamlike. I thought that I had constructed enough wards to fend the residual curses of Zhengyi, but I was wrong. All I know is that I was sick soon after back in my house. Olgerkhan brought Wingham and Mariabronne, and another, Nyungy the old bard."

"Wingham insisted that you come into the castle with us."

"There was no other choice."

"To destroy the book before it consumes you," Entreri reasoned, and Arrayan did not argue the point.

"You were sickly, so you said."

"I could not get out of my bed, nor could I eat."

"But you are not so sickly now, and your friend . . ." He glanced back at Olgerkhan. "He cannot last through a single fight, and each swing of his war club is less crisp and powerful."

Arrayan shrugged and shook her head, lifting her hands up wide.

Entreri noticed her ring, a replica of the one Olgerkhan wore, and he noted too that the single gemstone set on that band was a different hue, darker, than it had been before.

From the side, Olgerkhan saw the woman's movement and began stalking back across the room.

"Take care how much you admit to our companions," Entreri warned before the larger half-orc arrived. "If the book is draining you of life, then it is feeding and growing stronger because of you. We will—we must—find a way to defeat that feeding magic, but one way seems obvious, and it is not one I would expect you or your large friend to enjoy."

"Is that a threat?" Arrayan asked, and Olgerkhan apparently heard, for he rushed the rest of the way to her side.

"It is free advice," Entreri answered. "For your own sake, good lady, take care your words."

He gave only a cursory glance at the imposing Olgerkhan as he turned and walked away. Given his experience with the lich Herminicle in the tower outside of Heliogabalus, and the words of the dragon sisters, the answer to all of this seemed quite obvious to Artemis Entreri. Kill Arrayan and defeat the Zhengyian construct at its heart. He blew a sigh as he realized that not so long ago, he would not have been so repulsed by the idea, and not hesitant in the least. The man he had been would have long ago left Arrayan dead in a pool of her own blood.

But now he saw the challenge differently, and his task seemed infinitely more complicated.

"She read the book," he informed Jarlaxle. "She is this castle's Herminicle. Killing her would be the easy way to be done with this."

Jarlaxle shook his head through every word. "Not this time."

"You said that destroying the lich would have defeated the tower."

"So Ilnezhara and Tazmikella told me, and with certainty."

"Arrayan is this construct's lich—or soon to be," Entreri replied, and though he was arguing the point, he had no intention, if proven right, of allowing the very course he was even then championing.

But still Jarlaxle shook his head. "Partly, perhaps."

"She read the book."

"Then left it."

"Its magic released."

"Its call unleashed," Jarlaxle countered, and Entreri looked at him curiously.

"What do you know?" asked the assassin.

"Little—as little as you, I fear," the drow admitted. "But this . . ." He looked up and swept his arms to indicate the vastness of the castle. "Do you really believe that such a novice mage, that young woman, could be the life-force creating all of this?"

"Zhengyi's book?"

But still Jarlaxle shook his head, apparently convinced that there was something more at work. The drow remained determined, for the sake of purse and power alone, to find out what it was.

CHAPTER
IMPROVISING
16

With Entreri moving off ahead of them, the group passed swiftly out of the corner tower and along the corridors of the interior eastern wall. They didn't find any guardian creatures awaiting them, though they came upon a pair of dead gargoyles and a decapitated flesh golem, all three with deep stab wounds in the back.

"He is efficient," Jarlaxle remarked more than once of his missing friend.

They came to an ascending stair, ending in a door that stood slightly ajar to allow daylight to enter from beyond it. As they started up, the door opened and Artemis Entreri came through.

"We are at the joined point of the outer wall and the interior wall that separates the baileys of the castle," he explained.

"Stay along the outer wall to the back and the turn will take us to the main keep," Mariabronne replied, but Entreri shook his head with every word.

"When the gargoyles came upon us last night, they were not the castle's full contingent," the assassin explained. "From this point back, the outer wall is lined with the filthy creatures and crossing close to them will likely awaken them and have us fighting every step of the way."

"The inner wall to the center, then?" asked Ellery. "Where we debark it and spring across the courtyard to the keep's front door?"

"A door likely locked," Mariabronne reasoned.

"And locked before a graveyard courtyard that will present us with scores of undead to battle," Jarlaxle assured them in a voice that none questioned.

"Either way we're for fighting," Athrogate chimed in. "Choose the bony ones who're smaller in the biting!" He giggled then continued, "So lead on and be quick for it's soundin' exciting." The dwarf howled with laughter, but he was alone in his mirth.

"How far?" Mariabronne asked.

Entreri shrugged and said, "Seventy feet of ground from the inner gatehouse to the door of the keep."

"And likely a locked door to hold us out," added Ellery. "We'll be swarmed by the undead." She looked to Pratcus.

"I got me powers against them bony things," he said, though he appeared unconvinced. "But I found the first time that they didn't much heed me commands."

"Because they are being controlled by a greater power, likely," Jarlaxle said, and all eyes settled on him. He shrugged, showing them that it was just a guess. Then he quickly straightened, his red eyes sparkling, and looked to Entreri. "How far are we now to that keep?"

Entreri seemed perplexed for just a moment then said, "A hundred feet?"

"And how much higher is its top above the wall's apex here?"

Entreri looked back behind him, out the open door. Then he leaned back and glanced to the northeast, the direction of the circular keep.

"It's not very high," the assassin said. "Perhaps fifteen feet above us at its highest point."

"Lead on to the wall top," Jarlaxle instructed.

"What do ye know?" asked Athrogate.

"I know that I have already grown weary of fighting."

"Bah!" the dwarf snorted. "I heared ye drow elfs were all for the battle."

"When we must."

"Bah!"

Jarlaxle offered a smile to the dwarf as he squeezed past, moving up the stairs to follow Entreri to the outside landing. By the time the others caught up to him, he was nodding and insisting, "It will work."

"Pray share your plan," Mariabronne requested.

"That one's always tellin' folks to pray," Athrogate snorted to Pratcus. "Ye should get him to join yer church!"

"We drow are possessed of certain . . . tricks," Jarlaxle replied.

"He can levitate," said Entreri.

"Levitation is not flying," Canthan said.

"But if I can get close enough and high enough, I can set a grapnel on that tower top," Jarlaxle explained.

"That is a long climb, particularly on an incline," remarked the ranger, his head turning back and forth as he considered the two anchor points for any rope.

"Better than fighting all the way," said Jarlaxle.

As he spoke, he took off his hat and reached under the silken band, producing a fine cord. He extracted it, and it seemed to go on and on forever. The drow looped its other end on the ground at his feet as he pulled it from the hat and by the time he had finished, he had a fair-sized coil looped up almost to the height of his knees.

"A hundred and twenty feet," he explained to Entreri, who was not surprised by the appearance of the magical cord.

Jarlaxle then took off a jeweled earring, brought it close to his mouth and whispered to it. It grew as he moved it away, and by the time he had it near to the top end of the cord, it was the size of a small grappling hook.

Jarlaxle tied it off and began looping the cord loosely in one hand, while Entreri took the other end and tied it off on one of the crenellations along the tower wall.

"The biggest danger is that our movements will attract gargoyles," Jarlaxle said to the others. "It would not be wise to join in battle while we are crawling along the rope."

"Bah!" came Athrogate's predictable snort.

"Sort out a crossing order," Jarlaxle bade the ranger. "My friend, of course, will go first after I have set the rope, but we should get another warrior over to that tower top as quickly as possible. And she will need help," he added, nodding toward Arrayan. "I can do that with my levitation, and my friend might have something to assist . . . ?"

He looked at Entreri, who frowned, but did begin fishing in his large belt pouch. He pulled out a contraption of straps and hooks, which looked somewhat like a bridle for a very large horse, and he casually tossed it to the drow.

Jarlaxle sorted it out quickly and held it up before him, showing the others that it was a harness of sorts, known as a "housebreaker" to anyone familiar with the ways of city thieves.

"Enough banter," Ellery bade him, and she nodded to the north and the line of gargoyles hanging on the outside of the wall.

"A strong shove, good dwarf," Jarlaxle said to Athrogate, who rushed at him, arms outstretched.

"As I pass you," Jarlaxle quickly explained, before the dwarf could launch him from the wall—and probably the wrong way, at that! He positioned Athrogate at the inside lip of the tower top, then walked at a direct angle away from the distant keep. "Be quick," he bade Entreri.

"Set it well," the assassin replied.

Jarlaxle nodded and broke into a quick run. He leaped and called upon the power of his enchanted emblem, an insignia that resembled that of House Baenre, to bring forth magical levitation, lifting him higher from the ground. Athrogate caught him by the belt and launched him out toward the tower, and with the dwarf's uncanny strength propelling him, Jarlaxle found himself soaring away from the others.

Jarlaxle continued to rise as he went out from the wall. Halfway to the keep, he was up higher than its highest point. He was still approaching, but greatly slowing. The levitation power could make him go vertical only, so as the momentum of his short run and Athrogate's throw wore off, he was still twenty feet or so from the keep's wall. But he was up above it, and he began to swing the grapnel at the end of one arm.

"Gargoyles about the top," he called back to Entreri, who was ready to scramble at the other end of the rope. "They are not reacting to my presence, nor will they to yours, likely, until you step onto the stone."

"Wonderful," Entreri muttered under his breath.

He kept his visage determined and stoic, and his breath steady, but was assailed with images of the gargoyles walking over and tearing out the grapnel, then just letting him drop halfway across into the middle of the courtyard. Or perhaps they would swarm him while he hung helpless from the rope.

"Take in the slack quickly," Entreri said to Athrogate as Jarlaxle let fly the grapnel.

Even as it hit behind the keep's similarly crenellated wall, the dwarf began yanking in the slack, tightening the cord, which he stretched and tightly looped over the wall stone.

Off went Entreri, leaping from the wall to the cord. He hooked his ankles as he caught on, his arms pumping with fluid and furious motion. He hand-walked the cord, coiling his body, then unwinding in perfect synchrony, and so fast was he moving that it seemed to the others as if he was sliding down instead of crawling up.

In short order, he neared the roof of the keep. As he did, he let go with his feet and turned as he swung his legs down, gathering momentum. He rolled his backbone to gather momentum as he went around and back up, and he let go at the perfect angle and trajectory. Turning a half flip as he flew, drawing his weapons as he went, he landed perfectly on his feet on the wall top—just as a gargoyle rushed out to meet him.

The creature caught a sword slash across the face, followed by a quick dagger thrust to the throat, and Entreri followed the falling creature down, leaping from the wall to the roof in time to meet the charge of a second gargoyle.

"Come on, half-ugly," Athrogate, who was already in the housebreaker harness, said to Olgerkhan.

Before the half-orc warrior could respond, the dwarf leaped up to the top of the wall, grabbed him by the back of his belt, and swung out, hooking the harness to the cord as he went. With amazing strength, Athrogate held Olgerkhan easily with one arm while his other grabbed and tugged, grabbed and tugged, propelling him across the gap.

Olgerkhan protested and squirmed, trying to grab at the dwarf's arm for support.

"Ye hold still and save yer strength, ye dolt," Athrogate scolded. "I'm leaving ye there, and ye best be ready to hold a fight until I get back!"

At that, Olgerkhan calmed, and the rope bounced. The half-orc managed to glance back, as did Athrogate, to see Mariabronne scrambling onto the cord. The ranger moved almost as fluidly as had Entreri, and he gained steadily on the dwarf as they neared the growing sounds of battle.

Up above them, Jarlaxle lifted a bit higher, gaining a better angle from which to begin loosing his missiles, magical from a wand and poison-tipped from his small crossbow.

"Go next," Commander Ellery bade Pratcus. "They will need your magic."

She leaned on the wall, straining to see the fighting across the way. Every so often a gargoyle raised up from the keep's roof, its great leathery wings flapping, and Ellery could only pray that the creature didn't notice the rope and the helpless men scrambling across.

Pratcus hesitated and Ellery turned a sharp glare at him.

The dwarf grabbed at the rope and shook his head. "Won't be holding another," he explained.

Ellery slapped her hand on the stone wall top and turned to Canthan. "Have you anything to assist?"

The wizard shook his head. Then he launched so suddenly into spellcasting that Ellery fell back a step and gave a yelp. She turned as Canthan cast, firing off a lightning bolt that caught one gargoyle as it dived at Athrogate and Olgerkhan.

"Nothing to assist in the climbing, if that is what you meant," the wizard clarified.

"Whatever you can do," Ellery replied, her tone equally dry.

⊲━━━⊳

Entreri learned the hard way that his location atop the keep's roof had put him in close proximity to many of the gargoyles. He'd taken down three of them, but as four more of the beasts leaped and fluttered around him, the assassin began moving more defensively rather than trying to score any killing blows.

From up above, Jarlaxle took down one, launching a glob of greenish goo from a wand. It struck a gargoyle on its wings and drove it down, where it stuck fast, hopelessly adhered to the stone. A second of the gargoyles broke off from Entreri and soared out at the levitating drow, but before the assassin could begin to get his feet properly under him and go on the attack against the remaining two, another pair came up over the wall at him.

Muttering under his breath, the assassin continued his wild dance, using Charon's Claw to set up walls of opaque ash to aid him in his constant retreat. He glanced quickly at the rope line to note Athrogate's progress and had to admit to himself that he was glad to see the dwarf fast approaching—an admission he thought he'd never make where that one was concerned.

Entreri worked more deliberately then, trying not only to stay away from the claws and horns of the leaping and soaring foursome but to turn them appropriately so that his reinforcements could gain a quick advantage.

He started left, then cut back to the right, toward the center of the rooftop. He fell fast to one knee and thrust his sword straight up, gashing a dropping gargoyle that fast beat its wings to lift back out of reach. Entreri started to come back up to his feet, but a clawing hand slashed just above his head, so he threw himself forward into a roll instead. He came up quickly, spinning as he did, sword arm extended, to fend off the furious attacks. With their ability to fly and leap upon him, the beasts should have had him—would have had any typical human warrior—but Artemis Entreri was too quick for them and managed to sway the angle of his whipping blade to defend against attacks from above as well.

⊲━━━⊳

Hanging by the harness under the rope, Athrogate came right up to the keep's stone wall.

"Get up there and get ye fighting!" he roared at Olgerkhan.

With still just one arm, the dwarf hauled the large half-orc up over the lip of the stone wall. Olgerkhan clipped his foot as he went over, and that sent him into a headlong tumble onto the roof.

The dwarf howled with laughter.

"Go, good dwarf!" Mariabronne called from right behind him on the rope.

"Going back for the girl," Athrogate explained. "Climb over me, ye tree-hugger, and get into the fightin'!"

Not needing to be asked twice, Mariabronne scrambled over Athrogate.

The ranger seemed to be trying to be gentle, or at least tried not to stomp on the dwarf's face. But Athrogate, both his hands free again, grabbed the ranger by the ankles and heaved him up and over to land crashing on the roof beside Entreri and Olgerkhan. Athrogate couldn't see any of that, since he was hanging under the rope, but he heard the commotion enough to bubble up another great burst of laughter.

As soon as the rope stopped bouncing, the dwarf released a secondary hook on the harness and a few quick pumps of his powerful arms had him zipping back down the decline toward the others. He clamped onto the rope though, bringing himself to an abrupt halt when he saw Pratcus climbing out toward him. Unlike Entreri and Mariabronne, the dwarf had not hooked his ankles over the rope but was simply hanging by his hands. He let go with the trailing hand and rotated his hips so that when he grabbed the rope again, that hand was in front. And on he went, rocking fast and hand-walking the rope.

Athrogate nodded and grinned as he watched the priest's progress. Pratcus wore a sleeveless studded leather vest, and the muscles in his arms bulged with the work—and with something else, Athrogate knew.

"Put a bit of an enchantment on yerself, eh?" Athrogate said as Pratcus approached. Athrogate turned himself around so that his head was down toward the other dwarf, and reached out to take Pratcus's hand.

"Strength o' the bull," Pratcus confirmed, and he grabbed hard at Athrogate's offered hand.

A spin and swing had Pratcus back up high beyond the hanging dwarf, where he easily caught the rope again and continued along his way.

Athrogate howled with laughter and resumed his descent to the tower wall.

"Who's next?" he asked the remaining trio.

Ellery glanced at Canthan. "Take Arrayan," she decided, "then Canthan, and I will go last."

"We've not the time for that, I fear," came a voice from above, and they all turned to regard Jarlaxle.

The drow tossed a second cord to Athrogate, and the dwarf reeled him in.

"The castle is awakening to our presence," Jarlaxle explained as he descended. He motioned down toward the ground, some twenty feet below.

Athrogate started to argue but lost his voice when he followed Jarlaxle's lead to look down. For there was the undead horde again, clawing through the soil and moving out under the long rope.

"Oh, lovely," said Canthan.

"They're coming into the wall tunnels, too," Jarlaxle informed him.

"Ye think they're smart enough to cut the rope behind us?" Athrogate roared.

"Oh, lovely," said Canthan.

Jarlaxle nodded to Ellery.

"Go," he bade her. "Quickly."

Ellery strapped her axe and shield over her back and scrambled out onto the rope over the hanging Athrogate.

"Be quick or ye're to get me hairy head up yer bum," Athrogate barked at her.

She didn't look back and moved out as quickly as she could.

Take the half-orc girl and drop her to the horde, sounded a voice in Athrogate's head.

The dwarf assumed a puzzled look for just a moment, then cast a glance Canthan's way.

Our victory will be near complete when she is dead, the wizard explained.

"Come on, girl," the obedient Athrogate said to Arrayan.

Jarlaxle alit on the wall top beside the woman and grabbed her arm as she started for the dwarf. "I'll take her," he said to the dwarf, and to Canthan, he added, "You go with him."

Canthan tried not to betray his surprise and anger—and suspicion, for had the drow somehow intercepted his magical message to the dwarf? Or had Athrogate's glance his way somehow tipped off the perceptive Jarlaxle to his designs for Arrayan? Canthan used his customary sarcasm to shield those telling emotions.

"You can fly now?" the mage said.

"Levitate," Jarlaxle corrected.

"Straight up and down."

"Weightlessly," the drow explained, and he took the end of his second cord from Athrogate and looped it around the lead of the housebreaker harness. "We will be no drag on you at all, good dwarf."

Athrogate figured it all out and howled all the louder. Canthan was tentatively edging out toward him by then, so the dwarf reached up and grabbed the wizard by the belt, roughly pulling him out.

"Got me a drow elf kite!" Athrogate declared with a hearty guffaw.

"Hook your arms through the harness and hold on," Jarlaxle bade the wizard. "Free up the dwarf's arms, I beg, else this castle will catch us before we reach the other side."

Canthan continued to stare at the surprising drow, and he saw clearly in Jarlaxle's returned gaze that the dark elf's instructions had emanated from more than mere prudence. A line was being drawn between them, Canthan knew.

But the time to cross over that line and dare Jarlaxle to defy him had not yet come. He had kept plenty of spells handy and was far from exhausted, but trouble just then could cost him dearly against the castle's hordes, whatever the outcome of his personal battle with the drow.

Still staring at Jarlaxle, the wizard moved to the lip of the wall and tentatively bent over to find a handhold on Athrogate's harness. He yelped with surprise when the dwarf grabbed him again and yanked him over, holding him in place until he could wrap his thin arms securely through some of the straps. Then he yelped again as Athrogate planted his heavy boots against the stone wall, pushed off, and began hand-walking the rope.

Jarlaxle took up the slack quickly and moved to the lip with Arrayan.

"Do hold on," the dark elf bade her, and to her obvious shock, he just stepped off.

Perhaps to ease the grasping woman's nerves, the drow used his power of levitation to rise up a bit higher, putting more room between them and the undead monsters. Canthan had heard tell that all drow were possessed of the ability to levitate, but he suspected that Jarlaxle was in fact using some enchanted item—perhaps a ring or other piece of jewelry. He was well aware that the mysterious drow had more than a few magic items in his possession, and not knowing precisely what they were made the wizard all the more reluctant to let things go much farther between them.

"We're coming fast, Ellery!" Athrogate called to the woman up ahead. "Ye're gonna get yerself a dwarf head! *Bwahaha!*"

Ellery, no fool, seemed to pick up a bit of speed at that proclamation.

The rooftop was clear, but the fight was still on at the keep, for the undead had begun scaling the tower—or trying to, at least—and more gargoyles were awakening to the intrusion and flying to the central structure.

Mariabronne worked his bow furiously, running from wall to wall, shooting gargoyles above and skeletons scrambling up from below. Olgerkhan, too, moved about the rooftop, though sluggishly. He carried many wounds from the initial fight after Athrogate had unceremoniously tossed him over the wall, most of them received because the large warrior, so bone-weary by then, had simply been too slow to react. Still, he tried to help out, using gargoyle corpses as bombs to rain down on the climbing undead.

Artemis Entreri tried to block it all out. He had moved about eight feet down the small staircase along the back wall to a landing with a heavy iron door. The door was locked, he soon discovered, and cleverly so. A quick inspection had also shown him more than one trap set around the portal, another clear reminder that the Zhengyian construct knew how to protect itself. He was in no hurry, anyway—he didn't intend to open the door until the others had arrived—so he carefully and deliberately went over the details of the jamb, the latch, potential pressure plates set on the floor. . . .

"We've got to get in quickly!" Mariabronne cried out to him, and the ranger accentuated his warning with the twang of his great bow.

"Just keep the beasts off me," Entreri countered.

As if on cue, Olgerkhan cried out in pain.

"Breach!" Mariabronne shouted.

Cursing under his breath, Entreri turned from the door and rushed back up the stairs, to see Mariabronne ferociously battling a pair of gargoyles over to his right, near where the rope had been set. A third creature was fast approaching.

Behind the ranger, Olgerkhan slumped against the waist-high wall stones.

"Help me over!" the dwarf priest called from beyond the wall.

Olgerkhan struggled to get up, but managed to get his hand over.

Entreri hit the back of one gargoyle just as Pratcus gained the roof. The dwarf moved for Olgerkhan first, but just put on a disgusted look and walked past him as he began to cast his healing spell, aiming not for the more wounded half-orc, but for Mariabronne, who was beginning to show signs of battle wear, as claws slipped through his defenses and tore at him.

"We have it," the ranger cried to Entreri, and as the dwarf's healing washed over him, Mariabronne stood straighter and fought with renewed energy. "The door! Breach the door!"

Entreri paused long enough to glance past the trio to see Ellery's painfully slow progress on the rope and the other four working toward him in a strange formation, with Jarlaxle and Arrayan floating behind Athrogate and the hanging wizard.

He shook his head and ran back to the keep's uppermost door. He considered the time remaining before the rest arrived, and checked yet again for any more traps.

As usual, the assassin's timing was near perfect, and he clicked open the lock just as the others piled onto the stairwell behind him. Entreri swung the door in and stepped back, and Athrogate moved right past him.

Entreri grabbed him by the shoulder, stopping him.

"Eh?" the dwarf asked, and he meant to argue more, but Entreri had already put a finger over his pursed lips.

The assassin stepped past Athrogate and bent low. After a cursory inspection of the stones beyond the threshold, Entreri reached into a pouch and pulled forth some chalk dust. He tossed it out to cover a certain section of the stones.

"Pressure plate," he explained, stepping back and motioning for Athrogate to go on.

"Got yer uses," the dwarf grumbled.

Entreri waited for Jarlaxle, who brought up the rear of the line. The drow looked at him and grinned knowingly, then purposely stepped right atop the assassin's chalk.

"Make them believe you are more useful than you are," Jarlaxle congratulated, and Entreri merely shrugged.

"I do believe you are beginning to understand it all," Jarlaxle added. "Should I be worried?"

"Yes."

The simplicity of the answer brought yet another grin to Jarlaxle's coal-black face.

CHAPTER

CANTHAN'S CONFIRMATION

17

The door opened into a circular room that encompassed the whole of one floor of the keep. A basalt altar stood out from the northern edge of the room directly across from them. Red veins shot through the rock, accentuating the decorated covering of bas relief images of dragons. Behind the altar, between a pair of burning braziers, sat a huge egg, large enough for a man Entreri's size to curl up inside it.

"This looks like a place for fighting," Athrogate muttered, and he didn't seem the least dismayed by that probability.

Given the scene outside with the undead, the dwarf's words rang true, for all around the room, set equidistant to each other, stood sarcophagi of polished stone and decorated gold. The facings of the ornate caskets indicated a standing humanoid creature, arms in tight to its sides, with long feet and a long, canine snout.

"Gnolls?" Jarlaxle asked. Behind him, Entreri secured the door, expertly resetting the lock.

"Let us not tarry to find out," said Mariabronne, indicating the one other exit in the room: another descending stairwell over to their right. It was bordered by a waist-high railing, with the entry all the way on the other side of the room. The ranger, his eyes locked on the nearest sarcophagus, one hand ready on his sheathed sword, stepped out toward the center of the room. He felt a rumble, as if from a movement within that nearest sarcophagus, and he started to call out.

But they didn't need the warning, for they all felt it, and Entreri broke into motion, darting past the others to the railing. He grabbed onto it and rolled right over, dropping nimbly to the stairs below. Hardly slowing, he was at the second door in an instant, working his fingers around its edges, his eyes darting all about.

He took a deep breath. Though he saw no traps, the assassin knew he should inspect the door in greater detail, but he simply didn't have the time. Behind him, he heard his friends scrambling on the stairs, followed by the creaking sounds as the undead monsters within the sarcophagi pushed open their coffins.

He went for the lock.

But before he could begin, the door popped open.

Entreri fell back, drawing his weapons. Nothing came through, though, and the assassin calmed when he noted a smug-looking Canthan on the stairs behind him.

"Magical spell of opening?" Entreri asked.

"We haven't the time for your inspection," replied the mage. "I thought it prudent."

Of course you did, so long as I was close enough to catch the brunt of any traps or monsters lying in wait, Entreri thought but did not say—though his expression certainly told the others the gist of it.

"They're coming out," Commander Ellery warned from up in the room.

"Mummified gnolls," Jarlaxle said. "Interesting."

Entreri was not so interested and had no desire to see the strange creatures. He spun away from Canthan, drawing his weapons as he went, and charged through the door.

He was surprised, as were all the others as they came through, to find that he was not on the keep's lowest level. From the outside, the structure hadn't seemed tall enough to hold three stories, but sure enough, Entreri found himself on a balcony that ran around the circumference of the keep, opening to a sweeping stone stair on the northernmost wall. Moving to the waist-high iron railing, its balusters shaped to resemble twisting dragons with wings spread wide, Entreri figured out the puzzle. For the floor level below him was partially below ground—the circular section of it, at least. On the southernmost side of that bottom floor, a short set of stairs led up to a rectangular alcove that held the tower's main doors, so that the profile of that lowest level reminded the assassin of a keyhole, but one snubbed short.

And there, just at the top of those stairs, set in the rectangular alcove opposite the doors, sat the book of Zhengyi, the tome of creation, suspended on tendrils that looked all too familiar to Artemis Entreri. The assassin eventually pulled his eyes away from the enticing target and completed his scan of the floor below. He heard the door behind him close, followed immediately by some heavy pounding and Jarlaxle saying, with his typical penchant for understatement, "We should move quickly."

But Entreri wasn't in any hurry to go down the stairs or over the railing. He noted a pair of iron statues set east and west in the room below, and vividly recalled his encounter in Herminicle's tower. Even worse than the possibility of a pair of iron golems, the room below was not sealed, for every few feet around the perimeter presented an opening to a tunnel of worked and fitted stones, burrowing down into the ground. Might the horde of undead be approaching through those routes even then?

A sharp ring behind him turned Entreri around. Athrogate stood at the closed iron door, the locking bar and supports already rattling from the pounding of the mummified gnolls.

The dwarf methodically went to work, dropping his backpack to the ground and fishing out one piton after another. He set them strategically around the door and drove them deep into the stone with a single crack of his morning star—the one enchanted with oil of impact.

A moment later, he hopped back and dropped his hands on his hips, surveying his work. "Yeah, it'll hold them back for a bit."

"They're the least of our worries," Entreri said.

By that point, several of the others were at the rail, looking over the room and coming up with the same grim assessment as had Entreri. Not so for Arrayan and Olgerkhan, though. The woman slumped against the back wall, as if merely being there, in such close proximity to the magical book, was rendering her helpless. Her larger partner didn't seem much better off.

"There are our answers," Canthan said, nodding toward the book. "Get me to it."

"Those statues will likely animate," Jarlaxle said. "Iron golems are no easy foe."

Athrogate roared with laughter as he walked up beside the drow. "Ain't ye seen nothing yet from Cracker and Whacker?" As he named the weapons, he presented them before the dark elf.

"Cracker and Whacker?" the drow replied.

Athrogate guffawed again as he glanced over the railing, looking down directly atop one of the iron statues. "Meet ye below!" he called and with that he whispered to each of his weapons, bidding them to pour forth their enchanted fluids. With another wild laugh, he hopped up atop the railing and dropped.

"Cracker and Whacker?" Jarlaxle asked again.

"He used to call them Rotter and Slaughter," Ellery replied, and Entreri noted that for the first time since he had met Jarlaxle, the drow seemed to have no answer whatsoever.

But as there was no denying Athrogate's inanity, nor was there any way to deny his effectiveness. He landed in a sitting position on the statue's iron shoulders, his legs wrapping around its head. The golem began to animate, as predicted, but before it could even reach up at the dwarf, Cracker slapped down atop its head. The black iron of the construct's skull turned reddish-brown, its integrity stolen by the secretions of a rust monster. When Whacker, gleaming with oil of impact, hit the same spot iron dust flew and the top of the golem's head caved in.

Still the creature flailed, but Athrogate had too great an advantage, whipping his weapons with precision, defeating the integrity of his opponent's natural armor with one morning star, then blasting away with the other. An iron limb went flying, and though the other hand managed to grab the dwarf and throw him hard to the floor, the tough and strong Athrogate bounced up and hit the golem with a one-two, one-two combination that had one leg flying free. Then he caved in the side of its chest for good measure.

But the other golem charged in, and other noises echoed from the tunnels.

Mariabronne and Ellery, Pratcus in tow, charged around to the stairwell while Entreri slipped over the railing and dropped the fifteen feet to the floor, absorbing his landing with a sidelong roll.

Canthan, too, went over the railing, dropping the end of a rope while its other end magically anchored in mid-air. He slid down off to the side of the fray with no intention of joining in. For the wizard, the goal was in sight, sitting there for the taking.

He wasn't pleased when Jarlaxle floated down beside him and paced him toward the front alcove.

"Just keep them off of me," Canthan ordered the drow.

"Them?" Jarlaxle asked.

Canthan wasn't listening. He paused with every step and began casting a series of spells, weaving wards around himself to fend off the defensive magic that no doubt protected the tome.

"Jarlaxle!" called Ellery. "To me!"

The drow turned and glanced at the woman. The situation in the room was under control for the time being, he could see, mostly owing to Athrogate's abilities and effectiveness against iron golems. One was down, thrashing helplessly, and the second was already lilting and wavering as blast after blast wracked it, with the dwarf rushing all around it and pounding away with abandon.

"Jarlaxle!" Ellery cried again.

The drow regarded her and shrugged.

"To me!" she insisted.

Jarlaxle glanced back at Canthan, who stood before the book, then turned his gaze back at Ellery. She meant to keep him away from it and for no other reason than to allow Canthan to examine it first. Ellery stared at him, her look showing him in no uncertain terms that if he disobeyed her, the fight would be on.

He glanced back at Canthan again and grew confident that he still had time to play things through, for the wizard was moving with great caution and seemed thoroughly perplexed.

Jarlaxle started across the room toward Ellery. He paused and nodded to the stairs, where Olgerkhan and Arrayan were making their way down, the large half-orc practically carrying the bone-weary woman.

"Secure the perimeter," Ellery instructed them all, and she waved for the half-orcs to return to the balcony. "We must give Canthan time to unravel the mystery of this place." To Mariabronne and Entreri, she added, "Scout the tunnels to first door or thirty feet."

Entreri was only peripherally listening, for he was already scanning the tunnels. All of them seemed to take the same course: a downward-sloping, eight-foot wide corridor bending to the left after about a dozen feet. Torches were set on the walls, left and right, but they were unlit. Even in the darkness, though, the skilled Entreri understood that the floors were not as solid as they appeared.

"Not yet," the assassin said as Mariabronne started down one tunnel.

The ranger stopped and waited as Entreri moved back from the tunnel entrance and retrieved the head of a destroyed iron golem. He moved in front of one tunnel and bade the others to back up.

He rolled the head down, jumping aside as if expecting an explosion, and as he suspected, the item bounced across a pressure plate set in the floor. Fires blossomed, but not the killing flames of a fireball trap. Rather, the torches flared to life, and as the head rolled along to the bend, it hit a second pressure plate, lighting the opposing torches set there as well.

"How convenient," Ellery remarked.

"Are they all like that?" asked Mariabronne.

"Pressure plates in all," Entreri replied. "What they do, I cannot tell."

"Ye just showed us, ye dolt," said Athrogate.

Entreri didn't answer, other than with a wry grin. The first rule of creating effective traps was to present a situation that put intruders at ease. He looked Athrogate over and decided he didn't need to tell the dwarf that bit of common sense.

⊲══╼═╾══⊳

Strange that she should choose this moment to think herself a leader, the wizard mused when he heard Ellery barking commands in the distance. To Canthan, after all, Ellery would never be more than a pawn. He could not deny her effectiveness in her present role, though. The others didn't dare go against her, particularly with the fool Mariabronne nodding and flapping his lips at her every word.

A cursory glance told Canthan that Ellery was performing her responsibilities well. She had them all busy, moving tentatively down the different tunnels, with Olgerkhan and Arrayan back upstairs guarding the door. Pratcus anchored the arms of Ellery's scouting mission, the dwarf staying in the circular room and hopping about to regard each dark opening as Ellery, Entreri, Jarlaxle, Mariabronne, and Athrogate explored the passages.

Canthan caught a glimpse of Ellery as she came out one tunnel and turned into another, her shield on one arm, axe ready in the other.

"I have taught you well," Canthan whispered under his breath. He caught himself as he finished and silently scolded himself for allowing the distraction—any distraction—at that all-important moment. He took a deep breath and turned back to the book.

His confidence grew as he read on, for he felt the empathetic intrusions of the living tome and came to believe that his wards would suffice in fending them off.

Quickly did the learned mage begin to decipher the ways of the book. The runes appearing in the air above it and falling into it were translations of life energy, drawn from an outside source. That energy had fueled the construction, served as the living source of power animating the undead, caused the gargoyles to regenerate on their perches, and brought life to the golems.

Canthan could hardly draw a breath. The sheer power of the translation overwhelmed him. For some two decades, the wizards of the Bloodstone Lands considered Zhengyi's lichdom, his cheating of death itself, to be his greatest accomplishment, but the book . . .

The book rivaled even that.

The wizard devoured another page and eagerly turned to the next. In no time, he had come to the point where the lettering ended and watched in amazement as runes appeared in the air and drifted to the pages, writing as they went. The process had been vampiric at first, Canthan recognized, with the tome taking from the living force, but it had become more symbiotic, a joining of purpose and will.

The source of energy? Canthan mused. He considered Arrayan, her weakness and that of her partner. She had found the missing book, Mariabronne and Wingham had told them.

No, the wizard decided. That wasn't the whole of it. Arrayan was far more entwined in all of it than just having been drained of her life energies.

Canthan smiled when he finally understood the power of the tome and knew how to defeat it.

And not just defeat it, he hoped, but possess it.

He tore his gaze away from the page and glanced up the staircase to see Arrayan leaning back against a wall, watching Olgerkhan. She looked his way desperately, plaintively. Too much so, Canthan knew. There was more at stake for the young woman than merely whether or not they could find their way out of the castle. For her, it was much more personal than the safety of Palishchuk.

Entreri had shown them how to test each pressure plate safely, but Mariabronne needed no such instructions. The ranger had played through similar scenarios many times, and had the know-how and the equipment to work his way quickly down the tunnel he had chosen.

It had continued to bend around to the left for many feet, with pressure plates set between wall-set torches every dozen feet or so. Mariabronne lit the first by tapping the plate with a long telescoping pole, but he did not trigger the next, or the next after that, preferring to walk in near darkness.

Then, convinced all was clear, the ranger rushed back to the second set of torches and triggered the plate. He repeated the process, always lighting the torches two sets back.

After about fifty feet, the tunnel became a staircase, moving straight down for many, many steps.

Mariabronne glanced back the way he had come. Ellery had told them to inspect the tunnels just to thirty feet or so. The ranger had always been that advanced and independent scout, though, and he trusted his instincts. Down he went, testing the stairs and the walls. Slowly and steadily, he put three dozen steps behind him before it simply became too dark for him to continue. Not willing to mark his position clearly by lighting a candle or torch of his own, Mariabronne sighed and turned back.

But then a light appeared below him, behind the slightly ajar door of a chamber at the bottom of the stairs. Mariabronne eyed it for a long while, the hairs on the back of his neck tingling and standing on end. Such were the moments he lived for, the precipice of disaster, the taunt of the unknown.

Smiling despite himself, Mariabronne crept down to the door. He listened for a short while and dared to peek in. Every castle must have a treasure room was his first thought, and he figured he was looking in on one of the antechambers to just that. Two decorated sarcophagi were set against the opposite wall, framing a closed iron door. Before them, in the center of the room, a brazier burned brightly, a thin line of black smoke snaking up to the high ceiling above. Centering that ceiling was a circular depression set with some sort of bas relief that Mariabronne could not make out—though it looked to him as if there were egglike stones set into it.

Stone tables covered in decorated silver candelabra and assorted trinkets lined the side walls, and the ranger made out some silver bells, a gem-topped scepter, and a golden censer. Religious items, mostly, it seemed to him. A single cloth hung from one table, stitched with a scene of gnolls dancing around a rearing black dragon.

"Lovely combination," he whispered.

Mariabronne glanced back up the ascending corridor behind him. Perhaps he shouldn't press on. He could guess easily enough what those sarcophagi might hold.

The ranger grinned. Such had been the story of his life: always pushing ahead farther than he should. He recalled the scolding King Gareth had given to him upon his first official scouting expedition in eastern Vaasa. Gareth had bade him to map the region along the Galenas for five miles.

Mariabronne had gone all the way to Palishchuk.

That was who he was and how he played: always on the edge and always just skilled enough or lucky enough to sneak out of whatever trouble his adventurous character had found.

So it was still, and he couldn't resist. The Honorable General Dannaway of the Vaasan Gate had been wise indeed not to entrust Ellery to Mariabronne's care alone.

The ranger pushed open the door and slipped into the room. Gold and silver reflected in his brown eyes, gleaming in the light of the brazier. Mariabronne tried hard not to become distracted, though, and set himself in line with the coffins.

As he had expected, their dog-faced, decorated lids swung open.

As one gnoll mummy strode forth from its coffin, Mariabronne was there, a smile on his face, his sword deftly slashing and stabbing. He hit the creature several times before it had even cleared the coffin, and when it reached for him with one arm, lumbering forward, Mariabronne gladly took that arm off at the elbow.

The second was on him by then, and the ranger hopped back. He went into a quick spin, coming around fast, blade level, and the enchanted sword creased the gnoll's abdominal area, tearing filthy gray bandages aside and opening up a gash across the belly of the dried-out husk of the undead creature. The gnoll mummy groaned and slowed its pursuit. Mariabronne smiled all the wider, knowing that his weapon could indeed hurt the thing.

And the two undead creatures simply weren't fast enough to present a serious threat to the skilled warrior. Mariabronne's blade worked brilliantly and with lightning speed and pinpoint accuracy, finding every opening in the mummies' defenses, taking what was offered and never asking for more. He fought with no sense of urgency, as was his trademark, and it was rooted in the confidence that whatever came along, he would have the skills to defeat it.

A rattle from above tested that confidence. Both mummies were ragged things by then, much more so than they had been when first they had emerged from their coffins, with rag wrappings hanging free and deep gashes oozing foul odors and the occasional drip of ichor all around them both. One had only half an arm, a gray-black bony spur protruding from the stump. The other barely moved, its gut hanging open, its legs torn. The ranger led them to the near side of the room, back to the door through which he'd entered, then he disengaged and dashed back to find the time to glance up at the rattle.

He noted one of the egg shapes rocking back and forth above the brazier. It broke free of the ceiling and dropped to the flaming bowl. Mariabronne's eyes widened with curiosity as he watched it fall. He came to realize that it was not an egg-shaped stone but an actual egg of some sort. It hit the flaming stones in the bowl and cracked open, and a line of blacker smoke rushed out of it, widening as it rose.

Hoping it was no poison, Mariabronne darted back at the mummies, thinking to slash through them and get in position for a fast exit. He hit the nearest again in the gut, extending the already deep wound so thoroughly that the creature buckled over, folded in half, and fell into a heap. The other swung at Mariabronne, but the ranger was too fast. He ducked the lumbering blow and quick-stepped past, nearly to the door.

"You shall not run!" came a booming voice in his ears, and the ranger felt a shiver course his spine. Accompanying that voice was a sudden, sharp gust of wind that whipped the ranger's cloak up over his back.

Worse for Mariabronne, though, the wind slammed the door.

He rolled and turned as he came around, so that he faced the room with his back to the door. His jaw dropped as he followed the billowing column of black smoke up and up to where it had formed into the torso and horned head of a gigantic, powerful demonic creature that radiated an aura of pure evil. Its head and facial features resembled that of a snub-nosed bulldog, with huge canines and a pair of inward-hooking horns at the sides of its wide head. Its arms and hands seemed formed of smoke, great grasping black hands with fingers narrowing to sharp points.

"Well met, human," the demon creature said. "You came here seeking adventure and a test of your skills, no doubt. Would you leave when you have at last found it?"

"I will send you back to the Abyss, demon!" Mariabronne promised.

He started forward but realized his error immediately, for in his fascination with the more formidable beast, he had taken his eye off the mummy. It came forward with a lumbering swing. The ranger twisted and ducked the blow. But that second, cropped arm stabbed in, the sheared, sharpened bone gashing Mariabronne's neck. Again Mariabronne's speed extracted him before the mummy could follow through, but he felt the warmth of his own blood dribbling down his neck.

Before he could even consider that, however, he was leaping aside once more. The smoky creature blew forth a cone of fiery breath.

"Daemon," the beast corrected. "And my home is the plane of Gehenna, where I will gladly return. But not until I feast upon your bones."

Flames danced up from Mariabronne's cloak and he spun, pulling it free as he turned. He noted then that the pursuing mummy had not been so fortunate, catching the daemon fire full force. It thrashed about, flames dancing all over it, one arm waving frantically, futilely.

Mariabronne threw his cloak upon it for good measure.

Then he leaped forward and the daemon came forth, smoke forming into powerful legs as it stepped free of the brazier. It raked with its shadowy hands and its head snapped forward to bite at Mariabronne, but again the ranger realized at once that he was the superior fighter and that his sword could indeed inflict damage upon the otherworldly creature.

"Gehenna, then," he cried. "But you will go there hungry!"

"Fool, I am always hungry!"

Its last word sounded more as a gurgle, as the ranger's fine sword creased its face. In his howl of triumph, though, Mariabronne didn't hear the second egg drop.

Or the third.

CHAPTER

18

The sound of battle echoed up the corridor and into the main room of the tower. Canthan snarled at the noise but refused to turn away from the tome. He felt certain there were more secrets buried within that book. Energy made his skin tingle and hummed in the air around it. The book was magical, the runes were magical, and he had a much better understanding of how the castle had come about, about the source of energy that had facilitated the construction, but there was more. Something remained hidden just below the surface. The magical runes even then appearing on the page might prove to be a clue.

The ring of steel distracted him. He turned back to see an agitated Pratcus hopping from one foot to the other in the middle of the room. Ellery came out of one tunnel, and cut to the side from where the sound emanated. She looked at Pratcus as Athrogate emerged from a tunnel opposite. Up on the balcony, Olgerkhan and Arrayan leaned over the railing, looking down with concern.

"Who?" Ellery asked.

"Gotta be the ranger," Pratcus answered.

Ellery ran toward the sound. "Which tunnel?" she asked, for the torches in all had gone dark again, and the echoes of the sounds confused her.

All eyes went to the dwarf, but Pratcus just shrugged.

Then from above, Olgerkhan cried out, "Breach!"

The fight had come.

"Just keep them off me!" Canthan growled, and he forced his attention back to the open book.

Another egg fell and broke open, and that made five.

Mariabronne finished the first with a two-handed overhead chop, but he was too busy leaping away from fiery daemon breath to applaud himself for the kill.

He went into a frenzy, spinning, rolling, and slashing, scoring hit after hit, and he came to realize that the creatures could only breathe their fire on him from a distance. So he ran, alternately closing on each. He took a few hits and gave a few more, and his confidence only heightened when, upon hearing more rattling from above, he leaped over and shouldered the brazier to the floor.

The rattling stopped.

There would be no more than the four standing against him. All he had to do was hold out until his companions arrived.

He sprang forward and charged but skidded to a stop and cut to the side. He used the sarcophagi as shields and kept the clawing, smoky hands at bay.

His smile appeared once more, that confidence reminiscent of the young Mariabronne who had rightly earned the nickname "the Rover" and had also earned a rakish reputation with ladies all across Damara. His sense of adventure overwhelmed him. He never felt more alive, more on the edge of disaster, of freedom and doom, than he was in times of greatest danger.

"Are all of Gehenna so slow?" he tried to say, to taunt the daemons, but halfway through the sentence he coughed up blood.

The ranger froze. He brought his free hand up to his neck to feel the blood still pumping. A wave of dizziness nearly dropped him.

He had to dive aside as two of the daemons loosed cones of fire at him, and so weak did he feel that he almost didn't get back to his feet—and when he did, he overbalanced so badly that he nearly staggered headlong into a third of the beasts.

"Priest, I need you!" Mariabronne the Rover shouted through the blood, and all at once he wasn't so confident and exuberant. "Priest! Dwarf, I need you!"

Entreri and Jarlaxle rushed into the room to join the others. Sounds of fighting from above assailed them, and both Entreri and Athrogate started that way.

Then came the desperate call from Mariabronne, "Priest, I need you!"

"Athrogate, hold the balcony!" Ellery ordered. "The rest with me!"

Entreri heard Arrayan's cry and ignored the commander's order. In his thoughts, he pictured the doom of Dwahvel, his dear halfling friend, and so overwhelming was that sensation that he never paused long enough to consider it. He sprinted past the dwarf and hit the stairs running, taking them three at a time. He cut to the right, though the door and his companions were on the balcony to the left.

Then he cut back sharply to the left and leaped up to the slanted stairway railing in a dead run. His lead foot hit and started to slide, but the assassin stamped his right foot hard on the railing and leaped away, spinning as he went so that when he lifted up near the floor of the balcony, his back was to the railing. He threw his hands up and caught the balusters, and with the others on the floor below looking at him with mouths hanging open, Entreri's taut muscles flexed and tugged. He curled as he rose, throwing his feet up over his head. Not only was his backward flip over the railing perfectly executed, not only did he land lightly and in perfect balance, but on the way over he managed to draw both dagger and sword.

He spun as he landed and threw himself into the nearest gnoll mummy, his blades working in a scything whirlwind. Gray wrappings exploded into the air, flying all around him.

Down below, Jarlaxle looked to Ellery and said, "Consider the room secured."

Ellery managed one quick look the drow's way as she sprinted toward the tunnel entrances.

"Which one?" she asked again of Pratcus, who ran beside her.

"Yerself to the right, meself to the left!" the dwarf replied, and they split into the two possible openings.

Jarlaxle followed right behind them, but paused there. Athrogate rambled back from the stairs, trying to catch up.

Torches flared to life as Ellery ran through. A split second later, Pratcus's heavy strides similarly lit the first pair in his descending corridor.

"Which one, then?" Athrogate asked Jarlaxle.

"Here!" Ellery cried before the drow could answer, and both Jarlaxle and Athrogate took up the chase of the woman warrior.

In the other tunnel, Pratcus, too, heard the call, just as he passed the second set of torches, which flared to life. The dwarf instinctively slowed but shook his head. Perhaps his tunnel would intersect with the other and he wouldn't have to lose all the time backtracking, he thought, and he decided to light up one more set of torches.

He hit the next pressure plate, turning sidelong so that he could quickly spin around if the light didn't reveal an intersection.

But the torches didn't ignite.

Instead came a sudden clanging sound, and Pratcus just happened to be looking the right way to see the iron spike slide out of the wall.

He thought to throw himself aside but only managed to cry out. The spike moved too fast. It hit him in the gut and drove him back hard against the far corridor wall. It kept going, plunging right through the dwarf and ringing hard against the stone behind him.

With trembling hands, Pratcus grabbed at the stake. He tried to gather his wits, to call upon his gods for some magical healing.

But the dwarf knew that he'd need more than that.

Flames licked at Mariabronne from every angle. He drove his sword through a daemon's head, tore it free and decapitated another as he swung wildly. All the room was spinning, though, and he was staggering more than charging as he went for the last pair of daemons.

His consciousness flitted away; he felt the rake of claws. He lifted an arm to defend himself and a monstrous maw clamped down upon it.

Black spots became a general darkness. He felt cold . . . so cold.

Mariabronne the Rover summoned all of his strength and went into a sudden and violent frenzy, slashing wildly, punching and kicking.

Then the ranger's journey was before him, the only road he ever rightly expected while following his adventurous spirit.

He was at peace.

Blackness engulfed Arrayan as the mummy's strong hands closed around her throat. She couldn't begin to concentrate enough to throw one of her few remaining spells, and she knew that her magic had not the strength to defeat or even deter the monsters in any case.

Nor did she have the physical strength to begin to fight back. She grabbed the mummy's wrists with her hands, but she might as well have been trying to tear an old oak tree out of the ground.

She managed a glance at Olgerkhan, who was thrashing with another pair of the horrid creatures, and that one glance told the woman that her friend would likely join her in the netherworld.

The mummy pressed harder, forcing her head back, and somewhere deep inside she hoped that her neck would just snap and be done with it before her lack of breath overcame her.

Then she staggered backward, and the mummy's arms went weak in her grasp. Confused, Arrayan opened her eyes then recoiled with horror as she realized that she was holding two severed limbs. She threw them to the ground, gasped a deep and welcomed breath of air, and looked back at the creature only to see the whirlwind that was Artemis Entreri hacking it apart.

Another mummy grabbed at Arrayan from the side, and she cried out.

And Entreri was there, rolling his extraordinary sword up and over with a left-to-right backhand that forced the mummy's arms aside. The assassin turned as he followed through, flipped his dagger into the air and caught it backhand, then drove it right to the hilt into the mummy's face as he came around. Gray dust flew from the impact.

Entreri yanked the dagger free, spun around so that he was facing the creature, and bulled ahead, driving it right over the railing.

Arrayan sobbed with horror and weakness, and the assassin grabbed her by the arm and guided her toward the stair.

"Get down!" he ordered.

Arrayan, too battered and overwhelmed, too weak and frightened, hesitated.

"Go!" Entreri shouted.

He leaped at her, causing her to cry out again, then he went right by, launching himself with furious abandon into another of the stubborn gnoll mummies.

"Now, woman!" he shouted as his weapons began their deadly dance once more.

Arrayan didn't move.

Entreri growled in frustration. It was going to be hard enough keeping himself alive up there as more creatures poured in, without having to protect Arrayan. A glance toward the door inspired him.

"Arrayan," he cried, "I must get to Olgerkhan. To the stair with you, I beg."

Perhaps it was the mention of her half-orc friend, or perhaps the calming change in his voice, but Entreri was glad indeed to see the woman sprint off for the stairs.

The mummy before him crumbled, and the assassin leaped ahead.

Olgerkhan was losing badly. Bruises and cuts covered him by then, and he staggered with every lumbering swing of his heavy war club.

Entreri hit him full force from behind, driving him right past the pair of battling mummies, and the assassin kept pushing, throwing Olgerkhan hard against the back of the opened door. The door slammed, or tried to, for a gargoyle was wedged between it and the jamb.

But Entreri kept moving, right into the incoming creature. He ignored the mummies he knew were fast closing on him and focused all of his fury instead on that trapped gargoyle. He slashed and stabbed and drove it back.

Olgerkhan's weight finally closed the door.

"Just hold it shut!" Entreri yelled at him. "For all our sakes."

The assassin charged away at the remaining two mummies.

⊷══⊶

Ellery instinctively knew that she was in grave danger. Perhaps it had been the tone of Mariabronne's plea for help or even that the legendary Rover had called out at all. Perhaps it was the closed door at the bottom of the staircase before her, or maybe it was the sound.

For other than her footsteps, and those of the duo behind her, all was silent.

She lowered her shoulder and barreled through the door, stumbling into the room, shield and sword presented. There she froze, then slumped in horror and despair, her fears confirmed. For there lay Mariabronne, on his back, unmoving and with his neck and chest covered in his own blood. Blood continued to roll from the neck wound, but it was not gushing forth as it had been, for the ranger's heart no longer beat.

"Too many," Athrogate said, rambling in behind her.

"Guardian daemons," Jarlaxle remarked, noting the demonic heads, all that remained of the creatures, lying about the room. "A valiant battle."

Ellery continued to simply stand there, staring at Mariabronne, staring at the dead hero of Damara. From her earliest days, Ellery had heard stories of that great man, of his work with her uncle the king and his particular relationship with the line of Tranth, the Barons of Bloodstone and Ellery's immediate family members. Like so many warriors of her generation, Ellery had held up the legend of Mariabronne as the epitome of a hero, the idol and the goal. As Gareth Dragonsbane and his friends had inspired the young warriors of Mariabronne's generation, so had he passed along that inspiration to hers.

And he lay dead at Ellery's feet. Dead on a mission she was leading. Dead because of her decision to split the party to explore the tunnels.

Almost unaware of her surroundings, Ellery was shaken from her turmoil by the shout of Athrogate.

"That's the priest!" the dwarf yelled, and he charged back out of the room.

Jarlaxle moved near to Ellery and put a comforting hand on her shoulder.

"You are needed elsewhere," the dark elf bade her. "There is nothing more you can do here."

She offered the drow a blank look.

"Go with Athrogate," said Jarlaxle. "There is work to be done and quickly." Hardly thinking, Ellery staggered out of the room.

"I will see to Mariabronne," Jarlaxle assured her as she stumbled back up the corridor.

True to his word, the drow was with the ranger as soon as Ellery was out of sight. He pulled out a wand and cast a quick divination spell.

He was surprised and disappointed at how little magic registered on a man of Mariabronne's reputation. The man's sword, Bayurel, was of course enchanted, as was his armor, but none of it strongly. He wore a single magical ring, but a cursory glance told Jarlaxle that he possessed at least a dozen rings of greater enchantment—and so he shook his head and decided that pilfering the obvious ring wasn't worth the risk.

One thing did catch his attention, however, and as soon as he opened Mariabronne's small belt pouch, a smile widened on Jarlaxle's face.

"Obsidian steed," he remarked, pulling forth the small black equine figurine. A quick inspection revealed its command words.

Jarlaxle crossed the ranger's arms over his chest and placed Bayurel in the appropriate position atop him. He felt a moment of regret. He had heard much of Mariabronne the Rover during his short time in the Bloodstone Lands, and he knew that he had become party to a momentous event. The shock of the man's death would resonate in Vaasa and Damara for a long time to come, and it occurred to Jarlaxle that it truly was an important loss.

He gave a quick salute to the dead hero and acknowledged the sadness of his passing.

Of course, it wasn't enough of a regret for Jarlaxle to put back the obsidian steed.

"Aw, what'd ye do?" Athrogate asked Pratcus as soon as he came upon the dying priest.

Pinned to the corridor wall, his chest shattered and torn, Pratcus could only stare numbly at his counterpart.

Athrogate grabbed the spike and tried to pull it back, but he couldn't get a handhold. It wouldn't have mattered anyway, both of them knew, as did Ellery when she moved in behind the black-bearded dwarf.

"Bah, ye go to Moradin's Halls, then," Athrogate said. He pulled a skin from around his neck and held it up to the priest. "A bit o' the gutbuster," he explained, referring to that most potent of dwarven liquid spirits. "It'll help ye get there and put ye in a good mood for talking with the boss."

"Hurts," Pratcus gasped. He sipped at the skin, and even managed a thankful nod as the fiery liquid burned down his throat.

Then he was dead.

CHAPTER

CLEARING THE PATH

19

Leaning on each other for much-needed support, Arrayan and Olgerkhan inched down the staircase. Entreri came up and moved between them, pushing Olgerkhan more tightly against the railing and forcing the half-orc to grab on with both his hands.

Entreri turned to Arrayan, who was holding on to him and swaying unsteadily. He shifted to put his shoulder back behind her, then in a single move swept her up into his arms. With a glance at Olgerkhan to make sure that the buffoon wouldn't come tumbling behind him, the assassin started away.

Arrayan brought a hand up against his face and he looked down at her, into her eyes.

"You saved me," she said, her voice barely audible. "All of us."

Entreri felt a rush of warm blood in his face. For just a brief moment, he saw the image of Dwahvel's face superimposed over the similar features of Arrayan. He felt warm indeed, and it occurred to him that he should just keep walking, away from the group, taking Arrayan far away from all of it.

His sensibilities, so entrenched and pragmatic after spending almost the entirety of his life in a desperate attempt at survival, tried to question, tried to illustrate the illogic of it all. But for the first time in three decades, those practical sensibilities had no voice in the thoughts of Artemis Entreri.

"Thank you," Arrayan whispered, and her hand traced the outline of his cheek and lips.

The lump in his throat was too large for Entreri to respond, other than a quick nod of his head.

⊰━━━⊱

"That'll hold, but not for long," Athrogate announced, coming to the railing of the balcony overlooking the keep's main floor. From below, the dwarf's six remaining companions glanced up at him and at the continuing pounding and scratching on the door behind him. "More gargoyles than mummies," Athrogate explained. "Gargoyles don't hit as hard."

"The room is far from secure," put in Canthan, who still stood by the open book. "They will find a way in. Let us be on our way."

"Destroy the book?" Olgerkhan asked.

"Would that I could."

"Take it with us, then?" Arrayan asked, and the horror in her voice revealed much.

Canthan snickered at her.

"Then what?" Ellery chimed in, the first words she had spoken in some time, and with a shaky voice. "We came here for a purpose, and that seems clear before us. Are we to run away without completing—"

"I said nothing about running away, my dear Commander Ellery," Canthan interrupted. "But we should be gone from this particular room."

"With the book," Ellery reasoned.

"Not possible," Canthan informed her.

"Bah! I'll tear it out o' the ground!" said Athrogate, and he scrambled up on the railing and hopped down to the stairs.

"The book is protected," said Canthan. "It is but a conduit in any case. We'll not destroy it, or claim it, until the source of its power is no more."

"And that source is?" Olgerkhan asked, and neither Canthan nor Jarlaxle missed the way the half-orc stiffened with the question.

"That is what we must discern," the wizard replied.

Jarlaxle was unconvinced, for Canthan's gaze drifted over Arrayan as he spoke. The drow knew the wizard had long ago "discerned" the source, as had Jarlaxle and Entreri. A glance at his assassin friend, the man's face rigid and cold and glaring hard Canthan's way told Jarlaxle that Entreri was catching on as well and that he wasn't very happy about the conclusions Canthan had obviously drawn.

"Then where do we start?" Ellery asked.

"Down, I sense," said Canthan.

Jarlaxle recognized that the man was bluffing, partially at least, though the drow wasn't quite certain of why. In truth, Jarlaxle wasn't so sure that Canthan's guess was off the mark. Certainly part of the source for the construction was standing right beside him in the form of a half-orc woman. But that was a small part, Jarlaxle knew, as if Arrayan had been the initial flare to send a gnomish fire-rocket skyward before the main explosion filled the night sky with its bright-burning embers.

"The castle must have a king," the drow remarked, and he believed that, though he sensed clearly that Canthan believed it to be a queen instead—and one standing not so far away.

It wasn't the time and place to confront the wizard openly, Jarlaxle realized. The pounding on the door continued from above, and the volume of the scratching on the keep's main doors, just past Canthan and the book, led Jarlaxle to believe that scores of undead monstrosities had risen against them.

The room was no sanctuary and would soon enough become a crypt.

⊷═══⊶

Jarlaxle will peruse the book and you will guard him, Canthan's magical sending echoed in Ellery's head. *When we are long gone, you will do as you were trained to do. As you promised you could do.*

Ellery's eyes widened, but she did well to hide her surprise.

Another magical sending came to her: *Our victory is easily achieved, and I know how to do it. But Jarlaxle will stand against my course. He sees personal gain here, whatever the cost to Damara. For our sake, and the sake of the land, the drow must be killed.*

Ellery took the continuing words in stride, not surprised this time. She didn't quite understand what Canthan was talking about, of course. Easily achieved? Why would Jarlaxle not agree to something like that? It made no sense, but Ellery could not easily dismiss the source of the information and of her orders. Canthan had found her many years ago, and through his work, she had gained greatly in rank and reputation. Her skill as a warrior had been honed through many years of training, but that added icing, the edge that allowed her to win when others could not, had been possible only through the work of Canthan and his associates.

Though they were the enemies of the throne and her own relatives, Ellery knew that the relationship between the crown of Damara and the Citadel of Assassins was complicated and not quite as openly hostile and adversarial as onlookers might believe. Certainly Ellery had quietly profited from her relationship with Canthan—and never had the wizard asked her to do anything that went against the crown.

In her gut, however, she knew that there was something more going on than the wizard was telling her. Was Canthan seeking some personal gain himself? Was he using Ellery to settle a personal grudge he held with the dark elf?

Now!

Ellery jolted at the sharp intrusion, her gaze going to Canthan. He stood resolute, eyes narrow, lips thin.

A hundred questions popped into Ellery's head, a hundred demands she wanted to make of the wizard. How could she follow such an order against someone who had done nothing out of line along the expedition, someone she had asked along and who had performed, to that point, so admirably? How could she do this to someone she had known as a lover, though that had meant little to her?

Looking at Canthan, Ellery realized how she could and why she would.

The wizard terrified her, as did the band of cutthroats he represented.

It all came clear to Commander Ellery at that moment, as she admitted to herself, for the first time, the truth of her involvement with the Citadel of Assassins and its wizard representative. She had spent years justifying her secret relationship with Canthan, telling herself that her personal gains and the way she could use them would benefit the kingdom. In Ellery's mind, for all that time, she thought herself in control of the relationship. She, the relative of Tranth and of both King Gareth and Lady Christine, would always do what was best for Damara and greater Bloodstone.

What did it matter if the dark tendrils of her choices delayed her from that "moment of miracle" her relatives all enviously awaited, that release of holy power that would show the world that she was beyond an ordinary warrior, that she was a paladin in the line of Gareth Dragonsbane?

At that moment, though, the nakedness of her self-delusion and justification hit her hard. Perhaps Canthan was imparting truthful thoughts to her to justify her killing of the drow. Perhaps, she tried to tell herself, the dark elf Jarlaxle truly was an impediment to their necessary victory.

Yes, that was it, the woman told herself. They all wanted to win, all wanted to survive. The death of Mariabronne had to mean something. The Zhengyian castle had to be defeated. Canthan knew that, and he apparently knew something about Jarlaxle that Ellery did not.

Despite her newest rationalization, deep in her heart Ellery suspected something else. Deep in her heart, Ellery understood the truth of her relationship with Canthan and the Citadel of Assassins.

But some things were better left buried deep.

She had to trust him, not for his sake, but for hers.

⊷═╫═⊶

His eye patch tingled. Nothing specific came to him, but Jarlaxle understood that a magical intrusion—a sending or scrying, some unseen wave of magical energy—had just flitted by him.

At first the drow feared that the castle's king to whom he had referred might be looking in on them, but then, as Ellery remarked to him, "Do you believe you might be able to find some deeper insight into the magical tome? Something that Canthan has overlooked?" Jarlaxle came to understand that the source of the magic had been none other than his wizardly companion.

The drow tried not to let his reaction to the question show him off-guard when he lied, "I am sure that good Canthan's knowledge of the arts arcane is greater than my own."

Ellery's eyes widened and her nostrils flared, and the drow knew that he had surprised and worried her with his tentative refusal. He decided not to disappoint.

"But I am drow and have spent centuries in the Underdark, where magic is not quite the same. Perhaps there is something I will recognize that Canthan has not."

He looked at the wizard as he spoke, and Canthan gracefully bowed, stepped aside, and swept his arm to invite Jarlaxle to the book.

There it was, as clear as it could be.

"We ain't got time for that," Athrogate growled, and the thought "on cue" came to the drow.

"True enough," Ellery played along. "Lead the others out, Athrogate," she ordered. "I will remain here to guard over Jarlaxle for as long as the situation allows."

Ellery nodded toward the book, but Jarlaxle motioned for her to go first. He passed by a confused-looking Entreri as he followed.

"Trouble," he managed to quietly whisper.

Entreri made no motion to indicate he had heard anything, and he went out with Canthan, Athrogate, and the two half-orcs, moving down the tunnel Mariabronne had taken on his final journey.

Jarlaxle stood before the open book but did not begin perusing it. Rather, he watched the others head down the tunnel and stayed staring at the dark exit for some time. He felt and heard Ellery shifting behind him, moving nervously

433

from foot to foot. Her focus was on him, he understood; she was hardly "standing guard for him." Over him, more likely.

"Your friend Canthan believes he has figured out the riddle of the castle," the drow said. He turned to regard the woman, noting especially how her knuckles had whitened on the handle of her axe. "But he is wrong."

Ellery's face screwed up with confusion. "What has he said to you? How do you know this?"

"Because I know what he discerned from the book, as I have seen a tome similar to this one."

Ellery stared at him hard, her hand wringing over the handle, and she chewed her lips, clearly uneasy with it all.

"He told you to keep me here and kill me, not because he fears that I will prove an impediment to our escape or victory, but because Canthan fears that I will vie with him for the book and the secrets contained within. He is nothing if not opportunistic."

Ellery rocked back and seemed as if she would stumble to the floor at Jarlaxle's obviously on-the-mark observation. Jarlaxle wasn't fool enough to think he could talk the woman out of her planned course of action, though, so he was not caught off-guard when, just as he finished speaking, Ellery roared and came on.

A dagger appeared in the drow's hand, and with a snap of his wrist, it became a sword. He flipped it to his left just in time to parry Ellery's axe-swipe and he back-stepped just fast enough to avoid the collision from her shield rush. A second dagger spilled forth from his bracer, and he threw it at her, slowing her progress long enough for him to extract a third from his enchanted bracer and snap his wrist again. When the initial assault played out and the two faced each other on even footing, the drow was holding a pair of slender long swords.

Ellery launched a backhand slash and pressed forward as Jarlaxle rolled around the cut and thrust forth with his sword. Her shield took that one aside and a clever underhand reversal of her cutting axe deflected the thrust of the drow's second blade, coming in low, aimed for the woman's leading knee.

Ellery chopped down with her shield, spun a tight circuit behind it, and extended as she came around.

Jarlaxle threw back his hips then started in yet again behind the flashing axe. He stopped and flung himself out to the side as Ellery cut short her swing and came ahead in a rush, her powerful axe at the ready. She stayed right with him, step for step. An angled sword moved aside her powerful chop. Her shield tapped down on one sword, driving it low, came up to take the second high, then low again, then . . .

Jarlaxle was too quick with his second blade, feigning high once more but thrusting it down low instead.

But Ellery was quick as well, and the shield tapped down appropriately.

On came the woman with a growl, and Jarlaxle had to step back fast and spin out to the side. He brought both his swords in one desperate parry and accepted the shield bash against his arm, glad that the momentum of it allowed him to put some distance between himself and the surprisingly skilled woman.

"If I win again, will I find your bed?" he teased.

Ellery didn't crack a grin. "Those days are long past us."

"They don't have to be."

Ellery's response came in the form of another sudden charge and a flurry of blows that had Jarlaxle furiously defending and backing, stride after stride.

<hr />

Entreri rushed out past Athrogate. "I have the point," he explained. "Follow with caution, but with speed."

He sprinted down the corridor, pushing through the door and into the room where Mariabronne lay still, his sword held in both hands over his chest, its blade running down below his waist.

Entreri shook his head and dismissed the tragic sight. He went across the room to the other door, did a cursory check for traps when he saw that it had not recently been opened, and pushed through to find another curving, descending tunnel.

He sprinted down and carefully set the first torches burning by tapping the pressure plate. Then he turned and rushed back to the door, scrambling up beside it to the top of the jamb. Using just that tiny lip and the ceiling above him, the assassin pressed himself into place.

A few moments later, Athrogate moved out under him, followed closely by Olgerkhan and Arrayan, with Canthan moving last. They passed without noticing the assassin, and before they had even disappeared around the tunnel bend, Entreri hooked his fingers on the lip of the door jamb and swung down, launching himself and landing lightly back in the room with Mariabronne. He hit the ground running and ran back up the corridor.

<hr />

Her movements were very much in line with the fighting style and skill level she had shown to him in their sparring match those days before at the Vaasan Gate. Ellery was no novice to battle and had practiced extensively in single combat techniques. Her efforts tested Jarlaxle at every turn. He had beaten her then, however, and he knew he could beat her again.

She had to know that too, as Canthan, who had sent her, had to understand. Unless . . .

They were the "Citadel of Assassins," after all.

Ellery continued the flow of the fight, working her axe with quick chops and cuts, generally playing out more and more to Jarlaxle's right. She followed almost every swing with a sudden popping thrust of her shield arm, leaving no openings for the drow's swords and also balancing herself and her turns to keep her feet properly aligned to propel her side-to-side or forward and back as required.

She was good but not good enough, and they both knew it.

It almost slipped past the observant drow that Ellery had crossed her feet, so smooth was the transition. Even noting that, Jarlaxle was taken aback at how efficiently and quickly the woman executed a sudden spin, so that as she came around, her axe chopping hard, she was aiming back at the drow's left.

And he couldn't stop it.

Jarlaxle's eyes widened and he even smiled at the "kill swing"—that one movement assassins often employed, that extra level of fighting beyond anything any opponent could reasonably expect to see. Jarlaxle had expected something of that nature, of course, but still, as he saw it unfolding before him, he feared, he *knew,* that he could not stop it.

Ellery roared and chopped hard at the drow's shoulder. Jarlaxle grimaced and threw his swords across in an effort to at least partially defeat the blow and threw himself aside in a desperate effort to get out of the way.

But Ellery's roar became a scream, and in mid-swing her axe wobbled, its angle pulling aside, her arm falling limp, as Charon's Claw slammed hard atop her shoulder. Her fine silvery breastplate rattled and loosened as the shoulder cord tore apart under the force of Entreri's blow.

She staggered and turned, trying to come around and get her shield up to fend off the assassin.

Entreri's other hand was under her shield, however, and his dagger easily found the seam in her breastplate and slid in between the woman's ribs into the left side of her chest.

Ellery froze, helpless and on the precipice of disaster.

Entreri didn't finish the movement but held her there, his dagger in place. Ellery glared at him and he called upon the life-drawing powers of the weapon for just an instant, letting her know the complete doom that awaited her.

She didn't persist. She was beaten and she showed it. Her weapon arm hung limp and she didn't try to stop the axe as it slid from her grip and clanged against the floor.

"An interesting turn of events," Jarlaxle remarked, "that Canthan would move against us so quickly."

"And that a relative of the King of Damara would be an instrument for an assassin's guild," Entreri added.

"You know nothing," Ellery growled at him, or started to, for he gave the slightest of twists on his dagger and brought the woman up to her tip-toes. The commander sucked in her breath against the wave of pain.

"When I ask you to answer, you answer," Entreri instructed.

"I told you that Canthan was fooled," Jarlaxle said to her. "He believes that killing Arrayan will defeat the tower." He turned to Entreri. "She is the Herminicle of this castle, so Canthan believes, but I do not agree."

Entreri's eyes widened.

"This is beyond Arrayan," Jarlaxle explained. "Perhaps she began the process, but something greater than she has intervened."

"You know nothing," Ellery said through her gritted teeth.

"I know that you, the lawful representative of King Gareth in this quest, were about to kill me, though I have done nothing against the crown and risked everything for the realm's sake," Jarlaxle pointed out.

"So you say."

"And so you deny, without proof, because Canthan would be rid of Jarlaxle, would be rid of us," the drow added, "that he might claim whatever secrets and power Zhengyi has left in this place and in that book. You are a pawn, and a rather stupid one, Lady Ellery. You disappoint me."

"Then be done with me," she said.

Jarlaxle looked to Entreri and saw that his friend was hardly paying attention. He yanked free the knife and darted toward the tunnel exit and the four he realized he had foolishly left alone.

Her magical shield absorbed much of the blow, but still Canthan's lightning blast sent Arrayan flying back against the wall.

"It will hurt less if you drop your wards and accept the inevitability," the wizard remarked.

To the side, Olgerkhan once again tried to get at Canthan, and again Athrogate was there to block his way.

"She is the foundation of the castle," Canthan said to the large and furious half-orc. "When she falls, so falls this Zhengyian beast!"

Olgerkhan growled and charged—or tried to, but Athrogate kicked his ankles out from under him, sending him face-down to the floor.

"Ye let it be," the dwarf warned. "Ain't no choices here."

Olgerkhan sprang up and swung his club wildly at the dwarf.

"Well all right then," the dwarf said, easily ducking the lumbering blow. "Ye're making yer choices ye ain't got to make."

"Be done with the stubborn oaf," Canthan instructed, and he calmly launched a series of stinging glowing missiles Arrayan's way.

Again, the half-orc wizard had enacted enough wards to defeat the majority of the assault, but Canthan's continuing barrage had her backing away, helpless to counter.

For Olgerkhan, disaster was even quicker in coming. The half-orc was a fine and accomplished warrior by Palishchuk's standards, but against Athrogate, he was naught but a lumbering novice, and in his weakened state, not even a promising one. He swung again and was blocked, then he tried an awkward sidelong swipe.

Athrogate went below the swinging club, both his morning stars spinning. The dwarf's weapons came in hard, almost simultaneously, against the outsides of Olgerkhan's knees. Before the half-orc's legs could even buckle, Athrogate leaped forward and smashed his forehead into the half-orc's groin.

As Olgerkhan doubled over, Athrogate sent one morning star up so that the chain wrapped around the half-orc's neck, the heavy ball smacking him in the face. With a twist and a sudden and brutal jerk, one that snapped bone, Athrogate flipped Olgerkhan into a sideways somersault that left him groaning and helpless on the floor.

"Olgerkhan!" Arrayan cried, and she too staggered and went down to her knees.

Canthan watched it all with great amusement. "They are somehow bound," he mused aloud. "Physically, so. Perhaps the castle has a king as well as a queen."

"The human is coming," Athrogate called, looking past Canthan to the corridor.

Enough musing, the wizard realized, and he took the moment of Arrayan's weakness to fire off another spell, a magical, acid-filled dart. It punctured her defensive sphere and slammed into her stomach, sending her sitting back against the wall. She cried out from the pain and tried to clutch at the tiny projectile with trembling hands.

"Kill him when he enters," Canthan instructed the dwarf.

The wizard ran out of the room along one of the side corridors just as Entreri burst in.

Entreri looked at Athrogate, at Olgerkhan, and at Arrayan, then back at the dwarf, who approached steadily, morning stars swinging easily. Athrogate offered a shrug.

"Guess it's the way it's got to be," the dwarf said, almost apologetically.

Ellery held her hands out to her sides, not knowing what she was supposed to do.

"Well, gather up your weapon and let us be off," Jarlaxle said to her.

She stared at him for a few moments then bent to retrieve the axe, eyeing Jarlaxle all the while as if she expected him to attack.

"Oh, pick it up," the drow said.

Still Ellery paused.

"We've no time for this," said Jarlaxle. "I'll call our little battle here a misunderstanding, as I'm confident that you see it the same way now. Besides, I know your trick now—and a fine move it is!—and will kill you if you come against me again." He paused and gave her a lewd look. "Perhaps I will extract a little payment from you later on, but for now, let us just be done with this castle and the infernal Zhengyi."

Ellery picked up the axe. Jarlaxle turned and started away after Entreri.

The woman had no idea what to do or what to believe. Her emotions swirled as her thoughts swirled, and she felt very strange.

She took a step toward Jarlaxle, just wanting to be done with it all and get back to Damara.

The floor leaped up and swallowed her.

Jarlaxle turned sharply, swords at the ready, when he heard the thump behind him. He saw at once that those weapons wouldn't be needed. He moved quickly to Ellery and tried to stir her. He put his face close to her mouth to try to detect her breath, and he inspected the small wound Entreri had inflicted.

"So the dagger got to your heart after all," Jarlaxle said with a great sigh.

Entreri wasn't certain if Athrogate was incredibly good or if it was just that the dwarf's unorthodox style and weaponry—he had never even heard of someone wielding two morning stars simultaneously—had him moving in ways awkward and uncomfortable.

Whatever the reason, Entreri understood that he was in trouble. Glancing at Arrayan, he realized that her situation was even more desperate. Somehow, that bothered him as much, if not more.

He growled past the unnerving thought and created a series of ash walls to try to deter the stubborn and ferocious dwarf. Of course, Athrogate just plowed through each ash wall successively, roaring and swinging so forcefully that Entreri dared not get too close.

He tried to take the dwarf's measure. He tried to find a hole in the little beast's defenses. But Athrogate was too compact, his weapon movements too coordinated. Given the dwarf's strength and the strange enchantments of his morning stars, Entreri simply couldn't risk trading a blow for a blow, even with his own mighty weapons.

Nor could he block, for he rightly feared that Athrogate might tangle one of his weapons in the morning star chain and tear it free of his grasp. Or even worse, might that rusting sludge that coated the dwarf's left-hand weapon ruin Charon's Claw's fine blade?

Entreri used his speed, darting this way and that, feigning a strike and backing away almost immediately. He was not trying to score a hit at that point, though he would have made a stab if an opening presented itself. Instead, Entreri moved to put the dwarf into a different rhythm. He kept Athrogate's feet moving sidelong or had him turning quickly—both movements that the straightforward fighter found more atypical.

But that would take a long, long time, Entreri knew, and with another glance at Arrayan, he understood that it was time she didn't have to spare.

With that uncomfortable thought in mind, he went in suddenly, reversing his dodging momentum in an attempt to score a quick kill.

But a sweeping morning star turned Charon's Claw harmlessly aside, and the second sent Entreri diving desperately into a sidelong roll. Athrogate pursued, weapons spinning, and Entreri barely got ahead of him and avoided a skull-crushing encounter.

"Patience . . . patience," the dwarf teased.

Entreri realized that Athrogate knew exactly his strategy, had probably seen the same technique used by every skilled opponent he'd ever faced. The assassin had to rethink. He needed some space and time. He came forward in a sudden burst again, but even as Athrogate howled with excitement, Entreri was gone, sprinting out across the room.

Athrogate paused and looked at him with open curiosity. "Ye running or thinking to hit me from afar?" he asked. "If ye're running, ye dolt, then be gone like a colt. But be knowing in yer mind that I'm not far behind! *Bwahaha!*"

"While I find your ugliness repellant, dwarf, do not ever think I would flee from the likes of you."

Athrogate howled with laughter again, and he charged—or he started to, for as he began to close the ground between himself and Entreri, an elongated disk floated in from the side, stretching and widening, and settled on the floor between them. Athrogate, unable to stop his momentum, tumbled headlong into the extra-dimensional hole.

He howled. He cursed. He landed hard, ten feet down.

Then he cursed some more, and in rhymes.

Entreri glanced at the tunnel entrance, where Jarlaxle stood, leaning.

The drow offered a shrug and remarked, "Bear trap?"

Entreri didn't respond. He leaped across the room to Arrayan and quickly tore the magical dart from her stomach. He stared at the vicious missile, watching with mounting anger as its tip continued to pump forth acid. A glance back at Arrayan told him that he had arrived in time, that the wound wasn't mortal, but he could not deny the truth of it when he looked into Arrayan's fair face. She was dying, with literally one foot in the nether realm.

Desperation tugged at Entreri. He saw not Arrayan but Dwahvel lying before him. He shook the woman and yelled for her to come back. Hardly thinking of the movement, he found himself hugging her, then he pulled her back to arms' length and called to her over and over again.

Lying on the floor to the side, the dying Olgerkhan saw the fleeting health of Arrayan and understood clearly that much of his dear companion's current grief was being caused by her magical binding with him. As the rings had forced Olgerkhan to share Arrayan's burden, so they had begun to work the other way. Olgerkhan knew his wounds to be mortal, knew that he was on the very edge of death.

And he was taking Arrayan with him.

With all the strength he could muster, the half-orc pulled the ring from his finger and flicked it far to the side.

His world went black at the same time Arrayan opened her eyes.

Entreri fell back from her in surprise. She still looked terrible, weaker than anyone he had ever seen before, more—he could only describe it as thin and drained of her life energy—frail than any human being could be, much more so than she had been before the fight.

But she still had life, and consciousness, and so the assassin learned, rage.

"No!" the woman cried. "Olgerkhan, *no!*"

The tone of her voice showed that she was scolding the half-orc, not denying his wound. That, combined with her sudden return from the grave, had the assassin scratching his head. Entreri looked again to Jarlaxle, who studied the pair intently but seemingly with just as much curiosity.

Arrayan, so weak and drained and sorely wounded, dragged herself past Entreri to her half-orc companion

"You took off the ring," she said, cradling his face in her hands. "Put it back! Olgerkhan, put it back!"

He didn't, couldn't answer.

"You think to save me," Arrayan wailed, "but don't you know? I cannot be saved to watch you die. Olgerkhan, come back to me. You must! You are all I love, all that I have ever loved. It's you, Olgerkhan. It was always you. Please come back to me!"

Her voice grew weaker, her shoulders quivered with sobs, and she held on dearly to her friend.

"The ring?" Jarlaxle asked.

Arrayan didn't answer, but the drow was figuring it out anyway. He thought of all the times the two had seemed to share their pain and their weariness.

"So the castle does have a king," Jarlaxle remarked to Entreri, but the assassin was hardly listening.

He stood staring at the couple, chuckling at himself and all of his foolish fantasies about his future beside Arrayan.

Without a word of explanation, Artemis Entreri ran out of the room.

CHAPTER

20

Though he was confident that his job was done regarding Arrayan and Olgerkhan and that Athrogate would dispatch the assassin, Canthan glanced back many times as he ran down the descending corridor. Though his gaze turned to what lay behind him, his thoughts were on the future, for he knew that there was a great prize to be found in the pages of the Witch-King's book. His perusal of the tome had shown him possibilities beyond his imagination. Somehow within that book loomed the secret that would grant him ownership of the castle, without it taking his life-force as it had Arrayan's. He was certain of that. Zhengyi had designed it so. The book would trap the unwitting and use that soul to build the castle.

But that was only half the enchantment. Once constructed, the fortress was there for the taking—for one wise enough and strong enough to seize it.

Canthan could do that, and certainly Knellict, among the greatest of wizards in the Bloodstone Lands, could too. Had the Citadel of Assassins just found a new home, one from which they might openly challenge King Gareth's claim of dominion?

"Ah, the possibilities," Canthan muttered as he approached the next door.

The castle was either dormant or soon to be, he believed, or at least it was beyond regeneration given the fall of its life sources. Still the wizard remained at the ready.

He threw a spell of opening that swung the door in long before he physically entered the room. In the large chamber beyond, he saw movement, and he didn't even wait to discern the type of creature before he began his spellcasting.

A gnoll mummy came to the threshold. It served as the first target, the initial strike point.

A bolt of lightning arced onto its head then shot away to the next target, and on again. It diminished with each successive strike but jumped about several times. That first mummy smoked and unwrapped into a pile of smoldering rags, and Canthan was fast to the point, next spell ready. A quick survey of the large room showed him the course of his first strike, the chain bouncing across five targets, mummies all. The healthiest remaining creature had been the last hit, so Canthan reversed his line and made that one the first.

In the instant it took the second lightning chain to leap across the remaining mummies, all four went down, reduced to smoking husks.

Canthan rushed in and braziers flared to life. The wizard looked upward at the ceiling ten feet above and saw the tell-tale egg shapes of the guardian daemons nestled above each of the four braziers in the room.

Grinning, Canthan filled the upper two feet of the room, wall-to-wall, with strands of sticky webbing. It was a precaution only, he believed, for the castle had to be dead. The already animated monsters, like the mummies, might remain, so he thought, but with Arrayan gone, no others should animate.

The wizard paused to catch his breath and consider the situation. He hoped Ellery was done with the troublesome drow and Athrogate with the equally troublesome assassin. Mariabronne's death was good fortune for the Citadel. The troublesome but loyal ranger would have most assuredly handed Zhengyi's great gift over to King Gareth and the other fools who ruled Damara.

Canthan knew he still had to approach things with great care, though. He hoped his guess about the qualities of the castle was correct, for his task of truly deciphering the secrets of the book would be much more difficult if he had to spend half his time destroying monsters.

The wizard had to quickly gather Athrogate and Ellery back to his side and take some rest. He had nearly exhausted his magical spells for the day, and even though he believed the battle to be won, Canthan didn't like feeling vulnerable. His wizardry was his armor and his sword. Without his spells, he was just a clever but rather feeble man.

He didn't appreciate the view, then, when a solitary man stalked with great determination into the chamber.

Far from being dead, as Canthan had presumed, the outer walls of the great structure teemed with life. Gargoyles, regenerated from their previous night's battle on the hill, flew off with the sunset, speeding across the few miles to the walls of Palishchuk.

There the defenses had been set, and there the desperate battle began. But walls proved little impediment to the winged creatures, and they swarmed the city in search of easy targets.

In her room, Calihye heard the commotion beginning on the streets, the cries of alarm and the sounds of battle joined. She looked over at Davis Eng, his eyes wide, his breathing heavy with anticipation and stark fear. A twinge of sympathy went through her, for she could only imagine his terror at being so completely helpless.

"What is it?" he managed to whisper.

Calihye had no answer. She moved to the room's one window and pulled aside the drape. Out on the street below her, she saw the fighting, where a trio of half-orc guards slashed and rushed wildly after the short hops and flights of a single gargoyle. Calihye watched for a while, mesmerized by the strange sequence and dance.

Then she gave a shout and fell back as a gargoyle crashed through the window, scattering shards of glass, its clawed hands reaching for her throat.

The woman let herself fall over in a backward roll, and she came up lightly to her feet, reversing her momentum and leaping forward as the foolish gargoyle charged ahead, impaling itself on her blade.

But another was at the window, ready to take its place.

"Help me," Davis Eng cried out.

Calihye ignored him, except to think that if the situation got too desperate she might be able to use the man as an offering to the beasts while she made her escape out the door.

She was a long way from that unpleasant possibility, however, and she went forward to meet the newest invader, working her sword with the skill of a seasoned veteran.

"Be reasonable, my friend," Canthan said as he backed away.

Artemis Entreri, his face perfectly expressionless, walked toward him.

"The girl is dead?"

No answer.

"Be reasonable, man," Canthan reiterated. "She was the source of power for this place—her life-force was feeding it."

No answer. Soon Canthan had a wall to his back, and Entreri was still coming on, sword and dagger in hand.

"Ah, but you fancied her, did you not?" Canthan asked.

He laughed—a sound he had to admit to himself was for no better reason than to cover his sincere discomfort. For Canthan didn't have many spells left to cast, and if Entreri had found a way to defeat Athrogate, he was a formidable foe indeed.

Still no answer, and Canthan cast a quick spell that sent him in an extra-dimensional "blink" to the other side of the room.

Entreri did nothing but turn and continue his determined approach.

"By the gods, don't tell me that you slew Athrogate?" Canthan said to him. "Why, he was worth quite a bit to the Citadel—a favor I do for you in killing you now. However we might talk, I cannot forgive that, I fear, nor will Knellict!" He finished with a flourish of his arms, and launched a lightning bolt Entreri's way.

But it wasn't that easy. Entreri moved before the blast ensued, a sudden and efficient dive and roll out to the side.

Canthan was already casting a second time, sending a series of magical missiles that no man, not even Artemis Entreri, could avoid. But the assassin growled through their stinging bites and came on.

Laughing, Canthan readied another blast of lightning, but a dagger flashed through the air, striking him in the chest and interrupting his casting. The wizard was of course well warded from such mundane attacks, and even the jeweled dagger bounced away. He quickly refocused and let fly his blast at the man—or at what he thought was the man, he realized too late, for it was naught but a wall of ash.

Growing increasingly fearful, Canthan spun around to survey the room.

No Entreri.

He spun again, then stopped and muttered, "Oh, clever."

He didn't even have to look to understand the assassin's ruse and movement.

For in that moment of distraction from the dagger, in that reflexive blink of the wizard's eye, Entreri had not only swiped the sword and put forth the ash wall, but he had leaped up, catching himself on Canthan's webbing.

The wizard glanced up at him. The assassin was in a curl, legs tucked up tight against his chest, his hands plunged into the secure webbing. He uncoiled and swayed back, then toward Canthan. As he came forward, he flicked something he held in one hand—a simple flint and steel contraption. The resulting spark ignited the web and burned the entire section away in an instant, just as Entreri came to the height of his swing.

He flew forward, falling over into a backward somersault as he went, extending his legs and arms to control the fall. He landed lightly and in perfect balance right in front of the wizard, and out came his sword.

The skilled wizard struck first, a blast of stunning lightning that crackled all over Entreri's body, sparks flying from his sword. His jaw snapped uncontrollably, his muscles tensing and clenching, the fingers of one hand curling into a tight ball, the knuckles of the other whitening on the hilt of Charon's Claw.

But Entreri didn't fly back and he didn't fall away. He growled and held his ground. He took the hit and with incredible determination and simple toughness, he fought through it.

When the lightning ended, Entreri came out of it in a sudden spin, Charon's Claw flying wide. Given the sheer power of that blade, beyond the defenses of any wards and guards, Entreri could have quite easily killed the horrified wizard, could have taken the man's head from his shoulders. But Charon's Claw came in short in a diagonal stroke, cutting the wizard from shoulder to opposite hip.

Stunned and falling back, Canthan could not get far enough away as Entreri, his face still so cold and expressionless that Canthan wondered briefly if he was nothing more than an animated corpse, leaped high in a spin and came around with a circle kick that snapped Canthan's head back viciously.

Entreri retrieved his prized dagger and wiped the blood from his nose and mouth as he again stalked over to the prone Canthan. Face down, the man squirmed then stubbornly pulled himself up to his elbows.

Entreri kicked him in the head and kicked him again before Canthan settled back down to the floor. The assassin put his sword away but held the dagger as he grabbed the semi-conscious wizard by the scruff of his neck and dragged him back to the corridor.

"Surely you'll be reasonable in this regard," Jarlaxle, on his hands and knees and peering over the edge of the hole, said to Athrogate. "You cannot get out without my help."

Athrogate, hands on hips, just stared up at him.

"I had to do something," Jarlaxle said. "Was I to allow you to kill my friend?"

"Bah! Well I wouldn't've fought him if he hadn't've fought meself."

"True enough, but consider Olgerkhan."

"I did, and I killed him."

"Sometimes acts like that upset people."

"He shouldn't've got in me friend's way."

"So your friend could kill the girl?"

Athrogate shrugged as if it did not matter. "He had a reason."

"An errant reason."

"What's done is done. Ye wanting an apology?"

"I don't know that I want anything," Jarlaxle replied. "You seem to be the one in need, not I."

"Bah!"

"You cannot get out. Starvation is a lousy way for a warrior to die."

Athrogate just shrugged, moved to the side of the hole, studied the sheer wall for a moment, and sat down.

Jarlaxle sighed and turned away to consider Arrayan. She was still cradling Olgerkhan's head, whispering to him.

"Don't you dare leave me," she pleaded.

"And only now you realize your love for him?" Jarlaxle asked.

Arrayan shot him a hateful look that told him his guess was on the mark.

Noise from the corridor turned Jarlaxle's head, but not the woman's. In came Entreri, muttering under his breath and dragging Canthan at the end of one arm. He moved around the hole to Arrayan and Olgerkhan.

The woman looked at him with a mixture of surprise, curiosity, and horror.

Entreri had no time for it. He grabbed her by the shoulder and shoved her aside, then dropped Canthan before Olgerkhan.

Arrayan came back at him, but he stopped her with the coldest and most frightening look the woman had ever seen.

With her out of the way, Entreri turned his attention to Olgerkhan. He grabbed the large half-orc's hand and pulled it out over the groaning Canthan. He put his dagger into Olgerkhan's palm and forced the half-orc's fingers over it. He glanced at Arrayan then at Jarlaxle, and he drove the dagger down into Canthan's back.

He slipped his thumb free, placed it on the bottom of the dagger's jeweled hilt, and willed the blade to feed. The vampiric weapon went to its task with relish, stealing the very soul of Canthan and feeding it back to its wielder.

Olgerkhan's chest lifted and his eyes opened as he coughed forth his first breath in many seconds. He continued to gasp for a moment. His eyes widened in horror as he came to understand the source of his healing. He tried to pull his hand away.

But Entreri held him firmly in place, forcing him to feed until Canthan's life-force was simply no more.

"What did you do?" Arrayan cried, her voice caught between horror and joy. She came forward and Entreri did not try to stop her. He extracted his dagger from Olgerkhan's grasp and moved aside.

Arrayan fell over her half-orc friend, sobbing with joy and saying, "It was always you," over and over again.

Olgerkhan just shook his head, staring blankly at Entreri for a moment. He sat up, his strength and health renewed. Then he focused on Arrayan, upon her words, and he buried his face in her hair.

"Ah, the kindness of your heart," Jarlaxle remarked to the assassin. "How unselfish of you, since the contender for your prize was about to be no more."

"Maybe I just wanted Canthan dead."

"Then maybe you should have killed him in the other room."

"Shut up."

Jarlaxle laughed and sighed all at once.

"Where is Ellery?" Entreri asked.

"I believe that you nicked her heart."

Entreri shook his head at the insanity of it all.

"She was unreliable, in any case," Jarlaxle said. "Obviously so. I do take offense when women I have bedded turn on me with such fury."

"If it happens often, then perhaps you should work on your technique."

That had Jarlaxle laughing, but just for a moment. "So we are five," he said. "Or perhaps four," he added, glancing at the hole.

"Stubborn dwarf?" asked the assassin.

"Is there any other kind?"

Entreri moved to the edge of the hole. "Ugly one," he called down. "Your wizard friend is dead."

"Bah!" Athrogate snorted.

Entreri glanced back at Jarlaxle then moved over, grabbed Canthan's corpse, and hauled him over the edge of the hole, dropping him with a splat beside the surprised dwarf.

"Your friend is dead," Entreri said again, and the dwarf didn't bother to argue the point. "And so now you've a choice."

"Eat him or starve?" Athrogate asked.

"Eat him and eventually starve anyway," Jarlaxle corrected, coming up beside Entreri to peer in at the dwarf. "Or you could come out of the hole and help us."

"Help ye what?"

"Win," said the drow.

"Didn't ye just stop that possibility when Canthan put it forth?"

"No," Jarlaxle said with certainty. "Canthan was wrong. He believed that Arrayan was the continuing source of power for the castle, but that is not so. She was the beginning of the enchantment, 'tis true, but this place is far beyond her."

The drow had all of the others listening by then, with Olgerkhan, the color returned to his face, standing solidly once more.

"If I believed otherwise, then I would have killed Arrayan myself," Jarlaxle went on. "But no. This castle has a king, a great and powerful one."

"How do you know this?" Entreri asked, and he seemed as doubtful and confused at the others, even Athrogate.

"I saw enough of the book to recognize that it has a different design than the one Herminicle used outside of Heliogabalus," the drow explained. "And there is something else." He put a hand over the extra-dimensional pocket button he wore, where he kept the skull-shaped gem he had taken from Herminicle's book. "I sense a strength here, a mighty power. It is clear to me, and given all that I know of Zhengyi and all that the dragon sisters told me, with their words and with the fear that was so evident in their eyes, it is not hard for me to see the logic of it all."

"What are you talking about?" asked Entreri.

"Dragon sisters?" Athrogate added, but no one paid him any heed.

"The king," said Jarlaxle. "I know he exists and I know where he is."

"And you know how to kill him?" Entreri asked. It was a hopeful question, but one that was not answered with a hopeful response.

The assassin let it go at that, surely realizing he'd never get a straight answer from Jarlaxle. He looked back down at Athrogate, who was standing then, looking up intently.

"Are you with us? Or should we leave you to eat your friend and starve?" Entreri asked.

Athrogate looked down at Canthan then back up at Entreri. "Don't look like he'd taste too good, and one thing I'm always wantin' is food." He pronounced "good" and "food" a bit off on both, so that they seemed closer to rhyming, and that brought a scowl to Entreri's face.

"He starts that again and he's staying in the hole," he remarked to Jarlaxle, and the drow, who was already taking off his belt that he might command it to elongate and extract the dwarf, laughed again.

"We'll have your word that you'll make no moves against any of us," Entreri said.

"Ye're to be takin' me word?"

"No, but then I can kill you with a clearer conscious."

"Bwahaha!"

"I do so hate him," Entreri muttered to Jarlaxle, and he moved away.

Jarlaxle considered that with a wry grin, thinking that perhaps it was yet another reason for him to get Athrogate out and by their side. The dwarf's lack of concern for Canthan was genuine, Jarlaxle knew, and Athrogate would not go against them unless he found it to be in his best interests.

Which, of course, was the way with all of Jarlaxle's friends.

CHAPTER

21

Athrogate and Entreri eyed each other for a long, long while after the dwarf came out of the hole.

"Could've ruined yer weapon, ye know," Athrogate remarked, holding up the morning star that coated itself with the rust-inducing liquid.

"Could've eaten yer soul, ye know," the assassin countered, mimicking the dwarf's tone and dialect.

"With both yer weapons turned to dust? Got the juice of a rust monster in it," he said, jostling the morning star so that the head bounced a bit at the end of its chain.

"It may be that you overestimate your weapons or underestimate mine. In either case, you would not have enjoyed learning the truth."

Athrogate cracked a smile. "Some day we'll find out that truth."

"Be careful what you wish for."

"Bwahaha!"

Entreri wanted nothing more than to drive his dagger into the annoying dwarf's throat at that moment. But it wasn't the time. They remained surrounded by enemies in a castle very much alive and hostile. They needed the powerful dwarf fighting beside them.

"I remain convinced that Canthan was wrong," Jarlaxle said, moving between the two.

He glanced back at the two half-orcs, leading the gaze of the dwarf and the assassin. Arrayan sat against the wall across the way, while her companion scrambled about on all fours, apparently searching for something. Olgerkhan looked much healthier, obviously so. The dagger had fed Canthan's life energy to him and had healed much of the damage of Athrogate's fierce attacks. Beyond that, the great weariness that had been dragging on Olgerkhan seemed lifted; his eyes were bright and alert, his movements crisp.

But as much better as he looked, Arrayan appeared that much worse. The woman's eyes drooped and her head swayed as if her neck had not the strength to hold it upright. Something about the last battles had taken much from her, it seemed, and the castle was taking the rest.

"The castle has a king," Jarlaxle said.

"Bah, Canthan got it right, and ye killed him to death for it," said Athrogate. "It's the girl, don't ye see? She's wilting away right afore yer eyes."

"No doubt she is part of it," the drow replied. "But only a small part. The real source of the castle's life lies below us."

"And how might ye be knowin' that?" asked the dwarf. "And what's he looking for, anyway?"

"I know because I can feel the castle's king as acutely as I can feel my own skin. And I know not what Olgerkhan is seeking, nor do I much care. Our destiny lies below and quickly if we hope to save Arrayan."

"What makes ye think I'm giving an orc's snot rag for that one?"

Entreri shot the dwarf a hateful look.

"What?" Athrogate asked with mock innocence. "She ain't no friend o' me own, and she's just a half-orc. Half too many, by me own counting."

"Then disregard her," Jarlaxle intervened. "Think of yourself, and rightly so. I tell you that if we defeat the king of this castle, the castle will fight us no more, whatever Arrayan's fate. I also tell you that we should do all that we can to save her, to keep her alive now, for if she is taken by the castle it will benefit the construct and hurt us. Trust me on this and follow my advice. If I am wrong, and the castle continues to feed from her, and in doing so it continues to attack us, then I will kill her myself."

The dwarf nodded. "Fair enough."

"But I only say that because I am certain it will not come to that," Jarlaxle quickly added for the sake of Olgerkhan, who glared at him. "Now let us tend our wounds and prepare our weapons, for we have a king to kill."

Athrogate pulled a waterskin off and moved toward the two half-orcs. "Here," he offered. "Got a bit o' the healing potions to get yer strength back," he said to Arrayan. "And as for yerself, sorry I breaked yer neck."

Olgerkhan offered nothing in reply. He hesitated for a moment by Arrayan's side, but then moved back toward the side passage and began crawling around on all fours once more, searching.

Entreri pulled Jarlaxle to the far side of the room and asked, "What are you talking about? How do you know what you pretend to know, or is it all but a ruse?"

"Not a ruse," Jarlaxle assured him. "I feel it and have since we entered this place. Logic tells me that Arrayan could not have constructed anything of this magnificence, and everything I have seen and felt since only confirms that logic."

"You have told me that all before," the assassin replied. "Could you offer something more?"

Jarlaxle patted his button pocket, wherein he had stored the skull. "The skull gem we took from the other tower has sensitized me to certain things. I feel the king below us. His is a life-force quite mighty."

"And we are to kill him?"

"Of course."

"On your *feeling?*"

"And following the clues. Do you remember Herminicle's book?"

Entreri thought on that for a moment then nodded.

"Do you remember the designs etched upon its leathery cover, and in the margins on the page?"

Again the assassin paused, and shook his head.

"Skulls," Jarlaxle explained. "Human skulls."

"And?"

"Did you notice the designs on the book up the ramp, the source of this castle?"

Entreri stared hard at his friend. He had not actually looked at the book that closely, but he was beginning to catch on. Given his experiences with Jarlaxle, where every road seemed to lead, his answer was as much statement as question: "Dragons?"

"Exactly," the drow confirmed, pleased that Entreri resisted the urge to punch him in the face. "I understand the fearful expressions of our sister employers. They knew that the Witch-King could pervert dragonkind as he perverted humankind, even from beyond the grave. They feared the apparent opening of Zhengyi's lost library, as evidenced by Herminicle's tower. They feared that such a book as the one that constructed this castle might be uncovered."

"You doubt that Arrayan started this process?"

"Not at all, as I explained. The book used her to send out its call, I believe. And that call was answered."

"By a dragon?"

"More likely an undead dragon."

"Wonderful."

Jarlaxle shrugged against his companion's disgusted stare. "It is our way. An adventurous road!"

"It is a fatal disease."

Again the drow shrugged, and a wide grin spread across his face.

They continued on their way down the side passage Canthan had taken to the room where Entreri had defeated the battle mage. The magical webbing Canthan had created to prevent the daemon eggs from falling remained in place, except for the small area Entreri had burned away in his fight with the mage. Still, the five went through the room quickly, not wanting an encounter with those powerful adversaries. They all believed that the "king," as Jarlaxle had aptly named it, awaited them, and they needed no more wounds and no more weariness. The order of the day at that time was avoiding battles, and so with that in mind, Entreri took up the point position.

They made good progress for a short while along the twisting, winding corridor. No traps presented themselves, only the pressure bars that kept lighting the wall torches, and no monsters rose before them.

Around one particularly sharp bend, though, they found Entreri waiting for them, his expression concerned.

"A room with a dozen coffins like those of the gnoll mummies," he explained, "only even more decorated."

"A dozen o' the raggy ones?" Athrogate replied. "Ha! Six slaps each!" he said and sent his morning stars into alternating swings.

The dwarf's cavalier attitude did little to lift the mood of the others, however.

"There is another exit from the room, or is this the end of our path?" Jarlaxle asked.

"Straight across," said Entreri. "A door."

Jarlaxle instructed them to wait then slowly moved ahead. He found the room around the next bend, a wide, circular chamber lined, as Entreri had said, with a dozen sarcophagi. The drow took out the skull gem and allowed it to guide his sensibilities. He felt the energy within each of the coffins, vengeful and focused, hating death and envying life.

The drow fell deeper into the skull gem, testing its strength. The gem was attuned to humans, not the dog-faced humanoids wrapped in rags within the coffins. But they were not too far removed, and when he opened his eyes again, Jarlaxle drew forth a slender wand from its holster inside his cloak and aimed it across the room at the door. He paused a moment to consider the richly decorated portal, for even in the low light of the torches burning in the wall sconces behind him, he could see the general make-up of its design: a bas relief of a great battle, with scores of warriors swarming a rearing dragon.

The drow found the design quite revealing. "It was made of memories," he whispered, and he looked all around, for he was talking about more than that door; he was talking about the whole of the place.

The castle was a living entity, created of magic and memories. Its energy brought forth the gargoyles and the doors, the stone walls and tunnels complete with the clever designs of the wall torches and the traps. Its energy recreated its former occupiers, the gnoll soldiers Zhengyi had used as staff, only trapped in undeath and far more powerful than they had been in life.

And its energy had unwittingly tapped into the other memories of the place, animating in lesser form the many bodies that had been buried on that spot. Jarlaxle suspected then that those undead skeletons that had arisen against them in the courtyard were not of Zhengyi's design but were an inadvertent side effect of the magical release.

He smiled at that thought and looked ahead at the design on the door. It was no haphazard artist's interpretation. The scene was indeed a memory, a recording of something that had truly occurred.

The drow had hoped that the suspicions festering within him since crawling through the portcullis would prove accurate, and there was his confirmation and his hope.

He pointed his wand at the door and uttered a command word.

Several locks clicked and a latch popped. With a rush of air the door swung open. Beyond it, the corridor continued into darkness.

"Remain in a tight group and be quick through the room," Jarlaxle instructed the others when he returned to them a moment later. "The door is open—make sure it remains so as we pass. Come now, and be quick."

He glanced at the half-orcs, Olgerkhan all but carrying Arrayan, who seemed as if she couldn't even keep her head from swaying. Jarlaxle motioned for Athrogate to help them, and though he gave a disgusted sigh, the dwarf complied.

"Are you coming?" the drow asked Entreri as the others started away.

The assassin held up his hand, looked back the way they had come, and said, "We're being followed."

"Press ahead," Jarlaxle instructed. "Our road is ahead of us, not behind."

Entreri turned on him. "You know something."

"You hope I do," Jarlaxle replied, and he started after the trio. He paused a few steps down and glanced back at his friend and grinned sheepishly. "As do I."

Entreri's expression showed that the humor was not appreciated.

"We cannot go out, unless we are willing to let the castle win," Jarlaxle reminded him after they had taken a few steps. "And in that victory, the construct will claim Arrayan. Is that acceptable to you?"

"Am I following you?" Entreri remarked.

They passed through the chamber quickly and no sarcophagi opened and no eggs fell, releasing daemons to rise against them. Through the other door, they found a long descending staircase and down they went into the darkness.

Entreri took the lead again, inspecting every step and every handhold as the light diminished around them. Near to the bottom, he was relieved to see another of the pressure plates, and torches soon flared to life on the opposite walls at the sides of the bottom step.

The light flickered and cast long, uneven shadows across stone that was no longer worked and fitted. It seemed as if they had come to the end of the construct, to a natural winding tunnel, boring down ever deeper before them.

Entreri went ahead a short distance, the others moving close behind. He turned and went back past them to the last two torches. He inspected them carefully, expecting a trap or ten, and indeed on the left-hand one, he removed several barbed pins, all wet with some sort of poison. Then he carefully extracted the torches and carried them back to the others. He handed one to Olgerkhan and had thought to give the other to Arrayan. One look at the woman dissuaded him from that course, however, for she didn't seem to have the strength to hold it, and indeed, had it not been for Olgerkhan's supporting arm, she would not have been standing. He offered the torch to Athrogate instead.

"I got dwarf eyes, ye dolt," Athrogate growled at him. "I ain't needing no firelight. This tunnel's bathed in sunlight next to where me kin've dug."

"Jarlaxle needs both of his hands and Arrayan is too weak," Entreri said to him, thrusting the torch back his way. "I prefer to lead in the darkness."

"Bah, but ye're just making me a target," the dwarf growled back, but he took the torch.

"Another benefit," Entreri said, turning away and moving out in front.

The corridor continued to bend to the left, even more sharply, giving the assassin the feeling that they were in the same general area from which they'd started, only far below. The caverns were all of natural stone, with no more torches and no pressure plates or other traps that the assassin could locate. There were intersections, however, and always sharp turns back the other way as the other winding tunnels joined into this one, becoming one great spiraling corridor. With each joining, the passage widened and heightened, so that it seemed almost as if they were walking down a long sloping cavern instead of a corridor.

Trying to minimize the feeling of vulnerability, Entreri kept them near to the inner bending wall as he edged ahead, sword in one hand, dagger in the other. Their progress was steady for some time, and they put many hundreds of feet between themselves and the staircase. But then Olgerkhan's cry froze the assassin in mid-stride.

"It's taking her!" the half-orc wailed.

Entreri spun and ran back past the turning Athrogate. He shoved by Jarlaxle, needing to get to Arrayan. By the time he spotted her, she was down on the ground, Olgerkhan kneeling over her and whispering to her.

Entreri slid down beside her opposite the large half-orc. He started to call out to her but cut himself short when he realized that he was calling the name of a halfling friend he had left far back in the distant southern city of Calimport. Surprised and unnerved, the assassin looked from Arrayan to Jarlaxle, his expression demanding answers.

Jarlaxle wasn't looking back at him, though. The drow stood facing Arrayan with his eyes closed and his hand over the center of his waistcoat. He was whispering something that Entreri could not make out, and in looking from him back to the fallen woman, Entreri understood that the drow was trying to somehow intervene. Entreri thought of the skull gem and guessed that Jarlaxle was somehow using it to disrupt the castle's possession of the woman.

A moment later, Arrayan opened her eyes. She seemed more embarrassed than hurt, and she accepted Olgerkhan and Entreri's help in getting back to her feet.

"We are running out of time," Jarlaxle stated—the obvious for the others, but his tone explaining clearly to Entreri that he could not long delay the inevitable life-stealing process. "Quickly, then," the drow added, and Entreri gave a nod to Arrayan then left her with Olgerkhan and sprinted back to the front of the line.

He had to hope that there would be no more traps, for he did not slow every few feet to inspect the ground ahead.

The corridor continued to bend and spiral but began to narrow again, soon becoming a mere dozen feet across and with a jagged ceiling often so low that Olgerkhan had to crouch.

Entreri felt the hairs on the back of his neck tingling. Something was ahead, he sensed, whether from some smell or perhaps a sound barely audible. He motioned for the dwarf behind him to halt, then crept ahead on all fours and peered around a sharper bend.

The corridor continued for another dozen feet, then the stone floor fell away as it opened into a great chamber. He remembered Jarlaxle's words about the "king" of the castle, and he had to take a deep, steadying breath before going forward.

He crept ahead, belly-crawling as he exited the corridor into a vast cavern, on a ledge high up from the uneven floor. To his right, the ledge continued for just a short distance, but to his left, it continued on, sloping down toward the unseen cavern floor. It was not pitch black in there, as some strange glowing lichen scattered about the floor and walls bathed the stone as if in starlight.

Entreri crawled to the edge and peered over, and he knew they were doomed.

Far below him, perhaps fifty feet, loomed the king of the castle: a great dragon. But not a living dragon of leathery skin and thick scales but one made mostly of bones, with only patches of skin hanging between its wings and in patches across its back and head. The gigantic dragon carcass, mostly skeleton, crouched on the floor with its bony wings tucked in tight atop its back. If Entreri had any doubts that the creature was "alive," they were quickly dispelled when, with a rattle of bones, the great wings unfolded.

Swords, armor, and whitened bones littered the chamber all around the undead beast, and it took Entreri a few moments to sort out that that had been the spot of a desperate battle, that those weapons and bones belonged to warriors—likely of King Gareth's army, he realized when he gave it some thought—who had done battle with the wyrm in the time of Zhengyi.

Entreri started to back up then nearly jumped out of his boots when he felt a hand on his shoulder. Jarlaxle moved up beside him.

"He is fabulous, is he not?" the drow whispered.

Entreri shot him a hateful look.

"I know," the drow said for him. "Always dragons with me."

Down below, the dragon of bones and torn skin swung its head to look up at them, and though it had no physical eyes, just points of reddish light, its intimidating gaze rattled the companions.

"A dragon cadaver," Entreri said with obvious disgust.

"A dracolich," Jarlaxle corrected.

"That is supposed to sound better?"

The drow just shrugged.

And the dragon roared, its throaty blast reverberating off the stone walls with such power that the assassin feared the ledge he lay upon would collapse.

"That ain't right," Athrogate said when the echoing blast at last relented. The dwarf had come up as well, but unlike Entreri and Jarlaxle he wasn't lying on the stone. He stood at the lip of the ledge, staring down, hands on his hips. He looked at Jarlaxle and asked, "That the king?"

"One would hope."

"And what're we supposed to do with that thing?"

"Kill it."

The dwarf looked back down at the dracolich, which hunched upon its hind legs, sitting upright, head swaying, two-foot long teeth all too clear with little skin covering its mouth.

"Ye're joking with an old dwarf," said Athrogate.

He didn't rhyme his words, and Entreri knew that no "bwahahas" would be forthcoming.

Jarlaxle pulled himself up. "I am not," he proclaimed. "Come now, our time of trial is upon us. Run along, mighty Olgerkhan, for the sake of your lady Arrayan. And you, good Athrogate, fearless and powerful. Those brittle bones will turn to dust before your mighty swings!"

Olgerkhan roared and came out onto the ledge, then with strength and power they had not seen from him before, he took up his heavy club and charged down along the ledge.

"Ye're really not joking with an old dwarf?" Athrogate asked.

"Shatter its skull!" Jarlaxle cheered.

Athrogate looked at the drow, looked down at the dracolich, looked back at the drow, and shrugged. He pulled his morning stars over his shoulders and whispered to his weapons alternately as he ran off after Olgerkhan, bidding their enchantments forth.

"Fill yer teeth with half-orc bread," the dwarf yelled to the waiting beast, "while Athrogate leaps atop yer head! *Bwahaha!*"

"And now we leave," Entreri remarked, coming up beside Jarlaxle and making no move to follow his two warrior companions.

But then it was dark, pitch black so that Entreri couldn't see his hand before his face if he'd waggled his fingers an inch in front of his eyes.

"This way," Jarlaxle bade him, and he felt the drow's arm around his waist.

He started to protest and pull away, sheathing his dagger to free up one hand, though he dared not move too quickly on the ledge. But the assassin was caught by surprise when Jarlaxle pushed against him hard, wrapping him in a tight hug. The drow then fell the other way, off the ledge.

The dragon roared.

Entreri screamed.

But then they were floating as the drow enacted the power of his levitation, and as they set down on the cavern floor, Jarlaxle threw aside the stone he had enchanted with radiating darkness and let go of Entreri.

Entreri rolled to the side, putting some distance between himself and the dark elf. He got his bearings enough to realize that the dracolich wasn't looking at him and Jarlaxle, but was focusing on the half-orc and the dwarf as they continued their raucous charge down the sloping stone ledge.

Entreri had his chance to strike with the element of surprise. With the beast distracted, he could get past its formidable defenses and score a mighty blow.

But he didn't move, other than to look down at his weapons. How could he even begin to hurt something like that?

He glanced to the side and considered leaping over and stabbing Jarlaxle instead, but he found the drow with his eyes closed, deep in concentration.

Jarlaxle had some hidden trick to play, it seemed—or at least, that's what Entreri hoped.

But Entreri still did not charge in against the beast, as it was no fight that he wanted. He rushed away from the wall, weaving toward the far side of the cavern, putting as much distance between himself and the half-orc and dwarf as possible.

He glanced back as Olgerkhan cried out, and he nearly swooned to see a line of black spittle spraying from the dracolich's skeletal mouth. Though he was still fully twenty feet from the floor, the half-orc desperately leaped from the ledge ahead of that spit, which engulfed the stone and immediately began to melt it away.

"Once a black dragon," Entreri heard Jarlaxle explain in reference to the acidic breath weapon, trademark of that particular beast.

"It can breathe?" Entreri gasped. "It's a skeleton, and it can breathe?"

But Jarlaxle had closed his eyes again and was paying him no heed.

Entreri ran along faster, heedless of Olgerkhan's groans. He did glance back once to take note of the poor half-orc, crumpled on the floor, one leg bent out at a disturbing angle, obviously shattered. How ridiculous, he thought. For the first time, the half-orc had seemed as if he might be ready for battle, and there he was, out of the fight yet again before it had even begun. And he was Arrayan's "hero" and true love?

The momentary distraction cost the assassin dearly, for when he looked back, he saw the great bony tail swiping his way.

<hr />

Arrayan, too, fought a great battle, but hers was internal and not carried out with sword or wand. Hers was a test of will, a battle as one might wage with a disease, for like a cancer did the darkness of the Zhengyian construct assail her. It clawed at her life energy with demonic hands. For days it had pulled at her, thinned her, sapped her, and now, so close to the king of the castle, the monstrous beast she had inadvertently awakened, Arrayan had come to the final battlefield.

But she had no way to fight back, had no strength to go on the offensive against the dracolich and the continuing intrusions of the book. That was a physical battle for her companions to wage.

She had to just hold on to the last flickers of her life, had to cling to consciousness and identity. She had to resist the temptation to succumb to the cool and inviting darkness, the promise of rest.

One image, that of Olgerkhan, carried her in her battle though she knew it to be a losing cause. For all those years he had been her dearest of friends. He had tolerated her pouting when she couldn't unravel the mysteries of a certain spell. He had accepted her selfishness when all of her thoughts and all of her talk had been about her own future and dreams. He had stayed beside her, his arm offered in support, through every setback, and he cheered her on from afar through every victory.

And she had accepted him as a friend—but just as a friend. She had not understood the depth of his devotion and love for her. He had worn that ring, and though Arrayan had not been in on the placement and explanation, she understood the properties of physical arbitration the matched set had created. He had suffered, terribly so, so that she could get where she was, so that she would have her one chance, feeble as it seemed.

She could not let him down. She could not betray the trust and the sacrifice of the half-orc she loved.

Yes, loved, Arrayan knew beyond all doubt. Far beyond her friend, Olgerkhan was her partner, her support, her warmth, and her joy. Only when she had seen him near death had Arrayan come to fully appreciate that.

And she had to fight on.

But the darkness beckoned.

She heard the ruckus in the far room and managed to open her eyes. She heard the approach of someone from the other direction, but she hadn't the strength to turn her head.

They passed her by, and Arrayan thought she was dreaming, then feared that she had gone over to the netherworld. For those three, Ellery, Mariabronne, and Canthan, had certainly died, yet they walked past her, ran by her, the warrior woman hefting her mighty axe, the ranger holding his legendary sword, the wizard preparing a spell.

How was it possible?

Was this the reality of death?

"Bwahaha! Ye got to be quicker than that, ye bony worm!" Athrogate bellowed as he dodged past a slashing claw, dived under the biting fangs, and came up with a smashing swing that cracked hard against the dracolich's foreleg. Bone dust flew, but the leg didn't give out or crack apart.

Athrogate had put all of his weight behind that strike, had let fly with all of his magically enhanced might, and had used the enchantment of the morning star, the oil of impact coating it, for maximum effect.

He hadn't done much damage.

He hit the leg again, and a third time, before the other foreleg crashed against his shoulder and launched him into a flying roll. He bounced through the heap of bones, weapons, and armor, finally coming back to his feet just in time to leap aside to avoid the snap of the dracolich's powerful and toothy jaws.

"A bit o' help, if ye might!" the dwarf yelled, and that was as close to a call of panic as had ever been uttered by the confident Athrogate.

The dracolich bit at him again, and he dodged aside, and even managed to snap off a one-two routine with his morning stars, their glassteel heads bouncing alternately off the thick dragon bone.

The creature showed no sign of pain or fear, and the head pressed on, snapping at him over and over. He retreated and dodged, jumped back, and when the dracolich finally caught up to him, the dwarf leaped up high, just high enough to get above the thing's snapping maw. He was spared a deadly bite but was thrown back and to the floor.

When he landed and slid down onto his back, he noted Olgerkhan, still squirming and grabbing at his shattered leg.

"By the gods, ye dolt, get up!" Athrogate pleaded.

Entreri wasn't quick enough. He jumped and turned sidelong but got clipped by the swinging tail and spun halfway over. He kept the presence of mind to tuck his head and shoulders and turn all the way as he landed among the bones, but when he came back to his feet, he found that one ankle would hardly support his weight. He gave it a cursory glance to see blood staining the side of his boot.

He hopped and limped along, though, and still his thoughts were to simply find a way out of there. All along, Entreri had expected that Jarlaxle's thirst for adventure would eventually put them in a position where they could not win. That time had come.

He stumbled on a tangle of bones then threw himself flat as the dracolich's tail swung back his way but higher off the ground. He glanced back across the length of the undead beast to see Jarlaxle standing quietly off to the side, to see Athrogate's desperate struggle against the more dangerous weapons of the dragon, to see Olgerkhan squirming in agony, and to see . . .

The assassin blinked repeatedly, unable to comprehend the scene before him. Running down the slope to join in the fray was Ellery. Ellery! Supposedly dead at his hand. And behind her came Mariabronne, also dead.

Entreri snapped his glare back at Jarlaxle, thinking that his friend had deceived him. He hadn't seen Ellery's corpse, after all. Was it all just a lie?

Even as he contemplated abandoning his flight and rushing back to slaughter Jarlaxle, however, he realized that he had indeed seen Mariabronne lying in the utter stillness of death.

Entreri's gaze was drawn up to the small landing at the top of the ramp. There stood Canthan, waving his arms.

Now that man was dead, Entreri knew. More than dead, his soul had been destroyed by the jeweled dagger.

Yet here he was, casting a spell.

Farther down, still forty feet from the ground, Ellery took up her axe in both hands and leaped out into the air.

Suicidal, Entreri thought. But could it be suicide if she was already dead?

She soared from on high, her body snapping forward as she crashed down beside the dracolich, her axe slamming into a rib with tremendous force, taking a chunk of bone and tearing a long line of tough skin all the way down to the ground. She landed hard but came right back to her feet, swinging with abandon, without concern for any semblance of defense.

Behind her came Mariabronne, leaping far and wide. He slammed down on the dracolich's back face-first, and somehow held on, eventually bringing himself to a sitting position straddling the beast's huge spine. He locked his legs around a vertebra, took up his sword in both hands, and began slamming away.

The dracolich reared—and from above came a sudden and blinding stroke of lightning that crackled around the creature's head.

But if the lightning hurt the dracolich at all, the beast didn't show it.

It all made no sense to Entreri, so of course he glanced back at Jarlaxle. The drow just stood there, serene, it seemed, with his eyes closed in concentration. Entreri shook his head. That one always had a trick to play.

His sigh was one of disgust, his shrug one of helplessness, but Entreri changed direction and lifted Charon's Claw above his shoulder. Perhaps it wasn't the end after all.

The dracolich was focused on Canthan, and Athrogate charged back in from the front as Entreri limped in at the back. Ellery and Mariabronne pounded away with abandon. The assassin still shook his head, though, doubting that it would be enough.

He watched the serpentine neck lift the head fast toward the wizard. Canthan let loose a second spell and the dracolich's skull momentarily disappeared within the flames of a fireball. It came through smoking and blackened in spots.

With his free hand, Entreri pulled out the side of his cloak and whispered, "Red" into a pocket, then grabbed Charon's Claw with both hands, determined to make his first strike count.

Up above, the dracolich's head snapped Canthan from the ledge, its powerful jaws taking in the wizard to the waist and clamping hard. The beast swung its neck side to side and Canthan's lower torso fell free from on high as his upper body was ground into pulp.

Entreri wanted to scream.

But he growled instead and came up on the dracolich's rear leg, throwing all of his weight behind his strike.

He did some damage, but hardly enough, and it occurred to him that he would have to hit the creature a thousand times to kill it.

Canthan was already gone. The dracolich fell to all fours and swiveled its head around to spit forth another stream of acid, one that engulfed Mariabronne and melted him in place.

Entreri reconsidered his course.

Beside him, a skeleton rose, lifting a rusting broadsword. The assassin slashed at it, felling it with a single stroke. But all around him, more bones rattled, collected themselves, and rose. Entreri looked everywhere for some way out. He moved to strike at the next nearest skeleton, but he stopped short when he realized that he was not their enemy.

The skeleton warriors, formerly men of the Army of Bloodstone, attacked the dracolich.

Stunned, Entreri looked again to Jarlaxle, and his mind whirled with the possibilities, the insanity, as he noted that Jarlaxle stood with one hand extended, a purple-glowing, skull-shaped gemstone presented before him.

"By the gods!" Athrogate yelled from in front, and for the first time Entreri was in full agreement with the wretched little creature.

All around the great chamber, the Army of Bloodstone rose and renewed the battle they had waged decades before. A hundred warriors stood tall on skeletal legs, lifted sword, axe, and warhammer. They had no fear and only a singular purpose, and as one they rushed in at the beast. Metal rang against bone, leathery skin tore apart beneath the barrage.

Athrogate had no idea what was happening around him or why. He didn't stop to question his good fortune, though, for had the dead not risen, he undoubtedly would have met a sudden and brutal end.

The dracolich's roar thundered through the room and nearly felled the dwarf with its sheer power. A line of acidic spittle melted one group of skeleton warriors, but as the beast lowered its head to breathe its devastation, another group of warriors charged in.

Athrogate saw his opening. He called forth more oil of impact on his right-hand morning star and charged in behind the group of skeletons, pushing through them and letting fly a titanic swing.

The explosion shattered dragon teeth and took off a large chunk of the dracolich's jawbone, but before the dwarf could swing again, the great skull lifted up beyond his reach.

Then it came down, and hard, and Athrogate cried out and dived away. Skeletons all around him got crushed and shattered, and the dropping skull smacked him hard and sent him sprawling, his weapons flying from his grasp. He tried to rise but could not. He sensed the dracolich coming in at his back and knew he was doomed.

But first he was grabbed by the front by a stumbling half-orc who yanked him aside and drove him to the ground then fell atop him defensively.

"Ye still smell bad," the dwarf muttered, his voice weak and shaky.

Olgerkhan would have taken that as a thank you, except that the half-orc was barely conscious by that point, overwhelmed by the lines of agony rolling up from his broken leg.

⚔

Entreri slashed and bashed with all his strength, his mighty sword having some effect. The cumulative efforts of all the fighters was their only chance, he knew, and he played his part.

But not too well, for in Entreri's thoughts, first and foremost, he did not want to draw the dracolich's attention.

Wherever that attention went, the beast's enemies crumbled to dust.

And the great creature was in a frenzy by that point, its wings beating and battering, its tail whipping wildly and launching warriors through the air to smash against the chamber's distant walls.

But metal rang out, on and on, snapping against bones, tearing rotting dragon skin. One wing came down to buffet Ellery, but when it reached its low point, a dozen undead warriors leaped upon it and hacked away, and bit and clawed and tugged on bones with skeletal arms. The dracolich roared—and there seemed to be some pain in that cry—and thrashed wildly.

The skeletons hung on.

The dracolich rolled, and bones splintered and shattered. When it came around, the skeleton warriors were dislodged, but so was its wing, snapped right off at the shoulder.

The creature roared again.

Then it bit Ellery in half and launched her torn corpse across the room.

Stubbornly, relentlessly, the skeletons were upon it again, bashing away, but Entreri recognized that the ring of metal on bone had lessened.

A line of spittle melted another group of charging skeletons. Forelegs tore another undead soldier in half and threw its bones at yet another. The dracolich flattened another pair with a downward smash from its great skull.

All hope faded from Entreri. Despite the unexpected allies, they could not win out against that mighty beast. He looked over to Jarlaxle then, and for the first time in a while the drow looked back. Jarlaxle offered an apologetic shrug, then tugged on the side of his hat's wide brim. His body darkened, his physical form wavered.

The dark elf seemed two-dimensional more than three, more of a shadow than a living, breathing creature. He slipped back to the wall, thinned to a black line, and slid into a crack in the stone.

Entreri cursed under his breath.

He had to get away, but how? The ramp was no good to him with the large section burned out of it.

So he just ran, as fast as his wounded ankle could carry him. He stumbled across the room, away from the dracolich as it continued its slaughter of the skeleton army. He looked back over his shoulder to see the creature's massive tail sweep aside the last of the resistance, and his heart sank as those terrible red points of light that served as the beast's eyes focused in on him.

The monster took up the chase.

Entreri scanned the far wall. There were some openings but they were wide—too wide.

He had no choice, though, and he went for the narrowest of the group, a circular tunnel about eight feet high. As he reached its entry, he leaped to a stone on the side, grimacing against the stinging pain in his ankle, then sprang higher off of it, catching the archway with both hands. He worked his hands fast, hooking a small cord, then let go and ran on into the tunnel.

But it wasn't a tunnel, only a small, narrow room.

He had nowhere to run, and the dracolich's head could easily snake in behind him.

He turned and flattened himself as much as possible against the short tunnel's back wall. He drew his weapons, though he knew he could not win, as the creature closed.

"Come on, then," he snarled, and all fear was gone. If he was to die then and there, so be it.

The beast charged forward and lowered its head in line. Its serpentine neck snapped with a rattle of bones, sending those terrible, torn jaws forward into the tunnel, straight for the helpless Entreri.

The assassin didn't strike out but rather dived down, curled up, and screamed with all his strength.

For as the dracolich's skull came through the archway, came under the red-eyed silver dragon statuette that Entreri had just placed there, the devilish trap fired, loosing a blast of fire that would have given the greatest of red dragonkind pause.

Flames roared down from the archway with tremendous force, charring bone, bubbling the very bedrock. The dracolich's head did not continue through to bite at Entreri, but the assassin knew nothing but the sting of heat. He kept curled, his eyes closed, screaming against the terror and the pain, denying the roar of the flames and the dracolich. He felt his cloak ignite, his hair singe.

The defenders of Palishchuk fought bravely, for they had little choice. More and more gargoyles came in at them from out of the darkness in the latest wave of a battle that seemed without end. After the initial assault, the townsfolk had organized into small, defensible groups, tight circles surrounding those who could not fight. To their credit, they had lost only a few townspeople to the gargoyles, though a host of the creatures lay dead in the streets.

In one small room, a lone warrior found less luck and no options. For, like some of the other townsfolk who had fallen that night, Calihye had been cut off from the defensive formations. She battled alone, with Davis Eng helplessly crying out behind her. Three gargoyles were dead in the room, with two killed in the early moments of the long, long battle. After an extended lull, the third had come in against her, and it had only just gone down. Its cries had been answered though, with the next two crashing in, and Calihye knew that others were out there, ready to join the fray.

She dodged and stabbed ahead, and she thought she might win out against the pair, but she knew she couldn't keep it up much longer.

She glanced over at Davis Eng, who lay there with the starkest look of terror on his face.

Calihye growled as she turned her attention back to the fight. She couldn't leave him, not like that, not when he was so utterly helpless.

So she fought on, and a gargoyle went spinning down to the floor. Another came in, then another, and Calihye spun and slashed wildly, hoping and praying that she could just keep them at bay.

All thoughts of winning flew away, but she continued her desperate swinging and turning, clinging to the last moments of her life.

The gargoyles screeched so loudly, so desperately, that it stung Calihye's ears, and behind her, Davis Eng cried out.

But then the gargoyles were gone. Just gone. They hadn't flown out of the room. They hadn't done anything but disappear.

The gargoyle corpses were gone too, Calihye realized. She blinked and looked at Davis Eng.

"Have I lost my mind then?" she asked.

The man, looking as confused as she, had no answers.

Out on the street, cheering began. Calihye made her way to the broken window and looked down.

Abruptly, without explanation, the fight for Palishchuk had ended.

From a crack in the wall across the chamber, Jarlaxle had seen the conflagration. A pillar of fire had rained down from above, obscuring the dracolich's upper neck and head. The great body, one wing torn away, shuddered and trembled.

What trick had Entreri played?

Then it hit the drow. The statuette he had placed over their apartment door in Heliogabalus, the gift from the dragon sisters.

My clever friend, Jarlaxle thought, and he thought, too, that his clever friend was surely dead.

The flames relented and the dracolich came back out of the hole. Lines of smoke rose from its swaying head and neck, and when it turned unsteadily, Jarlaxle could see that half of its head had been melted away. The creature roared again or tried to.

It took a step back across the room. It swayed and fell, and it lay very, very still.

Jarlaxle slid out of the crack and rematerialized in the chamber—a room that had grown eerily quiet.

"Get off o' me, ye fat dolt," came Athrogate's cry, breaking the silence.

The drow turned to see the dwarf roll Olgerkhan over onto the floor. Up hopped Athrogate, spitting and cursing. He looked around, trying to take it all in, and stood there for along while, hands on his hips, staring at the dragon cadaver.

"Damned if we didn't win," he said to Jarlaxle.

The drow hardly heard him. Jarlaxle moved across the room quickly, fearing what he would find.

He breathed a lot easier when Artemis Entreri walked out from under the archway, wisps of smoke rising from his head and torso. In one hand he held the crumpled, smoldering rag that had been his cloak, and with a disgusted look at the drow, he tossed it aside.

"Always dragons with you," he muttered.

"They do hold the greatest of treasures for the taking."

Entreri looked around the bone-filled but otherwise empty room, then back at Jarlaxle.

The drow laughed.

CHAPTER

22

Olgerkhan grunted and groaned and held his breath as Athrogate tied a heavy leather strap around his broken leg. The dwarf looped the belt and held one end up near the half-orc's face.

"Best be biting hard," he said.

Olgerkhan looked at him for a moment, then took the end of the strap in his mouth and clamped down on it.

Athrogate nodded and gave a great tug on the strap, yanking it tight and forcing the half-orc's leg in line. The strap somewhat muffled Olgerkhan's scream, but it still echoed through the chamber. The half-orc's hands clenched and he pounded them on the stone floor.

"Yeah, bet that hurt," Athrogate offered.

The half-orc lay back, near to collapse. He flitted in and out of consciousness for a few moments, black spots dancing before his eyes, but then through the haze and pain, he saw something that commanded his attention. Arrayan appeared on the ledge. She stood straight, for the first time in so long, leaning on nothing.

Olgerkhan came up to his elbows as she met his gaze.

"And so it ends," Jarlaxle remarked, he and Entreri moving to the dwarf and half-orc. "Help him up, then. I will levitate you up to join Arrayan on the ledge one at a time."

Athrogate moved to help Olgerkhan stand, but Entreri just moved away to the wall, where he quickly picked a route and began climbing. By the time Jarlaxle made his first trip up, easing Olgerkhan down beside Arrayan, Entreri was nearly there, moving steadily.

When he finally pulled his head above the ledge, he found Arrayan fallen over Olgerkhan, hugging him tightly and professing her love to him. Entreri hopped up beside them, offered a weak smile that neither of them even registered, and moved off to check the ascending hallway.

He sprinted up some distance but found no enemies and heard no sounds at all. When he came back, he found the other four waiting for him, Olgerkhan leaning on the dwarf with Arrayan supporting him under his other arm.

"The corridor is clear," he reported.

"The castle is dead," Arrayan replied, and her voice rang out more strongly than Entreri had previously heard.

"Ye can't be sure," Athrogate replied.

But Arrayan nodded, her confidence working against the doubts of the others. "I don't know how I know," she explained. "I just know. The castle is dead. No gargoyles or mummies will rise against us, nor daemons or other monsters. Even the traps, I believe, are now inert."

"I will ensure that, every step," Entreri assured her.

"Bah, but she can't be sure," Athrogate reiterated.

"I do believe she is," said Jarlaxle. "Sure and correct. The dracolich was the source of the castle's continuing life, was giving power to the book, and the book power to the gargoyles and other monsters. Without the dragon, they are dead stone and empty corpses, nothing more."

"And the dragon was giving the book the power to steal from me my life," Arrayan added. "The moment it fell, my burden was lifted. I do not understand it all, good dwarf, but I am certain that I am correct."

"Bah, and I was just starting to have some fun."

That brought a laugh, even from Olgerkhan, though he grimaced with the effort. Jarlaxle moved out before the trio to join Entreri.

"We will move up ahead and ensure that the way is clear," the dark elf said, and he and Entreri started off.

They trotted along swiftly, putting a lot of distance between themselves and the others.

"The castle is truly dead?" Entreri asked when they were well alone.

"Arrayan is a perceptive one, and since she was inextricably tied to the castle, I would trust her judgment in this."

"You seem to know more than she."

Jarlaxle shrugged.

"No gargoyles and no mummies," Entreri went on. "Their source of power is gone. But what of the undead? Will we find skeletons waiting for us when we get back to the keep?"

"What do you mean?"

"Their master, it would seem, walks beside me."

Jarlaxle gave a little laugh.

"When did you become a necromancer?" Entreri asked.

Jarlaxle took out the skull gem.

"It was you back there, of course," the assassin said. "All of it."

"Not completely true," Jarlaxle replied. "I brought in our three lost companions, true. You did indeed hear them following us down."

"And left the fourth hanging on a spike?"

Another laugh. "He is a dwarf—the gem grants me no power over dead dwarves, just humans. So if you fall in battle. . . ."

Entreri was not amused. "You have the power to raise an army of skeletons?" he asked.

"I did not," the drow explained. "Not all of them. The dracolich animated them, or the castle did. But I heard them, every one, and they heard me, and heeded my commands. Perhaps they harbored old grievances against the dragon that had long ago slaughtered them."

They crossed the room where Entreri had battled Canthan and moved steadily along. No eggs fell from the ceiling carvings, releasing guardian daemons to terrorize them, and no sarcophagi creaked open. When they at last reached the main chamber of the keep, they found that the monsters had broken through the doors. But none remained to stand against them. Bones littered the floor, and a pair of gnoll mummies lay still on the stairs, but not a gargoyle was to be seen. Outside it was dark, for it was well into the night by then.

Jarlaxle paid it all little heed. His prize was in sight, and he was fast to the book, which still stood on its tendril platform. No mystical runes spun in the air above it, and the drow felt no tingles of magical power as he moved to stand before it. He looked over at Entreri then tore out a page.

He paused and looked around, as if listening for the rumble of a wall crumbling.

"What?" Entreri asked.

"The castle will not crumble as did Herminicle's tower."

"Why?"

"Because, unlike that structure, this one is complete," Jarlaxle explained. "And because the life-force that completed this castle is still alive."

"Arrayan? But you said . . ."

Jarlaxle shook his head. "She was nothing more than the one who began the process, and the castle leeched her for convenience, not for survival. Her death would have meant nothing to the integrity of the structure, beyond perhaps slowing the growth of the gargoyles or some other minor thing."

"Well, if not Arrayan, then who?" Entreri asked. "The dracolich?"

Jarlaxle tore out another page, then another. "Dracoliches are interesting creatures," he explained. "They do not 'die' as we know it. Their spirits run and hide, awaiting another suitable body to animate and inhabit."

Entreri's eyes went wide and despite himself he glanced around as if expecting the beast to drop upon him. He started to ask Jarlaxle what he meant by that but paused when he heard the others shuffling into the chamber behind him.

"Well met," Jarlaxle said to them. "And just in time to witness the end of the threat."

He stepped back from the book as he finished and tapped the tips of his thumbs together. Fingers splayed before him, he called upon the power of one of his magic rings. Flames fanned out from his spread hands, washing over the magical book and igniting it. Laughing, Jarlaxle brought a dagger into his hand and began tearing at the tome, sending blackened, burning parchment flying.

In that show, the drow found his treasure, and he slipped it into his sleeve under the cover of his slashing movements. He was not surprised by the sight of the prize: a purple glowing gem shaped like a skull. Not a human skull, like the one Jarlaxle already possessed, but the skull of a dragon.

Immediately upon closing his fingers on the gem, the drow felt the life-force of the great black dragon contained within.

He felt the hate, the outrage.

But most of all, he felt the dragon's fear.

He enjoyed that.

The five remaining party members did not have to go far to find more allies. With the defeat of the dragon, the defeat of the Zhengyian artifact, had come the defeat of the gargoyles. Guessing that something positive and important must have happened out there, Wingham had quickly led a contingent of half-orc soldiers out of Palishchuk's northern gate.

How pleased they were to see the five exiting through the hole in the port-cullis Athrogate had earlier made.

Pleased and concerned all at once, for four were missing, including a man who had been a friend to Palishchuk for decades.

Arrayan ran to Wingham and wrapped him in a great hug. Cheers went up all around the pair—for Arrayan and for Olgerkhan, with the occasional reminder thrown in to salute the other three.

Those cheers were fast tempered however, when Olgerkhan confirmed the deaths of Canthan and Ellery, of good Pratcus and of Mariabronne the Rover.

So it was a muted celebration, but a celebration nonetheless, for the threat had passed and Palishchuk had survived. After a short while of cheering and many prayers offered for the dead, Wingham demanded a complete recounting.

"There will be time for that when we return to Palishchuk," Jarlaxle responded, and the others, even ever-curious Wingham, quickly agreed. The castle might have been dead, but they were still deep in the Vaasan wilderness, after all.

"We almost lost her," Jarlaxle later said to Wingham, for he had made it a point to walk beside the old half-orc on their journey back. "Olgerkhan threw off his ring, and the sudden shock of bearing all the burden nearly overwhelmed the poor girl."

Wingham cast him a curious glance and nearly blurted out, "How do you know about that?" Jarlaxle figured, for he read it clearly on the old weapon dealer's face.

"When we could not find Olgerkhan's ring, we knew we had to move quickly. Fortunately, by that time, we were ready to do battle with the true king of the castle, a black dracolich of enormous size and power."

That widened Wingham's eyes. "You have a few stories to tell," he said.

"It has been a long day," Jarlaxle replied.

All of the city turned out that night, the old, the very young, and everyone in between, to hear the tales of the fall of the dracolich. Jarlaxle served as story-teller for the five, of course, for few in all the world could weave a tale better than the strange old dark elf. Athrogate got in a few rhymes and seemed to take particular delight in the groans of the onlookers.

Through it all, Entreri moved to the far side of the common room, trying to remain inconspicuous. He didn't really want to talk to anyone, didn't want any pats on the back, and had little desire to answer questions about the deaths of Ellery and Canthan in particular.

But he did see one face among the crowd, in the back and over by the door, which he could not ignore.

"Davis Eng?" he asked when he arrived by Calihye's side.

"Resting well," she curtly replied. "He nearly died when the gargoyles attacked the town, but I was there."

"Ever the hero."

Calihye turned a glare over him. "That would be your title, would it not?"

"We asked you to come along."

"To lie dead beside Ellery, no doubt."

Entreri merely smiled, bowed, and took his leave.

The cheering faded behind him as he walked out into the Palishchuk night. He was alone with his feelings, including a few that he hadn't even known he possessed. He pictured Arrayan's face then thought of Dwahvel Tiggerwillies. He considered his anger, his hurt, when Arrayan had professed her love to Olgerkhan.

Why had he felt that? Why so keenly?

He admitted to himself that he was indeed attracted to Arrayan, but he had been to Ellery and Calihye, as well, on that level. He didn't love the half-orc—how could he, when he didn't truly know her?

It all had him shaking his head, and as he considered it, with time to think and reflect, with no danger pressing and no distractions, he found his answer.

He drew out Idalia's flute and stared at it, then gave a helpless little laugh.

So, the dragon sisters—and his drow friend, no doubt—had conspired to manipulate him.

Strangely, at that moment of reflection, Artemis Entreri was not angry with them.

A wagon rolled out of Palishchuk three days later, carrying Entreri and Jarlaxle, Calihye, Athrogate, and Davis Eng. A handful of Palishchuk soldiers had agreed to serve as guards and drivers. Behind it came a second wagon, bearing the bodies of Pratcus and Commander Ellery. Of Mariabronne, they hadn't found enough to bury, and Canthan's lower torso, though supposedly retrieved by the Palishchuk guards who had returned to the castle, had not been placed in the cart. Whispered rumors said that it had been claimed and removed in quiet the day before, but even the ever-suspicious Jarlaxle and Entreri had put little credence in the confused reports.

"You would be wise to keep all curiosity seekers out of the castle," Jarlaxle told Wingham, who stood with Arrayan and Olgerkhan and a much older half-orc, who had been introduced as an old and renowned bard. "The book is destroyed, so the place should be dead, by all reasoning. But it was a Zhengyian artifact, after all, and we do not know what other surprises the Witch-King left in place."

"The soldiers who went in have told everyone of the fate of Pratcus," Wingham replied, "and that there was apparently no treasure to be found. The castle will remain as it is until King Gareth can send an appropriate force to investigate."

"Farewell then," the drow said with a low bow and a sweep of his great hat. "Expect my return here at Palishchuk, at a time when I might more fully peruse and enjoy the town."

"And you will be welcomed, Jarlaxle," Arrayan put in. "Though we'll not likely see you until the spring melt."

Jarlaxle smiled at her and held up the magical ring she had given him, on his request that he might study it further and perhaps replace its lost companion. Arrayan had no problem in handing it over after Wingham had agreed, for neither knew that Jarlaxle already had the sister ring in his possession. As soon as the others had left that room of battle, a quick spell had shown Jarlaxle its location, and the drow was never one to let such items go to waste.

"Winter is fast approaching," Wingham said. "But then, up here, winter is always fast-approaching, if it is not already here!"

"And you will be welcomed, as well, Artemis Entreri," Olgerkhan added.

Entreri locked stares with the half-orc then turned his gaze over Arrayan. Her smile was warm and friendly, and full of thanks.

Entreri reached into his cloak and pulled forth the flute of Idalia, then looked back to the pair. Feeling Jarlaxle's curious gaze upon him, he turned to the drow.

There was apprehension there, and Entreri got the sense that his friend was about to be quite disappointed.

He held up the flute but didn't toss it to Olgerkhan, as he had intended.

"Perhaps I will learn to play it well enough to entertain you upon my return," he said, and he saw the smile widen on Jarlaxle's dark face.

Entreri wasn't sure how he felt about that.

"I would like that," said Arrayan.

The wagons rolled away. Artemis Entreri spent a long time staring back at the half-orcs, and a long time letting his hands feel the craftsmanship of Idalia's work.

The rest of the day proved uneventful. Even Jarlaxle was quiet and left Entreri pretty much alone. They set their camp for the night, and Entreri chose one of the wagon benches as his bed, mostly because then no one was likely to sleep too close to him. He wanted very much to be alone again and only wished that he had been far enough away from all the others that he might take up the flute and try to learn more of its magic.

He found himself wishing he could be even farther away when, a short while into the quiet night, Calihye climbed up to stand beside him.

At first, he feared she might make a move against him. His dagger in hand, he knew he could easily defeat and kill her, but he did not wish to do that.

"The road will not be clear tomorrow," the half-elf said to him.

Entreri put on a puzzled look and swung around to sit up.

"Before mid-day, perhaps sooner, we will find pursuit, a band of riders coming with questions and accusations," she explained.

"What do you know?"

"The Citadel of Assassins wishes to know about Canthan," Calihye explained. "He was no minor player in that dark association, and now he is dead. Rumors say by your hands."

"Rumors say many things."

"Olgerkhan told of his near-death experience in the castle. He told of a dagger and of the fall of Canthan. Many ears beyond the small group of friends sitting beside the half-orc heard that tale."

Entreri stared at her hard.

"Archmage Knellict is not Canthan," Calihye went on. "Whatever success you found against that wretch will not easily be replicated where Knellict is concerned. Nor will he come alone, and the men beside him will not be novices to the art of murder."

"Why are you telling me this?"

The woman stared at him for a long while. "I will not live indebted to Artemis Entreri," she said and turned away.

Not for the first time, Entreri was glad that he had not killed her.

Dawn was still long away when Entreri and Jarlaxle moved out from the wagons.

"The word is 'Blackfire,' " Jarlaxle explained as he handed the obsidian figurine over to his companion.

"Black—" Entreri started to ask, but the drow interrupted him with an upraised hand and a word of warning.

"Do not speak the summons until you are ready to ride," Jarlaxle explained. "And place the figurine on the ground before you do, for it will summon an equine beast from the lower planes to serve you. I found it on the body of Mariabronne—a curious item for a goodly ranger of the Army of Bloodstone to carry."

Entreri started at him, then at the figurine.

"So if you are ready, we should go," Jarlaxle said.

"You will ride behind me?"

"Beside you," said the drow, and from yet another of his many pouches, he produced an identical item.

Entreri couldn't find the heart to even shake his head.

The cries of the nightmares split the night, awakened the others at the wagons, and reminded those who were supposed to be guarding the troupe that they were supposed to be guarding the troupe. By the time any of them got to the south side of the encampment, though, Entreri and Jarlaxle were long gone.

The wind whipped Entreri's hair and buffeted his cloak as the nightmare charged on, fiery hooves tearing at the soft tundra.

When dawn broke, the companions were still running, their steeds showing no sign of tiring though they had put many, many miles between themselves and the wagons.

Even with that, however, they found that they were not alone.

"The woman spoke truthfully," Jarlaxle remarked when a line of horsemen appeared behind them and to the side, riding hard and with purpose. "Let us hope that the Bloodstone Lands are filled with places to hide!"

The horses would not catch them, however hard their riders drove them. The hellish steeds were too powerful and did not tire. Soon the pair were running free again, and they knew they were much closer to the Vaasan Gate.

"We could seek the protection of King Gareth," Jarlaxle remarked.

"Until he learns that we killed his niece."

"We?"

Entreri turned his head, and if Jarlaxle hadn't been grinning at that moment, Entreri would have leaped across and throttled him.

"If the Citadel of Assassins hunts us, then King Gareth will likely embrace us even more," said the drow. "I am not fond of relying on such things, but until we can sort out the potential of our new power, it will have to do. Well, that and the dragon sisters, who I'm sure will look upon us with new respect."

"Respect or hatred?"

"They are not as different as you seem to believe."

Entreri moved to reply, but before he could get a word out, the air around the riding pair shimmered weirdly, like a wave of soft blue cloth.

Their summoned horses disappeared out from under them.

Entreri hit the ground hard, bouncing and rolling, scraping his face and nearly shattering his jaw. As he at last came around, finally controlling the roll, he saw Jarlaxle drift by, the drow still upright and levitating through the momentum of the fall.

"That was no accident, nor did the duration of the magic of the mounts run out simultaneously," the drow called back, from far ahead.

Entreri looked around, his hands going to his weapons.

"To the foothills, and quickly," Jarlaxle insisted. "The Citadel mustn't catch us out in the open."

They rushed back to retrieve their mounts, merely obsidian figurines once more. Then they scrambled to the west, where the ground began to slope up, and great tumbled boulders from the Galenas offered them some cover. They were still climbing when far in the distance to the north, they spotted the unmistakable dust and movement of many galloping horses.

"How did they do that?" Entreri asked when they pulled up with their backs against a huge stone for a much-needed break. "Was it an ambush? Is there a wizard about?"

"Was it even them?" Jarlaxle asked.

"If not, then this troupe should ride right past us," Entreri reasoned.

Both he and Jarlaxle took that cue to peer around the boulder down to the flat plain, where the truth of it all became quite evident. For the pursuers had slowed, with some already turning to the west and filtering into the foothills north of their current position.

"We should find a defensible spot," Jarlaxle suggested.

Entreri didn't blink. "When they close on us, you will just turn to shadow-stuff and melt into a crack in the stones, no doubt," he said.

Jarlaxle considered the words for a moment, but given the incident in the dracolich's cave, he really wasn't in any position to promise differently.

"Come," the drow offered. "All hope is not lost. There are caves, perhaps."

"None that will suit your needs," came a voice, and the two turned their heads very slowly to see an older man, well-groomed and dressed in splendid robes of purple and red, and with not a speck of mud on him. The way he held himself, the tilt of his head, and the obvious reverence with which those several guards around him, including a dwarf both of them knew too well, told them exactly who he was before he even introduced himself as Archmage Knellict.

"I do not know that I would name Canthan as a friend," Knellict said. "He was an annoying one, who seemed to find even more annoying companions."

"That'd be me," Athrogate proudly announced, and no one was amused.

"But he was an asset to my organization," Knellict continued. "A valuable one, and one lost to me."

"If I had known that, I would have let him kill me," Entreri quipped.

"Bwahaha!"

"Shut up, dwarf," said Knellict, and when Athrogate immediately buttoned his lip, shifted nervously, and averted his gaze to the ground, it occurred to Entreri and Jarlaxle that the archmage was all his reputation claimed, and more.

"Commander Ellery was no small asset, as well," Knellict said. "A liaison to the happenings of the crown—mostly an unwitting and stupid asset, but an asset nonetheless."

"Ah, and now you seek to reclaim that which you have lost," Jarlaxle replied.

"Do I?" Knellict began walking around to the side, studying them both as he went. "You were stronger than Canthan, obviously, since you vanquished him," he said. "And no doubt King Gareth will now welcome you into his court, since you have saved Palishchuk and defeated the magic of Zhengyi."

"I think we just volunteered," Entreri remarked.

"You prefer the alternative?" Jarlaxle came right back.

"I need not explain the details to you, of course," Knellict said. "You are both well aware of the rules. We understand each other?"

"I have created such organizations," Jarlaxle assured him.

Knellict burst into movement. Entreri went for his weapons, but Jarlaxle, recognizing the gesture, grabbed his friend's arm.

A great wind came up and dust swirled around them, blinding them momentarily. And when it was gone, the two stood alone.

"They were never really here," Jarlaxle said. "Knellict projected the image and sounds of the entire group to us. He is a powerful one."

"But we really had that conversation?"

"We heard them and they heard us," Jarlaxle assured him. The drow cast a few quick spells and tapped his eye patch more than once.

"And now we work for the Citadel of Assassins?" Entreri asked.

"And the dragon sisters. We would not be wise to forget that pair."

"You seem pleased by it all."

"The easiest road to gaining control is one walked beside those who currently rule."

"I thought it was Jarlaxle who was always in control," Entreri remarked, and his voice took a sudden sharp edge to it.

The drow looked at him curiously, catching that razor line.

"Even when he should not be in control," the assassin went on. "Even in those instances when he is taking control of something that does not concern him."

"When did you take to speaking in riddles?"

"When did you presume to so manipulate me?"

"Manipulate?" Jarlaxle gave a little laugh. "Why, my friend, is that not the nature of our relationship? Mutual manipulation for personal gain?"

"Is it?"

"Are we to spend this entire conversation asking questions without answers?" In reply, Entreri pulled forth Idalia's flute and tossed it at Jarlaxle's feet.

"I did not give you that," the drow stated.

"Truly?" asked Entreri. "Was it not a gift from the sisters, with Jarlaxle's understanding and agreement?"

"It is a precious instrument, a gift that most would appreciate."

"It is a manipulation of the heart, and you knew it."

The drow put on an innocent look but couldn't hold it and just gave a little laugh instead.

"Did you fear that I would not go into the castle unless I felt something for Arrayan?"

"I had no idea that there was an Arrayan," Jarlaxle pointed out.

"But you enjoyed the manipulation."

"My friend . . ." Jarlaxle began, but Entreri cut him short.

"Don't call me that."

Again Entreri's tone caught the drow by surprise, as if that knife's edge in his voice had developed a wicked, serrated blade.

"You still cannot admit the obvious, I see," Jarlaxle said. He took a step back, almost expecting Entreri to draw his sword on him.

The assassin looked around.

"Knellict and his minions are long gone," Jarlaxle assured him, and he tapped his enchanted eye patch to accentuate his certainty.

"Jarlaxle knows," Entreri remarked. "Jarlaxle knows everything."

"It keeps us both alive."

"And again, that is by the choice of Jarlaxle."

"You are beginning to bore me."

Entreri rushed up to him and grabbed him by the throat.

Jarlaxle dropped a knife from his enchanted bracer into one hand, ready to plunge it home. But Entreri wasn't pressing the case, other than to shout in Jarlaxle's face, "Are you my father, then?"

"Hardly that."

"Then what?" Entreri asked, and he let go, sending Jarlaxle stumbling back a step. "You manipulate and carry me along, and for what? For glory? To give a dark elf credibility among the humans? For treasures that you cannot carry alone?"

"No such treasures exist," came the dry reply.

"Then for what?" Entreri yelled at him.

"For what," Jarlaxle echoed, with another of his little laughs and a shake of his head. "Why, for anything and for nothing at all."

Entreri stared at him with a puzzled expression.

"You have no purpose, no direction," Jarlaxle explained. "You wander about muttering to yourself. You walk no road, because you see no road before you. I would be doing you a favor if I killed you."

That brought a look showing a complete acceptance, even an eagerness, for the challenge.

"Is it not the truth?" Jarlaxle asked. "What is the point of your life, Artemis Entreri? Is it not your own emptiness that led you all those years into desiring a battle with Drizzt Do'Urden?"

"Every time you mention that name, you remind me how much I hate you."

"For giving you that which you desired? For facilitating your fight with the rogue drow? Ah, but did I steal the only thing in your life giving you meaning, by giving you that which you said you desired? A pitiful state of the heart, would you not agree?"

"What would you have me say? I only know that which I feel."

"And you feel like killing me."

"More than you would understand."

"Because I force you to look at yourself and you do not like what you see. Is that a reason to kill me, because I am offering to you a chance to sort through your own emotions? That is all the magic of the flute did to you, I suspect. It offered you the opportunity to look past your own emotional barriers."

"Did I ask for your help?"

"Friends help when they are not asked."

Entreri sighed and shook his head, but he could not deny any of what the drow had said. His shoulders slumped a bit, and Jarlaxle let the dagger fall to the ground behind him, certain then that he would need no weapons.

A few moments passed between them until finally Entreri looked up at the drow, his face calm, and asked, "Who are you?"

Jarlaxle laughed again, and it was a sincere expression of joy, for that was where he had hoped it would all lead.

"Why, Artemis Entreri, do you not yet know? Have you not come to understand any of it?"

"I understand less each day."

"I am your muse," Jarlaxle announced.

"What?"

"I am he who will give meaning to your life, Artemis, my friend. You do not even begin to understand the breadth of your powers. You know how well you might skulk through the shadows, you know all too well your prowess with the blade, but you have never understood what those well-deserved, well-earned powers can bring you."

"You assume that I want anything."

"Oh, you do. If you can only dare to wish for it."

"What? Athrogate's Citadel of Assassins? Shall we move to dominate them?"

"Of course, to begin."

"Begin?"

"Think large, my friend. Make your goal expansive. Athrogate will give us the insight and bona fides we need to find a strong place within the Citadel's organization—we will quickly learn whether it is worth our time to overtly dominate the place or merely to covertly exert enough control to render them harmless to us."

"Couldn't we just kill the annoying little dwarf instead?"

Jarlaxle laughed. "There has been a void of power up here for many years."

"Since the fall of Zhengyi."

"Vaasa is ours for the taking."

"Vaasa?" Entreri could hardly repeat the word, and for one of the few times in all his life, he actually stuttered. "Y-you would go against King Gareth?"

Jarlaxle shrugged. "Perhaps. But there are other ways." He ended by holding up the dragon skull gemstone. "The sisters will learn of a new balance of power between us, to begin with. And within this stone lies control of the castle and a new ally."

"An ally that will bite us in half."

Jarlaxle shook his head. "Not while I am in possession of his phylactery. He and I are already in communication, I assure you. If I choose to let him out again, he will only do so with great trust in me, for if I destroy the phylactery, I destroy the dracolich's spirit. Utterly."

"Gareth will send soldiers to the castle."

"And I will let them stay for a while."

"Vaasa?"

"At least."

"You will go against a legendary paladin king?"

"Come now, can you not admit that it might be fun?"

Entreri started to speak several times, but nothing decipherable came forth. Finally he just shook his head, sighed, and turned away, moving back down toward the flat ground.

"Trust me," said Jarlaxle.

"My muse?"

"Your friend."

EPILOGUE

Did the fool human pass your silly little test?" Kimmuriel Oblodra asked Jarlaxle a few days later, off in the shadows beneath the Vaasan Gate.

"Do not underestimate Artemis Entreri," Jarlaxle replied, "or the value he brings to me—to us."

"And you should not overestimate the power of the skull gems you have found," Kimmuriel warned, for he had just finished inspecting the pair at Jarlaxle's request. He had spoken with the dracolich, Urshula by name, and had confirmed Jarlaxle's suspicions that the beast would not dare to go against the possessor of the phylactery.

"They are but the beginning," Jarlaxle said with a grin. "Artemis Entreri and I have an audience with the paladin king in two days, just south of here in Bloodstone Village. We will be received as heroes for our efforts in Vaasa and as solemn witnesses to the end of Gareth's heroic niece."

He couldn't help but chuckle at the irony of that last statement. If King Gareth only knew!

Kimmuriel looked at Jarlaxle, wary, recognizing that look of confidence and grandiose schemes in his eyes, for he had seen that look from his former master dozens of times over the centuries. But they were not in the Underdark, in Menzoberranzan where Bregan D'aerthe and Jarlaxle had held many secret trumps.

"Have you found another Crenshinibon?" the psionicist asked with obvious disgust and concern.

"I have found opportunity," Jarlaxle corrected.

"Bregan D'aerthe will not come forward in force against the likes of King Gareth Dragonsbane."

Jarlaxle stared at him with appreciation and said, "Glad I am that I had the wisdom to put Kimmuriel in control of my band," he said. "Of course you are correct in resisting this bold move. You are a fine leader, and I urge you to continue with all caution, but too with an open mind. There are many events yet to play out up here in this untamed land, and I am in control of most of them." He brought forth the dragon statuette. "My relationship with a pair of living dragons just changed in ways they cannot understand."

"More allies for your battle?"

"Allies? We shall see."

Despite himself, Kimmuriel could not help but offer a wry grin.

"You might find a way to fit in as events play out," Jarlaxle said to him. "I pray that Kimmuriel remains an opportunistic leader. The point of Bregan D'aerthe is more than survival, is it not? It is to grow in power."

"You nearly destroyed us in Calimport."

"Nay," Jarlaxle corrected. "It was an inconvenience to you. It was myself that I nearly destroyed."

"You and Entreri will take down a paladin king?"

"If it comes to that."

Kimmuriel didn't reply, other than to dip a respectful bow.

Muddy Boots and Bloody Blades had long since emptied out for the night, but Entreri had tossed the innkeeper enough gold to get the key for the door. He sat alone with his thoughts and a beer, considering the emotions that had accompanied him all the way to Palishchuk and back. On the table beside his flagon lay Idalia's flute, and Entreri wasn't yet certain if he hated the item or prized it.

It was all so very new to him.

He was to leave in the morning with Jarlaxle for a meeting with the king, where they would receive a commendation and an offer to join the Army of Bloodstone, so Honorable General Dannaway had informed them. As intriguing as it all was, however, Entreri's thoughts were much smaller in scope. He thought of the women who had accompanied him to the north, of how that innocent looking flute had given him a different way of viewing them.

That new viewpoint hadn't stopped him from killing Ellery, at least, and he took some comfort in that.

A soft footstep behind him told him that he was not alone, and from the sound of it, the assassin understood much. She had been watching him from across the room for most of the night, after all.

"I did not kill your friend," he said, not turning around. "Not with intent, at least."

The footsteps halted, still half a dozen strides behind him. Finally he did turn, to see that his reasoning was correct. Calihye stood there, her face very tight. Entreri was relieved to see that she did not have any weapon in her hands.

"Accept it as truth or do not," he said to her, and he turned back to his beer. "I care little."

He started to raise it to his lips, but Calihye came over quickly. Her hand grasped his wrist, stopping him and making him look back up at her.

"If you do not care whether I believe you or not, then why did you just tell me that yet again?" she asked.

It was Entreri's turn to stare at the half-elf.

"Or is it that you're simply afraid that you do care, Artemis Entreri?" Calihye teased, and she let go and stepped away.

Entreri stood up, his chair skidding out behind him, and said, "You flatter yourself."

"I am still alive, am I not?" Calihye reasoned. "You could have killed me back in Palishchuk, but you didn't."

"You were not worth the trouble," Entreri said. "A soldier of the crown was under your care."

"You could have killed me any time, yet I am still alive, and still, perhaps, a threat to you."

"You do flatter yourself."

But Calihye wasn't even listening to him, he realized as she stepped right up to him, her bright eyes staring into his.

"I assure you, Artemis Entreri, that I am always worth the trouble," she said, her voice turning husky, her breath hot on his face, her lips practically brushing his as she spoke.

"I did not kill your friend," Entreri reiterated, but his voice was not so strong and not so steady at that moment.

Calihye brought her hand gently up, brushing his chest and settling on his collar, where she grasped him tight.

"I accept that," she said, and she pulled him closer, pulled him right into her. She kissed him hard and bit at his lip. Her arms went around him and pulled him even closer, and Entreri didn't resist. His own arms went around the half-elf, crushing her into him. He brought one hand up to grab at her thick, silky black hair.

Calihye pulled him with her as she fell atop the table—or tried to, for the pair were too far to the side and the flimsy table overturned, dumping them against a chair, which went bouncing away, and they dropped down to the floor.

Neither cared or even noticed. They fumbled with each other's clothing, their lips never parting.

Artemis Entreri, surviving on the wild streets of Calimport from his boyhood days, had known many women in his life but had never before made love to a woman. Never before had the act been anything more to him than a physical release.

Not so this time.

When they were finished, Entreri propped himself up above Calihye and stared down at her in the quiet light of the low-burning tavern hearth. He brought his hand up to stroke the line of her facial scar, and even that didn't seem ugly to him at that moment.

But it was just a moment, for noise out in the corridor reminded the couple where they were and told them that the night had nearly ended. They jumped up and dressed quickly, saying not a word until they stood facing each other, with Calihye fastening the last buttons on her shirt.

"You are looking at my face and regretting your choice?" she asked.

Entreri put on an incredulous expression. "Do you think yourself ugly?"

"Do you?"

Entreri laughed. "You are a combination of talent and beauty," he said. "But if your vanity demands of you to coerce such compliments, then why not seek out a wizard or a priest to repair . . ." He stopped short, seeing the woman's scowl.

And Entreri understood. Without that scar, Calihye would have ranked among the most beautiful women he had ever seen. She was trim and fit, slight but not weak. Her eyes shone, as did her hair, and her features held just enough of an elf's angular traits to make her appear exotic by human standards. Yet she kept the scar and had worn it for years, though she certainly had the financial means, by bounties alone, to be long rid of it. He thought back to their lovemaking, to the frantic beginning, the very tentative middle, and finally, the point where they both simply let go and allowed themselves to bask in the pleasure of each other. That had been no easy break-point for Entreri, so too for Calihye, he realized.

So she could draw her sword and battle a giant without fear, but that more intimate encounter had terrified her. The scar was her defense.

"You are beautiful, with or without the scar," he said to her. "How ever much you wish it was not true."

Calihye rocked back on her heels, but as always, she was not long without a response.

"I'm not the only one hiding behind a scar."

Entreri winced. "I have killed people for making such presumptions about me."

Calihye laughed at him and stepped closer. "Then let me make another one, Artemis Entreri," she said, and she put her hands on his shoulders, then slid them up to cradle his face as she moved very near.

"You will never kill me," she said softly.

For one of the few times in his life, Artemis Entreri had no answer.

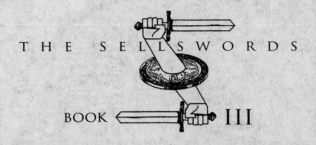

THE SELLSWORDS

BOOK III

ROAD OF THE PATRIARCH

PRELUDE

Yes, she is beautiful, Artemis Entreri thought as he watched the naked Calihye walk from the bed to the clothing rack to retrieve her breeches and shirt. She moved with the grace of a skilled warrior, one leg flowing effortlessly in front of the other, the soft pads of the balls of her feet coming down lightly and cushioning her step. She was of medium height, lithe but strong, and the few scars on her body did not detract from the graceful image of the tight cords of muscle. She was a creature of paradox, Entreri realized as he watched her, a being of fire and fluidity. She could be ferocious or tender, and she seemed to understand how to move between the two to the greatest effect when they were making love.

And no doubt she did the same on the battlefield. Calihye wasn't just a fighter; she was a warrior, a thinker. She knew her own strengths and weaknesses as well as any, but measured her opponent's better than most. Entreri had no doubt that the woman often used her feminine charms on unwitting opponents, throwing them off guard before eviscerating them.

He respected that; the image brought a smile to his often-scowling face.

It was a short-lived grin, though, as the man considered his own situation. On a peg near the clothes rack where Calihye dressed hung his small-brimmed black hat, the one Jarlaxle had given him. Entreri had found that the cap, like his drow companion, was much more than it seemed. It held many beneficial properties, magical and mechanical, including the ability to chill his body to better help him hide from eyes that sensed heat instead of light, and a wire inset into the band, easily retractable, that allowed the hat to fit so snugly that even a fall from a horse wouldn't dislodge it.

More than it seemed, Entreri thought. Wasn't everything?

He had slept soundly after his encounter with Calihye the previous night. Too soundly? Calihye could have killed him, he realized, and the thought flickered through his mind that perhaps the woman was using her charms on him. She had put him into more vulnerable a position than he had ever known.

No, he assured himself. Her feelings for me are genuine. This is no game.

483

Except, he noted, wouldn't that have been Calihye's strategy, to put him so completely off his guard that she could risk an attack upon him?

Entreri dropped his head into his hands and rubbed his bleary eyes. He shook his head as he did, and was glad that his hands covered his helpless chuckle. He would drive himself mad with such thoughts.

"Are you coming with me, then?" Calihye asked, drawing him from his reverie.

He lifted his head and looked at her again as she stood by the rack. She was still nude, though his eyes did not roam her body, but rather settled upon her face. By all measures, Calihye had once been a strikingly beautiful woman, with startling eyes that sometimes showed reflections of gray amidst their blue. At other times, depending on the background—the lighting, her clothing—those eyes glowed an exquisite shade of medium blue, and either way they always seemed striking because of their contrast with her raven-dark hair. Her face was symmetrical, her bone structure impeccable.

But that scar. It ran across her right cheek to her nose, then down through her lips to the middle of her chin. It was an angry scar, often inflamed and red. Calihye hid behind it, Entreri knew, as if in denial of her feminine beauty.

When she flashed her smile, though, so mischievous and dangerous, Entreri hardly noticed the tear in her lips. To Artemis Entreri, she remained beautiful, and other than to consider her motivations for keeping the scar and the deeper meaning it seemed to hold to her, he hardly noticed it. It did not detract in the least for him, so lost was he in the mysteries that simmered in her eyes. She shook her head and her thick hair rolled over her shoulders, and Entreri wanted to leap over and bury his face in that warm, soft mane.

"We agreed to eat," Calihye reminded him. She gave a sigh and began pulling on her shirt. "I would have thought you'd worked up a great and growling hunger."

As her head came up through her collar her eyes set on her lover, and Calihye's smile disappeared.

That flash of a frown clued Entreri in to his own expression. He was scowling. He didn't know why. There wasn't a singular thought in his mind that might bring a scowl to his face just then. Calihye wouldn't elicit such a thought from him, after all, for he considered her a bright spot in his miserable life. But he was indeed scowling, as her reflective frown revealed.

He wore that dour expression often of late—or had it been forever?—and usually for no apparent reason at all. Except, of course, that he was often angry—at everything and nothing all at once.

"We do not have to eat," the woman said.

"No, no, of course we should go and get some food. The morning is late already."

"What troubles you?"

"Nothing."

"Did I not please you last night?"

Entreri nearly snorted aloud at that absurdity, and he couldn't suppress a smile as he considered Calihye and recognized that she was simply goading him for a compliment.

"You have pleased me many nights. Greatly. And last night was among those," he offered to her, and he was glad to see her apparent relief.

"Then what troubles you?"

"I told you that I am not troubled." Entreri reached down and gathered up his pants and began pulling them over his feet. He stopped when he felt Calihye's hand on his shoulder. He looked up at her, staring down at him, a look of concern on her face.

"Your words do not match your expression," she said. "Tell me. Can you not trust me? What is it that so upsets the humors of Artemis Entreri? What is it about you? What happened to you, to ignite this inner fire?"

"You speak in foolish riddles of your own imagination." He bent down again to pull his pants on, but Calihye gripped him more tightly, forcing him to look back at her.

"What is it?" she pressed. "How is a warrior of such perfection as Artemis Entreri created? What history did this to you?"

Entreri looked away from her, looked down at his own feet. But he didn't really see them. In his mind's eye, Artemis Entreri was a boy again, barely more than a child, in the dusty streets of a desert port city that was full of the smell of brine or filled with stinging sand, depending upon which way the wind was blowing.

The wagons creaked even though they were not moving, as the sandy breeze sizzled against their wooden sides. A couple of the horses nickered uncomfortably and one even reared up as far as its heavy, tight harness would allow. The driver, a thin and sinewy man of harsh, angular features who reminded the boy of his father, wasted no time in putting the whip savagely to the frightened creature.

Yes, just like his father.

The fat spice dealer seated on one wagon stared at him for a long time. Those heavy-lidded eyes seemed to invite him to slumber, as mesmerizing as a swaying serpent. There was something there, he knew, some magic behind that gaze, some method of control that had allowed the pathetic, slovenly beast to rise to prominence among the troupe gathered for their seasonal caravan out of Memnon. The others all deferred to that one, he could see, though he was just a boy and knew little about the world or about the hierarchy of the merchant class.

But that one was the boss, to be sure, and the boy flushed, flattered that the leader of so many would spend time with him and his mother. That prideful flush became an open-jawed, wide-eyed stare of disbelief as the fat man handed over coins—gold coins! *Gold* coins! The boy had heard of them, had heard of golden coins, but had never seen any. He had seen silver once, handed by some stranger to his father, Belrigger, before the stranger went behind the curtain with his mother.

But never gold. His mother was holding gold!

How thrilling it had been, but briefly. Then Shanali, his mother, grabbed him roughly by the shoulder and pushed him to the fat man's waiting grasp. He wriggled and fought the hold. He tried to tug away from the sweaty arms, at least so that he could get some answers from his mother.

But when he finally managed to face her, she had already turned and started away.

He called out to her. He pleaded with her. He asked her what it all meant.

"Where are you going?

"Why am I still here?

"Why is he holding me?

"Mama-hal!"

And she did glance back, only once and only for a moment. Just long enough for him to see her sunken, sad eyes one last time.

"Artemis?"

He shook his memories away and looked at Calihye. She seemed amused and concerned all at once. Strangely so.

"Are you to sit there with a flute in your hands and your breeches about your ankles all morning?"

The question shook him, and only then did Entreri realize that he was indeed holding Idalia's flute, the magical instrument the dragon sisters had given to him. And yes, as Calihye had noted, his breeches were still rumpled around his ankles. He placed the flute down beside him on his bed—or started to, but found he couldn't quite let it go just then. With that realization came a sudden strength, and he dropped the flute, quickly stood, and pulled up his pants.

"So what is it?" Calihye asked him, and he looked at her with curiosity. "What is it that creates a perfect warrior such as Artemis Entreri?" she clarified.

His mind flashed back again to Memnon. An image of Belrigger flashed before him and he felt himself jerk.

He realized that he was holding the flute again.

Tosso-pash's one-toothed leer flickered before him, and he threw the flute down on the bed.

"Training? Discipline?" Calihye asked.

Entreri snatched his shirt up from the chair and moved past her.

"Anger," he said, and in such a tone that no further questioning would likely be forthcoming.

It stood as just another clay-stone rectangle in a sea of similar houses, an unremarkable structure a dozen feet across and half a dozen front-to-back. It had an awning, like all of its neighbors, facing the sea breeze that usually offered the only relief from Memnon's unrelenting heat. There were no walls partitioning the house. A single threadbare curtain sectioned off a sleeping area, where his mother and father, Shanali and Belrigger—or Shanali and someone who had paid Belrigger—slept. For the boy there was just the floor of the common room. Once, when too many bugs had crawled around him, the boy had climbed on the table to sleep, but Belrigger had found him there and had beaten him severely for the infraction.

Most of the beatings had blended together in the haze of passing time, but that particular one, Artemis remembered clearly. Drunker than usual, Belrigger had taken to his back and rump with a rotted old board, and the battering had left several splinters in Artemis's backside that had become infected and oozed white and greenish pus for days.

Shanali had come to him with a wet cloth to wipe those wounds. He remembered that. She had rubbed his backside gently, with motherly love, and though she had uttered a few scolding words, calling him foolish for not remembering Belrigger's rules, even those had come tinged with sympathy.

Was that the last time Shanali had treated him kindly? Was that the last gentle memory he had of his mother?

The woman who had handed him over to the merchant caravan a few months later hardly seemed like the same creature. She had even physically changed by that fateful day at the merchant's, had grown pale and sunken, and she couldn't speak a full sentence without pausing to catch her breath.

His mind recoiled from the image of that day, rushing back to Belrigger and Tosso-pash, the toothless and bristle-faced idiot who spent more time under Belrigger's awning than did Belrigger himself.

Tosso-pash came to him in flashing images—leering, always leering, and always leaning over him, always reaching for him. Even the man's words flashed in phrases Artemis had heard far too many times.

"I'm yer Papa-hal's brother.

"Ye call me Uncle Tosso.

"I can make ye feel good, boy."

Entreri's mind recoiled from those images, from those words, even more so than from the last image of his mother.

Belrigger had never done that, at least, had never chased him around the alleyways until his legs ached from the exertion, had never lain down beside him when he was trying to sleep, had never tried to kiss him or touch him. Belrigger hardly ever even acknowledged his existence, unless it was to administer another beating, or to lash out at him with a string of insults and curses.

He could only imagine that he had been a great disappointment to his father. What else could bring the man to such anger against him? Belrigger was embarrassed by the frail Artemis—ashamed and angry that he had to feed the boy, even if all he ever gave to Artemis was the stale crust of his bread or other morsels left over after he was done with his meal.

And even his mother had turned away from him, had taken the gold . . .

The fat merchant's flabby arms provided no warmth and no comfort.

Entreri woke in darkness. He felt the cold sweat all over his naked form; the blankets clung wetly to him.

The moment of panic subsided somewhat when he heard Calihye's steady breathing beside him. He moved to sit up, and was surprised to find that magical flute of Idalia lying across his waist.

Entreri picked it up and brought it before his eyes, though he could barely see it in the dim starlight slipping in through the room's single window. From its feel, both physically in his hands and in the emotional connection he had attained with it in his mind, he was certain that it was the same magical flute.

He paused for a moment to consider where he had placed the flute when he had gone to bed—on the lip of the wooden bed frame beside him, he recalled, and within easy reach.

· So he had apparently scooped it up during his sleep, and it had brought him to those memories again.

Or were they even memories? Entreri had to wonder. Were the images flashing so clearly through his mind an accurate recounting of his childhood days in Memnon? Or were they some devilish manipulation by the always-surprising flute?

He remembered clearly that day with the caravan, though, and knew his flute-enhanced images of it were indeed correct. That memory of Memnon, the final and absolute betrayal by his mother, had followed Artemis Entreri for thirty years.

"Are you all right?" Calihye asked softly as he sat on the edge of the bed. He heard her shift behind him, then felt her against his back, leaning on him, her arm coming around to rub his chest and hold him close.

"Are you all right?" she asked again.

His fingers moving along the smooth curves of Idalia's flute, Entreri wasn't sure.

"You are tense," Calihye noted, and she kissed him on the side of the neck.

His reflexive movement showed her that he wasn't in the mood for any of that, though.

"Is it your anger?" the woman prodded. "Are you still thinking of that? The anger that created Artemis Entreri?"

"You know nothing," Entreri assured her, and shot her a look that even in the darkness she could sense warned her that she was walking on ground uninvited.

"Anger at who?" she asked anyway. "At what?"

"No, not anger," Entreri corrected, and he was talking to himself more than to her. "Disgust."

"At?"

"Yes," Entreri answered, and he pulled away and stood up.

He turned to Calihye. She shook her head and slowly slid off the bed to move to stand at Entreri's side. She gently draped her arm behind his neck and leaned in close.

"Do I disgust you?" she whispered in his ear.

Not yet, Entreri thought, but did not say. But if you ever do, I will put a sword through your heart.

He forced that notion from his thoughts and put his hand over Calihye's, then glanced sidelong at her and offered a comforting smile.

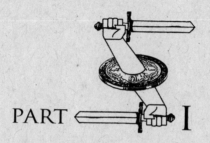

PART I

TIGHTROPE

A re they still together, walking side by side, hands ever near the hilts of their weapons—
to defend against each other, I would guess, as much as from other enemies?

Many times I think of them, Artemis Entreri and Jarlaxle. Even with the coming of
King Obould and his orc hordes, even amidst the war and the threat to Mithral Hall,
I find my thoughts often wandering the miles of distance and time to find in my mind's
eye a reckoning of the unlikely pair.

Why do I care?

For Jarlaxle, there is the ever-present notion that he once knew my father, that
he once wandered the ways of Menzoberranzan beside Zaknafein, perhaps much
as he now wanders the ways of the World Above beside Artemis Entreri. I have
always known that there was a complexity to this strange creature that defied the
easy expectations one might have of a drow—even that one drow might have for
another. I find comfort in the complexity of Jarlaxle, for it serves as a reminder
of individualism. Given my dark heritage, oftentimes it is only the belief in individualism that allows me to retain my sanity. I am not trapped by my heritage, by
my elf's ears and my coal-colored skin. While I often find myself a victim of the
expectations of others, they cannot define me, limit me, or control me as long as I
understand that there is no racial truth, that their perceptions of who I must be are
irrelevant to the truth of who I am.

Jarlaxle reinforces that reality, as blunt a reminder as anyone could ever be that
there resides in each of us a personality that defies external limitations. He is a unique
one, to be sure, and a good thing that is, I believe, for the world could not survive too
many of his ilk.

I would be a liar indeed if I pretended that my interest in Artemis Entreri only
went so far as his connection to the affirmation that is Jarlaxle. Even if Jarlaxle had
returned to the Underdark, abandoning the assassin to his lonely existence, I admit that
I would regularly turn my thoughts to him. I do not pity him, and I would not befriend
him. I do not expect his redemption or salvation, or repentance for, or alteration of, the
extreme selfishness that defines his existence. In the past I have considered that Jarlaxle
will affect him in positive ways, at least to the extent that he will likely show Entreri the
emptiness of his existence.

But that is not the impetus of my thoughts for the assassin. It is not in hope that I so often turn my thoughts to him, but in dread.

I do not fear that he will seek me out that we might do battle yet again. Will that happen? Perhaps, but it is nothing I fear, from which I shy, or of which I worry. If he seeks me, if he finds me, if he draws a weapon upon me, then so be it. It will be another fight in a life of battle—for us both, it seems.

But no, the reason Artemis Entreri became a staple in my thoughts, and with dread, is that he serves as a reminder to me of who I might have been. I walked a line in the darkness of Menzoberranzan, a tightrope of optimism and despair, a path that bordered hope even as it bordered nihilism. Had I succumbed to the latter, had I become yet another helpless victim of crushing drow society, I would have loosed my blades in fury instead of in the cause of righteousness—or so I hope and pray that such is indeed the purpose of my fight—in those times of greatest stress, as when I believed my friends lost to me, I find that rage of despair. I abandon my heart. I lose my soul.

Artemis Entreri abandoned his heart many years ago. He succumbed to his despair, 'tis obvious. How different is he than Zaknafein, I have to ask—though doing so is surely painful. It almost seems to me as if I am being disrespectful of my beloved father by offering such a comparison. Both Entreri and Zaknafein loose the fury of their blades without remorse, because both believe that they are surrounded by a world not worthy of any element of their mercy. I make the case in differentiating between the two that Zaknafein's antipathy was rightly placed, where Entreri is blind to aspects of his world deserving of empathy and undeserving of the harsh and final judgment of steel.

But Entreri does not differentiate. He sees his environs as Zaknafein viewed Menzoberranzan, with the same bitter distaste, the same sense of hopelessness, and thus, the same lack of remorse for waging battle against that world.

He is wrong, I know, but it is not hard for me to recognize the source of his ruthlessness. I have seen it before, and in a man I hold in the highest esteem. Indeed, in a man to whom I owe my very life.

We are all creatures of ambition, even if that ambition is to free ourselves of responsibility. The desire to escape ambition is, in and of itself, ambition, and thus ambition is an inescapable truth of rational existence.

Like Zaknafein, Artemis Entreri has internalized his goals. His ambition is based in the improvement of the self. He seeks perfection of the body and the arts martial, not for any desire to use that perfection toward a greater goal, but rather to use it for survival. He seeks to swim above the muck and mire for the sake of his own clean breath.

Jarlaxle's ambition is quite the opposite, as is my own—though our purposes, I fear, are not of the same ilk. Jarlaxle seeks to control not himself, but his environment. Where Entreri may spend hours building the muscle memory for a single maneuver, Jarlaxle spends his time in coercing and manipulating those around him to create an environment that fulfills his needs. I do not pretend to understand those needs where Jarlaxle is concerned. They are internal ambitions, I believe, and not to do with the greater needs of society or any sense of the common good. If I were to wager a guess based on my limited experience with that most unusual drow, I would say that Jarlaxle creates tension and conflict for the sake of entertainment. He finds personal gain in his machinations—no doubt orchestrating the fight between myself and Artemis Entreri in the replica of Crenshinibon was a maneuver designed to bring the valuable asset of Entreri more fully into his fold. But I expect that Jarlaxle would cause trouble even without the lure of treasure or personal gain.

Perhaps he is bored with too many centuries of existence, where the mundane has become to him representative of death itself. He creates excitement for the sake of excitement. That he does so with callous disregard to those who become unwitting principles in his often deadly game is a testament to the same sort of negative resignation that long ago infected Artemis Entreri, and Zaknafein. When I think of Jarlaxle and Zaknafein side by side in Menzoberranzan, I have to wonder if they did not sweep through the streets like some terrible monsoon, leaving a wake of destruction along with a multitude of confused dark elves scratching their heads at the receding laughter of the wild pair.

Perhaps in Entreri, Jarlaxle has found another partner in his private storm.

But Artemis Entreri, for all their similarities, is no Zaknafein.

The variance of method, and more importantly, of purpose, between Entreri and Jarlaxle will prove a constant tug between them, I expect—if it has not already torn them asunder and left one or both dead in the gutter.

Zaknafein, as Entreri, might have found despair, but he never lost his soul within it. He never surrendered to it.

That is a white flag Artemis Entreri long ago raised, and it is one not easily torn down.

—Drizzt Do'Urden

CHAPTER

LIFE AS USUAL?

1

It wasn't much of a door, actually, just a few planks thrown together and tied with frayed rope, old cloth, and vines. So when the ferocious dwarf hit it in full charge, it exploded into its component parts. Wood, rope, and vine went flying into the small cave, trailed by ribbons of cloth.

No fury summoned from the Nine Hells could have brought more tumult and chaos in the instants that followed. The dwarf, thick black hair flying wildly, long beard parted in the middle into two long braids flopping across his chest and shoulders, lunged at the poor goblins, twin morningstars spinning with deadly precision.

The dwarf veered for the largest group, a collection of four of the goblins. He barreled into their midst without heed for the crude weapons they brandished, blowing past their defenses, kicking, stomping, and smashing away with his devastating morningstars, their spiked metal heads whipping at the ends of adamantine chains. He hit one goblin square in the chest, crushing its lungs and lifting it into a ten-foot flight. A turn and duck put him under the thrust of a spear that was no more than a pointed stick, and as he rolled around, the dwarf brought his trailing arm up and across, hooking the goblin's arm and throwing it aside. The dwarf squared before the goblin, and two overhead swings crushed its shoulder and its skull. He kicked the creature hard under the chin as it dropped to the stone, shattering its jaw, though it was already so far gone from life that it didn't even scream.

The dwarf's braids whipped as he leaped and turned to face the two remaining goblins. They could not match that ferocity, could not seem to even comprehend it, and they hesitated just an instant.

An instant more than the dwarf needed.

Forward he raced, and each arm struck at the goblins. One hit squarely, the other a glancing blow, but even that second goblin stumbled under the weight of the assault. The dwarf rolled over the goblin, driving it down with kicks and chops.

He rushed past and broke for the door, leaping into a sidelong spin and coming around with a double swing that took one goblin in the back as it tried

494

to retreat through the door and back to the mountain slopes. Indeed, it got through the door, and much more quickly than it ever would have believed possible if it had been thinking of such things.

Its shattered spine took precedence, though, and as it crumbled to the dirt and stone, it felt . . . nothing.

The dwarf landed in front of the door, feet wide and steady. He went into a defensive crouch, eyes wild, braids bouncing, and arms out to his sides with the morningstar's heads dropping down low.

There had been at least ten of the creatures in the cave, he was certain, but with five down, he found only two facing him.

Well, at least one was facing him. The other banged frantically on a second door at the back of the cave, one more substantial and made of iron-bound hardwood.

The second goblin shrank against its companion, not daring to take its gaze from the furious intruder.

"Ah, but ye got yerself a safer room," the dwarf said, and took a step forward.

The goblin recoiled, small and pathetic sounds escaping its chattering teeth. The other pounded more furiously.

"Come on, then," the dwarf chided. "Pick up a stick and fight back. Don't ya be takin' all the fun out of it!"

The goblin straightened just a little bit, and the dwarf had seen enough of battle to catch the clue. He whirled around, launching a high-flying backhand that got nowhere close to hitting the sneaky goblin that slipped in the blasted door behind him. But it wasn't supposed to hit the creature, of course, merely distract it.

So it did, and as the dwarf strode forward and came around with his second swing, he found a clean opening. The goblin's face shattered under the weight of the morningstar, and the creature would have flown far indeed had not the jamb of the door caught it.

When the dwarf turned back, both goblins were pounding on the unyielding door with desperate abandon.

The dwarf sighed and relaxed, shaking his head in dismay. He walked across the room, and one, two, caved in the backs of the creatures' skulls.

He took up his morningstars in one hand and grabbed one of the fallen creatures by the back of the neck with his other. With the strength of a giant, he flung that goblin aside, throwing it the ten feet to the side wall with ease. The second then went for a similar flight.

The dwarf adjusted his girdle, a thick leather enchanted affair that bestowed upon him that great strength—even more than his powerful frame carried on its own.

"Nice work," he remarked, studying the craftsmanship of the portal.

No goblin doors those; the creatures had likely pillaged them from the ruins of some castle or another in the bogs of Vaasa. He had to give the goblins credit, though, for they had fit the portal quite well into the wall.

The dwarf knocked, and called out in the goblin tongue, in which he was quite fluent, *"Hey there, ye flat-headed walking snot balls. Now ye don't be wantin' me to ruin such a fine door as this, do ye? So just open it up and make it easy. I might even let ye live, though I'm suren to be takin' yer ears."*

He put his own ear to the door as he finished, and heard a quiet whimper, followed by a louder *"Shhhh!"*

He sighed and knocked again. *"Come on, then. Last chance for ye."*

As he spoke, he stepped back and rolled his fingers around the leather-wrapped handles of the twin morningstars, willing forth their magic. Liquid oozed from the spikes of each ball, clear and oily on the right hand one, and reddish and chalky on the other. He sized up the door, recognizing the center cross of perpendicular metal bands as the most important structural point.

He counted to three—he had to give the goblins an honest chance, didn't he?—then launched into a ferocious leap and swing, left morningstar leading, and connecting precisely at the juncture of those two critical iron bands. The dwarf kept jumping and turning and building momentum with his right-hand weapon, though he did whack at the door a couple of times with the left, denting wood and metal and leaving behind that reddish residue.

It was the ichor of a rust monster, a devilish creature that made every knight in shining armor wet himself. For within moments, those solid iron bands began to turn the color of the liquid, rusting away.

When he was convinced that the integrity of the iron bands had been fully compromised, the dwarf jumped into his greatest leap of all, turning as he went so that he brought all of his weight and all of his strength to bear as he finally unloaded his right-hand morningstar at the same exact spot. Likely his great might and impeccable form would have cracked the door anyway, but there was no doubt at all as the liquid on that second head, oil of impact by name, exploded on contact.

Sundered in two, both the door and the locking bar in place behind it, the portal fell open, half flopping in to the dwarf's right, still held awkwardly by one hinge, while the left side tumbled to the floor.

There stood a trio of goblins, wearing ill-fitted, plundered armor—one had gone so far as to don an open-faced metal helm—and holding various weapons, a short sword for one, a glaive for the second, and a battle-axe for the third. That might have given younger adventurers pause, of course, but the dwarf had spent four centuries fighting worse, and a mere glance told him that none of the three knew how to handle the weapons they brandished.

"Well, if ye're wantin' to give me yer ears, then I'll be lettin' ye walk out o' here," the dwarf said in heavily-accented Goblin. *"I'm not for givin' the snot of a flat-headed orc one way or th'other whether ye live or whether ye die, but I'm takin' yer ears to be sure."* As he finished, he produced a small knife, and spun it to stick into the floor before the feet of the middle of the trio. *"Ye give me yer left ears, and give me back the knife, and I'm lettin' ye walk on yer way. Ye don't, and I'm takin' them from yer corpses. Yers to choose."*

The goblin on the dwarf's right lifted its glaive, howled, and charged.

Just the answer Athrogate was hoping for.

Artemis Entreri slipped behind a dressing screen when he heard the dwarf pushing through the door. Never an admirer of Athrogate, and never quite trusting him, the assassin was glad for the opportunity to eavesdrop.

"Ah, there ye be, ye elf-skinny pretender to me throne," Athrogate bellowed as he pushed into Calihye's room.

The woman looked at him with a sidelong glance, seeming unconcerned—and a big part of that confidence, Entreri knew, came from the fact that he was within striking distance.

"So ye're thinking that ye got yerself a title here, are ye?"

"What are you talking about?"

"Lady Calihye, leading the board," Athrogate replied, and Calihye and Entreri nodded in recognition.

At the Vaasan Gate, a contest of sorts was being run by the many adventurers striking out into the wilderness. A price had been put on the ears of the various monsters roaming the wasteland, and to add to the enjoyment, the gate's commanders had put up a peg board listing the rankings of the bounty hunters. Almost from the start, Athrogate's name had topped that board, a position he had held until only a few months previous, when Calihye had claimed the title. Her fighting companion, Parissus, had been only a few kills back of the dwarf.

"Ye think I'm caring?" the dwarf asked.

"More than I am, obviously," replied the half-elf.

Behind the screen, Entreri nodded again, pleased with the response from the warrior who had become so dear to him.

Athrogate harrumphed and snorted, and roared, "Well, ye ain't for staying there!"

Entreri paid close attention to every inflection. Was the dwarf threatening Calihye?

The assassin's hands instinctively went to his weapon, and he dared move a bit farther behind the screen so that he could peek around the edge closest to the door, the angle of attack that would bring him in at the powerful dwarf's flank, if it came to that.

He relaxed as Athrogate brought one hand forward holding a small, bulging sack—and Entreri knew well what might be in there.

"Ye'll be looking at me rump again, half-elf," Athrogate remarked, and gave the bag a shake. "Fourteen goblins, a pair o' stupid orcs, and an ogre for good measure."

Calihye shrugged as if she didn't care.

"Ye best be winter huntin', if ye got enough dwarf in ye," Athrogate said. "Meself, I'll be goin' south to drink through the snows, so if ye're having some good luck, ye might get back on top—not that ye'll stay there more than a few days once the melt's on."

Athrogate paused there, and a wry smile showed between the bushy black hair of his beard. "Course, ye ain't got yer hunting partner no more, now do ye? Unless ye're to convince the sneak to go out with ye, and I'm not thinking that one's much for snowy trails!"

Entreri was too distracted to take offense at that last remark, however honest, for Calihye's wince had not been slight when Athrogate had referred to Parissus. The wound was still raw, he knew. Calihye and Parissus had been fighting side-by-side for years, and Parissus was dead, killed on the road to Palishchuk after she fell from the wagon Entreri drove from a horde of winged, snakelike monsters.

"I have little desire to go out and hunt goblins, good dwarf," Calihye said, her voice steady—though with some effort, Entreri noted.

The dwarf snorted at her. "Do as ye will or do as ye won't," he replied. "I'm not for carin', for I'll be takin' me title in the spring, from yerself or anyone else who's thinkin' to best me. Don't ye doubt!"

"Not to doubt and not to care," Calihye said, taking some of his bluster.

Indeed, Athrogate hardly seemed to have an answer for that. He just nodded and made an indecipherable sound, and shook the bag of ears at Calihye. Then he nodded again, said, "Yeah," and turned and walked out the door.

Entreri didn't note the movement at all, for he stayed focused on Calihye, who held her composure well though the weight of the dwarf's remarks surely sat heavily on her delicate shoulders.

CHAPTER

THE ROAD TO BLOODSTONE

2

The companions could not have appeared more disparate. Jarlaxle rode a tall, lean mare, seventeen hands at least. He was dressed all in finery—silk clothing, a great sweeping cloak, and a huge wide-brimmed purple hat, adorned with the gigantic feather of a diatryma bird. He seemed impervious to the dust of the road, as not a smudge or stain showed on his clothing. He was lean and graceful, sitting perfectly upright, appearing as a noble of great stature and breeding. One could easily imagine him as a prince of drow society, a dark emissary skilled in the ways of diplomacy.

The dwarf riding next to him, on a donkey no less, could never have been accused of such delicacies. Stocky and brutish, many might have confused Athrogate for the source of the road's dirt. To the obvious irritation of the poor donkey, he wore a suit of armor, part leather, part plated, and covered with a myriad of buckles and straps. He hadn't bothered with a saddle, but just clamped his legs tightly around the unfortunate beast, which poked along stiff-legged, giving the dwarf a jolting and popping ride. His weapons, a pair of gray, glassteel morningstars, rose up in an **X** from his back, their spiked heads bouncing with each of the donkey's jarring steps.

And of course, Athrogate's considerable hair, too, was so unlike the clean-shaven drow, whose head shone smooth and black beneath the rim of his great hat—and indeed, those occasions when Jarlaxle lifted the hat showed him to be completely devoid of hair on his head, save a pair of thin, angled eyebrows. Athrogate wore his mane like a proud lion. Black hair, lots of it, lifted wildly from his head in every direction, blending with an abundance coming out of his ears, and he had once more braided his great beard, with its customary part in the middle, each braid secured with ties that featured blue gemstones.

"Ah, but ain't we the big heroes," Athrogate said to his traveling companion.

Ahead of them on the trail rode Artemis Entreri and Calihye, with a couple of soldiers leading the way. Behind the drow and the dwarf came more soldiers, leading a caisson that held the body of Commander Ellery, the young and once-promising knight, niece of King Gareth Dragonsbane and an officer in the Army of Bloodstone. The people of the Bloodstone Lands mourned Ellery's loss. The heroine had been cut down in the strange castle that had appeared in the bog lands of Vaasa, north of the half-orc city of Palishchuk.

Jarlaxle was glad that no one other than he and Entreri knew the truth of her death, that it had come at Entreri's hand during a fight between Ellery and Jarlaxle.

"Heroes, indeed," the drow finally replied. "I prophesied as much to you when I pulled you out of that hole. Holding fast to your anger about Canthan's unfortunate demise would have been a rather silly attitude when so much glory was there for our taking."

"Who said I was angry?" Athrogate huffed. "Just didn't want to have to eat the fool."

"It was more than that, good dwarf."

"Bwahaha!"

"Your allegiances were torn—legitimately so," Jarlaxle said, and glanced at Athrogate to try to measure the dwarf's reaction.

Athrogate had been engaged in a fight to the death with Entreri when Jarlaxle had intervened. Using one of his many, many magical items, Jarlaxle had opened a ten-foot-deep magical hole at the surprised dwarf's feet, into which Athrogate had tumbled. Grumbling and complaining, the helplessly trapped Athrogate had been unwilling to join in and see the error of his ways—until Entreri had dropped the corpse of the dwarf's wizard associate into the hole beside him.

"Ye're not for knowing Knellict the way I'm for knowing Knellict," Athrogate leaned over and whispered. Again Jarlaxle was taken aback by the tremor that came into the normally fearless dwarf's voice when he mentioned the name of Knellict, who at that time was either the primary assistant of Timoshenko, the Grandfather of Assassins in the prominent murderers' guild in Damara, or—so hinted the whispers—who had assumed the mantle of grandfather himself. "Seen him turn a dwarf into a frog once, then another into a hungry snake," Athrogate went on, and he sat straight again and shuddered. "Halfway through dinner, he turned 'em back."

The level of cruelty certainly didn't surprise or unnerve Jarlaxle, third son of House Baenre, who, as a newborn, had been stabbed in the chest by his own mother—a sacrifice to the vile goddess who ruled the world of the drow. Jarlaxle had spent centuries in Menzoberranzan, living and breathing the unending cruelty and viciousness of his malevolent race. Nothing Athrogate had told him, nothing Athrogate *could* tell him, could elicit a shudder such as the one the dwarf had offered during his recounting.

And Jarlaxle had suspected as much about Knellict, anyway. Knellict was the darker background in an organization built in the shadows, the dreaded Citadel of Assassins. Jarlaxle knew from his own experience as leader of the mercenary band Bregan D'aerthe, that in such organizations the leader—in the case of the citadel, reputedly Timoshenko—played a softer, more politic hand, while his lieutenants, such as Knellict, were quite often the barbarians behind the throne, the vicious enforcers who made followers and potential enemies alike take some measure of hope in the leader's infrequent but not unknown smiles.

On top of that, Knellict was a wizard, and Jarlaxle had always found that type to be capable of the greatest cruelties. Perhaps it was their superior intellect that so divorced them from the visceral agony resulting from their actions. Perhaps it was the arrogance that often accompanied such great intellect that so allowed them to disassociate themselves from the common folk, as an ordinary man might step on a cockroach without remorse. Or perhaps it was because wizards usually attacked from a distance. Unlike the warrior, whose killing strike often soaked his arm in the warmth of his enemy's blood, a wizard might throw a spell from afar and watch its destructive effects divorced from their immediacy.

They were a complicated and dangerous bunch, spellcasters, aloof and ultimately cruel. In Bregan D'aerthe, Jarlaxle had often elevated wizards to lieutenant or higher posts for just those reasons.

And the dwarf beside him, the drow reminded himself, was not to be taken lightly either. For all his jovial and foolish banter, Athrogate remained a potentially dangerous and capable enemy, one who had put Artemis Entreri back on his heels in their battle within the Zhengyian construct. Athrogate was as pure an instrument of destruction as any assassin's guild—or any army, for that matter—could ever hope to employ. He had gained quite the reputation at the Vaasan Gate, bringing in the ears of bounty creatures by the sackload. And for all his passion, his bluster, and his raucousness, Jarlaxle saw a significant gulf in Athrogate's personality. However Athrogate might befriend Jarlaxle and Entreri, if the order came from on high to kill them, Athrogate would likely shrug and take on the task. It would be just business for him, much as it had been for Entreri for all those years he served the Pashas in Calimport.

"Is yer friend understandin' the honor he's gettin'?" Athrogate asked, nodding his chin toward Entreri. "Knight of the Order—ain't no small thing in the Bloodstone Lands these days, what with Gareth bein' the king and all."

"I am sure he does not, and will not," the drow replied, and he gave a little laugh as he considered Entreri's obstinacy. With the exception of the two half-orcs, Arrayan and Olgerkhan, who had remained in Palishchuk, the survivors of the battle with Urshula the dracolich and the other minions of the magically animated castle were being hailed as heroes in Bloodstone Village on the morrow. Even Calihye, who had not gone into the castle, and Davis Eng, a soldier of the Army of Bloodstone who had been wounded on the road out from the Vaasan Gate, were to be honored. Those two and Athrogate would be recognized as Citizens of Good Standing in Damara and Vaasa, a title that would grant them discounts from merchants, free lodging in any inn, and—most important for Athrogate—free first drinks in any tavern. Jarlaxle could easily picture the dwarf running from tavern to tavern in Heliogabalus, swilling down a multitude of first drinks.

For his part, recognized for a more important role, Jarlaxle was to be given a slightly higher title, that of Bloodstone Hero, which conveyed all the benefits of the lower medal, and also allowed Jarlaxle free passage throughout the burgeoning kingdom and granted the guarantee of Gareth's protection wherever it might be needed. While Jarlaxle agreed that his own role in the victory had been paramount, he had been a bit perplexed at first by the discrepancies in the honors, particularly between himself and Athrogate, who had battled the dracolich valiantly. At first he had presumed it to be the result of Athrogate's rather extensive and less-than-stellar public record, but after hearing of the honors to be given to Entreri, the actual slayer of the beast, Jarlaxle had come to see the truth of it.

These degrees of honor had been quietly suggested, whispered through appropriate and legitimate channels, by Knellict and the Citadel of Assassins. Knellict had already explained to Jarlaxle that his value to the guild would, in no small part, be due to his ability to fill the void left by the death of Commander Ellery, distant niece of King Gareth, who was also tied in with the citadel.

For Entreri, that one blow—luring the beast to thrust its head under the trap he had set in a side tunnel off the main lair—had changed the world. Entreri was the hero of the day, and accordingly, King Gareth would bestow upon him the title of Apprentice Knight of the Order.

Artemis Entreri, a knight in a paladin king's army . . . it was more than Jarlaxle could take, and he burst out laughing.

"*Bwahaha!*" Athrogate joined in, though he hadn't any idea what had set the drow off. Apparently catching on to that reality, Athrogate bit off his chortle and said, "So what's got ye titterin', coalskin?"

<hr/>

Low clouds in the west dulled the late afternoon sun, and the cool breeze comfortably tickled Master Kane. He sat cross-legged, hands on his thighs with his palms facing up. He kept his eyes closed, allowing his mind to focus inward as he consciously relaxed his body, using his rhythmic breathing as a cadence for his complete concentration.

One would not normally fly upon a magical carpet with his eyes closed, but Kane, former Grandmaster of Flowers at the Monastery of the Yellow Rose, was not concerned by trivial matters such as steering the thing. Every so often, he opened his eyes and adjusted accordingly, but he figured that unless a dragon happened to be soaring through the skies over Bloodstone Valley, he was safe enough.

So perfect was his mental count that he opened his eyes just as Bloodstone Village came into view far below him. He spotted all of the major buildings, of course, but they didn't impress him, not even the grand palace of his dear friend, Gareth Dragonsbane.

Nothing man-made could hold much of an impact over Kane, who had known the decorated corridors of the Monastery of the Yellow Rose, but the White Tree. . . .

As soon as the monk spotted it in the grand garden on the shores of Lake Midai his heart filled with serenity and the contentment that could only come from accepting oneself as a part of something larger, of something eternal. The seed for that tree, the Tree-Gem, had been given to Kane and his fellow heroes by Bahamut, the platinum dragon, the greatest wyrm of all, as a tribute to their efforts in defeating the Witch-King and his demonic associates and destroying the Wand of Orcus.

The White Tree stood as a symbol of that victory, and more than that, it served as a magical ward preventing creatures of the Abyssal planes from walking across the Bloodstone Lands. That tree showed Kane that their efforts had created not just a temporary victory, but a lasting blessing on the land he called home.

As he looked upon it, Kane reached to his side and picked up his walking stick, which had been fashioned from a branch of that magical tree. Smooth as polished stone and as white as the day he had taken it from the tree, for the dirt of no road could gray it, the jo staff was as hard and solid as adamantine, and in Kane's skilled hands, it could shatter stone.

With a thought, Kane veered the magic carpet toward the tree, gliding in to a smooth landing on the ground before its trunk. He stayed in his seated position, legs crossed, hands on his upturned thighs, the jo stick laid across his lap, as he offered prayers to the tree, and thanks to Bahamut, Lord of Goodly Dragons, for his wondrous gift.

"Well, by the blessings of the drunken god's double visions!" came a roar, drawing the monk from his meditation. He rose and turned, not surprised at all when Friar Dugald, nearly four hundred pounds of man-flesh, barreled into him.

Kane didn't move an inch against that press, which would have sent mighty warriors flying backward.

Dugald wrapped his meaty arms around the monk and slapped him hard on the back. Then he moved Kane back to arm's length—or rather, as he extended his arms, he moved himself back to arm's length—for again, the monk proved immovable.

"It has been too long!" Dugald proclaimed. "My friend, you spend all of your days wandering the land, or in the monastery to the south, and forget your friends here in Bloodstone Village."

"I carry you with me," Kane replied. "You travel in my prayers and thoughts. Never are any of you forgotten."

Dugald's flabby, bald head bobbed enthusiastically at that, and Kane could tell from the way he exaggerated his motions, and from the smell of him, that the friar had been consuming the blood of the vine. Dugald had found a kindred spirit within the Order of the God Ilmater in the study and patronage of St. Dionysus, the patron of such spirits, and Dugald was quite the loyal disciple.

Kane reminded himself that his own vows of discipline against such potent drink had been his conscious choice. He must not judge others based on his personal standards.

He turned away from Dugald to regard the tree, its spreading limbs framed by the quiet lake behind it. It had grown quite a bit in the two years since Kane's last visit to Bloodstone Village, and though the tree was only twelve years old, it already stood more than thirty feet, with branches wide and strong—branches it occasionally offered to the heroes that they might fashion items of power from the magical wood.

"Too long you've been gone," Dugald remarked.

"It is my way."

"Well, how am I to argue with that?" the friar asked.

Kane merely shrugged.

"You have come for the ceremony?"

"To speak with Gareth, yes."

Dugald eyed him with suspicion and asked, "What do you know?"

"I know that his choice of hanging a medal about the neck of a drow is something other than expected."

"More than Kane have said as much," Dugald said. "And this drow's a strange one, even by the standards of his lot, so they're saying. Do you know anything of him? Gareth knows only the stories coming from the wall."

"And yet he will offer this one the title of Bloodstone Hero, and award his companion status as a Knight of the Order?"

"Apprentice Knight," Dugald corrected.

"A temporary equivocation."

Dugald conceded the point with a nod. No one who had attained the title of apprentice knight had not then gone on, within two years, to full knight status—except of course for Sir Liam of Halfling Downs, who had gone missing, and was presumed slain, on the road home after attending his ceremony of honor.

"You have reason to believe that this drow is not worthy, my friend?" Dugald asked.

"He is a dark elf."

Dugald sighed and assumed a pensive, almost accusing stare.

"Yes, we have the sisters of Eilistraee as evidence," Kane replied. "It is a precept of the Monastery of the Yellow Rose to judge the actions and not the heritage of any person. But he is a drow, who arrived here only recently. His history is unknown and I have not heard a single whisper that he serves Eilistraee."

"General Dannaway of the Vaasan Gate is meeting with the king and Lady Christine even now," Dugald replied. "He speaks well of the exploits of this Jarlaxle character and the soon-to-be-apprentice knight."

"Formidable warriors."

"So it seems."

"Skill with the blade is the least important asset for a knight of the order," Kane said.

"Every knight can lay waste to his share," Dugald countered.

"Purity of purpose, adherence to conscience, and the discipline to strike or to hold in the best interests of Bloodstone," Kane came right back, citing the crux of the Bloodstone knight's pledge. "Honorable General Dannaway will attest to their feats in killing monsters beyond the Vaasan Gate, no doubt, but he knows little of the character of these two."

Dugald looked at his friend curiously. "I'll be guessing that Kane does, then?"

The monk shrugged. Before his journey to Bloodstone Village, he had spoken to Hobart Bracegirdle, the halfling leader of the war gang the Kneebreakers, who had been operating from the Vaasan Gate in recent days. Hobart had offered a few clues to the intriguing duo, Jarlaxle and Entreri, but nothing substantial enough for Kane to yet draw any conclusions. In truth, the monk had no reason to believe that the two were anything less than their actions at the gate and in the battle outside of Palishchuk seemed to indicate. But he knew, too, that those actions had not been definitive.

"I fear King Gareth's choice regarding these newcomers is premature, that is all," he said.

The friar nodded his concession of that point, then turned and swept his arm out to the north, where stood the grand palace of Gareth and Christine. Still under construction after a decade of work, the palace was comprised of the original Tranth home, the residence of the Baron of Bloodstone, expanded in width and with perpendicular wings running forward on either end. Most of the continuing work on the palace involved the minor details, the finishing touches, the decorative parapets and stained-glass windows. The people of Bloodstone Village—indeed, the people and artisans of the entire region known as the Bloodstone Lands—wanted the palace of their king to be reflective of his deeds and reputation. With Gareth Dragonsbane, that would prove a tall order indeed, and one that would take all the artisans of the land years to fulfill.

Side by side, the two went to see their friends. They entered without questions, past guards who bowed in deference at the appearance of the ragged-looking man. Anyone who did not know the reputation of Grandmaster Kane would have no way of looking at the man and suspecting any such thing. He was past middle age, thin, even skinny, with fraying white hair and beard. He wore rags and no visible jewelry other than a pair of magical rings. His belt was a simple length of rough rope, his sandals worn and threadbare. Only his walking stick, white like the wood of the tree from which it was made, seemed somewhat remarkable, and that alone would not be enough to clue anyone in to the truth of the shabby-looking creature.

For Kane, a simple wanderer, had been the one to strike the fatal blow and free the Bloodstone Lands from the grip of the Witch-King Zhengyi.

The guards knew him, bowed as he passed, and whispered excitedly to one another when he had gone by.

As the pair came upon the decorated white wooden doors—another gift of the White Tree—of Gareth's audience chamber, the guards posted there scrambling to open them, they discovered that another of their former adventuring band had come calling. The animated and always-excited ramblings of Celedon Kierney charged out through the doors as soon as they were cracked open.

"Gareth has put out the call to Spysong, then," Kane remarked to Dugald. "That is good."

"Isn't that what brought you here?" Dugald asked, for Kane, like Celedon, was part of the Bloodstone scouting network known as Spysong, with the monk serving as its principle agent in Vaasa.

Kane shook his head. "No formal call summoned me, no. I thought it prudent."

The doors swung wider and the pair stepped through the threshold. All conversation in the room stopped. A wide smile erupted on the handsome face of King Gareth. Dugald had been expected, of course, but Kane's arrival was obviously a rather pleasant surprise.

Beautiful Lady Christine, too, offered a smile, though she remained less animated than her passionate husband, as always.

Celedon offered Kane the raised back of his right hand, fingers stiffened, thumb straight up. He held it there for a moment, then turned his hand so that his thumb tapped his heart, the greeting of Spysong.

Kane acknowledged it with a nod, and moved forward beside Dugald to stand before the dais that held the thrones of Gareth and Christine. He immediately noticed the weariness in Gareth's blue eyes. The man seemed very fit for his forties. He wore a sleeveless black tunic, his bare, muscled arms showing no weakness. His hair was still much more black than gray, though a bit of the salt had crept in. His jaw line remained firm and sharp.

But his eyes . . .

The blue still showed its youthful luster, but Kane looked past the shine to the increased heaviness of Gareth's eyelids and the slight discoloration of the skin around his eyes. The weight of ruling the land had settled upon his strong shoulders, and wore at him despite his disposition and despite the love showered on him always by almost everyone in Damara.

Leadership with consequence would do that to a man, Kane knew. To any man. There was no escaping such a burden.

Court etiquette demanded that King Gareth speak first, officially greeting his newest guests, but Celedon Kierney moved in between the guests and the royals.

"A-a drow!" he yammered, waving his arms in disbelief. "Surely that is what brought Master Kane to court . . . his surprise—nay, astonishment—that you are doing such a thing."

Gareth sighed and shot a plaintive look Kane's way.

Kane, though, found his attention stolen by the crinkled nose of General Dannaway, who stared at him with obvious disgust. The monk, dressed in his dirty rags, was not unaccustomed to such expressions, of course, nor did they concern him.

Still, he met the man's gaze with an intense look, one so unnerving that Dannaway actually took a step backward.

"I—I must be going, my king," Dannaway stammered, and bowed repeatedly.

"Of course," Gareth replied. "You are dismissed."

Dannaway moved at once for the exit, crinkling his nose again as he passed near an uncaring Kane.

But Dugald, smile wide, was not so generous. He put a hand on Dannaway's elbow to halt the man and make him turn, then whispered—but loudly enough for all to hear, "He could insert his hand into your chest, pull forth your heart, hold it beating before your disbelieving eyes, then put it back before your body ever missed it." He ended with an exaggerated wink and the unnerved Dannaway stumbled away and nearly to the ground.

He rushed ahead so quickly that he overbalanced, and had not the guard at the white doors swung them wide at his approach, he no doubt would have barreled into them head-first.

"Dugald. . . ." Lady Christine warned.

"Oh, he should know," the fat friar replied, and he laughed, and so did Celedon. Gareth soon joined in, and even Christine could not completely hide her giggle. Kane, though, showed little emotion.

It was just the five friends, then, and all pretense and protocol could not hold against the bonds of their shared experiences.

"A drow?" Kane asked after the titters died away.

"Dannaway speaks highly of him, and of the drow's friend," Gareth replied.

"Dannaway sees it as a source of glory for his work at the wall," Celedon put in. "And a mitigation of the great losses incurred in the journey he instigated to the replica of Castle Perilous."

"Not much of a replica if these vagabonds so easily defeated it," Dugald scoffed.

"We do not know their worth," Kane said. "And I remind all that a great ranger fell at that castle. We know not its true nature, nor the depth of its powers. To that end, Spysong has dispatched Riordan to Palishchuk to begin a more thorough investigation."

The mention of Riordan Parnell brought nods all around. Another member of the band of seven who had defeated Zhengyi, the bard still served the land well with his uncanny ability to coax the truth from reluctant witnesses.

"Other investigations will be needed, of course," Kane said. "I suggest that our responses be kept to a minimum until they are completed."

"Never a moment to relax, eh, my friend?" asked Gareth.

"Riordan went at the request of the Duke of Soravia," the monk replied, referring to still another of the seven heroes, Olwen Forest-friend, a bear of a man whose laughter would often shake the walls of a tavern. "Olwen did not receive the news of Mariabronne's demise well."

"His protégé," Dugald remarked, nodding. "Mariabronne studied under him for so many years, and has lately spent much time at Olwen's side." He gave a sigh and shook his head. "I must offer Olwen comfort."

"The Duke of Soravia will not attend tomorrow's ceremony," Gareth said, nodding in agreement.

"He believes it to be premature, no doubt," said Kane.

"We have visiting dignitaries who wished to witness the event," Lady Christine said. "Baroness Sylvia of Ostel—"

"We cannot deny the accomplishments of this group," Gareth interrupted, but Kane continued to look at Christine.

"The Baroness of Ostel," the monk said. "Whose closest ally is . . . ?"

"The Baron of Morov," said Celedon. "Dimian Ree."

Gareth rubbed his chin. "Ree is an unseemly character, I agree. But he is, first and foremost, a baron of Damara." Celedon started to interrupt, but Gareth held up his hand to stop him. "I know the rumors of his relationship with Timoshenko," the king said. "And I do not doubt them, though none of us have found any solid evidence of corroboration between Morov and the Citadel of Assassins. But even if it were true, I cannot move against Dimian Ree. Heliogabalus is his domain, and it remains the principle city of Damara, whether I am there or here."

Gareth's point was well taken by all in the room. The Sister Baronies, as Morov and Ostel were often called, commanded the center of Damara, and Baron Ree and Baroness Sylvia had the unquestioning loyalty of more than sixty thousand Damarans, nearly half the population of the kingdom. Gareth was king and had the love of all, so it seemed, but everyone in the room understood the tentative nature of Gareth's ascent. For in unifying Damara under one ruler, he had reduced the power of several long-entrenched baronies. And in trying to bring Vaasa into his realm to create the greater Kingdom of Bloodstone, he was rattling the nerves of many Damarans, who had known untamed Vaasa as a source of naught but misery for all of their lives.

More talk went on outside of Bloodstone Village than within, Gareth and everyone else in the room knew well, and not all of that talk favored the creation of a greater Kingdom of Bloodstone, or even the continued unification of the previously independent baronies.

Though Baroness Sylvia and Lady Christine had forged something of a friendship over the past few years, no one in the room thought highly of Baron Dimian Ree of Morov, considering him to be the consummate self-serving politician. But none in the room dared underestimate him, either, given the volatile political climate, and so Gareth's words put a block in the path of the debate.

"The drow and his friend approach Bloodstone Village in the company of a dwarf," Kane said.

"Athrogate, by name," said Gareth. "A most unpleasant fellow, but a fine warrior, by all accounts. A second dwarf died in the castle, and will be honored posthumously."

"Athrogate is a known associate of Timoshenko and Knellict," said Kane. "As was the wizard, Canthan, who also fell in the castle."

"Master Kane, you have quite a conspiracy envisioned," said Christine.

Kane took the jab with good nature, and bowed to the Queen of Bloodstone. "No, milady," he corrected. "It is my duty to serve Gareth's throne and King Gareth, and so I do. The web of a potential conspiracy appears faintly visible if the light is just right, but it could be a trick of the sun, I know."

"Wherever we have seen a filament of a web, we have found a spider," Celedon interjected, rather loudly. "It is not right, I say. There is more here than we know, and we should not be offering such honors as apprentice knight of the order until the questions are answered beyond all doubt. I'll not—"

Kane stopped him with an upraised hand, right before Gareth could tell him to shut up. "The drow, his human companion, and the dwarf," the monk said in a quiet voice. "Be they friends, we have gained worthy allies. Be they enemies, and we have put them under our eye, clearly so. To know your enemy is a warrior's greatest asset. If you wish to remain as king, Gareth my friend, and hope to expand beyond the gate fortress north of here, then you need to know Athrogate and the creatures of the shadows who work his strings."

"And if these three, this drow, the dwarf, and the man on whom I will tomorrow bestow knighthood, are truly aligned with the Citadel of Assassins?" Gareth asked, though his grin betrayed the fact that he already knew well the answer.

Kane shrugged as if it did not matter. "We will reward them and honor them, and never allow them free passage to any place or position where they might do us harm."

Even Celedon calmed at that assurance, for when Kane offered such words, he always delivered on his promise.

Soon after, Celedon, Dugald, and Kane took their leave, promising to return later that evening for a feast in their honor.

"You're hoping to lure Olwen here with a grand table," Christine said to Gareth when they were alone—alone except for the guards, who had become such a fixture of their lives that they were all but invisible to the couple.

"Olwen can smell an orc from a hundred yards, so it is said," Gareth replied. "And so it is also said that he can smell a meal from a hundred miles."

"It is more than a hundred miles to Kinbrace," Christine reminded, referring to the seat of Soravia's power, where Olwen dwelt. "Even with his enchanted boots, even with his growling stomach urging him on, Olwen could not cover that distance in time for your feast."

"I was thinking that another might enjoy the reunion of the seven," Gareth slyly replied.

Christine rolled her blue eyes, for she knew of whom her husband spoke, and she wasn't thrilled at the prospect of entertaining Emelyn the Gray. The oldest of the band who had defeated Zhengyi, past his seventieth birthday, Emelyn's understanding of "civility" often tried Lady Christine's patience. Glad she was those years ago when the wizard announced that he would return to the Warrenwood ten miles southeast of Bloodstone Village, and happier still was she when it became apparent that he would rarely return for a visit.

Gareth moved out of the audience chamber to a side corridor that led to his private rooms. He entered a small anteroom to his bedchamber and moved to a desk set against the side wall, near his bedroom door. The back of the desk rose high above the writing table, and was draped with a silken cloth. Gareth pulled the drape free, revealing a mirror, framed in gold that was molded into exotic runes and symbols. From the side of the mirror, the king slid forth a six-inch red ball set in a golden base. He positioned it right before the mirror and lifted his hand as if to cover it.

"There is no other way?" Christine asked from the doorway behind him.

Gareth glanced back at her and offered a grin as she rolled her eyes yet again. He knew that she was only half-serious, for Emelyn was indeed a trial, and in all truth, Gareth had not been sorry at the wizard's announcement of his "retirement" with the centaurs of Warrenwood.

"We may be needing Emelyn's services soon enough," Gareth replied, and he placed his hand on top of the red ball and closed his eyes, picturing his old friend in his thoughts.

A few moments later, he looked into the mirror, and instead of seeing his own reflection, he saw a separate room. It was full of vials and skulls, books and trinkets, statues small and large, and a grand and ornate desk that seemed as alive as the white tree from which it had been fashioned.

At the desk with his back to Gareth sat an old man in satiny gray robes. His white hair, long and unkempt, hung down nearly to the desk—in fact its end strands showed that they had dipped into the inkwell more than once—as he hunched over his parchment.

"Emelyn?" Gareth asked, then more insistently, "Emelyn!"

The wizard straightened, glanced left, then right, then turned around to look behind him and across the room at the sister mirror set in his wall.

"Peering in uninvited, are we?" he said in a nasal and scratchy voice. "Hoping to catch a view of Gabrielle, no doubt." He ended with a cackle of delight.

Gareth just shook his head, and wondered again why such a beautiful young woman as Gabrielle had agreed to marry the old kook.

"Oh, I know your game!" Emelyn accused, wagging a gnarled old finger Gareth's way and flashing a yellow, gap-toothed smile.

"One you perfected, no doubt," Gareth dryly replied, "which is why I keep a shroud over my mirror."

The wizard's smile disappeared. "Never were you one to share, Gareth."

Behind the king, Lady Christine made her presence known by clearing her throat, loudly. Of course, that only made Emelyn cackle all the more.

"I was looking for you, my friend, though Lady Gabrielle is surely a more welcome sight before my eyes," said Gareth.

"She is in Heliogabalus, seeking components and potions."

"A pity, then, for I have come with an invitation."

"To see a drow honored?" Emelyn replied. "Bah!"

Gareth accepted that with a nod. He knew, of course, that Emelyn would have heard about the morning's ceremony. Surely the word was general all about Bloodstone Valley.

"Kane and Celedon have arrived in Bloodstone Village," Gareth explained. "I think it a good time for old friends to eat and drink, and speak of adventures past."

Emelyn started to respond, apparently in the negative, but stopped short and chewed his lip. A moment later, he rose from his chair and faced Gareth directly. "There is little I can do until Gabrielle's return, in any case," he said.

The mirror filled with smoke.

And so did the room, and both Gareth and Christine gave a shout and fell back.

The smoke cleared, revealing a sputtering Emelyn, waving his hands before his face to chase the fumes away.

"Never used to . . . create such combustion," Emelyn explained, coughing repeatedly as he spoke. At last he straightened and smoothed his robes. He looked alternately into the blank stares of Gareth and Christine, then back to Gareth. "So when do we eat?"

"I was hoping that perhaps you could retrieve Olwen before the meal," Gareth explained.

"Olwen?"

"The Duke of Soravia," Christine clarified, and Emelyn snapped a stare over her.

"How might we locate him?" Emelyn asked. "He is never near the six castles of Kinbrace of late. Always out and about."

"We could look," Gareth said. He stepped aside and waved his arm back at the scrying mirror.

"More than a meal?" Emelyn asked.

"You have heard of the goings-on in Vaasa?"

"I have heard that you mean to honor a drow, and that there is apparently a knight-in-waiting."

"A Zhengyian construct appeared north of Palishchuk," Gareth explained.

"They seem to be more common of late. There was a tower outside of Heliogabalus—"

"Mariabronne the Rover fell within the walls of this one."

That set Emelyn back on his heels.

"It was said to be a replica of Castle Perilous," Lady Christine interjected. "Alive with gargoyles, and ruled by a dracolich."

Emelyn's eyes, gray like his robes, widened with every proclamation. "And this drow and the others defeated the menace?"

Gareth nodded. "But the construct remains."

"And you wish me to fly to the north to see what I might learn," Emelyn reasoned.

"That would seem prudent."

"And Olwen?" Emelyn asked, but before Gareth or Christine could respond, the old wizard gasped and held up his hand. "Ah, Mariabronne!" he said. "I'd not considered Olwen's love for that one."

"Find him?" Gareth bade Emelyn, and again he indicated the mirror.

Emelyn nodded and stepped forward.

No one in Faerûn was better at preparing a banquet than Christine Dragons-bane. She was the daughter of Baron Tranth, the former ruler of the region known as Bloodstone Valley, which included Bloodstone Village. Growing up in the time of Zhengyi, in the noble House that controlled the sole pass between Vaasa and Damara, Christine had witnessed scores of feasts prepared for visiting dignitaries, both from the duchies and baronies of Damara and from Zhengyi's court. In the years before open warfare, much of the duplicity that had lured Damara into a position vulnerable to Zhengyi's imperialistic designs had occurred right there in Bloodstone Village, at the table of Baron Tranth.

The meal planned for that night held no such potential for intrigue, of course. The guests were the friends of Gareth, honest and true companions who had fought beside him in the desperate struggle against the Witch-King. Riordan Parnell wouldn't be there, as he was off to Palishchuk, which complicated things for Christine a bit. Had he been in attendance, Riordan, an extraordinary bard, would have provided much of the entertainment. And entertainment was paramount on Gareth's mind.

"This is a meal for solidarity of purpose and agreement of how we should proceed," he told Christine not long after Emelyn had magically flown out to Soravia. "But most of all it is for Olwen. He has lost a child, in effect."

"And we have both lost a niece," Christine reminded.

Gareth nodded, but neither of them were truly devastated by the death of Commander Ellery. She had been a relative, but a distant one, and one that neither Gareth nor Christine had known very well. Gareth had seen her only a few times and had spoken to her only once, on the occasion of her appointment to the Army of Bloodstone.

"This night is for Olwen," Christine agreed, and took her leave.

Soon after, though, they found out that they were both incorrect. Emelyn the Gray returned from Soravia, appearing in Gareth's audience chamber amidst a cloud of smoke. Coughing and waving his hands, more with annoyance than with any expectation that he would clear the cloud, Emelyn stood alone, shaking his head.

"Olwen is not in his castle," the old wizard explained. "Nor is he anywhere in the city, or in Kinnery or Steppenhall. He went out soon after the news of Mariabronne's fall reached Kinbrace, along with several of his rangerly ilk. Who knows what silliness they are up to."

" 'Rangerly'?" Gareth asked.

"Druidic, then?" Emelyn offered. "How am I to properly describe men who dance about the trees and offer prayers of gratitude to beautiful and benevolent creatures right before and right after they kill them?"

" 'Rangerly' will suffice," the king conceded, and Emelyn wagged his wrinkled old head.

"Do you have any notion of where they went?" Gareth asked.

"Somewhere in the northeast—some grove they have deemed sacred, no doubt."

"A funeral?"

Emelyn shrugged.

"And there was no way to find him?" Gareth asked.

Emelyn's look became less accommodating, his expression telling Gareth in no uncertain terms that if he could have found the man, Olwen would be standing beside him.

"Olwen has been an adventurer for most of his life," Emelyn reminded. "He has known loss as often as victory and has buried many friends."

"As have we all."

"He will overcome his grief," said the wizard. "Better, perhaps, that he is not here in the morning when you celebrate those who survived the trip to this Zhengyian construct. Olwen would have strong questions for them, do not doubt, particularly for the drow."

"We all have questions, my friend," Gareth said.

Emelyn eyed him with open suspicion, and Gareth couldn't hold back his smile from his ever-perceptive old companion.

"How could we not?" the king asked. "We had an unusual party travel north on our behalf, unbeknownst to us, and we are now left an unusual band of victorious survivors. We have a construct of unknown origin—"

Emelyn held up his hand to stop his friend. "I detest Palishchuk," he remarked.

Gareth's grin widened. "I could trust no other with this most important investigation. Riordan is already there, doing that which Riordan does best—interrogating people without them even realizing it—but he has no practical understanding of such creation magic as this."

"I am not fond of Riordan, either," grumped Emelyn, and Gareth couldn't contain a chuckle. "But he is a bard, is he not? Are bards not especially skilled at determining the origins and history of places and dweomers?"

"Emelyn. . . ." Gareth said.

The old wizard huffed. "Palishchuk. Oh joy of joys. To be surrounded by half-orcs and their unparalleled wit and wisdom."

"One of the heroes who defeated the castle's guardians was a half-orc wizard," said Gareth, and that seemed to pique Emelyn's curiosity for a moment.

A brief moment. "And I know a dwarf who dances gracefully," came the sarcastic reply. "For a dwarf. Which means that the area clerics need only repair a few broken toes among the spectators after each performance. Could a half-orc wizard be any more promising?"

"When the survivors returned to the Vaasan Gate, they reported that Wingham was in Palishchuk."

That did interest Emelyn, obviously so.

"Enough, my king," he surrendered. "You wish me to go, and so I go, but it will not be as brief a journey as my trip to Soravia, a land that I know well and can thus teleport to and from quickly. Expect me to be gone a tenday, and that only if the riddles presented by the Zhengyian construct are not too tightly wound. Am I to leave at once, or might I partake of the feast you promised in order to lure me here in the first place?"

"Eat, and eat well," said Gareth, smiling, then he paused and took on a more serious visage. "I trust that your magic is powerful enough to lift you and transport you when your belly is full?"

"If you were not the king, I'd offer a demonstration."

"Ah, but if I were not the king, then Zhengyi would not likely allow it."

Emelyn just shook his head and walked off to the guest rooms where he could clean up and prepare for Christine's table.

It was a night of toasts to old friends and old times. The five adventuring companions lifted their glasses to Olwen, most of all, and to Mariabronne, who had held such promise. They reiterated their goal of unifying the Bloodstone Lands, Damara and Vaasa, into a singular kingdom, and of defeating any and all remnants of the tyrant Zhengyi.

They talked of the next morning's ceremony, sharing what little they knew of the man who would be granted knighthood and of his strange, ebon-skinned companion. Celedon Kierney promised that they would know much more of the pair soon enough, a vow he made with a nod of approval from Kane. There was no disagreement at that table among the friends who had struggled hand-in-hand for more than a decade. They saw the challenges before them, the potential trouble, and the mystery of the newcomers, and they methodically set out their plans.

In the morning, after Friar Dugald offered a blessing for them all, Emelyn departed for Palishchuk and Celedon set out for Heliogabalus. Celedon asked Kane to accompany him, or to fly him part of the way on the magical carpet, but Kane declined. He wanted to witness the day's events.

And so as King Gareth and Queen Christine prepared for their ceremony, they knew that they were well flanked by powerful friends.

CHAPTER

3

S he exited the front door of her modest mercantile, a shop specializing in trinkets, around sunset, as she did every evening, handing the keys over to her trusted assistant. The sign over her head as she walked from her porch read Tazmikella's Bag of Silver, and true to the moniker, most of the items within, candlesticks and paperweights, decorative orbs and pieces of jewelry, were crafted of that precious metal.

Tazmikella herself had earned quite a handsome reputation among the merchant class of the circular road called Wall's Around in Heliogabalus, a cul-de-sac off the more major route, Wall Way, so named because of its proximity to the city's high defensive encirclement. The woman was rather ordinary looking and dressed simply. Her hair showed some of its former strawberry blond luster, but was mostly soft gray, and her shoulders appeared just a bit too wide in support of her smallish head. But she always had a kind word for her fellow merchants, and always a disarming smile, and if she had ever fleeced a customer, none had ever complained.

Unassuming and simple, with few needs and plain tastes, Tazmikella did not have a fancy coach awaiting her departure. She walked, every night, the same route out of the city and to an unremarkable cabin set on the side of a hillock.

The woman coming out of Ilnezhara's Gold Coins across the street from her could not have appeared more contrary. She stood straight, tall, and thin, with a shock of thick, copper-colored hair and huge blue eyes. She was dressed in the finest of threads, and a handsome coach driven by a team of shining horses awaited her.

"Can I offer you a ride, poor dear?" Ilnezhara asked her counterpart, as she did every evening—much to the amusement of the other merchants, who often whispered and chortled about the pair and their rivalry.

"I was given legs for a purpose," Tazmikella responded on cue.

"To the city gates, at least?" Ilnezhara continued, to which Tazmikella merely waved her hand and walked on by, as she did every night.

Any witnesses watching more closely that night might have seen something a bit out of the ordinary, though, for as Tazmikella passed by Ilnezhara's coach, she turned her head slightly and offered the tall woman the slightest of nods, and received one in return.

Tazmikella was out of the city in short order, moving far from the torchlit wall toward the lonely hill where she kept her modest home. At the base of that hill, in nearly complete darkness, she surveyed all the land around her, ensuring that she was alone. She moved to a wide clearing beyond a shielding line of thick pines. In the middle, she closed her eyes and slipped out of her clothes. Tazmikella hated wearing clothes, and could never understand the need of humans to hide their natural forms. She always thought that level of shame and modesty to be reflective of a race that could not elevate itself above its apparent limitations, a race that insisted on subjugating itself to more powerful beings instead of standing as their own gods in proud self-determination.

Tazmikella was possessed of no such modesty. She stood naked in that unnatural form, basking in the feel of the night breezes. The change came subtly, for she had long ago perfected the art of transformation. Her wings and tail began to grow first, for they were the least painful—additions were always easier than transformations, which included cracking and reshaping bone structure.

The trees around her seemed to shrink. Her perspective shifted as she grew to enormous proportions, for Tazmikella was no human. She had crawled from her egg centuries before beside her sister and sole sibling in the great deserts of Calimshan, far to the southwest.

Tazmikella the copper dragon lifted into the night air. She gained altitude quickly, flying away from the human city. The leaders of the land knew who she was, and accepted her, but the commonfolk would never comprehend, of course. If she revealed herself to them, King Gareth and his friends would be left with no choice but to evict her from the Bloodstone Lands. And she really didn't want a fight with that company.

She moved directly north, across the least populated expanse of Morov and into the even less densely populated Duchy of Soravia. She flew between the Goliad and the Galena Snake, the two parallel rivers running south from the Galena Mountains. And she continued to climb, for the thin air and the cold did not bother Tazmikella at all. A person on the ground might catch a fleeting glimpse of her, but would that person know her to be a dragon flying high, or think her a night bird, or a bat, flying low?

She was not concerned. She was naked in the night air, above such concerns. She was free.

Tazmikella crossed the mountains easily, weaving in and out of the towering peaks, enjoying the play of the multidirectional air flows and the stark contrast between the dark stones and moonlit snow. She entered Vaasa just to the west of Palishchuk, and turned east as she came out of the mountains. Within moments, she noted the lights of the half-orc city.

The dragon stayed up high as she overflew the city, for she knew that the half-orcs, living amidst the Vaasan wilds for so many years, knew how to protect themselves from any threat. If they saw the form of a dragon over-flying their city at night, they wouldn't pause to consider the color of the wyrm—nor would they be able to determine that in any case, under the light of the half-moon and stars alone.

Tazmikella used her extraordinary eyesight to scrutinize the city as she passed. It was late, but many torches burned and the town's largest tavern was bright and noisy. They still celebrated the victory over the Zhengyian castle, she realized.

She banked right, to the north, and began her descent, confident that none of Palishchuk's citizens would be out and about. Almost immediately, she saw the dark and dead structure, an immense fortress, a replica of Castle Perilous, only a few miles to the north of the city.

She came down in a straight line, too intrigued to pause and take a survey of the area. As she alighted, she changed back into a human form, thinking that anyone who subsequently spied her wouldn't feel threatened by the sight of a naked, middle-aged woman. Of course, if any lurking onlookers had watched her more closely, that image would have created more confusion than comfort, for she strode up to the huge portcullis that barred the front of the structure without pause. She considered the patchwork grate that had been chained over the break in the gate, where Jarlaxle and his companions had apparently entered. She could have removed that patch easily enough, but that would have meant stooping to crawl under.

Instead, the woman slipped her arms between two of the thick portcullis spikes, then pushed outward with both, easily bending the metal so that she could simply step through.

Unconcerned, Tazmikella strode right through the gatehouses and across the courtyard of torn, broken ground, littered with the shattered forms of many, many skeletons.

She found the great doors of the main keep repaired and secured by a heavy chain—one that she grabbed with one hand and easily snapped.

She found what she was looking for in the main room just beyond the doors. A pedestal stood intact, though blackened by fire near its top. The remnants of a large book, pages torn and burned, lay scattered about. Her expression growing more sour, Tazmikella went up to the ruined tome and lifted the black binding. Most of it was destroyed, but she saw enough of the cover to recognize the images of dragons stamped there.

She knew the nature of the book, a tome of creation and of enslavement.

"Damn you, Zhengyi," the dragon whispered.

The clues of Jarlaxle and Entreri's progress through the place were easy enough to follow, and Tazmikella soon entered a huge chamber far below the structure, where lay the bones of a long-past battle, and the debris of a more recent struggle. One look at the dracolich confirmed everything Tazmikella and her sister Ilnezhara had feared.

The dragon arrived back on the hillside outside of Heliogabalus shortly before the dawn. She dressed and rubbed her weary eyes, but she did not return to her home. Rather, she moved south to a singular tower, the home of her sister. She didn't bother knocking, for she was expected.

"It was that easily discerned that you did not even need a full day at the site?" the taller, copper-haired Ilnezhara said as soon as Tazmikella entered.

"It was exactly as we feared."

"A Zhengyian tome, animated by the captured soul of a dead dragon?"

"Urshula, I think."

"The black?"

"The same."

"And the book?"

"Destroyed. Torn and burned. The work of Jarlaxle, I would expect. That one is too clever to allow such a treasure to escape his greedy hands. He saw the truth of Zhengyian tomes when he destroyed Herminicle's tower."

"And we offered him too many clues," Ilnezhara added.

They both paused and considered the scenario unfolding before them. Ilnezhara and Tazmikella had been approached by Zhengyi those years before with a tempting offer. If they served beside his conquering armies, he would reward them each with an enchanted phylactery, waiting to rescue their spirits when they died. Zhengyi had offered the sisters immortality in the form of lichdom.

But the price was too high, they had agreed, and while the prospect of surviving as a dracolich might be better than death, it was anything but appealing.

"Jarlaxle understood exactly what was buried within the pages of Zhengyi's book, so we can only assume that he has Urshula now, safely tucked away in a pocket," Tazmikella said after a long while.

"This drow plays dangerous games," said Ilnezhara. "If he knows the power of the phylactery, does he also understand the magic behind it? Will Jarlaxle begin tempting dragons to his side, as did Zhengyi?"

"If he walks into Heliogabalus and offers us a dark pact toward lichdom, I will bite him in half," Tazmikella promised.

Ilnezhara put on a pouting expression. "Could you not just chain him and hand him to me, that I might use him as I please for a few centuries?"

"Sister. . . ." Tazmikella warned.

Ilnezhara simply laughed in response, but it was a chuckle edged with nervous tension. For both of them were beginning to understand that Jarlaxle, a creature they considered a minion, was not to be taken lightly.

"Jarlaxle and Entreri defeated a dracolich," Tazmikella stated, and there was no further laughter. "And Urshula the Black was no minor wyrm in life or death."

"And now he is in Jarlaxle's pocket, figuratively and literally."

"We should talk to those two."

Ilnezhara nodded her agreement.

Every so often in his life, the fiercely independent Artemis Entreri found himself in a time and place not of his choosing, and from which he could not immediately escape. It had been so for months in Menzoberranzan, when Jarlaxle had rescued him from a disastrous fight with Drizzt Do'Urden outside of Mithral Hall and had taken him back with the dark elves on their retreat from the dwarf lands.

It had been so quite often in his younger days, serving the dangerous Basadoni Guild in Calimport. In those early phases of his career, Artemis Entreri had done what he was told, when he was told. On those occasions when his assignment was not to his liking, the younger Entreri had just shrugged and accepted it—what else was he to do?

As he got older, more experienced and with a reputation that made even the Pashas nervous, Entreri accepted the assignments of his choosing, and no one else's. Still, every so often, he found himself in a place where he did not wish to be, as it was that morning in Bloodstone Village.

He watched the ceremony with a strange detachment, as if he sat in the crowd that had gathered before the raised platform in front of King Gareth's palace. With some amusement, he watched Davis Eng go forward and accept his honor. The man hadn't even made it to Palishchuk of his own accord. He had been downed on the road and had been carried in, a liability and not an asset, in the back of a wagon.

Some people will celebrate anything, Entreri mused. Even mediocrity.

Back on the streets of Calimport, a man who had performed as pathetically as Eng would have been given one chance to redeem himself, if that.

Calihye was called forward next, and Entreri watched that presentation more carefully, and with less judgment. The half-elf had refused to go into the castle, though she had agreed to stay with the wounded Davis Eng. She had broken her agreement with Commander Ellery, her vow of servitude to the mission, and still she was being rewarded.

Entreri merely smirked at that one and let the negative thoughts filter away, his personal feelings for the half-elf overruling his pervasive cynicism for the moment.

Still, it amazed him how liberal the king seemed to be with his accolades—because it was all for show, Entreri understood. The ceremony wasn't about Davis Eng or Calihye. It wasn't about the annoying Athrogate, who hopped forward next to receive his honor. It wasn't even about Jarlaxle and Entreri. It was about the people watching, the commonfolk of Bloodstone. It was all about creating heroes for the morale of the peasants, to keep them bowing and praising their leaders so that they wouldn't notice their own troubles. Half of them went to bed hungry most nights, while those they loved so, the paladin king and his court, would never know such hardship.

In the end, cynicism won over, and so when Entreri was called forward—the second time, for he had been too turned inward to even hear the first summons—he stepped briskly and didn't even hide his scowl.

He heard Jarlaxle's laugh behind him as he moved to stand before Gareth, and he knew that his companion was enjoying the spectacle. He managed one glance back at the drow, just to glare. And of course, Jarlaxle laughed all the more.

"Artemis Entreri," Gareth said, turning the man back to face him. "You are new to this land, and yet you have already proven your worth. With your actions at the Vaasan Gate, and in the north against the construct of Zhengyi, you have distinguished yourself above so many others. For your defeat of the dracolich, Artemis Entreri, I bestow upon you the title of Apprentice Knight of the Order."

A man dressed in dirty robes stepped up to the bald, fat priest at Gareth's side. The priest, Friar Dugald, offered a quick blessing over the sword then handed it to Gareth.

But as he did, the ragged man looked not at the king, but at Entreri. And though Gareth's complimentary words had been full of all the right notes,

Entreri saw clearly that this man—a dear friend of the king's, apparently—was not viewing Entreri in the same complimentary light.

Artemis Entreri had survived the vicious streets of Calimport with his skill at arms, but even more importantly, he had survived due to his ability to measure friends and enemies at a glance.

That man, slightly older than he, and no commoner despite his ragged dress, was no friend.

Gareth took the sword and lifted it high with both hands.

"Please kneel," Queen Christine instructed Entreri, who was still regarding the man in rags.

Entreri turned his head slowly to consider the queen, then gave a slight nod and dropped to his knees. Gareth laid the sword on his left shoulder, and proclaimed him an apprentice knight of the order. The fat priest began to recite all of the honors and benefits such a title bestowed, but Entreri was hardly listening. He thought of the man in rags, of the look that had passed between them.

He thought about how Jarlaxle was wrangling them both into places where they did not belong.

Far to the north of Bloodstone Village, the celebration in Palishchuk lasted long into the night, and Riordan Parnell continued to lead the way. Whenever things seemed to be quieting, the bard took up a rousing song about Palishchuk and its many heroes.

And glasses were lifted in toast.

Most of the town had turned out in the common room of the Weary Wanderer that night to honor—yet again—Arrayan and Olgerkhan, their brave kinfolk who had ventured into the castle. Several of the citizens had been killed and many more injured in the battle with the castle's gargoyles, who had flown through the dark sky to assault the town. To a man and woman, the half-orcs recognized that had Arrayan, Olgerkhan, and the others not proven victorious over the dracolich and its vile minions, their beloved city would likely have been abandoned, with refugees streaming south for the safety of the Vaasan Gate.

So the half-orcs were more than willing to celebrate, and when Riordan Parnell, the legendary bard and a charter member of King Gareth's court, had arrived in Palishchuk, the revelry had taken on new heights.

Seeing that his reputation had preceded him, Riordan was determined not to disappoint. He sang and played on his fine lute, backed by some fairly good musicians from Wingham's traveling merchant band, who—as good luck would have it, for Wingham and Riordan were old friends—happened to be in town.

Riordan sang and everyone drank. He sang some more, and they drank some more. Riordan graciously treated many of the dignitaries, including the two guests of honor, from his seemingly endless pouch of coins—for in his generosity, the bard could cleverly determine how much each was drinking. Initially, he had thought to keep Arrayan and Olgerkhan semi-lucid, for there was much more to that particular evening's celebration than merely the bard showing off his musical talents. Drunken people talked more freely, after all, and Riordan had gone there for information.

After seeing the pair of heroes, though, the bard had slightly altered his plans. One look at Arrayan's beautiful face had convinced him to make sure that Olgerkhan was getting the most potent of drinks, all the night long. Truly, Arrayan had caught Riordan off his guard—and that was not a common occurrence for the brash and charming rake. It wasn't that she was spectacularly beautiful, for Riordan had bedded many of the most alluring women in the Bloodstone Lands. No, what had so surprised the bard was that he found himself attracted to Arrayan at all. Her face was flat and round, but very pleasantly so, her hair lustrous, and her teeth straight and clean, so unlike the crooked and protruding tusks so prevalent in her orc heritage. Indeed, had he seen Arrayan walking the streets of Heliogabalus or Bloodstone Village, Riordan would never have guessed that a drop of orc blood coursed her veins.

Knowing the truth of it, though, the bard could see bits of that heritage here and there on the woman. Her ears were a bit small, and her forehead just a little sloped, up from a brow that was a hair too thick.

But none of it mattered to the whole, for the woman was pretty, and pleasant and smiling, and Riordan was intrigued, and because of that, surprised.

So he made sure, with a wink at the barmaid and an extra coin on her tray, that Arrayan's escort and fellow hero, the brutish Olgerkhan, was amply sauced. Soon enough, Olgerkhan fell off his chair and out of the picture entirely, snoring contentedly on the floor to the howls and cheers of the other patrons.

Riordan picked his time carefully. He knew that he couldn't outmaneuver Wingham, for the old half-orc was far too crafty to be taken in by a man of Riordan's well-earned reputation, and he saw that Wingham took quite the interest in Arrayan, who, Riordan had learned, was his niece. When he judged that an ample number of patrons were falling by the wayside, the bard changed the tempo of his songs. It was early in the morning by then, and so he began to wind things down . . . slowly.

He also began slipping a bit more enchantment into his tunes, using the magic of his voice, the gift of the true bards, to manipulate the mood of the slightly inebriated Arrayan. He put her at ease. He charmed her with subtle flattery. The background magic of his songs convinced her that he was her friend, to be trusted, who could offer comfort and advice.

More than once, Riordan noticed Wingham glancing his way with obvious suspicion. He pressed on, though, continuing his quiet manipulation while trying to find a plan to be rid of the too-smart old half-orc.

Even clever Riordan realized that he was out of his league, though. There was no way he was going to distract Wingham. During one of his rare pauses from song, the bard gathered a pair of drinks from the tavernkeeper and moved to Wingham's side. He was not surprised when Wingham dismissed the other three merchants who had been sitting at his table.

"You sing well," the old half-orc said.

Riordan slipped one of the drinks over to him then lifted the other in an appreciative toast. Wingham tapped one glass to the other and took a deep swallow.

"You know Nyungy?" he asked before he had even replaced his glass on the table.

Riordan looked at him curiously for just a moment. "The bard? Of course.

Who of my heritage and training would not know the name of the greatest bard to ever walk the Bloodstone Lands?"

"The greatest *half-orc* bard," Wingham clarified.

"I would not put such limitations on the reputation of Nyungy."

"He would tell you that the exploits of Riordan Parnell outshone his own." Wingham lifted his glass to lead the toast, and Riordan, grinning, tapped his glass to Wingham's.

"I think you flatter me too greatly," the bard said before he drank. After the sip, he added, "I played a small role, one man among many, in the defeat of the Witch-King."

"Curse his name," said Wingham, and Riordan nodded. "I stand by my comment, for I have heard those very words from Nyungy, and recently."

"He is still alive, then? Fine news! Nyungy has not been heard from for years now, and many assumed that he had passed on from this life, to a reward that we all know must be just."

"Alive and well, if a bit crotchety and sore in the joints," Wingham confirmed. "In fact, he warned me to be wary of Riordan Parnell when we learned that you were coming to Palishchuk, only two days ago."

Riordan paused and cocked his head, studying his companion.

"Yes, my friend, Nyungy lives right here in Palishchuk," Wingham confirmed. "Of course he does. Indeed, it was he who deciphered that Arrayan had unwittingly begun the cycle of magic of the Zhengyian construct. His wisdom helped guide me to the understanding that ultimately allowed Commander Ellery's group to defeat the construct and its hellish minions."

Riordan sat staring at the old half-orc through it all, neither blinking or nodding.

"Yes, you would do well to pay Nyungy a visit before you leave, since you have come to discern the complete truth of this construct and its defeat."

Riordan swallowed a bit too hard. "I have come to honor the exploits of Arrayan and Olgerkhan," he said, "and to share in the joy and celebration until King Gareth arrives from Bloodstone Village to formally honor them."

"And truly, what a fine honor it is that the king would even travel the muddy expanse of Vaasa to pay such a tribute, rather than demanding the couple travel to him in his seat of power."

"They are worthy of the honor."

"No doubt," Wingham agreed. "But that is far from the extent of it—for their visit and for your own."

Riordan didn't bother to deny anything.

"King Gareth is right to worry," Wingham went on. "This castle was formidable."

"The loss of Mariabronne, and Gareth's relative, Ellery, would attest to that."

"To say nothing of Canthan, a high-ranking wizard in the Citadel of Assassins."

The blunt statement gave Riordan pause.

"Surely you suspected as much," said Wingham.

"There were rumors."

"And they are true. Yes, my singing friend, there is much more for us—for you—to unravel here than the simple defeat of yet another Zhengyian construct.

Fear not, for I will not hinder you. Far from it, for the sake of Palishchuk and all of Vaasa, my hopes lie with Riordan and King Gareth."

"We have always considered Wingham a valuable ally and friend."

"You flatter me. But our goals are the same, I assure you." Wingham paused and looked at Riordan slyly. "Some of our goals, at least."

At that surprising comment, Riordan let Wingham steer his gaze across the way to Arrayan.

Riordan gave a laugh. "She is beautiful, I admit," he said.

"She is in love, and with a man deserving of her."

Riordan glanced at Olgerkhan, who lay under the table curled up like a baby, and laughed again. "A man too fond of the liquor this night, it would seem."

"With the help of a few well-placed coins and better-placed compliments," said Wingham.

Riordan sat back and smiled at the perceptive half-orc. "You fear for Arrayan's reputation."

"A charming hero from King Gareth's Court . . ."

"Has come to speak with her, as a friend," Riordan finished.

"Your reputation suggests a bit more."

"Fair enough," the bard said, and he lifted his glass in salute to Wingham. "On my word, then, friend Wingham," he said. "Arrayan is a beautiful woman, and I would be a liar if I said otherwise to you."

"You are a bard, after all," came the dry reply, and Riordan could only shrug and accept the barb.

"My intentions for her are honorable," Riordan said. "Well, except that, yes, I have indeed played it so that she is . . . less inhibited. I have many questions to ask her this night, and I would have her honest replies, without fear of consequence."

He noted that Wingham stiffened at that.

"She has done nothing wrong," said the half-orc.

"That I do not doubt."

"She was unwittingly trapped by the magic of the tome—a book that I gave to her," Wingham said, and a bit of desperation seemed to be creeping into his voice.

"I am less concerned with her, and with Olgerkhan, than with their other companions, those who made it out alive and those who did not," the bard assured the half-orc.

"I will tell you the entire story of the book and the creation," Wingham replied. "I would prefer that you do not revisit that painful experience on Arrayan, this night or any other. Besides, since she was in the thrall of powerful and manipulative magic, my observations will prove more accurate and enlightening."

Riordan thought it over for a moment then nodded. "But you were not with them inside the construct."

"True enough."

Riordan set his glass down on the table, and slid his chair back. "I will be gentle," he promised as he stood up.

Wingham didn't seem overly pleased by it all, but he nodded his agreement. He didn't have much of a choice, after all. Riordan Parnell, cousin of Celedon Kierney, friend of Gareth and all the others, was one of the seven who had brought Zhengyi down and had rescued the Bloodstone Lands from the hellish nightmare of the Witch-King.

The celebration was fine that night in Bloodstone Village, as well. Though many had little idea of what had transpired in Vaasa to warrant such a ceremony, or a knighting, the folk of the long-beleaguered land seemed always ready for a celebration. King Gareth told them to eat, drink, and make merry, so make merry they did.

A huge open air pavilion was set up on the front grounds of Castle Dragonsbane, to the side of the Palace of the White Tree. A few tents had been set about, but most of the people preferred to dance and sing under the stars that clear, dark night. They knew they wouldn't have many such evenings left before the onset of winter's cold winds.

For his part, Jarlaxle wandered in small circles around the table where Entreri, the hero of the day, sat with Calihye and some of the lesser lords and ladies of King Gareth's court. Every so often, Friar Dugald would wander by, offering a mug in toast, before staggering off into the crowd.

Many, of course, showed great interest in the drow as he glided about the perimeter, and he found himself tipping his hat almost non-stop. It was a practiced gesture, and one that served well to hide the truth of Jarlaxle's attention. For with a wave of his hand and a call to a small silver cone he held tight in his palm, the drow had created an area of amplified sensibilities, from himself to Entreri and the half-elf. People strode up before Jarlaxle and addressed him directly, even loudly, but he just nodded and smiled and moved along, hearing not a word from them.

But hearing everything said between Entreri and Calihye.

"I have no desire to winter in the tight confines of the Vaasan Gate," Entreri said to her, and from his tone, Jarlaxle could tell that he had spoken those very words several times already. "I will find work in Heliogabalus, if it suits me to work, and enjoy fine food and drink if not."

"And fine women?" Calihye asked.

"If you would accompany me, then yes," Entreri replied without hesitation.

Jarlaxle chortled upon hearing that, then realized that he had just confused, and likely insulted, a pair of young women who had approached him.

With an offer, perhaps?

He had to find out, so he abandoned Entreri's conversation just long enough to recognize that the moment had passed.

"Your pardon," he managed to say as the pair turned their backs and rushed away.

With a shrug, Jarlaxle summoned the cone again and tuned in.

". . . Parissus has unfinished affairs," Calihye was saying, referring to her dear friend who had been killed on the road to Palishchuk—a death that she had initially blamed on Artemis Entreri, and for which she had vowed revenge. It seemed that she had entertained a change of heart, Jarlaxle thought, unless she planned to love the man to death.

Jarlaxle smiled and nodded at that rather discordant thought. For some reason, he found himself thinking of Ilnezhara, his dragon lover.

"I am bound to her by years of friendship," Calihye continued. "You cannot deny me my responsibilities to see that her final wishes are carried out as she desired."

"I deny you no road. Your path is your own to decide."

"But you won't come with me?"

Jarlaxle couldn't help but smirk as he regarded that distant exchange, how Calihye gently placed her hand on Entreri's forearm as she spoke.

Ah, the manipulation of human women, Jarlaxle thought.

"Jarlaxle has been my friend for years, as well," Entreri replied. "We have business in Heliogabalus."

"Jarlaxle is not capable of handling your affairs alone?"

Entreri gave a chuckle. "You would have me trust him?"

Jarlaxle nodded his approval at that.

"I thought you were friends," Calihye said.

Entreri merely shrugged and looked back to his drink, set on the table before him.

Jarlaxle noted Calihye's expression, a bit of a frown showing around the edges of her mouth. As Entreri turned back to her, that frown disappeared in the blink of a drow's eye, upturning into a calming, assured smile.

"Interesting," the drow muttered under his breath.

"What is?" came a question before him, one that had him nearly jumping out of his boots. Before him stood a group of young men, boys actually, all of them staring at him, sizing him up from head to toe.

All of those stares reminded Jarlaxle keenly that he was out of his element, that he was among a suspicious throng of lesser creatures. He was a novelty, and though that was a position he had long coveted among the drow, among the surface races, it was both a blessing and a curse, an opportunity and a shackle.

"A good evening to you," he said to them, tipping his outrageous hat.

"They're saying ye killed a dragon," the same boy who had spoken before offered.

"Many," Jarlaxle replied with a wink.

"Tell us!" another of the group exclaimed.

"Ah, so many stories . . ." the drow began, and he started off for a nearby table, herding the boys before him.

He glanced back at Entreri and Calihye as he went, to see his friend with both hands wrapped around his mug, his head down. At his side, Calihye held his arm and stared at him, and try as he might, Jarlaxle could not read her expression.

Arrayan was thoroughly enjoying herself. All guilt had washed from her, finally. Even the defeat of the "living" castle had not allowed the woman to truly relax, for several people had died in battling that construct—a creation of her unwitting actions.

That was all behind her, though, for one night at least. The music, the drink, the cheers . . . had it all, just possibly, been worth it?

Sitting beside her, face down on the table—and that after clawing his way up from the floor—Olgerkhan snored contentedly. Dear Olgerkhan. He had been her truest friend when they had entered the castle, and had become her lover since they had left it. Soon they were to be married, and it was a day that could not come quickly enough for Arrayan. She had known the brutish half-orc for all of her life, but not until the crisis within the construct, when she had watched Olgerkhan sacrifice so much for her benefit, had she come to understand the truth of his feelings for her—and hers for him.

She reached over and tousled his hair, but he was too drunk to even respond. She had never seen Olgerkhan drunk before, for neither of them often partook of potent liquor. For herself, Arrayan had begun sipping her drinks more carefully hours before. She wasn't much of a drinker, and it hadn't taken a lot to set her head spinning. She was only just coming back to clarity, somewhat.

She was glad of that indeed when she noted the handsome and heroic bard striding her way, a huge smile on his face. Behind him, she caught a glimpse of her uncle Wingham, but the concern clearly stamped on his old face did not register with the tipsy woman.

"Milady Arrayan," Riordan Parnell said as he moved near to her. He dipped a graceful, arm-sweeping bow. "I feel that the warmth of the night has almost overcome me. I wish to take a short walk in the cool air outside, and would be honored if you would join me."

A flash of concern crossed Arrayan's face, and she was hardly aware of the movement as she looked to Olgerkhan.

"Ah, milady, I assure you that my intentions are nothing but honorable," Riordan said. "Your love for Olgerkhan is well known, and so appropriate, given the status that you two have rightly earned. You will be the most celebrated couple in Palishchuk, perhaps in all of Vaasa."

"Help me to rouse him, then," Arrayan replied, and she blushed as she realized that she slurred her words a bit. She reached over to grab Olgerkhan, but Riordan took her by the wrist.

"Just we two," he bade her. He glanced back over his shoulder, leading her gaze to Wingham.

The old half-orc still wore that grave look, but he nodded in response to Arrayan's questioning expression.

With a fair amount of potent liquor clouding Arrayan's thoughts, it was not hard for the powerful Riordan to weave a magical enchantment over her as they walked out of the tavern. By the time they'd moved only a block from the place, Arrayan had come to fully trust the handsome man from Damara.

In such a situation, it didn't take Riordan long to learn what he needed. He had heard of Mariabronne's demise already—that the ranger had been killed not by the dracolich, but by shadowy demons beforehand when he had been out scouting. Yet, strangely, Mariabronne's corpse had been found at the scene of the dracolich battle, bitten in half.

Riordan got the complete picture, including when three of the already dead companions—Mariabronne, Canthan, and Ellery—had walked past Arrayan to join in the fight. They had been animated by someone or something. Canthan had thrown spells in the dracolich fight, and the animated warrior and ranger had battled fiercely.

The magic that had brought their physical bodies to animation had been powerful, Riordan understood.

He listened intently as Arrayan lowered her voice and admitted the truth of Canthan's demise: that the man and the dwarf had turned on her and Olgerkhan, and had been stopped by Entreri and Jarlaxle. She lowered her voice even more as she recounted the last moments of Canthan's life, when Entreri's horrible, vampiric dagger had drawn forth his remaining life-force and transferred it to Olgerkhan.

Riordan's head spun. There was so much more to the whole business than anyone had understood. And what had happened to Ellery, Gareth's niece, a Commander of the Bloodstone Army? Even Arrayan didn't know, for the woman had remained behind the group with Jarlaxle, studying the tome, and had not returned with the mysterious drow to the room where Entreri had finished off Canthan.

And so Riordan's interrogation, for all the answers it provided, had only led him to so many more, and more intriguing, questions.

They were questions to which he would find no answers from either Arrayan or Olgerkhan, or anyone else in Palishchuk.

With so much to report, he escorted the woman back to the tavern and didn't even stay the night, collecting his mount from the stable and riding out into the darkness, galloping hard to the south.

At the same time, not far to the west, Emelyn the Gray, in the form of a night bird, sped the other way. The grumpy wizard had no intention of going into Palishchuk, so he skirted around the town to the west and veered back to the northeast. He found the castle easily enough and flew over the outer wall, reverting to his human form as he settled before the doors of the main keep. He took a moment to consider the broken chain on the doors.

"Hmm," he said, a sound he would repeat many times that night and the next morning, as he made his way through the Zhengyian construct.

CHAPTER

HOME, BITTER HOME

4

"You should put the dragon statuette back," Jarlaxle remarked as he and Entreri arrived at the door to their apartment in Heliogabalus, a modest affair set on the second story of an unremarkable wooden building. Modest from outward appearances, at least, for inside lay the spoils of the pair's successful ventures before their trip north to Vaasa. Entreri and Jarlaxle were very good at gathering coin, and Jarlaxle in particular was very good at spending it.

"I left it in the castle," Entreri replied, an obvious lie that brought a grin to the drow. Never would Entreri leave behind such a powerful tool as the statuette, which had proven instrumental in defeating the dracolich. That tiny, silvery item could be set as a trap, bringing forth the various breath forms of the deadly chromatic dragons.

"Perhaps I can persuade Tazmikella and Ilnezhara to provide us with another one," Jarlaxle said.

"And what else might you coerce from the dragon sisters?"

Jarlaxle feigned a wounded look.

"Now that you have proffered a bargaining chip, I mean," Entreri clarified.

Jarlaxle's expression shifted to one of confusion—again, obviously feigned.

"Immortality was the prize Zhengyi offered to the dragons," Entreri said. "The gem you took from the book—the second one, not the one from Herminicle's tower—would prove intriguing for our dragon friends, would it not?"

"Perhaps," the drow agreed. "Or perhaps they will find it revolting. Perhaps they will kill me if I even mention it, or if I reveal it but do not turn it over to them."

"Jarlaxle is nothing if not daring."

The drow shrugged and grinned. "Our dragon friends sent us to Vaasa to find just such a tome, and just such a phylactery. I am duty-bound to report to them in full."

"And to turn over the spoils?"

"The phylactery?" The drow scoffed. "I made no such agreement."

"They are dragons."

"And one is a fine lover. That changes nothing."

Entreri shuddered at the thought, which of course only made Jarlaxle smile all the wider.

"We were not sent to retrieve anything more than information, and so information I shall offer," said Jarlaxle. "Nothing less."

"And if they demand the phylactery?"

"It belongs to Urshula. I am simply holding it for him."

"And if they demand the phylactery?" Entreri asked again.

"They need not know—"

"They already know! They are dragons. They have lived in this region for centuries. They remember well the time of Zhengyi—perhaps they even fought beside him, or against him."

"Presumptions."

"They are dragons," Entreri said yet again. "Why do you not seem to understand that? You live through manipulation—never have I seen anyone better at playing the emotions of those around him. But these are *dragons*. They are not serving wenches or even human kings or queens. You play with a force you do not understand."

"I have played with greater, and won."

Entreri shook his head, certain then that they were doomed.

"Ever the worrier," said Jarlaxle. He had just hung his cloak on a hook, but took it back. "I will settle this, and calm your churning gut. Tazmikella and Ilnezhara are dragons—yes, my friend, I understand this—but they are *copper* dragons. Formidable in battle, of course, but not so much in the realm of the mind."

"You forget how they enlisted us in the first place," said Entreri.

Indeed, the dragon sisters had created an elaborate ruse to entwine the pair and to determine their intentions. Tazmikella had hired them, secretly and from afar, and when they had discovered the riddle of the woman—not that she was a dragon, but merely that she was the one who had hired them to acquire a certain candlestick—she had created a second ruse, claiming that Ilnezhara was her bitter and hated rival and that the woman was in possession of something that rightfully belonged to Tazmikella: Idalia's flute, the same magical instrument that had later been given to Entreri.

But the deception hadn't ended there, with a simple theft, for during that attempted robbery, Entreri and Jarlaxle had been shown the awful truth of Ilnezhara, revealed to them in her dragon form. Then she had wound a third level of intrigue, and yet another secret test, offering them their lives only on condition that they return to their former employer, Tazmikella, and kill her.

By any measure, even that of Entreri and Jarlaxle, the dragon sisters had played them for fools, and repeatedly.

Jarlaxle shrugged at the painful reminder and admitted, "A decent enough game they played, but one, no doubt, they had spent years perfecting. In Menzoberranzan, a ruse within a ruse within a ruse is an everyday affair, and usually spontaneously generated."

"And yet you were tripped up by theirs."

"Only because I did not expect—"

"You underestimated them."

"Because I believed them to be humans, of course, and it would be hard to underestimate a human."

"I am truly glad you feel that way."

Jarlaxle laughed. "I know they are dragons now."

"This woman you take as a lover," Entreri added dryly.

That gave Jarlaxle pause. "Because I love you as a brother, I pray that you will one day fathom the truth of it all, my friend."

"They're dragons," Entreri muttered. "And I know how drow love their brothers."

Jarlaxle sighed at his friend's unrelenting ignorance, then offered a salute embedded in a resigned sigh and slung his cloak over his shoulders. "I will return after sunset. Perhaps you would do well to run back to Vaasa and the castle and retrieve the statuette. And if you do, pray use the powers of white or blue. The fiery breath of a red dragon would not be wisely placed over our door—too much wood, of course."

⚬╪══╪⚬

The drow found his "employers" at Ilnezhara's tower. They always met there, rather than at the modest abode of Tazmikella. Perhaps that was an indication of Ilnezhara's haughtiness, her refusal to lower herself and venture to the hovel. Jarlaxle, of course, saw it a bit differently. Tazmikella's willingness to go to Ilnezhara's fabulous abode betrayed her true feelings, he believed. She pretended to care little for the niceties, but as with so many others who did likewise, it was a deception—a self-deception. So many people derided the materialistic tendencies of dragons, drow, humans, and dwarves . . . claiming that their own hearts were purer, their own designs more lofty and important, when in truth, they were merely deriding that which they believed they could not attain. Or if they could attain such things, they still used their "lofty" aspirations in the same manner the wealthy merchant used his gilded coach: to elevate themselves above other people.

That personal elevation was the true occupation of rational beings, even long-living creatures such as dragons.

"It was as we expected," Ilnezhara remarked after the initial greetings.

That it was she who had initiated the conversation and not the more typically forthcoming Tazmikella revealed the anxiety felt by both of the sisters.

"Your predictions that Zhengyi's library had been unearthed seem validated, yes," he answered. "You said there would be more constructs, and alas, that is what we found."

"One to dwarf Herminicle's tower," said Tazmikella, and the drow nodded.

"As a dragon might dwarf a human, in size and in strength," Ilnezhara added.

Jarlaxle didn't miss her point. The sisters knew that Zhengyi had enslaved dragons like Urshula the Black. They understood the magic that had created Herminicle's tower, and they had expected similar magic to reach to greater heights when fueled by a dragon.

So it was.

"The book was destroyed," Ilnezhara added.

"Unfortunately," said the drow.

"By Jarlaxle," the tall copper-haired creature said, and that put Jarlaxle back a step. "Or one like him," she quickly equivocated, "fast with the blade and with the spell."

Jarlaxle started to protest, but Tazmikella cut him short. "I went there," she said. "I ventured into the castle and found the podium in the main keep. I found the remnants of the book of creation, torn and burned."

Jarlaxle started to argue, then to deny, but he smiled instead, dipped a bow of congratulations to the deductive dragon, and said, "It had to be destroyed, of course."

"And the phylactery contained within?" asked Ilnezhara.

Jarlaxle's eyes shifted to take in the delicate creature, his lover, and his hand casually slipped near to the belt pouch on his right hip, wherein he kept a small orb that could blink him away from any threatening situation. Crushing that ceramic orb would throw him through the multiverse—to where, to which plane of existence even, he could not predict.

In that moment, he figured that there were few places in the multiverse more adverse than in the den of a pair of angry dragons.

"Zhengyi created many such phylacteries," Tazmikella explained. "He tempted every dragon in the Bloodstone Lands with his promises, we two included. Our guess is that the castle north of Palishchuk contained the phylactery of the dracolich Urshula the Black."

Jarlaxle shrugged. "The acidic breath of the creature we battled was consistent with that."

"And the dracolich was destroyed?"

"With help from the statuette you wisely gave to me."

"And the phylactery was removed," Ilnezhara said.

Jarlaxle held his free hand out to the side as if he did not understand.

"The phylactery that was embedded in the tome of creation, which was shredded by Jarlaxle, was, therefore, removed," the dragon clarified.

"By you," her sister added.

The drow stepped back and brought his hand away from his pouch and up to his chin. "And if what you say is true?" he asked.

"Then you possess something you do not understand," Ilnezhara replied. "You have made your way by playing your wits against those you encounter. Now you are playing with dragons—with dead dragons. That seems not a healthy course."

"Your concern is touching."

"This is no game, Jarlaxle," Tazmikella said. "Zhengyi wove a complicated web. His temptations were . . ." She looked to her sister.

"Potent," Ilnezhara finished for her. "Who would not wish immortality?"

"There are phylacteries for Tazmikella and Ilnezhara?" Jarlaxle asked, catching on to their anxiety, finally.

"We did not ally with Zhengyi," Ilnezhara stated.

"Not by the time of his demise," the drow replied. "I would guess that many of your kind refused the Witch-King, until . . ."

He let that hang in the air.

"Until?" Tazmikella's tone showed that she was in no mood for cryptic games.

"Until the moment of truth," Jarlaxle explained. "Until the moment when the choice between oblivion and lichdom was laid bare."

"You are a clever one," said Ilnezhara. "But not so if you think this a game to be manipulated."

"You demand the phylactery of Urshula the Black? You presume that I have it, and demand it of me?"

The sisters exchanged looks again. "We want you to understand that with which you play," Tazmikella said.

"We care nothing for Urshula, alive or dead," Ilnezhara added. "Never was he an ally, surely."

"You fear that I am unlocking Zhengyi's secrets," said the drow.

He paused for a moment, certain of his guess, and considered the fact that he was still alive. Obviously the sisters wanted something from him. He looked at Tazmikella, then over to his lover, and he realized that the dragons weren't going to kill him anytime soon. They knew he would come to a point of understanding—they *needed* him to come to a point of understanding—though it was a dangerous place for them.

"Zhengyi created phylacteries for you both," the drow said again, with more confidence. "He tempted you, and you refused him."

He paused, but neither dragon began to argue.

"But the phylacteries remain, and you want them," Jarlaxle reasoned.

"And we will kill anyone who happens upon them and does not turn them over immediately," Ilnezhara said with cold calm.

The drow considered the promise for a moment, and knew Ilnezhara well enough to realize that she was deadly serious.

"You would control your own destiny," he said.

"We will not allow another to control it," said Tazmikella. "A minor differentiation. The results will prove the same for any who hold the items."

"You sent me to Vaasa in the hope that I would learn that which I have learned," Jarlaxle reasoned. "You would have me find the rest of Zhengyi's still-hidden treasures, to return to you that which is rightfully yours."

They didn't disagree.

"And for me?"

"You get to tell others that you met two dragons and survived," said Ilnezhara.

Jarlaxle grinned, then laughed aloud. "Might I tell them of the more intimate encounters?"

The woman's return smile was genuine, and warm, and gave Jarlaxle great relief.

"And of Urshula the Black?" he dared ask after a few moments.

"We said we care nothing for that one, alive or dead," Ilnezhara replied. "But be warned and be wary, my black-skinned friend," she added, and she sidled up to the drow and stroked the back of her hand across his cheek. "King Gareth and his friends will not suffer a second Zhengyi. He is not one to underestimate."

Jarlaxle was nodding as she finished, but that disappeared in the blink of an eye as the dragon clamped her hand on the back of his cloak and shirt and effortlessly lifted him into the air, turning him as she did to face her directly.

"Nor would we suffer another tyrant," she warned. "I know that you do not underestimate me."

Hanging in the air as he was, feeling the sheer strength of the dragon as she held him aloft as easily as if he were made of feathers, the drow could only tip his great hat to her.

Entreri turned up the side of his collar as he walked past Piter's bakery, not wanting anyone inside to recognize him and pull him in. He and Jarlaxle had rescued the man from some highwaymen who had indentured him as their private cook. Then Jarlaxle, so typical for the drow, had set Piter up in Heliogabalus in his own shop. Ever was the drow playing angles, trying to squeeze something from nothing, which annoyed Entreri no end.

Piter was a fine baker—even Entreri could appreciate that—but the assassin simply wasn't in the mood for the perpetually smiling and overly appreciative chef.

He moved swiftly past the storefront and turned down the next side street, heading for one of the many taverns that graced that section of the crowded city. He chose a new location, the Boar's Snout, instead of the haunts he and Jarlaxle often frequented. As with smiling Piter, Entreri wasn't in the mood for making conversation with the annoying dregs, nor was he hoping that Jarlaxle would find him. The drow had gone off to see the dragon sisters, and Entreri was enjoying his time alone—finally alone.

He had a lot to think about.

He moved through the half-empty tavern—the night was young—and pulled up a chair at a table in the far corner, sitting as always with his back to the wall and in full view of the door.

The barkeep called out to him, asking his pleasure, and he returned with, "Honey mead."

Then he sat back and considered the road that had brought him to that place. By the time the serving wench appeared with his drink, he had Idalia's flute in his hands, rolling it over and over, feeling the smoothness of the wood.

"If ye're thinking to play for yer drink, then ye should be asking Griney over there," he heard the wench say. He looked up at the woman, who was barely more than a girl. "I ain't for making no choosings about barter." She placed the mead down before him. "A pair o' silver and three coppers," she explained.

Entreri considered her for a moment, her impertinent look, as if she expected an argument. He matched her expression with a sour one of his own and drew out three silvers. He slapped them into her hand and waved her away.

Then he slid his drink to the side, for he wasn't really thirsty, and went back to considering the flute and his last journey—truly one of the strangest adventures of his life. Entreri's trip to Vaasa had also been a journey inside himself, for the first time in more years than he could remember. Because of the magic contained in the flute—and he knew for certain that it was indeed the instrument that had facilitated his inward journey—he had opened himself to emotions long buried. He had seen beauty—in Ellery, in Arrayan, and in Calihye. He had felt attraction, mostly to Arrayan at first, and so strongly that it had led him to make mistakes, nearly getting him killed at the hands of that wretched creature Athrogate.

He had found compassion, and had done things for Arrayan's benefit, and for the benefit of her beloved Olgerkhan.

He had risked his life to save a brutish half-orc.

One hand still worked the flute, but Entreri brought his other up to rub his face. It occurred to him that he should shove this magical flute down Jarlaxle's throat, that he should use it to throttle the drow before its magic led him to his own demise.

But the flute had brought him to Calihye. He couldn't dismiss that. The magic of the flute had given him permission to love the half-elf, had brought him to a place where he never expected and never intended to be. And he enjoyed that place. He couldn't deny that.

But it is going to get me killed, he thought, and he nearly jumped out of his seat to see that a man sat at his table, across from him, waiting for him to look up.

No reminder that the flute was putting him off his normally keen guard could have been more clear to the assassin.

"I have allowed you to walk over unimpeded and unchallenged," Entreri bluffed, and looked back down at the flute. "State your business and be gone."

"Or you will leave me dead on the floor?" the man asked, and Entreri slowly lifted his eyes to lock his opponent's gaze.

He let his stare be his answer, the same look that so many in Calimport had experienced as the last thing they had ever seen.

The man squirmed just a bit, and Entreri could see that he was unsure if indeed he had been "allowed" to come over and sit down, and hadn't really caught Entreri by surprise as it had seemed.

"Knellict would take exception," the man whispered.

It took every bit of control Artemis Entreri could manage to not reach over the table and murder the man then and there, for even mentioning that cursed name.

"You put your threats away and you keep them away," the man went on, seeming to gain courage from the mention of the powerful archmage. He even shifted as if to point his finger Entreri's way, but Entreri's stare defeated that movement before it really got going. "I'm here for him, I am," the man said. "For Knellict. Ye thinking ye're in the mood for a fight with Knellict?"

Entreri just stared.

"Well? Ye got no answer for that, do ye?"

Entreri managed an amused grin at how badly the man was reading him.

The stranger sat up straighter and leaned forward, confidence growing. "Course ye got no answer," he said. "Ain't none wanting a fight with Knellict." Entreri nodded, his amusement growing as the fool's voice continued to mount in volume. "Not even King Gareth, himself!" the man ended, and he reached up and snapped his fingers before Entreri's face—or tried to, for the assassin, far quicker, grabbed the man by the wrist and slammed his hand down hard on the table, palm up.

Before the fool could begin to squirm, the assassin's other hand came up over the table, holding the jeweled dagger. Entreri flipped it and slammed it down hard, driving it into the wood of the table right between the fumbling fool's fingers.

"Raise your voice again, and I will cut out your tongue," Entreri assured him. "Your patron will appreciate that, I assure you. He might even offer me a bounty for taking the wagging tongue of an idiot."

The man was breathing so heavily, in such gasps, that Entreri half-expected him to faint onto the floor. Even when Entreri put his dagger away, the fool kept on panting.

"I believe that you have some information to relay," Entreri said after a long while.

"A-a job," the man stammered. "For yerself and just yerself, Apprentice Knight. There's a merchant, Beneghast, who's come afoul o' Knellict."

Entreri's thoughts began to spin. Had they arranged for him to attain a position of trust within the kingdom only to waste the gain for the sake of a simple merchant? However, the perceptive Entreri lost his surprise as the fool went on, clarifying the plan.

"Beneghast's got a highwayman laying in wait. Ye're to rush to Beneghast's rescue from our men."

"But of course I won't get there quite in time."

"Oh, ye're to get there soon enough to kill the merchant," the fool explained, and he grinned widely, showing a few rotten teeth in a mouth that was more discolored gum than tooth. "But we'll be blaming the thief."

"And I am the hero for apprehending the murderer," Entreri reasoned, for it was a ruse he had heard many times in his life.

"And ye just turn him over to the city guards, who'll come rushing yer way."

"Guards paid well, no doubt."

The man laughed.

Entreri nodded. He walked his thoughts through the too-familiar, and too-complicated scenario. Why not have the highwayman just kill the man and be done with it? Or have the guards "find" the body of Beneghast, right where they placed it after killing him?

Because it wasn't about Beneghast at all, Entreri understood. It wasn't payback for any wrong done Knellict. It was a test for Entreri, plain and simple. Knellict wanted to see if Entreri would kill, indiscriminately and without question, out of loyalty to the Citadel of Assassins.

How many times had Artemis Entreri facilitated something very much like this back in Calimport when he had served as Pasha Basadoni's principle assassin? How many new prospects had he similarly tested?

And how many had he killed for failing the test?

The fool sat there, wagging his head and showing that repulsive grin, and rather than dismissing him, Entreri stood and took his leave, shoving past and heading for the door.

"Wall's Around," the man called after him, referring to a section of the city the assassin knew well. Entreri could only shake his head at the courier's stupidity and lack of discretion.

The assassin couldn't get out of that tavern fast enough.

He headed down the street, pointedly away from Wall's Around at first. With every step, he considered the test, considered that Knellict would deign to test him at all.

With every step, he grew angrier.

CHAPTER

UNSHACKLED

5

To the outside world, even to Artemis Entreri, it was a simple bakery, the place where chef Piter worked his wonders. After the sun set over Heliogabalus, Piter and his workers went home and the doors were locked, not to be opened again until the pre-dawn hours each and every day.

Entreri likely understood that the place was a bit more than that, Jarlaxle realized. Its pretensions as a simple bakery served as a front, a token of legitimacy for Jarlaxle. How might Entreri react, the drow wondered, if he discovered that Piter's bakery was also a conduit to the Underdark?

It was after dark and the door was locked. Jarlaxle, of course, had a key. He walked past the storefront casually, his gaze sweeping the area and taking in his surroundings to be certain that no one was watching.

He walked past again a few moments later, after a second inspection of the area, and quietly entered and secured the portal behind him, both with his key and with a minor incantation. In the back room, the drow moved to the left-most of the three large ovens. He glanced over his shoulder one last time, then climbed almost completely into the oven. He reached up into the chimney, holding forth a small silver chime, and lightly tapped it against the brick.

Then he climbed back out and brushed the soot from his clothing—none of the soot was stubborn enough to cling to Jarlaxle's magical garb.

He waited patiently as the minutes slipped past, confident that his call had been heard. Finally, a form bubbled out of the oven's base, sliding effortlessly through the bricks. It grew and extended, seemed no more than a shadow, but gradually took on a humanoid shape.

Shadow became substance and Kimmuriel Oblodra, the psionicist who had been Jarlaxle's principle lieutenant in the mercenary band Bregan D'aerthe, blinked open his eyes.

"You keep me waiting," Jarlaxle remarked.

"You call at inconvenient times," Kimmuriel replied. "I have an organization to run."

Jarlaxle grinned and bowed in response. "And how fares Bregan D'aerthe, my old friend?"

535

"We thrive. Now that we have abandoned expansionist designs, that is. We are creatures of the Underdark, of Menzoberranzan, and there—"

"You thrive," Jarlaxle dryly finished. "Yes, I get the point."

"But it seems one that you stubbornly refuse to accept," Kimmuriel dared to argue. "You have not abandoned your designs for a kingdom in the World Above."

"A connection to greater treasures," Jarlaxle corrected, and Kimmuriel shrugged. "I will not repeat my errors perpetrated under the influence of Crenshinibon, but neither will I recoil from opportunity."

"Opportunity in the land of a paladin king?"

"Wherever it may be found."

Kimmuriel slowly shook his head.

"We are heroes of the crown, do you not know?" Jarlaxle said. "My companion is a knight of the Army of Bloodstone. Can a barony be far behind?"

"Underestimate Gareth and his friends at your peril," the psionicist warned. "I set spies to watch them from afar, as you instructed. They are not blind fools who accept your tales at face value. They have dispatched emissaries to Palishchuk and to the castle already, and they even now question their informants in Heliogabalus and in other cities, whose primary duties involve keeping track of the movements of the Citadel of Assassins."

"I would be disappointed if they were inept," Jarlaxle replied casually, as if it did not matter.

"I warn you, Jarlaxle. You will find Gareth and those adventurers who stand beside him to be the most formidable foes you have ever faced."

"I have faced the matron mothers of Menzoberranzan," the drow reminded him.

"Who were ever kept at bay by the edicts of Lady Lolth herself. Those matron mothers knew that they would displease the Spider Queen if they brought harm upon one she had so blessed as Jar—"

"I do not need you to recount my life's history to me."

"Do you not?"

The ever-confident Jarlaxle couldn't help but wince at that statement, for of course it was true. Jarlaxle had been blessed by the Spider Queen, had been ordained as one of her agents of tumult and chaos. Lady Lolth, the demon queen of chaos, had rejected Matron Baenre's sacrifice of her third-born son, as was drow tradition. Due to the work of one loyal to Lolth, Baenre's spider-shaped dagger had not penetrated the babe Jarlaxle's tender flesh, and when Lolth had magically granted Jarlaxle the memories of his infancy, of that fateful night in House Baenre, he had keenly felt his mother's desperation. How she had ground that spider-shaped dagger on his chest, terrified that the rejection of her sacrifice had portended doom for her supreme House.

"Matron Baenre learned centuries ago that her own fate was inextricably tied to that of Jarlaxle," Kimmuriel, one of only three living drow who knew the truth, went on. "Ever were her hands tied from retaliating against you, even on those many occasions she desperately wanted to cut out your heart."

"Lady Lolth spurned me long ago, my friend." Jarlaxle tried hard not to betray any emotions other than his typically flippant attitude, but it was difficult.

On his mother's orders, the failure of the sacrificial ceremony had been buried beneath a swath of lies. She had ordered him declared dead, then wrapped in a shroud of silk and thrown into the lake known as Donigarten, as was customary for sacrificed third sons.

"But Baenre never knew of your betrayal of the Spider Queen, and her rejection of you as her favored drow," said Kimmuriel. "To Matron Baenre, to her dying breath, you were the untouchable one, the one whose flesh her dagger could not penetrate. The blessed child who, as a mere infant, utterly and completely destroyed his older brother."

"Do you suggest that I should have told the witch?"

"Hardly. I only remind you in the context of your present state," Kimmuriel said, and he offered his former master a low and respectful bow.

"Baenre found me, and Bregan D'aerthe, to be a powerful and necessary ally."

"And so Bregan D'aerthe remains an ally to House Baenre, and Matron Mother Triel, under the guidance of Kimmuriel," the psionicist said.

Jarlaxle nodded. "Kimmuriel is no fool, which is why I entrusted Bregan D'aerthe to you during my . . . my journey."

"Your relationship with the matron mothers was not akin to the one you now seem determined to forge in the Bloodstone Lands," Kimmuriel stated. "King Gareth will not suffer such treachery."

"You presume I will offer him a choice."

"You presume that you will hold the upper hand. Your predecessor in this adventure, a Witch-King of tremendous power, learned the error of his ways."

"And perhaps I have learned from Zhengyi's failure."

"But have you learned from your own?" Kimmuriel dared to say, and for just a brief instant, Jarlaxle's red eyes flared with anger. "You nearly brought ruin to Bregan D'aerthe," Kimmuriel pressed anyway.

"I was under the influence of a mighty artifact. My vision was clouded."

"Clouded only because the Crystal Shard offered you that which you greatly desired. Is the phylactery you now hold in your pocket offering you any less?"

Jarlaxle took a step back, surprised by Kimmuriel's forwardness. He let his anger play out to a state of grudging acceptance—that was exactly why he had given Bregan D'aerthe over to Kimmuriel, after all. Jarlaxle had chosen a road of adventure and personal growth, one that could have proven disastrous for Bregan D'aerthe had he dragged them along. But with the possibilities he had found in Vaasa and Damara, was he, perhaps, dragging them right back into the path of ruin?

No, Jarlaxle realized as he considered his dark elf counterpart, the intelligent and independent psionicist who dared to speak to him so bluntly.

A smile grew upon his face as he looked over his friend. "There are possibilities here I cannot ignore," he said.

"Intriguing, I agree."

"But not enough to bring Bregan D'aerthe to my side should I need them," Jarlaxle reasoned.

"Not enough to risk Bregan D'aerthe. That was our agreement, was it not? Did you not install me as leader for the very purpose of building a wall between that which you created and that which you would gamble?"

Jarlaxle laughed aloud at the truth in that.

"I am wiser than I know," he said, and Kimmuriel would have laughed with him, if Kimmuriel ever laughed.

"But you will continue to monitor, of course," Jarlaxle said, and Kimmuriel nodded. "I have another duty for you."

"My network is stretched thin."

Jarlaxle shook his head. "Not for your spies, but for yourself. There is a woman, Calihye. She did not travel south with me and Entreri, though she is his lover."

"That one is not possessed of the frailties that would allow for such unreasonable emotions," Kimmuriel corrected. "She is his partner for physical release, perhaps, but it could be no more with Artemis Entreri. It is the one thing about the fool that I applaud."

"Perhaps that is the reason I find comfort around him. His demeanor reminds me of home."

Kimmuriel didn't react at all, and Jarlaxle figured the psionicist, so cunning regarding the larger issues of life but so oblivious about the little truths of existence, hadn't even realized the comparison of himself to Entreri.

"I see no incongruity between her actions and her professed intent," Jarlaxle explained, a code he had often used with his invasive lieutenant.

Kimmuriel bowed, showing his understanding.

"You will continue to monitor?" Jarlaxle asked.

"And to inform," Kimmuriel assured him. "I do not abandon you, Jarlaxle. Never that."

"Never?"

"To date," Kimmuriel said, and despite himself, he did chortle a bit.

"It could get very dangerous here," Jarlaxle finally admitted.

"You play dangerous games with dangerous enemies."

"If it comes to war, I am well-prepared," said Jarlaxle. "The armies of the nether world await my call, and Zhengyi left behind constructs that are continually self-protecting."

"You will claim the castle."

"I already have. I own he who owns it. The dracolich is mine to command. As I said, I am well prepared. Better prepared if Bregan D'aerthe offered support. Quietly, of course."

"If it escalates, I will watch and I will judge what is best for Bregan D'aerthe," said Kimmuriel.

Jarlaxle grinned and bowed. "You will offer me an escape, of course."

"I will watch and I will judge," the psionicist said again.

Jarlaxle had to accept that. His deal with Kimmuriel precipitated on the fulcrum of Kimmuriel's independence. Kimmuriel, and not Jarlaxle, ruled Bregan D'aerthe, and would continue to until Jarlaxle returned to Menzoberranzan and formally retrieved his throne. That was as they had agreed upon after the destruction of the Crystal Shard. Neither held any illusions about that agreement, of course. Jarlaxle knew that if he stayed away from his homeland for too long, allowing Kimmuriel to make inroads into the supportive relationships Jarlaxle had built within the City of Spiders, then Kimmuriel would not relinquish control of Bregan D'aerthe without a fight.

Jarlaxle also knew that calling upon Kimmuriel in times of desperation was a risky prospect indeed, for if Kimmuriel allowed him to fall, the psionicist would stand unopposed as leader of the profitable mercenary band. But Jarlaxle understood well the drow who served as his steward. Kimmuriel had never coveted power over other drow, as had Rai-guy or Berg'inyon Baenre, or any of the other notables in the band. Kimmuriel's designs dwelt in the realm of the intellect. He was a psionicist, a creature of thought and introspection. Kimmuriel preferred intellectual sparring with illithids to bargaining for position with the wretched matron mothers of Menzoberranzan. He would rather spend his day destroying brain moles or visiting the Astral abodes of githyanki than reporting his findings to Matron Mother Triel or maneuvering Bregan D'aerthe's warriors to capitalize on any dramatic events in the nearly constant intra-House warfare.

"You try to build here," Kimmuriel remarked even as he started into the chimney and his magical road back to the Underdark. "You grasp to create something on the World Above, yet no matter your success, it could not rival that which awaits you in Menzoberranzan. I try to understand you, Jarlaxle, but even my brilliance is no match for your unpredictability. What is it you seek here that does not already await you in our homeland?"

Freedom, Jarlaxle thought, but did not say.

Of course, Kimmuriel was a psionicist, and a powerful one indeed, so Jarlaxle never really had to "say" anything to him to get his point across.

Kimmuriel stared at him for a few moments, then slowly nodded. "There is no freedom," he finally said. "There is only survival."

When Jarlaxle didn't immediately respond, the steward of Bregan D'aerthe slipped into the chimney and melted into the stone.

Jarlaxle stood staring into the oven for a long while, fearing that Kimmuriel was right.

The roadway formed a wide circle inside the sharp right angle of Heliogabalus's wall, a cul-de-sac of mercantiles. Ilnezhara's shop was nearby, as was Tazmikella's. Dozens of chandlers, cobblers, blacksmiths, weavers, tailors, wheelwrights, importers, bakers, and other craftsmen and tradesmen of every imaginable stripe made Wall's Around their working home.

A large, three-tiered fountain centered the cul-de-sac, water dribbling from top to bottom without much energy, more of a continual rolling overflow. As he had envisioned it during his approach, Entreri had thought to use the fountain as his base, his vantage point to watch the scripted attack play out around him. But as he came through another alley to gain his third angle on the fountain, he realized that Knellict's hired highwayman had beaten him to it. The man was cleverly curled inside the second bowl, and only the uneven drip of the water had clued the assassin in to the fact that something was amiss.

He considered the highwayman's dark form and sensed patience and discipline—he was no novice.

With a nod, Entreri faded back into the shadows of the alley, grabbed a rail, and scaled the side of one shop, propelling himself to the roof. Low at the edge, he studied the fountain again, though he couldn't see the would-be assailant from that angle. Silent as a shadow, he slipped from roof to roof, circling the cul-de-sac, taking in a full view of the layout.

And noting two more figures lurking in the darkness under the porch of a darkened emporium.

The assassin froze in place then slipped lower on the roof, his gaze never leaving the two silhouettes. Those were Knellict's men, he knew, the wizard's insurance that nothing went amiss. Entreri couldn't make out many details, for they were well-concealed, but their lack of movement as the moments slipped past again spoke to him of discipline and training.

The easy course—to slay the merchant Beneghast and be on his way in Knellict's good graces—called out to him.

But Artemis Entreri had never been fond of the easy course.

The moment of truth, the time that Entreri had to ready himself one way or the other, slipped past, and the assassin transitioned into an almost unthinking, instinctual state. He had to move fast, back around the cul-de-sac, to put the fountain directly between himself and the two men under the porch. Roof to roof he went, fading back to the far side of each building, his body bending and twisting with each stride so that he seemed a part of the landscape and nothing more, and moving so silently that people in the buildings below his running feet wouldn't think that so much as a squirrel was skittering across their rooftops.

He came back down to the ground with equal grace, sliding flat at the eave, hooking his hand on the lip of the roof, and rolling over to extend himself fully before gently dropping to the alleyway.

He hesitated at the front corner of the building, for someone exited the door just a couple of steps to his left. That oblivious figure walked right past without taking any note of him, and continued on out of the cul-de-sac.

When a second figure appeared across the way and to his right, Entreri crouched a bit more. It was Beneghast.

The highwayman in the fountain would have noticed the merchant, as well, Entreri realized, and so he used that split second of distraction. He exploded into motion, running low and silently, then diving into a forward roll that brought him up against the lowest bowl of the fountain.

The man watched Beneghast's approach; the merchant would cross right by the fountain on the side opposite Entreri. The highwayman tried to find Entreri then, staying low and slowly swerving his head to take in as much of Wall's Around as possible, briefly locking his stare on this alleyway and that in search of the shadowy figure of the assassin he'd been told to expect.

Entreri quietly counted it out. He had already taken a measure of Beneghast's distance from the fountain, and could easily approximate the walking speed of the bent little man with a sack thrown over his shoulder.

The man in the fountain up above him was skilled, he reminded himself, and that meant that he would continue his scan for Entreri until the last possible second. But as Beneghast approached, the highwayman would have to shift his focus to the merchant.

That one moment, after the highwayman stopped his scan to look back at the target, yet before the highwayman actually found Beneghast again and moved to intercept, was Entreri's time.

He rolled up to a standing position, thin behind the stem of the fountain. He didn't allow Beneghast's approach to occupy a moment of his thought, but simply leaped up to the rim of that bottom bowl, a vertical jump of three feet. While his feet set quietly and surely on the slick, rounded rim, his left hand went out against the second bowl to secure his balance and his right hand, dagger drawn, struck hard and sure.

He felt the blade slide through the highwayman's ribs, and as soon as he noted the pressure of the initial contact, he came forward with it, releasing his grip on the second bowl and snapping his hand against the highwayman's head instead, driving him down below the water so that his cry became a burst of bubbles and nothing more.

Entreri felt the warmth of the man's blood rushing over his forearm, but the angle of the stab was all wrong for a quick in-the-heart kill. That mattered not at all to Entreri, though, for he summoned the vampiric powers of his dagger, drawing the highwayman's life-force into the magical blade, leaving him limp and lifeless in the bowl in a matter of a few heartbeats.

How convenient that the highwayman was wearing a mask, he thought, as he slipped the cloth free and quickly set it over his own face.

A short pause, a quick breath, and Entreri moved again, swiftly and grace-fully, barely making a splash in the bowl as he slipped up to the rim and sprang free, landing lightly in the street beyond the wider, lower level. Beneghast noted his approach, of course, but the assassin moved so fast that the poor merchant barely had the time to gasp.

Entreri was there with frightening speed, standing right before him, the tip of his dagger just below Beneghast's Adam's apple

He locked stares with the man, letting Beneghast see the intensity in his dark eyes, the promise of death. The merchant groaned and wobbled, as if his legs would simply give out beneath him—but of course, the dagger remained tight and held him upright. A slight grin appeared on Entreri's face, and he retracted the dagger just a bit.

"Oh, I am murdered!" the merchant squealed, and Entreri smiled wider and made no move to silence him. "Oh, fie, that my life should be taken by . . . by . . ."

"Ah, ah," Entreri warned, lifting one finger of his free hand up before Beneghast and wagging it back and forth.

The merchant fell silent, except for the short gasps of his breathing.

"Drop your sack behind you," Entreri instructed.

The satchel hit the ground.

Entreri paused, considering the two watching from under the porch. They were tense, he knew, on edge and ready to strike, and wondering where Entreri might be.

The assassin paced slowly around Beneghast, smoothly picking up the sack as he moved around behind the man. His eyes never left the merchant, but also, he looked past the man, noting movement behind the windows and open doors of several shops. A whistle in the distance told him that the city guard had been alerted. No doubt Knellict's paid stooges were fast approaching to arrest the murderous highwayman even then.

And no doubt, the two fools under the porch across the way were wringing their hands and cursing under their breath that Artemis Entreri had yet to make an appearance.

"If you want to live, you will do exactly as I instruct—and even then, I cannot guarantee that you will escape with your life," Entreri told Beneghast. The man yelped—or started to, before Entreri cut him short. "You have one chance. Do you understand?"

"Y-yes," the merchant stammered, nodding stupidly.

"A bit of discretion would go a long way toward keeping my dagger out of your heart," the assassin told him.

"Y-yes—yes—" Beneghast stammered, but then stopped and slapped a hand across his mouth.

"When I tell you to run, you will go straight ahead," Entreri explained. "Turn into the alley on this side of the emporium—do not pass the porch. Do you understand?"

The sound of shouting came to them, from down the straight road leading to Wall's Around.

"Run," said Entreri.

Beneghast leaped into motion, screaming and sprinting, stumbling like a fool and nearly falling onto his face. He veered out toward the center of the road and seemed as if in his panic he would run right past the porch—to his sudden demise, no doubt—but then he stumbled again at the last moment and came out of it running straight into the alley.

Whistles and shouts closed from behind, but Entreri didn't even glance that way. He watched the two forms rush out from under the porch, two men, one large, one small—or perhaps the small one was a woman. They both looked Entreri's way, to which he offered a simple shrug, then the large one charged down the alley behind Beneghast, while the smaller began gesturing as if casting a spell.

So intent was that one on the fleeing Beneghast, that she—for it was indeed a woman—never even noted Entreri's swift approach. Just as she was about to release her spell, a blade flashed down before her, trailing a line of magical ash that hung in the air, blocking her view.

"What—?" she gasped and fell back a step, turning to regard Entreri just as he pulled the mask down from his face.

"I just wanted you to see the truth," he said.

The woman's eyes popped open wide, and her jaw dropped.

Entreri stabbed her with his dagger—or tried to, for she had an enchantment about her that defeated the attack. It was as if he had struck the blade against solid stone.

The woman shrieked again and turned to flee, but Entreri smacked her with his sword, again to no avail, and kicked her trailing foot back over her leading ankle. She tripped up and fell flat, immediately rolling to her back and raising her hands defensively before her.

"Do not kill me!" she begged. "Please, I have wealth."

He hit her again, and again, and again. "How many will your shield stop?" he said as she thrashed helplessly below him.

Beneghast's cry echoed out of the alleyway.

Entreri kicked the female mage one more time, then leveled Charon's Claw at her, the magnificent red blade barely an inch from her wide eyes.

"Tell your master that I am not a pawn," he said.

The woman bobbed her head frantically, and Entreri nodded and ran off. He noted two guards passing the fountain in hot pursuit, but he outdistanced them, disappearing into the darkness of the alley. As he did, he threw the sack up to a roof and ran on. Past a pile of discarded boxes and a broken wagon, he came in sight of Beneghast, down against the wall and bleeding, one hand up before his face pitifully. Above him loomed the larger assassin from the porch, a warhammer raised for the kill.

Entreri's dagger flew down the alleyway, striking true in the side of the killer's chest. The man staggered a step but did not go down. He turned and offered a defensive stance, though he couldn't help but lurch to the side from the pain.

Charon's Claw in both hands, Entreri went in with sudden and overwhelming fury. He swiped across, right to left, and the murderer, no novice to battle, blocked and disengaged quickly enough to keep his hammer in front of him.

"You're mad," he gasped, intercepting an overhand chop.

Entreri noted how forcefully that hammer came up to parry, and was not surprised in the least when the man moved forward underneath the angle of Charon's Claw. Nor did Entreri try to prevent that movement, nor did he twist aside. He simply loosened his grip on Charon's Claw and went forward as well, coming against the big man, who tried to overpower him and bull rush him to the ground.

Except Artemis Entreri was much stronger than he looked, and also had his hand clamped around the hilt of the jeweled dagger. A slight twist stopped the momentum of the large man as surely as any stone wall ever could. The killer looked down at Entreri, his hammer falling free to clang to the ground beside the fallen Charon's Claw. A look of absolute horror crossed his face, a look that never failed to bring a grin to Artemis Entreri's lips.

Entreri twisted the dagger again. He could have drawn the man's life-force out, utterly destroying his soul, but he found a moment of mercy. Instead of utter annihilation, he settled for the simple kill.

Entreri eased the dying man to the ground, and picked up Charon's Claw as he did.

"You . . . he saved me," Beneghast said, and the change in pronoun clued Entreri in to the fact that they were not alone. He came up fast and spun, facing the two guards—men he knew to be in Knellict's employ.

The expressions on the faces of the two guards revealed their utter confusion. Entreri hadn't followed the script.

"Saved you?" Entreri scoffed at Beneghast. "No amount of your gold will make me follow you down your road of lies! Take this man," Entreri ordered the guards. "He murdered the merchant Beneghast and left him dead in the fountain. His companion lies dead here, by my own hand, and he has promised me riches if I feign ignorance of his murderous ways."

The guards exchanged confused looks and Entreri was certain that he could have knocked them both over if he merely blew upon them. To the side, Beneghast stuttered and stammered, spitting all over himself.

Entreri silenced him with a look, then reached down and grabbed him by the front of his tunic. As he roughly pulled the merchant to his feet, purposely bringing a concealing grunt from the man, he whispered into his ear, "If you wish to live, play along."

He stood straight and shoved Beneghast into the arms of the confused guards.

"Be quick and escort him away. There may be more murderers hiding in the shadows."

They didn't know what to do—that much remained plain on their faces. They finally turned and started away, Beneghast in tow. The merchant managed to look back at Entreri, who nodded and winked, then put a finger to his pursed lips.

Did the guards fall for the ruse, Entreri wondered? Did they know Beneghast and the Citadel of Assassins's killers? He had seen no recognition on their faces in the moment before he had made his choice.

And even if he was wrong, even if they knew the truth of Beneghast's identity and subsequently killed him, what did Artemis Entreri care?

He tried to tell himself that, over and over, but he found himself back up on the rooftops. He moved to retrieve the merchant's sack—no reason he shouldn't collect some reward for his good deed, after all—then slipped along the tops of the buildings, shadowing the movements of the guards and their prisoner. As he expected, the corrupted soldiers didn't stay out in the street, but turned down another alleyway, one that opened out the back end, where they and their "prisoner" could easily escape.

"Go on, then," Entreri heard one tell Beneghast.

"Knellict's not to like losing one of his men," the other remarked.

"Not our affair," the other said. "That merchant fellow is dead and this one's to leave. That's all we were told to do."

On the roof above them, Entreri smiled. He watched Beneghast stumble out the back side of the alleyway, running as if his life depended on it—for surely it did.

The two guards followed slowly, chatting amongst themselves. One of them produced a small bag and jiggled it to show that it was full of coins.

Entreri looked at the sack he carried, then glanced back at the pair. For the first time since he had entered Wall's Around, the assassin paused to consider the ramifications of his course. He knew that he had just bought himself and Jarlaxle a lot of trouble from a very dangerous enemy. He could have gone along with Knellict's orders so easily.

But that would have meant accepting his fate, admitting that he was reverting to the life he had lived in Calimport, when he had been no more than a killing tool for Pasha Basadoni and so many others.

"No," he whispered and shook his head. He wasn't going back to that life, not ever, whatever the cost. He looked at the departing guards again.

He shrugged.

He dropped the sack.

He jumped down between the guards, weapons drawn.

He left soon after, a sack over one shoulder, and a bag of coins tied to his belt.

CHAPTER

FRIGHTENED MICE, NERVOUS DRAGONS

6

The white cat dropped down from the windowsill and strode toward the disheveled merchant. Purring, the cat banged its head against Beneghast's leg.

"Ah, Mourtrue," the merchant said, sagging back against the wall and reaching down to pat his companion. "I thought I would never see you again. I thought I would never see anything again. Oh, but they were murderers, Mourtrue. Murderers, I say!"

"Do tell," the cat answered.

Beneghast froze in place, his words catching on the lump in his throat. He slowly lifted his hand away from the animal and shrank back against the wall.

Mourtrue began to grow.

"Please," the cat implored him, "do tell your tale. It is one that interests me greatly."

Beneghast gave a wail and flung himself aside—or tried to. A paw caught him and threw him back hard against the wall, the sharp claws shredding his good vest and overcoat in the process.

"I am not asking," the cat explained, grimacing as popping sounds erupted from all over its body. Bones broke and reformed, and skin stretched and twisted. The white fur shortened, became a bristly coat of fuzz, and disappeared.

Beneghast's knees went weak and he slumped to the floor. Knellict the wizard towered over him.

"You like cats," Knellict said. "That is a mark in your favor, for so do I."

"P-please, y-your magnificence," Beneghast stuttered, shaking his head so violently that his teeth chattered.

"You should be dead, of course."

"But . . ." Beneghast started, but he was too terrified to go on.

"But my men are dead instead," Knellict finished for him. "How is it that a foolish and flabby merchant could have done such a thing?"

"Oh, no, your magnificence!" Beneghast wailed. "Not that! Never! I struck no one. I did as I was told, and nothing more."

"You were told to kill my men?"

"No! Of course not, your superiorness. It was the masked man! Wicked with the blade, was he. He killed one in the alley that I saw. I know not of any oth—"

"The masked man?"

"The one with the red-bladed sword, and the dagger with the jeweled hilt. He caught me on the street and took my goods—your payment was in there. Oh please, your magnificence! I had your coin, and I wouldn't have been late but for the guards who came and took my gemstones. I tried to tell them that I needed the stones to—"

"You told city guards that you owed coin to Knellict?" the wizard interrupted, and his eyes flashed with the promise of death.

Beneghast got even smaller—Knellict didn't think that possible—and gave a strange squeaking sound.

"You killed my man in the fountain," Knellict accused, trying to break it down piece by piece to get a better sense of it all. Had his men provoked Entreri? Jailiana, who had survived, was just the type to have changed the plan, the impetuous little wench.

Beneghast shook his head violently. "There was no man in the fountain, except that the masked man came out of the fountain."

"The man with the red-bladed sword?"

"Yes," the merchant replied, bobbing his head.

"And that was when you were first accosted?"

"Yes."

Knellict pursed his lips. So, Entreri had betrayed him from the start.

"Please, magnificent sir," Beneghast whined. "I did nothing wrong."

"What of the two guards found at the other end of the alley?"

Beneghast's expression was all the answer Knellict needed, for the man obviously had no knowledge of that pair.

"You did nothing wrong?" Knellict asked. "Yet you were late in repayment."

"But . . . but . . ." Beneghast stammered, "but it's all here. All of it and more. And all for you."

"Get it."

The man moved fast, arms and legs flailing in all directions and ultimately doing little to get him out of the corner and off the floor. But then an invisible hand grabbed at him and hoisted him up, right off the ground.

"Where?" Knellict asked.

Hanging in midair, the terrified Beneghast lamely pointed at a dresser across the way. Knellict's telekinetic grip launched him that way, to crash into the drawers and crumble at the bureau's base. He only remained down for an instant, though, to his credit, and he yanked open a drawer so forcefully that it came right out of the dresser and fell at his feet. Clothes flew every which way and the merchant spun back, a large pouch in hand.

"All of it," he promised, "and more."

As Knellict reached out toward the merchant, a movement from the side caught both their attention. Into the room walked the real Mourtrue, looking exactly as Knellict had a moment before. The cat started for his master, but suddenly went up into the air, magically grasped, and flew fast to Knellict's waiting grasp.

"No!" the merchant wailed, lunging forward. "Please, not my Mourtrue."

"Commendable," said Knellict as he held and gently stroked the frightened cat. "You are loyal to your feline companion."

"Oh please, sir," said Beneghast, and he fell to his knees begging. "Anything but my Mourtrue."

"You love her?"

"As if she was my child."

"And does she return the love?"

"Oh yes, sir."

"Let us see, and if you are right, then I forgive your debt and your tardiness. In fact, if you have so garnered the loyalty of such a beautiful creature as this, I will return all of the coin in that purse tenfold."

Beneghast stared at him with confusion, not really knowing what to say.

"Fair?" Knellict asked.

Beneghast had no idea what to say, but he nodded despite himself.

Knellict began to cast a spell and Beneghast recoiled. It took some time for the wizard to complete the enchantment, finally waggling the fingers of one hand at the merchant, sending out waves of crackling energy.

Beneghast heard popping sounds—the sounds of his bones cracking and reshaping. The room got larger suddenly, impossibly huge, which confused poor Beneghast as much as did the fact that his breaking bones didn't really hurt.

He felt strange. His vision was black and white, and so many odors floated out at him they overwhelmed his sensibilities. He glanced left and right and saw white lines across his field of vision, as if he had . . . whiskers.

Mourtrue's growl turned his attention back to the wizard, who stood with gigantic, titanic even, proportions. In Knellict's arms, Mourtrue squirmed and twisted.

Beneghast started to question it all, but his voice came out as a chirp and nothing more.

Then he understood, and he glanced back to see his thin tail.

He was a mouse.

He snapped his gaze back to Knellict and Mourtrue.

"Shall we learn the depths of your cat's loyalty, then?" asked the smug mage.

He dropped Mourtrue to the floor, but it seemed to Beneghast as if the cat never even touched down, so graceful and fast was Mourtrue's leap.

"I guess not so deep," Knellict said.

Knellict left a short while later, the well-fed cat curled up against his shoulder, wondering what in the world he was going to do about this Artemis Entreri fellow.

Tazmikella knew who it was as soon as she saw the lean, late-middle-aged man walking slowly up the hill toward her front door. His threadbare and weather-beaten robes could have belonged to any of a thousand nomads who wandered the region, of course, but the walking stick, white as bone, belonged to one man alone.

A shudder coursed Tazmikella's spine and she couldn't help but wince at the sight of Master Kane. She hated the monk—irrationally so, she knew. She hated him because she feared him, and Tazmikella did not like "fearing" any human. But Kane was a monk, a grandmaster, and that meant that he could all too easily avoid the effects of her breath weapon, her greatest battle asset. Tazmikella didn't fear wizards, not even an archmage like Knellict. She didn't fear the paladin king, nor any of his heroic friends—not the ranger, priest, thief, or bard—save for one. The only humans—the only creatures of the lesser races, the drow included—who so unnerved the dragon were those strange ascetics who dedicated their lives to perfecting their bodies.

And Kane was no ordinary monk, even. In the martial sense, he was the greatest of the disciples in all the Bloodstone Lands and far beyond. So perfect was his understanding of and control over his body, that he could achieve a state of otherworldliness, it was said, where his physical form transcended its corporeal limitations to escape the very bonds of the Material Plane.

All of those rumors and whispers bounced about Tazmikella's thoughts as she watched the seemingly simple man's determined approach.

"Remember who you are," the dragon finally whispered to herself. She gave a quick shake of her head and her concerned look became a grimace.

"Master Kane," she said as the man neared her porch. "It has been far too long . . ." She meant to continue with an invitation for the monk to enter her home, but Kane didn't wait, walking right past her with only a slight nod of his head for acknowledgement.

Tazmikella paused at the door and didn't look back inside at the monk until she found the strength to wipe the sneer off her face. She reminded herself repeatedly that Kane was there at the request of King Gareth, no doubt.

"To what do I owe the honor of your presence?" she said, a bit too sweetly, as she turned and walked to her seat at the table opposite the monk. She noted his posture as she went, and that too only reminded her that the man was different. Kane did not sit with his feet on the floor, as others would. He had his legs folded tightly beneath him, feet under his buttocks, and with his back perfectly straight and balanced over the center of his form. He could move in a blink, Tazmikella realized, unfolding faster than any enemy, even a coiled snake, might strike.

"Your sister will join us presently," Kane replied.

"You expect Ilnezhara to arrive in a timely fashion?" Tazmikella asked, her tone light and sarcastic, and for effect, she rolled her eyes.

She might as well have rolled out of the chair and across the floor, for all the effect her humor had on Kane. He sat there, unblinking and unmoving. Not just unmoving, but utterly still, save the minor rise and fall of his breathing. The dragon paused, even shifted noisily a few times, leaning forward in anticipation, trying to prompt the monk to speak.

But he did not.

He just sat there.

Many moments slipped past, and he just sat there.

Tazmikella got up repeatedly and walked to the door, glancing out for any sign of her sister. Then she sat back down, offering both smiles and frowns. She asked a few questions—about the weather, about Vaasa, about King Gareth and Lady Christine, inquiring how they fared.

Kane just sat there.

Finally, after what felt like the whole of the morning to Tazmikella, but was in fact less than an hour, Ilnezhara arrived at the door. She came in and greeted her sister and the monk, who gave the slightest of nods in response.

"Do take care, good sister," Tazmikella dared to say, for she drew confidence with the arrival of a second dragon. "It would seem that my guest is not in good humor this morning."

"You were not at the ceremony honoring those returning from Vaasa," he said, addressing both.

"I did hear of that," Ilnezhara replied. "Those who investigated the latest Zhengyian construct, yes?"

Kane stared long and hard at her.

"Well of course, information travels slowly from Bloodstone Village to Heliogabalus, and we are not about to take wing."

"By order of King Gareth," Tazmikella added. "We would not wish to terrify half of Damara."

"Jarlaxle the drow and Artemis Entreri are known to you," Kane stated. "They were in your employ before their journey to Vaasa—a journey they took at your request, perhaps?"

"You presume much, Master Kane," said Ilnezhara.

"You deny little," Kane replied.

"We have had minor dealings with this drow and his friend," Tazmikella said. "You know our business. Who better to acquire goods than that pair?"

"You sent them to Vaasa," the monk said.

Ilnezhara scoffed, but Kane didn't blink, so Tazmikella remarked, "We suggested to Jarlaxle that his talents might serve him better in the wilderness, and that perhaps he would find adventure, reputation, and booty."

"There is an old saying that a dragon's suggestion is ever a demand," the monk remarked.

Tazmikella managed a weak grin, and looked to her sister. She noted the exchange of looks between Kane and Ilnezhara, bordering on threatening.

"We know Jarlaxle and Entreri," Tazmikella said bluntly. "They are not in our employ, but we have, on occasion, employed them. If you have come to question their bona fides, Master Kane, should you not have arrived before the ceremo—"

Kane stopped her with an upraised hand, a gesture that had the proud dragon fighting hard to suppress her anger.

"Your accommodations here are at the suffrage of King Gareth," Kane reminded her. "Never forget that. We are not enemies; we have welcomed both of you into the community of Bloodstone with open arms and trust."

"Your warning does not reek of trust, Grandmaster," said Ilnezhara.

"You repudiated Zhengyi's advances. That is not unnoticed."

"And now?" Ilnezhara prompted.

Kane unfolded suddenly, standing on the chair, and dipped a low bow. "I pray you understand that we are in dangerous times."

"You see the world from a human perspective," Ilnezhara cautioned. "You view disasters in the terms of years, at most, and not in terms of decades or centuries. It is understandable that you would utter such a silly statement."

Kane betrayed no anger at the statement as he sat again, but neither did he seem impressed. "The castle was no small matter, was perhaps the greatest manifestation of Zhengyi, curse his name, since his demise those years ago."

"Zhengyi himself was a small matter," Ilnezhara replied. "A temporary inconvenience and nothing more."

Even Tazmikella winced at the obvious and self-serving understatement. Both she and her sister had breathed much easier indeed when the Witch-King had fallen, and not since the time when Aspiraditus the red dragon and her three fiery offspring had flown into the mountains of western Damara four hundred years before had the dragon sisters been that concerned about anything.

"Perhaps we measure our catastrophes in the sense of tendays, or even years, good lady, because that is all we have," Kane countered. "Our time is short by your measures, but eternity by our own. I am not overly concerned about this latest Zhengyian construct, for it is dead now, and I am confident that whatever plagues the Witch-King left behind for us will be handled accordingly by Spysong and the Army of Bloodstone."

"And yet, you are here," reasoned Tazmikella.

"This is how we handle accordingly our catastrophes," Kane answered, and for the first time, a bit of emotion, a dry sarcasm, crept into his monotone voice.

"Then pray tell us of your catastrophe," Ilnezhara stated with a clear air of condescension.

Kane stared at her for a few moments but did not reply.

"Pray tell us why you have come to see us," Tazmikella intervened, guessing correctly that the monk wasn't willing to label the purpose of his visit as such.

"That this drow and human in your employ walked out of that castle, while King Gareth's niece, a knight of the order, did not, is worrying," the monk admitted. "That this drow and human walked out of that castle, while Mariabronne the Rover, a hero of the realm by all measures and a student of Olwen, did not, is worrying. I would be ill-serving my king and friend Gareth if I did not investigate the circumstances of his niece's death. And I would be ill-serving my friend Olwen if I did not investigate the circumstances of his student's death. It is no mystery why I have come."

The sisters looked at each other.

"Do you vouch for the character of the drow and human?" Kane asked.

"They have not disappointed us," Tazmikella said.

"Yet," added her sister.

Tazmikella looked from Ilnezhara to Kane, trying to judge the monk's response, but reading his emotions was like trying to find footprints on hard stone.

"We are not well acquainted with the pair, truth be told," Tazmikella offered.

"You were not responsible for importing them to Damara?"

"Certainly not," Tazmikella answered, and Ilnezhara echoed her words as she was speaking them. "We learned of them in Heliogabalus, and decided that we could put their talents to use. It is not so different from the methods of Spysong, and I am certain that if we had not hired the pair, your friend Celedon would have."

"They are talented at what they do," Ilnezhara added.

"Stealing?" asked Kane.

"Procurement," Tazmikella corrected.

Kane actually offered a bit of a smile at that equivocation. He snapped up to stand on the chair again, and dipped a low bow. Without another word, he turned and walked out of Tazmikella's house.

"Those two are going to get themselves killed," Tazmikella remarked when the monk was far away.

"At least," said her sister, with more concern than Tazmikella expected. She glanced over to see Ilnezhara staring at the open door and the back of the departing Kane.

Indeed, Tazmikella thought, few creatures in all the world could unnerve a dragon more than a grandmaster monk.

"You have heard about the fight at Great Fork Ford?" Ilnezhara said, obviously noticing Tazmikella's stare. "Two reds and a mighty white seemed about to rout one of Gareth's brigades."

"And Grandmaster Kane rushed in," Tazmikella continued. "He dared their breath, fire and frost, and avoided it all."

"And even deceived the dragons into breathing upon each other," Ilnezhara added.

"The white—Glacialamacus, it is rumored—was severely burned, and none know if she has survived her wounds. And both reds were wounded, by the frost and by the blows of Kane, followed by the charge of Gareth's warriors."

"It is all rumor, you know," Tazmikella remarked.

"Perhaps, but a plausible rumor, no doubt."

After a long pause, digesting the implications, Tazmikella added, "I grow weary of those two."

"Jarlaxle troubles me," Ilnezhara agreed.

"Troubles?"

"But he is a fine lover," Ilnezhara went on unabated. "Perhaps I should keep him close."

Tazmikella just rolled her eyes at that, hardly surprised.

From the outside, the black hole in the mountainside seemed like just another of the many caves that dotted the region of towering stones and steep facings of the high peaks of the Galenas, east of the Vaasan Gate. Anyone who entered that particular cave, though, would find it to be much more, full of comforts and treasures, inviting aromas and magically lit walkways.

Of course, anyone who entered it uninvited would likely find himself dead.

Chased from Heliogabalus after the fall of Zhengyi, Timoshenko, the Grandfather of Assassins, and his mighty advisor Knellict, had moved the band to their remote, well-defended location. Suites of rooms went far back into the mountain, some carved by hired stonemasons and miners, and many others created by Knellict's magic. Timoshenko's band lived in comfort and security, but were not too remote from their dealings in Damara, for Knellict and his mage companions had also created and maintained a series of magical portals to strategic locations within Gareth's kingdom.

Through one of those portals, Jailiana, the mage who had survived Entreri's betrayal at Wall's Around, had arrived back at the citadel, trembling with outrage.

She had delivered her report quickly, and had asked for support that she might go right back to Heliogabalus and slaughter the traitor. As angry as she was, however, Jailiana knew better than to act without the express permission of Knellict, and so when he had ordered her to stand down, she had quietly gone, sulking, to her chambers.

Knellict came out into the sunlight on the natural stone balcony of the cave, staring west along the northern foothills of the stony mountains. He still held Mourtrue, and had taken quite a liking to the purring cat, and was even considering creating a magical wizard-familiar bond with the animal.

It pleased Knellict to know that one of those who had tried to deceive him was making his way through this creature's intestines.

"Jailiana trembles with anger," came a voice behind him, one of his lieutenants, a dependable if unremarkable fellow named Coureese.

"I have a spell prepared that can cure that," Knellict absently replied. "Of course, it would freeze her solid in the process."

"She knows that she failed you," Coureese said.

"Failed?" Knellict turned, and Coureese looked at him, at the white cat, with obvious surprise. "She did not fail."

"She was to ensure the death of Beneghast."

"She was to witness the loyalty, or lack thereof, of Artemis Entreri," Knellict corrected. "She did not fail."

"But he got away, and two men were slain."

"Where can he run, I wonder? And we lose young recruits almost daily. There are always more to take their places, and if we did not lose so many, then how would we ever know which ones were worthy of our efforts to train them?"

Coureese's lips moved, but he didn't say anything, and Knellict smiled at the man's confusion.

"Perhaps I should go and tell Jailiana of your feelings," Coureese offered.

"Perhaps I should telekinese you over the cliff."

The man blanched and fell back a step.

"Let her stew in her anger," Knellict explained. "It is a fine motivator. And let us set an order of elimination on the head of dear Artemis Entreri. Perhaps our female friend would seek the coin."

"She would go after him for free," Coureese replied. "She would pay us for the opportunity."

"Well, that is her decision to make. She has seen this man at his craft. I would expect that a woman wise enough to dabble in the arcane ways would also be wise enough to recognize the difference between opportunity and suicide."

Coureese wagged his head for a few moments, digesting all of that. Finally, he asked, "The bounty?"

Knellict considered it for a moment, thinking it might be a good training exercise for the younger members, and a good way to truly measure the prowess of Artemis Entreri. "Fifty pieces of platinum," he replied.

Coureese licked his lips and nodded.

"Your thoughts?" Knellict prompted, seeing, and expecting, his discomfort. After all, a man of Entreri's reputation—even the little bit that was known in Damara, which was likely only a very minor piece of the intriguing killer's history—would normally bring a bounty of ten times that offering.

"Nothing, my lord Knellict. I will post the order of elimination." He bowed quickly and turned to leave. Before he reached the cave, however, the magical stone door slid out from its concealment at the side, sealing the entrance in a camouflaged manner that made it seem as if no cave existed there. Coureese spun back to face Knellict, for he knew that the archmage had closed that door with a minor spell.

"When I ask for your thoughts, you would do well to offer them," Knellict explained. "All of them."

"Your pardon, master," Coureese begged, bowing repeatedly and awkwardly. "I only . . ."

"Just speak them," the mage demanded.

"Fifty pieces of platinum?" Coureese blurted. "I had thought that I would try to collect this bounty myself, but to go after this Entreri—who walks beside a drow!—for such a price is not enticing."

"Because you are intelligent."

Coureese looked up at him.

"Only a fool would go after Artemis Entreri for this price, agreed. So let us see what fools we need to remove from our ranks. Or I should say, let us see what fools Entreri will eliminate for us. And in the process, perhaps he will leave a trail of bodies that King Gareth cannot ignore. We can only gain here."

"But Entreri will not likely be killed," Coureese dared to remark.

Knellict snorted as if that hardly mattered. "When I want him to die, he will die. Athrogate is close to him, do not forget, and the dwarf is loyal. Better to enrage Entreri—or should I call him 'Sir' Entreri?—and embarrass King Gareth. And perhaps one of those who seek him out will show unexpected promise and actually slay him. Or perhaps several will prove resourceful enough to work together to win the bounty."

Coureese began to nod, catching on to all the potential gains.

"Every so often, we must put such a test before our young recruits," Knellict explained and shrugged. "How else are we to know who is worthy and who should be dead?"

Coureese offered a final nod then, hearing the door magically sliding open behind him as Knellict simply waved a hand, he bowed and took his leave.

Knellict chuckled and stroked the purring Mourtrue. "Ah, cat, how am I ever to survive with such fools as that serving me? And he is one of the better ones of late!"

He went back to the ledge and stared out over southern Vaasa. He missed the days of glory when Zhengyi had occupied the troublesome Gareth and the Citadel of Assassins had thrived.

He hated living in a cave—even one magically furnished.

CHAPTER

SHADOWS

7

To a surface dweller, they were called shadows, patches of confusing darkness made all the harder to decipher because of the splotches of light beside them. But to Jarlaxle, who had spent centuries wandering the lightless abyss known as the Underdark, these "shadows" were really just dimmer areas of lightness. And so the drow had no trouble at all in discerning the man crouched beside a pile of debris in the alleyway beside the building where he and Entreri shared their second-story apartment. So painfully obvious was the fool that Jarlaxle had to work hard to keep from giggling at him as he walked past the alleyway to the wooden staircase that would take him to the outer door of his apartment.

At the foot of those stairs, the drow casually glanced all about. Sure enough, he spotted a second man, slipping along the rooftop of an adjoining building.

"What have you done, Artemis?" Jarlaxle whispered under his breath.

He started up the stairs, but stopped short and turned around, acting very much as if he had forgotten something. He even went so far in his deception as to snap his fingers in the air before starting off quickly back the way he had come. They were all watching him, he knew, and there were likely more than two.

But how could they question his decision to enter Piter's Bakery, given the sweet, sweet aroma emanating from its open door?

❈━❈

The drow's turnabout might have fooled the would-be ambushers, but it revealed much more to Artemis Entreri, who watched from his apartment, from the corner of the small window overlooking the street. He understood the significance of Jarlaxle's somewhat exaggerated movements: the finger snap and the feigned expression of forgetfulness.

Agents of the Citadel of Assassins were nearby, no doubt, and Jarlaxle had spied them.

After waiting a bit longer to see if anyone followed Jarlaxle's detour to Piter's shop—and no one did—the assassin moved back into the center of the room and considered his course. He was most certainly outnumbered, and the first rule when so outmanned was to never allow oneself to be cornered. He moved swiftly to the door, drew his sword and dagger, and kicked it open. He went through in a rush, speaking the command password, "White," so that the magic of his trap didn't kill him where he stood.

As he went under the arch of the door, he jumped up and hooked his dagger inside the looped silver chain that held a small statuette of a dragon rampant, its eyes shining like white moonstones. A flick of his wrist had the dragon safely dangling on the blade of his dagger, a second fluid twist dropped the figurine safely away in a pouch, and a third, executed with such precision and speed that it all seemed as one swipe, replaced the dagger in its scabbard with the fine chain from the statuette still looped around it.

Three running steps took Entreri down the hall, to the outer door, the balcony, then the stairway to the street. He thought to pause and inspect whether his uninvited guests had placed any traps on the door, but suspecting that he didn't have that much time, he just lowered his shoulder and crashed through. On the balcony, he cut fast to the left, to the stairs, and he started down—one, two, three strides. There, still more than halfway up, he slipped over the waist-high railing, catching it with his free hand, sliding down its angled decline for a moment, then dropping to the ground. He rolled as he landed to absorb the shock, and came back to his feet already into his run. As he ran across the street, he could feel the eyes of archers upon him.

A small two-wheeled cart of fruit had been placed across from Entreri's stair. The jovial vendor and his teenage son chatted easily with a young couple who were inspecting the wares—a scene very typical for the streets of Heliogabalus.

Or not so, Entreri realized as he approached, for he noted that the foursome were not fast to react to his sudden and unexpected appearance and his obvious urgency—or even to the fact that he held a red-bladed, fabulously designed sword in one hand. He locked stares with the bearded vendor, just for a moment, but that was enough for him to see a flicker of recognition in the man's dark eyes. Not the recognition of a common vendor who might have seen him pass by a dozen times, but the look of a man who had found what he was seeking.

Entreri broke into a charge just as he heard the click of a crossbow releasing from somewhere to the side—and he heard the bolt hum through the air right behind him. He drew his dagger back out as he went, but again kept the blade carefully tipped so that it did not allow the silver chain to slide off as he pulled the statuette free of the pouch.

The young couple next to the cart threw off their peasant cloaks and spun around, weapons at the ready, but Entreri charged through with a quick back-and-forth slash of his sword that had them both falling aside in opposite directions.

A leap brought Entreri to the edge of the cart. A second spring brought him past the "vendor" and the younger man, sailing through the entryway to the alley. Up snapped Entreri's dagger arm as he crossed just under a trellis beam that joined the buildings. He set his dagger into the wooden beam, the dragon statuette bouncing beneath it. He hit the ground in more of a dive than a run, for he understood how little time he had, how close came the pursuit.

And those pursuers, he knew, wouldn't utter the password, wouldn't properly identify the dragon.

He was still rolling and scrambling—anything to move down the alleyway—when the trap went off right behind him and he felt a blast of frost that chilled him to the bone and left a red burn on his trailing ankle. He tried to stand, but his leg had gone numb, and he quickly found himself face down on the cobblestones. He thrashed and rolled, sword slashing across, for he was certain that another of the killers would be fast upon him.

⊰═══⊱

Pie in hand, Jarlaxle leaned casually on Piter's counter and watched the couple, a man and his petite and pretty lover, come through the door. They looked into each other's eyes, giggling all the while.

Jarlaxle knew a put-on when he saw one.

"Ah, young love!" he cried dramatically. "Good Piter, I will gladly pay for their sweets."

The two looked at Jarlaxle, expressions correctly confused. He tossed the pie to the man, but up high. When the man went to catch it, the movement lifted up the hem of his waistcoat, revealing a pair of well-worn dagger handles.

The second pie Jarlaxle threw came in harder, and was not meant to be caught—except by the man's surprised expression.

"What?" the woman yelled as the pie splattered across her lover's face, and he gave a yell, as well, but one of pain.

"Jarlaxle, what are you about?" Piter demanded.

"I am killed!" the surprised man cried. He slapped at his face, sending cream flying and eventually revealing a small dart that had been concealed within the pie, protruding from his cheek. He reached for it, hands trembling, but he couldn't quite seem to grasp it.

Beside him, the young girl screamed and cried.

Jarlaxle had his arms bent, hands by his shoulders, ready to thrust them down and call forth a pair of blades from the magical bracers set on his wrists. He could summon daggers with a thought, then elongate the magical weapons into long swords with a snap of his arms.

But he didn't, because at least the girl's reaction was all wrong. The man, predictably, slumped down to the floor, his eyes rolling back into his skull, froth spilling from his slack jaw.

"Jarlaxle!" Piter cried, scrambling out beside his investor. "What have you done? Oh, Clairelle! Oh, Mischa!"

Jarlaxle cleared his throat as Piter wobbled his way to help Clairelle support the limp form of her lover.

"You know them?" the drow asked.

A troubled Piter looked back at him. "This is Maringay's daughter and her husband-to-be! They live right next to you. They are to be wed in the spring, and I am . . . I was to bake . . . oh, what have you done?"

"I have put him to sleep, and nothing more," Jarlaxle explained as he moved past the trio to the door. "Keep them inside, for there are killers about."

Clairelle slapped at him, then grabbed his pant leg as he moved past.

"It was for his own good," the embarrassed drow lied. "Your gallant lover would wish to play the role of hero, no doubt, and now is not the time. Lock your door, Piter, and keep all inside. On pain of death, do not go out!"

Jarlaxle tugged his leg away, spent the time to tip his hat at the distressed young lady, then quickly took his leave. He burst onto the street, suddenly doubting all that he had seen and inferred.

But he heard the tumult a bit farther down, across from his apartment. A man staggered out of the alleyway, white—frosted—from head to toe and walking awkwardly, stiffly. He crashed into the fruit cart, and the jolt sent a pile of apples spilling onto the street.

Apples frozen so solid that some of them shattered like glass when they hit the cobblestones.

"Entreri," the drow whispered.

He slipped a ring onto his finger and clenched his fist, releasing its magic. Up he jumped, a dozen feet and more, to land lightly on the roof of Piter's shop, where he fast melted from sight.

Entreri staggered down to the end of the alley, which was blocked by a wall and fronted by a pile of broken crates and some old wooden furniture. He had thought to use the pile to go over the wall and sprint out across the street parallel to his own, but his legs were barely working, one of them shifting from complete numbness to a pervasive, burning pain. He looked back to see the phony vendor and his "son" lying very still on the ground, covered in frost. A third killer, one of the pair who had feigned shopping at the cart, leaned up against the alley wall, seeming frozen in place, eyes open and unseeing, eyelashes white with ice. His companion staggered back out in the street behind him then tripped over the partially frozen fruit cart and tumbled hard to the cobblestones where he lay shivering and helpless, likely dying.

But more were coming, Entreri realized as a pair of forms darted left to right across his field of vision, on the other side of the street.

Entreri knew that he was in trouble. He used the pile of debris to pull himself up, and he tried to walk, but his numb foot flopped forward and he tripped over his own toes. He kept his balance, though, and did not fall down. Instead he used the stumble to propel himself back behind some of the crates, turning as he went.

A dark form slipped in around the left-hand corner of the alley exit, hugging the wall and using it for support as he inched down across the icy surface. A second killer came in a bit faster, and skidded across the ice. When his feet hit dry ground, he jolted forward several steps.

Had his legs been capable, Entreri would have leaped out to intercept, laying the overbalanced fool low before he ever came out of that bent-over stumble.

But his legs were not capable, and and he could hardly stand, let alone move to attack.

The man regained his balance and straightened to face the assassin, a gleaming long sword in one hand, a small buckler strapped to his other arm. He stayed out of reach and remained in a defensive crouch, glancing back repeatedly at his slowly approaching companion.

"Hurry it on, then," he whispered harshly. "We got the rat cornered."

"The rat that spews like a dragon of white," the other replied.

"Yes, come and freeze," Entreri bluffed.

He angled himself so that he did not appear as if he was leaning quite so heavily on the wall, but in truth, had it not been for that solid barrier behind him, Entreri would have toppled over. He brought his impressive sword out in front of him, waving the red blade tantalizingly.

The nearer man straightened a bit and took a step away.

"It was a trap set in the alley, and nothing he's got to play again," the man closer to Entreri deduced, calling the assassin's bluff.

"As you wish," Entreri said with an evil little chuckle, and he waved the blade in invitation.

He held his sigh of relief when the man backed another half a step, for he felt the tell-tale tingling in his legs to indicate that the feeling was beginning to return, that his blood flowed once more. It took all of his training to hold back his grimace in the next few moments, but he knew that he couldn't let on how weak he still was.

If they attacked boldly, he was dead.

"Knellict sent you, of course," Entreri said. "He promised me that he would utilize me as a trainer, though he may decide, after the six of you lie dead, that I take my task far too seriously."

The two men exchanged nervous looks. More importantly to Entreri, they held their ground and did not advance.

But then one of them, the second who had come in, straightened and relaxed, and began to laugh a bit. "He thinks there's but six of us," he said, and he slapped his friend on the shoulder, and that fool, too, began to giggle stupidly.

Entreri got the meaning, and he lamented that he would die in such a way—struck from above, no doubt, and without any means to defend himself from that quarter.

Despite his speed, despite his stealth, despite the uneven grades and facings of the various rooftops, Jarlaxle kept his bearings. He knew exactly where he was at all times, and when he saw the two men standing overlooking one alleyway, one hunched over and with crossbow in hand, aiming down, he could well imagine the target.

The drow's hand came up fast and steady from under his cloak, holding a favored weapon of his race, a hand crossbow. He let fly and watched with satisfaction as the archer twitched from the sting of the tiny bolt. The other man looked at the archer in surprise, but the crossbowman couldn't answer, for he was already swaying from the sleep poison, leaning forward, sure to tumble.

The other man grabbed at him.

Jarlaxle reached into himself, summoning forth his innate dark elven magic in the form of a globe of absolute darkness that covered both would-be killers.

Jarlaxle heard the shuffling, the grunt, and the shout. He was quite pleased, but hardly surprised when he saw the movement over the lip of the ledge, just below his stationary globe, as the archer pitched forward, taking his grabbing companion with him.

"Entreri, what have you done?" Jarlaxle whispered.

The drow faded into the shadows of the jumble of jagged, multi-pitched rooftops, looking for a way to get a safe view of the alley below.

◆━━━◆

Entreri reacted on instinct when he caught movement out of the corner of his eye. He threw himself across to the opposite side of the narrow alleyway. He took care to stay on balance, though, for the pair of ruffians advanced. Apparently emboldened by the arrival of their reinforcement, they charged.

Entreri started forward, sword leading, in a sudden rush. The newcomers crashed down beside him. He pulled up short, though, for his attack was no more than a feint, an attempt to buy time so that he could take care of the newest threat. Had he been a lesser fighter, a desperate charge would have been the only course, an attempt to burst through the pair and run off.

But Entreri wasn't about to flee any fight.

He nearly fell over when he stopped so abruptly, though, for the feeling had not yet fully returned to one leg. Still, he covered the stumble, falling against the wall of the alley, and bouncing back to center balance.

He spun around, and nearly froze in confusion when he noted the tangle of the two newcomers, who had crashed through some of the debris. One lay perfectly still and limp and the other squirmed in pain, grabbing at his wrist, ankle, and knee alternately, having done serious damage to all three. Entreri understood a moment later, when he glanced up from where they had come, to see a globe of enchanted blackness hovering in the air.

Jarlaxle.

With the other pair coming on fast, Entreri leaped at the reinforcements and stabbed hard, driving Charon's Claw right through the top, unconscious man and into the fellow below him. The first made no sound, as though he was already dead, but the bottom man screamed and thrashed.

Entreri had no time to finish him off. He yanked Charon's Claw free, a gush of blood following its retraction, and spun around. His blade crossed just in time to bat aside a thrusting sword then force the other man's dagger arm up and out. The assassin pressed his advantage, shuffling ahead and stabbing repeatedly, not in any real hope of scoring a hit on his skilled opponents, but more to drive them back and give him some room to maneuver—and to react in case the man on the bottom of the pile had any fight left in him.

He turned his back foot perpendicular to both enemies and to his front foot. He brought it forward and tapped his heel, then planted and stepped ahead. Then again and again, quick-stepping in perfect balance and driving the two killers back. He still couldn't feel one foot, but his every plant was solid and certain, and bolstered by the coordination of foot against foot, using the leg he could feel to guide the leg he couldn't.

559

Finally, and just before they hit the still-slick area where the white dragon's breath had struck, the pair managed to coordinate a counter stance. They moved wider apart, each turning slightly to better their angles of attack.

Entreri recognized that his momentum had played out. He fell back in a defensive crouch, legs wide and balanced, though one remained a bit stiff and more immobile than he let on.

"Ah, but he killed Wyrt!" cried the knave on the right, the one with the sword.

"Shut your mouth, fool!" his companion snapped at him.

"You'll meet him again, and soon," Entreri promised. He wasn't fond of speaking to his opponents in battle, but he had to buy time. His leg tingled and burned, and it was all he could do to hide his winces.

The man with the dagger lunged, and Entreri slapped Charon's Claw out to intercept. The man was fast, though, and he retracted his arm inside the reach of the sword, and came ahead with a cunning second strike.

He didn't understand.

For even on one leg, even distracted by the pain and the numbness and off balance, Entreri easily brought his blade back in—indeed, it moved to such a position even as his opponent began to pull the dagger back.

And Entreri knew that feint wasn't all of it.

To the side came the other man, sword thrusting, but Charon's Claw slashed across smoothly, slapping the blade and driving him back.

Entreri brought all his weight over his numb left leg. He had to trust it, and he locked it in place, pivoting his right leg back with the coming of the anticipated second dagger thrust.

The knife came in short, its tip just brushing his backing hip.

To the attacker's credit, the man recognized his miss quickly enough to leap backward from any coming counter.

That, too, Entreri anticipated, and instead of pursuing, he brought Charon's Claw back across the other again. Calling forth the magic of the sword, he hung a line of opaque ash in the air to shield himself from the swordsman's sight.

He knew the man would instinctively straighten before he managed to shuffle his feet back. In that instant, Entreri dropped to one knee and slashed his sword across under the wall of ash.

The assassin felt the impact, then the tug of ligament and bone resisting the cruel cut, and the swordsman howled in agony.

Entreri came up in a complete spin, around left to right, that left him squared up to the man with the dagger. A crash to the side told him that the swordsman had fallen back hard, and was out of the fight for a little while at least.

Entreri instinctively brought his sword across to block, and sure enough, the dagger flew at him, clanging harmlessly off of Charon's Claw's blood-red—and bloody—blade.

The killer drew another dagger.

Entreri grinned.

The man turned and ran, howling for mercy with every step. He only got a couple of strides before he hit the ice and went sprawling to the ground. Crying, screaming, and scrambling, he continued away as if expecting the killing blow to fall at any moment. He finally got back to dry ground, and went flailing down the street.

Entreri just stood there, amused.

A sharp cry from behind, followed by a gurgle, had him turning around. There stood Jarlaxle, wiping the blood from a dagger, having finished off the bottom man.

The drow looked at Entreri for a long while, silently asking him what it was all about. Entreri just returned the stare, offering nothing. Finally, Jarlaxle looked away, just a bit.

"Oh lovely," the dark elf said.

Entreri followed the drow's gaze to the side, where the ash wall began to drift apart. There, right where the man had been standing, remained both of his feet, severed at the ankles. The rest was back from there, slumped against the wall, bloody hands in the air, trembling. He didn't even try to stem the flow any longer.

Jarlaxle walked up to him and looked him over. "You are bleeding to death," he calmly explained. "It will be slow, but no more painful than that which you experience now. You will get cold, however, and do not panic when the world goes dark before your eyes."

The man whimpered, shaking his head, hands up, pleading.

"Perhaps if you are willing to divulge . . ." Jarlaxle started, and the man wagged his head furiously—or started to, until Entreri stepped up beside his friend and plunged Charon's Claw into the fool's heart.

Entreri pulled the sword free, glanced at Jarlaxle only briefly, and offered nothing more as he started out of the alleyway to retrieve his dagger and the dragon statuette.

"You seek no answers because you know them already, I must presume," Jarlaxle said.

Entreri kept walking, and fortunately, the feeling in his leg had returned enough for him to manage his balance across the slick surface of the frozen alleyway.

CHAPTER

TO SLEEP WITH DRAGONS

8

"B wahaha, ye just keep the drink flowing," Athrogate howled.

He hoisted his foamy mug and gulped it down in one swallow—at least the contents of it that didn't pour all over his braided black beard. He dropped the mug back on the table and drew his sleeve across his beard, taking only a bit of the foam from the frothy mess.

Jarlaxle started to slide the next mug of ale across the table. "I know they were Knellict's men," he said, holding the ale just out of Athrogate's reach. "Else, he has a rival band operating right in Heliogabalus."

"Goblin snot. Any rival band'd be lying dead in a day's time," the dwarf blustered, and gave an exaggerated wink.

Jarlaxle slid the ale the rest of the way, and the mug never even stopped in its slide before it went up into the air and overturned into the dwarf's mouth.

"Bwahaha!" Athrogate howled as he slammed it back down, gave an enormous belch, and slapped his arm across his mouth yet again. As he moved to retract his arm, he noted that the cuff of his sleeve was sopping wet, so he put it in his mouth and sucked the ale out of the fabric.

Jarlaxle shook his head, looked at the lines of empty mugs covering more than half the large tavern table, and nodded to the serving girl who watched him from the bar. He'd known he'd have to get Athrogate drunk to get his tongue wagging, of course, but he hadn't quite realized how expensive a proposition that might be.

"Shall I order more?" he asked, and the dwarf howled at the absurdity of the question.

Jarlaxle chuckled and held up his open hand, indicating five more of the large mugs, then saluted the nodding serving girl with a tip of his wine glass—the only drink he had imbibed while Athrogate had gone through a dozen ales.

"So it was Knellict, and the target was Artemis Entreri," Jarlaxle remarked.

"Never said it was Knellict," Athrogate corrected, and he belched again.

"A rival within the Citadel of Assassins?"

"Never said it weren't Knellict," Athrogate added with an even louder burp.

The waitress began placing the full mugs on the table then, so Jarlaxle paused and offered a disarming smile. She cleared her tray and began scooping some of the empties, and the drow dropped a pair of shiny gold coins on the platter beside them, drawing a wide smile from her.

"Then say," he said to the dwarf as soon as the girl had gone. The drow kept his hand tight on a mug, holding it hostage.

"Entreri got himself a job to kill a merchant," Athrogate said, then he paused to stare at the mug. After a moment, Jarlaxle slid the ale over, and Athrogate wasted no time studying it.

"Knellict believes that Entreri kept the spoils from that job?" Jarlaxle reasoned. "He would have no reason. We are still fat on the bounties collected in Vaasa, and as a knight of the order, coin is hardly Artemis Entreri's concern."

"*Bwahaha,* knight of the order!" the dwarf howled.

"Apprentice knight, then."

"*Bwahaha!*"

"He would have no incentive to keep the booty from the slain merchant," Jarlaxle said.

"Weren't no slain merchant, so I'm hearing," Athrogate replied. He motioned to another mug. Jarlaxle slid one to his waiting grasp, but he didn't flip it right up to his mouth. "Not until Knellict caught up to the merchant, at least. Seems yer friend got his identities all crossed."

"He killed the wrong merchant?"

"He killed a couple o' Knellict's men, sent to watch his work." Athrogate finished by emptying the mug then offering a resounding belch.

Jarlaxle sat back, letting it all digest. What have you done, Artemis? he thought, but did not ask aloud. Certainly his companion, as professional and fine an assassin as had ever walked the streets of Heliogabalus or any other city, could not have made such a grievous error as that.

So it was no error on Entreri's part. It was a statement. Of what? Independence? Stupidity?

"Tell me, Athrogate," Jarlaxle quietly and calmly asked, "is the bounty offered for Entreri enough to entice those morningstars from your back?"

"*Bwahaha!*" howled the dwarf.

"Is that why you have returned to Heliogabalus, instead of taking the road to Vaasa?"

"Winter's coming, ye dolt. Got no thoughts o' riding out Vaasan blizzards. Work through the summer, drink through the winter—now there's a formula for dwarven success."

"But if some easy work is to be found in Heliogabalus . . ." Jarlaxle teased. "An unexpected windfall, perhaps."

"For yer Entreri? *Bwahaha!* Would hardly cover the drink ye bought me here and now."

Jarlaxle slid another mug across as he furrowed his brow in confusion. "Knellict underestimates—"

"He wouldn't give yer friend the respect of a decent bounty," the dwarf explained. "He's knowin' that many'd take up the hunt for Entreri, on the gain to their reputation alone. To kill a hero knight? Now there's a feather to rival that thing you keep in yer stupid hat!"

"For an upstart, perhaps," the drow reasoned.

"Or as an insult. Whatever."

"But when Knellict realizes his error, and runs out of upstarts, he will reconsider the remuneration."

"I'd be agreeing, or not, if I knew what in a pig's nose ye was talking about," said Athrogate. "Remuner-what?"

"The payment," Jarlaxle explained. "When all those who try for Entreri are slain, Knellict will recognize the truth of this enemy and will offer a larger reward."

"Or he'll kill yer friend himself—course, I still ain't telling ye it's Knellict at all, now am I?"

"No, of course not."

Athrogate howled, belched, and downed another mugful.

"And if the reward goes higher, might Athrogate be tempted to try?"

"Meself don't ever *try*, black skin. I do or I don't."

"And would you 'do'? If the price were right?"

"No more or less than yerself'd do it."

Jarlaxle started to reply, and sharply, but he recognized that he couldn't honestly disagree with the proposition, though of course the reward would have to be exceedingly high.

"I like yer friend," Athrogate admitted. "Nine Hells, I like ye both."

"But you like gold more."

Athrogate lifted the next mug up high before him in salute. "I'm liking what coin buys me. Got meself one life for living. Could be over next tenday, or in three hunnerd years. Either case, I'm thinking the more time I'm spending drunk and fat, the better a life I'm living. And don't ye never doubt me, black skin, the better life I'm living is th'only thing what's really mattering."

It was a philosophy that Jarlaxle found hard to contradict. He motioned to the waitress again, indicating that she should keep the drink coming, then he fished out some more gold coins and dropped them on the table.

"I like you as well, good dwarf," he said as he rose from his seat. "And so I tell you in all seriousness, whatever bounty Knellict—yes, yes, if it is Knellict," he added, seeing Athrogate about to interject. "Whatever bounty you find on Artemis Entreri's head, it is not enough to make the attempt worth your while."

"Bwahaha!"

"Simply consider all the years of drinking you will forfeit. Let that be your guide." Jarlaxle winked, gave a slight bow and walked away, passing by the serving girl who was coming over with another full tray. He gave her a little pat on the buttocks as he passed, and she offered a promising smile in return.

Yes, he could understand why Athrogate would shy from Vaasa when the weather turned cold. Certainly he, too, would like to weather the winter in the more hospitable city.

Unless, of course, Artemis Entreri had worn through that hospitality.

Jarlaxle exited the tavern. The rain had ended, the heavy clouds blown away by a cold northern wind to reveal the faint first stars of evening above. So quickly had the chill come through that the puddles left over from the day's rain steamed into the night air, rising in ghostly wisps. Jarlaxle spent a while looking both ways along the boulevard, examining those wisps and wondering if killers lurked behind their gray veils.

"What have you done, Artemis?" he asked quietly, then he bundled his cloak around his neck and started off for home. He reversed direction almost immediately, though, having no patience for the events swirling around him.

By the time he got to Wall's Around, twilight had fallen across the city. A bank of clouds hanging along the western horizon defeated the last, meager rays of the sun, ushering in an earlier and deeper darkness. Thus, several of the mercantiles had candles burning, for though it was dark, it was not yet time for them to close their doors.

So it was for Ilnezhara's Gold Coins, where a single, multi-armed candelabra danced in the large window. All around it, crystals sparkled in the uneven light.

The little bell set upon the door sang out when Jarlaxle entered. The place was nearly empty, with only one middle-aged woman and a young couple walking the length of the showcases, and a single figure behind the counter across the way.

Jarlaxle took pleasure in the blanch of the middle-aged woman when she finally noticed him. Even more delicious, the younger woman slid a step to the side, bringing her much closer to her male companion. She clutched the man's arm so urgently that she roused him from his shopping.

The man's jaw drooped, stiffened suddenly, and he puffed his chest out. He gave a quick glance around, and led his companion toward the exit, moving past Jarlaxle, who politely tipped his hat.

The young woman gave a little yelp at that, and being on the side closest the drow, she shrank even nearer to her protector.

"I do so enjoy the taste of human flesh," Jarlaxle whispered as they passed, and the woman gave another little yelp and her brave friend moved even more furiously to the door.

Jarlaxle didn't even bother to glance back at them as they departed. The sharp ring of the bell was enough to amuse him.

And to draw the attention of the other two in the shop. The middle-aged woman he did not know stared at him—a bit fearful, perhaps, but seemingly more intrigued than frightened.

Jarlaxle bowed to her and when he came up, he worked his fingers through a simple parlor trick and produced a single flower, a late summer purple alveedum, a rare and striking Bloodstone spectacle.

He held it out to the woman, but she did not take it. She slid past him instead, staring at him every step of the way.

Jarlaxle's fingers worked fast and the flower disappeared. He offered the woman a shrug.

She just kept staring, and her eyes roamed up and down, sizing him from head to toe.

Jarlaxle moved to a nearby case and pretended to inspect several pieces of golden jewelry. He did not glance the woman's way, nor toward the proprietor behind the counter, but he covertly kept careful track of both of them. Finally, he heard the bell on the door tinkle, and he glanced that way to lock a final stare with the obviously intrigued woman. She betrayed her thoughts with a wry smile as she exited the store.

"The wife of Yenthiele Sarmagon, the Chief Gaoler of Heliogabalus and a close personal friend of Baron Dimian Ree," Ilnezhara remarked as soon as the door closed behind the departing woman. "Take care if you bed that one."

"She seemed quite boring to me," Jarlaxle replied, never looking up from the necklace he rolled through his fingers, reveling in the weight of the precious metal.

"Most humans are," Ilnezhara said. "I suspect it is their state of always being close to death. They are confined by fears of what may come next, and so they cannot step outside of their caution."

"But of course, by that reasoning, a drow is a much better lover."

"And a dragon better still," Ilnezhara was quick to respond, and Jarlaxle didn't dare question that statement. He offered a grin and a tip of his hat.

"But even the companionship of a dragon cannot sate the appetite of Jarlaxle, it would seem," Ilnezhara went on.

Jarlaxle considered her words, and the somewhat sour look that had come over her fair features. She crossed her arms in front of her—a most unusual gesture from this one, he thought.

"You do not think me content?" the drow asked, a bit too innocently, he knew.

"I believe that you stir."

"My contentment, or lack thereof, is compartmentalized," Jarlaxle explained, thinking that it might be wise to assuage the dragon's ego. "In many ways, I am indeed content—quite happy, in fact. In other ways, less so."

"You live for excitement," Ilnezhara replied. "You are not content, never content, when the road is smooth and straight."

Jarlaxle mulled that over for a few moments, then grinned even wider. "And you would live out the rest of your life in the bliss of buying trinkets and reselling them for profit," came his sarcastic reply.

"Who says I buy them?" Ilnezhara answered without hesitation.

Jarlaxle tipped his hat and offered a quick smile that did not hold, for he would not release the dragon from the bite of his sarcasm so readily as that.

"Are you content, Ilnezhara?"

"I have found a life worth living, yes."

"But only because you measure it by the short lifespan of King Gareth and his friends, whom you fear. This is not your life, your existence, but merely a pause for position, a plateau from which Ilnezhara and Tazmikella can move along to their next pursuits."

"Or perhaps we dragons are not as anxious and agitated as drow," the dragon replied. "Might it be the little things—a drow lover this tenday, salvaging a destroyed merchant ship next—that suffice?"

"Should I be insulted?"

"Better that than consumed."

Jarlaxle paused again, trying to get a reading on his most curious of counterparts. He couldn't rightly tell where Ilnezhara's jokes ended and her threats began, and that was no place he wanted to be where a dragon was concerned.

"Perhaps it is the excitement I can provide extraneous to our . . . relationship, that so enthralls you," he offered somewhat hesitantly a moment later. He put on his best cavalier effect as he finished the thought, striking a pose that evoked the mischievous nature of a troublemaking young boy.

But Ilnezhara did not smile. Her jaw tightened and her eyes stared straight ahead, boring through him.

"So serious," he observed.

"The storm approaches."

Jarlaxle put on an innocent expression and posture, standing with his arms out wide.

"You survived the trials of the castle of the Witch-King," Ilnezhara explained. "And it is not in Jarlaxle's nature to merely survive. Nay, you seek to prosper from every experience, as you did with Herminicle's tower."

"I escaped with my life—barely."

"With your life and . . . ?"

"If we are both to speak in riddles, then neither will find an answer, milady."

"You believe that you have found advantage in the constructs of Zhengyi," the dragon stated. "You have discovered magic, and allies perhaps, and now you seek to parlay those into personal gain."

Jarlaxle started to shake his head, but Ilnezhara would not be so easily dismissed.

"To elevate your position within the current structure of Damara—to be named as apprentice knight of the order, then to climb to full knighthood—is one thing. To elevate your position without, to aspire to climb a ladder of your own making, in a kingdom where Gareth reigns the fields and farms and Timoshenko haunts the alleyways and shadows, is to invite disaster on no small scale."

"Unless my allies are more powerful than my potential enemies," Jarlaxle said.

"They are not," the dragon replied without pause. "You reveal a basic misunderstanding of those you seek to climb beside, or above. It is not a misunderstanding shared by myself or my sister, at any level, be assured. I met with Zhengyi in the days before the storm, as did my sister. His name is reviled throughout the land, of course, but there was a brief period when he was highly regarded, or absent that, when he was powerful enough to destroy any who openly defied him. He came to us not with threats, but with powerful temptation."

"He offered you immortality," Jarlaxle said. "Dracolichdom."

"Urshula the Black was not alone in Zhengyi's designs," the dragon confirmed. "A hundred dracoliches will rise in turn because of the legacy of the Witch-King. A month from now, perhaps, or a hundred years or a thousand years. They are out there, their spirits patient in phylacteries set within tomes of creation, immortal."

"And of Ilnezhara?"

"I chose my course, as did Tazmikella, and at a time when it seemed as if Zhengyi could not be stopped."

She paused there, staring hard, and Jarlaxle silently recited the next logical thought: if Zhengyi could not tempt the dragon sisters back in the day when he seemed to be the supreme and unchallenged power in the Bloodstone Lands, how might Jarlaxle hope to tempt them now?

"My sister and I expect that your services will not be required through the quiet winter months," Ilnezhara said. "Nor those of Entreri. If you wish to journey out of Heliogabalus, mayhaps to rest from your recent trials in the softer climate of the Moonsea, then go with our blessing."

A knowing smile widened on Jarlaxle's face.

"If a situation arises where your particular skills might be of value, and you two are still about Heliogabalus, we will seek you out," the dragon went on, in a tone that made it clear to the drow that she had no intention of doing any such thing. He was being dismissed.

More than that, Ilnezhara and Tazmikella were running from him, distancing themselves.

"Take care, Ilnezhara," Jarlaxle dared to warn. "Artemis Entreri and I uncovered much in the northland."

Ilnezhara narrowed her eyes, and for a moment, Jarlaxle feared that she would revert to her true dragon form and assault him. That threatening stare flashed away, though, and she calmly replied, "Enough to garner attention, of course."

That gave Jarlaxle pause.

"Whose attention?" he asked. "Your own?"

"You had that before you went north, of course."

Jarlaxle let that digest for a moment. She was torn, he could see, and there remained in her a wistfulness toward him. She had dismissed him—almost.

"Ah, perhaps we will travel south," he said. "Weaned in the Underdark, I have little tolerance for winter's cold bite."

"That may be wise."

"I expect that I, and particularly Artemis, would do well to report our departure to King Gareth," the drow reasoned. "Though the journey north to Bloodstone Village is not one I care to take. Already the wind blows cold up there. Still, as I see this as our responsibility, I should send word, and it is not a message I wish to entrust to a city guardsman."

"No, of course not," the dragon agreed, in an almost mocking tone that conveyed to the drow that she was catching on to his little game.

"Perhaps if any of Gareth's friends are in town. . . ." the drow mused aloud.

Ilnezhara hesitated, locking stares with him. She smiled, frowned, then slowly nodded, making it clear to him that *that* favor was the last he should expect, her expression reminding him of, and confirming, the earlier dismissal.

"I have heard that Grandmaster Kane has been seen about Heliogabalus," she said.

"A remarkable character of unique disposition, I would gather."

"A vagabond in weathered and dirty robes," Ilnezhara corrected. "And the most dangerous man in all of the Bloodstone Lands."

"Artemis Entreri is in the Bloodstone Lands."

"The most dangerous man in all of the Bloodstone Lands," the dragon reiterated, and with a surety that Jarlaxle did not lightly dismiss.

"Grandmaster Kane, then," he said. "He will deliver my message, I am certain."

"He does not fail King Gareth," llnezhara agreed, and warned: "Ever."

Jarlaxle sat there nodding for a few minutes. "Perhaps he will be interested in some information regarding Gareth's dead niece, as well." The dark elf rose and offered a disarming smile to the dragon. He tried very hard to appear appreciative of the information she had just shared, and tried even harder to keep his supreme disappointment hidden.

He turned to go, but stopped in his tracks when the dragon said from behind him, "You weave webs that entrap. It is the way of your existence, from your earliest days in Menzoberranzan, no doubt. You play intrigue with characters like Knellict and Timoshenko, and it is a game in which you excel. But hear me well, Jarlaxle. King Gareth and his friends ride hard and straight, and bother not with the meandering strands of webs. Your weave will never be strong enough to slow the charge of Kane."

Out in the street, Jarlaxle quickly regained the spring in his step. He had gone to Ilnezhara hoping to enlist both her and her sister in his plans. Certainly he had to adjust his thinking and his immediate aspirations regarding Vaasa. Absent the dragons, his position was severely compromised—and even more so when he considered the mischief Artemis Entreri had apparently begun.

Caution told him he might do well to go to ground, perhaps even to take that holiday Ilnezhara had offhandedly advised—step away and reassess his opportunities against the seemingly mounting obstacles.

Never did Jarlaxle laugh louder than when he was laughing at himself.

"Caution," he said, letting the word roll off his tongue so that it seemed as if it was ten syllables instead of two. Then he offered the same treatment to a word he considered synonymous: "Boredom."

Every sensible bone in Jarlaxle's body screamed out at him to heed the advice of Ilnezhara, to remove himself from the web of intrigue that grew ever more intricate in the Bloodstone Lands. Truly, Jarlaxle realized that the current tide was pushing against him, that shadows gathered at every corner. A wise man might cut his losses—or winnings, even—and run for safer ground. For such "wise" men, Jarlaxle reasoned, though they didn't know it, death was irrelevant, redundant.

The tide swelled dangerously, to be sure. When facing a losing combination in *sava*, the wise player sacrificed a piece or surrendered.

But Jarlaxle, above them all, moved boldly in a way that seemed incongruous, even foolish. He bluffed harder.

"'Let a roll of chance's dice alter the board,'" he recited, an old drow saying that exalted in chaos. When dangerous reality closed in, so went Lolth's edict, the goal was simply to alter the reality.

His heels clicked loudly on the cobblestones—as he willed his enchanted boots to do—as he made his way down the cul-de-sac, with one name rolling through his thoughts: Grandmaster Kane.

Jarlaxle slept with dragons.

"Hang from the ceiling by yer toes, do ye?" Athrogate harrumphed. "Ye're bats!"

"They should not know?" the drow replied innocently.

"They shouldn't be knowing how Athrogate's knowing!"

"You believe that Spysong knew nothing of Canthan and his dwarf friend who accompanied him to the castle?"

Athrogate pursed his lips and seemed to shrink down in his seat. He alleviated his mounting fear with a mug of ale, dropped straight to the belly.

"Are you so naïve regarding your enemies?" Jarlaxle pressed.

"They ain't me enemies. Ain't done nothing against the crown, nor anyone else who didn't make me do it."

Jarlaxle smiled at the familiar words, spoken with Dwarvish flair but so similar to the claims of Entreri.

"The reckoning is coming fast," the drow warned. "Gareth's niece Ellery is dead."

"I'm still wondering how that might've happened."

"The details will matter not to Gareth's friends."

"Could say the same o' Knellict's friends if I'm doing what ye're asking me to be doing."

"The opposite, I would venture," said Jarlaxle. "The complicity of Ellery will mitigate the blow to Knellict. You will be doing him a favor."

Athrogate snorted, and a bit of ale spurted from his hairy nose.

"My little friend, you have thrived by remaining outside the web woven by your spidery friends."

"What in the Nine Hells are ye babbling about?"

"You are part of them, but removed from them," Jarlaxle explained. "You serve the Citadel of Assassins, but you do not plot with them. There is nothing in your past for which you will answer at the Court of King Gareth, else you would have been called to answer long ago."

"Would I, now?"

"Yes. You walk the edge of a coin, as do I, and now heads and tails are ready for a fight. How tight will our edge become when the blows begin to fall? Too narrow to tread, I expect, and if we must fall to one side or the other, which shall it be?"

"If ye're thinking Knellict's the tail, then yer friend's already jumped to the head," the dwarf reminded.

"This is not about Artemis Entreri," the drow replied. "It is about Jarlaxle, and Athrogate." He slid another mug Athrogate's way, and as per usual it never even stopped sliding before being scooped up and overturned into the dwarf's mouth.

Jarlaxle went on, "There is an old saying in my home, Menzoberranzan. *Pey ne nil ne-ne uraili.*"

"And here I'm thinking that ye looked funny. Next to the way ye talk . . ."

" 'In truth, the bonds are shed,' " the drow translated. "You feel the chains of worry now, my friend. Shed them."

"He won't be likin' the truth."

"But he is wise enough to lay blameless the messenger."

Athrogate took a deep breath then swallowed another ale. He slammed his hands on the edge of the table and pulled himself to his feet. "He's payin'," he said to the serving wench who turned his way, and he pointed to Jarlaxle.

"Pey ne nil ne-ne uraili," Jarlaxle whispered as Athrogate embarked on his mission to find Kane. His translation of the drow saying had been exact, if incomplete, for the bonds referenced were not the chains of worry, but the limiting boundaries of the flesh.

Announce yer arrival, Athrogate silently and repeatedly reminded himself. Surprising a grandmaster monk probably wasn't a wise choice. He placed the rickety wooden ladder before the wall of the inn and banged it loudly in place against the eave of the roof.

"Ye buy a room *in* the inn," he grumbled as he started up. "That's why they're callin' it an inn. Ye don't rent a bed *on* the durned inn. Ain't called an out!"

Every bootfall rang more loudly than the previous as the dwarf clumped his way up to peer over the edge.

A dozen feet from the lip, his back against the stone chimney, sat the monk. His legs were folded under him, his hands on thighs, palms upright. He sat with perfect posture and balance, and seemed more a fixture of the building, like the chimney, than a living creature.

Athrogate paused, expecting a response, but when the limit of his patience slipped past with no word or movement from the monk, the dwarf hauled himself up again, rolling his upper body awkwardly onto the slightly-sloping roof. He belched as his belly—grown more ample in just the few days he had been in Heliogabalus—wedged against the soffet.

"Are ye sleeping, then?" he asked as he pulled himself up to his hands and knees. One of the bouncing heads of his twin morningstars swung in and bashed him off the side of his face, but he just blew out the side of his mouth as if to push it aside. "I'm thinking a friend o' King Gareth'd have himself a better bed. King ain't paying ye much these days?"

Kane opened one eye to regard the dwarf.

"And I'm surprised that ye got no guards," Athrogate dared to say. The dwarf managed to stand up, and when he did, he realized that the slate shingles all around him were loose—no, not just loose, but were a false set of extra shingles set upon the real ones!

"Oh, by Clangeddin's fartin' arse," he managed to say as his feet slid out from under him, dropping him hard to his belly then off the roof entirely. He crashed into the debris-filled alleyway all entangled with his ladder, arms and legs flailing helplessly, morningstar heads bouncing and slapping around him.

He sprang to his feet and hopped about, eyes darting to every shadow. If anybody had witnessed that humiliation, Athrogate would have to kill him, of course.

When he was satisfied that his unceremonious fall had gone unnoticed, he slapped his hands on his hips and looked back up at the roof.

"Durned monk," he muttered as he collected his morningstars, set them back in place across his back, and untangled the ladder. A couple of the steps had been knocked out, but it would still suffice, he decided, so he propped it back in place and began his careful climb, again taking care to announce his arrival.

When he came up to the edge of the roof, he reached out and tested the remaining slate.

"It is safe now, dwarf," Kane said. He remained in the same position, eyes still closed.

"Clever trap," Athrogate remarked, and he came up slowly, inch by inch, feeling every bit of ground before settling his weight onto it. "Couldn't ye just hire a few guards and leave the traps for stinky thieves?"

"I need no guards."

"Ye're up here all alone—and why ain't ye in a room?"

"I am in the grandest room in all the universe."

"Lookin' like the rains're coming. Think ye'll be singing that then?"

"I did not invite you here, dwarf," Kane replied. "I do not welcome company. If you have purpose, then speak it. Or be gone."

Athrogate narrowed his eyes and crossed his burly arms over his chest.

"Ye know who I be?" he asked.

"Athrogate," the monk replied.

"Ye know the things I done?"

No answer.

"Ain't none killed more at the wall," Athrogate declared.

"None who bothered to count, at least," came the quiet—and infuriating—reply.

"I went to the castle north o' Palishchuk!" the dwarf declared.

"And that is the only reason I allow you to bother me now," said Kane. "If you have come to speak with me of that adventure, then pray wag. If not, then pray leave."

Athrogate deflated just a bit. "Well, good enough then," he said. "Weren't for that trip, then I'd be having no business with ye anyway."

"None that you would wish," Kane calmly and confidently replied, and the dwarf shrank just a bit more.

"I come to talk about Ellery."

Kane opened his eyes and turned his head, suddenly seeming very interested. "You saw her fall?"

"Nope," the dwarf admitted. "I saw Canthan fall, though. Fell at me feet, killed to death by Artemis Entreri."

Kane didn't blink. "You accuse him?"

"Nope," the dwarf clarified. "Was a fight Canthan started. Stupid wizard was tryin' to kill them half-orcs." The dwarf paused and collected his thoughts. "Ye got to know that Canthan weren't one to follow the lead o' King Gareth."

"He had ulterior motives in traveling to the castle?"

"Don't know what an 'ulterior' might be, but he was looking out for Canthan, and for his masters—and ain't none o' them sitting by your king, for the sake o' yer king." He ended with an exaggerated wink, but Kane didn't blink and Athrogate issued a frustrated sigh.

"He was part o' the Citadel of Assassins," the dwarf explained.

"That much was suspected."

"And known," said Athrogate, "by yer own Commander Ellery. And she knowed it well before she picked him to go along to the north."

"Are you saying that Canthan killed Ellery?"

"Nah, ye dolt—" Athrogate bit the word back as it escaped his flapping lips, but again, Kane showed no reaction. "Nah, none o' that. I'm saying that Ellery, yer king's blood kin, picked Canthan to go because she was told to pick him to go. Ye might be thinking her a paladin o' yer order, but ye'd be thinking wrong."

"You are claiming that Ellery had connections with the Citadel of Assassins?"

"I'm adding two fingers and three fingers and making a fist to whack ye upside the head. If yerself can't count, that'd be yer own problem."

"Spysong counts more proficiently than you can imagine, good dwarf. The strands of the citadel entwine many, it would seem, to varying degrees."

The level of threat in that statement was not lost on Athrogate, a sobering reminder of who he was dealing with, and of his own complicity—at least in the eyes of King Gareth's court.

"Well, I was just thinking ye should know," he said then backed to the ladder and eased one foot onto the top step. He didn't turn as he climbed down, though, preferring to keep his gaze squarely on Kane.

The monk didn't move, didn't stand, didn't react at all.

When he was back in the alley, walking briskly away, Athrogate puzzled over the wisdom of that meeting, and of betraying Knellict.

"Damned drow," he muttered, and suddenly every shadow seemed darker and more ominous. "Damned drink."

Those last words rang in his head, nettling his sensibilities.

"Think I'll go get me some," Athrogate added, compelled to offer a formal apology to his beloved ale.

CHAPTER

OUT THE GAUNTLET

9

B ah, ye're listenin' to the way I babble and ye're thinking I'm a stupid one, ain't ye, elf?"

"I?" Jarlaxle replied with mock innocence. He grabbed Athrogate's arm as the dwarf reached his hand into a pocket and produced some coin for the waiting serving girl.

Athrogate looked down at the drow's hand, tight around his wrist, then lifted his gaze to consider Jarlaxle eye-to-eye.

"Ye're asking me to go, ain't ye?"

"It is an offer of adventure."

Athrogate snorted. "Yer friend's tied Knellict's butt hairs in a knot and now yerself's flicking yer finger under the nose o' Kane hisself. Adventure, ye say? I'm thinking ye built yerself two walls o' iron, Jarlaxle, and now they're both to fall atop ye. Only question is, which'll flatten ye first?"

"Ah, but if they fall together, might they not impede each other's progress?" He held his hands up before him, fingers together and skyward, then dropped them in toward each other until the fingers tapped together, forming an inverted **V**. "There is room left between them, is there not?"

"Ye're bats."

Jarlaxle could only laugh at that observation, and really, when he thought about it, there wasn't much point in disagreeing.

"Ain't far enough in all the world to run from them," Athrogate said more solemnly, preempting the drow's forthcoming repeat of the offer. "So ye're to run from Heliogabalus, and a good choice that'll be—best ye got, anyway, though I'm not saying much in that!"

"Come with us."

"Ah, but ye're a stubborn one." The dwarf planted his hands on his hips, paused for just a moment, then shook his hairy head. "Can't be doing that."

Jarlaxle knew that he was beaten, and he couldn't rightly blame the pragmatic dwarf. "Well, then," he said, patting Athrogate's strong shoulder. "Take heart in my assurance that your tab here is paid the winter through." He turned to the tavernkeeper standing behind the bar and the man nodded, having obviously overheard. "Drink yourself into oblivion until the snows have receded and you return to the Vaasan Gate. Compliments of Jarlaxle. And visit baker Piter as you wish. Your coin will not be welcomed there, but your appetite surely will."

Athrogate pursed his lips and nodded his appreciation. Whether he wanted to get entangled with Jarlaxle or not, the dwarf wasn't about to turn down those offers!

"Eat well and drink well, good Athrogate, my friend," Jarlaxle finished, and he bowed.

Athrogate grabbed him hard by the arm before he could straighten, though, and pulled his ear close. "Don't ye be calling me that, ye durned elf. Least not when ears're perked our way."

Satisfied that they understood each other, Jarlaxle straightened, nodded in deference to the dwarf's demands, and left the tavern. He didn't look back because he didn't want Athrogate to see the sting of disappointment on his face.

He went out into the street and spent a moment surveying his surroundings. He tried to remain confident in his decisions even in the face of Athrogate's doubts. The dwarf knew the region well, of course, but Jarlaxle brushed it off as the dwarf underestimating him.

At least, he tried to tell himself that.

"You heard?" the drow asked the shadows, using the language of his Underdark home.

"Of course," came a reply in the same strange tongue.

"It is as I told you."

"As dangerous as I told you," the voice of Kimmuriel Oblodra replied.

"As promising as I told you."

No answer drifted to Jarlaxle's ears.

"One enemy is manageable," Jarlaxle whispered. *"The other need not be our enemy."*

"We shall see," was all Kimmuriel would offer.

"You are ready when the opportunity presents itself?"

"I am always ready, Jarlaxle. Is that not why you appointed me?"

Jarlaxle smiled and took comfort in those confident words. Kimmuriel was thinking ahead, of course. The brilliant psionicist had thrived on the treachery of Menzoberranzan, and so to him the games of humans were child's play. Entreri and Jarlaxle had become targets of the Citadel of Assassins and curiosities of Spysong. Those two groups would battle around the duo as much or more than they would battle *with* the duo. And that would present opportunities. The citadel was the less formidable, by far, and so it followed that they could be used to keep Spysong at bay.

Jarlaxle sensed that Kimmuriel was gone—preparing the battlefield, no doubt—so Jarlaxle made his way through Heliogabalus's streets. Lights burned on many corners, but they flickered in the wind and were dulled by the fog that had come up, so typical of that time of the year, where the temperature varied so greatly day to night. The drow pulled his cloak tighter and willed his magical boots to silence. Perhaps it was better that he blend in with his surroundings just then.

Perfectly silent, nearly invisible in his drow cloak, Jarlaxle had little trouble not only getting back to the stairs leading to his apartment in the unremarkable building, but he managed to do a circuit or three of the surrounding area, noting others who did not notice him.

A tip of the right side of his great hat lifted Jarlaxle's feet off the ground and he glided up the rickety, creaky staircase silently. He went inside, into the hallway, and moved up to his door in complete darkness.

Complete darkness for a surface dweller, but not for Jarlaxle. Still, he could barely make out the little dragon statuette trap set above the apartment door. He couldn't tell the color of its eyes, though.

He had told Entreri to keep it set at white, but was he to trust that?

Not wanting to bring up any light to alert the many suspicious characters he had noted outside, the drow reached into his hat and pulled forth from under its top a disk of black felt. A couple of roundabout swings elongated it enough and Jarlaxle tossed it against the wall beside the door.

It stuck, and its magic created a hole in the wall, revealing dim candlelight from within.

Jarlaxle stepped through to see Entreri standing in the shadows of the corner, at an angle that allowed him to peer out through the narrow slot between the dark shade and the window's wooden edge.

Entreri acknowledged him with a nod, but never took his eyes off the street outside.

"We have visitors gathering," the assassin whispered.

"More than you know," Jarlaxle replied. He reached up and pulled his disk through, eliminating the hole and leaving the wall as it had been before.

"Are you going to berate me again for angering Knellict? Are you going to ask me again what I have done?"

"Some of our visitors are Knellict's men, no doubt."

"Some?"

"Spysong has taken an interest," Jarlaxle explained.

"Spysong? King Gareth's group?"

"I suspect they've deduced that the fights with the gargoyles and the dracolich were not the only battles at the castle. After all, of the four who fell, two were to the same blade."

"So again, I am to blame?"

Jarlaxle laughed. "Hardly. If there is even blame to be had, by Gareth's reckoning."

Entreri moved closer to the window, slipped the tip of his dagger under the edge of the shade and dared to retract it just a bit to widen the viewing space.

"I do not like this," the assassin said. "They know we're in here, and could strike—"

"Then let us not be in here," Jarlaxle interrupted.

Entreri let the shade slip back into place and stepped to the side of the window, eyeing his friend. "To the dragons?" he asked.

Jarlaxle shook his head. "They will have nothing to do with this. Gareth's friends unnerve them, I think."

"Wonderful."

"Bah, they are only dragons."

Entreri crinkled his face at that, but wasn't about to ask for clarification. "Where, then?"

"Nowhere in the city will be safe. Indeed, I expect that we will find strong tendrils of both our enemies throughout all of Damara."

Entreri's face grew tight. He knew, obviously, what the drow had in mind.

"There is a castle where we might find welcome," Jarlaxle confirmed.

"Welcome? Or refuge?"

"One man's prison is another man's home."

"Another drow's home," Entreri corrected, eliciting a burst of laughter from Jarlaxle.

"Lead on," the assassin bade his black-skinned companion a moment later, when a sound from outside reminded them that it might not be the time for philosophical rambling.

Jarlaxle turned for the door. "White as we agreed?" he asked.

"Yes."

The drow opened the door then paused and glanced back. Holding the door wide, he stepped aside and motioned for Entreri to go first into the hallway.

Entreri walked by, over the threshold. "Blue," he said, and reached up to retrieve the dragon statuette.

Jarlaxle laughed all the louder.

⊷══╫══⊶

"It's Gareth's boys, I tell ya," Bosun Bruiseberry said to his companion. An incredibly thin and wiry little rat, Bosun seemed to move through the tightest of alleyways and partitions as easily as if they were broad avenues—which of course only frustrated his hunting partner, Remilar the Bold, a young wizard whose regard for himself greatly exceeded that of his peers and masters at the citadel of Assassins.

"So Spysong, too, has taken an interest in this Artemis Entreri creature," Remilar replied. He bit the words off short, nearly tripping as his rich blue robes caught on the jagged edge of a loose board on the side of Entreri's apartment building.

"Or an interest in us," Bosun said. "Seems that group across the street're watching Burgey's boys in the back alley off to the left."

"Competing interests," Remilar answered in a disinterested drawl. "Very well then, let us be quick about our task, and about our departure. I did not interrupt my all-important research to leave without that bounty."

"This one's dangerous, by all accounts, and his drow friend's worse."

Remilar gave a disgusted sigh and brushed past his cautious companion. He moved to the end of the alley, the front corner of the building, and glanced out at the street beyond.

Bosun moved up very close behind, even put a hand on Remilar's back, which made the mage straighten and offer another heavy and disgusted sigh.

"Quickly, then," he said to the young assassin.

"I can slip in and get behind the rat Entreri," Bosun offered. "Yerself'll distract them and me blades'll do the dirty task. I'll be taking his ear for proof."

If Remilar was impressed, his expression certainly didn't show it. "We've no time for your legendary stealth," he replied, and had Bosun been a brighter chap, he'd have caught the sarcastic tone in the adjective. "You are the decoy in this one. Right in through the front door you go. Draw him out—or them, if the drow is at home—and show him your blades. You need keep his thoughts and actions occupied for but a few seconds and I will lay him low with a blast of lightning and a burst of missiles to still his twitching. Be sharp and fast with your blade to retrieve the trophy—his head, if you will—and with a snap of my fingers, we will depart this place, teleporting back to the hills outside the citadel."

Bosun wore a stupid look as he digested all of that. He began to question the plan, but Remilar grabbed him by the front of the tunic and pulled him past, out into the street.

"You wish to do battle with Spysong, or to lose Entreri to other bounty-claimers?" the wizard asked.

A yell went up from a nearby building, and the pair knew they were out of time for their planning. Bosun stumbled to the door and reached up for the handle.

But the door exploded before his surprised face, torn from its hinges as out charged Entreri astride a tall, gaunt black stallion that snorted ebon smoke and wore cuffs of orange fire around its thundering hooves. The mount, a hellish nightmare, apparently didn't distinguish between barriers, for it treated the frozen-with-surprise Bosun in the exact same manner as it had the door.

Down he went under a sudden and vicious barrage of hooves. He hit the ground and squirmed, and good fortune turned him inside the thundering back hooves as the nightmare charged over him. That good fortune didn't hold, however, as the second nightmare exited the building, the dark elf astride. Poor Bosun lifted his head just enough to get it clipped, and to get his scalp torn away, by the fiery hooves of the second mount.

To the side, still in the shadows of the alley, Remilar the More-Smart-Than-Bold improvised, casting the third of his planned spells first.

Her hands trembled as she opened the small chest, for it was the first time she had dared to lift that cover since returning from Palishchuk. She had kept herself busy during her short stopover before going to Bloodstone Village for the ceremony, and mostly so that she could avoid that very thing. The task, necessary and painful, was something that Calihye could hardly bear.

Inside the small chest were trinkets and a necklace, and a rolled-up parchment with a sketch done by one of the merchants of a caravan that had spent some time on the Fugue. The artist had done a sketch of Calihye and Parissus, arm-in-arm. She looked at it and felt tears welling behind her blue eyes. The likeness was strong enough to elicit memories of her dear Parissus.

Calihye ran the fingers of one hand gently over the image. The pose was so natural for the pair, so typical. The taller Parissus stood firm, with Calihye's head resting on her shoulder. Calihye lifted a scarf with her free hand and brought it to her face. She closed her eyes, the image in the sketch firmly rooted in her thoughts, and breathed deeply, taking in the scent of her lost companion.

Her shoulders bobbed with sobs, tears wetted the scarf.

A few moments later, Calihye sorted herself out with a deep and steadying breath. Her lips grew very tight as she put both scarf and sketch off to the side. More trinkets came out: some jewelry, a pair of medals given to the duo by one of the former undercommanders at the Vaasan Gate, and a necklace of varied gemstones. The woman paused then pulled forth a fake beard and a cap of brown leather, a disguise that Parissus had often worn when she and Calihye had gone out tavern-hopping. Parissus impersonated a man quite well, Calihye thought, and she heard in her mind the husky voice her friend could assume at will. How they had played with the sensibilities of folks across the Bloodstone Lands and beyond!

The woman finally arrived at the item she had gone there to retrieve: a small crystal vial filled with blood: Calihye's and Parissus's, mixed and mingled, a reminder of their shared pledge.

"In life and beyond," she recited quietly. She looked at her dagger, which she had placed on a small table to the side, and continued as if addressing it, "Not yet."

Calihye produced a small silver chain from her pouch, an item she had purchased in Bloodstone Village upon her departure. She held the vial up before her eyes, turning it slowly so that she could see the tiny golden eyelet set in the back. With the fingers of an accomplished thief, Calihye threaded the chain through the eyelet then brought it up and set the unusual necklace around her delicate elf's neck.

She lifted her hand to cover the crystal vial then touched the scarf to her face once more and inhaled the scent of Parissus.

She did not cry again and when she removed the scarf, her face was devoid emotion.

Remilar nearly lost his train of thought, and his spell, when he noted Bosun crawling his way, blood streaming down his forehead. The garishly wounded man reached out a trembling hand Remilar's way, his look plaintive, confused, dazed.

In the midst of the spell, and unwilling to let it go, Remilar nodded furiously at the man, bidding him to hurry.

Somehow Bosun found a burst of energy, scrambling along, but he wouldn't get there in time, Remilar knew.

Across the street, agents of the Citadel of Assassins came out of the shadows to give chase and fire arrows and spells at the retreating duo. But to Remilar's horror, others came out of the shadows as well, and it only took the mage a moment to understand the identity of the second force.

Spysong!

Had the Citadel of Assassins been baited with Entreri and Jarlaxle? Had Entreri's treachery been nothing more than a ruse to lure the network into Spysong's deadly sights?

Remilar shook the thoughts from his head, and realized that he had lost his spell, as well. He motioned more vigorously to the crawling Bosun and began casting again.

Bosun got there in time, falling at Remilar's feet and hooking his arms around the mage's ankles. Remilar even reached down and grabbed the man's shoulder as his spell released, transporting them across space to a rocky hillside in southern Vaasa, a score of miles east of the Vaasan Gate.

"Come along, then," Remilar said to his prone companion. "It's two hundred yards uphill to the citadel, and I'm not about to carry you." He reached down and tugged at the man, and shook his head when he looked into Bosun's eyes, for the man seemed hardly conscious of his surroundings.

And indeed, Bosun was not even there behind that vacant gaze. He was lost in a swirl of gray mists and flashing, sharp lights, the confusion of the psionicist's mind attack as Kimmuriel Oblodra possessed his corporeal body.

The nightmares pounded down the cobblestones, smoke and gouts of flame flying from their otherworldly hooves. Jarlaxle led Entreri around one tight corner—too tight!—and his coal black, hellish steed brushed a cart of fresh fish. Patrons ran every which way and the vendor threw his arms defensively over the open cart. The look upon the middle-aged man's bloodless, open-jawed, wide-eyed face was one Artemis Entreri would not forget for many tendays to come.

The market parted before the charging pair, people scrambling, tripping, calling out for one god or another, even crying in terror. Mothers grabbed their children and hugged them close, rocking and cooing as if Death himself had arrived on the street that day.

Jarlaxle seemed to be enjoying it all, Entreri noted. The drow even pulled off his hat at one point and waved it around, all the while expertly weaving his mount through the dodging crowds.

Entreri spurred his steed past the drow and took the lead, then led Jarlaxle down a sharp corner to a quieter street.

"The peasants are cover for our escape!" Jarlaxle protested.

Entreri didn't answer. He just put his head down and spurred his nightmare on faster. They crossed several blocks, turning often and fast, frightening every horse and every person who viewed their fiery-hoofed nightmares. Pursuit rang out behind them, from the back and the sides, but they were moving too quickly and too erratically, and they had left too much confusion back at the initial scene, for anyone to properly organize to cut them off.

"We've got to make it through the gate," Entreri said as Jarlaxle pulled up even with him on one wide and nearly deserted avenue.

"And then my own," Jarlaxle replied.

Entreri glanced at him curiously, not understanding. He hadn't the time to contemplate it then, however, for as they came around the next corner, leaning hard and turning harder, they came in sight of Heliogabalus's northern gate. It was open, as always, but more than a few guards were already turning their way.

The reactions of those guards, sudden frantic running and screaming, led both riders to guess that the massive portcullis would soon lower, and the heavy iron gates would begin their swing.

Jarlaxle put his head down and kicked hard at the nightmare's sides, and the coal black horse accelerated, its hooves crackling sparks off the cobblestones. Rather than pace his friend, Entreri fell into line behind him, and similarly spurred on his mount. Jarlaxle waved his arms, and a globe of darkness appeared on the sheltered parapet above the open gates. The drow's arm went out to the side and Entreri saw that Jarlaxle held a thin wand.

"Wonderful," the assassin muttered, expecting that his reckless friend would set off a fireball or some other destructive magic that would bring a retaliatory hail of arrows down upon them.

Jarlaxle leveled the wand and spoke a command word. A glob of green goo burst forth from the item's tip and leaped out ahead of the riders, soaring toward a man who worked a crank at the side of the gate. Jarlaxle adjusted his sights and launched a second glob at the gates themselves, then spurred his nightmare on even faster.

The man working the crank fell back and cried out, pulling free the crank's setting pin as he went. The crank began to spin, and the portcullis started to drop.

But the magical glob slapped hard against the mechanism, filling the gears with the sticky substance. The spin became a crawl and the crank creaked to a halt, leaving the portcullis only slightly closed, with enough room for the ducking riders to get through.

The second glob struck its target as well, slapping into place at the hinge of the right-hand gate, filling the wedge and holding back the guards who tried to pull the gates closed. One of them turned for the glob, but then all of them cried out and scrambled aside as the riders and their hellish steeds bore down upon them.

Jarlaxle was far from finished, and Entreri was reminded quite clearly why he still followed that unusual dark elf. The wand went away and the drow switched the reins to his right hand. He brought his left hand out with a snap, and a golden hoop bracelet appeared from beneath the cuff on the sleeve of his fine shirt. That hoop went right over his palm, and he grabbed it and brought it in before his face.

An arrow arced out at the pair, follow by a second.

Jarlaxle blew through the hoop, and its magic magnified his puff a thousand-thousand times over, creating a barrier of wind before him that sent the arrows flying harmlessly wide.

"Stay right on my tail!" the drow shouted to Entreri, and to Entreri's horror, Jarlaxle summoned a second globe of darkness in the clearing between the narrowly opened gates.

Jarlaxle put his head down, and three powerful strides brought him under the creaking portcullis, straining against the strength of the goo. He plunged into the darkness, and Entreri, teeth gritted in abject horror, rushed in behind.

Then it was light again, or relatively so, as the normal night was as compared to Jarlaxle's summoned globes, and the pair galloped off down the road north of Heliogabalus. A couple of arrows reached for them from behind—one even managed to clip Entreri's horse—but the nightmares were not slowed, carrying their riders far, far away.

Some time later, the city lost in the foggy night behind them, Jarlaxle pulled up short and clip-clopped his nightmare off the road.

"We've no time for your games," Entreri chastised him.

"You would ride straight to the Vaasan Gate?"

"To anywhere that is not here."

"And Knellict, or one of Gareth's wizards, or perhaps both, will enact a spell and land before us, as happened on the road south of Palishchuk upon our return from the castle."

The drow dismounted, and as soon as he hit the ground he dismissed his nightmare then reached down and picked up the obsidian statuette and placed it safely in his pouch.

Entreri sat astride his horse, making no move to follow suit.

Seemingly unperturbed, Jarlaxle drew another wand out of a loop inside his cloak, one of several wands set in a line there. He held it up before him and offered a questioning look at his companion. "Are you meaning to join me?"

Entreri looked around at the drizzly, dark night, then sighed and dropped from his saddle. He spoke the command, reducing his nightmare to a tiny statuette, then scooped it up and shuffled toward the drow.

Jarlaxle held out his free hand and Entreri took it, and a moment later, colorful swirls began to fill the air around the pair. Streaks of yellow and shocks of blinding blue flashed all around, followed by a sudden and disorienting distortion of visual perception, as if all the light, stars and moon, began to warp and bend.

A sudden blackness fell over the pair, a thump of nothingness as profound as the moment of death itself.

Gradually, Entreri reoriented himself to his new surroundings, the nook where a great, man-made wall joined a natural wall of towering mountain stone. They had arrived at the westernmost edge of the Vaasan Gate, he realized as he got his bearings and noticed the tent city set upon the plain known as the Fugue.

"Why didn't you do that from the beginning?" the flustered assassin asked.

"It would not have been as dramatic."

Entreri started to respond, but bit it back, recognizing the pragmatism behind Jarlaxle's decision. Had the drow used his magic wand to whisk them out of the city, the remnants of the spell would have been recognized by their enemies, who might have quickly surmised the destination. Riding out of town so visibly, they might have bought themselves at least a little time.

"We should ride out to the north with all speed," Jarlaxle informed him.

"To hide in the castle?"

"You forget the powers of Zhengyi's construct. We won't be hiding, I assure you."

"You sound as if you've already put things in motion," Entreri remarked, and he knew, of course, that that was indeed the case. "I need some time here."

"Will you bring the half-elf along?" Jarlaxle asked, catching Entreri off his guard. "She might lack the common sense of Athrogate, after all, and out of misplaced loyalty to you decide that she should join us."

"And you think that would be foolish? Does that mean that you're not as confident as you pretend?"

Jarlaxle laughed at him. "She is not implicated in any of this. Not by Knellict and not by Gareth, whatever either side might know of your relationship with her. We would do well to put her at arms' length for a short time. Once we are established in the northland, Calihye can ride in openly. Until that time, she might prove more valuable to us, and will certainly remain safer, if there is distance between you two. Of course, I am presuming that you can suffer the pain in your loins. . . ."

Entreri narrowed his eyes and tightened his jaw, and Jarlaxle merely chuckled again.

"As you will," the drow said with a great flourish, and he walked off along the wall.

Entreri remained there in the shadows for a short time, considering his options. He knew where he would find Calihye, and soon enough, he decided on what he would say to her.

Her fingers trembled as she traced the delicate outline of Parissus's face in the precious portrait. Calihye closed her eyes and could feel again the smoothness of Parissus's cheeks, the softness of her skin above the hard and strong tension of her muscles.

She would never replace that feel, Calihye knew, and moistness came into her blue eyes once more.

She sniffed it away, dropped the portrait, and spun when her door opened. Artemis Entreri stepped into the room.

"I knocked," the man explained. "I did not mean to surprise you."

Calihye, so skilled and clear-thinking, forced herself up quickly and closed the ground to her lover. "I did not expect you," she said, hoping she hadn't too obviously exaggerated her excitement. She wrapped her arms around the man's neck and kissed him deeply.

Entreri was more than glad to reciprocate. "My plans have changed," he said after lingering about the woman's lips for a long while. "Again I find myself at the center of a storm named Jarlaxle."

"You were chased out of Heliogabalus?"

Entreri chuckled.

"By Knellict or Gareth?"

"Yes," Entreri replied, and he smiled widely and kissed Calihye again.

But the woman would have none of it. She pulled back to arms' length. "What will you do? Where will we go?"

"Not 'we,'" Entreri corrected. "I will go out to the north, straightaway. To the castle north of Palishchuk."

Calihye shook her head, her face crinkling with confusion.

"It will all sort out," Entreri promised her. "And quickly."

"Then I will go with you."

Entreri was shaking his head before she ever finished the thought. "No," he replied. "I need you here. It may well be that you will serve as my eyes, but that is not possible if you are known to be an associate."

"We have been seen together," the woman reminded him.

"Such liaisons are not uncommon, not unexpected, and not indicative of anything more."

"Is that how you feel?" the woman asked, a hard edge coming to her voice.

Entreri grinned at her. "How I feel isn't the point, is it? It is how we are, or will easily be, perceived, and that is all that matters. We engaged in a brief and intense affair, but we parted ways in Bloodstone Village and went on with our separate lives."

Calihye considered his words, considered all of it for a few moments, then shook her head. "Better that I come with you," she insisted, and she pulled away and turned for the rack that held her traveling gear.

"No," Entreri stated, his tone leaving no room for debate.

The woman was glad that her back was to him, else he would have seen her sudden scowl.

"It is not wise, and I'll not put you in such danger," Entreri explained. "Nor will I willingly relinquish the advantage I have with you as a secret ally."

"Advantage?" Calihye spat, turning to face him. "Is that the goal of your life, then? To seek advantage? You would forego pleasure for the sake of tactical advantage that you likely will not even need?"

"When you put it that way," Entreri replied, "yes."

Calihye straightened as if she had been struck.

"I'll not allow either my loins or my heart to bring us both to disaster," the assassin told her. "The road before me is dark, but I believe it is a short one." His voice changed, growing husky and serious, but no longer harsh and grave. "I'll not lead you to your doom out of selfishness," he explained. "We will not be apart for long—perhaps no longer than we had originally intended."

"Or you will die out in the northland, without me."

"In that instance, I would be doubly grateful that I did not allow you beside me."

Calihye tried to understand her own feelings well enough to respond. Should she be angry with him? Should she be insulted? Should she thank him for thinking of her above his own desires?

She felt like she was wrapping herself into winding webs, where even her emotions had to execute a feint within a feint.

"I did not come here to argue with you," Entreri said, his voice growing steady once more.

"Then why did you come? To have me one last time before you ride out of my life?"

"A pity, but I haven't the time," he answered. "And I am not riding out of your life. This is temporary. I owed it to you to keep you abreast of my travels."

"You owe it to me to tell me that you'll likely die by someone else's hand?" Calihye asked, and in a moment of particular wickedness, she wondered how Entreri might appear if he recognized the double meaning in her words.

He didn't, obviously, for he began shaking his head and slowly approached.

Calihye noted his belt and the dagger set there on his hip.

But the door opened then and Jarlaxle poked his head into the room. "Ah, good, you remain upright," he said with an exaggerated wink.

"You said I had time," a frustrated Entreri growled at him, turning to face him.

"I fear I underestimated the cleverness of our enemies," the drow admitted. "Kiss the girl farewell and let us be gone. Some time ago would have been preferable."

Entreri turned back to Calihye. He didn't kiss her again, but merely took her hands in his own and shrugged. "Not long," he promised, and he followed the dark elf.

Calihye stood there for a long time after the door had closed behind the departing pair, her emotions swirling from confusion to fear to anger and back again. She looked back at the portrait of her lost friend, then, and wondered if Entreri too would be lost to her in the Vaasan wasteland.

She found no options, though. She could only clench her fists and jaw in helpless frustration.

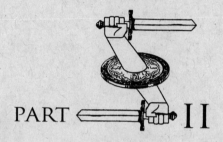

PART II

BY BLOOD OR BY DEED

I am not a king. Not in temperament, nor by desire, nor heritage, nor popular demand. I am a small player in the events of a small region in a large world. When my day is past, I will be remembered, I hope, by those whose lives I've touched. When my day is past, I will be remembered, I hope, fondly.

Perhaps those who have known me, or who have been affected by the battles I've waged and the work I've done, will tell the tales of Drizzt Do'Urden to their children. Perhaps not. But likely, beyond that possible second generation, my name and my deeds are destined to the dusty corners of forgotten history. That thought does not sadden me, for I measure my success in life by the added value my presence brought to those whom I loved, and who loved me. I am not suited for the fame of a king, or the grandiose reputation of a giant among men—like Elminster, who reshapes the world in ways that will affect generations yet to come.

Kings, like my friend Bruenor, add to their society in ways that define the lives of their descendants, and so one such as he will live on in name and deed for as long as Clan Battlehammer survives—for millennia, likely, and hopefully.

So, often do I ponder the ways of the king, the thoughts of the ruler, the pride and the magnanimity, the selfishness and the service.

There is a quality that separates a clan leader such as Bruenor from a man who presides over an entire kingdom. For Bruenor, surrounded by the dwarves who claim membership in his clan, kin and kind are one and the same. Bruenor holds a vested interest, truly a friendship, with every dwarf, every human, every drow, every elf, every halfling, every gnome who resides in Mithral Hall. Their wounds are his wounds, their joys his joys. There isn't one he does not know by name, and not one he does not love as family.

The same cannot be true for the king who rules a larger nation. However good his intent, however true his heart, for a king who presides over thousands, tens of thousands, there is an emotional distance of necessity, and the greater the number of his subjects, the greater the distance, and the more the subjects will be reduced to something less than people, to mere numbers.

Ten thousand live in this city, a king will know. Five thousand reside in that one, and only fifty in that village.

They are not family, nor friends, nor faces he would recognize. He cannot know their hopes and dreams in any particular way, and so, should he care, he must assume and pray that there are indeed common dreams and common needs and common hopes. A good king will understand this shared humanity and will work to uplift all in his wake. This ruler accepts the responsibilities of his position and follows the noble cause of service. Perhaps it is selfishness, the need to be loved and respected, that drives him, but the motivation matters not. A king who wishes to be remembered fondly by serving the best interests of his subjects rules wisely.

Conversely, the leader who rules by fear, whether it be of him or of some enemy he exaggerates to use as a weapon of control, is not a man or woman of good heart. Such was the case in Menzoberranzan, where the matron mothers kept their subjects in a continual state of tension and terror, both of them and their spider goddess, and of a multitude of enemies, some real, some purposefully constructed or nurtured for the sole reason of solidifying the matron mother's hold on the fearful. Who will ever remember a matron mother fondly, I wonder, except for those who were brought to power by such a vile creature?

In the matter of making war, the king will find his greatest legacy—and is this not a sadness that has plagued the reasoning races for all of time? In this, too, perhaps particularly in this, the worth of a king can be clearly measured. No king can feel the pain of a soldier's particular wound, but a good king will fear that wound, for it will sting him as profoundly as it stings the man upon whom it was inflicted.

In considering the "numbers" who are his subjects, a good king will never forget the most important number: one. If a general cries victory and exclaims that only ten men died, the good king will temper his celebration with the sorrow for each, one alone repeated, one alone adding weight to his heart.

Only then will he measure his future choices correctly. Only then will he understand the full weight of those choices, not just on the kingdom, but on the one, or ten, or five hundred, who will die or be maimed in his name and for his holdings and their common interest. A king who feels the pain of every man's wounds, or the hunger in every child's belly, or the sorrow in every destitute parent's soul, is one who will place country above crown and community above self. Absent that empathy, any king, even a man of previously stellar temperament, will prove to be no more than a tyrant.

Would that the people chose their kings! Would that they could measure the hearts of those who wish to lead them!

For if that choice was honest, if the representation of the would-be king was a clear and true portrayal of his hopes and dreams for the flock and not a pandering appeal to the worst instincts of those who would choose, then all the folk would grow with the kingdom, or share the pains and losses. Like family, or groups of true friends, or dwarf clans, the folk would celebrate their common hopes and dreams in their every action.

But the people do not choose anywhere that I know of in Faerûn. By blood or by deed, the lines are set, and so we hope, each in our own nation, that a man or woman of empathy will ascend, that whoever will come to rule us will do so with an understanding of the pain of a single soldier's wound.

There is beside Mithral Hall now a burgeoning kingdom of unusual composition. For this land, the Kingdom of Many-Arrows, is ruled by a single orc. Obould is his name, and he has crawled free of every cupboard of expectation that I, or Bruenor, or any of the others have tried to construct about him. Nay, not crawled, but has shattered the walls to kindling and strode forward as something beyond the limitations of his race.

Is that my guess or my observation, truly?

My hope, I must admit, for I cannot yet know.

And so my interpretation of Obould's actions to this point is limited by my vantage, and skewed by the risk of optimism. But Obould did not press the attack, as we all expected he certainly would, when doing so would have condemned thousands of his subjects to a grisly death.

Perhaps it was mere pragmatism; the orc king wisely recognized that his gains could not be compounded, and so he looked down and went into a defensive posture to secure those gains. Perhaps when he has done so, beyond any threat of invasion by the outlying kingdoms, he will regroup and press the attack again. I pray that this is not the case; I pray that the orc king is possessed of more empathy—or even of more selfishness in his need to be revered as well as feared—than would be typical of his warlike race. I can only hope that Obould's ambitions were tempered by a recognition of the price the commoner pays for the folly or false pride of the ruler.

I cannot know. And when I consider that such empathy would place this orc above many leaders of the goodly races, then I realize that I am being foolhardy in even entertaining these fantasies. I fear that Obould stopped simply because he knew that he could not continue, else he might well lose all that he had gained and more. Pragmatism, not empathy, ground Obould's war machine to a stop, it would seem.

If that is the case, then so be it. Even in that simple measure of practicality, this orc stands far beyond others of his heritage. If pragmatism alone forces the halt of invasion and the settling of a kingdom, then perhaps such pragmatism is the first step in moving the orcs toward civilization.

Is it all a process, then, a movement toward a better and better way that will lead to the highest form of kingdom? That is my hope: It will not be a straight-line ascent, to be sure. For every stride forward, as with Lady Alustriel's wondrous city of Silverymoon for example, there will be back-steps.

Perhaps the world will end before the goodly races enjoy the peace and prosperity of the perfect realm.

So be it, for it is the journey that matters most.

That is my hope, at least, but the flip of that hope is my fear that it is all a game, and one played most prominently by those who value self above community. The ascent to kingship is a road of battle, and not one walked by the gentle man or woman. The person who values community will oft be deceived and destroyed by the knave whose heart lies in selfish ambitions.

For those who walk that road to the end, for those who feel the weight of leadership upon their shoulders, the only hope lies in the realm of conscience.

Feel the pain of your soldiers, you kings.

Feel the sorrow of your subjects.

Nay, I am not a king. Not by temperament nor by desire. The death of a single subject soldier would slay the heart of King Drizzt Do'Urden. I do not envy the goodly rulers, but I do fear the ones who do not understand that their numbers have names, or that the greatest gain to the self lies in the cheers and the love fostered by the common good.

—Drizzt Do'Urden

CHAPTER

CASTLE D'AERTHE

10

The day had been mild of that time of year, though it was gray and with a persistent, soaking drizzle. The clouds had broken right before sunset, blown away by a north wind that reached down from the Great Glacier like the cold, dead fingers of the Witch-King himself. That clearing had afforded the townsfolk of Palishchuk a brilliant red sunset, but by the time the stars had begun to twinkle above, the air had grown so cold that all but a few had been driven indoors to their peat-filled hearths.

Not so for Wingham and Arrayan, though. They stood side by side on Palishchuk's northern wall, staring out and wondering. Before them on the dark ground, puddles and rivulets shone silver in the moonlight, like the veins of a great sleeping beast, frozen, as was the ground below.

"Do you think they will thaw again before the first snows?" Arrayan asked her much-older uncle.

"I have known the freeze to come earlier in the year than this," Wingham replied. "One year, it never actually thawed!"

"1337," Arrayan recited, for she had heard the stories of the two-year freeze many times from Wingham. "The Year of the Wandering Maiden."

The old half-orc smiled at her overly-exasperated tone and the roll of her eyes. "They say a great white dragon was behind it all," Wingham teased, the beginning of one of the many, many folktales that had arisen from that unusually cold summer.

Arrayan rolled her eyes again, and Wingham laughed heartily and draped his arm around her.

"Perhaps this winter will be one of which I will spin yarns in the decades hence," the woman said at length, and with enough honest trepidation in her voice to take the grin from Wingham's wrinkled and weathered face.

He hugged her closer, and she tucked her arms and pulled her fur-lined cowl tighter around her frosty cheeks.

"It has been an eventful year already," Wingham replied. "And one with a happy endin' . . ." He paused when she tossed him a fearful look. "A happy *middle*," he corrected.

592

For indeed, the adventure that they all had thought successfully concluded with the defeat of the dracolich had returned to them yet again with the arrival a few days earlier of Artemis Entreri and Jarlaxle. The pair had come riding in to Palishchuk on hellish steeds, coal black and with hooves pounding fire into the frozen tundra.

They had been welcomed warmly, as heroes, of course. They had earned the accolades for their work beside Arrayan and Olgerkhan, and they had been granted free room and board in Palishchuk at any time for the remainder of their lives. Indeed, when the pair had first arrived, several of the townsfolk had argued loudly over who would have the honor of boarding them for their stay.

How quickly things had changed from that initial meeting.

For the pair would not stay. They were merely passing through on their way to the conquered castle—Castle D'aerthe, Jarlaxle had named it. *Their* castle, the seat of their power, hub of the kingdom they planned to rule.

The kingdom they planned to rule.

A kingdom that by definition would surround or encompass Palishchuk.

There had been no answers forthcoming to the multitude of questions shot back at the surprising pair by the leaders of Palishchuk. Jarlaxle had nodded, and merely added, "We hold nothing but respect and admiration for Palishchuk, and we consider you great friends in this wondrous adventure upon which we now embark."

Then they had gone, the pair of them back on their impressive steeds, thundering out of Palishchuk's northern gate, and while some of the leaders had called for the pair to be detained and questioned, none had the courage to stand before them.

But they had returned, and the city's scouts had been filtering in and out with reports of shadowy figures moving about the castle's formidable walls, and of gargoyles taking flight only to crouch at another spot along the parapets and towers of the magical construct.

Arrayan glanced down the length of the wall, where a doubled number of guardsmen stood ready and nervous.

"Do you think they will come?" she asked.

"They?"

"The gargoyles. I have heard the tales of Palishchuk's fight while I was battling within the castle walls. Do you think this night, or tomorrow's, will bring another struggle to the city?"

Wingham looked back to the north and shrugged, but was shaking his head by the time his shoulders slumped back down. "The scouts have claimed sightings of gargoyles in the dark of night," he said. "I can imagine their fear as they crouched outside of that formidable place."

Arrayan looked at him at the same time he was turning to her.

"Even if it is true and Jarlaxle and Artemis Entreri have brought the castle back to life, I fear no attack from them," Wingham went on. "Why would they have bothered to stop in Palishchuk to proclaim their friendship if they meant to attack us?"

"To put us off our guard?"

With a nod, Wingham directed her attention back to the doubled sentries lining the wall. "Our guard would have been nonexistent had they just ridden by the city, to animate the castle and attack while we played under the delusion that our battle was successfully completed, I expect."

Arrayan spent a moment digesting that as she looked back to the north. She smiled when she met Wingham's gaze yet again. "Are you not curious, though?"

"More than you are," the old barker replied with a mischievous grin. "Fetch Olgerkhan, will you? I would appreciate his sturdy companionship as we venture to the home of our former allies."

"Former?"

"And present, we must believe."

"And hope."

Wingham smiled. "Castle D'aerthe," he mumbled as Arrayan started for the ladder. Even more quietly, he added, "It can only portend trouble."

Two sets of eyes looked back in the direction of Wingham and Arrayan, from far away and with neither pair aware of the other. On the southern wall of the magical castle north of Palishchuk, Jarlaxle and Entreri did not huddle under heavy woolen cloaks—nothing that mundane for Jarlaxle, of course, who had taken out a small red globe, placed it on the stone between them, and uttered a command word. The stone glowed red, brightly for a moment, then dimmed and began to radiate heat comparable to that of a small campfire. The northern wind rushing off the Great Glacier still bit at them, for they were thirty feet up atop the wall, but the mediating warmth sufficed.

"What now?" Entreri asked, after they had been up there for many minutes, staring in silence across the miles to the dim glow of Palishchuk's nighttime fires.

"You started the fight," Jarlaxle replied.

"We ran from the Citadel. Better that we fight them in the streets of Heliogabalus, one alley at a time."

"It is a bigger fight than just the Citadel," Jarlaxle calmly explained—and indeed, it was that tone, so self-assured and reasonable, that had Entreri on his edge. Whenever Jarlaxle got comfortable about something, Entreri knew from experience, big trouble was usually brewing.

"We have stirred the nest," Entreri agreed, "between the king and Knellict. So now we must choose a side."

"And you would select?"

"Gareth."

"Conscience?"

"Practicality," Entreri countered. "If there is to be an open war between the Citadel of Assassins and King Gareth, Gareth will win. I've seen it before, in Calimport, and you've known this struggle in Menzoberranzan. When a guild pricks too sharply at the side of the open powers, they retaliate."

"So you believe that King Gareth will obliterate Knellict and the Citadel of Assassins? He will wipe them from the Bloodstone Lands?"

Entreri mulled that over for a few moments, then shook his head. "No. He will drive them from the streets and back into their remote hideouts. Some of those will likely fall, as well. Some of the Citadel's leaders will be killed or imprisoned. But Gareth will never truly be rid of them. That is never the way." He paused and considered his own words, then chortled, "He wouldn't wish to be completely rid of them."

Jarlaxle watched him out of the corner of his eyes, and Entreri noted the little grin spreading on the drow's face. "King Gareth is a paladin," the drow reminded. "Do you doubt his sincerity?"

"Does it matter? Having the Citadel of Assassins lurking in the shadows is good for Gareth and his friends, a reminder to the people of Damara of the alternative to their hero king.

"He is no Ellery, perhaps, in that he won't deal with the Citadel, but he uses them all the same. It is the nature of power."

"You have a cynical view of the world."

"It is well earned, I assure you. And it is accurate."

"I did not say it was not."

"Yet you seem to think Gareth above reproach because he is a paladin."

"No, I think him predictable because he is guided more by principle—ill-reasoned or not—than by pragmatism. Gareth's end plan is always known, is it not? He may be served well by the Citadel, but he is likely too blinded by dogma to see that truth."

"You still have not answered my question," said Entreri. "What now for us?"

"It seems obvious."

"Enlighten me."

"Always."

"Now."

Jarlaxle gave an exasperated sigh. "We declare our independence from King Gareth, of course," he replied.

Far below the pair, very near the room where the bones of Urshula the dracolich lay, Kimmuriel Oblodra conferred with his drow lieutenants, laying out plans for the defense of the castle, for assaults from the walls and gates, and most important of all, for orderly and swift retreat back to that very chamber. Not far from the drow, a magical portal glowed a light blue. Through it came more drow warriors of Bregan D'aerthe, driving mobs of goblins, kobolds, and orcs bearing supplies, armaments, and furniture, fashioned mostly of sturdy Underdark mushrooms.

A continual line passed through the gate, and other drow went through in the other direction, back to the corresponding magical portal set in the maze of tunnels along the great Clawrift in Menzoberranzan, the complex that Bregan D'aerthe called home.

"The sooner we are gone, the better," one of Kimmuriel's lieutenants remarked, and though others nodded their accord, Kimmuriel flashed the drow a dangerous look.

"Do say," the psionicist prompted.

"This place is uneasy," the drow replied. "It teems with an energy that I do not recognize."

"And thus, an energy you fear?"

"The portcullis on the front gate . . . grows," another soldier added. "It was damaged by unwanted entry, and now it repairs itself of its own accord. This is no inert construction, but a magical, living creature."

"Is this place any different than the towers of the Crystal Shard?" said the first lieutenant.

"Is Jarlaxle, you mean," Kimmuriel remarked, and neither of the pair disavowed him of that notion.

"I do not know," the psionicist answered honestly. "Though I believe that Jarlaxle is acting of his own volition and wisdom here. If I did not, I would not have marched us to this wretched place." He led their gazes to the portal, and another group of goblins trudging through, bearing several rolled tapestries and carpets. "He recognizes equivocation . . ."

"An easy egress," one of the others remarked.

Beside them, a quartet of goblins tripped and stumbled, spilling a mushroom-fashioned hutch across the floor. Drow drivers stepped up, cracking their whips against the flesh of the miserable creatures, who all fell to their hands and knees to try to collect the broken pieces.

The soldiers beside Kimmuriel nodded, recognizing the truth of it all, that they weren't bringing anything of real value to the castle, just utilitarian furniture and simple dressings.

And fodder, of course. Goblins, orcs, and kobolds, all as easily expendable to the dark elves as a cheap piece of mushroom furniture.

<hr />

"Our independence?" Artemis Entreri answered after many stunned moments. "Could we not just leave the Bloodstone Lands?"

"And take this castle with us?"

Entreri went silent, finally understanding the drow's machinations. "You were serious when you warned Palishchuk to remain neutral?"

"We must pick a name for our kingdom," Jarlaxle said, ignoring the question and confirming it all at once. "Have you any suggestions?"

Entreri looked at him with complete incredulity.

"The gauntlet is down," Jarlaxle said. "You threw it at Knellict's feet when you did not kill the merchant."

Entreri looked away again, his lips going very tight.

"Was the man not worthy of your blade? Or was he not deserving of it?"

Entreri turned a hateful gaze the drow's way.

"I thought as much," Jarlaxle said. "You might have found a better moment to discover your conscience. But it does not matter, for it had to come to this in any event. Better now, I suppose, than when Knellict grew a better appreciation for what has truly come against him."

"And what might that be? A pair of impetuous fools, a small army of gargoyles and an undead dragon we can hardly control?"

"Look more closely," Jarlaxle said slyly, and he directed Entreri's attention to the watchtower off to the right of the gatehouse. A slender form moved there, silent as, and seeming no more substantial than, the shadows.

A drow.

Entreri snapped his gaze back over Jarlaxle. "Kimmuriel?"

"Bregan D'aerthe," Jarlaxle replied. "And ample slave fodder arrive regularly through magical gates. If you wish to start a war, my friend, you need an army."

"Start a war?"

"I had hoped that we could do this more easily, and more by proxy," Jarlaxle admitted. "I had hoped that we could get the two beasts—the king and the Grandfather of Assassins—to devour each other. You played our hand too quickly."

"And now you wish to start a war?"

"No," Jarlaxle corrected. "But it is not beyond the realm of possibility. If Knellict comes, we will drive him back."

"With the drow and Urshula and all the rest?"

"With everything at our disposal. Knellict is not one to be bargained with."

"Let us just leave."

That seemed to catch Jarlaxle off guard. He leaned on the wall, staring out at the south and the darkness that was interrupted only by the glow of a few fires burning in Palishchuk and the starlight. "No," he finally answered.

"There is a big world out there, where we might get lost—sufficiently so. It would seem that we have worn out our welcome."

"With Knellict."

"That is enough."

Jarlaxle shook his head. "We can leave whenever we wish, thanks to Kimmuriel. As of now, I do not desire to go. I like it here." He paused there and let his smile fall over Entreri until the man finally acknowledged it—with a derisive snort, of course. "Consider Calihye, my friend. Remind yourself that some things are worth fighting for."

"We make a stand where we need not. Calihye is not a plot of ground or a magically created castle. There is nothing to stop her from coming with us. Your analogy cannot hold."

Jarlaxle nodded, conceding the point. His smile told Entreri, however, that the point was moot. Jarlaxle liked it there; for the drow, apparently, that was enough.

Entreri looked over to the corner tower again, and though he saw no movement there, he knew that Jarlaxle's friends had come. He thought of Calimport and the catastrophe Bregan D'aerthe had wrought there, eliminating guilds that had stood for decades and altering the balance of power within the city with relative ease.

Would the same occur in the Bloodstone Lands?

Or was Jarlaxle's ambition even more ominous? A kingdom to rival Damara. A kingdom built on an army of drow and slave fodder, on undead servants and animated gargoyles, and forged in a bargain with a dracolich?

Entreri shuddered, and it was not from the cold northern wind.

"A gargoyle," Arrayan remarked, nodding toward the dark castle wall where a humanoid, winged creature had taken flight, moving from one guard tower to another. "The castle is alive."

"Curse them," Olgerkhan grunted, while Wingham only sighed.

"We should have known better than to trust a drow," Arrayan said.

"How often have I heard those words about our own half-orc race," Wingham was quick to answer, drawing surprised looks from both of his companions.

"The castle is alive," Olgerkhan reiterated.

"And Palishchuk has not been threatened," said Wingham. "As Jarlaxle promised."

"You would trust the word of a drow?" Olgerkhan asked.

Wingham's answer came in the form of a shrug and the simple reply of, "Have we a choice?"

"We beat the castle once," Olgerkhan growled in defiance, and he held a clenched fist up before him, the muscles in his arm bulging and knotting.

"You beat an unthinking animation," Wingham corrected. "This time, it has a brain."

"And one who has marched several steps ahead of us," Arrayan agreed. "Even inside, when they saved me from Canthan. When they brought you back to life through the vampirism of Entreri's dagger," she said to Olgerkhan, stealing much of his bluster. "Jarlaxle understood it all where I, and the wizard Canthan, did not. I wonder if even then his goal was not to destroy the construct, but to control it."

"His castle stands here, alive and strong, and King Gareth's is to the south," Wingham remarked. "And Palishchuk is in between them."

"Again," Arrayan said with great resignation, "as it was with Zhengyi."

⊟══╪══⊟

"I am no longer surprised by the clumsiness of the surface races," Kimmuriel Oblodra said to Jarlaxle. The two were very near the same spot on the wall where Jarlaxle had held his conversation with Artemis Entreri a short while before, and as with then, they looked out to the south. Not to Palishchuk, though, for Kimmuriel had directed Jarlaxle's attention to a copse of leafless trees a bit to the right, in the shadow of a small hill. Neither drow could make out the forms that Kimmuriel had promised his former leader lurked in there, a trio of half-orcs.

"There is a wizard among them," Kimmuriel said. "She is of little consequence and no real power."

"Arrayan," Jarlaxle explained. "She has her uses, and is comfort to weary eyes—as much as any with orc heritage could be, of course."

"Your promises did not hold much sway in the town, it seems."

"They are being careful, and who can blame them?"

"They will know that the construct is awakening," said Kimmuriel. "The gargoyles fly about."

Jarlaxle nodded, making it obvious that they did so at his behest. "Have they seen any of your scouts? Are they aware of any drow about other than myself?"

Kimmuriel scoffed at the ridiculous notion. Drow were not seen by such pitiful creatures as these unless they wanted to be seen.

"Show them, then," Jarlaxle instructed.

Kimmuriel stared hard at him, to which Jarlaxle nodded a confirmation.

"You would use terror to hold them at bay?" Kimmuriel asked. "That speaks of diplomatic weakness."

"Palishchuk will have to choose eventually."

"Between Jarlaxle—"

"King Artemis the First," Jarlaxle corrected with a grin.

"Between *Jarlaxle*," the stubborn Kimmuriel insisted, "and King Gareth?"

"I surely hope not—not for a long while, at least," Jarlaxle replied. "I doubt that Gareth will be quick to charge to the north, but the Citadel of Assassins is likely already infiltrating Palishchuk. It is my hope that the half-orcs will think it unwise to provide aid to Knellict's vile crew."

"Because they will be more fearful of Jarlaxle and the dark elves?"

"Of course."

"Your fear tactics will work against you when King Gareth comes calling," Kimmuriel warned, and he knew that he had struck a chord there by Jarlaxle's long pause.

"By that time, I hope to have Knellict long dispatched," Jarlaxle explained. "We can then build a measure of trust to the half-orcs. Enough trust coupled with the fear that will force them to keep King Gareth at arm's length."

Kimmuriel was shaking his head as he looked back to the southwest.

"Show them," Jarlaxle said to him. "And allow them to go on their way."

Kimmuriel wasn't about to question Jarlaxle just then, for his words to his doubting lieutenants just a short while before had been spoken sincerely. It was Jarlaxle's scheme, and in truth, Kimmuriel, for all of his growing confidence, recognized that standing beside him was a drow who had survived the intrigue of Menzoberranzan and elsewhere for several centuries. With the notable exception of the near-disaster in Calimport, had Jarlaxle's schemes ever failed?

And that near-disaster, Kimmuriel pointedly reminded himself, had been caused in no small part by the corrupting influence of the artifact known as Crenshinibon.

The psionicist could not manage a reassuring expression to his companion, though. For all of the history of successful manipulations Jarlaxle brought to the table, Kimmuriel had familiarized himself quite extensively with the recent events in the region known as the Bloodstone Lands, and had come to understand well the power King Gareth Dragonsbane could wield.

Jarlaxle's own actions showed him clearly that he was not alone in his fears, he realized. Jarlaxle had not reclaimed control of Bregan D'aerthe, though he had bade Kimmuriel to garner all of their resources. For all of his outward confidence, Jarlaxle was hedging his bets by allowing Kimmuriel complete control. He was protecting himself from that very confidence.

Understanding the compliment that Jarlaxle was once again paying to him, Kimmuriel offered a salute before going on his way.

CHAPTER

THE LURE

11

Jureemo Pascadadle put his back against the wall just inside the door of the tavern and heaved a great sigh of relief. Out in the street, several of his companions lay dead or incapacitated, and several others had been dragged off by the thugs from Spysong.

Glad indeed was Jureemo that he had been given the rear guard position, watching the back of his Citadel crew as they had closed in on the dark elf and the assassin. "Spysong," he muttered under his breath, his throat filling with bile.

The door burst open beside him and the man fell back with a shriek. In stumbled Kiniquips the Short, a slender—by halfling standards—little rogue of great renown within the organization. Kiniquips was a master of disguise, actually serving as a trainer of such at the Citadel, and was often the point halfling on Citadel of Assassins operations in Heliogabalus. He had spent the better part of two years creating his waif alter-ego. Watching him stumble through the common room, though, Jureemo knew that the halfling's cover had been blown. His shirt was ripped and a bright line of blood showed across his left shoulder, and it looked like a substantial part of his dark brown hair had been torn away, as well.

He glanced at Jureemo and the man nearly fainted. But Kiniquips was too much the professional to betray an associate, even with a glance, and so the halfling looked away immediately and stumbled on.

The air erupted with a shrill whistling in Kiniquips's wake, though, and a most unusual missile, a trio of black iron balls spinning at the ends of short lengths of rope flew past the startled Jureemo and caught the fleeing halfling around the waist and legs. The balls wrapped around the poor fellow and came crunching together with devastating efficiency, cracking bones and thoroughly tangling him up.

Kiniquips hit the floor in a heap, ending up on his side, writhing in pain and whimpering pitifully. Tables skidded every which way as the patrons of the tavern scrambled to get as far from him as possible.

For in came a pair of dangerous-looking characters, an elf and a human woman, both dressed in dark leather. The elf had thrown the bolos, obviously, and moved steadily to retrieve them, his fine sword set comfortably on his hip. The woman wore a pair of bandoliers set full of gleaming throwing knives and moved with the same grace as her companion, betraying a lifetime of training.

With brutal efficiency, the elf unwound and yanked the bolos free, and the halfling shrieked again in pain.

Jureemo looked away and headed for the open door. The woman called after him, but he put his head down and hurried around the open door, turning fast for the street.

And there he was blocked by a man in plain, dirty robes. Jureemo tried to push by, but with a single hand, the man stopped him fully.

Jureemo offered a confused expression and looked down at the hand.

With a subtle shift and short thrust, the man in robes sent Jureemo stumbling back into the room, uncomfortably close to the dangerous woman.

"Wh-what attack is this?" he stammered, looking plaintively about. His continuing protests stuck in his throat, though, as he locked stares with the woman.

"This one?" she asked, turning to the elf behind her.

In response, the elf leaned on the fallen Kiniquips's broken hip, and the halfling yelped.

"That one?" the elf asked Kiniquips.

The halfling grimaced and looked away, and grunted again as the elf pressed down on his hip.

"What is the meaning of this?" Jureemo demanded, and he cautiously stepped back from the woman. Others in the tavern stirred at that display of brutality, and it occurred to Jureemo that he might garner some assistance after all.

The woman looked from him to the man in the robes. "This one, Master Kane?" she asked.

The stirring stopped immediately, and a palpable silence, almost a physical numbness, fell over the tavern.

Jureemo had to remind himself to breathe, then he gave up trying when Master Kane walked over to stand before him. The monk stared at him for a long time, and though Jureemo tried to look away, for some reason he could not. He felt naked in front of that legendary monk, as if Kane looked right through him, or right into his heart.

"You are of the Citadel of Assassins," Kane stated.

Jureemo babbled incoherently for a few moments, his head shaking and nodding all at once.

And Kane just stared.

The walls seemed to close in on the trembling assassin; he felt as if the floor was rushing up to swallow him, and he hoped it would! Panic bubbled through him. He knew that he had been discovered—Kane had stated the fact, not asked him. And those eyes! The monk didn't blink. The monk knew all of it!

Jureemo didn't reach for his own knife, set in his belt at the small of his back. He couldn't begin to imagine a fight with that monster. His sensibilities darted in every different direction, instincts replacing rational thought. He cried out suddenly and leaped for the door . . . or started to.

A white wooden walking stick flashed up before him, cracking him under the chin. He vaguely felt the sensation, the sweet and warm taste, of blood filling his mouth, and he sensed that walking stick sliding under his armpit. He didn't see Kane grab its free end, behind his shoulder-blade, but he did realize, briefly, that he was airborne, spinning head-over-heels, then falling free. He hit the floor flat on his back and immediately propped himself up on his elbows—

—right before the walking stick, that deadly jo stick, cracked him again across the forehead, dropping him flat to the floor.

"Take them both to the castle," Kane instructed his minions.

"This one will require the attention of a priest, perhaps even Friar Dugald," replied the elf standing over the halfling.

Kane shrugged as if it did not matter, which of course it did not. Certainly the priests would make the little one more comfortable.

Perhaps he would even be able to walk up the gallows steps under his own power.

The creature was well-dressed by the standards of Damaran nobles, let alone the expectations aroused by his obvious orc heritage. And he carried himself with an air of dignity and regal bearing, like a royal courier or a butler at one of the finer houses in Waterdeep. That fact was not lost on the half-orcs manning Palishchuk's northern wall as they watched the orc's graceful approach. He walked up as if without the slightest concern, though several arrows were trained upon him, and he dipped a polite bow as he stopped, swinging out one arm to reveal that he held a rolled scroll.

"Well met," he called in perfect Common, and with an accent very unlike anything the sentries might have expected. He seemed almost foppish, and his voice held a nasal quality, something quite uncommon in a race known for flat noses and wide nostrils. "I pray you grant me entrance to your fair city, or, if that is not to be, then I bid you to fetch your leadership."

"What business ye got here?" one of the sentries barked at him.

"Well, good sir, it is an announcement of course," the orc replied, holding forth his hand and the scroll. "And one I am instructed by my master to make once, and once only."

"Ye tell it to us and we might let ye in," the sentry replied. "Then again, we might not."

"Or we might be getting Wingham and the council," a second sentry explained.

"Then again, we might not," the first added.

The orc straightened and put one hand on his hip, standing with one foot flat and the other heel up. He made no move to unroll the scroll, or to do anything else.

"Well?" the first sentry prompted.

"I am instructed by my master to make the announcement once, and once only," the orc replied.

"Well then ye've got yerself some trouble," said the sentry. "For we aren't letting ye in, and aren't bothering our council until we know what ye're about."

"I will wait," the orc decided.

"Wait? Ack, fullblood, how long are ye to wait, then?"

The orc shrugged as if it did not matter.

"We'll leave ye to freeze dead on the path before the gate, ye fool."

"Better that than disobey my master," the orc replied without the slightest hesitation, and that made the sentries exchange curious, concerned looks. The orc pulled a rich, fur-lined cloak tightly around his shoulders and turned slightly to put his back to the wind.

"And who might yer master be, that ye're so willing to freeze?" the first sentry asked.

"King Artemis the First, of course," the orc replied.

The sentry mouthed the name silently, his eyes widening. He glanced at his companions, to see them similarly struggling to digest the words.

"Artemis Entreri sent ye?"

"Of course not, peasant," the orc replied. "I am not of sufficient significance to speak with King Artemis. I serve at the pleasure of First Citizen Jarlaxle."

The two lead sentries slipped back behind the wall. "Damned fools meant it," one said. "They built themselves a kingdom."

"There's a difference between building one and just saying ye built one," the first replied.

"Well, where'd they find the page?" the other asked. "And look at him, and listen to him. He isn't one to be found wandering about in a fullblood hunting party."

A third guard moved up to the huddled pair. "I'm going for Wingham and the councilors," he explained. "They'll be wanting to see this." He glanced out over the wall at their unexpected visitor. "And hear it."

In less than half an hour, Wingham, Arrayan, Olgerkhan, the leadership of Palishchuk, and most of the town's citizens were gathered at the northernmost square, watching the strange courier prance in through the gate.

"I almost expect to see flowers dropping in his wake," Wingham whispered to Arrayan, and the mage giggled despite the obvious gravity of the situation.

Taking no apparent notice of any of the many titters filtering about the crowd, the fullblood orc moved to the center of the gathering, and with great dramatic flourish, an exaggerated flip of his wrist, he unrolled the scroll before him, holding it up in both hands.

"Hear ye! Hear ye!" he called. "And hear ye well, O good citizens of Palishchuk, in the land formerly known as Vaasa."

That started some stirring.

"Formerly?" Wingham whispered.

"Never trust a drow," Olgerkhan added, leaning past Arrayan, who was no longer giggling, to address Wingham.

"King Artemis the First doth proclaim full and unfettered rights to Palishchuk and the people therein," the orc went on. "His Greatness makes no claim over your fair city, nor a demand of tithing, nor does he deny any of you any passage over any road, bridge, or open land in the entirety of D'aerthe."

"D'aerthe?" Wingham echoed with a shake of his head. "Drow name."

"Excepting, of course, those roads, bridges, and open land within Castle D'aerthe itself," the orc added. "And even in there, Palishchukians are welcome . . . by specific grant of entrance, of course.

"King Artemis sees no enemy when he looks your way, and it is his fondest wish that his reign will be marked with fair trade and prosperity for D'aerthian and Palishchukian alike."

"What is he talking about?" Olgerkhan whispered to Wingham.

"War, I expect," the wizened and worldly old half-orc replied.

"This is insanity," Arrayan said.

"Never trust a drow," Olgerkhan lectured.

Arrayan looked to Wingham, who merely shrugged as the fullblood finished his reading, mostly reciting titles and adjectives—excellence, magnificent, wondrous—to accompany the name of King Artemis the First of D'aerthe.

As he finished, the orc flicked his wrist and let go with his bottom hand, and the formed parchment rolled up tight. With a swift and graceful movement, the orc tucked it under one arm, and stood again, hand on hip.

Wingham glanced across the way to a group of three of the town's leading councilors, and waited for them to nod deferentially for him to lead the response—a not surprising invitation, for the half-orcs of Palishchuk often looked to the worldly Wingham for guidance in matters outside of their secluded gates. At least, for matters that did not entail the immediate threat of battle, as was usually the case.

"And what is your name, good sir?" Wingham addressed the courier.

"I am of no consequence," came the reply.

"Would you have me speak to you as fullblood, orc, or D'aerthian Courier, perhaps?" Wingham asked as he stepped out from the gathering, trying to get a better take on the odd creature.

"Speak to me as you would to King Artemis the First," said the orc. "For I am but the ears and mouth of His Greatness."

Wingham looked to the town councilors, who had no insight to offer other than smirks and shrugs.

"We beg you look past our obvious surprise . . . King Artemis," Wingham said. "Such an announcement is hardly expected, of course."

"You were told as much less than two tendays ago, when King Artemis and the first citizen rode through your fair city."

"But still . . ."

"You did not accept his word?"

Wingham paused, not wanting to cross any unseen lines. He remembered well the battle Palishchuk had fought with the castle construct's gargoyles, and neither he nor any of the others wanted to replay that deadly night.

"You must admit that the claim of Vaasa—"

"D'aerthe," the orc interrupted. "Vaasa is to be used only when speaking of what was, not of what is."

"The claim of a kingdom here, by a king and a first citizen until recently unknown to all in the Bloodstone Lands, is unprecedented, you must agree," Wingham said, avoiding any overt concurrence or disagreement. "And yes, we are surprised, for there is another king who has claimed this land."

"King Gareth rules in Damara," the orc replied. "He has made no formal claim on the land once known as Vaasa, excepting his insistence that the land be 'cleansed' of vermin, including one race that you claim as half your heritage, good sir, in case you had not noticed."

That ruffled some feathers among the gathered half-orcs, and more than a few harsh whispers filtered about the uneasy crowd.

"But yes, of course, and your surprise was not unforeseen," the orc went on. "And it is a minor reaction compared to that which the first citizen expects will greet your courier when he travels to the D'aerthian, formerly the Vaasan, Gate and through Bloodstone Pass to the village of the same name." He snapped his arm out, handing Wingham a second scroll, sealed with a wax mark.

"All that King Artemis the First bids you, and of course it is in your own interest as well, is that you send a courier forthwith to King Gareth to deliver news of the birth of D'aerthe. It would do well for King Gareth to cease his murderous activities within the borders of D'aerthe at once, for the sake of peace between our lands.

"And truly," the orc finished with a great and sweeping bow, "such harmony is all that King Artemis the First desires."

Wingham hardly had an answer to that; how could he? He took the rolled parchment, glanced again at the strange seal, which was formed of some green wax that he did not recognize, and glanced again at the puzzled councilors.

By the time he looked back, the orc was already swaggering well on his way to the city's northern gate.

And no one made a move to intercept him.

"You enjoyed that," Jarlaxle said with a wry grin that was not matched by his psionicist counterpart.

"I will itch for a tenday from wearing the shell of an orc," Kimmuriel replied.

"You wore it well."

Kimmuriel scowled at him, a most unusual show of emotion from the intellectually-locked dark elf.

"News will travel fast to Damara," Jarlaxle predicted. "Likely Wingham will send Arrayan or some other magic-user to deliver the announcement before the way is sealed by deep snows."

"Then why did you not wait until the snows began?" asked Kimmuriel. "You will grant Gareth the time to facilitate passage."

"Grant him?" Jarlaxle asked, leaning forward on his castle parapet. "My friend, I am counting on it. I do not desire to have the fool Knellict here uncontested, and I expect that King Gareth will be more reasonable than the betrayed wizard of the Citadel of Assassins. With Gareth, it will be politics. With Knellict, it is already personal."

"Because you travel with a fool."

"I would not expect patience from a human," said Jarlaxle. "They do not live long enough. Entreri has moved the situation along, nothing more. Whether now before winter's onslaught, or in the cold rain of spring, Gareth will demand his answers. Better to pit him against Knellict outside our gates than to deal with each separately."

Athrogate's misery at being jailed was mitigated somewhat by the generous amounts of mead and ale his gaolers provided. And Athrogate never let it be said that he couldn't sublimate—well, he used the words, 'wash down,' since 'sublimate' was a bit beyond him—his misery with a few pounds of food and a few gallons of ale.

So he sat on his hard bed in his small but not totally uncomfortable cell, filling his mouth with bread and cake and washing it down with fast-overturned flagons of liquid, golden and brown alternately. And to pass the time, between bites and gulps and burps and farts, he sang his favorite dwarven ditties, like "Skipping Threesies with an Orc's Entrails" and "Grow Your Beard Long, Woman, or Winter'll Freeze yer Nipples."

He saved the latter for those times when a female elf or a human woman was set as guard outside his door, and he took special care to raise his voice to a thunderous level whenever he happened upon the refrain about "shakin' them by the ankles, so ye're seein' up their skirts."

For all of his bluster and belch-filled outward joviality, though, Athrogate could not truly ignore the continual hammering outside of his cell's small, high window. Late one moonlit night, when the lone guard outside his cell door breathed in the smooth rhythms of sleep, the dwarf had propped his angled cot against the wall and managed to get up high enough to peek out.

They were building a gallows, with a long trap door and no less than seven noose-arms.

Athrogate had been told his crime against King Gareth, and he knew well the penalty for treason. And though he was cooperating, and had surrendered several of Knellict's spies placed in Heliogabalus—men he had never really liked anyway—none of Gareth's representatives had given him any hint that his sentence might be put aside or even reduced.

But he had ale and mead and plenty of food. He figured he might as well be fat if the door dropped out beneath him so that his neck would get a clean break and he wouldn't be flailing about and peeing himself in front of all the spectators. He had seen that a few times, and decided it would not be a fitting end for one of so many accomplishments as he.

Perhaps he could even bargain to have his name kept on the plaque at the Vaasan Gate. . . .

He had that very thought in mind late one afternoon when his cell door swung open and a familiar figure strode into the room.

"Ah, Athrogate, it will take more than a Bloodstone winter to make you lean for the spring," said Celedon Kierney.

"Lean's for elfs," the dwarf grunted at the charming rogue who had more than a bit of elf blood in him. "For them who're needin' to twist and turn to get out o' the hammer's way."

"You don't think that wise?"

"Bah!" Athrogate blustered and puffed out his chest, smacking his balled fist against it.

"And what if that hammer was instead a fine elven sword?"

"I'd grab it and snap it, then take yer hand and pull ye close for a fine Athrogate hug."

Celedon grinned widely.

"Ye're not for believin' me, then? Well go and get yer fine elven blade. And bring a bow, and not the shooting kind, when ye do. I'll bend yer sword over and play ye a tune that'll put ye in a dancing mood afore I give ye the big hug."

"I do not doubt that you could do just that, Athrogate," Celedon replied, and the dwarf looked at him with complete puzzlement. "Your exploits in Vaasa have been sung across all the Bloodstone Lands. A pity it is, as I'm sure King Gareth will agree when he arrives this very night, that one so accomplished as Athrogate chose to collude with the likes of Timoshenko."

"The Grandpappy? Bah, never met him."

"Knellict then, and voice no denials."

"Bah!" Athrogate snorted again. "Ye got no course to hang me."

"Hang you?" Celedon Kierney replied with exaggerated incredulity—the animated rogue was good at that particular ploy, Athrogate recognized. "Why, good dwarf, we would never deign to do such a thing. Nay, we intend to celebrate you, in public, to honor you for your aid in capturing so many criminals of the dreaded Citadel of Assassins."

Athrogate stared hatefully at the man, at the threat that made hanging seem quite pleasant by comparison. The mere thought of an angry Knellict in that moment sent a shiver coursing up the dwarf's sturdy spine.

"There may even be a knighthood in it for Athrogate, hero of Vaasa, and now hero of the crown in Heliogabalus."

The dwarf spat on the floor. "Ye're a wretched one, ain't ye."

Celedon laughed at him, and walked out of the small cell. He paused at the door and turned back to the dwarf. "I will have a ladder brought with your breakfast," he said, glancing at the window. "Better than a leaning cot. We have prepared a ceremony for King Gareth, of course, as is right and just."

"Pleasure for ye, elf?"

"Practicality, good dwarf, and grim resolve. We've not enough cells, nor are they really called for on this occasion." He gave a wink and half-turned, before adding, "They attacked a knight of the order—an apprentice knight, to be honest. The case is clear enough, is it not?"

"Ye know it's more muddled than that," said Athrogate. "Ye know what happened at that castle, and what allegiances yer own king's niece struck on her own."

"I know of no such thing," Celedon replied. "I know only that order must be maintained, and that the Citadel of Assassins has brought this fate upon itself."

"And yer Lady Ellery's still dead."

"And Gareth is still the king."

On that definitive note, Celedon Kierney exited the room, banging the door closed behind him.

True to his word, Celedon had a ladder delivered to Athrogate that morning, along with his voluminous breakfast. The dwarf munched his food loudly, trying to drown out the ceremony playing outside his window, trying to ignore the reading of charges and the demands for confession, many of which were offered in pathetic, whining tones.

"Bah, just go with yer dignity, ye dolts," Athrogate muttered more than once, and he chomped down all the harder on his crusty cake.

Like a moth to the flame, though, the dwarf could not deny his curiosity, and he managed to set and climb the ladder just in time to see seven of the Citadel's men drop from the platform and sway at the end of a rope. Most died right away, Jureemo Pascadadle among them, and two, including a halfling Athrogate knew as Kiniquips the Short—*Master* Kiniquips—struggled and kicked for some time before finally going still.

Master Kiniquips, Athrogate thought as he climbed back down to his remaining portions.

Master of the Citadel.

Athrogate winced as he considered Celedon's threats.

Suddenly, and for perhaps the first time in his life, the dwarf didn't feel the desire to eat.

CHAPTER

CAT AND MOUSE

12

"What do I do?" the nervous woman asked the great mage.

Knellict eyed her sternly and she shrank away from him. It was not her place to ask such questions. Her duties at the Vaasan Gate were simple enough, and hadn't changed in five years, after all.

The woman chewed on her lower lip as she summoned the courage to press on—and she knew that if she did not, the danger to her would be greater than that of invoking the anger of the mage. "Pardon, sir," she said, working her way around the damaging words. "But people are hanging by their necks, o' course. Spysong's all about . . . here, too. They're finding our like and turning them on others, and them that don't turn're getting the hemp collar in the south, so it's said."

Knellict's returned stare was utterly cold, devoid of emotion. The woman, despite her fears, couldn't hold firm under that gaze and she lowered her eyes and assumed a submissive and contrite posture, and managed to whisper, "Beggin' yer pardon, sir."

"Consider that it is good that you know of no one here against whom you might turn," Knellict said to her. He reached over and cupped her chin in his hand and gently tilted her head up.

The woman's knees wobbled when she looked into the archmage's cruel face.

"Because of course nothing that Spysong might do to you would approach the exquisite agony you would suffer at my vengeful hands. Do not ever forget that. And if you find the noose about your slender neck, will yourself to sleep, to relax completely when the trap door falls out beneath you. The clean break is better, I am told."

"B-but sir . . ." The poor woman stammered. She trembled so badly that had it not been for Knellict's hand against her chin, she would have wobbled across the room.

Knellict stopped her by placing the index finger of his free hand over her lips. "You have served me well again today," he said, and no words ever sounded more like a condemnation to the fitful and terrified tavern girl. "As you have since you *chose* to enter my employ those years ago," he added, emphasizing her complicity.

"A little extra this time," the mage went on, smiling now—and that seemed even more cruel. He let the woman go and reached to his belt, producing a small pouch that rattled with coins. "All of it gold."

For a brief moment, the woman's eyes flashed eagerly. Then she swallowed hard, though, considering how she might explain such a treasure if Spysong came calling.

Still, she took the pouch.

⊕══╾══╌

A cloud of smoke and the sound of coughing told King Gareth and his friends that Emelyn the Gray had at last arrived in Heliogabalus. Surprisingly, the old wizard had chosen to teleport to the king's audience hall in the city's Crown Palace, rather than in the safer—for teleportation purposes—wizard's guild on the other side of the city. And even more surprisingly, Emelyn was not alone.

All eyes—Gareth, Celedon, Kane, Friar Dugald, and Baron Dimian Ree—turned to the pair, the old wizard and a pretty young woman with a round, flat face and fiery red hair.

"Well met, troublesome one," Celedon remarked dryly. "As always, your timing nears the point of perfection."

"I did not ask for your advice, and that alone would make any of my actions less than perfect in your self-centered thinking," Emelyn countered. "If all the world obeyed only Master Kierney, then all the world would be . . . perfect."

"He's learning, now isn't he?" Celedon asked the others, turning back to Gareth.

Emelyn grumbled and waved his hands at the rogue, and coughed again.

"In truth, I find your timing quite favorable," Gareth said. He looked from Emelyn to his guest, the Baron of Heliogabalus, who had long been a quiet adversary. For Dimian Ree, who led Damara's most populous and important barony, was rumored to be in league with the Citadel of Assassins to some extent, and so it didn't surprise Gareth and his friends to find the agitated man banging on their door that morning to complain vociferously about the multiple hangings that Gareth's men were carrying out in his fair city.

"Baron Ree," Emelyn said, rather coldly, and he did not dip a bow.

"Gray one," Ree responded.

"Our friend the barom has come to protest the justice we have brought to his city," Friar Dugald explained.

"I only just arrived," Emelyn prompted.

"Spysong has encountered many agents of the Citadel of Assassins," King Gareth explained. "They brazenly attacked an apprentice knight of the order."

"That Entreri creature?"

"Precisely him," said Gareth. "But our enemies overplayed their hand this time. They did not know that Master Kane and Celedon were about, along with many allies."

"And you're hanging them? Well, good! And what of this matter might Baron Ree find objectionable, I must ask? Are any of his former lovers swinging by their necks?"

"You would do well to weigh carefully your words before uttering them, gray one," Dimian Ree said, drawing a dismissive scoff from the archmage.

"And you would do better to remember that the only reason I did not utterly destroy you with the fall of Zhengyi was because of the mercy of that man sitting on the throne before you," Emelyn countered, beside him the woman shuffled and glanced about, nervous.

"Enough, Emelyn," commanded King Gareth. "And the rest of you." He looked at them all alternately and sternly, letting his gaze fall at last over the angry baron. "Baron Ree, Heliogabalus is your city, to be sure. But your city lies within my kingdom. I do not ask for your permission to enter."

"And you would always be welcomed as my guest, my king."

"I am not your guest when I come to Heliogabalus," Gareth answered. "That is your basic misunderstanding here. When your king comes to Heliogabalus, *you* are *his* guest."

That brought a widening of eyes all around the room, and Dimian Ree began stepping nervously from foot to foot, like a fox caught against a stone wall with dogs fast approaching.

"And when I offer my resources, as with Spysong, to aid you in keeping your fair city safe, you would do well to express your appreciation."

Dimian Ree swallowed hard and didn't blink.

But Gareth didn't blink, either. "Pray do so and be gone," he said.

Ree glanced about, mostly at Kane then Emelyn, the two members of Gareth's band most antagonistic toward him—openly at least.

"The king is waiting for you, fool," came a booming voice from the back of the hall, and all turned to see the bearlike figure of Olwen Forest-friend and the lithe Riordan Parnell, the missing two of Gareth's band of seven, standing by the door.

"Go on, then," Olwen commanded, coming forward with great, long strides, and seeming even more ominous because he carried his mighty axe Treefeller in one of his large hands. "Tell your king how grateful you be, and how all your city will dance the streets tonight knowing they are more safe because of his arrival."

Dimian Ree turned on Gareth. "Of course, my king. I only wish I had been invited to the hangings, or that my city guards had been informed of the many battles before they were waged about our streets."

"And they'd be flipping gold pieces to see what side to join," Emelyn muttered to the woman at his side, but loud enough for the others to hear, drawing muted chuckles from all—except for Gareth, and Dimian Ree, of course, who glared at him.

"And it would have been even more interesting to see how many of the doomed prisoners looked to their baron for clemency," Emelyn said, taking up the dare of that look.

"Enough," Gareth demanded. "Good Baron Ree, I pray you be on your way, and I thank you for your . . . advice. Your complaints are duly noted."

"And discarded," said Emelyn, and Gareth glared at him.

"And how long might Heliogabalus be honored by your presence, my king?" Dimian Ree asked too sweetly.

Gareth looked to Kane, who nodded. "Our time here is nearly ended, I expect," Gareth answered.

"Indeed," Emelyn added, turning Gareth his way yet again. The mage tilted his head to indicate the woman at his side, and Gareth got the message. "Baron," he said, and he stood and motioned toward the door.

Dimian Ree paused for just a moment, then bowed, turned, and walked from the hall. Before he had even departed, all of the friends descended on Olwen, patting him on the back and offering their condolences over the loss of Mariabronne the Rover, the ranger who had been as a son to him.

"I will know Mariabronne's final tale, in full," Olwen promised.

"And I have brought with me one who might tell you some of that tale," said Emelyn, and he led the others to look at the woman, who still stood off to the side. "I give you Lady Arrayan of Palishchuk."

"That's a half-orc?" Olwen blurted, and he cleared his throat and coughed repeatedly to cover his rather blunt observation.

"Arrayan?" said Gareth. "Ah, good lady, please approach. You are most welcome here. I had hoped to be in Palishchuk by now to present you with your well-deserved honors, but the situation here intervened, I fear."

Arrayan skittishly moved toward the imposing group, though she relaxed visibly when Riordan offered her a confident wink.

"We had been told that you would not be journeying south to the gates," Gareth said.

"And so I was not, good king," Arrayan replied, her voice barely above a whisper. She bowed, then curtsied, halfway at least, before turning it into another uncomfortable bow.

"Pray be at rest, fair lady," said Gareth. "We are honored by your presence." He turned to Dugald and Kane and added, "Surprised, but honored nonetheless."

Arrayan's glance at Emelyn, one full of nervousness, clued in Gareth and the others that she wasn't there merely as a courtesy.

"I did as you bade and traveled to the gates to see if our friends Jarlaxle and Artemis Entreri were there," Emelyn explained. "I found them."

"At the gate?" Gareth asked.

"Nay, they had already passed through, within hours of the skirmish here in Heliogabalus, so it seems."

"There is more magic about that pair than we know," Friar Dugald remarked, and no one disagreed.

"North?" Gareth and Celedon asked together.

"To Palishchuk?" Gareth added.

"Beyond," said Emelyn, and he looked to Arrayan.

When she hesitated, the old mage put his arm around her shoulders and practically shoved her forward to stand directly before the throne. Arrayan took a long moment to collect her wits then produced a parchment from a loop under a fold of her robes.

"I was bid travel here and read this to you, my king," she said in an uncharacteristically quiet voice. "But I do not wish to speak the words." As she finished, she reached out with the parchment.

Gareth took it from her and unrolled it, arching his thick eyebrows curiously and looking briefly to his friends. He silently read the proclamation of the Kingdom of D'aerthe and the rule of King Artemis the First, and his face grew dark.

"Well, what is it?" Olwen demanded of Emelyn.

The old wizard looked to King Gareth, who seemed to feel his gaze and at last lifted his eyes from the parchment. He regarded all of his six friends alternately and said, "Rouse the Army of Bloodstone, all major divisions. Within a fortnight, we march."

"March?" said a confused Olwen, perfectly echoing the thoughts of the others, other than Emelyn, who had seen the proclamation, and Kane, who, principal among them, was beginning to understand the complexity of the web.

Gareth handed the parchment to Dugald. "Read it to them. I go to pray."

<hr/>

"There is nowhere to run, I assure you," Knellict said to Calihye, after simply appearing before her in her private quarters. "And I would advise against going for the sword," he added when the woman's eyes betrayed her and glanced at her weapon, which lay against the far wall. "Or for the dagger you keep at the back of your belt. In fact, Lady Calihye, if you make any movement against me at all, I can promise you the most exquisite of deaths. You know me, of course?"

Calihye had to force the words past the lump in her throat. "Yes, archmage," she said deferentially, and she only then remembered to avert her gaze to the floor.

"You wanted to kill Entreri for what he did to your friend," Knellict said matter-of-factly. "I share your feelings."

Calihye dared to look up.

"But of course, you buried that honest desire for vengeance, silly girl." The archmage gave a great and exaggerated sigh. "The flesh is too, too weak," he said, and he reached out to stroke the trembling woman's cheek.

Calihye instinctively recoiled—or tried to, but Knellict waggled his fingers and a wind came up behind her, pushing her back to his waiting hand. She didn't dare resist any more overtly.

"You have taken one of my mortal enemies for your lover," Knellict said, shaking his head, and he added a few mocking "tsks."

Calihye's mouth moved weirdly, trying vainly to form words.

"Perhaps I should simply incinerate you," Knellict mused. "A slow burning fire, carefully controlled, that you might feel your skin rolling up under the pressure of its heat. Oh, I have heard strong men reduced to whimpering fools under such duress. Crying for their mothers. Yes, it is a most enjoyable refrain.

"Or perhaps for such a one as pretty as you—well, as you once were before a blade reduced you to medusa-kin . . ." He paused and mocked her with laughter.

Calihye was too terrified to respond, to show any emotion at all. She knew enough of Knellict to understand that they were by no means idle threats.

"Still, you are a woman," Knellict went on. "So you are possessed of great vanity, no doubt. So for you, perhaps I will summon a thousand-thousand insects, that will bite at your tender flesh, and some that will break through. Yes, your eyes will reveal your terror no matter how stubbornly you choke back your screams when you see the bulge of beetles boring underneath your pretty skin."

It proved too much for the warrior woman. She exploded into action, leaping forward at Knellict with raking fingers aimed at his smug expression.

She went right through him and stumbled forward. Stunned, off balance, Calihye tried quickly to re-orient. She spun around, focusing on the image, which was even then fading to nothingness.

"It was so easy to fool you," came the wizard's voice, over by her sword. She looked that way, but he was not to be seen. "You were so terrified by the thought of my presence that a simple illusion and an even more simple ventriloquism had you feeling my touch."

Calihye licked her lips. She shifted her feet beneath her, setting her balance for a spring.

"Can you get to the sword, do you think?" Knellict's disembodied voice asked, and it still seemed to be coming from very near the weapon.

Before he had even finished the sentence, Calihye's hand reached behind her, grabbed the dagger, and whipped forward, launching the missile at the voice. It seemed to stutter in its progress for just a moment, before pressing on with a flash of bluish light. Then it hung there, in mid-air, hilt tilted down as if it had struck into some fabric or other flimsy material.

"Oh, and it is a magical dagger," Knellict said. "It defeated the weakest of my wards!"

His position confirmed, Calihye swallowed her fear and darted for her sword. Or tried to, for even as she started, the archmage materialized. Her dagger hung limply, caught in a fold of his layered robes. He extended his arm toward her, finger pointing, and from that digit came a green flash of light. A dart shot forth to strike the woman in the midsection.

"My dart is magical, as well," Knellict explained as Calihye doubled over and clutched at her belly. Her grimace became a loud groan, then a continual scream, as the dart began to pump forth acid.

"I have found gut wounds to be the most effective at neutralizing an enemy warrior," Knellict said with detached amusement. "Would you agree?"

The woman staggered forward a step.

"Oh please, do press on, valiant warrior woman," Knellict teased. He stepped aside, leaving the path to her sword clear and visible before her.

With a growl of defiance, Calihye grasped the dart and tore it free of her belly with a bit of intestine, yellow-green acid, and bile dripping forth from the hole, followed by the bright red of blood. She threw the dart to the ground and grabbed for her sword.

As soon as her fingers touched the blade, a jolt of lightning arced from it and through her body, launching her back across the room and to the floor. She tried to curl, but her spasms allowed her no control of her body. Her hair stood out wildly, dancing from the shock. Her teeth chattered so violently that her mouth filled with blood, and her joints jolted repeatedly and painfully. She wet her breeches, as well, but was too agonized to even realize it.

"How did you ever survive the trials of Vaasa?" the archmage taunted her, and the sound of his voice told her that he stood right over her. "A first-year apprentice could destroy you."

The words faded along with Calihye's consciousness. She felt Knellict reach down and grab her hair. She had the thought that he would kill her conventionally—a knife across the throat, perhaps.

She hoped it would come that quickly, at least, and was relieved indeed when darkness descended.

The heavy cavalry were the first to come through the open gates into the frozen marshland of Vaasa. Four abreast they rode, breaking off two-by-two to the left and right, the plated armor of knight and horse alike gleaming dully under the heavy gray sky. The clatter of hooves continued for a long while, until a full square of cavalry, seven ranks of seven, had formed at each flank of the gate. Forty-five of the riders in each square were veteran warriors, trained in lance, bow, spear, and sword, and tested in battle. But every other row, one, three, five, and seven, was centered by a man in white robes, which, like the chestplates of the warrior's metal armor, was emblazoned with the White Tree symbol of the king. They were Emelyn's warriors, the wizards of the Army of Bloodstone, well-versed in defensive magic and well-trained to keep the magical trickery of an enemy at bay, while the superior warriors of Bloodstone won the day. Well-respected by the armored warriors who surrounded them, the wizards were affectionately known as the Disenchanters.

Behind the cavalry came the armored infantry, ten abreast, marching in unison and presenting a deliberately ominous cadence by thumping their maces against their shields with every other step. They did not veer to either side, but continued their straightforward march, until fifty full ranks had cleared the gate. There too, the ranks were speckled with Disenchanters, and few wizards in all the region could hope to get a spell, even a sorely diminished spell, through the web of defensive magic protecting King Gareth's men-at-arms.

Then came more riders, the mounted guard of King Gareth Dragonsbane, encircling the paladin king and his entourage of six trusted advisors, including the greatest wizard of all in the Bloodstone Lands, Emelyn the Gray.

The rest of the heavy infantry, fifty more ranks of ten, the core of the Army of Bloodstone, followed in tight and disciplined formation, similarly playing the cadence of mace and shield. As they passed out onto the field, the cavalry began its march again, riding wide and stretching the line to aptly protect the flanks of the core group, eleven hundred men and women, many the children of warriors who had fought with Gareth against the Witch-King.

If the infantry was the backbone of the force, and the cavalry its arms, and King Gareth and his six friends its head, then next came the legs: a second cavalry force, less armored and with swifter mounts. They were Olwen's men, rangers and scouts trained to act more independently. And behind them came still more infantry, lightly armored spearmen, mostly, serving as protection for the batteries of longbowmen.

On and on it went. More light infantry, battalions of priests with carts full of bandages, caravans of supply wagons, lines of strong men carrying ladders, horses towing rams and beams for siege towers. . . .

Men and women lined the top of the wall, watching the procession as it issued forth from the Vaasan Gate for hours, and when at last those great gates swung closed, the sun was beginning its western descent and more than eight thousand soldiers, the heart and soul of the Army of Bloodstone, marched out to the north.

"It surprises me that Gareth moved so quickly and decisively on this," Riordan Parnell said to Olwen and Kane, the three of them bringing up the rear of Gareth's diamond set between the main ranks of heavy infantry.

"That has always been his strength, as Zhengyi learned," Kane replied.

"To his great dismay," Riordan agreed with a wide grin. "Zhengyi's, I mean," he added when he saw that his two companions were not similarly smiling.

While the others rode, Kane walked, his face as stoic as always, his eyes set with his typical grim determination. On the far side of Kane, on his lightly-armored but large horse, Olwen obviously stewed, and his great black beard was wet around his mouth from chewing his lip.

"Still," Riordan argued, "we have merely a simple piece of paper. It might mean little or nothing at all."

Kane motioned forward with his chin, directing Riordan's gaze to Gareth and Dugald, and the two wizards, Emelyn and Arrayan.

"The half-orc woman was very clear that the castle had returned to life," the monk reminded. "Our apprentice knight and his dark elf cohort meddle with the artifacts of Zhengyi. That is not 'nothing at all.' "

"True," Riordan admitted, "but is it sufficient to rouse the Army of Bloodstone and abandon Damara at a time when we have gone to open war against the Citadel of Assassins?"

"The Citadel has been dealt a severe blow—" Kane began to answer, but Olwen cut him short.

"It's worth it all just to get the answers on the death of Mariabronne," he said, a throaty growl behind every word, so that it seemed to his companions as if he might use some ranger magic and turn into a bear at that moment.

It occurred to Riordan that the ranger's horse might not enjoy that experience, but the bard kept the thought to himself—though he did begin composing a song about it.

"Those two were involved, I'm sure," Olwen went on.

"Our information says they were not," said Kane. "Mariabronne scouted forward of his own volition, and contrary to the orders of Ellery. It is a convincing tale, particularly given Mariabronne's reputation for risk-taking."

Olwen snorted and looked away, his meaty hands working the knuckles white by clenching at the reins.

"Well, they are two people, and foolish ones at that," Riordan quickly put in, trying to get the conversation away from a subject that was obviously too painful for his ranger friend. "Even if they are dabbling in Zhengyian magic, as this report from Palishchuk and the words of the dragon sisters might indicate, are they truly such a threat that we should open our flank and our kingdom to the retribution of Knellict and Timoshenko?"

"Nothing is open," Kane assured him. "Spysong's network is fully ready to repel any moves by the Citadel, and if we are needed Emelyn can get us back with a wave of a wand."

"Then why didn't Emelyn just take us six there, leaving Gareth and the soldiers in place?"

"Because this is the opportunity our king has been patiently awaiting, to fully reveal his influence in Vaasa," answered another voice, that of Celedon Kierney. The eavesdropper slowed his horse to bring him in line with the three. "Gareth's aim here is not the castle—or at least, not the castle alone."

Riordan paused and considered that for a moment, then said, "Palishchuk." He glanced at Kane, who nodded knowingly. Olwen gave no indication that he was even listening. "He's showing Palishchuk that they are vital to his designs, and that when they are threatened, he will take that as seriously as if it were Heliogabalus itself under the Zhengyian shadow," Riordan reasoned on the fly.

The looks from Celedon and Kane showed him that he had correctly sorted the puzzle.

"That's why he's the king," Riordan added with a self-deprecating chuckle.

"I expect that by the time we return through the Vaasan Gate, the Kingdom of Bloodstone will be whole, Vaasa and Damara united under the banner of Gareth Dragonsbane," said Celedon.

Suddenly, to Riordan, the day seemed just a bit brighter.

CHAPTER

13

The half-orc city was on edge. And why not? Word had reached Jarlaxle, and so it had reached Palishchuk as well, that King Gareth was on the march, his formidable army rolling northward across the Vaasan bog to challenge the claim of King Artemis the First. The news had surprised Jarlaxle—who didn't much like being surprised. He hadn't thought Gareth would move so decisively, or so boldly. Winter was coming on, which alone could destroy an army in Vaasa, and Gareth was dealing with drow, after all. Gareth had no idea what Jarlaxle had arrayed against him—how could he? And yet he had marched out at once, and in force.

Jarlaxle's respect for the man had multiplied with the news. Rarely had he encountered humans with such confidence and determination.

He made certain his boots clicked loudly even on the slick, rain-soaked stones on the side of the hill. He did not want a fight with Wingham, and did not want to startle any of the nervous sentries surrounding the half-orc.

Wingham stood near a small fire at the center of the hillock's flat top, with another, larger half-orc—Olgerkhan, Jarlaxle realized—close beside him. They noticed Jarlaxle's noisy approach and turned to greet him.

As he neared the pair, Jarlaxle recognized the anxiety in their expressions. A bit of fear, a bit of anger, all very clearly revealed in the way they, particularly Olgerkhan, kept glancing around them. Olgerkhan even had his burly arms crossed over his chest, as sure a sign of resistance as could be offered. The differences in racial habits occurred to Jarlaxle at that moment. In Menzoberranzan, when a drow male crossed his arms over his chest, it was a sign of obedience and respect. On the World Above, though, and as with the drow matrons, it was a signal of steadfast defiance, or at least defensiveness.

"Master Wingham," he greeted sweetly. "I am honored that you answered my call."

"You knew I would come out," Wingham replied, his tone less diplomatic than usual. "How could I not, with the winds of war stirring about my beloved Palishchuk?"

"War?"

"You know that King Gareth has marched."

"To celebrate the coronation of King Artemis the First, of course."

Wingham put on a sour expression that seemed even more exaggerated in the dancing shadows of the small fire.

"Well, we shall learn of his intent soon enough," Jarlaxle offered. "Let us both hope that King Gareth is as wise as his reputation indicates."

"Why have you done this?"

"I serve the king."

"You challenge the rightful king," Olgerkhan interjected.

From under the great brow of his ostentatious hat, Jarlaxle narrowed his red-glowing eyes and thinned his lips, locking Olgerkhan in a stare that surely reminded the burly warrior of his recent adventure beside the drow. Olgerkhan's crossed arms slipped down to his side and he even stepped back a bit, the aggressiveness melting from his posture. With that one look, Jarlaxle had reminded him of Canthan, to be sure.

"The Bloodstone Lands were opened to you and Artemis Entreri both," Wingham said, forcing the drow to look back his way. "Opportunity awaited you. With respect and song, and the appreciation of all the people, you and Entreri could have had much of what you desire without this confrontation. Would King Gareth have denied you the castle?"

"I doubt he would approve of the magic it offers," the drow replied.

"Even without it! A knight of the order can lay claim to a barony that is as yet unclaimed and untamed. Negotiations with Gareth would have handed the castle to you, and would have earned you the allegiance of Palishchuk, as well, a friendship we were all too willing to extend. Likely, King Gareth would have been grateful to have such worthy warriors helping him to tame the northern wilderness."

"And why should we help Gareth extend his claim? Are you so willing to kneel, Wingham?"

Both half-orcs stiffened at the insult, but Wingham didn't back away. "Kneel?"

"If King Gareth tells Wingham to kneel, his knees will soil, no doubt."

"It is respect freely given."

Jarlaxle laughed at him. "It is the obedience of resignation."

Olgerkhan grumbled something indecipherable, shaking his head, and Jarlaxle wasn't really surprised that he had confused that one. Wingham, though, just continued to stare, his expression showing clearly that he wasn't buying the premise one bit.

"Ah well, it is a sad state, is it not?" Jarlaxle asked. "It is the way. The way it has been for millennia uncounted, and the way it will be until the end of time."

"And you accuse *me* of resignation?"

Jarlaxle laughed again. "I accept the truisms of ambition," he explained. "What is resignation to you is relished by me." He looked down and pulled his fine *piwafwi* open a bit to reveal his black leather trousers. "I do not dirty my fine clothes. Not for any man. Not for any king."

"King Gareth will tarnish them with your own blood!" Olgerkhan promised.

Jarlaxle shrugged as if it did not matter.

"You called us out here," said Wingham. "Is there more a point to it than this banter? When you came through Palishchuk, you asked nothing of us, and we were glad to offer you the same."

"But now King Gareth marches," Jarlaxle replied. "The situation is changed, of course. Palishchuk finds herself caught between the breaking waves of possibility. To remain between them as they crest is to be crushed by both. It is time to swim, Wingham."

Olgerkhan stood with his tusky jaw hanging open, a look upon his ugly face so perfectly blank that Jarlaxle nearly laughed out loud. Wingham, though, nodded as he grasped the analogy and its dire implications all too clearly.

"You would have us war with King Gareth, who saved us from the Witch-King and has been a great friend to us?" the worldly old half-orc asked.

Jarlaxle grinned knowingly as he weighed the determination in Wingham's words—a resolve that he knew he would not weaken however great the threat of Kimmuriel's drow armies. In fact, it was a resolve that he had counted on since he had learned of Gareth's bold initiative against the new King of Vaasa.

"Palishchuk will not betray King Gareth," Wingham stated, and the drow knew that he was speaking truth.

"We do not forget the time of Zhengyi," Wingham went on, and his need to justify his position amused Jarlaxle. "We remember well the darkness of the Witch-King and the light named Gareth who risked all, who risked his life, his friends, and all of Damara to ensure that we were not out here all alone against a foe we could not defeat."

"It is a fine tale," the drow agreed.

"We will not betray King Gareth," Wingham said again.

"I never said that you should," Jarlaxle replied, and Wingham's steely gaze melted into one of confusion. "The Army of Bloodstone has marched, with their fine glittering weapons and shining armor. A most impressive sight, to be sure. They come armed and armored, and with wizards and priests aplenty.

"And yet, on the other side, you are faced with the unknown," Jarlaxle continued. "Other than the reputation of my kin and what you so painfully learned of the powers of the Zhengyian castle. I do not make your choice for you, my friend. I only seek to explain to you that the waves are closing and you must swim into one or the other or be destroyed. The time of neutrality has passed. I had not thought it would come to this—not so quickly, at least—but it has, and I would be remiss as a friend if I did not help you to understand."

"A friend?" Olgerkhan roared. "A friend who brings war to Palishchuk's door?"

"My army is not marching," Jarlaxle remarked, and at his reference to an army, he noted Wingham's eyebrows arching just a bit.

"But you come with threats," said Olgerkhan.

"Nay, far from it," Jarlaxle was quick to reply. "King Artemis is a man of peace. Look to the south for the winds of war, not to the north." He turned from the brutish Olgerkhan to Wingham's doubting expression, and added, "It would seem that King Gareth is not a man who shares."

"With thieves?" Wingham dared to ask. "Who take that which is not theirs? Who lay claim to a kingdom without cause of blood or deed?"

"Deed?" Jarlaxle replied as if wounded. "We conquered the castle, did we not? It was King Artemis who slew the dracolich, after all. Your friend beside you can testify to that, though he lay on the ground helplessly when Artemis struck the fateful blow."

Olgerkhan bristled and seemed stung by the simple truth, but did not reply.

"So claim the castle, and bargain with King Gareth for a barony," Wingham suggested. "Avert the war, for the sake of all."

"A contract that would entail our fealty to Gareth, no doubt," the drow said.

"And did you not promise exactly that when you accepted the honors bestowed upon you at King Gareth's court?"

"A moment of duress."

Wingham's expression soured. "You have no claim."

Jarlaxle shrugged, again as if it did not matter. "Perhaps you will be proven correct. Perhaps not. Ultimately, the claim goes to the strongest, does it not? In the final sort of things, I mean. He who remains alive, remains alive to write the histories in a light favorable to him and his cause. Surely as worldly as you are, you know well the histories of the world, Master Wingham. Surely you recognize that armies carrying banners are almost always thieves—until they win."

Wingham didn't flinch, and Jarlaxle knew enough about him, about people in general, to understand that he clutched at the rather pitiful—from Jarlaxle's perspective—ideal of a higher justice, of a universal truism of right and wrong. No man could be more broken, after all, than he who at last must face the truth that his king, his living god, is flawed.

"Look forward, good Wingham," Jarlaxle offered. "The outcome is not known to you, but the result after the battle is indeed. The victor will determine which king rules the land of Vaasa. One wave will overtake the other, and will flatten all the water under its weight. That is the truth facing Palishchuk, however we might feel about it. And in that light, I would caution you to withhold your judgment about who rightfully—and more importantly, who practically—will rule in Vaasa."

Wingham seemed to blanch for just a moment, but he squared his shoulders and firmed his jaw, his round, flat face tightening with admirable determination. "Palishchuk will not battle against King Gareth," he stated.

"Neutrality, then?" asked the drow, and he let his expression sour. "Rarely is the course of the coward rewarded, I fear. But perhaps King Artemis will forgive—"

"No," Wingham interrupted. "You are right in one thing, Jarlaxle. Palishchuk must not let the events around her bury her under their weight. Not without a fight. We have survived by the sword for all of our history, and so it will be again. Kill me now if you will. Kill us all if you are so thirsty for blood, but understand that if King Gareth's horn calls out for allegiance, the warriors of Palishchuk will answer that call."

Jarlaxle's sudden smile took the half-orc off his guard, and the drow dipped a sincere and respectful bow. "I never said that you should not," Jarlaxle offered, and he turned and walked off into the night

He knew that the half-orc would misinterpret him, would think that his carefree attitude regarding any alliance Palishchuk might choose was a sign of supreme confidence.

Jarlaxle loved irony.

"King Gareth has reached Palishchuk," Kimmuriel informed Jarlaxle the following afternoon in large and airy foyer of the main keep of Castle D'aerthe. The room had become his audience chamber, in effect, though Artemis Entreri, the man Jarlaxle had named as king, hardly spent any time in the place. He was always out along the walls, in some odd corner with a stone wall sheltering him from the increasingly cold north wind. Jarlaxle understood that his human friend was trying to keep as far away as possible from Kimmuriel and the scores of other dark elves who had come in through the magical gate the psionicist and the wizards of Bregan D'aerthe had created.

The king's absence had not deterred Jarlaxle from playing the games of court fashion, however. Bregan D'aerthe had brought in furnishings that soon adorned every room of the keep. Jarlaxle sat on Entreri's throne, a purple and blue affair fashioned of a giant mushroom stalk and with the cap used as a fan-like backdrop. Other smaller chairs were set about, including the one directly before the throne, in which sat Kimmuriel.

All around them, dark elves tacked tapestries up on the walls, both to defeat the intrusion of stinging daylight and to steal some of the bluster of the biting breeze. Those tapestries showed no murals to the onlookers, however, just fine black cloth, for they were folded in half, their bottom hem tacked up with the top, Kimmuriel's expression, and those of the other dark elves, reminded Jarlaxle keenly that he was asking quite a bit of his former band in making them come up to such an inhospitable environment.

"He has made good time, given the size of his force," Jarlaxle replied. "It would seem that our little announcement made an impression."

"You waved a wounded rothé before a hungry displacer beast," Kimmuriel remarked, an old Menzoberranyr saying. "This human, Gareth, strikes with the surety of a matron mother. Most unusual for his race."

"He is a paladin king," Jarlaxle explained. "He is no less fanatical to his god than my mother, Lolth torment her soul eternally, was to the Spider Queen. More so than the dedication one might expect out of fallen House Oblodra, of course."

Kimmuriel nodded and said, "Thank you."

Jarlaxle laughed aloud.

"You anticipated this move by Gareth, then," Kimmuriel reasoned, and there was an edge to his tone. "Yet you allowed me to expend great resources in opening the many gates to this abysmal place? The price of the cloth will come out of your fortune, Jarlaxle. Beyond that, I have only a minimal crew operating in Menzoberranzan at the height of the trading season, and almost all of my wizards have been fully engaged in transporting goods, warriors, and fodder for your expedition."

"I did not know that he would march, no," Jarlaxle explained. "I suspected that it could come to this, though the speed of Gareth's response has surprised me, I must admit. I expected this decisive encounter to occur no earlier than next spring, if at all."

Kimmuriel stroked his smooth, narrow black chin and looked away. After a moment of mulling it over, the psionicist offered a deferential nod to his former master.

"There was great potential gain, and nothing to lose," Jarlaxle added.

Kimmuriel didn't disagree. "Yet again I am reminded of why Bregan D'aerthe has not seen fit to kill you," he said.

"Though you have come to see me as an annoyance?"

Kimmuriel smiled—one of the very few expressions Jarlaxle had ever seen on the soulless face of that one. "This will rank as no more than a minor inconvenience, with perhaps some gain yet to be found. Whenever Jarlaxle has an idea, it seems, Bregan D'aerthe is stretched."

"Dice have six sides for a reason, my friend. There is no thrill in surety."

"But the win must come from more than one in six," said Kimmuriel. "The Jarlaxle I knew in Menzoberranzan would not wager unless four of the sides brought a profit."

"Do you think I have so changed my ways, or my odds?"

"There was the matter of Calimport."

Jarlaxle conceded that point with a nod.

"But of course, you were caught in the thrall of a mighty artifact," said Kimmuriel. "You cannot be blamed."

"You are most generous."

"And, as always, Jarlaxle won out in the end."

"It is a good habit."

"And he chose wisely," said Kimmuriel.

"You have a high opinion of yourself."

"Little of what I say or think is opinion."

True enough, Jarlaxle silently conceded. Which was exactly why he had made certain that Rai-guy, the temperamental and unpredictable wizard, was dead and Kimmuriel was still alive and in charge of Bregan D'aerthe during Jarlaxle's sabbatical.

"And I must admit that your recent scheme has intrigued me," Kimmuriel said. "Though I know not why you insist on even visiting this Lolth-forsaken wilderness." He wrapped his arms around him as he spoke and cast a disparaging glance to the side, at a tapestry that lifted out from the wall under the weight of the howling wind rushing in through the cracks in the stone.

"It was a good chance," Jarlaxle said.

"It always is, when there is nothing truly to lose."

Jarlaxle sensed the hesitance in his voice, almost as if Kimmuriel was expecting a confrontation, or an unpleasant surprise. The psionicist feared, of course, that Jarlaxle meant to challenge him and order Bregan D'aerthe into battle against King Gareth.

"There are ways around Gareth's unexpectedly bold move," he said to reassure his former, and likely future, lieutenant.

"There are ways through them, as well," Kimmuriel replied. "Of course."

"The point of this wager is not to place too much on the table. I'll not lose a drow soldier here—and though I do believe that our fodder serve us well by charging into the chewing maw of Gareth's able army, in even that endeavor we must be stingy. I am not Matron Baenre, obsessed with the conquest of Mithral Hall. I do not seek a fight here—far from it."

"Gareth will grant you nothing in a parlay," said Kimmuriel. "You say that he is acting boldly, but no less so than you did when you sent word of the rise of King Artemis."

"He will not parlay," Jarlaxle agreed, "because we have nothing to offer to him. We will remedy that, in time."

"So what will you say to him now?"

"Not even farewell," Jarlaxle answered with a grin.

Kimmuriel nodded with contentment. He glanced again at the waving tapestry, and squeezed his arms just a bit more tightly around himself, but Jarlaxle knew him well enough to realize that he was at peace.

A few miles to the south of the castle, on a field outside of Palishchuk, another warrior was anything but at peace. Olwen Forest-friend stalked about the encampment, speaking encouragement to the men and women of the Army of Bloodstone. His forest-green cloak whipped out behind him as he strode briskly from campfire to campfire. His face flushed with passion and eagerness and his legendary war axe gleamed in the firelight. For many years, his favorite weapon had been the bow, but as his agility had decreased with age, he found that running along the fringes of the battlefield no longer suited him. It hadn't taken long for Olwen to discover the thrill of close combat, nor to perfect the technique.

"We press the walls tomorrow," he promised one group of young soldiers, who stared up at him in awe. "We'll be home through the Galenas in a matter of days."

Their eager and grateful responses followed Olwen as he moved on to the next group, dragging a second, far thinner and more graceful figure in his wake.

Riordan Parnell was usually charged with maintaining morale. Often in the calm before battle, the bard would entertain with stirring tales of heroic deeds and darkness shattered. But his planned performance had been sidetracked by the overwhelming presence of his ranger friend.

He caught up to Olwen before the ranger reached the next group in line, and even dared tug on the man's sleeve to halt him, or slow him at least. That brought a warning glare, Olwen locking his bright eyes on Riordan's grasping hand then slowly lifting his gaze to meet that of the bard.

"We have much yet to learn," Riordan said as he gently pulled away.

"I've not the time or the desire to read the history of King Artemis."

"It is all vague."

"They're for taking King Gareth's hard-won land," said Olwen. "They locked themselves in a castle, and we'll knock that castle down. I see nothing vague here. But don't you worry, bard. I'll give you a song or two to write." As he made the promise, Olwen brought his war axe over his shoulder and held it firmly before him. With a nod, the ranger turned to go.

But Riordan caught him again by the sleeve. "Olwen," he said.

The ranger cocked his head to consider the man.

"We do not know all of the details of Mariabronne's death," said Riordan.

Olwen's expression hardened. "Why are you bringing Mariabronne into this?"

"Because he fell in that castle, and you know that well. Nothing you do in there tomorrow will change that sad reality."

Olwen turned to face Riordan squarely, his muscular chest puffed out. He slipped the axe down at the end of one arm, but the movement did little to diminish his imposing posture. "I march to King Gareth's call, and not that of a ghost," he said, "to defeat a pretender named Artemis Entreri."

"Emelyn has been inside the castle," said Riordan. "And I have spoken with Arrayan and Olgerkhan of Palishchuk, and with Wingham. All of the indications and all of the stories—consistent tales, one and all—do not indicate treachery, but misjudgment, in the death of Mariabronne the Rover. We believe that he was felled by a monster's blow, and not due in any way to the actions, or even the inactions, of Artemis Entreri or the drow Jarlaxle."

"And of course, it wouldn't be the way of a dark elf to create any mischief."

It was hard for Riordan to hold his stance against that simple logic.

"Nor for the Witch-King," the bard finally managed to counter. "From all that we have learned, Mariabronne was slain by the enduring and dastardly legacy of Zhengyi."

"Speak not that name!" Olwen ground his teeth and the considerable muscles on his arms twisted as he rolled tight the fingers of his hands, one fist clenched on his right, the knuckles of his other hand whitening as they clamped on the axe handle.

Riordan offered a sympathetic look, but Olwen scowled all the more.

"And it might be that the dastardly and enduring legacy of Zhengyi is now in the hands of King Artemis," Olwen said and he brought his axe up before him to catch it again in both hands. He pulled it back a bit and slapped it hard into his right mitt for effect. "I've grown weary of that legacy."

As much as he wanted to argue that point, Riordan Parnell found himself without an answer. Olwen nodded gruffly and spun away, then launched into another rousing cheer as he approached the next group of soldiers in line, all of whom lifted their flagons to the legendary ranger and shouted out in unison, "For Mariabronne the Rover!"

Riordan watched his friend for a moment, but sensed the approach of another and turned to greet his cousin, Celedon Kierney.

"It is a cheer that will rush us to bloodshed," Celedon remarked. "Olwen will be in no mood for delay when we reach this Castle D'aerthe on the morrow."

"I cannot imagine his pain," said Riordan. "To lose a man who was as a son to him."

"I wish Gareth had bid him stay in Damara," Celedon replied. "He is as fine a warrior as I have ever known, but he is in no humor for this."

"You fear his judgment?"

"As I would fear yours, or my own, if I had just lost a son. And Mariabronne was exactly that to Olwen. When word reached his ears, he cast about like a lion on the rampage, so the story claims. He went to the druids of Olean's Grove outside of Kinnery and bade them to reveal the tale in full, and even, it is rumored, to inquire about the possibilities of reincarnation."

Riordan blanched, but was not really surprised. "And he was refused, of course."

"I do not know," said Celedon, "but I trust that the Great Druid of Olean's would not entertain such a notion."

"So he will assuage his pain with his axe instead," said the bard. "I hope that King Artemis has not grown too fond of his title."

"Or his head."

◄══╬══►

The next morning, Entreri and Jarlaxle stood on the southern wall of Castle D'aerthe, near the western tower that flanked the castle's main, south-facing gate. Behind and below them in the courtyard that had once teemed with undead monsters that had risen against their initial incursion into the castle, three hundred goblins and kobolds shifted nervously. None dared speak out, for around them stood merciless dark elf guards bearing long canes and drow priests with their trademark whips, the heads of which were living, biting snakes. Any kobold or goblin who shuffled too far out of line felt the sting of those bites, then squirmed and writhed in horrible, screaming agony on the ground before sweet death finally took it.

Entreri and Jarlaxle hardly paid any attention to the spectacle behind them, however, for before them came the Army of Bloodstone. The main infantry marched in tight ranks in the center, flanked by heavy cavalry to either side and with batteries of longbowmen grouped behind the front ranks. The many pennants of Damara, of the Church of Ilmater, and of King Gareth waved in the brisk morning breeze, and the cadence played out on the shields of the warriors, as they had drummed when leaving the Vaasan Gate less than a tenday earlier.

A mere fifty yards out from the castle, the procession stopped, and with remarkable precision, they moved into their defensive formations. Shields turned crisply and the front ranks fanned left and right, streaming in thin lines, then thickening again into defensive squares. Wizards danced about as if they were jesters in a court procession, waving their arms and enacting all sorts of wards and shields to deflect and defeat any incoming evocative magic. Just inside the infantry square, the archers formed their ranks, every bow with arrow ready. As the center of the line fully separated, the companions on the wall were treated to a view of the king himself, all splendid in his shining silver armor, and flanked by his powerful friends.

"Do you think they have come for a banquet in my honor?" Entreri asked.

"That would be my guess. Friar Dugald is dressed in finery, you see, and of course, the king shines as if the sun itself has settled upon him."

"And yet that one," said Entreri, nodding to indicate the man standing to Gareth's right, "seems ill-dressed for anything other than the ruts of a cattle trail."

"Master Kane," Jarlaxle agreed. "He truly is an embarrassment. One would think that the King of Damara would find someone to infuse some fashion sense into that fool."

Entreri smirked, remembering all the days on the road with Jarlaxle, when his companion had set out fine shirts for him. He thought of the night when Jarlaxle had returned with a new belt and scabbard for Charon's Claw and Entreri's jeweled dagger. That belt was a magnificent black leather affair, and as fine in design as in appearance, for it held a pair of small throwing knives, fully concealed, within its back length.

"Perhaps Gareth will hire you to instruct the monk," Entreri said.

626

Jarlaxle hesitated for a moment before responding, "He could do worse."

Six riders and Master Kane came forward from the line. The monk walked in front of Gareth, who was centered by Celedon Kierney and Olwen Forest-friend. Directly behind Gareth rode Riordan Parnell, the bard, strumming a lute and singing. Flanking the bard were Dugald and Emelyn, both quietly spellcasting, building defensive walls.

The group closed half the distance to Castle D'aerthe then stopped, and Riordan came out around his king and galloped the short expanse to pull up before the great gates. He noted Jarlaxle and Entreri and trotted his mount off to the side, to sit directly below them.

"Master Jarlaxle and Artemis Entreri, Apprentice Knight of the Order" he began.

"*King* Artemis," Jarlaxle corrected, loudly enough so that Gareth and his friends heard, and bristled—which brought a smile to the drow's face.

"Good subjects—" Riordan began again.

"We are not."

The bard stared hard at the obstinate drow. "You pair of fools, then," he said. "King Gareth Dragonsbane, he who defeated Zhengyi, who cast the Wand of Orcus across the planes of existence, who—"

"Spare us," Jarlaxle interrupted. "It is cold, and we have heard this litany before—in Gareth's own court, and not so long ago."

"Then your folly should be obvious to you."

"Someday I will tell you my own litany of deeds, good bard," Jarlaxle called down. "Then indeed will your friends label you as long-winded."

"King Gareth demands audience," Riordan called out. "If you refuse, then war is upon you." He looked to the east, and motioned with his right arm. Following that, the pair saw a light cavalry force flanking Castle D'aerthe, and a light infantry taking up defensive positions in its wake.

Riordan then motioned west, and the pair saw a similar scene unfolding in that direction.

"To grant audience or to accept a siege," Riordan said. "The choice seems quite obvious."

"Why would we not grant free and friendly passage to King Gareth of Damara," Jarlaxle asked him, "our sister kingdom, after all, and no enemy to the throne of Artemis? You need not come to us so formally, and with threats. King Gareth is ever allowed free and welcomed passage through our lands—though if he intends to be accompanied by so large a contingent, who will tramp down our flora and fauna, I do fear that I might have to impose a toll."

"A toll?"

"For smoothing the bog after your passage, of course. Simple upkeep."

Riordan sat perfectly still for a long while, clearly not amused. "Will you grant the audience?"

"Of cour—" Jarlaxle started to answer, but Entreri grasped his shoulder and shifted in front.

"Tell King Gareth that we do not enjoy the spectacle of an army at our doorstep unannounced," Entreri called down to Riordan, and again loud enough for Gareth, and perhaps even some of those in the ranks of the main force, to hear. Keeping his tone polite, and his voice loud, he continued, "But even so, Gareth may enter my home. We have many tall towers here, as you can see. Please tell Gareth, from me, that he is most welcomed to dive headlong off of any of them."

Riordan sat a moment, as if digesting the words. He even glanced at one of the towers. "You are besieged!" he declared. "Know that war has come to your door!" He expertly turned his mount and galloped it back to his group, who were already turning for the main force.

"That wasn't the wisest thing you've ever done," Jarlaxle remarked to his friend.

"Isn't this what you wanted?" Entreri replied. "War with King Gareth?"

"Hardly."

Entreri's face screwed up with doubt. "You thought to parlay our good deeds to an independent kingdom for Jarlaxle?"

"For King Artemis," the dark elf corrected.

"You believe that Gareth would allow a drow to rule a kingdom within that which he now calls his own kingdom?" Entreri went on, disregarding the correction. "You are a bigger fool than I once thought you—and on that previous occasion, you had the excuse of the lure of Crenshinibon. What is your excuse now beyond abject stupidity?"

Jarlaxle eyed him for a long while, his thin drow lips curling into a smile. He half-turned and looked to the courtyard below, then lifted his hand and clenched his fist.

The drivers snapped into action, cracking their whips and setting the fodder into a frenzy. A great crank creaked, chain rattling in protest, and the massive portcullis that blocked Castle D'aerthe's main gate lifted.

"I was shown two roads," Jarlaxle explained to Entreri. "One would lead me to operate in the shadows, much as I have always done. To find my niche here in the Bloodstone Lands in comfort behind the powers that be—perhaps to serve the Citadel of Assassins, though in a sense far removed from that which Knellict envisioned. Perhaps I would then convince Kimmuriel that this land was worth his efforts, and he and I would lead Bregan D'aerthe to grab at absolute leadership in the underworld of the Bloodstone Lands, similar to what we achieved back in Calimport for a short while, and certainly as we have created in the darkness of Menzoberranzan for nearly two centuries." He ended with a laugh, as he finished with, "It would be worth the effort, perhaps, merely to see Knellict beg for his eternal soul."

Jarlaxle stopped and stood staring at his friend. Beneath them, the gates of the castle swung open and the three hundred goblins and kobolds, the unfortunate shock troops who had only death and pain behind them and a waiting army before them, flooded out onto the field in full charge.

"And the other road?" Entreri finally, and impatiently, prompted.

"The one we have walked," Jarlaxle explained. "Autonomy. The Kingdom of D'aerthe, presented to King Gareth and the other powers of the Bloodstone Lands, aboveboard and with all legitimacy. A sister and allied kingdom to Damara's north, living in harmony with Damara, and with Palishchuk."

"They would accept a kingdom of drow?" Entreri made no effort to keep the incredulity out of his voice, which elicited a smirk from Jarlaxle.

"It was worth a try, as I found the other option . . . boring. Would you disagree?"

"You wanted it, not I."

Jarlaxle looked at him as if wounded.

"You led our adventures here," Entreri said. "You put us in the service of a pair of dragon sisters, and tricked me to Vaasa, knowing well, all the while, the destination of this road we walk and the inevitable ending."

"I could not have known that such an opportunity as Urshula would present itself so readily," Jarlaxle argued, but he stopped short and threw up his hands in defeat. "As you will," he said. "In any event, our time here is at its end."

⊕══════╼

"Beware the ruse!" Friar Dugald and his clerics shouted out the length of the line, using magic to enhance their shouts.

Before the heavy priest, King Gareth and the others coordinated the response to the monstrous charge. Left and right, great longbows bent back and volleys of arrows flew at the goblins and kobolds, the shots spaced properly so that a falling, dying target would not intercept a second arrow.

Emelyn the Gray and his wizards held back as the monstrous ranks thinned under the rain of arrows. "Minor spells only!" the archmage instructed his forces. "Keep your power in reserve. They are trying to exhaust us!"

"And to lessen the burden on their foodstuffs, perhaps," Kane quietly added. He was between Gareth and Emelyn when he spoke, and both caught his meaning well. "They expect a siege, we can conclude, and believe that they can outlast us with winter fast approaching."

Before them, those monsters who had somehow managed to avoid the arrows came on fast, and were met by a barrage of minor spells. Missiles of wizardly energy—blue, green, and red—shot out and swerved of their own accord, it seemed, unerringly blasting into the targeted creatures. When a pair of ambitious goblins drew too near, Emelyn waved away his charges and stepped forward personally. He touched the tips of his thumbs together, fingers spread wide before him, and spoke a simple command.

The goblins, more confused and terrified than bloodthirsty, could not pull up in time, and burst into flame as a wave of fire erupted from the wizard's hands, fanning out before him.

"Archers fire a volley over the wall!" Gareth called, and the order echoed down the line. Indeed, with the monstrous ranks so depleted, there was no need for another, point-blank barrage.

Out rode Gareth with Celedon, Olwen and Riordan beside him, and, amazingly, the monk Kane sprinted before the charging horses and was the first to engage. He leaped and fell straight out, feet leading, as he neared a goblin and kobold duo, taking the smaller, doglike kobold with a snap kick to the face and slamming the five-foot goblin with a solid hit to the chest.

Both shot back as surely as if a horse had kicked them.

Kane landed on his back, but moved so quickly and fluidly that many onlookers blinked and shook their heads. For he was up again, in perfect balance, almost as soon as the trailing folds of his dirty robes touched the ground. He stomped on the downed kobold's neck for good measure, then leaped ahead and to the side, spinning as he landed beside a surprised goblin. The creature took an awkward swing with its mace, one that Kane easily pushed up into the air as he came around. Not breaking the momentum of his turn, the monk snapped his arm back to the right angle and followed through with a jarring elbow, catching the goblin right below the chin and fully crushing its windpipe.

"He does steal all the fun," Celedon remarked to Gareth.

Gareth began to reply that there were plenty of enemies to be found, but he didn't bother. The infantry came on hard, and Emelyn's wizards continued their devastation, and the paladin realized that he would have to be quick if he intended to stain his brilliant sword, Crusader the Holy Avenger, in that initial battle. A quick glance at his friend Kane told him to veer in a different direction if he hoped to find a target.

Gasping for breath from the perfectly aimed, driving elbow, the goblin fell away, and before it had even hit the ground, Kane had already engaged another, his hands working furiously in the air before him, like great sweeping fans.

And it was all a ruse, designed to get the goblin leaning forward, to get its weapon shifted out just a bit to the side. As soon as that happened, Kane sprang forward, high and turning a somersault as he went. He hooked his leading forearm under the goblin's chin then planted his shoulder against the goblin's back as he came around and over. The monk landed on his feet back-to-back with the dizzy goblin, and as he continued forward, he pulled his arm up and over the goblin, forcing its head back and up.

Hearing the snap of the creature's neck bone, Kane quickly released, let the limp thing fall dead to the ground, and charged on.

The battle, the slaughter, was over in minutes, with the charge stalled and crushed, the goblins and kobolds lying dead or dying, other than a few who knelt on the ground, their arms up in the air, pleading for their lives.

Across the field, the portcullis had already fallen back in place and the gates had swung closed.

"Beware the following wave!" Dugald and others cried out. "Beware the gargoyles!"

But there were none. Nothing. The castle sat before them, enormous and deathly quiet. Goblin statues set along the wall leered out, but merely as unmoving, unthreatening stone. No figures moved behind them.

Another volley of arrows went over that wall, then a second, but if they hit anything other than the interior walls or the empty ground, no confirming cries of alarm or agony indicated it.

"Hold fire!" Gareth called as he and the other warriors turned back to reform their previous ranks. The paladin king cast a disparaging glance at the castle of King Artemis the First as he rode, thinking that Kane's observation had been quite on the mark.

But knowing as well that he had neither the patience nor the supplies to support such a siege.

⊷━━⊶

Entreri and Jarlaxle heard the arrows cracking on the front door of the main keep, and the assassin was glad that he had thought to close the repaired portal behind him as he had entered.

Inside the main room of the ground level, Kimmuriel and several other dark elves waited for the pair, and Entreri couldn't contain a sour expression at the sight of the hated creatures.

"They will not wait long," Kimmuriel told Jarlaxle in the drow tongue, and it bothered Entreri that he still understood that paradoxically lyrical language. How could creatures so vile sound so melodious? *"Gareth will show no patience with the winter winds blowing. As soon as they come to believe that our assault was not merely a diversion for a greater attack, expect that they will come on. They've dragged war engines across the miles, and they will not let the catapults remain silent."*

"We are well prepared, of course."

"We are the last," Kimmuriel replied. *"The gate is held fast in the lower chamber. It is time to choose, Jarlaxle."*

"Choose what?" Entreri asked his companion, using the common tongue of the surface world.

That didn't exclude the fluent Kimmuriel in the least. "Choose between flight and awakening the full power of the castle," he said in the same language, his inflection perfect. He seamlessly went back to the drow tongue as he added to Jarlaxle, *"Will you awaken Urshula?"*

Jarlaxle thought on that for a short while. Another volley of arrows streamed into the castle, some cracking against the keep's doors.

"We might fight a great battle here," Jarlaxle said. "With Urshula and the gargoyles, with the undead who will come to my call, we could inflict great misery on our enemy. And with Bregan D'aerthe's full power, there is no doubt that we would win the day."

"The gain would be temporary, and not worth the price," said Kimmuriel. "We have no reinforcements, yet Damara is a country of King Gareth's minions, who will not sit idly by. And Gareth likely has many treaties that would bring other nations against us in time."

Jarlaxle looked to Entreri. "What say you?"

"I say that I have traveled with an idiot," the assassin replied, and Jarlaxle merely laughed.

"Many dead dark elves have said the same," Kimmuriel warned, and Entreri shot him a threatening look.

But Jarlaxle's laughter defeated all of the tension. "It was a good attempt," he decided. "But now that we've seen the response, it is time to take our leave of King Gareth and his Bloodstone Lands."

He motioned for Kimmuriel and the others to lead the way into the tunnels, then waited for Entreri to walk up beside him before following. As they passed the mushroom throne, Jarlaxle tossed a rolled scroll, bound with two strings of gold, onto its seat.

Entreri turned as if to retrieve it, but Jarlaxle put a hand on his shoulder and guided him along.

They moved through the tunnels, to the room where Mariabronne had fallen to the daemons, then farther down the winding way. Dust fell from the ceiling as the bombardment began above in full. Finally they entered the chamber of Urshula, the scars of the battle bringing that deadly encounter clearly back into Entreri's thoughts.

And reminding him that, in his darkest hour, Jarlaxle had abandoned him.

At the back of the huge chamber, beyond the sprawled, bony corpse of the dracolich, its head and neck blackened from the fire of Entreri's killing trap, an ornate portal, a glowing blue doorway, loomed. While the walls of the chamber could be seen all around its edges, within the frame of the jamb there was only blackness.

One after another, the dark elf soldiers of Bregan D'aerthe walked through and disappeared.

Soon there were only three left, and Kimmuriel nodded to Jarlaxle then stepped through.

"After you," Jarlaxle invited Entreri.

"Where?"

"Why, in there, of course."

"Not that where," Entreri growled. "Where does it lead?"

"Where does it look like?"

"A place I do not wish to go." As he spoke the words, the truth of them assaulted the human assassin. It was time to leave Gareth and the Bloodstone Lands, so Jarlaxle had said, and that was a sentiment Entreri shared. But to leave with Kimmuriel and the Bregan D'aerthe soldiers implied something entirely different than what he had in mind.

"But the choice has been made," said Jarlaxle.

"No. That is the Underdark."

"Of course."

"I will not return there."

"You act as if there's an option to be found."

"No," Entreri said again, staring at the portal as if it was the gateway to the Nine Hells. His memories of Menzoberranzan, of his subjugation to twenty thousand cruel drow, of his understanding that he was no more than *iblith*, offal, and that anything he might do, anyone he might kill, would be completely irrelevant in altering that recognition of his worth, flooded back to him at that terrible moment.

And he thought of Calihye, the first woman he had loved both emotionally and physically, the first woman with whom the bond had become complete. How could he desert her?

But what choice did he have?

He took a step toward the doorway, and paused as he saw its lines waver, as he saw that the magic was fast diminishing.

During that pause came a second wave of memory, of pain, of regret, of anger. The doorway wavered again.

"No," said Entreri, and he put his hand on Jarlaxle's shoulder and guided his companion. "Go quickly. The magic is fading."

"Be not a fool," Jarlaxle warned.

Entreri sighed and seemed to deflate before the obvious indictment. He looked at Jarlaxle and nodded—just enough to get the drow to relax his guard.

In the blink of an eye, Entreri had the red blade of his sword up high, held in both hands over his front shoulder. He gave a growl and went into a sudden spin, bringing the blade around at waist height, an even slice that would have cut Jarlaxle in half.

The drow had no way to defend.

He offered a sneer as he fell away the only way he could, tumbling more than running into the gate. Jarlaxle winked away just ahead of the cutting blade.

Entreri stood there staring at the shimmering extraplanar opening for a few moments longer, but even had its magic not then dissipated, there was no way Artemis Entreri was returning to the Underdark, to Menzoberranzan.

Not even to save his life.

CHAPTER

OVERREACHING

14

As the castle fell quiet, the horns on the field began to blare and a great cheer swept through the line. "King Gareth!" the enthusiastic soldiers chanted, and nowhere was that cry more energetic and grateful than among the contingent from Palishchuk.

As heartwarming as it was, though, Gareth Dragonsbane was not amused. They had not lost a single man, and hundreds of monsters lay dead on the field, almost all of them felled before combat had even been engaged.

"That was not an assault, it was mass suicide," Emelyn the Gray commented, and none of the friends could disagree.

"It accomplished nothing, but to wipe a bit of the stain of goblins and kobolds from the world," Riordan said.

"And to strengthen our resolve and cohesion," Friar Dugald added. "A free moment of practice before a joust? Are our enemies so inept?"

"Where is the second assault?" Gareth asked, as much to himself as to the others. "They should have struck hard at the moment of our greatest diversion."

"Which was never so great at all, now was it?" asked Emelyn. "I expect that Kane was correct in his assessment—they were clearing out fodder to preserve their supplies."

Gareth looked at his wise friend and shook his head.

They waited impatiently as the moments slipped past, and the castle only seemed more inert, more dead. Nothing stirred behind the high walls. Not a pennant flew, not a door banged open or closed.

"We know that Artemis Entreri and Jarlaxle are in there," Celedon Kierney remarked after a long while had passed. "What other forces have they at their disposal? Where are the gargoyles that so threatened Palishchuk when first the castle awakened? Gargoyles that regenerate themselves quickly, so it was reported. An inexhaustible supply."

"Perhaps it was all merely a bluff," Friar Dugald offered. "Perhaps the castle could not be reanimated."

"Wingham, Arrayan, and Olgerkhan saw the gargoyles fluttering about the walls just days ago," Celedon replied. "Tazmikella and Ilnezhara clearly warned us that Jarlaxle has Urshula the Black, a mighty dracolich, handy at his summons. Is the conniving drow trying to draw us in now, where his magical minions will prove more deadly?"

"We cannot know," King Gareth admitted.

"We can," said Kane, and all eyes turned his way. The monk squared himself to Gareth and offered a slow and reverential bow. "We have been in situations like this many times before, my old friend," he said. "Perhaps this will be a matter for our army, perhaps not. Let us forget who we are for a moment and remember who we once were."

"You cannot expose the king," Friar Dugald warned.

Beside him, Olwen Forest-friend snorted in derision, though whether at Kane or Dugald, the others could not yet discern.

"If Jarlaxle is as wise as we fear, then our caution is his ally," said Kane. "To play the games of intrigue with a drow is to invite disaster." He turned to face the castle, compelling them all to look that way with his set and stern expression.

"We have been in this situation before," Kane said again. "We knew how to defeat it, once. And so we shall again unless we have become timid and old."

Friar Dugald began to argue, but a smile widened on King Gareth's face, a smile from a different time, a decade and more past, when the weight of all the Bloodstone Lands was not sitting squarely on his strong shoulders. A smile of adventure and danger that wiped away the typical frown of politics.

"Kane," he said, and the sly edge in his voice had half his friends grinning and the other half holding their breath, "do you think you could get over that wall without being seen?"

"I know my place," the monk replied.

"As do I," Celedon quickly added, but Gareth cut him short with an upraised hand.

"Not yet," the king said. He nodded to Kane and the monk closed his eyes in a moment of meditation. He opened them and gently swiveled his head, taking in the whole scene before him, absorbing all of the angles and calculating the lines of sight from any hidden sentries on the castle walls. He dropped his face into his hands and took a long and steady breath, and when he exhaled, he seemed to shrink, as if his entire body had become somehow smaller and less substantial.

He held up one hand, revealing a small jewel that glowed with an inner, magical fire, one that could flash to light at the wielder's desire. It was their old signal flare, a clear indication of Kane's intent and instructions, and the monk went off in a trot.

The friends watched him, but whenever any of them turned his gaze aside, even for a moment, he could not then relocate the elusive figure.

Sooner than anyone could have expected, even those six men who had spent years beside the Grandmaster, Kane signaled back to them with the lighted jewel from the base of the castle wall.

Kane moved like a spider, hands sweeping up to find holds, legs turning at all angles to propel him upward, even sometimes reaching above his shoulder, his toes hooking into the tiniest jags in the wall. In a matter of a few heartbeats, the monk went over the wall and disappeared from view.

"He makes you feel silly for using your climbing tools, doesn't he?" Emelyn the Gray said to Celedon, and the man just laughed.

"As Kane would make Emelyn feel rather silly and more than a little inept as he avoided all of your magical lightning bolts and fireballs and sprays of all colors of the prism," Riordan was quick to leap to Celedon's defense.

"That strange one mocks us all," Dugald agreed. "But he's too tight to down a belt of brandy, and too absorbed to bed a woman. You have to wonder when it's simply not worth the concentration anymore!"

That brought laughter from all the friends, and all those nearby.

Except from Olwen. The ranger stared at the spot where Kane had disappeared, unblinking, his hands tight on his war axe, his beard wet from chewing his lips.

Two flashes from the monk's jewel, atop the wall, signaled that the way was clear.

"Emelyn and Celedon," Gareth instructed, for that was the usual course this group would take, with the wizard magically depositing the stealthy Celedon to join up with Kane. "A quick perusal and raise the portcullis—"

"I'm going," Olwen interrupted, and stepped before Celedon as the rogue made his way toward the waiting Emelyn. "You take me," the ranger instructed Emelyn.

"It has always been my place," Celedon replied.

"I'm going this time," Olwen said, and there was no compromise to be found in his steady, baritone voice. He looked past Celedon to Gareth. "You grant me this," he said. "For all the years I followed you, for all the fights we've shared, you owe me this much."

The proclamation didn't seem to please any of the friends, and Friar Dugald in particular put on a sour expression, even shook his head.

But Gareth couldn't ignore the stare of his old friend. Olwen was asking Gareth to trust him, and what sort of friend might Gareth be if he would not?

"Take Olwen," Gareth said to Emelyn. "But again, Olwen, your duty is to quickly ensure that the immediate area about the courtyard is secure then raise that portcullis and open those gates. We will all be together when we face Artemis Entreri and Jarlaxle, and whatever minions they have hidden inside their castle."

Olwen grunted—as much of a confirmation as Gareth would get—and moved to Emelyn, who, after a concerned look Gareth's way, launched into his spellcasting. Olwen grabbed onto the wizard's shoulder and a moment later, with a flash of purple light, the pair disappeared, stepping through a dimensional doorway to the spot on the wall where Master Kane waited.

In the tunnels of the upper Underdark, far below the construct Jarlaxle had named Castle D'aerthe, the soldiers of Bregan D'aerthe set their camp, along with those fortunate slaves who had not been forced onto the field to face the might of King Gareth. Off to one side of the main group, in a short, dead-end corridor, Kimmuriel and a pair of wizards had already enacted a scrying pool, and by the time Jarlaxle caught up to them, they looked in on various parts of the castle.

Jarlaxle smiled and nodded as the image of Entreri moved through the dark waters of the pool. The assassin had traveled up from the dracolich's lair, back into the upper tunnels, near where he had battled Canthan the wizard.

"He tried to kill you," Kimmuriel said. "We cannot go back immediately, but if he somehow escapes this time, I promise you that Artemis Entreri will fall to a drow blade, or to drow magic."

Jarlaxle was shaking his head throughout the speech. "If he had wanted to kill me, he would have used his wicked little dagger and not his cumbersome sword. He was making a statement—perhaps even one of complete rejection—but I assure you, my old friend, that if Artemis Entreri had truly tried to slay me before the portal, he would now lie dead on the floor."

Kimmuriel cast a doubting, even disappointed look at his associate, but let it go. A wave of his hand over the pool brought a different, brighter image into focus, and the four dark elf onlookers watched the movements of three men.

"It is a moot point anyway," the psionicist said. "I warned you of these enemies."

"Kane," Jarlaxle said. "He is a monk of great renown." One of the drow wizards cast him a confused look. "He fights in the manner of the kuo-toa," Jarlaxle explained. "His weapon is his body, and a formidable weapon it is."

"The second one is the most dangerous," Kimmuriel said, speaking of Emelyn the Gray. "Even by the standards of Menzoberranzan, his magic would be considered powerful."

"As great as Archmage Gromph?" one of the drow wizards asked.

"Do not be a fool," said Kimmuriel. "He is just a human."

Jarlaxle hardly heard it, for his gaze had settled on the third of the group, a man he did not know. While Kane and Emelyn appeared to be searching about cautiously, the other was far more agitated. He held his large axe in both hands before him, and it was quite obvious to Jarlaxle that he desperately wanted to plant it somewhere fleshy. And while Kane and Emelyn kept looking toward, and moving in the direction of, the front gates, the third man's attention had been fully grabbed by the central keep across the courtyard.

Kimmuriel waved his black hand over the pool again, and the image shifted back to Entreri. He was in a chamber Jarlaxle did not recognize, with his back to the wall just beside an upward-sloping tunnel. He had not yet drawn his weapons, but he seemed uneasy, his dark eyes darting about the torchlit tunnels, his hands resting comfortably close to his weapon hilts.

He gave a sudden laugh and shook his head.

"He knows we are watching him," one of the wizards surmised.

"Perhaps he thinks we will come to his aid," remarked the other.

"Not that one," said Jarlaxle. "He saw his choices clearly, and accepted the consequences of his decision." He looked at Kimmuriel. "I told you Entreri was a man of integrity."

"You confuse integrity with idiocy," the psionicist replied. "Integrity is the course of protecting one's own needs for survival, first and foremost. It is the ulti-mate goal of all wise people."

Jarlaxle nodded, not in agreement, but in the predictability of the response. For that was the way of the drow, of course, where the personal trumped the communal, where selfishness was a virtue and generosity a weakness to be exploited. "Some would consider simple survival the penultimate goal, not the ultimate."

"Those who would are all dead, or soon to be," Kimmuriel replied without hesitation, and Jarlaxle merely continued to nod.

"We cannot get back to help him without great cost," Kimmuriel added, and from his tone alone, Jarlaxle understood that return was not an option in Kimmuriel's mind. The psionicist was not willing to bring Bregan D'aerthe back into the fray, clearly, and from his inflection—and perhaps he had added a telepathic addendum to his statement; Jarlaxle could never be certain with that one!—it was clear to Jarlaxle that if he tried to use the opportunity to assume the mantle of leadership over Bregan D'aerthe once more, and order a return to Entreri's defense, he would be in for a fight.

But Jarlaxle had no such intention. He accepted fate's turn, even if he was not pleased by it.

The courtyard remained visible in the scrying pool, but the three figures had moved out of view. Then movement at the side of the pool revealed one, the anxious man with the axe, as he briefly showed himself. He moved fast, from cover to cover, and given the angle in which he moved out of view again, it was clear that he was making his way fast for the door of the keep.

"Farewell, my friend," Jarlaxle said, and he reached forward and tapped his hand on the still water of the pool. Ripples distorted the image before it blacked out entirely.

"You will return to Menzoberranzan with us?" Kimmuriel asked.

Jarlaxle looked at his former lieutenant and gave a resigned sigh.

❖

No one in all the Bloodstone Lands was better able to discern movements and patterns better than Olwen Forest-friend. The ranger could track a bird flying over stone, so it was said, and no one who had ever seen Olwen's deductive powers at work ever really argued the point.

"They've got a gate," Olwen said to Kane and Emelyn when they came down from the wall into the main open courtyard of the castle. The tracks of the goblin and kobold army were clear enough to all three, the ground torn under their sudden, confused—and forced, Olwen assured his friends—charge.

The ranger nodded back toward the main keep of the place, a squat, solid building set in the center of the wall that separated the upper and lower baileys. "Or they've found tunnels below the keep where the monsters made their home," he said.

"No tracks coming in?" Emelyn asked.

"The goblins and kobolds came out that door," Olwen assured the others, pointing at the keep. "But they never went in it. And three hundred of them would have pressed the castle to breaking."

"There are many tunnels underneath it," replied Emelyn, who had been through the place before.

"Finite?" Olwen asked.

"Yes."

"You're certain?"

"I used a Gem of Seeing, silly deer hunter," the wizard huffed. "Do you think I would allow something as miniscule as a secret door to evade my inspection?"

"Then they have a gate," Olwen reasoned.

"Two-way, apparently," said Kane.

The ranger looked around at the emptiness of the place, and paused a moment to consider the silence, then nodded.

"Well, let us throw the place open wide, and inspect it top to bottom," said Emelyn. "King Artemis and his dark-skinned, fiendish friend will not so easily evade us."

Emelyn and Kane turned to the gates and portcullis, and to the room open along the base of the right-hand guard tower, where a great crank could be seen. But Olwen kept his gaze focused on the keep, and while his friends moved toward the front of the castle, he went deeper in.

He could move with the stealth of a seasoned city thief, and his abilities to find shelter in the shadows were greatly enhanced by his cloak and boots, both woven by elf hands and elven magic. He disappeared so completely into the background scenery that any onlookers would think he had simply vanished, and his steps fell without a whisper of noise. In fact, it wasn't until they noticed the keep's door ajar that Kane and Emelyn—who stood near the crank, trying to figure out how to reattach the broken chain—even realized that Olwen had moved so far from them.

"His grief moves him to recklessness," Kane remarked, and started that way.

Emelyn caught the monk by the shoulder. "Olwen blazes his own trails, and always has," he reminded. "He prefers the company of Olwen alone. No doubt his training of Mariabronne incited similar feelings in that one."

"Which got Mariabronne killed, by all reports," said Kane.

Emelyn nodded. "And Olwen likely realizes that."

"Guilt and grief are not a healthy combination," the monk replied. He glanced back behind them. "Fix the chain and bring our friends," he instructed, and he started off after Olwen.

The furniture and half-folded tapestries in the audience chamber didn't slow Olwen. He moved right to the multiple corridor openings on the far side of the room, all of them bending down and around. He crouched low and moved across them, finally discerning the one that had seen the most, and probably most recent, traffic.

Axe in hand, Olwen jogged along. He came through a series of rooms, slowly and deliberately, and the repetition did nothing to take him off his guard, to bring any carelessness to his step. Nor did the multitude of side passages distress him, for though there were few tracks to follow, he suspected that they were all connected. If he misstepped, he could easily regain the pursuit in the next room, or the one beyond that. Silent and smooth went the ranger, down another corridor that ended at an open portal, spilling into a candlelit room beyond. As he neared the doorway, along the right-hand wall, the ranger noted the fast cut of the tracks to the right, just inside the door.

Olwen crept up. Barely a foot from the opening, he held his breath and leaned out, just enough to see the tip of an elbow.

He looked back at the floor—one set of tracks.

With grace and speed that mocked his large form, Olwen leaped forward and spun, bringing his two-handed axe across for a strike that the surprised sneak couldn't begin to block. Satisfaction surged through the ranger as his perfectly-balanced, enchanted blade swiped cleanly through the air with no defense coming. It drove hard into the sneak's chest; there was no way for the fool to defend!

Off to the side of the portal where Olwen had abruptly and aggressively entered, in the shadows of another corridor, Artemis Entreri watched with little amusement as the ranger's weapon blew apart the chest of the mummy Entreri had propped next to the opening.

The weapon went right through, as Entreri had planned, to slice the securing rope set behind the perserved corpse, before finally ringing off the stone.

Across from the mummy, on the other side of the intruder, a glaive, released by the severing of the rope, swung down.

Entreri figured he had a kill, and that there was no turning back because of it.

But the burly intruder surprised him, for as soon as the ring of stone sounded, almost as soon as he had cut through the rope, the man was moving, and fast, diving into a sidelong roll. He tumbled deeper into the room, just ahead of the swinging glaive, and came back to his feet with such balance and grace that he was up and crouched before Entreri had even fully exited the side corridor.

And even though Entreri moved with unmatched silence, Olwen apparently heard him, or sensed him, for he leaped about, axe swiping across, and it was all Entreri could do to flip Charon's Claw up and over to avoid getting it torn from his hand.

Olwen cut his swing short, re-angling the axe with uncanny strength and coordination, then stabbing straight out with it, its pointed crown jabbing for the assassin's throat.

Entreri let his legs buckle at the knees, falling back as Olwen came on. He finally got Charon's Claw out before him, forcing the ranger to halt, but by that point he was so overbalanced that he couldn't hope to hold his ground. He just twisted and let himself fall instead, his dagger hand planting against the ground.

Olwen's roar signaled another charge, but Entreri was already moving, using those planted knuckles as a pivot and throwing himself out to the left over his secured hand, twisting and tucking his shoulder to turn a sidelong roll into a head-over somersault. He was up and turning before Olwen could close, coming around much as the ranger had done in dodging the glaive trap, with Charon's Claw humming through the air before him as he spun.

"Oh, but you're a clever killer, aren't you?" Olwen asked.

"Isn't that the difference between the killer and the deceased?"

"And Mariabronne wasn't so clever?"

"Mariabronne?" Entreri echoed, caught by surprise.

"Don't you feed your lies to my ears," Olwen said. "You saw the threat of the man—the honest man."

He finished with a sudden leap forward, his axe slicing the air in a downward diagonal chop, right to left. Olwen let go with his top hand, his right hand, as the axe swung down, and he didn't slow its momentum at all, turning his left arm over to bring it sailing back up, catching it again in his right with a reversed grip, then executing a cross-handed chop the other way.

Entreri couldn't begin to parry that powerful strike, so he simply backed out of reach. He planted his back foot securely as the axe came past, thinking to dart in behind it. As Olwen let go with his left hand, the axe swinging out to the right, his right hand gripping it at mid-handle, Entreri saw his opening. With the shortened grip, Olwen couldn't hope to stop him.

Artemis Entreri got his first taste of the true powers of the Bloodstone Lands then, the powers of the friends of King Gareth.

Olwen sent his right arm to full extension to the right, and loosened his grip on the axe so that it slid out to full extension. The ranger's freed left hand grabbed up a hand axe set in his belt, just behind his left hip, and as Entreri came on, a flick of Olwen's wrist sent the smaller weapon spinning out.

Entreri ducked and threw Charon's Claw up desperately, just nicking the spinning hand axe, defeating its deadly spin if not entirely its angle. He still got clipped, across the side of his head, but at least the weapon hadn't planted in his face!

Worse for Entreri, though, was Olwen's mighty one-handed chop, his powerful axe soaring back across with frightening speed and strength.

The only defense for Entreri was to go under that blow, turning as he went to absorb the impact.

For any other fighter, it would have been no more than a desperate and defensive turn, but Entreri improvised, flipping his weapons as he went. His left arm caught Charon's Claw, and his right hand deftly snagged and redirected his jeweled dagger. Even as he slowed the axe, Entreri was into the counter, stabbing ahead for Olwen's ample belly.

But Olwen's free hand came across to slap hard against Entreri's leading forearm, forcing the thrusting dagger to the side as the ranger turned away from the strike. With both his weapons to Olwen's right, and with the ranger turning, balanced, behind his shoulder, Entreri had no choice but to press forward even more forcefully, diving into a headlong roll and again coming to his feet in a sudden defensive spin.

He picked off another soaring hand axe, barely registering the silvery flickers of the blade, and he could hardly believe that Olwen had managed to square himself, pull another weapon and throw it with such deadly precision and fluidity.

"Akin to catching the greased piglet, I see," Olwen taunted.

"Which rarely gets caught, and oft makes a fool of the pursuers."

Olwen smiled confidently as he walked to the side, his battle-axe swinging easily at his right side, and retrieved the first hand axe he had thrown. "Oh, it takes a while to catch it," he said. "But the greater truth is that the piglet never wins."

"Those who rely on certainties are certain to be disappointed."

Olwen gave a belly laugh, and waved his hands at Entreri in an invitation. "Come along then, murdering dog, King Artemis the Stupid. Disappoint me."

Entreri stared at the man for a short while, watched him drop into a balanced defensive crouch, setting his axes, battle- and hand-, in fine position and with a comfort that showed he was not unused to two-handed fighting. The ranger apparently believed that Entreri had killed Mariabronne, a crime for which he was innocent.

He thought to protest that very point. He thought, fleetingly, of calming the fine warrior with—uncharacteristically—the truth.

But to what end? Entreri had to wonder. Jarlaxle had proclaimed him as King Artemis the First, a usurper of lands Gareth claimed as his own. That crime carried the same sentence the man was trying to exact, no doubt.

So what was the point?

Entreri glanced at his own weapon, the red blade of Charon's Claw, the glimmering jewels of a dagger that had gotten him through a thousand battles on the streets of Calimport and beyond.

"Oh, come on, then," his opponent teased. "I'm expecting more out of a king."

With a resigned shrug, an admission yet again that it was all just a silly and insanely random game, an admission and acceptance that, though he was for once being misjudged, there had been more than a few occasions when Olwen's verdict would have been quite fair, Artemis Entreri advanced.

The sounds of battle echoed up the corridors to the foyer, where Master Kane stood before the perplexing array of tunnel openings. Because of the design of the place, with all the tunnels curving the same way, there was no way for the monk to accurately discern which opening would lead him to the fight. Even the battle sounds clattered out of all the openings uniformly, as if they were joined by cross channels.

"You should have marked it, Olwen," he mumbled, shaking his head.

Kane tried to gauge the angle of the curve and the distance of the battle sounds. He moved to the second opening from the right. He paused for a moment, until he realized that his hesitation wouldn't grant him any more insight or any better guess. He reached into a pouch, produced a candle, and dropped it on the floor, marking the opening.

Down he ran, silently and swiftly.

Entreri thrust with his sword and Olwen's hand axe descended quickly to deflect it. The assassin retracted the blade, feinted with his dagger, and thrust again with the longer weapon. Olwen had to twist aside and bring his larger axe across from his right.

And again, Entreri retracted fast and shifted as if to bring his left foot forward and thrust with the dagger, which was again in his left hand. The ranger stopped in his twist and tried to re-align himself to the right, but Entreri came on with another thrust of Charon's Claw.

He thought the fight at its end—against a lesser opponent, it surely would have been—but then the assassin realized that Olwen had anticipated that very move, and that the ranger's twist back to the right had been no more than a feint of his own, one designed to line him up for a throw.

The hand axe spun at Entreri, and only the assassin's great agility allowed him to snap his jeweled dagger up fast enough to tip it up high as he ducked. Entreri kept his feet moving as he did, reshuffling fast so that as he went down low under the spinning missile, he also was able to dart forward, once again leading with Charon's Claw.

Olwen blocked it, but Entreri stepped right behind that parry—or so he thought—and thrust with the dagger.

For Olwen had to have parried with his larger axe, the assassin had believed, and so confusion enveloped him as his dagger thrust came up short, as Olwen, more squared to him than he had thought possible, managed to slide back a stride.

As it untangled, Entreri noted that the man had pulled a second hand axe, and that it, and not the larger weapon, had defeated his low thrust.

And he was too far forward and too low, his blades hitting nothing but air, and with Olwen recoiled, his large axe up high and back. Forward it came in a sudden and devastating rush.

Entreri fell flat to the floor, wincing as the air cracked above him. He planted his hands and shoved up with all his strength, and with a perfect tuck, tugging his legs back under him, he came up straight, his weapons circling in a cross down low before him and rising fast and precisely. The lifting Charon's Claw caught Olwen's following chop with the hand axe, the red blade locking under the curved axe head, and Entreri drove the ranger's arm up and out. Entreri dropped his left arm lower, to belt height, and thrust forth the dagger, pushing the ranger back, and forcing the man to drop his larger axe low to block.

That thrust only set up the real move, though, as Entreri hopped up and to the right, gathering leverage. With the better angle, he rolled Charon's Claw right over Olwen's small axe and stabbed it down, twisting the ranger's arm.

Olwen surprised him, by dropping the axe and punching out, clipping Entreri's chin.

He staggered back a step, but recovered quickly—and a good thing he did, for on came Olwen, chopping wildly with his battle-axe. Down it rushed, and around, a sudden backhand followed by another lightning-fast strike. Metal rang against metal, clanging and screeching as the axe head ran the length of Entreri's blades in rapid succession. And in the midst of that barrage, Olwen produced yet another hand axe and added to the fury, both hands chopping.

Entreri fought furiously to keep up, deflecting and parrying. For many moments, he found no opportunities to offer any sort of a counter, no openings for any strikes at all. It was all instinct, all a blur of movement—sword, dagger, and axes whipping to and fro.

And if Olwen was growing at all weary, he certainly didn't show it.

As he exited the tunnel where he had entered, Kane turned the candle to the side, so that it was parallel to the tunnel opening, a sign for Emelyn or anyone else who came in that he had explored the passage and was no longer within. He placed a second candle on the ground at the entrance to the next corridor in line, its wick pointing into the descending darkness, clearly marking his trail for his friennd, who knew how to read his signals.

He set off more speedily, both because he understood the general layout of the tunnel, given the other, and because he was certain that it was the one that would take him to Olwen and the fight.

And judging from the frenetic pace of the ringing metal, the tempo of that battle had increased greatly.

He knew the instant his red-bladed sword cut nothing but air that he had missed the parry, but without a split second's thought about it, without the hesitation of fear or dismay, Entreri followed with a perfect evasive maneuver, turning his hips toward the left, opposite the incoming axe strike, and thrusting his waist back.

He got clipped—there was no avoiding it—on his right, leading hip, Olwen's fine battle-axe tearing through the assassin's leather padding, through his flesh, and painfully cracking against his bone.

A wince was all Entreri allowed himself, for Olwen came on, sensing the kill.

Entreri cut a wild swing, from far out to his right and across with his mighty sword. Olwen, predictably, put his axe in line to easily defeat it. But the desperation on Entreri's face, and echoed by his seemingly off-balance swing, only heightened the feint, and the assassin dropped his swing short and used the momentum, instead of as a base to strike at Olwen, to spin himself to the side.

He sprinted off, limping indeed from his wound, but refusing to give in to the waves of burning pain emanating from his torn hip.

"You've nowhere to run!" Olwen chided, and he came in fast pursuit as Entreri sprinted for the doorway, where the glaive hung, its pendulum swing played out.

Entreri shoved the glaive out to the left and rushed past—or seemed to, but he pulled up short, spun, and whipped Charon's Claw in a downward strike. He called upon the magic of the blade as he did, releasing a trailing opaque wall of black ash that hung in the air.

Even as he finished the swing, the assassin simply let go of the sword and charged out to his left, opposite the glaive. His footsteps covered by the clanging of Charon's Claw on the stone floor, Entreri rolled around the wall, judging, rightly, that the visual display of glaive and ash would confound Olwen, albeit briefly. Indeed, the ranger sent his left arm out wide to interrupt the recoil of the glaive, and he pulled up short, astonishment on his face, to see the ash wall before him.

But he couldn't stop completely, and certainly didn't want to become entangled with the cumbersome glaive anyway, so he roared and rushed forward, bursting through the ash veil and into the tunnel.

And he froze, for no enemy stood before him.

A fine and sharp dagger came about to rest on Olwen's throat. A free hand tugged at his thick shock of black hair, yanking his head back, opening his throat fully for an easy kill.

"If I were you, I'd keep my arms out wide and drop my weapons to the floor," Entreri whispered in Olwen's ear.

When the ranger hesitated, Entreri tugged his hair again and pressed a bit more with his jeweled dagger, drawing a line of blood, and when Olwen still hesitated, Entreri showed him the truth of his doom, his utter obliteration, by calling upon the vampiric powers of the dagger to steal a bit of Olwen's soul.

The battle-axe hit the floor, followed by the hand axe.

"You multiply your crimes," came a calm voice from behind.

Entreri tugged Olwen around and pressed him through the ash and past the glaive, back into the room, to face Kane, who stood at the other open exit. The monk appeared quite relaxed, fully at peace with his arms hanging at his sides, his hands empty.

"The only crime I committed was to dare step out of Gareth's gutter," the assassin retorted.

"If that is true, then why are we in battle?"

"I defend myself."

"And your kingdom?"

Entreri narrowed his eyes at that and did not respond.

"You hold your blade at the throat of a goodly man, a hero throughout the Bloodstone Lands," Kane remarked.

"Who tried to kill me, and would have gladly cut me in half had I allowed it."

Kane shrugged as if it didn't really matter. "A misunderstanding. Be reasonable now. Allow your actions to speak clearly for you when you face the justice of King Gareth, as you surely must."

"Or I walk away . . ." Entreri started to say, but he paused as a second figure came into view, ambling down the corridor to stand beside Kane. Emelyn the Gray huffed and puffed and snorted all sorts of halting and sputtering protests at the unseemly sight before him.

"Or I walk away with this man," Entreri reiterated. "Without obstruction, and release him when I am free of the misjudgments of Gareth Dragonsbane and his agitated followers."

The wizard sputtered again and started forward, only to be intercepted by an outstretched arm from Kane. That only slightly deterred Emelyn, though, for he began waving his arms.

"I will reduce you to ash!" the wizard declared.

Entreri gave a crooked grin and willed his dagger to drink, just a bit.

"Stop!" Olwen bellowed, his eyes wide with terror, and indeed, that gave Emelyn and Kane pause. Olwen had faced death many times, of course, had faced a demon lord beside them, but never had they seen their friend so unhinged.

"You will not survive this," Emelyn promised Entreri.

Beside him, Kane lowered his arms and closed his eyes. A blue gemstone on a ring he wore flickered briefly.

"Enough!" Entreri warned, and he ducked aside, pulling Olwen with him, as a spectral hand appeared in the air beside him. "My first pain is his last breath," the assassin promised.

Kane opened his eyes and brought his hands up in a gesture of apparent concession.

The spectral hand swept down, lightly brushing Entreri but feeling as nothing more than a slight breeze as it dissipated to nothingness.

Entreri breathed heavily, a bit confused. He didn't want to play his hand; killing Olwen, of course, left him with no bargaining power. He tugged the man's head for good measure, drawing a pained groan.

"Turn and lead me out," Entreri instructed.

Emelyn did begin to turn, but he paused halfway, his gaze—and subsequently, Entreri's—going to the monk, for Kane stood perfectly still, his eyes closed, his lips moving slightly, as if in incantation.

Entreri was about to issue a warning, but the monk opened his eyes and looked at him directly. "It is over," Kane declared.

The assassin's expression showed his doubt.

But then, a moment later, that expression showed Entreri's confusion, for he felt very strange. His muscles twitched, legs and arms. His eyes blinked rapidly, and he snorted, though he didn't will himself to snort.

"Ah, well done!" Emelyn said, still looking at Kane.

"Wh-wh-what?" Entreri managed to stutter.

"You have within you the intrusion of Kane," the monk explained. "I have attuned our separate energies."

The muscles on Entreri's forearm bulged, knotting and twisting painfully. He thought to slice his prisoner's throat then and there, but it was as if his mind could no longer communicate with his hand!

"Picture your life energy as a cord," Emelyn explained, "stretched taut from your head to your groin. Master Kane now holds that cord before him, and he can thrum it at will."

Entreri stared in disbelief at his forearm, and he winced, nauseous, as he began to recognize the subtle vibrations rolling throughout his body. He watched helplessly as Olwen pushed his dagger-arm out, then reached up and extracted himself from Entreri's grasp all together.

To the side, Kane calmly walked over to the fallen Charon's Claw. Entreri had a distant understanding of some satisfaction as the monk bent to retrieve it, thinking that the sentient, powerful, and malevolent weapon would melt Kane's soul, as it had so many who had foolishly taken it in hand.

Kane picked it up—his eyes widened in shock for just a moment. Then he shrugged, considered the weapon, and set it under the sash that tied his dirty robes.

Confusion mixed with outrage in the swirling thoughts of Artemis Entreri. He closed his eyes and growled, then forced himself against the intrusion. For a moment, a split second, he shook himself free, and he came forward awkwardly, as if to strike.

"Beware, King Artemis," Emelyn said, and there was indeed a hint of mocking in his voice, though Entreri was far too confused to catch the subtlety. "Master Kane can cut that cord. It is a terrible way to die."

As if on cue, and still long before Entreri had neared the pair, Kane spoke but a word, and wracking pains the likes of which Artemis Entreri had never imagined possible coursed through his body. Paralysis gripped him, as if his entire body twitched in the spasm of a single, complete muscle cramp.

He heard his dagger hit the floor.

He was hardly aware of the impact when he followed it down.

CHAPTER

15

With Kane's strong arm supporting him, Entreri managed to get up again, but he had little strength and balance. There was no resistance within him as Olwen pulled his arms back behind him and bound them tightly with a fine elven cord.

"Where is Jarlaxle?" Emelyn asked him, and though the wizard moved very near as he spoke, his voice came to Entreri as if from far, far away. And the words didn't register in any cohesive manner.

"Where is Jarlaxle?" the wizard asked, more insistently, and he moved so close that his hawkish nose brushed against Entreri's.

"Gone," the assassin heard himself whisper, and he was surprised that he had answered. He felt as if his mind had disconnected from his body and was floating around the room like a bunch of puffy clouds, each self-contained with partial thoughts that might have once been connected to, but had come fully removed from, any of the thoughts flitting through the other clouds.

He saw Emelyn turn to Kane, who merely shrugged.

"I'll go check it," the distant voice of Olwen said.

"More carefully this time," said Emelyn.

The ranger snorted and walked past, directly in front of Entreri, and he paused just long enough to offer the beaten assassin a glare.

Kane took Entreri by the arm and led him off, with Emelyn coming close behind. As they entered the ascending corridor and wound their way up, the assassin's coordination, mental and physical, did not return, and on several occasions, the only thing that kept him standing was the support of Kane.

They found King Gareth, Friar Dugald, and many soldiers milling about the audience chamber. Gareth stood by one wall, hands on his hips and staring curiously at one of the tapestries, which had been unfastened to hang to its full length.

"Well, now," Emelyn muttered, walking by Entreri and stroking his beard.

"Ah, you have him," Dugald said, turning to see the trio. "Good."

"It is curious, is it not?" Gareth asked, turning to face his friends. "Can you explain?" he started to ask Entreri, but he paused and considered the man before turning a questioning stare at his two friends.

"Kane touched him in a special way," Emelyn said dryly.

Gareth slowly nodded. "Where is Olwen?" he asked, a sudden urgency coming into his tone.

"Confirming that the drow has departed."

"And he has," came the ranger's voice from the tunnel entrance. "Through a magical gate, I suspect. And if the tracks are any indication, and we all know that they always are, then Jarlaxle wasn't the only elf—probably drow—walking about the place. I'm thinking that our friend here, the King of Vaasa, will have some answering to do."

"He should start with this, then," said Emelyn, and both he and Gareth moved aside from the tapestry, revealing it fully to Entreri and his nearest captors. Behind the assassin, Olwen sputtered. Beside him, Kane offered no words, sounds, or expression.

As he gradually began to focus on the tapestry, Entreri became even more confused. The image seemed double, as if the tapestry was coming alive, its inhabitants stepping from the fabric into the chamber.

But then he realized, far in the recesses of his groggy mind at first, but gradually working its way into his general thoughts, that the people portrayed on the tapestry were the very same ones who stood beside him in the audience chamber. For the tapestry depicted the victory of King Gareth over Zhengyi the Witch-King, and with great and accurate detail.

"Well, King Artemis?" Gareth asked. "Why would you decorate your audience chamber with such depictions as these?"

Entreri stared at him, dumbfounded.

Kane pushed him to the side, then, and eased him into one of the mushroom thrones.

"He is not ready to speak yet," Kane explained to Gareth. "The mystery will hold for a bit longer."

"As will this one," Gareth replied, and handed Kane a rolled scroll, the same one Kane had noted on the throne in his passing. He took it from Gareth and unrolled it, and again showed no emotion, though the cryptic words were surprising indeed.

Welcome Gareth, King of Damara.
Welcome Gareth, King of Vaasa.

King of Vaasa, you are most welcome.

"What trick is this?" asked Emelyn, reading over Kane's shoulder.

Outside the audience chamber, a great cheer went up for King Gareth, led by the elated soldiers of Palishchuk.

All looked to Gareth.

"The threat to their fair city is defeated," he said.

Friar Dugald gave a great belly laugh, and several of the others joined in.

"And the drow is nowhere to be found," Emelyn said to Entreri. "Are you the sacrifice, then?"

"A great waste of talent," said Olwen. "He is a fine fighter."

"But not so fleet of foot," Dugald said. "But if we are done here, then let us return to Bloodstone Village. It's a bit too cold up here."

"Bah, you've enough layers of Dugald to fend off the north wind," teased Riordan Parnell, coming in the keep's open door. "Our friends from Palishchuk wish a celebration, of course."

"They always wish a celebration," Dugald replied.

"I do like the place."

"Straightaway, as soon as we are sure the threat here is no more, we turn for home," said Gareth. "We'll leave a contingent to remain in Palishchuk through-out the winter if our half-orc friends so desire, in case the drow has any tricks left to play. But for us, it will be good and wise to be home."

"And him?" Kane asked, indicating Entreri.

"Bring him," Entreri heard Gareth say, and Entreri was disappointed at that, wishing that it would just end.

"Home to Bloodstone Village, where your friend will be executed," Kimmuriel Oblodra said as they watched the exchange in the scrying pool.

"Gareth will not kill him," Jarlaxle insisted.

"He will have no choice," said the psionicist. "You declared Entreri King of Vaasa. If Gareth allows that to stand, he is diminished in the eyes of his subjects—irreparably so. No king would be foolish enough to suffer that sort of challenge to stand. It is once removed from anarchy."

"You underestimate him. You view him through the prism of experience with the matron mothers of our homeland."

"You pray that I do, but your reason tells you otherwise," Kimmuriel replied. "Step away from your friendship with the human, Jarlaxle, for it clouds your common sense."

Jarlaxle shifted back as the wizards ended their quiet chanting and the pool fell silent, its image beginning to blur. Jarlaxle was a drow who usually spoke with certainty, and who backed up that certainty with a generous understand-ing of others. But he was also one who long ago learned to trust in Kimmuriel's judgment, for never did that one let hope or passion cloud simple logic.

"We cannot allow it," Jarlaxle remarked, speaking as much to himself as to Kimmuriel.

"We cannot prevent it," Kimmuriel replied, and Jarlaxle noted that the wizards to the sides raised their eyebrows at that. Were they expecting a con-frontation, a battle for the leadership of Bregan D'aerthe?

"I will not put Bregan D'aerthe against King Gareth," Kimmuriel went on. "I have explained as much to you once already. Nothing that has happened has changed that stance, and certainly not for the sake of a pathetic human who, even if rescued, will be dead of natural causes anyway before the memory of this incident has faded from my consciousness."

Jarlaxle wondered at that last statement, in light of Entreri drawing a bit of the essence of shadow into his blood through the use of his vampiric dagger. He let that thought go for another day, though, and focused on the issue at hand.

"I did not ask you to wage war with Gareth," he said. "If I had wanted such a thing, would I have abandoned the power of the castle? Would I not have called forth Urshula to strike hard into Gareth's ranks? Nay, my friend, we will not battle the King of Damara and his formidable army. But he is, by all accounts, a reasonable and wise human. We will barter for Entreri."

A brief flash of expression across Kimmuriel's stone face revealed his doubt. "You have nothing with which to barter."

"You did not see King Gareth's expression when he viewed my gift?"

"Confusion more than gratitude."

"Confusion is the first step to gratitude, if we're clever." Jarlaxle's sly grin brought looks of concern from all around, except from Kimmuriel, of course. "The field of battle is prepared. We need only another point of barter. Help me to attain it."

Kimmuriel stared at him hard, and doubtfully, but Jarlaxle knew that the intelligent drow would easily sort out the still-unspoken proposal.

"It will be entertaining," Jarlaxle promised.

"And worth the cost?" Kimmuriel asked. "Or the time?"

"Sometimes entertainment alone is enough."

"Indeed," replied the psionicist. "And was all of this—the arrival of the troops, the death of the slaves, the magically exhausting withdrawal—worth the trouble for you, a simple game for your amusement merely to run away when the predictable occurred and King Gareth arrived at his door?"

Jarlaxle grinned and shrugged as if it did not matter. He pulled out a curious gem, one shaped as a small dragon's skull, and with a flick of his hand, sent it spinning to Kimmuriel.

"Urshula," Jarlaxle explained. "A powerful ally to Bregan D'aerthe."

"The Jarlaxle I know would not relinquish such a prize."

"I loan it to you as an asset of Bregan D'aerthe. Besides, you will undoubtedly learn more of the dracolich than I can, aided as you will be by priests and wizards, and even illithids, no doubt."

"You offer payment for our assistance in your next endeavor?"

"Payment for that already rendered, and for that which you will still provide."

"When we find your barter for the pathetic human?"

"Of course."

"Again, Jarlaxle, why?"

"For the same reason I took in a refugee from House Oblodra, perhaps."

"To expand the powers of Bregan D'aerthe?" Kimmuriel asked. "Or to expand the experiences of Jarlaxle?"

Kimmuriel considered it for a moment and nodded, and with a laugh, Jarlaxle answered, "Yes."

CHAPTER

16

As he neared the audience chamber in his Bloodstone Village palace, King Gareth heard that the interrogation of Artemis Entreri had already begun. He glanced to his wife, who walked beside him, but Lady Christine stared ahead with that steely gaze Gareth knew so well. Clearly, she was not as conflicted about the prosecution of the would-be king as was he.

"And you claim to know nothing of the tapestries, or of the scroll we found on the fungus-fashioned throne?" he heard Celedon ask.

"Please, be reasonable," the man continued. "This could be exculpatory, to some extent."

"To make my death more pleasant?" Entreri replied, and Gareth winced at the level of venom in the man's voice.

He pushed into the audience chamber then, to see Entreri standing on the carpet before the raised dais that held the thrones. Friar Dugald and Riordan Parnell sat on the step, with Kane standing nearby. Celedon stood nearer to Entreri, pacing a respectfully wide circle around the assassin.

Many guards stood ready on either side of the carpet.

Dugald and Riordan stood up at the approach of the king and queen, and all the men bowed.

Gareth hardly noticed them. He locked stares with Entreri, and within the assassin's gaze he found the most hateful glare he had ever known, a measure of contempt that not even Zhengyi himself had approached. He continued to stare at the man as he assumed his throne.

"He has indicated that the tapestries were not of his doing," Friar Dugald explained to the king.

"And he professes no knowledge of the parchment," added Riordan.

"And he speaks truly?" asked Gareth.

"I have detected no lie," the priest replied.

"Why would I lie?" Entreri said. "That you might uncover it and justify your actions in your own twisted hearts?"

Celedon moved as if to strike the impertinent prisoner, but Gareth held him back with an upraised hand.

"You presume much of what we intend," the king said.

"I have seen far too many King Gareths in my lifetime . . ."

"Doubtful, that," Riordan remarked, but Entreri didn't even look at the man, his gaze locked firmly on the King of Damara.

". . . men who take what they pretend is rightfully theirs," Entreri continued as if Riordan had not spoken at all—and Gareth could see that, as far as the intriguing foreigner was concerned, Riordan had not.

"Take care your words," Lady Christine interjected then, and all eyes, Entreri's included, turned to her. "Gareth Dragonsbane is the rightful King of Damara."

"A claim every king would need make, no doubt."

"Kill the fool and be done with it," came a voice from the doorway, and Gareth looked past Entreri to see Olwen enter the room. The ranger paused and bowed, then came forward, taking a route that brought him within a step of the captured man. He whispered something to Entreri as he passed, and did so with a smirk.

That smug expression lasted about two steps further, until Entreri remarked, "If you are to be so emotionally wounded when you are bested in battle, then perhaps you would do well to hone your skills."

"Olwen, be at ease," Gareth warned as he watched the volatile ranger's eyes go wide.

Olwen spun anyway, and from the way Celedon stepped aside, Gareth thought the man might leap onto Entreri then and there.

But Entreri merely snickered at him.

"We are reasonable men, living in dangerous times," Gareth said to Entreri when Olwen finally stepped aside. "There is much to learn—"

"You doubt my husband's claim to the throne?" Lady Christine interrupted.

Gareth put a hand on her leg to calm her.

"Your god himself would argue with me, no doubt," said Entreri. "As would the chosen god of every king."

"His bloodline is—" Christine started to reply.

"Irrelevant!" Entreri shouted. "The claim of birthright is a method of control and not a surety of justice."

"You impertinent fool!" Christine shouted right back, and she stood tall and came forward a step. "By blood or by deed—you choose! By either standard, Gareth is the rightful king."

"And I have intruded upon his rightful domain?"

"Yes!"

"King of Damara or King of Vaasa?"

"Of both!" Christine insisted.

"Interesting bloodline you have there, Gareth—"

Celedon stepped over and slapped him. *"King* Gareth," the man corrected.

"Does your heritage extend to Palishchuk?" Entreri asked, and Gareth could not believe how fully the man ignored Celedon's rude intrusion. "You are King of Vaasa by blood?"

"By deed," Master Kane said, and he stepped in front of the sputtering Dugald as he did.

"Then strength of arm becomes right of claim," reasoned Entreri. "And so we are back to where we began. I have seen far too many King Gareths in my lifetime."

"Someone fetch me my sword," said the queen.

"Lady, please sit down," Gareth said. Then to Entreri, "You were the one who claimed dominion over Vaasa, King Artemis."

The roll of Entreri's eyes strengthened Gareth's belief that the drow, Jarlaxle, had been the true instigator of that claim.

"I claimed that which I conquered," Entreri replied. "It was I who defeated the dracolich, and so . . ." He turned to Christine and grinned. "Yes, Milady, by deed, I claim a throne that is rightfully mine." He turned back to Gareth and finished, "Is my claim upon the castle and the surrounding region any less valid than your own?"

"Well, you are here in chains, and he is still the king," Riordan said.

"Strength of arms, Master Fool. Strength of arms."

"Oh, would you just let me kill him and be done with it?" Olwen pleaded.

To Gareth, it was as if they weren't even in the room.

"You went to the castle under the banner of Bloodstone," Celedon reminded the prisoner.

"And with agents of the Citadel of Assassins," Entreri spat back.

"And a Commander of the Army of Bl—"

"Who brought along the agents of Timoshenko!" Entreri snapped back before Celedon could even finish the thought. "And who betrayed us within the castle, at an hour most dark." He turned and squared his shoulders to Gareth. "Your niece Ellery was killed by my blade," he declared, drawing a gasp from all around. "Inadvertently and after she attacked Jarlaxle without cause—without cause for her king, but with cause for her masters from the Citadel of Assassins."

"Those are grand claims," Olwen growled.

"And you were there?" Entreri shot right back.

"What of Mariabronne, then?" Olwen demanded. "Was he, too, in league with our enemies? Is that what you're claiming?"

"I claimed nothing in regards to him. He fell to creatures of shadow when he moved ahead of the rest of us."

"Yet we found him in the dracolich's chamber," said Riordan.

"We needed all the help we could garner."

"Are you claiming that he was resurrected, only to die again?" Riordan asked.

"Or animated," Friar Dugald added. "And you know of course that to animate the corpse of a goodly man is a crime against all that is good and right. A crime against the Broken God!"

Entreri stared at Dugald, narrowed his eyes, grinned, and spat on the floor. "Not my god," he explained.

Celedon rushed over and slugged him. He staggered, just a step, but refused to fall over.

"Gareth is king by blood and by deed!" Dugald shouted. "Anointed by Ilmater himself."

"As every drow matron claims to be blessed by Lolth!" the stubborn prisoner cried.

"Lord Ilmater strike you dead!" Lady Christine shouted.

"Fetch your sword and strike for him," Entreri shouted right back. "Or get your sword and give me my own, and we will learn whose god is the stronger!"

Celedon moved as if to hit him again, but the man stopped fast, for Entreri finished his insult in a gurgle, as vibrations of wracking pain ran the course of his body, sending his muscles into cramps and convulsions.

"Master Kane!" King Gareth scolded.

"He will not speak such to the queen, on pain of death," Kane replied.

"Release him from your grasp," Gareth ordered.

Kane nodded and closed his eyes.

Entreri straightened and sucked in a deep breath. He stumbled and went down to one knee.

"Do give him a sword, then," Christine called out.

"Sit down and be still!" Gareth ordered. He from his chair and walked forward, right toward the stunned expressions of most everyone in the room—except for Entreri, who glanced up at him with that hateful intensity.

"Remove him to a cell on the first dungeon level," Gareth ordered. "Keep it lit and warm, and his food will be ample and sweet."

"But my king . . ." Olwen started to protest.

"And harm him not at all," Gareth went on without hesitation. "Now. Be gone."

Riordan and Celedon moved to flank Entreri, and began pulling him from the chamber. Olwen cast one surprised, angry look at Gareth, and rushed to follow.

"Go and ease his pain," Gareth said to Friar Dugald, who stood staring at him incredulously. When the friar didn't immediately move, he said, "Go! Go!" and waved his hand.

Dugald stared at Gareth over his shoulder for many steps as he exited the room.

"You suffer him at your peril," Christine scolded her husband.

"I had warned you not to engage him so."

"You would accept his insults?"

"I would hear him out."

"You are the king, Gareth Dragonsbane, king of Damara and king of Vaasa. Your patience is a virtue, I do not doubt, but it is misplaced here."

Gareth was too wise a husband to point out the irony of that statement. He didn't blink, though, and didn't nod his agreement in any way, and so with a huff, Lady Christine headed out the side door through which she and Gareth had entered.

"You cannot suffer him to live," Kane said to the king when they were alone. "To do so would invite challenges throughout your realm. Dimian Ree watches us carefully at this time, I am certain."

"Was he so wrong?" Gareth asked.

"Yes," the monk answered without the slightest pause.

But Gareth shook his head. Had Entreri and that strange drow creature done anything different than he? Truly?

You would think them wiser, Kimmuriel Oblodra signaled in the silent drow hand code, and the way he waggled his thumb at the end showed his great contempt for the humans.

They do not understand the world below, Jarlaxle's dexterous hands replied. *The Underdark is a distant thought to the surface dwellers.* As he signed the words, Jarlaxle considered them—the truth of them and the implications. He also wondered why he so often rushed to the defense of the surface dwellers. Knellict was an archmage, brilliant by the standards of any of the common races of Toril, a master of intricate and complicated arts. Yet he had chosen his hideout, no doubt looking east, west, north, and south, but never bothering to look down.

A mere forty feet below the most secretive and protected regions of the citadel's mountain retreat, ran a tunnel wide and deep, a conduit along the upper reaches of the vast network of tunnels and caverns known as the Underdark, a route for caravans.

An approach for enemies.

Do not forget our bargain, Kimmuriel signed to him.

The last time, Jarlaxle promised, and he tapped his belt pouch, which contained the magical item to which Kimmuriel had just referred.

Kimmuriel's return look showed that he didn't believe Jarlaxle for a minute, but then again, neither did Jarlaxle. The demand was akin to telling a shadow mastiff not to bark, or a matron mother not to torture. Controlling one's nature could only be taken so far.

Kimmuriel's expression reflected little beyond that initial doubt, of course, but in it, if there was anything, it was only resignation, even amusement. The psionicist turned to the line of wizards assembled at his side and nodded. The first rushed to Kimmuriel and pointed straight up. He quickly traced an outline, and as soon as Kimmuriel agreed, the wizard launched into spellcasting.

A few moments later, the drow completed his spell with a great flourish, and a square block of the stone ceiling twice a drow's height simply dematerialized, vanished to nothingness.

Without hesitation, for the spell had a finite duration, the second wizard rushed up beside the first, touched his insignia, levitated up into the magical chimney, and similarly cast. Before he had even finished, the third had begun levitating.

Twenty or more feet up from the corridor, the third wizard executed the same powerful spell.

With the next we will be into the complex, Kimmuriel's hands told the Bregan D'aerthe soldiers gathered nearby. *Fast and silent!*

The fourth wizard ascended, and with him went the first contingent, Bregan D'aerthe's finest forward assassins led by an experienced scout named Valas Hune. They were the infiltrators, the trailblazers, and they most often marked their paths with the blood of sentries.

They timed their rise perfectly, of course, and floated past the fourth wizard just as the stone dematerialized, so that without breaking their momentum in the least, the group floated through the last ten feet and into the lower complex of the Citadel of Assassins.

The first three wizards went up right behind them, and as soon as the scouts had gathered the lay of the region and had slipped off into the torchlit tunnels, the wizards cast again.

All through the lower reaches of Knellict's mountain hideaway, a mysterious fog began to rise. More a misty veil than an opaque wall, the wafting fog elicited curiosity, no doubt.

It also rendered the quiet footsteps of drow warriors completely silent.

It also dampened most evocative magic.

It also countered all of the most common magical wards.

More warriors floated through the breach and moved along with practiced skill. Jarlaxle tipped his great hat to enable its magical powers, and he and Kimmuriel came through, accompanied by an elite group of fighters. They swept up two of the wizards in their wake, the other two moving to their predetermined positions.

This was not strange ground to the dark elves. Kimmuriel's spying of the hideaway had been near complete, and at Jarlaxle's insistence, the maps he had drawn had been studied and fully memorized by every raider rising through the floor. Even the two guard contingents left in the Underdark corridor below knew the layout fully.

Bregan D'aerthe left little to chance.

To the head, Jarlaxle's fingers flashed, and his small, elite band slipped away.

Knellict was more angry than afraid. He didn't have time to be afraid.

Screams of alarm and pain chased him and his three guards down the misty hallway and into his private chambers. The guards slammed the door shut and moved to bolt it, but Knellict held them back.

"One lock only," he explained. "Let them try to get through once. The ashes of their leading intruders will warn others away." As he finished, he began casting, uttering the activation words for the many magically explosive glyphs and wards that protected his private abode.

"We should consider leaving," said one of his guards, a young and promising wizard.

"Not yet, but hold the spell on the tip of your tongue." He drew out a slender wand, metal-tipped black shot through with lines of dark blue.

An especially shrill scream rent the air. The sound of men running moved past the door, followed at once by the sound of a couple of small crossbows firing and of one man, at least, tumbling to the floor.

"Be ready now," Knellict said. "If they breach the door, the explosions will destroy them. Those in front, at least, but you must be quick to close it again and drop the locking bars into place."

His guards nodded, knowing well their duties.

They all focused on the door, but nothing happened and the sounds moved away.

Still, they all focused intently on the door.

So much so that when the wall to the next room in line, more than half a dozen feet of solid stone, simply vanished, none of them even noticed at first.

Jarlaxle's five warriors fell to one knee and fired the poison-tipped bolts from their hand crossbows. One of the wizards amplified the shots with a spell that turned each dart into two, so that each of Knellict's two guards was struck five times in rapid succession. For the wizard sentry, there came a missile of another sort: a flying green glob of goo, popping out from the end of a slender wand Jarlaxle held.

It hit the man, engulfed him, and drove him back hard into the wall where he stuck fast, fully engulfed, and he could move nothing beyond the fingers of one hand that was flattened out to the side, could not even draw in air through the gooey mask.

Knellict reacted with typical and practiced efficiency, turning his lightning wand to the side. The trigger phrase was "By Talos!" and so Knellict cried it out, or tried to.

His words hiccupped in his mind and in his larynx, and he said "B-by Thooo." Nothing happened.

Knellict called to the wand again, and again, his brain blinked in mid-phrase. For as fast as Knellict was with his wand and his words, Kimmuriel Oblodra was faster with his thoughts.

The wizard plastered on the wall continued to helplessly waggle his fingers and feet. The two warriors slumped down to the ground, fast asleep under the spell of the powerful drow poison.

And Knellict could only sputter. He threw the wand down in outrage and launched into spellcasting, a quick dweomer that would get him far enough away to enact a proper teleportation spell and be gone from there.

A burst of psionic energy broke the chant.

The eight dark elves confidently strode into the room, four of the warriors taking up guard positions at either side of the main door and either side of the magically opened wall. The fifth warrior, on a nod from Jarlaxle, crossed the room and cut the goo from in front of the trapped wizard's nose, so that the man could breathe and watch in terror, and little else. One of the drow wizards began casting a series of detection spells, to better loot any hidden treasures.

Jarlaxle, Kimmuriel, and the other wizard calmly walked over to stand before Knellict.

"For all of your preparations, archmage, you simply do not have the understanding of the magic of the mind," Jarlaxle said.

Knellict stubbornly lifted one hand Jarlaxle's way, and with a determined sneer, spat out a quick spell.

Or tried to, but was again mentally flicked by Kimmuriel.

Knellict widened his eyes in outrage.

"I am trying to be reasonable here," Jarlaxle said.

Knellict trembled with rage. But within his boiling anger, he was still the archmage, still the seasoned and powerful leader of a great band of killers. He didn't betray the soldiers who were quietly coming to his aid from the other room.

But his enemies were drow. He didn't have to.

Even as the dark elf warriors flanking the open wall prepped their twin swords to intercede, Jarlaxle spun on his heel to face the soldiers.

They yelled, realizing that they were discovered. A priest and a wizard launched into spellcasting, three warriors howled and charged, and one lightly armored halfling slipped into the shadows.

Jarlaxle's hands worked in a blur, spinning circles over each other before him. And as each came around, the drow's magical bracers deposited into it a throwing knife, which was sent spinning away immediately.

The drow warriors at either side of the opening didn't dare move as the hail of missiles spun between them. A human warrior dropped his sword, his hands clutching a blade planted firmly in his throat, and he stumbled into the room and to the floor. A second fighter came in spinning—and took three daggers in rapid succession in his back, to match the three, including a mortal heart wound, that had taken him in the front.

He, too, fell.

The wizard tumbled away, a knife stuck into the back of his opened mouth. The priest never even got his hands up as blades drove through both of his eyes successively.

"Damn you!" the remaining warrior managed to growl, forcing himself forward despite several blades protruding from various seams in his armor. Two more hit him, one two, and he fell backward.

Almost as an afterthought, Jarlaxle spun one to the side, and it wasn't until it hit something soft and not the hard wall or floor that Knellict and the others realized that the halfling wasn't quite as good at hiding as he apparently believed.

At least, not in the eyes of Jarlaxle, one of which was covered, as always, by an enchanted eye patch—a covering that enhanced rather than limited his vision.

"Now, are you ready to talk?" Jarlaxle asked.

It had all taken only a matter of a few heartbeats, and Knellict's entire rescue squad lay dead.

Not quite dead, for one at least, as the stubborn fighter regained his feet, growled again, and stepped forward. Without even looking that way, Jarlaxle flicked his wrist.

Right in the eye.

He collapsed in a heap, straight down, and was dead before he hit the floor.

The drow fighters stared at Jarlaxle, reminded, for the first time in a long time, of who he truly was.

"Such a waste," the calm Jarlaxle lamented, never taking his eyes off of Knellict. "And we have come in the spirit of mutually beneficial bargaining."

"You are murdering my soldiers," Knellict said through gritted teeth, but even that determined grimace didn't prevent another mental jolt from Kimmuriel.

"A few," Jarlaxle admitted. "Fewer if you would simply let us be done with this."

"Do you know who I am?" the imperious archmage declared, leaning forward.

But Jarlaxle, too, came forward, and suddenly, whether it was magic or simple inner might, the drow seemed the taller of the two. "I remember all too well your treatment," he said. "If I was not such a merciful soul, I would now hold your heart in my hand—before your eyes that you might see its last beats."

Knellict growled and started a spell—and got about a half a word out before a dagger tip prodded in at his throat, drawing a pinprick of blood. That made Knellict's eyes go wide.

"Your personal wards, your stoneskin, all of them, were long ago stripped from you, fool," said Jarlaxle. "I do not need my master of the mind's magic here to kill you. In fact, it would please me to do it personally."

Jarlaxle glanced at Kimmuriel and chuckled. Then suddenly, almost crazily, he retracted the blade and danced back from Knellict.

"But it does not need to be like this," Jarlaxle said. "I am a businessman, first and foremost. I want something and so I shall have it, but there is no reason that Knellict, too, cannot gain here."

"Am I to trust—"

"Have you a choice?" Jarlaxle interrupted. "Look around you. Or are you one of those wizards who is brilliant with his books but perfectly idiotic when it comes to understanding the simplest truism of the people around him?"

Knellict straightened his robes.

"Ah, yes, you are the second leader of a gang of assassins, so the latter cannot be true," said Jarlaxle. "Then, for your sake, Knellict, prove yourself now."

"You would seem to hold all of the bargaining power."

"Seem?"

Knellict narrowed his gaze.

Jarlaxle turned to one of his wizards, the one who still stood beside Kimmuriel while the other continued to ransack Knellict's desk. The drow leader looked around, then nodded toward the wizard trapped on the wall.

The wizard walked over and began to cast an elaborate and lengthy spell. Soon into it, Kimmuriel focused his psionic powers on the casting drow, heightening his concentration, strengthening his focus.

"What are you . . ." Knellict demanded, but his voice died away when all of the dark elves turned to eye him threateningly.

"I tell you this only once," Jarlaxle warned. "I need something that I can easily get from you. Or . . ." He turned and pointed at the terrified, flailing wizard on the wall. "I can take it from him. Trust me when I tell you that you want me to take it from him."

Knellict fell silent, and Jarlaxle motioned for his wizard and psionicist to resume.

It took some time, but finally the spellcaster completed his enchantment, and the poor trapped wizard glowed with a green light that obscured his features. He grunted and groaned behind that veil of light, and he thrashed even more violently behind the trapping goo.

The light faded and all went calm, and the man hanging on the wall had transformed into an exact likeness of Archmage Knellict.

"Now, there are conditions, of course, for my mercy," said Jarlaxle. "We do not lightly allow other organizations to pledge allegiance to Bregan D'aerthe."

Knellict seemed on the verge of an explosion.

"There is a beauty to the Underdark," Jarlaxle told him. "Our tunnels are all around you, but you never quite know where, or when, we might come calling. Anytime, any place, Knellict. You cannot continually look below you, but we are always looking up."

"What do you want, Jarlaxle?"

"Less than you presume. You will find a benefit if you can but let go of your anger. Oh, yes, and for your sake, I hope the Lady Calihye is still alive."

Knellict shifted, but not uneasily, showing Jarlaxle that she was indeed.

"That is good. We may yet fashion a deal."

"Timoshenko speaks for the Citadel of Assassins, not I."

"We can change that, if you like."

The blood drained from Knellict's face as the enormity of it all finally descended upon him. He watched as one of the drow warriors approached the wizard who bore his exact likeness.

A crossbow clicked and the man who looked exactly like Knellict soon quieted in slumber.

Mercifully.

* * *

"All hail the king," Entreri said when the door of his cell opened and Gareth Dragonsbane unexpectedly walked in. The king turned to the guard and motioned for him to move away.

The man hesitated, looked hard at the dangerous assassin, but Gareth was the king and he could not question him.

"You will forgive me if I do not kneel," Entreri said.

"I did not ask you to do so."

"But your monk could make me, I suppose. A word from his mouth and my muscles betray me, yes?"

"Master Kane could have killed you, legally and without inquiry, and yet he did not. For that you should be grateful."

"Saved for the spectacle of the gallows, no doubt."

Gareth didn't answer.

"Why have you come here?" Entreri asked. "To taunt me?" He paused and studied Gareth's face for a moment, and a smile spread upon his own. "No," he said. "I know why you have come. You fear me."

Gareth didn't answer.

"You fear me because you see the truth in me, don't you, King of Damara?" Entreri laughed and paced his cell, a knowing grin splayed across his face, and Gareth followed his every step warily, with eyes that reflected a deep and pervading turmoil.

"Because you know I was right," Entreri continued. "In your audience chamber, when the others grew outraged, you did not. You could not, because my words echoed not just in your ears but in your heart. Your claim is no stronger than was my own."

"I did not say that, nor do I agree."

"Some things need not be spoken. You know the truth of it as well as I do—I wonder how many kings, pashas, or lords know it. I wonder how many could admit it."

"You presume much, King Artemis."

"Don't call me that."

"I did not bestow the title."

"Nor did I. Nor does it suit me. Nor would I want it."

"Are you bargaining?"

Entreri scoffed at him. "I assure you, paladin king, that if I had a sword in hand, I would willingly cut out your heart, here and now. If you expect me to beg, then look elsewhere. The fool monk can bring me to my knees, but if I am not there of my own choosing, then calling it begging would ring as hollow as does your crown, yes?"

"As I said, you presume much. Too much."

"Do I? Then why are you here?"

Gareth's eyes flared with anger, but he said nothing.

"An accident of birth?" Entreri asked. "Had I been born to your mother, would I then be the rightful king? Would your mighty friends rally to my side as they do yours? Would the monk exercise his powers over an enemy of mine at my bidding?"

"It is far more complicated than that."

"Is it?"

"Blood is not enough. Deed—"

"I killed the dracolich, have you forgotten?"

"And all the deeds along your road led you to this point?" Gareth asked, a sharp edge creeping into his voice. "You have lived a life worthy of the throne?"

"I survived, and in a place you could not know," Entreri growled back at him. "How easy for the son of a lord to proclaim the goodness of his road! I am certain that your trials were grand, heir of Dragonsbane. Oh, but the bards could fill a month of merrymaking with the tales of thee."

"Enough," Gareth bade him. "You know nothing."

"I know that you are here. And I know why you are here."

"Indeed?" came the doubtful reply.

"To learn more of me. To study me. Because you must find the differences between us. You must convince yourself that we are not alike."

"Do you believe that we are?"

The incredulity did not impress Entreri. "In more ways than his majesty wishes to admit," he said. "So you come here to learn more in the hope that you will discern where our paths and characters diverge. Because if you cannot find that place, Gareth, then your worst fears are realized."

"And those would be?"

"Rightful. The rightful king. An odd phrase, that, don't you agree? What does it mean to be the rightful king, Gareth Dragonsbane? Does it mean that you are the strongest? The most holy? Does your god Ilmater anoint you?"

"I am the descendant of the former king, long before Damara was split by war."

"And if I had been born to your parents?"

Gareth shook his head. "It could not have been so. I am the product of their loins, of their breeding and of my heritage."

"So it is not just circumstance? There is meaning in bloodlines, you say?"

"Yes."

"You have to believe that, don't you? For the sake of your own sanity. You are king because your father was king?"

"He was a baron, at a time when Damara had no king. The kingdom was not unified until joined in common cause against Zhengyi."

"And that is where, by deed, Gareth rose above the other barons and dukes and their children?"

Gareth's look showed Entreri that he knew he was being mocked, or at least, that he suspected as much.

"A wonderful nexus of circumstance and heritage," Entreri said. "I am truly touched."

"Should I give you your sword and slay you in combat to rightly claim Vaasa?" Gareth asked, and Entreri smiled at every word.

"And if I should slay you?"

"My god would not allow it."

"You have to believe that, don't you? But humor me, I pray you. Let us say that we did battle, and I emerged the victor. By your reasoning, I would thus become the rightful King of Vaa—oh, wait. I see now. That would not serve, since I haven't the proper bloodline. What a cunning system you have there. You and all the other self-proclaimed royalty of Faerûn. By your conditions, you alone are kings and queens and lords and ladies of court. You alone matter, while the peasant grovels and kneels in the mud, and since you are 'rightful' in the eyes of this god or that, then the peasant cannot complain. He must accept his muddy lot in life and revel in his misery, all in the knowledge that he serves the rightful king."

Gareth's jaw tightened, and he ground his teeth as he continued to stare unblinking at Entreri.

"You should have had Kane kill me, back at the castle. Break the mirror, King Gareth. You will fancy yourself prettier in that instance."

Gareth stared at him a short while longer, then moved to the cell door, which was opened by the returned guard. Beside him stood Master Kane, who stared at Entreri.

Entreri saw him and offered an exaggerated bow.

Gareth pushed past the pair and moved along, his hard boots stomping on the stone floor.

"You wish that you had killed me, I expect," Entreri said to Kane. "Of course, you still can. I feel the vibrations of your demonic touch."

"I am not your judge."

"Just my executioner."

Kane bowed and walked off. By the time he caught up to Gareth, the man had departed the dungeons and was nearing his private rooms.

"You heard?" Gareth asked him.

"He is a clever one."

"Is he so wrong?"

"Yes."

The simple answer stopped Gareth and he turned to face the monk.

"In my order, rank is attained through achievement and single combat," Kane explained. "In a kingdom as large as Damara, in a town as large as Bloodstone Village, such a system would invite anarchy and terrible suffering. On that level, it is the way of the orc."

"And so we have bloodlines of royalty?"

"It is one way. But such would be meaningless absent heroic deeds. In the darkest hours of Damara, when Zhengyi ruled, Gareth Dragonsbane stepped forward."

"Many did," said Gareth. "You did."

"I followed King Gareth."

Gareth smiled in gratitude and put a hand on Kane's shoulder.

"The title holds you as tightly as you hold the title," Kane said. "It is no easy task, bearing the responsibility of an entire kingdom on your shoulders."

"There are times I fear I will bend to breaking."

"One ill decision and people die," said Kane. "And you alone are the protector of justice. If you are overwhelmed, men will suffer. Your guilt stems from a feeling that you are not worthy, of course, but only if you view your position as one of luxury. People need a leader, and an orderly manner in which to choose one."

"And that leader is surrounded by finery," said Gareth, sweeping his hands at the tapestries and sculptures that decorated the corridor. "By fine food and soft bedding."

"A necessary elevation of status and wealth," said Kane, "to incite hope in the common folk that there is a better life for them; if not here then in the afterworld. You are the representative of their dreams and fantasies."

"And it is necessary?"

Kane didn't immediately answer, and Gareth looked closely at the man, great by any measure, yet standing in dirty, road-worn robes. Gareth laughed at that image, thinking that perhaps it was time for the Bloodstone Lands to see a bit more charity from the top.

"Damara is blessed, so her people say, and the goodly folk of Vaasa hold hope that they, too, will be swept under your protection," said Kane. "You heard their cheers at the castle. Wingham and all of Palishchuk call to Gareth to accept their fealty."

"You are a good friend."

"I am an honest observer."

Gareth patted his shoulder again.

"What of Entreri?" Kane asked.

"You should have left that dog dead on the muddy lands of Vaasa," said Lady Christine, coming out of her bedchamber.

Gareth looked at her, shook his head, and asked, "Does his foolish game warrant such a penalty?"

"He slew Lady Ellery, by his own admission," said Kane.

Gareth winced at that, as Christine barked, "What? I will kill the dog myself!"

"You will not," said Gareth. "There are circumstances yet to be determined."

"By his own admission," Christine said.

"I am protector of justice, am I not, Master Kane?"

"You are."

"Then let us hold an inquiry into this matter, to see where the truth lies."

"Then kill the dog," said Christine.

"If it is warranted," Gareth replied. "Only if it is warranted." Gareth didn't say it, and he knew that Kane understood, but he hoped that it would not come to that.

He had just heard the report from Vaasa, where his soldiers held forth at Palishchuk, and motioned to the majordomo to bring forth the Commander of the Heliogabalus garrison, where promising reports had been filtering in for a tenday. But to Gareth's astonishment, and to that of Lady Christine and Friar

Dugald who sat with him in chambers, it was not a soldier of the Bloodstone Army who entered through the doors.

It was an outrageous dark elf, his bald head shining in the glow of the morning light filtering in through the many windows of the palace. Hat in hand, giant feather bobbing with every step, Jarlaxle smiled widely as he approached.

The guards at either side bristled and leaned forward, ready to leap upon the dark elf at but a word from their king.

But that word did not come.

Jarlaxle's boots clicked loudly as he made his way along the thickly-carpeted aisle. "King Gareth," he said as he neared the dais that held the thrones, and he swept into a low, exaggerated bow. "Truly Damara is warmer now that you have returned to your home."

"What fool are you?" cried Lady Christine, obviously no less surprised than were Gareth and Dugald.

"A grand one, if the rumors are to be believed," Jarlaxle replied. The three exchanged looks, ever so briefly.

"Yes, I know," Jarlaxle added. "You believe them. 'Tis my lot in life, I fear."

Behind the drow, at the far end of the carpet, the majordomo entered along with the couriers from Heliogabalus. The attendant stopped short and glanced around in confusion when he noticed the drow.

Gareth nodded, understanding that Jarlaxle had used a bit of magic to get by the anteroom—a room that was supposedly dampened to such spells. Gareth's hand went to his side, to his sheathed long sword, Crusader, a holy blade that held within its blessed metal a powerful dweomer of disenchantment.

A look from the king to the sputtering majordomo sent the attendant scrambling out of the room.

"I am surprised that I am surprising," Jarlaxle said, and he glanced back to let them know that he had caught on to all of the signaling. "I would have thought that I was expected."

"You have come to surrender?" Lady Christine asked.

Jarlaxle looked at her as if he did not understand.

"Have you a twin, then?" asked Dugald. "One who traveled to Palishchuk and beyond to the castle beside Artemis Entreri?"

"Yes, of course, that was me."

"You traveled with King Artemis the First?"

Jarlaxle laughed. "An interesting title, don't you agree? I thought it necessary to ensure that you would venture forth. One cannot miss such opportunities as Castle D'aerthe presented."

"Do tell," said Lady Christine.

A commotion at the back of the room turned Jarlaxle to glance over his shoulder, to see Master Kane cautiously but deliberately approaching. Behind him, staying near the door, the majordomo peered in. Then Emelyn the Gray appeared, pushing past the man and quick-stepping into the great room, casting as he went. He looked every which way—and with magical vision as well, they all realized.

Jarlaxle offered a bow to Kane as the man neared, stepping off to the side and standing calmly, and very ready, of course.

"You were saying," Lady Christine prompted as soon as the drow turned back to face the dais.

"I was indeed," Jarlaxle replied. "Though I had expected to be congratulated, honestly, and perhaps even thanked."

"Thanked?" Christine echoed. "For challenging the throne?"

"For helping me to secure the allegiance of Vaasa," Gareth said, and Christine turned a doubting expression his way. "That was your point, I suppose."

"That, and ridding the region immediately surrounding Palishchuk of a couple of hundred goblin and kobold vermin, who, no doubt, would have caused much mischief with the good half-orcs during the wintry months."

At the back of the room, Emelyn the Gray began to chuckle.

"Preposterous!" Friar Dugald interjected. "You were overwhelmed, your plans destroyed, and so now . . ." He stopped when Gareth held his hand up before him, bidding patience.

"I trust that none of your fine knights were seriously injured by the outpouring of vermin," Jarlaxle went on as if the friar hadn't uttered a word. "I timed the charge so that few, if any, would even reach your ranks before being cut down."

"And you expect gratitude for inciting battle?" Lady Christine asked.

"A slaughter, Milady, and not a battle. It was necessary that King Gareth show himself in battle in deposing King Artemis. The contrast could not have been more clear to the half-orcs—they saw Artemis hoarding monstrous minions, while King Gareth utterly destroyed them. Their cheering was genuine, and the tales they tell of the conquest of Castle D'aerthe will only heighten in heroic proportions, of course. And with Wingham's troupe in town at the time of the battle, those tales will quickly spread across all of Vaasa."

"And you planned for all of this?" Gareth asked, sarcasm and doubt evident in his tone—but not too much so.

Jarlaxle put a hand on one hip and cocked his head, as if wounded by the accusation. "I had to make it all authentic, of course," the drow explained. "The proclamation of King Artemis, the forced march of King Gareth and his army. It could not have been known a ruse to any, even among your court, else your own integrity might have been compromised, and your complicity in the ruse might have been revealed."

"I say foul," Lady Christine answered a few moments later, breaking the stunned silence.

"Aye, foul and now fear," Dugald agreed.

Gareth motioned for Kane and Emelyn to join him at the dais. Then he instructed Jarlaxle to leave and wait in the anteroom—and several guards accompanied the drow.

"Why do we bother wasting time with this obvious lie?" Christine said as soon as they had gathered. "His plans to rule Vaasa crumbled and now he tries to salvage something from the wreckage of ill-designed dreams."

"It is a pity that he chose the route he did," said Gareth. "He and his companion might have made fine interim barons of Vaasa."

All eyes turned to Gareth, and Christine seemed as if she would explode, so violently did she tremble at the thought.

"If Olwen were here, he would have struck you for such a remark," Emelyn said.

"You believe the drow?" Kane asked.

Gareth considered the question, but began shaking his head almost immediately, for his instinct on this was clear enough, whatever he wanted to believe. "I know not whether it was a ruse from the beginning or a convenient escape at the end," he said.

"He is a dangerous character, this Jarlaxle," said Emelyn.

"And his friend has no doubt committed countless crimes worthy of the gallows," Christine added. "His eyes are full of murder and malice, and those weapons he carries . . ."

"We do not know that," Gareth said. "Am I to convict and condemn a man on your instinct?"

"We could investigate," said Emelyn.

"On what basis?" Gareth snapped right back.

The others, except for Kane, exchanged concerned glances, for they had seen their friend dig in his heels in similar situations and they knew well that Gareth Dragonsbane was not a malleable man. He was the king, after all, and a paladin king, as well, sanctioned by the state and by the god Ilmater.

"We have no basis whatsoever," said Kane, and Christine gasped. "The only crime for which we now hold Artemis Entreri is one of treason."

"A crime calling for the gallows," said Christine.

"But Jarlaxle's explanation is at least plausible," said Kane. "You cannot deny that the actions of these two, whatever their intent, solidified your hold in Vaasa and reminded the half-orcs of Palishchuk of heroic deeds past and the clearest road for their future."

"You cannot believe that this . . . this . . . this drow, went to Vaasa and arranged all of that which transpired simply for the good of the Kingdom of Bloodstone," said Christine.

"Nor can I say with any confidence that what has transpired was anything different than exactly that," said Kane.

"They sent an army of monsters against us," Dugald reminded them all, but his description drew an unexpected burst of dismissive laughter from Emelyn.

"They called a bunch of goblins and kobolds to their side, then put them before us for the slaughter," said Gareth. "I know not the depths of Jarlaxle's foolishness or his wisdom, but I am certain that he knew his monstrous army would not even reach our ranks when he sent them forth from the gates. Much more formidable would have been the gargoyles and other monsters of the castle itself, which he did not animate."

"Because he could not," Dugald insisted.

"That is not what Wingham, Arrayan, and Olgerkhan reported," reminded Kane. "The gargoyles were aloft when first they went to see what mischief was about the castle."

"And so we are left with no more than the crime of inconvenience," said Gareth. "These impetuous two circumvented all protocol and stepped far beyond their province in forcing me north, even if it was for the good of the kingdom. We have no proof that what they did was anything more than that."

"They tried to usurp your title," Christine said. "If you are to let that stand, then you condone lawlessness of a level that will bring down Bloodstone."

"There are darker matters at hand," Emelyn added. "Let us not forget the warnings we were given by Ilnezhara and Tazmikella. This Jarlaxle creature is much more than he appears."

The sobering remark left them all quiet for some time, before Gareth finally responded, "They are guilty of nothing more than hubris, and such is a reflection of our own actions those years ago when we determined the fate of Damara. It is possible, even logical, that Jarlaxle's ruse was exactly as he portrayed it, perhaps in a clever—overly clever, for he wound himself into a trap—attempt to gain favor and power in the wilds of the north. Maybe he was trying to secure a comfortable title. I do not know. But I have no desire to hold Artemis Entreri in my dungeon any longer, and he has not proven himself worthy of the noose. I will not hang a man on suspicion and my own fears.

"They will be banished, both of them, to leave the Bloodstone Lands within the tenday, and never to return, on pain of imprisonment."

"On pain of death," Christine insisted, and when Gareth turned to the queen, he saw no room for debate in her stern expression.

"As you will," he conceded. "We will get them far from here."

"You would do well to warn your neighbors," said Emelyn, and Gareth nodded. The king pointed to Emelyn's robe, and the wizard huffed and pulled it open. He produced from a deep, extra-dimensional pocket the scroll they had found in the Zhengyian castle.

Gareth waved his friends back from the dais and motioned to the back of the room. A few moments later, Jarlaxle, his great hat still in his hands, again stood before the king.

Gareth tossed the scroll to the drow. "I know not whether you are clever by one, or by two," he said.

"I lived in the Underdark," the drow replied with a wry grin. "I am clever by multiples, I assure you."

"You need not, for it is exactly that suspicion that has led me to conclude that you and Artemis Entreri are guilty for your actions north of Palishchuk."

Jarlaxle didn't seem impressed, which put all of Gareth's friends on their guard.

"Exactly what that crime is, however, cannot be deduced," Gareth went on. "And so I take the only course left open to me, for the good of the kingdom. You are to remove yourself from the region, from all the Bloodstone Lands, within the tenday."

Jarlaxle considered the verdict for just a moment, and shrugged. "And my friend?"

"Artemis Entreri or the dwarf?" Gareth asked.

"Ah, you have Athrogate, then?" Jarlaxle replied. "Good! I feared for the poor fool, entangled as circumstance had made him with the Citadel of Assassins."

It was Gareth's turn to pause and consider.

"I was speaking of Artemis Entreri, of course," said Jarlaxle. "Is he under similar penalty?"

"We considered much worse," Christine warned.

"He is," said Gareth. "Although he was the one who assumed the title of king, I note that the castle was named for Jarlaxle. Similar crimes, similar fate."

"Whatever those crimes may be," said the drow.

"Whatever that fate may be," said Gareth. "So long as it is not a fate you discover here."

"Fair enough," Jarlaxle said with a bow.

"And if it were not?" said Christine. "Do you think your acceptance of the judgment of the king an important thing?"

Jarlaxle looked at her and smiled, and so serene was that look that Christine shifted uneasily in her chair.

"One more piece of business then," said Jarlaxle. "I would like to take the dwarf. Though he was entangled with the Citadel of Assassins, as you discerned, he is not a bad sort."

"You presume to bargain?" Christine asked indignantly.

"If I do, it is not without barter." Jarlaxle slowly pulled open his waistcoat and slid a parchment from its pocket. Kane shifted near as he did, and the drow willingly handed it over.

"A map to the hideout of the Citadel of Assassins," the drow explained.

"And how might you have fashioned or found such a thing?" Gareth asked suspiciously as his friends bristled.

"Clever by more ways than a human king could ever count," the drow explained. As he did, Jarlaxle shifted his great hat, turning it opening up. "Clever and with allies unseen." He reached into the hat and produced his trophy, then set it at the foot of the dais.

The head of Knellict.

After the gasps had quieted, Jarlaxle bowed to the king. "I accept your judgment, indeed," he said. "And would pray you to accept my trade, the map and the archmage for the dwarf, though I have already turned them over, of course. I trust in your sense of fair play. It is time for me to go, I agree. But do note, Gareth Dragonsbane, King of Damara, and now King of Vaasa, that you are stronger and your enemies weaker for the work of Jarlaxle. I expect no gratitude, and accept no gifts—other than one annoying dwarf for whom you have little use anyway. You wish us gone, and so we will go, with a good tale, a fine adventure, and an outcome well served."

He finished with a great and sweeping bow, and spun his feathered hat back up to his bald head as he came up straight.

Gareth stared at the head, his mouth hanging open in disbelief that the drow, that anyone, had brought down the archmage of the Citadel of Assassins so efficiently.

"Who are you?" Christine asked.

"I am he who rules the world, don't you know?" Jarlaxle replied with a grin. "One little piece at a time. I am the stuff of Riordan Parnell's most outrageous songs, and I am a confused memory for those whose lives I've entered and departed. I wish you no ill—I never did. Nor have I worked against you in any way. Nor shall I. You wish us gone, and so we go. But I pray you entrust the dwarf to my care, and do tell Riordan to sing of me well."

Neither Gareth nor Christine nor any of the others could begin to fashion a reply to that.

Which only confirmed to Jarlaxle that it was indeed time to go.

CHAPTER

OF LOVE AND HATE

17

E ntreri looked up as his cell door swung open and Master Kane entered, bearing a large canvas sack. "Your possessions," the monk explained, swinging the sack off his shoulder and dropping it on the floor at the man's feet.

Entreri looked down at it then back up at Kane, and said not a word.

"You are being released," Kane explained. "All of your possessions are in there. Your unusual steed, your dagger, your fine sword . . . everything you had with you when you were captured."

Still eyeing the man suspiciously, Entreri crouched down and pulled back the top of the sack, revealing the decorated pommel of Charon's Claw. As soon as he gripped the hilt and felt the sentient weapon come alive in his thoughts, he knew that this was no bluff.

"My respect for you multiplied many times over when I lifted your blade," Kane said. "Few men could wield such a sword without being consumed by it."

"You seemed to have little trouble picking it up," Entreri said.

"I am far beyond such concerns," Kane replied. Entreri pulled the *piwafwi* out and slung it around his shoulders in one fluid motion. "Your cloak is of drow make, is it not?" Kane asked. "Have you spent time with the drow, in their lands?"

"I am far beyond such questions," the assassin replied, mocking the monk's tone.

Kane nodded in acceptance.

"Unless you plan to compel me to answer," Entreri said, "with this sickness you have inserted into my being."

Kane stepped back, his hands folded causally at his waist before him. Entreri watched him for a few moments, seeking a sign, any sign. But then, with a dismissive snicker, he went back to the bag and began collecting his items, and kept a mental inventory all the way through.

"Are you going to tell me more about this sudden change of mind?" he asked when he was fully outfitted. "Or am I to suffer the explanations of King Gareth?"

"Your crime is not proven," said Kane, "since there is an alternative explanation of intent."

"And that would be?"

"Come along," Kane said. "You have far to go in a short amount of time. You are freed of your dungeon, but your road will be out of Damara and Vaasa."

"Who would wish to stay?"

Kane ignored the flippant remark and began walking up the corridor, Entreri in tow. "In a tenday's time, Artemis Entreri will enter the Bloodstone Lands only on pain of death. For the next few days, you are here at the sufferance of King Gareth and Queen Christine, and theirs is a patience that is not limitless. One tenday alone."

"I've a fast horse that doesn't tire," Entreri replied. "A tenday is nine too long."

"Good, then we are in agreement."

They walked in silence for a short while, past the curious and alert stares of many guards. Entreri returned those stares with his own, silent but overt threats that had the sentries, to a man, tightly clutching their weapons. Even the presence of Grandmaster Kane did not free them from the dangerous glare of Artemis Entreri, the look that so many had suffered, a foretelling of death.

Artemis Entreri was not in a generous mood. He felt the vibrations of Kane's indecent intrusion into his body, a swirling and tingling sensation that seemed like strange ocean waves caught within the uneven contours of his corporeal being, rolling and breaking and re-gathering as they swept about. Emelyn's explanation of an elven cord of energy pulled taut seemed very on the mark to the assassin. What he knew beyond that description was that this intrusion seemed in many ways as awful as the life-draining properties of his own prized dagger.

Entreri's hand subconsciously slipped to the jeweled hilt of that trusted weapon, and he considered the possibilities.

"Pause," Entreri said as the pair neared the king's audience chamber.

Kane obeyed and turned back to regard the man. The guards flanking the door leaned forward, hands wringing tightly around their adamantine-tipped halberds.

"How am I to trust in this?" Entreri asked. "In you?"

"There is an alternative?"

"You would have me walk out of here, judgment passed and rendered, and that judgment being banishment and not death, and yet you hold the cord of my life in the single puff of your breath?"

"The effects of Quivering Palm will wear away in a short enough time," Kane assured him. "They are not permanent."

"But while they last, you can kill me, and easily?"

"Yes."

As the monk spoke the word, Entreri swept into motion, drawing forth his dagger and closing the ground between them. Kane was not caught unawares, as Entreri had not expected him to be, and the monk executed a perfect block.

But Entreri wasn't trying for a kill, or for the monk's heart. He got what he wanted and managed to prick Kane's palm with his vampiric blade. He held the dagger against the monk's torn flesh.

He stared at Kane and smiled, to keep the monk curious.

"Am I to facilitate your suicide, then?" the monk asked.

In response, Entreri called upon the life draining abilities of his jeweled dagger. Kane's eyes went wide; apparently the monk wasn't beyond all such concerns.

Behind Kane, one guard lowered his halberd, though he wisely held back—if Grandmaster Kane couldn't handle the assassin, then what might he do, after all? The other turned to the door and shoved it open, shouting for King Gareth.

"An interesting dilemma, wouldn't you agree?" Entreri said to the monk. "You hold my life in your thoughts, and can paralyze me, as I have seen, with a simple utterance. But I need only will the dagger to feed and it will feed to me, in replacement, your own life energy. Where does that leave us, Master Kane? Will your Quivering Palm be quick enough to slay me before my blade can drink enough to save me? Will we both succumb? Are you willing to take the chance?"

Kane stared at him, and matched his unnerving smile.

"What is the meaning of this?" King Gareth said, coming to the door.

Beside him, Friar Dugald sputtered something indecipherable, and Queen Christine growled, "Treachery!"

"No more so than that shown to me," Entreri answered, his stare never leaving the gaze of Kane.

"We should have expected as much from a dog like you," Christine said.

Would that your throat had been in my reach, Entreri thought, but wisely did not say. Gareth was a reasonable man, he believed, but likely not where that queen of his was concerned.

"You were granted your possessions and your freedom," Gareth said. "Did Kane not tell you?"

"He told me," Entreri replied. He heard the shuffling of mail-clad feet coming up the corridor behind him, but he paid it no heed.

"Then why have you done this?" asked Gareth.

"I will not leave here under the immoral hold of Master Kane," Entreri replied. "He will relinquish his grip on my physical being, or one of us, perhaps both, will die here and now."

"Fool," said Christine, but Gareth hushed her.

"Your life is worth so little to you, 'tis apparent," Gareth began, but Kane held up his free hand to intervene.

The monk stared hard at Entreri the whole time. "Pride is considered the deadliest of the sins," he said.

"Then dismiss your own," Entreri countered.

Kane's smile was one of acceptance, and he slowly nodded, then closed his eyes.

Entreri rolled his fingers on the dagger hilt, ready to call fully on its powers if it came to that. He really didn't believe that he had a chance, though, even if it had been just him and Kane alone in the palace. The monk's insidious grasp was too strong and too quickly debilitating. If Kane called upon the Quivering Palm, Entreri suspected that he would be incapacitated, perhaps even killed, before the dagger could do any substantial work.

But only serenity showed on Master Kane's face as he opened his eyes once more, and almost immediately, Entreri felt his inner tide fall still.

"You are released," Kane informed him, and within the blink of an eye, the monk's hand was simply removed, gone, from the tip of the dagger. Too fast for Entreri to even have begun drawing forth with its vampiric powers had he so desired.

"You give in to such demands?" Queen Christine railed.

"Only because they were justly demanded," said Kane. "Artemis Entreri has been told of the conditions and granted his release. If we are not to trust that he will accept his sentence, then perhaps we should not be releasing him at all."

"Perhaps not," said Christine.

"His release was justly secured," said Gareth. "And we cannot diminish the importance of the rationale for such a judgment. But now this assault . . ."

"Was justified, and in the end, meaningless to us," Kane assured him.

Entreri slipped his dagger away, and Gareth turned and drove Christine and Dugald before him back into the audience chamber.

"Have I missed all the excitement?" came a voice from within, one that Artemis Entreri knew all too well.

"The bargainer, I presume," he said to Kane.

"Your drow friend is quite persuasive, and comes prepared."

"If only you knew."

Walking down the cobblestone road beside Jarlaxle a short while later, Entreri did not feel as if he was free. True, he was out of Gareth's dungeon, but the drow walking beside him reminded him that there were many dungeons, and not all were made of wood and stone and iron bars. As he considered that, his hand slid back to brush the flute he had tucked inside the back of his belt, and it occurred to him that he was not yet certain whether the instrument was, in and of itself, a prison or a key.

Entreri and Jarlaxle cast long shadows before them, for the sun was fast setting behind the mountains across the small lake. Already the cold night wind had begun to blow.

"So ye're to be walkin', and whistlin' and talkin', and thinkin' yer world's all the grand," a voice rang out behind them.

Jarlaxle turned, but Entreri just closed his eyes.

"While I'm to be sittin', and grumblin' and spittin', and wiggling me toes in the sand?" Athrogate finished. "I'd rather, I'm thinkin', be drinkin' and stinkin' "—he paused, lifted one leg, and let fly a tremendous fart—"and holdin' a wench in each hand! *Bwahaha!* Hold up, then, ye hairless hunk o' coal, and let me little legs catch ye. I won't be hugging ye, but I'm grateful enough that ye bargained me way out o' that place!"

"You didn't," Entreri muttered.

"A fine ally," Jarlaxle replied. "Strong of arm and indomitable of spirit."

"And boundless in annoyance."

"He has been sad of late, for the trouble with the Citadel. I owe him this much at least."

"And here I was, hoping that you had bargained for my freedom by turning him over instead," Entreri said, and Athrogate was close enough to hear.

"Bwahaha!" the dwarf boomed.

Entreri figured it was impossible to offend the wretched creature.

"Why, but I am hurt, Artemis," Jarlaxle said, and he feigned a wound, throwing his forearm dramatically across his brow. "Never would I abandon an ally."

Entreri offered a doubting smirk.

"Indeed, when I had heard that Calihye had been grabbed from her room at the Vaasan Gate by Knellict and the Citadel . . ." Jarlaxle began, but he stopped short and let the weight of the proclamation hang there for a few moments, let Entreri's eyes go wide with alarm.

"Traveling to Knellict's lair was no minor expedition, of course," Jarlaxle went on.

"Where is she?" the assassin asked.

"Safe and roomed at the tavern down the road, of course," Jarlaxle replied. "Never would I abandon an ally."

"Knellict took her?"

"Yup yup," said Athrogate. "And yer bald hunk o' coal friend took Knellict's head and put it on Gareth's dais, he did. *Bwahaha!* Bet I'd've liked to see Lady Christine's nose go all crinkly at that!"

Entreri stared hard at Jarlaxle, who swept a low bow. "Your lady awaits," he said. "The three of us are bound to be gone from the Bloodstone Lands within the tenday, on pain of death, but we can spare a day, I expect. Perhaps you can persuade Lady Calihye that her road runs with ours."

Entreri continued to stare. He had no answers. When he had forced Jarlaxle through Kimmuriel's magical gate in the bowels of the castle, he had expected that he would never see the drow again, and all of what followed, his release, the dwarf, the news about Calihye, rushed over him like a breaking ocean wave. And as it receded, pulling back, it dragged him inexorably along with it.

"Go to her," Jarlaxle said quietly, seriously. "She will be pleased to see you."

"And while ye're stayin' and gots to be playin', meself is thinkin' I got to be drinkin'!" Athrogate roared with another great burst of foolish laughter.

Entreri's eyes shot daggers at Jarlaxle. The drow just motioned toward the tavern.

Jarlaxle and Athrogate watched Entreri disappear up the stairs of the Last Respite, the most prominent inn of Bloodstone Village, which boasted of clean rooms, fine elven wine, and an unobstructed view of the White Tree from every balcony.

Both the dwarf and the drow were known in the village, of course, for Athrogate's morningstars had made quite an impression on the folk at the Vaasan Gate, just to the north, and Jarlaxle was, after all, a drow!

The glances that came their way that day, however, were ones full of suspicion, something that didn't escape the notice of either of the companions.

"Word of Gareth's pardon has not yet reached them, it seems," Jarlaxle remarked, sliding into a chair against the far wall of the common room.

" 'Tween't no pardon," Athrogate said. "Though I'm not for thinking that a banishing from the Bloodstone Lands is a bad thing. Not with the Citadel lookin' to pay ye back for Knellict and all."

"Yes, there is that," said the drow. He hid his smile in a motion to the barmaid.

The two had barely ordered their first round—wine for the drow and honey mead for the dwarf—when a couple of Jarlaxle's acquaintances unexpectedly walked in through the Last Respite's front door.

"Ain't many times I seen ye lookin' surprised," Athrogate remarked.

"It is not a common occurrence, I assure you," Jarlaxle replied, his eyes never leaving the new arrivals, a pair of sisters who, he knew, were much more than they seemed.

"Ye got a fancy, do ye?" Athrogate said, following that gaze, and he gave a great laugh that only intensified as the two women moved to join them.

"Lady Ilnezhara and dear Tazmikella," Jarlaxle said, rising politely. "I meant to speak with you in Heliogabalus on my road south out of the realm."

There were only three chairs around the small table, and Tazmikella took the empty one, motioning for Jarlaxle to sit down. Ilnezhara looked at Athrogate.

"We must speak with Jarlaxle," she told the dwarf.

"*Bwahaha!*" Athrogate bellowed back. "Well, I'm for listening! Ain't like he can make the both of ye grin, now can—?"

He almost finished the question before Ilnezhara grabbed him by the front of the tunic, and with just one hand, hoisted him easily into the air and held him there.

Athrogate sputtered and wriggled about. "Here now, drow!" he said. "She's got an arm on her! *Bwahaha!*"

Ilnezhara glared at him, and the fact that almost everyone in the tavern stared at the spectacle of a lithe woman holding a heavily armored, two-hundred-pound dwarf up in the air at the end of one slender arm seemed not to disturb her in the least.

"Now, pretty girl, I'm guessin' ye got yerself a potion or a spell, mighten even a girdle like me own," Athrogate said. "But I'm also thinking that ye'd be a smart wench to know yer place and put me down."

Jarlaxle winced.

"As you wish," Ilnezhara replied. She glanced around, seeking a clear path, and with a flick of her wrist, launched the dwarf across the common room where he crashed through an empty table and took it and a couple of chairs hard into the wall with him.

He leaped up, enraged, but his eyes rolled and he tumbled down in a heap. Ilnezhara took his seat without a second look at him.

"Please don't break him," said Jarlaxle. "He cost me greatly."

"You are leaving our employ," Tazmikella said.

"There is no choice in the matter," replied the drow. "At least not for me. Your King Gareth made it quite clear that his hospitality has reached its limit."

"Through no fault of your own, no doubt."

"Your sarcasm is well placed," Jarlaxle admitted.

"You have something we want," Ilnezhara said.

Jarlaxle put on his wounded expression. "My lady, I have given it to you many times." He was glad when that brought a smile to Ilnezhara's face, for

Jarlaxle knew that he was treading on dangerous ground, and with extremely dangerous characters.

"We know what you have," Tazmikella cut in before her sister and the drow could get sidetracked. "Both items—one from Herminicle's tower, and one from the castle."

"The more valuable one from the castle," Ilnezhara agreed.

"Urshula would agree," Jarlaxle admitted. "This Witch-King who once ruled here was a clever sort, indeed."

"Then you admit possession?"

"Skull gems," said Jarlaxle. "A human one from the tower, that of a dragon from the castle, of course. But then, you knew as much when you dispatched me to Vaasa."

"And you acquired them?" reasoned Ilnezhara.

"Both, yes."

"Then give them over."

"There is no room for bargaining in this," Tazmikella warned.

"I don't have them."

The dragon sisters exchanged concerned glances, and turned their doubtful stares at Jarlaxle.

Across the room, Athrogate pulled himself up to his knees and shook his hairy head. Still wobbly, he gained his feet, and staggered a step back toward the table.

"To escape King Gareth, I had to call upon old friends," said Jarlaxle. He paused and looked at Ilnezhara. "You are well versed in divine magic, are you not?" he asked. "Cast upon me an enchantment to discern whether I am speaking the truth, for I would have you believe my every word."

"The Jarlaxle I know would not readily part with such powerful artifacts," Ilnezhara replied. Still, she did launch into spellcasting, as he had requested.

"That is only because you do not know of Bregan D'aerthe."

"D'aerthe? Is that not what you named your castle?" Tazmikella asked as soon as her sister finished and indicated that her dweomer was complete.

"It is, and it was named after a band of independent . . . entrepreneurs from my homeland of Menzoberranzan. I called upon them, of course, to escape King Gareth's army, and to facilitate the release of Lady Calihye from the Citadel of Assassins."

"We heard that you delivered Knellict's head to Gareth," said Tazmikella.

Behind Ilnezhara, Athrogate lowered his head, and fell forward as much as charged. He ran into the woman's upraised hand, and stopped as surely as if he had hit a rocky mountain wall. He bounced back just a bit, standing dazed, and Ilnezhara faced him squarely and blew upon him, sending him into a backward roll that left him on his belly in the middle of the floor. He propped himself up on his elbows, staring incredulously at the woman, unaware of her real nature, of course.

"Got to get meself a girdle like hers, I'm thinking," he said, and collapsed.

"It was an expensive proposition," Jarlaxle said when the excitement was over. "But I could not let Lady Calihye die and I needed the bargaining chip to facilitate the release of my friend . . ." He paused and considered Athrogate. "My friends," he corrected, "from King Gareth's dungeon."

"You gave the skull gems to your drow associates from the Underdark?" Tazmikella asked.

"I had no further use for them," said Jarlaxle. "And the Underdark is a good place for such artifacts. They cause nothing but mischief here in the sunlit world."

"They will cause nothing but mischief in the Underdark," said Ilnezhara.

"All the better," said Jarlaxle, and he lifted his glass in toast.

Tazmikella looked to her sister, who spent a few moments staring at Jarlaxle, before slowly nodding.

"We will study this further," Tazmikella said to the drow, turning back.

Jarlaxle hardly heard her, though, for another call had come to him suddenly, in his thoughts.

"Indeed, I would be disappointed if you did not," he said after he sorted through her words. "But pray excuse me, for I have business to attend."

He stood up and tipped his hat.

"We did not dismiss you," Tazmikella said.

"Dear lady, I pray you allow me to go."

"We are tasked by Master Kane to fly you from these lands," said Ilnezhara. "At sunrise."

"Sunrise, then," said Jarlaxle and he stepped forward.

Tazmikella's arm came out and blocked his way, and Jarlaxle cast a plaintive look at Ilnezhara.

"Let him go, sister," Ilnezhara bade.

Tazmikella locked Jarlaxle with her gaze, the stare of an angry dragon, but she did drop her arm to allow him to pass.

"Do see to him," Jarlaxle bade the waitress, indicating Athrogate. "Put him in a chair when he awakens and dull his pain with all the drink he desires." He tossed a small bag of coins to her as he finished, and she nodded.

※

"He spoke truthfully?" Tazmikella asked as soon as she and her sister were alone.

"If incompletely, and I am not so sure about Knellict's fate."

"A wise choice by King Gareth to send that one on his way," Tazmikella said. "He remains in contact with the creatures of the Underdark?" She gave a derisive snort. "The fool, to be sure, but we are all better off if the skull gems are indeed removed from the lands. Perhaps good consequence can come from evil dealings, for that one is naught but trouble."

"I will miss him," was all that the obviously distracted Ilnezhara would reply, and she stared wistfully at the departing drow.

※

She swayed in the smoky candlelight, her hair rolling behind her, shoulder to shoulder. Sweat glistened on her naked form, and she arched her back and looked up at the ceiling of the inn room, breathing and moaning softly.

Beneath her, Artemis Entreri clutched that beautiful image in his thoughts, found respite from the frustration and anger. He was angry at being used by

Jarlaxle, and more so at being rescued by the drow—the last thing he wanted was to be indebted in any way to that one. And the road beckoned again, a road he would walk with Jarlaxle and the annoying Athrogate, apparently.

And with Calihye, he reminded himself as he reached up and ran his hand gently from the underside of the woman's chin all the way down to her belly. She would be his anchor, he hoped, his solid foundation, and with that firm footing, perhaps he could find a way to be rid of Jarlaxle.

But did he really want that?

It was all too confusing for the poor man. He glanced to the side, to where he had piled his clothes and other gear, and he saw Idalia's flute among that pile. The flute had done things to him, he knew, had pried open his heart and had forced him to ask for more out of his life than simple existence.

He hated it and appreciated it all at once.

Everything seemed like that to Artemis Entreri. Everything was a jumble, a confusing paradox of love and hate, of stoicism and desperate need, of friendship and the desire for solitude. Nothing seemed clear, nothing consistent.

He looked up at his lover and changed his mind on those last points. It was real, and warm. For the first time in his life, he had given himself fully to a woman.

Calihye rolled her head forward and looked at him, her eyes full of intensity and determination. She chewed her bottom lip a bit; her breath came in short puffs. Then she threw her head back and arched her spine, and Entreri felt her tighten like a drawn bowstring.

He closed his eyes and let the moment wash over him and take him with it, and he felt Calihye relax. He opened his eyes, expecting to see her crumbling atop him.

He saw instead the woman staring down at him, a dagger in her hand.

A dagger aimed for his heart.

And he had no defense, had no way to stop its deadly plunge. He could have brought his hand across to accept the stab there, perhaps, but he did not.

For in the split second of the dagger's plunge, Entreri understood that all of his hope had flown, that all of it, the entire foundation that held his sanity, was just another lie. He didn't try to block it. He didn't try to dodge aside.

The dagger could not hurt him more than the betrayal already had.

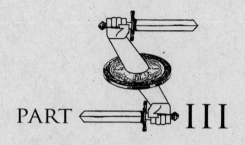

PART III

THE ROAD HOME

The point of self-reflection is, foremost, to clarify and to find honesty. Self-reflection is the way to throw self-lies out and face the truth—however painful it might be to admit that you were wrong. We seek consistency in ourselves, and so when we are faced with inconsistency, we struggle to deny.

Denial has no place in self-reflection, and so it is incumbent upon a person to admit his errors, to embrace them and to move along in a more positive direction.

We can fool ourselves for all sorts of reasons. Mostly for the sake of our ego, of course, but sometimes, I now understand, because we are afraid.

For sometimes we are afraid to hope, because hope breeds expectation, and expectation can lead to disappointment.

And so I ask myself again, without the protective wall—or at least, conscious of it and determined to climb over it—why do I feel kinship to this man, Artemis Entreri, who has betrayed almost everything that I have come to hold dear? Why do I think about him—ever? Why did I not kill him when I had the chance? What instinct halted the thrust of a scimitar?

I have often wondered, even recently and even as I ponder this new direction, if Artemis Entreri is who I might have been had I not escaped Menzoberranzan. Would my increasing anger have led me down the road he chose, that of passionless killer? It seems a logical thing to me that I might have lost myself in the demands of perfectionism, and would have found refuge in the banality of a life lived without passion. A lack of passion is perhaps a lack of introspection, and it is that very nature of self-evaluation that would have utterly destroyed my soul had I remained in the city of my birth.

It is only now, in these days when I have at last shed the weight of guilt that for so long burdened my shoulders, that I can say without hesitation that no, had I remained in Menzoberranzan, I would not have become the image of Artemis Entreri. More like Zaknafein, I expect, turning my anger outward instead of inward, wearing rage as armor and not garmenting my frame in the fears of what is in my heart. Zaknafein's was not an existence I desire, nor is it one in which I would have long survived, I am sure, but neither is it the way of Entreri.

So the worries are shed, and we, Entreri and I, are not akin in the ways that I had

681

feared. And yet, I think of him still, and often. It is, I know now, because I suspect that we are indeed akin in some ways, and they are not my fears, but my hopes.

Reality is a curious thing. Truth is not as solid and universal as any of us would like it to be; selfishness guides perception, and perception invites justification. The physical image in the mirror, if not pleasing, can be altered by the mere brush of fingers through hair.

And so it is true that we can manipulate our own reality. We can persuade, even deceive. We can make others view us in dishonest ways. We can hide selfishness with charity, make a craving for acceptance into magnanimity, and amplify our smile to coerce a hesitant lover. The world is illusion, and often delusion, as victors write the histories and the children who die quietly under the stamp of a triumphant army never really existed. The robber baron becomes philanthropist in the final analysis, by bequeathing only that for which he had no more use. The king who sends young men and women to die becomes beneficent with the kiss of a baby. Every problem becomes a problem of perception to those who understand that reality, in reality, is what you make reality to be.

This is the way of the world, but it is not the only way. It is not the way of the truly goodly king, of Gareth Dragonsbane who rules in Damara, of Lady Alustriel of Silverymoon, or of Bruenor Battlehammer of Mithral Hall. Theirs is not a manner of masquerading reality to alter perception, but a determination to better reality, to follow a vision, and to trust their course is true, and it therefore follows, that perception of them will be just and kind.

For a more difficult alteration than the physical is the image that appears in the glass of introspection, the pureness or rot of the heart and the soul.

For many, sadly, this is not an issue, for the illusion of their lives becomes self-delusion, a masquerade that revels in the applause and sees in a pittance to charity a stain remover for the soul. How many conquerors, I wonder, who crushed out the lives of tens of thousands, could not hear those cries of inflicted despair beyond the applause of those who believed the wars would make the world a better place? How many thieves, I wonder, hear not the laments of victims and willingly blind themselves to the misery wrought of their violation under a blanket of their own suffered injustices?

When does theft become entitlement?

There are those who cannot see the stains on their souls. Some lack the capacity to look in the glass of introspection, perhaps, and others alter reality without and within.

It is, then, the outward misery of Artemis Entreri that has long offered me hope. He doesn't lack passion; he hides from it. He becomes an instrument, a weapon, because otherwise he must be human. He knows the glass all too well, I see clearly now, and he cannot talk himself around the obvious stain. His justifications for his actions ring hollow—to him most of all.

Only there, in that place, is the road of redemption, for any of us. Only in facing honestly that image in the glass can we change the reality of who we are. Only in seeing the scars and the stains and the rot can we begin to heal.

I think of Artemis Entreri because that is my hope for the man. It is a fleeting and distant hope to be sure, and perhaps in the end, it is nothing more than my own selfish need to believe that there is redemption and that there can be change. For Entreri? If so, then for anyone.

For Menzoberranzan?

—Drizzt Do'Urden

CHAPTER

18

The end of the assault was no less brutal than the beginning. The man, past middle age, gyrated fiercely and growled and grunted with primordial savagery, and even slapped the young woman across the face once in his climactic delirium.

Then it ended, like the snap of fingers, and the man pulled himself off the young girl and lowered his many-layered red, gold, and white robes as he calmly walked away with not a look back at the deflowered creature. For Principal Cleric Yozumian Dudui Yinochek, the Blessed Voice Proper of the Protector's House, the most powerful man in at least one entire ward of the port city of Memnon, had not the time to consider the rabble.

His pursuits were intellectual, his obstacles physical, and his "flock" often more an inconvenience than a source of strength.

He walked stiff-legged and swayed a bit as he crossed the cluttered room, his energy spent. He considered the carts and the crates, the canvas sacks and piled tools. Rarely did he or any of the clerics of Selûne, who controlled the all-important tides, go to that room for purposes other than that one. The place was dirty and smelled of brine; it was a chamber for the servants and not the blessed clerics. The place had only a single redeeming quality: a fairly secretive door heading out to the street, through which "visitors" could readily be smuggled.

That thought turned the principal cleric back to the young woman, barely more than a girl. She cried, but was apparently wise enough not to whine too loudly and insult his performance. She was in pain of course, but it would pass. Her confusion and inner tumult would be more damaging than the sting of a punctured hymen, Yinochek knew.

"You performed a valuable service to Selûne this night," he said to her. "Free of my earthly desires, I can better contemplate the mysteries of paradise, and as they are revealed to me, the road to redemption will be better shown to you and to your failing father. Here."

He lifted a loaf of stale bread he had set on a cart by the hall door when he had entered, and gave it a shake to dislodge a few of the crawling creatures, then tossed it to her. She caught it and clutched it tightly, desperately to her breast. That brought a condescending chuckle from Yinochek.

"You treasure it, of course," he said. "Because you do not understand that your greater reward will be the result of my contemplations. You are so rooted in the needs of the physical that you cannot begin to comprehend the divine."

With a derisive snort at the blank, tear-streaked expression that came back at him, Yinochek turned to the door and pulled it open, startling a handsome young cleric.

"Devout Gositek," he greeted.

"My apologies, Principal," Papan Gositek said, crossing his arms at his belt and bending stiffly in supplication. "I heard . . ."

"Yes, I am finished," Yinochek explained, glancing back and leading Gositek's gaze to the woman, who slowly rocked and clutched at the bread. The principal cleric turned back to the younger priest.

"Your treatise on the Promise of Ibrandul awaits me in my quarters," he said, and the young priest beamed. "I have been told that your insights are nothing short of brilliant, and from what I have perused, I am finding that the rumors are credible. So misunderstood is that god, whose domain is death itself."

Gositek's teeth showed, despite his strenuous attempt at humility.

"Your work proceeds?" Yinochek asked, and he knew he had caught the young man in a prideful gloat.

"Y-yes, yes, Principal," Gositek stammered, respectfully lowering his gaze.

Yinochek hid his amusement. Pride was considered a weakness of course, even a sin, but Yinochek understood the truth of the matter: absent pride, no young man would undertake the rigors of such contemplation. He shifted aside just a bit as Gositek began to lift his head, allowing the man a view of the shivering girl.

Gositek's eyes, and even a little lick of his lips, betrayed his lust.

"Take her," Yinochek offered. "She is pained, if you care, but your work is more important than her comfort. Release your earthly passions and find a state of contemplation. I am beyond curious to view your thesis regarding the godly propaganda ploys of the Fugue Plane. The thought of the gods themselves vying for the souls of the uncommitted dead fascinates me, and presents opportunities for us to recruit for the worship of Selûne."

Yinochek turned to the girl. "Your dead mother has not yet attained paradise," he said, and he didn't even try to hide his contemptuous snicker. "Devout Gositek here," he stepped aside so that she could better see the man, "prays for her. Your attention to his needs will allow him to better assure her ascent."

He turned back to Gositek and shrugged. "It will be better this way," he said, and walked out of the room.

The girl was all but forgotten by Yinochek by the time he arrived at his chamber on the temple's third and highest floor. He moved past his wooden desk—polished and rich in hue, unlike the gray and grainy driftwood that was most often used in the desert port. The wood had been imported, as was the case with most of the implements, furniture, and decorations of the fabulous temple, by far the largest and most grand structure in the southwestern quarter of the sprawling city.

Divine contemplations required inspirational surroundings.

Yinochek moved to the western door, the one that led to the private balcony, in the great temple known as the Protector's House. There resided the priests of Selûne, the Moon Goddess, and their sister faiths of Valkur and Shaundakul. The single encompassing structure was the center of prayer and contemplation, with a growing library that was fast becoming the envy of the Sword Coast. That library had expanded considerably—and ironically—only a few years earlier, soon after the Time of Troubles, when a cult of the death god Ibrandul had been discovered in the catacombs of that very building. Flushed from their secrecy, not all of those rogue priests had been killed. Under the daring and bold command of Yinochek, many had been assimilated. "Expand the knowledge," he had told his doubting lessers.

Of course, they had done it secretly.

The balcony was shielded from the ever-prying eyes of idiot peasants who continually gathered in the square below, begging indulgences or healing spells when they had not the coin to pay. His other balcony didn't have the angled high railing to prevent those spiritual beggars from viewing him. Yinochek could view the harbor in full, a round moon setting beyond the watery horizon, silhouetting the tall masts of the great trading ships moored off the coast as they swayed with the rhythmic, gentle waves. That natural harmony reminded the principal cleric of his lovemaking that night, creating in him a connectedness to the universe and lifting him to thoughts of eternity and oneness with Selûne. He sighed and basked in the moment. Physically sated of base and corrupting urges, he soared among the stars and the gods, and more than an hour passed, the moon disappearing from sight, before he turned his thoughts to Gositek's brilliant thesis.

He had found inner peace and so he could find Selûne.

He couldn't even remember what his shivering vessel had looked like that night, nor did he care to try.

CHAPTER

19

Lady Christine, Queen of Damara, sat on the white, iron-backed stool before the grand, platinum-decorated mirror of her vanity. Before her rested an assortment of beauty treatments, jars, and perfumes she had been given as gifts from all over the kingdom, and from Impiltur as well. Her appearance was important, the ladies-in-waiting continually reminded her, for with her stature and with her magnificent husband, she held the hopes and dreams of women across the Bloodstone Lands.

She was an illusion, built to sustain the facade necessary for effective leadership.

Though she had been raised as a noblewoman, Christine was not comfortable with such things. In her heart she was an adventurer, a fighter, and a determined voice.

How thin her voice had seemed that day, when Artemis Entreri had been let go. She heard Gareth moving around the bedroom behind her, and saw him flitter across the image at the corner of her mirror. He was on edge, she knew, for her lack of conversation after the release of the assassin had told him clearly that she did not approve.

It was such a coy little game, she thought, the relationship called marriage. They both knew the issue at hand, but they would dance around it for hours, even days, rather than face the volatility head on.

At least, that was the usual way for most couples, but never had demurring been a staple of Lady Christine's emotional repetoire.

"If you would prefer a less opinionated queen, I'm sure one can be easily found," she said. She regretted the sarcasm as soon as the words had left her mouth, but at least she had started the dialogue.

She saw the image of Gareth behind her, and felt his strong and comforting hands come to rest upon her shoulders. She liked the touch of his fingers against her bare flesh, interrupted only by the thin straps of her nightgown.

"What a fool I would be if I desired to be rid of the closest friend and advisor I have ever known," he said, and he bent and kissed her on top of her head.

"I didn't suggest that you be rid of Master Kane," she replied, and she let Gareth see her smile in the mirror.

He joined in her laugh and gently squeezed her shoulders.

Christine turned in her seat and looked at him. "Yet you were quick to dismiss my advice throughout this ordeal with Artemis Entreri and that devilish drow."

Gareth's nodding sigh was one of both agreement and resignation.

"Why?" Christine asked. "What is it you know of them that the rest of us—other than Kane, it seems—do not?"

"I know little of either of them," Gareth admitted. "And I suspect that the world would be a better place with both of them removed from it. Certainly I find few redeeming qualities in the likes of Artemis Entreri or that confounding drow. But neither have I the right to pass such judgment. By all accounts they are innocent of any heinous actions."

"They committed treason to the throne."

"By claiming a land over which no man has rightful dominion?" Gareth asked.

"Yet you went to dethrone them, posthaste."

Gareth nodded again. "I would not let it stand. Vaasa will become a barony of Damara. Of that I am determined. And I am certain it will be done with the blessing and support of every city within our northern neighbor. Surely Palishchuk desires such a union."

"Then which is it? Treason? Or are you a conqueror?"

"A little of both, I suspect."

"And you believe the drow and his wild tale that this was all prearranged?" Christine did not hide her skepticism in the least. "That he planned for you to come so that you could be seen as a hero yet again to the folk of Palishchuk? He is an opportunist in the extreme, and only your quick action prevented him from securing his kingdom!"

"I do not doubt that," said Gareth. "Nor do I underestimate the threat from that one. For him to successfully infiltrate the Citadel of Assassins is no small feat, nor is retrieving the head of Archmage Knellict an action of one who should be easily dismissed. Spysong is watching them, and carefully, I assure you. They will be gone from the land within the tenday, as demanded."

"Or they will be killed?"

"Efficiently," Gareth promised. "Indeed, the dragon sisters have agreed to fly them far from our borders."

"Where they may wreak havoc somewhere else."

"Perhaps."

"And in that admission, do you believe that you serve Ilmater?"

"I often do not know," the man said. He turned away and paced back to the side of the bed.

Christine shifted her chair so that she could face him directly, and earnestly asked, "What is it, my love? What hold has this man upon you?"

Gareth stared at her and let a long moment pass silently, then said, "The experience with Artemis Entreri will make me a better king."

That proclamation made Lady Christine raise her eyebrows. "In that you are determined that you will not become akin to him?" she asked, and her inflection revealed doubt and confusion with every word.

"No, that is not the point," Gareth replied. "But in my private conversation with Artemis Entreri, he was correct in that neither blood nor a disconnected deed is the true measure of leadership. My actions now, and now alone, can justify this title I hold dear . . . and it is an empty title unless it is one that truly represents the hopes, dreams, and betterment of the people of the kingdom—of *all* the people of the kingdom."

"Artemis Entreri told you that?" Christine asked, not attempting to mask the doubt in her voice.

"I'm uncertain that he understood what he was asking," said Gareth. "But in essence, yes, that is exactly what he told—what he taught—to me. I rule Damara, and wish to bring Vaasa under my fold in the single Kingdom of Bloodstone. But that decision must be one that serves the betterment of the folk of Vaasa, else I am no more worthy to claim this title than—"

"Than Entreri, Jarlaxle, or Zhengyi?"

"Yes," said Gareth, and he nodded as he looked at her, his eyes set with determination, his lips showing that optimistic and hopeful grin that so endeared him to almost everyone who had ever looked upon him. Against that sincere expression, Lady Christine could not maintain her resentment.

"Then let the image of Artemis Entreri linger in your thoughts, my love, for the good of Damara and Vaasa," she said. "And let the man be far gone from here, his dark elf friend beside him."

"For the good of Damara and Vaasa," said Gareth.

Christine went to her husband, the man she loved.

She barely felt the dagger tip connect with his skin before she retracted her arm and stabbed him again, and again. In a wild, crying frenzy, Calihye struck at the helpless man. She felt the warmth of blood under her thigh and pumped her arm even more furiously, her eyes closed, tears streaming down her cheeks and crying for Parissus all the while.

Her anger, her frustration, her sadness, her remorse, and her explosion of desperation all played out, leaving her in a great physical weariness, and she looked down at the man who had been her lover.

He lay on his back, arms out wide and making no move to defend against her. He stared at her, his jaw clenched, his expression a mask of disappointment.

He didn't have a scratch on him. The blood on her thigh was her own, caused by a cut she had inflicted on one retraction of the blade.

"So predictable, these weak human creatures," Kimmuriel Oblodra remarked as he and Jarlaxle watched the spectacle playing out on Entreri's bed from an extra-dimensional pocket from which had opened a gate to the side of the room.

"She was so convincing," Jarlaxle said. "I never would have believed . . ."

"Then you have been around these fools too long," Kimmuriel said. "Are your judgments so impaired that I should not welcome you back to Bregan D'aerthe when you at last abandon this folly and return to Menzoberranzan?"

Jarlaxle glanced at the psionicist, a frozen look, a murderer's look, that reminded Kimmuriel in no uncertain terms who he was addressing.

But Jarlaxle didn't hold to the threatening stare, as he was drawn back to the spectacle on the bed. Calihye's expression had turned more to terror by that point, and she struck again, at Entreri's eye, as if she wanted so desperately to stop him from looking at her with his accusing gaze.

Entreri did flinch, but so remotely that Jarlaxle marveled at the sheer discipline of the man. He had ordered Kimmuriel to enact the psionic kinetic barrier, of course, for the psionicist had learned of Calihye's desperate plan. But Entreri could not have known that he was so protected, and yet he had not in any way tried to fend off the attacks.

Had Calihye coaxed him to a point of such vulnerability? Had her actions and soothing words so put Artemis Entreri off his guard?

Or did he simply not care?

"Fascinating," Jarlaxle whispered.

"It reminds you of your own birth, no doubt," said Kimmuriel, catching him off balance. He looked at his companion.

"No doubt," Jarlaxle replied, and since his companion had mentioned it, he could indeed picture a terrified and frustrated Matron Baenre plunging her spider-shaped dagger at his newborn breast. He imagined that her look must have been somewhat similar to Calihye's at that very moment, such a delicious mixture of a dozen conflicting emotions.

"You never did get the opportunity to thank my House's matron mother," Kimmuriel remarked.

"Oh, but I did," Jarlaxle assured him.

"When Baenre's Secondboy scooped you from the altar and all of the kinetic energy bound within your infant frame exploded into him and tore his chest apart," Kimmuriel agreed, recalling the stories of that distant time, tales that had been told and retold in House Oblodra over the centuries. "My grandmatron did have a way of removing her sworn enemies."

"Few could so fluster Matron Baenre as the matron mothers of House Oblodra," said Jarlaxle. "I am certain that Baenre keenly considered such insults as the power of Lolth flowed through her and offered her the power to tumble House Oblodra into the Clawrift."

Kimmuriel, ever so in control, did wince at that, and Jarlaxle smiled. For only a few short years before, Jarlaxle's mother had obliterated Kimmuriel's House in one devastating burst of power.

The two exchanged looks of mutual surrender, then turned their attention back to the room, where the stubborn and terrified Calihye lifted the dagger before her in both hands, clutched it tightly, and drove it at Entreri's heart yet again. He reached up and stopped her, and as she struggled to push through his powerful grasp, his other hand came up and slapped her hard. As he did that, he turned his hips and sent her tumbling off the far side of the bed.

"He knows what happened," Kimmuriel remarked. He led Jarlaxle's gaze behind them, to the brutish orc warrior patiently awaiting its orders.

"End the dweomer," Jarlaxle instructed, and he grabbed the orc's tether and pulled the creature behind him into the room. As Entreri jumped up from the bed to face them, Jarlaxle tugged the orc close and whispered, "Kill him," into its ear, then shoved it forward at Entreri.

The sight of a naked human, his right side red with blood from chest to hip, was all the encouragement the brutish beast needed. It charged Entreri and leaped for him.

With hardly an effort, only simple instinct, Entreri's hand came out hard to grasp the orc by the throat, and all of the energy that had been bound up kinetically within his frame, every one of Calihye's vicious strokes and stabs, flowed through that connection.

The orc's chest exploded with garish wounds; its left eye drove into its brain, blood spurting from the wound.

It spasmed and jerked, and tried to cry out in stunned horror.

But all it could do was gurgle on its own blood, and Entreri unceremoniously dropped the dead thing down to the ground.

He stood there on the edge of disaster, covered in blood, breathing deeply as if fighting for control.

Jarlaxle knew that the furious man wanted nothing more than to spring forward and strike at him, then. He also held faith that Artemis Entreri was too disciplined to do such a stupid thing.

Behind Entreri, Calihye rose and gasped at the sight of the dead orc and the two dark elves. Her arms went limp at her sides and the dagger fell to the floor.

"I am sorry," Jarlaxle said to Entreri.

The assassin didn't blink.

"It is not the way I wanted it to be," Jarlaxle said.

Entreri's look told him clearly that the man considered it none of Jarlaxle's business.

"I could not let her kill you, even if you seemed resigned to that fate," Jarlaxle explained.

Kimmuriel's fingers flashed disapproval in the air. *You spend too much time justifying yourself to your inferiors,* the psionicist scolded.

"And you spend too much time breathing," Entreri said to Kimmuriel, reminding the drow that he had learned to interpret that silent drow language during his stay in Menzoberranzan, even though his less delicate human fingers could not "speak" it well.

Jarlaxle put his hand on Kimmuriel's arm, a silent reminder to the psionicist that he did not have permission to kill Entreri.

Never blinking, never taking his awful stare off of Artemis Entreri, Kimmuriel obediently stepped back, prepared, Jarlaxle knew all too well, to cripple or even kill the human with a wave of psionic energy.

As Kimmuriel retreated, Calihye stumbled forward to Entreri's side. Her sobs genuine, she grabbed his arm and lowered her head to his shoulder in supplication, whispering that she was sorry over and over again.

"The poor thing has wound herself into an emotional collapse," Kimmuriel remarked.

"Shut up," said Entreri. He turned to Calihye and roughly pulled her back.

"It was Parissus," she blabbered. "And you were leaving. You can't leave . . .

I can't let you . . . I'm sorry."

Entreri's responding expression was, perhaps, the most profound look of disappointment and dismay Jarlaxle Baenre had ever seen. Entreri let out a long sigh and seemed to relax, and apparently bolstered by that, taking confidence that the moment of crisis had passed, Calihye dared to look up and say, "You will never hurt me." She even managed to put a weak, hopeful smile on her face.

She was trying to be cute, to be coy, to be playful, Jarlaxle recognized, but he saw, too, that to Entreri, she appeared as nothing but mocking.

He ran his hand down her cheek softly, then changed in a blink, his expression going hard, his hand grabbing at her chin. Her eyes went wide and she clutched and clawed at his unyielding wrist with both hands.

He drove her before him with two powerful strides and with frightening strength shoved her backward. She crashed through the shutters, she smashed through the glass of the window, and she shrieked only once as she tumbled over the pane to fall a dozen feet to the street below.

Entreri turned back to Jarlaxle.

"You should have killed her," the drow said, and in a voice dripping with sympathy and regret. "She is dangerous."

"Shut up."

Jarlaxle sighed.

"And if you slay her, I promise you that you will join her in death," Entreri added.

Jarlaxle sighed again. But of course, he could only blame himself for using the flute to manipulate the assassin, for prying open the heart of Artemis Entreri, which for so long had been shielded from the agony of love.

The cold began to overtake her. Blood flowed from a hundred cuts and when she tried to extract herself from the planking and broken glass, Calihye found that her leg would not support her.

She was dying, she knew. Miserable and alone in the biting cold, naked and bleeding before the world. She held no hope, and didn't want to live, anyway. She had failed, in all ways.

She had fallen in love with the man who had killed her dear Parissus, and that discordant reality had broken her. When faced with the thought of leaving her home, or of saying farewell to Entreri, she had found the options untenable.

So she had made her own course, reverting to her fierce desire for revenge, using her despair at the loss of her dearest love Parissus as armor against the heartbreak Entreri was about to inflict upon her by leaving her.

And she had failed.

So she was dying, and she was glad of it. She crawled through the glass in search of a suitable shard, agony burning, cold wind biting. She found a sizable chunk, elongated like a dagger's blade, and with it clutched in hand, she crawled around the side of the inn, into the alleyway where she could die, free from the intrusion of any curious eyes.

She barely made it in, and fell back into a sitting position against the wall. Her breathing came in rasps, and she coughed up some blood. She realized she didn't even have to put the shard to her throat to end it all; the fall had done the work.

But death from her wounds would be too slow, and it hurt too much.

Calihye lifted the point of the shard to her throat. She thought of Entreri, of their lovemaking, but she brushed it away. She pictured Parissus instead, and imagined her waiting in death, arms wide to embrace her dear Calihye again.

Calihye closed her eyes and stabbed.

Or tried to, but a stronger hand clasped her wrist and held it steady. Calihye opened her eyes, and they went all the wider when she realized that a dark elf held her wrist, and that other drow were about, all leering at her. In that instant of terror, the fog and the pain abandoned her.

"We are not finished with you quite yet," she heard from the back of the group, and the dark elves parted to reveal one of the drow she had just seen in the room above, the one Entreri had spoken of before and had named as Kimmuriel.

"Perhaps in time we will allow you to take your life," Kimmuriel said to her. "Perhaps we will even do it for you, though I doubt you will enjoy our technique."

A pair of dark elves forced her to her feet and a twist of her wrist made her drop the glass shard.

"But then, perhaps you will enjoy the Underdark even less," said Kimmuriel. "Fail in your duties, and we will be happy to determine which is the worst fate for Lady Calihye."

"Duties?" the stunned woman managed to whisper.

The drow dragged her away.

CHAPTER

DREAMS AND MEMORIES

20

He went looking for her," Jarlaxle said to Kimmuriel when the pair met up the next day in a shaded glen near the appointed rendezvous with the dragon sisters. Not far away, Entreri and Athrogate sat about a tumble of boulders in the middle of a rocky lea.

Kimmuriel had joined them, intending to prevent the conversation from veering toward Calihye. Jarlaxle, as if reading his mind, had led with a reference to the wretched human woman.

"It is typical of humans, is it not?" the psionicist answered. "To throw a lover through a glass window, then seek her out in remorse? Our way is much more straightforward and honest, I think. No drow matron would expel a male and let him live."

"With notable exception."

"Notable," Kimmuriel agreed. "Of course, in the instance to which you refer, Matron Baenre had little choice in the matter. Is it true that the Secondboy of House Baenre was the one commanded to rid the House of the cursed Jarlaxle, who lay on the altar without a mark despite the repeated stabbing of the mighty matron mother herself?"

"You know the tale," Jarlaxle replied.

"Yes, but I would like to hear it as often as you would deign to tell it. To see your mother's face twisted in exquisite frustration and horror when her blade would not bite into the infant! And then to see her expression of the sheerest terror, and that of Triel as well, when Secondboy Doquaio whisked you from the slab! He must have looked much like that bloody creature in Artemis's room when the infant Jarlaxle unwittingly released the captured energy into him."

Kimmuriel took hope at Jarlaxle's chuckle, an indication, perhaps, that he had deflected the conversation from Calihye.

"And of course, then Jarlaxle was no longer the third son, and no longer a fitting sacrifice," he rambled on.

"I haven't seen Kimmuriel bantering this much since you wagged your hands in trying to alleviate a cramp in your forearm," Jarlaxle said, and the psionicist's lips went tight.

"She was gone from the alley," Jarlaxle said. "She didn't crawl far, for the blood trail ended—and rather abruptly, and right near a place where the blood had pooled. She was sitting there, against the wall, of course, before she was taken away."

"Lady Calihye has made powerful enemies, and powerful friends," said Kimmuriel. "Perhaps it is a good thing that Artemis Entreri is leaving the realm, and quickly."

"And she has made friends of convenience," Jarlaxle remarked, staring his associate right in the eye. "Who will turn on her, no doubt, at the slightest hint of betrayal."

Kimmuriel didn't deny it.

"This place is worth the trouble of Bregan D'aerthe," Jarlaxle went on. "There is much to be found here, such as the bloodstone, a mineral we cannot easily procure in the Underdark. With Knellict serving our . . . *your* cause, you will find easy access to it and other valuables."

"You have explained it all, many times."

Jarlaxle clapped Kimmuriel on the shoulder, and the stiff psionicist just stared at him with awkward curiosity. Kimmuriel did intend to use Calihye and Knellict to create a network in the Bloodstone Lands, but in truth it was more for the preservation of Jarlaxle's reputation than for any monetary gains or increase of power the psionicist expected to make. Jarlaxle's reputation couldn't withstand another disaster like the one in Calimport, so close on the heels of that debacle, Kimmuriel believed, and the last thing he wanted was for Bregan D'aerthe to turn away from Jarlaxle. For Jarlaxle would one day return to Menzoberranzan and resume his mantle of leadership. Bregan D'aerthe needed that in order to keep Matron Mother Triel Baenre at proper distance and in proper humor, and more than that, Kimmuriel needed it. His pursuits of the purely intellectual were not served well by the responsibilities of maintaining Jarlaxle's band. He longed for the day when Jarlaxle returned and he could turn his attention more fully to the illithids and the mysteries of their expansive mental powers.

And turn his attention away from the concerns of the mercenary band, and away from protecting the increasingly renegade Jarlaxle.

"I know that you doubt," Jarlaxle said, again as if reading his mind, which the psionicist knew to be impossible. Kimmuriel was far too mentally shielded for any such intrusions. "And I am glad that you do, for else who would force me to question my every twist and turn?"

"Your own common sense?"

Jarlaxle laughed aloud. "My vision is correct," he insisted.

"Menzoberranzan demands our attention at all times."

Jarlaxle nodded. "But the day will come when the contacts we—the contacts *you* secure on the surface will prove invaluable to the matron mothers."

"What do you know?"

"I know that the world is in flux," said Jarlaxle. "Entreri and I were attacked by a Netherese shade, and he made it quite clear that he was not alone. If the shadows fall across the World Above, the matron mothers will not wish to remain oblivious.

"Furthermore, my friend, there is growing here on the surface a following of Eilistraee. Drizzt Do'Urden is hardly unique among surface drow, and he is finding more acceptance among the surface dwellers."

"Your former House—"

"I was never of their House," Jarlaxle corrected.

"House Baenre," said Kimmuriel, "will not go against Drizzt again, nor would they find any followers if they so decided. There are even priestesses postulating that Drizzt is secretly in the favor of Lolth."

"They said the same of me after the failed sacrifice."

"The evidence was strong."

"And I have never bended knee for the spider bitch. Nor has Drizzt Do'Urden. I am certain that if he learned that he was in Lady Lolth's favor, it would torment him more than a festering wound ever could."

"More the reason for the goddess to so favor him, then."

Jarlaxle merely shrugged at the inescapable logic. Such was the irony of following a deity dedicated to chaos.

"But I do not speak of Drizzt in any case," said Jarlaxle. "I find it unlikely that the Spider Queen will tolerate the worshipers of Eilistraee much longer, and when that day of reckoning befalls the dancing fools, their judgment may well be served by the Houses of Menzoberranzan. Bregan D'aerthe will prove invaluable at that time, of course."

"Even if it is centuries hence."

"Patience has sustained me," said Jarlaxle. "And our endeavors will be profitable in the meantime. In human parlance, that is known as a win-win."

"Humans often think they are winning until the moment they are thrown through the glass window."

Jarlaxle surrendered with another laugh and with the full understanding, Kimmuriel knew, that Bregan D'aerthe would indeed exploit the contacts made here in this rugged land of Damara and Vaasa.

Kimmuriel looked past Jarlaxle to the open field and nodded, and the other drow turned around.

"Your dragons approach," said Kimmuriel.

Jarlaxle turned back to him and extended his hand. "Then farewell."

Kimmuriel didn't shake the hand, and so Jarlaxle moved it to his belt pouch to show his lieutenant that he was carrying the item, as they had agreed. Kimmuriel nodded at that, and one hand came out from under his dark robes, bearing a small coffer that held three small vials.

Jarlaxle's eyes gleamed when he viewed them. "I have opened his heart, and now I will open his mind," he said.

"For reasons that no sane drow could ever fathom."

"Sane is boring."

Kimmuriel snorted derisively as Jarlaxle took the potions. "His mother, his childhood . . . these are the questions that will open Entreri's mind to you," the psionicist said, and as he retracted the empty coffer, he brought forth his other hand from under the folds of his robes, bearing Idalia's flute.

"The residual memories lingering within the flute showed you this?" asked Jarlaxle.

"You asked me to inspect it, and so I did. You asked me for the potions, and so they are yours."

Jarlaxle, smiling widely, took the flute.

"And now we are gone, Jarlaxle," said Kimmuriel. "I'll not heed your call again until our next arranged meeting."

"A long time hence."

"Rightly so—I've grown far too weary of this blinding surface world, and spent not enough energy heeding the needs of Bregan D'aerthe in Menzoberranzan. It is a city of chaos and constant change, and my former master taught me well that Bregan D'aerthe must change with it, or before it, even."

"Your former master was brilliant, I am told."

"So he often says."

Jarlaxle had rarely laughed as much in the presence of the dry-witted psionicist. "I am certain that I will find the band well tended when I return to Menzoberranzan," he said.

"Of course. And when will that be?"

Jarlaxle glanced back toward Entreri, who stood with Athrogate before Ilnezhara and Tazmikella. "A human's lifetime, perhaps."

"Or the remainder of this one's?"

"Or that. But recall that he was infused with the stuff of shadow. It could be a longer time than you believe." He looked back at Kimmuriel and offered a wink. "But I will indeed return."

"Don't bring the dwarf."

Yet another burst of laughter escaped Jarlaxle's lips, and Kimmuriel tightened his expression even more. Jarlaxle seemed almost giddy to him, and it was not a sight he enjoyed.

"Why, Kimmuriel, you lack imagination!" Jarlaxle declared dramatically. "Do you not see that Athrogate would be a fine gift for my sister, whichever one rules House Baenre, when I return?"

Kimmuriel didn't smile at all, and at that, Jarlaxle only laughed even louder.

<hr />

"Well, I ain't much for wizard teleportin'," Athrogate was grumbling when Jarlaxle joined the foursome at the boulder tumble in the small field. The dwarf blew a stray strand of black hair from his mouth and crossed his burly arms over his chest. For added effect, he stomped one foot, which set his morningstar heads bouncing at the ends of their respective chains, one over each shoulder as the weapons were crossed on his back. "Knew a halfling once joined a mage such. A skinny old wizard in need of a crutch. And his eyes weren't so good to the price o' their bones, for he shot a bit low and landed both in the stones! *Bwahaha!*"

Athrogate snapped off his knee-slapping laughter almost as soon as it began, re-crossed his arms and returned a scowl at Jarlaxle. "And I'm meanin' *in* the stones."

The drow looked to Entreri, who just stood there shaking his head and showing no interest in tipping the dwarf off to the reality of their impending journey. He turned to the dragon sisters, who seemed quite amused by it all.

"You think they have come to teleport us?" Jarlaxle asked. "You forget your flight across the tavern's common room."

"Ain't forgetting nothing," said the dwarf. "Wizard tricks . . . bah! They ain't to throw us across the damn sea. Though hell of a landing that might be!"

"Wizard?" the oblivious Entreri asked, for he had not witnessed the flying dwarf. "You think they mean to teleport us?"

"Well they ain't about to carry me, with skinny girl arms and skinny girl knees! *Bwahaha!*"

"Well maybe instead they'll tie you to a tree," rhymed Entreri, drawing curious, surprised stares from all the others. "Bend it to the ground and let it fly free. Launching you high to the clouds in the sky, and when you come falling we all hope you'll die."

Athrogate's lips moved as he digested the words by repeating them, and Entreri, his brow furrowed, for he was far from joking, wisely moved a hand to his sword hilt as if expecting the dwarf to launch himself forward.

But Athrogate exploded into laughter instead of into action. "*Bwahaha!* Hey, I'm stealin' that!"

"An appropriate price," Ilnezhara said. "Can we be on with this? I've a shop to attend in the morning."

"Of course, milady," Jarlaxle said with one of his characteristic, hat-sweeping bows. "But we must prepare our oblivious friend—"

"No, I don't think we shall," said Ilnezhara, and her voice changed abruptly in timbre and volume, cutting Jarlaxle short and sending Athrogate's jaw to his chest.

"I care not what he might say, and less that he runs away!" Ilnezhara roared, and the boulders shook from the strength of her voice.

Her jaws elongated, as if the sheer power of the words had pulled it forward, and a pair of copper-colored horns prodded through her golden hair and stretched upward. As she half-turned, a heavy tail thumped onto the ground and began to lengthen, as her torso stretched and twisted, bones popping into place.

"You thought we'd ride in a wagon," Entreri teased the mercifully speechless dwarf. "But instead we're flying a . . ." He paused and waved his hand to prompt the poet dwarf. "Yes, as I expected," Entreri remarked when no words came forth.

"Uh-uh," said Athrogate, his hands out in front of him and waving, and he began backing away.

Hardly noticed at the side, Jarlaxle produced a thin wand and pointed it at Entreri, then Athrogate, then himself, each time speaking the command word to enact its magic.

"Ah, but to soar to the clouds!" Jarlaxle said, and he moved around Ilnezhara. "May I mount you, good lady?" he teased, and Ilnezhara, her transformation continuing, her body elongating, roared in reply. Jarlaxle scrambled astride her scaly back just before two great leathery wings erupted from behind her shoulders, snapping out mightily to their full extension.

"Dragon," Athrogate muttered.

"You missed the cue, sorry," Entreri said to him, his voice mirthless though he enjoyed the spectacle of a befuddled Athrogate.

"Dragon," sputtered Athrogate. "It's a dragon. She's a wyrm . . . a dragon . . . a dragon."

"May I eat the dwarf?" Ilnezhara asked Jarlaxle as soon as her transformation was complete. She stood on four legs, a mighty copper dragon. "I will need sustenance for the journey."

Jarlaxle leaned forward and whispered into her ear, and her serpentine neck snapped her head out toward Athrogate, who blanched and nearly fainted. Ilnezhara hit him with a burst of her windy breath, a magical cone of "heavy" air. Suddenly Athrogate seemed to be moving much more slowly, and he turned as if running through deep mud.

But Ilnezhara had no such bonds on her, and she reared and leaped forward, a single snapping beat of her wings lifting her and her rider drow from the ground. They shot past Entreri, who fell away, and Tazmikella, who seemed to take pleasure in the sudden buffet of wind.

Athrogate dived aside—or was beginning to—when Ilnezhara passed over him, and her claw grabbed him hard and yanked him along. In a blink of the stunned and terrified dwarf's eye, he found himself fifty feet off the ground and climbing fast.

"I will miss you, Artemis Entreri," Tazmikella said when the two were alone on the field. "I grew fond of you, though I never came to trust you." She gave a little grin as her face started to twist and distort. "Perhaps there is something to this element of danger that my sister so enjoys."

Entreri wanted to remind her that she was a dragon, but it occurred to him that insulting such a creature might not be the smartest thing he ever did. As Tazmikella moved more fully into her transformation, he slipped around her side and onto her back, thinking to emulate Jarlaxle instead of Athrogate.

In a few moments, they were airborne, the wind whipping around them, the world spinning below in a dizzying blur. Entreri and Athrogate didn't know it, but Jarlaxle's use of the wand saved them from the killing bite of the winter wind. As the dragons climbed higher into the cold sky, the trio of lesser creatures would have frozen to death had it not been for the protective enchantment.

Artemis Entreri didn't notice any of that. His cape buffeted out behind him and the world below moved past at dizzying speed. Shortly into the flight, he could see the northern shore of the Moonsea.

Still the dragons climbed, so that any observers on the ground would think them nothing more than a bird. A short while later, to Entreri's surprise, they went out over the sea, and the sisters executed a right turn, veering west-southwest. They flew through the night and landed on a small island just before the break of dawn.

Entreri scrambled down from Tazmikella.

"Rest," the dragon instructed. "We will be up again at nightfall, to finish crossing the sea. We will set you down north of Cormyr, and there your road is your own."

Entreri noted the approach of Jarlaxle and Athrogate—mostly from the sputtering and grumbling of the obviously thoroughly shaken dwarf.

"Ought to hit 'em both," he mumbled. "Treatin' a dwarf like that. Just ain't polite."

Entreri could only hope that his threat was more than mere words. The spectacle of Tazmikella's giant maw closing over Athrogate was one the assassin surely would enjoy, but he let the pleasant image go and kept his attention on the dragon.

"I have coin," he said. "Some, at least." He gave a look to Jarlaxle. "I would ask that you take me farther along that course, to the southwest."

Jarlaxle came up beside him then, and offered him a curious glance. "Cormyr is a fine diversion," he said.

"I wish you well there, in that case," said Entreri, and Jarlaxle backed a step and blinked as if he had been slapped. "I've neither the time nor the desire."

"How far would you wish to go?" Tazmikella asked, keeping her dragon voice as quiet as she could so that it did not carry across the open water.

"As far as you will take me. My road is to Memnon, on the southern Sword Coast."

"That is a long way," remarked Ilnezhara.

Entreri looked to Jarlaxle. "Whatever my share is, give it to them."

"Share of what?" the drow replied. "We lost."

Entreri narrowed his eyes.

"I can arrange some payment," Jarlaxle said to the dragons. "How much will you require? Or perhaps there are other things for which you would barter. We can discuss it later."

The dragons exchanged wary looks, which struck Entreri as very strange, since they were, after all, dragons.

Except at that moment, Ilnezhara reverted to her human form, and bade her sister to do likewise. "In case the island has visitors," the blond-haired woman explained, though Tazmikella's look as she came out of her natural form showed that she understood Ilnezhara's ulterior motives all too well, particularly when Ilnezhara shot Jarlaxle a rather lewd wink.

"That, too, of course," said Jarlaxle. "Though I feel as if I should pay you even more."

"You should," said Ilnezhara.

Entreri's sigh showed that he had heard about enough of that nonsense. "Will you fly me?"

"Not all the way to Memnon, no," Tazmikella replied. "I've made enemies in the southern deserts that I do not wish to encounter. But we will see how far the winds will carry us."

"And what of you?" Ilnezhara asked Jarlaxle.

"And meself?" Athrogate asked hopefully.

Jarlaxle and the dragon looked at the dwarf.

"Well, ye taked me from the place I've known as home for many a year," Athrogate protested. "Ye can't be expecting me to just swim to Cormyr, now can ye?"

"We will stay together, we three," Jarlaxle answered both the dragon and the dwarf. "I would be grateful if you would fly me in the wake of your sister and Artemis."

If he was trying to gauge the reaction of the surprising Entreri as he declared his intentions, the drow was sorely disappointed, for Entreri, who simply did not care, had already started away.

Ilnezhara grabbed Jarlaxle by the hand and pulled him along. "Come and show me your gratitude," she bade him.

Jarlaxle followed without complaint, but he kept looking back at Entreri, who sat with his back against a rock, staring out at the dark and empty waters to the west.

"I remain surprised that you would provide such information," Ilnezhara said to Jarlaxle around noon the next day, when she awoke beside him. "Why would you trust me with such information after I sided with King Gareth against you? Or is it that you wish harm to befall this Kimmuriel creature and your former associates?"

"You will not see Kimmuriel, nor any of my Underdark brethren," a sleepy Jarlaxle replied. He yawned and stretched, and considered his surroundings. Waves lapped rhythmically at the rocky shores of the small island, drowned out intermittently by Athrogate's snoring. "They will work from the shadows below."

"Then why tell me?"

"They pose no threat to King Gareth," said Jarlaxle. "And now I know your loyalty there. Indeed, Kimmuriel will force Knellict to behave himself, so consider the efforts of Bregan D'aerthe to be a welcomed leash on the Citadel of Assassins. And an opportunity for you and your sister. Items we consider commonplace and cheap in Menzoberranzan will no doubt interest you greatly for your collections, and will bring a fine price on the surface. Similarly, you can barter goods that hold little value here but will light the red eyes of matron mothers in the city of drow."

"Bregan D'aerthe is a merchant operation, then?"

"First, foremost, and whenever the choice is before us."

Ilnezhara slowly nodded, though her expression remained doubtful. "We will watch them carefully."

"You will never see them," said Jarlaxle, and he pulled himself to his feet and gathered his clothing. "Kimmuriel is not skilled in the ways of polite society. Ever has that been my role, and of course your beloved King Gareth is too small a man to understand the worth of my company. Now, if you will excuse me, good lady. The day grows long already and I must go and speak with my associate." He finished with a bow, and pulled on his shirt.

"He surprised you with his request," Ilnezhara said as Jarlaxle started away. The drow paused and glanced back.

"Or are you simply not used to him leading?" Ilnezhara teased.

Jarlaxle grinned, shrugged, and walked off. He spotted Entreri, dozing against the same rock, shaded from the rising sun and with the western waters before him.

The drow looked all around, then quickly quaffed one of the potions Kimmuriel had given him. He waited a moment for the magic to settle in, then focused his attention on Entreri, considering the questions he might ask to spur the man's thoughts.

Jarlaxle blinked in surprise, for Entreri's thoughts began to crystallize in his intruding mind. The potions facilitated mind-reading, and as images of a great seaport began to flit through his thoughts, Jarlaxle realized that Entreri was already there, in Memnon, the city of his birth.

So clear were those images that Jarlaxle could almost smell the salty air, and hear the seabirds. Entreri's dream—was it a dream or a memory, the drow wondered—showed him a plain-looking woman, one who might have once been somewhat attractive, though the soil and dust, and hard living had taken a great toll on her. Her few remaining teeth were crooked and yellow, and her eyes, perhaps once shining black orbs, showed the listlessness of despair, the empty and weary eyes of a person who had suffered prolonged poverty. The world had broken that once-pretty woman.

Jarlaxle felt a tenderness emanating from Entreri as the man's dream lingered on her.

Then a cart, a priest, a young boy's screams . . .

Jarlaxle fell back a step as a wave of rage rolled out from Entreri to nearly overwhelm him. Such anger! Passionate, feral outrage!

He saw the woman again, receding into the dust, and sensed that he was on a cart rolling away from her. The tenderness was gone, replaced by a sense of betrayal that filled Jarlaxle with trepidation.

The drow came out of it, shaken, a short while later. He stood staring at Entreri, and he knew that what he had seen when he had insinuated himself into the assassin's dreams were indeed memories.

"Your mother," the drow whispered under his breath as he considered the image of the black-haired, black-eyed woman.

The drow snorted at the irony. Perhaps the kinship he felt toward Artemis Entreri was more rooted in common experiences than he had consciously known.

CHAPTER

NEVER THE SIMPLE COURSE

21

Entreri stood staring at the west, at a cluster of palm trees rising from the rolling dunes of sand. He nodded as he realized where they were, for he was quite familiar with the mountains south of their position. Not much of this region north of the divide was rolling white sand, though south of those mountains, closer to Calimport, the desert extended for miles and miles. The land was almost equally barren, but was more a matter of mesas and long-dead river valleys, but one stretch was the exception. They were along the trade route, and since the mountains stretched out, impassable, southeast of their position, Entreri realized that they were no more than a few days from Memnon. He looked back at the dragon sisters, who were preparing to depart, and offered Tazmikella, when she caught his glance, as close to an expression of gratitude as he'd ever offered anyone.

Off to the side of Entreri, Athrogate sat, spitting curses and pulling off his boots. "Rotten stuff," he said, pouring a generous amount of sand from one shoe. When they came in, Ilnezhara had skimmed low, and the rut the claw-riding Athrogate had cut in the coarse sand could be traced back many yards.

While the dwarf's discomfort pleased Entreri, he shifted his gaze to his other companion. Jarlaxle stood near the dragons with his back to Entreri, his hat far back on his head, completely obscuring the assassin's view of him. Something in the expressions of the two gigantic creatures clued him in that Jarlaxle had somehow caught them off guard. With a cursory glance at the complaining Athrogate, Entreri moved beside his long-time companion.

And saw a handsome elf, with golden skin and hair the color of the morning sun.

Entreri fell back a step.

"Although the hair suits you well, I prefer the drow image," Ilnezhara said. "Exotic, mysterious, enticing . . ."

"Dangerous," said her sister. "That is always the lure for you, dear sister, which is why we are farther into Dojomentikus's domain than I had desired. Come now, it is time for us to be gone."

"Dojo would not strike out at the both of us, sister," said Ilnezhara. She turned back to Entreri and Jarlaxle. "Such a petty beast, like most males. Imagine that just a few trinkets could invoke such wrath."

"A few trinkets and your refusal to breed with him."

"He bored me."

"Perhaps he should have donned a drow disguise," Tazmikella said, and Entreri realized that that should have been his line—except that he was hardly listening to the conversation, for he remained transfixed on Jarlaxle.

"You should close your mouth," Ilnezhara said, and it took Entreri a moment to understand that she had directed the comment at him. "The sand will blow in. It is most uncomfortable."

Entreri shot her a quick look, but turned back to his companion.

"Kimmuriel is often difficult in his dealings," Jarlaxle explained. "He conceded quite a bit, but demanded of me that I wear this mantle beyond the Bloodstone Lands, for all the rest of my days on the surface."

"Agatha's mask," Entreri realized, for he had once worn the magical item, many years before. With it, he had assumed the mien of Regis, the troublesome halfling, and had used the disguise to infiltrate Mithral Hall before the drow invasion. He shook that memory from his mind, for from that failed invasion had come his servitude in the city of drow, a place he did not like to think about.

"The same," Jarlaxle confirmed.

"I had thought it lost, or destroyed."

"Little gets lost that cannot be found, and no magic is ever truly destroyed for those who know how to put it back together." He smiled as he spoke, reached behind him, and brought forth a familiar gauntlet, the complimentary piece to Entreri's mighty sword.

"Kimmuriel managed to piece it back together; he is no fonder of magic-users than are you, my friend." He tossed the gauntlet to Entreri, who studied it for a moment, noting the red lines shot through the black material. He slipped it on his hand and clutched the hilt of Charon's Claw. The gauntlet minimized the magical connection. Kimmuriel, as always, had done well.

"Well now, I'd say that's better, but it'd be a lie," Athrogate said, walking up to join the group and taking a long look at the transformed Jarlaxle. "Any elf's but a girl making ready to cry. *Bwahaha!*" The dwarf waggled his bare toes in the hot sand as he laughed.

"And if you keep rhyming, you're going to die," Entreri said, and Athrogate laughed all the louder.

"No," Entreri said, his voice deadly even. Athrogate stopped and stared at the man and his undeniably grim tone. "There is no joke in my words," Entreri promised. "And the rhyme was coincidental."

Athrogate winced, but at the burn on the soles of his feet, not at the threat, and he hopped about. "Well, tell that one to quit inspiring me, then," he blustered, waving his arms at Jarlaxle. "Ye can't be expectin' me to behave when he's springin' such surprises on me!" He walked around Jarlaxle, inspecting him more closely, and even reached up with his stubby fingers and pinched the drow's cheek, then fiddled with the golden hair. "Bah, but that's a good one," he decided. "Good for getting into places ye don't belong. Ye got more o' that magic? Might be that if we find some orcs, ye can make me look like 'em so I can walk in before bashing?"

"That wouldn't take magic," said Entreri. "Just trim your beard."

Athrogate shot him a dangerous look. "Now ye're crossing a line, boy."

"I should have eaten him," said Ilnezhara.

"No, and all is quite well," said Jarlaxle. "Well met and well left, good ladies. I . . . *we* are most grateful for your assistance, and I speak truly when I say that I will miss your company. In all of my travels across the wide world, never before have I encountered such beauty and grace, such power and intelligence." He bowed low, his outrageous hat sweeping the desert sands.

"So you believe the tales that proclaim that dragons are weak for flattery?" said Ilnezhara, but her grin showed that she really was quite pleased with the drow's proclamation.

"I speak truly," Jarlaxle insisted. "In all things. You will find the Bloodstone Lands an interesting and profitable place upon your return, I believe."

"And we will see you again," said Tazmikella. "And I warn you, your disguises do not fool dragon eyes."

"But I cannot return, I fear," the drow replied.

"Dragons and drow live longer than humans, longer even than the memories of humans," said Ilnezhara. "Until we meet again, Jarlaxle."

"Durned wyrms!" Athrogate complained.

By the time the three got the sand out of their eyes and managed to look back, the sisters were no more than small spots in the distant east.

"Well, I won't be missing them two, but I'm not for walking on this ground," Athrogate muttered. He plopped back down on his butt and began pulling on his boots. "Too soft and unsure for me liking."

"I don't walk," Jarlaxle assured him. The drow-turned-elf reached into his belt pouch and pulled out a curious red figurine. He offered a wink at Entreri and tossed it to Athrogate.

The dwarf caught it and sat staring at the item: a small red boar. "Sculptor forget to put the skin on the damned thing?"

"It's an infernal boar," Jarlaxle explained. "A creature of the lower planes, fierce and untiring—a suitable mount for Athrogate."

"Suitable?" the dwarf asked, obviously perplexed. "Why, if I sat on it, I'd lose it up me bum! *Bwahaha!*"

"The figurine is a conduit," Jarlaxle explained, and he pulled out his own obsidian statuette and dropped it on the ground beside him. He called to the hellish nightmare, and in moments, the fiery steed pawed the soft ground beside him.

Athrogate gave him a crooked smile, then likewise dropped the red boar to the ground. "What do I call it?" he eagerly asked.

"Snort," Jarlaxle said.

Athrogate snorted.

"No, that is its name. Call to 'Snort,' and 'Snort' will come to your call, if you see what I mean."

Watching with little amusement and no surprise, Entreri brought his own mount, Blackfire, to his side. At the same time, Athrogate did as instructed, and sure enough, a large red-skinned boar appeared beside the dwarf. Steam rose from its back, and when it snorted, as it often did, little bursts of red flame erupted from its nostrils.

"Snort," Athrogate said approvingly. He moved beside the creature, which, like the nightmares, appeared with full saddle, but he hesitated before lifting his leg over it. "Seems a bit hot," he explained to his companions.

Entreri just shook his head and turned his nightmare around, starting off toward a distant oasis at a gallop.

Jarlaxle and Athrogate came soon after, and the smaller mount had no trouble pacing the nightmares, its little legs stepping furiously.

Entreri stayed in front of the others all the way to the last high dune overlooking the oasis. He stopped his mount and waited there, not out of any desire for companionship, but rather, because the sight below gave him cautious pause. He knew the ways of the desert, knew the various peoples who roamed the shifting sands. That particular stop along the trade route was classified as "*everni,*" which translated, literally, as lawless. An oasis such as that was under no formal control, with no governing militia in place, and by edict of the pashas of both Memnon and Calimport to the south, "unavailable to claim." Anyone who tried to set up a residence or fortress in such an oasis would find himself at war with both powerful city-states.

The obvious benefit to such an arrangement was that it prevented any tolls from being forced on the frequent merchant caravans traveling between the cities. The downside, of course, was that caravans often had to defend themselves from competing interests and bandits.

The wreckage of a trio of wagons beside the small pond in the shadow of the palms showed that one recent caravan had not done so successfully.

"Perhaps we should have bid the dragons stay beside us just a bit longer," Jarlaxle remarked when he and Athrogate came up on the bluff and looked down at the many white-robed forms milling about the place.

"Desert nomads," Entreri explained. "They hold no allegiance to elves or to dwarves, or even to humans who are not of their tribe."

"They sacked them wagons?" Athrogate asked.

"Or found them destroyed," said Jarlaxle.

"They did it," Entreri insisted. "That caravan was destroyed within the tenday, or else the wood would have already been scavenged. The night gets cold here, as you will learn soon enough, and wood is greatly treasured." He nodded to the south of the small oasis pond, where buzzards hopped about. "The carrion birds haven't even finished their feast. This caravan was sacked within the last couple of days, and there are your highwaymen, enjoying their respite."

"How long will they remain?" Jarlaxle asked.

"As long as they choose. There is no pattern to the nomads' wandering. They roam, they fight, they steal, and they eat."

"Sounds like a good life to me," Athrogate remarked. "Though I'd be looking for a bit o' the drink to top it all off!"

Entreri scowled at him.

"At least he's not rhyming anymore," Jarlaxle whispered. "Though his words tear no less."

"So if we go down there, we're looking at a fight?" Athrogate asked.

"Perhaps. Perhaps not," said Entreri. "Desert nomads fight for gain and gain alone. If they saw us as a threat, or as worthy victims, they would fight. Else, they would ask of us stories, and perhaps even share their spoils. They are an unpredictable lot."

"That makes them dangerous," said Athrogate.

"That makes them intriguing," Jarlaxle corrected. He slid down from his hell horse and dismissed it, pocketing the figurine.

"Ah well, if it's a fight, all the better," Athrogate said and began to dismount.

Jarlaxle stopped him, though. "Stay here and stay astride," the drow instructed.

"Yerself's going down there?"

"Us?" Entreri asked.

Jarlaxle considered the oasis and began a quick count. "There can't be more than twenty of the creatures. And I find that I am thirsty."

Entreri knew well that Jarlaxle could summon some drink if that were the case, or could create an entire extra-dimensional chamber full of food and fine wine if he so desired. "I did not come here to engage in random fights in the desert," he said, his expression sour.

"But you came here for information, or at least, you will need information to find that which you seek. Who better to tell us of the road to Memnon, or the current disposition within the city? Let us learn what we might."

Entreri stared at his troublesome companion for a long while, but he did indeed draw his foot over his horse and drop to the sand. He dismissed the nightmare and placed the figurine in his belt pouch, within easy reach.

"If we need you, charge in hard and fast," Jarlaxle said to Athrogate.

"Don't know any other way," the dwarf replied.

"Which is why I value your companionship," the drow said. "And you will find, I do believe, that your mount is possessed of the same fighting spirit—and a few tricks of its own."

Entreri looked to the dwarf as he sat astride that strange-looking, fierce war boar. He glanced back at the oasis and the white headgear of the nomads. He could well imagine where events were leading, but he found himself walking beside Jarlaxle down the western face of the high dune nonetheless.

"The nomads have been known to fill uninvited guests with arrows, then seek their answers in the items on the corpses," Entreri said as they neared the oasis—and already several sets of eyes turned their way.

Jarlaxle whispered something that the assassin could not make out, and Entreri felt a surge of warmth within him, rolling from his core to tickle all of his being, arms, legs, and head.

"If they let fly with their bows, they'll find only more questions," Jarlaxle replied.

"Questions in the arrows that will be lying at our feet?" Entreri rightly surmised.

"It will take a mighty bolt to get through that enchantment, I assure you."

Just before the duo stepped onto the sudden transformation of sand to grass, a pair of men rushed over to block their way. Both held wide-bladed weapons—khopesh blades, they were called—and with an ease that showed them to be quite skilled with them.

"You tink to joost walk trooh our camp?" one asked in the common language of the land, one that neither Entreri or Jarlaxle had heard in many months, and spoken with so severe an accent that it took both of them a moment to decipher the words.

"Show us the boundary, and we will walk around," said Entreri.

"De boundary? Why de boundary is de oasis, silly man."

"Ah, but if that is the case, then how are we to fill our skins from the pond?" Jarlaxle asked.

"Dat ees a problem," the nomad agreed. "But for you and not for me." Beside him, the other put his second hand to the long hilt of the great khopesh sword.

"We are not here to fight," said Entreri. "Nor do we care about your dealings with the caravan."

"Caravan?" the man echoed. "Dese wagons? But we found dem here. Poor men. Dey should take more care. Bandits, you know."

"Indeed," said Entreri. "And their ill luck is not my concern. We have come for some water, that we might be on our way. Nothing more"—he eyed the second nomad, who seemed quite eager to put his great sword into action—"and nothing less. By edict of the pashas of both Memnon and Calimport, these oases are open and free."

A dangerous grin creased the face of the first man.

"But we will pay anyway," said Entreri, similarly grinning. "We will take the water we need and in exchange we will entertain you with tales of our exploits beside Pasha Basadoni in Calimport."

The nomad's grin disappeared in the blink of an eye. "Basadoni?"

"Ah, Artemis, they know the name!" said Jarlaxle.

Both bandits blanched at the mention of Entreri's name, and the second one actually fell back a step, his hands loosening on the hilt of the khopesh.

"Well . . . yes," the first stammered. "We would not be friends of de desert if we did not accept barter, of course."

Entreri snorted and walked right past him, brushing him with his shoulder and pushing him aside. Jarlaxle kept close beside him the thirty feet to the pond's edge.

"Your reputation precedes you," the drow mentioned quietly.

Entreri snorted again as if he did not care, and bent low to put his waterskin in the cool waters. By the time he stood straight again, several other desert nomads approached, including an enormously fat man dressed in richer robes of white and red. Instead of the simple cloth hoods the others wore, he wore a white and red turban, stitched with golden thread, and he carried a jeweled scepter wrought of solid gold. His gold-colored shoes were no less ornate, with their toes stretching forward and rolling up into an almost complete circle.

He moved to stand a few feet from the pair, while his bodyguards fanned out in a semicircle about them.

"There is a saying in the desert that bold is once removed from foolish," he said in a dialect far more cultured and reminiscent of Calimport than the open sands.

"Your sentries appeared to have dropped their protestations," Jarlaxle replied. "We had thought a deal struck. Water for stories."

"I have no need of your stories."

"Ah, but they are grand, and the water will not be missed."

"I know a story of a man named Artemis Entreri," the boss said. "A man who served with Pasha Basadoni."

"He is dead," said Entreri.

The boss eyed him curiously. "Did he not name you as . . . ?"

"Artemis," Entreri confirmed. "Just Artemis."

"Of Pasha Basadoni's guild?"

"No," Entreri said, at the same time Jarlaxle replied, "Yes." The pair turned and looked at each other.

"I claim no allegiance to any guild," Entreri said to the boss.

"And yet you dare to walk into my oasis—"

"It is not yours."

"Your diplomacy skills are amazing," Jarlaxle muttered to Entreri.

The fat man held his scepter out before him horizontally. "Bold," he said and he tipped one end up slightly. "Foolish," he added, and he more than reversed the angle, as if weighing his words with a scale.

"My friend is weary from many days on the road, and in the hot sun," said Jarlaxle. "We are traveling adventurers."

"Blades for hire?"

Jarlaxle smiled.

"So you would offer your services in exchange for my water?"

"That would be quite a bargain for . . . ?"

"I am Sultan Alhabara."

"Quite a bargain for Sultan Alhabara, then," said Jarlaxle. "I assure you that our services are quite formidable."

"Indeed," said the fat man, and he gave a slight chuckle, which brought a response of laughter from the six men fanned out about him. "And what fee would be deemed appropriate for the services of Artemis and . . . ?"

"I am Drizzt Do'Urden," said the drow-turned-elf.

"By the balls of a castrated orc," muttered Entreri and he heaved a great sigh.

"What?" Jarlaxle asked, feigning innocence as he turned to him.

"We could not have just ridden by, could we?" Entreri replied. "Very well, then."

"Easy, Artemis," Jarlaxle bade him.

"Our fee is more than fat Alhabara can afford," Entreri said to the man. "More than stupid Alhabara can imagine. The water is free, in any case, by edict of Memnon and of Calimport. Can the criminal Alhabara understand that?"

Alhabara flashed a fierce scowl and the men around him sputtered with outrage, but Entreri didn't relent.

"And so I take what is free, without asking the permission of a common thief," he said and he swept his gaze out at the others as he finished, "And the first of you to lift blade against me will be the first to die this day."

The man in the middle of the trio to Entreri's left did draw on him, tearing a khopesh from his belt and waving it menacingly in Entreri's direction. The man even came forward a step, or started to, but a look from Entreri held him in place.

Alhabara, meanwhile, fell back several steps and lifted his scepter defensively before him.

"Rulership," Jarlaxle whispered to Entreri, correctly identifying the magical rod the sultan held, for it was one he had seen before, many times, among chieftains and tribal leaders. If it was akin to any of the similar rods Jarlaxle had known, such an item could enable its wielder to impose his will on his would-be subjects—those of weak mind, at least.

A moment later, both the drow and the assassin felt a wave of compulsion wash over them, a telepathic call from Sultan Alhabara to fall to their knees.

The pair looked to each other, then back at the man. "Hardly," Entreri said.

To either side of the companions, weapons came forth. Jarlaxle responded by plucking the feather from his cap and tossing it to the ground him. The item transformed into a gigantic, twelve-foot-tall creature known as a diatryma, a great flightless bird with short wings tucked in close to its sides, and a thick, strong neck and powerful triangular beak.

The six closest men screamed and fell back. Alhabara scrambled away and cried out, "Kill them!"

The man nearest the bird on the right tried to rush past it to get at the man and the elf, but the diatryma's powerful neck snapped as he passed, driving the beak into his shoulder with such force that it snapped bone and dislocated his shoulder so badly that it left his arm swinging numbly several inches down from its previous position, and far to the back. The man yelped and tumbled to the grass, howling pitifully.

Charon's Claw and his jeweled dagger in hand, Entreri leaped at the trio on the left. Back-to-back with him, Jarlaxle snapped his wrist, bringing a magical dagger into his hand from his enchanted bracer. A second snap elongated that dagger into a slender sword, which the drow flipped to his left hand and used to parry the nearest khopesh in the same movement.

His right hand snapped again and the bracer answered. While working his sword brilliantly and fluidly to keep that troublesome khopesh at bay, he retracted and flung the dagger at the last in line. Hardly slowing, he wrist-snapped, retracted, and threw again, and again.

The man was good with his blade and quite agile. After five throws, he only had one dagger-wound in one thigh, and that had been no more than a glancing blow. His friend tried to press the attack on Jarlaxle, but the agile drow easily held him at bay, even working his sword around the khopesh to stick him lightly in the ribs.

And all the while, Jarlaxle kept up the flow of daggers, spinning end over end and coming at the man high, low, and center with no discernable, thus no defensible pattern. The man couldn't anticipate, he could only react, and in that state, another blade got through, grazing the side of his face, then a third—a solid strike into the shoulder of his sword arm.

Worse for him, and for his friend, Jarlaxle's pet bird intervened, trampling the man as he pressed in on Jarlaxle. The man managed to bang his khopesh off the giant creature's leg, but the bird stomped him, then jabbed down with three hard pecks.

Jarlaxle sent it off after Sultan Alhabara, as he turned his attention to the remaining man. His next dagger came forth and he did not throw it, but snapped his hand to elongate it into a second, sister blade.

He stalked at his wounded opponent.

A trio of arrows soared in from the side, shot from a tree across the oasis. Jarlaxle saw them too late to avoid them.

Entreri turned left, then went that direction and forward, moving to the flank of the trio so that they all couldn't get at him at once. He led with an underhanded sweep of his dagger, one that, because of his bold stride forward, caught the swinging sword up near the hilt and allowed him the leverage to turn it out with just that small blade. Without room to maneuver his own sword, he came across with a right-hand punch instead, cracking Charon's Claw's pommel into the man's cheek.

He followed through with the punch past the man's broken face, extended his left arm, taking both the khopesh and the man's arm out wide with him, and rolled his sword arm over that extension then down and under.

Feeling pressure from a second attacker coming in behind him, Entreri rolled right over the arm, a complete flip that left him on his feet, and he came up strong, lifting his sword arm high, gashing the bandit's arm in the process. A twist had the man rolling over Entreri's hip, flailing helplessly.

"You are dead," Entreri promised, for the man had no defense at all. "Except . . ."

Entreri reversed his grip as he dropped his sword arm, and he stabbed out behind him as he did a sudden reverse pivot.

The blade drove into the gut of a second bandit, the one who had been in the middle of the trio, the one who had drawn first.

"I promised him that he would die first," Entreri explained. He kicked the prone man—who had dropped his khopesh to hold his badly torn arm—in the face and leaped past him, dagger and sword working in complimentary circles to foil the attack of the third man.

It was all going so smoothly and easily, he thought, but then he noted that dozens of others were closing in, hooting and raising swords and bows. A quick glance back showed him arrows diving for Jarlaxle. Beyond the drow, he saw his other companion, one better forgotten, roaring down the side of the dune on his war pig, holding tight with his powerful legs, his arms out wide and swinging morningstars left and right.

"Wahoo!" Athrogate yelled, the clear and steady tone of his shout defying the jolting, stiff-legged romp down the side of the dune. Despite those stiff legs and their shortness, Athrogate learned that his magical boar could cover tremendous ground.

The dwarf clamped his legs tight and sent his morningstars swinging wide left and right. He crossed from sand to grass, and the nearest bandits moved to intercept, a couple leveling spears.

Athrogate just howled louder and kept straight his course, thinking to pick off the prodding spears with his weapons. As he bore in, however, he found that his mount was more than a beast of burden. The boar had been summoned from the fiery pits of the Nine Hells, where battle was constant. Both its temperament and its armament were well suited to that harsh environment. It broke its stride only briefly, so it could snort and stomp a hoof, and as it did, a burst of orange flames rushed out from its body, a complete ring of wispy fire rolling away as it dissipated.

"Bwahaha!" Athrogate howled in gleeful surprise, and as the boar drove on, the dwarf clamped his legs tighter around it and adjusted the angle of his spinning weapons.

The bandits fell back and curled, shocked by the fiery burst. A bit of residual flame burned on one's robes, while the other had wisps of smoke rising from his singed hair. And both showed bright red skin where the flames had touched them.

Neither was really harmed by the burst, but as Athrogate rushed between them, the weight of his already heavy blows was only enhanced by the momentum of the boar. One man took a hit in the chest and went into a nearly complete backward somersault, except that he landed on his face instead of his feet. The other somehow maintained his footing after the strike.

But the morningstar had taken him across the side of his head, and though he was standing, he was far, far from consciousness. Athrogate was many strides away before he crumbled to the ground.

"Wahoo!" the dwarf roared wildly, thoroughly enjoying it all.

The arrows hit Jarlaxle's magical barrier barely an inch from the drow. They just stopped, in mid-air, and fell to the ground. The enchantment wasn't going to last, though, the drow knew, and so he looked out at the tree and the archers and used his innate magic to summon a globe of darkness over them.

"I'm blinded!" he heard one man cry, and he smiled, for he had indeed heard that false claim before.

The man before him was a stubborn one, he found, who came on yet again. With a sigh, Jarlaxle met his slashing khopesh, executing a downward diagonal, with a double-sword block. A turn to face the three locked blades gave him all the leverage he needed, and he easily drove the sword down.

He retracted suddenly, and the man nearly overbalanced. The drow began a "rattling parry," where both his swords rolled out a tapping drum roll on the blade. As his opponent finally began to compensate against the almost continual push, Jarlaxle side-stepped and with a sudden flourish rushed his sword downward, reversing the tip to point at the ground and taking the khopesh down with it.

The bandit pushed back, and found his blade climbing freely, but only because Jarlaxle had disengaged. The drow rolled his arms out wide, right blade closest to his opponent and angled out and down, left blade angled out and up. He tilted his body accordingly to provide maximum balance to the pose.

But it was a pose he held only briefly, for he drove his blades back in with sudden fury, the right blade coming up and under the khopesh down near the hilt, the left slamming down near the thicker end of the blade.

The bandit couldn't negotiate the alteration of pressure, and the drow's swipes tore the blade from his hands completely and sent it into a spin. Jarlaxle held that spin, the khopesh rotating around its hilt and the drow's right-hand sword.

The bandit stared at it as if mesmerized.

"Here," the gracious Jarlaxle offered, and he released the sword from its twirl, sending it up into the air back toward the bandit. The man looked up, his hands went up, and just before the khopesh landed in his grasp, the sole of the drow's boot landed against his face.

He hit the ground before the khopesh bounced atop him.

Jarlaxle glanced at Entreri. "Summon your . . ." he started to cry, but before he had even finished, Entreri's nightmare arrived on the scene, snorting fire and pawing the ground.

The poor remaining bandit on that side had already been stripped of his weapons, and the sight of the hellish horse stripped him of his sensibilities as well, apparently, for he blubbered something undecipherable and half-ran, half-crawled away, crying and screaming all the way.

Entreri leaped astride the powerful nightmare, and kicked the steed into a gallop that drove back the nearest group of approaching bandits. A pair of spears and an arrow came at him, but Jarlaxle's magical shield held them back.

Then Jarlaxle was up on his own black steed behind Entreri, who kicked his nightmare into a run. The two were swept up in Athrogate's wake, then thundered past the dwarf and his war pig. A battery of archers rose from behind one wagon, but almost as they stood, they, too, began screaming about blindness, as Jarlaxle's magical darkness engulfed them.

Behind the riding trio, Jarlaxle's diatryma continued its rampage, and the bandits had to settle for that fight.

Out the far side of the oasis, running free across desert sands once more, the three covered nearly a mile before Jarlaxle pulled up and bid his friend do likewise.

"Bwahaha!" Athrogate roared. "I can't ever be thankin' ye enough for me new pet! *Bwahaha!* Snort! *Bwahaha!"*

Jarlaxle offered him a smile, but turned on Entreri. "That went well," the drow said dryly. "All of my lessons in diplomacy were wasted on you, it seems."

Entreri started to respond, but he noticed then that a new feather was already growing inside the band on Jarlaxle's magnificent hat. He just shook his head and spurred his steed forward.

"We should be going back," said Athrogate. "More to hit!"

Jarlaxle never turned from the departing Entreri, and without a response, he kicked his nightmare into a run behind his departing companion.

"Bah," Athrogate snorted in disappointment.

He gave a wistful glance back toward the oasis, and reluctantly followed.

CHAPTER

22

W ell, now we're knowing why the last fool died," Athrogate said when he and his two companions entered the house that had been offered to them in the southwestern quarter of Memnon.

They had come into the city earlier that morning, and on Entreri's insistence—at least for himself—had eschewed the better sections of the port, where all the taverns were located, and had gone straight to a ramshackle district where the houses were no more than flimsy walls and floors of stone and dirt—and that was for the people fortunate enough to even have a shelter at all. Many of their neighbors, the poorest citizens by far in the city, slept on the side of the sandy avenues, often without even lean-tos to protect them from the occasional rains. A flash of gold from Jarlaxle had spared the trio that fate, at least, and the man, one of the clerks from the Protector's House, the temple of Selûne, had told them of their good fortune, for the owner of the house had recently departed the mortal world, leaving it open for the taking.

Jarlaxle groaned when he entered behind the dwarf, and knew he had greatly over-bribed the clerk. The place was no more than four walls, a roof that showed as much sky as reed, a floor of dirt, and a single table of piled stones so covered by crawling bugs—evil-looking reddish-brown critters with long pincers and an upward-curling tail—that it seemed obvious to the drow that the creatures had called the place home for a long, long time.

Athrogate walked over to the table and snorted, seeming amused. "Back home, we had a name for this," he said, and he extended one fat thumb and squished a crawler flat with a crunching sound. "Buffet."

"Do not dare eat that," said Jarlaxle, and Athrogate gave one of his characteristic *"bwahahas"* in reply.

Entreri walked in last. He glanced around and gave it all hardly a thought.

"Seemin' a bit too familiar to ye, by me own thinkin'," Athrogate teased.

Entreri looked at him out of the corner of his eye, but just shook his head and turned away. "They have midday services in the square overlooking the docks," he said to Jarlaxle. "I will be there, south side of the Protector's House." He turned and started back out the ill-fitting door.

"You are leaving us?" the drow asked.

"I never invited you here to begin with," Entreri reminded him as he walked away.

"*Bwahaha!*" roared Athrogate.

"Enough, good dwarf," Jarlaxle said, though he never took his eyes off the door. "This is difficult for our friend."

"Place didn't seem to bother him all that much," said Athrogate.

Jarlaxle turned to face him. "This?" he asked. "I suspect that Artemis Entreri is well acquainted with similar accommodations. But returning to this city, the place of his birth and early life, brings with it some painful memories, I would expect, which is why he needed to come here."

To Jarlaxle's surprise, Athrogate winced at that, and nodded but didn't otherwise reply, a very uncharacteristic response that revealed quite a bit to the perceptive, worldly drow.

"So are ye thinking the time's come to do some drinking?" the dwarf blurted. "I a'weighin' to go hear the prayin', or to make me a treat with these critters to eat! *Bwahaha!*"

"Is that all there is to Athrogate?" Jarlaxle asked in all seriousness, cutting short the dwarf's outburst. Athrogate stared at him hard, suddenly sobered.

"You are free of all feelings, it seems, other than your own humor," Jarlaxle pressed, and Athrogate's face tightened with every word. "Such as it is. Is there nothing but your pleasure?"

"I might be saying the same to yerself."

"You might, but my answer would involve a long history of explanation."

"Or ye might be telling me to mind me own business."

"Indeed, and which will you do, my hairy friend?"

"Ye're going to a place where ye don't belong."

"Your level of carefree is not attained without cause," said the drow. "Something to drink, something to hit, and a joke to make them groan—is that all there is to Athrogate?"

"Ye don't know nothing."

Indeed, Jarlaxle thought and smirked and decided to keep the irony of that double negative to himself. "So tell me."

Athrogate ground his teeth and slowly shook his head.

"Should I fill you with potent drink before I ask such things?" Jarlaxle asked.

"Ye do and ye'll find the ball end of a morningstar crunched into the side o' yer head."

Jarlaxle took the threat with a laugh, and let it drop. In discussion, at least, for in his thoughts he played it through over and over again. Something had created Athrogate as he was; something had broken the dwarf to that base level, where he had no emotional defense other than a wall of ridicule and self-ridicule, fastened by the occasional rap of a mighty morningstar and hidden by the more-than-occasional drink.

Jarlaxle nodded, thinking that he had just found something interesting, something he meant to explore, despite the dwarf's very serious threat.

The scene was all too familiar to Artemis Entreri and sent his thoughts careening back across the years. Before him, in the wide square that fronted the gigantic Protector's House, by far the largest structure in that part of the city, stood, sat, and lay the rabble of southwestern Memnon. They were the dispossessed, the poorest of the poor in the city, nearly all of them suffering the maladies so common among those who could not find enough to eat or drink, who could not keep clean, and who could not find shelter from the rain.

But they were not hopeless. No, the men on the eastern side of the square, richly dressed and bejeweled, would not allow for such a state of despair. They called out in melodic voices of the glories of Selûne and of the wonders that awaited her servants. Their pages went among the crowd, offering good news and good cheer, speaking of salvation and promises of an eternity free of all pain.

But there was more to this than cheerleading, Entreri knew all too well. There were promises of immediate relief from ailments, and even suggestions—normally reserved for grieving parents—that the afterlife for their dearly departed could be made even more accommodating than the promises of their god.

"Would you have your child suffer on the Fugue Plane a moment longer than he must?" one young acolyte said to a tearful woman not far from Entreri. "Of course not! Come along, good woman. Every moment we tarry is another moment your dear Toyjo will suffer."

It wasn't the first time the acolyte had pulled that same woman forward, Entreri could tell, and he watched as the pair shuffled through the crowd, the acolyte tugging her along.

"By Moradin, but yerselfs are calling me kin heartless," Athrogate muttered as he and Jarlaxle walked up beside Entreri. "Such a brotherhood ye got here. Makes me want to be findin' a wizard that'd polymorph me into a human." He ended with a fake sniffle, and wiped his eye.

Entreri flashed him a sour look, but as he was no more enamored with his fellow humans than was Athrogate, he really had no practical response. He looked to Jarlaxle instead—and did a double-take, still not used to seeing the drow with golden hair and tanned skin.

"You know this scene?" Jarlaxle asked.

"They are selling indulgences," Entreri explained.

"Selling?" Athrogate snorted. "These dirty fools got coin for spending?"

"What little they have, they spend."

Athrogate snorted as one particularly skinny man ambled by. "Ye might be better off in buying a cookie, if ye're asking me."

"The priests will heal their wounds for a fee?" Jarlaxle asked.

"Minor healing, and temporary at best," said Entreri. "Most who wish for physical heals are wasting their time. They are selling the indulgence of the god Selûne. For a few silver pieces, a grieving mother can spare her dead child a tenday in the Fugue, or can facilitate her own way when she dies, if that is her choice."

"They are paying for a priest's promise of such a thing?"

Entreri looked at him and shrugged.

Jarlaxle looked back over the throng—and it was indeed a throng of poor souls—then focused on the activity near the temple doors. Lines of dirty peasants waited their turn at the desks that had been set up. One by one, they walked forward and handed over a pittance, and one of the two men at the desk scribbled down a name.

"What a marvelous business," the drow said. "For a few comforting words and a line of text . . ." He gave an envious laugh, but to the side, Athrogate spat.

Both Entreri and Jarlaxle regarded the dwarf.

"They're telling them women that turning over their coins'll help dead kids?"

"Some," said Entreri.

"Orcs," muttered the dwarf. "Worse than orcs." He spat again and stormed off.

Entreri and Jarlaxle exchanged a confused glance, and Jarlaxle set off after the dwarf. Entreri watched them go, but didn't follow.

He remained at the square for quite a while, and every so often found his eyes drawn to a street entrance across the way, an avenue that wound down toward the docks.

A place he knew well.

"The Fugue Plane is a place of torment," Devout Gositek assured the nervous little man who stood before his desk. The man's hands worked feverishly about a tiny coin purse, rolling the dirty bag incessantly.

"I've not much," he said through his two remaining teeth, crooked and yellow.

"The charity given by the poor is more greatly appreciated, of course," Gositek recited, and the devout brothers standing guard behind him both smirked. One even winked at the other, for Gositek had done nothing but complain to them all morning, as soon as the listing had been pegged in the foyer, naming Gositek as one of the indulgence agents every day for the next tenday. He would spend his mornings, collecting coin, and his afternoons offering prayers for the paupers at the smelly graveyard. It was not an envied duty at the Protector's House.

"It is not the amount of coin," Gositek lied, "but rather the amount of *sacrifice* that is important for Selûne. So the poor are blessed, don't you see? Your opportunities for freeing your loved ones from the Fugue, and shortening your own visit, are far greater than those of the rich man."

The dirty old peasant rolled his tiny purse yet again. He licked his lips repeatedly as he fumbled about and extracted a single coin. Then, with a nearly toothless grin that spoke of lechery and deceit, he handed the coin to Devout Gositek's assistant, who sat beside him to watch over the heavy metal box, a slot in the top to accept the donations.

The peasant seemed quite pleased with himself, of course, but Gositek's glare was uncompromising. "You hold a purse," the devout said. "It bulges with coin, and you offer a single piece?"

"My only silver," the old peasant wheezed. "The rest're but copper, and just a score."

Gositek just stared at him.

"But my belly's growling bad," the man whined.

"For food or for drink?"

The peasant stammered and sputtered, but couldn't quite seem to find the words to deny the charge—and indeed, the stench that wafted from him would have made any such denial seem rather foolish.

Gositek sat back in his wooden chair and folded his arms in front of him. "I am disappointed," he said.

"But my belly . . ."

"I am not disappointed in your lack of charity, good brother," Gositek interrupted. "But in your continuing lack of common sense."

The peasant stared at him blankly.

"Twice the chance!" Gositek derided him. "Twice the opportunity to impress your devotion upon sacred Selûne! You can sacrifice greatly, for a pittance, and at the same time better your earthly standing by controlling your impure thoughts. Forsake your coin to Selûne, and forego your drink for yourself. Do you not understand?"

The man stuttered and shook his head.

"Each coin buys you double the indulgence and more," said Gositek, extending his hand.

The peasant slapped the purse into it.

Gositek smiled at the man, but it was a cold grin indeed, the smug grin of the cat dominating the mouse before feasting. Slowly and deliberately, Gositek pulled open the purse and dumped the meager contents into his free hand. His eyes flashed as he noted a silver piece among the two dozen coppers, and he looked up from it to the lying peasant, who squirmed and withered under that gaze.

"Record the name," Gositek instructed his assistant.

"Bullium," the peasant said, and he bobbed his head in a pathetic attempt to bow, and started away. He paused, though, and licked his lips again, staring at the pile of coins in Gositek's hand.

Devout Gositek pulled a few coppers from the pile, staring at the man all the while. He handed the rest to his assistant for the collection box, and started to put the others in the purse. He paused again, however, still staring at the man, and gave half of that pile to his assistant as well. Three coppers went into the purse, which Gositek handed back to the man.

But when the peasant grabbed it, Gositek didn't immediately let go.

"These are a loan, Bullium," he said, his tone grave and even. "Your indulgences are bought—a full year removed from your time on the Fugue Plane. But they are bought for the full contents of your purse, due to your reluctance and your lie about the second piece of silver. You have back three. I expect five returned to Selûne to complete the purchase of the indulgence."

Still stupidly bobbing his head, the peasant grabbed the purse and shuffled away.

Beside the wooden chair, Gositek's assistant chuckled.

⊷═══⊷

"You believe that Knellict and his band haven't done worse?" Jarlaxle asked when he at last caught up to the dwarf. They were almost back at their bug-filled shack by then.

"Knellict's a fool, and an ugly one, too," Athrogate grumbled. "Not much I'm liking there."

"But you served him, and the Citadel of Assassins."

"Better that than fight the dogs."

"So it is all pragmatism with you."

"If I knew what the word meant, I'd agree or not," said the dwarf. "What's that, a religion?"

"Practicality," Jarlaxle explained. "You do what serves your needs as you see fit."

"Don't everyone?"

Jarlaxle laughed at that. "To a degree, I expect. But few use that as the guiding principle of their lives."

"Maybe that's all I got left."

"Again you speak in riddles," said the drow, and when Athrogate scowled at him, Jarlaxle held up his hands defensively. "I know, I know. You do not wish to speak of it."

Athrogate snorted. "Ye ever hear o' Felbarr, elf?"

"Was he a dwarf?"

"Not a he, but a place. Citadel Felbarr."

Jarlaxle considered the name for a bit, then nodded. "Dwarven stronghold . . . east of Mithral Hall."

"South o' Adbar," Athrogate confirmed with a nod of his own. "Was me home and me place, and ne'er did me thoughts expect I'd ever be living anywhere but."

"But . . . ?"

"An orc clan," Athrogate explained. "They come in hard and fast—I'm not even knowin' how many years ago it's been. Not enough and too many, if ye get me meaning."

"So the orcs sacked your home and now you cannot but wander?" asked Jarlaxle. "Surely your clan is about. Scattered perhaps, but . . ."

"Nah, me kin're back in Felbarr. Drove them orcs out, and none too long ago."

Athrogate's face grew tight as he said that, Jarlaxle noted, and he decided to pause there and let Athrogate digest it all. He had started the dwarf down a painful road, he knew, but he did not want to press Athrogate too much.

To his surprise, and his delight, the dwarf went on without prodding, running his mouth as if he were a river and the drow had just crashed through the beaver dam.

"Ye got young ones?" Athrogate asked.

"Children?" Jarlaxle chuckled. "None that I am aware of."

"Bah, but ye're missing, then," said the dwarf.

To Jarlaxle's surprise, there was moistness about Athrogate's eyes—something he never thought he'd see.

"You had children," Jarlaxle surmised, gauging Athrogate's reaction to his every word before speaking the next. "They were slain when the orcs invaded."

"Good sprites, one and all," Athrogate said, and he looked away, past Jarlaxle, as if his eyes were staring into a distant place and distant time. "And me Gerthalie—what dwarf could ever be thinking he'd be so blessed by Sharindlar to find himself a woman o' such charms?"

He paused and closed his eyes, and Jarlaxle swallowed hard and wondered if he had been wise in leading Athrogate back to that place.

"Yep, ye got it," the dwarf said, eyes popping wide. All hint of tears were gone, replaced by the wildness Jarlaxle had grown used to. "Orcs took 'em all. Watched me littlest one, Drenthro, die. In me arms, he went. Bah, but curse

Moradin and all the rest for letting that happen!

"So we were chased out, but them orcs was too stupid to hold the place, and soon enough, they started fighting betwixt themselves. Me king called for a fight, and a fight he got, but meself didn't go. Surprised them all, don't ye doubt."

"Athrogate doesn't seem one to shy from a fight."

"And never's he been one. But not that time, elf. Couldn't go back there." He stood with his hands on hips, shaking his head. "Nothing there for me. They got their Felbarr back, but Felbarr's not me home no more."

"Perhaps now, after all these years. . . ."

"Nah! Ain't one o' them who was alive when the orcs come is still alive now. I'm old, elf, older than ye'd believe, but a dwarf's memory is older than the dwarf himself. Them boys in Felbarr now wouldn't have me, and I wouldn't be wanting them to have me. Dolts. In the first try on getting the place back, more than three hunnerd years ago, Athrogate said no. They called me a coward, elf. Yep, can ye be believing that? Me own kin. Thinkin' me afraid o' orcs. I ain't afraid o' undead dragons! But to them, Athrogate's the coward."

"Because you would not partake of the retribution?" Not wanting to break the dwarf's momentum, Jarlaxle didn't speak the other part of his question, regarding Athrogate's recounting of time. Few dwarves lived three centuries, and none, to Jarlaxle's knowledge, could survive for so long and still retain the vigor and power of one such as Athrogate. Either he was confused with his dates, or there was even more to the creature than Jarlaxle had assumed.

"Because I wouldn't be going back into that cursed hole," Athrogate answered. "Seen too much o' me dead kin in every corner and every shadow."

"Athrogate died that day the orcs came," said Jarlaxle, and the dwarf's look was one of appreciation, telling the drow that he had spoken the truth. "But if that was centuries ago, perhaps now. . . ."

"No!" the dwarf blurted. "Ain't nothing there for me. Ain't been nothing there for me in a dwarf's lifetime and more."

"So you set out to the east?"

"East, west, south—didn't much matter to meself," explained Athrogate. "Just anywhere but there."

"You have heard of Mithral Hall, then?"

"Sure, them Battlehammer boys. Good enough folk. They lost their place a hunnerd years after we lost Felbarr, but I'm hearing they got it back."

"Good enough folk?" asked Jarlaxle, and he filed away the confirmation of the timeline in his thoughts, for indeed, Mithral Hall had been lost to the duergar and the shadow dragon some two centuries before. "Or too good for Athrogate? Does Athrogate think himself unworthy? Were the barbs of your kin striking true?"

"Bah!" the dwarf snorted convincingly. "But what's good and what's bad? And what's mattering, elf? It's all a game with them gods laughing at us, ye're knowing as well as meself's knowing!"

"And so you laugh at everything, and hit whatever appears to need a hit."

"Hitting it good, too, but ain't I?"

"Better than almost any I've ever seen."

Athrogate snorted again. "Better'n any."

Jarlaxle received more than a few curious stares as he walked through the streets of the human-dominated city. They were not like the suspicious glares to which he had grown accustomed when he had walked as a drow, however, for there was no hatred, just curiosity, and more than a passing interest in his garments, which appeared far too rich for that poor section of Memnon.

In truth, the sum value of Jarlaxle's garments, just those he wore as he walked across the city, would have made a Waterdhavian lady of court jealous.

The drow shook all the distractions from his thoughts, reminding himself that the man he secretly followed was no novice to the ways of the thief. He knew that in all likelihood, Artemis Entreri had already detected the covert pursuit, but the man didn't show it.

Which of course meant nothing.

Entreri crossed the square before the temple with determined strides, making a beeline for an avenue on the southern side, a dusty way that sloped down and overlooked the southern harbor. With no cover available, Jarlaxle skirted the edge, and he feared that he'd lose the swift-moving Entreri because of his longer route. As he came around the southern edge of the square, though, he found that Entreri had slowed considerably. As the assassin made his way, Jarlaxle paralleled him, moving with all speed behind the row of shacks.

Within a few yards onto the avenue, Jarlaxle noted the visible change that had come over his friend, and never had he seen the sure and confident Entreri looking such. He seemed as if he could barely muster the strength to put one foot in front of the other. The blood had drained from his face, giving him a chalky visage, and made his lips seem even thinner.

With hardly an effort, the graceful drow climbed up to the roof of a shack, and shimmied across on his belly to overlook the avenue.

A few feet down the road, Entreri had stopped, and stood staring. His hands were by his sides, but they weren't at the ready near his weapon hilts.

Jarlaxle knew it beyond any doubt: Artemis Entreri, as he stood there, was helpless. A novice assassin could have walked up behind him and dispatched him easily.

That unsettling thought made Jarlaxle glance around, though he had no reason to suspect that any killers might be nearby.

He silently laughed at himself and his irrational fit of nerves, and when he looked back at Entreri, he only then fathomed the absolute strangeness of it all. He rolled over the edge of the roof, dropped lightly to his feet and walked over to stand beside Entreri—who didn't notice him until the very last moment.

Even then, Entreri never bothered to cast a glance Jarlaxle's way. His eyes remained fixed on a shack down the way, an unremarkable structure of clay and wood, and with the skeleton of a long-rotted awning jutting out in front. Beneath that, a ruined wicker chair was nestled against the shack, beside the open entrance.

"You know this place?"

Entreri didn't look at him and didn't answer. His breathing became more labored, however, telling Jarlaxle the truth of it.

This had been Entreri's home, the place of his earliest days.

CHAPTER

MISERY REVISITED

23

I f I am to help you, then I need to know," Jarlaxle argued, but Entreri's expression alone showed that the drow's logic was falling on deaf ears. They were back at the house with Athrogate, and Entreri had said not a word in the hour since they had rejoined their hairy companion.

"I'm getting the feelin' that he's not wanting yer help, elf," Athrogate said.

"He allowed us to come along on his adventure."

"I did not stop you from following me," Entreri clarified. "My business here is my own."

"And what, then, am I to do?" asked the drow with exaggerated drama.

"Live here in luxury, o' course!" said Athrogate, and he accentuated his point by slamming his hand down on the table, crushing a beetle beneath it. "Good huntin' and good food," he said, lifting the crushed bug before his face as if he meant to eat it. "Who could be asking for anything more? *Bwahaha!*" To Jarlaxle's relief, though Entreri hardly cared either way, the dwarf flicked the crushed beetle across the room instead of depositing it in his mouth.

"I care not at all," Entreri answered. "Go and find more comfortable lodgings. Leave Memnon all together."

"Why have you come here?" Jarlaxle asked, and Entreri showed the slightest wince. "And how long will you stay?"

"I don't know."

"To which."

Entreri didn't answer. He turned on his heel and stalked out of the house into the early morning sun.

"He's an angry one, ain't he?" Athrogate asked.

"With good reason, I presume."

"Well, ye said he growed up here," said the dwarf. "That'd put a pinch in me own butt, to be sure."

Jarlaxle looked from the open door to the dwarf, and gave a little laugh, and for the first time he realized that he was truly glad Athrogate had decided to come along. He considered his own role in this ordeal, as well, and he began to doubt the wisdom of entangling Entreri with Idalia's flute. Kimmuriel had warned him against that very thing, explaining to him that prying open a person's heart could bring many unexpected consequences.

No, Jarlaxle decided after some reflection. He was correct in giving Entreri the flute. In the end, it would be a good thing for his friend.

If it didn't kill him.

⊷══⊶

The compulsion that took him back to the sandy avenue that morning was so overpowering that Entreri didn't even realize he was returning to stand before the shack until he was there. The street was far from deserted, with many people sitting in the meager shade of the other buildings, and all of them eyeing the unusual stranger, with his high black leather boots, so finely stitched, and two weapons of great value strapped at his waist.

Clearly, Entreri didn't belong there, and the trepidation he saw in the gazes that came his way, and the background sensation of pure disgust, brought recognition and recollection indeed.

Artemis Entreri had seen those same stares during his days in Calimport serving Pasha Basadoni. The peasants of Memnon thought him a mercenary, sent by one of the more prosperous lords to collect a debt or settle a score, no doubt.

He relegated them to the back of his mind, reminding himself that if they all charged him together, he would leave them all dead in the dirt, then reminding himself further that those peasants would never find the courage to attack him in the first place. It wasn't in their humor—anyone with such gumption and willpower would have long ago left such a place.

It was even easier to dismiss them—in fact, it wasn't even a choice—when Entreri looked back to the ill-fitting door on the shack that had been his home for the first twelve years of his life. As soon as he focused on that place again, nothing else seemed to matter, as he fell into the same state of reflection that had allowed Jarlaxle to walk up right beside him unnoticed the night before.

Hardly aware of his movements, Entreri found himself approaching the door. He paused when he got there and lifted his fist to knock. He held it there, however, and reminded himself of who he was and of who these inconsequential, pathetic peasants were, and he just pushed through the door.

The room was quiet and still cool, as the morning sun hadn't yet come high enough over the hill to chase away the nighttime chill. No candles burned within, and no one was home, but a piece of stale bread on the table and a ruffled and tattered blanket in the corner told Entreri that someone had indeed been in the house recently. The bread wasn't covered in hungry beetles, even, and to Entreri, who knew the climate and the ways of Memnon, that was as telling as a warm campfire.

Someone lived in the house that had been his. His mother? Was it possible? She would be in her early sixties now, he knew. Was it possible that she still lived in the same place where she and his father, Belrigger, had made their home?

The smell told him otherwise, for whoever was living there took no care whatsoever in hygiene. He saw no chamber pot, but it wasn't hard for him to tell that one should have been in use.

That wasn't how he remembered his mother. She had barely a copper to her name, but she had always worked hard to keep herself, and her child, clean.

The thought came over him that the years might have broken that relic of pride from her. He grimaced, and hoped that it was not Shanali's home. But if that were the case, then she must have died. She could not have found her way out, he knew, for she was past twenty when he left. No one got out of that neighborhood past the age of twenty.

And if she was still there, then it must still have been her house.

The walls began to close in on him suddenly. The stench of feces assailed his nostrils and drove him back. He shoved through the door more forcefully than he'd entered, and staggered out into the street.

He found his breath coming in gasps. He looked around, as near to panic as he had been throughout his adult life. He saw the faces leering at him, glaring at him, hating him, and felt in that moment of uncertainty that the most frail among the onlookers could easily run up and dispatch him.

He tried to steady himself, but couldn't help but glance back over his shoulder at the swaying door. Memories of his childhood flooded his thoughts, of cold nights huddled on that very floor, brushing away the biting insects. He thought of his mother and her near-constant pain, and of his surly father and the pain he too often inflicted. He remembered those years in a way he hadn't in decades, and even thought of the few friends he had run the streets with.

There was a measure of freedom in poverty, he figured, and found some composure in that ridiculous irony.

He turned away again, thinking to plot his course, to find some way to move forward from there.

He found a faceful of wrinkled old woman instead.

"Byah, but ain't you the pretty one, with your shiny swords and fine boots," she cackled at him.

Entreri stared at the bent little creature, at her leathery face and dull eyes—a face he had seen a million times and not at all before.

"Ain't you the superior one?" she scolded. "Where you can just come down here and do as you please, when you please, no doubting."

Entreri looked past her, to the many eyes upon him, and understood that she spoke for them all. Even there, there was a collective pride.

"Well, you should be thinking your steps more carefully," the woman said more assertively, growing bolder with every word. She moved to poke Entreri in the chest.

That, Entreri could not allow, for he had known clever wizards to assume just such a guise as a pretense for touching an enemy, whereupon they could loose some prepared enchantment that would jolt their opponent right out of his boots. With uncanny reflexes and precision, and using his sword hand and the gauntlet Jarlaxle had reconstituted, he caught the thrust before it got near to him, and none-too-gently turned the woman's hand out.

"You know nothing of me," he said quietly. "And nothing of my reason for being here. It is not your affair, and do not interfere again." As he spoke, he looked past her to the many people rising in the shadows, all of them unsure but outraged.

"On pain of death," he assured the old wretch as he released her, shoved her aside, and walked past. The first one who came after him, he decided, would be put down in blood. If they kept on coming, the second one, he decided, he would cripple at his feet, and use the man to feed his health back to him through the dagger, if necessary. Two steps from the woman, however, he knew his planning unnecessary, for none would move on him.

But neither would the stubborn old woman let it drop. "Ah, but you're the dangerous one, ain't you?" she yelled. "We'll see how proud you puff your chest when Belrigger learns that you been in his house!"

At that proclamation, Entreri nearly fell over, his legs going weak beneath him.

He fought the urge to turn on the woman and demand more information, It was not the time, not with so many watching, and already angry at him. He studied the people around him more carefully as he made his way back to the square, in light of the knowledge that one of the old crowd, Belrigger, at least, was indeed still alive and about. Indeed, he started to notice more in-depth things about some—a tilt of the head, a look, the way one woman sat on her chair. A sense of familiarity came at him from many corners. So many people were the same ones Artemis Entreri had known as a child. Older now, but the same. And others, he thought, particularly one group of younger men and women, were people he had not known, but who showed enough similarities for him to guess that they might be the children of people he had.

Or maybe there was just a commonality of habit, and a shared manner of expression among all the peasants, he told himself.

It didn't matter, though, since in the end, Belrigger, his father, was alive.

That thought stayed with Entreri throughout the day. It followed him down the streets of Memnon, and all the way to the port. It haunted him under the bright, hot sun, and followed him, wraithlike, into the shadows.

Artemis Entreri had willingly, eagerly, stepped into mortal battle with the likes of Drizzt Do'Urden, but returning to his old home soon after sundown proved to be the most difficult challenge he had ever accepted. He used every trick he knew to get around to the back of the shack unnoticed, then quietly pried off a few planks of the back wall and slipped inside.

No one was home, so he replaced the planks and moved to the darkness of the back corner and sat down, staring at the door.

Hours passed, but Entreri remained on alert. He did not start, did not move at all, when at last the door swung in.

An old man shuffled in. Small and bent, his steps were so tiny that it took him a dozen to reach the table that was only three feet in.

Entreri heard flint hit steel and a single candle flared to life, affording the assassin a clear look at the old man's face. He was thin, so thin, emaciated, even, and with a bald head so reddened by the unrelenting Memnon sun that it seemed to glow in the faint light. He sported a wild gray beard and kept his face continually squinting, which jutted out his chin and made the facial hair seem even more pronounced.

He pulled out a small pouch with his dirty, trembling hands, and managed to dump its contents on the table. Muttering to himself the whole time, he began sorting through copper, silver, and other shiny pieces that Entreri recognized as the polished stones that could be found among the rocks south of the docks. The assassin understood, for he remembered well that some of the people of the neighborhood would venture there and collect pretty stones then sell them to the folk of Memnon, who paid for them as much to get rid of the annoying vagabonds as anything else.

Entreri couldn't be sure of the man's identity, but he knew that it certainly wasn't Belrigger. Age could not have bent his father so.

The man began giggling, and Entreri's eyes opened wide at the sound—one he had heard before. He rose without a whisper and moved to the table. Still unnoticed by the wretch, he slammed his hand down on the coins and stones.

"What?" the old man asked, falling back and turning on Entreri.

That wild-eyed look . . . the smell of his breath . . .

Entreri knew.

"Who are you?"

Entreri smiled. "You don't remember your own nephew?"

"Damn yourself, Tosso-posh," the man said as he entered the house an hour later. "If you're to shit yourself, then stay out of . . ." He was carrying a lit candle, and moved right for the table, but stopped just short as the door was pushed closed behind him—obviously by someone who had been standing behind it as it opened.

Belrigger took a step forward and spun. "You're not Tosso," he said as he took the measure of Entreri.

Entreri stared at the man for a few moments, for he surely recognized Belrigger. The years had not been kind to him. He looked drawn and stretched, as if he had been getting no nourishment other than the potent liquor he no doubt poured regularly down his throat.

Entreri looked past the man, to the far back corner, and Belrigger followed his lead and glanced back that way, bringing his candle around to illuminate the space. There lay Tosso-posh, face down, a small pool of blood around his midsection.

Belrigger spun back, his face a mask of rage and fear, but if he meant to lash out at the intruder, the sight of a long red blade leveled his way seemed to dissuade him more than a little.

"Who are you?" he breathed.

"Someone who just settled a score," Entreri answered.

"You murdered Tosso?"

"He's probably not dead yet. Belly wounds take their time."

Belrigger sputtered as if he simply couldn't find the words.

"You know what he did to me," Entreri stated.

Belrigger began shaking his head, and finally managed to say, "Did to you? Who are *you*?"

Entreri laughed at him. "I see that you hold no familial loyalty. I am hardly surprised."

"Familial?" Belrigger mouthed, and then his eyes went wider still as he asked again, "Who are you?"

"You know."

"I grow tired of your games," Belrigger said, and started as if he meant to leave. But the red sword flashed, tip coming in under his chin and stopping him in his tracks. With a slight twist of his wrist, Entreri forced the man back to the table, and then Entreri came forward and turned the blade again, angling Belrigger for a chair, where he fell back into a sitting position.

"Words I have heard before," Entreri said, and he pulled the other chair over and sat closer to the door. "Usually followed by the back of your hand. I would almost invite that slap now."

Belrigger seemed as if he could hardly breathe. "Artemis?" he asked, his voice barely a whisper.

"Have I changed so much, Father?"

After another few moments of gasping, Belrigger finally seemed to find his composure. "What are you doing here?" He glanced over the side of the table, at Entreri's fine sword and dress. "You escaped this place. Why would you come back?"

"Escaped? I was sold into slavery."

Belrigger snorted and looked away.

Entreri slammed his hand upon the table, demanding the man's full attention. "That notion amuses you?"

"It does nothing for me. It was not my decision, nor my care!"

"My loving father," came Entreri's sarcastic reply. To his surprise, and outrage, Belrigger laughed at him.

"Even Tosso didn't find such nerve as that," said Entreri, and his mention of Belrigger's dying friend sobered the man.

"What do you want?"

"I want to know of my mother," said Entreri. "Is she alive?"

Belrigger's mocking expression answered before the man ever spoke. "You went to Calimport, yes?"

Entreri nodded.

"Shanali was dead before you arrived there, even if the merchants drove their horses furiously," said Belrigger. "She knew she was dying, you fool. Why do you think she sold off her precious Artemis?"

Entreri's thoughts began spinning. He tried to recall that last meeting, and saw the frailty in his mother in an entirely new light.

"I actually pitied the whore," Belrigger said, and even as the word left his mouth, Entreri came forward with frightening speed and smashed him hard across the face.

Entreri fell back into his own seat, and Belrigger stared at him threateningly, and spat blood on the floor.

"She had no choice," Belrigger went on. "She needed coin to pay the priests to save her miserable life, and they wouldn't even take her diseased body in trade for their spells. So she sold you, and they took her coin. And still she died. I doubt they did anything to try to stop it."

Belrigger fell quiet, and Entreri sat there for a long while, digesting the surprising words, trying to find some way to deny them.

"Have you found what you sought, murderer?" said Belrigger.

"She sold me?" Entreri asked.

"I just told you so."

"And my dear father protected me," Entreri replied.

"Your dear father?" asked Belrigger. "And you know who that is?"

Entreri's face went very tight.

"Are you stupid enough to think me your father?" Belrigger asked with a laugh. "I'm not your father, you fool. If I was, I'd've beaten more sense into you."

"You lie."

"Shanali was fat with you when I met her. Fat in the womb from whoring herself out to those priests. Like all the rest of the girls. Might that you left too young to know the truth of it, but most of the brats you see running the dirty streets come from priest seed." He stopped and snorted, then laughed again. "I just gave her a place to live, and she gave me some pleasures in exchange."

Entreri hardly heard him. He considered again the scenes of his youth, when men came in and paid Belrigger, then went to Shanali's bed. The assassin closed his eyes, almost hoping that Belrigger would move fast in his moment of vulnerability. If Belrigger had come forward and taken Entreri's dagger, he wouldn't stop him, and would invite the blade into his heart.

But the man didn't move, Entreri knew, because he continued to laugh.

Until, that is, Entreri opened his eyes again and gave him that tell-tale stare.

Belrigger cleared his throat, obviously uncomfortable.

Entreri rose and sheathed his sword. One step brought him towering over the seated man. "Get up."

Belrigger stared at him defiantly. "What do you want?"

Entreri's fist crushed his nose. "Get up."

Bleeding, Belrigger rose, with one arm raised defensively before him. "What do you want? I told you everything. I'm not your father!"

Entreri's left hand snapped up and caught Belrigger's blocking hand. With the simplest of moves, the assassin bent Belrigger's hand over backward and wrenched the arm painfully to the side.

"But you beat me," Entreri said.

"You needed it," Belrigger gasped, trying to raise his other arm.

Entreri's free hand snapped out, slamming him in his already-bloody face.

"A tough life!" Belrigger protested. "You needed sense! You needed to know!"

"Say again that my mother was a whore," said Entreri. He twisted the bent arm a bit more, driving Belrigger to one knee.

"What would you have me say?" the man pleaded. "She did what she had to do to survive. It's what we all do. I don't blame her, and never did. I took her in when none would."

"To your own gain."

"Some," Belrigger admitted. "You cannot blame me for the way things are."

"I can blame you for every fist you laid upon me," Entreri calmly replied. "I can blame you for letting that filth"—he nodded his chin at Tosso-posh—"near me. Or did he pay you, too? A bit of coin for your boy, Belrigger?"

Gasping in pain, Belrigger furiously shook his head. "No . . . I didn't . . ."

Entreri's knee drove into Belrigger's face, knocking him to the floor on his back. Out came the jeweled dagger, and Entreri moved over the groaning man.

But Entreri shook his head. He put the dagger away, and walked out the door.

The old woman was out there again, having apparently heard the scuffle. Heard that and more, Entreri realized, as, instead of scolding him yet again, she said, "I knew Shanali, and I'm remembering yerself, Artemis."

Entreri stared at her hard.

"Did you kill Belrigger?"

"No," Entreri replied. "You heard our conversation?"

The woman shrank back. "Some," she admitted.

"If he lied to me, I will return and cut him apart."

The woman shook her head, a resigned look coming over her wrinkled old face. She nodded toward the chair set in front of her house, and Entreri followed her there.

"Your mother was a pretty one," she said as soon as she sat down. "I knew her mother, too, just as pretty, and just as young when she bore Shanali as Shanali was when she gave birth to you. Only a girl, doing th'only thing a girl down here can do."

"With the priests?"

"With whoe'er's the coin," the old one said with obvious disgust.

"And she really is dead?"

"Not long after you left," said the woman. "She was dying, and it got all the worse when she let her son go. Like she had no reason to keep fighting, not when them priests took her coins and cast their spells and said they couldn't do anything more for her."

Entreri took a deep, steadying breath, reminding himself that he expected from the beginning that he would not find Shanali alive.

"She's with the rest of them," the old woman said, surprising him, as his expression revealed. "On the hill, behind the rock, where they bury them that got no names worth remembering."

Like everyone who had spent his childhood in that part of Memnon, Entreri knew well the pauper's graveyard, a patch of dirt behind a large rocky outcropping that overlooked the southwestern most point of Memnon Harbor. Despite himself, he looked that way, and without another word to the old woman, and with only a final glance at the shack that had been his home, a place to which he knew he would never return, he walked away.

CHAPTER

24

Jarlaxle had his back to Entreri, pretending to look out the shack's front door at the early morning street. Athrogate snored contentedly in the corner of the room, his breathing interrupted at irregular intervals—Jarlaxle amused himself by imagining spiders climbing into the dwarf's open mouth.

Entreri sat at the table, his face tight and angry—the expression he had worn for most of the years he and Jarlaxle had spent together, one that Jarlaxle had hoped to replace forever with the use of Idalia's flute.

So much progress they had made, the drow silently lamented, but then that foolish woman had betrayed Entreri and torn a hole in his opened heart. And worst of all, what the drow knew but Entreri did not was that Calihye hadn't even wanted to attack him. Emotionally torn, confused by her loyalties and frightened of leaving the Bloodstone Lands, the woman had acted purely on impulse. Her strike was not wrought of malice toward Artemis Entreri, as it would have been in the early days of their relationship, but rather, was propelled by terror and grief and an anguish she could not overcome.

Jarlaxle hoped that someday Artemis Entreri might know that, but he doubted it strongly. Still, with Calihye safely under the control of Bregan D'aerthe, the drow knew better than to say "never."

The more pressing problem, of course, surrounded them in the hellish city of Memnon. Entreri had come home, though what that meant, Jarlaxle could not be sure. He glanced back at the grim man, who seemed not to notice him at all, not to notice anything. Entreri sat upright and his eyes were open, but he was no more aware, Jarlaxle reasoned, than was the sputtering dwarf in the corner.

His hands moving slowly and surely, Jarlaxle retrieved one of the small potion vials from his belt pouch. He stared at it for a long while, hating himself for having to so manipulate his friend yet again.

That thought surprised the drow; when in his entire life had he ever felt such a twang? In his betrayal of Zaknafein those centuries before, perhaps?

He looked at Entreri again, and he felt as if he was staring at his old drow companion.

I needed to do this, he reminded himself, and for Entreri most of all.

He quaffed the potion.

Jarlaxle closed his eyes as the magic settled in his body and in his mind, as he began to "hear" the thoughts of the other people in the room. He considered the life of Kimmuriel, who was always in such a state of heightened perception, and for an instant, he truly pitied the psionicist.

He shook his head and gave a great sigh, reminding himself that he had no time for such distractions. The potion wouldn't last long.

"So are you going to tell me where you went yesterday?" he said, turning to face the human.

Entreri looked up at him. "No."

But he was already telling Jarlaxle much more, for the question had elicited memories of the previous day's events: images of the street they had visited, of an old man lying on the floor holding in his spilling guts, of another man.

His father! No, the man he had thought his father, had known as his father for all his life.

"You have come here to find your mother. That much I know," Jarlaxle dared to say, though Entreri's expression grew more threatening from the moment he mentioned the lost woman.

An image flashed in Jarlaxle's mind, not of a woman, but of a view.

"You know, too, that I have told you that none of this is your affair," Entreri said.

"Why would you push an ally away?" Jarlaxle asked.

"You cannot help me in this."

"Of course I can."

"No!"

Jarlaxle straightened, assailed suddenly by a wall of red. He felt Entreri's anger more keenly than ever before, a razor edge that bordered on murderous rage. Images flashed too quickly for him to sort them and grasp them. He noted many of priests, of the great Protector's House, of the lines for indulgences playing out in the square.

Then just hatred.

Jarlaxle held up his hand defensively without even realizing it, though Entreri had made no move from the table.

The drow shook his head, to see the man staring at him curiously.

"What are you about?" the obviously suspicious Entreri asked.

"About tall enough to put me face between a woman's bosoms!" came a roar from the side, and Jarlaxle was truly relieved for the interruption at that particular moment.

Entreri cast a glance at Athrogate, then stood up quickly, his chair sliding out behind him. He stalked around the table, and never taking his stare off Jarlaxle, left the house.

"What's tyin' that one's armpit hair in knots?" Athrogate asked.

Jarlaxle merely smiled, glad that the potion's effects were already fading. The last thing he wanted was to be bombarded by the images that flitted through the mind of Athrogate!

Little life showed on the facings of the wind-swept brown rocks footing the mountains south of Memnon. There were a few lizards, though, sunning themselves or scampering from ledge to ledge, and so Jarlaxle knew that beneath the surface, deep in cracks or in caves formed by the incongruity of stone on stone, life found a way.

It always did—under the desert sun, or in the pits of the Underdark, where no stars shone.

A crude stone stair wound up the hundred feet or so around a large jut of rock, but Jarlaxle didn't use it. He moved off to the side, where the jag would keep him covered from view, and tipped his great hat to enact its levitation properties. He half-walked and half-floated up the sheer face. As he neared the top, he paused and glanced back behind him to view the distant harbor, and nodded with recognition in confirming that it was the same view he had seen in Entreri's thoughts when he had used the mind-reading potion.

Certain that Entreri was on the other side of the stone, Jarlaxle crept low as he went to the top.

Behind it was a flat patch of sandy ground, wider than the drow had expected. Many small and weathered stones littered the place—ancient gravestones, Jarlaxle realized. Across the sandy field directly south of his position, the drow noted a tarp-covered mound.

Bodies awaiting burial.

Entreri was indeed up there, walking among the stones, looking down at the sand and apparently lost in contemplation. Only one other man was about, a priest of Selûne, who stood at the westernmost edge, looking down at the harbor through a break in the brown stones.

It was a paupers' graveyard, where Entreri's mother was likely buried, Jarlaxle surmised. He retreated a bit over the far side of the rock and rested his back against it, considering it all. His friend was in turmoil, clearly. In breaking through Entreri's emotional wall, Jarlaxle had opened him to those painful memories.

He crawled back up and took one last look at Entreri, wondering what might result.

He floated back down carrying more than a little guilt on his slender shoulders.

"You'll not find any names on those stones," the priest said to Entreri as the assassin puttered about, coincidentally moving nearer to the man.

Entreri looked up and noticed the priest—the same one who had been collecting indulgences in the square that day—for the first time, really, so absorbed had he been in pondering the dirt and the many souls buried beneath it. He noted the man's defensive posture, and understood that the priest felt threatened.

He offered a helpless shrug and walked off a bit.

"It's not often that a man of your obvious means would come here," the priest persisted.

Entreri turned and regarded him again.

"I mean, these wretches don't get much in the manner of visitors," the priest went on. "Mostly unknown, unloved, and unwanted . . ." He ended with a condescending chuckle, which disappeared abruptly in light of Entreri's ensuing scowl.

"Yet you write their names on your scrolls when they give you their coins in the square," the assassin remarked. "Are you up here to pray for them, then? To fulfill the indulgences they purchased at your table?"

The priest cleared his throat and said, "I am Devout Gositek."

"You've confused me with someone who cares."

"I am a priest of Selûne," the man protested.

"You are a charlatan who sells false hope."

Gositek steadied himself and straightened his robes. "Beware your words . . ." he said, inquiring of Entreri's name with his expression and inflection.

Entreri didn't blink, and at first didn't respond at all. It was all he could do to keep from leaping across the ten feet that separated him from Gositek and throwing the fool from the cliff.

Entreri reminded himself to do nothing so rash. The young man was barely half his age and could not have been involved with his mother in any way.

"As I said, I am Devout Gositek," the man said again, apparently drawing strength from Entreri's snub. "A favored scribe of Principal Cleric Yozumian Dudui Yinochek, the Blessed Voice Proper, himself. Speak ill to me at your peril. We rule the Protector's House. We are the hope and prayers of Memnon."

He babbled on for a bit, but Entreri hardly heard him, for that name, Yinochek, sparked memory in him.

"How old is he?" Entreri asked, interrupting the fool.

"What? Who?"

"This man, this Blessed Voice Proper?"

"Yinochek?"

"How old is he?"

"Why, I don't know his exact—"

"How old is he?"

"Sixty years, perhaps?" Gositek asked as much as answered.

Entreri nodded as memories came back to him of a young and fiery priest, an oratory prodigy, a blessed voice proper, who had often delivered powerful homilies from the balcony of the Protector's House. He remembered viewing some of those beside his young mother, her eyes upturned, her heart uplifted.

"And this man has been at the Protector's House for many years?" Entreri asked. "And he has been known as Blessed Voice Proper . . ."

"From the beginning," Gositek confirmed. "And yes, he was a young man when first he came to join the priests of Selûne. Why? Do you know of him?"

Entreri turned and walked away.

"You used to live here," Gositek called after him, but Entreri didn't stop.

"What was her name?" the perceptive priest asked.

Entreri stopped, and turned to regard the man.

"The woman you seek here," Gositek explained. "It was a woman, yes? What was her name?"

"She had no name," Entreri replied. "None that you would remember. Look around you for your answers. Look at all their names, for they are etched on every stone."

Gositek straightened.

Entreri walked out of the graveyard.

◆━━━◆

Entreri hardly glanced at Jarlaxle as he took the bag of gold.

"You are welcome," the drow said, with more amusement than sarcasm.

"I know," was all he got in return.

The man's mood hardly surprised Jarlaxle. "I see that you are wearing your hat this day," he said, trying to lighten the mood, and referring to a thin-brimmed black top hat he had provided to Entreri, one with many magical properties—though not as many as Jarlaxle's great hat, of course! "I have not seen it on your head in many days." .

Entreri stared at him. The hat was tightly form-fitted, owing to a thin wire beneath its band. Entreri reached up and found the magical-mechanical clip, set just above his left temple. With a flick of his fingers, he disengaged it, and with a turn of his wrist, he removed the hat, tossing it to Jarlaxle, as if the reminder of where he had gotten the hat somehow sullied his desire to wear it.

That wasn't it at all, of course, as Jarlaxle clearly understood. Entreri had gotten exactly what he wanted from the hat, for it held much less rigidity, absent the wire. The idea of snubbing Jarlaxle had simply been an added bonus.

Entreri held stares with him for a moment longer, then hoisted the small sack of gold and walked out of the house.

"Must've had a bug crawl up his bum last night," said Athrogate, pulling himself up from the floor and stretching the aches from his knotty old muscles.

Still watching the departing man, and rolling the discarded hat in his hands, Jarlaxle answered, "No, my hirsute friend, it goes far deeper than that. Artemis has been forced to remember his past, and so now he has to confront the truth of who he is. Witness your own mood when speaking of Citadel Felbarr."

"I told ye I don't want to be talkin' about that."

"Exactly. Only Artemis isn't talking about anything. He's living it, in his heart. We did that to him, I fear, when he was given the flute." Finally, the drow turned to regard the dwarf. "And now we have to help him through this."

"We? Ye're pretty good with throwing around that word, elf. Course, if I knew what ye was talking about, I might be inclined to agree. Then again, I'm thinking that agreeing with ye is just going to get meself in trouble."

"Probably."

"Bwahaha!"

Jarlaxle knew that he could depend upon that one.

◆━━━◆

The scene at the square that morning was much as it had been when Entreri and Jarlaxle had first looked upon it, as it was almost every morning. The cobble-stones could hardly be seen beneath the hordes of squatting peasants, and the long lines leading to the two tables flanking the Protector's House's great doors.

When they arrived, Jarlaxle and Athrogate had little trouble picking Artemis Entreri out from that ragamuffin crowd. He stood in the line at the farthest table,

733

which struck Jarlaxle as odd until he noted the priest seated there, the same one he had seen in the pauper's graveyard the previous day. Entreri wondered if he had made a connection with the man.

Athrogate in tow, the drow cut through the first line of peasants and weaved across the way to move beside his companion. Those immediately behind Entreri protested the cut—or started to, until Athrogate barked at them. With his morningstars so prevalent, and a face scarred by a hundred years of battle, Athrogate had little trouble suppressing the protests of the paupers.

"Go away," Entreri said to Jarlaxle.

"I would be remiss—"

"Go away," the assassin said again, turning his head to look the elf in the eye. Jarlaxle held that stare for a few moments, long enough so that the line had time to thin ahead of them and when he disengaged the stare, Entreri was practically at the table. Entreri snorted at him dismissively, but Jarlaxle did not back off more than a couple of steps.

"First at a graveyard and now here," the priest, Gositek, said when Entreri's turn arrived. "You are truly a man of surprises."

"More than you can imagine," Entreri replied and he hoisted the sack of gold onto the table, which shook under its weight. As the bag settled, the top slipped open a bit, revealing the shiny yellow metal, and a collective gasp erupted from the peasants behind Entreri, and before, from the priest whose eyes widened so much that they seemed as if they might roll out onto the pile.

The guards behind Gositek came forward to hold back the pressing crowd, and Gositek finally sputtered, "Are you trying to incite a riot?" And it seemed as if he could hardly find breath for his voice.

"I am buying an indulgence," Entreri replied.

"The graveyard—"

"For a name long-forgotten by the priests of Selûne, their promises be damned."

"Wh-what do you mean?" Gositek stammered, and he worked to tighten the drawstring and hide away the gold before it could cause a stampede. As he moved to pull the sack toward him, though, Entreri's hand clamped hard and fast around his wrist, an iron grip that halted the man.

"Yes, the n-n-name . . ." Gositek stuttered, turning to his scribe, who sat with his mouth agape, staring stupidly. "Record the name—and a great indulgence it will—"

"Not from you," Entreri instructed.

Gositek stared at him blankly.

"I will purchase this indulgence from the blessed voice proper alone," Entreri explained. "He will receive the gold personally, will record the name personally, and recite the prayers personally."

"But that is not—"

"It is that, or it is nothing," said Entreri. "Would you go to your blessed voice proper after I have left with my gold, and explain to him why you could not allow me to see him?"

Gositek shifted nervously, rubbed a hand across his face, and licked his thin lips.

"I haven't the authority," the priest managed to say.

"Then go and find it."

The priest looked to his scribe and to the guards, all of them shaking their heads helplessly. Finally, Gositek managed to tell one of the guards to go, and the man ran off.

The line grew restless behind Entreri, but he wasn't moving for the short while it took before the guard returned. He pulled Gositek aside and whispered to him, and the devout came back to the table and sat down.

"You are fortunate," he said, "for the blessed voice proper is in his audience hall at this very time, and with a calendar that is not full. For the sake of an extreme indulgence—"

"For a sack of gold coins," Entreri corrected, and Gositek cleared his throat and did not argue the point.

"He will see you."

Entreri lifted the bag and stepped beyond the table, moving for the door, but the guards blocked his way.

"You cannot bring weapons inside the Protector's House," Gositek explained, rising again and moving to the side of Entreri. "Nor any magical items. I am sorry, but the safety of . . ."

Entreri unhitched his weapon belt and handed it back to Jarlaxle, who moved over, Athrogate still in tow—and with the dwarf still facing the crowd, holding them back with his snarling visage.

"Shall I strip naked here?" Entreri asked, pulling his *piwafwi* from his shoulders.

Gositek fumbled on that one. "Just inside," he said, motioning for the guard to open the door. Entreri went in with the priest, Jarlaxle, and Athrogate close behind.

"Your belt," Gositek instructed. "And your boots."

Entreri untied his belt and handed it to the drow, then pulled off his boots while Gositek began casting a spell. When finished, the priest scanned Entreri head to toe, and bade him to open his shirt. A nod from the priest to a burly guard had the man up close to Entreri, patting him down.

A few moments later, wearing nothing but his pants and shirt and holding a sack of gold, Entreri was escorted by yet another pair of armored soldiers through the next set of doors, disappearing into the Protector's House. In the anteroom, Jarlaxle bagged his belongings.

Gositek motioned for the elf and the dwarf to head back outside.

"There are many more bags of gold where that one came from," Jarlaxle said to the poor, stuttering priest. Noting Gositek's obvious interest, Jarlaxle gingerly reached back and pushed the door closed. "Let me explain," he said sweetly.

Some moments later, the crowd shifted uneasily as Devout Gositek walked out of the building. "Take care of their needs," he instructed the scribe and the two guards.

A flurry of protests erupted from the peasants, but the man held up his hand and cast a stern look at them to silence them. Then he disappeared back into the structure.

As the two sentries, their heavy armor clanking noisily, led him through the palace known as the Protector's House, Artemis Entreri's thoughts kept going back to his days in Calimport, serving the notorious Pasha Basadoni. For only there had Entreri seen so much gold and silver lining, and platinum artifacts and tapestries woven by the day's greatest artists. Only there had Entreri witnessed such grandeur, and hoarding of wealth. He was hardly surprised by the ostentatious decorations. Fabulous paintings and sculptures were each individually worth more coin than half the people gathered in the square could make in their lifetimes, even if they pooled all their wealth together.

Entreri knew the scene all too well. The wealth always flowed uphill and into the hands of a few. It was the way of the world, and whether it was facilitated by the threats and intimidation of the pashas of Calimport, or priests with their more subtle and insidious extortions, he had long ago ceased being surprised by it. Nor did he really care, except . . .

Except that part of the wealth that particular sect had taken from his mother had involved the most personal property of all. And she had since lay forgotten, in an unremarkable patch of sandy ground, hidden from the view of the city.

He looked at the sentries flanking him. It would would be his last walk, he knew, his last day.

So be it.

He came into a grand hall, with a ceiling that stretched up two score feet, and gigantic columns all carved and decorated with gold leaf standing in two rows, front to back. Between them lay a long and narrow bright red carpet, flanked every few feet by a soldier of the church in shining plate mail and with a halberd planted solidly at his side, its tip twice his height from the floor and tied with the banners of the principal cleric and his god, Selûne.

At the end of the carpet, perhaps thirty strides away, sat Principal Cleric Yinochek, the Blessed Voice Proper of Selûne, in a throne of polished hardwood, fashioned with white pillows shot with lines of pink and red. He wore voluminous robes, stitched with gold, and a crown of fabulous jewels rested on his head. He was indeed sixty or more, Entreri saw, though his eyes were still bright and his physique still hard and muscular. He even imagined that he saw a bit of his own features in the man, but he quickly dismissed that uncomfortable notion.

Before the throne stood three priests, two to the right and one to the left, and all half-turned to regard the approach of the man with his sack of gold.

Entreri felt the weight of their stares, their suspicions clear upon their faces, and for the flash of an instant, he believed himself too obvious, his intentions too clear. The wire of the hat band pressed in on him, and he nearly forgot himself and reached up to adjust it under his black hair.

But he stopped himself, then laughed at himself as he shook his head and glanced around, remembering who he was. He was not the bastard pauper child from the dirty streets—that was who he had been.

"I have come to purchase an indulgence," he said.

"We were told as much by Devout Gositek," one of the priests before the throne replied, but Entreri dismissed him with a wave of his hand.

"I have come to purchase an indulgence," he said again, his eyes set on, and his finger pointing at, the principal cleric, the blessed voice proper, who sat on the throne.

The four priests exchanged glances—more than one seemed out of sorts and seething.

"So we have been informed," Principal Cleric Yinochek replied. "And so we have welcomed you into our home, a place few people outside of the clergy ever see. And you speak directly to me, Principal Cleric Yinochek, as you requested." He motioned to the bag of gold. "Devout Tyre here will record the name of the person for whom you desire prayer."

"You will pray for her personally?" Entreri asked.

"Your indulgence is worthy of such, so I have been told," Yinochek replied. "Pray you leave the bag and offer the name. Then be gone in the comfort of knowing that the Blessed Voice Proper of Selûne prays for this woman."

Entreri shook his head and held the bag of gold close to his chest. "It is more than that."

"More?"

"Her name is—was, Shanali," said Entreri, and he paused and stared hard at the man, seeking a flash of recognition.

Yinochek wouldn't give him that satisfaction. If the principal cleric knew the name at all, he hid it completely, and when Entreri rationally considered the passage of thirty years and the reality of it all, he could only silently berate himself. Did the man even ask the names of the women he bedded? Even if he had, Yinochek couldn't likely remember them, the multitudes, if what the old woman had told Entreri was indeed the truth of it—and he knew in his heart that it was.

"She was my mother," Entreri said.

The looks that came back at him were of boredom, not interest.

"And she is deceased?" Yinochek asked. "As is my own mother, I assure you. That is the way of—"

"She has been dead for thirty years," Entreri interrupted, and Yinochek flashed a scowl and the other three priests and several of the guards bristled that the man would dare cut short the Blessed Voice Proper of Selûne.

But Entreri persisted. "She was a young girl—less than half my current age."

"It was a long time ago," Yinochek stated.

"I have been gone a long time," said Entreri. "Shanali—do you know the name?"

The man held his hands out helplessly and looked around at his similarly confused fellow priests. "Should I?"

"She was known among the priests of the Protector's House, so I am told."

"A noblewoman?" asked Yinochek. "But I was informed that you were at the cemetery on the rise—"

"Nobler than any in this room today," Entreri again interrupted. "She did what she had to do to survive, and to provide for me, her only child. I consider that noble."

"Of course," Yinochek replied, and he did well—better, at least—than the other three priests at hiding his amusement at the proclamation.

"Even if that meant whoring herself to priests in the Protector's House,"

Entreri said, and their mirth disappeared in the blink of an eye. "But you don't remember her, of course, though you were surely here at the time."

Yinochek didn't answer, other than to stare hard at the man, for a long, long time. "She has been dead for many, many years," he said finally. "Likely she has passed through the Fugue Plane in any case. Spare your indulgence for yourself, impertinent child, I pray you."

Entreri snorted. "Prayers to a god who would allow priests, even a blessed voice proper, to steal the dignity of the women of their flock?" he asked. "Prayers to Selûne, whose priests fornicate with starving young girls? Do you believe that I would wish such prayers? Better to pray to Lady Lolth, who at least admits the truth of her vile clergy."

Yinochek trembled with rage. At either side of Entreri, the guards stepped forward, weapons coming ready.

"Leave your gold and begone!" the blessed voice proper demanded. "It will purchase your life, and nothing more. And be glad that I am in a generous mood!"

"Go to your balcony," Entreri retorted. "Look out over them, Foul Voice Improper. How many are of your seed? Like myself, perhaps?"

"Remove him!" one of the priests before the throne yelled, but Yinochek stood up suddenly and shouted above them all, *"Enough!*

"You have tried my patience to its limits," he went on. "What is your . . ."

Entreri's scalp itched. He glanced around, measuring his strides, calculating the time his movements might bring. He stopped, as did Yinochek, as the door behind him banged open, forcefully, as if it had been kicked from up high.

"Wait! Your pardon and one moment, Blessed Voice Proper," said Devout Gositek, scrambling into the room. He held a wide-brimmed, feathered hat—Jarlaxle's hat.

"There is much more to this than our friend here, who consorts with elves who are much more than they seem," the man went on. As he finished he pulled something—a black fabric disk—from out of the great hat. "Much more than they seem," he said again.

Entreri's jaw dropped open at the reference, at the clue. He had his distraction.

Yinochek sat back down. "How dare you intrude, Devout Gositek?" he asked.

Gositek held up the disk of fabric, eliciting many curious stares.

Entreri leaped out to the side and smashed the guard across the face plate of his helmet with the sack of gold, launching the man to the floor. As he fell away, Entreri yanked the guard's halberd free, half turned, and launched it into the gut of the guard opposite, bending him double. His feet already moving, the assassin charged the throne, and when one of the three priests managed to react quickly enough to block his way, he threw the bag of gold into the man's face. Coins flew, and blood, and the priest fell back—even harder as Entreri planted a bare foot on his chest and leaped across.

He covered the distance to the throne in one stride, reaching up and pulling the slip-knot in the wire set under his hair. He swung it around as he went, catching the free end with his other hand, and with his fists outstretched before him, bore down on his prey. Yinochek lifted both hands defensively, but Entreri leaped headlong above the attempt to block him, snapped his hands down when they were behind the priest's defenses, then rolled over Yinochek's shoulder. Somersaulting and twisting as he went, Entreri brought his arm up and over his head so that as he descended he was back-to-back with the priest, the wire—the garrote—tight across Yinochek's throat.

Entreri used his momentum to yank the man away from the throne, hoping to snap his neck cleanly and be done with it.

But Yinochek was more stubborn and quicker than that, and he managed to come around with the flow of momentum. When it untangled, he remained very much alive, though Entreri was right behind him, tugging hard on the vicious wire, digging it into Yinochek's throat.

It would take too long, Entreri feared, expecting the guards and the priests to rush over him.

When he looked back, however, he pressed on with determination and hope that it would end then and there.

<hr />

Even as Entreri had first started his move, even as he had lunged to the right at the guard, the man on the carpet behind him, Devout Gositek by all appearances, flicked the oblong piece of fabric through the air. It elongated as it twirled, widening to several feet in diameter, and slapped against the side of one of the immense pillars lining the hall.

And it was no longer a piece of fabric at all, but a magical, portable hole, a dimensional pocket. From within it, almost as soon as it hit the wall, there came a tumult and a shout.

"Snort!"

The guards nearest the hole fell back as flames erupted from the blackness, and out leaped a red war pig, snorting fire, and with a hairy and no less fiery dwarf astride it. He passed between the nearest guards, morningstars whirling left and right, and landed a solid hit on both, launching them aside.

All across the room, guards and priests finally moved to respond, and yet another surprise caught them and held them momentarily, as Devout Gositek reached a hand under his chin and tore off the magical mask, revealing himself in all of his ebon-skinned glory.

Jarlaxle threw his hat to the floor, plucking free and tossing the magical feather as he did. His hands went into a rolling spin, summoning daggers into them from his enchanted bracers and launching them out in a steady line at the nearest guard. Even with those movements, the drow kept his wits about him enough to glance across the way, where Entreri knelt behind the blessed voice proper, who sat on the floor and clawed furiously at the assassin and at the wire that dug into his throat.

With but a thought, Jarlaxle summoned his innate drow magical abilities and brought a globe of darkness over the pair.

The armor worn by soldiers of the Protector's House was beautifully crafted and with few vulnerable areas, and so Jarlaxle's barrage did little real damage to the man. As that finally dawned on the sentry, he roared and lowered his halberd.

Jarlaxle snapped his wrists alternately, elongated daggers into swords, and even as one came into being, he parried across, turning the halberd, and leaped forward and to the side, right past the stumbling man.

The drow executed a perfect spin, and launched a backhanded uppercut that brought his fine blade under the rim of the guard's great helm, driving up into his skull.

Jarlaxle retracted it almost immediately and leaped away, gaining some time by finding Athrogate's swath of destruction, as the sentry went to the floor, flailing furiously and grabbing at the vicious wound.

Artemis Entreri understood Jarlaxle's tactical meaning in summoning the globe of darkness, of course, but it didn't suit him.

Not then.

He wanted to see Yinochek's face.

He rolled his legs under him and heaved backward, dragging the man out of the globe. As he came through the back limit of the darkness, he saw one of the priests, Devout Tyre, following his every move, the man's hands waving in spellcasting. Very familiar with clerical magic, Entreri knew what was coming, and he was not caught the least bit off guard as waves of compelling magical energy washed over him, an enchantment that could hold a man fast in place as surely as any paralysis.

Indeed, Entreri felt his arms go rigid, felt his body begin to deceive him.

But he conjured an image of Shanali, that last sight he had of her, and he imagined the man before him atop her, rutting like an animal, and thinking her no more than that.

His arms crossed more powerfully and Yinochek gave a pathetic wheeze.

But on came the other three priests and a pair of guards, and behind them lumbered . . . a gigantic bird?

Snort stomped and flames rolled out in a perfect circle, distracting the sentries, who were then swatted away by the wild Athrogate. His mighty legs clamping and twisting, he turned the boar at the next bunch to repeat the maneuver.

But the guards, well-trained men all, accepted the burst of flames and held their lowered halberds steady. Athrogate managed to drive one aside, but the other jabbed in at him, catching him just above the side seam in his metal breastplate. The fine tip drove through the leather under-padding and into the dwarf's armpit, and he had to throw himself back, letting Snort run right out from under him.

He fell hard to the floor, snapping the shaft of the halberd, but arched his small back and jerked his muscles in a single sudden spasm that propelled him back to his feet to meet the charge. Athrogate took some hope in the fact that the man's halberd had snapped, but it was short lived as the sentry, in one fluid motion, pulled a sword and slid a shield from his back. The man closed as if to run the dwarf right over.

From the other side came the second sentry, who similarly dropped his long weapon for sword and shield.

And Athrogate found he could hardly lift his right arm, blood running freely down his side.

Metal rang against metal as one long note across the way, closer to the door, as a pair of guards engaged the drow, and two more rushed in to join. Fighting defensively, diving into sudden rolls and using his lighter armor and better agility to keep ahead of the lunging men, Jarlaxle had little hope of scoring any solid hits against four skilled opponents. His swords whipped about every which way, seemingly randomly, but almost always deflecting a strike or forcing an attacker back.

Out in the hall behind him came many shouts, and the guards took heart.

So did the drow. And he rolled again, making sure that the approaching reinforcements could properly view the battle from the outside hall, and that they could see him, a drow, clearly. He wanted to hold their attention. He didn't want them to notice what was above the door jamb.

The release of fire, the breath of a red dragon, shook the structure with its sheer intensity as the leading guard passed under the archway. That man avoided most of the flames, but still came into the audience hall on fire, flailing. Behind him, for Jarlaxle had been sure to set the silver statuette with its little maw facing backward, the dozen men charging after him were not so fortunate, and were not about to rush through the tremendous force of that conflagration.

Fire rolled on for what seemed like many heartbeats, immolating the screaming sentries, ending any hopes of reinforcements and igniting tapestries, benches, carpeting, and the wooden beams of the structure.

Around Jarlaxle, the four sentries stared in disbelief—and though the distraction lasted for no more than perhaps two seconds, that was a second longer than Jarlaxle needed.

The drow came up from his roll, planted his feet, and propelled himself back the other way, into their midst. Out to the left slashed one blade, chopping hard on a sword arm and driving the weapon from the man's grasp. Out to the right stabbed the second sword, through a seam in armor and into the side of a man.

Out to the left leaped the drow, planting his feet on the chest of one guard and shoving off, launching the man to the floor and himself back and to the right, where he got up and over the blade of the fourth, turning as he went so that he was almost sitting on the man's shoulders. Jarlaxle dropped his bloody blades in a cross before the man's throat and slashed them out to their respective sides as he back-rolled over that shoulder, gracefully gaining his feet and spinning away.

The sentry grasped at his throat and sank to his knees.

"For Selûne!" the guard cried, thinking his victory at hand.

And under the cover of his shout, Athrogate called to his right-hand morningstar, enabling its magic, bringing forth explosive oil from its prongs. The dwarf snapped himself around, launching the head of the weapon at the guard's blocking shield. His arm was a limp thing, and there was no weight behind the strike, but when it connected with that shield, the oil exploded, shattering both the shield and the arm that held it and throwing the man back to the floor.

Athrogate fell off to the left, swiping across with his second weapon, one coated with the magically-duplicated ooze of a creature known to strike fear in the hearts of the greatest warriors: a rust monster. The initial contact of morning-star against shield did little to dissuade the oblivious attacker, who shield-rushed the dwarf and crashed his sword down hard on Athrogate's shoulder.

Roaring in pain, the dwarf sent his left arm in furious pumps, spinning the morningstar head in horizontal twirls, each connecting with the shield. So furious was his attack that the guard had to backtrack.

But the man seemed unconcerned, was even mocking the dwarf, as, bloody and battered, Athrogate turned to square up with him.

On he charged, and the dwarf spun left, his right arm swinging, his morn-ingstar coming at the shield with little power behind it.

It needed none, however, for the shield had turned to rust, and the impact blew it apart, red dust flying all over them both.

The guard paused in surprise, and Athrogate roared and spun the rest of the way around more furiously, his left coming across in a mighty backhand. His shield ruined, the guard had no choice but to spin away from the blow.

And Athrogate, leaping in that final turn, planted his leading left foot solidly and stepped into perfect balance with his right, halting his momen-tum with brutal efficiency. He stepped forward with his left foot, swinging his weapon, smashing the guard in the back in mid-turn, and sending him staggering forward.

Athrogate was with him, every stride, his left arm working left-to-right and down, then reversing right-to-left and over, the ball smashing against the man's back repeatedly, driving him forward in a stumbling run. Again and again the pursuing dwarf hit him, as if guiding him with the morningstar.

Headlong, face-first, into a stone pillar.

The guard's arms reflexively went around the thing as he slid down, though he was hardly conscious of the movement.

Athrogate whacked him again, just because. .

Entreri snapped his arms left and right as he drove up to his feet, drag-ging the poor Yinochek with him. He tried to break the man's neck, but had no leverage to do so, nor did he have the time to complete the strangulation. Reluctantly, angrily, he released the priest and shoved him forward at the nearest man, another priest, then rushed in hard behind and shoulder-blocked another aside. He spun out to the right in a dead run, hoping to get ahead of the stab of another man.

He wouldn't have made it, except that suddenly, instead of stabbing, the man was flying forward, launched by the powerful peck of Jarlaxle's dia-tryma. Entreri ran right by the giant bird as it plowed forward, trampling the fallen defender.

On Entreri sprinted, his bare feet slapping the stone floor. He cut and veered as guards closed in on him from both sides, but with a sudden burst, he got beyond them, diving into a headlong roll over the fallen chair. He came back to his feet with three men in close pursuit.

He noted Jarlaxle's sudden flurry, saw men falling every which way, and marked the fires raging out beyond the room, thick smoke starting to come in the door. None of it would help him, he knew.

He had to anticipate Jarlaxle, had to think like his drow companion.

He went straight for the extra-dimensional hole hanging on the side of the pillar.

With halberds reaching out just behind him, Entreri dived in and disappeared from sight.

He felt a body in there, one that moved and groaned, and he slugged the man across the face, laying him low. As he scrambled around, his hand closed on a pommel.

Kill them! came a message in his mind, one of eagerness.

Entreri wasn't about to disappoint the blade.

The three guards stood before the hole, rightly hesitating and tentative. Out came Entreri in a great leap, red-bladed sword in one hand, jeweled dagger in the other. He smashed Charon's Claw down atop the nearest halberd, to his right and before him, and drove the weapon down, but then rolled his sword underneath it as he landed and quick-stepped forward. He swung his arm back up and over his shoulder, taking the long, spearlike weapon with it, and swinging it out to intercept the thrusting sword of the next man in line.

At the same time, the assassin executed a reverse backhand parry with his dagger, driving the sword on his left out behind him. He turned as he did to face the man holding the sword, and lifted his left arm high, taking the sword with it, then thrust across with Charon's Claw, stabbing the man in the chest. As that one fell away, freeing up his dagger hand, Entreri threw himself backward and under the swipe of the cumbersome halberd. He fell into a sitting position, but kept turning, driving his jeweled dagger into the spearman's knee then rolling around as the man howled, tearing his dagger free. He slashed across with Charon's Claw, taking the man's legs out and toppling him to the ground. Entreri used the falling man as a shield, leaping back to his feet, but he needn't have, he realized, for the third had turned to run off.

Entreri leaped into pursuit, but pulled up short, his attention drawn across the room, where the three priests escorted the blessed voice proper out a back door.

"No!" Entreri yelled charging that way, though he knew he'd never get there in time to stop the escape. It couldn't happen like this! Not after all his effort, not after all the memories of Shanali had assaulted him.

Devout Tyre, in the lead, pulled open the door; Entreri did the only thing he could and launched his sword like a great spear.

"Ah, but ye're a good pig," Athrogate said to Snort. He leaned heavily on the boar, nearly collapsing from loss of blood, and directed the creature to the extra-dimensional pocket. As he neared the black hole, the dwarf noted a man crawling out.

Devout Gositek turned to him pitifully.

Athrogate slugged him hard, knocking him out, so that he was hanging by the waist over the lip of the hole, the fingers of his extended arms just brushing the floor.

On a word from the dwarf, Snort leaped back into the hole. Athrogate looked to Jarlaxle and saluted, though the drow hardly seemed to notice. Then the dwarf hopped into a sitting position on the rim of the dimensional pocket, grabbed Gositek by the scruff of his neck, and rolled back out of sight, taking the battered priest with him.

Out of the corner of his eye, Devout Tyre saw the missile coming. He fell back with a yelp, knocking his fellows into a stumble, with Blessed Voice Proper Yinochek, still gasping for breath, falling back against the wall. The red-bladed sword rushed past Tyre and hit the wood, the weight of the missile closing the door hard, and leaving the sword stuck there, quivering.

"Get him out!" Tyre commanded the other two, turning toward the charging Entreri. "I will finish this one."

With a snarl of defiance, the priest grabbed Charon's Claw and yanked it from the door.

Everything seemed to move in slow motion for Devout Tyre. He stumbled away from the door as one of his companions, Devout Premmy, tugged the portal back open. He saw the man Entreri, screaming in protest, still thirty feet or more away. He watched the man change hands with his remaining weapon, saw him leap high and far, planting his left foot as he came down.

Entreri's hips rotated to square with the door. His left arm swung out wide as he rolled his right shoulder forward, arm coming up and over in a mighty throw.

Tyre hardly registered the movement, the silver flickers of the missile, but he knew somehow exactly where it was heading. He tried to scream a warning, but his voice came out as a high-pitched shriek.

He hardly heard that, but instead heard Entreri's seemingly elongated cry of *"Shanali!"*

And as though with the snap of some unseen wizard's fingers, time sped up and the silver missile flashed past him. Devout Tyre turned and saw his Blessed Voice Proper, the Principal Cleric of the Protector's House, with his arms out before him, quivering, his face a mask of exquisite pain, the jeweled hilt of a dagger protruding from his chest.

And Tyre saw . . . white. Just hot white, as his sensibilities finally registered the excruciating pain that burned throughout his body and soul. He screamed again—or tried to, but his lips curled up over his teeth, and rolled back even farther as if melting away. Somewhere deep inside him, Tyre knew that he should drop the evil sword.

But his sensibilities were long gone by then, his thoughts no longer connecting to his body. Pain controlled him, and nothing more, as he felt a million stinging needles, a million burning bites, a fire within him as profound and devastating as the one that had exploded in the corridor across the way.

He fell to the floor but never knew it. He lay there trembling, his skin smoldering and crackling into charred bits as Charon's Claw ate him.

The throw—both of them—had come from somewhere so deep inside of him that Artemis Entreri had hardly even realized his actions. He had seen nothing but Shanali, frail and dying in the dust. He had felt nothing but his rage, his absolute fury that the vile priest would escape him.

The moment his dagger thudded into Principal Cleric Yinochek's heart, the spell was broken, and Entreri, running at the four priests, felt a flood of angry satisfaction.

He slowed his pace, noting movement from the side, then watched as two of the priests deserted Yinochek and rushed out the door, Jarlaxle's diatryma in close pursuit. There were soldiers coming toward the room down the hall beyond, he saw, but how they changed their attitude and their direction when that giant bird crashed out through the doorway.

Entreri rushed up and pushed the door closed. He glanced at the dying Tyre but paid him no more heed than that, moving instead to stand before the principal cleric.

"Do you know how many lives you have ruined?" he asked the man.

Trembling, sputtering, his eyes wide with horror, Yinochek's lips moved but no words came forth.

"Yes," Entreri noted. "You know. You understand it all. You know the wretchedness of your actions as you steal the coin of the peasants and the innocence of the girls. You know, and so you are afraid." He reached up and grabbed the dagger hilt, and Yinochek stiffened.

Entreri thought to obliterate the man's soul with his magical weapon, but he shook his head and dismissed the notion.

"Selûne is a goodly god, so I've heard," he said, "and thus will have nothing to do with the likes of you. I call you a fraud, and there is nowhere left for you to hide."

The man's eyes rolled back into his head, and he slumped to the floor.

"A better way to go than that one," Jarlaxle said, and only then did Entreri realize that the drow had come to his side. Jarlaxle's gaze led Entreri's to what remained of Devout Tyre, who lay on his back shaking wildly, his robes smoking and his face showing more bone than flesh.

With a growl, Entreri stomped hard on the man's forearm, crushing the burnt skin and bone, and the recoil lifted Charon's Claw into the air, where Entreri easily caught it.

He looked back at Jarlaxle as the drow settled the fabric patch back into his great hat.

The building shook violently, and across the room, a gout of flames rushed in.

"Come," Jarlaxle bade him, putting on his magical mask. "We must be away."

Entreri looked back at the blessed voice proper, sitting against the wall, his chest covered in blood, his eyes white.

He thought of Shanali one last time. He took a brief moment to consider the long and dirty road of his miserable life, which had ultimately brought him to that awful place.

EPILOGUE

The commotion behind him did little to take Entreri's gaze from the city below him. He stood on the jag of rock at the paupers' graveyard, staring down at the plume of smoke that hung lazily over the ruins of the Protector's House.

His vengeance had been sated, obviously so, but there was little left in the man. Finally he turned back to Jarlaxle, who had opened his portable hole against another stone, and stood with Athrogate beside him, staring into the darkness.

"Well, ye might as well be coming here," the dwarf recited. "Afore I find me way in there. In that case, yerself should fear, me pulling ye out by the tip o' yer ears!"

Entreri rubbed a hand over his weary face, and moved down from the perch as Devout Gositek, his face all bruised, crawled out of the hole.

"I am not afraid to die," he said, trembling so badly he seemed as if he was about to soil himself.

Jarlaxle turned deferentially to Entreri.

"Then get out of here," the assassin said.

Gositek's jaw dropped open.

"Generous," Jarlaxle remarked.

"Surprised," said Athrogate.

Gositek looked at the elf and dwarf, then scrambled for the stair. But Entreri intercepted him, and with frightening strength yanked him aside and ran him to the very edge of the hundred-foot drop.

"No, please!" the priest who was not afraid to die desperately pleaded.

"If you wish to remain alive, then look down there," Entreri growled in his ear. "Mark well the destruction of the Protector's House. You will rebuild it—you and your fellow priests?"

When Gositek didn't immediately answer, Entreri shifted him forward, almost off the ledge.

The terrified man yelped and blurted, "Yes!"

Entreri tugged him back. "And you will never forget their names again," he instructed. "Any of them. And you and your brethren will come up here, every

747

day, and pray for the souls of those who have gone before."

"Yes, yes, yes," Gositek stammered.

"Do you understand me?" Entreri roared, shaking him near the edge again.

"I do! We will!"

"I don't believe you," Entreri said, and the man began to cry.

Entreri threw him back from the cliff and to the ground. "Remember that view," he warned. "For if you forget your promise, you will see it again, with smoke once more rising from the ruins of your rebuilt temple. And on that next occasion, I will throw you from the cliff."

The man nodded stupidly as he crawled away. Finally, near the edge of the grave-yard, he managed to put his feet under him, and he scrambled down the long stair.

Entreri moved to the top of that stair and watched him run away.

"Are you satisfied now, my friend?" Jarlaxle asked.

Entreri put his head down and forced himself to remain calm then turned around, his expression revealing his emptiness.

Jarlaxle offered a shrug. "It is often the way," he said. "We've all demons needing to be put to rest, but the experience is not as rewardi—"

"Shut up," Entreri interrupted.

Athrogate laughed.

"We must be gone from this place," Jarlaxle said.

"I don't care where you go," Entreri answered. He reached into his pouch and pulled forth Idalia's flute, which he had broken into two pieces. He locked stares with the drow and tossed it to Jarlaxle's feet.

Jarlaxle gave a helpless chuckle, but there was no real mirth in it. Finally breaking Entreri's imposing stare, he bent and retrieved the flute. "A valuable item," he said.

"Cursed," came Entreri's reply.

"Ah, Artemis," said the drow. "I understand your wounds and your anger, but in the end, you will see that this was all for the best."

"You might be right, but that changes little."

"How so?" asked the drow.

Entreri pulled his pack around. He fished out the obsidian figurine and dropped it to the ground, calling forth his nightmare mount. As the creature materialized, Entreri pulled forth another object and sent it spinning at Jarlaxle.

A black, small-brimmed hat.

"I am finished with you," Entreri said. "Your road is your own, and I care not if it takes you to the gates of the Nine Hells."

Jarlaxle caught the hat and rolled it over in his slender hands. "But Artemis, be reasonable."

"I have never been more so," Entreri replied, and he put one foot in a stirrup and hoisted himself astride the tall black horse. "Farewell, Jarlaxle. Or fare ill. It matters not to me."

"But I am your muse."

"I don't like the songs you inspire."

Entreri turned his mount around, stepping to the stair.

"Where will you go?"

The assassin paused and looked back sourly.

"I can find out, in any case," Jarlaxle reminded him.

"To Calimport," Entreri answered, and he gave a helpless laugh at the truth of the drow's statement—and Jarlaxle took heart in that, at least. "To Dwahvel, and to a place I might call home."

"Ah, Mistress Tiggerwillies!" Jarlaxle said with sudden animation. "And will you seek to regain your status among the streets of that fair city?"

Entreri chortled and nodded toward the distant plume of smoke. "Artemis Entreri is dead," he said. "He died in the Protector's House in Memnon, chasing ghosts."

He turned his horse away, down the stairs and out of sight.

"Might that we should follow him," Athrogate said to Jarlaxle. "He'll be getting' hisself into trouble, no doubt. It's the way his blood's flowing."

But Jarlaxle, staring at the empty stair, shook his head with every word. "No," he said. "And no. I suspect that Artemis Entreri really is dead, my friend."

"Looked living to me."

Jarlaxle laughed, not willing to explain it, and not expecting that Athrogate, who had his own emotional barriers defining him, would begin to understand.

But Athrogate remarked, "Ah, he died the way meself died when them orcs come to Felbarr."

"More than three centuries ago?" Jarlaxle asked.

"Three and a half, elf."

"And yet you look so young."

"Might be that livin' long's a curse more than a blessing."

"A curse imposed by . . . ?"

"Ever twist the bum hairs of a wizard, elf?"

Jarlaxle rolled his eyes and laughed.

" 'Ill-argued and ill-met,' he told me. 'A pox on me bones for not payin' me debt. To grab the sun and not let it set, ye'll not die young, and ye'll never forget.' "

"That was his curse?"

"And after three hunnerd years, I'm tellin' ye it worked."

Jarlaxle nodded and considered the tale for a short while. Then, on a sudden impulse, he reached over and plopped the hat atop the dwarf's hairy head.

"Hey, now!"

"Yes," Jarlaxle said, nodding with admiration. "It suits you well."

As he spoke, the drow dropped a hand into his pouch, feeling the broken pieces of Idalia's flute and wondering how much it would cost him to get it repaired.

He winced just a bit, because he realized that Athrogate couldn't likely blow a note.

But he looked back to the empty stair, where Artemis Entreri had gone, and he reminded himself that sometimes you just had to play the hand you were dealt.

HOW TO READ THE

NOVELS OF
R.A. SALVATORE

Starting in March of 2004, Wizards of the Coast began reissuing all of the FORGOTTEN REALMS novels of R.A. Salvatore, bringing what used to be two trilogies and seven separate books into a cohesive series, THE LEGEND OF DRIZZT. The story of Drizzt Do'Urden continued in two subsequent trilogies: The Hunter's Blades and Transitions, and a spin-off trilogy The Sellswords. The Cleric Quintet was also reissued in the past couple years. And in October 2010, a new trilogy was launched with the Drizzt novel *Gauntlgrym.* This makes twenty-eight books in the expanded LEGEND OF DRIZZT series—and knowing where to start and where to go next can still be a little confusing, even with thirteen of those books clearly re-cast, and re-numbered.

This handy appendix should solve all those problems. All of the books listed below are in print and available from book stores everywhere, and often in more than one form—as individual paperbacks, e-books, or as part of three- or four-book collector's editions.

So then, where to start?

Begin at the beginning, with The Legend of Drizzt, Book I: *Homeland* (or *The Legend of Drizzt Collector's Edition,* Book I, which includes *Homeland, Exile,* and *Sojourn*).

Though *Homeland* was actually the fourth Drizzt book written, it began what was originally called The Dark Elf Trilogy: three prequel novels that went back in time to tell the story of the young Drizzt's childhood in Menzoberranzan, his exile from that evil city, and his first exploration of the World Above.

From *Homeland,* just keep reading the Legend of Drizzt series in order:

THE LEGEND OF DRIZZT

Homeland
Exile
Sojourn
or, *The Legend of Drizzt Collector's Edition,* Book I

The Crystal Shard
Streams of Silver
The Halfling's Gem
or, *The Legend of Drizzt Collector's Edition,* Book II
The Legacy
Starless Night
Siege of Darkness
Passage to Dawn
or, *The Legend of Drizzt Collector's Edition,* Book III
The Silent Blade
The Spine of the World
Sea of Swords
or, *The Legend of Drizzt Collector's Edition,* Book IV

These thirteen books bear the LEGEND OF DRIZZT series title and are clearly numbered, but you might want to pause somewhere around *Siege of Darkness* or *Passage to Dawn* and read:

THE CLERIC QUINTET

Canticle
In Sylvan Shadows
Night Masks
The Fallen Fortress
The Chaos Curse

This five-book series, also clearly numbered in new, revised paperback editions, are set around the same time, but introduce a whole new cast of characters, led by the scholar-priest Cadderly. Cadderly is mentioned in *The Silent Blade,* so having read the Cleric Quintet before you read *The Silent Blade* will keep you from wondering who this guy is! Anyway, you really want to read the Cleric Quintet before you get to *The Ghost King.* . . .

Once you've finished THE LEGEND OF DRIZZT series with *Sea of Swords,* pause again to read the spin-off series:

THE SELLSWORDS

Servant of the Shard
Promise of the Witch-King
Road of the Patriarch

Servant of the Shard was originally published between the LEGEND OF DRIZZT novels *The Spine of the World* and *Sea of Swords,* but was really more a sequel/spin-off from *The Silent Blade,* and features the drow mercenary Jarlaxle and his unlikely ally, the human assassin Artemis Entreri, as its principal protagonists. Their story continues into the next two Sellswords books. And trust me, the characters and situations from The Sellswords come full circle back into the ever-unfolding tale of Drizzt.

And back to Drizzt, then, with:

THE HUNTER'S BLADES TRILOGY

The Thousand Orcs
The Lone Drow
The Two Swords

Which leads directly to:

TRANSITIONS

The Orc King
The Pirate King
The Ghost King

Characters and situations from The Sellswords return to the fold in *The Pirate King*, and the Cleric Quintet is a must-read for you to have the full effect of *The Ghost King*.

Further, the short story "Iruladoon" in the anthology *Realms of the Dead* is a must-read sequel/epilogue to *The Ghost King*. Don't pass that up!

Characters and situations from The Sellswords continue on into *Gauntlgrym*, and onward from there into the Neverwinter trilogy as it continues in 2011 and 2012.

That might make it sound as if every single one of these books is a "must read," and that's only because, at least in my humble opinion, every single one of these books is a must read. Read them all, and I know you'll agree.

— Philip Athans
Senior Managing Editor
Wizards of the Coast

RICHARD LEE BYERS

BROTHERHOOD OF THE GRIFFON

NOBODY DARED TO CROSS CHESSENTA...

BOOK I
THE CAPTIVE FLAME

BOOK II
WHISPER OF VENOM
NOVEMBER 2010

BOOK III
THE SPECTRAL BLAZE
JUNE 2011

...WHEN THE RED DRAGON WAS KING.

"This is Thay as it's never been shown before ... Dark, sinister, foreboding and downright disturbing!"
—Alaundo, Candlekeep.com on Richard Byers's *Unclean*

ALSO AVAILABLE AS E-BOOKS!

Follow us on Twitter @WotC_Novels

FORGOTTEN REALMS, DUNGEONS & DRAGONS, WIZARDS OF THE COAST, and their respective logos are trademarks of Wizards of the Coast LLC in the U.S.A. and other countries. Other trademarks are property of their respective owners. ©2010 Wizards.

DUNGEONS & DRAGONS®

FROM THE RUINS OF FALLEN EMPIRES, A NEW AGE OF HEROES ARISES

It is a time of magic and monsters, a time when the world struggles against a rising tide of shadow. Only a few scattered points of light glow with stubborn determination in the deepening darkness.

It is a time where everything is new in an ancient and mysterious world.

BE THERE AS THE FIRST ADVENTURES UNFOLD.

THE MARK OF NERATH
Bill Slavicsek
August 2010

THE SEAL OF KARGA KUL
Alex Irvine
December 2010

The first two novels in a new line set in the evolving world of the DUNGEONS & DRAGONS® game setting. If you haven't played . . . or read D&D® in a while, your reintroduction starts in August!

ALSO AVAILABLE AS E-BOOKS!
Follow us on Twitter @WotC_Novels

DUNGEONS & DRAGONS, D&D, WIZARDS OF THE COAST, and their respective logos are trademarks of Wizards of the Coast LLC in the U.S.A. and other countries. Other trademarks are property of their respective owners. ©2010 Wizards.

WELCOME TO THE DESERT WORLD
OF ATHAS, A LAND RULED BY A HARSH
AND UNFORGIVING CLIMATE, A LAND
GOVERNED BY THE ANCIENT AND
TYRANNICAL SORCERER KINGS.
THIS IS THE LAND OF

CITY UNDER THE SAND
Jeff Mariotte
OCTOBER 2010

*Sometimes lost knowledge is
knowledge best left unknown.*

FIND OUT WHAT YOU'RE MISSING IN THIS
BRAND NEW DARK SUN® ADVENTURE BY
THE AUTHOR OF *COLD BLACK HEARTS.*

ALSO AVAILABLE AS AN E-BOOK!
THE PRISM PENTAD
Troy Denning's classic DARK SUN
series revisited! Check out the great new editions of
*The Verdant Passage, The Crimson Legion,
The Amber Enchantress, The Obsidian Oracle,*
and *The Cerulean Storm.*

Follow us on Twitter @WotC_Novels

DARK SUN, DUNGEONS & DRAGONS, WIZARDS OF THE COAST, and their
respective logos are trademarks of Wizards of the Coast LLC in
the U.S.A. and other countries. Other trademarks are property of
their respective owners. ©2010 Wizards.

RETURN TO A WORLD OF PERIL, DECEIT, AND INTRIGUE, A WORLD REBORN IN THE WAKE OF A GLOBAL WAR.

TIM WAGGONER'S
LADY RUIN

She dedicated her life to the nation of Karrnath. With the war ended, and the army asleep—waiting—in their crypts, Karrnath assigned her to a new project: find a way to harness the dark powers of the Plane of Madness.

REVEL IN THE RUIN
DECEMBER 2010

ALSO AVAILABLE AS AN E-BOOK!

Follow us on Twitter @WotC_Novels

A DUNGEONS & DRAGONS NOVEL

EBERRON, DUNGEONS & DRAGONS, WIZARDS OF THE COAST, and their respective logos are trademarks of Wizards of the Coast LLC in the U.S.A. and other countries. Other trademarks are property of their respective owners. ©2010 Wizards.

Want to Know Everything About Dragons?
Immerse yourself in these stories inspired by
The New York Times best-selling

A PRACTICAL GUIDE TO
DRAGONS

RED
Dragon Codex

978-0-7869-4925-0

BRONZE
Dragon Codex

978-0-7869-4930-4

BLACK
Dragon Codex

978-0-7869-4972-4

BRASS
Dragon Codex

978-0-7869-5108-6

GREEN
Dragon Codex

978-0-7869-5145-1

SILVER
Dragon Codex

978-0-7869-5253-3

GOLD
Dragon Codex

978-0-7869-5348-6

Experience the

power and magic

of dragonkind!

Follow us on Twitter @WotC_Novels

 DUNGEONS & DRAGONS, WIZARDS OF THE COAST, and their respective
logos are trademarks of Wizards of the Coast LLC in the U.S.A. and
other countries. Other trademarks are property of their respective
owners ©2010 Wizards.

Books for
Young Readers

Enjoy these fantasy adventures inspired by
The New York Times best-selling
Practical Guide series!

MONSTER SLAYERS

A Companion Novel to *A Practical Guide to Monsters*
Lukas Ritter
978-0-7869-5484-1
Battle one menacing monster after another!

NOCTURNE

A Companion Novel to *A Practical Guide to Vampires*
L.D. Harkrader
978-0-7869-5502-2
Join a vampire hunter on a heart-stopping quest!

Aldwyns Academy

A Companion Novel to *A Practical Guide to Wizardry*
Nathan Meyer
978-0-7869-5504-6
**Enter a school for magic where even the first day
can be (un)deadly!**

Follow us on Twitter @WotC_Novels

DUNGEONS & DRAGONS, WIZARDS OF THE COAST, and their respective
logos are trademarks of Wizards of the Coast LLC in the U.S.A. and
other countries. Other trademarks are property of their respective
owners ©2010 Wizards.

Books for
Young Readers